THE
AUSTRALIAN
TRILOGY

THE
AUSTRALIAN
TRILOGY

Bryce Courtenay is the author of *The Power of One*, *Tandia*, *April Fool's Day*, *The Potato Factory*, *Tommo & Hawk*, *Jessica*, *Solomon's Song*, *A Recipe for Dreaming*, *The Family Frying Pan* and *The Night Country*. He was born in South Africa, is an Australian and has lived in Sydney for the major part of his life.

BRYCE COURTENAY

THE AUSTRALIAN TRILOGY

VIKING

Further information about the author may be found at www.brycecourtenay.com

Viking
Penguin Books Australia Ltd
487 Maroondah Highway, PO Box 257
Ringwood, Victoria 3134, Australia
Penguin Books Ltd
Harmondsworth, Middlesex, England
Penguin Putnam Inc.
375 Hudson Street, New York, New York 10014, USA
Penguin Books Canada Limited
10 Alcorn Avenue, Toronto, Ontario, Canada M4V 3B2
Penguin Books (NZ) Ltd
Cnr Rosedale and Airborne Roads, Albany, Auckland, New Zealand
Penguin Books (South Africa) (Pty) Ltd
5 Watkins Street, Denver Ext 4, 2094, South Africa
Penguin Books India (P) Ltd
11, Community Centre, Panchsheel Park, New Delhi 110 017, India

The Potato Factory first published by William Heinemann Australia in 1995
Published by Mandarin Australia, a part of Reed Books Australia, in 1996
Published by Penguin Books Australia Ltd 1997
Tommo & Hawk first published by Penguin Books Australia Ltd 1997
Solomon's Song first published by Penguin Books Australia Ltd 1999
The Australian Trilogy first published by Penguin Books Australia Ltd 2000

1 3 5 7 9 10 8 6 4 2

Front cover image:
George Lambert (born Russia 1873, arrived Australia 1887, died 1930),
A sergeant of the Light Horse in Palestine 1920.
Oil on canvas, 77.0 × 62.0 cm, Felton Bequest, 1921,
National Gallery of Victoria, Melbourne. Reproduced by permission.
Maps by Craig McGill

Typeset in 10.5/13 pt Sabon by Post Pre-press Group, Brisbane, Queensland
Printed in Australia by Australian Print Group, Maryborough, Victoria

National Library of Australia
Cataloguing-in-Publication data:

Courtenay, Bryce, 1933– .
The Australian trilogy.

ISBN 0 670 89389 7.

I. Courtenay, Bryce, 1933– The potato factory. II. Courtenay, Bryce, 1933– Tommo & Hawk.
III. Courtenay, Bryce, 1933– Solomon's song. IV. Title.

A823.3

WRITERS' BLOC

THE READER IS ALWAYS RIGHT

www.penguin.com.au

THE
AUSTRALIAN
TRILOGY

❧

PART I

THE POTATO
FACTORY

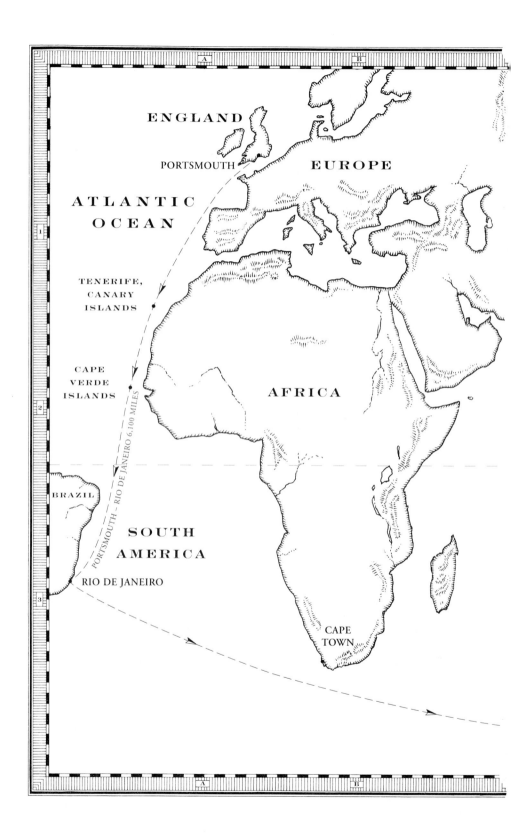

For my beloved wife, Benita, who always
had absolute faith and never failed to
wrap it in abundant love.

Acknowledgements

The first thing a writer learns is that real life contains far more coincidence than any he or she will ever be allowed to get away with in a fictional plot. Life is simply stranger than fiction. Almost at a glance any daily newspaper carries examples of character and plot well beyond the imagination of the boldest of fiction writers. Good, historical fiction may be said to be fact that went undiscovered at the time it happened and the historical novel is the writer's ability to dig deep enough to find some of the truth as it was at the time. To help me do this a lot of people gave generously of their knowledge, intelligence and time. Without them there could be no book. While they may appear below only as a list of names in alphabetical order, I count myself most fortunate to have known them all, for they are the fuel which fed the fire of my fiction.

Louise Adler, Jennifer Byrne, Adrian Collette, Benita Courtenay, David Daintree, Owen Denmeade, Margaret Gee, Alex Hamill, Jill Hickson, Elspeth Hope-Johnstone AM, Rabbi J. S. Levy, Dr Irwin Light, Larry Lyme, Libby Mercer, Essie Moses, Ross Penman, Jeff Rigby, Roger Rigby, Irene Shaffer, Michael Sprod, Paula Teague, Barbara and John Tooth. There are others who helped in smaller though no less important ways and I am grateful to you all.

There are always one or two people who need to be singled out for special mention. My editor Belinda Byrne qualifies as the star at the top of the tree, closely followed by Dr John Tooth and Paul Buddee AM. Also my publishers, Reed, who chewed their collective fingernails but kept their patience and their expletives to themselves when my manuscript was well past its promised deadline.

I thank you all.

Finally, I acknowledge my gratitude to all those writers and historians past and present who go before me; they are too numerous to mention and too wonderful for words.

Preface

Some people are bound to argue that this book is the truth thinly disguised as fiction and others will say I got it quite wrong. Both sides may well be correct.

That Ikey Solomon existed and was perhaps the most notorious English criminal of his day is not in dispute, and wherever possible I have observed the chronology of his life and that of his wife, Hannah, and their children. That Charles Dickens based the character Fagin in his novel *Oliver Twist* on Ikey Solomon is a romantic notion which I much prefer to believe. But the moment I allow him and all the characters in this book to speak for themselves I have created a fiction of the fact of their historical existence. By every definition this is therefore a work of fiction.

In reading it I ask you to take into account the time in which my story occurs, the first half of the nineteenth century. In these more enlightened times this book may be regarded as anti-Semitic; in the terms of the times in which it is written, it is an accurate account of the prevailing attitudes to the Jews of England.

These were dark times, bleak times, hard times, times where a poor man's life was regarded as less valuable than that of a pig, a poor Jew's far less valuable even than that. That Ikey Solomon's life could have happened as it did in fact, allows my fiction to exploit the ability of the human spirit to transcend the vile tyranny of which humankind has proved so consistently capable. In these terms Ikey Solomon was a real-life hero and my fiction cannot possibly do him justice.

In history there are no solitary dreams;
one dreamer breathes life into the next.

Sebastiao Salgado

Be This a Warning!

This little work is held up as a warning
beacon to keep the traveller from the
sands of a poisonous desert, or from
splitting upon the rocks of infamy.

It is necessary in such a case to point
out 'hells' and brothels, girls and bawds,
and rogues, by name and situation, not
as a direction for youth to steer towards
them, but that he may take the contrary
course – for no reasonable man would
enter a whirlpool, when he could pass
by it on the smooth surface o'
the reaches of a tranquil river crossing.

The life of Ikey Solomon is filled with
iniquitous adventure; he has acted with the
rope round his neck for twenty years,
but by his cunning always avoided being
drawn up to the beam, where he is
likely to end his infamous career.

We are duty bound to hold him up as a
depraved villain, whose conduct must
disgust, and whose miseries, with all his
wealth, will show how preferable a life
of honesty and poverty is to a guilty
conscience, and treasure gained by blood
and rapine.

From *Ikey Solomon, Swindler, Forger,
Fencer & Brothel Keeper,* 1829

BOOK ONE

LONDON

Chapter One

Ikey Solomon was so entirely a Londoner that he was a human part of the great metropolis, a jigsawed brick that fitted into no other place. He was mixed into that mouldy mortar, an ingredient in the slime and smutch of its rat-infested dockside hovels and verminous netherkens. He was a part of its smogged countenance and the dark, cold mannerisms of the ancient city itself. He was contained within the clinging mud and the evil-smelling putrilage. Ikey was as natural a part of the chaffering, quarrelling humanity who lived in the rookeries among the slaughterhouses, cesspools and tanneries as anyone ever born in the square mile known to be the heartbeat of London Town.

Ikey was completely insensitive to his surroundings, his nose not affronted by the miasma which hung like a thin, dirty cloud at the level of the rooftops. This effluvian smog rose from the open sewers, known as the Venice of drains, which carried a thick soup of human excrement into the Thames. It mixed with the fumes produced by the fat-boilers, fell-mongers, glue-renderers, tripe-scrapers and dog-skinners, to mention but a few of the stench-makers, to make London's atmosphere the foulest-smelling place for the congregation of humans on earth.

The burial ground in Clare Market was full to the point where gravediggers would be up to their knees in rotting flesh as they crammed more bodies into graves. Corpses piled on top of each other often broke through the ground emitting noxious gases, so that the stench of rotting bodies was always present in nearby Drury Lane.

Since infanthood Ikey had grown accustomed to the bloated effluence of the river and the fetidity that pervaded St Giles, Whitechapel, Shoreditch, Spitalfields and the surrounding rookeries. His very nature was fired, hammered and hardened within this hell which was the part of London he called home.

Ikey Solomon was the worst kind of villain, though in respectable company and in the magistrates' courts and the assizes he passed himself off as a small-time jeweller, a maker of wedding rings and paste and garnet brooches for what was at that time described as the respectable poor. But the poor, in those areas of misery after Waterloo, had trouble enough scraping together the means to bring a plate of boiled potatoes or toasted herrings to the table. If Ikey had depended for his livelihood on their desire for knick-knackery, his family would have been poorly served indeed.

In reality he was a fence, a most notorious receiver of stolen goods, one known to every skilled thief and member of the dangerous classes in London. In Liverpool, Manchester and Birmingham young pickpockets, footpads, snakesmen and the like referred to him in awed and reverent tones as the Prince of Fences.

Ikey Solomon was not a man to love, there was too much the natural cockroach about him, a creature to be found only in the dark and dirty corners of life. It might be said that Ikey's mistress loved him, though she, herself, may have found this conclusion difficult to formulate, love being a word not easily associated with Ikey. Mary wasn't Ikey's wife, nor yet his mistress, perhaps something in between, an attachment for which there is not yet a suitable name.

The doubtful honour of being Ikey's wife was reserved for Hannah, a woman of a most terrible disposition who did little to conceal her dislike for her husband. Such acrimonious sentiments as were commonly expressed by Hannah were usually forbidden to a woman, who was expected to accept with a high degree of stoicism her husband's peregrinations in life. A woman, after all, had no rights to carp or pout at the results of her partner's misfortunes. Nor decry his errors in judgment or his lack of moral rectitude but share the good, silently accept the bad and hope always for the best, which is the female's natural lot in life, though if this was ever made plain to Hannah, it had not sunk in too well.

Moreover, setting aside for a moment what might be considered formal filial duty, Hannah had a good case against Ikey. Their children also were on her side, both puzzled and somewhat ashamed of the curious man they took to be their father.

If Ikey understood the duties of a father he chose never to exercise them. To his children during the hours of daylight he was a dark, huddled, sleeping bundle wrapped in a large, extremely dirty coat from which protruded at one end strands of matted grey hair surrounding a mottled bald dome. Looking downwards, first there was a thick hedge of unkempt eyebrow and then a nose too long for the thin face from which it grew. Still further downwards in the area of the chin grew an untidy tangle of salt and pepper beard, thick in some parts and in others wispy, all of it most uneven and ratty in appearance.

From the other end of the greasy coat stuck a pair of long, narrow, yellow boots, their sharp snouts concertinaed inwards and pointed upwards. These boots were never seen to leave his feet and to the curious eyes of his children their dented snouts seemed to act as sniffing devices. With the first whiff of danger they would jerk Ikey from the horizontal into a wide-awake seated position, their snouted ends testing the air like truffle pigs, quickly establishing the direction from whence the danger came. Whereupon, Ikey's boots would become in appearance two yellow cockroaches, plant themselves firmly on the ground, then scuttle him away into some dark, safe corner.

Ikey was also a series of daylight noises to his children. A cumulation of slack-jawed snoring and wet spittle sounds issued constantly from a mouth clustered with large yellow and black teeth. Several appeared to be broken or missing, worn down by the gnashing and grinding of a torturous sleep which came to an end precisely at six-thirty of the clock in the evening.

At night Ikey's children, hugging each other for moral support, would watch wide-eyed from dark corners as he shuffled about the house, sniffing, snorting and whimpering as though expecting somehow to find it changed for the worse during his sleep. If Ikey should come across a clutch of children he would halt and stare momentarily as though curious to who they might be.

'Good!' he'd snort at them and shuffle away still sniffing and whimpering as he carried on with his inspection of the premises.

At seven of the clock precisely, the Irish woman who looked after the children in Hannah's absence would place in front of him a mutton and potato stew with a thick wedge of batter pudding. He'd eat alone in the skullery, his only implement a long, sharp pointed knife with which he'd stab a potato or a fatty piece of mutton and feed it into his mouth. Then, when the solid contents of the bowl were disposed of, he used the batter pudding to soak up the broth, polishing the bowl clean with the greasy crust.

Ikey's evening meal never varied. Neither beef nor fowl ever replaced the greasy mutton, and he would complete his repast with a bowl of curds swallowed in one long continuous gulp which made his Adam's apple bounce in an alarming fashion. Milk with meat was not kosher and Ikey, who had a regular seat in the Duke's Place synagogue, was a good Jew in all but this respect. With his hands, first the left and then the right, he'd wipe the remains of the frothy curd from his lips then run both greasy palms down either side of his coat, this action bringing scant improvement to either.

At this point the children listening at the door would strain their ears for the various oleaginous noises coming from his stomach. They'd hold their breath for the magnificence of the burp they knew must surely follow and the horrendous fart which would cap it, a single explosion which signalled the end of Ikey's repast.

His evening meal over, Ikey picked his teeth with a long, dirty fingernail. He would then take up Hannah's ledger and repair to his study. Before he unlocked the door he would pause and look furtively about him, then enter and immediately lock it, restoring the brass key to somewhere within the interior of his overcoat.

Ikey would light the two oil lamps in his study to reveal a smallish room thick with accumulated dust except within the precinct of his writing desk. This he kept pristine, the quill and blacking pot neatly lined up, a tablet of evenly stacked butcher's paper to the right.

Ikey would then take a cheap imitation hunter from the interior of his coat and lay the watch together with Hannah's ledger upon the desk. He then removed his coat and waistcoat, leaving him standing in his dirty woollen undershirt. The coat and waistcoat he hung upon the coat-stand, one peg of which already contained his flat-topped broad-brimmed hat. Then moving to one corner of the room, he sank to his knees and, in turn, pushed four knot-holes contained in the floorboards. These immediately sprang up an inch or so at one end, whereupon Ikey carefully removed the nails from the holes. He lifted the floorboards to reveal a small dry cellar no deeper than four feet and filled with ledgers. Ikey removed three and carefully clicked the sprung floorboards back into place, positioning the nails in the holes in which they belonged. He then crossed to his desk, placed the ledgers down, seated himself on the high stool and lit the lamp which hung directly above his head. Seated quiet as a mouse, he worked until midnight.

Precisely ten minutes later, the time it took to tidy his desk, return the ledgers to the cavity beneath the floorboards, get into his coat, fix his hat upon his head, douse the lamps, lock the door to the study, take Hannah's ledger back to the pantry and place it in the sack containing potatoes and leave the house, he slid furtively from a half-closed front door into the passing night.

Ikey wore his great coat buttoned tightly with the collar pulled high so that it wrapped around his ears. He pulled his hat down low across his brow and hardly any part of him was visible as he moved along, the hem of his thick woollen coat inches from the scuffed and dented caps of his scuttling yellow boots.

The irony was that Ikey's entire identity was revealed in his very self-concealment – his wrapping and scuttling, chin tucked in, head turned around at every half a dozen steps, dark eyes darting, as though seen through a brass letterbox slot; the crab-like sideways movement, stopping, sniffing, arms deep into the pockets of his great coat, instinctively seeking for a wall to sidle against, so that the shoulders of the coat were worn with scuffing against brick and rough stone.

These mannerisms clearly identified him to the street urchins and general low-life who used their rapacious eyes for observing the comings and goings of everyone they might prey upon. If Ikey had completely disrobed and walked, bold as a butcher's boy, in broad daylight, whistling among the stalls in the Whitechapel markets, this would have been a more complete disguise.

Perhaps the broad daylight aspect of such a disguise would have been the most effective part of it, for light in any form was repugnant to Ikey who, like Hannah, was nocturnal. Both were involved in duties best completed well after sunset, and before sunrise.

Ikey would be out and about after midnight, sniffing for business in the thieves' kitchens, netherkens and chop houses in the surrounding rookeries, while Hannah was the mistress of several bawdy houses which traded best as the night wore on.

Hannah had been born a beautiful child and lost none of her fine looks as she grew into a young woman, but then the pox had struck. Unable to restrain herself she had scratched at the scabs until the blood ran, leaving her pretty face and pubescent breasts badly and permanently pocked.

From childhood Hannah had imagined herself away from the hell of Whitechapel and occupying a small residence in Chelsea. She would be a courtesan, exquisitely perfumed and coiffured, dressed in fashionable gowns of shot silk. She would wear diamonds from Amsterdam and pearls from the South Seas which, naturally, were the grateful gifts of the young gentlemen officers of the Guards, the Blues and no other, or of the older, though equally handsome, titled members of the Tattersall Club. She would be seen at the opera and the theatre and remarked upon for her extraordinary beauty. Wherever Hannah went young swells and flash-men on the randy would evoke her name as one might a princess, knowing her to be beyond the reach of their impecunious pockets, dreaming of a windfall which might cause such unfortunate circumstances to be overturned.

Instead the dreadful scars had caused her to become a barmaid at the Blue Anchor in Petticoat Lane. Here her pretty figure and large blue eyes could have earned her a handsome enough living as a part-time prostitute, but the idea was repugnant to her. She was not prepared to deny her previous expectations to work on her back as a common whore.

Hannah's bitterness had left her moody and recalcitrant and the young men who paid her attention soon dwindled. Her tongue was too acerbic and her expectations too high for their aspirations or resources. Quite early in her pock-marked life she had conceived of the idea of owning a high-class brothel. She saw this as her only chance of resurrecting the original dream to associate with the better classes in dress and mannerisms, if not in respectability.

So she cast her eyes about for a likely patron. Perhaps an older man easily pleased with her generous hips and big breasts whose needs, after his nightly libation, were seldom onerous, satisfied after a half-dozen grunts and jerks whereupon he would fall back exhausted onto his duckdown pillow to snore and snort like the fat pig he undoubtedly was.

When Ikey, who at the age of twenty-one was already coming on as a notorious magsman and was thought not without spare silver jiggling in his pockets, came along, his very repulsiveness made him attractive to her. True, he was not elderly nor yet rich, but young, clever and careful, his dark eyes always darting. Appearing suddenly at the door of the Blue Anchor, he scanned the patrons, his eyes sucking in the human contents of the room before he entered. Hannah could sense that he was greedy, secretive, a coward and moreover he made no advances of a sexual nature during his pathetic attempt at courtship. What she had expected to find in an older man she now found in Ikey. Ikey would be her ticket to glory, the means by which she would achieve the remnants of her earlier ambition.

They were married in London in 1807 in the Great Synagogue at Duke's Place with all the trappings and regalia of the Jewish faith. It was a bitterly cold January morning, but it was well known that a morning ceremony was less costly and Hannah's father, a coachmaster, was not inclined to waste a farthing even on his family. If, by a little thought and negotiation, a small extra sum could be saved for ratting, the sport on which he chose to gamble most of his earnings, so much the better.

Hannah and Ikey were a well-suited couple in some respects and they shared a thousand crimes and ten thousand ill-gotten gains in their subsequent life together. As a consequence they became very wealthy, though Hannah had not achieved her ambition to mix with the male members of the best of society and be seen in the gilded boxes of the opera and theatre. Instead her bawdy houses were frequented by lascars and Chinese and black seamen from North Africa, the Indies and the Cape of Good Hope, and of course all the scum from the English dangerous classes. Panders, crimps, bullies, petty touts, bimbos, perverts, sharpers, catamites, sodomites and unspecified riff-raff, as well as the famine Irish with their emaciated looks and long thick swollen dicks. They were more in need of a feed than a broken-down tart, robbing their families of what little they had to boast of fornication with a poxy English whore.

Ikey counted himself fortunate to have found a wife as avaricious and morally corrupt as himself, yet one who could play the prim and proper lady when called upon to do so. Upon their marriage Hannah had adopted the demeanour in public of a woman of the highest moral rectitude with the strait-laced, scrubbed and honest appearance of a Methodist preacher's wife. This was only when she was in the presence of her betters and as practice for a time to come when, she told herself, she would run the most exclusive brothel in London Town.

Ikey's success as a fence had precluded such an establishment, designed, as it would be, to cater for the amorous needs of the better classes. It would be too public and draw too much attention. Hannah had reluctantly and temporarily put her ambitions aside. Instead, by working at the lowest end of the sex market, she often proved to be a useful adjunct to Ikey's fencing business.

This subjugation to her husband's needs did not come about from loyalty to him, but rather from simple greed. Ikey had been successful beyond her wildest expectations. Hannah began to see how she might one day escape to America or Australia, where she could set up as a woman of means and attain a position in society befitting her role as a wealthy widow with two beautiful daughters and four handsome sons, all eligible to be married into the best local families. It had always been quite clear in Hannah's mind that Ikey would not be a witness to her eventual triumph over the ugly scars which had so cruelly spoiled her face and with it, her fortune.

In the intervening period, Hannah felt that she had sound control of her husband. Her sharp and poisonous tongue kept him defensive and it was as much in her natural demeanour to act the bully as it was for Ikey to be a coward. She prodded him with insults and stung him with rude remarks as to his appearance. Ikey was constantly shamed in her presence. He knew he possessed no useful outside disguise to fool his fellow man and he greatly admired this propensity in her, who added further to his infatuation by giving him six children and proving his miserable, worthless and reluctant seed accountable.

Moreover, Hannah had gratified him still further, for none of his children had inherited any onerous part of his physiognomy and all took their looks strongly from her. She claimed that Ikey's puerile seed had been overwhelmed by her own splendid fecundity and, as he had no confident reason to doubt that this was true, he was grateful that she brought an end to his line of unfortunate looks. Hannah, who so clearly held Ikey in her thrall, had no cause whatsoever to suspect him capable of dalliance with another. The thought of a Mary or any other such female coming into Ikey's life was beyond even Hannah's considerable imagination or lack of trust in her husband.

Chapter Two

Temper and charm, it was these two contradictions in Mary's personality which were the cause of constant problems in her life. She showed the world a disarming and lovely smile until crossed. Then she could become a spitting tiger with anger enough to conquer any fear she might have or regard to her own prudent behaviour. In a servant girl, where mildness of manner and meek acceptance were the characteristics of a good domestic, Mary's often fiery disposition and sense of injustice were ill suited. However, without her temper – the pepper and vinegar in her soul – it is unlikely that she would have captured Ikey's unprepossessing heart.

Mary was the child of a silkweaver mother and a sometimes employed Dutch shipping clerk. She grew up in Spitalfields in pious poverty brought about by the decline in the silk and shipping trades in the years following Waterloo. Mary's consumptive mother was dying a slow death from overwork. Her despairing and defeated father sought solace in too frequent attention to the bottle. At the tender age of five Mary had learned to hawk her mother's meagre wares in nearby Rosemary Lane and to defend them from stock buzzers and the like. She quickly learned that a child faced with danger who screams, kicks, bites and scratches survives better than one given over to tears, though it should be noted that she was of a naturally sunny disposition and her temper was spent as quickly as it arrived.

Mary was also the possessor of a most curious gift. Although she could take to the task of reading and writing no better than a ten-year-old from the more tutored classes, she could calculate numbers and work columns of figures with a most astonishing rapidity and accuracy well beyond the ability of the most skilled bookkeeping clerk.

This ability had come about in a curious manner. Her father, Johannes Klerk, a name he'd amended simply to John Klerk when he'd come to England, had wanted Mary to be a boy and so instead of learning the art of silkweaving, as would have been the expected thing for a girl child to do, he had taught her the ways of figuring on an abacus. He learned this skill as a young man when he'd spent time as a shipping agent's clerk in the Dutch East Indies.

He had first come across the rapid clack-clack-clacking of beads sliding on elegant slender wire runners in Batavia. To his mortification, the framed contraption being used by the Chinee clerks in the spice warehouses soon proved superior in making calculations to his most ardent application by means of quill and blacking. Johannes Klerk soon learned that he could never hope to defeat the speed of their heathen calculations and so he determined to learn for himself the ancient art of the Chinese abacus. This curious skill, never developed to a very high aptitude in John Klerk, together with a few elementary lessons in reading and writing, was his sole inheritance to his daughter.

As an infant, the bright red and black beads had enchanted Mary and by the age of six she had grasped the true purpose of the colourful grid of wooden counters. By ten she had developed a propensity for calculation that left the shipping clerks at her father's sometime places of employment slack-jawed at her proficiency with numbers.

Alas, it was a skill which her family's poverty seldom required. But this did not discourage Mary, who practised until her fingers flew in a blur and her mind raced ahead of the brilliant lacquered beads. Despite her father's attempts to obtain a position for her as an apprentice clerk in one of the merchant warehouses on the docks, no such establishment would countenance a child who played with heathen beads. Added to this indignity, God had clearly indicated in his holy scriptures that those of her sex were not possessed of brain sufficient to work with numbers, and her ability to do so just as clearly indicated a madness within her.

When Mary was eleven, she was entered into domestic service by her father, her consumptive mother having died two years previously. John Klerk passed away not long after he'd secured employment for his daughter; he was a victim of a minor cholera epidemic which struck in the East India Docks.

Mary found herself quite alone in the world as a junior scullery maid in a large house where she was to begin what became a career, the outcome of which was determined more often by her fiery disposition than her maidenly demeanour.

Mary was popular among the below-stairs servants, well liked for her cheery disposition and bold intelligence, but her quick temper at some injustice shown to those unable to come to their own defence got her into constant hot water. She would inevitably alienate the cook or under-butler or coachman, those most terrible senior snobs in most households, who would thereafter wait for an opportunity to bring her undone. As a consequence Mary's career as a domestic servant was always somewhat tenuous.

At fifteen Mary was promoted above stairs, where she was a bedroom maid who would sometimes assist as lady's maid to her mistress. Her lively intelligence made her popular with her mistress, who felt she showed great promise as a future lady's maid. That is, until an incident occurred with a lady of grand title from Dorset, a weekend guest to the London house of her mistress to whom Mary was assigned as lady's maid.

Mary was most surprised when the very large duchess took her by the wrist after she had delivered her breakfast tray to her bed.

'Come into bed with me, m'dear. You will be well rewarded, now there's a dear. Come, my little cherub, and I promise you will learn one or two useful little things in the process!'

Whereupon the duchess, visibly panting with excitement, had pulled Mary off her feet so that she fell onto the bed across her large bosom.

'Oh I do hope you are a virgin, a nice little virgin for mummy!' the duchess exclaimed, planting several kisses on top of Mary's head.

Mary, a product of the Spitalfields rookery, wasn't easily given over to panic. She simply attempted to pull away from the fat duchess. Whereupon the huge woman, thinking this most coquettish, locked her arms about her and smothered her in further wet kisses. At this point Mary lost her temper. 'Lemme go, you old cow!' she gasped, still not taken to panicking at the mixture of sweet-smelling rouge and foul, dyspeptic breath which assailed her senses.

The duchess, much larger and stronger than the young servant girl, clasped her tighter so that Mary found her face smothered in heaving breasts and thought she might at any moment suffocate. She was no match for the strength of the duchess even though she fought like a tiger to break free.

'Such a silver tongue! Oh, you are a fiery little maidikins! A plump little partridge and all of it for mummy!'

With one huge arm the duchess continued to pin Mary down and with the other attempted to remove her bodice.

'Come now, darling,' she panted, 'be nice to mummikins!'

Mary, pushing away with her arms, momentarily managed to get her head free from the giant canyon of heaving flesh.

'You fat bitch!' she yelled. 'You keep your soddin' 'ands off me!'

It was to this last remark that her mistress, hearing the commotion, had entered the room. As a consequence, Mary lost her job, though her mistress was careful to furnish her with a good reference. It was well known in all the better houses that the duchess preferred her own sex to the wizened Duke of Dorset. She had, after all, come from poor stock, an ex-Drury Lane actress who had married the elderly and heirless duke and given him two sons in an amazingly short time, whereupon she had converted her stylish figure and good looks into lard and her taste from male to her own sex, with a decided preference for plump young servant girls.

In those late-Georgian times there remained in some London households a little of an earlier tolerance for the sexual proclivities, preferments and foibles of the nobility, and Mary's mistress was not as scandalised over the incident as might have been the case a little further into the century when the young Victoria ascended to the throne. Her parting words to Mary had proved most instructive to the young maidservant.

'You are a good worker, Mary, and quite a bright little creature, though you really must learn to respect the wishes of your betters and to control your peppery tongue. Have you not been instructed in your childhood in the manners required of your kind? Were you not taught by Mr Bothwaite the butler by heart the verse of the noble Dr Watts when you came into our employment?'

'Yes, ma'am.'

'And what does it say? Repeat it, if you please!'

Mary scratched around in her mind for the words to the catechism which every young domestic was expected to know upon commencement of employment in a big house. In a voice barely above a whisper she now recited the words to the verse:

Though I am but poor and mean,
I will move the rich to love me.
If I'm modest, neat and clean,
And submit when they reprove me.

'There you are, so very neatly put in a single verse by the great hymnist, you would do well to remember it in the future.'

Whereupon Mary's mistress gave her a not unkindly smile.

'Now you will not mention this unfortunate incident at your next position, will you? I have given you an excellent reference,' she paused, 'though it can always be withdrawn if it comes to my ears that there has been some idle tittle-tattle below stairs.' She placed her hand on Mary's arm. 'You do understand what I'm saying, don't you, my dear?'

Mary understood perfectly well. From the incident with the duchess she had derived several lessons; the first being not to resist the advances made to her, but instead to profit from them. The next, that a scandal, should she be caught with a member of the family or guest, gave her power to negotiate and so to leave her place of employment with her reputation intact.

Mary also understood the different standards which prevailed for promiscuous behaviour below stairs. Similar comportment involving a male member of the household staff would leave her without references, on the street, without the least prospect of obtaining a job in any respectable London house.

Mary even understood that she could learn to keep her big mouth shut. Though in this last endeavour she was never to prove very successful and she would privately, and to the secret delight of the junior maids below stairs, declare the verse by the great Dr Watts to be a load of utter shit.

Before her ultimate undoing she had served in two further households. In the first, the master of the house had left her several gold sovereigns richer, and in the second she had been promoted to the position of abigail, that is, lady's maid, and the youngest son in the family had been inducted by her into the delights of Aphrodite in return for lessons in reading and writing.

When two years later this scion of the family went up to Oxford, Mary was promptly, though discreetly, dismissed, again with an excellent reference and, as a result of her lover's tuition, a small knowledge of Latin and a facility at writing which was contained in a good copperplate hand studiously learned from a copybook he had bought for her. On return from the Michaelmas term her boy lover was said to have wept openly at the discovery that his dearest mumsy was now attended by a flaccid and cheerless personal maid in her late forties.

Mary's next billet was to prove her final undoing. Appointed as upstairs maid she soon found herself at odds with the family nanny, a middle-aged lady of imperious manner known as Nanny Smith. Well established in the family, the old woman exercised considerable power over all the other servants. She soon took a dislike to the new young maid, who seemed much too forward and confident around the male servants in the house and was not in the least afraid to speak before she was spoken to.

For her part Mary accepted Nanny Smith's carping instructions and held her tongue. But one day the old girl accused her of poisoning her cat, an aged tabby named Waterloo Smith who coughed up fur balls on the Persian rugs and stumbled about with a constant wheeze and permanently dripping nose. Mary had made no attempt to conceal her dislike for this creature, who returned the compliment by arching its back and hissing at her whenever they met along a corridor or in one of the many upstairs rooms.

'You ought to be dead and buried, you miserable moggy!' Mary would hiss back. Her abhorrence for Nanny Smith's cat was soon the joke of the below stairs staff and no doubt her dislike was soon communicated to Waterloo Smith's ill-tempered owner.

Then one morning Waterloo Smith went missing. Nanny Smith had placed him as usual on a broad upstairs window ledge to catch the morning sun and upon her return an hour later he was nowhere to be seen.

Mary, together with the second upstairs maid, was made to search every cupboard, nook and cranny and under each bed and, in the unlikely event that the disabled creature had somehow managed to negotiate the stairs, each of the four levels of the downstairs area of the house.

Bishop, the butler, had ordered the footman, the stable boy and Old Jacob the gardener to inspect the lavender bushes which grew forty feet below the window ledge where Waterloo Smith had been sunning himself. When this yielded nothing the speculation that foul play was involved started to grow. While nothing was said, Mary's well-known dislike for the cat made her the prime suspect.

By evening it became apparent that Waterloo Smith had disappeared quite into thin air, and his distraught owner retired to her bedroom, where her unconstrained weeping could be heard by all who worked above stairs.

Mary was given the task of taking a supper tray to the old lady and upon knocking on Nanny Smith's door the weeping from the other side immediately increased in volume.

'Come in,' the old woman's tremulous voice cried.

'Cook 'as made you a nice bit 'o tea and 'opes you feels better,' Mary said, placing the tray down beside Nanny Smith, who lay on the bed with a silk scarf covering her head.

At the sound of Mary's voice Nanny Smith sat bolt upright, the scarf falling to the floor. 'You did it, didn't you! You killed him!' she screamed, pointing a trembling finger at Mary.

Mary's jaw dropped in astonishment at this pronouncement and as she bent to retrieve the scarf the old woman continued, 'You horrid, horrid girl, pushed my pussy! I shall see that you are dismissed at once!'

Mary should have immediately panicked at Nanny Smith's words, for this time she was in no position to negotiate. The old cow's word against her own left her in no doubt as to who would prevail. Then Nanny Smith snatched the scarf from Mary's hands in such a rude manner that Mary lost her temper and a deep flush overtook her face.

'I never laid a finger on your bloody cat! Though I must say it's good riddance to bad rubbish, if you ask me, with 'im hissin' and wheezin' and doin' 'is mess all over the place! I 'ope 'e broke 'is bloody neck!' The offending words were barely out before Mary regretted them.

The following morning, in the manner to which his breed had been trained for countless generations, Samuel the family spaniel politely presented Waterloo Smith, stiff as a board, to Mrs Hodge the cook at the kitchen door.

Waterloo Smith's fur was matted and covered in fresh dirt, suggesting that Samuel, finding the dead cat in the lavender bushes, had contrived a hasty burial in some remoter part of the kitchen garden, but that later his conscience got the better of him and he'd repented by laying the dead cat at the feet of the cook.

Later at the inquest held in the library, Mr Bishop, seeking to console Nanny Smith, opened the proceedings by suggesting that the unfortunate creature might have died from natural causes – a fit, or convulsions or similar which had by natural movement catapulted Waterloo Smith from the window ledge?

However, the dead cat's distraught owner, red-eyed from weeping, wouldn't countenance this suggestion and declared flatly that her darling had been brutally murdered.

Nanny Smith glared meaningfully at Mary, who had been summoned to the library together with the other upstairs servants. 'We all *know* who the murderer is, don't we?' she sniffed and then buried her head in her hands and wept copiously.

Turning to Mary, Mr Bishop enquired, 'Mary, the room in which Waterloo Smith was last seen is your responsibility to clean. Did you see the cat on the window ledge?'

'I saw 'im, Mr Bishop! But I swear to Gawd I never laid a finger on 'im! I swear it on me dead mother's grave!'

With no further evidence to go on, Mr Bishop terminated the proceedings and Waterloo Smith's murderer, if such a person existed, was never apprehended. In fact, Mr Bishop had been correct in the first place; Waterloo Smith had suffered a violent fit followed by a stroke, the contractions of which had thrown him from the sun-bathed window sill to a merciful death in the lavender bushes four storeys below.

However, Nanny Smith was not to be thwarted and she caused such a disturbance with the master and mistress of the house that the butler was summoned and Mary, despite her protestations of innocence and Mr Bishop himself believing her not guilty, was stripped of her starched pinny and mob cap and banished below stairs to the laundry.

The laundry was the most onerous task among the skilled domestic duties and therefore the most humble and disliked. But Mary, who had never been afraid of work, discovered that if she worked hard she had time for reading and for practising her handwriting. Besides, the laundry was the warmest place in the big cold house and, like most children from the rookeries, she suffered greatly from chilblains.

Mary remained in the laundry for three years, even taking pride in her work, in starching and ironing, removing stains by bleaching with the juice of lemons and in mending, so that she became a useful, though not excellent, seamstress. By this time her reading and writing skills were much enhanced and she had graduated from the penny papers that pandered to the taste of the lower classes for bloodthirsty plots and overblown romances, to serious literature. Mr Bishop, feeling guilty for having politely complied with her demotion to the laundry without positive proof that she had pushed the cat from the window sill, negotiated for Mary to use the master's library. The master had agreed to this, providing the books were always taken from the shelves in his presence and after he had closely inspected the state of her hands.

It was in books that Mary discovered a world beyond any of her possible imaginings – Defoe's *Robinson Crusoe* and Jonathan Swift's *Gulliver's Travels* which she especially liked and read many times, quoting often from it to Mr Bishop; Thackeray, Macaulay, an excellent English translation of Cervantes' wondrously mad *Don Quixote*, Jane Austen and Fanny Burney. All these and a host of others she devoured with a great thirst for knowledge.

While reading became her abiding passion, Mary did not connect the lives of the people she read about in books with her own. Her earlier life had been difficult and the people about her for the most part poverty-stricken, dulled and witless from lack of proper sustenance and the absence of any education. That is, apart from the kind needed to survive among thieves, scoundrels and villains. From a young age she knew the world to be a wicked place and had learned to defend the small space she occupied in it with her teeth and nails.

However, the human mind has the fortunate capacity to forget pain and misery. Mary had been in the protected environment of a domestic servant in a big house from the age of eleven, so by the age of twenty she had all but buried the turmoil of her younger years. The sheltered life she now led meant she had gained little additional experience of the adult world other than the hurriedly taken copulative embraces thrust upon her by two of her past masters and the infinitely more pleasant, though inexperienced, couplings with the young master of the last employer.

Mary did not regard these hasty assignations as the same act of fornication she had observed against the walls in alleys or on the dark stairwells of shared lodgings or in the nesting midnight rooms, occupied by three destitute families, in which she and her father had been reduced to living in the years before she'd entered domestic service.

Some unknown affliction in childhood had rendered Mary sterile, not that she even equated the hasty love-making with her betters with the act of childbirth. Despite the presence of children in the houses in which she'd served, if she'd thought about it at all, she would perhaps have concluded that the idle rich had their children conveniently delivered by a stork, the evidence of this being ever present on the nursery wall. That the better classes should employ the same vile animal instincts which had been such a familiar aspect of her childhood would have seemed to her unthinkable.

In fact, Mary was both streetwise and naive all at once. While she longed for romance she knew in her heart that it was not intended for her kind, that *doing it* in some privacy with a clean and half-decent someone was the best she could hope for. Her body developed into a very desirable womanliness, and she would often feel the ache to use it other than by the deployment of her probing and urgent fingers.

Her moment came one morning at Shepherd Market in nearby Mayfair where she had been sent by Mrs Hodge to purchase the master's luncheon sole, Billingsgate being too far to walk and the coachman out with the mistress of the house all morning.

'Take the one wif the clearest eyes, lovey.' The young man pointed to a fish which lay upon a block of ice slightly to one side. 'That one! See the eyes, clear as a gypsy's crystal.'

Mary turned towards the voice and its owner smiled, showing two missing front teeth with the eye tooth on either side framing the gap and capped with gold. It was a smile devoid of any calculation, though mischievous enough.

Mary found herself smiling back, even though more prudent behaviour was called for from a servant girl in a nice house involved in a casual meeting with a strange man. She found herself immediately taken by the flash young man standing beside her and her heart beat in quite the strangest manner.

The possessor of these two astonishing gold teeth was flash in other ways too and wore a fancy corduroy waistcoat with a watch chain. His ankle boots, below a fashionable pair of breeches, were stitched with patterns of hearts and roses. His cloth coat with contrasting plush lapels was clean and carried large expensive pearl buttons and was cut to the back into heavily braided calf-clingers with an artful line of buttons at their extremity. On his head he wore a beaver-napped top hat that looked to be in excellent order, its nap neatly brushed and shining.

'Name o' Bob Marley, pleased to meetcha,' he'd said in a single breath, giving her another big grin which caused his incisor teeth to once more gleam and flash. 'Honoured to make yer acquaintance, Miss . . .?'

Mary had observed that he hadn't once taken his eyes away from her face and unlike most men with whom she had the slightest passing acquaintance, hadn't allowed his eyes to wander over those parts of her anatomy which usually brought a glazed look into their eyes and a gravel tone in their voices. His smile was ingenuous, quite open and impossible to resist.

'Mary,' she said simply. 'Them's lovely teeth,' she added, smiling.

Bob Marley jabbed a finger at his mouth, 'Like 'em does ya? Eighteen carat, that is! Pure gold, can't get none better!'

Bob Marley cast his eyes over Mary's firm breasts and trim waist, and in an unabashed voiced declared, 'What a corker! Care for a drop o' ruin?' He indicated the public house with a toss of his head. 'Come on then, I'll buy ya a taste o' whatever's yer fancy, gin is it, or a pint o' best beer?'

Mary, though sorely tempted, could not accept his invitation for fear of upsetting Mrs Hodge by being late and returning to the house with the smell of strong spirits on her breath. She was not accustomed to drink, though on the rare occasions when, on a public holiday, she'd ventured out with Mrs Hodge, she'd found gin left her very excited in a physical sort of way.

'I'll not be seen with a costermonger,' she said tartly, this seeming the best way to end a relationship where she was already beginning to feel at a distinct disadvantage. She noted too that her breasts were heaving and she was finding it difficult to breathe.

Bob Marley drew back with an exaggerated expression of hurt. Cocking his head to one side, his mouth turned down at the corner, he looked down at his chest as though closely examining his apparel. 'Costermonger? Not bleedin' likely, lovey.' He patted a velvet lapel. 'This is me disguise. I'm what ya might call an hoperator, I do a bit o' this and a bit o' that, finding' a bit 'ere and disposin' of it over there, if ya knows what I mean?'

'Oh, a tout?' Mary shot back, bringing her fingers to her lips as she tried to contain her laughter.

'Well not exactly that neiver, jus' . . . well . . . er,' he smiled his golden smile, 'an hoperator!' He seemed disinclined to further discuss the subject of his occupation. 'Well, what 'bout yer place, then?' Bob Marley said cheekily tugging on his watch chain and taking Mary by the elbow.

'Who do you think I am? I ain't no dollymop! Shame on you, Bob Marley!' Mary pulled her arm away from him. But then she laughed, enchanted by the young rogue standing beside her. 'You can walk me 'ome and no touchin', that's all I'll promise for now.'

By the time they reached the house in Chelsea Mary was completely smitten by the young rogue. She kept him waiting in the lane at the back of the house while she unlocked the stout door set into the kitchen garden wall, whereupon she went directly into the kitchen to deliver the sole to Mrs Hodge, who, predictably, scolded her for the time she had taken on her errand.

Mary's heart pounded in her breast as she returned down the garden path to open the garden door and let Bob Marley within the precincts of the kitchen garden. Quickly locking the door behind him, she led him into the laundry.

Now, with less than half an hour having passed, fat Mrs Hodge stood over Mary's half-naked body having hysterics and crying out in alarm at the astonishing gymnastics taking place on a pile of dirty linen at her feet.

Bob Marley was the first to react. Frantically pulling on his breeches and snatching up his embroidered boots, he jumped to his feet and fled the scene, knocking aside the stout cook with his shoulder and escaping into the kitchen garden. Not bothering to test the door set into the garden wall, he threw his boots over the top into the lane beyond and, quick as a rat up a drainpipe, scrambled after them, stubbing his toe badly in the process, pausing only long enough on the other side to retrieve his boots before making good his escape down the lane and into the Kings Road beyond.

Mary found herself dismissed from her place of employment

without references or even the wages due to her. Not an hour after her interrupted dalliance with Bob Marley she stood in the lane outside the rear of the large Chelsea house, her sole possessions the small wicker basket at her feet and her precious abacus under her arm. She glanced up at the big house and observed the odious Nanny Smith looking down at her from a top window. When the old woman realised Mary had seen her she leaned further out of the window and commenced to hiss in much the same manner as Waterloo Smith had done.

'The pox on you, you old cow!' Mary shouted up at her and then, picking up her basket, she proceeded to cross the lane. Then turning once again to look up at Nanny Smith, she yelled, 'I pushed your bloody cat off the window sill with me broom, it done two somersaults before it splattered on the ground!'

Then, head held high and withourt further ado, Mary proceeded in the direction of Hyde Park, not knowing why she'd bothered to lie to the old crone and not even sure why she had chosen this direction from any other, thinking only that she would find a quiet spot under one of the giant old beech trees and try to sort things out in her head.

Mary's future lay in tatters. She found a bench beside the Serpentine adjacent to a willow which hid her presence from passers-by. But no sooner was she seated than a dozen small brown ducks glided towards her, their webbed feet paddling frantically below the surface to give their smooth little bodies the look of effortless gliding. It was clear that they anticipated food from the wicker basket.

When Mary saw the ducks, quacking and fussing at the edge of the water, she realised Mrs Hodge hadn't even offered her a morsel to eat. A stern Mr Bishop had bid her pack her things and had shown her the door in the kitchen garden. Then, to Mary's enormous surprise, just as he was closing the door behind her, Mr Bishop pressed a small parcel upon her and announced in a deeply injured tone, 'You are ruined, my girl, utterly and completely ruined!' He paused and then added in the same melancholy voice, 'Now I simply cannot propose marriage to you.'

The door had closed behind her before Mary could fully comprehend this curious protestation. Mr Bishop had never entered the smallest part of her amorous imaginings, nor had he, perhaps with the exception of the obtaining of books from the master's library, shown any inclination to be especially kind to her. She placed the squarish parcel absently within her basket.

Now hungry and with nowhere to go, Mary started to weep softly. Although truthfully her tears were more for the warmth and security of Mrs Hodge's kitchen and the steaming plates of food so regularly placed in front of her than they were for love's labour lost with Bob Marley or, for that matter, Mr Bishop.

After a while Mary wiped her nose and dried her reddened eyes. 'C'mon, girl, cryin' never got a day's work done,' she said to herself, repeating a phrase she had heard so often as a little girl coming from her overburdened and sad-faced mother. She thought then for the first time about the parcel the butler had handed to her. Removing it from her basket she removed the wrapping to reveal the book *Gulliver's Travels*, quite her favourite. She smiled, feeling somewhat better towards life and the clumsy man whose marriage prospects she had so inadvertently ruined. Picking up her abacus and wicker basket, she crossed the park in an easterly direction to St Giles, where she knew from bitter experience she could obtain cheap lodgings.

Chapter Three

It would be nice to report that Mary's literacy skills and excellent penmanship, together with her wizardry with numbers, led to a new and fortunate life. Alas, these were not skills required of a woman at that time and most certainly not of a woman of her class. In the next six months she wore out a pair of stout boots in an effort to obtain employment as a clerk. She was always the lone woman in a long queue of applicants for a position advertised, and she soon became the butt of their cruel male jokes.

Furthermore, her abacus was the cause of much hilarity among the prospective clerks. Mary's persistent presence in the line of men would soon lead to her being known to them by the nickname Bloody Mary. This came about after an incident when a tall, very thin young man with a pale pinched face and sharp rodent teeth, wearing a battered top hat that resembled a somewhat misshapen chimney stack, snatched Mary's abacus from her. He held it in front of her face announcing to the men in the line, 'See, gentlemen, a monkey, a lovely little monkey in a cage playin' at being a clerk with pretty beads!'

It was a feeble enough joke but one which nevertheless brought some hilarity to the anxious line of unemployed men eager for any sort of distraction to alleviate the boredom. Mary snatched her abacus back from the ferret-faced clown and, lifting it, slammed it down upon the young comic's head, causing the top hat he wore to concertina over his eyes and halfway along his narrow snotty nose. This created a great deal more hilarity in all but the unfortunate owner of the hat who, upon removing the object of their mirth and pulling and bashing it back into some semblance of its original shape, placed it again upon his head, then delivered a vicious blow to Mary's nose before running from the scene.

Mary's nose had not yet stopped bleeding by the time it became her turn for an interview. The chief clerk, a coarsely corpulent man with a sanguine complexion and the remains of fiery red hair on the sides of a completely bald pate, looked at her with disapproval, shaking his head in a most melodramatic manner. 'What's the name, girl?' he asked.

'Mary, sir, Mary Klerk.'

'Bloody Mary, more like!' The men in the queue laughed uproariously at this joke. 'G'warn scarper! Be off with you, girl. 'Aven't you been told, clerkin's a man's job!'

The men clapped and cheered him mightily and pleased with their response the chief clerk played further to the crowd, for he'd witnessed the earlier incident with the clown in the top hat. 'What's to become of us if we allow a monkey on our backs?'

There is precious little charity in a queue of starving men, most of whom had a wife and young ones to feed, and soon upon Mary's arrival in any employment queue, a familiar chant would go up:

Mary, Mary, Bloody Mary
Who does her sums on bead and rack
Go away, you're too contrary
You're the monkey, the bloody monkey
You're the monkey on our back!

The chant was to become such an aggravation that few prospective employers were prepared to even grant her an interview for fear of angering the men. The men, in turn, found it impossible to understand why a woman with a trim figure, of Mary's young age and class, could not make a perfectly good living on her back. More and more they came to regard it as entirely reprehensible that she should attempt to steal the bread from their mouths and allow their children to starve and, moreover, that she should attempt to do so with the help of a foreign and heathen contraption made of wood, wire and beads. They told themselves that a screen that quivered and rattled and ended up doing sums had a distinct smell of witchcraft about it.

As the weather turned colder and the queue more desperate, the resentment against Mary grew out of all proportion. In the fevered imaginations of the unemployed clerks Bloody Mary's presence in a job queue soon took on all the aspects of a bad omen. When they returned home empty-handed to their ragged and starving families they had come to believe that her presence had 'soured the queue', so the luck they all felt they needed to gain a position had gone elsewhere.

Mary's face had grown gaunt for lack of sufficient nourishment and, in truth, there began to be a somewhat simian look about her. With her large green anxious eyes darting about and her head turning nervously this way and that, expecting danger from every corner, the men began to believe increasingly that she was an incarnation of some evil monkey spirit.

Her dress too began to be much the worse for wear and hung upon her thin frame to give Mary an altogether morbid appearance, her black cotton skirt and blouse, and modest bonnet and shawl, together with her worn boots peeping below the frayed edges of her skirt, all showed the wear and tear of the long hours spent standing patiently in every kind of inclement weather.

While there were tens of thousands of women in a similar state of dress, their own wives being of much the same appearance, they saw in Mary's forlorn and ragged clothing the black cloth of a witch's weeds. The monkey chant, as it became known, grew increasingly threatening in tone and it took the utmost stubbornness and will for Mary to present herself at an advertised location for a job interview.

Yet Mary persisted well beyond the dictates of commonsense and into the province of foolishness. The long hours spent at reading and writing and the childhood application she had demonstrated with the complexities of mathematics had somehow convinced her that within her capacity lay a destiny beyond her humble beginnings. Mary's father had told her almost from infancy that her abacus would be her salvation and she could not believe that she might end up like her consumptive silkweaver mother or the sad, destitute and drunken shipping clerk she knew

28

as her father. She saw herself achieving something well beyond the modest expectations of a laundry maid, though quite what this could be was past anything she could imagine. She felt certain that this destiny would all begin, if only she could obtain a position as a clerk.

After six months Mary had used up most of her savings and had repeatedly changed her place of residence, on each occasion moving to a cheaper lodging house, until she ended up sharing a foul room with a family of five in the very cheapest of netherkens in Shoe Lane.

She would wake at dawn each morning and, with no more than a drink of water and without allowing herself to think, set out to seek employment, fearful that, should she pause to contemplate her increasingly desperate position, she would give up altogether and take herself to Waterloo Bridge and commit herself to the dark, foul river.

One bitterly cold morning she left her miserable lodgings at dawn to be the first in line for a clerk's position advertised in a warehouse on the south bank of the Thames at Saviour's Dock. This was one of the vilest slums in London, and the mist lay thick on the river, and the streets were dimmed to near blindness by the sulphurous-coloured smog from the first of the winter fires.

Huddled at the entrance of the gate and near frozen, Mary was thankful that her presence would be concealed by the thick fog. The misted air about her was filled with the groans of masts and cross stays. In her imagination, the dockside took on the shape of a jungle filled with the wild and fearsome growls of fantastical creatures, while the howl of the wind through a dozen mizzen masts and the slap of loose canvas became the spirits of the dead which had come to protect her from the living, the men who would soon be lined up behind her and who had the capacity to frighten her beyond any perceived ghosts.

She had not eaten for two days and in her state of weakness must have fallen asleep, for she was awakened by the toe of the gateman's boot placed against her buttocks.

'Be up now, the gov'nor will be on 'is way soon!' a gruff voice demanded. Mary stumbled to her feet, clutching her shawl about her thin shoulders. 'Blimey, if it ain't a female!' the voice exclaimed in surprise.

A large man dressed in a military great coat with a shako,

polished like a mirror, upon his head stood towering over her. It was the shako cap, complete with its scarlet and white cockade and braid, otherwise devoid of any regimental insignia, that gave the man his fearsome authority. Mary had expected the customary gateman in cloth cap, woollen scarf, corduroy breeches and workman's boots, the advertisement having instructed simply that the queue would commence at the gate under the gateman's supervision.

'Yessir, I be enquirin' about the billet advertised. The one for a clerk?'

'Well then, I s'pose it ain't against the law now is it?' The gateman twisted the corner of his large moustache. 'It's a pretty rum turn, but I can't see that it be against the law. First is you? You shall 'ave your interview, miss.'

Glancing fearfully at the formless shapes of the men disappearing into the fog behind her, Mary felt suddenly safe and strangely hopeful. She told herself that such an unpropitious day must surely bring her luck. The first good omen had been that the men standing directly behind her were strangers and seemed not to recognise her. The ones behind them, pale shapes in the mist, would surely have among them a great many who were acquainted with her, but these had not yet become aware of her presence in the thick yellow fog.

The gateman turned away from her to address the vaguely defined line of men stretching away behind Mary.

'Now then, gentlemen, me name's Sergeant William Lawrence, late of the 40th regiment, veteran o' the Peninsular War, wounded in action at the Battle o' Waterloo. I am the gatekeeper 'ere and I'll brook no interference. It will be one at a time through the gate, no pushin' and shovin' and no idle chatter, if you please!'

There was a murmur in the crowd at the sound of a carriage rattling over distant cobblestones and then the rumble of its wheels as it drew onto the wooden dockside and shortly afterwards came to halt at the gate, the horse snuffling and shaking its head, blowing frosted air from its distended nostrils.

Mary, who stood close enough to see clearly, observed a small, very fat man alight. He was dressed in a heavy coat which swept to within an inch of the ground in the manner of a woman's skirt, his shoes being quite lost from sight. He wore a top hat which sat upon his head down almost to his eyes and rose alarmingly high into the air for a man so short. The remaining space between head and shoulders was wrapped in a woollen scarf so that in the uncertainty of the mist the whole of him took on the proportions of a very large perambulating bottle. The gatekeeper snapped to immediate attention and gave the bottle shape a rigid salute, his jowls and side-burns quivering with the momentum of it.

'Mornin', Mr Goldstein, sah!' Sergeant Lawrence shouted at the very top of his voice as though addressing the commander of a battalion of soldiers who was about to embark on a parade inspection.

'Goot mornink,' the bottle replied in a muffled voice. Then, without glancing at the line of men it entered the gate and waddled into the mist towards the unseen warehouse not twenty feet away.

The gatekeeper, pushing his hand between two brass buttons and into the interior of the great coat, pulled from within it a watch chain which soon enough produced a large, though not expensive-looking, watch. Glancing down at it from under his peaked cap he addressed the queue.

'I shall allow five minutes for Mr Goldstein to settle and then the first in the line will proceed through the gate to the door! You will oblige Mr Goldstein by knockin' on the outside door, whereupon you will remove your 'at and proceed in an inwardly direction and without waitin' for an answer! Mr Goldstein will be in the office to the left of the door upon which you shall again knock and then immediately enter! For them what is ambidextrous and 'asn't 'ad the misfortune to 'ave been trained in 'is Majesty's military forces, the left side is the side what's got the coat-stand!'

Anxious laughter came from the mist as men strained to catch every word, fearful of the consequences of making a mistake.

The imperious Sergeant Lawrence looked down at his watch again and then glanced sternly at Mary.

'Goldstein, you understand, miss? *Mr Goldstein*!'

Mary nodded, feeling herself beginning to tremble.

Mary knocked on the outer door of the warehouse and then, without waiting for a reply, did as she had been told and entered. To her left was a heavy, free-standing coat-stand on which hung the overgrown top hat together with its owner's coat and scarf. Behind it was a door with a frosted glass upper panel on which in gold relief lettering was the name *Jacob Goldstein, Prop.* The door seemed designed especially for Mr Goldstein, for it was not an inch higher than five feet though one and a half times as wide as one might normally expect an office door to be. Mary tapped nervously on the surface of the glass, her heart pounding in her ears, her knees feeling light, as though they might give at any moment, and the palms of her hands were wet.

'You must be here comink, please,' a voice answered in an accent which Mary immediately recognised. She had spent her childhood around Rosemary Lane and the Whitechapel markets and the accent was unmistakably that of a German Jew.

Mary entered and curtsied to the man, who sat well back from a large desk. He was dressed in a morning suit and his huge stomach, she felt certain, would not permit his very short arms to reach to the edge of the desk, the top of which contained a pot of blacking and a goose quill pen, a large writing tablet and a medium-sized brass bell of the kind a schoolmaster might use to summon his pupils from play.

'Good mornin', Mr Goldstein,' Mary said, summoning all her courage into a nervous smile.

Mr Goldstein seemed astonished to see her and commenced immediately to bluster.

'Ach! Vot is dis? A vooman? You are a vooman! Vot is vanting a vooman here? You are vanting to see me, ja?'

'I come about the job, sir. The assistant clerk . . . the position what was advertised?'

Mr Goldstein's bewilderment persisted and Mary added desperately, 'It were advertised on the 'oardings, sir.'

'You are a vooman and you vant you can be a clerk?' Mr Goldstein was now somewhat recovered, though still plainly bemused.

'I'm most 'appy to do a test, anythin' you want, sir! Please, your 'onour, er, Mr Goldstein, don't send me away, give me a chance, I can do it, gov . . . honest I can!'

Mary was suddenly conscious of Mr Goldstein staring at the region of her waist and that the merest semblance of a smile had appeared on his moon-round face.

'Abacus!' He pointed a fat finger at her midriff. 'You can use, ja?'

'Yes, sir, Mr Goldstein, your honour, since I was a brat . . . er child, give me a sum, any sum you like, sir.'

'In Armenia, also ven I vos a *Kind*! *Das ist wunderbar*!' he chuckled. 'You are vonting I should give you some sums? Ja, I can do zis!'

Whereupon, to Mary's astonishment, he pushed his chair violently backwards. She now saw it to be on tiny wheels and possessed of a seat which could swivel. She observed that the points of his highly polished boots only just touched the floor. Using them to gain a purchase Mr Goldstein spun himself around so that the chair, with his fat dumpling body within it, flashed past her astonished face fully four times, much like an egg in an egg cup turned into a merry-go-round.

When it came to a halt Mary could see that Mr Goldstein now sat considerably closer to the ground and that his boots were planted firmly upon it. Propelling himself towards the desk his stomach now fitted neatly beneath it, the desktop coming to just under his arms.

'A test? Ja, das is gut!' He pointed to the abacus. 'From vere are you learnink zis?'

'My father, sir. 'E were in the East Hindies.'

'He is Chinee man?'

'No, sir . . . er, Mr Goldstein, 'e were a Dutchie, from 'Olland.'

Mr Goldstein reached for his quill and dipping it into the small pot of blacking he hastily scrawled an elaborate equation on the pad in front of him. Then he pushed it over to Mary.

Mary examined the problem scrawled on the paper tablet. Then, laying it down, she placed her abacus beside it and began immediately to move the beads across the thin wire rails, her long, slender fingers blurring with the speed of her movements. She hesitated once or twice before once again sending the bright beads flying. In a short time she slapped the last bead into place and stood back looking down at Mr Goldstein. There had never been a more important moment in Mary's life.

She looked up to see that Mr Goldstein was smiling and holding a gold hunter open in his hand. Mary announced quietly, though her heart was once again pounding furiously and she fought to keep her breathing steady, 'Eight 'undred and sixty-two pounds . . . at eleven pounds, fourteen shillin's and sixpence ha'penny a case, sir . . . er, Mr Goldstein.'

'Gut! Gut, young lady, in vun half minute! Now ve can see, ja?'

He placed the watch down on the desk and sliding open a drawer produced a large ledger which he opened and examined for a moment, running his fat index finger down several columns until it came to rest.

'Ja! Das is gut! And also *schnell*!'

'Beg pardon, sir?'

'Very fast!' he beamed. 'You can write also in ledger?'

He pointed to the pad on which he'd written previously and returning his quill into the blacking pot he handed it to Mary.

'Please . . . Numbers, also vords, let me see?'

Mr Bishop had not only provided books for Mary from the master's library but, upon her beseeching him, had on several occasions found old ledgers for her to copy out. Mary had studied these assiduously, emulating their neat columns and precise language a thousand times until she knew the contents of every page in her sleep. Now she wrote carefully in the well-formed and almost elegant copperplate she had studied so hard at the hands of her young Oxford lover, and later for countless hours on her own, to perfect.

34 cases @ a total of six hundred and twelve pounds no shillings and eightpence = seventeen pounds, one shilling and sevenpence halfpenny per case.

Then she repeated the sum in neat numerals directly below this sentence. She handed the quill and pad back to Mr Goldstein.

Mr Goldstein examined Mary's writing for a sufficient period of time for her to grow anxious that she might have made a mistake. Then he looked up, his expression stern and businesslike, shaking a fat finger with a large gold ring directly at her as in admonishment.

'I pay eight shillink for vun veek and Saturday only no verk. Half-past seven you are startink, eight o'clock you are finishink. Tomorrow half-past seven o'clock report, if you please, Mr Baskin, who is also here the senior clerk.'

Mr Goldstein pointed his stubby finger at the abacus, 'Gut!' he said.

Unclenching his remaining fingers he patted the air in front of him as though he were patting the abacus in approval, giving Mary the distinct impression that he had not employed her, but her frame of wooden beads.

Mary had to restrain herself from bursting into tears of joy.

'Thank you, sir, Mr Goldstein! You'll not regret it! Thank you and Gawd bless you, sir!'

Mr Goldstein grunted and taking up the bell on the desk he rang it loudly several times. Mary now became conscious that, in the short time she'd been in Mr Goldstein's office, the warehouse had filled with the hum of people going about their work. Now the buzz and clatter stopped as the bell rang out.

'Mr Baskin!' Mr Goldstein shouted into the sudden calm.

Presently a tall and very thin, Ichabod-Crane-looking man, stooping almost double, opened the wide door and entered the office. Mr Goldstein, writing in the ledger, ignored his presence for a full minute while the man stood with his hands clasped in the manner of a mendicant, his head downcast and his eyes avoiding contact with Mary.

Looking up from his ledger Mr Goldstein pointed directly at the abacus.

'Tomorrow Miss . . .' he suddenly realised that he had not enquired as to Mary's name, '. . . Miss Abacus!' he added suddenly and smiled at Mary. 'Ja! I can call you this!' He returned his gaze to Mr Baskin, 'Tomorrow she is startink vork. You show her varehouse, please!'

'Very well, sir, at once, show her the warehouse is it, Mr Goldstein? I shall attend to Miss Aba . . . Abacus?' He paused. 'For what purpose may I ask? A visit is it?'

Mr Goldstein looked up. 'Clerk, she is new clerk!' he said impatiently and then returned his attention to the ledger.

'The position? A woman? New clerk?' Mr Baskin was clearly confused as though the three bits of information couldn't somehow be joined together in his mind.

'Ja, of course, *Dummkopf*! Next veek she is maybe havink your job!'

Mr Baskin stiffened to attention as the three bits of previously disparate information, with an almost audible clang, shunted into place in his mind.

Once outside the office and well clear she turned to the unfortunate Mr Baskin. 'Me name ain't Abacus, sir, it's Klerk, spelt with a "K", it's a Dutchie name, me father was a Dutchman.'

Mr Baskin looked directly at her for the first time. 'If Mr Goldstein says its Abacus, then that's what it be!' Mr Baskin sniffed. 'No arguments will be entered into and the contract is legal and binding.'

He paused and seemed to be thinking and, indeed, his expression suddenly brightened. 'Unless . . .' he began looking directly down at Mary again.

'What?' Mary asked suspiciously.

'You don't turn up for work tomorrow!' Mr Baskin's expression took on a most beseeching look and his voice carried a whining tone. 'It would be a most honourable and decent thing to do, Miss . . . Miss?'

'Klerk!'

'Ah!' Mr Baskin said pleased. 'Ah, yes, well that's it, then isn't it? That is precisely the situation! We have no position here for a Miss Klerk! No such person is known to us here! Mr Goldstein knows of no such person! I know of no such person! No such person exists, I'm very much afraid to say you're a missing person! You will not be commencing tomorrow, we shall not be expecting a Miss Klerk!'

Mr Baskin announced this as though Mary were some impostor whom, just in the nick of time, he had cleverly exposed and quickly undone.

Mary bristled. 'Why, sir, you can call me Miss Spotted Chamber Pot if you like, but this billet is the most important thing to 'appen to me in me 'ole bleedin' life! If I 'as to crawl over broken glass all the way from Whitechapel, you may be sure, sir, I'll be standin' 'ere large as life tomorrow an' all!'

Her change of name was not of great concern to Mary, for she had never been christened and her own surname had not served her particularly well in the past. Her new one, compliments of the little bottle-shaped man in the glass office, at the very least identified her with an object she loved. She decided she would happily become Mary Abacus.

'Mr Goldstein said as you should show me the ware'ouse, sir, Mr Baskin,' Mary now declared timorously.

Despite the sour reception she'd received from Mr Baskin, it was quite the happiest day of Mary's life. The large warehouse was stacked to the ceiling with goods of every description intended for America and the colonies and the chief clerk, despite his foul mood, seemed to take some pride in pointing out the extent of Mr Goldstein's venture into commerce and shipping.

Upon their leaving Mr Goldstein's office Mr Baskin had sent word to Sergeant Lawrence to disperse the waiting men and to announce that the very first candidate had been found suitable by the redoubtable Mr Goldstein.

At the end of the tour, Mr Baskin turned to Mary with a sniff.

'Right then. Half-past seven tomorrow and if you're so much as a minute late you'll not be starting here, miss!' Then he escorted Mary to the door, merely grunting as she bid him a polite and, in her heart, a most ecstatic farewell. All the chief clerks in the world couldn't have dampened Mary's elation – she'd turned the Klerk into a Clerk and fulfilled the dearest wish of her dead father. '*Learn it well, my dearest child, for the beads, the beautiful Chinee beads, will set you free!*'

To her surprise the sergeant seemed pleased to see her.

'Well then, miss, you could have blow'd me down with a fevva! Wonders will never cease, what a day an' age, eh?' He pointed to the abacus under Mary's arm. 'I mean 'is 'ebrew 'ighness takin' to your Chinee countin' machine contraption.' He seemed to know precisely what had taken place in the office with Mr Goldstein, though Mary couldn't imagine how this could possibly be.

''Ow did you know?' Mary asked happily, her eyes showing her surprise. 'The door was shut an' all!'

The old soldier patted her on the arm and then touched his forefinger to his nose.

'Never you mind that, miss! We 'ave ways an' means, ways an' means, there ain't much what escapes us!' He drew himself up to his full height. 'Mind, I can't say the gentlemen waitin' in line was too pleased, you getting the billet and being a woman an' all.'

He spread his hands and shrugged his shoulders. 'Don't suppose you can blame 'em, but it were curious, very curious, they 'ung about when I told 'em to scarper, then they done this chant, see, summink about a monkey. It were all very strange if you ask me, very queer indeed!'

Mary was only half listening, still feeling dizzy at her good fortune. 'I'm one now! Blimey! Fancy that, I'm a clerk!' Mary decided that she had never been quite as happy in her life.

And then the gatekeeper's words sunk in . . . *then they done this most curious chant . . . summink about a monkey . . .* The fog had cleared a little, though it was still not possible to see beyond a few feet. The chill returned to Mary's bones and she felt terrified to leave the gateman's side and enter the ghostly gloom of the docks.

She was about to ask if she could remain in the sergeant's hut until the fog lifted when he said cheerily, 'Go on, then, orf you go, miss. See you tomorrow! Mind your step now, men workin', lots of rope lyin' about.'

Mary had hardly walked for more than a minute when she felt the presence of people about her, fleeting shadows darting in front and to the side of her, boots scuffing on the wooden surface of the dockside. In the distance she heard the deep bray of a steamer groping its way up the Thames and the rattle and screech of cranes and winches and chains as they lowered cargo into and brought it out of invisible hatches. She was afraid to call out, thinking that the shadows about her might be dock workers. No noise other than fog-muffled footsteps came from the darting shapes around her, each of which seemed to be consumed by the mist before she could properly focus upon it. Somewhere a whistle blew three short peep-peeps, its shrill sound fattened by the thick air. A suffocating fear rose up within her and she felt the need to flee, though the fog was much too thick for her to attempt to do so. Then, so low that she thought at first she might have imagined it, she heard the hum of male voices and as suddenly the dark shapes looming formed a circle about her and the hum rose and rose and the monkey chant began:

Mary, Mary, Bloody Mary
Who does her sums on bead and rack
Go away, you're too contrary
You're the monkey, bloody monkey
You're the monkey on our back!

Mary froze, her throat constricted by terror. From within the thick fog strong hands grabbed at her and she was thrown to the ground.

She heard the clatter of her abacus as it landed somewhere near by. A scream rose within her, but a rough hand clamped down on her mouth. She felt a boot sink into her side, then another and immediately thereafter hands were everywhere as they tore at her bodice and skirt and grabbed at her legs, wrenching them apart. An excited, panting voice said into her ear, 'Scream and you die, Bloody Mary!' Then the hand was removed from her mouth and the weight of the first man thrusting between her legs pressed down upon her.

As each male completed and withdrew from her supine body he gave her a vicious kick or slapped her across the face with the back of his hand. Some loosened the phlegm in their throats and spat into her face.

Mary lay helpless, whimpering like a small wounded beast, her eyes wide open, though seeing nothing, the vile spittle running down her face and neck. She felt nothing, but the weight of the men pummelling her and the rasp of their foul breath was lost in the whirling confusion of shock. Even when they struck or kicked her, though she felt her body jar, no feeling followed.

She lay completely still while a dozen or more men mounted her. Then, with the chant continuing, they seemed to stop and her arms were torn roughly from where she held them stiffly to her sides. Strong hands stretched her arms out as though in a crucifixion, with the palms pressed flat against the wooden surface of the dockside. Two dark shapes pushed down on her, each with his knee pinning a shoulder and hand pressed down upon her wrists.

The shapes now stood in a dark circle, hovering over her, the yellow fog swirling about their heads. Two men stepped forward from the circle and stood to either side of her and as the chant rose, 'Mary, Mary, Bloody Mary . . .' they stamped down hard, crushing both her hands under the heels of their boots. The terrible pain cut through Mary's half-delirious state and a scream rose in her throat which was again cut short by the free hand of one of the men squatting to the side of her head. One after another the chanting men broke from the circle and stamped down upon her hands. Long before the last of the men had stamped and ground his heel into the broken and bloody flesh and bone, she had mercifully lost consciousness.

Despite her terror and revulsion, Mary would eventually overcome the physical invasion of her body. What broke her spirit was the wanton destruction of her beautiful hands. When the bones eventually knit she was left with blackened claws which more closely resembled those of an aged monkey.

For the remainder of her life, whenever Mary looked down upon her scarred and crooked hands, she would hear the monkey chant and see the dark shape of hate in the swirling, sulphur-coloured fog around her, on a day which had promised, upon leaving fat Mr Goldstein with his perambulating, merry-go-round chair, to be the happiest of her twenty-one years.

Chapter Four

Towards noon the fog had cleared sufficiently for two dock workers to discover Mary hunched in a dark corner, moaning. At first they thought her some drunken slut, her swollen face and broken lips the result of some gin brawl in the nearby and notorious public house, The Ship Aground, and so passed her by as they pushed their loaded barrow from a ship's hold to a nearby warehouse. Finally her continued and pitiful moans caused them to stop and examine her dark corner more closely. It was then that they observed that her skirt was wet with blood and saw her broken fingers pushed through the beads and bars of her abacus.

'Goldstein!' Mary groaned. 'Goldstein.'

The two men lifted her as gently as they could onto the barrow and wheeled her to Mr Goldstein's warehouse where they accosted the gatekeeper. 'She keeps callin' name o' Goldstein, ain't that yer gov, sergeant?'

Sergeant Lawrence nodded, then bending over Mary's body took in at once the nature of her injuries. 'Jesus Christ! The sharks, the bloody sharks got her!' He helped them lift Mary from the barrow and laid her down outside his hut.

Mary, who had long since given up any thought of God, would later in her life ponder on whether it had been divine guidance which had taken her to Mr Goldstein's gatekeeper. For at the great

Battle of Waterloo he had been seconded as sergeant to a platoon of stretcher bearers.

The veteran soldier sent the yard boy to the warehouse and the lad soon returned with a large bottle of oil of tar and a length of used canvas. Whereupon the sergeant tore strips from an old canvas sail and soaked them in a solution of oil of tar. He bound Mary's hands in the Waterloo manner, as was done when a cannoneer had burnt or lost his hands from a breech explosion, binding the hands together in a single parcel of coarse cloth.

'She needs a bone-setter or 'er 'ands ain't gunna be no good no more,' the gatekeeper said to those gathered around, then he lifted his chin and pointed to the twisted abacus beside Mary, 'no more Chinee counting contraption for the likes of 'er, ain't a bone what's left straight in them fingers, nor one what ain't broke!'

'Bone-setter? Ja, zis is gut!'

Mr Goldstein in his coat and top hat suddenly stood bottle-shaped beside the gatekeeper. He opened his dumby and from it withdrew a five pound note. 'You must be fixink!' he said to the gateman. 'You get better this younk lady.'

Mr Goldstein bowed stiffly to where Mary lay whimpering on the dockside.

'Such a pity, so *schnell* for vorkink sums! Accht! Maybe she can be vun day chief clerk, now finish, ticht, ticht.' He bowed formally again. '*Aufwiedersehen*, Miss Abacus.' Then turning on a precise little heel he allowed the coachman to hand him up into the waiting carriage.

Mr Goldstein's five pound note paid for the bonesetter and ten days in hospital plus several bottles of physic of opium to kill the pain of her mutilated hands. This left Mary a pound over which would allow her to live for two months in one of the foul netherkens in Rosemary Lane, existing on a single tuppeny meal each day. Though the tar oil had prevented infection, for some reason Mary's hands remained a peculiar blackened colour. They had been too badly damaged for the bone-setter to repair properly and when some movement eventually returned to her fingers, they were twisted and bent, like the tines of a tin fork, and hideous in appearance.

As soon as she could stand the pain Mary began once again to practise on the abacus. She would work on it for six years before she would once again regain her old skills, although the beauty of her movements was gone forever.

The six years which passed were not good ones. It was not long before Mary was standing on a street corner as a lady of the night. But other prostitutes ganged up on her, chasing her away. Mary moved on to meaner and meaner streets until there was no pavement or doorway left on which she could safely ply her trade. Eventually she was forced into a brothel.

Mary had still not learned to hold her tongue. When she was intoxicated she had even more difficulty concealing her bitterness and controlling her temper. And so she moved ever lower down the whore's ladder, until six years later only the dockside brothels and opium dens were left open to her. She had formed an addiction for opium from the physic she had obtained from the hospital while her hands were mending and now she craved the dreams and oblivion the pipe would bring.

She caught the pox and the brothel mistress, a vile, toothless hag, sent her to a pox doctor who treated her successfully, though at some considerable expense. The money was advanced directly to him by the old woman who, in turn, advanced the debt to Mary at the rate of interest of fifty percent on the principal amount per week.

Mary knew herself to be enslaved for it was a debt she could never hope to pay. She was on her back eighteen hours a day, and in what time was left to her she sought the comfort of the dreams the opium pipe brought. She knew that should she attempt to escape, she would be cut. The 'Slasher' would be sent after her with his cut-throat razor and sulphuric acid, and her face would be disfigured forever.

Nevertheless, as might be expected, Mary reached a point where she could no longer tolerate the old hag's greed. One evening, having shared a pint of gin with a customer and having been continually chastised by the old hag to get back on her back, Mary finally lost her temper. In the furious battle which ensued, for the old woman was well bred to fighting, Mary lashed out blindly and her sharpened talons raked across the old crone's cheek. Her hands went up to cover her face and in a moment Mary could see blood running through her fingers. Mary took up her abacus and fled from the brothel, running wildly into the dockland night.

The acid slasher found her two days later in a dark alley in Spitalfields, led to her by two street urchins. Mary had collapsed from hunger, fatigue and the vicious cramps resulting from the withdrawal of opium and she lay propped against a wall, her chin resting upon her chest. After examining her by slapping her face several times with the knuckles of his hand and discovering that this did not have the desired effect of reviving her, the slasher hesitated, fearing that cutting her in such a state might lead to her bleeding to death. The earnings from a simple slashing with a drop of acid added did not warrant the risk of a murder charge being brought against him.

The police would make a light search for the culprit of a prostitute knifing, but the law required a full and exhaustive enquiry into a murder victim. Murder was a crime of an altogether more serious nature, even when done to a poxed up prostitute. Furthermore, the slasher knew himself to have been seen and heard enquiring after Mary in several public houses and netherkens and in all of the central London rookeries.

Paying the older of the two street urchins a farthing to watch over Mary in case she should revive and attempt to move, the slasher left and soon returned with a small toke and a quarter pint of rough brandy. He lifted Mary's inert body to a seated position and poured a measure of brandy down her throat. Handing what remained of the brandy to the older of the urchins to hold, the slasher slapped her hard several times until Mary, taken in a coughing fit from the sudden burning of the brandy on her empty stomach, returned to consciousness. Then he fed her small pieces of bread soaked in brandy until she had the strength to sit up on her own.

He handed a second farthing to the younger of the two urchins, though he knew the bigger boy would soon enough take the coin from him.

'She's me wife and ya saw nuffink, see? If you speak o' this to any geezer what may be interested, I'll come after ya and cut yer bloody throats, ear to bleedin' ear!'

The folded razor with its white ivory handle suddenly appeared as though by magic in his hands and the slasher slowly opened its bright blade. 'Now scat!' the slasher commanded and the two boys took flight and disappeared down the darkened alleyway.

The slasher now turned back to Mary, ready to complete his original purpose.

Mary, by now sufficiently out of her daze to understand what was about to happen, stared mesmerised by the razor in the man's hand. She was too weak to fight, too exhausted even to resist, yet the spirit within was not yet willing to die. 'Fuck me, kind sir,' she said, her voice hardly above a whisper.

The slasher leaned closer to her, carefully inspecting her face as if deciding where to make the slash. 'Ya can make it easy on y'self, lovey, jus' close yer eyes and think of summink beautiful.'

Mary fought back her fear and smiled in a coquettish manner, her hands concealed behind her back.

'I'm clean, I'm not with the pox, you have my Gawd's honour!' Her smile widened and her green eyes looked steadily at him, 'G'warn, just one more time with an 'andsome gentleman so I dies 'appy, please, sir.'

'Tut, tut, yer too pretty to die, lovey, it's just a little scratch and a bit of a burn. A bit o' punishment, a permanent reminder, 'cause you've been a naughty girl then, 'asn't ya?'

Mary kept her voice light, though inwardly her bowels twisted with fright.

'You'll fuck me to be remembered by and I promise you, kind sir, you too will not quickly forget me lovin' ways!'

'No fanks, lovey, I don't mix business wif pleasure, know what I mean?' A slow grin spread upon his face, an evil grin but with some of the harm gone out of it. 'Yer game, I say that for ya, game as a good ratter and still a nice looker!'

'Game if you are?' Mary replied cheekily, knowing her life might depend on the next few moments. Though she had long since abandoned any faith in God she now made a silent prayer that, if she should survive, she would never again let strong drink or opium pass her lips.

'Tell ya what I can do,' the slasher said suddenly. 'I can give ya a bit of a kiss, ain't no harm in that is there?' He threw back his head and laughed. 'I'll not spoil yer gob, just a little slash, add a bit of character. It won't be the last time a man wants to kiss ya!'

For a fraction of a second Mary could not believe what she had seen. The slasher's laughter revealed that he was missing his two front teeth but to either side of the gap he sported gold incisors. Her heart leapt and started to beat furiously.

'If it ain't Bob Marley, last observed fleein' from the laundry of a certain Chelsea 'ouse, by means o' the garden wall with 'is breeches 'alf on and 'is boots carried, quick as a ferret down a rat 'ole you were, over the wall with your bum showin' where you 'adn't got your breeches fully up!'

Mary, though weakened by the effort this outburst required, held her smile. She had a good head for names and faces, though in the ensuing years both of them had changed greatly and for the worse.

''Ow d'ya know me name, then?' Marley demanded.

'The laundry maid? Remember? We met in Shepherd Market? Me buying fish, nigh eight year back! You 'ad a gold watch what had a brass chain. You was ever so posh! I took you back to me master's 'ouse. Remember, we done it on the linen pile. Well, not done it *really*. You see, before you'd 'ad your wicked way with me the bloody cook come in on us and you 'ad to scarper! Surely you must remember that, Bob Marley?' Mary, exhausted, lay back panting.

Bob Marley grinned broadly as he suddenly recalled the incident and the details of it flooded back to him. 'Blimey! That was you? You was the dollymop?'

He shook his head in wonderment. 'Well ain't that a turn up for the bleedin' books! I remember it now, I stubbed me big toe 'cause o' not 'avin' me boots on, all black an' blue it were, took bleedin' forever to come good so I could walk proper again. I've told that self same story a 'undred times or more. Oh, deary me, what a laugh, eh?'

Marley had closed the razor in his hand and now he slipped it into the pocket of his jacket.

They sat together in the alley and finished the brandy, talking of the things that had happened to them. Marley asked Mary about the abacus which lay beside her and she explained its use to him in accounting and numbers.

'Pity ya wasn't a man, lovey. I knows a gentleman, matter of fact I used to be 'is snakesman when I was a nipper, before I grow'd, I'd climb in an' out of 'ouses like a rat up a bleedin' drainpipe, thievin' stuff for 'im. This self same gentleman's got word out, very discreet mind, that 'e needs a clerk what 'e can trust. Someone wif a bit of form, if ya knows what I mean?'

Ikey Solomon, Marley explained, trusted no one and was loath to make such an appointment, but stolen goods were piling up unledgered and unaccounted for.

Bob Marley pointed to the abacus. 'Don't suppose 'e'd en'ertain a contraption like that,' he remarked gloomily, 'even if ya was a man. I think 'e's got more yer normal quill and blackin' pot in mind, some old lag what is a clerk and can be trusted never to talk to the filth and what can be suitably blackmailed into keepin' 'is gob shut.'

Mary explained to him that she could use a quill, ink and paper for clerking and that she knew how to write up a ledger. Bob Marley scratched his head, pushing his top hat further back in order to do so.

'If it were up to meself I'd give ya a go. "What's I got to lose?" I'd say. Nice lookin' tart like you, well worth a try, eh?' Marley mused for a moment. 'But then I got a kind 'eart and 'e ain't, 'e's an old bastard!' He looked up and smiled. 'I can give ya 'is address, confidential like, mind.'

He scowled suddenly. 'But if ya tells 'im who give it to ya, I won't take it kindly, know what I mean?'

Mary shook her head. 'Gawd's 'onour, Bob, I won't tell no one who it was what told me. I'm exceedin' obliged to you.'

Mary's hopes soared. Bob Marley was not going to kill her, or even mark her.

'It's Bell Alley, ya know, ring-a-ding-ding, bell, got it? Islington. I dunno the number, but it's got a green door wif a brass lion wif a loop through its nose, as a knocker, like. There's a lamp post in Winfield Street where ya turn into the alley, only light in the 'ole bleedin' street, but it don't work. Best time to catch 'im is dawn when 'e's coming 'ome. It's not 'is real 'ome, it's where 'e keeps 'is stuff and does 'is accounting like. Wait for 'im at the entrance o' the alley; 'e can't come no other way.'

Their conversation waned and then came to a complete silence. Bob Marley had shown no signs of producing the razor again, but the tension so overwhelmed Mary that she could not put the prospect of the razor aside and idle chatter between them became impossible for her.

'You ain't gunna cut me, then?' she asked finally, smiling disarmingly at the man squatting in front of her.

Marley coughed politely into his fist and looked up at Mary so that their eyes met again for the first time in a long while.

'I'm sorry, love, but I 'ave to.' He smiled in a sympathetic way, and his gold teeth flashed. 'I don't like doin' it in yer case, I sincerely don't!' Bob Marley shrugged and turned away.

Mary was flushed with the brandy, but with only a few mouthfuls of stale bread inside her stomach she felt it turn and she was sure she was going to be sick.

'Please don't cut me, Bob Marley,' she begged.

'I won't cut ya bad, lovey, just a straight slash what will 'eal quick, a slash and a little dab of acid to keep the scar permanent like and as witness that I done me job. Yer still a corker to look at an' all, I don't wanna spoil that, it don't say in the contract I gotta mutilate ya, I can make up me own mind 'bout that! Cut 'n acid, a slash 'n dab, that's all I gotta do accordin' to me code of efficks.'

Mary, attempting to hold back the bile rising in her throat, concentrated on looking into Bob Marley's eyes. She didn't see the razor come out of his pocket and she barely saw the flash of its blade when she felt the sharp, sudden sting of it across her cheek.

'I'm truly sorry, lovey,' she heard Bob Marley whisper. 'If ya move now I'll splash the acid, stay still, very still, so I don't 'arm yer pretty mug too much.'

Mary wanted to scream and vomit at the same time but she clenched her teeth and held on and then there was a second blinding, unbearable sting as Bob Marley pushed back her head and poured acid into the cut. She could no longer keep her hands behind her back and now she clasped them to her face.

'Jesus Christ! What 'appened to yer 'ands?' Bob Marley exclaimed, then he rose quickly and was gone before the scream was fully out of Mary's mouth.

Mary could scarcely remember how she survived the next three weeks. Despite her pain and misery she had determined she would somehow fulfil her promise never to drink again. Denying herself gin and the opium pipe to which she'd become accustomed sent her into fearful spasms and cramps. She sweated profusely so that her clothes were soaked and she was only dimly aware of her surroundings.

By the time she had set out to meet Ikey Solomon, though still shaky, she was over the worst of her tremors. The scar on her cheek, though not entirely healed, was free of scab. Bob Marley had done his job skilfully and her face, despite the scar, was not in the least misshapen, the parts of it remaining as is normal on a woman's countenance, nose, lips and eyes where they ought to be and perfectly intact.

Mary waylaid Ikey at dawn, just as Bob Marley had suggested. Standing in the shadows several feet into Bell Alley, she had seen him enter from Winfield Street and let him almost pass her before she stood suddenly in his path.

Ikey stiffened and gasped in fright, bringing his arms up to his face as Mary stepped out of the shadows, but then seeing it was a woman he lowered his hands, dug his chin deeper into his overcoat and proceeded on his way.

'Please, Mr Solomon, sir,' Mary called, 'can you spare just one minute of your time? I've waited 'ere all night with news that may be o' great benefit to you.'

'What is it, woman? 'Ave you got somethin' to sell?'

'Yes, sir, but I cannot speak of it here, you must grant me time to see you elsewhere. What I 'ave to offer is o' great value. You will wish to see a sample, I feel sure.'

'Where will I come? When? Be quick, it's late! I must be gorn. Where?' Ikey snapped, expecting to intimidate the woman who stood before him.

Mary had thought about this meeting too often to be thrown by Ikey's brusque manner. 'I shall come to you, sir,' she said calmly, though her heart was beating furiously. 'What I shall bring with me will be worth your while.'

'Bah, humbug!' It was unusual for a woman of Mary's standing to confront him unless she had some urgent business, probably of the stolen goods kind. Or she might be a spy of some sort, or a trap set by the runners.

'Who sent you? Who told you to wait 'ere?' Ikey asked.

'I cannot say, sir, I pledged to keep me gob shut, but it ain't no one what means you 'arm.'

'Hmmph! I cannot think that such a man exists,' Ikey sniffed, though his instinct in these things was usually sound and he could feel no malice of intent in the woman who stood before him. 'Very well, tonight, at seven o'clock precisely in Whitechapel. If you are late and not alone you will not be let in. You shall say one word, "Waterloo", to the woman what answers the door, "Waterloo" and no other, do you understand?'

Mary nodded, too nervous and overcome even to thank him as Ikey gave her the address of his home in Whitechapel.

'G'warn, be off with you now and don't you be late, you shall 'ave ten minutes tonight!' Ikey paused. 'That is, if you 'ave something of worth to show me, less, much less, I can assure you, if you doesn't!'

Without a word Mary moved past Ikey and into Winfield Street. She had succeeded in the first step, though she had done so with a trick, a deception, yes, but not a lie. Now she had given herself the chance to pick up the broken pieces of her miserable life and perhaps change it forever.

At seven o'clock precisely that evening Mary, carrying her abacus, tapped on the door of Ikey's Whitechapel home. It was not as big a house as any in which she had once worked, but imposing nevertheless and grand for where it stood one street from the Whitechapel markets. The door was answered by a raw-boned woman who appeared to be about forty and whose breath smelled of stale beer.

Mary, afraid even to offer the pleasantry of an evening greeting lest she betray Ikey's instructions, blurted out, 'Waterloo!'

'You're expected t' be sure,' the woman said in an Irish brogue. 'Will you be after followin' me then, miss?' The woman, taking a candle from a ledge in the hallway, then led Mary through the darkened house to the door of Ikey's study where she tapped three times and departed, leaving Mary waiting in the darkness. She had a sense of being watched and then she heard a sniff followed by the muffled giggle of a child, though she could see no one.

In a moment or so Mary heard the rattle of a key placed into the lock and the door opened, though only a crack. The light was behind Ikey's head and Mary could only just make out his long nose, a single beady eye and a scrag of beard in the space allowed by the opening. The door opened wider and Ikey silently stood aside for her to enter the small room beyond. The door closed behind her and she heard Ikey lock it once again.

Ikey brushed past where Mary stood, turned and surveyed her with his hands on his hips. He was wearing his great coat though he'd removed his hat and she now saw his face clearly for the first time. This she found the way she had imagined it to be. That was the point with Ikey's face – to those who saw it clearly it was exactly what you would expect his face to look like if you knew his vocation in life. Behind Ikey stood a coat-stand and beside it a high desk above which a lamp burned brightly. Two further lamps lit the room to give it an almost cheerful look which contrasted markedly with the general darkness of the house.

Ikey did not bid her to be seated, though there was a small table and single chair some four feet from the desk. Mary moved past Ikey and placed her abacus flat upon the table and then returned to where she'd formerly stood.

'Well, what is it? Why 'ave you come? Show me, I 'ave no time to waste.' Had she been a man who might be carrying news of a rich haul, Ikey might have been more circumspect, he might have smiled at the very least, ingratiating himself, but such pleasantries were not necessary for a woman of Mary's sort.

'Please, sir, you 'ave granted me ten minutes, it will take some of this time to tell you me story.'

'Story? What story? I do not wish to hear your story, unless it is business, a story o' the business o' profit, some for who it is who sends you 'ere and some for yours truly! Be quick. I am most busy of mind and anxious to be about me work.'

Mary smiled, attempting to conceal her nervousness. 'You will assuredly profit from what I 'ave to say, kind sir, but I begs you first the small charity of your ears, no more, a few minutes to 'ear a poor widow's tale.'

Mary then told Ikey how she had been recently widowed from a merchant sailor who had been swept overboard in the Bay of Biscay. How she, penniless, had been forced with her darling infant twins to share a miserable room with a destitute family of five and pay each day from her meagre salary for an older child to mind her precious children while she worked as a laundry maid in a big house in Chelsea. How the husband of the mistress of the house took advantage of her desperate circumstances to use her body for his pleasure whenever he felt inclined and without any thought of payment. How one night a most frightful fire had swept through the netherken where she slept with her baby infants and she had been dragged from the flames but had rushed back to save her precious children.

'I bear the marks, good sir, the marks of that terrible tragedy!' She gave a little sob and withdrew the woollen mittens from her hands, holding them up to reveal her horribly blackened and mutilated claws. 'It were to no avail, me little ones was already perished when I pulled them from that ghastly inferno!'

'Ha! Burnt into two roast piglets, eh?' Ikey snorted.

Mary ignored this cruel remark. 'I lost me billet as a laundry maid 'cause of me 'ands and being burned an' all and not even a sovereign from the master of the 'ouse to send me on me way!'

At this point Ikey waved his hands, fluttering them above his head as though he wished to hear no more.

'Enough! I 'ave no need for a laundry maid 'ere, missus. Be off with you, at once, you will get no charity from me!'

'No, sir, you are mistaken,' Mary hastily exclaimed. 'I want no charity. I 'ave come to apply for the position as clerk, the same as what you was lettin' out you wanted, a clerk well acquainted with all manner of bookkeepin'.'

Ikey's face took on a look of bewildered amazement.

'A clerk? You come 'ere to offer your services as me clerk? A woman and a laundry maid is a clerk? 'Ave you gone completely barmy, missus?' Ikey thumped the side of his head with the butt of his hand. 'Bah! This is quite beyond knowing or supposing!' He made a dismissive gesture towards Mary. 'Go away, I'm a busy man. Be off with you at once, you 'ave already taken up too much of me time. Shoo, shoo, shoo!' He made as though to move towards the door.

Mary took the abacus from where she had placed it on the table. 'Please, a moment, sir, Mr Solomon! I 'ave a gift with the Chinee abacus, sir.' She held the abacus up in front of her. 'A most extraordinary gift what will make you very rich, sir!'

'Rich? That thing? A Chinee . . . why, it be nothin' but a bit of wire and beads! Coloured beads! What manner o' trickery is this? Beads and laundry maids and 'anky panky, roasted twins and drownings, gifts and very rich! Bah! Go! Be off with you at once!'

'Please, sir, I beseech and implore you. I ask for no charity, not a brass razoo, only for a test.' Mary appealed to Ikey with her eyes. 'Me abacus, that is, me beads and wire, against your astonishin' and well-known and altogether marvellous way with numbers. Ways what people talk about in wonderment.' Mary gulped. 'While I know a poor clerk like me 'asn't got no chance against such as your good self, it's a fair chance I'm a better bet than most men who count themselves clerks.' Then she added, 'And I am trustworthy, most trustworthy and not known to the beaks, you 'ave me word on that, sir!'

'Ha!' Ikey barked. 'Trustworthy by your own word! I am the King o' Spain and the Chief Justice by my own word!'

'No, sir, but the Prince o' Fences and known chiefly for just dealin' by the admiring word o' others,' Mary said quickly.

Ikey, despite himself, was impressed with this quick wit. He knew himself to be a positive wizard with numbers and calculations, and enjoyed the flattery, though he knew it to be false. Ikey's heart had never so much as skipped a beat in the vaguest general consideration of charity or goodwill or justice, not ever, not even once since he'd been an urchin selling lemons on the streets of Whitechapel. Though he didn't believe a word of Mary's tale, even had it been true it would have drawn no emotion from him. Mutilation was so common in his experience that he hadn't even flinched at the sight of Mary's grotesque hands. Children being consumed by fire was a nightly occurrence as soon as the weather turned cold. The scar on her face told him all he needed to know about her. Moreover, it annoyed him that Mary had shown not the slightest sagacity in the concocting of the story she told. The least he would have expected from her was a letter from a screever, slightly worn and faded and perhaps even somewhat tearstained, purporting to come from the captain of the vessel from which her imagined husband had been swept overboard and to testify to this tragic event. Such a document would be readily available for a shilling or two from any forger, a fundamental requirement if the slightest degree of deception was to be practised. In Ikey's opinion Mary clearly lacked the most elementary criminal mind and he could waste no further time with her. The contest of numbers, an absurdity of course, was a quick way to be rid of her, to send her packing, for good and all.

'Bah! Beads and wire against me! Impossible, my dear, quite, quite absurd, ridiculous, improper and impossible!'

Mary sensed from this outburst that Ikey's curiosity had been roused and, besides, his voice was somewhat mollified. She smiled, a nice, demure smile.

'Announce me any five numbers in any number of digits in any combination of multiplication, division, addition and subtraction you please,' Mary challenged. 'If I best you in this purpose, then I pray you listen to me plea for a position as your clerk.'

'And what if I best you, me dear? What will you give me?' Ikey liked the idea of a challenge and the ferret grin appeared upon his face.

Mary smiled and her pale countenance was momentarily most pleasantly transformed, for she had an even smile that would light up her face and cause her lovely green eyes to dance, though this was beyond the ability of Ikey to notice. Po-faced once more, Mary stooped to lift the hems of her skirt and the two dirty calico petticoats beneath to just above her thighs. What Ikey witnessed was a pair of shapely legs quite unencumbered.

'It is all I 'ave to give, but I know meself clean, sir,' she said, trying to imagine herself a respectable though destitute widow so that her words carried sufficient pathos.

'Ha! Clean by your own word! Trustworthy by your own word! Bah! Not good enough for the master o' the 'ouse to pay for, but good enough for me, is that it, eh?'

Ikey, who had been standing in front of Mary now moved over to his clerk's desk. He removed the ledger from it and placed it on the ground, then reaching for a piece of paper from a small stack placed beside where the ledger had been he laid it squarely in the centre of the desk-top. Then he fumbled briefly within the recesses of his coat and produced a pair of spectacles which he took some time to arrange about his nose and hook behind his large hairy ears. Then he removed the coat and hung it upon the coat-stand.

The absence of his coat made Ikey look decidedly strange, as though he had been partly skinned or plucked. Mary was surprised at how tiny he appeared standing in his dirty embroidered waist-coat and coarse woollen undershirt beneath. It was almost as though Ikey wore the heavily padded great coat, which stretched down to touch the uppers of his snouted boots giving the effect of a much larger man, to conceal from the world his diminutive size. That he should choose to remove it now so that he could more rapidly move his arms to write indicated to Mary that he had taken her challenge seriously. Or, otherwise thought so little of her presence that he cared nothing for her opinion of his physical stature or the rank, ripe cheesy odour which came from his tiny body as he climbed upon the stool and hunched over his desk.

Ikey glanced scornfully at Mary over his spectacles as he took up his quill.

'You shall 'ave your challenge, my dear, and if you win, which I very much doubt, I shall make enquiries as to your past.' Ikey paused and shrugged his shoulders. 'If you pass you shall 'ave your billet, you 'ave me word for it.'

Mary laughed. 'And *your* word, it is to be trusted and mine is not, sir?'

Ikey did not reply, nor even look up, but he liked the point and the boldness it took to make it. He turned away from Mary's direction and briefly rubbed the tip of the quill with his thumb and forefinger, testing its sharpness, whereupon he dipped it into an inkwell and dabbed its point on the blotter which lay beside it.

'But if you lose . . .' Ikey looked down at the area of her skirt, now once again concealing her legs, and pointed the tip of his goose quill at its hemline. 'Lift, my dear, lift, lift, a little 'igher if you please!'

As Mary's skirts rose slowly to her thighs, she tried desperately to remember some past incident of embarrassment so that she would appear to flush with modesty. Instead she felt herself growing angry and fought to contain her temper while her face remained impassive. 'Now turn around, my dear, right around, that's it! Now lift, 'igher . . . Ah!' Mary now stood with her back to Ikey. 'That will do very nicely, my dear,' his voice grown suddenly hoarse. 'You may turn around again, though keep your skirt raised if you please.'

Mary's face was a deep purple as she beat back her rising anger. The display of her buttocks and now her cunny did not dismay her, it was the feeling of complete powerlessness which angered her. She was at Ikey's mercy. The billet he was empowered to give her could mean the beginning of a new life for her, but if he summarily dismissed her, she felt certain that she would not survive. She dropped her hands from her skirts and did not look directly at Ikey for fear her eyes might betray her anger.

'Ah, you 'ave done well to flush, my dear. A touch of modesty is most becoming in a laundry woman, even in a poor widow what 'as lost 'er darlin' 'usband and precious little ones, the one in water, the terrible stormy briny and t'others in a roastin' pit, the crackle o' hell itself!' Ikey paused and smiled his ferret smile. 'Perhaps you will make a modest clerk, a very modest clerk, so modest as not to be a clerk at all but altogether something else, eh? What do you say, my dear?'

'I shall be most pleased if you would give me your calculation, sir,' Mary said quietly. She kept her eyes averted, fearing that should she glance up she might lose control and spoil her chance to take him on at calculations.

Ikey leaned backwards in the high chair showing a surprisingly large erection through his tightly pulled breeches. He was most gratified at this unexpected event. He could not remember when he'd been so encouraged by a woman's display of immodesty, especially a woman such as the one who stood before him. Women and sex seldom entered his mind. He had thought simply to humiliate Mary and to erode her confidence before the contest by showing her he knew her to be a whore, yet she had stirred a part in him so seldom stirred that he had almost forgotten that it was possessed of a secondary purpose beyond pissing.

Ikey looked down at his swelling breeches with some approval, then looked up at Mary with a mixture of pleasure and fear. If anything, this woman, with her ridiculous contraption of wire and beads, had gained the upper hand and he knew he must do something at once to regain the advantage. The thought of losing to her caused an immediate diminishing within his breeches, but upon his becoming aware of this, the perverse monster came alive again, pushing hard against the cotton of his breeches.

Ikey concentrated desperately and cast his thoughts to embrace his wife Hannah, an act of mental flagellation which was at once sufficient to damp down the unaccustomed fire that burned in the region of his crotch.

Waving the goose feather quill in an expansive gesture above his head, Ikey announced to Mary, 'If you should lose, do not despair, my dear. Mrs Solomon, a woman of a most benign nature and generous heart, who 'erself is an expert on,' Ikey coughed lightly, '. . . er, *figures* . . . is in need of someone capable of your very well-presented, ah, hum . . . *figurations*.'

Ikey moved forward, leaning both his elbows on the desk so that the area of his loins was concealed. His bony shoulders were hunched up above his ears to make him look like an Indian vulture bird. 'You will do very nicely, my dear, very nicely indeed, my wife will be most pleased to make your acquaintance!' Ikey felt immediately better for knowing what Hannah might do to the woman who stood before him should she lose to him.

Mary remained silent nor did she change her expression, though she was acquainted with Hannah's vile reputation and Ikey's insidious suggestions were not lost on her.

'I shall need a surface upon which to place down me abacus,' was all she said in reply.

Ikey motioned her to a small table and chair and Mary seated herself, placing the brightly beaded abacus at the required distance in front of her. Her voice was hardly above a whisper. 'I am ready please, sir.'

'Mmph!' Ikey said in a tight voice. 'Ready you may be, but beat me you shan't, not now, not never and not likely!'

It is a matter of history how Ikey threw all sorts of mathematical computations at Mary and before he could properly ink his quill her flying fingers sped the coloured beads this way and that to find the answer. This she announced in a steady voice free of emotion, fearing to upset Ikey if she appeared too bold and forward with her triumph over him.

She need not have feared, for had she whispered the answers in a voice most demure and modest she would have upset Ikey no less. He soon grew furious and, it being in his nature to cheat, attempted to grab back the advantage by trying to think ahead the total of the sum before announcing it. Yet Mary bested him, beat him on every occasion, until finally he was forced to concede defeat. This he did with the utmost bad temper, claiming a headache, a blunt quill and the mix of blacking ink in his pot not to his usual liking.

'You 'ave won the first round, my dear,' he finally mumbled without grace. 'The second test remains.'

Mary held her gaze steady as Ikey continued. 'Now we shall 'ear of your past, my dear, for the position of my clerk is one requiring great trust and I shall want to know that your background is spotless, blameless and pure as churchyard snow.'

Mary knew the game was up. The hideous little man was playing with her. She now realised that he'd been playing with her from the beginning, though she felt sure she'd caught him by surprise with the abacus. Why, she now asked herself, had she not simply told him the circumstances of her life? Why would her feigning of respectability, a widow fallen upon hard times, have influenced this odious creature? Perchance he would have preferred the real story of her descent into debauchery and whoring. It was much more the world he knew and understood.

Mary could feel her temper rising, the heat of her anger suffusing her entire body. She rose without haste from where she was seated and, taking up her abacus from the table, moved in slow, deliberate steps towards where Ikey sat smiling triumphantly at the counting desk. She came to a halt in front of the desk and it seemed that she was about to beg him for his mercy, but instead she lifted the abacus above her head and swung it as hard as she might at the grinning little fence. The abacus caught him on the side of the head and sent him sprawling from the high chair onto the floor. Ikey's spectacles launched from his head and landed with a clatter in the corner behind him.

'You can keep your poxy job, you bastard!' she cried. 'Fuck you!'

'No, no! Please! Don't 'it me! Please, no violence! I beg you, missus! Anythin', take anythin', but don't beat me!' Whereupon he began to sob loudly.

'You shit!' she said disgusted, though the anger had already gone half out of her voice as she looked at the pathetic, whimpering weasel cowering at her feet.

Ikey, sensing the danger was over, let go of her leg. He scrambled frantically to his haunches and with his arms propelled himself backwards into a corner. He sat down hard upon his spectacles which promptly broke and pierced through his breeches and cut into his scrawny bum.

'Ouch! Fuck!' he yelled, then lifting his arse he felt frantically at the damaged area and his hand came away with blood on the tips of his fingers. He looked down at his bloody paw, his expression incredulous. 'Blood! Oh, oh, I shall faint! Blood!' he sobbed. 'I shall bleed to death!'

Mary moved towards him, the abacus raised above her shoulders ready to strike him again. Ikey, sobbing, pulled up his knees and covered his head with his arms.

'No, no! I'll pay you! Don't 'urt me! For Gawd's sake, I beg you! Don't 'it a poor man what's bleedin' to death!' Ikey, cringing in the corner with his arms about his head, waited for the blow to come.

'Get up, you gormless lump!' Mary snapped.

Ikey scrambled hurriedly to his feet, sniffing and sobbing, snot-nosed and flushed with fright. Mary grabbed him by his scrawny neck and steered him towards the counting desk, bending him over it so that his arms hung over the front and his head lay upon its writing surface. Then she placed the abacus on the floor beside the desk.

'Now be a man and don't cry while I remove the glass from your arse,' she laughed.

It was at that precise moment, crouched with his bleeding bum facing her and his miserable head face downwards on the desk that Ikey knew for certain he was deeply and profoundly in love for the first and only time in his life.

Chapter Five

Ikey found Mary to be a studious and diligent clerk, quick to learn even if somewhat lacking in experience. He also knew that working for him was Mary's only chance to make something of her life and that consequently she would work tirelessly to bring her change of fortune about. Ikey exploited the situation and he paid her little and worked her late with no thought of gratitude for her services, though, each week, he paid her the agreed sum without demurring.

Mary was content with such an arrangement. An amorous Ikey was only acceptable if the experience was infrequent and she soon realised that her skill at numbers made her indispensable to him and that she need no longer show her gratitude to him on her back. It did not take long for Mary's quick mind to grasp the peculiar language of Ikey's ledgers and to learn the ways of disposing stolen goods throughout Europe and America. She soon showed that her bookkeeping skills extended to a good head for business. Ikey found himself possessed of a clerk who managed his affairs exceedingly well, though it concerned him greatly that Mary had come in the process to know a disconcerting amount about his nefarious dealings.

It was time to put a little salt on the bread but he could not embrace the idea of raising her salary. Not only because he was exceedingly mean, but also because it involved the idea that he was pleased with her progress, or even that he admitted to himself that Mary had become indispensable to his wellbeing. To Ikey, who could flatter a penny out of a pauper's hand, the notion of openly caring for another human was the most dangerous idea he could conceive of, a weakness which would, he felt certain, lead inevitably to his demise.

As Mary's confidence grew her natural impetuosity returned and with it her lively temper which caused her to argue with Ikey, for she found him stuck in his ways and not readily open to new suggestions. She became convinced that Ikey's connections in Amsterdam and Brussels were cheating him in the melting down of silver and gold and the resetting and re-cutting of diamonds.

Ikey would say, 'It is appropriate that those who cheat should also be cheated. It is in the nature of thievin', my dear. There is a saying among my people, "Always put a little salt on the bread." It means, always leave a little something for the next man, leave a little extra, a little taste on the tongue, a reason to return. It is true in business and it is even more true in the business o' fencin'!'

How curious it was then that Ikey, who understood this principle so well, could not see how to bring it about with Mary, that is without perceiving himself as made impossibly vulnerable in his emotions.

Mary's mind lacked the subtlety of her opponent but she was not entirely without gall. She knew herself to be worked hard for very little remuneration and she expected no less. But by showing her concern for Ikey's interest in other matters, she was proving her loyalty to him.

Besides, she had a plan which concerned the house in Bell Alley and so she worked without complaint, becoming more and more indispensable to Ikey until she perceived his concern that he could no longer afford to be without her. Then she made the suggestion to Ikey that she work without salary at his bookkeeping and that, in addition, she be allowed to open a brothel in Bell Alley in partnership with him.

Ikey was delighted. It meant that she was fully compromised. She would do his bookkeeping and add even further to his gain and, at the same time, completely negate his fears. Mary, he told himself, knew decidedly more of whoring than of clerking, and as the mistress of a brothel as well as his bookkeeper she would be tied to him for ever. Greed was the only emotion Ikey trusted in himself as well as in others. An agreement was struck between them whereby Ikey would put up the capital for the brothel for which he would receive seventy percent and Mary thirty percent after the deduction of running expenses. Moreover, the house would still be a repository of stolen goods, it being possessed of a large attic, and the dry and commodious cellar would also be in Ikey's sole possession.

The last point was a master stroke on Ikey's part. Through Hannah he had met a notorious Belgian forger who had been forced to escape from the authorities in several European countries and had proposed a business deal. The forger, a man named Abraham Van Esselyn, was also a Jew. Moreover he was deaf and dumb and, if he was to make a living at his craft, needed a partner. Ikey was ideally suited to this purpose, for he could procure all the materials needed for a sophisticated forgery operation through his various contacts and had an established network of fellow Jews in Europe and America through whom the fake banknotes could be laundered. He would set up a printing operation in the cellar at Bell Alley.

Ikey now had the premises in Bell Alley working to his complete satisfaction. He hated waste and now he had turned every inch of space to profit – the cellar turning out counterfeit notes and, in daylight hours, printing handbills and pamphlets; the centre of the house supplying the physical and fantastical needs of bankers, lawyers, judges, magistrates and toffs in general; the attic serving as a counting house and storage for the rich fruits of his nocturnal harvesting.

Ikey was well pleased with himself. There remained no chinks in his emotional armour and he had kept Mary at his side by involving her in two of these activities. The forgery he shared with his wife Hannah and not with Mary, who did none of the bookwork involved.

Ikey had also persuaded Hannah never to venture near the premises at Bell Alley as implication in the forging of high denomination banknotes led to the death penalty. Ikey pointed out, though unnecessarily, that if they should both go to the gallows, all their property confiscated, their children would be alone and destitute in a cruel and uncaring world. Hannah needed no further encouragement to stay away. In this way Hannah was completely unaware of the existence of a high-class brothel at the

Bell Alley address nor was she aware of Mary, the second woman in Ikey's life.

Though Ikey hated Hannah, she owned half of his ready fortune. That is, his convertible wealth, the gold sovereigns and ingots, silver and precious stones, for Ikey believed in liquid assets of the kind you could pack into a smallish space when you beat a hasty retreat. They shared everything equally by means of each of them only knowing a half of the combination to the safe they kept under the floorboards in the pantry of the Whitechapel house, so both were required to be present to open it and neither could escape with the contents without the co-operation of the other.

This was an agreement Ikey had foolishly made in earlier years when he had first been released from a prison hulk and the money taken from Hannah's bawdy houses had supplied the cash he needed to start up in the fencing business. Hannah had insisted on the basis that if Ikey was arrested again he might, under duress, reveal the combination to the authorities or various villains. He now regarded it as the single most foolish thing he had ever done, but Hannah had been unrelenting in her insistence that the practice be continued. Ikey comforted himself that while this prevented him from stealing the contents some day and deserting his wife, Hannah was placed in the very same predicament.

Mary took to the standing upright part of her profession handsomely and developed clear ideas of how she would conduct her role as mistress of a whorehouse to the gentry. She successfully persuaded Ikey that they must go first class with no corners cut and create an establishment second to none in London.

She furnished the house much like the Chelsea one she'd been chased from after the aborted affair with Bob Marley, though with a distinctly oriental flavour she'd observed in a picture of a salon in the window of a printing shop and which she persuaded the proprietor to sell to her. Mary spared not a penny in making the premises in Bell Alley grandly ostentatious with a front parlour lavishly done out in silks and rare carpets as well as erotic statues showing every form of human copulation. Many of the statues were painted in gold and bedecked in coloured ostrich feathers to make a dazzling display of erotica.

Ikey was a rich man, a very rich man, but not one given to spending it upon others. But persuaded by Mary that the best of London's professional and commercial society would beat a path to her door, or more correctly between her expensive linen sheets, where they would be attended by the most skilled and beautiful young courtesans in return for large amounts of money, he opened his purse to the fullest. At the same time he allowed that Mary should owe him thirty percent of the total cost of refurbishing, to be paid off from her future brothel earnings.

Mary was delighted. For the first time she was in control of her own life and she did not regard Ikey's terms as onerous. On the contrary, she was aware that she owed him a great debt and was determined that she would repay it with the utmost loyalty. Ikey was the first person who had shown her the least charity and she would never forget this. A great deal would happen in the course of this strange partnership, some good and much bad, but Mary would never deny that Ikey had been the means of her salvation.

In Mary's bawdy house Ikey could take vicarious pleasure in observing the high and the mighty at work through a peephole in the ceiling. He found it ironic and immensely pleasing to think that one day he was bound to stand trial before a bewigged and scarlet-robed judge and have the image recalled of this same m'lord, without breeches, fat belly wobbling, rogering one of Mary's plump little pigeons.

Mary's establishment made Ikey feel clean and respectable and even somewhat superior for the first time in his life and he grandly imagined himself a member, if only by proxy and proximity, of London's professional classes. Indeed, it gave him the greatest possible satisfaction that it was lawyers, judges, magistrates and bankers who became Mary's regular clients, the very men who, throughout his life, had caused him so much anxiety.

For Ikey it was money well spent and soon it was money most easily earned as men of the bench and at the bar and in the city knocked discreetly at the scarlet door of Mary's Bell Alley brothel.

For the most part Mary's clients shared two characteristics: the sprightliness and easy randiness of youth had long passed, though the memory of it remained bright as a sunlit morning. They came to Egyptian Mary's, as it became known, to attempt to relive the past while indulging any current fantasies.

The story of Mary's missing hands, often told with great conviction, added greatly to her fame and customers believed that many of the sexual fantasticals available to them stemmed originally from her time spent in the mysterious orient. Mary took to wearing a turban of multi-coloured silks which did nothing to dispel the rumours and added greatly to her mystique.

Mary taught her girls the use of belladonna to lift their spirits and to enter with enthusiasm into the many bondages, recitations, titivations, dressing ups and stripping downs, spankings, pretendings, offendings, excitements, oral, anal, frontal and often curiously banal, which her ageing, mostly pot-bellied, clientele required. They learned to be extravagant in their compliments and the most inadequate sexual performance was built to high praise so that the ageing participant left Egyptian Mary's convinced of his renewed and awesome virility.

There were three things not on offer at Egyptian Mary's but which could be procured at any other London brothel. Mary did not trade in little boys or girls or in young men.

This was not because Ikey had any morality in regard to the exploitation of children or whoresons, but Mary did. She loved children and each day at noon the brats would be at the scullery door for soup and bread which she had cooked up in a steaming cauldron so that she would feed fifty or more. Though she took care not to show them more than a rough affection, she longed to take the smaller children into her arms and hug them. Street children, she knew from her own experience, were feral animals and must be treated as wild creatures that would always bite the hand that fed them. Mary expected nothing from them and somehow they knew she was their friend, and even perhaps that she loved them. She earned their loyalty slowly with food and some physic and an occasional dressing for a cut or yellow ointment for their eyes, and they repaid her with gossip. Should a constable appear to be snooping there was always a child at the back door to alert her.

Though a new client might occasionally demand the services of a child or a young boy, a common enough request in almost any London brothel, Mary would refuse him and often in the process offend some high-ranking toff. London Town was swarming with starving urchins who would go with anyone for twopence or a plate of toasted herrings. There was no class in that sort of rough trade which was more for the likes of Hannah to supply, which she did without compunction. Mary had no trouble convincing Ikey, who wanted no close attention from the law paid to the premises on Bell Alley and he knew, better than most, that children cause trouble when grown men of the middle and upper classes are involved.

Several hours past midnight, long after the customers had been gratified, satisfied, slumbered, sobered and finally put into carriages and sent on their way, when the clicking of Mary's abacus beads ceased and the accounting books were made up in straight lines and neatly squared columns, Ikey would arrive.

He would come in from his vile night abroad where he received and paid and argued and bartered for stolen property in dimly lit taverns and tap rooms, brothels, flash-houses, netherkens and thieves' kitchens and it was usual for him to drop into the Pig 'n Spit where he passed some time at the ratting. His life was populated by all manner of villains, thieves, swell mobsmen, flash-men, touts, pickpockets, pimps, itinerant criminals and scallywags. His last call before returning to Egyptian Mary's was always within the great St Giles rookery, known in the vernacular as the 'Holy Land', to a decaying building long vacated by its original occupants. Here he unlocked the door and in darkness crept up a set of rickety stairs to the very top where the damp and decay had not yet fully penetrated.

Within this building resided a gang of carefully chosen urchins, street children who had been trained to Ikey's ways and who did his bidding. The youngest of them were stock buzzers or smatter haulers, stealers of silk handkerchiefs known as kingsmen which, as was the fashion with toffs, were conveniently carried protruding from the coat tail. Ikey would pay ninepence each for these, though some were worth as much as three shillings when later sold in Rosemary Lane.

Ikey was always on the look-out for a talent, a boy with fingers light enough to make a tooler. A tooler was the most elite of the pickpockets, a planner and plotter, a boy with brains, daring and courage. At any one time Ikey hoped for four toolers in the making and two fully blown and working at the top of their trade. A great tooler could go on to be a swell mobsman, though most, even some of the best, got their hands to shaking from too frequent imbibement of gin or brandy or found their minds preoccupied and numbed to action by the fear of being caught and transported.

Tooling was where the real money lay in the art of pickpocketing and it required four boys, the tooler himself, a stickman and two stalls and, if available, up to four urchins to transport the goods from the scene of the crime as quickly as possible.

The first stall would go ahead, scanning the crowd for members of the law or even a group of workmen or a large shop boy who might give chase to a thief in return for the prospect of a reward. The second stall was on duty between the tooler and the stickman and was generally a larger boy who was required to impede the progress of any person in too hot pursuit of the stickman, who was the first to receive the article from the tooler and get the transportation of the lifted goods under way. The tactics followed were to set a pattern, a routine worked by Ikey until it became second nature to the boys.

Choosing a victim was a task not taken lightly, for the tooler was trained to observe human nature in the smallest detail, to watch the mannerisms of a chosen quarry, how each talked and walked and where they placed their hands, with whom they conversed and where they stopped. Ikey would demand patience and careful selection. A pogue taken from a dizzy shop-girl containing one silver shilling carried the same penalty at law as a dumby lifted from a rich toff stuffed with Bank of England longtails and jingling with gold sovereigns. A garnet brooch deftly unclipped from the bombasine blouse worn by a nanny earned a gaol term or transportion no different to the neatest unclipping of a diamond pin from the silk bodice of a duchess.

'It's quality we's after, lads. To be sent abroad for the lifting of a tin brooch is a sin of character what can't never be recovered from. A gentleman's gold 'unter or a diamond pin, now that's a lay worthy o' true respect!' Ikey would pause, taking in the eager faces around him. 'We does not sell ourselves cheaply, my dears. Tooling is a most ancient and noble art and we are artists. Our fingers play as lightly upon a purse or dumby, diamond clip or gold yack as the fingers o' the greatest virtuoso alight upon the ivories of a harpsichord at a concert in 'onour of the King 'imself.'

Sometimes a promising quarry would be watched for days until the tooler knew precisely how and where to make the pull. A lady might be taken while shopping in the afternoon, this being regarded as light-fingered practice for the more meaningful tooling of toffs and gentlemen during the evening to come. ''Umans is all predictable, observe the pattern and you know the mark,' Ikey would repeat ad nauseam to his dirty-faced pupils.

Ikey seemed never to tire of the training of these small boys. He started with them very young, not older than six or seven, for it was his belief that the lad who had not mastered the grammar of his art by the time his voice broke seldom reached any high degree of competence. He even taught them to cheat skilfully at the game of cribbage, for he understood that they would naturally grow up to be gamblers and he hoped to give his boys a better chance than most of keeping their ill-gained money in their own pockets.

In this respect and in many others he was known as the best and most famous of all the kidsmen and his toolers became the élite on the streets and in the busy arcades. Urchins would implore him to be enrolled in what Ikey referred to as the 'Methodist Academy of Light Fingers', a spoof on the Methodist Academy of Light, a salvationist school for the honest poor, situated in an adjacent slum court in St Giles.

While there were a great many kidsmen to be found, men who trained street urchins for snakesmen, pickpockets and as beggars, they were generally most harsh in their methods, ignorant men with a too frequent hard, flat, impatient hand to the side of an urchin's head. Should a boy fail to exhibit the required amount of tact and ingenuity in dipping it was the custom for him to be given a severe beating from the other boys or by the kidsman himself. To this punishment was added no food to eat until the hapless child improved his pickpocketing technique or simply starved to death.

Ikey, however, offered not harsh punishment but reward, a bright penny handed over, a large chop rimmed with fat added to a child's plate at supper, or even a glass of best beer given with a pat on the back. Ikey's thorough ways and his understanding of the competitive nature of small boys created the best toolers to be found in London, all most proud to be graduates of the Methodist Academy of Light Fingers, Proprietor, Isaac Solomon, Esq.

At practice Ikey would use a tailor's dummy set up in a pool of lamplight and dressed up with the garments most likely to be worn in the street. Sometimes these would emulate the attire of a toff, swell or country gentleman and at others, a grand lady, a doxy or, for the smallest of the children, a nanny or shop assistant. Into these clothes were sewn tiny bells that tinkled at the slightest vibration.

At the conclusion of each week it was the custom among Ikey's boys to take a vote decided by the acclamation of all. The most proficient boy at the practice of dipping was voted the title of Capt'n Bells, whereas the least competent was christened Tinkle Bell. The former was a title much prized among his young apprentice thieves, while the latter was worn with a fierce resolve to be 'unchristened' as speedily as possible.

Bob Marley had come from among these children and there were a number of talented magsmen, swell mobsmen and flash-men who could claim 'a proper education' by the redoubtable Ikey in the ways of thieving and disposing and the general nature of surviving in the trade of taking what rightfully belonged to others. It was this foundation, laid early and trained carefully, which later supplied much of the goods which Ikey would receive as a fence.

Ikey would arrive at the boys' squalid quarters around three in the morning, whereupon lectures and demonstrations on the art of light fingers and the brightening of minds took place. Afterwards those boys with goods to dispose of, such items as they might have taken on the street since the previous night's visit, would wait back while the remaining urchins would repair to a nearby chop house where a private room was held for them. Ikey would carefully examine the prize each offered, explaining its composition in stones or judging its value in precious metal or as an article alone.

'Know what you takes, my dear. A bit o' glass set in lead and gold dipped ain't worthy o' your knowledge, emeralds or diamonds set in gold is what your fingers is trained to lift. Watch the light, see it play, diamonds shoot, emeralds pulse, rubies burn, pearls glow. Judge the wearer, not the glory o' the gown, the toss o' the head, the modesty of eye. Fake pearls is more common than real and when worn on a bosom young, temptin' and firm, is most likely to be that of a tart playin' at courtesan than a lady o' quality. Judge the laughter – too shrill and too often is the 'abit o' the badly bred. Details, my dears, everythin' is in the details. Sniff the perfume, examine the nap o' the boots and the 'em o' the skirt for old dirt or much mending. If the gentleman's 'ands is too familiar with 'is escort then the lady is too cheaply bought. It's all there waiting for your eyes to measure and your mind to equate before you decides to make the vamp.'

Ikey would then pay them, naturally at a much reduced price to the street value of the goods, though never were the articles so cheaply purchased as to encourage a young lad to take the merchandise elsewhere.

The business of the night completed, Ikey would join the dozen or so boys who ranged in age from six to sixteen for a meal in the nearby chop house. Here they would all be fed from Ikey's purse, though in the order and quality of their performances. Those who had not done well at practice or failed to bring in any merchandise taken on the street would be denied a plate of chops or steak, meat being the reward for performance, though all were equally given a thick wedge of bread and a large bowl of thick steaming broth, enough to keep body and soul together. Ikey himself partook of a bowl of mutton and potato stew, followed by a dish of curds.

Some of the smaller boys, their bellies replete, would leave the chop house to crawl back into their squalid quarters and sleep until noon in a bed of dirty rags. Those who had money or friends who would share what they'd won would stay to grow drunk on a pint of gin or brandy.

During the progress of one night Ikey might be seen, his hands working in the gestures of unctuous trading, in the reeking hubbub of Rosemary Lane doing business among the festoons of second-hand clothes. Or if the tide was in and to run before dawn, he might be seen working his way to the river to the regions of Jacob's Island and those parts known as the Venice of Drains in Bermondsey, which he reached by traversing the impenetrable alleys, dives and runways round Leicester Square and the Haymarket, this part of the great rookery being the convenient asylum for the thieves, flash-men, touts and prostitutes working the rich fields of the West End. Here could be found the rakish members of the upper classes with their courtesans, their ears and necks and decolletage awash with diamonds and pearls, the starched young swells, toffs and codgers on the randy, the gamblers and cashed-up jockeys and the furtive old perverts from the privileged classes who mixed vicariously with the low-life. This place, too, was an essential nightly visitation for a fence of Ikey's status in the underworld.

Ikey could come upon these places from Whitechapel or Spitalfields along dark, fetid lanes, and through vile netherkens crowded to suffocation with thieves and beggars and the desparate, starving poor sleeping and copulating on straw-filled billets and bundles of rags.

Sometimes he moved along well-established paths formed over rooftops or through cellars and dark alleys, sliding past the stagnant open gutters which ran down the centre of these narrow filth-choked runways. Even in the dark he knew the whereabouts of the numerous cesspools which would trap many a gin-soaked hag, or drunkard who'd lost his way and having slipped on the surrounding excrement could not regain a foothold and would be sucked into the shit to drown.

Ikey knew with intimacy this great rookery of St Giles and many others, and was as much at home in them as the rats scurrying ahead of him along the soot-stained walls. He could reach the destination of his choosing without once crossing an honest thoroughfare or appearing within the light of a single street lamp, seen along the way only by the incurious eyes of beggars, thieves, night-stand prostitutes, petty touts, sharpers and the broken and desperate humanity who lived in these festering parts. Those who saw nothing unless they were paid to do so and who, upon being questioned by a magistrates' runner, knew nothing of a person's whereabouts, even if they had glimpsed them, bold as brass, not a moment beforehand.

On a rising tide Ikey might be seen furtively moving close to a wall or along a pier in the dock areas before disappearing below the malodorous deck of a boat. Before dawn's light it would slip its moorings and on the morning tide move silently down the river, its progress concealed by the sulphurous mist and smog that sat upon the Thames.

By sunrise this vessel, which outwardly carried hemp or tiles or any of the other miscellanea which made up the maritime drudgery of commerce between England and the continental ports, would be safely into the Channel. It carried about Ikey's consignments of stolen jewellery to be reworked in Amsterdam and Antwerp; parcels of Bank of England notes in every denomination to be laundered in Hamburg and Prague banks; silver and gold bound for Bohemia and Poland to be sold or melted down in the shops and workshops of various foreign Jews.

Ikey would arrive at Egyptian Mary's not a minute beyond five in the morning. He would greet Mary upon his return from the foulness of his peripatetic night and before anything else he would look at the house takings, always wheedling and quarrelling, as if the bitter bargaining of the night must be run down and unwound before he could be brought to a state of calm.

He would carp at the cost of a haunch of ham, or measure the level of the claret cask, as much to bring himself to an emotional repose as to attempt to gain more than his fair share of the night's profit. Thereafter he would unload the takings of his fencing business for that night, valuing each item expertly and suggesting what might become of them; a melting or resetting or re-cutting, what could be disposed of in London, what must needs be sent abroad.

Mary entered all this into her receivals ledger. Ikey also acquainted her of the whereabouts of heavier merchandise: bolts of cloth, linen and brocade, a handsome pair of Louis XIV chairs or a valuable tapestry. Mary would arrange to have these picked up and delivered at a time when they would arrive unobserved. In this last regard she would often use Bob Marley, the slash man, whom she trusted and who proved to be a careful and reliable go-between.

Ikey had a passion for order in his affairs and this had made him extremely rich. When this final task for the night was completed, Mary would place the books in a secret place, this task always overseen by Ikey. Then, at last, often just before dawn, they would pause to share a glass of chilled champagne in her little private parlour at the rear of the establishment.

This was the happiest time of Ikey's life and he composed an epigram which he would pronounce to Mary and which encapsulated the satisfaction he took from being the joint proprietor of Egyptian Mary's. Holding his glass of champagne to the light and watching the tiny beaded bubbles rise in straight and orderly lines to the surface he would announce, 'My dear, I 'ave a theory fantastic for the success of our enterprise. Shall I say it for you?'

'You certainly may, sir! You certainly may!' Mary would rise and top up his glass and then do the same to her own, whereupon she would seat herself again holding her glass and wait. Ikey would lower his glass and take a polite sip of champagne, then in a preacher-like manner, intone:

> *If the angle of the dangle*
> *is equal to the heat of the meat,*
> *then the price of the rise,*
> *is decided by the art of the tart.*

'There it be, my dear, the entire business of brothel keepin' contained in a simple rhyme.'

Simple as he claimed it to be, Ikey thought it exceedingly clever and never tired of the reciting of it. At the conclusion of the rhyme they would clink glasses and entwine arms, each taking a sip of champagne, whereupon Mary would say, 'May our bubbles keep risin'. Amen!'

It was as close as the two of them ever came to sentimentality of the kind which might be described as love.

For Mary the bawdy house on Bell Alley was a daily confirmation that she could be a woman of enterprise and that by her own wit and skill she could gain a security in life she had never known. Ikey was proving to be her way out of poverty, misery and an almost certain slow crippling death from syphilis, or a quicker one at the hands of some madman with a shiv in need of the means for an opium pipe. There were a thousand ways a prostitute could meet her death, but very few ways in which she could expect to remain alive much beyond her mid-twenties.

In gratitude Mary showed Ikey more tolerance than ill temper. She was often sorely tempted to screw his scrawny neck, but for the most part refrained from violence, boxing his ears only when provoked to the extreme. She knew him to be a coward, a cheat, a liar and, of course, a notorious thief, though this last characteristic she regarded simply as Ikey's profession.

Without the thief there would be no magistrate or judge or lawyer or half the regular clientele of her bawdy house. And so she had no reason to place Ikey's choice of vocation in any poorer light than that of her clients. When the poor embrace the tenets of morality it comes ready-made with misery as its constant companion. Mary counted herself fortunate to have Ikey in her life and very occasionally in her bed, which was as close as anyone had ever come to loving him, or she to feeling affection for any other person since her mother and father died.

But it is not in the nature of things to remain calm. Contentment is always a summer to be counted in brief snatches of sunlight, while unhappiness is an endless winter season of dark and stormy weather. The cold wind of Ikey's and Mary's discontent was beginning to howl through the rat-infested rookeries, sniffing at the mud and shit of the dark alleys and stirring the slime of the river into a foment of disaster which was about to wash over them both.

Chapter Six

At the end of a miserable night in December with the wind roaring and the snow swirling, Ikey was just turning into Bell Alley from Winfield Street when a figure leapt from the shadows directly into his path. Ikey jumped in fright as the dark shape presented itself through a sudden flurry of snow.

'It be friend!' Bob Marley shouted into the driving wind. 'A word is needed in yer ear, Ikey, an urgent word!'

Ikey relaxed. Bob Marley was to be trusted. As a young 'un he'd been a chimney sweep whom Ikey had plucked from his miserable trade to work for him as a snakesman. He recalled how he hadn't cheated the boy particularly and so had no reason to fear him. He was a likely lad in his day who seemed to be double jointed in all his connected parts, and could squirm and slide through apertures too small for a dock rat to enter. While he had remained small Ikey had profited well from his talent for entering property.

As a boy Marley had been intelligent and naturally cunning and would have made a good leader if he had not always been a loner. Though it was this very characteristic which meant he could be trusted not to open his gob or boast of his conquests to the other street urchins. With money in his purse for frequent visits to a chop house, the pocket-sized lad had grown quickly and was soon too big to be a snakesman. Ikey had trained him as a pickpocket but he never amounted to greatness for he refused to work in a team. He'd grown into a villain, dangerous if crossed, but known to work only for himself and only for gold. In the terms of the times and the kind with whom Ikey naturally mixed, Bob Marley was reliable as a new-minted sovereign. Ikey stepped deeper into the alley where the noise of the wind was less intense.

'I 'ave information important to ya, Ikey, most important, most important indeed! Yes! If I say so meself, information o' the kind a person doesn't come upon every day.' Marley paused and then added in an ominous voice, 'Thank Gawd!'

Ikey removed his hands from the pockets of his great coat and slipped off the filthy fur-lined glove of his right hand, then he re-entered the coat through an entirely different part of its anatomy and opened his dumby secretly. He allowed his fingers to slip through the coins in the leather purse until he sensed the warmer touch of a gold sovereign, whereupon his nimble fingers worked until they touched six sovereigns which he carefully pushed to one corner of the purse, then he took three. These he produced held between thumb and forefinger as though they were a single coin conjured from the air. He had already gauged the worth of Marley's information, which he'd set in his mind at six gold sovereigns. He knew from the tone of his informer's voice that the information was kosher. He'd think less of Marley if he didn't manage to extract another three sovereigns from him for its deliverance. He held the three gold coins out to the man in front of him.

'Three sov? Three bleedin' sov!' Marley removed the scarf that covered all but his eyes, looked at Ikey in disgust and then spat onto the snow at his feet. 'This ain't no bleedin' social call!'

But Ikey held the gold sovereigns in front of Marley until his fingers began to tingle with the cold and finally Marley, shrugging his shoulders, removed the woollen mitten from one hand and took them without a word, testing their weight in the palm of his hand before biting each in turn with a gold eye tooth. He grunted and placed them into his vest-pocket. Though he'd hoped for more, he'd been standing around in the bitter night for more than an hour, and he needed a large steak with relish and a pint of hot gin or he was sure he would perish from the cold.

'You've been shopped!' Marley said finally.

'Who done it?' Ikey asked.

'It come up from Rosemary Lane. No names. Just a good friend what's got an ear connected.'

'When?' Ikey asked.

'Termorra, early mornin', sparrow fart!' Marley paused, then added, 'After all the toffs 'ave scarpered from yer 'ouse of ill repute!'

'This mornin'! Oh Jesus! Oh me Gawd! Oh shit! This mornin'? This very mornin'?'

Bob Marley nodded and dug into the interior of his coat to produce a gold hunter at the end of a brass chain. Clicking it open, he examined its face.

'I'd say 'bout three 'ours, tosh!' He closed the lid of the watch with a flick of his thumb. 'Reckon they gotcha this time, me lovely!'

'Where?' Ikey asked tremulously. It was an important question, for if it was the house he and his wife Hannah shared he would be less concerned. The house in Whitechapel had been raided several times, but the trapdoor under Hannah's bed, which led to a large false ceiling in which his stolen property was stored, was so cunningly contrived as to be invisible to the naked eye. But the house at the end of the alley in which he stood was less well accommodated to the concealment of stolen goods. A raid on Mary's bawdy house, even if he could clear it of contraband in time, which hardly seemed possible, would be a disaster. Its basement contained the heavy mechanicals of the printing press which had been brought in, one piece at a time, over several months, to make up a press of a very peculiar kind, and such as would be of great interest to the law if examined with the printing of banknotes in mind. There could be no thought of its removal, which would take several days.

Bob Marley's hand went out and he rubbed his forefinger and thumb together. Ikey returned to the interior of the great coat and produced another gold sovereign. Marley pocketed it and simply jerked his thumb down towards the interior of Bell Alley. 'Right 'ere, me lovely.'

It was not possible for Ikey's sallow skin to grow more pale. ''Ere? Oh me Gawd! Not 'ere, not tomorrow!' He looked up at Marley in despair. 'Who? Who will it be?' Ikey produced a gold coin without Marley encouraging him.

Bob Marley took it with a grin. He'd hoped for five sov and

he'd got it. He was not to know that Ikey had reserved another but, given the nature of the news, would have paid five times as much for his information.

'Is it a question of *feeing* the officers, my dear?' Ikey's lips trembled as he asked. ''Ave they sent you? Is that why you've come? Do we 'ave any time? No, o' course not, no time, no time whatsoever and at all!'

Bob Marley shook his head slowly and replaced the woollen mitten, rubbing his hands together to restore the circulation in his recently exposed limb.

'No set up, Ikey. City!'

'City!' Ikey howled. 'Oh Gawd, oh mercy, oh no!'

''Fraid so, me lovely, it's them machines you got in the basement what's got you in this awful pre*dicta*ment!'

Ikey drew back alarmed. 'What's you know about that then?'

Marley chuckled. 'It's me business to know fings, ain't it? Just like I knows it's City what's comin' after yer!'

The single word 'City' had struck mortal terror into Ikey's heart. 'City' was simply another word for the Bank of England. For the private police force they ran who were said to be as remorseless as a pack of bloodhounds when they set upon a case.

Ikey's worst nightmare was taking place. He had been tempted into dealing with queer screens, the making of forged Bank of England notes, knowing it to be the most dangerous criminal vocation of them all. It was also as good a business as a villain could think about, providing you had the capital and the skill to set it up and the courage and wit not to be caught.

Forged English notes were laundered in Europe, mostly in Russia, Poland and Bohemia, where frequent enough commercial travel took place from England through the Hanseatic Ports. These countries, unlike France, Holland, Austria and Italy, were not sufficiently traversed for the smaller banks to be totally familiar with the larger denominations of English notes, so that a good forgery would more easily deceive their bank officials.

Ikey was making an enormous profit all round, paying for the European remodelling work on stolen jewellery with forged long-tails, this being a splendid way to launder the counterfeit English banknotes. It was also why he allowed Mary to chastise him for being cheated in his overseas transactions. Ikey was cleaning up at both ends.

Forgery was nevertheless an exceedingly dangerous endeavour. Ikey knew that no feeing or bribing of a Bank of England officer was possible and that once on his tail, the City police would not give up until they had him safely in the dock at the Old Bailey or, better still, posted for a hanging and locked in a condemned man's cell at Newgate.

Ikey had broken the first rule of a good fence, this being that a criminal endeavour in which bribery is not possible is the most dangerous of all possible pursuits and not, under any circumstances, to be undertaken. Ikey was not given to self-recrimination but now he castigated himself for the fool he had been. There were fine pickings elsewhere and he was already a rich man. Forgery carried the death penalty and no crime under English law was considered more heinous, for it attacked the very basis of property, the oak heart of the English upper classes.

Ikey mumbled his thanks to Bob Marley, who had started to move away.

'It's nuffink, me pleasure,' Marley called back laughing. 'I'll visit you in Newgate, me lovely, bring ya summink tasty, wotcha say then, jellied eels?'

''Ave you told Mistress Mary?' Ikey shouted at the retreating Marley.

'Nah!' His dark shape disappeared into Winfield Street.

Ikey waited a few moments before he too traced his steps out of the alley back into the gusting snow storm. In less than fifteen minutes he'd arrived at the netherken where his boys slept. Here he found two likely lads and sent them to Covent Garden to borrow a coster's cart narrow enough to move down the alley. Ikey arranged to meet the two boys at the Bell Alley brothel half an hour hence.

It was fortunate that it was Christmas and much of the goods, usually kept in the attic above the brothel, had been 'doctored'. That is, the monogram and other forms of identification removed and the goods sent back into the marketplace or to the continent, this time of the year being most expedient for the disposal of expensive merchandise. If Ikey could get the two lads back in time and the load of contraband away, at the very least, they would not be able to charge him for receiving.

Ikey was a deeply frightened man as he turned his key in the lock of the rear door of the Bell Alley premises and slipped quietly into the scullery. The house was still. The last customers had long since been sent home by carriage, and the girls put to bed with a hot brandy toddy into which Mary always mixed a sleeping draught.

He decided not to tell Mary of the events to occur but simply to say that he was unwell with a stomach ache and wished to take her ledger home with him so that he might go over it later. This had occurred once or twice before and she would not be overly suspicious at such a request. He would explain the removal of the stolen goods from the attic as goods sold in a bumper Christmas season.

However luck was on Ikey's side in the event that he discovered Mary asleep in her chair as he crept silently into her parlour. She was still seated in an over-stuffed chair wrapped about in a comforter with her chin resting on her chest. On the small table beside her was her ledger and to the side of it stood two pewter tankards and an open bottle of good claret wine. Ikey moved to the wall and turned the gaslight lower, then quietly lifted the ledger and one of the tankards together with its doily from the table and stuffed them into a pocket in his great coat.

Ikey worked quickly, using a bull's eye lamp he'd trimmed in the scullery, to move the stolen goods from the attic down to the small back room leading into the alley. He left a large square parcel carefully wrapped in oilcloth until last. Ikey was forced to rest several times as he struggled with it down to the scullery and, despite the cold, he was perspiring profusely by the time he heard the low pre-arranged whistle of one of the lads. The cart, the noise of its wheels padded by the six inch fall of snow, had arrived silently at the rear of the house. The two boys stood rubbing their hands and blowing into their mittens as Ikey opened the scullery door.

With the help of the boys the goods were quickly loaded, placing the square oilcloth parcel into the cart last before covering the whole load with a blood-stained canvas, the cart having been obtained from a mutton butcher at the Garden. Ikey gave each lad a shilling, with the promise of another to come, and asked them to await him at the Pig 'n Spit.

Ikey then let himself into the basement quarters down a short flight of stairs and through a door within the house to which only he had a key. Upon entering he became aware of a deep and resonant snoring coming from behind a curtained partition at the far end of the large room which his partner kept as his own quarters. He had no need to concern himself with careful movement since Van Esselyn, the deaf and dumb master forger, would not awaken unless shaken.

Ikey knew the room off by heart, having often enough visited it before dawn. The remainder of the room contained the engraver's bench with etching tools, a large lock-up cupboard for storing the special paper and precious inks procured from a source in Birmingham, a general work bench, hand press, guillotine, and finally the splendid Austrian-manufactured printing press.

Ikey quickly crossed over to the beautiful press and, kneeling beside it, he pushed down hard on what appeared to be a knot-hole in the floorboard. The board immediately snapped open an inch. Ikey repeated this with similar knot-holes in adjacent and parallel boards until the ends of four short boards stood raised an inch above those surrounding them. Ikey then removed the loose nails and lifted the boards to reveal a steel safe set into the floor, its door facing uppermost.

Ikey quickly worked the combination and removed five copper plates etched with the markings of Bank of England notes of various denominations. The etching for the Bank of England five pound note he immediately placed back in the safe. Then he removed all the counterfeit notes from the safe, save for a small bundle of five pound notes. He locked the safe again and carefully replaced the floor boards, clicking the knots back into place and pushing all but one of the nails back into their slots, so that it was once again firm underfoot. The nail he placed not quite beside the empty hole into which it belonged so that even the most careless searchers might eventually become suspicious.

Ikey spent several minutes more looking about the room and then quietly left, carrying the etching plates and counterfeit notes under his arm. He collected a hemp bag, into which he placed the copper plates and the larger denomination forged notes taken from the safe. Dipping into the interior of his coat he added Mary's ledger, the pewter tankard and the doily, and killing the wick of the bull's eye lamp, he returned it to the scullery, whereupon he let himself out into Bell Alley and back onto Winfield Street. He had less than an hour left before dawn, when the raid was due to take place.

The snow storm seemed to have abated, the wind had dropped

and now everything lay quiet, covered in a blanket of fresh snow. But Ikey, his yellow boots crunching on the carpet of white, saw none of the new innocence of his surroundings. Nor did he appreciate the crispness of the clean air which the wind had punched through the rookeries, replacing the foulness which lingered all year, trapped within vile-smelling yellow smog, until the first big snowfall froze the stench, covered the filth and banished the smog. Ikey's mind was otherwise occupied with the problems which lay ahead. In his entire life he had never faced a more difficult situation. If he were to be arrested and convicted on a conspiracy to defraud the Bank of England through forgery, he would be fortunate to escape the hangman's noose. But should this misfortune be avoided it would most certainly be replaced with 'The Boat'. He was sure to get life and be transported to Botany Bay or the new prison island of Van Diemen's Land.

It had been Hannah who had persuaded Ikey to deal in counterfeit money. Ikey recalled how he had at first been most reluctant, but eventually became pleased with the suggestion for all the wrong reasons, the major one used by a nagging Hannah being that the notorious Van Esselyn was deaf and dumb. This, to someone of Ikey's cautious nature, had been what had finally persuaded him.

At first Ikey had insisted on the most basic equipment for the forger, such as could be quickly disposed of in an emergency, but the Liverpool contact grew too greedy and demanded too great a share of the resultant notes. The decision to add the latest in printing machinery finally came about when Ikey discovered a method of obtaining the very paper used by the Bank of England. Furthermore, he had also located a source of inks from Birmingham which closely matched those needed for all the denominations of Bank of England banknotes. The temptation to print on his own had simply been too great and Ikey set about obtaining, mostly from Austria, the machine parts needed for a highly sophisticated press. The only drawback was that such specialised and large equipment could not be easily dismantled, or moved, nor could it be passed off as a press used for printing works of the usual everyday kind.

Ikey cursed his carelessness and his vanity. The location of his forgery business was another of his exquisite ironies. Often a rich banker would be in the process of dalliance, his fat bum pumping up and down, while directly under his squeaking mattress, separated only by a wooden floor, was a sophisticated printing press in the hands of one of Europe's most skilful engravers and designed to rob the very institution to which this pompous and randified gentleman belonged.

Ikey once confided in Mary that he had invented the three 'f' system of profit: 'A modern economic marvel, my dear, fencin', fuckin' and forgery. We take profits from the bottom, the middle and the top, an excellent arrangement, do you not agree? In the basement we make money, in the house proper we employ your plump little pigeons to make riches from downed breeches and at the very top, we store plate, silver and gold taken from the rich by the bold!'

Ikey, although in shit deeper than that which flowed from the two hundred sewerage outlets which spilled into the River Thames, was far from witless in this matter facing him. For example, he had all the documents of rent and receipts for the printing machinery made out in Van Esselyn's assumed name, this being Thomas Thompson. These were all signed by Van Esselyn. Nor did Ikey's name appear, other than as landlord, on any other documents of a formal nature. In the event of a raid, Abraham Van Esselyn, alias Thomas Thompson, would take the blame and Ikey would assume the unlikely role of a rather stupid absentee landlord, hugely astonished to find his premises, hired innocently to a simple printer, so ill-used by this rapacious and untrustworthy foreigner. The fact that the printing press was of such a specialised nature that it immediately condemned its owner as a high-class printer of banknotes he would claim was beyond his limited knowledge of mechanicals and machinery.

Ikey's genius for avoiding disaster was revealed in his arrangements to have the bank's people find Van Esselyn not only with the machinery to print forged notes but with a plate for a five pound note, the mixing inks and some of the notes themselves, though no paper. Van Esselyn was known to the Bank of England, and should he be found with the printing press but with no other evidence of forgery such as engraving tools, at least one etched copper printing plate and some samples of the completed notes they would be forced to conclude that Van Esselyn was not acting alone. That he was being supplied from elsewhere with the further materials needed to create forged banknotes.

This would immediately cast suspicion on his landlord as a known fence and receiver. But if they found the complete means of achieving a forged banknote under the one roof, and evidence that the process was undertaken alone by a known master forger, any barrister defending Ikey could argue that no proof of a conspiracy between the two men existed and that Van Esselyn had acted on his own accord.

Furthermore, while forgery of high denomination notes, those above five pounds, carried the death sentence, this especially for foreigners, the making of notes up to five pounds in value only carried a protracted prison sentence. Ikey had saved Van Esselyn's neck from the hangman's noose and at the same time probably his own.

It was nice planning, for in the eyes of the law and the officers of the Bank of England who wished to be seen accountable to their depositors, Van Esselyn's arrest would effectively put an end to the forgery operation and conveniently supply both a foreign victim and a successful prosecution. A foreign villain was always better news, and one who could be construed as French even more so. With a bit of luck the City might, in time, give up the quest to get Ikey arrested and even if not, once again, in the hands of a good barrister (Ikey could afford the very best), his prosecution in the Old Bailey could be made to look like blatant victimisation.

Ikey's relationship with Van Esselyn had, as far as he knew, never been witnessed by any other person. Though Mary knew of it, she had never actually seen the two men together. So only Van Esselyn and Mary could testify to the connection and both could, if the need arose, be declared hostile witnesses and have their evidence discounted.

Ikey knew full well that no judge would possibly believe this, nor any jury for that matter, but he knew also that the letter of the law was often in direct contrast to its spirit. In the hands of a talented King's Counsel, all the evidence could point to his being the *innocent* landlord. The paper submitted for scrutiny by his defence, the leases, receipts and ledgers would show clearly that he'd acted only as a property owner hiring his premises for commercial purposes. In fact, it was essential that Van Esselyn do all in his power to implicate Ikey as his partner in crime. In this way counsel could demand evidence to support this assertion, a receipt, note, possibly a witness who had seen them together. Even if the jury convicted Ikey, he would take his case to the Court of Appeal where his 'technical' innocence would be almost certainly upheld by a judge. Ikey's cool head and knowledge of the law had on more than one occasion saved his skin. But he had never before been up against the Bank of England.

Though he was most hopeful that he could make a case for his innocence regarding the printing press and Van Esselyn's forgery practice, the same was not true with Mary's occupation of the premises. While she too carried documents testifying that she rented the premises from him and that she was the sole owner of the business which she conducted within the house, it would be almost impossible to prove himself unaware of the nature of her vocation.

However, Ikey was almost certain that the City police would not be interested in arresting Mary as a brothel keeper. The premises were outside the City area and they were unlikely to stoop to such menial policing matters as the arrest of the mistress of a brothel. Besides, in the case of this particular house of ill fame, there was no knowing on whose potentially awkward toes they might be treading.

All things considered it was a neat enough arrangement, but by no means a plan without obvious flaws. Several occurred to Ikey's untrusting nature at once. For instance, who had shopped him? Would they appear as witness for the prosecution? Was Bob Marley reliable, or a part of the conspiracy? How drastically would Hannah react when she heard about the goings on in the house in Bell Alley and the existence of Mary? Ikey grew pale at the thought of her anger, for he feared Hannah almost as much as he did the law.

Ikey determined that he would secure the contents in the cart at his Whitechapel house and leave on the early morning coach for Birmingham, waking Hannah only to inform her that he would be gone for some time.

In Ikey's experience, a little seeking and finding always cooled matters down. The hullabaloo which the capture of a notorious international forger would make in both *The Times* and the penny papers would be sufficient initial glory for the bank, and he hoped they might keep his name out of it until they had more concrete evidence of his involvement, by which time he felt sure he would have constructed a web of outrageous circumstances to meet every question, legal or filial. But everything depended on the Bank of England police being forced to accept that Abraham Van Esselyn, alias Thomas Thompson, was a lone operator free of Ikey's influence.

He then ran a second scenario through his head, this being the possibility that he and Mary would be arrested and convicted as brothel owners. Ikey soon saw that there might be some advantage in this occurrence. He could readily admit to his partnership in Egyptian Mary's and would then be able to claim that the presence of a sample printing business on the premises was a ploy to conceal the existence of a brothel at the same address. It was a common enough occurrence, concealing an illegitimate business behind a legitimate one.

Being the silent partner in a whorehouse was a minor crime when compared to the crime of forgery of Bank of England notes. Again, with a good barrister, he might escape with a heavy fine and a couple of months in Newgate. Mary, alas, would almost certainly be transported. The female wickedness of running a brothel far transcended the loan of the finance to set up such a business, or even the crime of enjoying the profits resulting from such a loan. Many a magistrate or member of parliament was a slum landlord, investing his money for profit and not overly concerned about the purpose for which his premises were used, whether for a Sunday school or a brothel. Profit enjoys the divine blessing of the Church and was to be worshipped without question.

In England money and property were thought to be the business of God and both received His absolute sanction. But the corrupting of the young and the innocent by a madam in a bawdy house was a crime against the Almighty and His angels of the most heinous nature. Mary, Ikey knew, would be severely punished if she was convicted.

For the first time in his life Ikey found himself at odds with a conscience which he had hitherto not known to exist. His love for Mary was directly opposed to his greed and his greed was entirely tied up with Hannah and her children.

Ikey was well used to walking the thin line between safety and disaster, but he was getting older and was very much richer and, for the first time, happy with much of his life. It was a pity that Mary might need to be sacrificed, for she was in large part the cause of his contentment. But kind regard was such a recent experience in Ikey's narrow universe of feelings that he neither trusted it nor appreciated its worth. It was a sentiment he had never once felt directed towards himself, and even his children had shown him none, their mother careful, on the rare occasions they were together, not to allow him the slightest influence over them.

Ikey's low regard for himself meant it was impossible to contemplate that Mary might care for him in the least. His nature and the world he lived in allowed for neither sentiment nor pity. Survival was the only rule to which there was no exception. And so he felt some sadness at the possibility of losing Mary, an entirely new and alien experience, but in no sense did he feel remorse. In the most unlikely event of the brothel being included in the raid Mary must be sacrificed if he was to survive.

Besides, Ikey told his recently discovered conscience, it was far better for him to be on the outside so that he could secretly pay Mary's counsel and other legal fees and, if she was convicted, to fee the turnkeys and officials at Newgate prison in order to make her incarceration tolerable. Should she be sentenced to transportation and accommodated first, as was the custom, for several months in a prison at Chatham, Bristol or Plymouth or with luck on the Thames, the many bribes, remunerations and emoluments she would require to survive this experience would need to come from his unfortunate purse. Although the thought of parting with money, even in so noble a cause, filled him with an unhappy sense of himself being the victim, he decided he would accept this sacrifice as some sort of repayment for the time he had spent with Mary.

Ikey arrived at the Pig 'n Spit where the boys waited for him, jumping up and down in one spot and hugging themselves against the bitter cold. He lifted the canvas cover and removed the parcel wrapped in oilcloth, then sent the boys on their way, agreeing to meet them at his Whitechapel home in less than half an hour.

Struggling with the heavy parcel, Ikey walked down a small alley to the side of the building and into the skittle yard at the rear of the public house. He placed the parcel at the back door and walked over to the cellar chute, where he bent down and lifted the heavy wooden cover with some difficulty to reveal a further barrier, a set of iron bars which were locked down from within the cellar. Removing his boot, he rapped loudly on a single steel bar with its heel, at the same time calling out to the cellar boy to wake up and open the back door of the public house. In a few moments a lantern appeared at the base of the chute, though it was too dark in the cellar below to see the face behind it.

'Let me in, lad, it be Ikey Solomon,' he called, keeping his voice as low as possible. 'I 'ave most urgent business with your mistress. 'Urry now, I've no time to waste!'

Ikey left the public house less than ten minutes later. The streets and alleys were white with snow though a few early-morning market carts, and a small herd of scraggy-looking sheep being driven to a slaughter house were already beginning to turn it into slush. It was six o'clock in the morning and not yet light when he reached his house in Whitechapel and waited for several minutes in the freezing cold for the boys to arrive with the cart.

Ikey and the boys, their breath frosting from the effort, unloaded the contents of the cart and placed the load in the front parlour. Then Ikey paid the young lads a second shilling and sent them, well pleased, on their way.

Mary's ledger he took straightaways to his study and added it to those already concealed in the cavity below the floorboards. Then removing the counterfeit notes and copper etching plates from his bag he put each of the plates carefully aside. He then took up the notes, several thousand pounds of counterfeit longtails, which he placed in the grate and set alight, setting fire to the pile three times in all to make certain that there was nothing left but a handful of ashes. Whereupon he carefully swept the ash onto a piece of butcher's paper and put them into a small pewter tankard which he half filled with water, stirred well and swallowed.

Destroying the counterfeit banknotes was the most difficult thing Ikey could remember ever having to do – the notes were almost perfect and he might quite easily have allowed them into the London markets without fear of immediate discovery. But he was a consummate professional and in Ikey's mind releasing the notes in London was the equivalent of shitting on your own doorstep, in effect asking to be caught. Laundering the false notes through foreign banks was an example of the finesse which had earned him his title as the Prince of Fences. Though, having finally swallowed the contents of the mug, he allowed two silent tears to run down his cheeks and permitted himself the luxury of a single-knuckled sniff.

Ikey then took a needle and thread from the drawer of his desk and sewed the copper engraving plates into the hem of his great coat, first wrapping them carefully in four sheets of strong white paper. Each sheet was taken from separate books in a collection of several dozen handsome leather-bound volumes contained within a breakfront bookcase. Had any person been observing him they would have been curious at the manner of obtaining these squares of paper. Ikey removed the four volumes seemingly at random and opened them to the back cover where he carefully peeled back the endpaper. This revealed a second sheet of paper which Ikey now used as wrapping for the plates, first binding them with twine before sewing them into the hem of his coat.

All this activity took longer than he had intended and Ikey was anxious to make good his escape. He climbed the stairs and shook Hannah awake so that she might help him carry the stuff from the parlour, to be hidden within the false ceiling. Hannah, naturally cantankerous and more so by having been awakened after less than two hours of sleep, cursed Ikey, though she was not unaccustomed to this sort of disturbance. Ikey was known to use several places to store goods at this time of year and sometimes they needed to be hastily moved. Neither was she surprised when after the task was completed Ikey grunted a brusque farewell, explaining only that he had decided to travel to Birmingham. News of a rich haul had come to him and seeking to amuse her so as not to arouse the least suspicion he added a sentiment she loved so much to hear: 'Ah, my dear, the gentile scriptures are *not* correct. Even at Christmas time it is *never* better to give than to *receive!*'

Chapter Seven

Ikey arrived at the coaching post at Whitechapel markets just as the coachman's call to climb aboard was heard, and he seated himself beside the far window so that he could look outwards with his back turned to the other passengers. He pulled his head deeply into the lapels of his great coat so that his hat appeared to be resting upon its upturned collar. Thus, cut off from the attentions of his fellow passengers, he fell into deep cogitation on the matters which had unfolded in Bell Alley in the earlier hours of that morning.

It was not long before his ruminations allowed him to see the entire affair in an altogether different light, and Ikey suddenly felt himself ennobled by his sacrifice on Mary's behalf.

As he sat hunched in the coach, with its rattle and bump and clippity-clop, the general rush and rumble of wheels on flinted stone, rutted road and hard white gravel, and watched the country racing past, from deep within his great coat Ikey felt the warm glow of goodness enveloping him.

This sense of saintly satisfaction was not one Ikey could previously remember experiencing, for it is an emotion which comes to a man who has sacrificed his own needs for those of another. It contained a strange feeling of light-headedness and was an experience Ikey was not entirely sure he would like to repeat.

While he knew himself very fond of Mary, he was quite inexperienced in matters of the heart, and was therefore unable to recognise that strange emotion which sentimental women referred to so knowingly as true love.

He had once, as a boy of eight selling oranges and lemons on the street, bought a secondhand halfpenny card from a barrow in Petticoat Lane. The card was braided along its edges with pink ribbon and showed a circle formed of tiny red roses at its centre, and within the circle two blue doves perched side by side upon a silver branch, their heads touching. Above the circle and below the braided ribbon was the legend, *To my one and only true love*. Ikey had carried the card with him until he was twenty-two years old, convinced that one day he too would find his one and only true love.

At twenty-two, and quite soon after he had married Hannah, he was convicted of stealing a gentleman's purse. He was sentenced at the Old Bailey to transportation for life and removed to the hulks at Chatham. Here he was to remain for six years, avoiding transportation to Australia through the influence of an uncle who was a slops dealer at the port, and who pleaded directly and successfully to the naval authorities for him to remain in England.

While on the hulks Ikey made the aquaintance of a convicted forger named Jeremiah Smiles, who had taken to being a tattoo artist and proved to have an exceedingly fine hand at the matter of ink rubbed into human flesh. Ikey had paid him to tattoo the design on the card onto his upper arm. The card, by this time much faded and worn, had lost, by means of a missing portion, the last two words of the legend and it now read, *To my one and only* . . .

Ikey explained that the two missing words were *blue dove*. Smiles, like all forgers, was not a man of great imagination. His aptitude being for detail and accurate copying of the known rather than depicting in fantasy the unknown. 'Humph!' he snorted. 'Them's birds, doves most likely. Birds don't love and doves ain't blue!'

Ikey was never lost for an explanation. 'It be a well-known curiosity that doves o' this particular and brilliant hue takes only one partner in their life,' he lied. 'Should one dove die then the other will remain faithful to its memory, takin' no other partner to itself ever again.'

'Blue doves? Bah! Ain't no such creatures, doves is grey and piebald and brown, speckled and pure white if they be fan-tails, but they ain't blue. There never was, nor ever will be, blue doves!'

'Ah, but you're wrong my dear!' Ikey announced. 'Quite wrong and emphatically incorrect and absolutely misinformed! In Van Diemen's Land there is a great wilderness which begins at the edge o' the clearing to a prison garrison place name o' Cascades.' Ikey sighed heavily. 'Gawd forbid, we may yet see it in our lives. It is to the edge o' this clearin' that the blue doves come at mornin's light, each paired and seated with their 'eads together. They sit and coo softly in the 'igh branches o' the blue gum trees and should they witness a convict fellow at work on the ground below, it is reliably told that they cry human tears for the misery they sees and the compassion they feels for the injustice done to all of us who suffer in the name o' the unjust and 'einous laws o' Mother England.'

Ikey paused, for he could see the beginning of contrite tears in his listener's eyes.

'When a convict dies from an act o' violence, such as a floggin' with the cat o' nine, or a beatin' by an officer or by means of a hangin' or starvation or from a charge o' shot while attemptin' to escape, then a blue dove dies with 'im, dies of a broken 'eart.'

By this time Smiles, seated on his haunches on the deck in front of Ikey, was sobbing unashamedly.

'There is told of a tree at this vile place,' Ikey continued soulfully, milking the moment to its extreme, 'an old tree without leaf, its bark peeled and its branches pure silver, where at sunrise the blue doves come in such numerosity that they become the very leaves o' the tree. The tree becomes a shinin' blue thing in the antipodean sunlight. But, if you should observe with careful eyes, you will see no two doves are perched with 'eads together. No dove is partner to another, for each o' these doves is the partner of a blue dove who 'as died when a convict 'as violently perished.'

Ikey lowered his voice to a whisper. 'It is said that the blue doves that sit upon that great silver tree are too numerous for any man to count!'

Much taken with this story, Jeremiah Smiles had faithfully rendered onto Ikey's upper arm the circle of roses and within it the two blue doves, whereupon he had inscribed above the heart the words: *To my one and only blue dove.*

Now, nearly twenty years later, on his way to Birmingham, the thought crossed Ikey's mind that Mary was his one and only blue dove and he grew suddenly greatly sentimental at this thought.

Ikey told himself he would take good care of his little blue dove, and that no violence would come to her, as she would not lack the means to bribe and pay her way. Should she be arrested, convicted in due course and, as was most likely, transported to New South Wales, he would pay for her continued good treatment in prison and upon her eventual transportation she would lack for nothing.

It was at this point in his rumination that an idea of startling magnitude came to him, one so bold that it caused his head to pop completely up and out of his great coat to see whether the nature of things had changed so entirely that he was not, as he supposed, on the coach to Birmingham, but on some celestial flight of fancy – a voyage of the imagination which had taken himself out of himself and transformed him into another creature of an altogether different nature and disposition.

But all he could see upon his tortoise-like emergence was a line of stringy winter willows tracing the path of a stream, the familiar dotting of black-faced sheep upon the rise, and a solitary crow high on a winter-stripped branch of a sycamore tree. Upon the road, wrapped in rags and skins, their breath clouding in the cold, trudged the usual conglomeration of feckless wanderers, gypsies, tinkers, navvies, moochers, beggars and tradesfolk.

Moreover, the people within the coach seemed the same as those with whom he had embarked at Whitechapel markets. There was a fat woman in mourning, her poke-bonnet festooned in black dobbin and upon her lap a very large wicker basket. Beside her sat two gentlemen from the city, Tweedledum and Tweedledee, square-rigged in black with coloured waistcoats, their top hats pulled over their eyes, bearded chins upon their breasts asleep.

On the same side as Ikey, but at the opposite window, occupying fully the space for two passengers, sat an enormously stout red-bearded countryman. He wore a rough tweed jacket and breeches, and a pair of enormous countryman's boots. The colour of his clothes was matched by his wildly gingered chin, upon which the stem of a curved pipe was gently cushioned, the tobacco of his choice being particularly acrid and rank smelling.

At the ginger man's feet lay a large hound with one eye missing, its head upon its paws, its single cyclops eye fixed balefully upon its master, who being a jolly fellow had purchased a ticket for the dog which entitled it to human passage, but then, in a gesture of goodwill, had invited the other passengers to place their feet upon its large, furry carcass. This the woman and two city gentlemen had promptly done as there was no possible alternative, the great lolling dog having filled most of the floor space available.

On a warm summer's day the foul pipe and the presence of the large panting creature who undoubtedly carried a host of fleas upon its back would have proved most onerous for a person delicate of stomach, but on this bitterly cold December afternoon it made for a certain snugness, even an unspoken friendly fugginess within the coach.

Ikey was now much alarmed, for he was sure some mental aberration had struck his febrile brain, and now the banal scene about him seemed to contradict this very supposition.

There had risen up in Ikey's fevered mind the idea that he would reform, take on the mantle of respectability and the strictures of moral rectitude, forsake his born ways and take ship to Australia where he would establish himself as a gentleman and tend to Mary's needs until she received her ticket of leave and was able to join him. Her head and his touching, blue doves together again.

It may cause surprise that Ikey could think in such a mawkish manner, but even in the foulest heart there lies a benign seed of softness. It may long lie dormant, but if given the slightest chance will swell to fecundity and surprise all who have previously known its owner. Was this not the very point made by the salvationists who despair for no man and follow their hopes for redemption to the gates of Tyburn and to the knotted cord and final trapdoor itself?

It must also be remembered that Ikey's potential metamorphosis did not include his wife Hannah or his children. The milk of human kindness had not entirely washed away the stains of his known and expected character and he felt no compunction about deserting his wife and children providing he could contrive to take his money with him. This Ikey knew to be an unlikely circumstance as he was made to account to Hannah for almost all the transactions which passed through his hands. Besides, she held the second half of the combination safe under the pantry floor.

Ikey's obsession with bookkeeping was his downfall. He had trained Hannah to keep books on her five brothels and these he inspected every evening before leaving home, entering the profits in a ledger of his own. Hannah, who pretended to the outside world that she was illiterate, demanded the right to see Ikey's ledgers, which she understood to a degree which often frustrated him.

Ikey could not bear for anyone to know his business and the ledgers Mary kept so diligently for him consisted only of the merchandise coming in, a stocktaking list and first evaluation of stolen and fenced articles, not a final accounting. So she never entirely knew the state of his affairs.

Ikey's ledgers were of the final reckoning of profits cross-referenced in astonishing detail; the what, why, when and where of every stolen article, so that no two articles from the same source would appear for sale in the same market. These great books were an extension of his mind, a beautiful reckoning of the results of his every business endeavour. Each ledger was a tangible proof that he existed, the strong vellum pages, the stoutly bound cover of softest calf leather with his name embossed in gold upon it, the squareness of the corners and the beautiful marbled endpapers. These all spoke of strength, respectability and an ordered and handsome masculinity.

Ikey's ledgers were everything he couldn't be and when he wrote within them in his neat copperplate hand, each entry adding to the sum of his wealth, in his mind the ledger became himself, brave, strong, valuable, clean, permanent, respectable and accepted. Ikey's ledger was an addiction as necessary to him as an opium pipe is to the captain of a China clipper.

For a man whose every instinct was to conceal his affairs, his compulsion to record everything was a terrible weakness which Hannah had exploited to the fullest. His year-end ledgers, which contained all the profits made from both his work and his wife's, were kept in a large safe built into the floor of a small basement chamber. Its casual appearance resembled a cold storeroom for provisions, being without windows and fitted with a stout iron door to resist rats, and it was referred to as the pantry.

Indeed, Hannah kept potatoes, flour and apples within it and from the ceiling hung the papery white carcasses of dried cod and a large bunch of Spanish onions. The safe was concealed in exactly the same manner as the one in Van Esselyn's printing shop and in Ikey's own study. Along with the ledgers, it contained a vast amount of paper money as well as gold, mostly in sovereigns, though some melted down bars, and several small velvet bags of precious stones worth a king's ransom. So cunningly was the safe hidden that several raids on the house had not come even close to discovering its whereabouts.

Alas for Ikey, Hannah's insistence on them each knowing only half the combination meant that neither could open the safe without the presence of the other. Thus the bulk of their fortune could never be removed from the safe without their mutual agreement.

It was against this background that Ikey found himself lost in the imaginings of escaping to New South Wales with the eventual prospect of uniting with Mary. Now, as the coach drew to a halt at a staging post to allow its passengers to take refreshment, he realised that he must have momentarily lost his sanity.

Ikey's wealth was irrevocably tied up with Hannah's, and though he surprised himself by still determining secretly to help Mary should she be arrested, there was no reconciliation possible between them. Mary would forever remain the sweetest passage in Ikey's life, but if it came to a choice between riches and sentiment then, Ikey reasoned, the short journey they'd taken together in life was already concluded.

Mary had spent an eventful day. She had been awakened, considerably confused by the noise in the basement and, lighting a candle, hurried downstairs to investigate, only to be met by a stout policeman shining a torch into her eyes. He promptly ordered her back upstairs, though in a remarkably polite tone.

'We'll be up shortly, madam, to search your premises, but we'll not be making any arrests of your good self or your girls. Would you be so kind as to wait upon our attentions and make a large pot of strong black tea with sugar added.'

'Tea be too expensive for the likes of you lot,' Mary retorted, 'you will 'ave to be satisfied with beer!'

Mary had hurriedly retraced her steps to her little parlour. She thought only of the concealment of the ledger and was struck with panic when she entered the room to see that it no longer rested on the table beside the bottle of claret. Then she noticed the absence of the second tankard, and with a grateful sigh concluded that Ikey had been and had removed the ledger.

But after a moment she became bewildered. Why had Ikey not wakened her? Had he known of the raid and betrayed her? Mary, her head filled with the anxiety of the moment, made her way to the kitchen where she filled a large jug with beer and set it upon the table. Then she took half a dozen pewter mugs from a cupboard and placed them around the jug. She walked into the scullery and noticed the bull's eye lamp lying on the stone sink. She picked it up – it was still slightly warm to the touch. Ikey had most assuredly been, but why would he need the lamp? A gas light was kept burning low in all the passages except the attic and he would need only to have turned these up to see his way perfectly. Besides, Ikey seemed to see like a cat in the dark while others would tread fearfully with their arms stretched out in front of them.

'Jesus! The attic!' Mary exclaimed aloud.

The police were about to search the house and they would find the attic filled with stolen articles. Mary, now fully awake, raced up the stairs leading into the attic when she realised that only Ikey kept a key to the door. Then she saw that the door was slightly ajar. She opened it and sufficient pale light filtered through the barred dormer window to reveal that the attic was empty. Not a bolt of linen or brocade, no silver candelabra or plate, or fancy clocks, nothing remained.

Mary felt suddenly completely betrayed. She was not the kind to sob, but a great hollowness filled her being. Why had Ikey not alerted her? She sat heavily upon a step on the narrow stairway leading up to the attic door. Then she recalled the officer's words of a few minutes previously, '*We'll not be making any arrests of your good self or your girls!*'

Mary felt herself filling up with joyous relief. He'd fee'd the law. Ikey had bribed the officers not to arrest her! Mary felt a great warmth go out towards him. He loved her! The miserable sod *actually* loved her! Mary was suddenly as happy as she had been in her entire life, as happy even as she had been on the morning Mr Goldstein had hired her as a clerk. She hurried downstairs to stoke the embers and add coal to the stove, and then to make a large pot of sweet tea for the law. Her head whirled with the discovery that someone cared about her, that Ikey had escaped before being arrested for forgery, but first he had seen to it that she was safe! Mary vowed that she would never forget his loving act towards her.

The arrest of notorious forger Abraham Van Esselyn, alias Thomas Thompson, was a triumph for the bank officers. Though they had found no evidence in the form of large denomination forged banknotes, the discovery of an etching plate for the five pound denomination, together with a small stack of freshly minted counterfeit five pound notes taken together with the implements of forgery, the Austrian printing press, inks, though no paper, was sufficient to incarcerate him for the term of his natural life. Nonetheless, the City police were bitterly disappointed. They wanted Ikey Solomon, and they knew he had escaped.

The search of Egyptian Mary's had revealed nothing, though it had been thorough in the extreme. The beds and closets of the startled girls were overturned, mattresses ripped open, floorboards removed, false walls looked for and ceilings holed and tapped. The tiniest apertures were poked into and closely examined, even the coal had been removed from the scuttle, and the peephole Ikey used to spy upon Mary's clients was examined in the hope that it might reveal some secret hideaway. But at the end of a full morning's search, accompanied by Mary's repeated protests that Ikey was simply her landlord and that she knew the business in the basement to be a printing press and no more, nothing was found in the brothel part of the premises, nothing which could connect Ikey Solomon to forgery or, for that matter, to any other crime beyond that of allowing the premises he owned to be used as a brothel and his basement as a printing press.

Under normal circumstances Ikey's landlord activities might still have been sufficient to arrest him on a charge of conspiracy to defraud the Bank of England by allowing the printing of forged notes on property he owned. But the bank's officials knew Ikey could afford the best King's Counsel London could furnish and nowhere in the world was there better to be found. They needed much more than a possible charge of complicity. They needed traceable, verifiable stolen goods and banknotes which proved to be forgeries and which were found to be in his possession or concealed on premises where he was known to live.

Furthermore, Van Esselyn seemed not in the least inclined to bear witness against his landlord, though he had yet to be thoroughly worked upon. A deaf mute who purported to write only in the French language was, at best, a dubious witness. But even if his confession proved compelling, evidence taken from a forger of Van Esselyn's reputation could, they knew, be easily negated in cross-examination by any half-competent barrister with half a wig on his head.

Late that afternoon, as Ikey's coach was rumbling across the countryside, a meeting took place at the Bank of England on Threadneedle Street between its directors and various officers and in the presence of the Upper Marshal of the City of London. It was here a decision was quietly taken that Ikey Solomon must, by all means available, be apprehended and permanently removed from London's criminal society. A decision was also passed with a show of hands, and therefore not entered in the minutes, that should any emoluments be incurred in this endeavour, they would be met by the bank and dispensed through the services of a reliable go-between, so that these 'expenses' were not traceable back to the officers of the bank nor to any person acting on their behalf.

The task of apprehending Ikey and building a watertight case against him was made the personal responsibility of the Upper Marshal of London, Sir Jasper Waterlow. Sir Jasper was a member of the Select Committee on Police which was about to look into the whole question of policing in London. There was already a great deal of speculation about the formation of a Metropolitan Police Force to replace the corrupt and inadequate magistrates' runners and Sir Jasper could see himself as the head of such a body, a position which must inevitably lead to a peerage and a seat in the House of Lords. The additional responsibility for apprehending the notorious receiver and now head of a conspiracy to defraud the Bank of England was an unexpected turn of good fortune, and he was well pleased with the bank's nomination.

With this decision to persist in the hunt, Ikey Solomon became, at once, the most wanted man throughout the length and breadth of Britain, even though no actual warrant existed for his arrest.

Chapter Eight

It did not take long for Hannah to learn of the arrest of Abraham Van Esselyn and the reason for Ikey's hasty departure to Birmingham. Not more than an hour after Ikey had departed an officer from the City police had knocked loudly on the front door of their Whitechapel home. 'Name o' Ikey Solomon. Is this 'is 'ouse?' he demanded.

Hannah, who was accustomed to both rudeness and crisis, nodded calmly and invited the officer into her front parlour. 'Shall I take yer coat and mittens, officer?'

'Gloves, they's gloves,' the policeman corrected her. 'Thank 'e kindly, I'll stay put.'

Hannah smiled. 'And what brings ya out at the crack o' dawn, officer? Bit early to come callin', ain't it?' Without waiting for the policeman's reply, she rubbed her hands together against the cold, ''Ave a pew, officer, make y'self at 'ome, don't blame ya for stayin' with yer coat and mittens, cold as charity in 'ere, 'ang on a mo, good idea, I'll light the grate.' She said all of this with such rapidity that the policeman hadn't yet mustered sufficient wit to reply to her original question. He cleared his throat, preparing finally to answer, but Hannah turned her back on him and kneeling in front of the fire-place struck a lucifer to the kindling in the grate.

'Sit, sit, officer,' Hannah said. A tiny curl of yellow flame licked between the dark lumps of coal and a wisp of smoke followed it up the chimney.

The policeman, a stout, heavily jowled man with a bushy black moustache, lowered himself slowly into the chair. 'Your 'usband, madam, we should like to talk to 'im on a matter 'o some urgency.'

Hannah rose from the fireplace and turned towards him, her expression most conciliatory. 'What a bloomin' shame, you've come all this way for nuffink! 'E's gorn, sir, 'fraid 'e's not 'ere.'

'Gorn?' The policeman looked quizzical. 'Madam, I must inform you, we 'ave the 'ouse surrounded.'

'That won't 'elp none, you could 'ave the bloomin' 'ousehold cavalry outside, 'e still ain't 'ere. 'E left three days ago on business.'

'And where might 'e 'ave gorn, madam?' the police officer demanded. He was aware of Hannah's reputation and would not normally have appended the word 'madam' to his questions, the criminal classes being best addressed in the bluntest possible way. But such is the regard of the English for property that he was in truth paying his respects to the imposing three-storey residence and the expensive furnishings, in particular the magnificent Persian carpet upon which his large feet rested. He hadn't expected anything like this, and they demanded a courtesy which he knew the frumpy whore in curling papers, who hadn't even bothered to wear a mob cap, should be emphatically and officially denied.

Hannah's face puckered into a frown. 'I beg ya to understand, sir. I cannot tell ya the whereabouts of me 'usband. These are 'ard times and 'e is on the road seekin' customers for 'is bright little bits!'

The officer now leaned forward feigning exasperation, raising his voice and speaking in an imperious manner.

'Come now, we all know your 'usband's vocation, don't we! 'E ain't no jeweller sellin' 'is wares at country fairs an' the like, now is 'e, madam?'

Hannah shrugged her shoulders, wondering briefly why they'd sent this clumsy man to interview Ikey. She felt vaguely insulted – they deserved better, a more senior man who spoke proper and who would be a fair match in the wits department for Ikey or herself. She could almost see the cogs turning in the big policeman's head.

'I dunno what ya can possibly mean, sir! 'Onest to Gawd, officer, I swear I dunno where 'e is.' She folded her arms across her chest and pouted, 'He scarpered three days ago, that's all I can tell ya.' She gave the police officer a brief smile. 'Shall I tell 'im ya called when 'e returns?' Hannah raised her eyebrows slightly. 'Whenever, from wherever? What shall I tell 'im it's in connection with? Shall I tell 'im you've a warrant out?'

The policeman ignored Hannah's questions. 'Scarpered? You mean 'e's left you, done a runner on you and the kids?'

Hannah smiled, inwardly relieved. She knew from the policeman's reply that Ikey wasn't yet under arrest, they hadn't taken out a warrant nor had they a search warrant for the house. 'Nah! I mean 'e's just gorn. 'E'll be back. Sellin's 'is trade, ain't it? When 'e's sold 'is stock 'e'll be back orright, grumblin' and cantankerous,' she sighed, 'just like 'e never left.'

The policeman sniffed. 'Receivin', more like! Gorn to Birmingham or Manchester then, 'as 'e?'

Hannah shrugged again, though she was slightly more impressed. At least the officer had done some homework. 'What you take me for, a bleedin' clairvoyant? I told you, I dunno nuffink about where me 'usband's gorn, for all I knows 'e's gorn to Windsor Great Park to see the giraffe what the Mohammedan from Egypt give to the King!' Hannah's expression brightened at this bizarre thought and she added, 'Perhaps 'e's stayed to play a game of battledore and shuttlecock with 'Is Majesty? Wouldn't put it past 'im.'

The policeman sighed heavily and rose from the chair, pointing a stubby finger at Hannah. 'We've got the Froggie and we'll get Ikey! You can quite be sure o' that! This ain't no normal enquiry from the magistrates' runners, this is City, Bank o' England!' He sniffed again and turned towards the front door. 'We'll be back with a warrant, you may be sure o' that!'

'Always welcome, I'm sure,' Hannah said, smiling brightly at the officer. 'Next time, stay for a cuppa.' She arched an eyebrow and sniffed. ''Ardly worth lightin' the fire, that was, the price of a lump o' coal bein' what it is!'

Despite her outward calm, Hannah was far from in possession of her wits. The single word 'City' followed by the three others 'Bank of England' had struck terror into her heart, for they told her all she needed to know. They'd arrested Van Esselyn, and now they were after Ikey. The house in Bell Alley must have been raided and Ikey had somehow been informed just in time to make good his escape.

Hannah knew the seriousness of the situation, but she also knew her man and unlike Mary she did not for a single moment think he'd either betrayed or deserted her. Not when all their wealth was still sitting in the basement safe. Ikey had made no attempt to take a large sum of money with him, therefore he was not planning to escape to America as he'd often speculated they would do if there was no hope of either of them beating a rap.

Hannah would have liked to go to Australia where John and Moses, their two oldest sons, had been sent, well capitalised, to establish themselves in respectable vocations in Sydney Town. But she knew that New South Wales was not beyond the reach of the law or, even more so, the wrath of the Bank of England.

Hannah wanted her children to have a better life than her own. For them to be accepted as respectable members of society, even if it was only colonial society, was uppermost to her ambitions. The idea that they should follow in the path of their loathsome father was unthinkable. Curiously, Hannah did not see herself as an example of moral degeneration. She was, in her own eyes, a good girl turned temporarily aside by the events which Ikey had caused to happen to their family. Hannah saw her immorality as an expedient to be discarded as easily as a petticoat when the time came to lead a respectable middle-class life.

Left destitute as a young wife with two small children by a husband imprisoned on a hulk as a common thief awaiting transportation to Australia, Hannah had been forced to survive on her wits. The brothels she now owned were simply the end result of her determination not to be destroyed. She had even come to think upon herself as a necessary component in a complex but predestined society. The gin-soaked whores, starving brats, the deformed, witless, the whoresons, freaks, cripples, catamites and opium addicts, they all came to her and, if she thought she could convert their tortured minds and broken bodies into a cash flow, she employed them. Hannah took a secret pride in the fact that she was called 'Mother Sin, The Queen of the Drunken Blasphemers', in a popular Wesleyan tract widely issued by the salvationists. To her this inglorious title meant she had earned her place in life's rich tapestry, that she had triumphed within a social structure not of her making, and had overcome obstacles which would have defeated most other young women saddled with two infant mouths to feed.

Hannah saw herself as a good mother who worked hard and selflessly so that her children might grow up to have both the trappings and the virtues of respectability. She told herself it was all for them, John and Moses, who were already on their way in life, and David, Ann, Sarah and baby Mark. She was convinced that while they remained in England they would be regarded as the bottom of the social heap, the criminal poor. She was quite unable to recognise that she was already in possession of a grand fortune, that her children would never starve again.

The capacity to delude herself had been a part of Hannah's personality from a very young age, and her subsequent social disintegration had become so complete that she felt not a morsel of shame for her actions. Her life, she told herself, had been a bitter disappointment, meaningful only in the fact that she had been blessed with children, so she extracted, and continued to extract, her revenge upon it. Hannah was a woman who was possessed by hatred which had long since consumed her conscience. The only purity in her life was her offspring, the precious fruit of her loins, and the major object of her hate was their father.

It was quite clear to Hannah that Ikey would be returning and that he must have already evolved a plan to beat any indictment against himself for forgery. Although she loathed him, she respected his brains and his ability to make money and even, in a perverse sort of way, she enjoyed the 'respectability' he gave her as a criminal of international repute who carried the undisputed title of Prince of Fences.

Long after the departure of the police officer, Hannah continued to sit with her hands cupping her chin, staring into the fireplace which now filled the little parlour with its warmth. Her first task, she told herself, was to determine precisely what had happened earlier that morning. She could not go around to what she now thought of as the deserted house in Bell Alley, though she would need to ensure that it was securely bolted against intruders. She had often witnessed how the desperate poor could strip a deserted house of its contents, then occupy it in a matter of hours and destroy its worth in a matter of days. Of course, she knew nothing of Mary and imagined the property completely vulnerable, doors left off their hinges by an uncaring City police, windows thrown open to create a deliberate deadlurk. Hannah determined to send a dozen street brats immediately to scatter throughout the surrounding rookeries to find Bob Marley who she knew, given sufficient incentive, could be relied upon to see that the house was made safe against intruders.

To put this thought into action Hannah simply walked down the hall, opened the front door, put two fingers to her mouth and let out a piercing whistle. It was a trick she'd been taught by her coachman father as a child and was a well-known signal to any children in the neighbourhood. In a matter of moments two ragged urchins appeared and Hannah instructed them to gather ten of their mates. The boys soon returned with well in excess of this number.

Hannah explained what she wanted. Marley was well known in the Whitechapel markets and in Rosemary Lane where the local urchins looked up to him as a flash macer and both feared and greatly admired his reputation as the acid slasher.

'Me, missus, me!' they shouted, jostling each other. 'Please, missus, I'm yer man, I knows 'im, I knows 'im well! This Bob Marley cove, I knows where 'e lives, missus, 'onest I does! Please, me, me!' they yelled, clamouring around the front step, their skinny arms protruding from the tattered rags they wore.

Hannah selected ten helpers. Then she went into her kitchen and put a dozen apples into her pinny together with a sharp knife. From each apple she cut a single wedge a different size and handed the smaller piece, one to each of the selected boys, returning the apple to her pinafore pocket.

'I must 'ave Mister Marley 'ere on me doorstep in one 'our, no more, mind!' she instructed, then added, 'The boy what Mister Marley 'imself declares found 'im, gets a silver shillin'!' The urchins around her gasped and Hannah continued, 'The rest gets tuppence for yer 'ard work 'o lookin', can't be fairer'n that now, lads, can I?'

'No, missus, that's fair!' they chorused.

Hannah waved her forefinger and admonished the children standing directly below her. 'Don't no one eat the piece o' apple what 'e got, not even a tiny bite, if the piece ya brings back don't fit what I got in me pinny, ya don't get bugger all!'

'Does we get to eat the 'ole apple too, missus?' one of the urchins asked hopefully, his breath frosting in the air about his dirty little face as he pointed at Hannah's bulging pinny.

Hannah laughed. 'Cheeky bugger!' she looked down at the

tiny, malnourished child standing below her with his arms folded across the dirty rags covering his chest. Cold sores festered around his mouth and his nose ran so that he was constantly sniffing. Hannah saw none of the collective misery contained in the urchins crowded at her steps, they were all the same to her, dirty, ugly, starving, cruel, thieving and drunken and to pity them was a waste of time and sentiment. 'I'll 'ave to think about that,' she said at last. 'Make a nice apple pie these apples would.'

'Can we 'ave a penny now, missus? In advance, like?' the urchin tried again.

Hannah looked down at him in horror.

'You again! Well I never 'eard o' such a cheek! Think I was born under a cabbage leaf, does ya? Give ya a penny and 'ave ya all go out an' get a tightener or a mug o' gin and yours truly never sees 'ide nor 'air of any of ya brats again. Think I'm bleedin' barmy or summink?' Hannah looked down scornfully at the hungry, eager faces looking up at her. 'Righto, you lot! Tuppence and ya all gets the 'ole apple thrown in, that's the deal! Now scarper, before I changes me bleedin' mind!'

With the immediate details taken care of Hannah returned to the parlour to think, though moments later she was called to the front door by the arrival of the wet nurse to feed and care for baby Mark.

Hannah stood at the door and made the woman bare her breasts and squeeze them with both hands so that she might see her lactate. She wasn't paying for a wet nurse who was short of milk. Then she made the woman open her mouth and she smelt her breath to see if it carried the fumes of brandy or gin. The woman's teeth were rotten and her breath was foul, further burdened with the sour smell of the ale she'd had for breakfast, though nothing else. She allowed her to enter.

The children hadn't risen yet, though she knew the nurse would tend to them when they did. She instructed the woman not to disturb her or allow the children to do so and returned to the parlour, asking only that the woman bring her a cup of tea before she fed the baby.

The wet nurse was one of two selected for their milk. One stayed with the children at night while Hannah was at work and the other took care of the baby during the day and also tended to the house. This one, as well as breast feeding Mark, was employed for the rough work. Both women, Hannah knew, ate her out of house and home, but short of catching them stealing food for their own young 'uns, she didn't mind. The food they consumed, she told herself, went into making milk for baby Mark.

Hannah, only slightly comforted by the fact that no warrant existed for Ikey's arrest, was nevertheless fearful of what the future might hold and she knew she would need to make plans. She had endured one six-year period with almost no means when Ikey had been imprisoned. Now they were rich and they should think about going to live in America or, if Ikey should escape the forgery charge, Sydney Town, though she was realistic enough to know that this was unlikely.

On the rare occasions Hannah had discussed the consequences of crime with Ikey, he had pointed out to her that the crime of forgery carried the hangman's noose, the death penalty. Hannah dared not think further on that matter.

However, she was not above thinking that the ideal situation was to see Ikey transported for life to Botany Bay, leaving her to settle in America with their total assets in her sole possession, though she could think of no way to bring this about. If Ikey avoided being indicted for forgery but was arrested as a fence and proved unable to fee the arresting officers, then she too could be implicated and would receive a similar sentence of transportation. In the unlikely event that she was able to prove her innocence, Ikey knew she could easily live off the proceeds of her six bawdy houses and, while the hope of completing his sentence existed, would never agree to giving her control of their combined resources.

Even if she should contemplate divorce, by definition of law the wealth they'd accumulated together remained the property of the husband. Hannah was quite unable to contemplate such an outcome. In the event of a separation, she would be rendered virtually penniless. Yet in Hannah's mind, all the money rightfully belonged to her. Ikey was no more than a retriever is to a hunter, the dog that brings in the bird and who has no subsequent rights to the spoils from the day's shooting.

In this Ikey seemed to support Hannah's expectations, for he had no apparent need for money. He spent none on himself – even his watch and chain were of very little value lest he be robbed for it. He had only one small personal indulgence, this being the sport of ratting. He kept three of the best rat-killing terriers in England, cared for by a trainer, a butcher in the village of Guildford. But even in the ratting pit he would bet modestly.

Ratting was a sport which involved every grade of society, the ordinary poor, criminals, shop assistants, servants, toffs and even occasionally some of the nobility on the slum, each gambling according to his own means. Or, as Ikey hoped, beyond his means. Ikey saw the rat-pit as another opportunity to make money. There were very few seasoned gamblers at the rat-pits on Great St Andrews Street who, at some time or another, were not in debt to him.

With little taste for the sport of gambling itself, but with a fondness for the game little terriers, ratting was the closest Ikey ever came to being of a charitable nature, for should a client owe him a considerable sum of money, he would extend him a further loan against the odds given on one of his own terriers. This was considered most generous in the circles of ratting, for should his terrier win the bout then Ikey accepted the winnings as part or full payment of the loan.

However, if Ikey's terrier lost, then the money loaned would be added to the gambler's outstanding debt. Ikey's charity was limited to a single attempt to wipe out a gambling debt and, as often happened, if the debt was a large one and the gambler, being as gamblers are, bet sufficient on one of Ikey's terriers to eliminate the money owed, and the terrier lost, then the debt naturally doubled. When this happened it was generally agreed that the offender should forfeit goods or services to cover the outstanding money. Many a toff or member of the moneyed classes lost an item of value from his household in this manner, the convenience and advantage that Ikey was a fence and the article could be handed straight over to pay the debt without first being converted to cash.

Common criminals who had given their marker to Ikey undertook many a burglary and handed the contents of their night's work over to him, whereupon their marker was returned so they would remain in good standing for a future loan.

It was generally conceded in ratting circles that Ikey's terriers, which came from the Forest of Dean on the Welsh border, were exceedingly well bred and highly trained for courage and of the very best disposition for the rat-pit. The little black and brown terriers, usually the smallest dogs brought to the rat-pits, more often than not took the prize from bigger and more naturally brutal animals. Ikey's sparing use of his terriers to regain money lost by his clients was well regarded in the sport, and it was the only endeavour in Ikey's life where those about him did not look upon him as a rapacious and vile member of the Christ-killing race.

However, Ikey's reluctance to let his little terriers into the pit too often had nothing whatsoever to do with his desire to be well regarded, but was in a great part due to a sentimental consideration for them. Sewer rats give dogs canker, which is eventually the death of them. After each killing in the rat-pit Ikey would rinse the pretty pink mouths of his tiny terriers with peppermint and water and return them to their trainer with instructions to carefully tend the rat bites they had sustained. It was a tenderness he had never shown his children or any other living person, not even Mary, whom he would have been quite unable to stroke or touch as he did the little dogs he owned.

Ikey, like every other dog owner in England, dreamed of one day owning another Lord Nelson, a legendary ratter. Lord Nelson was so small he used to wear a lady's jewelled bracelet as a collar, weighed but five pounds and a half and had once killed two hundred rats in a single evening. It was said that, at times, some of the sewer rats pitted against him were his equal in size. But there was never a one or even a dozen together in the rat-pit who could bring the little terrier to a halt or bail him up. Ikey dreamed of owning a dog such as Lord Nelson though, for once, not for the money it could wring from the rat-pit. It was because he was so small, the smallest ratter ever to win in the pits, yet this miniature terrier, like Lord Nelson himself, who stood at only four feet and ten inches, contained a courage greater per pound of weight than any dog that had ever lived to kill a rat.

Ikey, too, was small and thought of himself as weak and a coward. A dog such as Lord Nelson proved the exception to the rule that the small and the weak must always eat shit. Had another such as Lord Nelson presented itself for sale, then Ikey might for the first time have understood a reason for money beyond avarice. He would be prepared to pay a king's ransom for a dog like-proportioned to Lord Nelson and as well proven in the pits.

Even the sport of ratting could not claim to involve Ikey in the need for money, since the costs of keeping the dogs fit for ratting constituted only a small part of his total earnings from the sport.

Ikey didn't need or use money for the material things it could buy, he simply accumulated it. When he required clothes or boots, he bought them secondhand in the markets around the corner or in Rosemary Lane, bargaining fiercely for an embroidered, long-sleeved waistcoat, or a pair of well-worn boots from a secondhand shoe dealer in Dudley Street. Ikey couldn't abide new shoes or even new hose and preferred his stockings to be well darned at the heels and knees. Only his great coat was purchased new, made bespoke of the finest wool to his own precise instructions with a hundred concealed pockets, the whereabouts of which required an exacting layout memorised in his mind.

In fact, this coat represented the very nature of Ikey Solomon. He, himself, was a hundred pockets, each concealing hurt: some contained past abuse, some inadequacies and some were stuffed with deformities of thought. In others past injustices rattled, yet other pockets contained abnormalities and social obscenities. A host of pockets were filled with past woundings which rubbed raw against insults, hatreds and peculiar malice. Ikey carried all the sins and bitter blows, pocks and pits of his wandering kind in the pockets of his mind. They became the total of who he was, the whole, concealed by a cloak of indifference to the outside world.

The sole importance of money to Ikey was protection. Money bought sycophancy and this passed well enough for respect. Money kept those who would destroy him at a proper arm's length. Money was the lining of the protective coat which concealed him from a dangerously cold and malevolent world.

For Hannah no such problem of concealment with a metaphorical garment existed. Her loathing of Ikey was the centre of her everyday preoccupation, and his accumulation of wealth her single reason for their coupling. Hannah saw Ikey as a servant to her ambition, and his wealth the means to purchase the social aspirations she so earnestly desired for herself, and for the futures of her six children. She had invested in Ikey as one might in the cargo of an opium clipper, and her expectation was for a handsome end profit.

Chapter Nine

Two days later Hannah received a very discreet messenger sent by the Upper Marshal of the City of London, Sir Jasper Waterlow. The messenger, a small, polite man in a frock-coat and top hat, somewhat too big for his head, stated that Sir Jasper wished to see her on a matter to her great advantage. She was naturally filled with apprehension though it did not occur to her to refuse his request, especially as the messenger had gone to great pains to assure her that she was not under arrest. She was to present herself at the Blue Wren coffee house in Haymarket on the following day, at precisely two o'clock.

Dressed in her Sabbath finery and having purchased a new best bonnet in the latest style, she pulled up at the Blue Wren, her barouche, hired by her father for the occasion, arriving at the coffee house door at precisely the appointed hour.

She announced herself to the surly proprietor, who took her cloak and ushered her to a small room to the rear of the premises where Britain's senior policeman, Sir Jasper Waterlow, waited for her. He neither rose from his chair nor took her hand at her entry. His expression was most acidic, as though the task at hand caused a sour taste in his mouth. Hannah thought this appropriate enough, expecting no different from the law.

Sir Jasper pointed to the remaining chair, there being but two upright chairs and a small table in the room. 'Sit, Mrs Solomons. I know you are aware of who I am, so I shan't introduce myself. Ceilings in such places have ears and the walls act as veritable trumpets for the deaf.' Then he added, 'It is not one's custom to be seen *or* heard in such an establishment and so I shall come directly to the point.'

The Upper Marshal of London was a small man though with a markedly large egg-shaped head. Its surface, including his chin, was quite free of hair but for three separate places: a very handsome black moustache curled and waxed at the ends, his eyebrows, equally dark and shaggy to the extreme and a pair of elaborate side whiskers which appeared to have been hot tonged and curled to resemble two dark tubes. They rested upon his jowls as though convenient handles to lift his over-sized head from his exceedingly narrow shoulders. His eyes were tiny, almost slits and his lips so narrow and straight that they suggested themselves as a single bluish stripe under his moustache. Indeed, had it not been for the large unlit cigar clamped between them, his mouth might have gone unnoticed. The only feature not yet remarked upon was his nose. It seemed a creature of independent life, large, bulb-shaped and wart-textured, and all together of a purplish hue. It sat upon his smooth, pink face like a conglomerate of several noses, where it twitched and snorted and seemed to wiggle continuously as though in great disagreement with the circumstances in which it now found itself.

This large head with its impatient, alienated nose was attached to a small, thin, short-legged body not more than five feet one inch in height. However, seated as he was with the cloth of his breeches pulled tight at the front, Hannah's practised eye observed that he carried the bulge of a surprisingly large engine for so small a man.

Sir Jasper was dressed in a dark cutaway coat above pale trousers and elegant boots, the heels of which were higher by a good two inches than might be normally supposed to be correct for the fashion of the day. A white silk choker finished off what Hannah knew to be the street uniform mostly favoured by men of the upper classes. Finally, Sir Jasper's very tall top hat had been placed with its brim uppermost on the small table between Hannah and himself, so that to observe the Upper Marshal she was forced to slightly crane her neck and look past the black hat's brim.

'So, madam, you are the spouse of the notorious criminal, Ikey Solomons?'

'Solomon, sir, it don't 'ave an "s",' Hannah corrected him, her heart fluttering at the presumption. Then she looked slightly bemused. 'Married yes, but as to criminal, not that I knows of, sir.' She drew a breath and then continued, 'Me 'usband, Ikey, 'as served 'is time, one year in Newgate and then on a hulk at Chatham. After six years 'e received the King's pardon.' Hannah paused again. 'Since then one or two small offences in the petty sessions, but nuffink what you might call *notorious* or *criminal*, if ya knows what I mean, sir?'

The officer sighed, 'Mrs Solomons, do not treat me like a simple-minded Bow Street runner or you could find yourself implicated in this unfortunate business.'

'And what unfortunate business is that?' Hannah asked politely, maintaining her calm.

'Forgery, madam! Defrauding the Bank of England by the printing of large denomination counterfeit notes of astonishing artistry to be passed through European banks and exchanged for foreign currency, and then re-converted to English currency again, though this time as the absolutely genuine article!'

'Me 'usband can do that?' Hannah asked, incredulously. 'Me 'usband can make money out o' scraps o' paper?' She shook her head. 'You 'ave the wrong man, sir, me 'usband is but a poor jeweller what makes a small and 'onest profit from sellin' o' betrothal and weddin' rings and bright little brooches for servant girls, shop assistants, country folks and the likes!'

'Ha! And how, pray tell, does he come to own the salubrious premises in Bell Alley?'

'Salubrious? 'Ardly that, sir, modest 'ouse to say the least. An uncle in Chatham, a slops dealer by trade, who passed away, Gawd rest 'is soul, a good man, sir, who left me 'usband a small legacy what we used to buy the 'ouse for rentin' purposes to decent folk. Our own little nest egg against 'ard times.'

'A modest house? Decent folk? A bawdy house in partnership with a well-known madam. A high-class establishment fitted out at great cost and with a printing press of the latest design in the basement, a nest all right, a nest of vipers!'

He pointed his unlit cigar at Hannah. 'Mark you carefully, we have arrested . . .' He hesitated and then removed and unfolded a small slip of paper from a pocket in his waistcoat. 'Damned silly names these Froggies . . . ah yes, Van Esselyn . . . Abraham Van

Esselyn, a notorious forger whose services do *not* come cheaply, and who is *not* paid in the currency his nimble hands create, but with the *real* thing!'

The nose on Sir Jasper's face looked at Hannah in a decidedly smug manner. Then, without so much as a moment's warning, Sir Jasper pushed back his chair, rose and banged his fist down on the table, causing the top hat upon it to jump and wobble, then fall to its side.

'Damn you, woman! Do you take me for a complete fool? I will have the truth, do you hear me!'

At first Hannah thought it must all be a mistake. They had somehow confused her own brothels with an imaginary one in Bell Alley. After all, Bob Marley, whom she had commissioned to report on the aftermath of the raid, had said nothing of a brothel at Bell Alley. But the information on Abraham Van Esselyn was perfectly correct. And who was the woman who ran the fashionable brothel which now seemed to exist at the Bell Alley premises?

Hannah needed time to gather her wits and to conceal her surprise at Sir Jasper's astonishing news. There was more going on at Bell Alley than she knew about. She told herself that if some other woman, with an eye to her husband's considerable fortune, was trying to gain his good favour, both this whore and Ikey would be made to suffer a consequence far worse than the noose at Tyburn.

'Yes, sir, no, sir, but I dunno what it is ya want me to say, sir,' Hannah blustered as she set about gathering her inward composure. 'You seems to want me to say me 'usband's guilty, is that it? A wife turnin' against 'er innocent 'usband and the law makin' up all sorts o' lies about brothels and mistresses to make 'er do so. Me a faithful wife and lovin' mother what cannot tell a lie without blushin' summink awful.'

'Mrs Solomons, I'm sure you are aware that a wife cannot testify against her husband. Only those frightful frogs across the Channel have such a damned stupid law, which, I'm led to believe, leads to all manner of female revenge, not at all in the interest of male justice! Sanctity of marriage, my dear, it's the foundation of British justice!'

Hannah's lips started to tremble and a muscle on her left cheek to twitch. She brought her hands up to cover her eyes so that the absence of tears could not be seen, although, when needed, they would come soon enough.

'I dunno what it is ya want from me, sir. Me what's got four little mouths to feed, you wants to take me darlin' 'usband away! 'Im what's done no 'arm to no one! Where's the British justice in that?' Hannah choked out the words and then began to sob miserably. 'When I come 'ere it was to a promise o' reward! But when I gets 'ere, all I 'ears is talk o' brothels and mistresses and takin' away me poor 'usband what's done nuffink to deserve no punishment!' Hannah commenced to howl loudly for some time, real tears now running down her cheeks, judging the Upper Marshal's patience carefully.

'For God's sake woman, stop your damned caterwauling!' Sir Jasper demanded, banging his tiny fist once more down upon the table. 'I want your co-operation! I'm willing to pay a very handsome price for it!'

Perhaps it was the words 'pay' and 'very handsome price' that Hannah's ears, always alert to a matter of profit, picked up. Her distress died down to a whimper and her head lifted, her large, tearful eyes peeping through her fingers. ''Ow much?' she asked in a broken, tiny voice, throwing in a loud sob for good measure.

Sir Jasper immediately relaxed and digging into the pocket of his coat produced a box of matches and commenced at last to light his cigar. Then he leaned back so that his chair rested against the wall balanced on its rear legs, the front ones being raised from the floor. Blowing a most satisfactory cloud of cigar smoke to the ceiling, he addressed Hannah in a calm voice.

'Mrs Solomons, we have the luxury of a choice – we can either offer your husband's mistress an incentive to co-operate with our enquiries or you may, with some little encouragement, decide to . . . er . . . help.'

'Beg pardon, sir, me 'usband ain't got no mistress! 'E ain't the sort. All along I been thinkin' you must 'ave the wrong man, now I'm certain in me own mind.' She smiled ingenuously, her eyes bright from recent tears. 'Maybe the person what yer looking for is *Solomons*. Common as dirt, they is, everywhere! We is *Solomon*, no "s". Me darlin' 'usband is very particular on that point, you see it means summink entirely different, it's not so kosher with an "s". Cohen is priests, Levy also, but Solomon, that's yer actual royalty, that is! That's yer Royal 'Ighness, yer genuine King Solomon, ya know the geezer what met the Queen o' Sheba? 'E wasn't called King Solomons, was 'e now? Nobody ain't never 'eard o' the wisdom o' *Solomons*, 'as they?'

'What on earth are you talking about, woman?' Sir Jasper leaned forward so that the front legs of his chair clunked to the floor. 'Whatever you're called, does it really matter?' He waved his cigar in the air. 'You are from the criminal classes and so your name, whatever it happens to be, spells thief, villain, ruffian, rascal! Solomons, Cohen, Levy, they all spell damned Israelite!

'Now, where was I? Oh yes, indeed! There is no possibility of a mistaken identity, I assure you, Mrs Solomons, and as to the other matter, I cannot vouchsafe that your husband is paramour to Egyptian Mary. But that she is his tenant we have from the woman's own lips. She has confessed, in a signed statement, that she rents the premises in Bell Alley from Isaac Solomons. Three of her strumpets have also made statements to the effect that your husband is a part owner, quite sufficient evidence to get him apprehended for allowing a bawdy house on the premises he owns or, even more compelling, being in partnership with another in this tawdry business.'

Hannah knew now with certainty that Ikey had betrayed her. She knew that Ikey would never simply rent out premises for a brothel without owning the larger part of the enterprise. Her first impulse was to feel an absolute fool, but then a darker anger rose within her. With great effort she fought it down and forced herself to concentrate on what the policeman was saying, though she was unable to control her rising voice, her venom turned to scorn.

'What? Do me a favour? On the evidence o' three tarts?' Hannah threw back her head and laughed. 'Even if me 'usband was convicted, which ain't likely, with a sharp counsellor 'e'd get no more than a drag. What good's a three month sentence gunna do ya? Ya must be jokin', sir?'

'Joking? Well no, not really,' Sir Jasper blew smoke towards the ceiling. 'Keeping a bawdy house is a perfectly indictable crime. But I'll grant you, madam, you do have a point, prostitutes make poor witnesses.' He glanced irritably at Hannah, suddenly deciding to take her into his confidence. 'It's damned messy really, not the sort of stuff the bank goes in for as a rule.'

'If it's a 'igh-class establishment, never know who comes and goes, does ya?' Hannah said cheekily, then added, 'Could be dodgy, knows what I mean?' She paused, once again in control of her emotions. Her anger, now well bedded down, would keep for another time. 'So what's ya want from me? Can't rightly see 'ow I can 'elp ya.'

'Yes, well, frankly you're right, it's not much to take before the bench.' He looked up at her and seemed for a moment to hesitate, then added, 'We also have a problem with the damned frog forger chappie we arrested in the basement of your husband's premises.'

'Oh, the geezer what's got the printer? What's the problem?'

Sir Jasper drew on his cigar and threw Hannah a dark look. He appeared to be thinking, his eyes narrowed, his head only half visible in a miasma of cigar smoke. 'Unfortunately he's deaf and dumb!'

The Upper Marshal batted away the smoke from his eyes, looked at Hannah and smiled, seeming for a moment genuinely amused. 'Ideal for a man of his occupation, eh? Most decidely nimble of hand and eye, though deaf and dumb. Not much chop in the witness box, though.'

'Three tarts and a madam in the Old Bailey and a bludger what's deaf an' dumb, it ain't much to go with, is it then? I'll bet ya London to a brick that in ten minutes I can find you four tarts who'll swear on the 'Oly Bible, even swear on their dyin' muvver's 'ead, that yer forger geezer just recited the ten commandments personal to 'em, forwards and then backwards and finished it orf with a rendition of 'Andel's 'Allelujah Chorus, and this Van Summink's a Jew as well!'

'Well, yes, you might be right! What we need is *someone* or *something* else.'

''Ere, wait a mo!' Hannah, astonished, exclaimed. 'Yer not askin' me to invent evidence against me 'usband, is ya?'

'Well, no, not precisely.' He arched one of his magnificent eyebrows. 'That would simply be making five witnesses of a kind!' Sir Jasper's nose suddenly came alive again, delighted at the tartness of this last remark. 'As you so wisely observed, women of your vocation will swear to anything on the heads of their dying loved ones.' He pulled at his cigar, satisfied that he had once again achieved the upper hand.

Hannah's hidden frustration at the news of Ikey's betrayal suddenly overwhelmed her sense of caution. She wanted to bite back and Sir Jasper was available. 'It takes a whore to know one! Whore's ain't only of one sex!'

Sir Jasper shot upright, the legs of the chair hitting the floor with a crack. 'Madam!'

To Hannah's surprise, after this single admonishment, Sir Jasper returned his chair to its former two-legged position and smiled, a small secret smile. With the sharpness quite gone from his voice he said, 'I'm grateful we've reached common ground at last, madam. Down to brass tacks, eh? I was hoping we might not have to raise the matter of the five, or is it six brothels *you* own?' His voice grew suddenly sharper again. 'Correctly prosecuted, you should receive more than a drag or even a stretch, transportation, fourteen years at the very least, Botany Bay or perhaps Van Diemen's Land.'

He waited for a reaction from Hannah and when none was forthcoming he cleared his throat and continued, 'Why, madam, such would seem the only possible sentence. You shall have fourteen years to regret your lack of co-operation! Do you not think you ought to think upon this? Or is your loyalty and affection to Mr Solomons of such a purity that you would protect him at the cost of a dark, rat-infested prison at the other end of the world for much of the remainder of your miserable life?'

Sir Jasper waited, removed the cigar from his mouth and examined it at arm's length. Hannah saw that it had become dark stained with his spittle at the sucking end, while it carried a full inch of spent ash at the other. She observed his cigar, not from any personal interest, but because her wits had temporarily forsaken her, and she knew herself to be hopelessly trapped and entirely at the mercy of the small, cigar-toting policeman.

Curiously, it did not occur to her to blame the smug little knight for her predicament. Nor did she recall that it was she who had persuaded a reluctant Ikey to employ Abraham Van Esselyn. All she could think was that it was Ikey who had once again caused her downfall. He had absconded and left her as his hostage. He had betrayed her with a whore and robbed her of a prize which was rightfully hers. Come what may, she would make him pay! She would not take a moment's punishment for the miserable, sodding shit.

'I should remind you that you will never see your darling children again,' Sir Jasper added. 'What do you say to that, Mrs Solomons?'

Hannah inhaled sharply and then in a low voice asked, 'Now, sir, what was it ya jus' said about it 'aving to be, ya know, *someone* or *summink else* what is needed for the case at 'and?'

Sir Jasper, now also smiling, leaned a little closer and placed his hand on her knee.

'Well done, my dear, how very sensible of you. I feel sure we can come to some satisfactory arrangement, what?'

Hannah looked up suddenly. 'Could we not leave England, scarper, never come back no more?'

'Why, madam, that's preposterous! Simply unthinkable!'

'Why?' Hannah asked simply.

'Justice, there must be justice! Good God, woman, where would we be if we simply let our hardened criminals escape to other societies. What would they think of the English?'

'They probably don't think all that much of 'em as it is,' Hannah said laconically.

'Balderdash! There's not a civilised man on earth who doesn't wish he was an Englishman! An arranged escape? Unthinkable and positively unpatriotic!'

Hannah cleared her throat, averted her eyes and spoke in a small, almost girlish voice. 'We could probably leave a little bequest, a little summink to remember us by, a little personal summink what we could leave to yer discretion to use for whatsoever good you might consider in yer wisdom can be done for Mother England?' She paused and looked furtively up at the policeman. 'If you knows what I mean, sir?'

The cigar fell from Sir Jasper's lips, 'Good God, woman! Are you attempting to bri–'

At this point Sir Jasper leapt from his chair with a terrible yowl, upsetting the table and sending his top hat flying across the room as he frantically beat at the front of his trousers. The cigar, nowhere to be seen, must have fallen through his waistcoat and down into the interior of his trousers, for Sir Jasper continued to beat at his crotch, while turning in small agitated circles, his legs pumping up and down as though dancing on the spot. Then his foot caught the leg of the upturned table and, losing his balance, he landed in Hannah's voluminous lap. His head fell upon her breast and his now panicked nose was inches from her own. But for the fact of the room being so small, and that the back of her chair was placed almost against the wall, Hannah, together with Sir Jasper, would have turned topsy-turvy, landing on the floor in a heap of kicking legs, petticoats, pantaloons and flailing arms.

Hannah was the quicker of the two to recover. She looked

down at the hapless Sir Jasper, who was flapping, whimpering and snorting, and observed the smoke rising from that area of his trousers which is known to be most delicate when assaulted. With one arm she pinned him to her breast and with her free hand hastily undid the last two buttons of his waistcoat, shot into the front of his trousers, and plucked the offending cigar from within.

Hannah's shameless sense of humour overcame her as she held up the still smouldering cigar. 'There were two of them little devils down there, sir. I chose the bigger one!' she cackled. Then, the gravity of the situation reasserted itself and she released him, and clamped her hand over her mouth to smother any possibility of a further outburst.

If Sir Jasper was conscious of this coarse attempt at humour he gave no sign of it. As though caught within a collapsed tent he was struggling wildly to find his way out of the folds of Hannah's commodious skirts. He regained his feet finally and, clutching his singed and painful scrotum in both hands, he roared at Hannah, 'You have not heard the last of this, madam! By God! I shall see you and your husband hanged at Tyburn yet!'

He removed a hand from his crotch and grabbed the cigar from Hannah, throwing it to the floor and stamping on it several times until it became a soggy, pulpy mess. Removing his hands he glanced down upon his recently violated area and observed a hole in the light coloured material not larger than a sixpenny bit, but in a strategically awkward area. Again clasping both his hands over it he backed away from Hannah.

'Damnation and blast! I have an appointment at four of the clock and cannot first go home!' Sir Jasper cried.

'Why, sir, it is not much of a mend,' Hannah remarked calmly, 'an 'ole no larger than the tip o' me tongue, and what might come about if a gentleman could 'ave took forty winks in his club chair with 'is pipe or cigar in 'is mouth. You must let me attend to it at once – I am a clever seamstress who will soon repair it invisible.'

'Keep your filthy harlot's hands off me!' Sir Jasper said fearfully, backing still further away from Hannah, so that he now stood in the corner with his back against the wall like some miscreant schoolboy who has failed at spelling.

'Tut, tut!' Hannah clucked. She was accustomed to crisis and mostly took immediate possession of the situation. 'Come now, sir, it ain't that bad!' She rose from her chair. 'See I shall move yer chair and sit upon it and you shall stand behind me back, remove yer trousers and pass 'em to me across me shoulder. I 'ave needle and thread with me and I am trained as a seamstress.' She smiled brightly, acting quite unconcerned and natural in her manner.

Sir Jasper looked at Hannah suspiciously, then he turned slightly away and uncupped his hands briefly to observe the damage once again. 'Very well, madam,' he said, the sulkiness still contained in his voice, 'but this service rendered does not alter your predicament! Attempting to fee an officer of the law is a very serious offence!'

Hannah chose, for the moment, to ignore this remark. A man without his breeches, she reasoned, is much more amenable to compromise. She rose and placed the table upright, then crossed to his chair and turned it so that when seated her back was towards him. She sat down and arranged her skirts.

'Come now, sir, it is to mendin' we must now pay our attention.' She waited with her hand placed on her shoulder ready to receive the recently damaged garment.

Sir Jasper found it impossible to be in opposition to Hannah's calmly stated demands. His imagination took flight and he was once again a small boy intimidated by his nanny. Standing with only a woollen vest above his waist as she chided him for some small misdemeanour, running her hands down his thighs and massaging his buttocks as she threatened him with the back of her hairbrush, then kissing and fondling his tiny waterworks, which, now in its adult proportion, was growing at a quite alarming rate.

Sir Jasper, quite breathless, seated himself upon Hannah's recently vacated chair and hurriedly removed his boots and then his trousers, releasing his engine with a spring as the restraining cloth passed beyond it. Whereupon he replaced his high-heeled boots upon his feet.

'Quickly! We must 'urry to mendin', or you'll catch yer death,' Hannah said solicitously, her fingers fluttering impatiently upon her shoulder.

She had already prepared the needle and thread from her bag. Now she took the trousers from Sir Jasper, and quickly turning them inside out blew the cigar ash from the surface of the cloth, and commenced to work upon the hole, gathering its edges together and stitching it in the manner of a sutured wound, this being much the quickest and neatest way under the prevailing circumstances.

From the corner of her eye she now observed that Sir Jasper had come to stand close to her shoulder and was breathing heavily. She turned slightly towards him and was confronted by his stiffened prod almost touching the edge of her bonnet.

'Well, well, what 'ave we 'ere?' Hannah's vast experience of men made her summation almost instinctive. 'A little boy what's 'urt 'imself? A little boy who wants nanny to kiss 'im better?'

'Yes, yes, please, nanny, it hurts a lot, please can you kiss it better!' Sir Jasper gasped urgently, his voice a mixture of fear and anticipation.

Hannah laid down her needlework, took the pins from her best bonnet and removed it, placing it on the table, whereupon she unpinned her hair and shook her head, so that her hair fell to her shoulders in a cascade of brilliant titian-coloured curls. Her movements were deliberate and calculated to excite him even more. Then, with Sir Jasper wincing and groaning at her shoulder, she took his manly pride between her thumb and forefinger. Moving her head closer, she ran the point of her clever tongue around the underside of its purpled cap at the point where it joined the manly thrusting stem.

'Ooh! Oooh! Oh, God! Oooh!' Sir Jasper moaned.

Then she withdrew her tongue. 'We'll not be 'earing any more of bribery charges, will we now, ya naughty boy?' Hannah cooed.

'No, nanny! I promise! Please, please, I beg of you, suck upon me! Oooh!'

Hannah smiled and licked her lips, and took him once again and brought him to the ultimate point before she withdrew her tongue again. 'And no more of 'anging?'

'Oh, Jesus! No! No more of hanging!' Sir Jasper whimpered. 'I beseech yoooou!'

'Swear it as an English gentleman, upon the 'ead o' the King 'imself!' Her tongue flicked out and licked invitingly at her lips then, darting further, playing mischievously with the tip of her nose.

'I swear as a gentleman, upon His Majesty's head,' Sir Jasper gasped. 'Please, nanny, do me! Do me now, I beg of you. I cannot bear it a moment longer, suck me dry, ooooh!'

Whereupon Hannah took Sir Jasper into her mouth and, with the help of her lascivious tongue, proceeded to satisfy him beyond his wildest fantasies. Completely exhausted, he reeled back and collapsed, gasping and panting. Half sprawled upon the chair, his pot belly was an incongruous helmet placed upon his otherwise skinny frame, his naked, hairless legs, encased at their ends with high-heeled boots. Hannah noted with satisfaction that his nose, now flat and pale as a badly risen scone, cowered against his florid, sweating face.

'Yer trousers,' Hannah said, rising and covering his nakedness by placing the garment across Sir Jasper's lap. 'I apologise most 'umbly,' she said, grinning wickedly, 'I made much too light of yer other cigar, it is a most worthy smoke, sir!'

Sir Jasper looked up at Hannah and gave her a small smile, his tiny obsidian eyes expressing a much becalmed disposition.

'If we are to be *friends*, m'dear,' he panted, 'it is best that I state the terms right off.' He sat up, clutching his trousers to his crotch, attempting to sound businesslike in his manner. 'I can do nothing for your husband other than attempt to forestall his march to the gallows. We can enter a plea that no long-tailed notes were found in his possession, only those of five pound value, though these are of exceptional quality and most numerous. The judge may, with a little persuasion, come eventually to see that transportation rather than hanging is in order.'

Sir Jasper grunted, and bent down to remove his boots. Arising, he proceeded without shame to reappoint his trousers to his skinny frame, and then, seated once more, returned his boots to his small stockinged feet.

'We shall, of course, need your co-operation in the matter of the counterfeit fivers,' he said, looking up at Hannah for her confirmation.

'An' me?' Hannah asked. 'What's to 'appen to me?'

Sir Jasper rose from the chair and stood once more trousered and confident. His recent intimacy and claims of friendship seemingly quite forgotten, and with his thumbs hooked into the lapels of his cutaway coat, he declared, 'Ah, yes, the sewing woman! We must reward the sewing woman.'

He glanced down at his front, admiring the tiny, almost invisible finger pluck seam where the cigar hole had previously been.

'A capital job, m'dear, and most skilfully completed!'

He glanced slyly at Hannah, so that his double meaning would not be lost to her.

'Yer most welcome, I'm sure, sir,' Hannah said, returning his knowing look. 'Yer always welcome to me 'umble mouth!'

Sir Jasper pulled himself up to his full height, which was by no means impressive. 'Mrs Solomons, I must remind you, each of us has our place and you would do well to remember yours! Let me be quite clear, we shall have no blackmail here, do you hear?'

Hannah had half expected his return to pomposity, for she was well aware that the masculine mind is directed largely from below the waist, and that there is nothing so restoring to the male ego as the return of his trousers. Even so, she was not of a mind to apologise. She knew enough of these matters to be certain that the priggish policeman would be back for more in due course. The next time she would tempt him further with a good spanking. The back of the hairbrush on his noble little botty. Hannah felt confident that her relationship with the Upper Marshal was far from over.

Hannah answered sweetly, 'Blackmail, sir? I can't rightly say that I knows what ya is talkin' about.' Then abruptly changing the subject Hannah looked ingenuously at Sir Jasper. 'Ya ain't answered me question sir. What shall become of our 'umble family? If me 'usband should be transported, 'ow shall we live?' She lowered her voice and its tearful character returned. 'With 'im gorn yer condemning us to the work'ouse!'

'Why, Mrs Solomons, you are by all accounts a resourceful woman. I feel sure your, er . . . dockside establishments bring you a handsome return?'

Hannah feigned surprise. 'I'm sure I don't knows what ya mean, sir. If what ya said was goin' on, but what I said wasn't, but could be, that is, if a person was forced into supportin' 'er four starving kids without an 'usband, if such establishments were to 'appen to be about to . . . open?'

'Yes, well, I dare say if you are prepared to co-operate fully, the bank isn't too interested in your, er . . . *other* businesses.'

Hannah sniffed, reaching into her handbag for a dainty handkerchief and touching it to each eye in what she supposed was a genteel gesture, she looked imploringly up at Sir Jasper. 'Am I so bold as to believe, sir, that ya would turn the self-same blind eye to the establishment what is at me poor 'usband's 'ouse in Bell Alley?'

'The printing shop or the brothel?'

'No, sir, not the printin', definitely not the printin'. Me, what can't read nor write 'as no use for a printin' shop.'

'Ah! You are sprung, madam!' Sir Jasper laughed. 'So you *do* know Egyptian Mary? You wish to continue your husband's partnership? Two sows in the same trough, eh?' Sir Jasper chuckled at his own joke. 'Well, well, well, well! I would be surprised if Egyptian Mary would countenance such an arrangement, she is a woman of some pepper. Still, I guess you would know, eh?'

'No, sir, I does *not*!' Hannah snorted. 'Ya quite mistake me meanin'. I want me 'usband's so *called* partner arrested! It were 'er what turned 'im to queer screenin' and printin' unlawful paper, if such a thing 'as been done by 'im! It ain't fair if she goes free! That's a blatant miscarriage o' justice, that is!'

'But there is no evidence to implicate her in his forgery,' Sir Jasper said frowning. 'We can't let you continue to run six bawdy houses and arrest her for running but one! Why, madam, we'd be the laughing stock of the City!'

'It ain't the same!' Hannah countered. 'I takes me earnin's from the criminal classes, the filth! Them what don't know, and never can know any better! What I does is as natural to them as stealin', they's born to it, it's a social 'abit, normal as breathin', I cater for them what doesn't 'ave no 'ope of risin' up from a life o' crime and grog!'

'I can't possibly entertain such a preposterous idea, Mrs Solomons!' In point of fact, though, Sir Jasper, who shared the contemporary social views that the criminal poor were born and not created by environment or circumstances, was not unimpressed with Hannah's argument. 'I must remind you, justice is blind. Running a bawdy house of whatever kind is an equal crime against the law. If we are to overlook the one kind, *your* kind, we must do the same for *her* kind, what?' Sir Jasper lifted his chin and looked down at Hannah across his florid nose. 'British justice must prevail, there's an end to it now, the matter bears no further discussion!'

Hannah was not prepared to concede. 'Yer actual law, yes! That I'll grant ya is the same! But what about yer lot, the upper classes? What about *yer* morals? What about *yer* standards o' society? Me 'umble customers can't get no better. They ain't got no morals and they ain't got no standards what can be upheld. But what o' *yer* lot? What this Egyptian whore is runnin' is causin' the destruction of the moral standards o' the better classes! Them what's born to morals and standards and must set an example for the 'onest poor!'

'Clever argument, as a matter of fact, dashed clever!' Sir Jasper seemed genuinely impressed. 'Madam, I commend you for your reasoning, but . . .'

Hannah's interruption was of perfect timing. 'I really don't think I could give me complete co-operation, me absolute best o' information and 'elp in the matter o' me 'usband and the printin' press, if ya was to turn a blind eye to this den of iniquity and sinfulness what 'as caught me darlin' Ikey in a web spun by this 'orrible, 'eathen, Egyptian whore!'

Sir Jasper, taken aback by this sudden change of attack from Hannah, seemed momentarily lost for words. He paced the few steps left to him in the tiny room. 'Hmm! Very awkward.' He glanced at Hannah. 'I don't suppose it would make any great difference if I told you Egyptian Mary is English? Her name is Mary Abacus. Not her real name, carries an abacus see, damned clever at calculations, London as the bells of St Clements, not a drop of wog in her, born in Rosemary Lane, tough as a brigade boot, lots of ginger, hands deformed, some sort of bizarre accident down at the docks on Jacob's Island.'

Hannah was now breathing heavily. The Mary she knew, who carried the Chinee contraption wherever she went, was a drunken whore who had also taken to the opium pipe, usually the end of the road for her kind. Hannah was an expert in such women. Their last stop was a brothel such as hers, thereafter they would be soon dragged from the river with a boatman's hook, or found with their ears and nose and fingertips eaten by rats, their body submerged in some putrid cesspool or rotting in a dark, evil smelling alley. It was almost beyond believing that this Egyptian whore might be the same Mary. That bastard Marley knew all the time – the miserable sod owed her two sov! Ikey had chosen this *nemmo* scumbag above his own wife to partner him in the high-class brothel of *her* dreams. The humiliation was too impossible to bear!

Now Hannah, visibly shaking, glared at Sir Jasper. 'If that filthy whore don't *get the boat* then ya can stick yer threats up yer arse! I'll take me chances with the law. This very night all six o' me places shall become netherkens where the desperate poor can stay for tuppence a night, you'll 'ave to prove otherwise and all I can say is you'll 'ave a bleedin' 'ard time doin' it!'

Sir Jasper, much taken aback by Hannah's fury, brought his hands up to his chest as though to protect himself from the battery of words she hurled at him.

'Hush, hush, m'dear, you'll do yourself a harm,' he cried in alarm. 'I shall see what we can do!'

'Not good enough, sir!'

'Hell hath no fury, eh?'

Sir Jasper was sufficiently sensitive to realise with some delight that Hannah's venom was largely directed towards her husband. Now she confirmed this, her scorn evident as she spoke. 'Ya can 'ave 'im, 'e ain't no good to me no more, I 'ope the bastard rots in 'ell!'

Sir Jasper smiled. 'Mary Abacus will be arrested, I promise.'

'And transported?'

'I can't influence the judge, m'dear.'

'Ya can 'ave 'im a word in the ear o' the judge, like you said ya could in the matter of Ikey's 'anging!' Hannah said tartly.

The little man sighed heavily. 'That being a civil crime, this, madam, would be a social one!' As though to explain he shrugged and added, 'A crime against the people.'

'Swear it!' Hannah demanded.

'You strike a hard bargain, Mrs Solomons.' Sir Jasper paused. 'Very well, I swear I shall arrest Mary Abacus and cause her to be transported, though it will not be a popular idea in the City.'

Hannah, vastly relieved, sighed heavily. She had been angry, but now she found herself excited at the prospect of the demise of the whore with the beads and, even more thrilling, her nicely contrived revenge on Ikey. She loved the feeling of power it gave her. It was more than simply revenge on two people who'd dared to cross her, it was a portion of repayment for the bitter disappointment of her life.

But then, like a thunderbolt, it struck her that she had once again been denied. Hannah realised that she must forgo the sweetest part of her vengeance. She could not let Ikey know it had been she who had brought about his downfall. If Ikey knew she had betrayed him he would never agree to give her his half of the combination to the safe. He would rather rot in hell than see her benefit a single penny from his plight.

Hannah looked up knowingly and smiled indulgently at Sir Jasper. 'Men got weaknesses what they can't rightly be blamed for.

I implore ya, sir! For the sake o' me young 'uns, I don't want me 'usband to know it was me who shopped 'im!'

Sir Jasper took a gold hunter from his waistcoat and clicked it open. He was anxious to conclude the business at hand. 'No, of course, Mrs Solomons, there is absolutely no need for your husband to know of your co-operation with the authorities.' He returned his watch to his waistcoat. 'Under the circumstances it is most honourable of you to spare his feelings.'

'Kindness 'as always been me great downfall,' Hannah, her eyes cast downwards, said modestly.

Sir Jasper cleared his thoat. 'Now, this is what we want and, I must warn you, I shall brook no altercation on the matter. We shall raid your premises in Whitechapel and we shall expect to find a number of counterfeit five pound notes well concealed. The money we find will be some portion of the counterfeit notes we discovered in the basement premises at Bell Alley.'

'The money? In me 'ouse? You must be completely barmy, that makes *me* guilty too, don't it?' Hannah cried. 'Complicity in 'elping to conceal stolen goods? I ain't as *meshuggah* as I may look, ya know!'

'I have already given you our assurance as an officer of the law and a gentleman on that matter, madam.'

Hannah laughed. 'With the greatest respect, sir, what 'appens if ya drop dead? When I'm standin' in the dock in the Old Bailey and the judge passes sentence on me, what am I goin' to say? Oi! That's not fair, yer worship! Him, what's the Upper Whatsit, told me I 'ad 'is personal guarantee as a gentleman and officer o' the law that I can't be nicked!' Hannah rose indignantly from her chair and placed her hands on her hips. 'Ha! The bleedin' judge will think I've gorn soft in the bloomin' 'ead, *and* 'e'd be right too, allowin' counterfeit money to be found in me own 'ouse.'

Hannah sat down again, huffing and snorting. She needed a moment to think, for she had a secondary reason for not wanting the police to raid her Whitechapel home. Though well concealed in the false ceiling under the floor of her bedroom, the house contained goods of great value. There was also the matter of the safe. The City police were an entirely different kettle of fish to the usual, dim-witted magistrates' runners. Hannah didn't want to take the chance that in the bogus search for the counterfeit banknotes, this too might be discovered.

Sir Jasper was visibly growing impatient. 'You will have to trust me, madam!' he said sharply.

'It ain't a matter o' trust, sir. It's a matter o' natural caution, a matter of survival. I wouldn't trust me own rabbi from shoppin' me if 'e was to find counterfeit money in me 'ouse! Stands to reason, don't it? In the eyes o' the law, Ikey and me, we'd both be guilty!' She paused and smiled at the police officer. 'May I suggest summink more appropriate?'

The Upper Marshal banged his fist down hard upon the table. 'No, madam, you may not! I hardly think a woman of your background could improve on our methodicals! This plan is the work of experienced officers, it requires no alteration, being quite perfect as it is!' He folded his arms across his chest and glowered at Hannah in a most imperious manner.

Hannah remained silent until she gauged that Sir Jasper's exasperation had somewhat calmed, then she persisted. ''Is coat. Sew the money in the linin' o' his coat, then nick 'im on the street, away from 'ome, away from me and the young 'uns!'

The police officer, despite his irritability, looked up at her in surprise. 'I say, do you think you could do that?' Then he rested his chin on his chest and mused, as though to himself, 'Lining of his coat? Caught red-handed with the money on his person, in his possession?' He looked up and smiled at Hannah. 'By, Jove, that's perfectly splendid! No way of wriggling out of that, eh?' Sir Jasper rubbed his hands gleefully together, completely mollified. 'Perfect! Why, it's quite, quite perfect, m'dear!'

'Not so perfect, already!' Hannah scowled. ''E don't ever take 'is coat orf, not never and not particular never at this time, when the weather is inclement and comin' up to Christmas.' She cocked her head and thought for a moment, 'On the other 'and, if 'e don't ever take orf 'is coat . . .' she paused, thinking again, 'then the only person what would 'ave put the money there is 'isself, ain't that right, then?'

Sir Jasper clapped his hands in delight. 'I say, that's damn clever, m'dear! Capital, how very wise of you!'

Hannah knew the task of apprehending Ikey away from home would be a most difficult one. Ikey's mode of travel through the rookeries was nocturnal and shadowy, never tiring in the task of concealment. No magistrates' runner or Bank of England law officer could ever hope to follow him, or even dare to enter those parts where his crepuscular fellow creatures engaged in business with him.

Ikey's coat was a very elusive target and the more she thought about it the less confident she was that such a scheme could be made to work. But with the knowledge that all the stolen property concealed in her Whitechapel home would come into her possession while she was, so to speak, under the protection of the law, Hannah possessed a powerful additional incentive to succeed.

'When will ya let me 'ave the false finnies, sir? I needs no more than two.'

'Finnies? Oh, you mean the five pound notes? You shall have them promptly on the morrow.'

'In the afternoon, if ya please. I needs me beauty sleep!' Hannah smiled and then, with one eyebrow slightly arched and her head cocked to one side, her expression coquettish, 'Perhaps you would like to bring 'em y'self, sir?'

Sir Jasper Waterlow's complexion turned a sudden deep purple and his nose began to twitch alarmingly. Avoiding Hannah's eyes he gathered up his top hat from the table and moved towards the door where he paused, and slid the slender fingers of his left hand into a bright yellow leather glove. He was quite exhausted and in urgent need of a stiff brandy.

His expression now somewhat composed, he looked directly at Hannah. 'I shall require you to wait five minutes before leaving,' he grunted, then added, 'I should also be very careful not to *lose* the five pound notes I shall send you. It would be most difficult to convince me that such a calamity was honestly come about.' He pulled the second glove on and glanced briefly at Hannah from under the rim of his top hat. 'Though, of course, in such an event, we do have others.' Then he touched the brim of his hat. 'Good day to you, Mrs Solomons,' Sir Jasper said and, passing through the doorway, closed the door behind him.

Hannah smiled. She could hear the clatter of his mincing high-heeled steps in the hallway and then the silence as he stopped to retrieve his cloak from the proprietor, then a few more steps as he departed the Blue Wren. 'That's gratitude for ya,' she said to herself. 'But that one will be back soon enough for a good spankin' from 'is adorable nanny, nothin' surer.'

Not long after this meeting, Hannah once again summoned Bob Marley. He was surprised to be contacted by Hannah so soon after it would have been apparent that he had duped her in the matter of the raid on the premises in Bell Alley. Hannah was not known for her forgiving nature. Marley was therefore understandably suspicious at her openly friendly manner. She sat him in the parlour where a bright fire blazed and where she had laid out a single glass and fresh bottle of brandy with a plate of oat cakes.

Apart from his initial greeting Bob Marley remained silent, pouring himself a large glass of brandy and helping himself to a couple of the cakes.

'It weren't nice what ya done, Bob Marley,' Hannah began. 'Takin' advantage of a poor woman what was 'elpless.'

Marley, with a mouth full of cake, stopped chewing and rose from his chair as though to leave. 'No, don't go!' Hannah added hastily, smiling. 'We got things to talk about what could be to yer advantage.'

Bob Marley swallowed the cake in his mouth and took a gulp of brandy to wash it down. 'It were you who called me, remember? All I done was take advantage of a situation what was not o' me makin'!' He was still holding the glass and, bringing it up to his lips, paused. 'It would 'ave been unprofessional not to 'ave done what I did. People might 'ave thought I was losin' me grip o' things!'

Hannah refrained from reminding him that there was only herself involved. When she thought about it, she supposed she too would have thought less of him if he hadn't exploited such an opportunity to benefit from her predicament. It was this very self-serving aspect of Bob Marley's nature which she now wished to use to her advantage.

'I needs a job done, no questions asked,' Hannah said finally.

Marley gave her a bemused look. 'There's always questions, lovey.'

'What I means is, I don't want to talk about me motives, I wants ya to accept 'em, no questions asked.'

'No questions costs more money, it means I can't measure the exact amount o' risk involved.'

'No more risk than if ya knew everyfink, you 'ave my word on that.'

Marley waited, saying nothing, and Hannah continued. 'Ikey will come back to London, reasons that don't matter to ya, but 'e'll be back. He can't come 'ome, too dangerous. 'E'll need a place to 'ide and somebody 'e can trust to find it for 'im and act,' she paused and looked at Bob Marley, 'sort of as a go-between 'tween me and 'im.'

Marley took a long swig at the brandy in his glass, prolonging his lips on the rim of the glass longer than would have seemed necessary, as though he was thinking carefully on the proposition. Finally he looked up at Hannah. 'There's a big reward out – I'd 'ave to be paid 'least that, and expenses, mind. Findin' a deadlurk what will keep 'im safe wif 'arf the bleedin' world keepin' a greedy eye out for 'im ain't goin' to be easy!'

Hannah had already taken herself through the process of having to pay Marley the equivalent of the reward on Ikey's head, but she was nonetheless shocked at the prospect when she heard it coming from Marley's own mouth. She swallowed hard, 'For that sort o' money I'd want more,' she said, her gaze steady.

'More? What's ya mean?'

'I wants ya to plant some fake stiff on Ikey.'

Marley brought his palms up in front of his face. 'Hey now, Hannah, we's family people! Ya going to shop Ikey by plantin' snide on 'im, that ain't nice. That ain't nice at all?'

Hannah stiffened. 'Remember, I said no questions. I 'as me reasons, Bob Marley.'

Marley whistled. 'I bet ya 'as, lovey.' He sighed and looked directly at Hannah, 'Sorry, I don't do domestics.'

'I'm not askin' ya to take sides! Jus' to plant some fake soft.'

'I'll not shop 'im, Hannah. I'm no copper's nark.'

'I didn't ask ya, did I? Just to do a plant, that's all.'

Marley looked up. 'Jus' the plant?' He seemed to think for a moment. 'It'll cost extra.'

Hannah laughed and then shook her head. 'Sorry, love, when ya asked for the reward, that be the limit. There's 'undred pound on Ikey's 'ead and I'll pay that, but not a farthin' more.'

Chapter Ten

Since time out of mind, long before the coming of the great belted engines with their hiss and suck of steam and whirr of wheels and pistons, before the city provided warmongery to the world with its mountains of iron ore, furnaced, hot rolled, steam hammered, pressed, poured and moulded into the fiery spit and spite of small arms, Birmingham had always been the Babylon of baubles. It was here that goldsmiths and silversmiths, in a thousand tiny workshops, made jewellery so wickedly extravagant as to turn many a fine lady into a whore, and many a whore into a fine lady.

As may be expected, where there is gold, silver, plate and wicked little stones with nimble fingers to shape and polish them, there are gentlemen with even lighter fingers to fleece them from their rightful owners into the greedy hands of the unctuous fence.

Ikey arrived in Birmingham at eight o'clock in the morning of his second day out from London, not stopping to pass the night in a comfortable tavern, though several of these establishments existed for this sole purpose – inns where a weary traveller could expect a crackling fire, a sizzling pot roast, a pewter mug of good mulled claret and, upon a quiet word into the landlord's ear, a bed warmed by a ploughman's daughter, a wench with ivory skin and thighs as creamy to the sight as fresh churned butter. It was common enough talk among those who often travelled these ways that the yokel's daughter, so lasciviously described, had indeed been much ploughed and so often seeded as to sprout half the snot-nosed bumpkins in the parish.

It was most surprising that Ikey chose to continue on the smaller, faster night coach to Birmingham. He was, after all, a natural coward and it being the Christmas season the danger of meeting a highwayman or footpad on the road was greatly increased. Only a fool or a traveller with most urgent business would think to travel with a mail-coach running hard through the night. But Ikey, a creature of the dark hours, felt most vulnerable when exposed to the brightness of sun-pierced light and, in particular, within a restricted location such as a coach. He had sat miserably all day trapped and huddled in the corner of the day coach from London, the collar of his coat pulled high and his hat placed deep-browed upon his head, with his face turned outwards to the passing countryside. Should his fellow passengers have wished to observe him they would have seen only the collar of his coat and the broad-brimmed hat which appeared to rest upon it.

To all appearances these aforementioned fellow passengers looked innocent enough: the ginger-bearded horse dealer with his shaggy one-eyed dog, the two long-fenced clerical types in dark cloth, only the colour of their waistcoats telling them apart, and of course the monstrously fat woman in widow's weeds, a human personage so big she could easily turn a living in the grand freak show at Southwark Fair. But Ikey was taking no chances and said not a single word all day, not even allowing the most banal of courtesies.

When evening came and his fellow passengers left the coach for the comforts of a night spent in a village tavern, the opportunity to continue on alone was presented to Ikey by the departure of a lighter and faster mail-coach travelling through to Birmingham. It contained sufficient room for four passengers, though he seemed to be the only one to purchase a ticket from the coachman.

It was a most bitter disappointment to Ikey when Tweedledum, the red-waistcoated clerk, climbed unsteadily into the coach. He smelled strongly of cider and barely nodded as he found his seat at the window opposite but on the same side as Ikey, so that their eyes could not meet. Now they both faced in the direction in which the coach was travelling. Ikey had not thought of him as separate, but as one component of a two-part presence in red and yellow, and it disturbed him to think that he'd made such an unthinking assumption based simply on their attire.

Ikey's first instinct was to become immediately suspicious of the man's presence. But if Tweedle was an officer of the law sent to keep an eye on him, his recent intake of the local cider had rendered him ineffective, for Tweedle was becoming increasingly cross-eyed, his head lolling with the delayed effects of the local scrumpy.

The ostler had all but completed checking the harnessing and the coachman was already aboard, whip in hand, when the fat widow, clutching her large hamper to her bosom, emerged panting from the tavern and came towards them.

The coach was delayed ten minutes as the ostler and the coachman pushed and squeezed, panted and shoved to fit the giant woman through the door of the smaller carriage. Once contained within its interior it would have been quite impossible for any further souls to occupy the remaining space, of which there was now very little. The lighter mail coach, though harnessed with a full team of horses, was built for speed and not for the comfortable accommodation of passengers. The gargantuan woman filled one entire side of its interior, her fat knees occupying the corridor between them, and her hamper taking up the centre of the opposite seat with the silently drunken Tweedle at one side, and Ikey huddled tightly into the corner at the other.

It was snowing quite hard, though the road was still clear and the post-chaise set off at a brisk pace into the night. The widow completely ignored Ikey's presence and shortly after they reached the first toll-gate she reached over for the hamper, placed it on her lap and clamped her fat arms around its lid. Then she fell into an immediate and seemingly deep slumber.

Ikey hoped to do the same, for he was desperately tired and had been awake more than twenty-four hours, and with the absence of the hamper the seat beside him promised to make an excellent bed. But Tweedle, as if struck by a blow from an invisible hand, collapsed into the space left between them. The cider had finally rendered him senseless.

Ikey turned up the collar of his coat and, pulling its lapels around his chest, settled down to sleep. Alas, the widow soon put this prospect from his mind, for she caused a great deal more trouble for Ikey asleep than ever she'd done in a state of wakefulness.

During the day Ikey had observed from the corner of his eye and by a direct assault on his nostrils, that the widow had partaken of several large meals, the fare coming out of the seemingly inexhaustible larder on her lap.

Now, as she snored, her tightly compact innards fought back with a series of combustible noises. From her vast interior oleaginous gases rumbled in ferment. After a period of time all these internally combusted sounds combined to reach a climax. It seemed that at any moment the pressure within her would become so great that a cork must surely pop from her navel, cause a huge efflux and send coach and horses, Ikey and the unconscious Tweedle all the way to kingdom come.

Ikey sat huddled in his corner with the collar of his coat and the brim of his hat tightly pushed against his ears, though the sounds prevailed, penetrating the protection of his cupped hands. Just as he supposed he could stand it no longer, when the noises and fumes of regurgitated gases and thunderous farts became too noxious even for his seasoned nose, with a soft sigh the widow quietly awakened and proceeded to open the hamper on her lap.

A small lantern swinging from the coach roof cast a to-and-fro shadow across the interior of the cabin, so that the widow would disappear into the complete darkness and then a moment later appear again, lit by the dim light of the swaying lamp.

Ikey watched from the inside of his coat as food began to appear. First was the smaller part of a haunch of ham, one side showing white to the bone and the other plump with pink meat. From it the widow carved, at the very least, a pound of pig flesh and proceeded to layer it upon a thick crust of bread. This she sprinkled with a generous pinch of salt, swiped with a blade of yellow mustard and garnished with pickle forked from a large jar. Finally she added to the conglomeration several thumps of thick, dark, treacle-like sauce.

Each meal was taken precisely on the hour, each different; a mutton pie large enough to feed a hungry family, a plump chicken and a raisin tart, a turkey leg and a pound of white breast meat, a large cold sausage and apple pie, a slab of cold roast beef and several boiled potatoes. A large pork and leek pie was the last but final means of satisfying the giant woman's voracious appetite.

Ikey, thoroughly miserable, watched as a cold blue dawn appeared over the gently rolling countryside, the tops of the low rounded hills blanketed with snow. He was desperate for sleep and his small belly, so seldom demanding of food and having observed so much of it during the night, now rumbled with the need for sustenance, though even now food was not his greatest need and he would willingly have remained hungry for another day in exchange for two hours of uninterrupted sleep. He envied Tweedle who seemed not to have stirred on the seat beside him.

With no further food to consume, the widow settled down to finish off the demijohn of gin. She seemed unaware of the sleeping shape of Tweedle, whose face lay only inches from her plump white knees, but fixed Ikey with a stern and disapproving eye, or rather, she fixed her disapproval on the dark, silent upright bundle in the corner. Holding the neck of the demijohn in her fat fist, she brought it to her lips, and with a tolerable level of sucking and lip smacking and occasional bilious burps the widow proceeded to get very drunk. Ikey, at last, was able to fall into an exhausted sleep.

He was awakened three hours later by the sound of giggling accompanied by several sharp prods in the region of his chest and stomach. 'Wake up! We be in (hic!) Brummmagen soon.' The widow was jabbing at him with the stick and giggling, her fat head wobbly with her mirth and she drooled like a well-fed infant. 'Wakey-wakey!'

Ikey sat up quickly, dazed from insufficient sleep. It was by no means the first time in his life that he'd been prodded awake with the point of a stick, and he immediately imagined himself to be in a prison cell, for the smell was much the same and the ride had become unaccountably smooth, so much so that, to his blunted senses, the coach appeared not to be moving at all.

In fact, the coach was completing the last mile into the centre of Birmingham by way of the new road composed of a material known as macadam. This was a tar-like substance as used for caulking vessels. It was heated until it was treacle-like and ran easily, whereupon it was poured upon a bed of small stones (the men who mixed it might use no stone larger than one they could roll on their tongue and still repeat: 'God save the King!'). The substance was soaked into the stony surface and while steaming was compressed with a large steamroller and allowed to dry smooth and hard. The result was a surface impervious to the most inclement weather and upon which any manner of wagon or coach wheel could travel. All was made without the need for skilled labour and at a fraction of the cost of the quarrying, shaping and laying of cobblestones.

Ikey's mind was not tuned to dullness and he was soon aware of his surroundings. The widow, satisfied that she'd done her Christian duty and wakened him, did the same for Tweedle. He sat up groaning and holding his head in both hands, eyes bloodshot and his hair standing up in untidy tufts. 'Oh my Gawd!' he moaned.

Ikey stared out of the coach window at the houses, some with chimneys already smoking in the early light, growing more and more numerous and close-built as they approached the city centre and the coach terminus. Staging posts, particularly at the terminus from one great metropolis to another, were much inhabited by the watchful eyes of the law as well as those of informers hoping to earn a few shillings for spotting a known villain. Ikey's fondest hope was that he would be allowed to skulk unnoticed from the scene into the nearest darkened lane, and thereafter to a nearby rookery where he would be free from the ever curious attentions of any members of the law or the under-world.

He now became concerned with the presence of Tweedle. His earlier anxiety returned and Ikey imagined him to be a law man who would elicit the aid of a waiting law officer from the Birmingham constabulary to arrest him, his task while on the coach simply being to keep a watchful eye on him lest he take his departure before reaching the city.

Ikey was tired and his senses somewhat blunted. He told himself one moment that he was imagining the danger, and the next that he should have reasoned it out long before this and left the coach when they'd stopped to change horses at a village during the night. Caution, with its partner suspicion, being his more natural instinct, Ikey decided he would make a dash for it the moment the coach drew to a complete standstill.

Ikey carried no personal baggage. In fact, Ikey's taking a chance that a highwayman might waylay the coach during the night journey was not as courageous as it might have outwardly seemed. Highwaymen seldom shoot their victims and Ikey had no fear of robbery, for he'd carried in his purse coin sufficient only to purchase the coach ticket and to eat frugally and pay for his accommodation for a day or two upon his arrival, with a little left over for miscellaneous expenses. A secret pocket under the armpit of his coat contained fifty pounds, though a highwayman would need to remove the coat and most carefully dissect its lining to find this. To be robbed of what he superficially possessed would have been no serious matter. He carried only a cheap watch and chain and a small cut-throat razor and the deeds to the house in Bell Alley, a paper which would make no sense to a common robber. Also resting in a pocket was the key to his home in Whitechapel.

It being so close to Christmas, this absence of serious cash on Ikey would have been somewhat surprising. Anyone who knew him was aware that he would often carry a thousand pounds on his person, for the season's pickings would be exceedingly good and ready cash was what was needed to make the most of the many opportunities certain to come his way. But, this time in Birmingham, Ikey was playing for much bigger stakes than the fencing of a few bright baubles taken in the Christmas crowds.

The coach drew at last to a standstill, the coachman laying aside his horn and shouting, 'Whooa! Whooa!' to the wild-eyed beasts in the time-honoured way. The horses thus brought to a stop shook their heads in a jingle of brasses, champed at the bit and stamped their feet on the hard surface of the road. Their coats were lathered with sweat from their final gallop and their nostrils snorted smoky air.

The coach official opened the door on the widow's side. 'Oh me Gawd!' he exclaimed fanning his nose. He immediately turned to the waiting crowd. 'Anyone come for a show freak?' he yelled. 'If 'e is, she be blind, 'opeless drunk! Need ter fetch cart and oxen, or special sprung carriage. She'll not be walkin', I can tell 'e that for sure and absolute certain!'

The widow reached out and took the unfortunate official by the collar of his coat and pulled the top half of him backwards into the coach so that his head lay upon her lap. ''Ullo, dearie, fancy a kiss?' she said, then burped loudly into the man's astonished face.

Ikey glanced quickly at Tweedle, who sat frozen upright looking directly out of the window, trying to ignore the bizarre antics of the drunken woman and the wildly struggling and whimpering official.

Taking advantage of the confusion, Ikey quietly unlatched the coach door on his side, leaving it ajar. Then he rose and lifted the still surprisingly heavy hamper and placed it down upon an astonished Tweedle's lap, quite preventing him from rising in pursuit should he take it in his mind to do so, whereupon he pushed the door open and stepped through it. But alas, his coat caught on the sharp corner of the small door and pulled him back. Ikey pulled desperately at the coat and a six-inch tear appeared in the thick wool as he wrenched it free, and then dashed into the dark shadow cast by the terminus building. In a few moments he had escaped up a narrow alleyway which ran between the stage coach terminal and the building beside it.

Ikey's immediate destination in Birmingham was not, as might normally have been the case, one of the more notorious flash-houses nor thieves' kitchens where he might be expected to take up temporary residence, but to a stabling property on the outskirts of the city.

This large, unprepossessing building of rough-hewn stone had all the appearances of a farmhouse. It was set on the road to the village of Coleshill, with stables on the ground level for several horses and above it two additional storeys, which a visitor might naturally suppose was the owner's residence. However, in this instance, the large building was much, much more than a simple farmhouse and might even have been called a kind of factory, a paper and ink factory to give this most improper and anonymous business a proper name.

The property belonged to Silas Browne Esq., outwardly a respected horse dealer but to those in the know, one of the greatest forgers of soft in the land. He was a man of great ingenuity and reputation known to all who dealt in a serious manner in good forged banknotes throughout England and continental Europe.

Birmingham was the chief centre of the production of good hard, this being the name for counterfeit coin. Since it had always been a place where fine jewellery, watches and military medals were made, it was easy enough for Birmingham craftsmen to turn to this illicit trade. The same was not necessarily true for the forging of banknotes, and had it not been for the remarkable talents of Silas Browne and his wife Maggie the Colour, the city might not have become a recognised centre for banknote forgery.

While the city supported a great many clandestine coining workshops it contained only a handful of talented engravers. These mostly derived from men who had been decorators of gold and silver plate. Though these few very skilled men together gave it an acknowledged presence in banknotes and forged letters of credit, and even some work on share certificates, their efforts were no greater than other major English cities.

Etching was an exacting task and a superior engraver might take a year or more to perfect the plates required for a single banknote, so that these men needed to be financed and carefully safeguarded by those who profited most from their skills. Silas Browne and Maggie the Colour were known to employ the very best engravers. But to the engraver's skill they added two ingredients which gave Birmingham an advantage in the forged banknote trade. The house to which Ikey now hurriedly set out was used for making this paper and ink.

Silas Browne, though seeming a ponderous and somewhat befuddled man, made the best counterfeit paper in England and his wife, Maggie the Colour, the best inks. This combination, together with the fact that Silas financed most of the more skilled engravers and so came into possession of the best engraved plates, made them very wealthy. It was claimed they had a share in every forgery printing operation in Birmingham and, as well, sold ink to Manchester printers and even to some of the better London operators.

Maggie the Colour was the daughter of a Manchester dyemaker and possessed a talent for mixing inks and dyes and an eye for subtle colour, shading and gradations, which was truly remarkable. She was known to use mostly local tinctures, some from plants and herbs she collected in the surrounding countryside, the juice of mulberry and pomegranate imported from Spain, as well as tannins from various types of wood. These she mixed with the exotic pigments and dyes available on the English market, but which came from India, China and from Dutch Batavia used by the silk makers in Macclesfield and the cotton spinners of Manchester. Any forger worthy of his name would use no other ink, the powdered galls mixed with camphor supplied by Maggie the Colour were so good that even the officials at the Bank of England could find no major fault with her product.

Given the very best engraver's plates, expertly prepared paper, perfect ink matching and superior printing, the work done by Silas Browne and Maggie the Colour was among the finest in England. But it fell short of perfection because the paper used for bills simply could not be reproduced, and the plates used for banknotes above the ten pound denomination were thought to be too complicated for a single engraver, and could never hope to deceive even the most casual banker's eye.

Abraham Van Esselyn's forged plates were near to being the exception. They were the very finest of their kind available, perhaps in the entire world of forgery, so perfect that they might have been prepared by the Bank of England's own engravers. These plates, now about to be offered by Ikey to Silas Browne, were the work of a single man of undoubted genius and moreover, each was perfect to the point of almost any magnification. This made them of the greatest possible value to a team like Browne and his wife, Maggie, though, of course, it was not concerning these alone that Ikey had come to see them.

Ikey, having walked for almost an hour, came at last to the end of the city's sprawling slums, and soon found himself in more open ground where cottages rested separately, some with small gardens to the front or back. Ikey disliked space of any sort and his eyes darted hither and thither. He shied away from a barking dog, and jumped wildly at the sudden crow of a cockerel or the hissing of a goose. Some of the lanes along which he passed contained hedges on either side which provided some concealment, though nature's walls of hawthorn thicket did very little for Ikey's peace of mind. Strange things went click and buzz and chirp within them, and none of these noises equated to the myriad sounds to which Ikey's highly particular ear was tuned.

It was coming up mid-morning when he finally reached the open field in the centre of which stood the house of Silas Browne. Ikey was in a state of high nervous tension. The daylight hour, though some snow had started to fall, coupled with the open terrain through which he had been forced to travel on this final part of his journey, had brought him very close to complete panic. He was hungry but so single-minded in his mission that he hadn't even thought to enter a chop house for a meal. Now he stopped and rested at the gate leading into the field and, removing his neckcloth, wiped the nervous perspiration from his brow and the back of his neck.

The large treeless field appeared to be flat and, but for a dozen or so horses grazing about it, completely empty. Ikey expected that the moment he entered the gate someone would appear from the house to meet him. In fact, this is what he hoped might happen before he'd intruded too far into the large field, and so was unable to retreat to the gate should a savage hound, designated for this very purpose, be set upon him. An envoy sent from the house would give him an opportunity to explain his reason for coming, and to send ahead of him a sample of his credentials for perusal by the redoubtable Silas Browne and his wife.

Ikey entered the field, his eyes darting everywhere, forwards and backwards and to either side. To his dismay no one came from the distant house and he was forced to move ever closer to it. Therefore it came as a fearful surprise to him when his hat was tipped over his eyes from behind, and a voice declared.

'Don't turn around, sir!'

Ikey, despite the fright he'd received, was of course an expert on young boys, and this voice was no more than ten or eleven years of age. This didn't do a great deal for his confidence, however, as street children of this age were as tough as grown men. Besides, they were sometimes larger than himself. He removed his hat and replaced it squarely back on his head.

'A penny for a word then, my dear,' Ikey said slowly, digging into his coat to find a copper coin which he held between finger and thumb and proffered behind his back.

His unseen assailant snatched the coin from Ikey's hand.

'Where does you think you're goin' then?' the boy enquired.

'Silas Browne! I begs to see Mr Silas Browne. That is, with your permission o' course, your very esteemed permission, my dear.'

'Mr Silas Browne, is it? 'Ow does you know such a name, then?'

'Business! We is in the exact line o' business. Mr Browne is what you might call a colleague, though, I'll freely admit, I 'aven't exactly 'ad the pleasure of 'is personal acquaintance.' Ikey shrugged his shoulders. 'You see, we share what you might call a vocation. Yes, that's it, precisely and nicely and most specifically put, my dear, an exact and precise and similar vocation!'

'Oh, a voca . . .' the voice gave up trying to pronounce the word, 'and what line o' business does you share, then?'

Ikey was surprised at the sharpness of the boy. He'd come across similar boys before, but these were few enough to be an exception. Most street lads this age were already dulled from gin and the lack of proper nourishment, and would not have the wit to become involved in a conversation the likes of which the two of them were now conducting. This one would have made an excellent addition to his Methodist Academy of Light Fingers.

Now that he'd properly gathered his wits Ikey was impressed at the boy's sudden appearance behind him, seemingly rising out of nowhere. Ikey's eyes missed very little and even though he was unfamiliar with open terrain and the lack of shadow in daylight to reveal the bumps and undulations in the grassy field, it was no simple task to deceive him. The boy who crept up could not have followed him for any distance, for Ikey was in the constant habit of glancing over his shoulder. He must have walked right past the boy without seeing him, and this Ikey found both admirable and very disconcerting.

'The copper business . . . copper plates that is.' Ikey paused, 'Also, you could say, also the paper and inks business. I can say no more, from this moment me lips is sealed and can only be opened by Mr Silas Browne 'imself!'

'Does you 'ave an affy davy to say who you is, then?'

'Affidavit?' Ikey held an additional penny behind his back, wiggling it invitingly, but the boy did not take it this time. 'Most certainly and o' course absolutely right and correct to ask, my dear! An affy davy you shall 'ave, right away and immediately, for 'ow would your master know the manner o' person who 'as come so far and taken so many risks to talk with 'im? 'Ow indeed? All the way from London, that is, with barely a wink o' sleep and not a morsel o' nourishment from sunrise to sunset. I asks you, 'ow is 'e to know the 'umiliations and vicissitudes inflicted or the extreme importance o' the mission? Quite right of you to ask, quite right and proper.'

'Your affy davy,' the boy repeated bluntly, seemingly unimpressed by Ikey's verbosity and still not taking the proffered coin. 'Give't me, sir, or you get nowt more from us!'

Ikey carried no personal identification whatsoever, and even if he had papers to prove himself, he would not have willingly let them into the boy's hands, especially without having first seen his face. He was on the run, and young likely lads like this one schooled in the rookeries learned early the value of informing, of keeping their eyes peeled for the opportunity of a little crude blackmail.

The engraved plates he carried concealed in the lining of his coat would be instantly recognised as masterpieces by any competent forger and a glimpse at one of them, Ikey knew, would be likely to have Silas Browne scurrying out to meet him, his voice a bluster of apology and his hands all apatter. But if he let the boy have only one plate as a proof of his integrity, and if his master should choose not to see him nor to return it, the single engraved plate in the right hands was still worth a considerable fortune.

'I shall give you a piece o' paper, a small piece o' paper you must promise to take to your master, to Mister Silas Browne 'imself and to no other. Do you understand, my dear?'

'It'll cost,' the boy added cheekily.

Ikey sighed and retrieving the copper coin he held it once more behind his back.

'A sprat! Cost you a sprat or nowt 'appens.'

'Sixpence!' Ikey howled, though he did so more for the form of it than anything else. The boy was good, very, very good and he wished he could have him under his tuition. The boy reminded Ikey of the young Bob Marley, same cheek and quickness of mind. He smiled to himself, for he knew he could now trust him to take the paper directly to Silas Browne. Ikey returned the copper coin to his dumby and found a silver sixpence which he handed backwards to the boy.

'This paper what I want you to take to Mr Silas Browne, it is concealed upon me person. I shall need to stoop down to reach it and to cut open the 'emline o' me coat to remove it. I 'ave a small razor to do so, but my dear, do not be in the least alarmed, we, that's yours truly, is not at all a creature o' violence and disputation.'

'Don't turn about now!' the boy said threateningly, trying to put a deeper tone into his voice.

'No need, absolutely no need! No need in the least, you have my guarantee upon that, my dear.'

Ikey reached for the cut-throat razor in his pocket and opening it he stooped down and cut quickly at the line of the hem, though above the hidden plates, and only a cut wide enough to ease one of the plates sideways through the slit. He untied the twine and removed the wrapping from around the engraving. With the razor he sliced a small triangular corner from the square of paper, which he handed backwards to the boy.

'Take the paper to Mr Silas Browne, my dear, it's me affy davy.'

Ikey waited.

'Hey, mister, 't ain't say nowt onnit!' the boy exclaimed. 'It be blank paper what's got nowt writ onnit!'

Ikey chuckled. 'On the contrary, my dear, it speaks most eloquent to those what knows 'ow to read its message.'

There was silence behind him and Ikey imagined the confusion the boy was feeling. Seeking to put the lad out of his agony, he added, 'It's invisible like, but to such as Mr Silas Browne Esquire who knows the trick o' reading it, it's a magical paper.' Ikey spread his hands. 'Trust me, my dear.'

'You'll stay 'ere, see! You'll not be doing nowt 'til I returns!' The boy added threateningly, 'There's dogs, big bastids what can be let loose and sent after you in a twinklin', you'll not get t'gate before they's torn you t' bits!'

'Not a muscle, my dear, not a single twitch, not a cat's whisker, not a scintilla o' movement until you gets back. Quiet as a mouse, silent as a ferret in a chicken coop, that's yours truly, Ikey Solomon, late of London Town. Tell your master there's more, much more where that come from, 'eaps and 'eaps more! 'E'll be most pleased, most pleased indeed to know that.'

The boy ran past Ikey and towards the house, laughing, not caring now whether Ikey saw him. He carried a long stick which he waved in the air. He was tiny, small enough even for Ikey to box his ears or place a sharp-toed boot into his scrawny little arse.

The boy, at first delighted to have made sevenpence so easily, grew anxious at his own reception as he drew nearer to the house. Silas Browne and the half dozen men and boys who worked with him stood waiting at the head of the ladder for him to climb into the room above. The lad, afraid he might lose the paper, held it between his lips as he climbed the ladder.

'Wotcha got then, Josh lad?' Silas Browne asked as the boy stepped from the ladder into the room.

Together with the others he'd stood watching from the windows at Ikey's original approach. They'd seen the boy Joshua, who'd been earlier sent on an errand, waylay Ikey from behind, before they could send an adult out to accost the stranger. Josh, though only ten years old, was known to be bright enough to make a judgement, yet young enough not to arouse any suspicion if the stranger was thought to be from the law. Silas knew that if the lad decided the man was up to no good he would drop his stick on the ground and then pick it up again. Whereupon he'd send one of the other lads down and set the dogs after the intruder to see him off their land.

One of the men pulled the ladder up after the lad had climbed clear and closed the trap door behind him, bolting it firmly back into place. The boy Joshua looked somewhat sheepish at the greeting given by his master and, removing the tiny slip of paper from between his lips, handed it to Silas Browne.

"Tain't much, sir, but 'e sayed it was magical like, that you'd understand immediate like?' The boy, a most concerned expression upon his face, looked up at Silas Browne. 'Did I do wrong, sir?'

Silas Browne took the paper and rubbed it for a moment between his forefinger and thumb, whereupon he jerked back in surprise.

'No, lad, methinks you done good!'

He moved immediately to the window, where he held the paper up to the light.

'Jaysus!' he exclaimed.

"E says there's more, lot's more where't come from, Mr Browne, sir,' Josh shouted across the room, much relieved at this reception.

'Bring sponge, lad . . . a wet sponge!' Silas Browne shouted at one of the boys nearest to him. "Urry!'

In a few moments the boy returned and handed Silas Browne a damp sponge. Placing the scrap of paper again against the window glass, Silas wiped carefully over it several times. Then he lifted it from the window with the edge of his thumbnail and called for a pair of tweezers. Holding the paper at one corner with the tweezers, he walked over to a hearth where several cast-iron pots of blacking plopped slowly on the open coals. He held the pincers and paper to the heat of the embers, and the tiny scrap of damp paper took only moments to dry. Silas Browne returned to the window and held the paper once again to the light.

'Jaysus, Mary and Joseph!' he shouted, "Tain't possible, watermark's stayed! Bloody watermark's stayed put right 'ere on paper! Quick! Call Maggie!'

Another young lad dashed off while the rest of the men gathered around, astonished to see that the faked Bank of England watermark had remained undamaged, as though it was woven within the very substance of the paper.

'What's 'is name, Josh?' Silas demanded.

'Ikey . . . Ikey Sausageman, sir . . .' Josh looked uncertain. 'Sonomins, summit like that, sir.'

'Ikey Solomons! Jaysus Christ!' Silas pointed to one of the men. 'Go with the lad, Jim, bring 'im along, 'e be famous like in London!' He looked around impatiently. 'Where's bloody Maggie?'

Not twenty minutes later Silas and Maggie looked on in amazement as Ikey produced the first of the engravings. Ikey unwrapped the watermarked Bank of England paper covering the copper rectangle, and leaving it lying in the centre of the paper he straightened out the sheet, smoothing its sides with the edges of his palm without touching the shining copper plate, so that the rectangular etching lay pristine, a precious slab of polished metal catching the light. Then Ikey tried to lift the etched copper plate from the centre of the paper but his hands were too cold and his fingers were quite unable to function. Maggie, seeing his distress, bid him warm himself at the hearth while she brought him a plate of bread and a deep bowl of beef and potato broth.

'There you be, then, Mr Solomons, a bowl of broth will soon warm you proper well!'

While Ikey greedily slurped the creamy broth, thick almost as a good Irish stew, Silas and his wife, who, in her wooden clogs, stood as tall as her husband, examined the etching but did not touch it or the bill paper on which it lay. Halfway through the large bowl Ikey stopped and pointed to the sheet of paper with its corner missing, and nodded to Maggie the Colour. 'Take a good look then, my dear! Never was there a better drop o' paper for your marvellous colours and tinctures, and never a plate etched more perfect!'

Maggie picked up the etched copper plate while Silas examined the paper, neither saying a word, as Ikey went back to slurping his soup. Maggie the Colour handed the copper plate to Silas, holding it carefully between her fingers at each end and took the paper Silas had placed back on the table and walked over to the nearest window. She carefully flattened a portion of it against the window pane.

After a few moments she turned to Silas. 'What you think, then?'

'Never seen nothin' the likes o' this engravin' before!

Never . . . and that's Gawd's truth!' exclaimed Silas, examining the plate through an eyeglass.

'The paper?' Maggie asked, turning now to Ikey.

''Ow'd you do it, Mr Solomons?'

'Solomon, it don't 'ave no "s",' Ikey said, placing down his spoon, the bowl close to empty. He was suddenly aware that hunger and cold had driven him to show too much without the attendant patter required to work them up to the first unveiling. He had neglected the basic tenet of business, to reveal only a little at a time, enough to whet the appetite, so to speak, while holding sufficient back to feed the urgency of the bargaining that must inevitably follow. Now he attempted to recover somewhat from this poorly managed beginning.

'I've 'ad the pleasure o' being a regular customer for your work, my dear. Marvellous! Ain't no personage in England, perhaps even the world, what can mix tinctures, colours and gradations as subtle as you. Work o' pure genius, madam! Pure and simple and undisputed genius, no less.'

Maggie the Colour smiled thinly and looked down, embarrassed. 'Now, Mr Solomons, 'tain't *that* good!'

'Not a scrap less praise and 'onour is due to you!' Ikey declared. 'Them colours is o' the 'ighest possible magnitude, the work of a genius!' Ikey cleared his throat and grinned at Maggie. 'Now supposin' I was to ask you 'ow you come about them colours, asked Maggie the Colour the secret o' her dyes and tinctures and the mixtures for your ink galls? What say you then, my dear?'

'Quite right!' Silas Browne laughed and with the eyeglass still clamped in his eye, clapped his hands. 'You'd be gettin' nowt from our Maggie! Them inks and dyes, tinctures and juices, they be 'er secret to 'er final dyin' breath, till grave an' beyond!'

'Ah, you see?' Ikey exclaimed. 'A secret is only a secret when it remains in the 'ead of one person. Share it with another and it ain't a secret no more. You can kiss it goodbye, my dear, it's gorn forever. It's like a bloomin' swallow what's left England for warmer climes when winter approaches. Next thing you know it's on the other side o' the bloomin' world, darkest Africa or wilds o' South America! Good secrets all 'ave a price and the tellin' o' them is never cheap!' Ikey resumed slurping his soup, satisfied that he'd somewhat recovered the initiative.

'Do we take it you 'as a proposition to make, like?' Silas Browne asked, carefully placing the plate he'd been examining back on the square of paper which Maggie had returned to the table.

Ikey's untidy eyebrows lifted halfway up his brow and his eyes widened in pleasant surprise, his spoon poised in mid-air.

'A proposition? Why sir, that is exactly and precisely and unequivocally what I 'ave! A proposition, a business proposition, a remarkable opportunity, a proposition the likes o' which may never come your way again. A truly great conjunction of opportunities, of copper and paper and ink, an opportunity not never to be matched in its potential for wealth! A proposition you say! Why, I couldn't 'ave put it no better meself.'

Ikey went back to the remainder of his soup, and when the scraping and rattling of his spoon had ceased he further stalled the opportunity for an answer from his hosts by wiping the interior of the bowl clean with the last of the bread. 'A proposition as delicious, madam, as this bowl of excellent broth!' he finally concluded.

Maggie the Colour smiled at the compliment, knowing it to be the first thrust in the bargaining to come. 'Where shall we begin, then . . . paper or plate? I can see the plate but paper be but one sheet and cut at corner like?'

'Paper's good, but 'ow much? 'Ow much 'as you got?' said Silas Browne, repeating his wife's question.

Silas was not a man inclined to much subtlety nor one to beat about the bush, and he'd already spent as much good humour as he was known to offer anyone. Ikey, seeing him for the more clumsy of the two, had hoped that he might be the mouth. But it took him only moments to realise that Maggie the Colour's smile was a clear indication of where the brains in their partnership lay.

'Depends o' course what denominations you want to print, my dears.'

'Denominations?' Maggie the Colour looked at Ikey curiously. 'This plate is for ten pounds.'

Ikey jabbed a finger at her. 'That it is, my dear, but it could be supposed that there might be others if an interest is shown in what 'as already been revealed and remarked upon? There could be a plate to the astonishin' denomination of one 'undred pounds!'

'One 'undred pounds? You say engravin' be for one 'undred!'

Silas said scornfully. 'Bullshit! 'Undred pound engravin' be too 'ard for single engraver, too 'ard by 'arf and then some! 'Undred pound engravin' take four scratchers, maybe five. 'Tain't humanly possible!'

Ikey shrugged. Things were beginning to go to plan; show the top and the bottom of a proposition, the extremities of the deal, and the middle. The details, could usually be relied upon to take care of themselves.

He reached into his coat pocket and withdrew the small cut-throat razor and opening it slowly, he stooped down, lifted the hem of his great coat and laid it with the dirty lining facing upwards on the table. Then he carefully extended the previous slit he'd made by perhaps three further inches. His thumb and forefinger acting as pincers entered the slit and soon withdrew a second wrapped plate. How Ikey knew this to be the hundred pound plate is a tribute to his very tidy brain, and an indication that he'd secured the four etchings in the lining of his coat before leaving London.

Now he handed it to Maggie the Colour, who carefully opened up the neat little parcel to reveal the plate for a one hundred pound Bank of England note. Ikey let the hem of his coat drop back to the floor as Silas Browne swept up the copper rectangle, this time making no pretence at care, so that Ikey was seen to wince. He twisted the eyeglass back into his head and commenced to examine the plate. As he did so, his breathing increased until he was positively panting in surprise. 'Jaysus! Jaysus Christ!' he said.

He laid down the plate, this time with care. ''Tain't possible,' he turned to his wife, 'but it be there and it be nigh perfect!'

'Does we take it the paper and the plates go together, like?' Maggie asked, 'the ten pound and 'undred pound plates and you ain't said 'ow much paper you got?'

Ikey chuckled and spread his hands wide. 'And I ain't told you 'ow many o' these little copper darlin's we've got, my dear!'

'Four,' Maggie said calmly. 'You 'ave four.'

Ikey's eyebrows shot up. 'Well done, my dear, you 'ave turned my supposin' into proposin'. Indeed I 'ave four.' Ikey pulled the hem of his coat back onto the table, and his long dirty nails disappeared within the slit he'd previously made and withdrew each of the remaining parcels.

'Twenty and fifty, I do declare!' Ikey announced triumphantly and laid the two parcels on the table. Maggie the Colour sucked at her upper lip and commenced to untie each of the small parcels, not opening either until the twine had been removed from both. Then she revealed the etchings, leaving each on its own square of bill paper.

Ikey took a corner of each sheet and pulled them together then added the wrapping from the hundred pound plate, and the original piece with the corner removed, so that the four pieces of paper formed a rectangle two feet wide and three square.

'There you are, one complete sheet? Big enough, if I may say so, to make three dozen banknotes of any denomination you likes, my dears.' He paused and then added, pointing to the square made from the four separate sheets of paper, 'We 'as the pleasure o' makin' available to your good selves one 'undred and ten sheets o' the very same watermarked and quite perfect paper!'

Maggie the Colour snorted. 'And at what sort o' risk do these one 'undred and ten sheets come to us? Too 'ot to touch, I should think!'

'I shall sell you one 'undred and ten pristine sheets o' this bill paper without any risks o' the source becomin' known, this bein' me available stockpile. Then, if the paper proves to your likin', I could offer you a continuin' supply at the rate of one 'undred sheets per annum, the delivery to be made at eight sheets per month and paid in gold sovs on delivery.' Ikey was not sure how he would bring this about, but as the business opportunity presented itself so neatly he found it impossible not to capitalise on it.

'Eight sheets per month, that be only ninety-six sheets, not one 'undred!' Maggie snapped.

Ikey laughed, impressed at her quick calculation. 'Madam, we 'ave a sayin': "Always leave a little salt on the bread!" You gets the extra four sheets as a Christmas gift, compliments o' the 'ouse o' Solomon!'

'The paper, it's too good, you didn't make it did you, it's the real thing, ain't it?' Maggie said pointedly.

Ikey touched his finger to his nose and sniffed. 'Well I must most reluctantly confess, my dear, you've hit the nail on the 'ead. It's the same what the Bank of England uses, not a scintilla different, not a smidgin, not one jot or tittle different from what they uses to print their own longtails.'

'And the watermark?'

'The same! Woven in, my dear, the very innermost part o' the bill itself. Can't be removed no matter what you does, stamp, wash, bite, tear, while the paper remains, the mark is there!'

'And you've got one 'undred and ten sheets o' same?' Silas Browne asked again.

Ikey picked up the plate for the hundred pound Bank of England note and cackled, showing his yellow teeth. 'Or three 'undred and sixty thousand pound worth o' paper if you've a mind to use only this little beauty, my dear!'

'Why 'ave you come to us, Mr Solomons?' Maggie asked. 'Why 'as you not gorn into business y'self like?'

Ikey shrugged his thin shoulders and spread his palms and smiled.

'I only works with the best. It ain't me line of business, see. Ain't me expertise, ain't what I knows best. A man must stick to what 'e knows, the cobbler to 'is last, the butcher to 'is block, the poacher to 'is traps. These,' he pointed to the copper plates, 'they come about in the business o' receivin'. Receivin' and disposin' is me business, my dear, I received these and now I am disposin' o' them. Simple arithmetic, if you knows what I mean?'

'Aye, 'e be the prince of all the London fences,' Silas Browne agreed, glad to find a way back into the conversation. 'I knows him for that reputation.' He looked directly at his wife. 'That be the truth Maggie m'dear, Mr Solomons 'ere is a well-regarded London fence, also known and trusted in these Midland parts.'

Maggie the Colour sniffed. 'And the paper? That be fencin' business too?'

Ikey looked amused. 'If you 'as the right connections, my dear, everything Gawd made on this earth is fencin' business! All it takes is a little cash and a mind for makin' a connection 'ere, another there. Innovation is what some modern folks calls it. Let me give you an example. A lovely little silver candlestick goes missing from Mrs A's 'ouse and is brought to Mr B, what is me, yours truly. I knows Mr C, who will melt it down and sell the silver content to Mr D, a most excellent silversmith who is innocent of all guile. He will craft it into a fish server what might then be bought again by Mrs A to console 'erself over the tragic loss of 'er lovely little silver candlestick!'

Ikey clasped his hands together and dry rubbed them. 'All because o' the noble art o' ready cash and steady connections the world o' trade goes round and round, and we all profits nicely on that particular merry-go-round. What say you, my dear?'

'You may speak for y'self,' Maggie sniffed. 'We are not accustomed to the ways o' stealin'.'

Ikey smiled. 'Quite right, my dear, only from the banks who can afford it, ain't that so? Forgery ain't fencin', that's the truth, forgin' is the veritable Robin Hood profession, almost Christian, a perfect example o' robbin' the rich to pay the poor, an honourable profession it is to be sure.' He paused to take a breath. 'But one what also requires from time to time a connection or two? Maybe a paper connection what come from A to B, what's me, and then goes on to C, what's thee!' Ikey clapped his hands, pleased with his neat little summary.

'Aye, it be good paper, the best, that I admit,' Silas Browne said, 'though we'd be more friendly disposed if we knew more about where it come from.' He pointed at the bill paper. 'Paper the quality of your'n, tha' be mill, tha' be special!'

Chapter Eleven

It had all begun when a carpenter and works mechanic named George Betteridge, who was much taken by the game of ratting, fell into debt to Ikey. Despite two separate attempts with Ikey's own little terriers to get back his promissory notes, he still owed a considerable sum. Ikey, as was the custom, requested that he pay up by the following week, either in cash or in kind to the value of what he owed, a debt of nearly ten pounds. The hapless Betteridge confessed that he was penniless. He had a wife and seven children, lived in a single rented room in a village in Hampshire, and possessed nothing of sufficient value to match the debt. Furthermore, he saw no prospect of obtaining goods to the required value as a petty thief. Nor was he placed in a position to steal from a rich master, being employed as a carpenter doing general maintenance work for a paper mill in the village of Whitechurch.

'Paper is it? What sort o' paper?'

It was a routine question. Ikey was accustomed to probing into the unused corners of the minds of men who lack imagination, and who are unable to see the opportunities for profit right under their bumpkin noses.

'All sorts o' paper, all special,' the carpenter replied.

'Special is it? What's its name then?'

'Name o' Laverstoke Paper Mill, very reputable, been making particular papers for nigh sixty years, they 'as.'

'Laverstoke eh? By particular, does you mean expensive?'

'No, no, it ain't paper you can buy, like!' Betteridge corrected then lowered his voice and cupped his hand to the side of his mouth. 'Paper for bills, banknotes, very secret it is, very 'ush-'ush!'

Ikey concealed his excitement. 'May I ask you a question, Mr Betteridge? Does you know, or could you make the acquaintance, o' someone what works in this section what you says is strictly private. That is, the particular section what makes your actual paper for these . . . er, bills?'

The carpenter scratched his head, thinking. After a moment he volunteered, 'Me wife 'as a second cousin, a young cove what goes by name o' Thomas Tooth. Methinks 'e works in one o' the sections by front office, though I can't say for sure, 'e being a clerk an' all and me only 'umble carpenter and mechanic.'

'This second cousin o' your dear wife, this Mr Thomas Tooth, do you think 'e might be partial to a night o' rattin' and a good tightener at a chop 'ouse after? Or even two tickets to the Adelphi Theatre in the Strand, compliments o' yours truly with a nice little doxy thrown in for 'is particular amusement?' Ikey looked at Betteridge slyly and spread his hands. 'We'd be most honoured, my dear, and 'ighly complimented to 'ave 'im as our esteemed guest!'

The young Thomas Tooth proved to be everything Ikey had hoped for, naive but not without a certain arrogance, married with two children and another in the oven. He was also ambitious to improve his lot in life, resentful that he was being held up by a doddery chief clerk by the name of Seth Robinson, a Quaker, and entirely trusted by his masters at the Laverstoke Mill.

Ikey was careful to build up his confidence in the game of ratting and to guide him in the ways of the sport, even teaching him a few of the finer points, until the young Thomas Tooth felt compelled, through Ikey's generosity and good spirits towards him, to trust him completely as a friend and confidant. The first requirement of the sharper, the confidence man, is complete trust from the dupe, and it did not take Ikey long to have this condition firmly in place in the mind of the young clerk.

The more serious sharping now began and Ikey elicited the help of Marybelle Firkin, the mot of the Pig 'n Spit, the public house where the ratting took place in St Giles. With her went the aid of George Titmus the rat master.

Ikey was therefore absent on the earlier part of the night when Thomas Tooth was finally netted, this action being almost entirely left to the enormous lady publican and her diminutive rat master.

Marybelle Firkin was a very large woman, said to consume an entire saddle of the roast beef of old England at one sitting, whereas George Titmus, her rat master, was four feet eight inches tall and weighed eighty-five pounds wringing wet, though this did not happen very often as he had not taken up the habit of cleanliness. Working with rats and blood made him stink to high heaven, but he sensibly reasoned that should he wash it would occur all over again at the very next evening's fights. His skill with rats was such that his stench was tolerated among the punters, most of whom were themselves none too keen on the deadly touch of water from the Thames.

Both Marybelle and George worked well together on the magging of Mr Thomas Tooth of Laverstoke Mill, Whitechurch, Hampshire, chubbing him along and building his self-esteem the entire evening until there was only one more contest to come, and young Tooth was twenty pounds behind.

This last contest was between a little black and white terrier named Valiant, a good fighter who wore the champion's silver collar around his tiny neck. The young terrier was known to possess an excellent ratting technique and could usually be depended on to make a kill of thirty to thirty-five rats in a timed spell. The odds were called very short so that there were no punters save Thomas Tooth interested in betting.

The young country clerk, though too drunk for his own good, and heedless of the peril he faced should he lose, nevertheless knew the odds to be wrong and asked for better, for an evens bet.

'Gentlemen there is no sport in you!' Tooth cried. 'Will you not take a chance? Thirty pounds on an *evens* bet!'

Thirty pounds was a very big bet, and the crowd grew silent and waited to see if a bookmaker would accept the offer. Instead one of them laughed and waved Thomas Tooth away with the back of his hand. 'G'warn, be orf with you, lad, go on 'ome and kip it orf!'

Thomas Tooth, swaying slightly, took out his dumby and made as though he was looking into the depths of his wallet at a fortune lying at its bottom. 'My credit is good, I swear it!' Tooth cried, persisting with the lie. 'Who will take my marker?' He turned to look at the four bookmakers. 'If I should lose I swear I shall settle before the midnight hour.'

The young clerk looked desperately over at George Titmus the ratting master who had earlier been so free with his compliments. 'Who'll take evens, thirty pounds on Valiant to kill thirty rats, small rats . . . no sewers, cess or docks?'

Titmus nodded, seeming to take the young gambler seriously. 'Small it is, sir. I've a nice sack o' small 'ouse and country, just right for the little fella 'ere.' He glanced in the direction of the dog Valiant held in his owner's arms. 'Should do 'is thirty rodents easy enough, strong little fella, known to be most game!'

The punters around the ring grew silent, looking towards the bookmakers to see what would happen next. Tooth had called for small rats, house and country, which was a fair enough call as some sewer, cesspool and dockside rats were almost as large as the little terrier himself. The rat master had accepted, the contest was fair game.

From the darkness of the stairway leading to the ratting room and to the backs of most of the punters a booming voice rang out. 'Aye, I'll take it! I'll take ye marker evens on thirty rodents killed! Settlement afore midnight, did ye say?'

'Ah, a sporting man, at last!' the young gambler cried, turning to face the darkened stairway. 'Certainly, midnight! Payment you shall have precisely at the striking of the hour, my good sir!'

'Aye! May the devil hisself help ye if ye doesnae pay, laddie!'

There was a surprised gasp as the owner of the voice stepped out of the gloom into the room. The brutish, broken face which moved into the light was well known to be Dan Figgins, ex-heavyweight boxing champion of Glasgow and London, now a bookmaker with a reputation for very rough and unfavourable handling should his clients fail to settle on time.

Dan Figgins was not a regular at the ratting ring, being a horse man and well known, even by the aristocracy, at his betting box at Newmarket and Ladbroke Grove. Thomas Tooth, almost alone in the room, was unaware of this infamous pugilistic personage and besides, was now too desperate and too drunk to care. He scribbled his marker for thirty pounds and handed it to Figgins. Whereupon the rat master called for the rat boy to bring the ratsack, shouting: 'Mixed smalls, country and 'ouse, bring out the ratsack!'

This was where the final phase of the sharping began. The rat boy, a tiny, ragged lad of about ten years old, his dirty face and mucoid nose not having felt the touch of soap for a year or more, had prepared a bag of thirty-five large sewer rats to earlier instructions.

The rat master, cupping his hands to his mouth called again to the rat boy. 'Ring in the rats and shake out the tails!'

The boy, dragging the rat bag, which was tied with twine about its neck, brought it over to the outside edge of the ring. He hopped nimbly over the three-foot wall of the small circular enclosure and the bag of rats was handed to him by Titmus. The boy dropped the sack in the ring and placed his boot onto the centre of the jumping sack, which immediately calmed the rats within. The boots he wore were greatly oversized and the property of the house and were crusted with the dried blood of the night's previous bouts.

'Slap, shake and pat a rat!' George Titmus called. 'Step up the gentleman what's makin' the touch! All's fair what finds no sneaks or squeaks!'

Thomas Tooth, being the only punter, stepped into the ring to do the honours. Puffed with drunken self-importance, he commenced to beat solidly at the boy's threadbare coat, slapping hard into his skinny ribs and pummelling his shoulders and thighs in such an enthusiastic manner as to cause the lad to wince at his careless blows. Finally he required the urchin to hold his arms downwards and away from his body and, first feeling down the length of each arm by squeezing tightly across the bicep and forearm along the greasy sleeve towards the boy's wrists, he then demanded that the lad shake both sleeves vigorously. This deployment was intended to remove any rats which might miraculously have escaped the previous rigorous inspection.

Tooth, now finally satisfied, gave a nod to the rat master, who pronounced on the punters, 'All's clean what feels clean, nothin' squeaked, nothin' seen!' He turned to the rat boy. 'Sample the show, three in a row!'

The boy bent over and taking up the bag at his feet, began to untie the twine, though mid-way through this task he appeared to have acquired an itchy nose. He held the top of the bag with his left hand and scratched his nose with the other, finally wiping the copious snot from under it into his open palm and appearing to wipe his hand on his matted and greasy hair. His hand disappeared completely beneath his very large cap seemingly for this very purpose.

His sniffing and scratching finally over, the rat boy returned his attention to opening the bag and without as much as a glance inwards plunged his arm into the bag of squeaking rats and brought up the first 'show', a rat selected blind to show that the bag had been called correct, and selected as specified, 'small, house and country'.

'One-o!' he shouted holding a small house rat up above his head and then dropping it into the ring at his feet before plunging his arm back into the bag and withdrawing it again. 'Two-o!' The second rat was almost identical in size to the first. Once again his arm entered the rat bag, which was now jumping and bumping around his boots 'Three-o!' the boy finally yelled, holding a third rat above his head.

'All's fair what's shown fair! Ring the rats and free the tails!' the rat master shouted.

Whereupon the boy upended the entire bag of rats into the ring and they fell in a large tail-twisted and squirming clump. The rat boy commenced to sort them out, untying their tails and scattering them helter-skelter about the ring. Free to sniff and scratch while their eyes grew accustomed to the bright light, they seemed now to be quite calm. The rat boy climbed out of the enclosure as George Titmus rang the starting bell and the terrier, Valiant, straining in his master's arms and yapping in great excitement, was dropped in among the rodents.

What Thomas Tooth hadn't witnessed was that the three sampling rats the boy appeared to have pulled at random out of the rat bag, in fact came from under his large cap. These three small house rats, so ceremoniously shown, had been nestling quietly in his hair. They had been trained to the smell of mucus on his hand, and upon it entering his cap they had slipped down his coat sleeve where he'd concealed a crust of bread. So that he now only had to put his hand inside the bag and let a rat drop down his sleeve into it, whereupon he would withdraw it again to show that the rats in the bag had been selected small. He repeated this twice more to show three small rats in what was seen to be an honest call.

The rats which were upended into the ring from the bag stank of the river and the sewers, a particular smell no person experienced in the game of ratting could possibly mistake. Their bite was most infectious and often quite deadly, and they were larger by as much weight again as the three smaller house rats the boy had 'shown', though a direct comparison was no longer possible as all the rats in the ring now appeared to be of similar size.

This was achieved by a second clever ploy, though it would take a more sober man than Thomas Tooth to see the trick. The rat boy, having emptied the rats from the bag, scattered them about the ring, though a moment before doing so he had again wiped his nose. The three smaller house rats in the ring, trained to the smell of the mucus on the boy's hand, once again darted up his sleeve, leaving only the larger rats behind.

Moreover, while Thomas Tooth was busy patting and slapping at the boy in the ring, behind his back the silver collar was taken from the dog Valiant's neck and placed around the neck of a second terrier of similar markings. This second ratter, a bitch named Rose, cankered from rat bites, was a sister to Valiant from an older litter. Enfeebled from the gnawing of the canker, she could no longer fight well, even though her canine instinct and eagerness to fight remained, and to all appearances she was equal to the task.

Rose worked briskly, picking up a rat and shaking it, biting deep behind its head to snap its neck and then drop it, immediately grabbing at another. Blood dripped to the floor and the little canine was soon slipping as she scrambled to snatch at the now panicky rats. The terrier lunged at a very large rodent, slipped in the blood on the ring and missed. The rat, panic stricken, bit deeply into the little bitch's nose and hung on. Rose, who had already killed twelve rats, was beginning to tire. She tried to shake the large rat off, but it held fast and soon the little bitch's slender neck started to drop. As though by some primeval instinct, the remaining rats rushed at the weakened ratter and pulled her down. She tried to rise but the rats smothered her, tearing at her tiny black and white pelt.

The bell sounded and the rat master shouted: 'Rats high, dog low! Take yer dog or let it go!'

The rats had won and the rat boy, wearing a thick leather mitten, for the rats were now maddened by the taste of blood and would bite at anything, jumped into the ring and pulled a frenzied rat from the still alive terrier's body and threw it back into the ratbag. Some of the rats held on so tenaciously that the boy had to grab about their blood-matted stomachs, lifting the terrier's body with the rat still attached to it. With a twist of the wrist he removed the rat, leaving its teeth embedded in the pelt, as the little bitch fell back into the ring to be smothered again by the feeding rodents.

With the rats finally safely in the bag, the boy tied the top and lifted it out of the ring. The blood-crazed rats would continue to attack each other inside the bag in a squeaking feeding frenzy until only one was left alive. Such a rat was tagged and much prized as a symbol of luck and, should it recover from the numerous bites to its body, was eagerly sought by a keen ratter as a pet.

The rat boy climbed from the ring, the ragged ends of his trousers and the toes of his boots soaked with fresh blood. The stench of death was everywhere and the punters, the fun over for the night, began to leave. As was the custom, most of them repaired downstairs to Marybelle Firkin's public house where the gin whores would be carousing and the fiddler would be playing a merry jig on a gypsy fiddle.

Marybelle Firkin's inglorious establishment was well known for both ratting and whores and was well frequented by gonophs and macers and magsmen, and all manner of thieves and villains. Towards the latter part of the evening, when the ratting was over, the Pig 'n Spit became a place of great merriment and fornication with every dark corner as well as the skittle court behind the public house taken up with thrusting bodies and much loud groaning. Lust and loving was bought here for the price of three drams of gin. Hence the people in the surrounding rookery took much amusement by referring to both Marybelle Firkin and the Pig 'n Spit as 'Merry Hell Fucking at the Pig 'n Shit'.

George Titmus, the last to leave the ratting ring, turned the lamps down low. Rose, the little terrier, tried to rise, but slipped on the blood-stained floor. She tried again and this time got shakily to her feet, whimpering and looking up with trusting eyes to see if she could find her master. But she lacked the strength to hold herself up and collapsed back among the dead rats. She was dead before her owner sneaked back up the stairs to retrieve the silver collar about her neck.

With the contest declared in favour of the rats, Thomas Tooth owed thirty pounds to Dan Figgins to be paid by midnight. The fish was landed.

Dan Figgins' small, cold, agate-blue eyes, only just visible within the multiple folds of scar tissue surrounding them, grew sharp as pin-points as he heard Tooth explain his inability to pay up at the appointed hour.

'There's naeone t' blame for tha' except yourself, laddie,' Figgins growled.

Thomas Tooth grinned foolishly and with some courage from the brandy yet within him said, 'I cannot pay you, sir, you will simply have to wait!'

'Nay, laddie, ye doesnae understand, ye'll nae be breathin' God's breath beyond the midnight hour!'

Thomas Tooth shrugged. 'Methinks you cannot get blood from a stone now, sir, can you?'

The crowd gasped at his temerity.

'Aye, that I can, laddie!' He turned to the crowd. 'You cannae blame us for givin' him a doing, it wasnae our fault he couldnae pay, was it?'

The drunken crowd murmured their approval and someone shouted, 'Drub 'im, Danny boy!' Then added in a dismissive tone, 'Cheeky bastard!'

'Ye shouldnae have said tha', Mr Tooth. I'm a patient mon, but tha's gone a wee bit too far, I cannae let ye get away wi' it!' Dan Figgins smashed his huge fist into the young clerk's face, breaking his nose in a gush of blood and sending the hapless Tooth sprawling across the room. He knocked into a whore, who careened backwards screaming as she bumped against the far wall, and slid to the floor with the young gambler's bloody head imprisoned between her thighs.

This created uproarious laughter from the crowd who quickly gathered around the huge fighter, who was now standing with his fists balled above the young drunk.

Dan Figgins reached down, preparing to jerk the sniffing and whimpering Thomas Tooth to his feet, when he felt himself propelled backwards and then turned completely around by an arm the size of a doxy's leg.

As if by some peculiar magic the huge shape of Marybelle Firkin was suddenly seen to stand in front of him. Her great ham-like arms were now folded across her huge bosom. The congregation of drunks and whores grew silent as the giant mot and the fierce Figgins locked eyes, hers bigger and even more blue than his own.

The fiddler leaped upon a table beside the huge woman and pulled a long melancholy note from his fiddle, then he tapped her lightly on the shoulder with his bow. Marybelle sighed at his touch then smiled a most beatific smile at Dan Figgins, dropped her arms to her side, and in a voice astonishingly sweet and pure started to sing.

> *Fine Ladies and Gents*
> *come hear my sad tale*
> *The sun is long down and*
> *the moon has grown pale*
> *So drink up your gin*
> *and toss down your ale*
> *Come and rest your tired heads*
> *on my pussy . . . cat's tail!*

The crowd, delighted and immediately distracted, took up the merry ditty and started to sing it over and over again as they cavorted around the tables and the fiddler sawed his bow across the gut, raising his knees high, prancing nimbly on the table top. The gin whores and the younger doxies danced with the drunks and the place was soon grown most merry again. Even Figgins was taken up by two whores, who whirled him across the room and planted copious kisses upon his broken face.

Ikey arrived back at the Pig 'n Spit shortly before midnight to find the miserable young Tooth seated in a corner sniffing and blubbing, now rapidly come to realise that he would not see another sunrise. Just when he thought he might try to bolt, hoping to escape into the darkness, Ikey tapped him on the shoulder.

Thomas Tooth, reduced to tears of drunken self-pity, clutched at the sleeve of Ikey's great coat and begged him to save his life by making good his debt to the awesomely ferocious Dan Figgins, who was threatening to take his life on the stroke of midnight.

'O' course, my dear.' Ikey spread his hands. 'What are friends for? A friend in need is a friend indeed! Do not fret, all's well what ends well!'

161

The arrangements which followed over the next couple of weeks between Ikey Solomon, the contrite young gambler and the carpenter George Betteridge, would prove to be one of the best investments Ikey was to make in his entire life of crime and punishment.

In the testing laboratory at the Laverstoke Mill, Thomas Tooth explained to Ikey, some thirty sheets of the bill paper used for banknotes were brought twice weekly to be submitted for testing and verification of their quality.

It was Thomas Tooth's task to count the sheets against the number which originally arrived for testing. Then he had to enter his count into the receivals and exit ledger before taking them across a large quadrangle and through a maze of buildings to where the furnace was located, at the opposite end of the mill from the laboratory.

Ikey had George Betteridge build a false floor into a cupboard under a stairway which Thomas Tooth had to pass on his way to the furnace. A single floorboard was hinged so that it lifted neatly up at one end if correctly touched. In a matter of moments Thomas Tooth could conceal two sheets of rolled paper under the floorboard as he passed.

Later, Betteridge, on the pretence of going about some small maintenance task, would retrieve the paper, conceal it in his tool box and take it out of the mill gates under a pile of wood shavings and off-cuts. As a mill carpenter, he was entitled to sell or take these home for his own use as kindling.

The Laverstoke Mill was a quietly run business where standards of workmanship were the preoccupation of the partners. The familiar and trusted local employees were often represented by three generations working at the mill, and not subject to the slightest suspicion. Security measures in this country backwater plainly left something to be desired, but any systems beyond the ones which had existed for more than sixty years seemed entirely unnecessary.

This scam soon proved so successful that Thomas Tooth repaid his gambling debt to Ikey, and agreed to be paid in gold sovereigns for each sheet subsequently delivered. Five sovereigns to himself and two to George Betteridge, whose anxiety that his good fortune might come to an end caused by some impropriety from Thomas Tooth caused him to watch carefully over the younger man so that no errant bragging should bring about their mutual downfall.

The method by which the paper came to Ikey was simple enough. The money would be left with George Titmus at the Pig 'n Spit, and the paper delivered to him concealed within one of the two similarly constructed long thin wooden boxes and tightly sealed so that the rat master did not know its contents. An empty box would then be returned with the receipt of the one containing paper, whereupon both men would repair to the rat ring where the young Thomas Tooth, for the most part, would be fleeced of the greater portion of his payment while his carpenter cousin kept a steady eye upon his drinking.

It was late into the evening when Silas Browne and Maggie the Colour finally concluded a deal for the paper and plates of twenty thousand pounds and agreed to a cash deposit of five hundred pounds. While Ikey knew this to be but a fraction of the true value of the merchandise, it was better than he'd expected.

Five hundred pounds was sufficient for Ikey to purchase a passage to New York and allow him to live for a few weeks while he learned the layout of the new city and made acquaintance, by means of some lavish entertainment, with the right connections.

The remainder of the money for the remaining bill paper Ikey requested to be in the form of a letter of credit from a thoroughly reputable Birmingham bank, one acceptable to Coutts & Company, 59 the Strand, London, so that when Ikey presented it to the great London bank they would transfer the money into an account in his name to a bank in New York, without questioning the credit of the bank of original issue.

Maggie left the parlour and shortly after returned with five hundred pounds in Bank of England notes. Ikey examined each of these using Silas's eyeglass. When he was satisfied to their authenticity, he handed over the four sheets of billpaper, requesting only the return of the small corner he'd cut away for the boy Josh to deliver earlier.

'And now for ongoin' paper supply, how will 'e do it?' Maggie asked.

Ikey hesitated. 'It's late, my dear, perhaps we can talk about that at some other time?'

Maggie the Colour was adamant. 'Now is as good as any other. We likes to know where we stands in business o' money, Mr Solomons.'

Ikey felt immediately frustrated; his presence in America would not allow him to negotiate a further supply of bill paper from Thomas Tooth and personally gain from such a transaction. But he also knew that life has a way of twisting and turning back to bite its own tail, and he was reluctant to close the door on the prospect of a future sale, so he proceeded to negotiate as though his life should depend on the outcome.

Finally, after a great deal of bargaining, an agreement was reached whereby Silas and Maggie would pay one hundred and fifty pounds a sheet for any future paper supplies. This was a much lower price than they'd paid for the stockpiled paper, but Maggie insisted that it involved them in a far greater risk of being caught.

Ikey requested a needle and cotton and a pair of scissors, and when Maggie brought these he removed a large silk scarf from somewhere within the interior of his coat and cut it into four similar sized pieces. Then using the twine from the previous wrapping he rewrapped the plates, each in a square of silk, and returned them to the hem of his coat, making a fair hand at sewing them back within the lining.

Then, thinking to avail himself of the means of sewing, he attempted to stitch together the rip made in his coat when he'd caught it in the door of the coach earlier that morning. The needle proved too small for the heavy felt and would not easily pass through the thick, greasy material, the thread breaking each time and rendering his efforts fruitless. Ikey could feel Maggie's mounting impatience and finally she remarked curtly, 'Will you be long, Mr Solomons? It is late and well past time we were abed.'

Ikey finally gave up the task of mending the tear and placed the needle and cotton down on the table. Rising, he walked over to the window and put his nose to a pane, looking out into the darkness where the winter wind howled and buffeted, rattling the stout window frame.

'I needs to sew them plates in the hem o' me coat to 'old me down against the blast o' the bitter wind what's blowin' in the dark and stormy night outside!' He turned and looked at Silas Browne and pointed to the fire. 'O' course, a night's lodgin's spent in a warm chair beside your hearth could leave these 'ere plates on the premises where you'd know they'd be safe from robbery?' He looked querulously at Silas. 'I could be gorn before the sparrows wake, my dear, one o' your likely lads paid a 'andsome sum to deliver me to me lodgin's?'

Maggie the Colour shook her head and spoke sharply. 'No offence, Mr Solomons, we be glad to do business with you, but we'll not 'ave a Jew sleepin' under our roof!' She cast a meaningful glance at Silas. 'That be bad luck brought upon our 'eads by our own stupidity!'

'Aye, we'll not be doin' that!' Silas Browne confirmed.

Ikey was aware of the common country superstition that a Jew sleeping under a Christian roof brought the devil into the house. It even existed in some of the smaller country taverns where he'd been turned away in the past. Nevertheless he was greatly in need of sleep and very wearied. The prospect of returning on foot, in the dark, along the way he'd earlier come was a daunting, if not to say, dangerous one.

'No offence taken to be sure, my dear!' Ikey said hastily. 'We all 'as our own little ways, but I caution you to think upon the matter a moment longer. If I should use shank's pony to get back to me lodgin's, it could turn out most dangerous at this time o' night.' He flapped the lapel of his coat meaningfully.

'We'll 'ave a boy take you in 'orse and trap,' Maggie snapped. 'You'll be back 'ere day after tomorrow, at night if you please, with remainder of paper and plates, one 'undred and ten sheets by the count, then we'll do further letter o'credit business, right?'

'No! No, my dear, beg pardon for abusin' your sensibilities on that question. You 'ave all day tomorrow and all night and part o' the following' mornin'. Then if you'll be so kind to send young Josh to the coach terminus to be there at ten o'clock in the mornin' with a note what contains the name o' the bank, which must be of excellent standing, and the time o' the appointment and such other details as what I'll need. The appointment is to be made the afternoon o' the day after tomorrow, the paper and the plates to be 'anded over in the bank after you 'as 'anded over the irrevocable letter o' credit made out in me name to Coutts & Company, the Strand, London.'

''And over plates and paper in bank? Are you daft?' Silas exclaimed.

'What better place, my dear? We simply asks the bank official for a private room to view the merchandise. It be none of 'is business what the package contains.'

Maggie the Colour sniffed. 'Don't you trust us to do it 'ere, then, Mr Solomons?'

Ikey laughed. 'You 'as your bad luck what you just described as a Jew spendin' a night under your roof, this you claims is *deliberate stupidity*. We also 'as a similar superstition, my dear. We believes that to practise *deliberate stupidity* is worse than witchcraft, and superstition and, most decidedly and emphatically, brings about a great deal o' bad luck to the person what is stupid!'

'The coach terminus, ten o'clock, mornin' day after tomorrow then,' Maggie the Colour snapped.

'That be quite right, my dear. Young Josh will give the letter of instructions to someone what might come up to him and say politely, "Dick Whittington's 'ungry cat 'as come to fetch a juicy rat".'

Maggie's head jerked in surprise. 'Beg pardon?'

'The passwords, my dear, 'case I can't make it meself, other pressin' business intervenin'.'

Maggie the Colour sighed, her patience close to ending. 'Password? Bah, what rubbish! Anyway, what's wrong with a single word, like "copper" or "'orse" or if you must, "cat"? Them words about Dick Whittington's cat, that be proper nonsense!'

Ikey smiled. 'You're quite right, my dear, rubbish it is, but it be more excitin' for a small lad what's intelligent! Much more excitin' to carry more than one word in 'is little 'ead as he sets out upon such a grand adventure. It is properly suitable to an occasion such as what we've been discussin', and what is worthy o' much more than a single word like "copper" or "'orse" or "cat"!'

Ikey was tired and a little testy but he'd deliberately created the nonsense about the cat to frustrate Maggie the Colour's desire to see him depart. It was a small revenge for her rudeness, but sweet enough at that for the lateness of the hour. Now, with the prospect of being taken into the city in a pony trap, he was as anxious to depart as she was to see him go.

Chapter Twelve

It was just past midnight when Ikey fought his way against the buffeting wind and sudden flurries of snow to a Birmingham netherken where he was well enough known. It was as foul a place as you could expect for a shilling a night, but by no means at the bottom of the rung. The wind howled about the eves and the windows rattled as Ikey hammered on the door to be allowed to enter.

The landlord, carrying a candle cupped with his hand against the wind, welcomed him with a scowl, which changed into a sycophantic smile when Ikey stepped out of the dark into the dim candlelight.

'Oh it's you! Welcome back to our ever so 'umble abode, Mr Solomon. We 'ave much improvement since your last stay. New straw stuffed only last week, like goose down them beds is, and the room I have selected for you is near empty with only two other fine gentlemen sharin'!' He sucked air through his rotten teeth. 'Two shillin' a night and summit to eat in mornin'! There, couldn't be fairer than that now, could there, sir?'

Ikey handed him a shilling. 'Master Brodie, your straw's damp with piss and alive with all manner o' vermin, and it ain't been changed in three months. A bowl o' cold gruel in the mornin' ain't what you calls "summit to eat" and I'll wager the two villains what's sharing the room 'as paid no more'n sixpence apiece for the privilege!'

Brodie tested the coin Ikey had given by biting down on it, then he shrugged, placed it in the pocket of his filthy waistcoat and beckoned for Ikey to follow him. They made their way through the dark shapes which seemed to be lying in every available space, some penny-a-nighters asleep seated, while tied about the neck with heavy twine to the banisters of the rickety stairs.

Panting with the effort, Brodie halted as they came to the upper reaches of the house and stopped outside a door no more than four feet in height.

'It be top room and there be no grate in there, so you'll be wantin' a blanket. That'll be sixpence extra.' Brodie pulled open the door to reveal a tiny attic with a dirty dormer window through which a pale slice of moon was shining across a window ledge crusted with snow. The window rattled loudly, and Ikey felt the freezing draught as the wind forced its way through the cracks in the frame. One of the men at his feet ceased snoring and moaned, then commenced to snoring again. The rhythm of the two men's rough breathing filled the space around them, so that there seemed not an inch left for another person to occupy. Ikey, observing the moon, sensed that time was running out for him, that before it reached its fullness he should be safely on a ship to America.

Ikey declined Brodie's offer of a blanket, knowing it would be infested with vermin. He stepped over the two sleeping bodies to reach the straw pallet nearest the window where the cold seemed at once to be at its greatest. His nocturnal perambulations had been thrown into disarray for a second day running as Ikey lay down on the filthy straw. Wrapping his coat tightly about his aching body, he fell into an exhausted sleep.

The following day Ikey went out early and purchased quill, blacking, paper and sealing wax, whereupon he hired the landlord Brodie's tiny private parlour for a further shilling, with sixpence added for a fire in the hearth to burn all day.

Ikey had also arranged with a small jeweller's workshop to make him a copper cylinder nine inches long by an inch and a quarter wide in its interior, with a cap to fit over one end rounded in exactly the same manner as the end of a cigar cylinder. Ikey stressed that the cap should screw on and when tightened fit so snugly that it had the appearance of being one object with no separation, that should a finger be run over the point where the cap fitted to the body it would barely discern the join. Ikey instructed that the cylinder be ready late in the afternoon of the following day.

Despite his outward appearance of complete disarray, Ikey was possessed of an exceedingly tidy mind. He liked his affairs to be well ordered, and the fact that he'd been forced to leave London at a moment's notice left him with a great deal undone, the most important being the fortune which lay beyond his grasp within the safe in his Whitechapel home.

For almost the entire coach journey to Birmingham his mind had been preoccupied with thoughts of how he might get his hands on all of the money he and Hannah jointly owned, leaving only the house and the stolen goods stored within it for her and the children.

Ikey's greatest fear was that she would send him packing without divulging her half of the combination of the safe, and then later have it drilled and tapped so that she might possess its entire contents. Genuine tears of frustration ran down his cheeks as he contemplated this ghastly possibility.

Ikey sat down to the task of tidying up his affairs before leaving Britain. There would be no time in London, which he might be forced to leave after only a few hours. There were the little ratting terriers he kept, he must take care of their welfare; instructions for Mary should he not see her again; and letters to his contacts in London and on the continent. On and on he worked in his arachnoid hand, and it was quite late in the afternoon when Ikey had finally completed these business matters. He placed the letters in his great coat and went looking for the landlord. Ikey found him over the communal hearth stirring a large cauldron of cabbage soup, and carrying a steaming kettle in his free hand.

'Ah, there you are,' Ikey exclaimed. 'It might be most profitable for you to step into your own little parlour, if you please, Mister Brodie.'

'What? Right now? This very moment?' Brodie answered, without looking up. 'Can't now! This soup what is blessed with 'erbs and spices and all manner of tasty ingredients is about to come to the simmer. Then I must add a fine shank o' veal and extra onions and potatoes to gift 'er with a most delicate degustation.'

Ikey laughed. 'All you've ever added to your cabbage soup is the water what's in that kettle! Come quickly, Mr Brodie, or you may be poorer to the tune of five shillings!'

Brodie almost dropped the kettle in his haste to place it back on the hob and follow Ikey into the parlour.

'Master Brodie can you repeat: "Dick Whittington's 'ungry cat 'as come to fetch a juicy rat!"? Can you say that?'

'Dick Whittington's angry cat come to fetch a Jewish rat!' Brodie repeated, then looked bemused at Ikey. 'That's daft, that is! Rats is rats, ain't no Jewish rats, leastways not in Brum, that I can assure you! Rats 'ere is Christian or not at all!'

Ikey corrected Brodie and repeated the phrase, making the landlord say it over several times before asking him to go to the coach terminus the following morning at precisely ten o'clock, to spend the password he'd just rehearsed on Josh and to receive a note from the boy to be returned to him.

Brodie scratched his head, bemused. 'When I done this you'll give me five shillin's?' He was plainly waiting for some catch.

'If you takes a most round-about route 'ome and makes sure you ain't followed there'll be two shillin's additional comin' to you, Master Brodie!'

'You've found yer man, 'ave no fear o' that – I can disappear in a single blinkin' and you wouldn't even know I was gorn. Ain't no lad on Gawd's earth could 'ave the cunnin' to follow me,' Brodie bragged.

Ikey left soon afterwards to visit an eating establishment in an adjoining rookery only slightly less notorious than the one in which he was staying. Here Ikey had often done deals with thieves and villains and the landlord welcomed his custom and willingly allowed him credit, his bills to be paid at the end of each visit.

This time, though, as Ikey greeted him he seemed less sure, and asked if he might have some money on account as the debt for food supplied to Ikey's guest was mounting by the hour.

The small room to which the landlord escorted him was almost completely occupied by the corpulence of Marybelle Firkin who sat at a table strewn with bones and crusts and empty dishes, as well as the half-eaten carcass of a yellow-skinned goose. She welcomed Ikey with a chop rimmed with a layer of shining white fat held in one hand, and a roasted potato in the other. Ikey looked around anxiously and was most relieved to see the hamper occupying one corner of the room. Marybelle pointed the chop directly at Ikey and spoke with her mouth crammed, a half masticated potato dropping into her lap.

'It was marvellous, eh, Ikey? If I says so meself, that performance on the coach were fit to be seen by the bleedin' Prince o' bleedin' Wales!' She cackled loudly, more food tumbling from her mouth. 'Better than any I performed on the stage in me 'ole career. What say ya, lovey? Was it the best ya seen?'

Ikey smiled thinly, his hands expanded trying to match her enthusiasm. 'What can I say, Marybelle? You was magnificent, my dear, the performance of a lifetime by a thespian o' rare and astonishin' talent!'

Marybelle blushed at the compliment and swallowed, her mouth empty and her voice suddenly soft and low. 'Ah, that's nice, Ikey. 'Ere, 'ave a pork chop, do ya the world, skin 'n bone you is, there ain't nuffink to ya!'

Ikey winced and drew back. 'No thanks, it ain't kosher!'

'Suit yerself, lovey, there's a lot o' nourishment in a pork chop and very little in religion!' Then, pointing to the hamper, she declared, 'All be safe. Paper's come to no 'arm.'

Ikey nodded. 'Thank you, my dear, I am most obliged, most obligin'ly obliged.'

Ikey appeared to hesitate, then continued, 'Marybelle, I needs a favour done and in return I shall put you in the way o' a nice little earner.'

'That's nice, lovey. What is it ya want, then?' She pointed at his coat. 'Sew up the tear in yer coat? I ain't much of a dab 'and at sewin' I warns ya.'

Ikey grinned, though in a feeble way. 'A bigger favour, my dear.'

'Bringin' yer paper, that *weren't* favour enough?'

'Yes, my dear, and you shall be paid the fifty pounds I promised you.'

'And this favour, it's worth more'n fifty pounds?'

'Much more, if you plays your cards right!'

It is only necessary briefly to describe the scene which took place in the bank, and the look of consternation on the faces of Silas and Maggie the Colour when Marybelle Firkin arrived in Ikey's place. She carried a letter from Ikey stipulating that she should act as his negotiating agent for the business at hand and the letter further asked that the banker, Mr David Daintree, sign the letter and return it to Marybelle as proof that she had been present. The letter also required the signatures of Silas and Maggie Browne.

Indeed, Ikey was wise to seek proof that the meeting had taken place, for the husband and wife team had conspired to rob him. They had concluded that he had no ongoing supply of paper, but only what he would bring to the bank. If they could rob him of the letter of credit and the money on his way back to London, or even at his place of residence in Birmingham – after all, he was not the sort who could go to the police – then they would possess the plates and the paper without having paid for them.

Mr Daintree, impressed with the handling of so great a sum of money, conducted the proceedings with the utmost rectitude, carefully pointing to where Marybelle should sign her name. When Marybelle handed the hamper over to Silas and Maggie he retired, as had been arranged, to a small inner chamber, while the two of them closely examined the hamper's contents.

Maggie then took a sheet of paper from the banker's desk and using his quill filled nearly half a page in her neat handwriting. Then she dusted the paper and allowed it to dry, whereupon she handed it to Silas. He read it, smiled, nodded and returned it to her, whereupon she indicated that he call the bank officer to return. Neither Silas nor Maggie passed so much as a single word in Marybelle's direction. Marybelle sat patiently, thinking about Ikey's promise of a fortune and trying to imagine how much nourishment it might buy. How many roast beef sides, fat geese, plump partridges, chops and pies and every manner of sweet dish known to the human species.

With the return of Mr Daintree the couple allowed that the credit note be duly signed in her presence by the bank officer. But before handing it to Marybelle, Maggie placed the page of writing on the desk in front of her.

'This be the document we wish to 'ave Mrs Firkin sign before we 'ands over letter o' credit,' she said bluntly, her eyes challenging the banker.

The letter simply stated that as Ikey had not arrived at the bank himself to collect the letter of credit and as Silas and Maggie the Colour had no way of knowing whether Marybelle was not an impostor, the letter of credit could only be presented in London by Ikey himself. If the Coutts & Company Bank in London did not inform Mr David Daintree of the Birmingham City and County Bank that Mr Ikey Solomon had himself presented the letter of credit within one week of the date which appeared on it, then the money should be returned to Silas and Maggie Browne and the goods returned. But Mr Ikey Solomon himself and no other.

'Is what they done against the laws of England?' Marybelle asked the bank officer.

Daintree frowned, pinching the brow of his nose. 'No, not strictly. A credit note issued in a contract involving two specific parties and identifying one specific party to another specific party and not redeemable by a third party is not uncommon,' he replied, though he was clearly bemused.

Marybelle shrugged. The implications were not lost on her. The husband and wife team would attempt to rob Ikey of the letter before he arrived back in London. She well recalled the look of consternation on their faces when she'd entered the banker's personal chambers. Any plans to retrieve the money and letter of credit, or to harm Ikey, would be based on someone identifying him as he came out of the bank. She, on the other hand, was unknown to any potential robbers.

Marybelle was a brave and tough woman not accustomed to being threatened and she set great trust in Ikey's cunning, so she comforted herself with the thought: *Since when is two clumsy bloody country bumpkins a match for two London Jews, fuck their goyim eyes!*

'Where does I sign?' Marybelle asked smiling.

'Really, Mrs Firkin, I should caution you, this may not be in Mr Solomon's interest!' the banker exclaimed.

Maggie the Colour jumped from her chair and accosted the man from the bank. 'Really, sir! We don't know *who* this woman be! We've never laid eyes on 'er before today! We 'ave no specimen o' Mr Solomons' signature, not the least identification, maybe the letter what introduced 'er is a trick? Maybe she stole the merchandise what we just paid for? We'd be plain daft if we took chance with letter o' credit!' Maggie the Colour's brittle tone suddenly softened and she smiled. 'You see, sir, Mr Solomons is much respected by me 'usband and me. If this woman is an impostor and 'as done him wrong, then, at great personal expense to ourselves, we 'ave protected 'is interests with the letter what I just wrote?'

'What about the small scrap o' paper what was in yer letter? Ikey said it were 'is affy davy, what made everyfink kosher?'

'Paper?' Maggie held up Ikey's letter. 'This be no proof 'e wrote it. It could be plain and simple forgery!'

'Not that! The small piece o' paper what was a triangle shape come wif that?'

Maggie the Colour looked at Mr Daintree and then at Silas, her expression plainly bemused. She shook her head slowly. 'Paper? What was triangle shape? That be plain daft for letter writin'. Small piece you say, triangle shape?' she repeated and held up Ikey's letter again. 'This be the only paper Mr Solomon sent and it be rectangle, not triangle and not small neither. I doesn't know what you can possibly mean, Mrs Firkin.'

Mary sighed, her huge bosoms quivering. 'Give us the quill then. Yer a right pair o' villains, you two!' She reached out for the paper which now lay on the desk in front of the banker. 'Be so kind as to show us the exact place where I puts me mauley, Mr Daintree, sir.' Then she looked up and asked, 'Is the address of 'er and 'er 'usband on this 'ere letter?'

Mr Daintree glanced at the letter and pointed to the left-hand corner. 'It's right there where it should be,' he confirmed.

'Will ya read it out loud, lovey? We don't want them two doin' a runner if they's up to some monkey trick!'

The banker, somewhat bemused, read the address out aloud.

Marybelle looked at Silas and Maggie Browne. 'I'll remember that I will, make no mistake!' Whereupon, her pink tongue protruding from the corner of her mouth, she tediously applied her signature to the letter. 'There you are, missus,' she said at last, and then cast a second malevolent glance at the husband and wife. 'Be that good faith enough for the likes o' you lot?'

Maggie the Colour sniffed, and gave the letter to the banker to apply his signature, and thereafter she made Silas do the same. Marybelle recognised in him the same tedious effort in signing his name and concluded that he too had difficulty with writing.

Marybelle then addressed the banker. 'Now, if ya please, sir, I requests the pleasure o' the monickers o' them two on the letter what Mr Solomon gave me what states my position as negotiator on 'is be'arf!'

Daintree attempted to conceal his grin. 'Of course, Mrs Firkin, it is completely in order for you to do so.' He picked up the letter

174

from where it lay on the desk and handed it to Maggie the Colour who read it with her lips pursed and an altogether sour expression upon her face.

'Humph!' she said finally and took the quill up again, signing the letter, as did Silas and Daintree, who blotted it carefully, before handing it back to Marybelle.

Maggie the Colour then asked the banker if he would be so good as to have a clerk make two fair copies of the letter she had written, this to be on bank stationery. When these arrived back she read both carefully, they were duly signed again by all four people present and the original given to the banker for safekeeping. A fair copy was handed to both Marybelle and the Brownes.

With this seemingly watertight agreement in their possession, Maggie and her husband could now set about the task of preventing Ikey from ever presenting their letter of credit. The total cost to them of the paper and plates would be five hundred pounds, though, if they could apprehend him soon enough, the larger part of this too might be recovered.

Marybelle Firkin was helped to her feet by a triumphant Silas Browne and a smiling Maggie the Colour. A concerned David Daintree placed the letter of agreement, Ikey's returned letter and the letter of credit in a heavy linen envelope, sealed it and pressed the bank's insignia into the hot wax. Then he rose and took Marybelle by the arm and guided her to the doorway. Marybelle paused at the door and turned to face the smug-looking couple. She smiled sweetly. 'I wish ya both *meesa meschina*!' she said, a Yiddish expression meaning, 'I wish you sudden death'.

Mr Daintree handed Marybelle the envelope, first cautioning Maggie the Colour and Silas Browne to remain seated in his chambers until he returned, then he walked Marybelle across the marble foyer of the bank chambers to the front door.

'Ten minutes it says in the letter? You'll not let them two miserable bastards out o' yer chambers for ten minutes, will ya?' Marybelle paused. 'Mind, I'd be right obliged if you'd make that a bit more, wotcha say, lovey?'

Mr David Daintree, member of the board of Birmingham City and County Bank, smiled. 'My pleasure, Mrs Firkin, fifteen minutes at the least, what?' He turned and instructed the guard at the door to see Marybelle safely to her carriage where two footmen with red rosettes on their top hats waited to work her enormous frame through the carriage door and safely into the interior.

Before pulling away the coachman reported quietly to Marybelle that four horsemen of rough looks and a young lad of about ten were waiting under a group of elm trees not fifty feet from the bank, and that he'd taken the trouble to make a casual enquiry to the doorman who'd indicated that they'd arrived shortly after two in the afternoon.

'Watch to see if they follow us,' Marybelle instructed.

After an hour the coachman stopped at a village inn and Marybelle was helped from the carriage into the hostelry, and taken immediately to a small room which contained only a table and two chairs. The room was fuggy with the steam of dishes covering the table. The landlord bid Marybelle *bon appetit* and bowing, backed out of the door, locking it behind him. A few minutes later she heard the rattle of a key again and Ikey stepped into the room and locked the door behind him.

'Loverly grub! I got to 'and it to ya, Ikey, ya knows a good nosh 'ouse when ya sees one.' Marybelle pointed to the envelope which sat on the only corner of the table not covered in dishes. 'There you are, lovey, signed, sealed and delivered by yers truly!'

Ikey snatched at the envelope and tore it open. 'You wasn't followed, was you, my dear?'

Marybelle's mouth was already full with a bite from a large chicken pie, and she shook her head unable to answer. Ikey waited until she could speak. 'Nobody followed us, but in the bank, there was complications.' She pointed to the envelope in Ikey's hand. 'Inside is a letter what I didn't know what to do about, so I signed.' Marybelle looked concerned. 'I only 'opes I done right?'

Ikey opened the sealed envelope and examined the letters within. He shook his head and grinned in admiration as he read Maggie the Colour's letter. Ikey looked up at Marybelle, who once again had her mouth full. 'You done good to sign, my dear.'

Marybelle swallowed, and with her mouth now empty she reached for a chicken leg and waved it in Ikey's direction. 'They be after ya, Ikey Solomon.' Still holding the chicken leg, she took up a roasted potato, popped it into her mouth and continued talking, with her mouth full. 'We wasn't followed 'cause the people they sent didn't know to follow me.' She frowned. 'But they'll be lookin' for ya, mark me words, they's a right pair o' villains them two!' She giggled. 'I wished them *meesa meschina!*'

Ikey laughed. 'More like they wished me!' he said.

Marybelle sucked the flesh of the entire chicken leg from the bone with a soft plop and commenced to chew. Ikey's hand went into his coat, and he withdrew it holding the copper tube he'd ordered in the shape of a cigar container, though somewhat thicker and longer. He placed it on the table beside the letter of credit.

'They aim to do ya in before ya gets 'ome wif that there letter o' credit. That's what 'er letter was all about, weren't it, Ikey? Do ya in, steal yer letter and then claim the contract's been broken!' Marybelle cocked her pretty head to one side and gave Ikey an ingenuous look. 'What's an irrevocable letter o' credit? What's all the fuss about, any'ow?' She pointed to the letter on the table. 'That don't look like no paper what's worth dying for!'

'It's money promised what can't be unpromised once it's been presented from one bank t'other,' Ikey said, trying to stay vague. 'You're perfectly right, my dear, they'll be after trying to stop me gettin' to a bank in London.' Ikey shrugged. 'It's only natural ain't it? You did good not to be followed, my dear. I 'ave made plans, we will make good our escape.'

Marybelle smiled, shrugged her shoulders and looked expectantly at Ikey. 'Ya said I done good, we wasn't followed, so where's me fortune what ya promised?'

Ikey dry-soaped his hands, his shoulders hunched. 'You've done special good you 'ave, my dear, you've done it perfect and exact and splendid. I couldn't 'ave asked for no more, 'cept one small thing?'

'What?' Marybelle asked suspiciously, holding another large piece of chicken poised in front of her greasy mouth.

Ikey reached across the small table, picked up the copper cylinder and unscrewed the smoothly fitting top. He carefully rolled the letter of credit into a tight cylinder itself, which he then neatly slipped into the copper container and screwed the top back on.

'Will you take this letter o' credit back with you to London tonight, my dear?'

Ikey placed the cylinder in front of Marybelle, then he announced he was giving her the rights to future instalments of paper from Thomas Tooth and George Betteridge. 'Until I returns to London to live, my dear, though I daresay that be never.'

'This bill paper to come, is it still kosher? I knows yer doin' a runner, Ikey. The law ain't on to it is they?'

Ikey cleared his throat and answered truthfully. 'They is and they isn't, I expects. O' course now, at this very moment, I suppose the Bank o' England will be goin' over the mill at Laverstoke with a fine-toothed comb, though I'll vouch if them two, Tooth and Betteridge, 'ave the good sense to lie low for a while, they'll find nothin'. Give it two months, maybe three or even four to be completely on the safe side, and the scam can be brought back intact. Clean as a whistle, free as a bird, kosher as the Beth Din! The bill paper be worth a king's ransom, keep you in nosh for the rest of your life!'

'Only if you knows 'ow to get rid of it, Ikey. I ain't got no contacts what wants bill paper.'

Ikey raised his eyebrows in surprise, 'Why, my dear, you sells it to them two you met in the bank today!'

'What? Do business wif that filth?'

Ikey shrugged. 'They's villains, but the best, my dear. We're all villains, given 'arf a chance, everyone in the whole world is villains. But in me experience there be two kinds o' villain, them what's got a bit o' class and them what ain't.' Ikey's dark eyes shone. 'That letter Maggie wrote today, that be most excellent. That be topnotch thinkin', nacherly nasty nogginin', my dear!' Ikey spread his hands wide. 'That's a rare combination what you doesn't find too often in the business o' villainy, brains and the stomach to act.' He paused, scratching the tip of his nose. 'You take my word for it, they be your natural customers, my dear! All you does is wait a year, then come down here with the bill paper what you 'as accumulated, startin' again in four months.' Ikey leaned back. 'You'll make thousands, my dear, thousands and thousands. Your table will be the envy o' dukes and duchesses. The King himself, I dare say, will come to 'ear o' your fine banquets.'

Marybelle picked up the cylinder and waved it at Ikey. 'And what if some villain they send catches me wif this on me way to London?' She drew the cylinder across her throat. 'That's what 'appens.'

'They won't find it will they?' Ikey said puckering his lips. He pointed to the cylinder. 'It be made to be put in a place what a man 'asn't got and a lady 'as. A place where your average villain ain't likely to go pokin' about without your express permission, if you knows what I mean, my dear?'

Marybelle's pretty blue eyes grew large and then shone with

delighted surprise. She gave a little squeal, running her fat, greasy fingers along the cylinder's smooth surface.

'Jesus, Ikey! You bleedin' thinks o' everyfink.' In between her laughter she managed to gasp. 'Methinks it will be a tight fit . . . *ha-ha-ha-ha*! But wif all the bumpin' o' the coach to London . . . *ha-ha-ha-hee-hee*! . . . I daresay it will bring a lady o' me proportions, oh, goodness lummy, oh, oh . . . a good deal o' pleasure on the . . . *ha-ha-hee-hee*! . . . journey 'ome!'

Chapter Thirteen

Ikey returned to London three days after he had left Marybelle Firkin at the inn with a pork pie stuck in her gob and his precious cylinder safely tucked away elsewhere on her large person. Waiting in the back room of a chop house in Houndsditch until well after dark when a light snow storm, churned with frequent wind flurries, began to fall and which he judged would further conceal his passage, Ikey slipped into the rookery of St Giles and soon thereafter let himself into the seemingly abandoned building which housed the Methodist Academy of Light Fingers.

Creeping up the rickety staircase, he appeared suddenly and to the utmost surprise of half a dozen boys who were playing a game of cribbage by the light of a solitary candle. Huddled beside the hearth directly behind them were as many boys again wrapped in rags and old blankets against the bitter cold.

'Now 'ow many times 'as I told you, keep a sharp eye!' Ikey admonished. 'The lad what's supposed to be watchin' out is asleep on the landin', lushed out and smellin' o' gin!' Ikey sucked at his teeth and wagged a mittened finger at the urchins seated crosslegged around a box. 'Gentlemen, gentlemen! Cribbage in this kind o' light ain't no good for the senses. You'll lose your touch, the light of a candle dulls the mind and makes it too easy to palm a card or deal a crooked 'and. Brightness be what's called for, where everything can be seen, clear as daylight, open and negotiable as a whore's cunny.'

The boys laughed loudly at this last remark but Ikey held up his hand for silence. 'A cardsharp to be warranted any good must make 'is play in the best o' conditions. We'll 'ave no second-rate broadsman spreadin' the flats in darkness in my school o' learnin'! A trade ain't worth 'avin' if you're not the best there is at it.'

His young pupils crowded about him. 'There's a people what's lookin' for ya, Ikey, is ya in lavender then?' a young tooler named Sweetface Mulligan enquired.

'Perhaps I is and perhaps I ain't, it all depends on who is lookin' and whether it be opportunity knockin' or disadvantage breakin' down the door.'

'It's Bow Street! Some say it be City police! All about Petticoat Lane they is! Anyone seen ya, they asks! Rewards is offered! Never seen so much law about, 'as we lads? Wotcha do, Ikey? Murder was it? There's talk o' forgery! Millions o' pounds! There be a poster o' yer gob pasted everywhere! We's proud to know ya, Ikey!' All this and more they chorused crowding around Ikey, the smaller ones hopping up and down and jumping on the backs of the larger boys to get a closer look in the semi-darkened room.

'And Mistress Hannah!' a boy they called Onion, whose birth name was Pickles, shouted. 'She been lookin' for ya an' all!'

Ikey shrugged his shoulders. 'It's true, my dears, the constabulary 'as a sharp eye peeled for me.' He looked around slowly, spread his hands and his face took on a look of regret. 'O' course I apologises for scarperin' without informin' you, gentlemen. A matter of urgent expediency, you understand? No offence intended and I 'opes none is taken. No time to pay me respects or bid you all adieu.'

They nodded, happy at the compliment he'd paid their mutual fraternity. Ikey rolled his eyes and seemed to look at each of them in turn. 'Now we 'asn't seen me, 'as we, lads? I means, no seein' to the degree o' not seein' nothin' at all!'

Ikey's fingers flicked heavenwards as though to expel the memory of having seen him completely from their minds. He stopped and lifted the candle from the box, the hot glass warming his mittened fingers. Holding the lighted jar before him, he inspected each boy's dirty face, watching as they solemnly nodded acquiescence. 'We doesn't want no pigs sniffin' round askin' awkward questions now does we, my dears?'

It was not Ikey's intention to stay long at the Academy of Light Fingers, although he did not indicate this to the urchins around him. While they were well trained in all matters of villainy and each had a healthy disregard for the constabulary, he knew he could ill afford to trust them. They were 'street Arabs' seldom allowed the importance of being noticed and any one of them with three or four noggins of gin to loosen his tongue would not be able to resist the urge to boast of his knowledge of Ikey's return. Ikey needed them now for only one purpose, to find Bob Marley as quickly as possible.

Under normal circumstances there were half a hundred places in the surrounding rookeries where Ikey might indefinitely conceal his presence, though he was not foolish enough to suppose that these would now apply. As a Jew in trouble with the law he was fair prey for all but his own kind. Even though his standing as the Prince of Fences was considerable, they would come snarling in for the kill, the promise of a large reward sufficient to overcome their normal tendency to remain stum. Ikey was aware the criminal code of honour was a fragile thing and would always buckle with the opportunity for a quick profit or a favour returned. He knew this as a certainty, for he was himself no different.

With the promise of a good tightener washed down with a pint of best beer at the nearby chop house, and with the further inducement of a shilling for all and a gold sovereign for the boy who turned out to be the fortunate finder, Ikey sent his young associates off into the winter streets. He directed them to the Haymarket at the popular West End to find and bring Bob Marley back to him.

'When you finds 'im, ask for 'is ear, very quiet mind, say that Ikey Solomon requests the pleasure of 'is company.'

It was not an hour later when Ikey, drowsing at the hearth, was awakened in a great start by a small urchin named Sparrer Fart, a tiny lad of ten with an open angelic face which, together with his size, gave him the appearance of being much younger. He showed all the makings of becoming an expert tooler, with fingers light and sticky as cobwebs and the fearless disposition of the young.

'I brung 'im, Ikey. I found Mr Marley. Can I 'ave the sov what's mine?' Sparrer Fart stuck out his dirty hand and grinned. 'Much obliged, I'm sure!'

'Where?' Ikey cried, shocked at the sudden awakening and

alarmed that he hadn't heard the boy ascend the stairs, though the howl of the winter wind and the natural creaking and groaning of the ancient building would have masked Sparrer's light footfall.

''E won't come up them stairs.' Sparrer grinned. 'Too dane-gis, 'e reckons.'

Ikey, by now fully recovered of his senses, removed a gold sovereign from the interior of his coat and held it out to the youngster, pulling it out of the reach as the urchin snatched at it. Ikey shook his head. 'Tut, tut! First principle o' business, Master Sparrer Fart! Seein' is believin', always inspect the merchandise before you pays fer it, my dear.' Bending to retrieve the candle, he rose from where he was seated on the cribbage box and proceeded carefully down the stairs.

Bob Marley was waiting in the darkness of the tiny downstairs hallway which was now clearly lit by the light of Ikey's candle. He wore a heavy dark coat which fell almost to his ankles with a pair of stout boots protruding from trousers of rough corduroy. A tartan scarf was wrapped about his face so that only his eyes showed between the scarf and the rim of his battered top hat. He removed the scarf at Ikey's approach and stuffed it into the pocket of his coat.

This form of attire was unusual for Marley, who liked to be seen about the town as a proper swell, dressed in the latest fashion. Ikey's keen eye noted this disparity in his dress and concluded that Marley had not been found by Sparrer Fart in the Haymarket, where a man of his reputation would not venture dressed in so poor a manner.

Ikey turned to look sternly at Sparrer Fart. 'We went off to spend our shillin' on a tightener and a noggin o' gin then, did we? We went local and not to the Haymarket did we? We didn't do no lookin' at all!' Ikey glanced at Bob Marley and winked. 'Methinks, we chanced upon Mr Marley 'ere by sheer luck and great good fortune and because we 'as a greedy guts!'

The boy shuffled, looking down at his feet. 'I found 'im di'nt I? I done good!' He moved up to Ikey and began to clutch imploringly at his coat. 'It were a fair find an' all!' he whimpered into the folds of Ikey's greasy coat.

Ikey clucked, wrapping his free arm around the boy's shoulder. 'We all needs a bit o' luck, my dear. Gawd knows yours truly could use a speck o' good fortune right now.' He pushed the young lad gently away and his hand went into his coat and a moment later appeared with half a sovereign held between forefinger and thumb. 'I tell you what I'll do, we'll keep 'arf a sov back on account of 'ow you disobeyed instructions and I'll give you 'arf a sov for deliverin' the goods. Punishment and reward both at the same time, now what could be fairer than that, my dear?'

The small boy looked doubtful. 'It ain't fair, I done what ya asked! Ya said a sov for 'im what found 'im!' He moved close to Ikey plucking at his coat. 'It ain't fair, I done what ya asked, I found 'im.'

This time Ikey pushed him away roughly, but the boy grabbed onto the coat and Ikey smacked him across the ear. 'Disobedience! Discipline! 'Arf a sov and you're lucky to be keepin' it, boy!'

Marley's hand shot out and snatched the coin from Ikey's fingers. ''Arf a mo, Ikey, one sov was promised the lad, one sov must be given!'

'Lessons! Boys must learn lessons! Obedience, discipline,' Ikey whinged.

Marley laughed. 'Promises! Boys must 'ave promises kept.' He tossed the half sovereign into the air and caught it. 'This'll pay for the inconvenience o' crossing the lane,' he said, pocketing the coin. 'Ya owe the brat a sov, so pay up, Ikey Solomon!'

Ikey's eyes widened in surprise. 'You was in the Hare and Hounds?' he exclaimed, naming the flash-house across the lane.

Marley nodded. 'Ya was due back 'bout now, ya couldn't 'ave gone to too many places what wouldn't 'ave shopped ya, this were one,' he explained simply, giving Ikey a slow smile. 'How may I be o' service to ya?'

Ikey turned to Sparrer Fart and handed him a sovereign. ''Ang about and you might learn something, me boy! See what we just seen demonstrated?' He turned and gave Bob Marley an oily smile, returned his gaze to the small boy and stooping low he pushed the candle close to his dirty little face. 'See? Discipline!' He tapped the side of his forehead with his forefinger. 'Use o' the noggin, thinkin'! That's trainin', my dear, that's discipline, that be what makes a great tooler into a swell mobsman, an aristocrat o' the art o' pickin' pockets!' Ikey straightened up, satisfied that he'd recovered his dignity by making his original point and at the same time had sufficiently softened Bob Marley with his flattery. Patting Sparrer Fart on the head, he said, 'You 'as just 'ad the benefit o' the wisdom o' Solomon, my dear!'

Sparrer Fart looked up and pointed to Bob Marley and then to Ikey. 'Oh yeah, 'ow come Mr Marley's got 'arf a sov what's yours and I've got a sov? Be that the wisdom o' Solomon?'

The boy ducked as Ikey swatted at his head with his free hand.

Marley laughed, delighted at the boy's quick mind. 'You've not lost yer touch, Ikey, yer still the best o' the kidsmen, there ain't no one knows better 'ow to pick the fly ones!' He too patted the top of Sparrer Fart's greasy cap. 'Stay away from the gin, you've got all the makin's, son.'

Sparrer hadn't moved. 'What about t'other lads, Ikey? You promised them a shillin' fer lookin' and a good tightener wif a pint o' best beer to follow.'

Marley looked suspiciously over at Ikey. 'That true?'

Ikey gave him a sheepish grin and a reluctant hand went into the interior of his coat and shortly returned with two sovereigns which he handed to Sparrer. 'Mind you give this to Sweetface Mulligan to share out. He's the kidsman when I'm away. Now scarper! Bugger orf!' He turned to Marley. 'Shall we go upstairs, there's a fire in the 'earth.' Then remembering Marley's reluctance he added, 'It ain't dangerous, only a tad rickety but the stairs be solid enough.'

'What, up them?' Marley said in alarm and pointed above to the dark shape of the stairs where Sparrer Fart had disappeared as though swallowed into a deep black hole. 'Not bleedin' likely! We'll talk down 'ere if ya don't mind.'

Ikey clasped his hands together in front of his chest. 'I needs a lair, a place where somebody what's lookin' 'ard and knows what they's lookin' for, can never 'ope to discover who it is they wants to find.'

'Hmm, a good 'iding place o' that nature, cost ya 'eaps,' Marley said speculatively. 'Big reward out, Ikey, 'arf London Town's lookin' for . . .' grinning he quoted *The Times*, 'the Jew what's financially undermine England!' Marley shook his head in a melodramatic way. ''Fraid ya ain't got no friends no more. City police is spreadin' five pounds notes about just for keepin' a sharp eye out. There's a fortune on yer 'ead.' Marley paused and gave Ikey an evil grin. 'Matter o' fact, I could be interested meself!'

Ikey reeled back in horror, his eyes large with fright. 'Don't talk like that, Bob Marley! I taught you everythin' you knows. Was I not your kidsman?' Ikey smiled, his voice somewhat calmer as he remembered. 'You was a good snakesman though, that I'll freely admit. In and out o' the smallest openin's, a natural eye for good stuff too!' Ikey spread his arms and smiled disarmingly. 'Look at you, my dear! Not a copper's dirty great 'and on your shoulder in all these years. Never stood in front o' the bench, never seen the judge's dreaded gavel come down pronouncing a sentence, nor 'as you 'ad the misfortune to look out from the inside o' the bars o' a Newgate cell.'

Ikey paused to emphasise his point, jabbing his forefinger at Bob Marley. 'That don't come natural, my dear! That's trainin', expert trainin', what you got young from a certain someone what is present and is beseechin' you to offer an 'elping hand in 'is hour o' most urgent need!'

Ikey cleared his throat and his tone became unctuous. 'I'm a bit short at the moment, unforeseen expenses and the like, but you knows me credit to be good. Me lovin' wife Hannah will pay you when she comes to see me.'

Marley shook his head. 'Don't know 'bout lovin' wife, Ikey. Yer missus weren't none too pleased findin' out 'bout Mary and yer high-class brothel in Bell Alley an' all!'

'Oh shit, she knows about Mary? 'Ow'd she know about Bell Alley then?'

Marley laughed. 'S'pect she read it in *The Times*. The 'ole of London's talkin' 'bout you, Ikey. What ya done an' all, inta-nash-nil forgery ring, plots to send the 'ole country broke wif fake English longtails floodin' the European market. Britain's credit in question by the Frenchy parley-ment! Austry-'Ungarian empire financially embarrassed and undermined! Yer a right notorious bastard, you is. If ya wasn't in so much shit you'd be the bloomin' toast o' the London criminal class. You is the biggest thing what's 'appened since Queen Caroline's trial!'

Ikey ignored Marley's exaggerated banter. 'Well, you may be sure Mary will pay you, then,' Ikey whined.

'Mary? Mary's in Newgate! She's been in front o' the beak and is awaitin' sentencin' at the Old Bailey. She's Botany Bay bound for sure.' Marley sniffed and looked ominously at Ikey. 'City arrested 'er three days after ya scarpered, charged 'er wif runnin' a bawdy 'ouse, but that were only the excuse.'

'Oh Jesus!' Ikey cried. 'Mary get the boat for runnin' a bawdy house? It ain't possible, runnin' a respectable brothel ain't no crime what merits transportation!'

'That's what folks is sayin' in the Lane. There's talk she'll get the full fourteen years.' Then Marley added darkly, 'On account of you, ya bastard. City ain't convinced she don't know nuffink 'bout that printin' press and what you've been up to wif the deaf and dumb Frenchy.'

Ikey looked up astonished. 'She kept stum? She didn't bleat?' If Mary had turned King's evidence and Ikey were caught there wasn't a judge in England who wouldn't find her information damning.

'She didn't say nuffink to nobody! That's a bloody good *nemmo* that is.' Marley jabbed a finger into Ikey's scrawny chest. 'Better'n what the likes o' you deserves, Ikey Solomon.'

Marley paused and shook his head. ''Fraid I can't give ya no credit, Ikey. I can't take no chances.' He shrugged. 'So that's it, it's all a matter o' business, knows what I mean? Pay up and I 'elps you to escape, don't and I marches ya straight to the City constabulary and collects me considerable reward for the heroic happrehension of England's number one notorious villain.'

Ikey examined the tops of his mittened hands, shook his head slowly, then looked up at Bob Marley accusingly. 'You got a bet each way, is that it!' In a broken whisper he added, 'Shame on you, Bob Marley!'

Bob Marley shrugged. ''Fraid so, me old matey. Business is business!' He paused, grinning. 'Now who was it taught me that?'

''Ow much?'

'Twenty sovs down.'

'Twenty sovs!' Ikey wailed. 'That be pure daylight robbery!'

Marley, not bothering to reply, shrugged and held out his hand. 'Fifteen? Fifteen sovs!'

Marley shook his head slowly. 'I'd like to, Ikey, but this ain't no ordinary deadlurk what's needed. I got expenses. Twenty sovs now and ten fer every week what I keeps ya safe in 'iding.'

Ikey made one final attempt. 'Twenty and five!'

'Twenty and ten, take it or leave it. I 'asn't got all night.'

Ikey sighed and, turning his back to Bob Marley, he foraged deep within his great coat and fished into a bag of coins which he knew contained two hundred and seventeen gold sovereigns, the last of the money Silas Browne and Maggie the Colour had paid him in cash for the Bank of England watermarked paper.

Getting back from Birmingham had proved an expensive

business. Twice he'd had to pay heavy bribes when he'd been recognised from his picture on posters which seemed to be sprouting like crocuses in April on the walls of every village or town through which he passed on his circuitous route to London.

Ikey slowly counted the twenty sovereigns into the slasher's hand. Marley counted the coins for himself, biting every second one as a test. Satisfied, he placed them in the pit pocket of his vest, then held his palm out to Ikey, wiggling the ends of his fingers.

'What?' Ikey asked, his eyes large and innocent.

Marley wiggled his fingers again. 'The ten sovs what's the first week's rent in advance,' he said quietly.

Ikey seemed at the point of tears as he counted ten more coins into Marley's outstretched maw.

'Cheers, Ikey!' Marley said, acknowledging the payment, then added, 'I got a nice little place, a deadlurk on Jacob's Island what is perfect for the purpose o' bein' in lavender. Lots o' bolt holes. Mind, 'iding a man o' yer extreme notoriety what everyone's lookin' for ain't easy and is very dangerous to me own safety.'

Bob Marley, now all business, placed his hands on his hips and looked quizzically at Ikey. 'You'll not be goin' out wif me dressed like that. Ain't a magistrates' runner or nark in London wouldn't recognise ya in an instant in that *schemata*. Buggered if I know 'ow ya got this far. Ya stick out like a bloomin' whore at a christening, ya does!'

Ikey opened his arms wide, palms outwards, and looked down at his chest in surprise. He had always assumed himself totally disguised in his long coat with his wide-brimmed hat pulled low over his forehead. 'I'm as invisible as the very night itself, my dear,' he said, clearly bemused at Bob Marley's uncharitable remark.

'Quite right! Invisible as the bleedin' 'arvest moon on Chatham Common.' Bob Marley pointed at Ikey's coat. 'Take your'n orf and put mine on.' Then removing his battered top hat he retrieved a cloth cap from within it and placed this upon his own head. Removing Ikey's hat, he dropped it gingerly to the floor, replacing it with the top hat which he set firmly on to Ikey's head, giving its crown a solid thump. The brim immediately dropped over Ikey's eyes and kept sliding until it stopped, trapped halfway down Ikey's nose.

Ikey gave a small squeak of alarm. 'Not me coat, I can't take leave o' me coat, not now, not never!' he pleaded.

'Christ, Ikey. I'll wear it! Ya won't lose it!' Marley said impatiently. 'Ya can 'ave it again when we gets to the isle.'

Ikey now pushed the top hat furiously off his head so that it tumbled backwards bouncing on the floor and rolling. 'Never, not ever, no, no no, not me coat!' he moaned.

Marley watched in amazement as Ikey clasped his arms about his chest hugging his coat, whimpering and rocking as though his life depended on it remaining on his back.

Which, of course, in Ikey's eyes was most certainly the case. Without his coat Ikey considered himself skinned and in no way different to an animal being led to the slaughteryard. Once skinned of his coat he believed he'd soon enough be hooked and hanging like some freshly peeled beast.

Marley appeared to be thinking, his hand cupped to his chin, 'I tell ya what . . .' He was about to say something, then changed his mind, paused and looked at Ikey. 'But it will cost ya another two sov.'

'What?' Ikey asked tremulously, backing away. 'You'll not have me coat, Bob Marley!'

'It be cold enough outside to freeze ya balls orf, but ya can wear me coat over your'n.' Bob Marley gave Ikey a fierce look. 'Mind, if I catches me death of this act o' extreme generosity, I'll cut yer bleedin' throat, Ikey Solomon!' He began once more to remove his coat, though first he removed the woollen scarf from its pocket and placed it about his neck.

For once, at the mention of money, there was no hesitation from Ikey. Almost before Bob Marley had ceased speaking, and long before he'd removed his coat, Ikey held out the two extra gold coins. 'Not me coat,' he whimpered. 'Not never me coat!'

Marley's coat proved sufficiently voluminous to accommodate Ikey within his own, but when it was fitted to his tiny body it dragged nearly ten inches on the ground. Furthermore, the sleeves extended six inches beyond Ikey's mittened fingers. Though this was of little consequence, the hemline of the coat dragging on the floor made it almost impossible for Ikey to walk at anything but a snail's pace.

Bob Marley looked puzzled, then suddenly he grabbed the back of the collar of the outer coat and lifted the entire garment so that the collar dropped over the top of Ikey's head in the manner of a monk's cowl. With his whiskers mostly concealed behind the lapels of the borrowed coat, Ikey now looked like an old crone.

Marley then produced a large silk handkerchief and, twirling it from corner to corner, tied it about Ikey's neck so that the hoisted top of the coat would not slip from his charge's head. This gave Ikey an even greater likeness to the shape of an old woman who, if casually observed in the darkness of the street, might be thought to be wearing a shawl about her head. Furthermore, with the lifting of the coat over Ikey's head, the sleeves now almost fitted, the tips of Ikey's mittened fingers protruding from the ends. It was an altogether admirable arrangement and Bob Marley stood back and felt well pleased with himself.

'Perfect! Even if I says so meself. If we're stopped by a crusher, you is me dear old muvver what's come up from the country. 'Ere, wrap this around yer gob so they won't see no whiskers if the law wants to take a closer gander at ya.' Marley handed Ikey the woollen scarf which hung from his neck.

Ikey reached out for the scarf. But with two coats on his back he could barely move his arms, much less wrap the scarf about his already tightly cowled head. Bob Marley grabbed the scarf and wound it around the bottom half of Ikey's face so that all that showed were the bright points of Ikey's bloodshot eyes.

''Ullo, old darlin',' Marley said and blew a kiss in Ikey's direction. His expression became suddenly impatient. 'C'mon, then, let's scarper. I'm ready so chilled me arse'ole thinks it's suckin' on a lemon!'

'What about me 'at? You've left me 'at!' Ikey cried in a muffled voice, pointing at his hat discarded on the floor.

Marley walked over to the banister and retrieved the candle. 'Fuck yer 'at, Ikey!' he said, kicking the hat into a dark corner. 'Fer Gawd's sake let's be rid o' this place before the law adds two and two and comes up wif a very popular arrest!' He rolled the jar containing the smoking candle back into the hallway and closed the door behind them.

Outside the wind howled and a sudden flurry of snow beat down on them, so that neither man heard the door open and then close again, or noticed the small shape of Sparrer Fart as he too left the Academy of Light Fingers. Under his arm, its broad brim almost touching the ground, the urchin carried Ikey's hat. He watched carefully as the two men turned towards Rosemary Lane and then he began to follow them into the bitter London night.

Hannah was woken to the loud knocking at the door of her Whitechapel home. The knocking seemed to have been going on for some time for she remembered it in her sleeping as she struggled to emerge from her laudanum-induced stupor. She'd returned home from the last of her brothels in the dock area just hours before dawn and had expected to sleep until midday.

She was too bleary-eyed to think why the Irish maid-of-all-work who slept with the two younger children hadn't responded to the knock. Wrapping herself in a blanket and thinking only that the slut had probably been at the gin again, having first fed it to the children to quieten them for the night, Hannah made her way down the stairs. She opened the front door to see Sparrer Fart standing on the snow-covered bottom step clutching what appeared to be a large hat.

At first the small urchin holding the hat made no sense. The street about her was transformed from its usual greyness and was white and clean from a fresh snowfall. It was still too early for people to be making their way to the Whitechapel markets around the corner, so that the street had the quality of a dream, enhanced further by the residual effects of laudanum. Hannah's face screwed up in vexation at the sight of the small boy who had the temerity to hammer at her door. She was about to send him packing with an oath when he stammered, 'Itttt's 'bbbout Ikkkey Ssssolmon, mmmissus!' Then slowly, her confused mind focused on the shape of Ikey's hat clutched under the urchin's arm.

Hannah rubbed her eyes, now suddenly fully awake, though the vestiges of the drug caused her words to slur when she spoke. 'Ikey? Ya got news?'

'Iiiit's urrrrgent, mmmmissus!' the small boy managed to say through half-frozen lips, his breath smoking in the freezing air.

'Come in, boy!' Hannah opened the door wider to let Sparrer Fart pass into the hallway. 'Keep walkin' to the kitchen in the back, I'll not 'ave such as you in me parlour.' Her head was surprisingly clear as she directed the urchin to the rear of the house.

'We ggggot 'immmmm missus!' Sparrer said, turning to her as they reached the kitchen.

'Got 'im, who's got 'im? Who's we?'

But the boy now seemed in a state too frozen to communicate further. He silently held up the hat for Hannah to see. He was shivering violently, his teeth chattering so furiously that it was plainly impossible for him to talk. Ikey's hat jerked and shook as though it might jump of its own accord from his tiny fist.

Hannah took a key from around her neck and opened a cupboard from which she took a quart bottle of brandy. She unhooked two small pewter mugs from the dresser, poured a small splash into one and handed it to Sparrer Fart. ''Ere, get that down yer gob, do ya the world.'

Sparrer dropped Ikey's hat and grabbed the mug with both hands, gulping greedily at the raw liquor. He began to choke and cough as the fiery liquid hit his stomach and chest, though he showed that he was well enough accustomed to such a reaction. Soon enough he took a second, more cautious, sip from the mug.

Hannah, clutching the blanket around her with one hand, poured a dash of brandy into the second mug and seated herself at the table.

'Well, what 'as ya to say for y'self, boy?' she demanded, pointing to Ikey's hat. 'No way Ikey would o' parted with 'is 'at.' She looked suspiciously at Sparrer, who was still shaking and clapping at himself. 'Ya ain't done Ikey no 'arm now, 'ave ya?' she demanded.

Sparrer shook his head and lifted the mug to his still chattering teeth for another sip.

Hannah sighed and reluctantly took the blanket from around her and handed it to the urchin who grabbed it gratefully, wrapping his diminutive body into its warmth. Hannah wore a thick red woollen nightdress which reached down to her ankles which, in turn, were encased in bedsocks and a pair of fleece-lined slippers. Warmed by a second sip of the brandy, she rose and went to the kindling box and laid a fire in the hearth, adding a few lumps of coal to the twigs before lighting it.

'Can I 'ave some more, missus?' Sparrer held out the pewter mug.

The tiny boy had consumed a good half inch of brandy which, apart from having restored his voice and stopped his shivering, appeared to have had no measurable effect on him. 'Got yer tongue back 'as ya, boy? Sorry, no more, not 'til after you've said what ya come for. What's yer name?'

'Sparrer, missus, Sparrer Fart, but they jus' calls me Sparrer.' He put the mug down on the table, licking the brandy taste from his lips. 'I'm 'ungry, missus, I ain't et since yesterday mornin'.'

Hannah sighed. She was growing impatient. 'What ya think this is, a bleedin' chop 'ouse? I ain't givin' you nuffink to eat until ya tells me what ya come for!' She pointed to the hat on the table. 'Ya can start with that!'

'It be Ikey's. Ikey Solomon! Honest, missus, I wouldn't tell you a lie!'

'I know that, but where'd you get it, boy?'

Sparrer, sensing Hannah's anxiety for an answer, looked suddenly forlorn. 'I'm 'ungry, missus, real 'ungry I is.'

Hannah realised she'd get no more from the urchin until she'd fed him, so she fetched a plate of cold salt beef from the cupboard and cut two large hunks from a loaf of yesterday's bread. Then she filled a bowl with curds and placed the offering in front of the small boy, who immediately began to devour the food.

In between mouthfuls Hannah got the story from Sparrer. Hannah listened as he told her how, a day or two back, he'd attempted to lift a kerchief from Bob Marley's pocket in the Hare and Hounds. How Marley had caught him at it and after boxing his ears for being clumsy had found that Sparrer was one of Ikey's brats.

'Maybe I could use ya, 'e says. 'Ow good are ya as a tooler, boy? I just caught ya, that ain't a good sign. I'll give ya a test, fail and ya gets yer arse kicked!' Sparrer cleverly mimicked Bob Marley's voice.

Bob Marley had watched as Sparrer demonstrated his skill on several of the patrons of the house, returning with a cheap watch, two snot rags and no value except as a demonstration of Sparrer's light fingers and a fob chain, also of little value, as it was made of brass. Marley had been sufficiently impressed to recruit Sparrer for what the urchin, imitating Bob Marley again, described as, 'A little job what may or may not 'appen, but is the very opposite to what you 'as been trained to do.' He had not said anything more except to instruct Sparrer to check into the Hare and Hounds late every afternoon to see if Marley had left a message for him.

'Then Ikey comes back. One moment 'e's not nowhere and the next there 'e is standing in the Academy in front o' all the lads. Then 'e says 'e wants us to find Bob Marley.' Sparrer stopped and thought for a moment. 'No 'e don't, first 'e starts puckering 'bout cribbage, 'ow we mustn't 'andle flats in the dark. Then 'e asks us to find this cove Bob Marley. Ikey says to us there's a sov for 'im what finds this cove, and a shilling and a tightener for all what goes lookin'. 'Cept he says Bob Marley will be in the Haymarket when I knows perfectly well that's where 'e ain't!' Sparrer, feeling very pleased with himself, looked up at Hannah. 'So they all scarpers, pushin' and shovin' to get down the stairway first so it nearly come down!'

'Yes, yes, go on,' Hannah said impatiently.

'So I goes back to where I seen me friend, Mr Marley, a couple o' hours before. To me surprise, 'e were still there an' all! I taps 'im on the back. Mr Marley, I says, Ikey Solomon asks for the pleasure of yer company.'

Sparrer laughed. '"'Ow'd you know I was lookin' for him?" Mr Marley says.' Sparrer looked pleased with himself. 'I didn't know 'e was lookin' for Ikey, but I ain't gonna tell 'im that, am I? I stays stum, don't I?' Sparrer paused and Hannah nodded her approval. '"Ikey, what's picture is on all the posters, ya means 'im?" Mr Marley asks again. I nods, the very same person, 'e's our kidsman. "Blimey!" 'e says. "Miracles will never cease!"'

Sparrer could see Hannah was intrigued. 'Mind if I 'as another drop o' brandy, missus?'

'No more mecks, ya ain't no use to me drunk!' Hannah said, her lips tight.

Sparrer picked up the mug and looked into it disappointed, but then continued to talk. '"Want to make 'arf a sov, Sparrer?" Mister Marley asks me. "Nacherly," I says. "Righto, Mister Sparrer Fart, let's see 'ow good a tooler ya is!" An' 'e 'olds up these two five pound notes.'

'Two?' Hannah interjected. 'Two five pound notes?'

'Yeah, that's right, then 'e give me instructions like, he says, "When we goes back and meets wif Ikey Solomon I wants you to plant these on 'im, Sparrer." Now I finks to meself, queer, even queerer than queer, all me life I 'as been practising to lift stuff, now this cove wants me to plant perfectly good soft on Ikey Solomon, the same person what's done all me trainin' in toolin'. It don't make no sense if ya asks me.'

Hannah was breathing fast. 'Well? Did ya do it?'

Sparrer, grown more loquacious with the brandy and enjoying his own story, continued without replying. '"I'll try, Mr Marley, sir," I says. 'E grabs me by me coat. "No! Just don't fail! If it don't look like ya can do it, don't take no chances, ya hear me boy?"'

Sparrer's imitation of Bob Marley was near perfect. "'E 'ands me 'arf a sov. "Money in advance, win or lose, do it right or not at all! Ya understand?"' Sparrer straightened up in his chair and unconsciously stuck out his chest. 'Blimey, missus, 'e's paid me before I done the job. Win or lose I wins! "I'll do me best," I says. "Seein' 'ow you trusts me an' all."'

Hannah grabbed the mug out of Sparrer's hand and banged it down onto the table. 'For Gawd sakes stop muckin' about, did ya or didn't ya?'

Sparrer jumped and pulled his head back instinctively, expecting to be hit. 'What did I do?' he exclaimed in alarm.

Hannah felt suddenly foolish but, unable to explain her agitation, attacked further. 'Yer lyin'!' she shouted, trying to recover her composure. 'Ain't nobody could plant nuffink on Ikey Solomon. Leastways, no tooler what's just a brat!'

Sparrer rose to the bait. 'I did so! It were easy, missus!'

Hannah laughed. 'Easy was it? You think Ikey is some moocher what's just come in town from Shropshire?'

Sparrer explained how Ikey had tried to welsh on the sovereign he'd promised, offering him half a sovereign instead. Hannah nodded. This part was familiar enough.

'So I starts to blub, see. "It ain't fair!" I says and goes up and 'angs onto Ikey's coat, cos I seen this tear in the front what 'asn't been mended yet, so I keeps blubbin' and pluckin' on 'is coat which he thinks is me beggin' for the other 'arf sov what he owes me. So I tucks the soft what Mr Marley give me inside the tear and rightaway it falls down into the lining.' Sparrer grinned. 'It were easy as pie!'

'So, tell me,' Hannah asked, 'Bob Marley gets ya to plant the soft on Ikey's person, real money what's valuable. Why would 'e do that? It don't make no sense now do it?'

Sparrer scratched his head. 'Buggered if I knows, missus.' He thought for a moment. 'Maybe it were a trick an' all. A joke or summink.'

Hannah said nothing until the boy grew uncomfortable under her steady gaze. Sparrer looked up and shrugged. 'I don't know why 'e done it, missus,' he said, ashamed that he could come up with no adequate explanation.

Hannah began, her voice soft at first, then building in volume, 'Let me tell ya summink for nuffink, Mr Sparrer Fart!' She pointed at the hat on the table. 'I think ya found Ikey's 'at, I dunno 'ow and I dunno where.' She reached over and picked up the hat. 'Look! It's got dust on it, 'ere look, on the brim, where it's been lyin' somewhere what's dusty! Ya found Ikey's 'at and ya thinks, "'Ullo, 'ullo, this be worth summink", so ya comes round 'ere and makes up some cock 'n' bull story about fivers what ya planted on me 'usband's person, stories what is ridiculous and stupid even for a brat the likes of you!' Hannah's voice rose even higher. 'I don't think you've seen Ikey Solomon. I think you've only seen 'is 'at!'

'It ain't true! It ain't true what ya says, missus! I knows where Ikey is, where 'e be 'iding. I can show ya!' Sparrer protested.

'I suppose Bob Marley showed ya?' Hannah sneered.

'No! I followed them two. When they left the Academy last night. I followed them to the Isle! It were snowing, they didn't see me.'

'The Isle?'

'Jacob's Isle, Ikey's got a deadlurk there.'

'Ha! Jacob's Island! Fat chance! That be docks and 'ouses what's mostly condemned!'

'C'mon, then, I'll show ya, missus!' Sparrer challenged, caught up in the argument and forgetting that his purpose for coming was to try for a couple of sovs in exchange for Ikey's whereabouts.

Hannah's expression changed suddenly and she smiled disarmingly then gave Sparrer a supplicating look. 'Please, Sparrer, don't fool with me poor broken 'eart. I loves me 'usband. I know 'e ain't much, but I loves 'im. If ya knows where Ikey is, I must go to 'im, 'e needs me.' She leaned forward and took Sparrer's dirty little hand in both her own. 'Look at me, a poor woman what's 'usband is in mortal danger. Please Sparrer, if ya 'as any loyalty to Ikey what's taught ya all ya knows, you'll let 'is poor, miserable wife visit 'im.'

Hannah's change of mood quite took Sparrer by surprise. The fact that she appeared suddenly to believe him, combined with the feel of his hand cradled in the warmth of her own, caused his eyes to fill with tears of relief.

'I can show ya, missus, the exact place,' he said.

Hannah went to the cupboard and returned with the plate of salt beef and what remained of the bread. She placed a knife beside Sparrer. ''Elp y'self, love, I won't be long.' She took the bottle of brandy and locked it in the cupboard, replacing the key around her neck and tucking it into the bodice of her nightdress. Then she took Ikey's hat. 'I'll be back in two shakes of a duck's tail. Be me guest, make y'self completely at 'ome.'

By the time Hannah had dressed for the street and returned to the kitchen, Sparrer was asleep, his arms on the table with his head cradled within them. It took a considerable amount of prodding and shaking to wake him. Hannah was anxious to be away before the early morning market crowd began to fill the streets. At last she got the urchin to his feet and escorted him to the front door.

'Ya go first, Sparrer, to the Pig 'n Spit and wait for me outside. I'll be along shortly in a hackney. We'll ride most o' the way, then, when we gets near the Isle, we'll walk.' Hannah gripped Sparrer's shoulder at the door. 'Be sure ya isn't followed, pigs in any number could be watchin' the 'ouse.'

Sparrer, after running most of the way to keep warm, had not long been waiting at the Pig 'n Spit when Hannah called to him from the interior of the hackney. The driver slowed down and Sparrer jumped into the small cabin and sat beside Hannah.

'When we gets close, but not too close, give me a nudge and we'll get out and walk. 'Ere, sit up close to me so I feels ya,' Hannah whispered. Sparrer moved up against Hannah's heavy woollen coat. Warmth and comfort seemed to emanate from her plump person. It stirred long forgotten memories in the child so that the tears began to run down his dirty cheeks and he became momentarily lost in the past. Consequently they found themselves closer to Ikey's deadlurk than was perhaps prudent before Sparrer finally nudged Hannah.

They walked onto the Isle and Sparrer led Hannah by a circuitous route to an area where the houses seemed deserted and were so closely packed that they appeared to be leaning on each other for support. They walked down an alley, wide enough to take a wagon, which was strewn with debris and foul with mud and evil-smelling puddles some of which appeared to carry a thin veneer of ice. Hannah had cause to lift her skirt and, despite the care she took, her boots sank into the stinking ooze, often almost to their tops. Sparrer, who walked ahead, came to the end of the alley and put his hand up to signal Hannah to stop. Then he called her forward with a flick of his fingers, indicating that she should move slowly and without making a sound. Hannah came towards him more carefully than ever, though the squelch and sucking of the mud, and crunching of thin ice under her feet seemed to be announcing her every step.

When she reached the far end of the alley Hannah discovered that it led to a small loading yard in the form of a quadrangle. It appeared to have once been paved with flagstones, though most of these had been removed and were piled high into one corner and partly covered with snow. The building which occupied three sides of the quadrangle had once been a fairly large warehouse backing on to the river. The warehouse seemed to have been deserted for a long time and its few windows and the main doors, big enough to take a horse and cart, were boarded up. The urchin put his finger to his lips and pointed to the pile of snow-covered flagstones.

'Entrance be there, missus,' Sparrer whispered. 'Be'ind them stones.'

Hannah's heart pounded furiously. She stood a few feet back from the entrance and deep within the shadows so that she could not possibly be seen, but she nevertheless imagined she could feel Ikey's eyes boring into her from a gap between two planks which boarded up the hoist door, set high up into the roof of the three-storey stone building. Hannah could sense Ikey crouching on his knees, wild strands of greasy hair flying from the sides of his head, his shiny bald pate vulnerable for want of the security afforded by his broad-brimmed hat. She could almost feel his eyes glued to the gap between the boards, willing her to come to him, though too fearful to call out lest her presence be some sort of trap.

She waited until she felt her breathing grow calmer then placed her hand on Sparrer's shoulder and gave it a tiny squeeze. Sparrer turned his head and looked up at her.

'Come!' she whispered and, turning about, began to retreat down the muddy alley. She walked ahead of Sparrer until they were well clear of the buildings. Not a soul had appeared in all the while they had been in the vicinity of the derelict row of houses. The part of the island they were on seemed to be totally desolate and their footsteps showed clearly in the snow, but it had begun to snow lightly again and they would soon be concealed. A low pewter-coloured sky added to the sense of isolation and misery of the broken-down surroundings. Hannah let out a discernible sigh of relief once she considered they had retreated sufficiently far from the deserted houses to communicate.

'Ya sure that be it, Sparrer? Gawd's truth, that old ware'ouse be Ikey's deadlurk?'

Sparrer looked hurt. 'Yes, missus, 'course I is. I knows these parts like the back o' me 'and. Before I growed up, Jacob's be where I come from.'

Hannah walked with Sparrer to the small causeway connecting Jacob's Island to the city side of the Thames. Here she opened her purse and took out two single pound notes and held them up in front of Sparrer.

'Ya never seen me, ever, ya understand? If ya tells a single livin' soul about Ikey's deadlurk I'll tell Bob Marley ya followed 'im and 'e'll come after ya with 'is razor and cut yer bleedin' throat from ear to ear!' Hannah ran a mittened hand across her throat for emphasis. 'You 'as never seen me, we's never met, ya understand, Sparrer?' Sparrer nodded, his eyes fixed on the money she held in her hand. 'Good!' She handed him the one pound notes. ''Ere, for yer trouble. Now disappear, scarper, I never seen ya, whoever you are.'

Sparrer placed one of the pound notes between his lips which were beginning to tremble from the cold again, then using both hands, he held either end of the second note and brought his fists together then snapped them suddenly apart pulling the banknote taut to test its strength. Satisfied as to the quality of the bank paper he held the note up to the sky to examine the Bank of England watermark. He seemed pleased with what he saw, but opened his mouth, the remaining note sticking to his bottom lip as he wet his fingers with spittle and rubbed the watermark on the note with his wet fingers to see if it would disappear. Sparrer then tried to remove the remaining note from his bottom lip, but it had frosted to the skin and he pulled gingerly until it finally came away, leaving a bright smear of blood where the paper had removed the skin. He folded both notes together and pushed them somewhere deep within the interior of his tattered coat.

Then, his breath making smoke in the cold air, Sparrer scanned the desolate surroundings at some length, then brought his gaze back to Hannah's face, his eyes showing no recognition.

'I must 'o been dreamin',' he declared in an exaggerated voice, ''cause I could o' sweared there was a woman standing right 'ere in front o' me not a moment ago!' He turned and began walking away from Hannah, not once looking back.

Hannah crossed the causeway and stopped at a hoarding where a man was busy pasting up a poster for Madame Tussaud's Travelling Waxworks. She purchased a handful of torn poster paper for a halfpenny and, seated on a low stone wall, she commenced to clean her muddy boots. Soon thereafter she hailed a hackney. 'Take me to Threadneedle Street, Bank o' England,' she instructed the driver.

Chapter Fourteen

Ikey was arrested by the City police in the early afternoon of the day Hannah visited Jacob's Island with Sparrer Fart. He was taken to Lambeth Street Police Office and bound over. After a thorough search of the inner parts of his body and clothes the two counterfeit five pound notes were discovered in the lining of his overcoat. Thereafter he was taken to Newgate, where he was lodged in a single cell reserved for prisoners thought to be dangerous.

'Oh shit! I 'as been shopped!' was all he was heard to cry when the fake soft was found. The senior constable, who went by the unpropitious name of George Smith and who had searched him, looked disgusted. A notorious old hand at the searching of suspects, he was known to any who had 'passed through his hands', as 'The Reamer', for he would delight in prodding his victims. Two great sausage-like fingers with fingernails grown long and filed sharp as a mandolin player's thumb entered their rear passage with a jabbing and stabbing that left them bleeding for days.

'Yer full o' shit, Ikey! But clean o' contraband!' he'd exclaimed in a booming voice, much to the delight of the constables who were holding down the screaming, blubbing Ikey with his breeches pulled down below his skinny white thighs. Then, after first having gone through the amazing configurations of pockets, slots, tubes and hiding places within Ikey's coat and eventually finding the two offending notes secreted within the innocuous tear on its outside, the senior constable held up the counterfeit notes and, shaking his head, declared, 'It ain't worthy o' you, Ikey, me boy, I expects much better from the likes o' you! Summink more ingenious, a hiding place what could challenge yours truly! A glorious adumbration to bedazzle the mind!' The Reamer waved the two notes in the air above his head and grinned. 'You'll be the laughin' stock o' Newgate Gaol, me boy!'

Ikey immediately concluded that Bob Marley had betrayed him and by means of half a sovereign placed into the hand of a turnkey sent urgent word for Hannah to come to Newgate. Here he had been placed in a cell on the third floor of the central block where, if he stood on the stone bed, he could catch a glimpse through the small barred window of the great dome of St Paul's. Though the stench was no better at the top of the building, some natural light penetrated into the cell. Moreover, the floor and walls, while of stone, were not covered with faeces, urine and the evacuation of drunken stomachs as in the dungeon cages. Nor were they especially damp, so that the fear of gaol fever, now known as typhoid, and which was said to be carried by the appalling fumes into every cell, was less likely to strike.

Ikey's more private incarceration was not intended to indicate his superior status but rather his notoriety. It was designed to keep him from being murdered in a public cell where drunkenness, fornication, starvation and every form of despair and degradation did not preclude a peculiar loyalty to the King of England.

It is an English paradox that prisoners who are flogged and starved in the name of the Crown and treated far worse than a barnyard pig by the society in which they live, remain loyal subjects to the King. The scurrilous and exaggerated stories of Ikey's attempt to bring financial ruin to the Bank of England were as well known in the dark public cages of Newgate as elsewhere, and should he have been thrown among these poor wretches it was feared that he would not live to face the full force of British justice.

Ikey, always the perfectionist, was as much dismayed as the senior Bow Street constable had pretended to be that someone had managed to plant the two five pound notes within the tear on his coat. He cursed himself bitterly for neglecting, after escaping from the coach in Birmingham, to immediately sew up the offending rip. It was just such lack of attention to detail which leads to downfall and, Ikey told himself, if a mistake of the same magnitude of neglect had occurred with one of his urchins, the young tooler would have been most severely punished.

Ikey's disappointment in himself was therefore profound. He prided himself on being alert to the lightest of fiddling fingers. So how had Bob Marley managed to plant the fake soft on him? Ikey knew Marley was no tooler. The slasher's fists were ham-like and would not have had the skill required to plant the notes within the coat.

Finally, after a process of elimination in which his careful mind examined every detail of his escapades over the past two days, Ikey arrived at the correct solution. Sparrer Fart had been the perpetrator. Ikey recalled how the young pickpocket had moved close, begging for the half sovereign he withheld from him. Such was the curious nature of Ikey Solomon's mind that he congratulated himself for having trained both Marley and Sparrer Fart – Marley for the foresight he showed in recruiting the urchin and young Sparrer for the way he had executed the plant.

Ikey was aware that he had finally come to the end of the line, which, in this event, was dangerously close to the end of a rope. All of England was braying for the noose to be placed around his scrawny neck, the public having believed the scurrilous twaddle in the penny sheets. Ikey's nefarious plans to undermine the very throne of England itself with fake currency, its distribution undertaken by a gang of international Jews and spread across all the capitals of Europe, was discussed in even the poorest netherkens. All of London wanted the case dealt with in a summary manner and damn the due process of the law. 'Hang the Jew bastard now!' was the popular call of the day. There were even some among the better classes who paid a reserve price for a window overlooking the scaffold erected in Newgate Street outside that notorious gaol. The only question which remained was the date on which Ikey's execution would be celebrated.

In Ikey's mind, though, there was a more urgent need in his life than the business of avoiding the hangman. He must, at all costs, contact Marybelle Firkin and retrieve the letter of credit for delivery to the bankers Coutts & Company before the seven days for its presentation expired. Ikey faced what appeared to be an impossible task. He had just three days to lodge the note in person and found himself trapped, a prisoner of His Majesty, locked in a guarded cell.

Moreover, and to Ikey's enormous chagrin, if he failed to present the letter of credit and lost the money he would not even be permitted to enjoy the satisfaction of shopping Silas and Maggie the Colour. To inform on them would be to indict himself as surely as if he had been caught with the bill paper in his possession. Ikey, for once in his miserable life, had been simply and elegantly foiled by a man with a mind like a suet pudding and a woman who wore wooden clogs.

However, having paid much for it in a lifetime outside the law, Ikey was possessed of a good mind for legal procedure. He knew that in England a man could be sentenced in a magistrate's court to be transported for stealing half a crown or a fat goose. But should he be able to afford the costs involved in a rigorous defence in a higher court, he had a much greater chance of avoiding transportation even though the crime committed be a hundred times more extravagant in its nature.

Ikey comforted himself that it could be argued by a good barrister that the two fake five pound notes found in the lining of his coat might well have been planted, the offending and obvious tear in his coat being the evidence to show how simply this might have been done without his knowledge.

This argument, if successful in casting some doubt in the mind of the judge, could be further supported by a timely stroke of great good fortune. Abraham Van Esselyn, who had taken full advantage of his twin afflictions and admitted nothing in his trial, had been sentenced to fourteen years transportation and had hanged himself in Cold Bath Fields Gaol just three days previously. The deaf mute, never able to share the joy of social intercourse with his fellow man, had finally decided to take his leave of the silent world around him. Ikey's defence could therefore proceed unencumbered by evidence of collaboration with his erstwhile partner.

Ikey's case could be built around the premise that he, a simple man, inexpert in the ways of machinery, was merely the landlord of the premises, unaware that amazing works of counterfeiting longtails were being created by the Frenchy foreigner, a deaf mute unable to communicate in the English language. Ikey had merely knocked on the door of the basement premises, accepting the rent due to him in an incurious and routine manner early each Friday morning.

Similarly, Mary Abacus had declared Ikey to be her landlord and her testimony had implicated him in no other way. It was on this issue of being the duped landlord for both prisoners that Ikey's case would depend. In this way the burden of proof lay with the prosecution and, as always in such cases, the silver tongue of an expensive advocate could be used to its greatest effect.

It was a neat enough argument, though as an initial defence Ikey knew it had little chance of working at his first trial in the magistrate's court. Here he would almost certainly be indicted. The scuttlebutt in the penny papers would have long since pronounced him guilty.

However, in the Court of Appeal at the Old Bailey where a fair trial could be guaranteed, and in the hands of a good barrister, this argument could be made to seem most compelling, or, at the very least, it would cast some doubt on the serious nature of the case against Ikey.

Ikey had just three days to contact Marybelle Firkin and lodge the letter of credit. To a man of less fortitude this might have seemed somewhat of a forlorn hope. But Ikey had been in more than one tight spot in his life and, in his mind, formulated a plan which, with Bob Marley no longer his go-between, depended almost entirely on Hannah, her coachman father, Moses Julian, and two carefully selected members of Ikey's own family. The first was an uncle who happened to be of similar age to Ikey, with a striking family resemblance around the eyes and nose. He possessed a small reputation as an actor and a slightly larger one as a broadsman, a card sharp, cheating at cribbage being what he did during the frequent 'resting' periods of his capricious career. His name was Reuban Reuban, a moniker which would have been better suited to a more illustrious thespian. Though he affected the manners of an actor, he was clean shaven and dressed sharp. The second was Ikey's cousin, a young tailor by the name of Abraham Reuban. Actor father and tailor son both had cause in the past to be grateful to Ikey and resided near the Theatre Royal in the Haymarket, this being in close enough proximity to No. 59, the Strand, the home of the bankers Coutts & Company.

To bring to fruition his plan to lodge the credit note on time

Ikey was obliged to tell Hannah of its existence. She would therefore know soon enough the extent of the funds Ikey was proposing to transfer to New York. This was a major concern to Ikey. If Hannah suspected that he had been funding his escape without her knowledge she would not reveal her part of the combination to the Whitechapel safe, which, of course, amounted to a great deal more in value than the nineteen thousand, four hundred pounds he was sending to New York.

Ikey would therefore need to concoct a story which convinced Hannah that the credit note was to their mutual benefit. He would have to persuade her that he had gone to Birmingham at great danger to himself, when he could just as easily have escaped to America immediately he knew of the raid. He would express in most compelling terms his reason for not so doing, his only thought having been to add to the funds they would have when she joined him with the children in New York.

Alas, his escape had been thwarted by his betrayal and premature arrest and it was Hannah who was now free to act in the matter of their mutual fortune. He would convince her that he must escape in order to lodge the letter of credit with Coutts & Company and so ensure the money would be transferred to New York.

Hannah, Ikey felt confident, would co-operate. Her greed would convince her as well as the knowledge that Ikey, should his escape prove successful, would not leave her without the prospect of his share of the Whitechapel safe. Their mutual assurance lay in each keeping their part of the combination secret from the other.

On her arrival at Newgate, Hannah was escorted by the keeper himself to Ikey's cell, being quite puffed by the steep stairs. Outside the door of the cell sat a turnkey, a large, slack-jawed, vacant looking man with very few teeth, chosen no doubt for his strength and not the wit at his command. Hannah waited for the gaol officer who had acted as her guide to depart before she fee'd Ikey's guard a fushme.

'I begs ya to stand well clear o' the grille, mister. I 'as things to do what a wife is obliged to do for 'er 'usband and what ain't respectable to be within the 'earin' or seein' of.' She looked boldly at the turnkey. 'If you knows what I mean?'

The man nodded and grinned, showing the stumps of four yellow and black teeth. Pocketing the five shillings she'd given him with obvious delight, the usual fee for 'showing a blind eye' being sixpence, he fumbled with a set of keys hanging from a large ring, which, in turn, was attached to a stout brass chain affixed to his belt.

'I'll be down the corridor a bit, missus,' he said, then making a small ceremony of unlocking the cell door, he added, 'Take yer time, now, I ain't goin' orf for two 'ours yet.' He let Hannah pass through into the cell, then locked the door behind her, making no attempt to search her hamper or, as was the usual case, to extract the larger share of its contents for himself.

Ikey was seated on his stone bed and did not rise when Hannah entered. She placed the basket down and immediately fell upon him, her demeanour most sorrowful and sympathetic.

'My poor Ikey, they 'ave caught ya and locked ya up!' she moaned. She grabbed Ikey and held his head clasped to her breast. 'My poor, poor darlin'!' she exclaimed, rocking his head in her arms.

Ikey grew much alarmed at this unexpected attack. Hannah had not placed a loving hand on him for years. Even their coupling had been completely without emotion, she taking him while he was piss-erect and half asleep, her single purpose to become impregnated with the minimum of time and effort. Before coming to visit him in gaol she had splashed some vile-smelling potion between her breasts and Ikey felt sure he must suffocate with the effect of this noxious perfume. He struggled frantically and managed after a few moments to extricate himself from Hannah's smothering grasp.

'For Gawd sakes, woman, leave orf!' he exclaimed as he backed away from his wife, adjusting the bandana he wore in the manner of a seaman's scarf and which had slipped to the back of his head from Hannah's embrace.

'Oh, Ikey, what shall we do? We are destitute! I am a poor woman with four small children, now deserted! Oh, oh, woe is me! What shall become of us?' Hannah cried, this time so loud that the turnkey, now seated at the opposite end of the corridor, could plainly hear her.

Then, as sudden as this surprising outburst, her voice dropped to a loud whisper. 'Ya bastard, ya piece of crud, who is this Mary, this whore ya give a 'igh-class brothel to?' Her expression had changed to a snarl. Then, stepping back, she slapped the seated

Ikey so hard across the face that his head was thrown against the wall of the cell, and for a few moments he thought he would lose his wits completely. 'Ya shit, you will pay for this!' Hannah spat, though none of her furious invective carried much above a hoarse whisper.

Ikey pulled his legs up onto the stone shelf that served as his bed and backed himself into the furthermost corner, his hands protecting his face. After a few moments he parted his fingers and peeked at Hannah, who stood with her arms folded, nostrils flared, snorting like a bull halted at a turnstile.

'Please my dear, don't 'it me!' he whimpered. 'It were business, that be all it were! Business to our mutual benefit, my dear,' Ikey wailed plaintively.

'Ya fucked her, didn't ya? Ya fucked that *shiksa* bitch!'

Ikey looked genuinely alarmed. 'Shhsssh! No, no, my dear, not ever, not once, not possible, you knows me, it were business, it were no more,' he lied.

'Humph!' Hannah snorted, then added, once again in a rasping voice, 'Well the whore got what she 'ad coming to 'er, at least there be some justice in this world!'

'We's in *shtunk*, my dear. I've been blowed and planted,' Ikey said, hoping to change the subject.

'What! Who blowed ya? Planted? What with?'

'Soft, two fives.' Ikey reached down and pulled at his coat and pointed to the tear eighteen inches up from the hem. 'Young tooler planted 'em in there, Bob Marley were the blow!'

'Marley?' Hannah, feigning surprise, shook her head. 'Nah! Not 'im, not Bob Marley, 'e's family!'

''E done it, couldn't 'ave been no one else.' Ikey shrugged. ''E were the only one what got close enough and knowed about the longtails, 'im with the kid what did the plant.'

''E wouldn't 'ave told no kid, not Bob Marley! Too careful. It must o' been someone else.'

'No, my dear, it were 'im. Kid would 'ave thought the bills were genuine.'

Hannah was, of course, thrilled. Ikey did not in the least suspect her. It had turned out exactly the way she had hoped. She took a kugel cake from her basket and handed it to Ikey who absent-mindedly broke a piece off and handed the remainder back to Hannah.

Ikey then told Hannah about the case he thought he could mount with a good barrister and her heart immediately sank. Although Hannah despised her husband, she had never underestimated his cunning. If Ikey should prove himself innocent of no more than being the negligent landlord of the premises in Bell Alley, he would receive only a short sentence, at most a stretch. In twelve months he would be out and her plans for the future of herself and her children would be in tatters.

'I must escape, it be a matter o' the utmost importance, I must get out of 'ere!' Ikey suddenly declared.

'Get out? Escape?' Hannah looked puzzled. 'But ya jus' said – ya jus' told me yer a good chance to beat the rap?'

Ikey then proceeded to tell Hannah about the letter of credit and asked her to visit Marybelle Firkin at the Pig 'n Spit and retrieve it. He also asked her to have Reuban Reuban and his son Abraham come to visit him. Then he carefully outlined the plan for his escape. As he spoke he pushed tiny lumps of the cake into his mouth, so that by the end of his lengthy instructions the piece of cake he'd broken off seemed to be much the same size as when he'd started.

'Whatsamatter? You ain't 'ungry?' she said, trying to collect her thoughts.

Ikey shook his head. 'Your father must be standin' exactly where I said, on the exact spot what I told you outside the Pig 'n Spit. A hackney what can take four, doors both sides o' the cabin.'

Hannah nodded, though her head was in a whirl. She thought Ikey's plan too far-fetched to succeed, but on the other hand she wanted him to lodge the letter of credit. It represented a great deal of money, enough in itself to set her up in America even without the contents of the Whitechapel safe, though it was unthinkable that she would not have this as well. In her mind she too began to formulate a plan.

Ikey's plan was based on the writ of *habeas corpus*, that is, the right of every Englishman to apply for bail to be granted until his case came up for hearing. In order for this to happen he would need to appear before a judge at the King's Bench court at Westminster, where he would be granted a hearing. This would entail being escorted by two turnkeys to the court and would allow him to travel outside the confines of the gaol.

It was standard procedure for two turnkeys to escort a prisoner by foot to the Court of King's Bench, which was situated not more than a mile from the gates of Newgate, though it was not unusual for a prisoner with funds, wishing to keep his identity and his shame from the passing crowd, to offer to pay for a carriage to be escorted in privacy to the courts.

Ikey had applied for bail the moment he had been bound over at Lambeth Street and the hearing was set for two days after Hannah had visited him. Reuban Reuban and his son Abraham, alerted by Hannah, had arrived during that afternoon. Ikey had spoken to them at length and Abraham had taken several measurements of Ikey's person.

At half-past nine on the morning of the hearing two turnkeys marched Ikey through the gates of Newgate. It was the custom for turnkeys who had been on duty to take the extra duty of escort to court hearings so that the day staffing would not be disrupted. This was an unpopular rule, as it attracted no extra stipend for working, at the least, half of the day shift, or even more if the court was delayed. The two men who escorted Ikey were therefore tired and somewhat dulled from the frequent tots of cheap gin and Spanish brandy they had received from prisoners during the night and were not inclined to treat him with respect.

The King's Bench in Westminster was a steady half an hour's walk from Newgate and was scheduled to commence at half-past the hour of ten o'clock. It was a week before Christmas and while no snow had fallen during the night a chill wind blew in from the North Sea. It brought with it a light fog which, added to the smog caused by the winter fires, made the streets as dark as the night itself. Moreover they were packed with Christmas shopping crowds and the smoking flares carried by the coaches and brandished by messenger boys dodging through the crush of people and between carriages added to the general annoyance and difficulty of conditions on foot.

It seemed almost a miracle when a hackney coach appeared through the gloom and appeared to be empty.

'Shall I 'ave the pleasure, gentlemen, of offerin' you a ride?' Ikey asked. He silently congratulated Hannah's father, Moses Julian, for his expertise in having the coach so 'fortuitously' available. Ikey's two escorts needed no further persuasion and he hailed the hackney with a sharp whistle.

'Where to, guv?' the coachman called down to them.

'Westminster!' Ikey called back. 'King's Bench!'

'We'll 'ave to go 'round back way, guv, through Petticoat Lane. Coaches jammed tight as fiddlesticks from 'ere to Westminster. It be the bleedin' fog,' he pointed his whip into the barely visible crowd milling along the pavement, 'and them bleedin' Christmas shoppers.'

Ikey glanced questioningly at the senior of his two escorts, a coarse looking man with a bulbous nose to rival that of Sir Jasper Waterlow, upon the tip of which resided a large wart not unlike a woman's nipple in appearance. It was therefore truly astonishing that his name was Titty Smart, though it may be supposed that this was a sobriquet and not his christian name. He was also the senior of the two men, much experienced and seventeen years in the prison service, and he now grunted and frowned saying gruffly, 'Mr Popjoy and I accepts.'

Ikey, with both his hands shackled, one to a wrist of each man, was held steady at the rear by the younger Popjoy as he climbed with difficulty into the interior of the hackney. The coach turned off the Strand at the first convenience and into a lane which despite its narrowness immediately seemed to improve their progress. The lighted flares stuck to each side of the hackney momentarily turned the drab grey walls of the smog-shrouded buildings into a bright mustard-coloured burst of light as they passed, giving the effect of magic lantern slides changing with rapidity. This flickering effect and the rocking of the coach soon began to have an effect on the weary turnkeys. Ikey watched as their chins sank to their chests and their eyelids rolled shut, only to jerk open every once in a while until the effort became too great and they could no longer stay awake.

The coach turned into Petticoat Lane and then into Rosemary Lane and, as they were about to pass the Pig 'n Spit, Ikey called loudly to the coachman to halt. The two turnkeys wakened with a start and their free hands went immediately to their truncheons.

'Gentlemen, you are wearied from your duties as good men should be what have spent the long night in the service o' the King.'

Ikey dragged the arm of Albert Popjoy with him as he took his watch from his fob pocket and clicked it open, examining its face briefly. 'We are makin' excellent progress and will arrive at the

King's Bench well before the time we are to be called before 'is worship.' He nodded towards the window. 'This 'ostelry, a tavern o' most excellent reputation, be closed to all at this hour, though I assure you it is open to us at any hour. 'Ere be a supply o' brandy the likes o' which may not be found anywhere in the kingdom. A veritable elixir of a miraculous nature what is said to heal the sick and cause the lame to walk again! A tonic extracted from the finest Frenchy vines, matured in English oak for twenty year or more, to render it now more British in its character than ever it were French. It can be mulled in old pewter and be used with great purpose to warm the cockles and keep the eyes brightly open! What say you, gentlemen?'

The thought of a pewter of mulled French brandy, expensive at the best of times, was too much for an old soak such as Titty Smart to refuse. 'The one. We'll have the one and then be off.' He looked at his partner, the younger Albert Popjoy, whose expression seemed doubtful. 'The one, it can't hurt to have the one, lad, now can it?' Smart sniffed, snorted and then rubbed his nose furiously with the edge of his forefinger, as though awakening it to the delicious prospect of the delectable brandy fumes.

'Pull in around the back,' Ikey instructed the coachman.

The coachman touched his whip to the horses and the hackney moved into the small lane which led to the courtyard behind the Pig 'n Spit, drawing up beside the back door. Smart opened the door on his side of the coach to see the head of the cellarman's boy suddenly appear through the open barrel chute at ground level. 'We be closed, sir, we opens again four o'clock. Four o'clock 'til four o'clock o' the mornin',' he yelled, squinting up at the turnkey.

Ikey stood up and leaning over the lap of the still-seated Smart stuck his head out of the coach door. 'Open, my dear, it be urgent business with your mistress!'

The boy's head disappeared underground again and a couple of minutes passed before he opened the back door. He wore a leather apron and carried a cooper's hammer and, judging from his height, appeared to be about fourteen years old. 'Who be it what's come callin'?' he asked.

'Call your mistress, my dear. Tell 'er, Ikey Solomon.'

The boy stood his ground. 'She won't take kindly, sir, she ain't been aslumber more'n two hour.'

'There'll be a shillin', lad,' Ikey said, then repeated, 'Call

Mistress Marybelle, tell 'er Ikey Solomon and friends 'as come 'round to pay their respects.'

The expression on the boy's face remained dubious but finally he nodded his head and closed the door. The three men climbed from the coach and the coachman moved the hackney to a tethering post. Several minutes later, which they spent waiting, with their breath smoking the air around their heads and their feet stamping the frosted ground, the door was once again flung open. Filling its entire frame was the giant shape of Marybelle Firkin. She was clad in a bright red woollen dressing gown which gave the immediate effect of a giant tea cosy with a pretty porcelain head in curling papers sewn upon its top as an ornament of decoration.

'My Gawd, bless me if it ain't you! Ikey Solomon! What a bloomin' pleasure!' There was no hint of annoyance in Marybelle's voice at the early hour. Had the turnkeys been more alert they might have wondered why this was so. A woman who has been up all the night to the boisterous demands of her drunken customers is not usually wakened as easily or in a mood of such pleasant alacrity. They might also have questioned why, when the tavern had been closed to patrons a good five and some hours, a hearty fire blazed in the private parlour with the mulling tongs in place between the coals.

'Come in, come in gentlemen,' Marybelle invited, turning and waddling down a passage, leading the way into a bright, warm room. 'Welcome to me 'umble parlour, make y'selfs comfortable.' Then, seeing the three men standing huddled close together at the door, she pointed to the leather chairs beside the fire. 'Sit, make yourselves at 'ome. Ikey sit 'ere, love.' She patted the back of a comfortable leather club chair nearest to where she stood.

Ikey lifted his arms, at the same time lifting the arms belonging to each of his gaolers, displaying the manacles for Marybelle to see. He looked at her sheepishly, raised his eyebrows and shrugged his shoulders in a mute explanation of the predicament in which he now found himself.

'Blimey, o' course! The pigs, they's nabbed ya!' Marybelle folded her great arms across her bosom and glared at Titty Smart and Albert Popjoy.

'Now listen to me, gents, this be me private parlour.' She pointed to the panelled walls. 'See it ain't got no windows for boltin', and there be a key in the door what ya can use to lock it!'

She walked over to where they stood and removed the large brass key from the stout oak door and handed it to Titty Smart. 'Yer welcome to me best brandy and the warmth o' me 'earth, but ya ain't welcome wif yer manacles in me tavern!' She pointed at Ikey. 'Mr Solomon 'ere be me right good friend what's me guest. I'll thank ya kindly to remove them pig's bangles from 'is wrists or ya can fuck orf right now!'

As she spoke the boy who'd earlier been sent to waken Marybelle came to the door followed by the coachman. The lad carried a cask of brandy and waited as Ikey and company moved further into the small room before he pushed past them and seated the small barrel of brandy carefully in a cradle placed on a carved oak dresser. On the shelf above the barrel were several rows of pewter mugs.

'Well?' Marybelle asked. 'What's it to be?' She moved over to the cask and taking a pewter tankard from the shelf above it placed it under the spout and allowed just a splash of the golden brown liquid into the tankard. Then she walked over to the fire and removed the mulling iron which she plunged into the interior of the tankard. Immediately a ribbon of flame leapt from the tankard almost to the height of the heavy oaken mantelpiece and the room was filled with the inviting fumes of good French cognac.

The effect on Titty Smart's nose was too much to bear and he reached into his pocket and quickly unlocked the manacle attached to Ikey's wrist and thereafter his own. His partner, perhaps not quite as taken with the need of strong drink and pyrotechnics, hesitated a little longer.

'Just the one, lad!' Smart grunted. 'Just the one for keeping us alert an' all.'

'It ain't regular,' Popjoy muttered, though in an undertone. 'There's regulations.'

Titty Smart glared at his partner. 'We ain't be paid for this escort, this ain't our shift, we be nights, not day, this be our own time what the bastards 'ave robbed from us, you can stuff yer regulations up yer arse, lad!'

Before his young partner could protest further Ikey interjected, clucking the two men to silence. 'What the 'ead keeper don't see 'e don't 'ave to grieve about, now does 'e?' He rubbed his left wrist with his right hand, deliberately pulling Popjoy's arm across with him in order to do so. Then he pointed to the parlour door which still stood ajar and grinned. 'Better lock the door 'case I takes a runner!'

Albert Popjoy, shaking his head in silent disapproval, unlocked the manacle on Ikey's wrist while leaving the one on his wrist. Titty Smart walked over to the parlour door, locked it, and placed the key in his pocket.

Marybelle pointed to the manacles dangling from the wrist of Albert Popjoy and laughed. 'Don't look cosy, knows what I mean? Official. We don't go much on duty 'ere.' She cocked her head to one side and grinned at the younger turnkey. Albert Popjoy, embarrassed at the attention, took the key from his pocket and unlocked the manacle around his wrist, placing the set within his coat pocket. 'That's it, lads, nice 'n cosy, take a pew, make y'selfs at 'ome.' She looked at the coachman. 'You too,' then she took up four pewter tankards and turned again to the now seated men, arched her eyebrows and nodded her head in the direction of the cask. 'A drop o' me very best brandy for all, is it then, gentlemen?'

It came as some surprise when no more than twenty minutes later, the mulled brandy having warmed, refreshed and lighted that small, bright flame that sputters in the stomach until temporarily doused with a second drink, Ikey suggested that they must depart and offered his wrists to the two turnkeys so that they might manacle them once more.

Titty Smart nodded to his partner. 'I told you, just the one and that will do for the manacle too.' The younger man fished into his pocket and produced his set of manacles and attached them once more to Ikey's and then his own wrist.

Ikey felt momentarily triumphant. 'One down, one to go!' he thought. He felt almost free with only one wrist attached to Albert Popjoy.

Marybelle Firkin saw them to the back door and placed her hands on Ikey's shoulders. 'Cheerio, lovey,' she said and Ikey was surprised to see the brightness of moisture in her large blue eyes. She paused and grinned, though when she spoke her voice was serious. 'Yer wife told me everyfink, good luck, Ikey.' Then she turned to Smart and Popjoy, ignoring the coachman who had taken his brandy but had said no single word except to nod his thanks while he had been in the parlour. 'Always welcome, I'm sure,' she said to the two turnkeys.

She stood at the door, her red dressing gown once again filling its entire space, her pretty head almost touching the lintel. 'Come back soon, gents!' she called at the departing hackney.

To Ikey's surprise, Titty Smart licked his lips and rolled his eyes. 'Ooh, ah! I'd like to be up to a bit o' fancy 'anky panky with the likes of 'er, I would an' all!' He turned to Ikey and added, 'That be damned good Frenchy brandy, just like what you said.'

Albert Popjoy looked out of the window of the carriage and smiled in a supercilious manner, which Smart must have observed, for he turned to his partner and barked, 'Wipe that smile orf yer gob, lad. Lady like that be much too good for the likes o' yer poxy little prick!'

They arrived at the courts in Westminster with a good twenty minutes to spare. 'Would you wish me to wait, guv?' the coachman asked. 'It ain't much point in this weather toutin' for a fare. I could drive you back afterwards, no trouble and no extra fare charged, 'cept o' course for the run back and a sixpenny bag of oats for me 'orse while we's waiting.'

Ikey nodded his agreement and the three men entered the precincts of the court to be met at the steps leading into the Westminster courts by Hannah and several of Ikey's associates, most of whom were Jews from the Whitechapel markets, Petticoat and Rosemary Lanes. Their attendance was less a show of loyalty than a favour returned for a similar attendance by Ikey and Hannah at some past occasion when each of those present had faced an indictment. This was because of the well-established fact that, should a Jew be in the dock, the likelihood of a conviction was near five times that of any other Londoner. It became therefore the custom to try to fill the court with 'sympathetic voices' so that the mood of the rabble in the gallery would not influence the judgment.

In Ikey's present predicament this was of overwhelming importance, the fear being, that if news of his application for bail should spread, the court would soon be filled with the rabble from the streets howling for his blood and the judge, sensitive to the animosity of the public at large, might think it safer for all concerned for Ikey to remain behind bars until his trial came up.

But when the time came for Ikey's hearing to be called the clerk of the court informed Titty Smart that the judge was in his chambers. He said there would be a delay of at least an hour, taking the hearing almost to the noon hour. The man, his lips pursed, had consulted his watch, whereupon he had shaken his head. 'No time, gentlemen, at noon his worship takes luncheon at the Athenaeum Club, he'll not return until two o'clock at best!' This meant that Ikey's writ of *habeas corpus* would therefore not be served until the early part of that afternoon.

Ikey suggested that he stand his two keepers a good tightener at a local chop house and requested that his friends be allowed to accompany them.

'I could go a good tightener and a jug o' best ale,' Titty Smart agreed, patting his large stomach without his mandatory show of reluctance. His attitude to Ikey had considerably softened following the time spent at the Pig 'n Spit and now he turned to Albert Popjoy. 'Drop o' fodder can't 'urt, now can it, lad?'

Popjoy nodded. He too was hungry and the idea of a plate of meat – mutton chops surrounded by a generous collar of yellow fat – was a most enticing prospect. It was difficult for him to maintain his official demeanour and not show his pleasure at the anticipation of such an unexpected treat.

'That be fine,' he said in a brusque voice, though he was salivating at the thought of the tightener to come at Ikey's expense.

'My pleasure, entirely, gents,' Ikey said with great alacrity.

Hannah, who stood close to her husband, shook her head. ''Ang on a mo'! We go into a chop 'ouse round these parts, in fact, any parts, there's plenty what will want to do Ikey an 'arm!'

A look of mutual disappointment crossed the faces of the two turnkeys, although Ikey could scarcely believe his luck. 'Gentlemen, what's to worry? Mistress Marybelle will welcome us back to the Pig! There be a dozen chop 'ouses in Rosemary Lane what can send in a banquet to suit the fancy o' the most particular appetite.' He spread his arms wide. 'What it is my great pleasure to satisfy.'

The matter was quickly settled and fifteen minutes later the three men arrived back at the Pig 'n Spit followed shortly afterwards by two hackney coaches containing the six others eager to avail themselves of Ikey's generosity. Hannah, though, protested to Ikey that she would follow a little later as young Mark had a bad cough and she must fetch some physic for him before joining them.

The fog had lifted somewhat, but the ever present miasma at rooftop level and the winter smog kept the day sombre and the visibility low. Therefore none but Ikey noted the outline of a gentleman's coach with four horses which had followed them and now passed them as they turned into the rear of the Pig 'n Spit. Nor would they have seen that it too came to a halt only a few yards further along the road.

Marybelle, now dressed, welcomed them with the same equanimity as on the earlier occasion. Upon entering the parlour Titty Smart, observing Marybelle's previous demand, had unmanacled Ikey and Popjoy had done likewise. Waiting for the other guests to enter the room, the older of the turnkeys once again locked the door and dropped the key into his coat pocket.

The parlour, if they should stand in a rather close-packed manner, was only just large enough to accommodate them all. In fact, the near proximity of Ikey's guests to each other, the warmth of the excellent fire in the hearth and the dispensing of generous quantities of Marybelle Firkin's best brandy coupled with her friendly banter added greatly to the jollity of the occasion. Ikey's two keepers were soon as loquacious as any in the room as they continued to imbibe the excellent brandy. But their stomachs were empty of food as Marybelle had delayed, by an hour, its delivery from a nearby chop house.

At last the food arrived and at the same time Hannah appeared. Titty Smart, Ikey noted, had with some difficulty inserted the key into the lock, to allow the trays to be brought into the room. Two large trays of chops, aproned with deliciously crisped fat and at least a dozen plump whole carcases of spatchcock stuffed with chestnuts together with mounds of golden roasted potatoes were hoisted above the heads of the guests and placed upon the dresser. Ikey watched again as the older turnkey made several unsuccessful thrusts at the lock before pausing to carefully place his tankard of brandy on the floor between his legs. Then with the key held in both hands, and squinting fiercely at the key hole, he finally managed to lock the door.

The smell of the roasted meat appeared to have much the same effect on Titty Smart as had been the case earlier with the flaming brandy fumes. Forgetting the half-filled tankard on the floor between his legs he kicked it over as he rudely pushed his way through the throng towards the trays of steaming food. As he passed, Ikey simply dipped his hand into the turnkey's coat pocket, and in a foolishly simple example of the art of tooling retrieved the key to the door.

While a mood of genial drunkenness overtook the room, Ikey retained a completely sober disposition. Marybelle pretended to frequently fill his pewter but, instead, merely splashed a lick of cognac into the bottom of his tankard, which was not sufficient to cause a comfortable night's sleep to a teething infant.

Ikey measured the cacophony of the room. It was, after all, filled with people who were easily inclined towards talking over each other in a manner seldom confidential, and when it seemed all were shouting and none were listening, he prepared to make his move. First he checked the whereabouts of Albert Popjoy and found him pinned to the wall by two *shmatter* traders from the Lane both battering him with expostulating words too mixed in the general banter to hear. Popjoy's eyelids seemed heavy with fatigue and he appeared to find it difficult to focus on the two men. Ikey moved towards the door and carefully unlocked it, whereupon he slipped quickly through to the other side, closed the door quietly and locked it again, placing the key above the lintel.

He made his way down the passage to the back of the Pig 'n Spit and was about to step into the courtyard when the cellarman's apprentice made an appearance.

'Me shillin'? You promised us a shillin', Mr Ikey.'

Ikey looked behind him in a panic, but he and the boy were alone. He fished into his coat for his dumby and from the purse produced two single shillings. Ikey dropped one of the shillings into the lad's hand and held the other up between forefinger and thumb and whispered urgently, 'There, a deuce hog, one for the promise and t'other for not seein' nothin' what's happenin' in front of your eyes at this very moment. Does you understand, my boy?'

The boy nodded and Ikey dropped the second shilling into his dirty hand and scuttled across the yard to the street entrance. In a matter of moments he was beside the coach where Moses Julian, who had followed them from the courts, had been waiting for him.

'Quick, Moses, be orf!' he said in a loud whisper, clambering into the carriage. 'To the 'ouse o' Reuban Reuban.'

Chapter Fifteen

On Ikey's arrival at the lodgings of the actor and his tailor son there was soon a frenzy of activity as Reuban Reuban clipped and trimmed Ikey's hair until it was short and much to the latest fashion, brushed close and forward to the forehead. Then he trimmed the sideburns in the shorter vogue allowing an inch or more between the side whiskers and the commencement of the beard, which he then clipped short and close to the face. With expert hands he shaved the remaining whiskers from Ikey's face and completely removed his moustache. The result was such a transformation of appearance that Hannah herself would have had great difficulty recognising her husband. Ikey had shed fifteen years in age and his appearance was of a man of handsome demeanour. His looks, occasioned by the wildness of his hair, scraggy beard and length of the nose which rose from his hirsute face like a mountain peak above the forest line, now looked well proportioned and passed well for that of an upper-class English gentleman.

It was Abraham who was next to work upon the transformation of Ikey. He stripped him quickly, though Ikey whimpered at the removal of his beloved coat, until Ikey stood stark naked, his only adornment a chain to which was attached a small medallion of gold which hung about his neck. Commencing with woollen long johns, piece by piece Abraham refurbished him from his under garments to a fine frock coat until his subject stood before him square rigged and every inch the prosperous City gentleman. Ikey, shown his new visage in a mirror, came near to fainting from the shock of witnessing the remarkable re-creation of his personage. Abraham's final act of sartorial brilliance was to produce a top hat and silver-topped malacca cane. Carefully brushing the nap of beaver fur with the elbow of his coat, he placed the hat upon Ikey's head, whereupon he handed him an elegant pair of pigskin gloves and the cane.

'Blimey! You looks a proper toff, Uncle Isaac!' Abraham exclaimed, well pleased with his work. 'You could pass for the Guv'ner o' the Bank o' England, walk right through the door, you could, no questions asked!' He turned and shouted to Reuban Reuban who, shortly after having trimmed and shaved Ikey, had departed to another room. 'Come see, father!'

'Me coat, where's me coat?' Ikey called out in alarm.

'Your coat? Why it be upon your back, Uncle Isaac!' Abraham's expression changed and showed sudden consternation. 'You'll not be wearing *that* coat?' He pointed to the greasy heap upon the floor. 'That'd be dead give away, that would an' all!'

''Ang it up! 'Ang it up!' Ikey commanded in an agitated voice, dancing from one foot to the other in his shiny black gentleman's boots.

Abraham looked momentarily confused, but then hastily took the coat hanger from which had hung the frock coat Ikey now wore, fitted the collar of Ikey's coat about it and suspended it from a hook behind the door.

'Now leave us, if you please!' Ikey said, his composure regained.

Abraham, in somewhat of a sulk, left the room. He was disappointed at Ikey's complete lack of interest in his clever tailoring and the remarkable change he'd brought about to such an unpropitious subject.

Ikey quickly rummaged through his overcoat, putting the contents of all its secret places into the few available pockets in the frock coat. All the bits and pieces that had a known and accustomed place. Cards, promissory notes, pencils of red and blue, string, wire, keys of innumerable configurations, money in small denominations, purses of various sorts containing various amounts, some filled with sixpences, others with shillings. Money in soft and hard, betting slips and receipts for the care of his two little ratters, the terriers he would so sorely miss, a magnifying glass and an eye piece for the assessment of jewellery, spectacles, pincers, pliers, tongs and probes. Each piece filed in its own place was now removed and flung onto a horrendous junk pile within his frock coat pockets, as though they were to be discarded willy-nilly as fuel to a bonfire of Ikey's past.

Finally Ikey took the long cigar-like cylinder containing the letter of credit from the breast pocket of his coat. He folded the letter neatly, added it to several other documents which Reuban Reuban had obtained and placed them in a leather wallet stamped with his monogram in gold on the outside cover. This was yet another small detail prepared by the actor, who had already put a small silver card container beside the wallet which carried the precise cards Ikey had instructed him to print. This too carried the letters I S inscribed upon it.

Whimpering like a newborn puppy, Ikey took leave of his coat. The loss of his beloved coat seemed almost more than Ikey could bear, for his new outfit felt altogether alien to him. It stiffened his joints and rubbed in strange places, so much so that he thought of himself as being not just transformed but as if somehow he had sloughed his old body, and mysteriously come upon a new one. One moment he was Ikey Solomon and then, with a little trimming, shaving and the application of new linen and half a bolt of suiting, he had been created into some curious unknown personage.

The smell and touch of the new cloth enveloped Ikey's bony body and added to this strange feeling of otherness. He wondered for a moment whether it all might drive him mad, his urgent mission with Coutts & Company quite forgotten as his newly tonsured head was utterly confused.

It was at this precise moment that Ikey saw himself in his old personage walking into the room, with wildly flying grey and gingered hair, scraggly beard and untidy, shaggy brows, his nose rising majestic between two small obsidian eyes looking directly at him. He saw old Ikey reach behind the door and take his beloved coat from its hook and place it upon his thin, angular body. He observed himself at once become stooped, his neck lowering itself tortoise-like into the shiny collar of the coat. His chin came to rest upon his breast, and, most remarkably, how, with all this doing, a sly, furtive expression had crept upon his former face.

Suddenly his nephew appeared in the doorway, a rude intrusion standing directly behind the vision. Abraham placed a flat-topped, broad-brimmed hat upon the apparition's head identical to the one Bob Marley had discarded at the Academy of Light Fingers. Ikey now observed himself standing in front of himself so completely that he pushed the fingers of both hands deep into his mouth. The astonishing manifestation before him was a more perfect likeness of himself than he knew himself to be.

'Not the fingers, Uncle Ikey! No gentleman swallows 'is fingers,' Abraham cried.

'What say you, Ikey?' Reuban Reuban asked. 'Do I well fit your personage? Is the likeness true, my dear?' His voice was thin and carping in the exact timbre of Ikey's own and his hands imitated perfectly the other's mannerisms.

It was not a moment more than half an hour later when Moses Julian, dressed in the expensive livery of a private house and accompanied by Abraham, similarly dressed as a footman, drew their carriage to a halt in a lane leading directly into the Strand. Inside sat Ikey and his remarkable likeness to his former self, Reuban Reuban, who touched Ikey's knee in a quick salute and slipped out of the coach even before it had completely come to a halt. Whereupon Moses urged the horses on and the coach moved away and soon enough came to the end of the lane and turned into the Strand.

The afternoon was already beginning to darken from the smog and the general effects of the fog so that the thronging humanity who moved along the crowded sidewalk were of a mind much occupied with their own progress in the failing light, so took no interest in the Jew as he made his way among them.

Nor, within a moment of turning into the Strand, could the coach have been recognised in the numerousness of similar carriages and coaches and hackneys that jammed and pushed their way along the great choked thoroughfare where they were yet further hidden by the smoke from the flares that ostensibly guided their way.

Abraham had the previous morning posted himself outside the bank to observe the protocol of a gentleman's manner of entering the premises. Thus he observed that, alighting from his coach, a person of quality would be greeted by the doorman, who would summon an usher from the interior of the bank. This bank officer, in all appearance a man of some mature age and authority, dressed in a frock coat and square rigged in the best of form, would immediately appear armed with a small silver salver which he would proffer in an obsequious manner while requesting the gentleman's personal card be placed upon it. At this point, of course, the doors were once again closed and Abraham had no way of knowing the manner of the client's further progress within the august establishment.

Abraham had returned home by way of Newgate Gaol, where he had informed Ikey of the manner of obtaining entry to the bank and Ikey had instructed him in the exact manner of the cards he required Reuban Reuban to have printed for the occasion.

It was just before the hour of two o'clock in the afternoon and the more important officers of the bank were returning to work from luncheon at their club when Ikey's carriage approached Coutts & Company on the Strand.

Abraham looked to see whether Reuban Reuban had arrived on foot. When he spotted him standing close to the wall of the bank, half concealed behind a Doric column, he tapped the roof of the carriage to tell Ikey that all was in order, and waited for Ikey's return tap to tell him to signal to Reuban Reuban to proceed. The two return taps came promptly and Abraham signalled to his father to proceed by appearing to rub an itchy nose and then smacking his gloved hands together as though against the cold.

Reuban Reuban commenced to walk boldly up the steps of the bank to where the doorman waited. Though boldly is perhaps an exaggerated description for he walked in the manner of Ikey, which none could even in their wildest imagination call bold. Ikey, watching from the interior of the carriage, saw the doorman stiffen slightly as Reuban Reuban drew nearer. Ikey, his instincts sharpened by a lifetime of experience with the mannerisms of a policeman, knew at once that he was a member of the constabulary. In as much as it was possible from the interior of the carriage he looked about to see if there were others, but could see no suspicious characters who might be miltonians, that is to say, policemen out of their official uniform.

Reuban Reuban halted beside the doorman and while Ikey could not hear what he said the doorman allowed that he should enter without apparently requesting his personal card or summoning an usher or in any manner following the form which Abraham had so carefully observed the previous morning. The door opened and Reuban Reuban disappeared into the interior of the building followed closely by the doorman. A few moments passed and a new doorman was seen to take the place of the old one, a man who stood more easily and assumed more naturally the accustomed nature of his task.

The interior of the bank comprised a large central hallway which at first seemed entirely composed of marble, with huge pillars of the same material supporting two storeys of gallery above which the offices of the partners were located and where the clerks worked at their ledgers. At one end of the impressive hallway were a set of brass tellers' cages and a stairway leading downwards, presumably to the underground vaults. At the other end was a similar stairway, though this one led upstairs to the galleries and carried a heavy banister of gleaming brass and was carpeted in brilliant red. Brass rods secured the carpet to the hinge of each step and they too shone with a brightness which gave the effect of a pathway leading heavenwards to untold wealth.

Reuban Reuban barely had time to take all of this in when he was accosted by an officer of the bank whose quick, sharp steps tapped out on the marble floor showed him to be most purposeful in his confrontation. Reuban Reuban was also aware that the doorman had remained and stood directly behind him as though to block any retreat he might contemplate. Several other men seemed now to have mysteriously emerged from behind the marble columns and were seen to be pacing the polished marble floor, although no work of banking seemed to be taking place in his immediate vicinity.

'Good day to you, sir,' the bank officer greeted Reuban Reuban. 'May I be of service?'

Reuban Reuban smiled unctuously and shrugged his shoulders in an admirable imitation of Ikey. 'Some other time maybe. I 'ave just remembered, uh . . . all of a sudden, if you knows what I mean. With the greatest respect to yourself, sir, I 'ave urgent business I must complete elsewhere!' Reuban Reuban turned towards the door again, only to see several of the men who had but a moment ago been contemplating their own business converge on him. He started to run towards the door but in a moment was grabbed from behind. It took only a few moments longer for several of the men to reach him and he was thrown roughly to the floor where he was quickly manacled by the doorman.

Reuban Reuban was pulled to his feet and immediately observed a small man with a very large red nose wearing a top hat exceedingly tall for the remainder of his size, approaching him.

'Ikey Solomons, in the name of the law, I arrest you,' Sir Jasper Waterlow shouted, so that his voice echoed through the hall and up into the galleries.

As they led Reuban Reuban away the galleries overlooking the entrance hall were soon filled with clerks and bankers observing the dramatic arrest. Even the partners had emerged from their offices to share in the excitement.

Sir Jasper Waterlow, not wishing to let the auspicious moment pass without some show on behalf of the Bank of England and his own future prospects, had deliberately shouted his orders of arrest at the uppermost tone of his voice so that all within the Coutts & Company bank might witness his triumph over Britain's most notorious villain and know that the Bank of England, like God, is not mocked.

Indeed, Sir Jasper Waterlow had just reason to congratulate himself. He had only a matter of some two hours to prepare his entrapment of Ikey. Hannah had informed him of the possibility of Ikey's escape that very morning, after Ikey had left the King's Bench courts upon the postponement of his hearing. By pre-arrangement she had met Sir Jasper in a coffee house on the Strand and acquainted him of Ikey's intended escape and his need to visit the premises of a certain bank, though she did not inform him of the name of the establishment until she had extracted in writing from Sir Jasper certain assurances and conditions. The first of these was that Ikey should be allowed to visit the bank and transact his business and that he would be arrested only on his way out. The second was that regardless of the outcome of Ikey's trial for forgery, he receive a sentence of transportation for his attempt to escape from custody.

Sir Jasper had no choice but to accept. The sentence Hannah had asked for was more or less a foregone conclusion and so presented no barriers. Furthermore, an arrest made after they had Ikey trapped within the confines of a building which could be easily surrounded, with additional men also placed within its interior, seemed much the better method of operation. Therefore, he issued Hannah with the written assurances she required. He told himself that she had previously delivered Ikey, as she had promised, with the counterfeit notes planted on his person. Now, when he might well have successfully escaped, she was once again informing on her husband. He therefore had no reason but to accept her information as genuine.

Sir Jasper told himself that whatever Ikey's business with Coutts & Company, it could hardly be the concern of the Bank of England. He had therefore given the chairman of Coutts & Company permission to process the transaction. This had occurred in a hastily contrived briefing when he had arrived at the bank with twenty City policemen in plain clothes. The senior bank officers were to allow Ikey to enter the premises and to afford him the normal protocol involved in making a transaction. Sir Jasper insisted that refusal by the bank to comply with this instruction would only be permitted if the transaction Ikey Solomon required was not a legitimate request for the bank's services, or would in some way threaten or undermine the safety or finances of Coutts & Company or of the Bank of England itself.

To ensure that the staff would go about their business in a normal manner Sir Jasper requested that one of his policemen, dressed in the uniform of a doorman of the bank, should replace the doorman on duty and that the doorman, along with the remainder of the bank's staff, be told nothing, other than that he should resume his normal duty when the policeman at the door was seen to escort Ikey into the interior of the bank.

The arrangements had all been finalised in great haste and Sir Jasper had no opportunity to consult the directors of the Bank of England. He was well aware that his instructions to Coutts & Company might have been beyond his authority as chief City policeman and Upper Marshal of London. With Ikey's sudden and most fortuitous panic and resultant attempt to escape the premises of the bank, Sir Jasper had even more reason to be pleased with himself. There would now be no awkward official enquiries as to why Ikey, upon visiting the illustrious private bank, had been allowed to make a transaction which, in every likelihood, resulted in remuneration to him as a consequence of a crime against the people. He had fully met Hannah's requirements, both as a gentleman and a police officer, and it had cost him no compromise with the law.

Moreover, there was much talk in parliament by the supporters of Sir Robert Peel of the organisation of a new police force, and Sir Jasper could see his candidacy for the position of its head much improved by both the first and second arrests of Ikey Solomon.

Ikey watched from the carriage as Reuban Reuban was led out of the bank manacled and surrounded by a dozen police officers out of uniform. A black maria, that is to say, a horse van drawn by two well-conditioned horses and built in the manner of a closed box with a door at the rear and no windows excepting narrow ventilation slits, appeared from the alley beside the building. Reuban Reuban was unceremoniously bundled into the back of it, whereupon the door was locked and three of the policemen mounted the platform protruding from the back of the van to further guard the villain residing within.

The crowd had halted and immediately formed around the van and on the steps of the bank and someone shouted, 'It be 'im, Ikey Solomon, the Jew forger!'

Almost at once the crowd grew angry and converged on the black maria. Despite the plain-clothes policemen who attempted to protect the van, part of the crowd pushed past and beat their fists against and commenced to rock the black maria, threatening to overturn it, so that the horses grew restless and began to stamp upon the ground and throw their heads up in alarm. The three men on the platform at its rear were forced to use their truncheons with fierce abandon, raining blows down upon the shoulders and heads of the angry attackers. The crowd had commenced to chant, 'Ikey! Ikey! Ikey!' and the coachman, working his police rattler so that the other coaches in the vicinity might move clear, finally managed to get the horses underway and direct the van into the stream of passing traffic. Though several urchins, skilled in the ways of dodging the traffic, followed the police van, they were quickly discouraged by the three policemen protecting the artful Reuban Reuban within.

Ikey watched until the crowd began to disperse, but with the sidewalk still somewhat crowded, Moses Julian moved Ikey's carriage forward to come to a halt directly outside the bank, whereupon Abraham alighted from the rear of the carriage, opened the door and with some ceremony, took Ikey's elbow in his white-gloved hand and guided him with care to the surface of the cobbled pavement.

Ikey moved quickly up the steps to the doorman, who, as is the nature of his profession, had been alert to his arrival at the moment his coach had pulled up. He had tugged at the lapels of his overcoat and adjusted his gold-braided top hat, conscious of the well-polished carriage and the livery of its retainers, and was therefore hardly surprised at the conservative, well-dressed gentleman who stepped from it onto the sidewalk.

'Good afternoon, sir!' he had offered in a manner akin to the military and which suggested both efficiency and respect, saluting Ikey.

Ikey grunted, though it was a well-modulated and upper-class grunt. 'Foreign transactions?' he asked, in a clipped and imperious voice.

'I shall call you an usher at once, sir.' The doorman opened the door, lifted his hand and crooked a finger to denote a requirement from someone within, whereupon he further opened it for Ikey to pass through.

It had all occurred just as Abraham had suggested and was quite unlike the reception Reuban Reuban had received. Ikey breathed a silent sigh of relief; the bank, it seemed, had assumed its normal routine. It felt like his lucky day.

Nathaniel Wilson, Coutts & Company's foreign transactions officer, had spent the morning with the ambassador from Chile, who had wanted to discuss the final interest rate for the public issue of a loan for his government, a part of which was being underwritten by the bank. The ambassador had plied him with glasses of an atrocious sherry he claimed was the pride and joy of the pampas and Wilson, who had finally departed to take luncheon alone at his club, in an attempt to be rid of the taste of bad sherry had imbibed rather too generously of a bottle of excellent burgundy, and followed it with two glasses of vintage port. The wine had left him thoroughly disgruntled and a little inebriated. The ambassador had demanded a shaving of one-tenth of one per cent of interest off the loan and towards the end had stamped his feet and brought his fist down several times hard upon the table and behaved in an altogether inappropriate manner. Wilson did not find foreigners in the least agreeable. Furthermore, he was not looking forward to facing the bank's senior partners with the Chilean ambassador's demand. He had returned only a few minutes after Reuban Reuban had been taken away in the police van and, as was his usual custom, entered the building through a private entrance to the side of the bank. He had repaired directly to his office on the first gallery, taking the back stairs used by the staff, and was therefore quite unaware of the excitement which had taken place in the bank before his return.

The usher knocked on Nathaniel Wilson's door, the two rapid knocks required to indicate a bank employee of inferior status to the occupant.

'Come!' the banker called.

Wilson looked up as the elderly usher opened the door and observed that he was carrying a salver.

'What is it, Coote?' he said with annoyance. 'I was not aware of any appointment at this hour.'

'No, sir, gentleman says he's from Germany.' Coote placed the salver containing Ikey's card on the desk. 'He requests an urgent interview, sir.'

Wilson reached for the card with obvious distaste. Ikey's card was well printed on expensive board and, in the manner of a man confident of his position in life, it contained no detail other than a name and address.

Herr Isak Solomon
114 Bunders Kerk Strasse, Hambourg

Nathaniel Wilson looked up at Coote. 'German Jew?'

'No, sir, English. Well spoken, proper gentleman.'

Nathaniel Wilson threw Ikey's card back into the tray. 'You will inform Mr Isak Solomon that I shall see him, but that I regret it must be a short interview as his appointment comes as an unexpected but not entirely convenient pleasure.'

Coote returned shortly with Ikey and Nathaniel Wilson rose from behind his desk to greet him. 'Ah, Mr Solomon, are you aware that the name Solomon has much been in the news lately?' He offered his hand to Ikey. 'Indeed a coincidence, what?'

Ikey removed his pigskin gloves, then his top hat and placed the gloves within the interior of the hat and gave it to Coote together with his cane, deliberately keeping the banker waiting. 'Oh? And why is that, Mr Wilson?' he replied in an incurious voice as he moved forward and finally took Wilson's hand, barely touching it before releasing it again.

'Ikey Solomon, or is it Solomons? Notorious forger chap. Arrested several days ago for counterfeiting, it seems he got away with a fortune in sham Bank of England notes, devil of a mess, what?' Wilson concluded.

'Really?' said Ikey in bored tones. 'I've been abroad, you see. Now, I am aware you do not have much time, so I shall be brief. I wish to lodge a letter of credit with you from the Birmingham City and Country Bank and require you to transfer these funds to the First Manhattan Bank on New York Island.' Ikey withdrew an expensive leather folder from the interior pocket of his frock coat and placed it on the desk in front of him.

Nathaniel Wilson opened the leather folder and quickly examined the documentation, his eyes seeking the letter of credit. He was immediately struck by the large amount of money involved. His time would not be wasted, as the bank's commission from the transfer transaction would be considerable. It was therefore in a much more respectful manner that he conducted the remainder of the negotiations and verifications.

Not more than twenty minutes later, with the Coutts & Company certificate of deposit safely in the folder, and with effusive assurances from the banker of the utmost of service available at any future occasion, Ikey was escorted by Coote down the red-carpeted stairway with its brass banister, across the hall of polished marble, through the imposing doors and down the steps to where Abraham and Moses Julian waited beside the carriage. Ikey paused as Abraham held open the carriage door for him and handed Coote a sovereign.

'Good day to you, Coote,' he said in his newly acquired accent.

'Bless you, sir,' the old man replied warmly. 'It's been a pleasure.'

The notorious luck of Ikey Solomon had once again held. With a pinch more, a *soupçon* of the same, he was on his way to America.

In his mind there formed yet another conclusion which he was most hard put to ignore any longer.

It was Hannah who, on both occasions, had betrayed him.

The thought of Hannah's betrayal brought Mary to Ikey's mind, Mary who had not betrayed him when she could have turned King's evidence and given witness most damaging to his case and, by so doing, spared herself the boat.

Ikey now felt a rare and genuine pang of conscience within his breast. Mary was in Newgate, incarcerated in a dungeon cage with a dozen other foul wretches and he had made no attempt to acknowledge her presence. This sharp stab of guilt almost immediately transformed itself into a surprising softness of feeling for Mary. It was an emotion not altogether different to the crisis of feeling which had overcome him in the coach to Birmingham. Ikey wondered in some panic whether there was a connection between the interior of coaches and his soft-headedness, for he was possessed suddenly by a compelling need to send fifty pounds to Mary so she might ameliorate the rigours of her transportation and be supplied with the necessities required on the troublesome and dangerous voyage to Van Diemen's Land. He would urge Abraham to seek her out in Newgate, acquaint her of his good wishes and give her the money as a token of his great esteem.

Ikey was uncertain as to whether this generosity came about because of the tender feeling for Mary which had come so overwhelmingly and unexpectedly upon him, or whether he wished only to ensure the continuance of his luck by putting right his bad conscience towards her. He knew only that he felt compelled to comply with this strange dictate which otherwise made no sense to his head and yet seemed so powerful to his heart. He told himself, though to no avail, that he was being foolishly generous with a gesture which could show him no future profit as he would not, in the further course of this life, see Mary again.

This last thought left Ikey in a surprisingly melancholy mood, for he realised how the routine of his life had been brought undone and how much a sustaining and pleasant part of it Mary had become.

This further onrush of sentiment led to an even more surprising gesture than the money Ikey told himself he had effectively thrown away. In fact, so foolish was the new thought that he feared some mischievous *golem* had possessed him. Around his neck he wore a gold chain from which was suspended, in the exact size and weight of gold in a sovereign, a medallion which commemorated the battle of Waterloo, and which carried a likeness of the Duke of Wellington on one side and a crescent of laurel leaves on the other. Nestled in the centre of this leafy tribute, fashioned in a small pyramid of words, was inscribed:

I
Shall
Never
Surrender

Ikey, shortly after his release from the hulk in Chatham and while working with his uncle, a slops dealer, that is to say a dealer in workmen's and sailor's clothes, had won the gold medallion at a game of cribbage from a sergeant in the Marines. It had been won fair and square and also while Ikey was legitimately employed, a conjunction of events which was never to occur again in his life, and so the medallion was a significant memento and had come to assume an importance to him. He always wore it under his woollen vest, where the warmth of its gold lay against his scrawny chest unseen by any other. Like the tattoo of the two blue doves on his arm, which, as a young man, had signified his secret and now entirely forsaken hope that one day he might find his one and only true love, the Wellington medallion was his special talisman.

At each narrow escape from the law or at the hands of the various people who would harm him, he had come to think of it more and more as the reason for his luck. Now he decided that if his luck should hold to the point when later that very night he would slip aboard a cargo vessel bound on the rising tide for Denmark, Mary should have his Wellington medallion.

Ikey, having determined this course of action, tapped on the roof for the coach to come to a halt, whereupon he bade Abraham come and sit beside him in the interior. As the coach moved on towards the docks he told Abraham in great detail what he was to do and say to Mary, his speech punctuated with a sentimentality Abraham had not thought possible in the man he knew Ikey to be. Ikey then took the medallion from about his neck and handed it, together with fifty pounds, to the young tailor to deliver to Mary.

In truth, it must be supposed that the concerns of the past few hours had greatly affected Ikey's mental state, for at the moment of this decision, if he had paused to consult his head and not pandered to the susceptibility of his heart, it would have declared him insane.

Ikey was giving Mary his luck.

Chapter Sixteen

Mary had been cast into a communal cell in Newgate to await her sentencing. Charged before a magistrate for running a bawdy house and with moral corruption, she was bound over in Newgate to await trial at the Old Bailey.

She had good reason to hope that her sentence might be a lenient one. Prostitution and earning a living off prostitutes did not generally earn the penalty of transportation. Indeed one might venture to say that 'moral corruption' was a fair description of the institution of the State itself.

The hard times which followed the Peninsular War against Napoleon, the effects of factory-produced cotton from Manchester on the wool and silkweaving cottage industries, and the migration of the Irish to England during the famines, created untold misery in the rural population. Their desperate migration in search of work caused calamity in the cities and, in particular, London, where among the poor prostitution, though not officially stated as such, was looked upon as a legitimate occupation for women who would otherwise be destitute, reduced to the workhouse or left to starve.

Mary had every reason to feel confident that she would receive perhaps as little as three months and no more than twelve months. Prior to her trial she had been approached by a City police officer to turn King's evidence against Ikey. But she had not implicated him, insisting that their relationship had been one of great circumspection and that he was merely her landlord.

Mary had invested ten pounds of her limited resources on a lawyer and hoped that the judge would see through the hypocrisy of her arrest, or, in any event, judge her most leniently. The lawyer, too, was confident and assured her of a speedy trial with, at most, a short sentence.

'Why, my dear, there is every chance that the judge has himself enjoyed the tender ministrations of your young ladies and behind his worship's wig and po-faced visage he bears you nothing but goodwill!' He was pleased that so simple a case to plead had earned him so generous a fee, for had Mary claimed hardship, he would happily have taken a case so free of conjecture for half the amount she had paid him.

It was therefore a shock beyond any imagining when Mary, arraigned before a judge she did not recognise at the Old Bailey, listened in increasing consternation to the clerk of the court. He, having read the original indictment, paused and informed the judge that the prosecution wished to add a further two charges, requesting the court's permission to do so. The judge agreed to add a further two counts and issued the warrant returnable immediately.

Mary listened in horror while the new charges were read out: 'That the accused had wilfully and maliciously killed the pet cat of Miss Maude Smith, nanny to the house of Sir James Barker of the King's Road, Chelsea. Furthermore, and in the second indictment, that she did steal a book, to wit, *Gulliver's Travels*, loaned to her through the negotiations of Thomas Bishop, the butler to Sir James, who had sought the co-operation of his master to make his private library available to the accused.'

Mary's lawyer immediately entered a plea asking that the two additional charges be set aside for a later hearing, pointing out that his client had not been apprehended for either supposed crime.

The prosecution then presented a warrant for Mary's arrest and the judge agreed that it be served on her within his court, whereupon he ruled that both new charges could be included with the original indictments and that they could be heard concurrently.

In discovering the details of Mary's background Sir Jasper Waterlow had proved himself a clever detective. At the same time he had met Hannah's conditions without the need for complicity with a member of the bench. While the charge of running a bawdy house was unlikely to receive a sentence of transportation, this was not the case with the new charges.

It was during the hearing of the second set of indictments that Mary's life came suddenly and irrevocably unstuck. Despite her desperate pleas from the dock that she had not put a hand on the ageing, nose dripping, fur shedding, pissing, fur ball vomiting Waterloo Smith and, furthermore, that the book, *Gulliver's Travels*, had been a parting gift from Thomas Bishop himself, it soon became obvious that she had no hope of being believed by the court. Both Nanny Smith and Thomas Bishop appeared as witnesses for the Crown, and while Nanny Smith was triumphant in her testimony, Bishop spoke quietly with downcast eyes throughout the hearing.

Whether the judge was a cat lover or a bibliophile, or both, is not known, but he seemed to be strangely agitated by the evidence he had heard. Before pronouncing sentence he saw fit to deliver, to the increasing delight of a cackling Nanny Smith, a lengthy address on Mary's moral turpitude.

'I find myself unwilling to grant leniency in this case before me, as it strikes at the very heart of civilised behaviour. It is common enough in the assizes to confront a person, a yokel who may have stolen a sheep, or pig or poached game, a fat pheasant or a clutch of partridge eggs, from his master's estate. Heinous as these crimes may be, it can be argued that the poor wretch may have had need of the flesh of these beasts or birds to feed a hungry family. While his be no less a crime in the eyes of the law, it is one which, in some instances, is worthy of our compassion, if not our mercy.'

The judge sniffed and looked about the court, finally allowing his eyes to rest again upon Mary. 'A sheep or a pig or a game bird, though valuable to its owner, is seldom an object of great love unless it be a champion.' He paused and looked about him as though he were delivering his message at the Lord Mayor's Banquet. 'But a cat? A cat is another matter. A cat to its owner can be an unquestioning and loyal friend when no other may exist. That the cat in question, so brutally disposed of in this case, was an object of great love and comfort to its owner is not, for one moment, to be doubted.' He looked across at Mary again. 'You did cold heartedly and with malice aforethought do away with one

Waterloo Smith, a cat owned by the plaintiff, Miss Maude Smith.' He wagged an admonishing finger at Mary. 'This court cannot take lightly such a callous and deliberate action to bring about the death of one of God's innocent creatures.' The judge paused and glared at the jury, who had previously found Mary guilty. It was as if he felt that guilty was probably not sufficient, that perhaps they should have pronounced her 'Very guilty' or 'Guilty beyond normal guilt'. He turned again to Mary. 'You have been found guilty and I choose therefore to sentence you in exactly the same way as if you had stolen and killed a prize sheep, or bull, or pig, or poached a brace of pheasants from the country estate of an honest gentleman.'

The judge brought his gavel down as though he were about to pronounce sentence, but, in fact, the judicial hammer was intended to serve only as a punctuation. Warmed to the task of castigation, he now continued:

'As to the second charge against you. You found yourself in a position of great privilege in the home of Sir James Barker who, due to the kind interceding on your behalf of his butler . . .' The judge paused to look at his notes, 'er . . . Thomas Bishop, it was agreed by Sir James that you should have the full use of his considerable library. In this one magnanimous gesture he was, in effect, opening up to a mere servant girl, if I should not be mistaken a laundry maid, the whole sublime world of literature and learning. It appears that you did not with honesty and a full heart, mindful of the great privilege accorded you, take advantage of this opportunity. On the contrary, in the face of such remarkable generosity, you chose instead . . .' he paused, searching for the correct words. 'You who have shown intelligence enough to have mastered reading and writing, to plunder this depository of knowledge by stealing from it one of its most precious jewels!'

The judge now brought his gavel down three times and in an even more sonorous voice than he had previously employed picked up his written judgment and commenced to read it.

'Mary Klerk, also known as Mary Abacus, it be therefore ordered and adjudged by this Court, that after having served three months in Newgate Gaol in accordance with the previous judgment of this court, you be transported upon the seas, beyond the seas, to such as His Majesty King George IV, by the advice of his Privy Council, shall see fit to direct and appoint, for the term of seven years!'

The judge's gavel rose up and went down upon its block one last time. The sound of it reverberated around the dusty, close-smelling and largely empty courtroom, and Mary's life was once again plunged into the darkest despair as she was manacled and led from the dock to the public cells, the 'bird cages' in the dungeons of Newgate Gaol. For Mary it was a descent back into hell.

It was her companions, those women with her in the cage, against whom she knew she must needs take the greatest care. There were few who would not tear her eyes out for the promise of a tot of gin and, in their drunken state, when the candles burned down, she would need to constantly defend herself against the groping hands that would possess her. At night, the grunting, panting cries of the fornicating women intensified when the younger women were seduced or raped by the larger 'bull whores' who owned the darkness.

Mary attempted to keep to herself, occupying one small corner of the large cell which contained eleven others. She had been placed with prostitutes who had been caught at various crimes – thieving, drunkenness and destroying public or private property. At the approach of a drunken woman Mary would reveal her blackened talons and snarl. But it soon became apparent that she could not remain separate. In a gaol cell it is the strong who rule and the weak who must be made to submit. The time would come, Mary knew, when she would be subjected to the needs of the strongest in the cage. Mary waited until her fellow inmates were drunk and distracted and then she bribed a turnkey to have a tinsmith visit her.

She instructed him to make four brass rings half an inch in breadth which fitted tightly to the topmost knuckle of the second and third fingers of each hand. Mary then told the tinsmith to fashion from each band a metal talon, sharpened to a point and arched, an inch beyond the extremity of each finger, to give the effect of four vicious nails. The tinsmith delivered them the next day, demanding an extortionate price in return for his speedy workmanship. But he had created weapons for her hands most fearsome to behold and Mary was happy to pay.

Mary attached the lethal hooks to her fingers and saw that they fitted well, then she placed them in the pocket of her pinny. The final meeting with the tinsmith had taken place in the morning before

eight of the clock while her cell mates still slept, snoring and
blubbering and often shouting in some nightmarish dream, unaware
of her newfound protection. She knew that they would soon awaken
and scream for water to quench their parched tongues and cool their
throbbing brows. She was now ready to make her presence felt.

Mary paid the turnkey twopence for a large bucket of water
and a ladle which she placed in the corner beside her. The water
was their daily entitlement, an allowance of three gallons for each
communal cell. The turnkeys demanded payment for it, although
it was intended that it should be free. There was very little that
came free in Newgate, and starvation was as much a cause of death
within its walls as was gaol fever or brutality. If the twopence was
not paid the turnkey would sell the bucket of precious water for a
penny to an adjacent cage or, if there was no hope of gain, place it
at his feet and piss into it before handing it into the cell.

Mary waited for the first of the women to wake up. It was Ann
Gower, who couldn't remember when she hadn't been on the
streets. She was probably still in her thirties but the effects of gin
and her brutal life had left her looking twenty years older. Two of
her front teeth were missing and matted brown hair hung over her
eyes, which she was now in the process of knuckling in an attempt
to clear her head of the gin she'd swallowed the previous night.

'Water, where's water?' she mumbled, as she stumbled over to
the bars of the bird cage. Grabbing them she shouted, 'Bring the
fuckin' water!' The shrill sound of her own raised voice caused her
to hold her head and groan in agony.

''Ere,' Mary said, 'Over 'ere, love.'

Ann Gower turned slowly and looked at Mary through
bloodshot eyes. 'You? Little Miss 'Orner what sits in a corner?'

Mary laughed, surprised at the woman's wit considering the
state of her health.

'Wotcha fuckin' laughin' at?' the other woman snarled.

Mary, still with a smile on her face, dipped the ladle into the
bucket and held it up towards Ann Gower. 'Drink.'

Ann Gower's hands were shaking as she took the large wooden
spoon. She brought it unsteadily up to her lips and managed to
spill a good portion of it down the front of her dirty pinny and
upon the floor. The remainder she drank, slurping greedily. 'More!'
she demanded, handing the ladle back to Mary.

'Sorry, love, that be it, there ain't no more.' Mary calmly put the ladle back into the bucket and stood up with one hand behind her back.

'Who says?' Ann Gower advanced menacingly towards Mary.

'I says,' Mary said, keeping her voice calm. 'That be your lot, Ann Gower.'

'I spilled 'arf of it!' Ann shouted.

'That be your problem, love. Next time be more careful.' Mary's voice remained steady and betrayed none of the fear she felt in the pit of her stomach. She was ready when Ann Gower lashed out at her and her hand came swiftly from behind her back, the two brass hooks at the end of her fingers cutting a double streak of crimson straight across the line of Ann Gower's jaw.

'Jesus!' she gasped, clutching at her face in surprise. 'The fuckin' bitch cut me!'

'Don't fuck with me, Ann Gower,' Mary said defiantly.

Ann Gower took one of her hands from her cheek and saw that it was covered with blood. 'Jesus! I'm bleedin'!'

'Next time it be your eyes.'

'I only wanted some water, wotcha do that for?' Ann Gower whined.

Mary forced a grin. 'Teach you some manners, darlin'.'

Mary was only five feet and two inches and carried no lard and Ann Gower was half as heavy again and at least three inches taller. But the larger woman, her head pulsating, and her cheek burning from the savage cut to her cheek, knew the ways of the street and realised she must make her move now or be beaten. The look in Mary's clear, cold green eyes told her that she had met a formidable opponent.

'You takin' charge, then?' Ann Gower said in a much mollified voice, one hand still clutched on her bleeding face.

'Somethin' like that,' Mary said.

Ann Gower smiled, the gaps in her teeth showing as she appeared to accept. 'Can I 'ave some water then?' she said, looking directly at Mary.

'No!'

Mary's eyes held the other woman's gaze and Ann Gower took two involuntary steps backwards. The fight was over, Mary had won. She had shown she was strong enough, hard enough to win the other woman's respect, or whatever passed for respect among the dispossessed.

Mary had also proved to herself that she had not forgotten the harsh lessons of the street and now indicated the sleeping women in the cell with a jerk of her chin. 'Wake them lot up, will you, tell 'em there's water, show 'em your face, tell 'em there's more where that come from if any should want it.'

Though Mary now controlled the cell she did not try to convert it to better ways. The women became drunk at any opportunity they could get their hands on a quart of gin and the nocturnal couplings continued. But the bullying stopped, the water was equally shared among all, and the cell was cleaned.

She was challenged on several occasions by older women, emboldened by a pint of gin in their bellies. But they stood little chance against her ferocious claws, and soon the rumour grew in Newgate Gaol of Mother Mary Merciless, who sat like a vulture in a corner of the whore cage cleaned of shit and dirt. It was said that she possessed the blackened talons of a great bird of prey and, if one should venture near, great slabs of flesh would be torn off in a single terrible swipe to feed her need for fresh blood and live human flesh.

A report which appeared in the *Newgate Calendar*, itself treated with gross exaggeration, was turned into a scurrilous and wholly lurid pamphlet sold in the streets and at fairs and in the Vauxhall Gardens and which was entitled: '*Mother Mary Merciless, the flesh eating demon of Newgate Gaol!*' It sold ten thousand copies at the full price of a penny ha'penny.

Though her infamous name did nothing but good for her reputation, increasingly Mary came to impress her cell mates with her tongue, sharp eyes and the agility of her mind. They marvelled at the rapidity with which she worked the beads and boasted to the other inmates that she could do any calculation which might come into their minds. The number of days Methuselah had lived, and then the hours and minutes. Or if an ounce of dried peas should contain one hundred peas, how many peas would there be in a two-hundred-pound sack? Though they had no hope of verifying the answers, it was the speed of Mary's fingers as they flew across the wire slides to push the blurring beads this way and that which confounded and fascinated them. With such skill, they reasoned, the answers she gave must be correct. Furthermore, if any should have any unseemly ideas, hands so cruelly tortured which could move so fast were a reminder to them all that the dreaded claws could strike before they had a chance to blink.

They became like small children, enchanted and silent when Mary read to them by the light of the candle from *Gulliver's Travels*. For the much-worn volume, which, in the end, cost her so dear, like her precious abacus had seldom left her side.

Mary also read to them from the Bible. But they were stories of conquests and the persecution of the Israelites and the wonders of the land of Canaan. She did not read to them of Christ's love and salvation, sharing with them the lack of enthusiasm for this particular God of love, and much preferring the one of wrath who practised revenge and waged war in the hurly-burly of the Old Testament.

Mary took to writing petitions for prisoners and preparing their pleas to be read in court, for few could afford the fees of even the most down-at-heel lawyer or screever. She would write letters to the authorities about husbands and the welfare of children of inmates carted off to orphanages. Or she would write to loved ones, this latter in particular for the Irish, who placed great store in the mystical properties of the written word. While they, and those who received their letters, could neither read nor write, the priest in their parish could, and so the entire parish would know of their love and tenderness. They fervently believed that writing a letter was a divine affair which would bestow good fortune and protection upon those they loved who still lived in the sad and broken places they had fled from in Ireland. A letter of love, they most fervently believed, had the spiritual substance to prevent these same loved ones from suffering the sad fate to befall its sender.

Mary would always begin an Irish letter with the same words, for it was this single opening sentence which inevitably brought those on whose behalf she wrote to swoon with the ecstasy of its poetry.

> *My dearest beloved,*
> *The prayers of a sincere heart are as acceptable to God from the dreary Gaol as from the splendid Palace. The love of a prisoner as pure and sweet as that of a prince . . .*

The cost in delivering such a letter to Ireland was prohibitive and would often mean that the sender must sell all that she possessed. But for the comfort it brought her, and the gift of love it was thought to bestow on the receiver, it was thought among the Irish women to be but a pittance to pay.

The inmates, usually the women, would often bring their squabbles to Mary to settle. Her judgments, using the peculiar logic of the criminal, left each with a portion of self-respect, and neither party's guilt confirmed. This would indubitably stop further trouble in the bird cages. When Mary was forced to judge one or another to be guilty this was seen as an exception, and her verdict, with the penalty she imposed, accepted by all and duly carried out.

This did not stop the drunkenness and lechery, the fighting and the cruelty, for these things were as much a part of Newgate as the bricks, and damp, the excremental filth and the gaol fever. But there was observed to be some small measure of calm about the bird cages. Mary was tough and her talons fierce and she was one of their own kind. Hers was a light which had not been dimmed and was a great source of courage to them all.

The most cherished moment of Mary's life came the day Abraham Reuban arrived at Newgate to visit her.

The excitement of Ikey's escape from custody was on everyone's lips that day, the story of his escape having spread like gaol fever among the inmates. The tale of how he had persuaded the two turnkeys to take a coach which had been 'conveniently upon the spot' when it was needed, and how he had persuaded both turnkeys to unlock his manacles and be his guest at the Pig 'n Spit was the cause of great laughter in Newgate. The simple device of picking the pocket of Titty Smart, the fat turnkey, and letting himself out of the door of Marybelle's parlour, leaving the key on the lintel, was told with glee and constantly repeated with not a little admiration for his brazenness.

Ikey Solomon had, after all, escaped from the most notorious gaol in Britain without resort to violence and had been gone a full hour or more before the dunderheads realised anything was amiss. Moreover, the cunning of Ikey had seen to it that Popjoy, the more diligent turnkey, with the help of a strong potion, was locked in the arms of Morpheus, slumped in the corner of Marybelle Firkin's parlour, while his older partner was too drunk to take two steps in pursuit of a quarry without falling full upon his own face. By the time the constabulary was alerted, as one of the penny papers reported:

Ikey Solomon was allowed time enough to row himself to France with sufficient over to fish midstream for a rack of herring to sell in Paris to the Frenchies!

Moreover, when the police had been alerted, they had immediately contacted the City division who had informed them, somewhat pompously, of the Bank of England's recapture of the villain. It had been a full eight hours later before Reuban Reuban revealed his true identity, and at least nine or ten since Ikey's initial escape from the Pig 'n Spit. By the time the hunt for him was under way again, Ikey had already slipped down the Thames, his ship long buried in the coastal mist as it headed for the North Sea and the kingdom of the Danes.

In fact, even at the point when Reuban Reuban had revealed his true identity, the City police officials on duty that night had not believed him, thinking that Ikey had merely shaved his head in some clever ruse. But no amount of logic applied to the conundrum could reveal what intention this clever ruse might serve. Ikey had, after all, presented himself as himself at the premises of Coutts & Company, and if this be a ruse it was a most mysterious one. It was only then that Sir Jasper Waterlow had been visited at his home in Kensington and aroused from his bed to be informed of the presence in the cells of the duplicate Ikey.

Ikey's double had been duly charged with complicity but this was small consolation for Sir Jasper who knew that, unless he brought the true Ikey Solomon to trial, his hopes for an illustrious future as Britain's foremost police officer, and ultimately a seat in the House of Lords, had been completely dashed.

He swore silently that Hannah, whom he immediately believed responsible for his humiliation, would pay dearly for her husband's escape, though, on further thought, this conclusion made little sense, for his detective's mind reasoned that if she *had not* told him of Ikey's intended escape she would have been thought by him to have been equally guilty of complicity. Sir Jasper was therefore reluctantly forced to conclude that Hannah had been telling the truth and that the cunning Ikey had outsmarted them both.

The curious thing was that neither *The Times* nor any of the penny papers made mention of Ikey's subsequent visit to Coutts & Company in the guise of a gentleman of means returned that very day from abroad.

It may only be supposed that the directors of the bank, not wishing to be the laughing stock of all England, had remained silent about the presence in the bank of the real Ikey and the transaction he had made. In fact they had suggested to *The Times* that the abortive ruse by Reuban Reuban was merely an attempt to gain notoriety. He was not to know at the time that the real escape of the notorious fence was taking place. A difficult coincidence to believe, but a coincidence nonetheless, life itself being so often stranger than fiction.

In actual fact, the Bank of England had deliberately conspired with Coutts & Company not to release the story of the real Ikey's visit in the supposed interest of national safety, thus making the story of the hapless actor's attempt at publicity necessary to explain the arrest of Reuban Reuban. In any event, Ikey's transaction was allowed to go through without hindrance to New York and the banker, Nathaniel Wilson, found himself somewhat of a hero for the manner in which he had conducted himself.

Furthermore, Sir Jasper Waterlow, conscious that royalty itself made use of the great private bank, was not in the least keen that the notorious Ikey Solomon's patronage of the same facility be known to the public at large. He had therefore dropped the conspiracy charges against Reuban Reuban, merely holding him in solitary confinement for a week, charged with being a public nuisance. When the greater part of the public furore over Ikey's escape had died down, he was sentenced to twenty-five lashes and released on the condition that he would say nothing more to the newspapers than was already known.

This was thought by Reuban Reuban to be the mildest of sentences. He had received the sum of one hundred pounds for his role as a thespian, the highest salary he would ever be paid for plying his craft. Realising that he had just completed the greatest performance of his life in a real life drama, Reuban Reuban hit upon the idea of using the money Ikey had paid him to mount a grand theatrical production in which he starred and was titled: '*The Jew who Bankrupted England!*'

Though this, when the sensibilities of the times changed under the new young queen, would be altered on the poster hoardings and outside the theatre to read:

'The Man who Bankrupted England'
※ ※ ※ ※
Presenting, in the title role:
The great Reuban Reuban himself!
The original and real life impersonator
in the escape of the notorious Ikey Solomon!

His role playing Ikey Solomon, Prince of Fences, in his own production was to earn the previously struggling actor a handsome living for the remainder of his career.

When Abraham announced his visit the day after Ikey's escape, Mary withdrew with him to a dark corner of the dungeons, taking a candle so that she might see the truth in his face. It was here that he told her the entire story, though the young tailor omitted the details of Ikey's passage on a Danish ship carrying ballast back to Denmark. Instead, he suggested that Ikey had left their coach on the road to Southampton and had been met by another, which was presumably to take him to a ship bound for America.

He told Mary of Ikey's most earnest resolve that she should have money to facilitate her voyage to Australia and that it was Ikey's fondest hope and desire she should lack nothing in order to extract the maximum comfort from so arduous and unpleasant an experience upon the high seas.

Abraham stressed Ikey's most heartfelt regrets at what had happened to Mary, and then took great pains to explain Ikey's reasons for making no attempt to contact Mary while they had both been incarcerated in this very same gaol – the explanation being that Ikey, thinking only of Mary's personal welfare, was mindful that their past association might reflect badly upon her and cause needless suffering and humiliation.

It was a succinct enough explanation and Abraham, who had watched his father at rehearsal since he had been a small boy, delivered Ikey's message with sufficient ardour to suggest that he might himself have enjoyed a career upon the stage.

Mary became at once so bemused with Abraham's message containing Ikey's solicitude that she could scarcely believe her ears. It was with great difficulty that she forced into her mind the true picture of the rapacious, greedy, whingeing, entirely selfish and self-serving Ikey she knew as her erstwhile partner.

'What does 'e want?' she demanded sternly, pushing the candle close to Abraham's face.

'In truth, I swear, he seeks only your high regard, Mistress Mary,' the young tailor protested, much enjoying the sound of such highminded phrasing. 'Those are the words from his own dear lips,' he added.

'Ha!' Mary replied. 'Ikey never done nothin' in 'is whole life what wasn't for profit! 'Igh regard, you says? Where's the profit to be found in that?'

'His sentiments were most soft in your regard, most spontaneous soft, Miss,' Abraham protested again. '"Abraham, my dear," he says to me, "you must convince Mistress Mary of my high regard, my most 'umble 'igh regard!" He said it three times, I swear it, Mistress Mary. There was tears in his eyes when he spoke them words and then he handed me the soft. "You must give 'er this fifty pounds, for she 'as been done a great wrong and it is I who is responsible!" That's what he says to me, Gawd's truth!' Abraham concluded.

Mary looked genuinely startled. 'Ikey said that? Ikey said it were 'im what was responsible?'

Abraham nodded. 'He was most sad, most very sad indeed at the inconvenience he'd caused your fair self.'

'Gawd 'elp us! Miracles will never cease!'

Despite her deep suspicion, Mary could think of no way that Ikey, at the moment of his escape, could possibly profit from her by a further penny. So why, she asked herself, had he parted with a small fortune? Could it possibly be for the reasons Abraham had given? Had Ikey grown a conscience? She could not imagine a repentant Ikey, nor one who was capable of feeling the slightest remorse for a fellow human. We all want to feel the love of another and Mary had not been loved since she had been a small child, when she had briefly known the tenderness of a consumptive mother. Did Ikey really love her, not simply regard her as a profitable partner, as she had always quite contentedly supposed? It seemed too bizarre for words that he might do so, or for that matter, that she could harbour in her breast, unbeknownst to her, a love for him in return.

Love was not a word in the vocabulary which had existed between Mary and Ikey. Even on those rare occasions when she had taken him to her bed, there had been no thought of love. Mary had long since packed that hope away, concealing it in the darkest corner of her soul. Love was not for such as her. And so she simply shook her head, silently forcing back a tear, truly not knowing what to think of the whole matter of Ikey's amorous protestations brought on the importuning lips of a young man with a strong sense of melodrama.

At that moment Abraham Reuban produced Ikey's Duke of Wellington medal.

'Ikey wishes you to have this as a further token of his most remarkable esteem, Mistress Mary,' he said, holding the medallion and chain against the light of the candle. 'It be pure gold an' all!'

'So, where'd 'e steal it, then?' Mary asked tartly, though her heart thumped within her breast at the sight of the medallion.

'No, no, missus, it be his luck, what be called his talisman!' Abraham then told Mary the story of the medallion as Ikey had related it to him in the coach.

Mary had a dim recollection of having once observed a gold chain about Ikey's neck. Stripped down to his vest and long johns, the gold chain had disappeared into the top of his tightly clinging woollen upper garment so that she had no knowledge of what might be contained at its extremity. Now the thought that it might be his medallion, Ikey's talisman, opened her heart like a summer rose. She took the Wellington medallion from Abraham and, turning it over, read the inscription nestled between the garland of laurel leaves. Whereupon Mary's broken hands pressed Ikey's talisman to her bosom and she knew with a fierce certainty that she would survive, that she would never surrender and that somehow she had inherited Ikey's uncanny luck.

At that moment, despite his innumerable faults and thinking him no more than she knew him to be, Mary loved Ikey Solomon.

Chapter Seventeen

Mary was to spend five months in Newgate Gaol, two months longer than her original sentence, this to await a convict ship bound for Van Diemen's Land. On the 15th of May 1827, with eighteen other female convicts, she was placed in light irons and transported by open cart to Woolwich, where the convict ship *Destiny II* was berthed to await its full complement of female convicts.

The weather was grand, the winter frost well past, the elm and larch and sycamore, the bright green oak, in new leaf all. The orchards showed a bedazzlement of white and pink, the fancy dress of pear, apple, cherry and of summer's blood-red plum to come. The woods through which the cart rumbled were carpeted with bluebells and the yellow splash of daffodil, in an England ablaze with bud and blossom and the joyous fecundity of spring.

Several of the convicts were heard to sigh that this was a poor time to leave the shores of England, their most ardent wish being to make their last farewell in the fiercest needle sleet and howl of north wind. This, so their memories might be consumed by the bitter gales and so send them, half cheerful, on their way to the hell of Van Diemen's shores.

This sky of clear blue with the high call of larks and the singing of thrush in the hedgerows was too much a bittersweet parting.

This single memory of the darling buds of May would linger with them for the remainder of their lives. They would hold their grandchildren in their laps under a different sky, and tell of the soft shining of the English countryside. They would remember these two days, when they had rocked and bumped in shackles along a rutted road, as if, for this short space in time, they had been transported through the gates of paradise itself.

It was an unbearable wrench for several of the younger women, who wept piteously for the time it took to arrive at Woolwich, where *Destiny II* creaked and groaned to the slap of the tide. They came upon it suddenly at the turn of a large warehouse and they immediately forsook the rattle and rumble of the cobblestones and turned into the quay, where the wheels of the cart squeaked and lurched along the uneven dockside timbers. Only then, with the cart drawn to a halt beside the squat vessel and with the sudden silence, into which dropped the call of a gull and a soft *phlurrr* from the nostrils of one of the cart horses, did the finality of the sentence of transportation come to each of them.

Standing on the dockside next to the gangway was a diminutive male in frock coat, dirty shirt with a sweat-soiled neckerchief, breeches, hose and tiny brass-buckled shoes much in need of repair. His hair was cropped, though not evenly or in the convict style, and stuck up in raggedy bits an inch or so all about his skull, with whiskers, once dark and now densely speckled with grey. These also stuck out and framed his face from sideburns to the circumference of his chin. Heavy tufted eyebrows, black as pitch, seemed to entirely encase his small bright eyes. Jutting at right angles to this furry visage were two large thin-skinned ears to which the light from the sun behind him gave a bright crimson glow. The total effect was of a remarkable likeness to a simian creature, a monkey dressed in a frock coat, breeches and hose.

'Gawd, look at that!' Mary exclaimed.

The tiny man chuckled and threw an arm upwards pointing to the sky. ' "Gawd", now that be a partickler name what Mr Smiles don't like folks to take in vain! That be three punishments all at once!' He tapped the first finger of his left hand with the forefinger of the right. 'Short rations and no port wine for the father!' He tapped the finger beside it. 'Two days' bread and water in the coal hole, for the son!' He tapped the third. 'Attendance to Bible study for a month, that be for the Holy Ghost!' He looked up at Mary.

'Swear away, me dear, help yourselfs, last chance afore comin' on board to be rid of all that bile! What's your name then?'

'Mary Abacus. What's it to you if I swear?' Mary challenged.

'Ah, yes! For me? Well it be a delightful hopportunity, Mary Habacus. A most pleasant task to do you . . .' He paused in mid-sentence and pointed to the abacus under Mary's arm. 'What be that? A contraption is it? Them black and red beads, it ain't witchcraft is it?'

'Abacus. It be an abacus.'

'A habacus, eh? An' pray tell us, what be an habacus if it ain't your name what is also Habacus?'

Before Mary could reply Ann Gower asked, 'What day o' the month and year ya born in, then, mister?'

The small, hairy creature thought for a moment, then decided to co-operate. 'April seven in the year o' our Lord, seventeen seventy-six or near enough, I reckons.' His voice had a cackle to it, his words sharp and fast and somewhat high-pitched like Chinese crackers going off in a bunch.

Ann Gower turned to Mary and whispered from the side of her mouth, 'Show lover boy, darlin'.'

'Lover boy, is it?' The little man had the most astonishing acuteness of hearing, for Mary had barely heard Ann's whisper herself.

Mary shrugged. She was manacled but the clamps were on either end of a good twelve inches of chain so that her hands were more or less free to work the abacus. She rested it on the side of the cart and instructed Ann to hold the abacus firmly. A moment later her twisted fingers began to fly in a clicking and clacking so rapid that the red and black beads slid across their wire runners faster than the eye could possibly follow them. After what seemed only a few minutes she stopped and read the beads.

'You been alive eighteen thousand, six 'undred and sixty-four days. You was borned on a Sunday.' Tapping the abacus, Mary added, 'That be what me abacus does, it counts things.'

'Ho, ho! We's got us a smart one 'as we? A Jack 'n a box what springs out above others! Well, Mary Habacus what's got an habacus what counts, pleased to meetcha, me name's Potbottom, Mister Tiberias Potbottom, that be the full complement o' me cartouches.' He spread his hands and grinned disarmingly. 'They calls me, "The Scrapins"! Now can you imagine why that could possibly be, eh?' His head jerked enquiringly from one woman to another, waiting for the women in the cart to acknowledge him with a laugh or some sign of acquiescence. But no laughter or even a nod was forthcoming, for Mary sensed a trap and the others had held back, waiting for her reaction. She remained stony faced looking down at the diminutive creature on the dock.

All at once the bright eager to-and-fro of Potbottom's head ceased and he looked down at his scuffed and worn shoes. His head began to nod slowly as though it were coming to some sort of conclusion. His dark eyes moved to each of the women above him, lingering as though taking in all their details, as if, in his observance, he had suddenly learned much about them and what he found was of the utmost disappointment. His eyes came last to Mary and held her gaze as he spoke.

'Ha! What about leap years, then? Your habacus didn't count no leap years, now did it?' He pointed a sharp finger at Mary and jumped from one foot to the other. 'Ho, ho, habacus ain't such a clever Dick now is it?'

The female convicts all looked questioningly at Mary.

'What you takes me for, an idjit?' Mary sniffed. 'There be eleven in all, they's all counted, leap years and even this mornin's included in.'

The women in the cart clapped and yelled their approval and there was much rattling of chains and laughter at Mary's sharp rejoinder.

'Well, well, we'll soon see about this mornin' included in, won't we?' Potbottom said, his lips drawn to a tight line. 'Welcome aboard His Majesty's convict ship, *Destiny II*. Destiny be a good name,' he jerked his thumb over his shoulder at the boat, 'for her gracious ladyship. You see, if you be o' the kind what trusts to destiny to supply yer needs, I is most pleased to inform you that you has got it exactly right! On board we supplies all the misery yer heart could desire, lashin's and lashin's o' the stuff, and, as well, we tops it up with despair, more of it than what you could possibly digest in one plain sailin'!'

Mary laughed nervously and the others followed, a titter ran through the cart.

'Oh, *now* we laughs, does we?' Potbottom's eyes narrowed. 'I knows not how many days you has been alive on Gawd's sweet earth, Mary Habacus, but I makes you this most solemn promise.'

Potbottom's eyes held Mary's. 'The worse ones hasn't yet come for you!' He paused and gave her a malevolent smile. 'But they will. Oh deary me, yes! They will, they will!'

Tiberias Potbottom turned his back on them and hurried up the gangway, his short bandy legs making his shoulders jump from side to side, his long arms hanging loose, so that he lurched along very much like the monkey creature he so closely resembled. It was only then that they noticed that one shoulder was higher than the other, that there was a hump, though not overly large, resting behind it. Tiberias Potbottom was a hunchback.

'Blimey! Who'll be touchin' that one's hump for luck,' Mary exclaimed softly.

The women in the cart giggled and watched as Potbottom disappeared on to the deck above them. 'Jesus!' Ann Gower said in a loud whisper. 'Talk about 'ot an' cold! What were that all about?'

'Whatever it were, it ain't good news for me,' Mary sighed. She turned to one of the two turnkeys who'd escorted them on the trip down and who had just that moment returned from reporting to the ship's surgeon-superintendent, the already infamous Joshua Smiles. Neither of their guards had witnessed the exchange between the convict women and Potbottom, who'd brushed past them just as they'd reached the top of the gangway.

'Can you take off our irons now, Mr Burke, we be exceeding tired o' standin'?' Mary asked politely.

'Not till you 'as been counted and numbers taken,' Burke said. 'Sorry, that be regulations.'

A murmur of dissatisfaction came from the cart which caused the second of their guards to raise both hands and pat the air in front of him. 'Now, now, girls, you been good so far, don't you go spoilin' things now!' He smiled up at the women in the cart, 'Besides, Mr Potbottom, what be assistant to ship's surgeon, be 'ere soon enough to count and take your numbers.'

An hour later with the spring sunshine turned unseasonably hot and uncomfortable they still remained standing in the cart. The female convicts had no protection but for their mob caps, their ankles were swollen and painful from standing and their throats were parched for want of water. Many of the older women were close to swooning in the heat. They commenced to shouting, demanding and begging from all who mounted the gangway to

253

release them from their chains and allow them to step down from the cart and into the shade cast by the ship's side. When they were ignored by the coming and going throng they cussed loudly, calling out obscenities. Finally two jack tars appeared at the top of the gangway, the one carrying a small table and the other a chair. They walked down and placed them in the shade on the dock.

'Call the bleedin' baboon what's meant to count us!' Mary shouted angrily at the two tars, her temper quite lost. 'There's some near dyin' for want of a drop o' bloody water!'

'Baboon, is I? Well thank you very much!' Potbottom said, appearing at the top of the gangway. 'A baboon what can count and take numbers, an extraordinary baboon what is blessed with a very long memory for the slightest slight and insults what injure!'

'Oh shit!' Mary said in a loud whisper.

Tiberias Potbottom, a small smile on his face, walked down the gangway and skipped lightly on to the dockside where he continued on to the table and chair.

'Shit it be, but not for me! Shit it be for such as thee!' He smirked.

He was carrying a large ledger under his arm which seemed to raise his hunched shoulder even higher and now he took it and opened it on the table to show one of its two opened pages half filled with writing. From the side pocket of his worn frock coat he produced a pot of blacking and, undoing its cap carefully, placed it beside the ledger. Then he took a goose feather quill from an inside pocket and this too he laid beside the book. Having completed this task he stepped to the front of the table and placed his hands behind his back, whereupon he commenced to rock on the back of his heels looking up at the women in the cart.

'Has we had enough, then? Enough profanity to last us all the ways to Hobart Town?' He did not wait for their response, but continued. 'Or does we stay another hour and get the rest o' the bile out of our vile hearts?' He paused and this time waited. 'Well?' he finally asked.

'Enough, sir,' Mary said, her eyes suitably downcast and her hands clasped in humility in front of her. The others nodded eagerly. 'We's 'ad enough o' cussin', sir,' Mary repeated. 'Can we step down now, if you please, sir, Mr Potbottom?'

Potbottom squinted up at Mary and, shaking his head slowly, said, 'Oh, I very much hopes so, Mary Habacus, I very much hopes so! You see, Mr Smiles don't take kindly to profanity and me,' he shrugged, 'I is his sharp eyes and his large ears and I must warn you!' He paused and chuckled. 'Me eyes is exceedin' good and . . .' he touched one of his ears lightly, '. . . me ears is even much better'n that!'

From his back pocket he produced a large red silk handkerchief and held it open in front of him, the silk hanging limp from one corner. 'Sailing is Gawd's breath,' he began, as though he were about to give a lecture, which indeed was his intention. 'When the sails lay limp that means Gawd has taken away his breath and we is becalmed.' He glanced at them as though to assure himself of their attention. 'Becalmed, that be an awesome thing. To be upon the ocean without Gawd's breath, to be forsaken by the Almighty.' Potbottom's small body seemed to shudder at the very prospect. 'That be a time for the devil to skip across the flat sea and come aboard.' He waited for the effect of his words to sink in and then, with his free hand, he took up a second corner of the scarf so that it hung square in front of his face, whereupon he blew upon it so that the silk billowed away from him. 'Gawd's gentle and steady breath be everythin' to them what sails upon the oceans wide. It be His gift to us for observin' His ways, ways you lot has long since forsaken!' Potbottom suddenly flapped the scarf furiously and his voice rose in pitch. 'You makes Gawd angry! Terrible angry! And when He be angry, His breath be angry! His angry breath be a storm at sea, a hurricane what takes small ships and drives 'em up high onto the furious waves and dashes them down, and breaks their backs and smashes 'em to tinder, and sends 'em to the bottom o' the ocean!' His voice lowered. 'Planks and carcases and barrels and bilge, spat up later on some distant and forsaken shore!'

Tiberias Potbottom, breathing heavily through his nostrils, crumpled the cloth into his hand and stuffed it angrily back into the pocket of his breeches. He appeared quite overcome, struggling to contain himself.

The women in the cart watched silently. Potbottom swallowed twice, his Adam's apple jumping along his scrawny neck, then he spoke slowly and quietly. 'That's why we talks to Gawd in prayer and meditation, we asks Him for His fair and lovely breath upon our voyage. When we uses profanity, when we take His name in vain, He will take His breath away, or, if He be angry, sufficient enough angry, if the blasphemy be too great, He will blow and blow until we is doomed upon the calamitous waves!'

Potbottom, his hands now once again clasped behind his back and his demeanour recovered, walked around the cart so that the prisoners within it were forced to follow him with their eyes and turn as he moved. The chains of their manacles rattled and clinked. Finally the tiny man came to stand directly in front of Mary.

'Me remarkable ears, Gawd's special gift, can hear a whisper o' profanity in the full face o' the Roarin' Forties! I am Gawd's watchman! When you's spewin' yer heart out in the sea sickness what's soon to come, if one of you so much as moans, "Oh Gawd!" I'll have you on bread 'n water in leg irons.' He looked at each of them in turn and then suddenly shouted, 'We only have Gawd's sweet breath to save us! And with your kind on board we places our lives in great jeopardy! Mr Smiles will not have no whore language, no profanity, no blasphemy on board, does you understand?' His voice lowered and spitting each word out as though it caused a bad taste in his mouth he added, 'Does-I-make-me-self-per-fekly-clear?'

Potbottom did not wait for any of the female convicts to nod but turned and moved around the table to sit down on the chair. Seated, he looked up again and addressed himself to the two turnkeys, who had been standing, eyes downcast, more or less at attention, beside the cart.

'Unshackle!' he instructed, taking up his quill and dipping it into the pot of blacking in front of him. Then he looked back up at the women and jabbed the quill at Mary and then at Ann Gower. 'Them two shall be last!'

Mary brought her hands up and placed them over Ikey's medallion until she felt the comfort of the small gold object in the centre of her flattened palm. The long hard voyage to Van Diemen's Land had begun. Ikey's medallion, his luck, she suddenly knew, was intended for the second great passage of her life. She must survive.

It was three weeks before all the female convicts had arrived from gaols as far away as Scotland, Ireland and Wales. The bright spring weather had turned into a wet, miserable early summer. Many of the convicts arrived with coughs, colds and bronchial infections, and a number of the older women suffered profoundly with the added affliction of rheumatism which often bent them double and made them seem like old crones twice their age. The children's dirty faces were pinched and wet with a constant flow of mucus leaking from their nostrils, and many were consumed by high fevers.

As each cartload, or coach, unloaded, Mary watched from the deck as Tiberias Potbottom met them, hopping and jumping about and, in general, making their arrival as difficult and fearful a prospect as he possibly could.

Upon coming aboard the *Destiny II* they had been taken directly to Joshua Smiles and his assistant, who had given them a medical examination of a most cursory nature, but carefully documented down as though of the utmost importance. A lifting of the bottom and top eyelids, a probing in the ears, an inspection of the tongue and a tapping of the chest for the almost certain signs of bronchial infections. This was followed with a more thorough inspection a week later which became known on shipboard as 'Bloody Pusover'.

Each week prisoners were examined for blood and pus in the ears, in the mucus, in the eyes, in the nose and mouth, and finally in the cunny for the glim or syphilis. There was little notice taken when an infection was discovered, though, apart from it being written in the surgeon's book with details of a most generously prescribed medication. This medication, though well conceived according to the contemporary dictates of treatment, was never administered.

Upon completion of the very first medical examination Joshua Smiles, in a burst of volubility not to be repeated outside of his prayers, explained the rules to be followed during the voyage. He then launched into a lengthy dissertation which included much comment about the dangers of immoral behaviour, the need for cleanliness and the benefits and rewards of a religious life. He left until last his admonition that profanity and blasphemy would earn the harshest of punishments and warned any female prisoner to bring the name of the Almighty God upon her lips in no other manner but in prayerfulness.

Mary and her intake were divided into two groups, each of which was termed a mess. From each mess a monitor was chosen to speak for all. Mary was elected monitor by the insistence of all in her group. Ann Gower was also selected as monitor in the second mess, which contained six convicts who were from Dublin, they being whores and thus thought to be most compatible to the other members.

The prison uniform consisted of a coarse parti-coloured cotton shift, two petticoats and two sets of ill-fitting undergarments, a pinny, with a spare, and two mob caps. The women's own clothes were washed by three members of each mess, hung out on the deck to dry then dry packed away in boxes with camphor balls. The idea behind imposing uniformity of dress was to eliminate a natural pecking order derived from the status of possessions – rags or fine gowns, tortoise shell brushes or combs of ox bone, bottles of perfumes or tincture of lavender water, a fine brooch or merely a few bright buttons or a single trinket. These were all placed on the mess inventory and packed away, so that those wearing a silver brooch and fancy outfit could not earn precedence over rags and a simple garnet pin. Upon arriving in Van Diemen's Land their belongings would be handed to the matron of the Female Factory in the presence of their owners to be kept until their release.

The money they had brought with them in gold, silver, copper and soft was ordered to be handed to the surgeon-superintendent, who entered the amounts into his cash book and, upon arrival, lodged these funds with the authorities in Van Diemen's Land. They were to be returned to the owners at the completion of their sentences.

This inventory of cash was undertaken by Tiberias Potbottom and such became Mary's fear that she would never again see what rightfully belonged to her, that at the risk of the most severe punishment if she should be discovered, she elected to keep her small personal horde of gold coins. Fifteen gold sovereigns remained from Ikey's gift and this she kept in her 'prisoner's purse' along with Ikey's medallion.

The prisoner's purse, readily obtained for a few shillings in any English gaol, consisted of a small metal tube of brass with a fitted cap and rounded end. It was fashioned in much the same manner as the cigar-shaped container Ikey had caused to be made and which had carried his letter of credit, so comfortably worn by Marybelle Firkin when she had travelled from Birmingham to London. Only, the prisoner's purse of the kind Mary wore was much smaller and made to fit, without too much discomfort, in either of the 'treasure caves' that is to say, the rear or front orifice, convenient places to bury contraband on a female person.

On bloody pusover days Mary would transfer the brass container to within the rear cave, which although uncomfortable was safe from Potbottom's supervision, and the probing fingers of the convict matron who would examine that other part of her anatomy and report it free of infection to the surgeon's assistant. He hovered behind her with quill and ledger in the hope that he might be able to record a finding of pus to transform into profit.

From the time the prisoners began to arrive the Ladies' Committee commenced to visit the ship. Mary, suspicious by nature of charity, was at first wary of these high-minded women, but she soon grew to respect them. Though pious in their ways they earnestly sought to alleviate the discomfort of the voyage and could, on occasion, become quite cantankerous if they found a facility in the prison which did not adhere to the prescribed regulations.

Potbottom did his unctuous best to earn their approval, dancing attendance like some small simian creature trained especially for the task of serving, assuring them with much dry-soaping of hands and nodding of head and frequent obsequious expression of his utmost co-operation. He insisted that any complaint they might make would be his personal pleasure to attend to in the time it took to snap his greedy fingers.

Nevertheless the formidable Mrs Fry and her Ladies' Committee were not easily deceived and they soon earned the approbation of all but the hardest and most recalcitrant female convicts. Though the world of the two classes of women was divided by a chasm too wide to leap, or even for one to imagine the life of the other, these committee women were not from the authorities, nor were they easily intimidated by them. Furthermore, they laboured trenchantly and with goodwill on behalf of the female convicts. They showed themselves as women who cared greatly for their unfortunate sisters. By notable contrast, with the exception of many of the surgeon-superintendents who often took the utmost care of their convicts (Joshua Smiles and some few others being the exception), the male administrators were, for the most part, totally indifferent to their welfare. In fact, most went to great pains to indicate that they cared not a rat's tail for the wellbeing of their charges but, instead, regarded every female prisoner as a whore transported to keep the men, both convict and free, sated.

Mary's misshapen hands did not allow for needlework but to her great delight, along with cloth and thread, the resourceful Quaker ladies had supplied a small library. While there were no novels, plays or other improper books, the single box contained, as well as religious works, travel, biographies and history books and poetry. This last gave Mary a new-found pleasure, and was to bring her considerable joy for the remainder of her life.

Most of the convicts on board adapted to the order and routine the Ladies' Committee established at the commencement of the voyage, and those within Mary's mess, though all of them prostitutes, encouraged by her, soon proved eager to take up needlework. They were frequently rewarded for their diligence by Mary with readings while they worked, but this was not true of Ann Gower's mess.

These were the women who were branded by the authorities within the surgeon-superintendent's report at the conclusion of each voyage with words such as, 'notoriously bad', 'disorderly', 'profligate wretches', 'quarrelsome', and for those with a flair for invective and a good, well-inked goose feather quill, 'the basest and most abominable wretch of a woman', or 'scheming, blasphemous vixen and prostitute' – this last description being appended to Mary's name by Tiberias Potbottom on the very first evening of her coming on board. When the ship arrived in Hobart, this single entry in the surgeon's report resulted in her being incarcerated in the Female Factory instead of being assigned as a servant to a settler. In truth, with the exception of theft and blasphemy, fighting and the urgent couplings which took place at night, most of the offences committed on board were minor breaches of discipline such as insolence and refusal to obey orders, howling and singing a hymn or prayer to the tune of a well-known bawdy and sentimental song.

In the week before the departure of the vessel the relatives of those convicts on board began to arrive to farewell their wives and daughters. Mary, having no family of her own, witnessed the piteous sight of parents parting from their daughters with no likelihood of ever seeing them in this life again. The deck of the *Destiny II* was washed with the tears of country folk who had seen their dear daughters leave home to find work as servants or some form of livelihood in the city only to end up, unbeknown to them, selling their bodies on the streets of London, Dublin, Glasgow or

Liverpool or resorting to petty crime in order to stay alive. These were good, honest people, who, for the most part, worked at backbreaking labour to earn barely enough to put bread and broth upon the table. They brought what they could as gifts, though frequently this was no more than the tears they shed and the love they bestowed for the last time upon their unfortunate and wretched offspring.

The *Destiny II*, flying the red and white pennant, 'the whip' which denoted a convict ship, sailed with the evening tide on the 14th of June amid the dreadful cries of distress from both those on board and the ones they'd left behind forever. The wind was from the nor'west, the temperature 68 degrees Fahrenheit and the sailing down channel was steady and most pleasant until about midnight when the winds changed to the west. This brought choppy seas and frequent squalls and the weather billowed into gales and huge seas by the time they entered the Bay of Biscay.

By midnight, when the prisoners had long since been confined below decks, almost the entire complement of convicts became sick to the point of frequent vomiting and nausea. They commenced to howling and blaspheming until no strength existed for these bitter emotions, whereupon they lay in their own vomit and moaned, willing themselves to die in the insufferable atmosphere of the water-logged prison.

The *Destiny II* was a 'wet' ship, that is to say, when the huge waves washed over the decks the water poured down into the prison quarters so that not a single flock mattress, pillow or blanket or anything contained within the female prison, including the convicts themselves, remained dry. The swinging stoves were hung in the prison to help dry the prison quarters but to no effect. The constant downpour of water rushing in from the deck above caused the contents of their stomachs to somewhat dilute, and with the hatches tightly closed, by the time dawn's light came the stench and the mess from the swill at their feet was beyond any possible description.

Sea sickness has no medication other than a tranquil sea and the weather remained inclement for the following week and then continued foul with intermittent calm of no more than, at most, a day, until they reached Tenerife, twenty days after departing from Woolwich.

At almost the moment they made the harbour at Santa Cruz at

seven of the clock on a Sunday morning with the church bells summoning worshippers to early mass, the wind died and the sun blazed up to chase away all signs of the threatening cumulus cloud gathered above the high conical peaks above the town. While there was no thought that the convicts might be allowed to go ashore, they rested for several days while the ship took on new provisions. The women were allowed fresh fruit bought from the various boats which pulled to the side of the vessel and all were kept occupied at cleaning-out below decks and drying their bedding, clothes and personal effects.

As each cloudless day passed, the women became more hysterical at the prospect of leaving. On the third day, as they up-anchored in preparation to depart, the convicts went berserk and were confined to below decks with the hatches of the prison quarters securely locked. This was for fear that they might riot at the expectation of atrocious weather such as they'd endured during their first month at sea.

Only Tiberias Potbottom and Joshua Smiles seemed content to be on their way again. God had blessed the voyage with gale force winds and stormy seas, though not sufficient of either to cause harm to the *Destiny II*, and this was seen by both men as a blessing breathed upon their journey to the other side of the world.

Soon the routine on board ship assumed a semblance of normalcy. Most of the women were allocated jobs on board which helped somewhat to alleviate the long empty hours. Some of these positions carried the promise of a small reward while others were reward enough by helping to pass the hours between six o'clock muster when they rose and the time, roughly twelve hours later at dusk, when they were confined below decks. Most, being experienced in domestic service, adjusted easily enough to the routines on board and took readily to the added pleasures of sewing and needlework. They were not averse to working as servants in the kitchens and hospital or in other menial tasks of cleaning and labouring. Mary asked that she might teach those who wished to learn to read and write. She was the only one among the female convicts with sufficient learning to impart this knowledge to others and the Ladies' Committee had encouraged the formation of a school. But this was refused as a duty, in Joshua Smiles' name, by Potbottom and so Mary was obliged to run her school during the afternoon. Potbottom saw to it that she was on constant duty cleaning out the prison each morning, dry scrubbing the deck with holystone and sand and washing down and refilling the water closets, these being the most menial and hated tasks on board ship.

Moreover, at every opportunity, Potbottom would try to humiliate Mary and at each bloody pusover he would make cruel jokes about her hands or comment on the scar upon her face, or make her linger longer before the matron with her skirts held above her waist and her flannel undergarment removed. On two occasions, when he had caught her in utterance of bad language, he had caused Mary to be placed in a scold's bridle, a strap worn tightly over the mouth, tied at the back of the neck and which made it quite impossible to speak, nor, for the space of one week, was she allowed to read from a book, a punishment she found far more onerous than the silence the bridle enforced.

The increasing tropical heat did not help the disposition of the convicts or that of the officials and crew who, increasingly, tormented them. Each passing day the breeze seemed to slacken a little more and the sun to grow hotter as it beat down on deck from a sky too high and blue for anything in their previous comprehension.

The women wakened each morning in a lather of perspiration with no breeze at all coming in from the hatches and the portholes, which were thrown wide open. Even the scuttles were opened, the sea being calm enough to allow it, but this too was to no avail. Nor was there a breath of air from the supposed 'ventilation shafts' in which the ship's officers had shown no trust. These wind sails and shafts were designed to blow cool air below decks, but such was their scorn for this new-fangled idea that the crew purposely neglected to adjust them according to instructions.

Soon it made no difference whether they had it right or wrong, for the ship had entered the equatorial doldrums in the Atlantic Narrows and the sails, whatever their purpose, lay limp and useless. Joshua Smiles watched the topgallant with increasing fear, for even this tiny sail trapped not the slightest breath of wind and the red and white 'whip' hung flat against the topmast.

With the sea totally calm and the heat each day climbing, a hellish invasion overtook the vessel. Hordes of vermin, once snug within the cracks and crannies in the woodwork and the bilges – cockroaches, bedbugs, lice and fleas and whole colonies of rats – emerged from the crevices and dark holes to attack the human inhabitants of the *Destiny II.*

The crew and officers were not spared in this, for if the vermin knew not convict from free man and spared not the one in preference to another, nor did the incredible stench, which pervaded the prison and the apartments of crew and officers alike.

For Mary the real hell of the outward journey to Van Diemen's Land was about to begin at the hands of Tiberias Potbottom. The assistant to the surgeon-superintendent, whether at the behest of his master or by his own decision, came to conclude that the becalming of the vessel and the invasion of the pestilence from the cracks and the bilges, which had in itself a biblical connotation as if one of the plagues upon Egypt, had come about because of the blasphemy of the whores on board. That God, in His righteous wrath, had withdrawn His breath, demanding that those who mocked Him should be punished.

With the extraordinary heat it was decided that the convict women might bring their bedding and sleep on deck, occupying the poop and quarter decks which could be safely enough guarded from the crew. Though the nights were exceedingly hot and and the air still, this was a most pleasant experience compared with the furnace of the prison quarters below decks, and the prisoners received this concession to their comfort with great joy.

'All may sleep on deck except the whores!' Potbottom had declared. 'These be the orders o' the surgeon-superintendent!'

There was a howl of consternation from Ann Gower's and Mary's groups.

'All what's declared whores on ship's manifest will take their beddin' down below after evening muster,' Tiberias Potbottom continued. Then he grinned. 'This be a little taste o' hell, a sample o' what's comin' to them what mocks the Lord Jesus Christ or takes His name in vain! Gawd is not mocked!' he repeated.

'We ain't done nothin'!' Mary shouted. 'Why pick on us, then? We ain't taken nobody's name in vain!' She turned to her group and then to Ann Gower's group. ''As we, ladies?'

'Oh, be that so?' Potbottom exclaimed. 'And I says different and surgeon thinks different and . . .' he pointed upwards to the limp sails, 'evidence says different!'

Mary showed her indignation, bringing her hand to her hip and throwing her shoulder forward. 'It ain't *our* fault there be no bleedin' wind!'

'Ah! That be a matter of opinion, Mary Habacus, Gawd's

opinion, surgeon's opinion and me own opinion, we all be against your single opinion!'

'Not single, mine too!' Ann Gower shouted. 'It ain't fair! We done no 'arm, we done nuffink wrong! It weren't Gawd what made them sails still, it be 'em doll drums!'

'That's right, it be the doldrums!' Mary shouted in support. 'They be perfectly natural, a phenomenon what sometimes happens near the equator!'

'Oh it be clever Miss Jack 'n a Box again! Phenomenon is it?' Potbottom paused. 'And Gawd! Is He not a phenomenon? Is He not the creator o' the heavens and the earth? The rain and the glorious clouds what is His billowin' breath!' Tiberias Potbottom stopped again and looked about him at the women assembled for muster. He finally fixed his eyes on Ann Gower and then again on Mary, and began to speak, this time most rapidly and in a high-pitched voice. 'Without His breath to drive the clouds there be no rain, without the rain there be starvation upon the face o' the earth! Gawd's breath be the breath of all life itself and when Gawd takes His breath from us it be a sign o' His anger!' He pointed upwards to the limp sails above his head and spoke more slowly. 'Gawd has taken His breath away from us! Doldrums just be another name for Gawd's anger!' Then Potbottom brought his hand down again and pointed to the group of convict women gathered around Mary. 'And we all knows the reason for it, don't we!'

'That be a whole 'eap o' bilge water!' Mary shouted angrily.

'Ha! And that be blasphemin'! Callin' Gawd's breath bilge now, is we?' Potbottom shouted triumphantly. 'You'll all go below right now, all the whores and blasphemers! We'll put the lid o' hell on the Jack 'n a Box and all her consorts, in the name o' Jesus Christ our Lord and Saviour!'

Ann Gower's group and Mary's group were sentenced to be locked in the prison below decks for three days on half rations, but with the full daily allowance of two pints of water, this ration not halved, for it would likely have caused them to perish.

The heat below decks was so intense and the vermin so prolific that the women were soon forced to remove their clothes and after several hours below they could think of nothing but the need for water. Many were so overcome that they fainted away, these faintings frequently terminating in fits. At night the portholes as well as the hatches were closed and by morning the following day many of them were delirious, wandering about unable to recall their own names.

By midday, when the sun was at its zenith, the heat upon the blazing deck would cause the pitch between the deckboards to melt. This molten hell would drop onto them in the prison below where it would bubble upon their flesh, the fiery pitch sticking long enough to arm or leg or back or head to burn savagely through the skin or scalp and deep into the flesh, so that they were permanently scarred from its effect.

On the afternoon of the second day Ann Gower, maddened by the circumstances below decks, attacked Mary, accusing her of causing the calamitous situation they found themselves in. Mary had been sitting alone in a corner against the bulkhead, clasping her legs together with her head resting on her knees when Ann Gower approached and stood over her.

'It were you, not us! It were you the sod wanted!' Ann began. 'All along it be you givin' 'im lip! In the wagon 'an all, when we first come. Then on an' on an' on, always makin' it 'ard for us. You what thinks you is better than a whore. Ya think 'cause ya can read that ya be clever, that ya knows everyfink! Well let me tell ya, all ya knows is 'ow to make trouble for all of us wif that fuckin' gob o' yers! Now Potbottom's gettin' 'is own back and it's us what's sufferin'! It were you, Mary Abacus, what done this to us and I reckons you 'as to pay!' Ann Gower turned and faced the others. 'What do ya say, girls, the bitch 'as gotta pay for our misery!' She indicated the prison around them. 'For this!'

As Ann Gower spoke Mary's hands were under her skirt, for she was one of the very few who had not removed her clothes, which hung soaking from her body. Suspended from a string about her waist was a small bundle of cloth concealed in her flannel undergarment which contained her brass talons. Mary's twisted fingers worked frantically at the knot, but it was too tightly bound to open without some persistent plucking and pulling. Long before it had yielded Ann Gower's right hand swept down and knocked Mary's mob cap from her head. She gripped a fistful of hair in her left hand and pulled Mary squealing to her feet. Balling her hand into a fist, she struck Mary a violent blow which broke her nose.

At the sight of the blood spurting from Mary's nose the other women seemed to go berserk. Howling, they rushed at her, tearing and pulling and pushing her to the deck. They kicked and jumped on Mary and drove their fists into her face and body, raking her with their nails in a furious frenzy of fighting.

So intense were the screams and caterwauling and hysteria that the hatches were hurriedly opened and three guards and Potbottom rushed below. At the sight of Potbottom the women turned like a pack of howling wolves and made towards him. The two prison guards were barely able to retreat and hold them off sufficiently long for Potbottom to beat a hasty retreat, his tiny bow legs propelling him as fast as they could carry him back on to the deck.

More guards arrived together with the prison matron and two of her assistants, and it took fully ten minutes before any order was restored and they were able to gain control of the hysterical women.

When the matron came upon Mary she lay unconscious, one of her purpled and twisted hands clasped tightly into a ball and resting on her bloodstained breast. She was carried to the hospital where she was washed and her wounds dressed, though every attempt to open her left hand failed. Her fingers seemed to have clamped shut with the shock of the beating she had taken, and had the appearance of the claws of a great bird of prey pulled tightly inwards as though in death.

Mary regained consciousness an hour later and took water from the matron which she drank greedily, asking for more in a hoarse whisper affected by her cut and swollen lips. She was still groggy and not fully possessed of her wits, unsure where she was and with both her eyes closed unable to see the woman who nursed her.

Mary was awakened by someone shaking her roughly and then she heard the cackle of Potbottom's voice, 'Wake her, matron, she has slumbered enough! Wake her at once, this be no inn for gentlefolks!'

Mary attempted to open her eyes and while the right eye still remained tightly closed the left had improved somewhat and she could see with a measure of clarity. Potbottom sat beside her bunk, perched on a stool with his hands clasped to his breast. He seemed to be positively shaking with excitement. One hand suddenly jerked out and a finger prodded into the side of Mary's ribs. A sharp pain shot into her lungs where the ribs had been broken.

Potbottom's hand shot back to be clasped again by the other in their former position. 'Wake up! Wake up at once! Say somethin'!'

'Mornin',' Mary said through her cracked and bulbous lips, and then added, 'Miszer Pobothum, sir,' in a voice slurred and hardly above a whisper.

'That's better, much better, you'll soon be well again, me dear.' He dry-soaped his hands. 'Well enough for bread 'n water and a bit o' loverly solitude in the coal hole!' he cackled. 'Guilty o' startin' a riot we is.' He clucked his tongue several times. 'Now that be most wicked. Mr Smiles don't like that, no he don't, indeed we don't tolerate no riot on Gawd's ship.'

Mary groaned and lifted the hand which was still fisted shut and Tiberias Potbottom gasped and reeled back, thinking she might hit him, though she barely had strength sufficient to lift her arm. 'No!' Mary rasped and tried to lift and shake her head. But the pain of it was too much to bear, and she winced and her head fell back and her hand fell limply by her side.

'No, says you! Yes, says I! Startin' a riot, now that be a most serious offence what will earn a floggin' if I be not mistaken. Surgeon-superintendent don't like that, no he don't, I'll vouch for that, not like it, not one little bit!'

Mary tried once again to move her head. 'No!' she managed again. She was suddenly aware of a strange sound and at the same time the vessel shuddered and then rolled slightly. 'Wind?' Mary whispered.

'Oh yes, wind! Glorious wind! Gawd's breath is back with us, Mary Habacus!' Tiberias Potbottom said triumphantly then pushed his ugly little monkey face close to Mary's. 'Gawd is not mocked!' he said, spraying her face with his fierce spittle. 'You have been punished and He has restored His precious breath to us!'

Tears ran from Mary's swollen eyes and she drew blood as she bit her top lip in an attempt to stop them. She did not want to show her physical pain, nor her confusion and agony of mind to the creature perched on the stool beside her.

'What's this then?' Potbottom asked suddenly.

Mary made no attempt to look, thinking him to be making comment over her distress. Instead she kept her lumpy eyes closed fighting back the tears that threatened to grow into a desperate sobbing. They were stupid tears, tears that showed Potbottom that he'd won, that he'd broken her spirit, tears for the past and the present and the future, tears that washed over her awful life.

'What be this I'm holdin', eh!' Potbottom asked again, and this time his demanding impatient tone caused Mary to open her one good eye. Tiberias Potbottom held up a prisoner's purse. 'Never know what you'll find when you looks, does you, me dear?'

Mary's hand went instinctively to her cunny but she knew before she reached it that her prisoner's purse was no longer hidden there. The brass tube Tiberias Potbottom held contained her fifteen sovereigns and Ikey's precious Waterloo medallion and chain and Mary began to sob uncontrollably.

'Shall we see what we's got, then?' Potbottom said gleefully. His small hands twisted the brass cap, removed and upended it, tapping it into the centre of his palm. 'Very curious,' he said, 'it don't have nothin' in it!' He tapped the tube once more in the same manner then held it with the open end facing Mary. Potbottom raised his dark, bushy eyebrows, his tiny black eyes shining. 'A pleasurin' device is it? A poor convict woman's comfort for the dark lonely nights at sea?' Potbottom shook his head and clucked his tongue several times. 'I don't think Mr Smiles will take kindly to such a device. Not kindly at all!' He replaced the cap and, leaning over Mary, he placed the small metal tube on her chest. As he did so, Ikey's medallion fell from within his linen shirt and dangled on its chain directly above Mary's breasts. Then, without a further glance at the hapless, sobbing Mary, he scuttled out of the hospital, leaving her to contemplate the loss of everything she possessed in the world.

Mary had secretly dared to hope that her life might change, that despite the hell of Van Diemen's Land she would survive and that something good, no matter how small, might come of it. Now she knew that she had been deluding herself all her life, in truth, the flame of her existence had been blown out the very moment she had been born. As she lay in the prison hospital Mary craved emptiness, to feel nothing, to walk upon the earth as a shadow until death came as yet another misadventure upon her senseless life. Her past filled her up, taking possession of every corner of her soul to make her life a dark, repugnant experience. Where others might have craved Christian salvation, Mary asked only for emptiness, for all feeling to be taken from her. She wanted neither God nor the devil, but what lay between. Without feeling, she told herself, she could continue to exist; with it, she wanted only to die.

Soon her tears dried up. They were pointless. To cry was to mourn and to mourn was to care and caring was what had always destroyed her. She cursed her mouth and its ability to find trouble; others knew their place and remained silent with their heads bowed in obsequious obedience. It was her big mouth which had destroyed her life. If she could empty out all that had happened to her, she would grow silent forever, not be seen or heard, or be there at all, her lips frozen forever.

But instead of emptiness, as Mary lay perfectly still, there grew slowly within her a great anger and then through the anger came pain, a sharp throbbing in her left hand. She tried to ignore it, but it was too alive and demanding, and soon the pain within the centre of her hand burned as though it were a fire kindled there, a furnace of white heat expanding and filling her, roaring at the very centre of her being. She could no longer ignore it. Mary lifted her hand to within the line of her vision and perceived for the first time that it was held tightly in a claw-like grip, its dark twisted fingers resembling, not a human hand, but an ugly, twisted knot. Within the knot a searing, leaping, roaring flame called out to her for revenge.

Mary attempted to open her hand but the fingers would not respond to her will and the pain caused by the effort brought her close to fainting. But she persisted, and after several minutes, her stiffened and contorted fingers broke loose sufficiently to reveal within them the small knotted rag bundle containing her brass talons. Mary started to weep again, but this time with a sense of great relief, for she knew instinctively that she would recover, and that the odious little monkey creature had not broken her spirit. She knew that the hatred in her would restore her health, though to be God's or the devil's child she knew not, and cared even less.

Chapter Eighteen

Mary's punishment was not completed with her beating and admission to hospital. A week after being released she was paraded on the prisoners' deck and charged with causing a riot within the prison. This was too grave an offence for Tiberias Potbottom to resolve by the usual proxy of his prayerful master, and Joshua Smiles himself was required to preside. With a charge of inciting a riot, the safety of the ship had been placed in jeopardy and the ship's master and those officers not on duty were required to be in attendance.

A muster of all the prisoners was called mid-morning with Mary standing with her head erect before the pale and mournful Smiles. The surgeon-superintendent, as was his usual habit, was dressed completely in black. This colour included both his blouse and neckerchief and a top hat of unusual height. The total effect gave him the appearance of being perhaps on stilts. He towered over the remainder of the prisoners, matrons, guards and even the tallest of the ship's officers present, and Mary was seen to come not much above the waist of his frock coat.

In a tone incurious to the consequence of his words he read out the charges against Mary and then, without raising his voice or heightening the inflections placed upon his words, he pronounced sentence. It was a noticeable contradiction to the blandness of his voice that throughout his reading the surgeon-superintendent, on no single occasion looked up or at the prisoner, and his hands shook as though in a tremor as they held the paper from which he read.

'. . . Mary Abacus, I, Joshua Jeremiah Smiles, under the authority given to me by the Admiralty and further, under the provisions of the Home Department and in the name of His Majesty King George IV, sentence you to twenty-five strokes of the lash to be administered at one time. Whereupon you shall have your hair shaved and be placed in solitary confinement within the coal hole and shall remain there for one week, this to exclude the Sabbath. During this time you shall be given bread and water as your only sustenance. I further order that the sentence be carried out immediately by Mr Tiberias Potbottom and that all prisoners and those who be in charge of them, and therefore under my authority, shall bear witness to these proceedings.'

There was a gasp from the prisoners, for even the whores felt great remorse at what they'd done to Mary.

'Ya bloody bastard!' a voice shouted from the centre of the crowd.

'Who said that?' Tiberias Potbottom called out, jumping up and down to try to see into the lines of assembled women.

'I did, ya fuckin' ape!' Ann Gower called as two guards moved into the crowd of suddenly thronging and excited women and grabbed her. 'You murderers!' she shouted again as she was pulled away and led from the deck. 'May ya rot in 'ell!' A guard struck her on the side of the head with his truncheon, so that she fell to her knees and was dragged down the hatchway.

Mary was placed over an empty barrel, her arms and legs held by the wrists and ankles, each limb by a separate male prison guard. The matron of the hospital, who had so recently nursed her back to health, was then required to fully expose her back. Mary was given a small square of folded cloth to place between her teeth.

The sky above was brilliant blue with no cloud to interrupt its surface, a storm having come up during the night so that the ocean and the sky seemed to shine in a world washed clean. The ship sailed steadily at eight knots to a breeze from the south-west, its prow cutting majestically through the waves. Even the sun, though warm, was not torturous, the breeze cooling the deck where Mary lay sprawled over a barrel in preparation for 'the Botany Bay dozen' – that is, twenty-five strokes of the lash. Potbottom stood over her wielding the dreaded cat. He was so tiny that the lash, with its three knotted leather straps attached to a wooden handle, seemed too big in his hand.

That he should have been allocated such a task was unusual in the extreme. Had such a need befallen a male convict ship there would have been some person skilled in the use of the whip. But flogging was exceptionally rare on female convict ships, and no such expert existed on the *Destiny II*.

While Potbottom gleefully held on to the whip handle with both hands, he was not himself sure quite how it should be used for maximum effect, so he slapped it down upon the deck at his feet to get the hang and angle of its correct use.

Meanwhile Joshua Smiles produced from the pockets of his top coat the two small knee cushions, 'Jesus' and 'Saves', which he had carefully strapped to his legs so that the two words embroidered in red against a white canvas background might be clearly seen by all. With his back turned to Mary and his eyes fastened upon the topgallant sail, he kneeled upon the deck, having first respectfully removed his top hat and placed it beside him.

Potbottom, the awkward whip in hand, observing the surgeon-superintendent to clasp his hands in prayer and then, no doubt by pre-arrangement, to briefly nod, brought the lash up above his shoulders and hard down upon Mary's back.

'Oh merciful God forgive this poor wretch her transgressions,' Joshua Smiles loudly intoned, his voice directed upwards at the topgallant sail.

He paused after delivering this single sentiment, then once more nodded. Whereupon Potbottom again wielded the lash.

'Oh Lord Jesus may she repent her sins and accept your merciful forgiveness!'

Pause, nod and Potbottom's lash came down a third time. Thin welts like the beginnings of a spider's web now began to rise on Mary's back.

Thus the prayers, the nods and the whipping continued until the twenty-five strokes were completed. Mary's back was now bleeding profusely and covered with ugly welts, much to the satisfaction of Potbottom.

Many of the convict women were weeping as Mary was lifted to her feet and the gag removed from her lips. Sobbing and sniffing, both her eyes still ringed purple from the beating she'd taken, her clawed and withered hands clasped to her trembling breast, Mary was in all appearance a most forlorn and heart-rending sight.

Witnessing her misery and dejection the convicts increased the volume of their weeping. Mary was pushed back on to her knees and the prison matron stepped up to her and commenced to crop Mary's hair close to her scalp. The soft, pale hair fell to the deck, where a sudden zephyr blew it about and then carried it out to sea.

When this initial cropping was completed a bowl of soapy water was produced by one of the prison assistants, who proceeded to lather the hair remaining on Mary's head. The matron then exchanged her scissors for a cut-throat razor and shaved Mary's head, the uncaring blade removing the crusted scabs where her hair had been previously yanked out from her scalp, so that the blood, turned pink with the foamy lather, ran down Mary's face and neck.

The howling of the convict women increased in intensity and, while prison guards drew closer with their truncheons at the ready, Potbottom jumped and skipped beside them, bringing the lash down upon the deck as a gleeful warning to any who would promote a further mischief.

Mary was taken to the hospital and made to wash. Her uniform was stripped from her and she was given an old and tattered garment to wear. It had been washed soft, ready to be used as a rag, and so brought some comfort to her burning back. When her blood-stained uniform was returned to the mess a quarrel broke out among the whores, each of whom wanted to wash and repair it. Mary was then taken to the coal hole, the darkest and gloomiest part of the ship, where she was locked up with the supply of coal used in the vessel's kitchens.

There is nothing as destructive to the mind as complete darkness and silence. If there be a hell then eternal fire would come but a poor second to an eternity filled with complete solitude, for humans are gregarious creatures, in the main, and not designed to be alone. Soon the will to live breaks down and the mind ceases to see things rational and coherent; instead, nightmares grow out of a darkness populated with beasts and demons and hob-goblins with sharpened teeth and long treacherous claws.

It was most fortunate therefore that a prison guard, bringing

Mary's ration of water and ship's biscuit, took pity on her and agreed to bring her abacus to her. Had it not been for this, the week spent in the coal hole might well have robbed Mary of her sanity. In the pitch darkness she would work the beads until her fingers were raw. Her mind grew to memorise the numbers of red and black upon the wire rails, and she spent hours making the most bizarre calculations to keep her mental condition sharp. She knew the height and width and circumference of the dome of St Paul's, and worked out the number of bricks it would have taken to build it. She knew the width and the length of the Mall and estimated the size of a single cobblestone, whereupon she worked out the number of these contained in the entirety of this regal way. It was with this kind of foolishness that she remained fully possessed of her wits in the darkness and silence of the dreadful hole into which she had been cast.

Sometimes Mary's hands became too painful and she was forced to leave her abacus alone. When she did so, her mind became filled with the spectre of Tiberias Potbottom, who now possessed her luck.

Mary was philosophical about the fifteen gold sovereigns he had stolen from her, but this was not the case with the medal. Potbottom's wearing of Ikey's talisman was an abomination. The usurping of her future luck was not a robbery but a snatching of her very soul. The legend inscribed upon it, '*I shall never surrender*', was a determination she now regarded as endowed to her along with the luck it possessed. Mary told herself that without this talisman, her life upon the Fatal Shore was most surely doomed. She had convinced herself that without the determination it engendered and the luck it brought as a consequence she would be helpless. It also concerned her that in wearing the medal, Potbottom's own determination, the very power and potency of his evil, was greatly enhanced.

Mary truly believed that what had befallen her on board ship was simply a continuation of her previous life. The *Destiny II* was still in her mind English territory, thus resulting in English circumstance. The luck Ikey's talisman contained was hers for a foreign land and remained Ikey's until she reached her destination. Lying in the darkness of the coal hole, Mary became obsessed with the urgency of retrieving the medal, for while Potbottom wore it about his neck, Ikey, wherever he might be, went unprotected.

Furthermore, if she arrived in Hobart without the blessing of the golden charm, she would have no reason to live, her dreadful fate having been already sealed.

Mary had a naturally observant nature and now as she lay in the dark she tried to think of all the daily movements of Potbottom about the ship. She earnestly contemplated his habits, those small things which appeared consistent in his daily routine. Alas, she found that, in contrast to his master, he was most gregarious, seldom alone or still for one minute at a time and not at all consistent. At muster, in the hospital or during bloody pusover he was always amidst a group and the centre of attention. Into this daily routine Mary silently followed Potbottom in her mind, but never could she discover a time when he was on his own.

And then she remembered that during her two days in the prison hospital the hatch was unlocked an hour earlier than that of the prison itself to allow Potbottom to enter. It was his habit to send the convict night assistant and the hospital assistant up on board while, on behalf of the surgeon-superintendent, he made an inventory of the medication in the small dispensary.

In fact, although this could not be known to Mary, what he was occupied in doing each morning was removing and packing the physic and medication prescribed and written in the ledger at the previous day's sick call or at the weekly bloody pusover. He would carefully remove from the dispensary the amounts prescribed for each treatment in the surgeon's ledger, packing the unused medicine into a small leather portmanteau. Then he would repair to his cabin where the contents of the case would be added, each medication to its own type, to the stock already accumulated on the voyage.

This contraband medicine, intended for the sick on board, would eventually be sold for a most handsome profit when the ship berthed in Rio de Janeiro. Potbottom also saw to it that some small part of the profit was paid to the hospital matron, a professed Christian, who had a most remarkable propensity to see no evil when to be blind was to her benefit.

It was a foolproof method, for when the medical supplies remaining were checked by the authorities in Hobart Town against the surgeon-superintendent's prescription ledger and subtracted from the amount placed on board at the port of embarkation, the amounts would tally perfectly. If any convict should complain to the authorities that she had not received medication for an illness, the hospital matron would swear that this was a lie. Furthermore, if a member of the crew or prison staff required attention while on board they would be treated most generously with whatever physic was required, so that they would readily testify to the probity of the ship's surgeon and the diligence of its hospital matron.

The dispensary was situated in a small cabin behind a bulkhead at the end of the hospital and Mary, while recovering from the attack on her in the prison, had observed that Potbottom entered it alone each morning, leaving the door slightly ajar. He worked there unobserved and, at the same time, allowed sufficient air into the tiny room which lacked a porthole of its own.

Mary tried to recall every detail of Potbottom's early morning entry. He had never spoken, which was unusual, for his busy cackle was as much a part of him as his quick, nervous movements. He was a prattler of exceptional talent. Yet he would enter the hospital silently and, Mary now realised, in a most agitated state fumble the key into the lock of the dispensary as though he were on a most urgent mission.

However, when some time later he emerged he would be his usual vile self, cackling and quick-tongued, small cruel eyes sparkling as he stood at her berth to say something unpleasant. He would leave the hospital in a fine mood, delighted with himself, eager to embrace the task of making those around him afraid of the consequences of doing anything which might displease him.

Mary's berth had been almost beside the door of the dispensary and on the second morning in hospital Potbottom had entered in an even more agitated state than usual. His arms were clasped tightly across his chest and he shivered as though he were very cold. His tiny claws scratched with great irritation at the topmost part of his arms. Mary observed that his lips were cracked and without colour, a thin line of white spit bubbles stretching the length of his mouth. Feigning sleep, she watched as his hands fumbled to unlock the door to the dispensary. In his haste to enter he left the door somewhat more ajar than usual, and by craning her neck Mary could see into the tiny cupboard-sized cabin.

Potbottom, his hands trembling, quickly mixed an amount of raw opium in a small glass container into which he poured what looked to be a syrup from its distinctive blue bottle. Mary was most familiar with opium, it having come close in the past to taking her life. The syrup she took to be laudanum, a mixture of opium dissolved in alcohol, used by prostitutes on the way down. Only those most heavily addicted would think to use more opium in their laudanum, as she herself had done in that darkest time of her life.

Mary watched as the surgeon's assistant hastily swallowed the liquid and then waited, with eyes closed, for it to hit. She knew exactly how he felt. The jangled nerves suddenly straightened, the tension relaxed and his mind and thoughts once more collected. The muscles of his arms and legs no longer jumped and as his craving body received the devil's tonic the dreadful itching under his skin mercifully melted away.

Mary knew at once that Tiberias Potbottom was a helpless victim of the oriental poppy and, judging from the amount of opium grains he'd mixed with the laudanum, he was greatly dependent upon its effects and well accustomed to its constant use.

As Mary lay in the darkness of the coal hole a plan slowly began to emerge in her mind. She prayed that some small part of all her future luck, the golden luck which now dangled around the little monkey's scrawny neck, might be granted to her on credit. Her prayers were directed at whomsoever cared to hear them, whether God or the devil, she didn't much care.

After her flogging and the week spent in isolation, Mary became the subject of great admiration among the convict women. They had greatly missed Mary reading to them in the hot afternoons and the wry and cryptic comments she made about many of the morally uplifting books the Quakers had so generously supplied. Mary's readings of faraway places and of great journeys undertaken allowed for pictures to grow in their minds. And when she read of the lives of great men, for there were no biographies of women, the prisoners felt as though they too were a part of the grand story of the human race and not merely the scum and sweepings of a society which had rejected them. The children on board would clamour around her the moment she was free from her work, plucking at her skirt. 'Please, Mistress Mary, a story!' they would beg, pestering her until she would relent and gather them around her in a corner of the deck and read to them from *Gulliver's Travels* or from the books left for children by the Quakers.

Mary would also sometimes talk of the great journey they were themselves making. She would recount it, not as though it were themselves taking part, but as if it had happened to a group of intrepid adventurers cast adrift and sailing at the merciless whim of the winds to the outer reaches of the universe. Mary's story filled them with pride and hope at their own resolve, and told how the women in this strange and magnificent adventure would one day tame a wild land. Their eyes would shine as she envisaged how they would make this wild frontier a safe place for their sons and daughters, who would be free men and women possessed of handsome looks, sturdy of body and mind, prosperous in every circumstance.

Mary had also taken on the task of running the school for those who wished to learn to read and write, and her pupils, including the eleven children on board, had missed her greatly. For while Mary was a strict task mistress, they had almost all progressed and took great confidence from the new light which was beginning to shine within their minds.

Potbottom insisted that Mary still be allocated the most menial of tasks for her morning duties. She persuaded the matron of the prison hospital to allow her to be a cleaner, this being in return for reading religious tracts to the patients for half an hour each day. The matron, Mrs Barnett, readily agreed, as Mary had been prepared to accept the most onerous of tasks, to clean out the water closets and to act as the laundry maid.

Mrs Barnett had no cause to be suspicious as Mary's request was a common one, given that rations for the sick were greatly superior to the food served to the other prisoners and included preserved tinned vegetables and rice. Those prisoners who were fortunate enough to work in the prison hospital would sometimes benefit from the scraps and scrapings left in the pots or on the plates. Or, on a propitious day they might come upon half a mug of beefy broth with golden gobbets of fat swimming on its surface, or a portion of food left by a patient who was too poorly disposed to eat. In contrast to their usual fare, which consisted of salted beef or pork, or a helping of plum pudding, all of which was served with a portion of weevily ship's biscuit, the heavenly taste of an ounce of tender preserved beef, a mouthful of peas or a spoonful of rice gathered a few grains at a time from several plates, was well worth the lowliest task required in the hospital.

Mary soon ingratiated herself with Mrs Barnett, who mistook her beautiful readings of the religious tracts to mean that Mary had seen the light and had herself embraced the Lord. Such was the tenderness of her rendering of the gospel that often those who lay sick in the hospital would weep openly for their sins and beg to be granted God's forgiveness. Mary, who could see no harm in it, would happily grant salvation to those who so earnestly sought it. But when one of her redeemed souls passed away from bronchial pneumonia she worried that her credentials as a Salvationist might not be acceptable at the heavenly portals, and that the poor woman might be sent elsewhere.

Matron Barnett, impressed with Mary's sanctity and often enough herself brought to tears by the readings, soon came to see her in an entirely new light. Mary was taken off cleaning the hospital closets, excused from laundry duties and made a convict assistant to the matron. It required only one small step for Mary to be allowed to be the convict assistant who slept in the prison hospital at night, and this privilege was soon enough granted her by the redoubtable Mrs Barnett. Mary had managed, in the space of four weeks and on the eve of the ship's arrival at the port of Rio, to find herself exactly where she needed to be when Potbottom entered the prison hospital each morning. All she now needed was a few moments access to the dispensary.

The ship lay anchored at sea and then sailed into Rio harbour with the evening tide as the sun set over the magnificent mountains that rose above the bay. The prisoners were allowed a brief glimpse of this paradise before they were sent below, the hatches closed while the jack tars stood with the hawsers and the capstans.

They would stay a week to make repairs and take fresh supplies on board. Of this land of church bells and beautiful dark-skinned people, of bright parrots and macaws and baskets laden with exotic fruit, the hapless convict women would see nothing. They would spend the entire time in the convict prison with the hatches closed.

Fortunately they benefited from excellent beef and fresh vegetables and fruit, in fact all the fruit they could eat, so that Rio became for them a place of fruit. They tasted the exotic mango and the pink-fleshed guava, supped on melons with tiny jet-black pips set into blood-red meat and gorged on papaya, a fruit with a soft, sweet orange flesh that proved most calming and efficacious to constipation and agreeable to the digestion.

At night, across the water, they could hear the drums beating out a rhythm that sent the blood racing and sometimes, if they lay awake late at night, a lone troubadour would come to the dockside and with an instrument resembling a mandolin play love songs in the strange, haunting language of the Portuguese. Playing to the silent ship, his brown naked chest, dark hair and seductive smile, all glimpsed in the moonlight by those who were fortunate enough to have a porthole facing the dockside above their berth, invited them to indulge with him in hot, tropical lovemaking. The convict women allowed that Mary should take her position at the porthole closest to the singer so that she might tell of him in future days, and weave his songs, laughter and the soft, sensuous swinging of his hips into her stories as they journeyed onwards to the hell of Van Diemen's Land. Rio would always remain in Mary's mind as a place of exotic fruit, love songs and of a young man of giant stature and ebony beauty.

On the evening of the final night in Rio, for the *Destiny II* would sail on the morning tide, the captain and surgeon-superintendent were dining ashore with the British consul when the police brought to the ship a cartload of seven sailors who had been gathered from the premises of a notorious brothel on the Rua do Ouvidor. They had been in a fight and from all appearances had received the worst part of it. Their blouses were red with blood from multiple lacerations to their bodies. Potbottom had also gone ashore, ostensibly to sell the prisoners' quilts and handiwork, and was not yet returned to the ship. The only medical authority on board was Mrs Barnett, who was summoned by the officer of the watch and instructed to make the hospital ready. Mrs Barnett called at once for all assistance, which included the convicts who worked in the hospital, and so Mary was called to duty.

The men were in an advanced state of drunkenness having consumed greatly of the local firewater, the deadly *aguardiente*, and had not yet come to their senses or seen how badly lacerated and beaten they were. Great confusion reigned in the hospital as the matron tried to clean away the blood and stitch and dress the stab wounds. Mary too was kept busy as several of the jack tars started to vomit. She was on her hands and knees cleaning up beside the dispensary door when she observed it to be open. Mrs Barnett had rushed in to fetch medication, and in her haste to get back to the injured sailors had left the door ajar.

Mary glanced quickly around to see the whereabouts of the matron and her assistants and, observing that they all had their backs to her, she hurriedly entered the dispensary. The candle the matron had earlier lit was still glowing so she lifted it and quickly found what she wanted, the blue bottle she'd seen Potbottom use. She sniffed it and established immediately that it was laudanum. Mary soon found the pewter box from which the surgeon's assistant had obtained the opium, and she transferred a sufficient quantity into the bottle of laudanum to make a most powerful mixture, in fact twice the strength she'd observed Potbottom make for himself. No more than a minute had elapsed before she was back on her knees cleaning the hospital decking some distance from the dispensary door, only to see Mrs Barnett enter the dispensary, blow out the candle and lock the door. Should the matron's life depend on it, she would have sworn that no person but herself had entered the dispensary.

It took several hours to attend to the wounded men before they were dispatched back to their own apartments on the ship. Mrs Barnett and her hospital assistants were in a state of extreme fatigue and when Mary had made them a cup of tea she bade them goodnight and returned to the prison. The hospital contained no prisoners at that time, as none had been poorly disposed with the ship's arrival in Rio. This meant Mary could not sleep in the hospital, and she dared not ask Mrs Barnett for fear that she might refuse or, worse still, agree and then remember later that Mary had been the only one within the hospital when Potbottom arrived in the morning.

Mary wondered desperately how she might be at hand when Potbottom arrived without causing any suspicion, but could think of no way to bring this about as the prison hatches were opened a full hour after those of the hospital. The solution she chose was simple enough, but fraught with the danger of discovery. She climbed the stairs leading to the hatchway, making sure that the sound of her footsteps on the ladder was clearly audible. At the open hatchway she sat upon the topmost step and quickly removed her boots, whereupon she climbed silently downwards again and into the hospital, concealing herself under one of the berths adjacent to the stairway. After a short while Mary saw the feet of the weary women pass and heard them climb towards the hatchway. Shortly afterward she heard the bolt slide behind them.

In the dark she removed her prisoner's purse from its snug hiding place and took from it the four brass talons which she now fitted, two to each hand. It was nearly dawn and she would have less than two hours to wait until Potbottom arrived at seven to attend to his urgent need for the fruit of the Chinese poppy.

Mary must have dozed off for she awoke to the sound of the bolt being pulled back, and then she heard the slight creak of the hinges as the hatch was pulled upwards. Her heart was suddenly beating so hard that she felt sure Potbottom must hear it as one might a drum on the dockside at Rio de Janeiro. His tiny feet soon scuttled past where she lay and she could hear though not see him fumbling with the key as he unlocked the door to the dispensary. She hadn't long to wait, perhaps no more than two or three minutes, when she heard what sounded like a loud gasp followed shortly thereafter by a dull thud as Potbottom hit the deck.

Mary crawled out from under the berth and crept silently to the dispensary door. Potbottom lay with the top half of his body outside the small room, as though he had turned to leave just as the effects of the opium hit. Mary bent over him and peeled back his eyelids, observing that his pupils had constricted and his dark eyes showed no movement. She shook him several times but he was as limp as a wet mop. Potbottom was unconscious.

Mary rolled Potbottom onto his stomach, being careful to place his head to the side so that he could continue to breathe. Then she removed the talons from her left hand and, lifting his head slightly, she took the chain and medallion from around his neck and clasped it to her bosom. The feel of the precious medallion in her hand was too much to bear, and tears ran from Mary's eyes.

There is something perverse in the nature of humans, stubborn and quite nonsensical to the intelligence, where we will do something impulsive which may culminate in the most dire consequences, but which, at the time, we cannot seem to prevent. It is an action of the heart which temporarily overpowers any recourse to the head.

Mary, her luck restored to her in the form of the Waterloo medallion, had need only to make her escape. Should Potbottom regain consciousness he would have no cause to be suspicious, or even, in the unlikely circumstances that he should be, would have no way of proving that the dosage had been tampered with, without revealing his own addiction. Mary had committed the perfect crime, providing she could escape from the prison hospital unobserved, and conceal herself until morning muster where she could simply join the other women prisoners on deck.

She wiped the tears from her eyes and was about to remove the brass talons from her right hand when she looked down again at Potbottom's unconscious form. All the anger and humiliation he had caused her suddenly coalesced within her breast as though it were a great fist which squeezed her heart. Mary took the remaining talons from her right hand and placed them on the deck beside the body where she'd left the others. Now she rolled Potbottom onto his back, quickly unbuttoned the front of his worn and greasy frock coat and opened it wide, whereupon she rolled him back onto his stomach. She then stripped the sleeves from his limp arms and pulled off the jacket. Mary was panting loudly, both from the effort of manhandling him and from her tremendous fury. She laid the coat aside and pulled the dirty blouse he wore from the top of his breeches and lifted it high over his back and the back of his head. This action completely exposed his back and with it the hump which now seemed larger than when it was concealed beneath his coat. Mary was whimpering as she replaced the talons onto her left hand, and with them she drew a long deep stroke across Potbottom's back, weeping afresh with a volatile mixture of anger, spite and despair. She was doing to someone else what had been so often done to her. Coldly, precisely, she carved twenty-five lines across the surgeon-assistant's hairy back, in a random criss-cross fashion, sparing not even the ugly hump.

'That be your twenty-five lashes back, Tiberias Potbottom! Gawd is not mocked, you 'ear?' Mary laughed, though somewhat hysterically, for she felt no humour in it. 'That be one stroke for every whore aboard and one for me, you cruel bastard! That be *our* Botany Bay dozen!' Panting with the emotional effort, Mary began to weep softly as the anger left, completely spent by her revenge.

After a few moments Mary ceased crying, sensing her own imminent danger. She sniffed and wiped her nose on the sleeve of her smock. She now felt strangely calm and pulled Potbottom's blouse down over his back, tucking the ends neatly into his broad leather belt. Bright crimson designs of a random pattern seeped through the dirty cloth.

Mary could feel the ship moving as she lifted Potbottom to a seated position so that he was propped against a berth. She then calmly returned his jacket to his person, buttoning it up as before and adjusting his neckerchief, whereupon she laid him back with his broken little buckled boots placed within the door of the dispensary. The remainder of his body was lying within the main cabin of the hospital. Then she took the bottle in which she'd mixed the opium and the laudanum and emptied what remained of its contents in the slop bucket and, stepping over her victim, returned it to the shelf in the dispensary. Mary then quickly checked that Potbottom was still breathing and, gathering up the two remaining talons, left by climbing up through the open hatchway onto the deck, where she threw the vicious brass claws over the side.

The rising sun caught the small brass objects and for a moment the wicked claws winked and then fell into the trough of a wave. It was a small enough thing to do and some might say Mary was simply destroying the evidence of her perfidy, but this was not the case. With the dreaded hooks went the past, that hard dark passage of time which was not of Mary's making. Ahead lay another life. And though Mary would enter her new land in captivity, she felt herself to be free at last.

The *Destiny II* had reached the entrance to the harbour between Fort San Juan and Fort Santa Cruz, so that the crew's attention was to the foredeck looking out to sea. With the prisoners still below decks, there was no one to observe her as she moved aft.

Mary moved rapidly to the stern of the vessel and up onto the poop deck where, as soon as the vessel was safely out to sea, morning muster would take place. She squeezed behind two barrels lashed to the deck and crouched there. High above her a flock of macaw parrots flew across from the headland, their brilliant plumage flashing in the early morning sun. Mary could see the high peak of the Sugar Loaf above the sweep of the bay and the dark green jungle which grew upon its slopes and almost to the pinnacle of the great mountain. She would always remember the immense height of the tropical sky and its infinite blueness so much sharper, brighter, fiercer than the English sky.

Potbottom was not missed at morning muster, for it was not unknown for him to be absent. But he would always surface later when sick call was made directly after muster, and those prisoners hoping to escape for a few days of improved rations remained behind on the poop deck endeavouring to persuade Mrs Barnett, or even the ship's surgeon, that they were right poorly disposed.

On the morning of sailing from Rio, Joshua Smiles had himself attended the sick call, and it had been assumed that Potbottom must have returned from ashore in the early hours of the morning and was still abed. But when the surgeon-superintendent asked for him a guard was sent to rouse him from his cabin.

However, before the guard could return one of the hospital assistants came up to the poop deck and from her demeanour she was seen to be most distressed. She went directly to Mrs Barnett, but because the surgeon was busy with his ear to the chest of one of the convict women the matron hushed her attempt to talk by placing a finger to her lips. When Joshua Smiles withdrew his ear the assistant, a rather fat young girl with an ugly pock-marked face, was wringing her hands and blurted out.

'Mr Smiles, excuse I, sir, Mr Potbottom be dead on 'ospital floor!'

It took several hours before Tiberias Potbottom regained consciousness. In truth he had been conscious a full hour before he allowed that this be known. By which time he was aware both from the pain and from the talk about him, of the mutilated condition of his back.

Joshua Smiles, more pale than usual and in a state of considerable distress, sat beside him praying, imploring the Lord Jesus to save his precious and diligent servant. By the time Potbottom was prepared to squeeze the hand of his mentor, to indicate his return to life, he had well grasped the nature of his own dilemma, and had concocted a story which explained his situation in the dispensary. This took several hours to emerge and came out in half-coherent snatches, whether due to his latent condition or a deliberate ploy is not known. By the end of that day he told a story of having been given some strange draught. 'In one o' them *bodegas* what they's got and where I stopped to partake o' a bowl o' the strong black coffee what they serves with the juice o' the cane plant.'

'Mescaline!' Joshua Smiles announced triumphantly. 'The juice from cacti, a most stupefying narcotic. They put mescaline in your coffee!'

'That be dead right, Mr Smiles, sir!' Potbottom exclaimed, delighted to have a name to add to his plot. 'Mescaleen eh? That be for sure as I were not aware o' what befell me after, save to know that me purse be stolen and a valuable gold chain and medal were taken from about me neck. Though how this came about I truly cannot say, I awoke in me own cabin in the early part o' the mornin' not knowing how I got to the ship and with me head poundin' something horrible and feelin' in every part a great discomfort.'

'And the lacerations to your back, can you perchance venture as to how they happened?' the surgeon asked.

'That I can't, sir. How it come about I haven't the slightest knowledge of,' Potbottom replied and then continued where he'd left off. 'But I looks at me watch what I had the good sense to leave aboard and sees it be time for me to attend dispensary.' Potbottom looked up beguilingly. 'As is o' course me daily duty and one which I takes most conscientiously.'

'Indeed, we are all most grateful for your diligence, Mr Potbottom,' Mrs Barnett said.

Potbottom ignored her remark and continued. 'I makes me way to the hospital when I perceived me back were hurtin' somethin' horrible, so I goes to make a physic of anodyne for the pain, like.' He looked soulful. 'That be all I remembers, nothin' more till I feels your blessed hand in mine,' Potbottom choked back a tear, 'and hears your generous prayers to the Almighty for me safe recovery, sir.'

'God has been good, Mr Potbottom. He has restored you to us to continue your good works among the heathen and the rapscallions.' Joshua Smiles paused and slowly shook his head and a small smile played upon his lips. 'We are all mightily blessed by His glory and compassion.'

He clasped his hands together and, looking up at the bulkhead as though the Almighty could be clearly seen seated upon its heavy cross beam, commenced to pray loudly and fervently, giving thanks for the recovery of God's most precious child, Tiberias Potbottom.

Mary's luck had held. Potbottom, whatever he thought, could make no open enquiries as to his misadventure for fear that his addiction to opium be discovered. While he subjected Mary to a great deal more persecution, confiscating her twice weekly ration of port and sending her back to work in the prison closets and to scrubbing and holystoning the interior of the prison and the decks, he could find no way of proving that she was the one who had brought about his undoing.

At each subsequent bloody pusover he had subjected Mary to the indignity of a front and rear inspection, though he was unable to discover the whereabouts of the chain and medallion. Once, when he had undertaken a surprise medical inspection, he had found her prisoner's purse and confiscated it only to find it disappointingly empty.

In fact, Mary had removed the sole of her boot, hollowed it out and placed her precious luck within it. She wore her boots all day and at night, as was the habit of the prisoners, she tied them about her neck so that they would not be stolen.

Weeks of great tedium passed as the *Destiny II* neared her destination, the tiny ship often climbing to the crest of waves that saw it half a hundred feet above the level of the ocean, and then sinking into the trough of a great wave where the ocean rose to the height of the topmast. The great swells of the Indian Ocean caused many to return to their previous sea sickness, but they were fortunate that they did not encounter a great storm at sea.

Of the trip, it can be said that it was not remarkable but typical of any other transport carrying female convicts. Two prisoners had died, an aged woman who was said to have a condition of the heart and an infant only just weaned, who had come aboard with bronchial pneumonia. They were most ceremoniously buried at sea with a consideration they had not known in their mortal lives.

Perhaps the one thing that might be said to have been remarkable about the voyage was the schooling Mary had given during the hot afternoons. Though schooling was encouraged on convict ships, it was usually conducted by an educated free passenger or the surgeon-superintendent. It achieved good, though often somewhat dubious, results, for the art of reading was often construed as having been achieved when a prisoner could recite a psalm while holding the Bible and appearing to be reading from it.

Mary's teaching was different, for she taught the rudiments of writing as well as reading, insisting on phonetics until her pupils could identify each letter with a sound and connect them with another to make a word. By the time they had reached their destination, fifty-five of the one hundred and twenty-six female prisoners who had come on board without a knowledge of reading would disembark with an ability to read individual words from a page and connect them aloud and continuously to make sense. Though this was done slowly and often with great movement of their lips and expostulations of breath, it was nevertheless the precious gift of the printed word.

Thus Mary, though the surgeon's report would place her in a most reprehensible light, was regarded by the female prisoners as a person of goodness, the best most of them had encountered in all of their unfortunate lives, while the children openly loved her. She was not the sort of pious personage they had been accustomed to regard as a saint, some creature whom they might have seen within the configurations of a stained glass window, with an aura about her head, clad in a diaphanous gown with her feet floating above the ground. Or some curate's daughter who saw her cunny only as an affliction and a shame and not as a delight. Nor did she resemble, in the least, the Quakers of the Ladies' Committee.

Mary was like themselves, hardened by the vicissitudes of a poverty-stricken life, though unlike themselves, not beaten by it. She was a woman who spoke her mind, had a tongue as harsh and foul as many, but who could not be easily led and who intuitively knew her own mind at all times. She could laugh and cry with the best of them and, most importantly of all, she showed that she believed in them.

Mary had demanded their attention at learning and had done so with a mixture of patience, encouragement, mockery, harsh words and foul language. The stories she read to them over the long, hot afternoons had opened their minds. And her great spoken story of their own voyage across the seas to the furthest ends of the earth had given them hope for the future. The women would be eternally grateful to Mary for bringing light into their lives where before there was only ignorance and darkness.

On their last night at sea Ann Gower called all to attention in the prison. 'We 'as one last duty to perform afore we goes ashore termorra, ladies!' Ann Gower shouted. 'Would ya be kind enough to be upstandin', then!' The women climbed from their berths and stood jam packed within the corridor, smiling and nudging each other for what they knew was about to happen.

'Afore we goes to Gawd knows where in the mornin' we 'as a

crownin' to do!' Ann Gower then produced a crown made from paper mashed with flour, covered most decorously in cloth sewn about with small, diamond-shaped patches for the rich jewels. It was embroidered with tiny flowers, bluebells and crocus, daisy and honeysuckle, garlands of cottage roses and all the flowers of England. Many loving hands had worked on the crown in secrecy and with great skill to fashion it quite perfectly.

Ann Gower held the beautiful crown high above her head for all to see and they sighed with the pleasure of their own creation.

'Mary Abacus, we crowns ya 'er Royal 'Ighness, Queen Mary, Queen o' Van Diemen's Land!'

There was much clapping and laughter as Ann Gower placed the crown upon Mary's head. 'Blimey, it don't 'arf grow fast do it?' she said, pointing to Mary's scraggy fair hair, now two inches grown about her head and a most unsightly thing to behold. 'Soon be able to braid that ya will, honest!'

She looked about her and shouted once again, 'Never were a crown what was better deserved to an 'ead!' There was a roar of approval from the prisoners and Ann Gower waited for it to die down before addressing Mary.

'One question please, yer most gracious majesty! 'Ow come Potbottom got twenty-five beautiful, deep an' permanent stripes upon 'is back? Be it a coincidence that it be the same number as there is whores on board plus countin' yer good self?'

There was a loud gasp from the surrounding women, and then an excited murmur.

'Shush!' Ann Gower called and waited for the excitement of this new speculation to die down. 'Be it also a coincidence that you was called from the prison to do duty in the 'ospital that very night and that we knows about yer talons o' brass?'

There was a hush as everyone waited for Mary to answer. She was silent for a good while, the beautiful crown resting on her head. Then she looked up and her lovely green eyes seemed to dance with the mischief of her thoughts. 'I can't say as I knows and I can't say as I doesn't know, it be a secret, Ann Gower.' She paused and then gave a little laugh. 'A royal secret what's treason to tell about!'

There was much laughter and banter at this reply and Mary had never felt as loved or wanted. She knew herself to be a leader and now she also knew she had the courage to demand from life more than she had hitherto been given. She looked at the women surrounding her; like them, she was going into a new life and fate would play its hand, but she was different from them too. She would make her own luck, for she had seen the distant shore not as a place of servitude, but as a conquest, a place to be taken with a full heart, where the shadows of the past were leached out by a brighter sun. She would live under a higher sky washed a more brilliant blue, a heaven against which green parrots flashed like emeralds. She could make something of this place. Tomorrow, when the *Destiny II* sailed the last leg of the voyage up the Derwent River and she went ashore in irons with Ann Gower, she would wear Ikey's Waterloo medallion about her neck. For she knew, whatever happened to her, she would survive, the words '*I shall never surrender*' inscribed not only on Ikey's medal, but forever on her heart. They would bring Mary Abacus to a new and astonishing beginning upon the Fatal Shore.

BOOK TWO

VAN DIEMEN'S LAND

Chapter Nineteen

The *Destiny II* lay at anchor in the D'Entrecasteaux Channel waiting for the morning tide to take it up river to Hobart Town. They had lain at anchor during the night, for the often shallow and treacherous channel waters, even though they appeared calm under the bright moon, were not to be embarked upon beyond sunset.

The morning was a smoky colour with a thin mist shrouding the surface of the water, and the prisoners, gathered on deck for muster, clasped their arms about their chests against the cold. They had been roused at dawn with the familiar 'Rouse out there! Turn out! Turn out! Huzza huzza!' and the words new to their ears resounded through the boat: 'Goin' ashore, huzza for the shore!' This was the last muster of the voyage and the cold could do nothing to conceal their excitement.

On the starboard side the Black Rocks and the cliffs of Bruny Island appeared most forbidding and their uninviting nature seemed to pervade the leaden-coloured landscape on either side of the ship. But when the sun came up not much past the hour of six, the sky was soon a clean high blue, somewhat darker than the tropical skies they'd grown accustomed to, and colder, a touch of ice in its high dome. The incoming tide was beginning to slap at the stern of the *Destiny II* when Joshua Smiles, with the ever-present Potbottom at his side, stood to address the female prisoners.

Smiles constantly rubbed his palms down the front of his frock coat, avoiding direct eye contact with any of the prisoners. From his coat he produced a tiny square of paper folded many times upon itself, which he commenced to unfold in a slow and tentative manner, each corner lifted as if he expected the words to leap off the paper and harm him. The women in the front row observing him at this silly task began to giggle. Finally, with the page fully opened, he began to read in a most lugubrious voice.

'I, Joshua Templeton Smiles, surgeon-superintendent of the prisoner ship *Destiny II*, do on this 18th day of October in the year of our Lord 1827 declare . . .' He glanced up from the page, his height enabling him to look over the heads of the assembled convicts towards an unseen Hobart thirty miles away. Then he slowly brought his eyes back to the pages held in his fist. '. . . that with the notable exception of a handful of refractory and turbulent spirits you have behaved well and I have marked your reports accordingly.' He paused again and cleared his throat. 'But for two prisoners who have shown themselves to be profligate wretches and designing blasphemous whores throughout this voyage.' Pleased to have surmounted this last statement he continued more slowly. 'I have therefore made recommendation to His Excellency Colonel Arthur, lieutenant governor of Van Diemen's Land, that with the exception of these two prisoners, you all be placed into service with the families of settlers as soon as this may be conveniently arranged.'

There was a collective gasp and then a swelling murmur of excitement among the female convicts, who had not known what to expect upon arrival but who had, as is usually the case, feared the worst rumours circulated on board during the voyage. Many of the convicts had worked as domestic servants in England and saw this arrangement as ideal, their immediate hope being that they might attract a considerate and kind master.

'Those two prisoners who will not be granted this privilege will be conveyed in light irons to the Female Factory where their vile natures and ardour of their blasphemous utterances might be cooled to a more silent, pleasing and obedient temperature. These two wretches, who Mr Potbottom informs me are well acquainted to you all as trouble makers, will *not* be granted the privilege of remaining on deck to witness our arrival, nor allowed to be present at the governor's inspection, but will be placed instead in the coal hole as a final gesture of our Christian contempt!'

'I am not mocked saith the Lord,' Potbottom shouted gleefully, 'Mary Habacus and Ann Gower now step you forward at once!'

A flock of bright green parrots flew over the ship calling raucously as though in a mocking welcome. Mary, determined to show no emotion, watched as the rising sun caught the gloss on the wings of the beautiful birds as they drew away from the ship.

She had seen a flock of parrots fly overhead as they sailed out of Rio de Janeiro. Now here they were again. Mary smiled as Ann Gower came up to her. Then she opened her arms and embraced her, the smaller woman holding the much larger one clasped to her thin chest.

Mary looked over Ann Gower's shoulder at Joshua Smiles and to her own surprise she heard herself say, 'Hear you, Joshua Smiles, we are the women o' this new land! You cannot defeat us, because we will never again surrender to the sanctimonious tyranny o' your kind!' She paused momentarily and pointed her crooked finger at the surgeon-superintendent. 'Gawd is not mocked!'

It was late into the afternoon when the hatch to the coal hole was opened and Mary and Ann Gower were allowed to emerge onto the deck. Their eyes, grown accustomed to the pitch darkness, were at first blinded by the brightness of the afternoon light.

The *Destiny II* had anchored late in the morning in Sullivan's Cove and the last of the prisoners were being cleared to disembark. Now as Mary and Ann Gower stood on the deck they observed a town of quite harmonious appearance. Built on the water's edge and rising steeply back from the Government Wharf, Hobart contained many well constructed buildings of stone and brick, and its streets were straight and broad. Several large native trees, saved from the builder's axe, gave the town an appearance of permanence which belied its recent development.

It was then that Mary, her eyes adjusted to the spring sunshine, glanced well beyond the waterfront to where Hobart Town climbed upon an even steeper slope, and saw the mountain. It rose into the ice-blue sky fully four thousand feet above her, its great rounded dome covered in late snow.

Mary gasped, bringing her hand to her chest, her heart pounding. This morning she had seen the parrots fly over her head and now, as in Rio de Janeiro, she had been given the gift of the great mountain. 'It all begins now, with the green birds and the magic mountain,' she whispered to herself. 'The luck begins for me. Whatever may follow, I swear I shall never knowingly surrender it again.' As if it was a catechism, she repeated the words on the Waterloo medal, 'I shall never surrender'.

What followed was a most tedious induction by the muster master, who sat at a table further along the deck, a canvas canopy having been built above his bald head to keep the sun at bay. He was in a most churlish mood, having been at his task several hours, and snapped at the two convicts to step forward.

Each in turn was made to stand before him while he completed their records. They were fortunate to have missed the visit on board by the lieutenant-governor, for it proved a tedious and longwinded occasion. The prisoners had been paraded on board and made to stand a full hour on deck before the great man, seated on a handsome black stallion, arrived at the Government Wharf. Colonel George Arthur dismounted to a short, sharp roll from a kettle drum and a salute by a platoon of troopers in scarlet jackets. Ignoring the large crowd, he stepped into a longboat where he stood upright in a stiff military manner as he was rowed to the vessel.

Once on board he lost no time with pleasantries, nodding brusquely at the master and officers and grunting, 'Well done!' Then turning to Joshua Smiles he shook his hand in a cursory manner, acknowledging him with the single word, 'Surgeon!' This may well have been a deliberate attempt to exert his authority for Colonel George Arthur was short in stature and came not much beyond the belt of the surgeon-superintendent. Although his exceedingly short legs did not hinder him in a frock coat, whenever he appeared in full vice-regal uniform or in a military deck-out his sword would drag along the ground as he walked. He was a man of rigid formality who would not entertain the possibility of a sword trimmed to less than regulation size, and so he always inspected his troops on horseback, selecting a large and fiery stallion for this purpose.

The governor tucked his small hands beneath the tail of his deep blue frock coat and commenced to stride up and down the assembled ranks of convicts.

'The hearts of every man and woman are desperately wicked and there is but one means of salvation, this be to have faith in the

Lord and in Christ's crucifixion! You will attend church regularly and twice on Sunday, that is an order!'

All his entreaties and warnings were completed crisply and without prevarication, enumerating in exact detail what he regarded as both good and bad behaviour and giving a dozen examples of each. The ultimate result of good behaviour was the prospect of an early ticket of leave; of bad, the certain demise of the repeatedly offending prisoner.

Suddenly, Arthur stopped pacing and pointed across the narrow strip of water separating the ship from the shore, to beyond the crowds waiting on the wharf, and further still to some point imagined on the steep road leading up the hill.

'As you come ashore on the way to the Female Factory you will pass a gibbet. There you will observe that the two corpses which hang from it are male. We have not yet on this island hanged a woman by the neck, but that is not to say we cannot.' The governor paused for the effects of his words to sink in. 'I implore you all to look well how they hang and to take great care to ensure that your destiny upon this island does not converge with that of these two unfortunate wretches.' Colonel Arthur pulled himself to his full stature. 'I will have you know that since I assumed this office, fully one hundred and fifty prisoners have been capitally convicted and executed! I tell you now, I am a fair man, but there is no mercy for those who will not observe the spirit and the letter of the law in its most infinite detail!' Colonel Arthur cast a cold eye over the prisoners. 'Do not disappoint me, for I warn you, I am not a man who takes well to disappointment!'

Now, several hours after the governor had departed, Mary and Ann Gower were subjected to a most thorough interrogation by the muster master, no doubt occasioned by his fear of the governor himself. He was a small, balding, bespectacled man of a most pernickety clerical appearance with an abundance of grey hair sprouting from his ears, who scratched the answers to his sharp and practised questions in a large black book which bore upon its gold-embossed cover the title: *Conduct Register*.

It was this book which ruled the lives of every prisoner on the island and from whence came the expression, '*I am in his black books*', to mean that things do not go well for someone.

Colonel Arthur fervently believed that every convict should be strictly accounted for and that the course of their lives, from the day of a prisoner's landing to that of their emancipation or death, should be written down. It was necessary therefore that every particular concerning a convict should be registered on their day of arrival and before they were taken ashore.

Mary's description was accordingly written down: *Light straw coloured hair, green eyes – placed wide apart, scar on left cheek, brow high, hands badly deformed – black/blue in colour, height 5 feet and 2 inches, skin fair, face clear – no pox pitting, comely in appearance.*

Next followed details on her crime and the events surrounding it, her non-marital status, date and place of birth, trade, next of kin and religion. Mary's literacy and numeracy were noted and both these tested and a sample of her handwriting added to the records. At the conclusion of her writing and numeracy test the muster master had said not unkindly, 'I 'ope you be'aves yourself, Prisoner Abacus. Orphans' school be most pleased to 'ave you, they would.'

'Orphan school?' Mary said, suddenly alert. 'There be a school 'ere for brats what's not owned?'

'Wesleyans, not Church of England. Don't know that much teachin' be done, though. I could put in a word?' He paused and then added, 'Got any,' he coughed lightly and grinned, 'gold . . . a sovereign perhaps?'

Mary sighed, 'Blimey! For a moment there I thought you was all 'eart, sir!'

The muster master shook his head, 'No 'eart to be found in these parts, only money! All the 'eart you wants if you can pay for it!' He cleared his throat and pursed his lips, suddenly conscious of his position, then he resumed writing.

'Be there a library, sir?' Mary asked.

The muster master looked up over the top of his spectacles. 'Mrs Deane runs the Circulating Library, books to hire. There's no books for convicts though, Mrs Deane don't 'ave no dealings with convicts.'

At the conclusion of the interrogation Mary was allocated a police number. Being kindly disposed to numbers she was delighted to find hers was No. 7752. In her mind she immediately converted this to three 7s which she knew to be astonishingly good luck. Abacus, Mary – Female Convict, No. 7752 became, together with the name of her ship, as affixed as her surname for the entire period of Mary's sentence.

Once these preliminaries were completed, Mary and Ann Gower were issued with new clothing. This consisted of a cotton gown of cheap, coarse material, a petticoat, jacket and apron, and a straw bonnet. Large yellow Cs were marked in a prominent place upon each article of clothing, though this was not necessary, the outfit itself bespoke a prisoner as surely as if it had been patterned with arrows. Those possessions they still had on board were taken from them though Mary was careful to conceal Ikey's medal in her prisoner's purse safely tucked away in its usual place. She was able to persuade the prisoner matron to allow her to retain her beloved abacus and her papier mâché crown, but her precious copy of *Gulliver's Travels* was taken from her.

The two women were then placed in light irons and ferried ashore. Here they were met by a lone trooper and marched under guard up Macquarie Street to the Female Factory. On the way they passed the two men hanging from a gibbet, though Mary did not look. Her mind was filled with anticipation of a new land and she did not need so ready a reminder of where she had come from.

'Poor bastards!' Ann Gower spat. 'Looks like nothin' 'as changed.'

'No, Ann, you must see it differently. Everythin' 'as changed for us, everythin'!' Mary said.

The Female Factory was abutted to the male gaol forming a part of it and separated by a twelve foot wall. In all, it consisted of only four rooms. Two sleeping rooms had a total capacity of fifty women, thirty in one and twenty in the other, the sick room could accommodate another nine bodies and the work room another forty. At this point, the Factory was fully accommodated in terms most onerous to the comfortable accommodation of the inmates. With the addition of the women and children from the *Destiny II*, it was crowded almost to the point of suffocation. The prison yard could hold forty prisoners at one time, but could not be used at night for the cold and, besides, was at all times most dreadfully befouled.

Mary and Ann Gower soon found themselves placed without ceremony or further processing, beyond their names being registered, in the larger of the two sleeping rooms which contained fifty of their shipmates, all of whom, it became immediately apparent, were in a high state of excitement. They had been told that they would be assigned and collected the very next day, each to the family of a married settler, where they would work their sentences out as domestic servants, cooks, dairymaids or nursemaids.

As these vocations were to be readily found among their numbers, they had cause to entertain great hopes for a good future. Even those not previously exposed to the particularities of domestic work were confident that they would soon learn the tricks of the trade, having been put to scrubbing, cleaning, sewing and laundry work on board ship.

The women loudly cheered Mary and Ann Gower as they entered, crowding around them and offering their sincerest condolences for the severity of their sentences. But it was apparent that, while both women were greatly admired for their courage, each convict thought herself fortunate not to be sentenced to remain as a refractory prisoner in the Female Factory.

On that first overwhelmingly happy evening ashore, despite the insalubrious environment, the prospect of a good, clean life seemed very possible. Each silently marvelled at the good fortune that had landed her upon the Fatal Shore. They did not yet comprehend that the settler became their absolute master and they his official slaves, a system which openly encouraged the most shocking abuse. The masters of Van Diemen's Land counted few among them who contained a tincture of compassion in their callous and self-serving natures.

The penal system was designed from the beginning to work in three ways, all of which were intended to place the least expense upon the government. The first was to put the responsibility for the care and maintenance of convicts into private hands. This saved money and provided the second advantage, a source of cheap labour for the free settlers who were largely responsible for opening up the land. Finally it was intended to be a useful tool of reform by removing the convict from others of her own kind, separating her from the temptations, bad influences and vices which inevitably flowed from close confinement with her sisters.

In this way it was argued that the convict woman would be given the opportunity to gain self-respect, mend the error of her ways and re-enter society as a sober, God-fearing and useful citizen.

The convict prisoner had no set working hours, was not allowed out at night, must reside in her master's house, could not labour for herself in her free time, if ever such were granted to her, and could not move off the master's property without a pass. She must wear at all times a convict's uniform, though most seemed to find a way around this.

To all this was added the single concession, that a master could not punish his convict servant but had recourse to a magistrate should he have cause for complaint. The prisoner had little redress of her own. Though permitted to give evidence against her master, she was seldom believed unless a free settler was prepared to bear witness for her cause. This was a situation which rarely prevailed, while its converse, brutality and exploitation, was a daily occurrence.

But here too lay a paradox. While *only* magistrates could punish, most officers of the law were in a quandary to know what to do with females who required punishment. Constant and severe punishment as might have been the case in England would have defeated the unwritten reason why women were sent to Van Diemen's Land – to stabilise the colony through marriage and concubinage. It was silently held that the crimes a female committed brought little permanent harm and posed no danger to society, consisting mostly of absconding, being drunk and disorderly, insolence, fighting, refusing to work, being out without a pass after hours, immoral conduct and minor pilfering.

Whereas a male convict might be given two hundred lashes of the cat o' nine until his flesh was flayed from his back for minor offences, a female convict could not be flogged. Under Governor Arthur's rigid system of order, punishment for a crime other than stealing the property of another was seldom physical. Instead, confinement to gaol and hard labour were imposed. This largely consisted of working at the male prisoners' wash tub, or cleaning the prison slop buckets and water closets. If harsher punishment were deemed necessary, a female convict would receive solitary confinement on bread and water for a week, the cropping of her hair, and be placed in the public stocks for an hour or two. For the truly incorrigible, when all of these remedies had failed, an Iron Collar, a device which fitted about the prisoner's neck and weighed seven pounds, was worn for two days to publicly point to the infamy of the wretch who carried it.

These remedies, when compared to the treatment of convict men, were undoubtedly exceedingly mild, especially as it was generally held that the female convict was far more difficult to reform than the male, her general characteristics being immodesty, drunkenness and foul language, though, of course, this was a male assertion and not to be entirely trusted.

While official leniency may have existed for the female of the species, no such thing was true of the unofficial behaviour of men towards women. Van Diemen's Land was a brutal society and violence towards women was so common as to place a female convict, who was thought to be of little worth, in constant jeopardy. Rapes were frequent and brutal bashings of females were as commonplace as a Saturday night tavern fight. Settlers, returning home drunk, would beat their female servants, sometimes crippling or even killing them. The body was usually dumped on the outskirts of Hobart Town and the murder would then simply be explained by reporting the prisoner as missing.

It is doubtful that the less stringent laws Arthur imposed on females were very successful in reforming them. But there was danger enough abroad for any convict woman, and fear of the law was the least of her concerns, nor observance of it likely to make her life any easier. Only the threat of being sent to the interior seemed to have any real effect. No greater fear existed in these city-bred women than that they should find themselves in the wilderness of the interior, where the cruelty of the men who lived as woodcutters in the forests was the subject of many fearful and gruesome tales told in the taverns and the disorderly houses of Hobart Town.

In short then, although Mary's confinement to the Female Factory might have seemed the harsher sentence, assignment to a settler was not the easy ride so fondly imagined by Mary's shipmates.

The moment Mary had heard of the existence of the orphans' school she had determined to gain a post within it as a teacher. The orphans' school housed the children who, shortly after birth, had been separated from their mothers. They were, for the most part, the children of assigned convicts. The women were routinely returned to the Female Factory by their masters, always with the story that the prisoner had been absent without a pass and had become pregnant while whoring. Hobart was full of orphan brats who bore a remarkable resemblance to many a settler's family.

The child would be born at the Factory, which also acted as a maternity hospital, and taken from its mother the moment it was weaned. Arthur considered the female convicts the very last persons to whom children ought to be entrusted. The mother would then be detained in the Female Factory to be punished for her licentious and drunken ways, and after serving her additional sentence either returned to her original master or assigned to another.

The children who had come to the island with their convict mothers and who were not convicts themselves were simply allowed to stay in the Factory with their mothers, as few settlers would entertain the prospect of another mouth to feed. They became wild creatures who wandered about the town and learned to pick pockets, bring in contraband, mostly tobacco and grog, and soon became rapscallions and petty thieves of the worst possible kind. Many of them were hardened criminals before they had reached the age of ten.

Mary would capture the hearts of these prison children with her stories and teach those who would submit to learning to read and write. She would also use them in quite another way, which was to earn her great power and respect among the other female inmates.

Mary was put to work in the prison bakery. This was not brought about by her intelligence or any skill she possessed, but because of her hands. They were thought to be too mutilated to be useful at any of the other tasks, while kneading dough was considered within her limited capacity.

It was a decision which, together with the requirement that Mary work two afternoons a week in the prison allotment, would give the direction to her future life. The allotment, an acre on the slopes of Mount Wellington, was used to grow potatoes, cabbages and some Indian corn, two of these, most fortuitously, being vegetables with a use beyond the platter, though a use not in the least contemplated by the prison officials.

Chapter Twenty

Ikey had eight hundred and thirteen pounds on him. Some of this was the remainder of the money paid to him in Birmingham by Maggie the Colour and Silas Browne, and some furnished by Hannah as a ploy to convince him of her sincerity in aiding his intended escape. It was sufficient to pay his fare to America from Denmark, as well as allowing him to stock up on merchandise likely to be in short supply in the New World.

Ikey, always a dreamer and schemer, saw America as a land of rich pickings for a man of his character and talent. It was his intention to land with a portmanteau stuffed with merchandise to confound the locals.

Alas, this was not to be, the prices for these articles in Denmark being too high at the shopfront and, besides, it was against Ikey's principles to purchase goods which afforded only a small margin of profit. It had not occurred to him that the Danish Jews might not speak Yiddish or contain a Jewish criminal class who would furnish the merchandise he required direct from the fob pockets of the unsuspecting citizenry, and therefore at prices a lot more competitive than those obtainable in wholesale jewellery emporiums.

So Ikey took the first ship he could find bound for New York. Though his hands were empty his head was full of plans for a life lived on the straight and narrow path as a merchant jeweller.

The crossing was rough and utterly miserable. In late February the Atlantic swells were large and frequent gales whipped the tops of the steel-coloured waves into a fury of howling white spray. The small three-masted packet was tossed like a cork seemingly all the way to the mouth of the Hudson River.

On a cold March morning, with dirty islands of late ice still floating on the river, the ship anchored at the immigration wharf at Castle Gardens. By early afternoon Ikey had paid his entry fee, been subjected to a smallpox vaccination and was allowed to step onto the streets of New York as free as an English lark.

It is a part of the human imagination to carry in our minds pictures of places we have heard or read about, pictures which have no substance other than the bricks and mortar of pure speculation. Ikey had expected New York to be a city not unlike London, though perhaps more primitive, for New York too lay on a great river and spoke the English tongue with a strange half-Irish intonation.

As an English Jew Ikey had assumed that he would fit in snugly enough. After all, the Jews of his world were street traders and merchants and of a naturally talkative and friendly disposition with the inclination to congregate together, marry among themselves, and on those several pious occasions such as Passover, Rosh Hashanah and Yom Kippur to share their faith. They would also attend synagogue on the Sabbath as brothers according to the ancient laws of Abraham, the prophets and the rabbinical creed.

Being a Jew, while being a matter of religion and orthodoxy, was also one of temperament. A Jew does not expect any but his own kind to understand him. Being Jewish is not something you wear outwardly like a badge, rather it is something you feel inwardly. It is as if your heart beats to a different cadence. This is as true of the Jew who is a villain as it is of one who is a rabbi. The smell of a chicken soup fart with noodles is absolutely one hundred per cent unmistakably Jewish. If you should be making chicken soup, delicious chicken soup, and you wish to make it Jewish, maybe you could try making these noodles.

Beat two eggs with a bit of pepper and salt. Add flour until it is a stiff paste. Flour a cutting board, then roll out the paste until it is very thin. Allow to dry for two hours. Now cut the dough into strips about three inches long by one inch wide. Stack and cut again into matchlike strips.

*Separate them by tossing, and spread them out to dry.
Then toss them with boiling chicken soup and boil for ten
minutes. Guaranteed to produce first-class farts when
added to chicken soup!*

New York, Ikey told himself, would have its own Rosemary and
Petticoat Lanes, its rookeries with noxious smells and a low-life
similar to St Giles, Whitechapel and Shoreditch, and a population
composed from rags to riches which seemed to live the one on top
of the other. This was the situation in London, Amsterdam and
Hamburg and, in fact, wherever European urban Jews could be
found. A Jew was not a part-time Jew or a sometime Jew or a non-
observing Jew, he was Jewish for the duration of his life. This gave
a wandering Jew a strength and unity he could depend on
wherever he found a congregation of his own people.

Ikey had not stopped to think that being a Jew also made him
accountable to the dictates and rituals of his community. In the
matter of being Jewish he was expected to act in a prescribed
manner, but not necessarily as a good man. In the good man
business, the ritualised and formal nature of the English and
European Jewish code of behaviour had allowed the form to
become more important than the function, Jewishness being more
important than goodness.

Ikey never missed going to the synagogue, where he gained a
reputation for being a devout man and an Israelite without guile. In
the synagogue each has a separate seat with a box where he deposits
his holy books and locks them up until he returns to worship. Ikey
frequently made use of his box for the most unhallowed of purposes,
concealing within it items which if discovered would have sent him
'across the water' several times over.

Yet Ikey was an excellent example of a pious, if not strictly
orthodox, Jew. While he did not observe the dietary laws, mutton
stew followed by a dish of curds being his most frequent repast, he
never worked on the Sabbath. He paid his tithes, contributed to
Jewish charity, took his seat in the synagogue and observed with a
full heart Rosh Hashanah, Passover and Yom Kippur.

Therefore it came as a great surprise to him to find that what
he had always taken for granted was no longer the case in New
York. Being a Jew was none, or very few, of the mystical things
he'd always supposed it to be, nor was it any longer the secret

satisfaction, despite the eternal suffering of the Jews, to be gained from being one of the chosen people.

The New York Jews neglected the Sabbath and many of them were now taking their rest on Sundays without the slightest show of guilt. The lighting of Sabbath candles and the singing of the Sabbath song was seldom practised. Secular learning of a pragmatic nature was regarded as more important than the study of the Torah. Moreover, philosophical thinking, based on the precepts of freedom and emancipation, was being given precedence over rabbinical discussion. The rebbe was not the centre of the universe nor did he settle all the arguments on behalf of Jehovah. The new *Bnai Jeshurun* synagogue on Elm Street contained only a handful of worshippers on any given Sabbath morning.

However, if the loss of the rituals and strictures of orthodoxy defined the American Jews, it did not lead to a corresponding loss of ideals, moral misconduct and social irresponsibility. In all this secular speculation, they had not given up a belief in Jehovah or the responsibility of God's chosen people to behave in a moral and honest way. Instead they rejected meaningless ritual and accepted natural goodness as the central tenet of their faith.

To be a good Jew meant to be a good man. What all this amounted to was that Ikey could no longer hide behind his observance of Jewish ritual while continuing to behave in an altogether reprehensible manner. While he had determined to turn over a new leaf in America, this realisation nevertheless came as a profound shock to him.

Ikey was also astonished to find that New York had few poor Jews and that the Jewish community lived openly in the mid-town area spread on both sides of Broadway. New York contained only five hundred Jewish families. Most were American-born and had formed into a community over the past one hundred and fifty years. There was none of the frantic struggle to gain a foothold in a new society or the clash of contradictory cultures between the immigrant and native-born children. The Jews of New York were an established, sober, moral and well-integrated minority population, most of whom had been in America before the War of Independence. They all seemed to know or be on nodding terms with each other, and had excellent business and social relations with their gentile neighbours.

Ikey had timed his arrival badly, for if he had landed in New York ten years later he would have found some forty thousand

European Jews in New York, and their numbers would continue to grow hugely for the remainder of the century. The dreadful slums, starvation, poverty and crime of the Lower East Side would come to exist as poor Jewish immigrants came to *Goldeneh medina*, 'The Golden country'. Alas, in Yiddish *Goldeneh medina* had a second meaning and was the name also given to a 'fool's paradise', a false gold, bright but worthless.

In this fool's paradise Ikey would have been completely at home. But he was totally at odds with the calm and ordered society he now found himself in, despite his determination to lead a sober and respectable life. Ikey's notoriety had not escaped the notice of the Jews of New York and the tight-knit community immediately closed ranks against him. England's most notorious Jewish criminal was not given a warm welcome. Ikey, despite his apparent wealth and appropriate philanthropy, found himself largely ostracised by his own kind.

Even those contacts to whom he had previously shipped stolen watches and silver objects had conveniently come to see these consignments as having been legitimised by the fact of arriving on American soil. They saw themselves as moral men, albeit practical, who had asked no questions of the origin of the merchandise and so heard no lies, their guilt assuaged.

But while they chose to believe that the stolen merchandise Ikey had sent them had somehow been 'washed' in the Atlantic crossing and thus transformed into honest goods, they were unwilling to accept that, by the act of the same crossing, Ikey had converted from being a criminal to an honest man. They felt morally obliged not to encourage a notorious criminal to establish himself in business in their own city or neighbourhood.

They would not recommend Ikey to wholesalers or to jewellery craftsmen, the greatest majority of whom were Jewish. Diamond merchants would not trade with him and the gold and silversmiths found themselves regrettably short of supplies or lamented that their consignment books were filled with orders beyond their expectations to complete. Despite his offer to pay them in cash, even in gold, their doors were closed to him. The few goods Ikey managed to assemble he sold only to gentiles. His poor selection, together with the used nature of his merchandise, attracted little attention and earned him a reputation not much beyond that of an enterprising pawnbroker.

The only respect Ikey commanded was from the First Manhattan Bank of New York where the manager, wreathed in unctuous smiles, would come out of his office to greet him personally. On the Sabbath, Ikey sat, a stranger in a strange land, alone in the bright new synagogue on Elm Street. The psalms the cantor sung were old, but the feeling of complete and abject loneliness was new.

Ikey had always thought of himself as a loner, a solitary soul who kept his own counsel. In his own eyes, but for his money, he was a worthless person. But now he began to realise that he had lost the human infrastructure, the supporting cast of thieves and shofulmen, card sharps, pimps, whores, actors, street urchins, his Academy of Light Fingers. How he missed the coarse company around a ratting circle, the hustle of Rosemary Lane, the rank humanity of the poor and hopeless, the tinsel and despair of the West End, the pickpockets and swells, beggars and noblemen who made up the street community of his native London.

America was proving completely alien to his past, his talents and to his very demeanour. Ikey's fortune and life had been developed on the mean dark streets and in the chop houses, taverns and thief dens of the grandest and most woebegone city on earth. He was by nature a creature of the night, wrapped in his familiar coat of secret pockets and accustomed to skulking within the dark shadow cast by a flat-topped, wide-brimmed hat.

Now all that had been forsaken for shopkeeping in daylight on Broadway, dressed in a suit of good American broadcloth which constantly scratched and itched. Ikey was a deeply unhappy man, but one determined to redeem himself in the eyes of his fellow Jews in his new country. Ikey was in search of personal redemption, but first he had to save himself from himself. He must separate from Hannah without losing the fortune contained in the Whitechapel safe. Four months after arriving in New York, he sat down to write to his wife in London.

My dear Wife,

America has proved a most pleasant place and the prospects for the advancement of our ambition is most encouraging. With the early summer come to us, at last the climate is most salubrious. You will take kindly to the air and space and the houses are of a solid brown stone and well proportioned. There is a spacious central park with room enough for children to play to their hearts content in safety. It is as though they should find themselves in some country dell. I have opened a jewellery establishment with excellent fittings on Broadway, a location which shows the promise of good trading if goods to the liking of the population can be offered at a price to be afforded. The craftsmen here are not of a sufficient standard to be desired, or of the same quality to be found in London, there being a notable shortage of finely made fashionable jewellery, the Americans being behind in what is of the latest mode in London and Paris. There is here also a great shortage of good watches of the medium quality variety and I beseech you to obtain quantities of the same. I have reason enough to believe I can turn these to good account, though I charge you to send me none but 'righteous' watches and not to touch even one what has been gained 'on the cross'. I shall require these to be of an assortment of nickel plate, sterling silver and gold. I believe these will here obtain up to six times the price of the watches purchased by you on the straight. My greetings to your children.

I am, as ever, your humble husband,

Isaac Solomon.

Ikey took care to be cheerful in his letter, though not overly so, for he knew that Hannah might smell a trap, the discussion of cheerful subjects and outcomes not being the usual nature of their conversation together. His mention of children and the park was sufficient to alert her to his desire to have her join him. He also deliberately refrained from sending a money order for the goods, giving her to understand that she should finance the purchase herself for their future mutual benefit. This thought being conveyed with the single sentiment '... *for the advancement of our ambition . . .*' She would receive the letter and see it clearly as a test of her intention to follow him to America, in which case, provided she co-operated with him, he would eventually send her his part of the safe combination.

By using Hannah as his purchasing agent Ikey was putting into place yet another plan. If the wholesale merchants and jewellers in New York would not take his custom then he would import all his merchandise from London. The passage across the Atlantic had been reduced to a little less than a month and the superior craftsmanship of the London and Paris workshops and their lead in the fashions would soon establish him in the forefront of Broadway jewellery establishments. He would deal in only the best merchandise, all of it initially honestly purchased. An evaluation and certificate of authentication would be issued with the more valuable pieces.

Ikey was determined to continue to obtain his merchandise through Hannah and always without payment, forcing her to finance the orders he placed by enclosing a signed I.O.U. for the amount against the time she would arrive in America. He intended this debt to accumulate until it matched half the amount of cash in gold sovereigns which Hannah knew to be contained in the safe of their Whitechapel home. Ikey knew full well that Hannah would not accept his I.O.U.s without knowing them to be covered by his share of the gold coin.

The deposit of thirty thousand pounds in sovereigns was by no means the most valuable part of their joint fortune. Within the safe lay precious stones: diamonds, rubies and emeralds contained within beautiful brooches, pins, necklaces and rings, and a double strand of exquisite South Seas pearls taken from the home of the Duke of Devonshire. There were also several hundred heavy fob chains of eighteen carat gold, a quantity of silver and gold plate and a dozen exquisite jewelled watches with rare movements. Finally, encased within a velvet-lined box and further protected by a chamois leather pouch, a jewelled and enamelled French carriage clock said to have belonged to Louis XIV. These objects, collected over fifteen years of fencing, represented much the greater part of Ikey and Hannah's personal fortune.

However, almost all the pieces were marked goods so particular in character that they dared not be presented in the London market where they would be instantly recognised. Even on the Continent they would need to be most carefully arranged within the world of the demi-monde if they were to escape detection. The best chance by far lay in the American market where new wealth was eager to acquire the trappings of an old culture and families such as the Astors and the Vanderbilts possessed the money to purchase it without asking too many awkward questions.

Hannah did not have the experience to value correctly this merchandise, nor did she have the knowledge to dispose of it discreetly. The precious stones could be removed from their casings and sold separately and the gold chains melted down, but not without a thorough knowledge of how this should be done to prevent the attention of both the underground and the police.

No middleman in the thief kingdom of London had the resources to pay or the foolhardiness to dispose of such a haul in under a year at the least. And even then each stone, if it were not cut into smaller specimens, would need to be entered onto the market with the greatest possible discretion. Therefore the chances of a gem stone of note being discovered and traced back to Hannah was exceedingly great. Indeed, even in America, it would take all of Ikey's considerable skill and the shopfront presented by a thriving and outwardly respectable jewellery establishment on Broadway with a reputation for straight dealing to judiciously dispose of the contents of the safe to the richest of the American gentiles.

In his subsequent letters Ikey decided he would increase his caution to Hannah to always buy 'righteous' goods, emphasising the great risk that she would be caught if she attempted to do otherwise. He knew that she would take this warning to include the disposal of the contents of the safe, this risk being even greater than the purchase of stolen merchandise should Hannah be foolish enough to try to act as a fence. Ikey was conscious that Hannah cared about her children more than anything else and the prospect of being transported and losing them was the one great fear he had to exploit in her.

Ikey also knew that if he should give Hannah the combination to the safe she might be tempted to abscond with only the money, the value of the gold chains and the proceeds obtained from the sale of their two London properties. The rest of the hugely valuable haul she might wait to dispose of at another time in some foreign country of her choice.

He had therefore determined on a ploy which, over a series of letters, would let her know that he was negotiating the sale of the pearl necklace to an American of great wealth. When he came close to the limit of his credit with her he would reveal this personage to be the redoubtable John Astor, said to be the richest man in America, 'American Royalty' as the saying went. The pearls were worth one hundred thousand pounds and Ikey was confident that Hannah's greed would persuade her to come to America with the contents of the safe.

Of the two of them, Ikey was the more vulnerable. Hannah would continue to exist whatever might happen, for Hannah hated not herself, only everyone else, and Ikey was simply the incarnation of everything she despised. Ikey, despite the fact that he might yet make a new and separate wealth in America, saw Hannah's determination to rob him of his fortune as an action more hellish in its nature than if she had plotted to murder him. If she were to succeed in stealing his fortune she would have won, not just his wealth, but his very existence. Her victory, and the hate contained within it, would destroy him completely. Victory over Hannah and therefore over himself lay in his retaining the contents of the safe. Hannah was playing a game with her husband for his money and because he was the perfect focus for her extraordinary resentment against the world. Ikey was playing a game with his wife for his very life.

Alas, the best laid plans . . .! Ikey was not to know that his luck was on its way to Van Diemen's Land and, at the moment of Hannah's receiving his letter in London, it was dangling freely on its gold chain about the scrawny neck of Tiberias Potbottom.

Chapter Twenty-one

The London police records of the time show that a large consignment of watches, said to be more than one hundred, were stolen from the premises of a wholesale merchant in Cheapside. This coincidence was to completely change the lives and luck of Hannah and Ikey Solomon.

A theft of such proportion would soon be known in the Whitechapel markets and in Rosemary and Petticoat Lanes and around the Haymarket, where there would be much discussion as to who might have brought it about and who might be capable of fencing such a 'delicate' haul.

It might at first be supposed that it would be simple enough to bring a consignment of new watches back onto the market, but such was not the case. The numbers and markings of the watches were all furnished to the police, being available from the manufacturer, and so each watch would need to be carefully 'christened', that is, the number altered and the name upon the face carefully removed or the face itself replaced. This was a task which took some skill and, moreover, time and was not often worthy of completion on a fob watch that was not of gold or silver. The watches taken were of a varying assortment, but mostly at the cheaper end of the quality market. This meant that such merchandise, while cheaply procured by a fence, was difficult to place into circulation – a trickle placed here and there in market towns and country fairs and all of this over a lengthy period of time, so that the risk of discovering the source of the trickle was greatly decreased.

Hannah, hearing of the theft, was quick to realise that it matched almost precisely the consignment Ikey had commanded her to obtain. Accordingly, and contrary to Ikey's instructions that '. . . *none but "righteous" watches be sent and not to touch even one what has been gained "on the cross"* ', Hannah sent for Bob Marley.

It was late afternoon when Marley knocked on the door of Hannah's Whitechapel home. He was dressed as a regular toff, ready for an evening of jollifications in Drury Lane and the Haymarket, and did not even bother to remove his top hat as he entered the house. This was an intended insult, designed to go along with his failure to greet Hannah as he brushed past her into the familiar parlour. Here he appropriated a glass of the good brandy Hannah had got in and took a bagel from the plate. He commenced to chew with his mouth open; his two gold eye teeth showed clearly as he stared blankly at Hannah, who had followed him silently into the parlour.

'Long time no see, eh, Bob?'

Marley took a gulp of brandy then pushed what remained of the bagel into his mouth. He did not acknowledge her greeting, sucking the crumbs from his fingers as he continued to stare at Hannah.

Hannah smiled ingratiatingly. 'Now, don't be like that, Bob, it were only business.'

'Humph!' Marley grunted.

'Ya done me one in the eye when they made the raid on Bell Alley, ya took me money under false pretences!' Hannah shrugged. 'So I got me revenge.' She grinned. 'That's all, it were tit f' tat!'

Marley swallowed, his Adam's apple bouncing. 'Ya made me look like a copper's nark! That's not the same thing! Me, a man o' me word, I gave Ikey me word, I took his contract!' He paused and took a slug of the brandy. 'Ya done in me fuckin' reputation!'

Hannah laughed uneasily, but then brightened. 'Well Ikey escaped anyway, no 'arm done, in the end ya done 'im a big favour, know what I mean?'

Marley jumped suddenly from the chair and grabbed Hannah by the throat with one large hand. 'Fuck Ikey! It were me reputation ya destroyed! Me a copper's nark, a fuckin' informer!' He shook Hannah, almost lifting her feet from the ground. 'Ain't nobody what trusts me no more!' His fingers tightened about her neck and Hannah's face grew purple, her eyes almost popping from their sockets. 'Don't never try that again, ya 'ear? You'll be dead meat!' Bob Marley released Hannah, who sank to her knees clutching her neck with both hands, forcing herself not to sob. Bob Marley held an open razor in his right hand.

Marley flicked the razor closed and placed it in the pocket of his coat, then threw back his head and swallowed the rest of his brandy. He thumped the glass down upon the table and started towards the door.

'I trusts ya, Bob,' Hannah said in a hoarse voice, rising slowly to her feet. 'Please wait.'

Bob Marley turned at the door and gave a short laugh. 'Ya trusts me! Well ain't that a fuckin' caution!'

Hannah moved up to him and touched him on the sleeve. 'Please?' she smiled again, her throat aching. 'G'warn, 'ave another brandy, a nice bagel, do ya good. I can explain everyfink, honest.'

Marley, eyeing the bottle of excellent brandy, hesitated. 'Explain what?' He crossed back to the bottle. 'Ain't nuffink to explain, ya fucked me reputation, that's all!'

'It ain't true, Bob. You is the best. Ya always was, ya still is. The best there be. Ikey always says, "'E's the best, 'e is, always use the best, Hannah". I says so too, the best o' the best!'

Bob Marley looked up at Hannah, his expression slightly mollified. 'What's ya want?'

'Watches!' Hannah removed Ikey's letter from within her bodice and waved it. 'Ikey wants watches in America.'

Despite himself Bob Marley was impressed. 'Jesus! 'E made it, eh? Cunnin' bastard!' He poured more brandy into his glass and glanced up at Hannah. 'Fencin' then is 'e?'

Hannah was reluctant to explain. 'Yeah, sorta.' She replaced the letter. 'Them watches what's been lifted from Cheapside, know anyfink?'

Marley shook his head. 'Too 'ot, 'Annah, they's got to cool down first, ain't nobody goin' to handle them yet. They's numbered and all, mostly cheap shit, not worth christenin'.'

'Could ya find 'em?' Hannah asked. 'Make a good buy? I'll take the lot if the askin' price be right.'

Marley shook his head. 'Too dangerous. I told ya, watches be too 'ot to touch!'

'I'll pay fifty per cent o' the shop price,' Hannah said quickly, knowing this to be a generous offer, also knowing that she would charge Ikey the full retail price for the watches.

'Sixty! Sixty per cent o' the retail, take it or leave it. And I'll need twenty sovs down payment,' Marley said emphatically. 'There's expenses, ya understand?'

Hannah nodded but inwardly she was concerned that Marley was losing his grip, that perhaps he *had* lost his reputation and therefore his old, greedy confidence. His sudden attack on her had left her frightened, but in the peculiar way of villains, it had also given her confidence in him. You knew where you stood. She'd fully expected to pay sixty per cent of the full price of the watches, but she'd also set aside fifty gold sovereigns as the down payment.

'Sure, I understand,' she said. 'Gimme a mo', I'll fetch it fer ya.'

'Mind, I can't take no chances,' Marley said. 'It may take a while to get to them yacks.' This was said almost as an aside.

Hannah turned at the door. 'Not too long, Bob. Ikey 'as great expectations.'

Marley frowned and shook his head slowly. 'If I 'as to take chances, make indiscreet enquiries like, that's no good fer me 'ealth! Pigs is everywhere, the Lane's tight as a duck's arse!' He looked over to where Hannah was standing and sighed. ''Fraid that kind o' haste is gunna cost you forty sovs extra on the down.'

Hannah smiled inwardly, her mind put at rest. She was dealing with the same dead cunning Bob Marley. She was anxious to get the watches and so impress Ikey with her diligence and continuing goodwill towards him. She was not foolish enough to imagine that he would send her his half of the combination after only one such consignment, but her heart had lifted at the opportunity his letter presented. She had high hopes that Ikey must eventually send her the combination to the safe when she pleaded impecuniosity, his debts incurred by his orders having become too large for her to carry any further on her own. Whereupon she would be rid of him forever.

But Hannah had completely underestimated Bob Marley. She'd quickly come to see his attack on her as a show, a token effort to assert his male pride, give her a fright, as he had well succeeded in doing. She didn't think for a moment he would have used the

319

razor. Marley, Hannah felt certain, could always be bought with gold.

She was wrong, however. Marley would have used the razor on her as lightly as he would have smiled. Hannah was unable to see the proud man who despised his fellow villains and thought himself quite different. She did not comprehend that, in his own eyes (and no others counted), she had damaged his reputation and done him irreparable harm. When she'd shifted the blame for betraying Ikey to the police onto him, she had delivered a blow to his pride which could entertain no possible forgiveness. Marley did business only for solid gold, for that is how he saw his reputation. And he always delivered. Hannah had compromised him, and because he always delivered, she would be no exception. The wolf would tear her flesh as well as any other.

Bob Marley made no attempt to locate the whereabouts of the watches stolen from Cheapside, this being much too dangerous. Instead he made directly for a jeweller of his acquaintance in the Haymarket, a Polish Jew by the name of Isaac Isaacson whom Ikey had used regularly when Marley had been his snakesman as a child. It was Isaacson who had moulded and created Marley's two gold teeth and so it came as somewhat of a surprise when his visitor bid him find one hundred mixed watches of brand new quality and all righteously purchased. They haggled at great length to finally reach an agreement of a thirty per cent reduction off the retail price of the proposed consignment.

Bob Marley was about to leave the premises reasonably well satisfied with the negotiations when Isaac Isaacson beckoned him to come closer. He explained in an urgent whisper that he was long owed a certain sum of money for a gold and diamond bracelet sold to a Miss Myrtle Manners, the governess of a well-known brothel in the Strand known appropriately enough as 'Girls with good Manners'. This 'Governess o' whores', he claimed, had flatly refused to pay him the final two instalments, a sum of three hundred pounds, claiming he had overcharged her and pointing out, with the least amount of subtlety, that she enjoyed the special patronage and protection of a senior police officer in the Haymarket watchhouse.

'You can cut, maybe a little, this person, ja?' Isaacson enquired of Bob Marley.

'Most certainly!' Marley replied. 'It'd be me pleasure to be o' service, Mr Isaacson.' He paused and scratched his eyebrow with the tip of his forefinger. 'Though it'll cost ya anuvver ten percent orf the cost o' the yacks. O' course, if ya wants a really nasty acid job, right down a cheekbone, and includin' a little turn o' the blade to slice away the corner o' the gob so it don't fit proper no more, it could be a little extra.'

Isaac Isaacson grew suddenly pale and threw his hands up in alarm. 'No, no! Ten per cent, no more, please, I beg you! A small violence only, if you please!'

Bob Marley grinned. 'Fer ten percent I can do ya a nice little job, Mr Isaacson. Gimme two days. Reckon you'll 'ave the yacks ready by then?'

The jeweller nodded, hunched his shoulders and spread his hands. 'A little cut, no more!' he begged again.

Bob Marley left the Haymarket and made his way to the Hare and Hounds in Rosemary Lane almost directly opposite the Methodist Academy of Light Fingers. He had not long to wait before he observed a boy leave the Academy in an old coat that fell to beyond his knees, the sleeves rolled up to fit his scrawny arms, bare feet showing below ragged trousers. The brat crossed the street to enter the tavern and Marley observed him to be snotnosed, dirty and small, with the pinched, rodent-like features of a street urchin. He appeared to be about ten years old as he placed two pennies down on the counter and ordered a daffy of gin.

'Make that a shant, m'dear!' Marley called to the barmaid.

The barmaid and the urchin both looked up at Marley. 'Suit yerself,' she said, picking up a bigger glass.

'And a double o' yer best brandy, love. I'll pay fer the lad's.'

The boy looked up at Bob Marley. 'You a turd burglar, mister?' he asked, swiftly taking up the two pennies on the counter and dropping them into the pocket of his coat.

Bob Marley enquired if the urchin knew Sparrer Fart.

'Maybe I does and then maybe I doesn't,' the boy replied cheekily.

'Tell 'im I wants to see 'im, two o' the clock termorra, in 'ere. Tell 'im no 'ard feelin's, I wants a job done, Bob Marley wants a job done. Got it?'

The boy nodded.

Marley lifted his head and called to the barmaid. 'Another gin fer the lad, love!' Then he placed a shilling on the counter and without a further glance at the boy he left the tavern.

Sparrer Fart was waiting for Marley when he entered the Hare and Hounds the following day. He was wearing a slightly battered top hat, coat and breeches all of which fitted him surprisingly well, though his entire outfit, including his shirt, neckerchief and scuffed boots, bore the signs of having been placed upon his tiny body some months previously and not having since been removed for the purposes of laundering. His face seemed also to have missed this opportunity to wash. Sparrer looked somewhat apprehensive as Bob Marley approached, backing into the safety of a group of men standing at the bar and glancing quickly over his shoulder to ascertain the shortest escape route should he have to make a sudden dash for it.

Bob Marley pushed into the group and extended his hand, smiling. 'I oughta beat the livin' shit out of ya, Sparrer!' Sparrer Fart backed away, ready to make a run for it. The barmaid looked at Marley questioningly. 'Brandy, love, the best o' the 'ouse!' Marley turned back to Sparrer, who now stood alone. 'What's your poison, gin is it?' The urchin nodded.

'C'mere, I'm not gunna 'arm ya,' Marley said, walking over to where Sparrer stood. The barmaid brought their drinks over. ''Ow's the fingers?' Marley enquired. 'Not drinkin' too much is ya? 'Aven't lost yer touch, I most sincerely 'opes?'

Sparrer Fart took the gin the barmaid placed in front of him, then he looked up at Bob Marley, his eyes large, his expression most contrite. 'I'm sorry what I done, Mr Marley,' he said tentatively.

Bob Marley lifted his drink and held it up. 'Cheers! Never say you is sorry, boy! Sorry be the sign o' a weak man!' He up-ended the glass and swallowed its contents in one gulp. 'Ahh! Same again, love!' he shouted to the barmaid.

'I wouldn't 'ave! I swear I didn't know she was gunna shop Ikey!' Sparrer said.

''Course ya didn't! 'Ow much she give ya?'

'Four quid,' Sparrer lied.

'Ya was robbed! Sovs or what?'

Sparrer shook his head. 'Soft. It were good paper though, not fake.'

Marley clucked his tongue. 'Never take no paper money, boy! Gold! Don't never take nuffink else, that is, if ya wants respect.'

'I don't think as I can afford respect what's always gold,' Sparrer said softly, taking a tiny sip from his gin.

'Lemme see yer 'ands. 'Old 'em out, spread yer fingers.'

Sparrer held his hands out and spread his fingers. They were tiny, dirty and beautiful, and they remained perfectly steady.

'Nerves! 'Ow's yer nerves?'

'I'm still the goodest, still the best o' everyone!' Sparrer boasted.

'Oh yeah? 'Ow does I know that?' Bob Marley challenged, amused at Sparrer's confidence.

Sparrer Fart dipped into the side pocket of his jacket and produced Bob Marley's gold hunter, handing the watch back to him.

'Jesus!' Marley exclaimed. He shook his head admiringly. 'Didn't never feel ya touchin' me! You're good, Sparrer, I'll give ya that!'

Sparrer shook his head. 'Nah! If ya was Ikey, he'd o' caught me. We don't get 'nuff trainin' since 'e's gorn away.' He took a sip from his gin and looked up at Bob Marley with big eyes. 'Academy's fucked!'

'You'll do nicely, lad,' Marley said, giving Sparrer's shoulder a comforting squeeze. 'Very nicely.' He explained what he required. 'There's three sovs in it fer ya, plus the worf o' the lift, three sovs in gold, what's got the King's 'ead on it,' he emphasised. He stabbed a finger at Sparrer Fart. 'But mind ya bring me silver, a good 'un!'

Marley met Sparrer in the Hare and Hounds at ten the following evening. In a leather satchel he carried the one hundred fob watches Isaac Isaacson had obtained for him.

'Well then, lad, 'ow'd ya go?'

Sparrer dug into his pocket and produced a silver hunter which he handed to Bob Marley.

'Like ya said, Mr Marley, not too cheap not too 'spensive, sterlin' silver, worf fifteen sovs new!' Sparrer declared expertly.

Bob Marley examined the watch. 'Jesus, Sparrer, it be monogrammed! Look, J.R., that be the 'nitials o' the cove ya nicked it from!'

Sparrer shrugged. 'Ya didn't say nuffink 'bout that. Do I still get me five sovs then?' he asked hopefully.

Bob Marley counted five gold sovereigns into Sparrer's tiny hand, then added three more.

'Ya done good, lad. I didn't say nuffink 'bout no 'nitials.'

Sparrer looked pleased. He was rich enough to eat and get drunk for a week and sit in on an endless game of cribbage. 'Thanks, Mr Marley, I done me best, sorry I fucked up.'

'Got a yack o' yer own, then?' Bob Marley asked suddenly.

Sparrer shook his head in alarm. 'Too dangerous in me profession! Pigs might find the cove I nicked it from, it'd be the boat fer me, fer sure!'

Bob Marley's hand went into his pocket and produced a handsome nickel-plated fob watch which he placed on the bar counter. Then he pulled out a watch chain and dropped it beside the watch.

'Take it, it be your'n.'

Sparrer looked confused. 'Huh?'

Marley laughed. 'A present, fer yer birfday!'

'I don't 'ave no birfday,' Sparrer said quietly, still bemused. 'Ya didn't nick it, did ya? Cos, if ya nicked it I can't 'ave it.'

'Nah, it were a bonus for doin' a job, a little favour fer a friend like.' He pushed the watch over to Sparrer. 'G'warn, take it, everybody's got a birfday even if they don't know when it be.'

Sparrer picked up the watch in one hand and the chain in the other, appearing to weigh both in his hands. 'I ain't never before seen a new one what's not nicked.'

'Guaranteed, honest to Gawd nab proof that is. Pig come up to ya, ask ya where ya got it, tell 'im it's kosher, Isaac Isaacson o' Drury Lane, "Jeweller to Thespians and Gentlemen, Established 1792"!'

Sparrer's eyes shone as he realised that the watch was safe for him to own. 'Thanks, Mr Marley, thanks a lot!' he said clicking open the lid and looking at the pristine face of the watch. Then he closed it and clipping the watch onto the chain placed it into his fob pocket, looped the chain over his tiny belly and fitted the crossbar at its other end into its appropriate buttonhole. The chain was much too long for his narrow torso and dangled in an arc to below his crutch. 'I never 'ad a watch o' me very own,' Sparrer said excitedly.

'Mazeltov!' Bob Marley said, patting him lightly on the shoulder. 'One good turn deserves anuvver!' He pointed to Sparrer's fob pocket. 'What's the time then?'

Sparrer took the watch from its pocket and expertly clicked it open again. ''Arf past ten o' the clock,' he said proudly.

'Read what it says,' Marley demanded.

The boy looked up at Bob Marley, then down at the inscription inside the watch cover as though he had seen it for the first time. He touched it lightly with his forefinger tracing the words inscribed into the metal as though by feeling them they might reveal their meaning to him. Bob Marley cleared his throat.

'No, don't read it, Sparrer! Lemme tell ya what it says,' he said quickly, rescuing the urchin. 'I sort o' composed it meself, see. So it be better said than read, knows what I mean?' Bob Marley leaned back as though thinking for a moment. 'It says: "To S.F. – A man's repitashin be more valiable than gold! B.M."'

'What's S.F. and B.M. mean?' Sparrer asked.

'S.F. stands fer Sparrer Fart, that bein' you . . . and B.M., why that's yers truly, the same what's talkin' to ya and whose repitashin be more valiable than gold!'

'Thanks, Mr Marley.' Sparrer touched the inscription again with his forefinger. 'S.F., eh? Blimey, that be me!'

Marley laughed and pointed to the watch. '*Tempus fugit*, that means "Time flies", I gotta scarper.' He threw down what remained of his brandy. 'Ya done good, Sparrer, cheer'o then.'

Sparrer didn't quite know why, but as he watched Bob Marley's back retreat out of the tavern door he wanted to bawl.

At near enough to ten o'clock the following morning, Bob Marley knocked on Hannah's door. Hannah's expression was at once anxious when she saw who it was.

'Bob!' Then she added quickly, but in a whisper, 'You 'asn't got 'em, 'as ya?'

Marley grunted and held up the bag.

Hannah, unable to conceal her excitement, invited him into the parlour. 'Wait, I'll get brandy! 'Ere, sit. 'As ya eaten?' She didn't wait for Marley's reply but left the parlour and moments later appeared with a large biscuit tin, a glass and a bottle of brandy. ''Elp yerself, love, I'll fetch yer money,' she said, leaving the room once more.

Half an hour after Marley had left the police arrived at Hannah's house with a search warrant, discovered the watches and arrested her on suspicion of obtaining stolen property. She arrived at the watchhouse where she was to be retained overnight to hear that Bob Marley was also being held by the police.

Both of them were arraigned before a magistrate the following morning, Hannah being the first to stand in the prisoner's dock, where she pleaded not guilty. She asked for the clerk of the court to bring her Ikey's letter which she'd caused to be held in evidence. 'See 'ere, yer worship, where it says in me 'usband's letter,' she commenced to read the lines '. . . "*I charge you to send me none but 'righteous' watches and not to touch even one what has been gained 'on the cross'. I shall require these to be of an assortment of nickel plate, sterling silver and gold. I believe these will here obtain up to six times the price of the watches purchased by you on the straight.*" '

The magistrate read Ikey's letter for himself and then looked up at Hannah. 'Hmm, I see that we shall not have the privilege of supplying your husband with accommodation in one of His Majesty's antipodean hostelries. We can only hope that the Americans may prove more successful at this task, eh, madam?'

Hannah smiled weakly at the judge. 'Yer worship, I 'as always been a good and obedient wife and I would not think to go against me 'usband's wishes and commands.' She dropped her gaze, wringing her hands piteously. 'I's a poor woman with four brats to feed and 'ousework to do.' She looked appealingly at the magistrate. 'What does I know about findin' one 'undred watches what's been nicked?'

'And how do you suppose these watches came into your possession then, madam?' the magistrate asked sternly.

Hannah pointed to Bob Marley, manacled and seated between two constables in the court. ''Im! I asks 'im to purchase on be'arf o' me 'usband one 'undred watches what's kosher, what's not nicked, but what's bran' new. 'E said 'e done it, but 'e didn't, did 'e? 'E gorn and got 'em on the cross!' Hannah suddenly clasped her hands together in front of her breasts and burst into tears. 'Oh, what shall become o' me children?' she wailed.

'You may stand down, Mrs Solomon.' The magistrate was not in the least affected by Hannah's tears. 'I shall presently call you to stand before me again.' He nodded at the clerk of the court, who rose from his seat and proclaimed.

'Robert Matthew Marley will take the stand!'

Hannah listened with increasing bemusement as Marley proved conclusively that the watches he'd obtained for her were unencumbered and purchased legitimately. To further support his case the respectable Haymarket jeweller, Isaac Isaacson, appeared as a witness for Marley, showing the number and names of the watches purchased by the accused as matching exactly the wholesaler's invoice. Bob Marley then produced in evidence Isaac Isaacson's own receipt to him. Furthermore, the Crown now admitted that none of the watches matched the serial numbers of those taken in the notorious Cheapside robbery.

The charges against Marley were summarily dismissed and the magistrate called for Hannah to appear before him again, whereupon he commenced to remonstrate severely with her for accusing the said Robert Matthew Marley, a man who had never been before the courts and whose reputation she had needlessly and maliciously impugned.

Hannah protested vehemently. 'Yer worship it were the police! They said them watches was stolen! I 'mediately supposed they was! I supposed that Mr Marley'd gorn an' nicked 'em, 'oping to profit from chargin' me the full price while 'avin' got 'em at a thief's rate!'

'And you did not think to ask Mr Marley for a receipt as proof that he'd made a legitimate purchase as you requested?'

'Yer worship, I were most pleased what Mr Marley 'ad done, knowin' as 'ow I 'ad served me 'usband's request wif promptness and exactitude. I am not accustomed to the ways o' doin' business, bein' a poor woman what knows nuffink about such things as bills and receipts and the general goin's on o' commerce!'

The magistrate snorted loudly. Hannah's reputation as a businesswoman was well known to the court.

Hannah, though appearing distraught, was delighted with the altogether surprising outcome. She had considered herself already bound for Botany Bay, but now Bob Marley's innocence conclusively proved her own. She waited impatiently for the miserable beak to conclude his tirade and to dismiss the case.

Finally the magistrate picked up a document and began to read.

'Hannah Margaret Solomon and Robert Matthew Marley you have been jointly charged with having obtained and, or, being found in possession of, a consignment of one hundred watches thought to have been stolen from an establishment in Cheapside. This has subsequently been proved to be incorrect and you, Mr Marley, have been cleared by this court of any charges relating to that robbery.' He looked up at Hannah, who smiled back at him. 'You too, madam, are free of this charge.'

'Thank you, yer worship,' Hannah said primly, preparing to step down from the dock.

But the magistrate held up his hand to stay her. 'If you please . . .' He picked up another document and began to read again. 'Hannah Margaret Solomon, you are further charged with being in possession of a sterling silver watch known to be the property of Joseph Ridley, the said watch being discovered concealed in a biscuit tin in the pantry of your home.' The magistrate looked up sternly. 'How plead you to this charge, guilty or not guilty?'

Hannah's mouth opened in astonishment and she glanced quickly to where Bob Marley sat, but all she could later remember seeing was the dark gap between his two shining gold teeth as he grinned at her.

'Not guilty, yer worship,' she said, then added in a whisper, 'Oh, me Gawd!'

Chapter Twenty-two

The first of the autumn leaves were starting to turn in Hyde Park and the geese on the Serpentine, plump with summer feeding, were increasingly feeling the primal urge to migrate to a warmer clime. On the 13th of September 1827, Hannah, a bird of a quite different feather, was sentenced to a less voluntary migration, though also to a warmer climate.

If her sentence at the Old Bailey to fourteen years' transportation appears rather too harsh for a crime so small, it may be supposed that much frustration had gone before it in the many unsuccessful attempts to trap both Hannah and Ikey. The law has a duty to be both parent and teacher and sometimes, in order to wipe the slate clean, a recalcitrant child must be dealt with more harshly than a particular crime seems to merit, in order to compensate for successful crimes which have gone unpunished. Hannah's conviction may well have rendered an opportunity to balance the scales of justice.

Ikey's escape to New York, as proved by the evidence of his letter to his wife, was reported in *The Times* and was blown up to exaggerated proportions in the penny dailies, where it created much merriment in the rookeries and even some grudging admiration among the lower classes. The law is blind only when it does not wish to see and the embarrassment to the City police and directors of the Bank of England caused by Ikey's gaolbreak may well have condemned Hannah to a harsher sentence.

To Hannah's fourteen years' transportation was added the condition that she never be permitted to return to her native land.

On hearing her sentence Hannah brought her hands up to her face and wailed, 'Oh! Oh! What shall become o' me precious mites?'

Whereupon the judge, to prove that the severity of the law may be tempered by compassion, gave permission for her children to accompany her to Australia so as to be under her fostering care.

The *Mermaid*, carrying Hannah and her four children together with ninety other female convicts, some also with children, sailed from Woolwich on the 10th of February 1828.

The voyage proved no better or worse than most. There was the usual sea sickness, bouts of catarrh and rheumatism brought about by the dampness between decks on the voyage to Tenerife. These ailments soon yielded with the coming of the sun, though an obstinate form of constipation remained. This was thought to be due to the fact that the Irish women on board, as was the custom in Irish prisons, received only gruel and milk. Now the introduction of salt and beef and pork to their shipboard diet proved most deleterious to their unaccustomed stomachs.

As is always the case, bickering, fights, bad behaviour and thieving among the women prisoners were much in evidence. In the matter of whoring, though, which was known to plague even the most watchful of voyages, Hannah was to play a part so skilful that the surgeon-superintendent would state in his report that the prisoners had co-operated well and had shown little pernicious disruption and almost none of the moral turpitude so commonly experienced on a convict ship carrying female prisoners.

This 'co-operation' had come about when Hannah, soon determining the nature of the voyage, grew fearful for the health of her children and concluded that the only advantage to them could be brought about by the chief steward.

Other than in matters of punishment, there are only two other aspects of life on board a convict ship which it is in the power of someone to improve, these being the daily tasks allocated to the prisoners and the nature of the food. Hannah soon ascertained that by greatly increasing the 'comfort' of the officers and certain members of the crew, and by enriching the chief steward in the process, both these rewards could be enjoyed by herself and her children.

It was a relatively easy matter for her to be appointed a monitor in charge of the more profligate and wayward of the female prisoners. The next step was one to which she was most accustomed as a whore mistress and governess of a brothel. She quickly organised a discreet service in which the chief steward acted as go-between and which both the co-operating prisoners and crew soon found to be greatly advantageous. The officers and crew received sexual favours which were arranged with a simple payment to the steward, and the prisoner-prostitutes were allocated pleasant duties and extra rations of food and beverages.

Hannah needed the surgeon-superintendent to turn a blind eye, so she set about the task of satisfying his desire while allowing him to maintain the utmost celibacy demanded of him in his position as disciplinarian, surgeon, superintendent and as His Majesty's representative on board ship.

This Hannah did not with her hips, but with the same 'Sir Jasper-like' employment of her skilful lips. In this way the surgeon-superintendent could not be accused of indulging in fornication or of the slightest neglect of his moral duty.

Hannah had found the key to a more comfortable voyage for herself and her children and was rewarded with special food and a plentiful supply of liquid refreshment. The importance of this arrangement cannot be stressed enough. While the food was monotonous it was deemed to be adequate to the prisoners' needs. It was liquid refreshment which was especially craved, particularly when the *Mermaid* lay becalmed on a shining tin-flat sea and the prisoners were possessed of a tropical torpor as they lay gasping below decks.

It was then that they would implore the steward for a drop of water to cool their parched tongues. But he would answer with an aggrieved shake of the head.

'Can't do it, allowances have been had.'

Hannah entered into business with the steward, who saw to it that 'hospital extras' were given to her and her four children. Indeed, it must be said, due to the importuning talents of their mother, these brats enjoyed every advantage to be obtained on the voyage. When Ann, Hannah's daughter, went down with the fever for a period of two weeks she was favoured with the most delicious diet and the tender ministrations of the surgeon-superintendent. She was also given a berth directly below a porthole to catch the clement breezes. Baby Mark, on the sick list for five days with diarrhoea (no doubt from an excess of rich rations), received the same conscientious attention and hospital food, served each day in an adult portion so that it might be shared by his brother and sisters.

Hannah was the matriarch of the first contingent of her tribe of Solomon to arrive in Van Diemen's Land on the 27th of June 1828, where they were to prove to possess stubborn and hardy roots. They would do much of both good and evil to shape the destiny of this new land, and would add their ancient faith to a burgeoning new culture.

A pause is necessary to contemplate a singular phenomenon. In every convict ship which carried Britons, from the First Fleet onwards, there were Jews to share their fate. In this haphazard way Australia was to become the only community of European people in which Jews were present from the moment of inception. For nearly nineteen centuries the Jews had not enjoyed a permanent welcome in European lands. Now, though only a tiny contingent, they were nevertheless a noticeable part of the convict community. Here they were regarded no differently from their fellows, a condition which has continued to exist in this the most egalitarian country on earth, where Jack is thought to be as good as his master, though it should in fairness be added that, at the time Hannah arrived in Van Diemen's Land, neither Jack nor his master were thought to be much good. Furthermore, the contention still persists, though noticeably among the English, that in the intervening years, nothing much has changed.

The new Female Factory was not yet fully constructed and Governor Arthur had allowed that a prisoner who had shown exemplary behaviour on the way out should be processed on board ship and then permitted to go directly to the home of a settler as an indentured servant.

Hannah and her children were consigned immediately to the home of Mr Richard Newman, a police officer of Hobart Town, who greeted her on the dock with the utmost civility as though she were of equal status and not a convict wretch with the additional burden of four extra mouths to feed.

This was thought most surprising, for Newman was said to be

a happily married man of small means, so there could be no thought of concubinage, nor was there any profit to be gained from the labours of the two older children, David and Ann, as they were not convicts and so not obliged to work under his roof.

It soon became apparent that Hannah did not intend to be burdened with the duties of a servant or suffer the instructions of a master. She did nothing except loll about the cottage, dawdling through the most undemanding tasks. Her quarrelsome ways soon alienated all who came in contact with her. It was often observed that Mrs Newman, a quiet soul, was the real servant and Hannah the mistress of the house. It was never suggested that this had come about because the convict had ensnared her master with her feminine guile, as Mrs Newman was both pretty and of a most cheerful nature and Hannah was not burdened with either of these pleasant characteristics.

The truth of the matter was rather more simple. Ikey had made arrangements ahead of Hannah's arrival, and Richard Newman was most handsomely recompensed for the accommodation of Hannah and her children.

This convenient arrangement may well have been beyond the talents of a man less enterprising than Ikey Solomon, who had heard about Hannah's arrest in a letter from Abraham Reuban, the son of the actor Reuban Reuban who had been a part of the great bank scam.

Abraham Reuban's letter, sent on the first packet bound for New York, arrived in Ikey's hands not more than twenty-six days after the conclusion of Hannah's trial. Furthermore, Ikey was kept abreast of the court case in *The Times*, news of the arrest and subsequent trial of the wife of the notorious Ikey Solomon being much in demand.

Ikey's most immediate concern was for the safe in the Whitechapel home. He hastily dispatched a letter to young Reuban by the next ship bound for London and enclosed with it sufficient money for the windows of the Whitechapel house to be bricked up and the doors to be boarded up.

Ikey was so certain that Hannah had been compromised in the matter of the watch that he was under no illusion that she might be acquitted. He knew she was capable of disobeying his instructions in the matter of purchasing the consignment of watches. But, when it transpired that the one hundred watches had been honestly purchased by Bob Marley, he knew immediately that she would not, under any circumstances, include a watch gained on the cross in the same shipment. Hannah was greedy and wilful but never stupid. She had been set up, either by Bob Marley, or the Law itself, of that much he was entirely convinced. It remained only for him to know whether she would be transported to Van Diemen's Land or to New South Wales for him to spring into action.

With the news that Hannah was to be transported to Van Diemen's Land, Ikey sent a letter by means of a certain Captain Barkman, master of a whaler sailing out of Boston and bound for Sydney, and then directly to Hobart where it would commence upon a whaling expedition in Antarctic waters. In his letter Ikey instructed his eldest son John to take passage with the captain to Hobart Town, and there to negotiate whatever comforts or conditions would be to the benefit of his mother and his brothers and sisters.

John Solomon arrived in Hobart Town not two weeks prior to Hannah's arrival on the *Mermaid*, and was quickly acquainted with Governor Arthur's desire to place female prisoners with settlers or emancipists in a manner most favourable to the containment of government expenses. Arthur ran the colony like a small-town grocer, aware of the cost of every tin, jar and package on his colonial shelves. Even a single night's detainment in the Female Factory meant a debit in the government books.

Richard Newman, an emancipist and police officer, with a third child on the way, was easily enough convinced by John Solomon that he should apply for Hannah to be assigned as his servant. The formalities were arranged with the authorities, who sought to look no further than sparing the government the responsibility and expense of accommodating and feeding not one, but five additional mouths.

John Solomon arranged for a monthly stipend to be paid a year in advance to Richard Newman, and thereafter to be subject to renewal only if Hannah found the arrangements to her personal satisfaction. In paying the money to the policeman he had demanded a receipt, which had been foolishly supplied without thought for what this might mean at a future time.

It was an unfortunate arrangement from the very first, and the policeman and his long-suffering wife were often to contemplate that all the riches in the world could not make up for the presence of Hannah Solomon and her children under their roof.

Without Hannah in London, Ikey's plans for his Broadway business had to be severely curtailed, and he decided that he had but one card left to play. He must immediately go to Van Diemen's Land and convince Hannah to let him have her half of the combination to the safe. If he could assure her of his constant concern for her welfare while supplying her with every creature comfort, he was confident of an early success. He told himself that his wife would soon come to see the utmost sense in his retrieving their now securely bricked-up fortune so that he might establish a prosperous platform against the time of her release. Perhaps in Canada, the West Coast of America or even the Cape of Good Hope where the English were beginnning to settle in some numbers.

Ikey had made several speculative purchases of land in New York, most of these on the island of Manhattan and in the Bronx. He now set about feverishly turning these back into liquid assets, accepting far less for a quick sale than the true worth of the property.

Ikey managed finally to sell all his interests with the exception of one half-acre corner block in Manhattan which in a moment of weakness he had leased to the Council of American Jews for the Land of Ararat. This was in order that they might build a hostel and reception centre for Jews fleeing from persecution in Europe and the Orient. The buildings were to be of impressive proportions and would be known as the Mordecai Manuel Noah, Ararat Foundation.

Mordecai Noah was a prominent American Jew who had been the consul to Tunis. During his travels he had discovered the plight of the homeless Jews in the Orient and Europe. He dreamed of seeing Palestine returned as a homeland for the Jews, but as a diplomat he was conscious of the impossibility of achieving this mission among the Arab rulers. His thoughts then turned to the great open spaces of America and upon his return from Algiers in 1825 he purchased a tract of seventeen thousand acres on Grand Island on the Niagara River near the city of Buffalo. This he nominated as the site for the temporary Land of Israel and declared himself Governor and Judge of Israel, issuing a manifesto to Jews all over the world to come and settle in the new land which would guarantee them freedom under the protection of the constitution and laws of the United States of America.

Whether the Jews of New York saw this new and temporary Israel as a holy mission worthy of their support, or simply regarded it as an effective way to keep the immigration of undesirable European and Oriental Jews out of their city is not known, but they determined to build an impressive reception centre for the 'New Israelites' so that they could be expedited as speedily as possible to the Land of Ararat. It was the real estate for this centre which Ikey had agreed to lease to the council for a period of fifty years.

This was the most generous gesture Ikey had made in his entire life but it gained him no favour in the eyes of his American co-religionists. They felt that it showed his true criminal rapacity, for they maintained that a good Jew would have donated the land to them free of all encumbrances and conditions.

However, for a man of Ikey's background and temperament this was simply not possible. He could not bring himself to give away something he owned, despite the fact that he did not give a fig for his heirs and was quite aware that he would be long dead before the land reverted to them. Perhaps, had they agreed to call it The Isaac Solomon Welcoming Centre for the Land of Ararat, or some such fancy name to honour his donation, he might well have relented. Men do strange things to perpetuate their importance. However, this too is unlikely given Ikey's nature and the fact that his instincts told him the great Mordecai Noah was a dreamer of dreams and not a creator of schemes. In this he proved to be entirely correct for not a sod was ever turned in the Land of Ararat, nor a brick placed upon its welcoming gate.

Ikey was well supplied with funds, despite having lost considerably on the resale of his land, and he spent a short time stocking up on goods to sell in Hobart Town. He also purchased a large quantity of tobacco from Virginia and cigars from the Cuban Islands. He planned to sell the hard goods as quickly as possible upon his arrival on the island and thereafter to open a tobacconist shop so that he might pose as a legitimate merchant.

Ikey reasoned that tobacco, like grog, was a commodity which would always be in demand in a society where men greatly outnumbered women. For this reason he did not venture to take with him a quantity of jewellery. He quickly surmised that trinkets and rings and bright shining things would not be so much sought after on an island consisting largely of convicts, emancipists and troopers. Furthermore, those free settlers who had made Van Diemen's Land their home had done so because their limited resources precluded the purchase of land and influence in the more civilised climes of the West Indies, Canada, America or the Cape of Good Hope.

Ikey took a ship in New York bound for Rio, where he hoped to join a vessel from England bound for New South Wales. In later years he would talk of this voyage as a moment when he thought the end was nigh. The ship had no sooner passed the island of Trinidad, in the temperate latitudes of the Caribbean, than the mercury in the barometer dropped alarmingly and the vessel became becalmed. Ikey would recall how there was a complete stillness as though the silence impregnated and thickened the air. There was no breath of wind and the sea grew flat as a sheet of rolled metal until not even the single slap of a wave upon the prow of the ship could be heard.

The captain, no stranger to conditions in these parts, ordered the portholes to be shut, hatches battened down and new rope was brought to secure what cargo remained on deck. Then he furled canvas and waited for the tropical cyclone to hit.

Slowly a sound, as though the sea itself had given off a soft sigh, grew into an ear-splitting whistle and soon became a ferocious howling. It was as though the forces of chaos had gathered above the ship to plan its total destruction.

The flat sea rose suddenly to mountainous proportions. An aft stay snapped like a twig though no responding crack was heard to penetrate the wail of the wind. The ship, a cork upon the sea, plunged deep into each troughed wave and then rode towards its crest seventy feet above the prow.

Huge seas smashed over the vessel so that below decks the wash came up to the waist and all felt they must surely perish, though sickness forbade them contemplating their lives. Besides, they knew with desperate certainty that no God existed with power sufficient to hear their repentant cries above the raging gale.

On the morning of the third day the cyclone left them and, once again, a benign sun twinkled on the calm blue waters of the South Atlantic. While no single pieces of cargo lashed to the deck remained, the damage to the vessel was surprisingly slight. The repair of several broken stays and rigging was all that was necessary to allow them to continue the voyage. Ikey arrived in Rio much shaken by the experience though none the worse for wear.

Of Rio we have spoken before and Ikey, ever active in 'turning a penny', spent his time selling the trinkets he had been unable to dispose of before closing his Broadway shop.

He thought little of the Latinos and even less of the mosquitoes which swarmed in from the surrounding mangrove swamps at night. Ikey had no eye for the watery plumes of splashing fountains, and even the dirt and squalor to be found in the wide avenues was not to his familiar taste. It was therefore with alacrity that he accepted passage, despite some inconvenience of arrangement, on the *Coronet*, an English ship bound most fortuitously for Van Diemen's Land.

Ikey boarded the ship under the name of Sloman, and it must be assumed that he crossed the palm of the captain most generously, for no berth remained on board. Dr William Henry Browne, LL.D., soon to be Hobart's colonial chaplain, was on deck taking morning prayers when his tiny cabin was forced open on the captain's orders and a berth added to accommodate the generous Mr Sloman.

Dr Browne arrived back to find his books and baggage piled in a most haphazard manner to one side of the tiny cabin, and a Hebrew personage ensconced where they had once lain in a well-ordered convenience. The clergyman, who was of a naturally choleric disposition, demanded that Ikey be removed, though without success, whereupon he took great umbrage and showed no grace or charity whatsoever towards his fellow passenger, who meanwhile remained quietly seated with his arms folded and said not a syllable to offend during the cleric's entire conniption.

However, Ikey's mute tolerance was not to last. While he was well accustomed to the slings and arrows of outrageous fortune, a long and tedious voyage is best peppered with an ongoing debate, whether this be an acrimonious or a pleasant one. Therefore Ikey, unable to win his cabin partner with affable conversation, amused himself by baiting the learned Dr Browne with matters of the Anglican religion, of which Ikey knew a surprising amount. This vexatious debate, in which Ikey did not fail to score some telling points on the resurrection and the Holy Trinity, did nothing to improve the temper of God's representative on board. No sooner had the clergyman landed in Hobart than he hastened to Colonel George Arthur with a burden of bitter complaint against the vile Mr Sloman.

This proved an altogether disastrous beginning for Ikey, as it brought the full attention of the governor to his presence on the island. Colonel Arthur, himself a devout believer, accepted Dr Browne's version of the voyage without question and promised that the blasphemous newcomer would be watched with an eagle eye.

Nor did it take long for Ikey to be discovered for his true self. He foolishly moved in with the Newmans as a lodger, where his very presence with Hannah in the tiny cottage caused jocular speculation about the nature of the bed he occupied. As soon as he walked the streets there were people who were quick to recognise him, Hobart Town being the enforced home of many of his old colleagues and not a few of his former customers.

'Oh, Ikey me boy, me boy! How are ya? Blow me down, but I'm glad to see ya! What a cursed lucky fellow yerv been, escapin' the rope and thereafter the boat. How are ya, m'boy?'

Other remarks were not as well intended. 'I say, there goes Ikey Solomon – he used to fence me swag, the cursed rogue! Were it not for him I should not be here now!'

Ikey, though his intelligence must have warned him otherwise, chose to ignore these remarks, walking on without appearing to recognise his verbal assailant or, if forced to respond, he would look upon the speaker with incurious eyes.

'You're quite mistaken, my dear, very much and entirely mistaken. I am not him whom you suppose I am, though I am pleased enough to make your acquaintance.' He would extend a long, thin hand. 'Sloman, recently off the *Coronet*, tobacconist by way of trade. A fine display of Cuban cigars and other inhalatory delights await your pleasure in my Liverpool Street establishment.'

Ikey had lost no time opening up as a tobacconist and all at once he became the best of his kind in town, his American stock being far superior to the leaf grown on the mainland of Australia, or imported from Dutch Batavia or the Cape of Good Hope. When complimented over his cigars he'd roll his eyes and grin knowingly. 'Ah, the secret be they roll 'em on the sweat of a nigger girl's thighs!'

However much Arthur might fume, his solicitor-general advised him that there were no grounds available for Ikey's arrest unless he committed a felony on the island. Until Colonel Arthur had written to England and acquainted the under-secretary of the colonial office of Ikey's whereabouts so that a warrant could be issued for his arrest in the colony, his iniquitous quarry was as free as a lark.

Ikey, most eager to show Hannah that he had turned over a new leaf and was determined to become a devoted family man, bid his two elder sons leave New South Wales and join their mother in Hobart Town. He then set up John, the eldest, as a general merchant, with Moses his brother as his junior partner. Their establishment was stocked mostly with the hard goods Ikey had transported from America.

John and Moses Solomon would soon prosper, though gratitude would not be Ikey's reward for so swiftly reuniting his family and increasing their material well-being. Their indifference to their father is not impossible to understand, as they had no opportunity in their childhood to know Ikey, nor were they ever given a single reason to love him. They had, however, been instructed in every possible vilification of their father by their much beloved mother.

Almost from Ikey's arrival, Hannah commenced to quarrel with her husband, drawing her family into the arguments on her side. She had become convinced, and soon convinced them, that she had been made a scapegoat and was carrying Ikey's sentence.

With that peculiar logic of which women are sometimes capable, Hannah had also convinced herself that Ikey had somehow bribed Bob Marley to plant the stolen watch in the biscuit tin. Though no possible logic could explain such a bizarre scheme, Hannah was nevertheless quite blind to reason on this issue, and saw it as part of Ikey's grand plan to get her to part with her half of the combination to the safe. Thereafter, she knew with certainty, he would abscond with the contents, leaving her, whether free or convict, as a destitute prisoner on this God-forsaken island.

Affairs in the Newman household soon reached a point where Hannah's disagreeable manner even overcame the patience of the mild-mannered Mrs Newman, who demanded of her husband that he ask Ikey to leave and that he send Hannah back to the Female Factory. Richard Newman was, it must be supposed, either a weak or an honest man, the latter being so unusual in a police officer as to make it reasonable to suggest that the first quality formed a large part of his nature. If he returned Hannah to the authorities he would be obliged to return an amount of twenty pounds in lieu of the remaining three months of the accommodation agreement he had struck with John Solomon. If he should return Hannah, he found himself open to blackmail as he had been foolish enough to issue Ikey's eldest son with a receipt which would now prove his complicity.

Newman begged his wife to allow the Solomon family to remain for the three months. He pointed out that he had already spent the whole amount of the year's stipend on extensions to their cottage, and had no way of paying back the twenty pounds. In addition, he observed that Ikey's contribution of rent was paying for furnishings which they could otherwise not contemplate owning. Mrs Newman, a good and faithful woman, agreed that they should honour the agreement until it expired, whereupon, she made her husband promise, Hannah and her children would be returned to the authorities and Ikey asked to leave.

Hannah heard of Mrs Newman's plans and in a state of intoxication she confronted her, shouting wildly and accusing her of ingratitude while, at the same time, threatening to tell the authorities of the unlawful financial arrangement her husband had entered into with Hannah's son.

As with many mild-mannered people who are finally provoked, this was the straw that broke the camel's back. Mrs Newman flew into a fit of fury such as had never occurred in her life and she struck Hannah repeatedly with a broomstick and drove her screaming from the cottage.

This was the moment for which the officials had been waiting. Under the governor's instructions they had been watching the goings-on in the Newman household and, at the first reasonable opportunity, had been instructed to move against the Solomons in the hope of ensnaring Ikey in some public misdemeanour. Hannah was arrested and taken to the Female Factory and her children, as they were still assigned to her care and therefore the responsibility of the authorities, taken to the orphanage.

An official investigation followed where it was convincingly shown that Hannah had never been treated as an assigned servant and that Newman, a constable and guardian of the law, had not reported as living under his roof a 'suspected' criminal who, though not positively confirmed, was thought to be the runagate Ikey Solomon.

While this was a slender enough accusation and one which would scarcely have withstood the scrutiny of even a colonial magistrate, it was sufficient to frighten Newman. In order to avoid possible censure, he claimed that Hannah's behaviour had greatly changed since the arrival of Ikey, who had on several occasions boasted to him that he had plans to take her out of the colony at the first opportunity. Newman completed his statement with the words: 'He told me that even should she be placed in the Female Factory he would use sufficient influence to free her again'.

This attempt to implicate Ikey in a conspiracy failed, but the colonial secretary, hearing of this boast by Ikey to bring about the escape of his wife, ordered that Hannah be closely confined within the Factory and never assigned as a family servant again.

Hannah once again took this to be Ikey's work, her reasoning being that, despite his constant supplications, her continued refusal to give him the combination to the safe had caused him to punish her further. Though she truly dreaded the prospect of the Female Factory, it was the loss of her children which caused her to hate Ikey even more, and she swore she would rather die than allow him the use of a single penny of their combined fortune.

Ikey, who still went officially under the name of Sloman and so was not permitted to attend the hearing, was greatly distressed at the outcome. Hannah was slipping further and further from his grasp. Though they had quarrelled incessantly since his arrival, he was certain she would eventually be persuaded to his cause. Now, with her incarceration in the Female Factory after nearly a year of freedom, her children taken from her, he knew the likelihood of his gaining her co-operation in the matter of the numbers to be severely diminished.

Ikey decided to throw all caution to the wind and appeal to the English weakness for an act of selfless nobility, and Arthur's strong desire not to waste the financial resources of the colony. He wrote directly to Arthur, dropping the name of Sloman and admitting to his real identity.

Hobart

His Excellency Colonel George Arthur

Lt. Governor of Van Diemen's Land

> *Sir, I beg to State the following for Which I most Humbly hope that Your Excellency will be pleased to take into Your Consideration.*

While in America I have read of my wife's unfortunate situation and, acting solely from those natural causes, feeling and affections unnecessary, I trusts, to explain to Your Excellency, I have travelled 30,000 miles, expressly to settle and pass the remainder of my life in the bosom of my family. I therefore beseech Your Excellency most humbly that You may allow my beloved wife to be assigned to me as servant as I am certain that a woman of her refined nature and frail disposition will not long survive the place of oblivion in which she is now confined to the utter discomfiture and bereavement of your memorialist.

I wish to explain to Your Excellency that in the matter of Mr R. Newman of which You are well acquainted, were it not for his constant demands for money there would be no such trumped up complaint as was brought before You. With the result that my beloved wife has been torn from the arms of her precious children and sent to that dreadful confinement which is worse than death.

I further promise Your Excellency that should You release my wife to my care I shall be happy to enter into a bond of indemnity to prove my utmost good faith on this matter.

I have the honour to Subscribe – Your Excellency's Most Humble Servant

Isaac Solomon.

Arthur's reply was a blunt and unequivocal refusal: '. . . *the ends of justice would be entirely defeated, if his wife, so soon after her transportation to this colony, should be assigned to her husband.*'

Meanwhile, Ikey, all his life a cautious man who seldom made mistakes of judgement concerning the law, seemed so entirely obsessed with the desire to get the information he needed from Hannah that he did not appear to realise he had come to the end of his efforts and ought to be making a hurried departure from Van Diemen's Land.

Caution, and the knowledge that opportunities are seldom singular and that another occasion will always arise to gain your purpose, had always been Ikey's favoured philosophy. This patience and trust in his luck had served him well in the past. Now it seemed as if, by giving his Waterloo medal to Mary, he had sacrificed his sound judgement and good sense. It was almost as though he was under a delusion that even the determined arm of the law was not long enough to stretch across the twelve thousand miles separating London from Hobart Town.

But stretch it did and its fingers began to close around Ikey with the necessary documents relating to the issue of a warrant for his arrest arriving in Hobart.

Time has warped the facts of Ikey's arrest and different versions have come to exist to satisfy the appetites of amateur historians bent on intellectual booty. The Sydney *Monitor* of 17th March 1830 reported Ikey's arrest thus:

At about 2 p.m. two constables, in the disguise of out-settlers, came into the shop, one of whom said he wanted some tobacco and the other a pipe. On coming in they asked for the old gentleman, as they preferred dealing with him to the young ones. Ikey, who was behind the counter, started up and said: 'I am the person,' and instantly one of the men seized him and said: 'You are the person we want.' On this apprehension, Ikey turned as pale as death, and after recovering from the stupor of a few moments exclaimed: 'So help me Heaven! I am a done man now; it's all over for me; I am done for!' He made a rush towards a desk at the upper end of the counter, on which there was lying a penknife, which he endeavoured to seize hold of, no doubt for the purpose of committing suicide, but was prevented in the attempt by the constables, to whose assistance four of the military, who were stationed outside, came with drawn bayonets and fire arms. Having rendered him powerless, they hand-cuffed him, and brought him before the Police Magistrate of the Colony. After identification as Isaac Solomon, he was committed to gaol, where to guard against the possibility of escape, he was heavily ironed.

It is on such dull documentation that history must build its case.

Mary would come to tell of it differently, for she had it from one of the prison urchins she taught in the Female Factory who was in the shop at the time.

Children have a better ear for the truth and can repeat quite clearly what they have seen and heard. This is particularly true of the street urchin, who must depend on his ears and his eyes to avoid trouble from shopkeepers, officials, grown-ups in general and, of course, the law. The boy, who stood in the corner of Ikey's shop unnoticed while the arrest took place, told it as an amusing piece in which two bumble-mouthed constables made a proper mess of the arrest procedure.

The young lad had barely entered the door when he was brushed aside by two settlers dressed in the rough manner of workmen from the bush. Ikey, who was trimming a split thumb nail with a small penknife, looked up and seeing the two men approach immediately placed the knife down upon the counter to give his two out-of-town customers his attention. His shopkeeper's smile appeared and his hands spread wide to welcome them.

'Gentlemen, a pinch of snuff, compliments o' the 'ouse, American, Kentucky blend and not to be sneezed at!' Ikey cackled at his own tired joke, expecting his grateful customers to do the same.

The two men became confused and then looked the one at the other.

'Go on, 'elp yourselves, lads, it be a custom o' the 'ouse when strangers comes to town.' Ikey pushed the yellow snuff tin along the counter towards the two men, one of whom gave a small shrug and took a useful pinch, first to one nostril and then the other. His partner did the same and almost at once their nostrils were seen to dilate, their mouths to open, eyes to close and their heads to draw back, whereupon the sneeze arrived at almost the identical moment for each. Their heads were thrown forward so that they were taken to bending quite involuntarily at the waist, so mighty was the report from their nostrils.

After a few moments they looked up at Ikey through watery eyes and the larger of the two men sniffed and wiped the mucus from his nose with the back of his hand. Ikey now stood most casually with both hands placed flat upon the counter.

'A king o' sneezes, say you not, my dears? A prime example o' the veritable art o' the most honourable Chinese emperor, Ah-Tishoo! That sniff o' snuff be the best in the colony, though a humble enough sample o' me wares and quite nothing compared with the Cuban cigars or blends o' baccy we 'as for pleasing those who come from out o' town. What say you, gentlemen, how may I serve you?'

'Ikey Solomon?' the second bushman said.

'To whom does I 'ave the pleasure?' Ikey asked pushing his long thin fingers across the counter.

'We 'as come to arrest thee, sir!' the man with the snotty hand said, not shaking Ikey's extended hand.

Ikey pulled back and clasped both his hands to his chest in a show of horror, his eyes rolled and his expression was most comic afraid, then he picked up the penknife and held it with the tiny blade pointed towards his heart. 'Oh, woe is me, so help me heaven,' he said looking towards the ceiling, 'I am a done man now!' He grabbed at his throat with his free hand and made a strangling sound, his tongue protruding. 'Aargh! I shall take me own life rather than be taken alive!'

It was a most amusing display and Ikey, seeing the urchin standing at the door, winked broadly at him. Children, he understood, were much more intelligent of wit than those who have lost the enchantment of pantomime.

'Arrest is it? How very amusing, gentlemen, shall you chain me now?' Ikey extended his wrists to beyond the counter, his hands clasped together. Then, as though suddenly grown tired of the childish game, he withdrew them and clasped the edge of the counter. 'What is it I can get for you, gentlemen? I have much to do in this pretty day.'

'A clay pipe!' one of the men shouted, and Ikey jumped at the boldness of his voice.

'An ounce o' shag!' the other shouted equally loudly, causing Ikey to throw up his hands in consternation at the manner of their delivery which, curiously, had not been directed at him but in the direction of the door.

Almost at once four troopers with drawn bayonets affixed to their firearms elbowed their way through the door in a clatter and banging of barrels and butts, the clinking of metal and thump of heavy boots. They wore their red coats and had polished their brasses in anticipation of the grand occasion.

'You are under arrest, Ikey Solomon!' the constable who'd earlier wiped his nose shouted, and this time produced a pair of police manacles from the pocket of his jacket.

'Ikey's luck 'as finally run out,' Mary said solemnly, after the boy returned in great excitement to the Female Factory to tell his story. She clasped the Waterloo medal to her bosom, the gold metal warm in her twisted hand. 'He should 'ave tried to see me, if only just to greet me!' Then she turned away so that the boy could not see her tears and in a voice too soft for him to hear she said, 'Stupid old sod! Maybe he could've shared some o' me luck.'

Chapter Twenty-three

Mary moved from the old Female Factory where she had spent the past eighteen months to the new one where, for a short period, she returned to work in the bakery. If new meant a larger factory it did not mean a better one. The new female house of correction was a remodelled distillery, secured cheaply by the government, and its site in the damp valley of the Hobart Town rivulet, under the shadow of a large hill which blocked almost all direct sunlight for a large part of the year, was most unsuitable. It was damp and dark and so unhealthy that during the first winter in the new Factory eighteen inmates and twenty-seven newborn babies died from bronchial illnesses.

While the kneading of dough was hard work, Mary found it pleasant enough. The ovens were warm on the cold days of drizzle and sharp, cutting winds which blew up the wide Derwent River from the coast in winter. Van Diemen's Land has a contrary climate and lies sufficiently close to the Antarctic Circle to have at least one of its toes permanently in ice. No local would be brave enough to pronounce a part of any day of the year safe from sudden bone-chilling cold, when summer's blue brilliance is turned, with a malevolent growl from atop the great mountain, into the misery of a winter gale.

The year and a half spent in the old Female Factory had not, at first, been easy for Mary. The overcrowded conditions, the constant fighting among the prisoners and the fact that the Factory was as much a brothel as a prison, made the day-to-day effort to survive most onerous. But Mary, convinced that her luck in life had changed the moment she had set foot in Van Diemen's Land, set about the task of surviving until she was granted her ticket of leave.

Life in a female gaol is no different from that of a male one – dominance and strength are usually all that matter. With Ann Gower at her side, Mary set about the conquest of her fellow inmates. She grew her nails until her twisted hands had the appearance of wicked claws. Ann Gower let the stories of Mary in Newgate and the raking of Potbottom's back be known. She also conveyed the fact that Mary had been crowned queen of the prisoners on the voyage because she had defied the authorities, earned a flogging and won the day. This was sufficient to make Mary Abacus greatly feared and respected among the prisoners without ever having to fight any of the inmates.

The prisoners at the Female Factory soon came to realise that Mary was on their side and was not a leader simply so that she might benefit herself or her cronies at their expense. The authorities also accepted that Mary's leadership was not necessarily to their disadvantage. She did not directly challenge their authority but, instead, organised the prostitution and the distribution of grog and tobacco in the Factory. Mary's past experience of running a brothel and organising the lives of the girls within it made life in gaol a great deal more bearable for all.

It was the custom of the Factory to elect female overseers and task mistresses from the prisoners and the superintendent of the Factory begged Mary to take such a position but she refused. They were obliged to accept that Mary carried more unsanctioned authority than those prisoners they had trusted with such a position. They also knew that those convicts appointed overseers would answer to Mary before them.

Payment by the troopers for services from the prison whores was now, as it had been at Egyptian Mary's, made not to the individual whore, but directly to Mary. She in turn negotiated the price of tobacco and grog among the corrupt turnkeys and, provided they did not become too greedy, paid them what they demanded. Mary retained a small percentage of the capital earned and paid the remainder to the prisoners who were owed it. This she did in money or in kind.

The clicking of her abacus could often be heard late into the night as she reconciled her ledgers. Mary's calculations were scrupulously correct and, while there are always those in a mutual society who whisper that the bookkeeper is a cheat, the ten percent she took from each transaction was considered by most to be fair for the task she undertook.

In fact, it had been an attempt by the prison officials to squeeze too great a profit from the prisoners which had consolidated Mary's position and proved the value of the ten percent levy. Those who profited dishonourably from the poor wretches under their care demanded an even higher price for their tobacco and grog. Mary refused and at the same time withheld the services of the prostitutes to the government troopers.

The Female Factory was unofficially endorsed by the military command as a soldier's brothel, and when it ceased to work the prison officials were forced to admit, in answer to the discreet though annoyed enquiries from the military command, that they could not alleviate the situation. This was the cause of much private embarrassment although, publicly, Governor Arthur had used it to his benefit. In fact, with much pomp and ceremony he had presided over an official commendation to the chief gaoler for having successfully put down prostitution in the Female Factory. In the same hour of the governor's departure the barracks commander had demanded, supposedly with the blessing of the governor, that 'the good work on behalf of my troopers be resumed at once!'

During the two-week strike Mary used the funds she had accumulated from taking her ten percent cut to purchase grog and tobacco which she dispensed to the workers while they were unemployed.

By organising the prison urchins, who could come and go as they pleased and, besides, had no problems evading the porter at the gate, Mary showed the corrupt officials that she had the means of bringing in adequate supplies of the commodities they had fondly imagined they exclusively controlled. Pressure continued to mount from the troopers who had come to see the Female Factory as their rightful source of recreation and so it was not long before commonsense prevailed. The turnkeys asked that the former prices should be maintained.

But Mary demanded the prices come down. She was sentenced to solitary confinement on bread and water on a trumped-up charge, but this manoeuvre was an abject failure. The prisoner whores refused to co-operate, although in all other things their behaviour was exemplary. In a pact which they named 'Legs crossed for Mary' they refused to lie on their backs on behalf of the Crown, and the authorities, fearing a public outcry, could not be seen to punish them.

Mary was released from solitary after only two days and a fair deal was struck with the turnkeys. Nothing like this had ever happened before. The fact that Mary had been prepared to be punished for their ultimate benefit deeply impressed the prisoners, and she now possessed their loyalty.

Mary also concerned herself with the prison urchins, and conducted a school for them for an hour each day in which they were taught to read and write. This ragged school was a great pride to the mothers of the children and also to many of the other prisoners, who were generally illiterate. They took comfort in the fact that ignorance was not, as they had been so often told, a permanent curse placed upon their kind by a malevolent God. Even the whores looked with satisfaction upon the slates the children carried and regarded these as a positive proof that their work was not unworthy.

However, it should not be construed that Mary's presence in the Female Factory had turned it into a place of calm and order. Prison is still an institution where the back is broken with hard labour and the soul is destroyed by despair. Despite Mary's efforts, this vile degradation had not changed in Van Diemen's Land. Sadness and despair are ingredients without which the recipe of prison cannot be made acceptable to society. If the old Female Factory had never worked better than under Mary's leadership, this was only that it was a lesser kind of hell on earth. One of the most palpable examples of this misery was the inevitable consequence of institutionalised prostitution, the illegitimately born child.

A great many of the children did not survive long. The poor diet in the Female Factory resulted in serious malnutrition and many mothers could not produce sufficient breast milk to feed their babies. Those infants which did survive were removed from their mothers as soon as possible after birth and sent to the orphanage, which was known as 'the nursery'. One of the most commonly heard sounds in the Factory was of a mother wailing at the enforced loss of her child, for it cannot be supposed that the whore has less love for the miracle within her womb than does the wife of a preacher.

However, this was not thought to be the case by the authorities and many of the population and proof thereof was rendered when a female convict, Mary McLaughlan, was executed for killing her newborn baby. Though children died like flies from the lack of food, hygiene and warmth in the Factory, this was thought to be quite in order, whereas the act of a mother putting her tiny infant out of misery, so that it should not suffer longer than its day of birth, was regarded as a crime so gross that the whole island was deeply shocked at this example of the brutalised convict mind. When Mary had gently asked her namesake why she had taken the life of her infant the little Scots woman had wept bitter tears. 'Acht, I couldnae bear the bairn t' suffer. I had nae milk in me teets nor ought t' save its wee life.'

The Reverend William Bedford, the drunken chaplain to the convicts who, in God's name, had been among the large concourse assembled to witness the last moments of Mary McLaughlan, preached a sermon while almost sober in the prison chapel on the Sunday following the hanging.

'She stood dressed in a snow-white garment with a black ribbon tied about her waist and a certain hope of forgiveness supported her in her final hour and, it is my belief, she died contrite and resigned.' Bedford looked about his congregation. Not all were prisoners and the townsfolk sat separated from the lewd looks of the male convicts by a curtain. 'On the falling of the drop, the instant before her mortal scene was closed, she did utter but three words of penitence, "Oh! my God!" though this may well have been a curse, I have chosen to see it as a plea to heaven for forgiveness! Hers was the dreadful crime of murder, the cold-blooded killing of the little innocent offspring of her own bosom.' He paused again, for he was in good form and had for once the complete attention of his congregation. 'Well has this first step to error been compared to the burning spark which, when lighted, may carry destruction to inconceivable bounds. But will mankind take a lesson from this?' He shook his head slowly then banged his fist upon the pulpit. 'Cannot the horrible tenacity be broken with which the Devil keeps his hold, when once he has put his finger on his victim?' The Reverend Bedford let this last sentiment reach the minds of his congregation before he added in a voice both sorrowful and low, 'I think not'.

And so the act committed by a desperate woman was entered into the history of the island as the most heinous of all crimes committed in that place of infamy.

Mary had always had a great love for children, though she would never be able to bear one of her own. She came to look upon the children in the orphanage as belonging to the women in the prison and therefore as her responsibility. Her heart seemed torn asunder when each newly weaned infant was taken away from its mother. On many occasions she had begged the prison authorities to allow the infants to stay, or even that the mothers might be allowed to visit their children at the orphanage on the Sabbath.

The reply had always been the same. The prisoner mother had no rights to a child born out of wedlock, nor could the prison authorities accept responsibility for its care. The best interests of the newborn infant were served away from the malignant pollutants of the prison atmosphere, where under the supervision of a benign government, a child would benefit from a Christian upbringing in the Reverend Thomas Smedley's Wesleyan Orphanage.

And so Mary had passed the first year and a half of her sentence in Van Diemen's Land, though one more aspect should be added which was to be of paramount importance to her future. She was naturally inclined to gardening, though she couldn't think why this should be, as her life had been spent almost entirely on cobblestones in decaying courts and alleys devoid of even a blade of grass. The names of flowers were quite unknown to her, but for the daffodil, rose and violet, and these three only because urchins sold them on the streets of London.

She loved to work in the potato patch and never failed to be surprised when, upon pulling up a dark green, hairy-leafed plant she would find attached to its slender roots great creamy orbs fit for the plate of a king. A little further digging would reveal more of the wonderful tubers and her hands, buried in the rich, damp soil, would for a moment seem whole, her long, slender fingers restored and beautiful.

In the new Female Factory her knowledge and disposition for gardening were recognised, and she was allowed to leave the bakery and spend all her prison working hours at this task. Mary talked to the Irish women in the Factory about the manner of growing potatoes, and learned much from them which improved the crop grown in the prison gardens. This, in particular, from Margaret Keating, who added further to her knowledge with information on the making of poteen, sometimes known as 'Irish whisky'. This is usually made from barley, but potatoes may be used instead. Though each kind has an altogether different taste, both are most astonishingly intoxicating.

Mary soon showed that her proficiency with potatoes carried over to Indian corn, cabbage, carrots and other vegetables. She asked that Ann Gower be allowed to work with her as well as several of the Irish women accustomed to working the soil, including Margaret Keating. She also asked that a good-sized shed be built so that the garden implements could be safely stored and the seeding potatoes successfully propagated. Behind this shed she proposed to build a hothouse for propagating seeds. This, she convinced the prison authorities, was because of the unpredictable weather, where frosts and cold snaps late into spring and early summer could destroy half an acre of vegetable seedlings overnight. This second project was considered to be outside the authority of the prison as it involved the purchase of glass, and was referred to the chief clerk of the colonial secretary's department, Mr Emmett.

Mary had greatly impressed Mr Emmett, who saw her use her abacus to calculate the cost of losing two crops as they had done the previous year to sudden cold snaps. She had offset this against the price of the materials, all of which, but for the glass used in the construction, were made by the male prisoners with only the smallest cost to the treasury.

For the hothouse Mary proposed a clever modification. She planned to build into one of the brick end walls a kiln which could be worked from the outside of the building. Ann explained to the authorities that one of the Irish women, skilled in the making of pots, had discovered a clay pit near the rivulet. The clay there was thought to be of excellent quality for pots. Mary proposed that they would produce water and plant pots for sale to the townsfolk and, with the advent of the hothouse, ornamental plants could be grown. The profits from this enterprise would go directly to the coffers of the colony. The chief clerk now took a keen interest in the hothouse as if the idea had been his own. He accepted the proposal and agreed that the hothouse should be built, together with the abutting kiln, a pottery drying shed and two wheels for turning the clay.

Mary had yet another modification in mind, though not one she thought to mention to the chief clerk. She requested of the prisoner bricklayer to construct a wide hearth on the inside of the end wall of the hothouse, which contained the kiln on its outside. This would be back-to-back with the kiln, so that there would be a fireplace with a good platform, wide working mouth and a double chimney flue shared by both hearth and kiln.

When, to Margaret Keating's precise instructions, the structure was complete, they had the basis of a first-class poteen still. The kiln could be fired separately from the outside and the hearth, if needs be, made to carry a fire of its own on the inside. Mary had a carpenter construct a door to the opening of the hearth, which had four stout wooden shelves built into its outside surface. If the authorities should arrive unexpectedly when the still was in progress the fire could be quickly doused, and the door closed to conceal it. Numerous pots containing plants could be hastily placed upon the shelves as though this was their permanent resting place. Smoke from the recently doused fire would carry up the chimney, where it could always be explained as being caused by the operation of the outside kiln.

All that was now required was the equipment needed to place within the hearth. This consisted of the numerous thin copper pipes which would be fed through the back wall of the hearth into the kiln so that they would be further heated by it, as well as the two chambers needed for the condensation and distillation of the spirit. These copper chambers would reside within the mouth of the hearth, where only a very small fire was needed to keep the water within the main cylinder producing the steam required for the distillation of the potatoes which had been set to ferment.

Ann Gower, who had not the slightest inclination to use a hoe or break her back in a potato patch, was nevertheless perfectly willing to work in a trade she knew best. Whoring in prison gained only a sixpence at a time, whereas in the private enterprise of the prison gardens she could command a quick shilling. She was given the task of procuring the pipes, cylinders and other equipment required for the still.

Ann took up permanent residence in the newly completed shed, where she soon attracted a regular clientele. She quickly discovered those among her clients who had the means to steal, or the skill to fashion and install what Mary required in pipes and cylinders, valves and taps.

They had been most fortunate to chance upon a randy mechanic who was masterful in his knowledge of pipes and pressures. By employing his considerable engineering skill Mary constructed a still which, with the turning of no more than half a dozen nuts, could be disassembled and quickly hidden in a specially constructed cavity, which was revealed by lifting one of the large flagstones which comprised the floor of the hothouse.

In return for their services, those few men who had been involved in supply and construction of the still were happy enough to be repaid in a free weekly fulfilment from Ann Gower for the period of 'snow to snow'. This was the time from the last snowfall on Mount Wellington to the first of the following winter, or, if they were exceedingly unlucky, to a summer fall, which was not unknown in these parts.

Mary Abacus and Ann Gower, with the help of Margaret Keating, had created the two things most in demand on the island, strong drink and lewd women, and both at a price most attractive to the customer.

Governor Arthur was determined to stamp out drunkenness within the female prison, and his orders were that any turnkey caught selling grog was to be instantly dismissed and severely punished with three hundred strokes of the lash. While it had been comparatively easy to use the children to smuggle tobacco and liquor into the old Factory, it was considerably harder in the new, where they were regularly searched by the guards at the gates.

Now Mary and her partners could not only sell grog to the free population but they could also bring into prison significant quantities of the fiery poteen concealed in the loads of vegetables delivered to the kitchen each evening.

The three women worked well together, Ann Gower being utterly loyal to Mary and Margaret Keating being a quietly spoken and sensible woman who was a political prisoner. Within six months of the completion of the still, having served three years in prison, she was assigned to an emancipist of good repute who offered at the same time to take her as his wife.

To her husband's surprise she brought with her a small but much-needed cash dowry, the source of which he was sufficiently prudent not to enquire about. And so Margaret Keating left her two erstwhile partners to enjoy a life of hard work and the utmost respectability, where she would lose one child and raise four others in the happiest of family circumstances. Mary took over the working of the poteen still.

Both Mary and Ann Gower knew well enough that whoring and strong drink taken together spelled trouble, so they were careful not to create a convivial atmosphere about the running of their business. Hobart Town abounded in sly-grog shops where all manner of homemade liquor could be obtained. This was a most potent and dangerous concoction and often laced with laudanum. When the revellers became too drunk and noisy they were given a finishing glass which consisted of a strong poison and was designed to render the drinker unconscious so that he might more easily be thrown out onto the street or, if he was a whaler with a pocketful of silver American dollars, robbed of all he possessed.

Men were not permitted to congregate or drink on Mary's prison vegetable plot, but only to use Ann's services or make a purchase of grog. A single transaction, the purchase of a 'pot', as a small container of poteen became known, took two minutes. A double transaction, a 'pot 'n pant', took no more than ten, a shilling being paid for each service, after which the recipient was required promptly to scarper from the premises.

Mary's poteen soon earned a reputation for its excellent quality and as men must always put names to things, this being especially true for things clandestine, where a wink and a nod may be involved, or a euphemism employed, some began to call the enterprise 'The Potato Patch'.

'Where are you going, mate?' a man might enquire of another.

'To the Potato Patch,' would be the reply.

However, late one winter's afternoon a trooper, not a usual customer, after obtaining his two shillings worth demanded company to go with his proposed drinking. When promptly ordered to leave he grew most cantankerous and, stumbling away, he turned and yelled at Mary.

'This place be shit! It be nothing but a damned potato factory!'

The name stuck and Mary's still became known as 'The Potato Factory'. It was a name thought most excellent to those who used its services, for it contained some character and style, which is an essential ingredient in any decent man's drinking habits, the Potato Patch always having had about it a somewhat base and primitive feel.

Now it might be supposed that an operation such as this would soon enough be the subject of the tattle tongues to be found in great numbers in a women's prison, and that the prison officials would soon come to know about it. But Mary and Ann Gower saw to it that the prisoners had drink sufficient to keep them happy, and that their children had clothes and physic when they had colic or were otherwise taken with sickness. Mary reigned as Queen no differently in the new Female Factory than she had done in the old.

Similarly, it must be expected that a customer of the Potato Factory would at some time reveal its whereabouts to such as an undercover plainclothes constable set about gathering useful information within the premises of a brothel or a tavern. Gossips and narks are among the most virulent forces at work in any convict community, but no sooner had one sly-grog outlet closed down than another would spring up in its place.

Even if human weakness is more often exercised than human strength, a community such as was to be found in Hobart Town could keep its secrets well. Most of the people who walked the streets were either emancipists, ticket of leavers or active prisoners, and all felt they had just cause to resent authority and to keep some things secret from the free settlers whom they disliked almost as much.

Mary saw to it that the troopers connected with the Female Factory were kept silent with a regular supply of poteen. Furthermore, several key members of the local constabulary would receive a pint-sized 'pot' with a tight wooden cork, brought in by a street urchin each week. And, at least one magistrate was known to consider Mary's poteen 'The purest water o' life itself!' and took pains not to ask his clerk, who declined to take payment for it, where he habitually obtained it.

Mary's vegetable garden and pottery continued to prosper and the prison authorities had no cause to complain. Abundant vegetables and sacks of splendid potatoes arrived at the Female Factory kitchen and, while much of this fresh produce never found its way onto the prison tables, being appropriated by those in charge, this did not concern Mary. She well understood that those in charge had even further reason not to look too closely behind the cabbage leaves.

From time to time, the chief clerk, Mr Emmett, would receive a reasonable sum of money, being the proceeds for the sale of plant and water pots. He would receive the funds together with a summary of what had been sold, to whom and at what price. A clerk sent about the town confirmed Mary's reconciliation correct to the penny – all this in Mary's neat hand, the columns precisely drawn and the addition and subtraction without error. The payment would always come together with a handsomely turned pot which contained some exotic forest bloom, Mr Emmett being famous for his garden and his cottage, Beauly Lodge, was considered the most beautiful in Hobart Town. Once, for his daughter Millicent on her tenth birthday, Mary sent a standard rose, a veritable pin cushion of tiny, perfectly formed pink blooms.

Mr Emmett, observing the honesty and integrity of Mary Abacus, called on the Female Factory to offer her the position of a clerk with the colonial secretary's department. But, though Mary had declared herself most flattered, she declined the offer.

'Do you not understand, Mary, that there are no women in my department or, I dare say, in any other? You should perceive this as a great honour.' Mr Emmett smiled and then resumed. 'No woman, I'll wager, and *never* a convict woman has been placed in so great and fortunate a position of trust on this island, my dear!'

Mary wondered how she could possibly think to refuse. Then she looked down at her twisted hands and her eyes filled with bitter tears at the memory of the cold winter morning in London's docklands, when she had left Mr Goldstein's warehouse with her heart singing. How in the swirling yellow mist the male voices had risen to envelop and crush her . . .

> *Mary, Mary, Bloody Mary*
> *Who does her sums on bead and rack*
> *Go away, you're too contrary*
> *You're the monkey, the bloody monkey*
> *You're the monkey on our back!*

The harsh memories flooded back and Mary was most hard put to restrain herself from weeping.

'I'm sorry, sir, I may not accept. There be reasons I cannot say to you, though me gratitude be most profound and I thank you from the bottom o' me 'eart.' Then she looked up at Mr Emmett, her eyes still wet with her held back tears. 'I prefers the gardens, sir. The air be clean and the work well disposed to me ability.'

Mr Emmett made one last effort to persuade her. It was apparent that he did not like being refused and now spoke with some annoyance. 'There are few enough on this cursed island who can read or write, let alone reconcile a column of figures! Good God, woman, will you not listen to me? You are . . .' he took a moment to search for words, '. . . wasted in this . . . this damned potato patch of yours!'

'Then let me teach, sir!' Mary pleaded urgently. 'So that we may make more of our children to read and write and meet with your 'ighest demands!'

'Teach? Where? Teach who?'

'The orphanage, sir. The prison brats. If I could teach three mornings a week I could still manage the gardens.'

Mr Emmett looked bewildered. 'Your suggestion is too base to be regarded with proper amusement, Mary. These are misbegotten children, the spawn of convicts and drunken wretches!' It was apparent that he had become most alarmed at the thought. 'They cannot be made to learn as you and I may. Have you no commonsense about you, woman?' He shook his head and screwed up his eyes as though he were trying to rid his mind of the thought Mary had planted therein. 'First you refuse my offer, now this urchin-teaching poppycock! These children cannot possibly be made to count or write! Surely you know this as well as I do? Have you not observed them for yourself? They are creatures damned by nature, slack of jaw and vacant of expression, the cursed offspring of the criminal class. I assure you, they do not have minds which can be made to grasp the process of formal learning!' He smiled at a sudden thought. 'Will you have them to do Latin?'

'*Ergo sum*, "I am one",' Mary said quietly. 'I were born a urchin same as them, slack-jawed and vacant o' face the way you looks when you be starvin'!' She cocked her head to one side and attempted to smile, though all the muscles of her lips could manage was a quiver at the corners of her mouth. She reached up to her bosom and clasped the Waterloo medal in her hand. 'Only three mornings?' she pleaded. 'I begs you to ask them folk at the orphanage, sir.'

The chief clerk seemed too profoundly shocked to continue and for some time he remained silent. 'Hmmph!' he growled at last. 'I shall see what I can make of it.' He shook his head slowly, clucking his tongue. 'Clerks out of street urchins, eh? I'll wager, it will be as easy to turn toads into handsome princes!'

A week later Mary received a message to see the Reverend Thomas Smedley, the Wesleyan principal at the orphanage in New Town which had been given the surprising name of the King's Orphan School, though no teaching whatsoever took place in the cold, damp and cheerless converted distillery which served as a home for destitute and deserted children. With this invitation came a pass to leave the prison garden so that she might attend the meeting scheduled for the latter part of the afternoon.

The Reverend Smedley was a short, stout man, not much past his fortieth year, who wore a frock coat and dark trousers, both considerably stained. Neither was his linen too clean, the dog collar he wore being much in need of a scrub and a douse of starch. He wore small gold-rimmed spectacles on a nose which seemed no more than a plump button, and the thick lenses exaggerated the size of his dark eyes. Though it was a face which seemed disposed to be jolly, it was not. Any jollity it may have once possessed was defeated by a most profoundly sour expression. The Reverend Smedley was clean shaven and his cheeks much crossed with a multiplicity of tiny scarlet veins, a curious sanguinity in one so young and not a drinking man. He was a follower of Charles Wesley and, unlike his Anglican counterparts, was sure to be a teetotaller. Instead of adding a rosy blush, these scrambled veins upon his fat cheeks exacerbated further his saturnine expression. It seemed as though he might be ill with a tropical fever, for apart from his roseate jowls, his skin was yellow, while a thin veneer of perspiration covered his podgy face. To Mary he looked a man much beset by life who was in need of the attentions of a good wife or a sound doctor.

'What is your religion, Miss . . . er, Abacus?' Mary had been left to stand while Thomas Smedley had flipped the tails of his frock coat, and sat upon the lone chair behind a large desk in the front office of the children's orphanage.

'I can't rightly say, sir. I don't know that I 'as one.' Mary paused and shrugged. 'I be nothin' much o' nothin'.'

'A satanist then? Or is it an atheist?'

'Neither, sir, if you mean I believes in the opposite or not at all.'

The Reverend Thomas Smedley looked exceedingly sour and snapped at Mary in a sharp, hard voice which contrasted with his flaccid appearance.

'Do you, or do you not, have the love of the Lord Jesus Christ in your heart? Have you or have you not, been washed in the Blood of the Lamb? Are you, or are you not, saved of your sins? If not, you *may* not!' These three questions had been too rapid to answer each at a time and his voice had risen fully an octave with each question so that the last part was almost shrill, shouted at Mary in a spray of spittle.

However, at their completion he seemed at once exhausted, as though he had rehearsed well the questions and they had come out unbroken and, to his surprise, much as he had intended them to sound. Now he sat slumped in his chair and his head hung low, with his chin tucked into the folds of his neck, while his chubby hands grasped the side of the desk and his magnified eyes looked obliquely up at Mary as he waited for her reply.

'May not what, sir?' Mary asked politely.

'Teach! Teach! Teach!' Smedley yelled.

'I do not understand, sir? I shall not teach them either of lambs or washing of blood, or sins and least of all of God, but of the salvation of numbers and letters, sir.'

The clergyman looked up and pointed a stubby finger at Mary. 'I am not mocked saith the Lord!' he shouted.

Oh, Gawd, not another one! Mary thought, casting her mind to the dreadful Potbottom, though outwardly she smiled modestly at the Reverend Smedley. 'I had not meant to mock, sir, my only desire is to teach the word o' man and leave the business o' Gawd to the pulpit men, like yourself.'

'God is not business! God is love! I am the way, the truth and the light saith the Lord! Unthinkable! Quite, quite, unthinkable!' His eyes appeared to narrow and his fat fist banged down upon the desk. 'Unless you are born again we cannot allow you to teach children! How will you show them the way, the truth and the light? How will you example the love of Jesus Christ?'

'Who is teaching them now?' Mary asked, hoping to change the subject.

'They have religious instruction twice each day,' the principal shot back angrily. 'That is quite sufficient for their need.'

362

'Oh, you have used the Bible to teach them to read and write,' Mary said, remembering this was how the Quaker women had suggested they perform this task on board ship.

'We teach salvation! The love of the Lord Jesus and the redemption of our sins so that we may be washed clean, we do not teach reading and writing here!' the preacher barked. 'These children shall grow up to be hewers of wood and drawers of water, that is the place for which they are destined in the Scriptures. They are no less the sons of Ham than the blacks who hide in the hills and steal our sheep. These orphan children are loved by the Lord, for He loves the sparrow as well as the eagle, the less fortunate as well as the gifted child.'

'Then, with Gawd's permission and your own, I will teach them to be more fortunate, sir. Surely Gawd will see no 'arm in such tinkering?'

Reverend Smedley looked up at Mary who stood with her back directly to the open window so that the light from behind flooded into the tiny room to give her body a halo effect, though, at the same time, it caused her features to darken, so that, to the short-sighted clergyman, she seemed to be a dark, hovering satanic form.

'Tinkering? Permission? God's permission or mine, you shall have neither. You shall have no such thing! You are *not* saved, you are *not* clean, you are *not* born again, you are an unrepentant and dastardly sinner whom I have every right to drive from this temple of the Lord!'

Mary sighed. The worst that could happen to her was that she be sent back to the Female Factory and to the prison gardens and this was no great matter. She was not in the least afraid of the silly little man who yapped at her like an overfed lap dog. Her fear was for the orphan children, for the child she had been herself, for the fact that had it not been for the Chinee contraption of wire and beads she would have remained in darkness. Her fear was that if she were not permitted to teach these orphan children they would grow up to perpetuate the myth that her kind were a lower form of human life, one which was beyond all salvation of the mind and therefore of the spirit.

'What must I do to be saved?' she asked suddenly.

The clergyman looked up surprisd. 'Why, you must repent, of course!'

Mary shrugged and raised her eyebrows. 'Then I repent,' she announced simply.

Smedley sat up, suddenly alert. 'That's not proper repenting. You have to be sorry!'

'So, I'm sorry, sir,' Mary sighed. 'Most sorry.'

'Not me! Not sorry to me, to the Lord Jesus! You have to go down on your knees before Him and repent!'

'Repent or say I'm sorry? Which is it to be?' Mary asked.

'It's the same thing!' Thomas Smedley shouted. Then abruptly he stood up and pointed to the floor at Mary's feet, where he obviously expected her to kneel.

'No it ain't! It ain't the same at all,' Mary said, crossing her arms. 'I could be sorry and not repent, but I couldn't repent and not be sorry, know what I mean?'

'On your knees at once. The glory of the Lord is upon us!' the Reverend Smedley demanded and again jabbed a fat, urgent finger towards the bare boards at Mary's feet.

Mary looked about and indeed glory had entered the tiny room. A shaft of pale late afternoon sunlight lit the entire space, turning it to a brilliant gold, and small dust motes danced in the fiery light.

Mary looked directly at the clergyman. 'If I repent, can I teach?' she asked.

'Yes, yes!' Smedley screeched urgently. 'Kneel down! Kneel down at once! His glory be upon us!'

Mary knelt down in front of the desk and the Reverend Smedley came around from his side and placed his fat fist upon her head. 'Shut your eyes and bow your head!' he instructed. Then he began to pray in a loud and sonorous preacher's voice which Mary had not heard before.

'Lord I have brought this poor lost lamb to Thee to ask Thee to forgive her sins, for she wishes to repent and accept Your Glorious salvation and receive life eternal so that she may be clasped to Your glorious bosom and receive Your everlasting love.' There was a silence although it was punctuated several times with a loud sucking of the clergyman's lips as though he were undergoing some mysterious ecstasy. Then suddenly his preacher's voice resumed. 'Thank you precious Jesus. Hallelujah! Praise His precious name!'

Mary felt his hand lift from her head and in a tone of voice somewhat triumphant but more or less returned to its former timbre the Reverend Smedley announced calmly, 'Hallelujah, sister

Mary, welcome to the bosom of the Lord Jesus Christ, you are saved, washed in the blood of the Lamb! You may rise now.'

Mary rose to her feet. 'That was quick,' she said brightly. 'When can I start, then?'

The Reverend Smedley smiled benignly. 'You have already started on the journey of your *new* life. God has forgiven you your sins, you are a born again Christian now, Mary!'

'No, no, not that,' Mary said impatiently. 'When does I start with the brats?'

For a moment the Reverend Thomas Smedley looked deeply hurt, but then decided not to turn this expression into words. He had scored a direct hit with the Lord and saved another sinner from hellfire and he was not about to cruel his satisfaction.

'Why, tomorrow morning. You will be here by eight o'clock and will have fifty pupils.' The Reverend Smedley paused and looked at Mary. 'Though we have no slates, or bell, or even board or chalk and nor shall we get them if I know anything of the government stores!' The irritable edge had returned to his voice.

Mary turned to leave. 'Thank you, sir!' she pronounced carefully. But she could barely contain her excitement and took a deep breath, though she was unable to conceal her delight. 'Thank you, I'm much obliged, sir.' She held her hand out and the Reverend Smedley shuddered and involuntarily drew back, so that Mary's crippled paw was left dangling in the air. Then he scuttled to the safety of his side of the desk and opened the ledger to reveal a letter which had been placed between its covers. He spoke in a brusque voice, attempting to conceal his terror at the sight of Mary's hands.

'It says here in your letter of appointment from the governor that you are to take the noon meal with myself and my sister. Have you learned proper table manners, Miss Abacus?' It was obvious to Mary that the image of her hands at his table was the focus of Smedley's question.

Mary suddenly realised that her appointment to the school was not the decision of the irritable little clergyman at all, but that Mr Emmett had independently secured her position from Colonel Arthur himself. The interview with the Reverend Smedley was simply a formality.

'Blimey, sir, I ain't been born again no more'n two flamin' minutes, I ain't 'ad no time to learn proper christian manners!' She held up her hands. 'They ain't pretty but they works well enough with a knife and fork and I knows what spoon to use for puddin'.' She turned and took the two steps to the door then turned again and grinned at the preacher. 'See you tomorrow, then!'

Mary had no sooner escaped through the front door than she reached for the Waterloo medal and, clutching it tightly, rushed down the path away from the orphanage. She should have told the fat little bastard to sod off, but her heart wasn't in it. A little way down the road she turned and looked up at the great mountain towering above the town.

'Thank you,' she said quietly to the huge, round-shouldered mountain, then she threw caution to the winds. 'Thanks a million, rocks and trees and blue skies and Mister oh-so-magic Mountain!' she shouted at the top of her voice. Mary remembered suddenly that yesterday had been her birthday and that she was twenty-nine years old, though for a moment she felt not much older than the children she would begin to teach in the morning.

'Go on, then, send us a nice bright day tomorrow, will you, love?' she shouted again at the mountain. To Mary's left, high above the massive swamp gums, a flock of brilliant green parakeets flew screeching upwards towards the summit of Mount Wellington. 'Tell 'im I want a real beauty! A day to remember!' she yelled at the departing birds. 'Thanks for the luck!'

Chapter Twenty-four

Ikey arrived back in London on the *Prince Regent* on the 27th of June 1830. He was accompanied on the voyage by the chief constable of Van Diemen's Land who was under instructions from Governor Arthur not to let Ikey out of his sight, even to attend to his needs at the water closet.

On board ship Ikey had set about the task of starving himself and no manner of coaxing could bring him to eat a sufficient amount to sustain normal health. He would go for days on end sipping water alone and then he would add a few spoonfuls of gruel to his diet in order that his frail heart should continue to pump. He seldom spoke to anyone and allowed his hair and beard to grow again so that the former fell to his shoulders and the latter almost to his chest.

If this was intended to make the citizenry of the great metropolis sympathetic towards him, the ploy did not work. In every tavern, dance emporium, club and home London celebrated his capture and the City police took on the mantle of the heroes. It was as if they had hunted their quarry to the ends of the earth and brought him back in chains to face the full retribution of British justice. At no time was any credit accorded to Colonel Arthur. The governor of an obscure convict colony was simply not grand enough for such a prominent capture.

Though retired, Sir Jasper Waterlow travelled up to London to ascertain that it was indeed Ikey Solomon who had been returned, and he was rumoured to have visited him in Newgate to shake his hand.

This time Ikey was placed in a cell in the very centre of Newgate Prison. He was guarded twenty-four hours a day and allowed no visitors except for the barrister, Mr Phillips, whom he had briefed to represent him. He was arraigned at the Old Bailey and charged with seven additional counts of theft on top of the original charge of forging Bank of England five pound notes.

These additional charges had come about when, following Hannah's sentence, the police had observed that Ikey's home in Whitechapel was in the process of being bricked up. They had immediately served a search warrant on Abraham Reuban and thoroughly ransacked every room. They found the trapdoor under Hannah's bed and within it the false ceiling which contained a small fortune in stolen goods. When Abraham Reuban was finally permitted to brick up the windows and doors, only the safe under the pantry floor remained undiscovered.

Eleven days can make a marked difference in the appearance of a man and Ikey still had a sufficient sum to treat himself well in prison and pay for the best legal advice in England. He abandoned his hang dog demeanour and hirsute looks and ordered a new suit of clothes and linen from a tailor, though not from Abraham Reuban, who was not permitted to see him. A gentleman's barber from the Haymarket was brought in to cut his hair and to trim and shape his ragged beard. With ten days of good food in his belly Ikey was much improved in every circumstance but that of hope. When he stood in the dock at the Old Bailey to hear the reading of the indictments against him he was thought by many to be a man of handsome appearance.

The scene of the day of the trial, consequently much exaggerated by Grub Street hacks, is best described by reading from the eminently respectable *Morning Post* of the following day.

. . . shortly, after the opening of the Courts, every avenue leading to the New Court, in which the case was appointed for trial, was thronged almost to suffocation. The decided majority of the crowd seeking admittance was evidently the descendants of the patriarchs. As was but naturally expected the utmost anxiety was evidenced on the part of all those of the Jewish persuasion to catch a glimpse of the person and the features of the prisoner. At 8 a.m. the Common Sergeant took his seat on the bench and shortly afterwards Ikey was placed at the bar. In the Newgate Calendar he was described as a dealer and the age given as 45. He did not, however, appear nearly so old. During the time the indictments were read, he frequently and piercingly surveyed the persons in the body of the Court as if he were prepared to find an accuser in everyone his eyes rested upon.

Five of the eight indictments read out in court carried with them capital offences and Ikey, it was supposed, could not bring himself to hope that he might escape them all and so save his neck from the gallows. It was often enough reported that since his arrival in this country he had suffered considerable dejection of the mind, but there was no sign of this in court. When the indictments were completed and the prisoner allowed to answer them he spoke calmly and in a voice devoid of despair.

'Your honour, it is my modest hope that the jury will find me innocent and that under all circumstances His Majesty's Government will be induced to spare my life, and permit me to join my wife and family who are still residing in Van Diemen's Land.'

This little speech, short and sweet, when picked apart seems somewhat confused. It claims his innocence, then asks to be spared the rope *under all circumstances* so that he be allowed to go free to join his wife and family. It is most doubtful that there existed in court, or anywhere in England, a person unaware of the notorious Hannah Solomon. Yet Ikey spoke of his wife as if she were some contented colonial settler's spouse waiting patiently for her loving husband to return home having been exonerated of all crimes by a just and benign English legal system.

The overcrowded court and the mayhem in the streets outside had delayed proceedings, but Mr Phillips, Ikey's barrister, was crisp on the uptake and the first two charges, neither of which were capital offences, were dealt with in a summary manner. Ikey, who naturally denied everything, was found not guilty by the jury.

Then three of the capital charges were heard and disposed of with equal speed. Thus in the process of one morning five of the charges against Ikey were dismissed. Mr Phillips had proved himself an able defender of his celebrated client and Ikey, standing in the dock, appeared almost nonchalant. He did not evince the slightest pleasure at the 'not guilty' verdict. It was as if he had not been possessed of the smallest doubt as to the outcome of each hearing. Though it was always allowed that the first five cases were weak in point of proof, three of them were also invalidated by the ruling that a person could not be called upon to account for the possession of goods found in his custody three months after they had been stolen.

However, the noose was not yet removed from Ikey's scrawny neck. The court was adjourned to the 12th of July, when the remaining three indictments would be heard. Two of these were capital charges and the evidence available for the prosecution was most compelling. All of London was ablaze with gossip and every tavern and chop house produced any amount of boisterous speculation. Customers with not a scintilla of knowledge of the law turned into street lawyers who waxed more wise with each jug of ale or snifter of brandy. A great deal of money was laid in bets as to whether the eventual outcome would be the rope or the boat. Only the most foolishly optimistic accepted the odds of a hundred to one on Ikey's ability to beat the rap entirely.

When Ikey returned to the Old Bailey the crush of people wishing to get in was even greater than on the first occasion. A near riot occurred when the court attendants attempted to close the doors to the New Court, there being not room enough for a dormouse to squeeze into the public gallery. Ikey was brought back to the bar of the court to face the final three charges against him.

The first charge to be heard, the only one of the three that was not a capital offence, was the one brought against him by the Bank of England and involved the forgery of banknotes of five pounds denomination. Sir Reginald Cunningham, a Scot and a barrister of the highest repute, led the prosecution. He proceeded to lay out in chapter and verse the story of Abraham Van Esselyn who was in partnership and under the influence of the notorious Ikey Solomon. Finally he had shown in evidence the result produced by

Ikey and his Belgian partner. Sir Reginald then asked that he might present the two fake five pound notes to the judge together with two of legitimate currency, with the further request that the jury might be allowed to examine them thereafter.

In a dramatic gesture Sir Reginald handed the judge a large magnifying glass and begged him to choose the fake from the real. While the judge examined the banknotes Sir Reginald, in a further dramatic thrust, asked the judge to examine the watermarks on all of the notes, pointing out that they were all identical in nature, the paper used being the very same as was employed by the Treasury. The great barrister paused and waited for complete silence, then he added in a stentorian voice, 'I need hardly remind this court that the theft of paper used in the manufacture of banknotes is a crime against the Crown and the Treasury and therefore punishable by death!'

There was a murmur of astonishment from the public gallery, for in one stroke the Bank of England's case had been turned into a capital crime and Ikey seemed certain to hang.

'I should remind the prosecution that the decision as to whether a crime is a capital offence most fortunately does not rest with the prosecution but with this bench. If it did not I fear that the least of crimes would earn the ultimate sentence!' It was plain that the judge was not pleased with Sir Reginald's final remark. He then caused the notes to be handed to the jury, and it might have been supposed that Ikey had, in the truest sense of the words, finally met his Waterloo. With the exception of his last statement, Sir Reginald appeared not to have put a foot wrong.

The noose was drawn tight and it seemed the trap door had all but sprung as Sir Reginald Cunningham retrieved the banknotes from the jury and held up two of them.

'These are the five pound notes on the person of the accused! They were printed from a five pound etched copper plate discovered in the Bell Alley basement premises owned by the accused.' He paused and then ended with a flourish. 'They were printed on the very same printing press also lodged at that address!'

Ikey's barrister, Mr Phillips, now rose to his feet. 'Can my learned friend please tell us how these two particular notes were discovered and by whom?'

'Your honour, we request permission to call up a witness, Mr

George Smith, senior constable at the Lambeth Street watchhouse who will answer my learned friend's question.' Sir Reginald was well pleased with himself and his tone was most accommodating.

The clerk of the court stood up and called upon Senior Constable George Smith to take his place in the witness box.

'Mr Smith, is it not true that you go by another even more familiar name?' asked Mr Phillips.

The senior constable looked confused. 'Beg pardon, sir? I don't rightly know what you mean.'

'Let me put the question another way then. Is it true that you are referred to with the sobriquet, "The Reamer", in criminal circles?'

George Smith cleared his throat. 'I can't rightly say what the criminal classes calls me.' There was a buzz of amusement from the court and the policeman seemed to gain confidence from this for he grinned and added, 'And I don't think I cares that much neither.'

There was further laughter and the judge banged his gavel.

'Then let us suppose that the name "The Reamer", which you state is of no consequence to you, is in fact the name used by what you refer to as *the criminal classes*. Can you venture to guess how this name came about?' His hand rose to prevent George Smith from answering. 'Before you answer, would you agree that a reamer is a sharp object placed into a narrow aperture which is used to scrape it clean of impediment?'

George Smith shrugged. 'If you say so, sir.'

'Mr Smith, would you kindly hold up the forefinger of your right hand.'

The policeman looked at the judge. 'Must I do this, your honour?'

'Is this request important to your line of enquiry, Mr Phillips?' the judge asked. 'I must say it doesn't seem to be leading anywhere.'

'Your honour, I intend to show that this witness is not accustomed to acting within the rules of the law and cannot be relied upon to act in the best interest of the truth.'

'That is a serious accusation to make against an officer of the law, Mr Phillips. You will need to be most careful how you proceed further.' He turned to the policeman in the witness box. 'You will hold your right forefinger up to the jury, Mr Smith.'

George Smith held up his forefinger which appeared normal in all aspects and there was a bemused titter from the crowded court.

'Whatever can you have in mind, Mr Phillips?' the judge asked frowning at Ikey's barrister.

A high-pitched voice suddenly sounded from the public gallery and an urchin in a top hat jumped up from his seat. ''E bit it orf. I seen 'im! 'E bit 'is nail orf while the judge were talkin'. 'E bit it orf and spat it out!' Sparrer Fart jumped to his feet in the public gallery and yelled at the top of his voice.

'Yeah, yeah we seen it!' several other urchins, seated around Sparrer, nodded their heads violently, confirming his outburst. Other members of the public gallery now shouted in agreement, so that the court was filled with their protestations.

The judge banged his gavel. 'Silence! I will have silence in my court!' he demanded. 'You will remove that small personage please, constable!' He pointed to the policeman nearest Sparrer Fart.

Sparrer was led out of the gallery, where the police constable cuffed him behind the ear before roughly throwing him out onto the street on his arse, though the other members of the Methodist Academy of Light Fingers were permitted to remain.

Sparrer had barely landed when he felt a strong hand grab him by the collar and lift him to his feet. All he could see was the man's waistcoat and fob chain as he frantically struggled to free himself.

'Steady on, lad, I mean you no harm,' a calm voice directly above him announced.

'Lemme go!' Sparrer yelled.

To his surprise the hand holding him released its grip. 'That was a brave thing you did in there,' the voice added.

Sparrer was about to run but then recognised the man as someone who had been seated near him in court. Sparrer dusted his coat and the seat of his pants. 'Stupid, more like!'

'What's your name, boy?' the man asked.

'I ain't done nuffink, mister,' Sparrer whined.

'On the contrary, you may have saved a man from the gallows.'

'You a detective then?' Sparrer asked, still suspicious of the stranger.

'No, no, a reporter.' He stuck out his hand. 'Charles Dickens. I thought I might do a small piece on you in the paper.'

'Blimey! In a newspaper?' Sparrer wiped his hand on his greasy lapel before taking the reporter's hand. 'Pleased to meetcha, Mr Dickens.'

'Well yes, likewise lad. What you did took real gumption. Would you *like* to be in the newspaper?'

'No thanks. Ikey says incognito be best, you don't want no name in the papers.'

'Incognito eh, that's a big word. Do you know Ikey Solomon?'

Sparrer squinted up at the reporter. 'Maybe I does and maybe I doesn't.' His confidence restored, he now stood with one foot placed on the boot cap of the other and with both his hands jammed into the pockets of his coat.

Charles Dickens took out his purse and offered a shilling to Sparrer.

Sparrer sniffed. 'Bloody 'ell, fer a shillin' I never seen 'im afore in me life, mister!'

Charles Dickens smiled and dropped the shilling back in his purse.

'Fer a shillin' ya gets me name,' Sparrer added quickly, realising he'd overplayed his hand.

'Your name? Is that all?' Charles Dickens laughed.

'For the newspaper! Ya can put me name in yer newspaper.'

The reporter took the shilling out of his purse again and handed it to Sparrer Fart. 'What's your name then, lad?'

Sparrer thought desperately. When he performed well at the Academy of Light Fingers Ikey would turn to the other lads and say, 'Look at Sparrer, a veritable dodger, nimble as a ferret!' Then he would pat him on the head and say, 'Well done, dodger, a most artful dodgin' performance, my dear!'

'They calls me the Artful Dodger,' Sparrer replied.

'And you know Ikey Solomon, Mr Artful Dodger?'

'That's fer me to know and you to find out,' Sparrer said cheekily, the shilling now safely deposited in his pocket.

Charles Dickens sighed. 'And how much will it take to find out?'

'It be a long and fascinatin' story what can't be told straight orf, it'll cost ya a daffy and a sov.'

'I'm not sure I have a sovereign on me.' Dickens reached again into his coat for his purse.

'What's the time then?' Sparrer said, pointing to the reporter's waistcoat.

With his free hand the reporter reached down to his fob chain and then more frenetically patted the lower part of his waistcoat.

'This yers then, mister?' Sparrer asked. The hint of a smile played on his pinched little face as he held up a gold hunter by its chain. 'Worth a lot more than a gold sov, now, don't ya think?'

'How the devil!' Dickens expostulated.

'Gotta be careful who ya picks up when they's fallen down on the pavement, mister. Grab a boy by 'is collar and 'e's got both 'ands free, ain't 'e now?'

Charles Dickens grinned sheepishly as Sparrer returned his watch to him. 'A daffy and a sovereign it is then. I do hope it's a good story, Mr Artful Dodger.'

'Best ya ever 'eard, mister,' Sparrer Fart shot back as he dodged into the oncoming traffic in Newgate Street to cross to a tavern on the far side.

Meanwhile in the New Court of the Old Bailey, Mr Phillips addressed the judge on the matter of Sergeant George Smith's missing fingernail.

'Your Honour, I request that the witness box be searched for a fingernail belonging to the witness.'

There was much laughter from the gallery at this notion, for most of the public had not understood the meaning of Sparrer's shouted accusation.

Sir Reginald rose quickly to his feet. 'With the greatest respect, your honour, the defence is both confused and confusing?' He glared at Mr Phillips. 'My learned colleague had first requested that the witness accept a new name, that of "The Reamer" and then asks that Mr Smith thrust his forefinger in the air. A most curious request to say the least! But then, when he perceives it to be a perfectly normal finger with a perfectly normal fingernail upon it, he demands that we all go on our hands and knees and look for a missing and imaginary finger part!'

There was a roar of laughter from the court and this time the judge threatened to remove all from the public gallery if the misbehaviour continued. Then he looked impatiently at Mr Phillips.

'Is that not substantially correct, Mr Phillips? Or do you have some motive which is beyond us in this court? Already you try my patience to a most precipitous point.'

'Your honour, it will take but a moment. I crave your

indulgence. What I hope to find is of the greatest significance to this case. It is my intention to show that the word of Senior Constable George Smith is not to be relied upon.'

The judge looked stern. 'I have already cautioned you against this sort of imputation and warn you that you will be charged before the bench with misconduct if you do not satisfactorily resolve the accusation you are making against Mr Smith. You may search the witness box with an officer of this court in attendance.'

Ikey's barrister leaned over and spoke quietly to his instructing solicitor who, accompanied by a constable, entered the witness box. It took only a moment for the police officer to find the torn part of a fingernail which had fallen to the floor at the feet of George Smith. The piece of nail was filed to a point and appeared to be almost an inch and a half long. He handed it to the solicitor, who then took it across to the clerk of the court.

'Your honour, I suggest that the portion of fingernail which I now submit as evidence can be shown to have been formerly attached to the forefinger of the witness. I have several witnesses, including my client, who are willing to testify that the offending forefinger, with nail attached, was used for the purposes of searching the back passage of prisoners for contraband. It was intended that this action of reaming would render grievous bodily harm to the victims of this odious search. It is for this reason that the witness has been christened "The Reamer"!'

'I object, your honour. This matter of nicknames has nothing whatsoever to do with the case at hand. I refer to my learned colleague's original question which, if I recall correctly, was how the notes were discovered on the person of the accused!'

'Your objection is sustained, Sir Reginald,' the judge said and turned to the jury. 'You will ignore the imputation made by Mr Phillips as to the usage of the fingernail, and reference to it will be struck from the record.' He looked at Ikey's barrister. 'You will restrict yourself to asking direct questions, Mr Phillips. I shall not warn you again!'

'Yes, thank you, your honour, you are most gracious,' Mr Phillips said, appearing not the least chastened by the judge's warning. 'Mr Smith, can you tell this court whether the man you searched, known as Ikey Solomon, is in this court?'

The senior constable nodded and pointed to Ikey. 'That be him, sir.'

'Thank you. And you conducted a thorough . . . er . . . *body* search upon this person?' There was a roar of laughter in the court and the judge banged his gavel again.

'It were the normal search, sir, for what we calls routine contraband.'

'Where did you find the two counterfeit notes? Can you tell me precisely their location, Mr Smith?'

'They were in the lining o' the coat, sir.'

'In the lining? In the lining of whose coat?'

'The accused, sir, he wore a coat on the night 'e were brought in.'

'An expensive coat? Sewn into the lining?'

'Yes, sir it were a good coat but no, not sewn, there were a tear in it. The notes were pushed down the tear into the lining, like.'

'Isn't that a little obvious, constable? Would you concede that a large tear which had not been repaired on an expensive coat was a rather too obvious place to hide the notes?'

'That's not for the likes o' me to say, sir. That be where them notes were found and I did not say it were a large tear, sir,' George Smith said tartly.

Mr Phillips wheeled around and pointed directly at George Smith. 'No, sir, with the greatest respect, I submit to you that the two five pound notes were *planted*!' Mr Phillips turned towards the jury. 'How very convenient to make a tear in his coat, the coat which the accused was *forced to remove* while he was undergoing a thorough *body* search! A tear into which, *abracadabra*, the two five pound notes suddenly appeared, politely stuffed within the lining of the coat to make the evidence your masters requested appear in the most convenient manner! Is this not a much more reasonable explanation of what happened, Mr Smith?'

'No sir, it is not! The notes be found just like I said.'

'Then you will demonstrate how you found these two notes please, Mr Smith.' Ikey's barrister turned to the clerk of the court. 'We have asked that the accused's coat be brought in evidence. Would you please identify it and hand it to the witness?'

The clerk of the court stood up and turned to the judge. 'Your honour, the coat in question was not taken in evidence from the prisoner at the time of his arrest.'

The judge looked astonished and then addressed George Smith. 'Mr Smith, did you not say that the counterfeit notes were found in the lining of the coat and that they had been so placed by means of a tear in the outer material?'

'Yes, your honour.'

'Am I to believe that the coat was then allowed to remain with the accused and was not confiscated as evidence?'

George Smith looked decidedly sheepish. 'We forgot, your honour, it were a cold night.' Then he pointed at Ikey in the dock. 'He were wearin' it when he made his escape.'

'Thank you, Mr Smith, you may step down,' Mr Phillips said.

In his summary of the evidence the judge pointed out that the absence of the coat and the subsequent denial of the accused that a tear had ever existed in it constituted 'reasonable doubt' as to whether the banknotes had been placed in the lining by the accused or by the actions of some other person or persons unknown. Furthermore, without the evidence of the two notes there appeared to be nothing which linked Ikey with the crime of forgery. The etched plate and printing press found in the basement premises proved nothing beyond the fact that Ikey was the landlord and the forger Abraham Van Esselyn his tenant. He noted that all the receipts for the printing press and subsequent forgery materials were in the name or pseudonym of Abraham Van Esselyn whom, he reminded the jury, had been previously tried and found guilty. Finally, there existed not a shred of evidence to show how Ikey might have procured the Treasury paper on which the forged notes were printed.

The jury took less than an hour to dismiss the charges of forgery against Ikey and the judge pronounced him not guilty for lack of evidence. Ikey's coat of many pockets had saved his life.

Only two more charges remained, those involving the purchase of goods known to have been stolen, and both were capital offences. Alas, with these Ikey's luck finally ran out and he was found guilty on both charges. The hangman had secured his man at last. But the judge did not place the black hood upon his head; instead he sentenced Ikey to fourteen years' transportation. This amelioration of Ikey's sentence may well have come about to prove to the barrister that the judge was independent of the pressure which might be placed upon him by those fronting the bench, though to this sentence of transportation was added the clause that Ikey was not permitted to return to England after he had served out his time in Van Diemen's Land.

But the redoubtable Mr Phillips had not entirely given up. Ikey's barrister instituted several legal quibbles on his client's behalf, the majority of which concerned the disposition of stolen property, and challenged the various Acts of Parliament involved in Ikey's conviction. This legal nitpicking served the purpose of postponing Ikey's transportation for nearly a year, though during this period Ikey was not, as was the usual custom, sent to a hulk on the Thames estuary but remained under close guard in Newgate.

The final outcome of this delay was that Ikey's prison expenses for food and drink and other luxuries, namely *The Times* and reading matter on a variety of subjects, coupled with the exorbitant fees Mr Phillips imposed for his services, finally exhausted the funds Ikey had brought with him from Van Diemen's Land. For the first time since he had been a young flash-man, Ikey had not a penny to his name.

On the 31st of May 1831, Ikey Solomon, his spirit broken and his body in chains, set sail for Van Diemen's Land on the *William Glen Anderson*.

Chapter Twenty-five

A large crowd gathered at Sullivan's Cove to witness Ikey's arrival on the 1st of November 1831, but Hannah was not among them. She thought of herself as very badly done by, and she blamed Ikey for necessitating her departure from the Newman household and for her present incarceration.

In fact, she had been rather fortunate, for she was not sent to the Female Factory but to the Cotton Factory, this second institution being somewhat better in its treatment of prisoners. Hannah was employed as a seamstress to make prison garments. Thus she was able to avoid meeting Mary Abacus. But this did not prevent her from constantly speaking of Mary as the person who had seduced her husband, and brought about the present and calamitous destruction of her entire family. She vowed loudly and often that she would wreak revenge on Ikey's erstwhile mistress, whatever the price.

For Mary, Hannah's existence on the island hardly mattered. She heard from time to time of Hannah's threats, but she expected no less from Ikey's wife and thought little of them. She was unaware that Hannah had a new and powerful reason for hating her, one which had nothing to do with their shared past. Hannah's children – her ten-year-old son David, Ann, who had just turned eight, Sarah six, and Mark four – were placed in the Reverend

Smedley's orphanage. David, Ann and Sarah found themselves in Mary's classroom where they felt as much loved by her as any of the other orphans. Hannah's children, the apple of her eye, were under the direct influence of the woman she hated more than any other, and there was nothing she could do about it.

Mary delighted in her task as teacher. Although many of the children were undernourished and stunted in their growth and so proved difficult to teach, some were bright and eager. But there were none so willing to learn as Ann, and none so naturally intelligent as her brother David. Both had received some schooling in England and so were much ahead of the other pupils, and Mary used them to instruct the younger children while, at the same time, giving them her special attention.

From the outset David was fascinated by Mary's abacus and begged to be allowed to use it. He had proved himself clever with numbers and could do much of the arithmetic Mary taught him mentally, not bothering with the slate on his lap. Ann, on the other hand, while competent with numbers, begged to be allowed to read. Finding books for an eight-year-old child was not an easy matter and the Reverend Thomas Smedley, still undecided about the merits of teaching the children God had intended to be the drones in the hives of life, did nothing to help the situation in the school.

Saving souls was clearly the major work of God and, he told himself, was as freely available to the poor as it was to the rich, to the clever as well as the stupid. In his infinite wisdom God made his salvation unstintingly available to all. But at this point God's universal design came to a halt. The qualities He gave to humans were dispensed, according to the needs of English society, which Smedley naturally accepted as being the closest to the divine intention.

To some God gave wisdom, for the wise are needed in some small proportion. Some He made clever, for these too are a necessary ingredient in the proportions of a just society. Others are possessed of natural skills to furnish the whole with artisans, teachers, clerks and shopkeepers, but most He made to be hewers of wood and drawers of water. They were the necessary human clay and had been allotted the largest and lowest space in the human family. By tampering with God's natural ordination Mary was attempting to change the balance of nature, and no good could possibly come of it. The saving of minds, Thomas Smedley concluded, was more likely to be the work of Satan than of a benign and loving God. The example he most often used to support his argument was that of the noble savage.

Mary took the midday meal with the preacher and his spinster sister. Elspeth, a quiet soul, was not able to counter her brother's aggressive nature and mostly kept her silence at the table. She was an excellent cook and took some care to see that Mary was well fed, always treating her with the utmost politeness though without venturing beyond the daily pleasantries.

Smedley more than made up for his sister's reticence. He possessed a viewpoint on all subjects except those which might interest a woman, and his opinions could almost certainly be counted upon to be of a negative persuasion. He used the dinner table as he might have done a pulpit, expounding on any subject he felt inclined to embrace without expecting argument or rebuttal from the two women who shared it with him.

The followers of John Wesley are of a naturally zealous disposition, the threat of fire and brimstone being the major part of their catechism. They hold that God's anger should be given precedence over His mercy and love, and agree that the fear of hellfire is the principal motivation for driving wicked people to salvation.

Thomas Smedley was well suited to this uncompromising faith, but his superiors nevertheless thought his nature too bitter to preach from an English pulpit, and so he had been sent to Van Diemen's Land where God's cause was secretly thought to be a hopeless one, except for the early salvation of its plague of illegitimate children.

Elspeth had accompanied him on his mission as housekeeper for, like Mary, she possessed a passion for children. She was much aggrieved by her brother's insistence that his charges be treated as creatures of little worth, with strict instructions that they be shown no outward sign of love. This cruel directive caused her to live in a clandestine way, loving the forlorn little creatures whenever she could clutch them unobserved to her bosom.

For a while Mary was willing to hold her tongue. She much enjoyed the food at Elspeth's table, which she took care to supply with fresh vegetables from the prison gardens so that she should not be at the mercy of the preacher's reluctant charity. She had been made to feel an uninvited guest from the very first meal when, after a prolonged and stony silence, the small, fat preacher suddenly threw down his napkin, slid back his chair and stormed from the room with the words, 'Vile claws!'

At the following midday meal Mary had come to the table to find a pair of white lace gloves placed between her knife and fork. For a moment she felt that her anger would cause her to explode. Her talons, grown in the prison, had been neatly cut to the perimeters of her fingers when she had come for her interview. But now she wished them long again so that she might rake the fleshy face of the preacher until the blood gushed from his rubicund cheeks to soak the napkin tied about his neck. As her anger abated she was overcome with humiliation. She fought to control her sobs, her face cast downwards and her poor, broken hands concealed upon her lap. A silent tear ran down her cheek and fell onto the gloves, placed so that the longest fingers appeared to be pointing accusingly at her.

'My dear Miss Abacus,' she heard Elspeth Smedley say in an unusually loud voice, 'I must apologise for my bad manners. I had quite forgotten to place gloves at the table for yesterday's luncheon. Can you possibly forgive me? It is all the fashion these days, but as Smedley and I eat mostly alone, I have grown careless of convention.'

Mary looked up slowly to be met by a smile from Elspeth who, she now saw, wore a pair of gloves identical to her own.

'I have made a brisket of beef with a tarragon sauce in the hope that you will forgive my appalling oversight.' Then Elspeth Smedley added lightly, 'The soup is made of the beautiful watercress you brought this morning from the rivulet. It is my favourite and I must thank you. Smedley does so much enjoy it too.'

It was the longest speech Mary had ever heard from the shy and naturally retiring Elspeth, and she felt sure that no person had ever addressed her with such kindness and compassion.

'Thank you, ma'am,' Mary murmured as she reached for the gloves in front of her.

'No, no, my dear, you must call me Elspeth, for you are as welcome at our table as any of our other friends.'

Though never in the least pleasant to her, the Reverend Thomas Smedley grew accustomed to Mary's presence at lunch.

He placed little store in her opinions but, unlike his sister, Mary was not willing to listen in silence to his tirades or accept his pronouncements as though they were infallible. After a few weeks she was beginning to get results from several of the children in her class, and she was convinced that she could fill their small minds with a love of learning.

Smedley, though pretending to evince no interest in Mary's progress, would command her to debate him, often interrupting her, and when she made a point worthy of consideration he dismissed it with a flick of his wrist and the expostulation 'Bah!' On one occasion he had followed this with the words, 'They are nothing but savages to be likened to the black creatures that crawl like vermin among the hills.'

'We are but the creatures we are permitted to be, sir,' Mary protested. 'This is as true for the orphans as it is for the savage. Our nature is not formed within the womb but by what 'appens to us beyond it!'

'Ah! But you are quite wrong!' Smedley replied. 'The pig is happiest in its own mud! When rescued from his natural ways and habitat, the noble savage, no longer covered in the stench of fish oil but bathed and dressed in linen, is soon forlorn and woebegone. If you would have your Van Diemen's savage dine at the table of the governor, the food would prove unsuitable to his digestion, the linen chafing and uncomfortable to his skin, his posterior quickly wearied by the gilt chair and the custom of knife and fork and spoon likely to confound his primitive mind. How then by means of books and slate can you change this repulsive creature for the better? How indeed, hmm, Miss Abacus?'

'Sir, I know nothing of savages, it be the young minds of little 'uns of our own kind I seek to change. They are not by nature consigned to the pig sty, but are born the same and washed as clean o' the blood o' their birth as any noble child. If perchance they was placed in the nursery of a grand manor, there's none would know the difference and they would carry their proxy nobility as well as any Lord or Lady.'

'Oh, but you are quite wrong again, Miss Abacus! You have observed them in your own class, the close-set eyes, the sloping, beetle brows, the vacuous and slack-jawed visage with no dawn of comprehension seen to rise up into their dulled, indifferent eyes. These are not the substitute sons and daughters of the decent classes, they are already well branded to the bottom class, marked every bit as surely as the black skin of the aboriginal savage marks him to his sub-human species!'

It was true enough that several of the children in Mary's class had the precise appearance described by the Reverend Smedley and true, also, that not a flicker of comprehension seemed to show in their eyes when they were presented with an idea which required the smallest conjecture. But they sang and clapped with gusto and were much entertained with simple games and Mary, in many ways, loved them most of all.

'That ain't fair, sir!' she exclaimed hotly. 'I've worked in big houses in my time, and heard tell of others where wrong 'un's, idjits, are born to the gentry. King George himself, Farmer George, he had more than one loose screw rattlin' about in his royal noggin! You're quite right, there be some in me class won't take much to learnin' but most o' them make progress and will in time come to somethin'!'

'Ha! If we cannot save their souls in time, Miss Abacus, all they will come to is corruption and licence, drunkenness and thieving!' Thomas Smedley jabbed a fat finger at Mary. 'You will know that your school is not of my making. Should I have my way I would wish it gone in an instant! My work, Miss Abacus, is God's work, and when you interfere with God's natural laws and would think to change the clay from which each of us is formed, I can clearly enough see the devil's hand in it!'

'Sir, the devil has no monopoly on brains!' Mary replied, looking into her napkin and holding down her anger.

'Oh?' Thomas Smedley snorted, pointing at her again. 'Then is it the Lord God who sends a brothel keeper and a whore to my orphanage to teach His precious children?'

The three mornings Mary spent at the orphan school soon became four and then five. Mr Emmett would sometimes call around and watch as the children sang or recited a poem for his benefit. He had seen to it that blackboard, slates, chalk, paper, quills and blacking and even a few children's books were made available. There were never sufficient books, for Mary believed that reading was the basis for any education and would lead naturally to the desire to write, and created in a child the thirst for knowledge of every description.

She had even persuaded Mr Emmett to get the authorities to return her battered leather-bound copy of *Gulliver's Travels*. She used this to create in the breasts of her older children a sense of social justice, so that they might understand that it is the strong who manipulate the weak, and that bondage and poverty are not a natural state ordained by God, but imposed by those who enjoy wealth, privilege and power upon those who have no means to resist or overcome poverty and servitude.

In this way unknowingly perhaps, Mary began to teach the tenets of freedom upon which a community of convict slaves became the most egalitarian nation on earth. Mary and her class of fifty orphan children, together with one hundred and sixty thousand convicted thieves, whores, forgers, conmen, blasphemers, political dissenters, the diseased, illiterate, mentally handicapped flotsam and jetsam upon the sea of English and Irish life, formed the basis of this new nation. Undoubtedly this was the most unpropitious human raw material ever gathered in one place, yet it would be forged into a free and equal people who would never again tolerate a despotic regime or accept that any man's station is above that of any other.

In the matter of books for her pupils Mary enlisted the help of Elspeth Smedley, who rented books in large numbers from the Hobart Town Circulating Library. This institution was presided over by the stern-faced Mrs Deane who, had she known their destination, would not have permitted the books to be released from her possession. Convicts were not allowed to rent books and the thought of orphans reading them, with their dirty little hands, would have caused a great fuss in the small community. As it was, Mrs Deane marvelled at Elspeth Smedley's ability to read so many volumes on every subject, and judged her quite the best-informed woman on the island. Privately she thought the parson's sister's reading was most eclectic, in some things juvenile to the greatest degree while her other tastes were distinctly scholarly. But she did not make the obvious connection that the books were being used in the orphanage. The very idea that the illegitimate brats of convicts and whores might be brought to learning was less believable than the notion that the moon was composed of green cheese.

The money for the books came, of course, from Mary's Potato Factory, and while Elspeth Smedley may herself have pondered the source of Mary's seemingly unlimited resources, she would not have dreamed of asking her for an explanation. Mary had encouraged Elspeth to become a teacher herself, and in this matter the gentle and retiring spinster sought to stand up to her bucolic older brother.

When confronted with Elspeth's request, Thomas Smedley ordered that she withdraw from the wicked influence of 'the Factory whore', as he had come to call Mary in private. He had long since cancelled Mary's salvation. She had clearly shown by her lack of humility and contrition, and by her willingness to argue with him on every conceivable subject, that her redemption had been nothing but a ruse to win his approval for her orphan school. He forbade Elspeth to enter Mary's class, or even to converse with her at the midday meal.

Elspeth had not disobeyed her brother's instructions. She found, however, that her extreme disappointment at his decision had entirely erased the numerous recipes she carried in her mind, save only for a recollection of how to boil potatoes.

For two weeks, morning, lunch and tea she served boiled potatoes and small beer until Thomas Smedley could stand it no longer, the demands of his stomach finally overcoming his principles. He had become quite pale and listless, and when the pangs of hunger and the desire for red meat could no longer be contained he had taken to walking down into Liverpool Street to take a meal at a chop house. He was a man who loved his food, and the boiled and fried mutton and badly prepared kangaroo flesh available as cheap fare in an eating house, though preferable to boiled potatoes, was not in the least to his liking. Elspeth was most grudgingly allowed to teach with Mary in the orphan school.

It was a decision which possessed the divine power to recall Elspeth's memory. That very night a splendid pot roast, garnished with tiny spring onions and a boat of rich gravy at its side, with a dish of rice and another of vegetables, was placed steaming upon the table, proving once again that principle is soon swamped by the gravy of greed.

David and Ann Solomon had not been to school since leaving England. An attempt had been made to enrol Ann in Mrs Bamber's boarding school for young ladies when Hannah had been assigned to the Newman family, but her application had been refused on the basis of breeding. The learning levels of both children were three years behind what might have been expected had they remained in England but the general intellectual fare served up at the orphanage was still not sufficient to occupy their minds. Mary had eventually allowed David to learn to work her abacus. Ann, too, had begged to be allowed to play with Mary's beads, insisting she also could make the numbers work. But Mary, sensing David's pride that he alone had been permitted to use her precious abacus, would not allow his sister the same privilege.

'Ann, you are our best reader and it be with books that you excel. David already knows the big numbers and can divide and multiply and add and subtract to make our very 'eads spin. Your turn will come when you be a little older and learn the bigger numbers.'

'It's not fair!' Ann protested, stamping her foot. 'I know a big number and I can write it too!' Whereupon she took up her slate and wrote the number 816.

'What number does that say, Ann?' Mary asked.

'Eight 'undred and sixteen, miss,' she exclaimed, then added triumphantly, 'See! I told you I can do big numbers!'

Mary took up the child's slate and, transposing the numbers, wrote 618 upon it. 'What is this number then?' she asked Ann. 'Say it in 'undreds again, like the last.'

The child stared without comprehension at the new number on her slate. 'It's not fair, I could learn it, I could so!' Ann began to sob, though more in anger at not getting her way, than in distress.

Mary, laughing, took Ann into her arms. 'Eight 'undred and sixteen be a lovely number, Ann. We will soon enough teach you others just as grand.'

Ann pulled away from Mary's embrace, her blue eyes large in her pinched little face as she pronounced, 'Anyway, our mum says it's the only big number we needs to know, and whatever should 'appen to 'er, we must never, never forget it!'

At this sudden recollection of her mother, Ann began to sniff and then to cry softly and although she was eight years old she was no bigger than a child of five or six and Mary took her once again onto her lap and this time she rocked her and kissed the centre parting of her lovely auburn hair and held her tight until she became calm.

Mary thought little more of the incident until the number 816 began to occur regularly in David's work on the abacus. He would often divide into it, subtract from it or find the various multiples of it.

'What be it with the number eight 'undred and sixteen, David?' Mary had finally asked. 'Were it perchance the number of your 'ouse in London?'

David flushed deeply and with a vigorous, though unconvincing, shake of his head replied, 'No, Miss, it be just a number. I didn't know as I were usin' it particular.'

But Mary noted that David Solomon never used the number again, while Ann continued to write it upon her slate when she appeared distracted. Later, when Ann had progressed and learned her multiples of ten and then of a hundred, the number 816 would still occur frequently in her arithmetic.

Though Mary had no time to ponder this childish conundrum she nonetheless tucked the number 816 away. She would not forget it, if only because her mind was so trained to numbers that no digit brought to her attention, for whatever purpose, was ever again forgotten.

Chapter Twenty-six

Ikey saw very little of Hobart Town upon his arrival back in Van Diemen's Land. He was taken directly to Richmond Gaol, some twenty miles out of town, where convicts were put to work upgrading the road to Colebrook. A huge penal settlement was being built to house the influx of convicts now that New South Wales was becoming a popular destination for free settlers from England.

'G'warn, get yer backs into it, yer miserable bastards!' Harris, the overseer of the road gang, liked to shout. 'Governor Arthur 'imself told me 'e needs a new place o' misery to 'ang ya and flog yer useless 'ides!'

In fact, Richmond Gaol served as much to hold the convicts building a road to Arthur's private property, Carrington, as for any other purpose. Governor Arthur abolished land grants to emancipists first, and then altogether, but had nonetheless awarded himself a great acreage, without the payment he demanded from everyone else. He then directed the ceaseless labour of convicts to be lavished upon it, equipping Carrington with a fine stone residence and outer building, fences and roads, all of which were the envy of the wealthiest free settler and worthy of any country estate in England. It was upon Arthur's own road near Richmond that Ikey found himself harnessed to a cart.

Much has been made of the Van Diemen's Land convict being made to pull the plough though, in truth, it was more as a cart horse than as an ox that he was customarily employed. The cart was as integral a part of the road gang as the pick-axe, shovel and wheelbarrow, and much the most onerous of the tasks allotted to a convict.

These carts, measuring six feet in length, two in depth and four and a half in width, were pulled by four men, as it was mistakenly calculated that this amount of human muscle is the equivalent to one well-conditioned cart horse. This might have been so if the men had been in excellent health and were the stature of a giant, six feet or more. But the prisoners were of an average English height, not much more than five feet and three inches and they were malnourished and scrawny. The four team members had leather collars which were attached by ropes and a hook to the cart. Near the extremity of the central harnessing pole were a pair of cross-bars which, when gripped, allowed for two men on either side of the pole to pull the cart. It was mandatory to fill the cart, usually with rocks and dirt, to the point of overflowing, which made it a herculean task to move.

Ikey had at first been given a pick-axe, a tool with which he was entirely unfamiliar. Besides, his confinement in chains on board ship had enfeebled him and his hands were as tender as an infant's. Despite being instructed by the more experienced lags to piss upon each hand to harden the surfaces of his palms, on Ikey's first day of labour his hands soon blistered. On the second day, the skin peeled away from the entire palm and even from between his fingers, and his fingernails were ripped off as a consequence of being made to labour with such a rough and heavy tool. But he was forced to labour for two more days until the handle of the pick was stained with his own blood, and particles of flesh remained upon it whenever he withdrew his hands. The pick itself was too large for even a robust man of his height, and Ikey was reduced to whimpering with each downward strike. Finally, an hour before sundown on the fourth day, he collapsed.

Several kicks of a more than tentative nature, administered by the overseer, Harris, failed to get Ikey to his feet. It was only when he was observed to cough blood that he was placed in a wheelbarrow after the day's work and several convicts, cursing him loudly, were made to take turns wheeling him back to Richmond Gaol.

That night the doctor was called to examine him. He thumped Ikey on the chest, and peeled back his eyes to peer at the jellied orb, whereupon he made him drop his breeches and, weighing his balls in his hand, commanded him to cough. Finally he squeezed Ikey's thigh and calf muscles. Standing up again he declared him fit to work.

'It be nothing but the softness of the voyage. This one will soon enough harden to labour. Put him back to work I say!' He seemed annoyed at being called out after supper for a matter so inconsequential and the superintendent felt compelled to apologise to him, explaining that Ikey was a prisoner of some renown or he would not have disturbed the good doctor.

Ikey groaned and held the lumps of raw flesh up for the surgeon to see. 'What about me hands?' he pleaded.

'Piss and spit soon fix them, my boy!' the doctor said, then turned to the superintendent. 'Tell the overseer to put this prisoner on carts – his legs be well muscled and strong enough by all accounts.'

Though the work on the carts was harder, each team being required to pull ten loads each of a mile every day, it suited Ikey better. Years of walking about the London rookeries at night had made his legs strong, and the strength of a prisoner's legs played the major function in pulling the brutal cart.

To add to the humiliation of the work, Harris thought it high jinks to place beside Ikey at the cross-bar a black boy named Billygonequeer, who was captured as a lookout while other members of his Stoney Creek tribe were said to be raiding sheep. Billygonequeer had been in captivity three years when Ikey joined the road gang, and his major claim to fame was that he had received the most stripes to his back of any in their company. He would work as hard as any man at pulling the cart and no prisoner could fault him for not doing his share. But every few weeks, as though he sniffed something in the air, he grew most melancholy, would take no food, and refused to work by standing rigid in a single place. This was known to all in the road gang as 'Billy gone queer' and so the black boy had received this strange appendage to his name.

At night it was not customary to lock Billygonequeer in the cells. For if he should be placed in close confinement he would commence to shout all night so that no prisoner could sleep a wink. And so, summer and winter, with only a blanket to cover him for the coldest part of the year, he would be chained to a ring set into an outer wall which formed part of the courtyard of the gaol. Here he would sleep like an animal on the hard cobblestones.

But when Billygonequeer went queer, he would stand all night and look upwards at the stars and howl exactly like the Tasmanian tiger, the thylacine, a creature dog-like in appearance and extremely shy of humans. This beast, only seldom glimpsed in the outer camps and always in the depths of the forest where it would come to stand just beyond the edge of the firelight at night, was familiar to timber workers and road gangs for its dreadful howl. It was a hollow sound that came from inside, as though vibrating from deep within the chest, and was most disconcerting to the ear. Billygonequeer did not so much appear to make the sound as to *be* the sound. His eyes seemed to turn yellow and catch the light in the darkness, and his jaws unlocked and widened as the terrible creature cacophony came from him. They had tried to gag him once but this proved to no avail – the sound continued as though it emanated from his chest and sought no expulsion from his lips.

When morning came Billy still would not move and it was impossible to imagine that a man could stand so rigid and so long in one spot. If he should be knocked down by the overseer, as often happened, he would not cry out, but would get back to his feet and stand as before, impervious to pain.

Harris, despite having seen Billygonequeer go queer on numerous occasions, could not bring himself to accept his condition. He was a stickler for the rules and greatly afraid of the wrath of the authorities, and on each occasion he would cause Billy to be dragged before the district magistrate. Here Billy would stand before the beak, his dark eyes glazed over as though he were in some distant place of his imagining. Nor would he respond to questions, though his comprehension of English was said to be quite sufficient to this task. Finally, the magistrate, partly angered and bemused and in all parts impatient, would declare himself compelled to obey the law. He would hand down the most severe punishment for refusing to work, a sentence of one hundred lashes with the cat o' nine tails.

A month after Ikey had been put to the cart beside Billy, following the eating of their midday rations, Billy had suddenly turned his head in the direction of a breeze which had that very moment blown up and commenced to sigh high in the giant gum trees. He jumped to his feet and seemed to breathe deeply, pulling the air into his nostrils so that his broad nose flattened upon his face. In great agitation he began to tear his clothes from his slim body, as though some vicious biting insect were to be found within them. As each garment was removed he flung it into the bushes. Then he gave a great sigh and, naked as the day of his birth, stood rigid with his arms to his sides, the pale palms of his hands turned outward. His only movement was the distension and retraction of his nostrils as he pulled the wind into him, as though it were some invisible musk sent from heaven.

'Jaysus Christ! Billy's gone queer,' Seamus Calligan shouted. 'Sniffin' in the wind and that. I'll be damned if he'll not soon be standin' still as a bloody fence pole!'

Michael Mooney, Calligan's partner on the front cross-bar, cautioned Ikey not to catch the attention of Harris the overseer. 'Let him be a while, poor bugger will suffer enough soon as bloody Harris comes.'

'We'll not pull the cart with only the three of us,' Ikey ventured.

'We'll have to. Billygonequeer will not be comin' back these three weeks or more,' Mooney replied.

They left Billy standing and walked back to the cart. They were loading rock for gravel that day and the cart was almost too heavy for four men to pull. Now with only the three of them they were forced to lessen the load. Harris, seeing them pass with the load not extended beyond the rim of the cart, was soon alerted. Then he saw Ikey was alone at his cross-bar.

'Where's the nigger?' he shouted, using an expression he had picked up on an American whaling ship.

The three men brought the cart to a standstill. 'Billy's gone queer,' a reluctant Seamus replied.

Harris grinned. 'Oh 'e 'as now 'as 'e, that be most considerate o' the black bastard!' He turned and called another convict over to harness up beside Ikey. Then, rubbing his hands gleefully, he set off for the camp where the prisoners had taken their midday rations.

When the team returned for the evening muster they found Billy in the same spot as they'd left him. He was rigid as a well-rooted sapling, but with one eye half closed, and the blood from his nose caked upon his smooth ebony chest. His shoulders, too, were crimson caked, and it appeared as though the back of his head had been smashed with some sharp object. A great cloud of flies had settled about his shoulders and eyes, and swarmed about his wild black head. Billygonequeer did not appear to notice the presence of either the flies or the men standing around him.

The men did not ask how his injuries occurred. Those who had worked on the road gang for some time knew Harris to be a coward and a bully, and when Billy went queer it was always an occasion for sadistic gratification on Harris's part.

Billy, still rigid, was wheeled back to Richmond, his thin legs, like two black poles, sticking out beyond the front lip of the wheel-barrow. No prisoner complained of the extra effort, even though each was himself exhausted from the day's toil. Ikey knew this was most peculiar. Compassion for another was not a part of the convict nature. To feel for another was to put oneself in danger. A singular and ruthless attention to one's own survival was paramount in all matters concerning the convict's life. Ikey understood these rules better than anyone, for he had always lived in accordance with them. Yet no one complained at the need for Billygonequeer's wheeled transportation back to Richmond Gaol.

Billy spent the night in the courtyard standing without the slightest movement, though once every few minutes he emitted the long, lonely howl of the forest dog creature.

Ikey found it impossible to sleep that night. He cursed himself quietly for his insomnia, and wondered how he could possibly feel disquiet and sorrow for the plight of a black savage. Ikey remembered only once before experiencing such a stirring of compassion, when he had impulsively given Abraham Reuban money and his Waterloo medal to give to Mary. Now he felt it again for his black partner, and felt ashamed that he should do so. Morning found him hollow-eyed and still despairing of Billy's plight. He tried all day to convince himself that such was not the case, but the feeling of deep, instinctive sorrow would not go away.

Ikey sensed that Billy was mourning, though how this could have been brought about by a sudden shift of the wind on a day which seemed to Ikey like any other, was a mystery. But he was a Jew and he knew instinctively about loneliness and terror, and the evil golem that comes at times to molest and disturb the soul. The mischievous ghost of the past who comes to make a Jew feel guilty when, seemingly, with a shift of the winds of terror, those who would destroy him arrive, even when he has done nothing to deserve this fate. There is this eternal conundrum for every Jew who is *not* guilty but nevertheless feels guilty. Guilty of what? Guilty how? But guilty nonetheless.

For centuries the elders and the rabbis have questioned how it is that the victim should think himself to be guilty. How can a man feel guilty when it is his own blood, and the blood of his wife and children which has been spilled? Only the Jew knows how this can be done. But even a Jew does not know why he must be made to bear the shame of his own persecution.

Ikey could see in Billygonequeer the same mysterious forces, the same looming tragedy, the fear that a sudden change in the wind might bring with it a great destruction of his people. But he knew also that Billy's people had nowhere to go, no opportunity for a diaspora. No borders to steal across at night, no river to wade with forlorn bundles on their heads or mountain to scale with safety promised on the leeward side, no corrupt officials to bribe to gain a temporary haven. Billy's people had been placed at the ends of the earth. Now, with the coming of the white man, they would be pushed over its edge to oblivion, where only the ghosts of the eleven lost tribes of Israel dwell in the howling, mournful, swirling mists of eternity.

When Billy had gone queer and thrown off his clothes, Ikey had seen his back. The lines of scar tissue joined in a contorted lunar landscape of ridges and troughs, so that no single piece of clear black skin remained. Billy had been beaten so often that his back looked like a shiny, carelessly plaited garment of hide pitted with a dozen small craters of yellow pus.

They left Billygonequeer behind that day at Richmond Gaol in order that he might be taken before the district magistrate. A police magistrate alone could order only three dozen lashes and this, Harris felt, was insufficient to curb the black man's constant rebellion. When the men returned that night they found Billy in the courtyard still standing rigid, his yellow palms turned outward, chained to the ring set into the prison wall. Harris informed them jauntily that they would not muster as usual at dawn, but would be allowed to rest until nine of the clock, and thereafter would be required to march to the nearby courthouse where the triangle stood and where they would witness Billygonequeer's sentence of flogging – one hundred strokes of the cat. The men cheered, for a late rising was like a holiday.

'Be there a man among you who will volunteer to be the flagellator?' Harris asked.

'Where be Rufus Manning?' someone called.

'Gorn to Hobart to do a floggin'. There be twelve men called to the triangle there and only two to flog the livin' daylights out o' them,' Harris explained, then added, 'It's double rations for him what volunteers to flagellate the nigger!'

There was a murmur among the prisoners though none stepped forward. Harris watched them, his eyes seeming to fix on each man before travelling on. Billygonequeer stood rigidly behind him in chains. The overseer saw the reluctance in each pair of eyes. 'Double rations and the 'arf day orf!' he now added.

The men shuffled and murmured among themselves. It was a prize each of them was much tempted to possess, and had it been any other man who was to be flogged, few would have hesitated. No man among them could remember when last he had felt his stomach contented. But they all felt differently about Billygonequeer, differently and afraid. Two flagellators who had whipped him in the past had died shortly afterwards, and were rumoured to have howled as they died, making the same dog-like noise as Billygonequeer. Afterwards the surgeon could find no cause of death, though there had been a look of great terror on their faces and both had torn at their guts until they drew deep furrows of blood. They did not for a moment believe that Manning had gone to Hobart. He had taken cover. Life on a road gang was not much to contemplate, but to die howling like a dog with some great terror ripping the life out of you from within, and all for the sake of half a day's rest and a good tightener, was a more fearful prospect.

'You do it, Mr 'Arris!' one of the prisoners shouted. 'G'warn, you flog 'im, you flog Billygonequeer!'

Harris grew suddenly pale, and while he tried to laugh off the suggestion, the corners of his mouth seemed for a moment out of control. 'It's not me job,' he finally muttered.

'It's not ours neither!' several of the men volunteered and there was a knowing snigger among the prisoners.

Suddenly Billy's arm rose stiff as a ramrod and pointed directly at Ikey, and from his throat came the howl. Harris turned to see the wild-eyed black pointing at Ikey's breast. Billy howled once more, then let his arm fall slowly to his side.

Ikey looked fearfully about him and then at the overseer and vigorously shook his head. 'Who, me? No, no, not me!' he said, taking a backwards step and bumping into the man behind him. 'Mercy be! I hates violence of any sort. Please, I begs you Mr Harris!' Ikey's eyes had grown wide with fear. 'No, no!' he repeated shaking his hand in front of his face. 'I cannot do it, I simply cannot, I should faint at the very prospect, I cannot abide the sight o' blood.' Ikey let out a sudden wail and fell to his knees at the overseer's feet. 'I begs you, no!' he sobbed.

The assembled prisoners were convulsed with laughter. Blood was such a common substance in their lives, they thought it hilarious that Ikey should declare his abhorrence to it. Before he had completed his prison sentence they knew he would see rivers of blood, until this substance would seem no more strange to him than the spittle on a man's tongue, or the beads of sweat gathered on his brow.

'Well now, you'll do nicely, it will be an excellent 'nitiation for ya, Ikey Solomon.' Harris smiled. 'Yer most fortunate, you are. You'll come to blood the easy way, not from the fresh opening of yer own Jew back, but upon the back o' the nigger!'

The gang mustered and was issued with their morning skilly and then marched by the three troopers who constantly guarded them to the nearby courthouse where the triangle stood.

The triangle, the dreaded flagellation post, was built of strong scantlings, that is to say posts or purlins of about five inches in width. They were placed so as to form a space about ten feet square at the bottom, and secured by pins into the ground in a slanted manner so that they rose to meet at a point in the centre. Horizontal bars were fastened to these posts, each about two feet apart, and it was to these that the person to be flogged was secured. He faced inwards, his back outwards, with his ankles, knees and outstretched arms tightly bound to the bars. The victim of the triangle was stripped, either to the waist or, more often, naked, this so that the blood would not damage his clothes, which were government property. Eight or ten men could be fastened to a single triangle, and several flagellators employed to beat them. These were usually ticket of leave men, expressly appointed to the position, and many took great pride in their work. Prisoners could also be selected if they were sufficiently robust to lend some weight to the task.

Ikey did not fit the bill in the least. Puny, with narrow sloping shoulders and delicate arms, in his hands the cat o' nine appeared to be a most incongruous instrument. Ikey carried the whip of many tails awkwardly, as though it were repulsive to him, and the knotted ends of the cutting cord drooped to the ground at his feet. Ikey's limbs appeared to tremble of their own accord, and his knees shook violently. There was no doubt in the mind of those brought in to bear witness that Billygonequeer was in for a soft time, a mere tickle of the flesh, and this prospect immensely cheered those who watched.

'You will put yer back into it, ya hear, Solomon? Step up and lay the cat square an' 'ard or, I swear, you'll receive the same yerself!' Harris shouted. He reached out, grabbed the knotted whip from Ikey's reluctant fingers, and demonstrated how it should be used. The cords whistled through the air and landed with a single hard smack across the smooth wood of one of the triangle's posts. Ikey's eyes screwed up in horror, and he trembled more than ever.

Harris handed him the whip and turned to the doctor. 'We are ready to yer count, sir.'

The doctor nodded to Ikey to commence and Ikey, uttering a low moan, raised the whip and brought it down upon Billygonequeer's back. The blow was so ineffectual that it brought a sudden gale of laughter from the onlookers. One of the knots at the end of the cord must have entered a festering pit in Billy's back, for a thin trickle of blood ran from it. Ikey gave a soft moan and fainted dead away to the hilarious laughter of the prisoners.

The doctor examined Ikey then took smelling salts from his bag which revived him. But it was clear Ikey was not up to the task of flagellation. The doctor turned to Harris.

'We do not have a trooper who is corporal by rank among us. You will have to complete the flogging yourself.' There was a sudden and complete silence among the prisoners as they watched Harris.

'I am not inclined, sir. Can it not wait for Mr Manning? Some other day perhaps?'

'Nonsense, man! I have just seen how well you take to the task by the way you approached the whipping post. Get to it. I have but little time to waste in this tedious matter.'

'Sir, I shall lose respect among my men,' Harris tried again.

'Nay!' several prisoners shouted. 'That you will not! G'warn, Mr Harris, do the deed!'

'Be silent, you!' Harris snarled at the ranks, grateful to have a chance to vent his spleen.

'There you are, Harris, you have the full support of your men.' The doctor stooped and picked up the cat o' nine tails. 'Can't ask for more than that now, can you?' He handed the whip to Harris. 'Be a good person and do your duty in the name of the King.'

Harris seemed suddenly to lose all control and his face took on a fierce and desperate look. He lifted the whip and ran at Billygonequeer, and brought the cat down with all his might across the black man's back. He rained blow after blow on Billy, grunting and frothing at the mouth, so that long before he had completed the one hundred strokes he was exhausted and bowed down for want of energy. His hands were clasped upon his knees and his breath came in great gasps. Specks of flesh and blood splattered his blouse and face and hair.

'Why you are the consummate flagellator, Mr Harris. Taken to the art like a duck to water, eh?' the surgeon said calmly, then added, 'That be quite enough, cut the prisoner down.'

Throughout the terrible beating Billygonequeer did not once flinch or cry out. Nor did he register any expression when a trooper splashed his back with brine before cutting him from the triangle. He spat the leather mouthpiece out, strips of raw flesh hanging from his back, and stood rigid, eyes glazed, the yellow palms of his hands turned outwards. He then howled three times, the eerie call of the Tasmanian tiger dog, and the Irishmen among the prisoners were seen to cross themselves.

Billygonequeer was not placed in solitary confinement, as was the custom after a flogging, but chained once again to the wall in the courtyard. He stayed there for two weeks on bread and water until his back was sufficiently healed for him to return to the cart.

Each evening Ikey would go to the gaoler Mr Dodsworth and beg for liniment and clean rags, and he would clean out the wounds on Billy's back and to the back of his head, wincing and gagging as he cleared the maggots the flies had laid in the festering craters during the day. Billy had long since come out of his trance and he would smile as Ikey approached. Silently he'd allow Ikey to clean his wounds and rub the sulphur ointment into his back without flinching, though the pain must have been excruciating.

Ikey could not explain to himself this voluntary act of caring. He knew it to be completely contrary to his character and he was not aware of having undergone any change in his nature. In fact he seldom thought of Hannah and his children, and cared even less about their welfare. He would lie awake at night plotting to get Hannah's set of numbers for the safe, and told himself that, if ever he should succeed, he would escape his wife forever.

Occasionally, in a moment of sentimentality, he thought fondly of Mary, though he harboured no future ambitions for a reunion with her. He told himself he wished only for a future life as a rich man, a life far removed from any he had previously led, and he was determined not to bring any of the past into his future.

Though it may be said that every heart on earth is kindled to love, Ikey had so early in his life been denied affection that he was dulled to its prospect. He had never felt the singular need to love. He felt he had loved Mary, if only briefly, but he had no notion of what he might expect from such an emotion. He did not care if he himself were liked, for he had come to expect the opposite. Now that the sycophancy on which he depended as a rich man was no longer available to him, he fully expected that he would be greatly disliked. That he himself should be loved was not a thought which ever entered his head. And so Ikey's feelings for Billygonequeer were hard for him to understand, and filled him with apprehension.

Almost every day as he laboured at the cart he would decide to ignore the black man on his return to the prison that night. But he was never able to do so. Billygonequeer would smile at him, his gleaming white teeth filling his astonishing coal-black face, and Ikey, inwardly cursing himself for his foolishness, would be off to Mr Dodsworth for liniment and cloth.

Ikey, as was his natural manner, talked to Billygonequeer at great length. To this torrent of words Billy would sometimes grunt, or smile, adding little more than sounds and nods to this one-way dialogue. Occasionally Billy would clutch Ikey's hand or pat him on his face and say, 'Good pella, Ikey.' Then he might grin and repeat, 'Much, much, good pella, Ikey.' It was as though, by Ikey's mannerisms and the few words Billy had at his disposal, he could grasp what his companion was saying.

Sometimes Billygonequeer would hear a bird cry and say aloud its Aboriginal name until Ikey could pronounce it clearly. He'd gather fruit or nuts, or grub for roots, and always share what he found. Ikey got used to the fat white grubs Billy would find under the bark of fallen trees and found them delicious when roasted. Whenever they came upon wild honey they would feast on it secretly for days. In these ways Billy supplemented their prison diet with bush tucker, and there were some days on the road gang when the four men on the cart counted their stomachs more full than empty. It was a wondrous thing to see Billy's willingness to share everything he found, and the smallest wild morsel would be meticulously divided.

Ikey had spent his life in acquisition, sharing as little as possible, and keeping as much for himself as he could. It would be nice to think that Billygonequeer might have changed this aspect of his nature, that the primitive savage could teach Ikey the highest achievement of civilisation, the equitable sharing of the combined resources of any society.

Alas, this is not the lesson Ikey took from the black man. Instead he came to realise that it was this very characteristic which would lead to the ultimate demise of the Van Diemen's Land savage. The rapacious white tribe who were arriving in increasing numbers, not only as convicts but also as settlers, wanted to own everything they touched. They slashed and burned the wilderness so that they might graze their sheep and grow their corn. They erected fences around the land they now called their own and which henceforth they were prepared to defend with muskets and sometimes even their lives. They built church steeples and prison walls and homes of granite hewn from the virgin rock and timber cut from the umbrageous mountain forests. They possessed everything upon the island, the wild beasts that grazed upon its surface, the birds that flew over it, the fish that swam in its rushing river torrents and the barking seals resting in the quiet bays and secluded inlets. Everything they thought worthwhile was attached to the notion of ownership.

Against this urgent and anxious desire for appropriation stood a handful of savages who seldom even built a shelter against the weather. They dressed in a single kangaroo skin, and believed that all they could see and walk upon was owned by all who moved across the land, and yet by none. A people who did not comprehend that one person could own, or wish to own, more than any other.

Ikey understood at once that the Aboriginal tribes in Van Diemen's Land must surely perish because they lacked the two things that had made human progress possible, the existence of greed and the desire to possess property. Ikey understood acquisition as the only guarantee of his survival. He saw that Billygonequeer's people were doomed, for they had not learned this fundamental lesson. Without the need to own there is no need to compete and an uncompetitive society can only exist if it is allowed to develop in isolation. For Billy's people, the isolation had come to an end.

Ikey was aware that Billygonequeer probably did not understand what he was saying, but he said it nonetheless. He would talk as he cleaned Billy's wounds and rubbed salve into his back. 'You must become like us, you must learn our ways, your ways are over, my dear!' Ikey would repeat this over and over, but all he got from Billygonequeer was a big smile. A big white smile in a very black face and always the same response.

'You good pella, Ikey!'

It was not three weeks after Billygonequeer had taken his place again beside Ikey on the cart when Harris began to suffer stomach pains. He would be shouting at the prisoners, or simply walking along, when suddenly he would grab at his stomach, doubling over with pain as each spasm came to him.

The road gang did not need to be told that he was dying. 'Harris's gone queer,' they'd say gleefully among themselves. A month later the overseer was dead, and it was rumoured that all the same symptoms, self-laceration of the stomach and howling in the manner of Billygonequeer, were in attendance at his death bed. Furthermore, the coroner conducting the autopsy could find no fault with his stomach and intestines.

The gang was now working too far from Richmond Gaol to return at night so they proceeded from a new out station, a series of rough buildings erected beside the road. These were infested with lice and fleas, with the addition of other vermin when the weather grew colder. A new overseer, James Strutt, who had come out from Launceston, proved not too harsh by the standards of the day, dealing with trouble only when he found it.

It was from Strutt that Ikey first learned the true extent of the range war which was being waged against the island's native people. Strutt was a member of a part-time militia unit, formed independently of the government troopers, and he spoke with great enthusiasm of the tactics to be employed in the killing of blacks. He had been a member of the Black Line in October the previous year, and spoke disparagingly of the bumbling manner in which this manoeuvre had been conducted. The Black Line was a government sponsored operation intended to drive the Aboriginals out of the settled areas. The plan was to drive the blacks south and east towards East Bay Neck, through the Forestier Peninsula, and into the Tasman Peninsula, where it was proposed a permanent Aboriginal reserve would be set up.

The task force consisted of two thousand men, five hundred of these soldiers, seven hundred convicts and eight hundred free settlers and involved a thousand muskets and three hundred pairs of handcuffs. Three weeks later this avenging army returned having captured one old Aboriginal man and a young boy.

Strutt dismissed the operation as an example of how not to go about the task of eliminating the blacks. 'Government and soldier be not the way. It be a question of us agin them, free men agin savages and, by God, we'll settle it soon enough!' he'd boast.

The Church talked of the salvation of the noble savage. For its part, the government talked increasingly of saving these primitive creatures from extinction by rounding them all up and placing them on a suitable island, which was yet to be found, where they would be out of harm's way.

It was estimated that a thousand natives still existed of the original three thousand who were thought to be on the island when it had been declared a penal settlement. As it turned out, this calculation was incorrect. A white man's respiratory disease had struck the tribes and only a few hundred Aboriginals still existed on the land they had traditionally occupied.

But it should not be supposed that the Tasmanian native was without courage. With wooden spears against muskets they valiantly fought back and caused great consternation among the settlers. During the four-year period of martial law they killed eighty-nine Europeans, while of the two hundred Aboriginals thought to be within the settled areas, fewer than fifty survived.

The government now believed that the natives might be persuaded to accept a safe haven. They appointed George Augustus Robinson, a religious zealot who spoke the main Aboriginal language, to peaceably round up what remained of the tribes for resettlement. In this task Robinson enlisted the help of an Aboriginal female, Truganini. She was his guide, and it was her influence which he hoped might persuade her people to capitulate, though the settlers thought the word 'guide' a very curious one for what they insisted was the true relationship between Robinson and the young and shapely Aboriginal woman.

If Church and State professed compassion for the Van Diemen's Land natives, the settlers held no such Christian or noble motives. They called openly for the elimination of the Tasmanian Aboriginal race and, in that duplicity so common to government, where a wink is as good as a nod, the authorities turned a blind eye as the settlers worked to bring that elimination about.

Governor Arthur issued a famous poster, which was nailed to trees in the wilderness, in which he showed the Aboriginals, by means of comic pictures, that there would be equal justice under British law. That a native killed by a white settler would see the culprit hanged as surely as if a black were to murder a white. Yet although hundreds of Aboriginal women and children were openly slaughtered, not a single European settler was ever hanged for the murder of a black.

Martial law was declared in 1828 which gave the military the right to apprehend or shoot on sight any Aboriginal found in the settled areas. The military proved ineffective in this task, and roving parties of settlers were formed under the pretence of a militia such as the one to which Strutt belonged. A bounty was introduced for the capture of Aboriginals, five pounds being paid for every adult and two pounds for each child. It was open season, and though few natives were captured, many were murdered with as little concern for the consequences as if they were kangaroos or a flock of marauding cockatoos.

To the settlers, Robinson, 'the Black Shepherd', was a bad joke and Strutt would often expostulate, 'While that Abo fucker George Robinson be playing sheepdog we be playin' huntin' dog. Before he can muster them black bastards, they'll all be on the roll call for the dead. They's vermin, scum, they's not human like us, a single fly-blown sheep be worth five o' them and a good huntin' hound worth ten!'

Whereupon Strutt would tell with alacrity one of his numerous stories of the hunting trips undertaken to kill the blacks. The men in Ikey's road gang thought these stories a great entertainment.

Two favourites were the tale of Paddy Hexagon, a stock-keeper who lived near Deloraine, who shot and killed nineteen Aboriginals with a swivel gun filled with nails, and another which the prisoners on the road gang called 'Stuffing Leaves'.

'G'warn then, Mr Strutt, tell us the one about the woman and the stuffin' o' leaves!' one of the prisoners asked one night when they'd moved from Richmond Gaol, and were accommodated at the out station in the bush.

They were sitting around a fire, Ikey seated next to the always silent Billygonequeer. Billy appeared not to listen to or even understand these horror stories. Instead he sat on his haunches with his back turned to the fire, and seemed more interested in the sound of the wind in the gum trees and the call of the frogs from a nearby stream.

This stream ran into a small wetland and Billygonequeer seemed to take an unusual interest in the frogs which resided there. Every once in a while he would cup his hands to his mouth and precisely imitate a call, though at a slightly deeper pitch. Whereupon all the frogs would grow suddenly silent. Then he would carry on in a froggy language as though he were delivering an address, pause, then deliver a single, though somewhat different note, and the frogs would continue their croaking chatter.

At first this was seen by the men as a great joke. But Billygonequeer would continue in earnest conversation in frog language until the gang got so used to his nightly routine of croaking and ribet-ribet-ing with nature that they took no more notice than if a loud belch or fart had taken place among one of their number.

'Oh aye, the woman with leaves, that be a most pleasin' hunt,' Strutt chuckled in reply. 'The women be the worst. They'll scratch your eyes out soon as look at you.' Strutt stroked his beard as though reviewing all the details of the tale before he began. 'There be three of us, Paddy Hexagon, Sam O'Leary and yours truly, and we's huntin' kangaroo in the Coal River area when we seen this gin who were pregnant like. "Oi!" we shouts, thinkin' her too fat to make a run for it, and five pound in the bounty bag if you please and very nice too! And if the child be near to born, another two for what's inside her belly.' He paused and the men laughed and one of them, a wit named Cristin Puding, known of course as 'Christmas Pudding', made a customary crack.

'That I needs to see! A government bounty man what pays two pound for what's not yet come outside to be properly skinned and cured!'

'Well we shouts again,' Strutt continued, casting a look of annoyance at Puding, for he did not wish him to steal even the smallest rumble of his thunder, or tiny scrap of the laughter yet to come. 'And she sets off, waddlin' like a duck and makin' for the shelter o' some trees not twenty yards away. She's movin' too, movin' fast for the fat black duck she's become.' This brought a laugh, for the gang had heard it often enough and were properly cued to respond.

'We sets off to get to her, but the grass 'tween her and us be high and she be into the trees. By the time we gets there she ain't nowhere to be seen. High 'n low we searches and we's about to give it away when we hears a cry up above. We looks up and there she be, up fifty feet or more in the branches of a gum tree, well disguised behind the leaves and all. How she gone and got up in her state I'm buggered if I knows. It were no easy climb.'

The road gang grew silent and even Billygonequeer ceased making his frog sounds.

'There she be, high up in the fork o' the tree and, by Jaysus, the child inside her is beginnin' to be borned! She's gruntin' somethin' awful, snuffin' and snoofin' like a fat sow and then it's a screamin' and a caterwaulin' as the head and shoulders come to sniff the world outside! "Here's sport for all!" Sam O'Leary, me mate, shouts. "We'll wait this one out!"'

'Wait this one out!' Cristin Puding shouted, turning to the others. 'Get it? Wait this one *out*!' But the other prisoners hushed him fast, anxious for the story to continue.

'Well, you'll not believe it,' Strutt continued, once again ignoring Puding, 'though I swear on me mother's grave it be true! Out come the bloody mess. The child's got the birth cord twisted round its neck and stranglin' him, only later it turns out to be a her, a little girl, and it's hangin' itself in the air, and the black gin's tryin' to hold onto the cord, but it's slippin' through her hands. "Five shilling to him what shoots it down first!" Paddy Hexagon shouts.'

Strutt stopped suddenly and rocked back on the log he'd sat on and then began to chuckle softly.

'Well you never seen such a loadin' and firin' and missin' and, all the time, the cord stretchin' longer and longer with the black woman holdin' on to it at her end and screamin' blue murder! Then Paddy takes a bead and fires and the little black bastard explodes like a ripe pumpkin! There be blood rainin' down on us! Jaysus! I can tell you, we was all a mess to behold. "Bastard! Bitch! Black whore!" O'Leary shouts at the gin screamin' and sobbin' up in the tree.' The foreman laughed again. 'His wife just made him a new shirt and now it be spoiled, soaked in Abo's blood! Paddy and me, we damn near carked we laughed so much!'

He paused, enjoying the eyes of all the men fixed upon him. '"You'll pay fer this ya black bitch!" O'Leary shouts upwards at her, shakin' his fist. Then he takes a careful shot. Bullseye! He hits the gin in the stomach. But she don't come tumblin' down, instead she starts to pick leaves from the tree and stuff them in her gut, in the hole what O'Leary's musket's made. We all shoot, but she stays up, and each time a shot strikes home she spits at us and stuffs more leaves where the new holes be. There we all be. Us shootin' and her stuffin' gum leaves and screamin' and spittin', the baby lyin' broke on the ground. It were grand sport, but then I takes a shot and hits her in the head, dead between the eyes, and she come tumblin' down and falls plop, lifeless to the ground.'

The men around the overseer clapped and whistled. Only Ikey and Billygonequeer remained silent.

Ikey turned and spat into the dark, thankful that Billygonequeer would not have understood a word of the foreman's grisly tale. Then someone threw a branch on the embers, and the dry leaves crackled and flared up and in the wider circle of light cast by the fire Ikey saw that tears were flowing from Billy's dark eyes. Large silent tears which ran onto the point of his chin and splashed in tiny explosions of dust at his feet. The fire died back to normal, and in the dark Ikey reached out and touched Billy's shoulder and whispered softly.

'You *got* to learn to be like us, Billygonequeer!' Then he added, 'Not like them. Jesus no! Like a Jew. I'll teach you, my dear. You could be a black Jew. All you got to learn is, when you've got suffering you've got to add cunning. Suffering plus cunning equals survival! That be the arithmetic of a Jew's life!'

Billygonequeer turned slowly and looked directly at Ikey, sniffing and wiping the tears from his eyes with the back of his hand.

'You good pella, Ikey,' he said, his voice hoarse and barely above a whisper. Then, 'You gib me name, Ikey!'

Ikey looked momentarily puzzled. 'You've already got a name, my dear. It ain't much, but it serves as good as most.'

Billygonequeer shook his head. 'Like Ikey. Name same like white pella.'

'Oh, you wants a proper name? Is that it, Billy?' He pointed to the men around the fire. 'Like them pella? Puding, Calligan, Mooney? Name like so?'

Billygonequeer nodded and smiled, his sad, teary face suddenly lighting up.

Ikey considered for a moment. After promising to turn Billygonequeer into a Jew he thought to give him a Jewish name, but then changed his mind. It would take too much explanation and might get Billygonequeer into even more trouble.

'William Lanney!' he said suddenly. It was the name of a carpenter mechanic who owed Ikey five pounds from a bet lost at ratting, a debt Ikey now knew he would never collect. 'Will-ee-am Lan-nee,' Ikey repeated slowly.

'Willeeamlanee!' Billygonequeer said in a musical tone as though it were the sound of a bird cry.

'No.' Ikey held up two fingers. 'Two words. William. Lanney.'

Billygonequeer was not only a dab hand at mastering frog calls, for he seemed now to grasp the pronunciation of his new name quite easily, 'William Lanney . . . William Lanney,' he said, with tolerable accuracy.

Ikey laughed. 'Good pella, Mr William Lanney!'

Billygonequeer stretched out and touched Ikey's face as though he was memorising his features through the tips of his long, slender fingers. 'You good pella, Ikey! Much, much good, pella!' He tested his new name. 'William Lanney!'

It was time for the evening lock up. The prisoners were led to their huts, mustered, and then each was manacled to his bunk and all locked in for the night, except for Billygonequeer, who was manacled and chained to a large old blue gum to sleep the night in the open.

At dawn Ikey wakened as the javelin man, the trusted prisoner in charge, entered the hut and called over for the man to come and unlock his shackles so that he might go outside to take a piss.

Ikey walked out into the crisp dawn. Above him, where the early sunrise touched the top of the gum trees, he could hear the doves cooing. When he'd emptied his bladder Ikey strolled over to the tree where Billygonequeer had been chained for the night. Here he stopped in surprise. The shackles, still fixed in their locks, lay upon the ground, but Billygonequeer was missing.

Ikey stood for a moment not fully comprehending. He wondered if Billygonequeer might have already risen, though it was customary to unchain him last of all. Then he noticed that the manacles and shackles had not been opened, and that there were bloodstains on the inside surfaces.

Ikey felt a great ache grow such as he had not felt before. A deep heaviness which started somewhere in his chest, and rose up and filled his throat so that he was scarcely able to breathe. He could hear his heart beating in his ears, his head seemed for a moment to float, and he was close to fainting. He stood very still, and he could hear the burble of water flowing over rock, and the wash of the wind in the leaves above him. Ikey, the most solitary of men, now felt more completely alone than ever before.

'May Jehovah be with you, Billygonequeer,' Ikey said, the words hurting in his throat as he spoke to the chains which lay unopened in the beaten grass where his friend had last lain. Then he began to rock back and forth and at the same time to recite the Kaddish, the prayer for the dead. Hot tears rolled silently down his cheeks and disappeared into his scraggly beard as the words of the ancient prayer frosted in the cold morning air.

And may he walk continually in the land of life,
and may his soul rest in the bond of life.

Then he leaned against the smooth, cool bark of the gum tree and sobbed and sobbed. High above him in the silver gum trees he could hear the blue doves calling to their lost partners.

Chapter Twenty-seven

Imprisonment is intended to break the spirit, to render harmless those who are thought to be harmful. Such is the human condition that it will endure the brutal lash and the bread and water of society's pious outrage, but is finally broken by the relentless boredom of prison life. The blankness of time, the pointless repetition, the mindless routines undertaken in a bleak and purposeless landscape addles the brain and reduces a person to whimpering servility. Humans best survive when they are given purpose; a common enemy to defeat, revenge to wreak or a dream to cling to.

Mary survived her sentence because she had a dream. She saw her incarceration in the Female Factory as her apprenticeship out of the hell of her past. Henceforth, she determined that she would be judged by her competence and not doomed by the circumstances of her birth. Here, under the shadow of the great mountain, she would take her rightful place in life.

During the four grim years she spent at the Female Factory Mary knew that she had taken the first steps in her great good luck. The Potato Factory in the prison vegetable gardens had prospered and when she was granted her ticket of leave to live outside the prison she had accumulated the sum of five hundred pounds. Ann Gower also now possessed sufficient money, saved for her by Mary, to achieve an ambition she talked of a great deal, open a bawdy house on the waterfront area of Wapping.

The King's Orphan School had achieved exemplary results, with most of Mary's pupils numerate and literate and some beginning to show a most gratifying propensity for learning. So impressed was Mr Emmett, the chief clerk, that he persuaded Governor Arthur to offer Mary the position of headmistress. This independent position meant that she would no longer be under the baleful eye of the Reverend Smedley, and would be entitled to a small salary. Much to the dismay of Mary's sponsor, she had once again refused his generous offer.

'What ever shall we make of you, Mary Abacus? Will you never learn what is good for you? A more stubborn woman would be most difficult to find upon this island! If you were a man you would be quickly dismissed as a complete fool!'

Mary, who had the greatest respect for Mr Emmett, was sorry to be the cause of his disappointment. In the three years she had been teaching he had come to support her keenly and had seen to it that she was supplied with equipment from government stores, and that the Reverend Smedley did not unduly interfere with or undermine her work.

'Mr Emmett, sir, I thank you from the bottom o' me heart for the trust you have shown in me, but I must remind you, I am a teacher only for the lack o' someone more qualified. You gave me the position only because I believed the brats could take to learning.'

'I'll give you that, Mary, I'll give you that,' Mr Emmett repeated, somewhat mollified. 'You've proved us all wrong and a salutary lesson it has been, I agree.'

Mary smiled. 'You're very kind, Mr Emmett, but it be time for you to make a proper appointment. There be a widow, Mrs Emma Patterson, a free settler out from England, a Quaker I believe. She has excellent references and is well trained to her vocation. She has applied to us for a billet and she is much superior in her knowledge and methods to me or Miss Smedley.' Mary paused. 'You would do well to grant her the post in my stead.'

'Oh Mary, Mary, quite contrary, what shall we do with you?' Mr Emmett asked.

Mary grinned, thankful that he seemed reconciled to her decision. 'A reference, sir. I intend to apply for a clerking position, with some bookkeeping, just as you would have me do for the government, but in commerce. Will you grant it me?' She tilted her head and gave Emmett a most disarming smile. 'Please?'

The chief clerk tried his utmost to appear disapproving, but finally nodded his head. 'It will do you no good, my girl,' he said.

The position of headmistress of the orphan school was duly given to Mrs Patterson who, together with the patient and loving Elspeth Smedley, would ensure that the future for Mary's pupils was a bright one.

On the day before her ticket of leave was granted Mary took a tearful farewell from her orphans and cried all the way back to the Female Factory. She loved her children and had watched them grow and take pleasure in learning. Mary felt sure that some, at last, would have respectable lives. She wondered how she could possibly have given up her post, for the children loved her, gave her a purpose and had confirmed her as being a natural teacher. But deep in her heart she knew that teaching would not fulfil her ultimate ambition, that her skill with numbers and her abacus was meant for a different purpose.

With the Potato Factory, Mary had gained a further sense of business and was reminded again that the rules of supply and demand work best when they are predicated against the innate weakness of men. The brothel in Bell Alley and the supply of poteen from the Potato Factory both demonstrated this fundamental principle. To this end Ann Gower had begged that once they were free of the Female Factory they do more of the same. She also suggested they take the still with them so that they might continue in the trades that had been so lucrative for them in the prison vegetable gardens.

But Mary had resisted her friend's offer. She wanted no more of the criminal life, and was determined to be as free as the brilliant green parrots which had welcomed her to Van Diemen's Land. Freedom meant a great deal more to her than the opportunity to live a respectable existence in a new land, where old beliefs and habits were applied to circumstances which had greatly changed. She would use her freedom as though it were truly the gift of being born again to a new life. Mary's conviction that destiny had called her to something more than a life of drudgery had persisted, and she responded to it with a full heart and the unstinting application of her nimble mind. Her body had grown strong on a diet of fresh vegetables and from working in the open air, and she was ready to make whatever sacrifices were necessary.

Mary's ticket of leave included a probationary period of three years and then her sentence would be completed. She wished to use this time to learn a new trade, so she would be ready when she was permitted to go into business on her own. She would take a billet where she might learn the intricacies of trade, and her first task had been to purchase a copy of the *Colonial Times* so that she might peruse the advertisements for employment. The number of these which requested the need for a bookkeeper, eight in all, filled her heart with joy. But before she set about walking to each address she had a promise to keep to herself.

She had been escorted to the gates of the Female Factory by the keeper, Mr Drabble, not much past six in the morning. To Mary's surprise he had taken her hand.

'You have served your time, Mary Abacus, and I wish you well. It is my most earnest hope that you shall never return to this place.'

Mary smiled. 'Not as earnest as mine, Mr Drabble. You'll not see hide nor hair of us again!'

Mary had left without Ann Gower, who was to serve an extra week in solitary on bread and water for insubordination when drunk. Mary was somewhat relieved, for though she loved Ann she feared that she would never change, that she would always be, as the popular expression went, 'A nymph o' the pave', though such a description of Ann Gower would have been a gross underestimation of her rapidly growing size. A diet consisting largely of grog and potatoes had caused her to grow exceedingly gross, which Ann described to her customers as 'the luxury o' comfort on the ride', and she would have charged an extra sixpence if she could have gotten away with it. Mary had been reluctant to hand Ann the money she had saved on her behalf, though she told herself she could no longer be responsible for her friend. She had also given the still to her partner, to be secretly dismantled when Ann left the Factory. If Ann should show the minimum of good sense then she had the means to prosper well on the new waterfront area of Wapping.

Mary did not go directly into the town when she left the Female Factory. Carrying her bed roll, a clay pot, her abacus and a small cloth satchel, she climbed the hill immediately behind the Factory and headed towards the great mountain. Sometimes, on her way to the orphan school, she would divert into the tall trees growing on the slopes of Mount Wellington. Along a secret path of her own making she had discovered a small stream, though stream was too grand a word for the trickle of sweet, clear water which came from a large overhanging rock.

Mary now made her way to the secret rock set into the mountain side, which was flat at its top and made an ample ledge. She would sit on a carpet of moss surrounded by fern and look out beyond the shadow cast by the rock to where clumps of brilliant yellow wattle grew under the gum trees. The air around her was scented with blossom. Mountain blueberry, the berries ripe and brilliant, twisted and trailed over the smaller trees and shrubs, and every once in a while she would see a splash of wild fuchsia or a clump of pale pink and lilac early snowberries.

On hot summer days it was cool under the shelter of the rock, which was scarred with lichen and pocketed with moss. On mild winter days Mary would climb on top of the rock ledge and the sun would dapple through the leaves to warm her.

Mary imagined sleeping on this ledge so that she might see the stars at night. Slowly the desire grew in her and she would think upon this prospect as she lay in the stale dormitory filled with the tainted breath of forty other prisoners, a heaving, snoring body on either side of her. Finally she had determined that she was going to spend her first night of freedom on her secret rock under the stars.

Mary arrived at the rock no later than seven in the morning. She removed a clump of moss from deep within the recesses of the overhanging rock and carefully buried the clay pot. Inside it was the five hundred pounds she had saved. She replaced the moss and marked the spot with a handful of small pebbles which appeared to be resting naturally. Mary paused only to take a drink of water and wash her hands before leaving. With her she took her abacus and the small satchel in which she carried a pound in copper and silver and Mr Emmett's letter of recommendation. She walked further up the mountain slope, making a wide arc well away from her rock, until she found a woodcutter's path which led down to the precincts of Hobart Town.

She walked down Macquarie Street and into the centre of the town. Every inch of ground was taken up with some small business concern. Even the fronts of the houses and business establishments for some yards were taken up by traders with stalls and hastily

415

erected sheds of canvas and hoarding. There were lollipop shops, oyster shops, barber shops and butcher stalls where flies hummed about the carcasses of lamb and kangaroo. Men and women shouted their wares at every approach with extravagant promises. 'Oyster the size of a plate!' one would shout. 'Fat lamb that weighs heavy to the pound!' cried a bloody-aproned butcher. 'Birds, song birds, what whistle hopera!' called a boy carrying a cage of yellow canaries.

At eight o'clock in the morning she was waiting at the doorway of the London & Overseas Insurance & Shipping Company, the first of the business concerns which had advertised for a bookkeeper clerk. Mary had arrived early, anxious to be the first if there should be a crowd of applicants. But she had no need to worry – Hobart Town had more billets for clerks than applicants to fill them.

By six o'clock that evening Mary had presented herself at each potential place of employ, dutifully proffering her letter of reference from Mr Emmett. Nothing had changed from her days in London. Mary was a woman, and a ticket of leave convict, and there had scarcely been a rejection of her services couched in even modestly polite language.

The first interview, which had taken place a few minutes after nine in the morning with the insurance and shipping company, had been no better or worse than the last. The manager, a tall, thin and exceedingly pompous chief clerk with the unprepossessing name of Archibald Pooley had looked askance at Mary, his eyes fixed on her mutilated hands. 'Be off with you, miss! I doubt that you could count to ten, but it would try my patience to test you even in this.'

'Please, sir, I have a reference.' Mary smiled brightly and proffered Mr Emmett's letter to the thin-lipped clerk.

He took the letter and held it up to the light. 'Ha! A forgery! No doubt about it!' He handed it back to Mary. 'Count yourself most fortunate that I do not have you arrested! Chief clerk of the colonial secretary's department, eh? You are not only forward but also most stupid. If this letter of reference had been from a lesser mortal than the inestimable Mr Emmett I might have believed in it.' Pooley wore an expression of utter disdain and now he tilted his head backwards as though assaulted by some odious smell. 'You reek of the Female Factory and you expect one to think you honest? Do you take me for a fool, miss?' He sniffed. Then his eyebrows shot heavenwards. 'Good God!' he exclaimed, pointing to Mary's abacus. 'What on earth is that?'

'Me abacus, sir. Please would you let me do a reckonin' for you, any calculation what is a part of your business?'

'Reckoning? On that contraption?' Pooley snorted. 'I sincerely trust you are not serious.'

Mary placed the abacus on a small table close to her and smiled.

'Any reckoning what pleases you, sir,' she said brightly, trying to hide her nervousness. 'As complicated as you wish.'

Pooley ignored Mary's request. 'That be a Chinee contraption, an abacus, is it not?'

'Yes, sir, and well able to do sums o' the most complicated nature,' Mary repeated.

'Not here it isn't!' Pooley said, alarmed. 'Beads for counting in my office? We do not count with beads here, just as we do not count with our fingers!' Then he brought his hands to his head. 'A woman *and* a convict who plays with beads thinks to clerk for me!' He spoke this at the ceiling and seemed for a moment genuinely upset that Mary should think so low of him. 'Your kind are made to be washer women not bookkeepers! Be gone, you have tried my patience long enough!'

As Mary left the scene of each not dissimilar rejection she could hear the words as they had reached her through the swirling, yellow mist of the London East India Docks:

> *Mary, Mary, Bloody Mary . . .*
> *You're the monkey on our back!*

She walked in some despair to the edge of Hobart Town and then, looking carefully lest she might be followed, veered into the shadows of a stand of tall trees that led to her rock. A chill autumn wind blew down from the mountain and the light was fading under the trees as she made her way to her secret sanctuary.

She had bought a small loaf of bread and a tiny jar of maple syrup. She'd not had anything to eat since her bowl of gruel at daybreak, her last meal at the Factory. Mary would have loved to stop at the orphanage, if only for a few moments, to regain her courage. She suddenly longed to have her children skipping around her anxious to be held and loved, she yearned to hold a child in her arms and feel its tender skin against her cheek. She knew she would also greatly miss Elspeth Smedley's midday meal which, despite the tedious presence of Thomas Smedley, had always caused her to feel less a prisoner and more like a civilised person. For the better part of an hour each day she could pretend to be normal. Now she was back to being dirt on the street. Although she had earned her ticket of leave she was still regarded as convict scum and she longed for the comfort of Elspeth's quiet voice. 'I fear a little too much salt in the gravy, Mary. Will you forgive my clumsiness?'

Elspeth had invited her to eat at the orphanage any time she wished, but Mary knew that the resources of the Reverend Smedley were meagre enough and that Mrs Emma Patterson would now take her place at the table. Besides, Mary told herself, she could no longer return Elspeth's generosity. The bountiful supply of vegetables she had brought from the prison garden was no longer available to her, and her pride would not allow her to arrive empty-handed. Now, seated under the rock where it was already dark, she devoured the loaf which she had soaked in maple syrup. By the time she was finished her hands and face were sticky but she could not remember a treat more sumptuous. It was Mary's first meal free of the shackles, and if it had been a banquet set for a queen it could have not tasted better. Mary washed, the icy mountain water leaving her poor, twisted hands aching with the chill and her face devoid of feeling, then climbed to the top of the rock to spread her mattress roll and blanket.

Mary, who had spent many a dark night alone in some foul corner of a London alley, had never before slept open to the elements. Above her myriad stars frosted the dark sky. Though she felt some trepidation at so much open space, and though it was cold under the thin blanket, she was stirred by a strange feeling of happiness. She was free at last, born again under the crystal stars of the great south land, a child of the green parrots and the great mountain. Somewhere high up in the trees she heard the call of a nightjar and before she fell into an exhausted sleep she determined that in the morning she would once again visit Mr Emmett. She smiled to herself at the thought of the exasperation she would see on his small face, though she knew her benefactor was most fond of her.

As Mary had predicted, Mr Emmett at first professed himself annoyed at her return. 'Mary Abacus, you have twice rejected my charity and now you ask again. I repeat my offer. You may come to work in the government as a clerk. We have a great need for your skill at numbers and ability to write up a ledger, and I shall see that you are treated fairly.'

'Sir, please, I should learn nothing working for the government but the task o' working for the government. There be new settlers coming in greater numbers each year to make their homes on the island and I feel certain there will be abundant opportunity for trade. If I should learn an honest profession, it would be greatly to my advantage. I wants a man's work at clerking and I begs you to make enquiries on my behalf.'

'Mary, you are a woman!' Mr Emmett protested. 'It will be no easy matter to find you a position in any trade as a clerk.' Emmett looked at Mary steadily. 'You see, my dear, even though I trust you, few others would. They would think they take a double risk, both a woman *and* a convict, it is too much to ask of them. A woman and a convict put to the task of preparing their ledgers would be an abomination!'

Mary sighed. 'Will you not help me then?' She explained how she had been rejected at eight separate places the previous day.

The chief clerk looked at Mary without sympathy. 'Help you? How can I help you? I have tried everything I know to help you! You have rejected my offer to be a clerk with me and then another as a teacher! All that's left for your kind is scrubbing, working in the kitchen or as a washer woman!' He thought for a moment, then added, 'You cannot even work at a market garden as it is forbidden for you to own property.' Then, as if an idea had suddenly occurred to him, Mr Emmett brightened. 'Though perhaps you could rent it. There are plenty here who have property they are too idle to till, your skill with vegetables is well known and your fresh produce will find a ready sale in the markets.' He clapped his hands, delighted that he had solved Mary's problem. 'That's it! I shall make enquiries at once!'

Mary shook her head. 'I am truly grateful, sir, but I have worked as a kitchen maid, lady's maid, laundry maid, and in the Factory as a gardener.' She lifted her crippled hands. 'Me hands won't stand for it and nor will me head.' Mary looked pleadingly at the little man. 'I wants to learn a trade, Mr Emmett! Something to sell what people must have and what uses numbers and me own good sense!'

'And what of your sly grog, will that not profit you handsomely as a trade?' the chief clerk demanded suddenly.

Mary was greatly shocked and began to tremble violently. She was not aware that the chief clerk of the colonial secretary's department had known about the Potato Factory. Fortunately Mr Emmett did not thrust the barb further but waited for her to defend herself. Mary knew not to deny her guilt. Mr Emmett was not a cruel man and he did not listen to idle tittle-tattle. He would have been certain of his information before he sought to employ it against her.

'Sir, that were different,' she stammered. 'I were in the crime class and might as well be hung for a sheep as a lamb, there weren't nothing to lose.' Mary felt more in control of herself as she continued. 'It were good grog what didn't rot your guts like what's sold elsewhere, even in respectable taverns.'

'My dear, in Hobart Town there are no respectable taverns. Besides, if you had been caught, it might well have caused your sentence to be doubled!' Mr Emmett said sternly.

Mary looked appealingly at him. 'I owes you me life, sir. I don't think I could have endured without what you done for me at the orphan school. Now I owes you this too! For keeping stum! I thank you from the bottom o' me heart. Please, sir, I ain't never going back to the Female Factory. I don't want to start me new life as a mistress o' sly grog. I ain't so stupid as not to know that, sooner or later, I'd be caught and sent back to the Factory! I couldn't stand that, honest, I couldn't!'

Mr Emmett sighed. 'I'm most glad to hear that, Mary. I shall make enquiries, though I should not hold out any hopes if I were you.' He paused. 'Remember, I make no promises. You have seen for yourself how difficult it will be to persuade any business to take you on.' Then he added, shaking his head, 'You are a most stubborn woman, Mary Abacus. What will you do now? Have you a place to go?'

Mary remained silent and dropped her eyes.

'Well?'

Mary looked up slowly and smiled. She knew she could not remain camped under the rock. It snowed on the mountain in winter and she would freeze to death. Her green eyes rested on the chief clerk. 'I could tend your garden, sir, and sleep in your potting shed, if you was to give me rations.'

Emmett shook his head slowly. 'You take me to be too soft, Mary Abacus. Perhaps even an old fool to be used by a pretty woman. You refuse to be a market gardener, yet you would tend *my* garden?'

'Not soft, or a fool, Mr Emmett, but a person what's been wise and kind and most generous beyond anyone I've ever known.' There were tears in Mary's eyes as she said urgently, 'I shall repay your kindness, I swear. The time will come, I know it!' Mary blinked away her tears. 'It would only be a short while, sir. Until your enquiries prove fruitful, which I know they shall. All speak of you with great respect!'

Emmett looked doubtful and Mary hastily added, 'With the season changing, your roses need pruning and there be much clearing to be done so that your plants may catch the weaker winter sun, and your cold weather vegetables are not yet planted nor straw cut for the seed beds against the coming frost.'

'The potting shed?' Mr Emmett hesitated. 'It's not very big. I daresay we could find a corner for you in the servants' quarters.'

Mary laughed. The previous night spent under the stars had been cold but tolerable, and she had woken to a bright autumn morning with the raucous call of parakeets feeding on the nectar of the butter-coloured eucalypt blossom in the trees above her. Mary knew she had spent her last night with dirty snoring bodies squeezed hard against her sides.

But she hesitated, thinking that to object to this arrangement might cause Mr Emmett to decline her proposition altogether. Finally she found herself saying, 'Sir, I ain't got fancy notions about meself, but I ain't no servant ever no more! The potting shed be more than I'm used to. I have no wish to disturb your household. I have a blanket and mattress roll and will be glorious comfy.'

Mr Emmett looked at her in surprise but then a small smile played at the corners of his mouth. 'Very well, Mary, I shall tell cook to issue you with rations.'

Mary, of course, had sufficient money to live comfortably had she wished to siphon off only a small amount from the contents of the clay pot. She could have stayed in one of the numerous cheap boarding houses which took in ticket of leavers, though the idea did not occur to her. Comfort was not a consideration in her life, and the money she had made from the Potato Factory was to be used only to make a new life. Mary was determined she would have a profession. When she'd earned out her ticket of leave and was free, she would start on her own in business. She didn't much care what business except that it should cater for people's essential needs. She would not touch a penny of the five hundred pounds for any other purpose.

Mary could not light a fire in the tiny potting shed so she spread straw over the cold brick floor. At night she stuffed her clothes with newspaper and in this way remained tolerably warm. During the day she worked in Mr Emmett's garden. He would sometimes visit her when he returned home from work in the early evening, and twice he had brought her a glass of fruit punch flavoured with the heavenly taste of fresh apricots. Mary had scarcely wished to accept the delicious concoction for fear that it might corrupt her resolve.

Mr Emmett always came upon her in the same way. As though to dispel any anticipation Mary might have at his approach, he would precede his arrival by shouting the selfsame words. 'Not much luck, my dear. If I may say so, no blasted luck at all!'

Mary would look up from where she was working and attempt a smile. 'I am much obliged to you, sir,' she would say, standing up at his approach and trying not to show her disappointment.

Mary took two hours each day to try to secure a position on her own, trudging into town if she should see an advertisement in the *Colonial Times*. This was the only money she spent, sixpence every week to purchase the newspaper. While there were vacant positions aplenty, none of those advertising for a clerk bookkeeper required a female bookkeeper who was a ticket of leave convict. Mr Emmett's letter was beginning to look weary at the folds and greasy at the edges, as though it too was possessed of a forlorn and hopeless disposition.

Mr Emmett tried again to get Mary to join him in the employ of the government but she would not surrender.

A month passed and Mr Emmett's garden was now well prepared for winter. Neat rows of winter cabbage and cauliflower seedlings filled their beds in the vegetable patch. The soil around the standard roses and young fruit trees had been dug around, aired and then bedded down with straw and the garden was now completely cleared of summer's dead leaf. Mary woke one chilly morning and went to the door of the potting shed. The grass outside was silver with hoar frost and, as was her habit each morning, she looked up at the great mountain. Snow had fallen during the night and had turned it into a veritable Christmas pudding. Above it an icy, cobalt sky stretched high and, though she could not see them, she could hear a flock of cockatoos in the trees near by.

'Please, mountain, let something happen today!' Mary appealed to the snow-covered monolith towering above her. 'The work be done in Mr Emmett's garden and I cannot accept no more charity.'

'Mary, Mary! Come here, girl!' She could hear Mr Emmett's excited voice before he reached her. It was just before sunset on the same day and Mary was planting lemon grass. 'Mary, where are you? It's good news at last!'

Mary stood up at Mr Emmett's approach.

'Good news, my dear!' he said a little breathlessly, flapping his arms as he came up to her. 'Mr Peter Degraves the sawmiller is building a brewery at the Cascades and he needs a clerk!'

Mary dropped the trowel she was holding and looked querulously at her benefactor. 'A woman, sir?'

'They'll take a chance on a woman . . . on you!' Mr Emmett laughed, well pleased with himself.

'Have you told them I be ticket o' leave, sir?'

'Yes, yes, everything! Do not fret yourself, my dear. Mr Degraves has been in debtor's prison himself. He sees nothing to harm him in your past.' Mr Emmett grinned at Mary. 'I daresay those silly Chinese beads of yours will be just the very thing for counting bricks and timber eh?'

'A brewery is it? Will he keep me on when the building is complete?'

'If you serve him well, I don't see why not.'

Mary, unable to restrain herself, burst into tears and Mr Emmett, no taller than she, even by an inch, stood beside her. He patted her clumsily on the back. 'Now, now, my dear, it isn't much, an outdoors job with winter almost here, among crude men loading drays, I doubt it will exercise your skills to any extent.'

'Gawd bless you, sir!' Mary whispered, her voice choked with relief.

'Tut, tut, you have little to thank me for, Mary Abacus. My garden is splendidly prepared for winter and I reward you with nothing but the smell of hops in your nostrils and the cussing of rough men in your ears. I think it a poor exchange indeed!'

'Thank you, sir, I will not forget this.'

'There is little for you to remember on my behalf, my dear,' Mr Emmett said gently. 'You are worthy of much, much more, Mary Abacus.'

The chief clerk of the colonial secretary's department was not to know that on the brisk autumn evening in late May 1831, he had watched a small woman with large green eyes, bright with recent tears, take the first tentative step in what would one day be a vast brewery empire that would stretch around the world. Mary Abacus had discovered the commodity men could not live without and yet was not condemned or forbidden by society.

The dream was in place, the new life begun, and Mary's great good luck had persisted. In the gathering darkness she could only just make out the frosted top of the mountain.

'Thank you!' Mary whispered, clasping Ikey's Waterloo medal tightly to her breast.

Chapter Twenty-eight

It is one of the great paradoxes in human migration that new beginnings often take with them old and often undesirable social customs. Those fleeing affliction or a hierarchical system for a new and free environment soon develop tyrannies and pecking orders of their own. Though in a penal colony one might expect a clear distinction between the convict and the free, the dichotomies of class in Van Diemen's Land were far more complicated and carefully graded. The relationship Mary enjoyed with Mr Emmett was all the more remarkable for this.

The first two great class distinctions were, of course, the free and the prisoner populations. This was a divide so wide that it was almost impossible to leap, even in exceptional circumstances. Mary had never been inside Mr Emmett's home, nor had she been introduced to his wife, Lucy. Occasionally they would meet in the garden, but Mary would stand with her head bowed and hands clasped in respectful silence while the grand lady passed by.

Lucy Emmett's pretty daughter, Millicent, had once stopped to talk with Mary, who was pruning and shaping the standard rose she had given Mr Emmett for his daughter's tenth birthday.

'Why! That's *my* rose!' Millicent exclaimed. 'I had quite forgotten it. Will you shape it well and make it beautiful again?'

'Yes, Miss Millicent, it will be perfect for the summer to come. It be robust enough and not much neglected.'

'Good! It was a present from Papa and grown just for me by a drunken wretch in the Female Factory!'

'Is that what your papa told you?' Mary asked softly.

'No, Mama told me that! Papa said there's good in everyone. But Mama said the women in the Female Factory were too low to be included in *everyone* and were long past being *good*.' Millicent tilted her head to one side. 'I think there is, don't you?'

'Is what, Miss Millicent?'

'Good in everyone.'

Mary gave a wry laugh. 'I've known some what could be in doubt and they didn't all come from the Female Factory neither.'

'Millicent! How *could* you! Come along *at once*!' Lucy Emmett's cry of alarm made her daughter jump.

'Coming, Mama!' Millicent called back. She cast a look of apprehension at Mary and fled without saying another word.

Mary could hear Lucy Emmett's high-pitched chiding for several minutes afterwards. Some time later Mr Emmett's wife entered the garden and passed by where Mary was weeding. At her approach Mary rose from her haunches with her hands clasped and head bowed. Some paces from where she stood Lucy Emmett halted as if to admire a late-blooming rose.

'You will be sent away at once should you venture to talk to Miss Millicent again,' she hissed. She did not look directly at Mary and it was as though she were talking to the rose itself. Then she turned abruptly and left the garden.

Because Lucy Emmett's husband worked in the government, she was considered a 'true merino' by the free inhabitants of the colony – that is, they were among the first in point of social order. This circumstance was considered sufficient grounds for keeping aloof from the rest of the community. In fact it was considered degrading to associate with anyone who did not belong to her own *milieu*.

The government class were somewhat jeeringly known by the next order as the 'aristocracy'. This next, or second, order, more numerous and certainly wealthier and more influential in the colony, were the 'respectable' free inhabitants, the merchants, bankers, doctors, lawyers and clergymen who had no connection with the government above being required to pay its crippling taxes.

Below them came the free persons of low station, clerks and small tradesmen, butchers and bakers, who serviced the daily lives of the first-rate settlers. They had little chance of rising above their stations in life and were collectively possessed with an abiding anxiety that they might, through bankruptcy or some other misfortune, sink to the lowest but one level, that of the labouring class.

Below even the labourer was the emancipist, though this group was perhaps the most curious contradiction in the pecking order. Emancipists could, and often enough did, rise through the bottom ranks, past the labouring class and into the ranks of clerks and tradesmen.

The sons of emancipists, if educated in a profession and if they became immensely rich, could rise beyond even the third rank. Daughters had greater opportunities, if they were pretty and properly prepared. That is to say, if they attended the Polyglot Academy, where French, Italian and Spanish were taught by Ferrari's Comparative Method. They would also need to have been instructed by Monsieur Gilbert, a Professor of Dancing, before being considered sufficiently 'yeasted' to rise upwards.

No young woman, even if she was exceptionally beautiful and possessed the most elegant manners, could think to enter society without a comprehensive knowledge of the steps in all the new dances being practised in the salons of London and Paris.

Only then, and only if she should bring with her the added incentive of a great deal of money, was it possible to rise in due course to the ranks of a first rater. But even when the children of a successful emancipist achieved such Olympian heights, their flawed lineage remained and the whispers of the crinolined society matrons would continue for the next two generations.

The bottom station was, of course, the prisoner population and it included the ticket of leavers such as Mary. Between this class and all others, a strict line was drawn. In the presence of any free person in the community, prisoners were as if struck dumb. It was considered correct, even by the lowest of the free orders, to regard them as invisible, ghosts in canary-yellow jackets who laboured on the roads or at tasks beneath the dignity even of the labouring class. And, of course, if they were assigned as servants in a household, they were expected to exercise the minimum speech required to perform their daily duties.

Mr Emmett's courage and generosity of spirit can now be properly appreciated. He, a member of the first station, not only acknowledged the existence of Mary, a convict, but consistently helped her. Emmett was also something of a dreamer for supposing that Mary might be accepted by even the lowliest of government clerks had she taken up his offer to work in his department.

The marked contrast of Lucy Emmett's attitude towards Mary should not be drawn as an example of uncharitable behaviour. To speak to a prisoner, albeit a ticket of leaver, was beyond the imaginings of a pure merino woman, a nightmarish confrontation not to be contemplated even in the most unlikely social circumstances.

Thus, the likelihood of Mary securing a billet as a clerk in Hobart Town was very much in the order of impossible. Not only was she a woman, but such a position lay strictly within the precincts of the third class whereas she was condemned to work within the lowest of the low, the sixth class. It can only be supposed that, in bringing about Mary's appointment, Mr Emmett had favoured Peter Degraves with a government contract, or perhaps waived some building dispensation for the construction of his new brewery, or even invoked a Masonic rite in his position as Grand Master of Hobart's secret order of Free and Accepted Masons.

The gamble Peter Degraves took on Mary soon paid off. She was quick to learn, arrived early and worked late, and took no nonsense from the men, who eventually came to call her, with much admiration, Mother Mary of the Blessed Beads.

It was not only Mary's skill at bookkeeping that impressed her employers, but also her plain sense mixed with some imagination. Mary was soon aware that pilfering on a building site by the labourers was costing the owners a considerable amount each month, and that the men regarded this scam as their natural right. She requested an appointment with Peter Degraves at his office higher up the slopes of the mountain, where he and his brother-in-law owned the concession to cut the timber right up to the rocky outcrop known as the organ pipes.

Degraves kept Mary waiting a considerable time before he called her into his small, cluttered office. A large cross-cut saw of the type used by convicts leaned against one wall, its blade buckled into a gentle curve. The room smelled of sawdust and the sap of new-cut wood. Peter Degraves was a tall, fair, clean-shaven man, not given to lard as were so many men in their forties. He sat in his shirt sleeves with his waistcoat unbuttoned and his clay-spattered boots resting upon a battered-looking desk.

'Take a pew, Miss Abacus,' he said, indicating a small upright wicker chair. 'What brings you to the sawmill?'

'Sir, I would speak to you about the site.'

'Ah! It goes well, Miss Abacus, the foreman says we are ahead in time and I know our expenses are well contained. You have done an excellent job.'

'Not as excellent as might be supposed,' Mary answered.

Degraves looked surprised. 'Oh? Is there something I ought to know about, Miss Abacus?'

'The pilfering, sir . . . on the site. It be considerable.'

Degraves shrugged. 'It was ever thus, Miss Abacus. Petty crime within the labouring class is as common as lice in an urchin's hair.' He spread his hands. 'We live, after all, in a penal colony.'

'Mr Degraves, sir, I have an inventory and we are losing materials at the rate o' fifty pounds a week, two thousand seven hundred and four pounds a year. That be a considerable amount, would you not say?'

'Aye, it's a lot of money, but I've known worse in the sawmilling business.'

'We have one 'undred workmen on the site, each earns fourteen pounds a year in wages, that be . . .'

'Fourteen hundred pounds and, as you say, we are losing nearly double that! Just how would *you* prevent this, Miss Abacus?' Degraves asked in a somewhat patronising manner.

'The value o' the material what's nicked and sold in the taverns and on the sly be one-fifth o' the market value, no more'n ten pounds.'

'And just how do you know this?' Degraves asked, removing his feet from the desk. He pulled his chair closer and leaned forward, listening intently.

'I took various materials from the site and flogged them,' Mary replied calmly.

'You what? You stole from my site!'

'Not stole, sir, it all be written in the books. It were a test to see what the value o' the materials were on the sly.'

Degraves sat back and laughed. 'Why, that's damned clever!

Ten pounds eh?' He paused then said, 'Well, that's the labouring class for you, not only dishonest but easily gulled and stupid to boot.'

'Let's give 'em the ten pounds, sir, or a little more, fifteen. That be three shillings per man per week extra in his pay packet, seven pounds two shillings and sixpence per year.'

'But, Miss Abacus,' Degraves protested, 'that's half again as much as they are paid now.'

'Sir, it ain't all the men what's stealing, most is family men as honest as the day. We make the money a weekly bonus, given a month in arrears and when we've determined no pilfering has taken place.'

'No pilfering?' Degraves laughed. 'Not a single nail or plank or brick or bag of mortar! I think you dream somewhat, Miss Abacus!'

'Well no, sir. I have allowed five pounds, that will be sufficient tolerance,' Mary said firmly.

'Twenty pounds and we save thirty, I'm most impressed! Do you think it can be made to work?'

'No, sir. It will not work with money,' Mary replied.

'Oh? How then?'

'In rations! A food chit issued to the labourer's wife what is worth three shillings a week. We pay the men on Saturdays and most of it be in the tavern keeper's hands by Sunday night with the brats starving at home for the rest o' the week. If there be the prospect o' three shillings worth o' rations from the company shop on a Monday, the family will eat that week.'

'Company shop? May I remind you, Miss Abacus, I am a sawmiller who is building a brewery, not a damned tradesman! Who will run this cornucopia of plenty?'

'I will, sir! There be enough money to pay the salary of a good shop assistant if we buy prudently and sell at shopkeepers' rates, and I will keep the books.'

'And will there be a further profit?' Degraves asked shrewdly.

'Yes, sir, to be used for the purchase of books for the orphanage school, as well as a Christmas party given to them by the brewery.'

Degraves laughed. 'Chits for workers' wives, company shops, books and Christmas parties for orphans, when will these fantasies end?' He grew suddenly stern. 'Miss Abacus, I am a practical man who has worked with rough men all my life. Mark my words, they will take your chit and steal as before. You cannot prevent a labouring man from stealing from his master.'

'You are perfectly right, sir. *You* cannot. *I* cannot. But his *wife* can! It's she who will be your policeman, she who will make her man deal with the thief what thinks to take advantage of all the other men by stealing from the site. Wives will make their husbands punish the guilty, for I guarantee she will let no villain take the bread out o' her little ones' mouths.'

Degraves leaned back into his chair. 'It be most clever, Miss Abacus, but I'm afraid it cannot be done. What of my reputation with my peers? Those who, like me, employ labour? They will not take kindly to the raising of a labourer's annual salary by more than fifty per cent! Let me tell you, there will be hell to pay!'

'Sir, heaven forbid! Raise in wages!' Mary appeared to be shocked at such a notion. 'It be a feeding scheme for the worker's family. The Church and the government will soon enough come out in support of you for such an act o' Christian charity!' Mary, afraid she might lose his support for fear of his peers, thought desperately. 'May I remind you that we have a large community o' Quakers what does not condone strong drink *and* there is them Temperance lot just started, the Van Diemen's Land Temperance Society. They's already kickin' up a fuss about the distilleries in the colony. But who will speak badly of a brewery what looks after workers' brats and cares about the education of orphans?'

Degraves smiled. There had already been several raised eyebrows in society concerning his intention to build a brewery. 'A model works, eh?' He frowned suddenly. 'Do you *really* think it will work, Miss Abacus?'

Mary knew she had won, and she was unable to conceal the excitement in her voice so she spoke quickly. 'Better than that, Mr Degraves, sir. We'll end up with the best and most honest workers in the colony on account o' the excellent family conditions what the boss o' the brewery Mr Peter Degraves has put into place!' She took a gulp of air and to this breathless sycophancy she added, 'Thank you, sir, I think it be most clever of you to think up such generous plans for those of us who is privileged to work for you!'

Degraves again looked surprised for a moment, then smiled. He was impressed. 'Why thank you, Miss Abacus, it's not a bad solution, even if I did not think of it myself.' His expression was whimsical when he added, 'You will, of course, let me know when I should reveal this brilliant new plan of mine to the men.'

'And to the *Colonial Times*, sir. The feeding scheme for workers' brats.'

Degraves nodded as he replaced his feet on the desk. 'Though I see little gain in helping the orphanage with the business of learning. These children are the illegitimate spawn of the island's scum and no good will come of it, I can assure you. Besides there is more ridicule in it than there be praise.'

'Sir, sometimes we may be allowed to take credit where no credit is due, and sometimes we deserve much more than we get. Besides, I were just like them poor little brats once.'

Degraves sighed and dismissed Mary with a backward wave of his hand. 'As you wish, Miss Abacus, I can see you do not surrender easily.'

Mary smiled and lowered her eyes to show her respect, though she laughed inwardly, thinking of the motto inscribed on her Waterloo medal. 'Thank you, sir, you have been most gracious,' she replied.

Degraves threw back his head and laughed. 'Prudent, Miss Abacus! Prudent to the tune of thirty pounds a week! I shall not think well of you if this turns out badly, and there will be little graciousness about my manner as I dismiss you from service.'

Mary continued to work for the brewery after its completion and by the time she had served out her ticket of leave she was intimate with every step in the process of making beer. She had been correct. Good men came from everywhere to seek employment at the new brewery where the practice of issuing ration chits had been continued and, as had also been the case on the work site, pilfering was reduced to insignificant proportions.

Written into the wrought-iron gate of the brewery were the words 'Happy workers make happy beer' and this motto also appeared on the labels of the bottled product. The beer they produced at the Cascades Brewery was of a light colour and very pure and, while there were a dozen other breweries in Hobart, none could match the quality of Peter Degraves' excellent light ale and pilsener-style beer. Such was its superiority that it quickly became popular all over the island and ships carrying the company's timber to New South Wales increasingly came also to carry barrels of Cascade beer to Sydney.

Mary soon realised that the difference in the beer was the quality of the malt they used and the pure mountain water. Peter Degraves had sited his mill near the confluence of the Hobart and the Guy Fawkes rivulets, damming them both to make a series of small lakes of pure mountain water. In addition to this he ran a pipeline from Strickland Falls, about a mile further upstream, which was the source of the purest water of all. The crystal-clear waters fed from a spring which began near the summit of the great mountain, well above its winter snowline.

Strickland Falls was not far from Mary's secret rock and she was determined to own the land on which the rock stood and also have access to the water in the falls. In the third year of her employment at the brewery she marked out approximately ten acres which included her beloved rock, and which led down to the bank on the opposite side of the falls to the brewery pipeline.

In 1824 Governor Arthur had granted Peter Degraves two thousand acres on the side of the mountain for saw milling, and with a further grant taken together with several judicious purchases, he and his brother-in-law Hugh McIntosh now owned the entire side of Mount Wellington. Mary was resolute that she must somehow purchase these ten acres from Degraves and his ailing brother-in-law, though even if they should agree to sell it to her, she was still a ticket of leave convict and could not legally own property.

Once again Mary went to see Mr Emmett. They stood in his garden while she explained what she wanted.

'Mary, by all accounts you have done exceedingly well and Mr Degraves has often enough thanked me for recommending you to him. I daresay, if I can find a plausible reason for the purchase of this land, he may be friendly enough disposed to sell it, always supposing that he should receive a good price. But what possible reason could I have to purchase ten acres of useless land on the slopes of Mount Wellington?'

'You could tell him that you want some day to build a home and wish to secure a small part of the creek bank below the falls, sir.'

Mr Emmett shook his head. 'I have been to the falls but once. It is quite an expedition and, as I recall, they make a fearful racket. I should be the laughing stock of the free settlers and no one in their right mind would build among the trees so far from civilisation with the din of a waterfall drowning all conversation. Besides, I am known for the excellence of my garden and you know as well as I do that the soil under gum trees is leached of all its goodness and is infertile and not in the least suitable for the cultivation of an English garden.'

'A retreat, a place in nature to go to, sir?' Mary suggested a little lamely.

Mr Emmett ignored this remark. He was still taken up with the absurdity of the whole notion. 'Furthermore, the big trees in the area you speak of have already been cut. I would be buying a pig in a poke, half-grown trees and red gum scrub. People, who already count me odd, would think me gone quite mad! My wife would not be able to tolerate the shame of so foolish a decision.'

'Could you not do the transaction in secret, sir? Mr Degraves knows you not to be a fool and would not judge you one for this!' Mary brightened with a sudden thought. 'You could offer him a little more than what the land be worth and ask him to stay stum, I mean, remain silent. He is a man with a good eye for an extra shilling made and, as you say, he has already made his profit from the area we speaks of.'

Mr Emmett scratched the top of his head and looked vexed. 'Can you not wait, my dear? It is only a year before you obtain your freedom, and it is most unlikely that land so far from the town will prove any more attractive to a buyer in the meantime.'

Mary's eyes welled with tears. 'It be the rock, sir!' she suddenly announced.

Mr Emmett was unaffected by Mary's distress – he had seen Mary's tears before when she wanted something from him. 'The rock? What on earth are you talking about?'

Mary knuckled the tears from her large green eyes and sniffed. 'It be a rock on the mountain, a magic rock, I simply must own it!'

'A rock! Own a rock! Magic? You really do try my patience, Mary Abacus!' But she could see that Mr Emmett was curious and prepared to listen to her explanation.

With a fair degree of sniffing, Mary began, swearing Mr Emmett to secrecy for the silliness of it. She told him how she often went to the rock for comfort and how, when the blossom was out and the berries ripe, she would lie on the rock and watch the green parakeets feeding and squabbling in the trees and surrounding bush. 'Not parakeets,' Mr Emmett corrected, 'rosellas, my dear, green rosellas, they are native to this island.' Finally Mary told him how she had slept upon the rock under the stars the first night she had been released from the Female Factory.

This last pronouncement astonished Mr Emmett who, though a nature lover, had acquired a healthy respect for the Tasmanian wilderness. Mary's admission filled him with alarm. It was not uncommon for people who were inexperienced in the ways of the bush to be lost on the mountain slopes, some even perishing in a fall of rock or a sudden snowstorm. Besides the slopes were used by dangerous men who hid from the law during the day and crept down into the town at night.

It had already been noted that Mr Emmett was an unusual man and something of a dreamer, and now he listened attentively as though Mary's preposterous story made more sense to him than any logical reasons she might have. Finally, though cautioning her against the notion, he agreed to approach Peter Degraves and attempt to purchase the ten acres on the mountain on Mary's behalf.

Degraves drove a hard bargain, for despite their friendship, Emmett was a government man and no settler would wish to be bested by the government, even in a private transaction. He finally agreed to sell the title to the ten acres of light timber and scrub for forty pounds, a sum somewhat in advance of the current value of the land.

Mr Emmett had confided in him that as he grew older and the mountain became safer a small cottage in the woods seemed an attractive place for a retreat, where he might stay for short periods alone to read and write. Degraves, aware of the gossip to which such a peculiar notion might give rise in the society of the pure merinos, agreed to keep the land transaction secret and asked surprisingly few questions.

Mr Emmett handled the registration of the title deeds himself so that the purchase was not published in the *Government Gazette* until two years later, when it was transferred into the name of Mary Abacus, emancipist, resident, Mount Wellington Allotment No HT6784, Hobart Town District, Van Diemen's Land. With the property came the rights to use the pathway created along the Cascade Brewery pipeline in perpetuity.

In digging up and breaking open her clay pot to give Mr Emmett the forty pounds, plus two more for stamp and registration duty, Mary had taken the first proprietorial step in her new life. The money made from the Potato Factory not only allowed her to acquire a small piece of her magic mountain, but with it came the purest commercial source of water for the brewing of beer available in the colony.

Mary determined that, when the time came, she would clear and use only what land she needed for a water mill, malt house and small brewery. Though this dream was well beyond the resources she ever seemed likely to acquire, she could see the brewery clearly in her imagination, the stone buildings sitting among the trees. The rest of the land would be left as nature intended, so that tree and bush would grow to splendid maturity, giving an abundance of blossom and fruit to attract the flocks of green parakeets Mr Emmett called rosellas.

Mary remained with the Cascade Brewery for another year after she had obtained her freedom. Peter Degraves was not concerned when he eventually heard that Mr Emmett had sold his land on the mountain to Mary. He had long since decided that Mary was rather strange and that she should wish to live alone on the mountain did not greatly surprise him. With the brewery's reputation established, he had turned to another grand adventure, building a theatre for the benefit of the citizens of the town, and he was also expanding into shipbuilding and flour milling.

Degraves was happy to know that Mary was the bookkeeper and accountant at the brewery as he had come to absolutely trust her financial judgement in all matters. But he did not estimate her above his own needs. And, if he thought about it at all, he would have expected Mary to regard her security of employment at the brewery as above the price of rubies, and consequently to show her gratitude in a lifetime of faithful and uncomplaining service to him.

He was greatly surprised, therefore, when in the spring of 1836 Mary resigned. The previous year, that is the year she had gained her freedom, had been a busy one for her. She had cleared the land for almost a quarter of an acre around as a fire break, leaving some of the tallest trees in place. With a fast-running stream fronting the clearing and the rush of water over rock, the leafy glade Mary had created for herself was to her mind as close as she was likely to get to heaven on earth.

In truth the mountain, while a paradise of nature, was a

dangerous place for a lone woman. Fire was always a threat and could sweep through the forest without warning. The weather on the mountain was unpredictable; sudden mists could move down the slopes, closing in the mountain and making visibility impossible. As the felling of the tall timber increased, mud slides and falling rocks became commonplace during winter storms.

But it was from man that the greatest danger lay. The mountain was also home to desperate men, the dregs of the colony's society who were frequently on the run from the law. In the summer months they would sleep on the mountain during the day and creep back into town at night to rob and steal so that they might frequent the drinking dens, sly grog shops and brothels. There they were served with raw spirits made on the premises which often enough killed them and more usually sent them mad.

Those who could still walk when daylight came would drag themselves into the bush on the slopes of the mountains to sleep until nightfall when they would re-emerge. Though most were harmless enough, their brains addled with alcohol, pathetic, shambling creatures, some were dangerous. Mary could not hope to construct a hut on her property where she might safely live, even though she had taken the precaution of learning how to fire a pistol which she always carried in her bag when she visited her clearing among the trees.

Mary was tempted to call her idyllic surrounding by some romantic name gathered from a book or taken from her native England, but in the end she chose, for reasons of sentiment and luck, to call her brewery The Potato Factory.

Mary argued to herself that the poteen still had been the true start of her great good luck. It had earned her a reputation for a quality product. Most of the sly grog available in the drinking dens and brothels of Hobart Town was more likely to kill the customer than to send him on his way happily inebriated. Her experience at the Cascade Brewery had shown her once again that quality was of the utmost importance, and she was adamant that it would become the hallmark of everything she did. When the time came to build the second Potato Factory she would boast that her beer was made from the finest hops and malt available, and brewed from the purest mountain water in the world.

If the association with the humble potato was a peculiar inheritance for a beer of quality this did not occur to Mary. While she had a very tidy mind she was still a creature of intuition, and she did what felt right to her even when logic might suggest she do otherwise. Mary was wise enough to know that few things in this world are wrought by logic alone, and that where men are often shackled by its strict parameters, women can harness the power of their intuition to create both surprising and original results.

In her mind Mary saw the chiselled stone of her malt house and the larger building of the brewery beside it with its enormous brick chimney rising above the trees. She would sometimes stand beside the falls which thundered so loudly they drowned out all other sound, and within the silence created by this singular roar, she would conjure up the entire vision. Mary could plainly see the drays lined up around the loading dock, hear the shouts of the drivers to make the great Clydesdale horses move forward, their gleaming brasses jingling as they left the Potato Factory to take her barrels of ale and beer to tavern and dockside. She looked into the bubbling water which rushed over smooth stones at her feet and saw it passing through imaginary sluice gates and along some elevated fluming and into the buckets of a giant iron water wheel which would power the brewery machinery. And sometimes, when the dream was complete, she would smack her lips and, with the back of her hand, wipe imagined froth from her mouth as though she could truly taste the liquid amber of her own future creation.

This world is not short of dreamers, but to the dreamer in Mary was added a clever, practical and innovative mind which once committed would never surrender. All ground schemes, she told herself, may be broken down to small beginnings. Each step she took, no matter how tentative it might seem, would be linked to her grand design and would always be moving towards it, if only a fraction of an inch each time. This was a simple and perhaps naive philosophy based on perseverance, on knowing that the grandest tapestry begins with a single silken thread. And so the first thing Mary did upon leaving the Cascade Brewery was to apply for a licence to sell beer. And here, once again, she had prevailed on the long-suffering Mr Emmett to help her with the recommendations she needed to obtain it.

Mary decided that even though she lacked the resources to start her own brewery she had sufficient to rent a smallish building which had once been a corn mill at the mountain end of Collins Street and which backed directly onto the banks of the rivulet. She named it the Potato Factory and converted it into a home brewery. In the front room she created a shop where citizens could buy a bottle of beer to take home. She used a small rear room in the building as her sleeping chamber and paid one of the mechanics at the Cascade Brewery to construct a small lean-to kitchen at the back. The remainder of the space in the old mill was given over to making beer.

The malt and yeast Mary used were of the highest quality, and she bought her hops from a wholesale merchant who imported it from England, as the product grown in the Derwent Valley was not yet of the highest standard. She made a light beer with a clean taste which was much favoured by the better class of drinker among the labouring classes, tradesmen and the respectable poor, and she soon attracted the favourable attention of the Temperance Society. Temperance members agreed to abstain entirely from the use of distilled spirits, except for medicinal purposes, so the society actively encouraged the drinking of beer, though in the home and not in public houses where, in the boisterous company of fellow drinkers, they might enter into the numerous evils, both moral and physical, which follow the use of spirits.

Her beer did not have 'the wallop' to appeal to the majority of drinkers, but the Temperance movement was growing rapidly in numbers, and right from the outset Mary prospered. She soon put a product on the market which she labelled 'Temperance Ale', and in six months it had become her mainstay. Mary, if only in the smallest way, was up to her eyes in the beer business, and at the same time she was favoured by the authorities for the quality of her product and the prompt manner in which she paid her taxes. There were even those within the third class, the tradesmen, clerks and smaller merchants, who considered that some day she might be admitted into their lofty and hallowed ranks.

But if Mary's great good luck had well and truly begun, the opposite to it lay waiting at her doorstep. Hannah and, eighteen months later, Ikey, were released into the community as ticket of leave convicts.

Ikey barely survived his seven years until he received his ticket of leave. He had neither hate nor dreams but only greed to keep him from despair.

Money had never meant anything to Ikey except as a means to

an end. He played for the sake of the game – money was simply the barometer to show when he had won. He wasn't a gambler, for he figured his chances most carefully, weighing the odds to the most finite degree. Now, with seven years of penal servitude behind him, the game was no longer worth the candle. If he should return to his old life of crime and be caught again he knew he would certainly die, either in servitude or by means of the dreadful knotted loop.

Ikey told himself that, should he obtain the second half of the combination to the Whitechapel safe, he would retire to some far haven where he would live in peace and run a small tobacco business, with perhaps a little dabble here and a little negotiation there. But secretly he knew that he was a creature of London and captive to its crepuscular ways. He had disliked New York, and Rio even more, and judged the world outside England by these two unfortunate experiences. He knew that a return to crime in any significant way in Hobart Town would be both foolish and short-lived. Ikey was a marked man in the colony.

Three years on the road gang and two years thereafter as a brick maker in the penal settlement of Port Arthur, and another two returned to Richmond Gaol had been quite enough for him. His health had been destroyed in the damp road camps and in the brick pits. He had lost the courage for grand larceny, his bones ached with early rheumatism and his brain creaked for lack of wily purpose.

All that was left for Ikey was the determination to get from Hannah her half of the combination to the safe. He would lie in his cell at night and his heart would fibrillate with terror that he should not succeed in this. He knew that Hannah would have the support of her children when she received her ticket of leave, but that he might well be destitute, for he could not hope for mercy from his alienated family. But what Ikey feared most in all the world was not their rejection, or being forced into penury, but that people might see Ikey Solomon, Prince of Fences, had entirely lost his courage.

Chapter Twenty-nine

Hannah received her ticket of leave in early November 1835, with the proviso that she be restricted to the district of New Norfolk, a small country town on the banks of the Derwent River, some twenty-five miles upstream from Hobart Town. Her behaviour as a convict had proved troublesome for the authorities and they wished to remove her from the boisterous atmosphere and temptations of Hobart.

Hannah had objected strongly to this assignment as she was of a good mind to enter her old profession. Hobart was host to the American whaling ships during the season, as well as to sealers and convict transports, and to this itinerant population was added a large underclass of criminals and society's dregs well suited to Hannah's style of bawdy house.

She had pleaded her case to remain in Hobart because of her children, which was not an untruthful assertion. She asked for custody of Sarah and Mark from the orphanage, and begged that they might all be allowed to live with David and Ann, who now resided in the tiny cottage which had once been Ikey's tobacconist shop.

The chief magistrate finally agreed to a compromise. Ann was now fourteen and David sixteen and they were considered adults who no longer required the ministrations of a mother. But as Sarah had only just turned twelve and Mark was ten years old, they were allowed to accompany their mother to New Norfolk.

Being a practical woman Hannah soon enough adapted, taking up with a certain George Madden, an emancipist who had become a wealthy grain merchant, and also acted as a district constable.

Hannah was happy enough to swap bed for bread in preference to finding employment as a servant in the small town and Madden, who had a reputation as an energetic though often difficult man, also felt himself well served. He had gained the services of a skilful concubine in exchange for two children accustomed to life in an orphanage, who knew to stay well away from irascible adults.

Living with Madden allowed for a lazy life and Hannah was content to lord it over most of the locals as a grand lady on the arm of a wealthy and handsome man. That there was a good deal of gossip from the country folk regarding her lewd behaviour troubled her not at all. The people of New Norfolk were of no consequence to Hannah. They were emancipists who had served their sentences on Norfolk Island and later settled New Norfolk, and in the peculiar pecking order of the Van Diemen's Land convict, they were considered below the station of a main islander.

As for the few free settlers in the town, Hannah knew that no amount of airs and graces or playing at the *grande dame* could persuade them to include her in their society. So she made no attempt to enter it. Besides, New Norfolk was only a temporary expedient forced upon her, and Madden a most convenient happen-stance. She dreamed of securing the fortune which lay waiting for her in the safe in Whitechapel and moving to Hobart Town, or perhaps even the mainland. There her wealth would soon secure good marriages for her two pretty daughters and sound careers for her two remaining sons.

Hannah also knew that sooner or later she would be confronted by the irksome presence of Ikey Solomon. But she comforted herself with the fact that he would need to serve at least seven years before he could expect his ticket of leave. This left her two years to contemplate her future, and to put into place several plans in order to defeat Ikey in that singular purpose which would preoccupy their lives the moment he was released.

Ikey must somehow be lulled into giving her his part of the combination. Hannah knew he would only do this if he felt completely confident about their shared future, and controlled their joint fortune. To accomplish the task of gaining Ikey's complete confidence, she needed to gather her family together and win back the affection of David and Ann, her two elder children. In particular David, who would play an important part in the plan to undermine her husband.

However, there was another reason why Hannah wished to regain the esteem and love of the two elder children still in Van Diemen's Land. She was determined to destroy any affection they might feel for Mary Abacus. Hannah was convinced that Mary had sought revenge for being transported. She felt certain that Ikey's scar-faced *goyem shiksa* whore had deliberately set out to steal the hearts and minds of her children, and turn them against their own flesh and blood.

Of course, this was entirely untrue. Mary was not even aware that Hannah had been the cause of her downfall. But no amount of persuasion would have convinced Hannah this was so. She had brooded on the matter too long, and what she had imagined in the dark recesses of her own vengeful mind had become an unshakable truth. Hannah had also concluded that Ikey and Mary were the collective cause of her demise, and it was a matter of personal honour to regain the love of David and Ann. She vowed to live long enough to punish Mary for plotting against her, and stealing her children's love.

Hannah intended to persuade David to win the complete trust of his father, while secretly maintaining his loyalty to her. After contriving a reconciliation with Ikey and convincing him that they should serve out their old age together, Hannah presumed David would logically be chosen to return to London, open the safe, and bring the contents back to Van Diemen's Land.

To this end Hannah needed David and his sister to settle in New Norfolk. She planned that they would take up a separate residence there so that when Ikey obtained his ticket of leave she would appear to leave Madden out of loyalty and affection for her real husband, and welcome Ikey back into the bosom of a loving and united family.

Hannah immediately set about cultivating the affection of her two elder children, who were frequently invited upriver to New Norfolk. This had not been a difficult thing to achieve. Ann had acted as a mother to young Mark and had always cared for her younger sister, and when Hannah had removed them from the orphanage Ann had been broken-hearted. She persuaded David that they should take the boat to New Norfolk and pay their respects to their mother, so that they might visit Sarah and Mark.

The first visit had been highly successful and was followed at regular intervals by others. Hannah was always sure to pay their two and sixpenny each-way ticket on the boat, and to furnish their return to Hobart with a handsome hamper, its crowning glory being a large fruit cake with sugar icing. She knew this to be a special favourite with David, who craved sweet things.

George Madden, too, seemed taken with Hannah's elder son. Hannah was pleasantly surprised when he offered David a position as a clerk in his grain business. Ann, most anxious to be close to her siblings, had pleaded with David to accept the offer. David, who was too bright for the dullards who were his superiors at the Hobart Water Works, and flattered by Madden's interest, accepted the position with alacrity. David rented the cottage in Liverpool Street, and brother and sister moved to New Norfolk.

Hannah had achieved her initial purpose with a minimum of fuss. There now remained plenty of time for her to win David's loyalty and affection before revealing her grand plan to sabotage Ikey.

But Ikey, as usual, was unpredictable, and he was released not five months after Hannah, rescued from servitude by a high-ranking government official who wished to remain anonymous. The official offered surety for Ikey and the government accepted his bond, whereupon Ikey left Port Arthur where he had served the past year of his sentence. He appealed to the reviewing magistrate to allow him to serve the first three years of his ticket of leave in New Norfolk.

'To live peaceably with my dear wife and children in New Norfolk, your honour. So that we may regain the lost years and grow old in love and kindness to each other.'

The magistrate who had signed Ikey's ticket of leave papers, a man known for his brusque manner, was quick to reply.

'There is much in your record of arrest of this kind of mawkish pronouncement, but very little demonstration of its successful consequence! I trust that on this occasion your high-blown rhetoric means more than the empty words of sentimental balderdash they have been in the past.'

For a moment Ikey's courage returned to him and he begged leave to make a statement. With an expression of deep hurt he offered the following pious testament.

'Your worship, I must beg to defend myself. My record will show that I escaped from custody in England to the safe and welcoming shores of America where no rules of extradition applied to send me back to England. Here I was immediately successful in matters of business but so missed the company of my dear wife and children that I risked all to walk back into the jaws of the English lion in order that we might be reunited.'

'A most fortunate circumstance for justice, but nonetheless a very foolish decision,' the magistrate interrupted.

Ikey continued. 'A decision of the heart, your worship. A decision made by a husband and father who could not bear to be parted from his loving wife and six children. I have suffered much for what your worship calls my mawkish sentimentality, but I would do it again if it should put me even a mile nearer to my loved ones!'

'Methinks you might have made an excellent barrister, Mr Solomon,' the magistrate replied, then added, 'Neither fish, nor flesh, nor good red herring!' He looked sternly at the prisoner. 'Hear me well now, Isaac Solomon, I should advise you not to return to this court. My patience is well nigh worn through!'

The *Colonial Times* reported Ikey's little oration and many a tear was shed by every class of woman in the colony. Ikey's testament was held up as the epitome of a husband's love for his wife and children. Officers of the court were never popular, even with the free settlers, and the acerbic tongue of the reviewing magistrate served only to enhance the heroic nature of Ikey's charming speech. Despite his notoriety, there were those in the colony who would forever remain most kindly disposed to a man who could sacrifice his own freedom and welfare for the love of his family.

It was this same reportage in the *Colonial Times* that alerted Hannah to Ikey's imminent return. She scarcely had time to extricate herself and her two youngest children from the home of George Madden and take up residence with David and Ann before Ikey appeared on the doorstep.

Whatever may have happened to Ikey and Hannah in the six years they had been parted, their low regard for each other had changed little. After the initial euphoria of homecoming, much pretended by both, the curmudgeonly Ikey and the vociferous, sharp-tongued Hannah were soon back to their old ways.

Hannah denied Ikey her bed either as a place for rest or recreation. This did not unduly upset Ikey, whose libido had not increased any during his captivity. He was forced to sleep in a corner of their tiny bedroom on a narrow horsehair mattress not much better than the one he'd recently vacated in Port Arthur. When their relationship had settled back into their customary mutual dislike, Hannah had forced him from this space as well. Ikey's adenoidal snoring kept Hannah awake at night, so he was banished to a tiny compartment in the sloping roof where his nocturnal melodies had the advantage of rising heavenwards.

Several months went by, though there was not a day among them that was not fired with vitriol from one or both partners. Ikey had somewhere picked up the habit of drinking, without learning the knack of holding his drink. A mere tipple would send him home cantankerous, with the inevitable result of a dreadful fight with Hannah.

The four children kept their own counsel. They were reared as orphans and knew when to keep out of the way. Nevertheless, David and Ann did not take easily to Ikey treating them like children and, what's more, in a rude and imperious manner. Ikey failed to grasp this; as a child of eight he had been on the streets selling oranges and lemons and his father had beaten him severely if he held back a single penny earned. Now he demanded only that David give him a half portion of his salary. He expected Ann, who had obtained work as a shop assistant, to hand over her entire wage.

They found Ikey smelly and dirty and, as he seldom addressed them by their names, they had little reason to feel he cared for them. In fact, for the most part, he seemed to forget who they were, frequently referring to the nearest child as, 'You, c'mere!' The two younger children were terrified of him and fled at his approach.

Hannah had taken David aside when Ikey first arrived and carefully explained the reason why he should always appear to side with his father. David immediately understood the future advantage to him so he readily agreed. He capitulated to Ikey's demands for money, and dutifully took Ikey's side in his parents' frequent arguments.

But Ikey was not an easy friend to make, and he considered his son a fool to be exploited and humiliated. The young man's patience was growing increasingly thin. He had never liked Ikey, but now he found that he loathed him. David warned his mother that, whatever the reward, he could not take much more.

Hannah, aware that time was running out, decided to broach the subject of the Whitechapel safe with Ikey. She cooked him a mutton stew well flavoured with rosemary, and followed it with fresh curds. She then joined him at the kitchen table after he had pronounced the meal much to his liking.

'Ikey, it's six months we've been together.' Hannah smiled brightly and spread her hands. 'And,' she sighed, ''ere we still are!'

Ikey let out a loud burp. 'So?'

'Well, we should begin to, you know, make plans, don't you think?'

'Plan? What plans?'

'The safe?'

Ikey picked at his teeth with the sharp nail of his pinkie, retrieved a tiny morsel of meat, glanced at it briefly, then placed his finger back into his mouth and sucked the sliver from it. 'We can't do nothing until I have a full pardon, my dear. It would be too great a risk if we were to be seen to come into a great fortune while we are both still ticket o' leave lags.'

'We could send David to England. 'E could return with the money and purchase property on the stum and to yer instructions,' Hannah suggested.

'And just 'ow would we send 'im?' Ikey asked, a fair degree of sarcasm in his voice. Then he shrugged. 'We are penniless, my dear, stony broke and without a brass razoo!'

'The cottage in Hobart – we could sell it. That would be sufficient with some to spare.'

'And 'ow do we know we may trust him?' Ikey asked.

'But 'e's our son!' Hannah protested.

'So?'

''E's our own flesh and blood, and a fine young man what we should be proud to call our own!'

'Is that so, my dear? 'E were a boy when 'e went into the orphanage, and 'e came out a man. But what sort of man, eh? We don't know, we ain't been there to watch 'im grow. What sort of boys do you think come from orphanages then? I know boys well,

447

very well! Let me tell you somethin' for nothin', boys what has been in an orphanage are good for bloody nothin' and not to be trusted under any circumstances.'

'David be a lovely boy, Ikey! 'Ard working and most clever with numbers!'

'I don't like 'im, too clever for 'is own good, and there is much of the weasel in 'im.' Ikey paused. 'It be 'is smile, all friendly like, but it comes with eyes 'ard as agate stones. Orphanage boys be all the same, dead sneaky and not to be trusted at all and under no circumstances whatsoever!'

'Well then, what about John or Moses?' Hannah asked. Her two sons in Sydney had always been a part of her contingency plan. 'They could leave from Sydney, nobody'd know, come back, invest the money like ya say they should, and when we gets our pardon it's happily ever after fer us, ain't that right, lovey?'

'Those two useless buggers!' Ikey exploded. 'Soon as we were nicked they scarpered, gorn, back to Sydney! No stickin' around to bring comfort, or to see if you or I could be assigned to them as servants. They simply sells up the shop,' Ikey thumped his chest several times, 'what *yours bloody truly* bought for 'em in Hobart and buggers off with the money, leaving us to fend for ourselves!'

'That's not fair, Ikey!' Hannah exclaimed. 'They tried to get me assigned, but the magistrate wouldn't 'ave no bar of it. John first, then Moses later, both tried.'

'Bullshit! They didn't try 'ard enough. What about me? They didn't try to get me assigned to them, did they? Not a letter, not a morsel o' concern these six years!'

'Ikey, you was road gang! You couldn't be assigned to nobody now could ya?'

'They could 'ave tried, anyway,' Ikey growled. 'They're no bloody good, spoilt by their mother they was! I wouldn't trust 'em further than I could blow me snot!'

'What then?' Hannah said exasperated. ''Ow are we gunna get the stuff out o' the peter if we can't trust our own kind to fetch it? You tell me.'

'I got a plan. You give me your set o' numbers and I'll take care of it,' Ikey said morosely, though suddenly his heart started to beat faster.

'What's ya take me for, *meshugannah* or summink?' Hannah asked, astonished. 'What plan? Let me hear yer plan, Ikey Solomon.'

'I can't tell you, it involves someone what has agreed to co-operate and what must remain a secret.'

'Secret, is it?' Hannah stood up abruptly from the table, her chair scooting off behind her. 'Some person what's secret? You've told some person what's secret 'bout the bloody safe, 'ave ya?' She paused, her nostrils dilating as her temper rose. But when she spoke again her voice, though menacing, remained even. 'It's 'er, ain't it?'

Ikey looked up at his wife in surprise. ''Er? What do you mean, 'er?'

'It's 'er, it's Mary bloody Abacus, ain't it!' Hannah leaned forward, pressing her palms down flat on the table, her shoulders hunched directly over the seated Ikey.

'Of course not! Whatever gave you such a peculiar notion, my dear?' Ikey tried to keep his voice calm, though Hannah's presence so near to him was unsettling.

Hannah's eyes narrowed and her face, now pulled into a furious expression, almost matched her flame-coloured hair.

'You bastard! Ya want me fuckin' numbers to give to that *goyim* slut, don't ya? That fuckin' dog's breath was gunna be the one to knap the ding!'

Hannah looked about her for something with which to strike Ikey, and he, sensing it was time to escape, fled from the room and out into the street.

'You bastard, you'll get nuffink from me, ya 'ear!' Hannah screamed after him, shaking her small fist at Ikey's rapidly diminishing back.

Ikey made for the nearest public house, ordered a double brandy and found a corner to himself. He had never been a drinking man and a double of brandy was usually more than enough to put him on his ear. But this time the liquor seemed to act in a benign way, bringing back into focus that glorious time when he was a leading member of London's criminal class. 'Practically the Lord Mayor o' thieves and villains. Prince o' Fences!' he mumbled pitifully to himself. It had a grand ring to it. Though now, on this miserable little island, it all seemed to be spun from the gossamer of an excitable imagination.

As the brandy worked its way through Ikey's bloodstream he began to imagine that it *had* been another life altogether. A primary existence, lived before this one of endless misery and despair, where his money had bought him respect and the royal title of thieves. Men had touched the brim of their cloth caps and mumbled a respectful greeting as he passed by or stood beside the ratting ring. Now he was reduced to human vermin, dirt, scum, the dregs of society, less even than the crud that clung to the hairy arses of the settlers who had the nerve to call themselves gentlemen.

And then the fiery liquid began to dance in his veins and Ikey cast his mind back seven years to when, in a flush of foolish sentiment, he had sent money and his Waterloo medal to Mary in Newgate. He'd all but forgotten Mary's existence, and Hannah's reminder had come as a shock. Occasionally, when he had first worked in the road gang, and especially when Billygonequeer had been with him, he would think of Mary with a sense of longing. But it was always in the past tense, as though she was dead, used up in his life. Ikey never thought that they might meet again, and after a while Mary had simply come closest to the words '*To my one and only blue dove,*' which were inscribed about the circle of roses surrounding two blue doves tattooed on his scrawny upper arm. The brandy in Ikey's blood settled into a mellow fluidity, and he grew sentimental, imagining what it might be like if he should find Mary again.

But at this point he made the fatal error of ordering a second glass of the fiery grape. The moment of sentimentality soon passed, and was replaced with an unreasoning rage. Stumbling home Ikey proceeded to yell violent obscenities until Hannah, David, Ann and Sarah collectively surrounded him. But after four years on a road gang cart, the former weakling was greatly increased in strength and each of them received several bony blows from Ikey's elbows before he was finally subdued.

Young Mark took off with great speed and shortly afterwards returned with George Madden who, acting in his capacity as a constable, arrested Ikey and locked him in the gaol house. Here Ikey shouted and screamed all night, cursing the perfidy of his family, with particular reference to the sexual prowess of 'the grand whore to whom I have the misfortune to be married'.

The police lock-up stood only a few yards from a public house. Ikey's boisterous remarks carried clearly into the street and quickly attracted the drinkers inside. Soon a fair crowd had gathered. By morning the small town of New Norfolk was agog with the whispered tales of Ikey's night in gaol. Ikey's family had finally had enough, and David caused him to be brought before the deputy police magistrate, where he was charged with drunkenness and violent conduct.

The case must have seemed clear enough to blind Freddy. But such is the nature of small towns, and so deep was the resentment held by the good burghers over Hannah's adultery with George Madden and, perhaps more precisely, her subsequent snooty behaviour towards all, that the charges were dismissed. The deputy police magistrate ruled that equal blame was attached to both parties. He warned both husband and wife that should such disorderly proceedings be repeated they would be returned to prison. Then, to the chagrin of some, and great amusement of most, he charged the assistant district constable, George Madden, to keep an eye on both husband and wife.

With the protection of George Madden, Hannah and David could do more or less as they wished and they lost no time in reducing Ikey to a most perilous state. He was unable to obtain work of any sort, though in this endeavour he did not seem to try very hard, and a word from the wealthy and influential Madden put a stop to any employer hiring him. David had also spread the word around that Ikey cheated at cribbage, which was true enough, so that there were none who would play with him, and this dried up Ikey's traditional source of drinking money.

Finally a desperate Ikey was provoked into prosecuting his wife. The deputy district magistrate, not at all pleased with the return of the miscreant couple to his court, to the delight of the townsfolk, brought in a verdict that the charge of disorderly conduct and the use of obscene language was proved. He ordered that Hannah be returned to the Female Factory for a period of three months.

After many such disputes, the authorities became thoroughly disenchanted with 'The tribe of Solomon' as the chief probationary officer was wont to call Ikey's family. After some interdepartmental discussion, the authorities made one final ruling. The family should attempt a reconciliation in New Norfolk. But, if this should not come about, either husband or wife, but not both, must move to Hobart Town, with or without the remainder of the family. Having moved, they would not be permitted to return to New Norfolk until they received a conditional pardon. The authorities saw this as a clause so onerous that the quarrelsome couple would make every possible effort to reconcile their differences.

But, of course, no such thing happened. At first Hannah tried to persuade George Madden to move to Hobart, but he refused. He had obtained a five-year contract from Peter Degraves of the Cascade Brewery for the excellent barley grown in the area which would allow him to build his own mill. Hannah, faced with this logic, was forced to capitulate. Somehow she must force Ikey to move to Hobart, and in this endeavour she received the full co-operation of her family.

With no recourse to the law, Ikey was a doomed man. Hannah ordered him out of the house first thing each morning and he was not allowed to enter it again until curfew in the evening. His only sustenance was a small plate of boiled potatoes, and no member of the family would deign to talk to him.

Each day Ikey became more of the vagabond. His bald pate went unprotected from the sun and the unkempt hair either side of it now fell to his shoulders. Somewhere he had acquired a great coat which he tied about his waist with coarse string. This ragged garment served him in appearance as his splendid bespoke great coat had once served him in England. But whereas a glance at the greasy original would have revealed the quality of the wool and sound workmanship beneath the dirt, this equally dirty coat was poorly made and threadbare. Ikey's yellow London boots now became his prison shoes, scuffed and broken away at the toe.

Ikey Solomon, Prince of Fences, the most celebrated criminal of his time, was brought to his knees, not by the vicissitudes of a prisoner's life, but by the unforgiving judgements of his wife and children.

Hannah was now frequently seen in the company of George Madden, though she had not yet moved back into his spacious home. She waited until Ikey had reached a point of abject despair and then offered him an ultimatum; he must give her the combination and also sell the cottage in Hobart so that David might use the money to go to England to open the Whitechapel safe. But to this she added a new clause. Ikey would not receive half of their shared fortune, but only one-eighth.

Hannah had decided that the entire fortune was to be divided equally between the two of them and their six children. She knew that a one-eighth share of the contents of the safe was still sufficient for Ikey to live in comparative luxury for the remainder of his life in Van Diemen's Land. With seven-eighths of their combined fortune under her direct control, Hannah told herself she was willing to sacrifice an estimated fifty thousand pounds, 'for being well rid of the mangy bastard'.

If he did not agree to these conditions, Hannah told him, he could go to hell. She would live with George Madden and wait for Ikey to die. Whereupon she would send her sons to England to remove the safe and bring it to Van Diemen's Land, where they would eventually find some way to open it. Ikey knew this threat to be idle, the safe having been fixed into a block of mortar too large to lift and, besides, it was fitted with a German combination lock of the same type used by the Bank of England, and no cracksman in Britain could ever hope to open it. But he was possessed of a morbid foreboding of his own death, and Hannah's willingness to wait until it occurred meant that he might die a pauper, a useless old lag, never able to enjoy the revenge of his wealth.

Ikey knew he should leave New Norfolk and move to Hobart. But he could not bring himself to do so for he lacked the necessary courage to cut himself off from his family. Ikey, the rich loner with a family for whom he cared not at all, was a far cry from Ikey, the poor loner with no future prospects, who lacked the internal fortitude and even the energy to begin again in the chancy business of crime.

Ikey tried to convince himself that Hobart was too small for a fence of his reputation, but he knew this to be only an excuse. His bones ached and the yellow teeth rattled in his head, and he saw death in every sunset. Ikey knew he would not survive another sentence. Fear gripped at his bowels and sucked the marrow of resolve from his bones, until it was better to get drunk than to think at all.

Sometimes, when the sun shone brightly and warmed his creaking bones, Ikey would consider his prospects in a more sober frame of mind. He could go kosher, that is to say, above board and respectable, a small businessman, perhaps a return to his tobacco shop. The sale of the cottage would supply the capital needed. But he knew in his heart that this was simply a quicker and quieter way to die.

Ikey loved the nocturnal life, the whispers and the knowing

looks of criminal intrigue, the hard-eyed bargaining, the joy of a deal well struck and the satisfaction of a neatly laid-out ledger which marked in numbers the progress of his private war against those who would bring him undone. He thought of himself as the enemy, and expected to be taken seriously by the rich and mighty. He was the destructive element in a world carefully constructed to benefit the self-serving better classes. Ikey had beaten the law dozens of times in a system that thought nothing of hanging a boy for stealing twopence. And now the same system had beaten him, not with imprisonment, but by stealing his courage. Ikey knew that, without courage, there is no luck and no hope. He who dares, wins. For him to become a respectable small businessman on an island steeped in the blood and sorrow of the outrageous system against which he had always pitted his cunning and his wits would be the greatest defeat of all.

Ikey needed the fortune which lay in the Whitechapel safe to publicly proclaim the victory of his salvaged wealth. He knew he had been defeated. But the money he had stolen would at least allow him to flaunt his pyrrhic victory and so hide the immensity of that defeat, whereas meek respectability would forever emphasise his complete destruction.

This was the state of Ikey Solomon in October 1837 when he sat alone on the banks of the Derwent River watching a cormorant on a rock some distance off, its wet wings opened wide to the heat of the late morning sun.

'Mr Solomon?' The voice of a small boy came from behind him.

Ikey turned to see an urchin of about twelve standing a few feet to his left. The Ikey of old would have long since sensed the approach.

'Mr Ikey Solomon?' the boy repeated.

'You knows it's me, boy, so why does you ask?' Ikey said gruffly.

'I was told I must,' the boy replied.

'Told was you? And who might it be what told you?'

'I runs errands, sir,'

'Runs errands?' Ikey's voice changed to a more friendly tone. 'A working boy, a respectable boy, a boy what's not footloose and up to no good!' Ikey held a dirty hand out in the direction of the boy. 'Ah, I don't believe we 'as been introduced, my dear.'

'I knows who you is,' the urchin said, not taking Ikey's hand and seeing no reason to proffer his own or give Ikey his name.

'Ha! So you knows who I is. But you *asks* who I is. Is that not a curious thing to do? Askin' and knowin'?' Ikey returned his hand to his side.

'Them what give me the letter said I must ask first.'

Ikey's eyebrows arched in surprise. 'A letter! You 'as a letter for Ikey Solomon? I don't recall as I've 'ad a letter recently. Would you 'ave it in mind to tell me who gave you this precious letter?'

'Why?' the boy asked. Ikey immediately marked him as intelligent, a rare enough occurrence among the dull-brained urchins who roamed the streets of New Norfolk throwing stones at dogs and chickens.

'A very good question, my dear! An excellent and most perspicacious question! You see, my dear, there are some letters you will receive in life what are not to your advantage, a letter, for instance, what might contain a summons or a warrant. A letter is not always best opened or even received, if you takes my meaning.'

'I've never 'ad a letter,' the boy replied, unimpressed by this first cautionary lesson in life.

'That's a bloomin' shame, boy!'

'Not if you can't read, it ain't,' the urchin shot back.

What a waste of a boy! Ikey thought. How well this one would have done at the Academy of Light Fingers.

'Who? Who was it gave you the letter what I might take, or I might not? Being as I might be Mr Isaac Solomon, and yet I might decide not to be!'

'It come off a boat from 'Obart. The cap'n. 'E asks if I knows you and when I does 'e give me an 'apenny and . . .' the boy dug into the interior of his shirt and produced an envelope, '. . . 'e give me this 'ere letter.'

'What does it say on the envelope?' Ikey asked.

The boy shrugged. 'I already told you, I don't do no readin'.' He took two steps closer to the seated Ikey and proffered the envelope.

'Well that be another shame, boy, a bright lad like you what can't read? Tut, tut, must learn to read, boy. There are no prospects for a lad what can't read, no prospects whatsoever, and never to be 'eard of!' He glanced up at the urchin. 'Do you hear me, boy?'

'Don't you want your letter?' the urchin said and then added, 'I ain't no toff what needs to learn to read.'

455

Ikey still refrained from taking the letter. 'Can you count, boy?' It had been several days since he had sustained any sort of conversation, and the bright morning sun had ironed out some of his aches and pains, and it was like old times talking to the urchin standing beside him.

'Yessir, I can count real good.'

'Pennies in a shilling?'

'Twelve!' the boy snapped back.

'Shillings in a pound?'

'Twenty,' the boy said with alacrity, then added spontaneously, 'Four farving in a penny and two 'a'pennies, a guinea be a pound and one shillin' and I can count good to one 'undred and poss'bly even a thousand, but I ain't tried yet!'

'Bravo!' Ikey exclaimed and clapped in applause. 'Bravo! Methinks you should still learn to read, but you've got the right idea.' Ikey smiled at the boy. 'I'm sorry, lad, but I 'aven't got a ha'penny nor even a farthing to give you for this splendid delivery of yours.' Ikey now finally took the letter from the boy's hand.

'That's orright, sir,' the boy replied. Then he cocked his head to one side and squinted down at Ikey. 'You ain't got even a farving, eh?' he asked somewhat incredulously.

Ikey shook his head, ashamed. 'Nothing, lad . . . I'm sorry. Next time I sees you I might 'ave one, or even a penny and you shall 'ave it!'

The boy dug into his trouser pocket and produced a sixpence which he rested on his thumb and forefinger and then flipped high into the air. The sunlight caught the bright silver coin as it spun, arched and descended and the boy slapped it onto the back of his hand and glanced down at it.

'It's 'eads! You lose!' he proclaimed happily. Then pocketing the coin he squinted at Ikey again. 'I suppose you is now gunna tell me you earned your present fortune 'cos you was so good at readin'?'

'Cheeky bugger!' Ikey shouted and made as if to rise. But the boy had already turned on his heels and was running up the steep bank of the river, his bare feet sending small pebbles and clods of red earth rolling into the water below. 'You'll go far, lad, that I'll vouch!' Ikey called after him, laughing.

'Cheer'o, mister,' the boy shouted back. 'See you in the library, then!'

Ikey looked down at the envelope in his hand. *Mr. Isaac Solomon Esq.*, was all it said, in an annoyingly familiar copperplate script. Ikey opened it very slowly, as though it might explode in his hands, and carefully unfolded the note. To his surprise it contained two one pound notes. He held each note in turn up to the sunlight to ascertain that they were genuine, then he began to read.

Hobart Town.

25th October 1837

Dear Mr Solomon,

I have need of a good clerk who can keep an accurate ledger. If such a position should interest you, I urge you to come to Hobart and to make yourself known to the undersigned. I enclose the sum of two pounds to defray any expenses involved.

I remain, yours sincerely,

Mary Abacus (Miss).

The Potato Factory.

Chapter Thirty

Mary's first triumph in the brewing of beer did not come from the amber liquid itself, although it was conceded by most to be an excellent ale, crisp and clean to the taste and light on the stomach, but came instead from the label she placed on each bottle. As labels go it lacked any sign of the artistic but made up for this with words that caused the Temperance Society to recommend her product to all who had taken 'The Pledge'. Those of her customers who could read took great pleasure in the story on the label, and those who could not would soak the label off and have someone read it aloud so that they might share the exquisite feeling of righteousness it gave them.

Sold into Slavery

'Tom Jones is sold into slavery!' said a man to me the other day.

'Sold into slavery!' I cried. 'Is there anything like that now-a-days?'

'Indeed there is,' was the answer.

'Who bought him, pray?'

'Oh, it's a firm, and they own a good many slaves, and more shocking bad masters.'

'Can it be in these days? Who are they?' I asked.

'Well they have agents everywhere, who tell a pretty good story, and get hold of folk; but the name of the firm is Messrs. Rum, Gin & Spirits.'

I had heard of them, it is a firm of bad reputation, and yet how extensive are their dealings! What town has not felt their influence? Once in their clutches, it is about the hardest thing in the world to break away from them. You are sold and that is the end of it; sold to ruin sooner or later. I have seen people try to escape from them. Some, it is true, if they should take 'The Pledge', do escape to find the heavenly delights of Mary Abacus' most excellent and unadulterated Temperance Ale, sold at threepence half-penny a bottle, or threepence if the previous bottle be returned empty.

The Potato Factory.

Mary's Temperance Ale became such a success that the large Hobart breweries decided at once to bring out a version of their own. But here again Mary was not caught napping. With the help of Mr Emmett she had registered the names Temperance Ale and Temperance Beer, and also Pledge Ale and Pledge Beer, so that these names could be used exclusively by the Potato Factory.

This caused great annoyance among the beer barons, and they thought to take her to court for registering a name which they claimed was in common usage. But the advice of their various lawyers was to leave well alone.

The label also caused great annoyance to the local importers of rum, gin, brandy and sweet Cape wine, as well as to the local manufacturers of the various ardent spirits available on the market. But the more they belly-ached, and shouted imprecations against Mary in the newspapers, the more popular her Temperance Ale became, not only among those customers who had signed the pledge and sworn off spirits, but also among those who liked a drop of the heavenly ambrosia as a matter of preference.

There was nothing the common people liked more than a poor, defenceless woman, only recently granted her conditional pardon, winning a point of law against the first raters, the whisky and beer barons, who grew rich on the pennies of the poor. To keep up demand, Mary was obliged to take on additional help. Soon she had three men working for her, as well as a girl of fifteen who came directly from the orphanage and who possessed the pretty name of Jessamy Hawkins.

Late one morning at the Potato Factory Jessamy came to Mary while she was testing the fermentation levels in the hop tanks.

'Mistress Mary, there be an old man what's called to see you.' The young maid looked concerned. 'I told him to go away, but he says he knows you, says he has a letter.' Then she added gratuitously, 'He's most smelly and has a shaggy beard and long hair, but is also bald and wears a coat what you might expect on an old lag what's a proper muck snipe, not ever to be redeemed.'

'Hush, Jessamy, do not speak like that, for all you know he could be a most loving father!'

'Gawd! I hope he's not mine!' Jessamy said, alarmed at the thought.

Mary laughed. 'Old lag what's a drunk, that description could fit half the bloomin' island. So, where be the letter, girl?'

'No, Mistress Mary, it weren't no letter what's *for* you! It were a letter he said he got *from* you. He says he comes because o' the letter you sent.'

Mary's heart started to pound. 'Dirty is he? And ragged?'

Jessamy nodded, brought her thumb and forefinger to her nose and pulled a horrid face.

'It's Ikey!' Mary said and her poor, crippled hands were suddenly all a-flutter, touching her hair, patting her apron, her hips, not quite knowing what they should do next. 'Bring my cotton gloves!' she commanded of Jessamy. Then she thought better of this. 'No, I'll get them, you take him into the bottle room and give him a glass of beer, tell him I'll be along presently.'

Mary removed her apron and ran her fingers through her hair, fluffing it as best she could in the absence of a mirror. Then she found a pair of clean cotton gloves and, with a feeling of some trepidation, entered the bottle shop.

Ikey crouched on a stool, clutching a glass of ale in both hands. He gasped as Mary entered, and his hands jerked upwards in alarm sending half the contents of the glass into his lap.

'Oh, Jesus! Oh, oh!' he exclaimed, looking down at the wet patch on his dirty coat and the mess at his feet. He wiped his hands on either side of the threadbare coat.

'Ikey? Ikey Solomon? It's you all right, Gawd help us!' Mary laughed, the spilt beer overcoming her nervousness. 'You always were a most nervous old bugger!'

Ikey grinned, which was not a pretty sight. Mary had forgotten how tiny he was, and he appeared to have lost several teeth and looked a great deal older than his fifty-two years. Jessamy was right, he stank to high heaven, even by the high standard of stink set by much of the local population.

'Nice to make your acquaintance again, my dear, news o' your remarkable success grows far and wide,' Ikey cackled. He looked around at the barrels of beer, and the racks of bottled ale stacked to the ceiling, as though weighing and valuing the contents to the last liquid ounce.

'Nonsense! News o' my remarkable success goes all the way down Liverpool Street and into Wapping, and not much further.'

'I is most proud of you, proud and honoured and most remarkably touched, my dear, and oh . . .' Ikey dug into the pocket of his coat and produced a pound. 'This be what's left o' the money you sent in your most kind letter, after the boat ticket and vittles eaten and five shillings paid for a week's board and lodging 'ere in town. That is, only until I can get back into my own 'ouse.'

'Change? You giving me change?' Mary looked incredulous. 'My goodness, we has reformed, hasn't we, then? Whatever could have come over you, Ikey Solomon?'

Ikey gave a phlegmy laugh and shook his head slowly. 'I admits, honesty ain't a habit what's come easy, Mary, my dear.' Mary saw that his back had become more hunched, though now he pulled himself as straight as he was able, wincing at a stab of rheumatism in his hip. Then he jerked at the ragged lapels of his coat and grinned, pushing his chin into the air.

'What you sees here, my dear, is a reformed man, honest as the day be long, reliable to the point o' stupidity and a ledger clerk what's to be praised for neatness, accuracy and the most amazing sagacity, experienced in all the ways o' gettin' what's owed to one quickly paid, and what one owes to others most tedious slow to be proceeded with!' He bowed slightly to Mary, bringing his broken shoes together. 'Isaac Solomon at your 'umble service, madam!'

'You'll need to sign the pledge and agree to take a bath once a month,' Mary said, unimpressed.

Ikey clutched at his chest. 'You knows I don't drink, least only most modest and circumspect, my dear! Bathe? Once a month?'

His eyebrows shot up in alarm. 'Does you mean naked? No clothes? But, but . . . that be like Port Arthur again! That be ridiculous and most onerous and unfair, and 'as nothing to do with clerking nor keeping ledgers fair and square!'

'Once a month, Ikey Solomon!' Mary repeated. Ikey could see from the tightness at the corners of her mouth that she meant it.

Ikey smiled unctuously. 'Tell you what I can do for you, my dear. I could wash me 'ands!' He held his hands up and spread his fingers wide. Mary observed them to be a far cry from clean. 'Not once a month, mind, but *every* time I works on the ledgers, once a day, even more, if you wishes! 'Ow about that, my dear?'

Mary shook her head and then folded her arms. 'Bathe once a month and take the pledge. I smoked you, Ikey, and I be most reliably informed that you has grown fond 'o the fiery grape!'

'Reliably informed, is it? That be most malicious gossip and not to be trusted at all and in the least! A little brandy now and again to calm me nerves in the most unpleasant times experienced in New Norfolk, that were all it was, I swear it, my dear!'

'Well, then you will have no qualms about signing the pledge,' Mary replied calmly. 'You can drink beer here, and if you works well your nerves won't need no calming with the likes of us, Ikey Solomon.'

Ikey hung his head and sucked at his teeth, and seemed to be considering Mary's proposition. Finally, as though coming to a most regrettable decision, he shook his head slowly and in a forlorn voice said, 'Hot water, mind? In a room what's locked and no soap! Soap makes me skin itch somethin' awful!'

'Soap, but not prison soap,' Mary said, remembering well the harsh carbolic soap issued once a fortnight in the Female Factory which caused the skin to burn and itch for hours afterwards.

Ikey, of course, did not fit in well. He was not the sort to be put on a high stool with a green eyeshade to labour at ledgers while the sun shone brightly. Sunshine was a most abhorrent spectre for Ikey and had been one of the more difficult aspects of his imprisonment. Daylight was a time when Ikey's internal clock ran down, and Mary soon realised this.

After Ikey had bathed and signed the pledge, she had taken him to Thos Hopkins the tailor. Now everyone, even the most ignorant, knows that 'Thos' stands for Thomas at his christening, so that he was forced to spend his whole life explaining that his name was not Tom or Thomas but Thos. He was small and plump, somewhat irritable and a dreadful snob, but a very good bespoke tailor, and quite the most expensive in Hobart Town. He used only the best imported worsteds and demanded three fittings at the very least.

Thos Hopkins had recently signed the pledge and become a most enthusiastic user of Mary's Temperance Ale, to the point of half a dozen bottles taken most evenings. But he soon revealed that behind his snobbish façade lay an impecunious state of affairs, and he owed Mary nearly five pounds in credit. Were it not for the mounting debt he would not have permitted Ikey to enter his establishment.

Mary replaced Ikey's clothes, and had the bootmaker make him a pair of pigskin boots with long, narrow toes which served as yellow snouts in exactly the same manner as the pair he'd owned in England. The coat was made to Ikey's precise instructions. Half a hundred pockets appeared in the most peculiar places, so that the redoubtable Mr Hopkins eventually cried out at the very sight of Ikey entering his establishment. 'Bah! More pockets, I will not tolerate more pockets!'

Eventually the coat was completed and after seven years Ikey was back to something like his old self, which included a return to his nocturnal ways. He would appear at six of the evening at the Potato Factory, just as the other workers were departing, and work until midnight. At the stroke of twelve he would creep away, heading for Wapping and the docks to spend the night in the public houses, sly grog dens and brothels inhabited by sailors, whalers, drunks, thieves and the general riff-raff of Hobart Town.

Though Ikey was no longer in the crime business he could still be persuaded to pay out on a watch temporarily loaned and returned for a small commission added. This was merely the business of being an itinerant pawnbroker conveniently on the spot when a drunk or a sailor found himself without funds in the early hours of the morning. More importantly, Ikey now carried a large basket over his arm filled with various types, sizes, packets and prices of snuff, cigars and pipe baccy, and he moved from place to place selling his wares. If there was only a small profit to be made from this trade it did not overly concern Ikey because it gave him an excuse to spend the hours of the night at perambulation. Once again he was a creature of the dark hours.

This suited Mary perfectly, as in daylight hours Ikey proved a difficult proposition. He would argue with the men at the slightest provocation, and had an opinion about everything. What's more, he was a tiger when it came to debt.

A great many of Mary's customers came from the dockside area of Wapping, the place in Hobart Town where the poor and the broken lived. Customers who required a drop of credit were a frequent and normal part of Mary's life. But Ikey, who had spent his life among the congregation of the unfortunate, had a very low opinion of the credit rating of the poor, and constantly grumbled and groused at the idea of giving them grog on the slate. Sometimes, when they came to the Potato Factory to beg a bottle or two for the night in advance of their weekly wages, he would soundly dress them down. A penny owed to Mary would irritate him until it was paid. While Mary found it difficult to argue with Ikey's diligence on her behalf, she knew how hard it was for many of her customers to stay on the pledge and not drink the raw spirit made by the sly grog merchants which would rot their stomachs, send them blind or even kill them.

Ikey had become more and more fidgety, often not appearing at the Potato Factory until mid-morning, and even then still bleary eyed. Finally, at about the time his new coat had acquired a suitably greasy patina, Mary tackled him as to the reason for his behaviour.

'It be the sunlight, my dear, seven years o' sunlight, too much o' the bright. Bright be always cruel, in the bright light the evil things done to a man is seen to be normal. I craves the dark. What a man does in the dark is his personal evil, what 'e does in the light 'e does in the name of truth, and that often be the most evil of all. People do not see clearly in the light, but they look carefully into the shadows. In the night I am a natural man, given to the feelings of honesty or deception, quite clear in the things I do, whether for good or for bad. In the light I am confused, for the most awful crimes are committed in the name of truth, and these always out loud, in the blazin' sunlight. It is a feeble notion that good is a thing of the light. Here, in the name of justice, property and ownership, poverty and starvation is considered a natural condition created for the advantage of those who rule, those who own the daylight. The poor and the miserable are thought to exist solely for the benefit of those who are born to the privilege.' Ikey paused after this tirade. He had surprised himself with his own eloquence. 'Ah, my dear, in the dark I can clearly see good and evil. Both can be separated like the white from the yolk. In the light I am blinded, stunned, eviscerated, rendered useless by the burning malevolence which blazes upon the earth with every sunrise.'

Mary had never heard Ikey talk like this, and she did not pretend to understand it all. She knew Ikey for what he was, a man possessed of cunning and greed, not given to the slightest charity. But now she became aware that Ikey had always exploited the rich and she could think of no instance where he had profited by robbing the poor. It was true that, as a fence, he had depended on the desperate poor to do his dirty work, but he had paid promptly and well for what they brought him. Even the brothel in Bell Alley had been for the gentry, where he caused the collective breeches of lawyers, magistrates, judges, barristers and bankers to be pulled down to mine the profit of their vanity, and milk their puny loins and their vainglorious attempts to recapture an imagined youth long since lost to rich food and port wine.

And so Ikey had returned to his old ways, and life at the Potato Factory continued without his avuncular interference, but with the advantage of his instinct for a bad debt approaching, and his sharp eye for any unscrupulous trader's attempt to bring Mary undone.

Mary spent the first hour with Ikey each evening before he started on the ledgers, and she served him the mutton stew and dish of fresh curds he loved. After he had wiped the foam from his beard, and in general declared the satisfaction of his stomach by the emission of various oleaginous noises, she would seek his counsel in those matters of immediate concern to her.

Their relationship was not in the least romantic, and Ikey would never again share Mary's bed. Mary had brought him back into her life because she earnestly believed his gift of the Waterloo medal was the reason for her good fortune in Van Diemen's Land. And it was Ikey who had given Mary her first chance at a decent life.

Mary never forgot a good deed or forgave a bad one, and she repaid each with the appropriate gratitude or retribution. She had always lived in a hard world where no quarter was given; now she realised that an even harder one existed. She had discovered that those who possessed wealth and property were dedicated to two things: the enhancement of what they owned, and an absolute determination never to allow anyone below them to share in the spoils, using any means they could to dispossess them. Mary had not accepted this rich man's creed. She was determined that those who helped her would be rewarded with her loyalty whether they were king or beggarman, while those who sought to cheat her would eventually pay a bitter price.

Against his better judgment she had persuaded Mr Emmett to apply in his own name for Ikey's release and had, through the chief government clerk, secretly paid the bond and secured Ikey's early ticket of leave. In doing this Mary did not seek Ikey's gratitude, but was merely repaying a debt. In offering Ikey the position as her clerk Mary was not seeking to gloat at the reversal of their roles. She was simply keeping faith with her own personal creed.

It should not be imagined that Mary and Ikey formed an ideal couple. They quarrelled constantly. Ikey's imperious ways and scant regard for the proprieties of a relationship where he was the employee often left Mary furious. He was careless about her feelings and often disparaging of her opinions. But whereas the old Ikey may have caused her in a fit of temper to throw him onto the street, she soon discovered that the new Ikey was unable to make a decision. Mary came to see him as the devil's advocate, useful for his incisive mind but now without the courage of his convictions.

Mary was growing in prosperity and she soon had the money to construct a water-powered mill and malt house on her land at Strickland Falls on the slope of Mount Wellington. Although she was still a long way from owning her own brewery, she already sold her high-quality barley mash and malt to some of the smaller breweries, as well as using her superior ingredients to increase her own output.

To her now famous Temperance Ale she had added an excellent bitter, a dark, smooth, full-bodied beer with a nice creamy head when poured well from the bottle. It was rumoured that many of the island's nobs and pure merinos would send their servants to purchase her excellent bitter ale for their breakfast table. This new beer came in a distinctive green bottle and, in marked contrast to the verbosity of the Temperance Ale label, had an oval-shaped label which featured two green parakeets seated on a sprig of flowering red gum. In an arch above them was the name 'Bitter Rosella', which soon became known by all as 'Bitter Rosie', and in the curve below were the words 'The Potato Factory'. Underneath this ran the line which would one day become famous throughout the world: *'Brewed from the world's purest mountain water'*.

Chapter Thirty-one

In the general course of events, the meeting of an acquaintance sixteen thousand miles from where you had last known them would seem to be a miracle. But in the penal colonies of New South Wales or Van Diemen's Land, it was a very common experience. The under class of London, Manchester, Birmingham, Glasgow and Belfast were transported in their thousands. Men and women who had lived in the same dark, stinking courts and alleys, who had, as children, starved and played in the same cheerless streets, might run into one another in a tavern crowd in Hobart Town. An old accomplice might tap one on the shoulder and claim a drink and a hand-out, or simply an hour's gossip of people and places known in a past now much romanticised by time and absence.

Ikey came to expect a familiar yell across a crowded room from someone who recognised him from London or the provinces; though in truth, he was previously so well known by reputation that there were some who merely imagined a past association with him. It did not come as a total shock, therefore, when Ikey one night entered the Hobart Whale Fishery, a tavern frequented by whalers, and heard a high sweet voice raised above the noise of the crowd as it sung a pretty ditty. He had last heard that tune at the Pig 'n Spit, and knew at once that the voice belonged to Marybelle Firkin.

Fine Ladies and Gents
come hear my sad tale
The sun is long down and
the moon has grown pale
So drink up your rum
and toss down your ale
Come rest your tired heads
on my pussy . . .
come rest your tired heads
on my pussy . . . cat's tail!

Jack tars of every nation joined in the chorus so that the tavern shook with their boisterous singing.

Come rest your tired heads
on my pussy . . .
Come rest your tired heads
on my pussy . . . cat's tail!

Ikey listened as Marybelle Firkin now added a new verse to the song.

Whaleman, whaleman
To Hobart you've come
The hunt is now over
the oil in the drum
So lift up your tankards
and drink to the whale
Come rest your tired heads
on my pussy . . .
Come rest your tired heads
on my pussy . . . cat's tail!

The notorious tavern on the Old Wharf was crowded with whalemen returned from Antarctic waters with a successful season's catch behind them, and their canvas pockets bulging with silver American dollars, French francs and the King's pound.

The tars spent wildly at their first port of call in months, and the shopkeepers rubbed their hands in glee. But it was at the Hobart Whale Fishery where most of the money was spent. This was the tavern most favoured by the thirsty and randy jack tars, and it was here also that some of the more expensive of the town's whores gathered.

It was almost sunrise before Ikey was able to greet Marybelle Firkin, who loomed large, bigger than Ikey had ever imagined, holding a tankard of beer. Around her on the floor washed with stale beer and rum lay at least a dozen jack tars, quite oblivious to the coming day.

Marybelle Firkin, who now called herself Sperm Whale Sally, put down her tankard of Bitter Rosie and swept Ikey into her enormous arms, lifting him from the ground in the grandest of hugs, until he begged her for mercy.

'Oh Ikey, it is you!' she screamed with delight. Then she placed Ikey down and held him at arm's length. 'You 'aven't changed at all, lovey, 'andsome as ever!' She pointed to Ikey's bald head. 'No 'at! Where's your lovely 'at?'

Ikey touched the shiny top of his head as though he had only just noticed the absence of his broad-brimmed hat. 'It ain't kosher to wear a Jew's 'at here, my dear, and I have yet to find another I prefers.'

Ikey and Marybelle resumed their friendship, though in truth Sperm Whale Sally, as Marybelle now insisted she be called, had fallen on hard times. Though Ikey was largely, though indirectly, responsible for this, she bore him no malice. Her involvement on the morning of his notorious escape had brought her to the attention of the police, and the blind eye previously turned to the existence of the ratting den upstairs was now withdrawn. As a consequence the profits of the Pig 'n Spit had greatly decreased. With the closing down of the ratting ring, Thomas Tooth and George Betteridge had taken it into their minds to find another buyer for their Bank of England bill paper, no longer trusting Marybelle Firkin as their intermediary. When the two men were arrested they had named her to place bond for them, threatening to tell of her involvement if she did not acquiesce. At the plea of *Habeas Corpus*, the judge had set the bond very high and when this had been paid Marybelle Firkin found herself under suspicion and at the same time robbed of all of her available resources.

It was not long before she received a visit from a police sergeant whom she had regularly paid to overlook the existence of the ratting ring. Now, after first extorting a tidy bribe from her, he warned that she was about to be investigated by the City police over the matter of the bank paper.

Marybelle had left that same night under the assumed name of Sally Jones, taking the first available boat from Gravesend, which happened to be sailing on the morning tide for Van Diemen's Land. She had arrived in Hobart Town almost penniless, and had found that the only way she could maintain her voracious appetite was to join the ranks of the world's oldest profession. She had soon enough been christened Sperm Whale Sally by the jack tars who came off the whaling ships. She begged Ikey never to reveal her proper name, lest news of her presence in Hobart Town reach England.

'That be my story, Ikey,' Sperm Whale Sally concluded. 'Sad, but no sadder than most and not as sad as many a poor wretch.' She chuckled and placed her boot on the stomach of an unconscious tar under the table at her feet. 'It were pretty bad at first, ain't too much call for an 'arf crown Judy. I grow'd most skinny them first months. Not every whale man likes a four 'undred pound cuddle!' Sperm Whale Sally hooted with laughter. 'It's the 'Mericans what most favoured me, but they ain't always in port. But then, three year ago. I come up with this Blue Sally lark, and now I eats well with a bit to spare for when the whalin' ships be out to sea.' She nudged the man at her feet with the toe of her boot. 'I loves these whalemen, Ikey. They come in from the cruel, cold sea proper starvin' for a bit o' love and cuddlin'.' She started to positively wobble with laughter, 'and I 'as a lot of lovin' to give 'em if they got the stamina to win it!' She lifted her tankard of Bitter Rosie and swallowed half of it in one great gulp. 'Ikey Solomon, we goes back a long ways, it be most lovely to see you again!'

The Blue Sally Challenge was a grand contest known to the crew of every whaling ship that sailed the Pacific Ocean. The Blue Sally was treasured among whalemen above anything else they took to sea, and some of the more superstitious considered it a matter of life or death that the vessel they sailed in carried it flying from the topmast, even though it was nothing more than a modest piece of bunting, a white flag with the outline in blue of a sperm whale stitched upon it. It was common enough in whaling ports around the world for a ship's master or agent recruiting whalemen for the season to be asked two questions: the crewman's share of the catch and, 'Capt'n, do she sail under a Blue Sally?' So important had the flying of the Blue Sally become that a whaling ship sailing into a Pacific port without the blue and white bunting flying from her masthead was the subject of more than a little raucous innuendo as to the masculine nature of the men aboard her.

How this peculiar and unique contest first came about is a story best told by Sperm Whale Sally herself. She recounted it to Ikey early one morning when she was sufficiently sober, having eliminated that night's Blue Sally challenger with such a degree of ease that she was still happily tucking into a leg of pork alone at the challenge table, her opponent stretched out unconscious under it, both arms folded across his chest.

'As you knows, lovey, eatin' is me passion, and drinkin' is me Gawd given gift! So I decides to combine both in a grand competition. If them fuckers won't pay 'arf a crown for me body, they'll do so for me north and south, for me great cake 'ole.' Sperm Whale Sally laughed.

'I needs a story, whalemen being most superstitious and given to legends and the like. So I invents me own. It be a real beauty, lots of adventure and a grand opportunity for me voice, me bein' an actress an' all. I even invents a song what goes with it. That done the trick, the song, the sea shanty what o' course you've heard a hundred times or more.'

Sperm Whale Sally began to sing in the clear, sweet voice the whalemen loved.

> Come gather around me, you jack tars and doxies
> I'll sing you the glorious whaleman's tale
> Let me tell you the story, of death and the glory
> of Rackham . . . who rode on the tail of a Whale
>
> So take up your doxy and drink down your ale
> And dance a fine jig to a fine fishy tale
> We'll fly the Blue Sally wherever we sail
> and drink to the health o' the great sperm whale!
>
> It started at dawn on a bright Sabbath morning
> When Lord Nelson's body came 'ome pickled in rum
> Every jack tar mourned the great British sailor
> And drank to their hero as church bells were rung

I be born to the sound o' the bells of St Paul's
Where they buried the sealord all solemn and proper
That very same day harpooner John Rackham
Rode the tail of a whale around Davey Jones' locker

The watch up the mainmast gave out a great shout,
'A six pod to starboard all swimming in strong!'
So they lowered a whale boat, harpoon gun and line
Three cheers for the crew then the whale hunt was on

John Rackham, he stood to his harpoon and line
'Row the boat close, lads, 'til we see its great chest
Steady she goes now, keep the bow straight
Or this great fearless fish will bring all to their rest!'

The boat's bow, on a crest, held still for a moment
Sufficient for Rackham to make good his aim
Then the harpoon flew screaming to carry the line
And buried its head in a great crimson stain

'Steady now, lads, let the fish make his dive
Then he'll turn for the top and the fight'll begin
Ship your oars, boys, take the ride as he runs
For the sperm has a courage that comes from within'

Ten fathoms down the fish turned from its dive
As the harpoon worked in, on the way to his heart
Then he spied the boat's belly directly above him
And he knew they'd pay for this terrible dart!

Fifty tons rose as the fish drove like thunder
Like a cork in a whirlpool the boat spun around
The jaws of the whale smashed through its planking
And the sharks made a meal o' the pieces they found!

John Rackham was saved as the fish drove him upwards
he found himself up on the nose of the whale
With a snort he was tossed sky high and then backwards
and landed most neatly on the great creature's tail

'Let me live! Master Whale, I've a child to be born!
Spare my life and I promise to name it for you!'
'That's a fanciful tale,' cried the furious whale
'But how can I know what you say will be true?'

John Rackham he pondered then started to smile
'Not only its name, but its soul to you too!
And we'll make a white flag with your picture upon it
A great sperm whale emblazoned in blue!'

The great fish turned and swam straight to the ship
With a flick of his tail threw him safe in a sail
Then the deadly dart finally pierced his great heart
Now we fly the Blue Sally to honour the whale!

So take up your doxy and drink down your ale
And dance a fine jig to a fine fishy tale
We'll fly the Blue Sally wherever we sail
and drink to the health o' the great sperm whale!

Sperm Whale Sally started to laugh. 'It were the song and the story. Some likes the song and others the story. Whalemen loves to dance a jig and sing a shanty and they loves a good story too, and so I made 'em two o' the very best I could!'

Sperm Whale Sally always told the story with the utmost sincerity so that the whalemen, anxious for a new sea legend, wanted to believe it and many of them did. Sperm Whale Sally never told the story without singing the song about her dearest papa, whaleman John Rackham, and how he had been nearly killed and then saved by a great sperm whale while hunting in Antarctic waters on the same day that she had been born and Lord Nelson was brought back to England from Cape Trafalgar in Spain, his body pickled in rum to preserve it.

Though Sperm Whale Sally had been born a normal size baby, she immediately started to grow at an alarming rate, and she needed the breasts of four wet nurses to keep her satisfied. Her concerned mother took her to see a Romany woman who told her that she saw death and life in the form of a great fish. That the fish was her child's birth sign and it had stolen her spirit and exchanged it for its own, so she had a whale as a child, which would continue to grow, and nothing could stop her.

The gypsy prophesied that one day 'the child of the Great Fish' would return to the hunting grounds where the nearest of all fish were to be found. That her fish spirit, looking to find its natural home so that her own human spirit might return to her, would guide the hunters in their quest for the whale. But this only if there was one among them who could match the strength and endurance of the great female fish, and consummate this by entering her. This man would earn for his crew a talisman in the form of the fish flag. Those who flew it would be protected at sea and have bountiful luck in hunting the great sperm whale.

'Ah, Ikey, lovey! It were a feeble enough legend and a not very good song, both most contrived to begin with, but you know 'ow these things grow with a little bit added 'ere and a bit more there. The first season I were dead lucky, the ships o' Black Boss Cape Town and Tomahawk were the only two that 'ad earned a Blue Sally, though thank Gawd there were a great many others who tried and met with the greatest o' good luck. They took the biggest catches o' the season and not a jack tar among them were lost overboard or killed in a whale boat.'

Sperm Whale Sally laughed uproariously. 'That were all it took! When the *Sturmvogel* and the *Merryweather* come into port flyin' the Blue Sally, the legend were truly born. Suddenly I were the reincarnation o' the great fishy, the talisman, the good luck a whaleman takes to sea.' Sperm Whale Sally's great carcass wobbled again as she laughed. 'Blimey, it were on for one an' all!' She paused and wiped the sweat from her brow and sighed. 'Thank Gawd it ain't stopped since and I eats like a queen, and when the whalin' ships are in I earns sufficient to live well after they be gorn orf again to 'unt.'

The rules of the contest had formed over the years Sperm Whale Sally had been playing it, though, for all this, it remained much the same. The crew of a whaling ship would issue their challenge and nominate their man as challenger. They would pay their dues, half a crown per man on board the vessel, and the master would sign a statement that his crew, or the vessel itself, would meet the costs of the food and the drink consumed by Sperm Whale Sally and her challenger.

It was not unusual for a ship's master to be present at such a contest and it was often claimed that the Blue Sally meant so much to the crew of a whaling ship that some captains would advertise in their ports of origin for a crew member of sufficient size and drinking reputation to join, with an extra bonus promised if he should win a coveted Blue Sally for his vessel.

With the challenge formally made and payment guaranteed, the crew would choose pork or mutton, and the nature of the challenger's drink, this being a choice of rum, brandy, whisky or gin. Sperm Whale Sally's nomination was always ale. The rules required that her drink be matched with a strong spirit and that each contestant drink one kind of drink followed by the other. Thus a pint of ale, followed by a tot of rum, was matched by both contestants drink for drink.

In addition, a roasted sheep or pig was placed on the table together with a barrel of ale and one of the challenger's nominated spirit. The publican, or the ship's master if he'd agreed to be present, would act as the meat carver, drink dispenser and master of the ceremony. His task was to pour the drinks openly so all might see they were not spiked to the disadvantage of the challenger. He would also carve equal amounts from the carcass and add the same number of roasted potatoes from a dish of one hundred equally sized.

Precisely two hours was allowed for the contest and if, after this time, the challenger was not 'under the table', that is to say unconscious, then he was led by Sperm Whale Sally to the beach some fifty yards from the Whale Fishery. This final ceremony was known as 'the Beaching of the Whale' where the victor was invited to mount and consummate his 'taking of the flag'.

Only in this way could a Blue Sally be won for a whaling ship and when the fleet was in, no night passed without a challenger. But when the fleet put back to sea there were very few 'who newly flew the Sally Blue', and many who swore they would return to try again.

There were also a few greatly envied ships who flew a 'Two Sally Blue', a flag which sported upon it two sperm whales, indicating successful challenges on two separate occasions.

And then there were the two vessels, the *Sturmvogel* and the *Merryweather*, who flew the 'True Blue', a Blue Sally which carried stitched against its white background three great sperm whales. Each one had been won by the ship by the two giant men, the negro, Black Boss Cape Town, who claimed to come from a tribe deep in the African wilderness somewhere north of the Cape of Good Hope, and Tomahawk, the Red Indian, a Cheyenne from the American wilderness. Both men stood six feet and seven inches tall and could not walk frontways through the door of the Whale Fishery without touching the posts on either side.

In the manner of sailors there were some men, big men too, who when drunk enough would challenge the 'nigger' or the 'injun savage', but none were known who had remained on their feet beyond a blow delivered from the giant fist of either man. As winners of the True Blue they were occasioned the favours of Sperm Whale Sally without payment whenever they were in port. Although this had never occurred simultaneously, there was much speculation among whalemen as to what would be the consequence if this should happen, as everyone agreed, sooner or later, the two men must meet in combat.

The whaling season that year was a good one and the ships came into port, their holds fully loaded with whale oil and the promise of a big payout for the crews. The whole of Hobart Town prepared for the windfall of several hundred whalers let loose on the town with cash jingling in the pockets of their canvas ducks.

When the *Sturmvogel* came in on the morning tide and the *Merryweather* on the evening, both flying the True Blue, it was Pegleg Midnight who was the first to alert Sperm Whale Sally as she struggled to alight from a hired landau at ten o'clock of the night when her day began. Among much giggling and moaning she locked her great arms about the shoulders of the diminutive driver who, as she finally alighted, was momentarily obscured, smothered in a mountain of baby blue satin and pink flesh.

'Better stay home tonight, Sperm Whale Sally,' Pegleg shouted across to her.

'What, and starve to death!' Sperm Whale Sally called back. 'What be the matter, lovey?'

'Black Boss Cape Town and Tomahawk both be in town!' Pegleg said.

Sperm Whale Sally looked back at the landau. It took four men to load her but only one to set her down, so she shrugged. The two whaling vessels might be in for a fortnight or more, besides she hadn't been eating much all day, and had already been booked for a Blue Sally contest. And so she laughed and shrugged her shoulders. 'Ah well, may the best man win!' she said cheerily, then made her way slowly towards the Whale Fishery where a light supper of a roast leg of mutton and a dish of potatoes awaited her ravenous attention.

Pegleg Midnight, known by all to be a terrible gossip, was, surprisingly, not yet motherless drunk. Before the evening was an hour older he had caused word to be spread around all the dockside pubs, brothels, cock fights, sly grog shops and gaming dens, that Black Boss Cape Town and Tomahawk would square off at midnight, their prize the singular favours of the giant whore Sperm Whale Sally.

Chapter Thirty-two

Evening has a short stay in Hobart Town, a soft, still light that squeezes in between day and night as the great mountain sucks the last splash of sun into its rounded belly. Far below the wide river lies flat, like a sheet of tin, and the hills on its distant shore grow smoky and vague to the eye. Then night comes quicky, as though there should be a clap of thunder to accompany such wizardry.

It is as if the town sits in the hollow of a great hand which snaps its malicious fingers shut and crushes it into darkness. Voices grow still, dogs cease to bark and the wash of the incoming tide slaps hard and cold to the ear.

And then a silver glow rises across the river and comes to dance upon the fist of blackness and, as though cajoled by the light, the hand slowly opens to the candle of a rising moon. New stars pin themselves to the cold, high firmament and the night in Hobart Town is begun.

Such was the night when Tomahawk, the giant Red Indian, met Black Boss Cape Town in the Whale Fishery for the exclusive rights to the fair hand of Sperm Whale Sally.

Both men were legends in South Pacific and Antarctic waters, harpooners with a hundred and more kills to their name, and each had earned the True Blue which flew with pride from the masts of their ships.

Luck is a curious companion, it comes to those who believe they hold it, and is an elusive servant to those who doubt they possess it. The conviction that luck is your willing partner brings with it a sharper eye, a keener spirit, a willingness to take more chances, work harder, start earlier and work later. Luck bears the nostrils of success, for it can smell good fortune at a distance and leads those who possess it as surely to its source as a Sabbath roast does to the nose of a pious verger.

The men who sailed on the *Merryweather* and the *Sturmvogel* thought themselves blessed with good fortune and so their catches seemed blessed and a cut above the rest of the whaling fleet.

Moreover, the Americans on the *Merryweather* regarded their crew to be of an even higher status than the Danish ship, for it was rumoured that Sperm Whale Sally carried a tattoo on her enormous right breast which bore the name Tomahawk. It had alway been obvious to them that she favoured their man, and therefore their ship, above any other. Now, when they heard that this was not so, that the giant whore had issued a challenge to see who would win her favour, they had grown most indignant and then angry. They were convinced that their harpooner must teach Black Boss a lesson, and establish for all time their supremacy in the South Pacific.

On the *Sturmvogel* a similar dilemma existed. They knew about the tattoo, and reckoned how the Americans, known in Hobart Town as 'Jonathans', would think their man most especially favoured by Sperm Whale Sally.

They were first to arrive at the Whale Fishery, preceded by Pegleg Midnight who hobbled in on his dummy leg playing his fiddle at a furious pace so that almost all turned their heads. Pegleg continued to play until he reached the huge chair at the end of the challenge table and which was known as 'the Whale's Tail'. It was made of solid Tasmanian oak with the scene of John Rackham riding on the tail of a sperm whale, carved into its backrest. It was where Sperm Whale Sally always sat. Another identical chair, adorned with a carving of the Blue Sally, stood at the other end of the table and was known as 'the Flagging Chair', which was where the challenger sat. Pegleg Midnight brought his fiddle to a crescendo before abruptly stopping in the middle of the highest note.

'They be comin', Black Boss Cape Town and the crew and

master o' the *Sturmvogel*, and by all appearances they be most angry!' he shouted.

He had hardly completed this announcement when Black Boss Cape Town's giant body filled the doorway of the Whale Fishery. He stooped and pushed himself through the door, his shoulders touching either side of the door frame. Black Boss Cape Town walked over to where Sperm Whale Sally sat and upon his dark face was a most mischievous and charming grin. Then he stooped, and in a single movement picked her up and swung her around to face the astonished onlookers. Sperm Whale Sally squealed, but when she realised she was held securely her cries changed to delight. 'Goet, goet, much goet, Sperm Whale Sally!' the giant black man announced, and then swung her around again and deposited her neatly back into the chair.

Sperm Whale Sally, somewhat flustered and red in the face, declared 'I guarantee 'e be a most pleasin' 'arpooner!' and wobbled with laughter. The tension was broken, and those who had come to witness the great bout were swept up in her merriment. Finally she jiggled to a halt and smiled sweetly at Black Boss Cape Town. 'Welcome, lovey, it be grand to see you safe returned! I trusts the True Blue flew true for you and that all your barrels be full o' the good oil?' She turned to the master of the *Sturmvogel*. 'Evenin', capt'n', then shouted towards the bar. 'Betsy, lovey, bring a double pint tankard o' Bitter Rosie for Mr Black Boss Cape Town, please, and a noggin o' best rum for the good capt'n!'

'We have come to fight!' Captain Jorgensen said suddenly in a raised voice. 'But also we must have a condition, if you please!'

Sperm Whale Sally looked up, shocked. 'Fight? What fight may that be then, capt'n?'

Jorgen Jorgensen drew back, momentarily nonplussed, having assumed everything to be settled, and that the idea of the fight had come from Sperm Whale Sally herself.

'You said, may the best man win!' Pegleg Midnight chipped in. 'Black Boss Cape Town 'ere come to fight the injun! They 'as to fight to see what ship lays the top claim to you, to the luck o' the great sperm whale!'

'Fight? For me?' Sperm Whale Sally drew herself against the back of the huge chair and brought both her hands to her breasts. 'There'll be no fights for me, lads!' She shook her head. 'Not on your bloomin' nelly!'

'We must fight!' Jorgensen repeated, banging his fist on the table.

Sperm Whale Sally looked up in alarm at the anger in his voice. 'Whatever for, capt'n? You both flies the True Blue most proud!'

Captain Jorgensen was not used to explaining himself, and warily looked about the crowded room which had grown completely silent. He seemed conscious that what he was about to say might sound rather foolish. 'We want to have . . .' he paused and lightly tapped his heart with his forefinger. 'We fight for . . . your titty!'

'Huh?' Sperm Whale Sally's mouth fell open. A ripple of surprise came from the crowd and then silence as the onlookers waited for the response. She glanced down at her breasts, touching each with the tips of her fat fingers before looking up at Jorgensen. 'One or both?' she asked.

There was a howl of laughter from the crowd, but the master of the *Sturmvogel* was not amused.

'Starboard only!'

Sperm Whale Sally looked down at her right breast, then at the left one and then back up at the captain. 'So, what be wrong with me other titty?' she enquired mischievously, enjoying the captain's embarrassment and finding it difficult to restrain her laughter.

'Portside belong to Jonathan! *Sturmvogel* wants boarding rights on the starboard titty!' He turned and motioned to a jack tar who stood near to come forward. 'We'll fight the Jonathan injun and when Black Boss Cape Town beats him, Svensen here make a tattoo o' the *Sturmvogel* on your starboard titty.' He held out his hand to the jack tar and the man he'd called Svensen placed a small piece of paper in it. Captain Jorgen Jorgensen took three steps towards Sperm Whale Sally and handed her the paper. 'A picture o' the ship, most excellently drawn, Svensen will make a good artwork of it.'

Sperm Whale Sally looked at the picture of the Danish whaling ship and thought the pretty drawing would look most handsome on her breast. But she did not indicate this to the captain. Instead she slowly undid her bodice and peeled back the material covering the vast expanse of her left breast, stopping just short of the rosy sphere around her nipple. Resting high upon it was a crude tattoo of the head of an Indian chief and the single word, 'Tomahawk'.

Those in the crowd standing close enough to see the tattoo

gasped. The rumour that she favoured the huge Indian was confirmed. Sperm Whale Sally seemed somewhat surprised herself at the presence of the tattoo, as if she had quite forgotten it existed.

And indeed she confirmed this, 'Blimey! I quite forgot it be there!' She covered the tattoo with her bodice and slowly did up the buttons. 'That be there since I were a young 'un, long before I come to Van Diemen's Land!' she said to Captain Jorgensen. 'That be there,' she began and then stopped suddenly, and looked up at Jorgen Jorgensen and added, 'I don't rightly remember . . .' her voice trailing off.

In fact she remembered it well. She'd been just fifteen years old, a young actress in a Drury Lane play named 'Trooper of the King', a story about the war against the American colonists. Cast as an Indian maiden, with no more than a walk-on part, she had become completely smitten with an actor playing the part of an Indian guide named Tomahawk. He had wined and dined her in the West End the night after the final performance. They caroused until the early hours and she had been too drunk to remember how or where she had been with him. All she recalled was waking up on a straw mattress in a cheap lodging house shortly before midday the following day to discover her erstwhile lover had departed and left his mark on her young breast in the form of a dark blue and very new tattoo.

'It 'as been there near all me life, capt'n! It ain't got nothin' to do with Mr Tomahawk the whaleman!' Sperm Whale Sally protested.

Jorgen Jorgensen shook his head, plainly not believing her. 'You been smoked, Sperm Whale Sally, we know it be there for the *Merryweather* and the injun savage.' He pointed at Sally's left breast. 'Portside be the *Merryweather* titty, now the starboard for Black Boss Cape Town and the *Sturmvogel*!'

'Three cheers for Black Boss Cape Town!' Pegleg shouted and the tavern resounded with three cheers for the giant black man who now stood with his arms folded, the front of his canvas shirt spread open to expose his immense barrel chest shiny with sweat.

'Oi! Remember me?' Sperm Whale Sally suddenly shouted. 'Ain't nobody gunna tattoo nothin' on me tits, you hear!'

There was a hushed silence and then someone shouted, 'Here they comes! The Jonathans are coming!'

All eyes turned to the doorway of the public house, though

most could only see the crown of a top hat, because Captain Alexis 'Blackmouth' Perriman, who led the Americans, stood no more than five feet and three inches. Unlike Jorgen Jorgensen, who wore the clothes of a sailor coming ashore, a rough woollen suit of little style and most shabbily turned out, the captain of the *Merryweather* was dressed in a well-pressed top coat, clean linen, breeches, hose and well-shone buckled shoes. He was also clean shaven, but for a small tuft of dark beard stiffened with whale grease which grew at the point of his chin and was joined by a thin moustache which circled from either side of his top lip to meet the tuft. Within this hirsute oval stretched a small, thinly drawn mouth, downturned, so that it gave the impression of a vinegary disposition. He carried an ebony cane two-thirds as tall as himself with a whale bone carving of a sperm whale at its head, its eyes sparkling with what was claimed to be two blood red rubies.

Despite his appearance, he was a skipper who drove his men hard, was not himself backward in derring-do, and had a record as a whaling captain which was second to none. Following him were the crew of the *Merryweather*, mostly Jonathans, though there were several of the Irish among them. The last to enter the tavern was Tomahawk, the giant Red Indian. His hair was parted at the centre and had been braided in a single plait which fell five inches beyond his shoulders. He was as tall and as big around the shoulders as Black Boss Cape Town but did not possess a similar girth. Instead he tapered down to a slim waist, so that he gave the appearance of being the younger, stronger man.

Black Boss Cape Town carried three black stripes of a tribal cicatrisation down either cheek, and fitted into the stretched lobes of his ears were round discs the size of a silver dollar made of whale bone. In the centre of each was an inset of the outline of the sperm whale with its tail held high, carved of black horn.

Tomahawk wore no ornamentation save for his facial skin, which was completely tattooed with swirls and dots. Of the two savages he had the more fearsome appearance. Moreover, he did not smile as he walked over to the table to stand beside the master of the *Merryweather*. Tomahawk, dressed as a jack tar, folded his arms about his chest and looked directly ahead, as though he were there for the purposes of his own sweet repose, quite alone with his eyes inwardly cast.

Captain Perriman bowed his head slightly to Sperm Whale

Sally and, turning, did the same to Captain Jorgen Jorgensen. 'Greetings captain,' he drawled.

Sperm Whale Sally smiled. 'Pleased to meetcha, capt'n!'

Jorgen Jorgensen went to extend his hand towards the American, but thought better of it and withdrew, then he nodded his head and grunted. 'Capt'n.'

Captain Perriman smiled thinly. 'Well, it be a fight then?' It was not so much a question as a statement. 'There should be rules,' he announced.

'Rules?' Jorgen Jorgensen looked puzzled. 'Whalemen do not fight to rules!'

'Aye, well, both are valuable men, captain. I feel sure you would not want your man killed nor even maimed, he be a harpooner be he not?'

Jorgensen pondered for a moment, and Sperm Whale Sally pushed herself up from her chair and pointed at the two captains. 'You listen to me, you pair o' right bastards!'

They both looked at her in surprise, as though they had quite forgotten she existed. 'What be it, woman?' Captain Perriman asked in an offhand and irritated voice.

'I already told you there ain't gunna be no fight and no one's gunna put a pitcher o' his ship on me tits!'

'But it is quite decided, Mistress Sally!' Jorgen Jorgensen replied, bemused by her sudden recalcitrance.

'Oh I see,' Captain Perriman said, smiling knowingly. He winked at the Danish captain and took his purse from his jacket and from it took a ten dollar American bill. Then he walked over to Sperm Whale Sally and threw it on the table in front of her.

Sperm Whale Sally looked at the bill. She might possibly have agreed to the tattoo for such a price but she wasn't going to be patronised by the supercilious Jonathan. Her voice was angry and aggressive. 'Now 'ang on a mo, capt'n! It ain't just the flamin' tattoo! It's me boys!' She pointed to Black Boss Cape Town and then to Tomahawk. 'They both o' them true blues, they both done what's needed, there ain't nothin' more they needs to do.' In a sudden impatient gesture she pushed the ten dollar bill away. 'You can stick yer Yankee money up yer tiny Jonathan arse!'

'My God, I do not believe my ears, a whore who turns down money?' Captain Perriman said, one eyebrow slightly arched.

'Well you 'eard of one now, Capt'n Blackmouth!'

Captain Jorgensen suddenly threw back his head and laughed. Then he took his purse from his jacket and added five English pounds to the American money. 'Be reasonable, Sally. You says you loves them both, but only one o' them be an owner of your titty!' He paused and spread his hands. 'Now that ain't fair!'

'Nobody owns me titty less they pays for it, and then it be only temporary!' Sperm Whale Sally said, eyeing the money on the table.

Jorgen Jorgensen pointed at his American counterpart. 'The *Merryweather* has got a titty permanent and the *Sturmvogel* ain't! If, as you says, they earned a True Blue the same, then we be entitled to one titty each. Now that be a fair proposition!'

'No!' Sperm Whale Sally shouted. 'And don't call me Sally, that be the privilege o' me friends!'

'Then will you cross it out?' Jorgen Jorgensen snapped back. He made an X in the air with his fingers. 'Svensen can put an X through that name, then the matter be finished and all's fair and square.'

Captain Perriman banged his ebony cane on the table and pointed to Sperm Whale Sally. 'Oh no you don't!' he cried. 'That tattoo on your portside titty belong to us and we ain't giving it up! No ma'am, not now, not never!' Then he turned and glared at the master of the *Sturmvogel*. 'We be rightfully the best ship, captain, and we aims to stay that way!'

The master of the *Sturmvogel* took out his wallet and threw it onto the pile in front of Sperm Whale Sally. 'You said it don't mean nothing, so now I'm paying you to cross it out!'

'Certainly!' Sperm Whale Sally said reaching over and picking up the ten English pounds, and leaving the American ten dollar bill on the table.

Captain Perriman went to his pocket and produced two more ten dollar bills and placed them on the table.

Jorgen Jorgensen matched him with another five pounds. 'Now we fight!' he said.

At that very moment Ikey arrived, pushing his way through the crowd, his basket bouncing on his arm. Sperm Whale Sally saw him coming and threw up her arms and shouted, 'Ikey Solomon, thank Gawd you come! I needs a spruiker what's gunna stop murder happenin'!'

Ikey looked about him and put his basket under the table. 'What's going on? There is nobody nowhere except here, my dear!

The brothels are all closed, the cock fight's over early, all the other public houses be empty.' He pointed to the money on the table. 'Jesus! Who belongs to that?'

Sperm Whale Sally shook her head and quickly whispered the story to Ikey.

'Leave the details to me, my dear. I thinks we're going to be rich before this night be out!' Ikey said and then straightened up. 'It's me rheumatism, lift me up on the table please, my dear,' he requested.

Sperm Whale Sally rose slowly to her feet, and picked him up and placed him on the table.

'Ladies and gentlemen.' Ikey paused and grinned. 'That is if any here has the right to be called by either salutation!' This brought a laugh from the crowd and he waited for it to die down then paced the length of the table as though deep in thought. Finally he lifted his head and addressed the crowd.

'What we has here be a puzzlement and a problem, a bedevilment o' purpose and a contradiction o' temperament, what can be summed up and put together as a conundrum what is not easy to solve, my dears.' He spread out his hands and wiggled his long fingers as though they were groping for an invisible object. 'We got two tits! One what's snowy white and t'other what's got an Indian head and Tomahawk wrote all over it!' He paused to accept the laughter of the crowd. 'One what's occupied and one what's vacant! One what's rented and one what's seeking a tenant. And that be the conundrum!'

Ikey paused and pointed to Tomahawk, who seemed not to have moved a muscle since he'd arrived. 'We have here this most honourable Red Indian gentleman by the name o' Mr Tomahawk! And . . .' he pointed to Black Boss Cape Town, 'the most worthy gentleman of African extraction by name o' Mr Black Boss Cape Town. Both is true blue and much loved by our very own Sperm Whale Sally!'

There was a cheer from the crowd at the mention of Sperm Whale Sally's name followed by some laughter at this amorous *ménage à trois*.

Ikey held his hand up for silence. 'Hands up them who wants to see these two lovely whalemen in a contest o' strength for the gaining o' tenancy to the two most beautiful and imposing and desirable areas o' mammary accommodation in the Pacific Ocean?'

There was a roar from the patrons and, seemingly, the hands of almost all the drinkers shot up. Ikey turned slightly and from the corner of his mouth whispered, 'Count the money, my dear.'

Sperm Whale Sally reached over and gathered up the money. She had long since counted it, but now she pretended to do so again.

'We have here some stiff what could be used as prize money if the two captains here agrees,' Ikey said. The crowd roared their approval and he turned to Jorgen Jorgensen and Blackmouth Perriman. 'What say you, gentlemen?'

They immediately agreed and Ikey turned to Sperm Whale Sally. 'What be the wager, my dear?'

'Fifteen pounds English, thirty Yankee dollars, lovey.' It was enough to feed her for several months and she was filled with consternation that Ikey might be giving it away as the wager.

The crowd gasped, it was a huge amount of money, more than double what a crew member received for a season of whaling. Ikey looked over the heads of the crowd until he saw Michael O'Flaherty. 'Publican! Your presence please!' he called.

Ikey turned and addressed both captains again. 'Michael O'Flaherty be as good a man as ever tapped a barrel of ale, gentlemen. Will you accept him to hold your money? If you do not agree to accept the rules o' the contest, then you shall have every penny back.'

Both captains nodded and O'Flaherty gathered up the money on the table. Ikey held his hand up until he had absolute silence.

'Ladies and gentlemen, as you knows Sperm Whale Sally will not tolerate violence.' He pointed to Tomahawk and Black Boss Cape Town. 'And no harm is to come to her true blue lads.' He paused so the full effect of his pronouncement could be heard. 'So, I now announces a grand contest of Indian arm wrestlin'!'

There was a groan from the crowd. Their minds were intent on the idea of a bloody fight between the two giant savages, and though a contest of arm wrestling would decide equally well who was the superior of the two, there is nothing like the taste of blood to excite a crowd.

Captain Perriman tapped his long stick on the table. 'And what about the money?' he demanded.

Ikey shrugged his shoulders and spread his hands. 'Why, my dear, the winner takes all!'

Sperm Whale Sally looked as though she might faint away and

standing up shakily she slapped at Ikey's ankle. 'Oi! You gorn mad or somethin'?' she said in a loud whisper.

Ikey bent down so that only she could hear his reply. 'Trust me, my dear.' Then he straightened up and addressed the crowd. 'The winner o' the grand arm wrestlin' stakes all his winnings on the second grand contest o' the night!'

'Two contests?' Captain Jorgen Jorgensen asked. 'Why does not one decide?'

'Two grand arm wrestlin' contests!' Ikey replied, ignoring him. 'But first the rules and conditions! If Tomahawk should win then he will be given a chance to enter a second arm wrestlin' challenge, and if he should win this too, then the *Merryweather* tattoo stays!'

There was a roar of approval from the crowd. It meant that the Tomahawk tattoo would be truly earned in virtuous combat.

'If Black Boss Cape Town wins then we crosses out the tattoo and he may challenge again, and if he wins again then he will have a tattoo of the *Sturmvogel* placed upon the breast of Sperm Whale Sally!'

'And if each should win one contest?' Captain Perriman asked.

'That won't be possible, Captain,' Ikey said firmly. 'The second contest will be followed immediately after the first and will be against the wrestlin' arm o' Sperm Whale Sally!'

There was a moment of astonished silence, then the crowd burst into laughter at such an absurd idea. Ikey avoided looking at Sally so he did not see the look of utter dismay on her face. Had she been an integral part of some elaborate scam where she was required to act out her consternation in order to gull her mark, she could not possibly have performed better. She had trusted Ikey and he had caused her to lose a fortune.

Ikey turned to the two masters. 'Are you agreed, gentlemen?'

'That be most fair,' Captain Perriman, the first to recover from the surprise at this absurd idea, replied.

'Aye, it be right by us,' the master of the *Sturmvogel* said, still smiling at the idea of arm wrestling the giant whore.

'Mr O'Flaherty, will you please bring the stools and table for the contest?' Ikey asked. Then he announced to the crowd, 'Ladies and gentlemen, I shall be running a book, though only for your sporting interest, so that some o' the fine gentlemen here tonight might double their money!' He paused and took a breath, 'It's evens I offers on both contestants!'

What this meant, of course, was that Ikey could make no profit from the betting and this was thought most sporting by all, so there was considerable applause. 'One more detail, my dears!' Ikey shouted. 'I shall be offering twenty to one odds on Sperm Whale Sally, and two to one on whoever wins the first contest! As this contest will take place immediately after the first you should lay your bets for both now!'

There was a general guffaw. Had the odds even been two hundred to one placed on Sperm Whale Sally, only a fool would have ventured a shilling on the likelihood of her winning. But the chance of doubling their money on either Black Boss Cape Town or Tomahawk was a most attractive proposition. It is a testimony to greed that, in a room full of cut throats and thieves, no one paused to suspect Ikey's motives or ask how he would pay his bets if Sperm Whale Sally lost.

Meanwhile, Sperm Whale Sally was quite beside herself. 'You'll not count me in on the betting, Ikey Solomon!' she said, her voice fraught with anxiety. 'I can't cover no losses.'

'Has I ever let you down in the past, my dear? Have you not profited gloriously in our mutual dealings?'

'Ha! That were before! But now I thinks you've gorn *meshugannah*! We've lost all that lovely money, now you's making barmy bets and I'm gunna end up with some bastard writin' all over me tits with a bloody needle!'

'Trust me, my dear, leave it all to your Uncle Ikey! At worst, maybe a little scratch on your titty. But there be a lot o' stiff to be won.' He paused and added, 'That reminds me, my dear, naturally we goes fifty-fifty with the winnings?'

'What bleedin' winnin's! You just gave the bloody money back to them two bastards!' She stabbed a finger in the direction of the ships' masters. 'You said winner takes all!'

'Only temporarily, my dear. Only for the Irishman to hold so everything looks kosher, above board, and exceedingly honest, and not to be doubted. In truth *our* winnings, my dear? Do you agree, fifty-fifty?'

'Jesus!' Sperm Whale Sally threw up her hands. 'Yes! Fifty-fifty o' fuck all! 'Elp your bleedin' self!' She looked as though she might cry. 'Ikey, how am I gunna arm wrestle one o' them monsters?'

'Now don't you fret, my dear, it be so easy it ain't even a proper scam worthy o' my intelligence!'

The table and stools were set in place for the contest, and the two giants made to take their seats. Michael O'Flaherty was given the role as the referee and the two masters were appointed as judges.

The rules of arm wrestling are universal and simple enough. The first man to push the back of the hand of his opponent to the table and hold it there for a count of three would be declared the winner. Ten minutes was allowed for the two contestants to tune up their muscles by building up a proper resistance against the arms of members of their own crew.

Ikey used the time to make book and as he expected, after each punter had bet on his favourite, he bet his winnings to continue on the winner of the first bout so that not a single bet was placed on Sperm Whale Sally.

Two glasses of fiery Cape brandy were brought and placed in front of Tomahawk and Black Boss Cape Town. Tomahawk had not uttered a word all evening and his silence, contrasted with the ebullient black man, had made him the favourite to win, the strength of silence being reckoned greater than the force of bombast.

Black Boss Cape Town lifted the brandy in his left hand, and bending his right arm showed his huge bicep to the crowd. 'We fight!' he said looking directly at Tomahawk and then threw back his head and tossed down the fiery drink in one gulp.

Tomahawk picked up his glass and for the very first time he looked at the huge black savage seated opposite him. 'You die, nigger!' he said and he too tossed down his brandy.

Black Boss Cape Town smiled and placed his glass down and reached out and patted Tomahawk on the top of his head. 'Goet boy!'

The Red Indian shot up from his stool and grabbed the throat of the huge black man. But Black Boss Cape Town had anticipated the move and his own hand moving from Tomahawk's head simultaneously clasped around the throat of the American savage. Then Tomahawk's left hand, still holding the brandy glass, slammed down on the edge of the table and in a flash the raw edge of the broken glass smashed into the face of his opponent. A huge crimson arc appeared under Black Boss Cape Town's eye as the jet black skin of his face opened up.

Black Boss Cape Town did not appear to flinch nor even

lighten his grip on Tomahawk's throat, but his left fist swung around and smashed against the side of Tomahawk's face. A great hammer blow which felled the Red Indian. The big black pushed the table over and raised his boot to kick Tomahawk in the face when he was suddenly jerked backwards off his feet by a huge arm which gripped him about the neck in a wrestler's stranglehold. Thrown off balance, he could do nothing as Sperm Whale Sally's arm tightened about his throat.

'Now, now, there's a good gentleman, we'll have none o' that!' she hissed into his ear. She held Black Boss Cape Town in a lethal grip as the crew of the *Merryweather* hurried to pull the bewildered Tomahawk to his feet. Sperm Whale Sally increased her grip on Black Boss Cape Town and addressed the two startled captains. 'You will have your men arm wrestle or not at all, there will be no fights, do you understand, gentlemen?'

Black Boss Cape Town was near to fainting from the pressure she applied and should he have tried to regain his feet his neck would have snapped like a twig. Both captains nodded and Sperm Whale Sally spoke to her captive. 'Do you understand, Mr Black Boss Cape Town?'

An almost imperceptible sound came from the black man's throat. 'Bring me some sea sponges, Bridget!' she shouted towards the bar. 'And a bucket o' salt water!' She turned to Black Boss Cape Town. 'Sit down, lad, lemme fix your ugly gob!' Then Sperm Whale Sally released the huge harpooner from her deadly grip and pushed him into her whale's tail chair. 'Be there a doctor?' she shouted as she took a sponge from Bridget and applied pressure to the wound on Black Boss Cape Town's face.

It was not unusual for a member of the medical profession, either surgeon or dentist, to be present in a public house. And in a few moments, Surgeon Balthasar Tompkins stepped from the crowd and waddled towards where Sally sat. It was obvious he was somewhat the worse for wear and he rocked on his heels as he examined Black Boss Cape Town's face.

'Horsehair!' he bellowed. 'Horsehair and needle!'

In a few moments his young male assistant appeared carrying a bag and it was he who appeared to be doing all the work. But then he handed the needle and horsehair to the physician, who stitched the wound with surprising dexterity, neatly snipping each knot as he worked.

Throughout the procedure Black Boss Cape Town remained calm, only flinching slightly during the suturing. Finally the fat physician completed the task and Sperm Whale Sally wiped what remained of the blood from his face. It was a crude enough job, but it held well and there had not been sufficient blood loss for Black Boss Cape Town to have lost any of his strength.

At that moment Ikey's small frightened face appeared from under Sperm Whale Sally's Tasmanian oak table and, seeing all was well again, he emerged completely and assumed a nonchalant position.

'The bets are laid. The Indian arm wrestle contest be still on!' he shouted at Michael O'Flaherty. 'What say you, gentlemen?'

The crowd yelled their approval, and the two ships' masters glanced at each other and after a few moments nodded their consent. Ikey breathed a huge sigh of relief. He felt quite weak at the knees at the thought of losing the money.

The two men walked slowly back to the stools. 'To your positions, please,' O'Flaherty called. The Irishman held up a large red bandanna. 'Take the strain. Go!' he shouted, dropping the cloth.

The two men's arms stiffened as they took the strain, one then the other making his play. Pressure was slowly applied which would bend one arm close to the surface of the table while the onlookers screamed their encouragement to the man on whom they had placed their bet. Sweat fell from their faces and chests, and the linen of their coarse shirts was soaked through, but still there was no advantage to either. Sometimes they would rest in the centre, and then one would try a sudden lunge to catch the other by surprise. But while both came close to victory, neither could lay the other's hand down upon the table.

After forty minutes it was obvious that the strength was leaching from both men, though it appeared that Tomahawk was gradually gaining the advantage. The Red Indian was the younger man and, in the end, it seemed he would prove the stronger. The muscles on both their arms strained mightily, and at one point the biceps of Black Boss Cape Town started to cramp and he knew he must surely lose. The strain as he held his opponent's arm was so intense that the blood started to pump from between the sutures on his face and run down his cheek. Then, just as he felt his strength finally deserting him, the Red Indian's eyes suddenly filled with pain as he, too, was gripped by a violent muscle spasm and his huge biceps convulsed and his nose started to bleed copiously.

Still they held on, the Indian forcing the black man's hand almost to the table top, before it would be slowly lifted, each movement greatly taxing both wrestlers. The punters had taken to screaming with each turnabout as though, by their voices alone, they could add strength to the man they had backed.

Finally Tomahawk began to sense he had the black man's measure. The front of both their shirts was now drenched with blood as well as sweat. Beads of perspiration shone in the crinkly hair of Black Boss Cape Town, and the smooth dark hair of his opponent lay soaked against his coppery skin. Slowly, agonisingly slowly, Tomahawk worked his opponent's arm, forcing it towards the surface of the table. Black Boss Cape Town's hand was no more than an inch from the table when he spat into Tomahawk's face.

The shock was so great that the giant Red Indian lost control, and Black Boss forced his hand back to the upright position, and then over to the other side so that Tomahawk's hand was now only an inch from the table on the African's side.

Suddenly there rose in Tomahawk's throat a cry that seemed to come from deep within his belly as the black man's bloody spittle ran down his face. His eyes burned in his head as his hand rose and rose, pushing the negro's fist to the upright position and then slowly down, until, with a second great wail, he smashed the top of Black Boss Cape Town's hand onto the table. It was all over. Tomahawk had won the contest, though both men were too exhausted to lift their heads, and their arms lay limp and useless on the table.

Sperm Whale Sally moved across to where Tomahawk sat and gently raised his head. With a wet sea sponge she wiped his face clean. Then she did the same for Black Boss Cape Town, wiping the blood from his cheek. 'You both true blue, both my good lads!'

Ikey had somehow climbed back onto the table, and now he began to wave his hands and shout until the pandemonium ceased. 'I can't make no payment on the bets until the contest be complete!' Finally the crowd noise calmed down sufficiently for him to be heard. 'Tomahawk be the declared winner o' the first contest, now he must arm wrestle against Sperm Whale Sally!' He turned to the master of the *Sturmvogel*. 'Please captain, move your man!' Ikey pointed at the black man.

493

'Ikey! Whatever are you doing? These boys be exhausted,' Sperm Whale Sally shouted up at him.

'Yes, yes indeed, my dear, we must hurry, sit, sit, there is no time to waste!'

Sally suddenly realised what Ikey was up to, and as quickly as possible for someone her size, adjusted her massive bottom upon the vacated stool opposite Tomahawk.

'Will you get your hand up now, lad!' Michael O'Flaherty said to the exhausted and bewildered Red Indian.

Tomahawk raised his hand and Sperm Whale Sally grabbed it and held it steady while both their elbows were pressed down on the table.

'Lady and gentleman, take your positions, please! May the best, er . . . contestant win.' O'Flaherty again held up the red bandanna. 'Take the strain. Go!'

Tomahawk had regained a surprising amount of strength in the few minutes he'd been allowed to rest and tried to force his opponent's hand down in one great effort. This was a big mistake. Sperm Whale Sally's hand dipped and then lowered almost to the surface of the table, but there it held, draining the Red Indian of all his remaining strength, then she forced it back to the upright position and started to push downwards. As publican of the Pig 'n Spit she had been required to stack and lift beer barrels on the full, and her fat was deceptive. She was very strong. What new strength Tomahawk had recovered was entirely spent on his first onslaught and not five minutes later Sperm Whale Sally slammed the back of the exhausted harpooner's hand onto the table.

It was a fitting ending. For generations whalers would tell the story of how the two greatest harpooners in the world had fought for the right to challenge the spirit of the great sperm whale. How after a great fight lasting several hours, between two of the strongest men in the world, the American Red Indian had won over the African giant. Then he pitted himself against the spirit of the great whale and was crushed in less than ten minutes. But the spirit of the great sperm whale would never desert them, nor any of the ships that flew the Blue Sally. But the greatest of the catch seemed always to go to the *Merryweather* and the *Sturmvogel*. Or so the legend goes.

It was all over. Ikey and Sperm Whale Sally had made a killing. Not only did they possess the money from both the *Merryweather* and the *Sturmvogel*, but they cleared nearly twenty pounds on the bets placed by the drinkers. Ikey could not remember when he had enjoyed himself as much, though he was a trifle disappointed when Sperm Whale Sally insisted that they buy drinks for the crews of both ships. Then to much shouting, joshing and general banter, Sperm Whale Sally bared her left titty and allowed Svensen, the tattoo artist from the *Sturmvogel*, to tattoo an X, cancelling the name Tomahawk.

'It be better this way, my lovies,' Sperm Whale Sally announced to the crew members who stood around her. 'Now you both be equal true blue! Both be equally blessed by the great good luck o' the spirit o' the sperm whale!' She paused, for she could see that the men from the *Merryweather* did not look altogether happy with this pronouncement and seemed reluctant to accept her blessing. 'One more thing be essential if we is to repair what happened tonight,' she announced solemnly. 'If you wishes to keep the luck o' the great sperm, you must do the spirit a final bidding.' She looked at Black Boss Cape Town and then at Tomahawk. 'You two must shake hands. Make peace the pair of you! You has broken your luck with your hatred and there is only one way to regain it. You must be friends.' She grinned and waited a moment and then said, 'As friends, together you must beach the whale tonight!'

There was a sudden howl of approval from both crews as the tension between them dissolved and they began to shake hands and drink to the health and happy hunting of both ships. Black Boss Cape Town extended his hand to Tomahawk, who took it and smiled, 'Good man!' he said. Black Boss Cape Town threw back his head and laughed. 'We fight!' he boomed happily, toasting the giant Red Indian.

Sperm Whale Sally took both giants by the hand and led them out of the Whale Fishery and into the dark towards the small beach that lay not fifty yards away.

The moon had climbed to its zenith, a bright silver coin suspended high above the great mountain. A million stars pricked a sky now closer to morning than to midnight. As Sperm Whale Sally sat upon the soft sand, a gentle wave washed into shore and she waited for the sound of it to retreat before she pointed to the giant African.

'Black Boss Cape Town, you be first and don't squeeze me left titty, it be most tender!' She laughed and then turned her head towards the Red Indian. 'You follow quick, Tomahawk. It must be done quick, the one after t'other, so the spirit o' the great sperm whale will reach you both in equal portion, and bring you the same great good luck in the next whalin' season!'

Sperm Whale Sally sighed and lifted her skirts above her gargantuan thighs. 'Jesus, I be starvin' hungry,' she thought as she fell on her back into the soft sand and watched the stars. 'The things a girl has to do to make a shillin'! I hope that bastard O'Flaherty ain't cancelled tonight's Blue Sally challenge, or I'll be obliged to eat both these bloody savages!' She guffawed inwardly at the notion as the shape of Black Boss Cape Town blotted out the moon. 'Oh Gawd, 'ere we goes again,' she thought. 'Lie back and think of a nice little pot roast, my girl!'

Chapter Thirty-three

The scam which Ikey perpetrated on the evening that Tomahawk and Black Boss Cape Town met became quite famous and was known among the local wags as the glorious night of 'Tit for Tat'. This incident had further enhanced the legend of Sperm Whale Sally and made the acquisition of a Blue Sally talisman even more desirable among the men of the whaling fleet. But it also served to benefit Ikey's own career. He was soon invited to become involved in the local gambling scene, in particular, in the sport of horse racing, which was just then becoming popular in the colony.

Ikey could now be seen at the horse races on a Saturday afternoon where he set up in a small way as an on-course bookmaker, but this did not curtail his nocturnal wandering. It was still his custom to perambulate from one waterfront dive to the next selling his tobacco, and he always finished up at the Whale Fishery to spend the last hour of each night in contented conversations with Sperm Whale Sally, happily recalling old times.

Ikey would sip at a glass of well-watered rum and Sperm Whale Sally would nurse her final quart pot of Bitter Rosie for the night. It was a time when Ikey felt almost like his old self, for Sperm Whale Sally never treated him any differently and did not seem to notice or care about his change in fortune. They were two old friends with a common past, content to be in each other's company, whether silent or merry, both calmed by the presence of the other after a loud and tiring night on the waterfront.

At the end of their hour together, around five of the clock in the morning, and with the help of four cellarmen from the Whale Fishery and Ikey's own puny contribution, which consisted mostly of meddlesome instructions, Sperm Whale Sally was lifted and manoeuvred and finally loaded into a waiting cart and transported by her driver Dick Smith to her rooms in Wapping scarcely half a mile away. Whereupon Ikey would make his way up the hill to the Potato Factory where, half an hour before sunrise, he would habitually take the first meal of the day with Mary.

Both Ikey and Sperm Whale Sally, the former as thin as a rake and plagued by rheumatism, and the other grown even larger than she had been on the night of the tit for tat scam some nine months previously, enjoyed rude good health by the standards of the day. They could be utterly relied upon to be a part of every Hobart night, but for Sunday, when the public houses were closed for the Sabbath.

Ikey therefore felt some concern when he arrived as usual at the Whale Fishery at four o'clock on the morning of the third Tuesday in November to find Sperm Whale Sally absent.

'Where be Mistress Sally?' Ikey asked a cellarman named Orkney, who was sweeping the spent sawdust from the floor. The Whale Fishery was almost empty, with only a handful of whalers still at the bar. Four drunken sailors sat slumped with their heads in their arms over various tables around the room, and two lay unconscious on the floor among the spew, piss and spilt ale. Orkney stopped sweeping and looked about the room.

'She be here earlier, guv, but be gorn a good hour since.'

'What, home?' Ikey queried in surprise.

'I expects not, guv, there were no cart.' He continued his sweeping, clearly having no more to add to the conversation.

Ikey walked over to the long bar where a weary Bridget was washing and stacking pewter tankards along the counter.

'Where be Mistress Sally, Bridget?' Ikey asked again.

The barmaid glanced over to Sperm Whale Sally's customary spot. 'Well I'll be blessed! She were there to be sure an' all, I seen 'er meself, I took 'er a quart pot o' bitter not a half hour since.' Bridget thought for a moment. 'Mind, she were off 'er grub tonight, I don't believe she ate more'n a couple o' legs o' mutton.

Weren't no whaler gentleman eating neither, she paid for 'er victuals 'erself.' Noting the concerned look on Ikey's face, she smiled. 'Don't fret, Ikey love, she most probably just gorn outside to do a bit o' woman's business, if you knows what I mean.' Then she added, 'I seems to recall she said she 'ad a bit of a stomach ache an' all.'

Bridget took down a small pewter tankard, filled it to a third of its volume from a small casket of rum and then topped it almost to the brim with water. 'Here you are then, Ikey, your usual.' She smiled and in a comforting voice added, 'Now you sit down, Ikey Solomon. Your friend Sally be back soon with no 'arm done I expects.'

Ikey sat in the flagging chair until Orkney had almost completed sweeping the large expanse of the floor. He pushed the foul sawdust into a large pile which blocked the doorway. This was a signal to anyone seeking a last drink before dawn that they were not welcome to enter. A good hour had elapsed since Ikey's arrival, which meant Sperm Whale Sally had been gone at the very least two hours by the cellarman's earlier reckoning.

'She must have gorn 'ome!' Bridget called over several times. Two of the barmaids who had been clearing up the kitchen had meanwhile been consulted, but both confessed they had not seen Sperm Whale Sally leave.

'It be half a mile to Wapping,' Ikey pointed out. 'She can't walk 'alf a mile home and it takes four people to lift her into a carriage, my dear.' Ikey was irritated at their apparent lack of concern. 'You would have seen her go if she'd been picked up by Dick Smith, besides, he always stops in for a pint before they leaves, don't he?'

Bridget was too tired to respond with any further sympathy and simply shrugged. 'She'll be back, I expects.' Ikey rose from the chair and, slinging his tobacco basket over his arm, asked Bridget for one of the lanterns which hung from the wall behind her.

'I'm going to take a look,' he announced.

'We'll be closing in half an hour,' Bridget said as she unhooked a lantern and handed it to Ikey. 'You be sure and bring it back, Ikey Solomon! Leave it at the back door. Mister O'Flaherty will dock me pay if it don't come back, 'e be most strict about not taking down no lamps from the wall!'

Ikey only grunted, upset that they did not share his concern for Sperm Whale Sally. He stepped gingerly through the pile of putrid sawdust at the door and walked out into the last vestiges of the night. It was half past four of the clock, with the sunrise less than an hour away.

The late spring night was cool, as it always is an hour before dawn, and a chill breeze blew in from the hills across the Derwent River. Ikey searched the dark corners and alleys along the waterfront, and checked under the hulls of two fishing boats pulled up onto a slip for scraping. Then he moved towards the small, dark beach where the doxies took sailors for 'sixpenny quick times' and which Sperm Whale Sally herself used for the consummation of a Blue Sally.

The beach was deserted. Ikey's boots squeaked as he trudged along the sand towards a wooden fisherman's jetty which ran some distance out into the river. Even when the tide was in, a small ramp built over a pipeline directly below the jetty provided a dry platform where drunks would sometimes take shelter from the rain. It was not a good place to sleep as the pipelines carried the entrails, fish heads and scales from a public fish market into the cove, and was notorious for the bravery of the rats who infested it at night when the tide was out. Many a sailor or hapless drunkard, falling into a stupor, had woken in the morning to find half an ear or nose missing, or his toes a gory, bloody mess where the rats had chewed through his leather boots.

Ikey stopped just short of the jetty and placed his basket on the sand. Then he climbed up onto the dark platform, which stank of rotting fish. The lantern cast only a small circle of light and he could hear the rats squeaking and see their darting black shadows as they scurried from the lighted perimeter back into the darkness.

Ikey was not repulsed by the stench or the rats. Rats were not only an integral part of the gaming ring, but an everyday occurrence in Ikey's life. In the rookeries of London rats and foul smells were a given, hardly to be remarked upon.

He moved deeper into the darkest part of the jetty so that the light from his lantern cast a wider glow. What he saw almost made his heart stop beating. A dozen rats sat on the giant shape of Sperm Whale Sally, who lay grotesquely huge and still upon the platform. Ikey let out a terrible moan, for he knew instantly that she was dead.

The rats scuttled away as Ikey plunged forward, missing his footing to land on his knees beside the giant shape of Sperm Whale

Sally. Overcome with grief, he laid his head on Marybelle Firkin's cold breast and started to wail.

'Wake up!' he called desperately time and time again, shaking Sperm Whale Sally's massive shoulder. 'Wake up please, my dear!' Ikey sobbed wildly, the intensity of his grief totally unfamiliar to him. After a long while, he gradually became possessed of his wits again and he slowly recited the words of the Jewish prayer for the dead, even though he knew his friend was not of the Jewish faith.

Not since the departure of Billygonequeer had Ikey felt such a terrible loss and now he lay panting on the sand, too weak even to resolve to rise to his knees. People are people through other people; we constantly seek confirmation of our own existence by how we relate to others. In losing Sperm Whale Sally, Ikey was losing a part of both his present and his past. Only two people in his life had neither judged him nor made demands on him: Billygonequeer and Marybelle Firkin. They had accepted him for what he was and in doing so they had defined a softer, more vulnerable Ikey no one else knew. Both had given his life meaning beyond sheer greed and survival, and now both were gone. Ikey had lost more than two friends, he had lost himself; the Prince of Fences was finally dead.

Only Mary Abacus remained. Yet Mary, with her thriving business and her ambition, was growing more and more impatient with him. Ikey knew she now thought him an old man who argued too much and who had little of value to offer her.

The death of Marybelle Firkin filled Ikey with a terrible fear. He thought of himself dying, quite alone, with no one to mourn him and not even a minyan of ten good Jews to lay him properly to rest.

It was at this moment of his own extreme anxiety that he heard the mewling cry of an infant. At first he thought it to be the rats grown bold and moving closer, or some creature crying out in the night. But soon it came again, faint, muffled, but close at hand. Ikey rose unsteadily and held the lantern above the body of Sperm Whale Sally. One side of her bodice had been pulled away so that a great breast lay exposed. It was as if she had been in pain and had ripped at her bodice in some sudden agony. Above the surprisingly small areola of her pink nipple Ikey saw the tattoo of the Indian chief's head and the word Tomahawk crossed through with the blue X, which Svensen of the *Sturmvogel* had tattooed to cancel its potency as the symbol of the *Merryweather*.

501

Ikey now saw that her dress was soaked in blood, and that the pathetic whimpering sounds came from below her blood-stained skirt.

He quickly sought the hem of her skirt and petticoat and gingerly pulled them over her thighs. Something was moving beneath the sodden cloth and, expecting rats, he jerked the material upwards. What an astonished Ikey saw squirming between the gigantic thighs, were two newborn infants. He gasped, reeling back in shock, and it took a moment for him to recover sufficiently to take a closer look. The tiny bodies were sticky with blood, but he saw that one was the reddish white of any newborn child, while the other was black as the devil himself.

Ikey's heart commenced to beat rapidly, thumping in his chest as though it might jump entirely from his person, for he could see that both infants were alive, their tiny fists tightly clenched and their little legs kicking at the stinking air about them. Each was still attached to the umbilical cord, and from the black one's mouth popped tiny bubbles of spittle. Ikey reached inside his coat and pulled out a length of twine and a small knife he used for cutting plugs of tobacco for his customers. He cut the twine into two pieces about six inches long, tied off the umbilical cord at the base of each tiny navel aperture and then, some six inches higher, severed each of the bloody cords with the sharp blade. He had witnessed this procedure in a hundred netherkens in the rookeries of London where birth was often enough a public occurrence, and onlookers were charged a halfpenny for the privilege of attendance. But he was nevertheless surprised at how well he was coping with this startling emergency.

With this messy task completed, Ikey walked to the water's edge and washed the blood from his hands and from the blade of his knife, then retrieved the basket from where he had left it on the beach. He hastily emptied it by stuffing what remained of the contents into a dozen or so of the pockets in the lining of his coat.

The sun had started to rise and the body of Marybelle Firkin was now clearly visible in the dawn light. Ikey closed his friend's beautiful blue eyes. Then he removed the cloth which lined his tobacco basket, picked up each tiny infant and placed them carefully inside the basket.

The moment they were lifted the babies began to scream and Ikey panicked and swung the basket one way and then another as if it were a cradle. 'Shssh . . . shssh,' he repeated several times. But when the crying continued he placed the basket down on the sand and instantly a dozen or more flies settled on the babies, attracted by the blood which still covered them. He picked up the cloth and flapped it to set the flies to flight, then covered the basket. To his surprise, the crying stopped. Ikey hastily pulled the hems of Marybelle Firkin's bloody petticoat and skirt back down to her ankles, and covered her exposed breast with the torn bodice. Then, squinting into the early morning sun, he took up his basket and trudged heavily back along the beach towards the Whale Fishery.

It was completely light when Ikey passed the front door of the public house which was now firmly shut, the last of the drunks and drinkers having been evicted. Ikey walked around the back and left the lantern on the back doorstep. He checked the basket, lifting a corner of the cloth to see that both tiny infants seemed to have fallen asleep, and as quickly as his human burden allowed, made his way up the hill to the Potato Factory where he knew Mary Abacus would be long awake, grown impatient and somewhat cantankerous that he was late.

Ikey tried to picture Mary's surprise. She would, he knew, have cleaned the cold ashes from the hearth, set and lit a new fire and then taken the pot of oats which had been left to soak all night on the shelf above and hung it over the flames to boil. Small beer and a loaf of yesterday's bread would be waiting for him on the table, the meal they shared together every morning when he arrived back from what Mary called his 'caterwauling'. But today would be different and Ikey smiled to himself, not thinking for a moment that Mary might not take kindly to the gift of life he carried in the basket so innocently slung over his arm.

Ikey entered the gate to the Potato Factory and passed down the side of the old mill building to the rear where a small wooden annexe had been built. This contained an accounting office Ikey himself used in the evenings, Mary's bedroom, and the kitchen in which they ate, all facing onto a backyard piled high with beer casks, and which led directly down to the rivulet. The kitchen door was open, and he entered to see Mary stirring the pot of oatmeal porridge with a long-handled wooden spoon.

'Don't turn about, my dear, I have a surprise.'

'Humph! The best surprise you could give me, Ikey Solomon, would be to be on time!' Mary sniffed the air without looking up from the pot and brought her finger and thumb to her nose. 'And the next is to wash! Wherever you 'as been, you stinks worse than ever this morning!'

Ikey ignored her remarks and continued in a merry voice. 'A surprise what is a wish and a desire and a whole life of hopes and dreaming! A surprise what surpasses all other surprises and a delight you never thought you'd experience, my dear!' Ikey started to do a small jig in the doorway.

Mary was not accustomed to mirth from Ikey at such an early hour, and now turned at last towards him. 'Is you drunk, Ikey Solomon?' She placed her hands on her hips, still holding the porridge spoon. 'Surprise is it? No surprises if you please. Sit down and eat. I have a long busy day to begin, while you be soon snoring your head off!'

While she often talked in such a stern manner to Ikey, Mary's remonstrations were seldom intended to be hurtful. She looked forward to his presence first thing in the morning, for he often brought with him bits of juicy gossip passed on by the servants of the pure merinos and the uppercrust in Hobart Town society. Mary had little time to listen to gossip during the day and Ikey often brought her both merriment and useful information.

'Come and see, my dear, come and see what Ikey has brought for you!' The excitement was apparent in his voice as he took three paces towards Mary and then, like a magician at a country fair, whipped away the cloth from the top of his tobacco basket.

Mary reeled backwards, dropping the spoon, her hands clawing at her breasts. 'Oh Jesus! Oh Gawd! What 'ave you done?' she cried.

Ikey laughed and took another step towards her so that Mary now looked directly into the basket. 'This little one be Tommo!' he said, pointing to the tiny pink creature in the basket, then his long dirty index finger moved to the opposite end. 'And this big little 'un be Hawk! A black child to bring you luck and great good fortune, my dear!' Ikey turned and placed the basket on the table. 'What say you, Mary Abacus, my dear?'

The names of the two infants had come to him without any thought, though later he would congratulate himself at the clever notion of splitting the word tattooed on Marybelle Firkin's breast.

Mary was not naturally given to panic and now she again placed her poor broken hands on her hips and looked most sternly at Ikey. 'Ikey Solomon, I hopes you has a very, very good explanation!' she shouted. But while her expression was grim, her heart was beating fast as her mind raced to embrace the notion of keeping the two infants. 'Dear God, how could such a thing be possible?' she said inwardly, her thoughts a whirl of confusion and hope. 'Where? How? Whose be they?' she demanded of Ikey.

Ikey placed the basket on the table and calmly breaking a piece of bread off the stale loaf popped it into his mouth. 'Why, they's yours, my dear!' he said, beginning to chew. He explained to Mary what had occurred. 'Nobody knowed that Sperm Whale Sally were pregnant, my dear, it be possible that she herself did not know,' Ikey concluded.

'Ha! When they find her they'll know!' Mary replied, now somewhat recovered, then she added, 'What about the afterbirth?'

Ikey swallowed the crust he was chewing. Already the terrible private grief he felt at Marybelle Firkin's death was hidden completely from view. 'Rats, my dear, there be scores o' rats by the fish pipe. By now there will be precious little o' the birth bits left. They'll think she been gorn an' haemorrhaged, you know, internal like, and that be the cause o' her death. The coroner ain't going to look too close, she were a whore after all! Natural causes, my dear, that be what he'll say. With twice as much government money to be spent on a double-sized pauper's coffin he won't want no further complications or expenses!'

'She'll be buried proper, Ikey, in St David's burial ground. You'll see to that!' Mary instructed. She ran her hand across her flat stomach. 'But it don't solve nothing. How did I give birth to twins overnight when yesterday I weren't even pregnant?'

'Left on the doorstep, my dear,' Ikey said blandly. 'The men and young Jessamy, they'll stay stum, or even believe it if you say that be how it happened! Plenty o' whores don't want their newborn brats.' Ikey shrugged his thin shoulders. 'You are well known for your charity at the orphanage.' Ikey paused and looked directly at Mary, his scraggy right eyebrow slightly arched. 'O' course, my dear, if you don't want them two, I could always take them off to the foundling home and tell them there what happened this morning.'

Mary gasped. 'You'll do no such thing, Ikey Solomon! That be a death sentence – more newborn brats dies in the Foundlin' than lives to see their first week!' This was true. The first hour of almost every day saw Reverend Smedley officiating at the burial of foundling infants who had not survived their first few days at the home.

Mary had not taken her eyes off the two tiny babies and now she lifted the black one Ikey had named Hawk out of the basket and held him against her bosom. Hawk's tiny mouth, feeling the skin of her neck against his lips, started to suck. That was all it took for Mary to fall utterly and completely in love. 'Give me t'other, Ikey,' she begged, her voice grown suddenly soft. Ikey plucked Tommo from the basket and laid him against her other breast where he too started to suck at the side of her neck. Mary knew, with a sudden, fierce happiness, that she would let no one take her new-found children from her.

Mary looked up at Ikey and tears gathered in her eyes. 'Thank you, Ikey,' she said tenderly. 'Thank you, my love.' Then Mary kissed the fine, matted hair on the infants' tiny heads and started to weep softly. She carried Tommo and Hawk into her bedroom, wrapped each of them in a blanket and placed them in the centre of her narrow bed. She told herself she must prepare hot water to wash away the blood, and tie down their little belly buttons with a strip of linen, then find two good wet nurses from the Female Factory. But for the moment all she could think to do as she looked down at the tiny creatures wrapped in the blanket was to clutch the Waterloo medal around her neck so tightly that the edges of the small medallion cut into the skin of her clenched fist. She turned to the window where the early sun touched the craggy top of the great mountain. 'Please,' she begged softly. 'Please let me keep them! Let them be mine forever!'

After a while she stopped crying and released her grasp on the medal. In the centre of her misshapen hand was a small cut where the edge of the medallion had punctured the skin, and from it oozed a bright drop of blood. Mary, not quite understanding what she was doing, dipped her forefinger into the blood and then returned to where the infants lay on the bed and touched the tip of her bloodied finger to their foreheads, first Tommo, then Hawk.

'You be my life's blood,' she cried. 'You be my everything, I shall never let you go!'

Chapter Thirty-four

For nearly four years Mary had been processing her own malt in her malthouse at Strickland Falls, crushing and preparing the barley mash using the power from the water mill she had constructed. At last she had the money to erect the first of her brewery buildings and to begin work on the chimney stack which would eventually be required. The chimney needed bricks and the skill of a master builder, so it could only be constructed a small section at a time as money became available. The other buildings were made of stone quarried on her own property. Mary's plan was that one day the quarry would become a small lake to store water for the brewery and lend further beauty to the woodland surroundings.

She still lacked the means to create a complete commercial brewery and it seemed unlikely that she would ever possess them. The steam turbines and huge fermenting vats and giant casks she required to compete against the likes of Peter Degraves' modern Cascade Brewery needed the kind of finance she could only hope to raise with a wealthy partner.

It was not a prosperous time in the colony. Several of the smaller banks had collapsed and more than half of the free colonists were insolvent. The Bank of Van Diemen's Land would not readily invest in emancipists, particularly women, unless they had assets to secure the loan well in excess of the amount they wished to borrow. While there were private investors which a sharp lawyer might find in England, they usually demanded a controlling interest and Mary was determined that she would never allow anyone to threaten her independence.

The new buildings gave her the capacity to make much larger quantities of beer using the crystal-clear water that flowed from the falls. Furthermore, using time-honoured methods, she knew she would eventually own a small complete brewery which produced ale of a very high quality.

Though Mary was not considered a serious threat to any of the larger breweries, her Temperance Ale and Bitter Rosella had earned a reputation in the colony for their quality and some of the public houses not tied to the mainstream breweries now accepted Bitter Rosie by the barrel, which was a major boost to her production. In the past she had relied on supplying her beer in jugs brought by the purchaser, or in bottles. This had severely curtailed her output, for glass was a scarce commodity almost entirely imported from England.

However, it was through the production of bottled beer that Mary was to make her reputation. Ikey's nocturnal habits and excellent nose for gossip meant he was always the first to know what was contained in the manifest of any ship arriving into port. If there should be a consignment of bottles on board Mary instantly knew about it and purchased the lot before other merchants were any the wiser. She would also buy any bottles the ship used during the voyage, and many a ship's master knew her as Queen Bottle. In addition, any urchin who could lay his dirty little hands on a bottle knew it would fetch him a halfpenny at the Potato Factory.

Soon Mary had sufficient capital to order from England her first consignment of green quart beer bottles, which she used for her Temperance Ale, and so the Potato Factory became the first brewery to offer its product in sealed bottles to be consumed in the home. This meant that working folk, who could not afford to buy beer by the barrel, could purchase their beer not, as was the custom, by the jug, so that they had to hurry home in haste to keep the benefit of its good, creamy head, but in a sealed bottle to be enjoyed at their leisure.

The other brewers sneered at this nonsensical notion. They

sold their beer in barrels to be consumed in public houses, and those who wished to take it home could bring their jugs to the ale house to be filled. They felt certain that quantities as small as a quart sold in expensive glass bottles would never catch on with the poor, who were the largest portion of the population who drank beer. They also thought Mary's Temperance Ale label another silly affectation as paper was relatively expensive, and a label on a bottle of three-penny beer was regarded as an outrageous waste.

Although Mary was prepared to take a lower profit for her beer by bottling and labelling it, she would not compromise on its quality. The people of Hobart Town, and those who lived further out in the country, immediately saw the benefits of what they called 'picnic beer', which could be transported in small quantities and drunk at leisure.

People soon realised that while they initially paid an extra halfpenny for the bottle, if they returned the empty for another full one they paid only the usual price of threepence for their beer. Furthermore, if they wished to surrender an empty bottle without buying an additional bottle of beer, Mary refunded the halfpenny they'd paid on the original deposit.

Soon Mary was selling all the beer she could make, and it was only the lack of glass bottles which prevented her from selling more. Thus Mary invented the concept of bottled beer with a paper label to indicate its quality and brand which would in time become commonplace on mainland Australia.

Six years had passed since Mary had been granted her unconditional pardon, and she now found herself welcomed into the society of tradesmen, clerks and the free settlers of smaller means who were collectively known as third raters. As an emancipist Mary rightfully belonged two social ranks further down the ladder. But her great business success, ardent support of the Temperance Society, stubborn courage against the beer barons and quiet manners, together with her charitable work for the orphanage, elevated her to the lofty heights of the third social position in the class ranking of the colony, this, despite the knowledge that she employed the odious Isaac Solomon, whom it was rumoured as common scandal had once been her paramour.

Any other woman of Mary's dubious background would have greatly cherished this unexpected promotion to the better classes. Hannah, for instance, would have made much of the opportunity.

But Mary was far too busy to profit from the social advantages of her newly acquired status. This was just as well, for it was soon enough to be taken away from her.

Before long the rumours concerning Tommo and Hawk were spreading among the tattle-tongues of Hobart Town. The very idea that Mary, an unmarried woman, should take in as her own children these so-called twins, said to have been left on her doorstep, and the fact that one was obviously of aboriginal extraction, horrified the respectable classes. The infants had only been with Mary two months when she was summoned to see Mr Emmett at his offices.

She was ushered into his chambers by a clerk, who silently indicated the chair in front of a large desk and immediately left. Mr Emmett was working on some papers and did not look up at Mary, who was uncertain as to whether she should wait for permission to be seated. She thought this most unusual for they had been friends a long time and, besides, he was an unfailingly courteous man.

'Sit down please, Mary,' Mr Emmett said, still not looking up. He continued to write for a full minute, so that Mary could hear only the scratching of the goose-feather quill against the paper and the slow, measured tic-toc of the pendulum from a wall clock to the left of his desk.

Mary sat quietly in the chair with her hands folded in her lap. She was not accustomed to meeting Mr Emmett in this manner. She always accorded him the respect he deserved as a first rater and high official of the government, but their relationship over the years had become a warm and familiar one. Mary was also aware that he took secret pride in what she had achieved and he would visit the clearing on the mountain to watch each new construction. He had been very useful in the obtaining of various licences, and a positive stalwart in her fights with the beer barons and others who did not like to see an emancipist and, in particular, a woman succeed at what they felt was most decidedly the province of a man.

Finally, and to Mary's relief, Mr Emmett looked up and smiled. 'Good afternoon, sir,' she said also smiling. Mary was still a pretty, slender woman, and today she was wearing a neat dress and best bonnet of a russet colour which complemented her lovely green eyes.

'My dear Mary,' Mr Emmett began, 'it is always such a pleasure to see you, though perhaps today is a somewhat less pleasant occasion.'

'Oh?' Mary exclaimed. 'Is there something I has done wrong, sir?'

Mr Emmett spread his hands and leaned back slightly, both gestures intended to relax her. 'You have done so well, Mary, and there are many, even in the government, who think most highly of you. I am sure you know how I feel about your success. We are good friends, do you not agree?'

'I take it a great honour to be counted your friend, sir.'

Mr Emmett cleared his throat and now leaned slightly forward across the desk. 'Mary, you must listen to me. It is not right that you should take these children to be your own. They do not have the right blood and it will turn out badly for all concerned.'

'Tommo and Hawk?' Mary exclaimed in surprise.

'Yes! If that be their names, you must be rid of them!'

Mary had never before heard such a harsh, uncompromising tone in Mr Emmett's voice. 'But why, sir?' she pleaded. 'They just be orphans, there be hundreds like them.'

'They will destroy you! We cannot have it!'

'Destroy me? But I loves them like me own!' Mary cried.

Mr Emmett shook his head impatiently. 'Mary, I will not lie to you, they be of an inferior species and the Lord God would not have us to mix with them. You have seen how the aboriginal people of this island are. There can be no place for them in this society. I beg you to see reason. This child will destroy you and the other, though thought to be white, is, I am told, a twin and therefore of the same stock!'

'Mr Emmett, you must help me please. These are my children and I wish them to be given my name!'

Mr Emmett shook his head. 'You were always of a most stubborn nature, Mary Abacus, but this time I am right! You cannot keep them. Besides, in the matter of a name, it can only be that of their father.' Mr Emmett was not a cruel man, but now he paused and raised one eyebrow. 'And God alone knows who he might be! The children of a whore and a nigger are not to be given a decent English name.'

'If I adopt them they shall have mine, it be decent enough!' Mary said defiantly.

'Should you be married, yes, that might be possible, but you are a spinster woman and the law will not allow you to adopt them.' The chief clerk paused and looked at Mary, whom he could see was deeply distressed. 'Do not try, Mary, it will be to no avail and I would personally interfere in the matter!'

Mary stood up and moved to where Mr Emmett sat behind his desk. She knelt beside him and held him by the sleeve with both her hands. 'Please, Mr Emmett, they be my children. I loves them as though they were my very own flesh and blood. You *must* help me, I begs you!'

'Mary, do not distress yourself so! And please be seated,' Mr Emmett said sternly. 'We are not in my garden now or in the woods at Strickland Falls.' He pulled his arm away, forcing Mary to rise and return to her chair. 'I have consulted the attorney general on this matter. You simply must give up these children, Mary. You have technically conspired in their abduction and, while God knows it is as much a technical crime as real on this island with the mother dead and the father unknown, it is a crime nonetheless. The children are wards of the State and must be given over to the foundling home.'

Mary half rose in her chair. 'But . . . but, they will die! I have seen what happens!'

'It is for the best, my dear. You will soon enough forget them.'

'And if I should find someone willing to adopt them?' Mary asked, a heartfelt sob escaping from her.

'What do you mean? Someone to adopt them, then give them over into your care?'

Mary nodded and sniffed. 'I loves them more than my life, sir.'

'Mary my dear, listen to me. They are scum! They will grow to be idiots! You have seen the vile offspring of harlots for yourself, the urchins in the streets in dirty rags, who grunt and snort like pigs, their minds not able to fully comprehend. These two of yours will be the same, even worse. They do not have the advantage of a full measure of English blood, but carry in their veins the instincts of the African savage, and God knows what else!'

'Sir, I were meself born o' the poorest class, the hopeless, the scum, as you calls it! I were myself a harlot! You have seen how in the orphanage we have brought children to learn, children what you said was hopeless, was scum, found bright and keen as any other. You said yourself you was wrong!'

'I am not wrong in this, Mary!' Mr Emmett said tersely. 'They were not black! Listen to me, please! There is more to this matter. The coroner thought not to make public his report of the results of the death of the prostitute known as Sperm Whale Sally, but it was his positive opinion that she died in childbirth. These are the two infants, the twins, born to her, are they not?'

Mary opened her mouth to reply and Mr Emmett lifted his index finger. 'Please do not lie to me, Mary. You and I have always spoken the truth.'

Mary sighed and looked directly at Mr Emmett, tears streaming down her cheeks. 'Ikey brought them home,' she said in a faltering voice.

'The morning the corpse was discovered?'

Mary nodded, biting her lower lip. Then she looked down at her hands, which were folded in her lap. Her shoulders shook as she sobbed.

'He stole them, Mary,' Mr Emmett said quietly. 'That is abduction. You helped in the kidnapping of two children and will be charged with complicity. If convicted you will both receive fourteen years!' He leaned back. 'For God's sake, woman, give them up now and nothing further will come of it!'

Mary felt the anger rising deep within her. On the streets of Hobart Town there were gangs of urchins in rags who were treated no better than stray dogs. It was so common to hear of street urchins of three and four years old found murdered having been brutally buggered, that the *Colonial Times* did not even make mention of it. These were the lost children of the island, so low in human reckoning that they barely existed in the minds of the general population. If they survived to the age of eight or nine they became hardened prostitutes, both male and female. Beyond the age of eleven, if they hadn't died of syphilis or some other infectious disease, most became drooling idiots or desperate criminals. Many were hanged before they reached fifteen years of age.

Newborn children, left by their destitute mothers on the steps of the foundling home, died more often than not and this was quietly condoned by the authorities. The King's orphanage could accommodate only a certain number, and was already thought to be a most onerous drain on the government coffers. Now the person Mary trusted more than any other in the world had turned against her, and was threatening her with prison for having saved two such children from certain death.

Mary knew that she was on her own again, that nothing had really changed. Her hand went to the Waterloo medal about her neck, and she held it tightly before looking up at Mr Emmett.

'You are wrong, sir! Ikey Solomon be their father!' Mary heard herself saying.

Mr Emmett's mouth fell open in astonishment. It was such a ludicrous assertion that he could not believe his ears. Several moments passed before he was able to speak. He shook his head in bewilderment.

'Mary Abacus, that is outrageous!' he cried. 'Ikey Solomon is a Jew!'

Mary looked directly into Mr Emmett's eyes. 'Hawk be a throwback, sir, on the maternal side.'

Mr Emmett remained quiet for a few moments and then he threw back his head and began to chuckle. Before long this had turned into genuine laughter. Eventually he stopped, removed his glasses and dabbed at his eyes with his handkerchief. 'And Ikey is the willing and happy father, is he?'

Mary could no longer restrain herself. 'I don't know, sir. I ain't told him yet!'

With this they both commenced to howl with laughter. Mr Emmett was now quite beside himself with mirth, and it took several minutes to regain his composure.

'Mary, I shall speak to the attorney general.' He looked most fondly at her. 'I fear you will suffer greatly in the choice you have made. The respectable class will not forgive you for this great indiscretion, my dear.'

'And you, sir?' Mary asked. 'Will you?'

Mr Emmett looked suddenly most awkward and picked up his quill and twirled it in his fingers. Without looking at Mary he declared, 'Me? Oh I am simply an old fool who is too easily led by the nose by a pretty young woman.'

Mary smiled, though her eyes filled again with tears. 'And if they be proved idjits, Mr Emmett, sir, they will be as equally loved as if they were the brightest o' brats!'

There is not much that can be said about the first few years of a child's life. They all seem to grow alarmingly quickly, and if they are loved and healthy they are usually of a pleasant enough disposition. They are a source of great pleasure as well as of moments of great anxiety when they suffer from the multitudinous childhood complaints every parent must of necessity endure. But the pleasure of infants is only known to those who are with them daily; to others, children only become interesting when they can think and ask questions.

Mary was a dedicated mother to Tommo and Hawk, and the two little boys returned her love with affection and trust. Sometimes, when she was busy at other tasks, the mere thought of them would overwhelm her and she would burst into tears of sheer joy for the love she felt for them. Mary was sure that life could bring her no greater moments of happiness than when the little boys were tugging at her skirts and demanding affection. Had she given birth to them she felt she could not have loved them any more deeply.

From the outset it became apparent that they would be quite differently sized. Tommo, considering his gigantic parents, was small boned and delicate in appearance, though not in the least sickly, and Hawk was large and seemed to grow bigger each day. As a baby Tommo seemed content with the single breast of his wet nurse, while Hawk would take all he could extract from his own and then greedily feed on the remaining breast of the woman who suckled his brother.

Jessamy Hawkins had grown into a pretty young lady, much sought after by young men. But she was of a sensible and independent mind, quick witted and with a laconic humour, and she doted on the two infants. She called Hawk 'Dark Thought', and Tommo 'After Thought'.

Tommo seemed the more adventurous of the twins. He was always into some sort of mischief and, more often than not, Hawk would be the one caught with his fingers deep in the jam pot after being led there by Tommo. But Hawk questioned everything and, even as a small child, would not be put off by an incomplete answer.

Throughout their childhood they refused to be separated and Hawk sensed the need to protect the smaller Tommo against all-comers, dogs or other children who might want to harm him. Even if Mary grew angry with Tommo for some mischief and he fled from her, Hawk would stand in her way until, impatient and frustrated, she would slap him. The moment she did so, Hawk would stand firm and grin up at her. 'That's for Tommo, Mama!' he'd declare. 'He be punished now!'

Ikey, to his great surprise, confessed to being most fond of Mary's brats, but had nonetheless made Mary pay him ten pounds for each before he agreed to perjure himself by swearing he was their father. He protested that, as the world had never before heard of a black Jew, but with Hawk and Tommo given the name of Solomon, it was not appropriate that they be gentiles. Nevertheless, his conscience would be assuaged, he assured Mary, if she gave a donation of fifteen pounds to a fund created by Mr Louis Nathan to establish a synagogue for the four hundred and fifty Jews known to live in the colony. Ikey was getting older and increasingly he gave thought to his immortal soul. He thought it worthwhile to be in good standing within his faith. The remaining five pounds he wanted for an addition to Sperm Whale Sally's headstone.

Mary had paid for the burial of Marybelle Firkin, alias Sperm Whale Sally, who now rested among the respectable dead in St David's burial ground with both her names on her marble headstone, but she soon enough recouped the money.

Michael O'Flaherty, the proprietor of the Whale Fishery, had opened a fund for this purpose, and every whaleman who entered the port of Hobart in the year that followed had willingly given something towards Sperm Whale Sally's funeral expenses.

Sufficient money was raised to repay Mary and also to erect a handsome headstone made from expensive pure white marble imported from England. In fact, so grand was the headstone that it caused a furore among the church elders and the congregation, who felt it unbefitting that a whore should have a more impressive tombstone than the respectable and pious merchant John Rutkin who had been buried on the very same day.

There were even some who tried to insist that Sperm Whale Sally's grave be moved from consecrated ground, and there was talk of a petition to Governor Franklin, who had replaced Colonel Arthur.

But in the end the vicar, in a stirring sermon, pointed out that within his churchyard lay villains far greater than the giant whore, and that Mary Magdalene had herself been a scarlet women and had received the love and compassion of Jesus Christ. This had silenced the hotheads and, at the same time, caused a better quality of headstone to appear in the churchyard, the respectable classes not able to bear the shame of sealing their dead beneath a less imposing stone.

But despite the grandness of the memorial to Sperm Whale Sally, Ikey, in a rare display of sentiment, expressed his displeasure. He persuaded the stone mason who created the tombstone to procure a slab of rare bluestone and to carve from it the shape of a great sperm whale, and to inlay this onto the face of the existing white marble. Beneath this he caused to be engraved the words:

> *So take up your doxy and drink your own ale*
> *And dance a fine jig to a fine fishy tale*
> *We'll fly the Blue Sally wherever we sail*
> *And drink to the health o' the great sperm whale!*

It pleased Ikey greatly to know that the Blue Sally would forever fly above Sperm Whale Sally's grave and Mary was happy enough to meet the bill. Apart from Ikey's renewed religious scruples, she understood his sentimental desire to perpetuate in stone the spirit of the great sperm whale so that it might guard the grave of the mother of her two adopted sons.

And so yet another myth was born. At the beginning of the winter whaling season, for as long as men hunted the whale in the South Seas and came into port at Hobart Town, the captains and men of the great fully rigged brigantines and barques and the smaller local bay whalers would gather together at St David's church for a blessing of the whale fleet. After the blessing the ships' masters would pay for a barrel of rum to be consumed at the grave of Sperm Whale Sally. Each whaleman present would take a glass of rum and drink what became known as 'A Sally Salute', a tribute to the spirit of the great sperm whale. Then they would link arms, the Yankees and the British, Swedes, French, Portuguese and the islanders, and form a circle around the grave of Sperm Whale Sally and sing the Blue Sally shanty. This they sang with a great deal more gusto than the dreary rendition of The Sailor's Hymn they had earlier been required to render within the church. It was claimed that there were whalemen who spoke no English but who could sing this elegy to the whale perfectly, having learned it by rote from some old tar during the lonely nights at sea.

517

Mary nurtured only one great anxiety during the first two years of raising Tommo and Hawk, which sprang from the damning words of Mr Emmett. '*Mary my dear, listen to me. They be scum! They will grow to be idiots!*' She watched them intently in the cradle to see if their eyes followed her or whether they might be made to grab for some object she held or respond to some loving nonsensical sound she made to show a growing awareness. Her fears proved groundless. Tommo and Hawk cried and laughed, slept and ate and fell and walked and played like any other happy, healthy infants.

Mary left nothing to chance, though, and as soon as they could comprehend in the slightest she began reading to them. At four years old they could recite a host of nursery rhymes, the one closest to Mary's heart being Little Jack Horner, for it contained the two things she was most determined to give her children, good food and an education.

> *Little Jack Horner,*
> *Sat in the corner,*
> *Eating a Christmas pie;*
> *He put in his thumb,*
> *And pulled out a plum,*
> *And said, 'What a good boy am I!'*
>
> *He was feasting away,*
> *And 'twas late in the day;*
> *When his mother, who made it a rule*
> *Her children should ever*
> *Be learned and clever,*
> *Came in to prepare him for school.*

Mary was also determined that their morals should be of the strictest rectitude and they would be most severely punished should they not tell the truth. She had sent to England for a book with the rather long title, *The Good Child's Delight; or, the road to knowledge. In short, entertaining lessons of one or two syllables; Nursery morals; chiefly in monosyllables.* This she read to them so many times that Hawk, at the age of five, could recite the entire book. Others she bought from the Hobart Town Circulating Library, where she drove the stern-faced Mrs Deane quite mad with her requests for children's books. One of the boys' favourites, for they cried at each reading, was *The Happy Courtship, Merry Marriage, and Pic Nic Dinner, of Cock Robin, and Jenny Wren. To which is added, alas! the doleful death of the bridegroom.*

On their cots Mary constructed strings of wooden beads in the same configuration as an abacus, so that their earliest memories would be of the rattle and touch of the red and black beads in their tiny hands.

At five both children were well acquainted with the alphabet and could read well and write simple words upon their slates. Tommo was clever enough but would quickly become impatient, while Hawk seemed much more interested. At the age of seven, when Mary took them to Mrs Tibbett's primary school, an establishment which took the young children of the tradesmen rank, both Tommo and Hawk proved well in advance of other children in their class. Hawk was not only the largest child among his age group, he also stood out as the most intelligent.

Though children are not concerned with colour, their parents soon enough perceived the presence of Hawk and it did not take them long to complain about the black child. Mary was asked by Mrs Tibbett to remove Hawk and Tommo from the school.

It was a fight Mary knew she could not win, and she saw no point in venting her spleen on the hapless Mrs Tibbett, who seemed genuinely distressed that she was forced to make the demand. Besides, Mary felt that the school was holding back her children for the benefit of other children less well prepared.

So she determined that she would continue as she had begun and personally attend to the education of her two children. In this she had elicited Ikey's most reluctant assistance, particularly as she required that he teach them nothing in the way of dishonest practices. Ikey protested that he knew of no other way to teach an urchin, and that if he should be forbidden to teach Tommo and Hawk the gentle art of picking a pocket, or show them how to palm a card or otherwise cheat at cribbage, pick a simple lock, short change a customer, successfully enter a house though it be securely locked, or doctor a stolen watch, there was nothing contained in his lexicon of knowledge which he believed could be useful to them.

'You will teach them of human nature! They must grow up

able to read a man or woman the way you do. How they stand or use their hands or smile or protest, how to know the fool from the villain and the good from the bad. Who to trust and who should be avoided. The manner o' the confidence man and the language o' the cheat and the liar. That is what I want them to know, Ikey Solomon!'

Ikey laughed. 'They are not Jews, my dear, they are not the raw material it has taken a thousand years and more to breed, so that this kind of wisdom is ingested without the need to think.'

'You must teach them, Ikey. Hawk most of all, for I fear greatly for him in this world where the dark people suffer even though they commit no crime, where the lowest wretch thinks himself superior to a black skin. You must teach Hawk to be a good reader of human nature.'

Ikey soon discovered that children with full bellies who are surrounded by love and attention make poor observers of human nature. Children learn the lessons in life by being thrown into life, and so he decided to take Hawk and Tommo to the races each Saturday. But first he taught them a new language. He found that both boys enjoyed the finger and hand actions which comprise the ancient silent language used among the traders in Petticoat Lane, Rosemary Lane, Whitechapel, Covent Garden and the other London markets. It is said that it is a language used by the Jews since the fall of the great temple of Solomon. That the Jews brought it to England in the Middle Ages and it became a language used in English prisons and had been brought to Port Arthur, where prisoners were not permitted to talk to each other. It was also most useful at the race track, where bookmakers talked to each other, setting the odds and laying of bets across the paddocks, and there it was commonly known as tic-tac.

Tommo and Hawk, like all young children, quickly learned the rudiments of this language and it did not take long before they added some of their own unique signs and devices, which meant they could silently communicate to each other on any subject.

Ikey was delighted with their progress, and when they were seven he would take them to the races, where they would move from one on-course bookmaker to the other sending back the odds to Ikey so that he was seldom caught short or 'holding the bundle' as it is known in racing parlance. In exposing them to the myriad people to be found at the Hobart races he was able to begin teaching Tommo and Hawk the lessons Mary wanted them to learn. Ikey taught them how to look at a crowd and break it into its various components.

'If you knows what you're looking for in a crowd, my dear, then you can read it like a book.' He looked down at Hawk. 'A crowd be composed o' what, Mr Dark Thought?'

Hawk looked at Ikey with his big serious eyes. 'Folks?'

'Folks! That be a right and splendid answer, very clever indeed!'

'What sort o' folks, Mr After Thought?' he asked Tommo.

'Very ugly ones what stinks!' Tommo replied, waiting for the giggle to come from Hawk.

'Well, well, well and we are the pretty ones what smells perfect are we then?' Ikey said. 'I stinks meself and I am not very pretty I admits. So be the crowd all like me? Like Ikey Solomon?'

'All sorts of different folks,' Hawk replied for Tommo.

'Yes! With all sorts o' different needs and deeds,' Ikey replied. 'Needs and deeds, that be what you have to learn, my dears. If you knows what folks needs, you can begin to understand their deeds.'

Ikey would patiently teach them how to spot the pickpocket, and to listen to the chatter of a tout, to notice the gestures and the patterns of speech of the confidence trickster, how to know when a man was a liar or a cheat. How body language was almost always the first way to judge a man.

'Then, when you've seen how he stands or sits or walks or uses his hands and his head, and he fits into a pattern, then, when you talks with him you listens with your stomachs, my dears.'

'Your stomach!' Tommo laughed. 'Be me belly button me new ear then?'

'That be most clever of you, Mister After Thought, most clever and to be remembered. "Let your belly button be your most important ear!"'

'Have you got a very big belly button then, Ikey?' Hawk asked. 'Big as your ear?'

'Huge, my dear!' Ikey slapped his pot belly. 'Nearly all be ear what's constantly listening.'

The two boys found this very funny. 'So what does you do with your ears on your head?' Hawk asked.

'Now that be another most clever question, Mister Dark Thought.' Ikey pulled at both his ears. 'These be your listening eyes.'

'Eyes can't listen!' both the boys shouted.

'Oh yes they can! If they be ears!' Ikey said solemnly.

'But ears can't see,' Hawk said emphatically.

'Oh yes they can! If they be eyes! Ears what is eyes and eyes what is ears is most important in the discovery o' human nature!'

'How?' they both chorused.

'Well, human speech be like pictures, only word pictures. When we speaks we paints a word picture what we wants others to see, but we only paints a part o' the picture what's in our heads. The other part, usually the most important part, we leaves behind, because it be the truth, the true picture. So your ears have to have eyes, so they can see how much o' the real picture what be in the head be contained in the words!'

'How then are eyes become ears?' Hawk asked.

'Well that be more complicated, but the way we moves our hands and heads, and folds our arms or opens them up, scratches our nose or puts our fingers over our lips, tugs our ear, twiddles our thumbs or fidgets, or puts one foot on the instep o' the other like Tommo be doing right now, that be what you calls the language o' the body. If you listen to the language o' the body with your eyes and sees the picture in the mind with your ears, you begins to get the drift o' the person, that is if you listens . . .'

'Through the ear in your belly?' Hawk shouted, delighted.

'Bravo! If he don't feel good in your stomach, then always trust it, my dears! Bad stomachs and bad men go well together!'

Tommo appeared to pay less attention to these lessons, but Hawk silently absorbed everything Ikey told him. Unlike his previous pupils in the Academy of Light Fingers, neither Tommo nor Hawk suffered from hunger and cold, homelessness or a lack of love. Privileged children only embrace the more difficult lessons in life when their survival is threatened and then it is often too late.

Both Mary's boys showed an early proficiency in numbers and constantly used the abacus, but once again it was Hawk who most quickly mastered the mysteries of calculation. By the time Ikey took them to the Saturday races Hawk carried his own small abacus and could calculate the odds in an instant and send them by sign language to his brother. Tommo would stand well outside the betting ring but where Ikey could glance up at him while he worked, and as he began to prosper as a bookmaker he came to rely increasingly on the two boys.

Mary spent as much time as she could spare with the boys tramping on the great mountain, and at Strickland Falls, and soon they knew the deeply wooded slopes and crags well enough to spend long hours exploring on their own. They hunted the shy opossum, who slept during the day in hollow tree trunks, and searched for birds' eggs, though Mary forbade them to gather the eggs or trap the rosellas and green parrots not yet able to fly, but which were sufficiently well feathered to sell in the markets.

Once, close to Strickland Falls, Hawk had his arm deep within the hole in a tree trunk looking for birds' eggs when he was bitten by a snake. Within a couple of minutes he had presented his puffed and swollen forefinger to Mary, who was fortunately working at the new buildings for the Potato Factory.

Mary lost no time and, consulting Dr Forster's *Book of Colonial Medicine*, she applied a tourniquet high up on Hawk's arm and sliced open the bite with a sharp knife, drawing a deep line down the flesh of his forefinger while ignoring his desperate yowling. Then she sucked the poison from the wound, spat it out, and applied a liberal sprinkling of Condis Crystals or, as it was called in the book, Permanganate of Potash. Though Hawk's hand remained swollen for a week, his forefinger recovered well, the scar from Mary's over-zealous cut being more damaging and permanent in its effect than the serpent's bite itself.

Mary was a strict mother who expected them to work. They gathered watercress and learned to tickle the mountain trout, and hunt for yabbies, the small freshwater crayfish abundant in the mountain streams, so that they would often bring home a bountiful supply. Sometimes they sold what they caught or gathered at the markets. They collected oysters off the rocks in the bay and set lobster traps, and both boys could swim like fish by the time they were five years old. At seven they were independent and spirited and in the rough and tumble of life in Hobart Town, where children of the poor grew up quickly and street urchins scavenged to stay alive, they mostly held their own. Though they would often enough come home to Mary torn, bleeding and beaten, robbed of the pennies or even a mighty sixpence they had earned.

Hawk's dark colour was almost always the problem, with the street urchins taking great delight in going after him. If Tommo and Hawk saw one of the gangs approaching and escape proved impossible, they ran until they found a wall and then, with their backs to it, would turn and fight their opponents. If they were not outnumbered they gave as much as they got and more. The street urchins learned to regard them with respect and to attack only in sizeable numbers, engaging the two boys just long enough to steal their catch, a brace of wood pigeons or several trout, a clutch of wild duck eggs or a couple of opossum.

Mary would patch them up, but offered little in the way of comfort. She loved her precious children so deeply that she often felt close to tears when they returned home with a black eye, bleeding nose or a thick lip. But she knew it was a hard world, and that they must learn to come to terms with it.

It was Ikey who finally gave them the key to a less eventful life. The two boys appeared at breakfast one morning, Tommo with both eyes shut and a swollen lip, and Hawk with one eye shut and a bruised and enlarged nose.

'Been in the wars, has we, then, my dears?' Ikey said.

'They've been fighting again,' Mary said, placing two bowls of porridge on the table. 'A couple o' proper hooligans, them two!'

'It were not our fault, Mama, it be the wild boys again!' Tommo said indignantly.

'You must run, don't fight them, just run,' Mary said emphatically. 'It's not cowardly to run, only prudent.'

'We had a bag of oysters what took two hours to collect,' Hawk protested. 'It were fourpence worth at least!'

'You can't run with a bag of oysters!' Tommo explained further.

'Well they got the oysters and you both got black eyes and fat lips and a bleeding nose, where's the sense to that?'

'We ain't scared, Mama,' Tommo said. 'Hawk hit three o' them terrible hard and I kicked one o' them in the shins so he went howling!'

'Of course, my dears, fisticuffs be all very well,' Ikey said, picking his teeth. 'But a much sharper sword would be your tongue!'

If the eyes of both boys had not been so well closed they would have rolled them in unison.

'They be idjits, Uncle Ikey. You can't try no reasoning on them, they not like us decent folks,' Tommo said.

'Don't you speak like that, Tommo Solomon!' Mary

remonstrated. 'They be poor brats what's had no chance in life. They does the best they can to stay alive! They be just as decent as us given half a chance!'

'Talk to them, my dears, use your wits,' Ikey said. 'Wits be much more powerful than fists.' He rose from the table and stretched his arms above his shoulders. 'I'll be off, then. No lessons today, your Uncle Ikey's had a long, hard night.'

Later that morning the two boys were sitting on Mary's magic rock on the slopes of the mountain when Hawk turned to Tommo. 'What's you think Ikey be on about this morning?' he asked.

Tommo shrugged. 'It be Ikey stuff we be supposed to understand but can't.'

'I got an idea,' Hawk said.

Two days later the two boys found themselves accosted by five street urchins. They'd just returned from their lobster traps and their sack was bulging and bumping with six live lobsters they were hoping to sell to Mrs McKinney's fish shop for threepence.

Hawk looked at Tommo and the smaller boy nodded.

'Wotcha got?' the biggest of the urchins demanded.

Tommo and Hawk remained silent, and the snot-nose who had asked the original question made a grab for the bag in Hawk's hand.

'Careful,' Tommo shouted. 'They be magic lobsters what can curse you!'

The boy drew back confused. 'Wotcha mean?'

Hawk opened the bag, brought out a plump lobster and held it up above his head. The creature's claws and feelers waved wildly in the air.

'They can read your mind, them lobsters!'

The boys standing around jeered. 'That be fuckin' stoopid!' the first boy answered. 'Lobsters what can read me mind!'

Hawk pushed the live lobster into the face of the boy, who reeled back.

'Yeah, bullshit!' another of the urchins shouted. 'Ain't no lobsters what can do that!'

'Not your ordinary lobsters, that I admits, but these be special magic ones,' Tommo said quickly. 'It be the secret curse o' the people from Africa!'

'Who, him? The nigger?' the boy said, pointing to Hawk.

Hawk grinned. 'Black magic!' he said.

'Wanna see?' Tommo asked.

The urchins had now forgotten their original intention to rob Tommo and Hawk of the bag. 'Yeah!' they chorused.

'You brave enough to take the chance to be cursed by the great African lobster what swum all the way to visit us from the Cape o' Good Hope in Africa?' Tommo asked the eldest of the boys.

The urchin hesitated but then, seeing the others looking at him, said, 'It be stoopid! That be a fuckin' lobster like any uvver what's in the river.'

'G'warn, show us the magic!' the urchins challenged Tommo.

'Don't be cheeky!' Tommo said to the bunch of skinny boys standing around him. 'Or we'll curse the lot of you, not only him.' He scowled at the boy who had first accosted them and beckoned to the gang in a low voice. 'Come here where that African lobster creature can't hear what you is saying! Come right away all of you to that tree.' He pointed to a swamp oak about fifty feet away.

The urchins and their leader followed Tommo and stood beside the tree. 'Now I wants you each to whisper your name in me ear, one at a time, and then we'll ask the magic lobster to tell me brother what knows lobster language to tell us what your name be!' Tommo pointed to their original attacker. 'You what be double cursed already for saying it be a lobster what come from the river, you go first. Whisper your name in me ear with your back to the magic African lobster me brother's holding.'

Tommo knew the boy was known as Boxey, because his head was almost square. 'George,' Boxey whispered slyly into Tommo's ear, though loud enough for those gathered around to hear him. There was a giggle from the others at their leader's foxy trick.

Tommo stood facing Hawk fifty feet away and signalled him using the silent language. Hawk held the lobster up to his ear and appeared to listen. Then he shook his head and then the crustacean, and listened once more. Suddenly a big smile appeared on his face. 'The magic African lobster says the name given be George, but Boxey be the name what's real!' he shouted back at them.

The mouths of the urchins standing around Tommo fell open, and Boxey became very red in the face.

'You be careful, mate!' Tommo growled. 'Or you could be in real big trouble!'

Hawk suddenly held the lobster back to his ear. 'The magic African lobster says if any boy gives him a wrong name again they be double cursed to drown at sea!' he shouted.

There was a further gasp of astonishment from the boys.

'You!' Tommo said, pointing to a skinny urchin who was dressed in rags with great holes showing through, 'Come and whisper your name.' The boy, even smaller than Tommo, looked up at him terrified. 'I dunno what's me real name, they calls me Minnow.' His eyes pleaded with Tommo. 'I don't wanna be cursed, please!'

'Yeah, well I'll do me best,' Tommo said. 'But I can't make no promise. Turn your back to the magic lobster so he can't see your lips,' he commanded sternly. The urchin, shaking all over, did as he was told.

Moments later Hawk called back, 'Minnow!'

Tommo turned to the leader of the gang. 'Boxey, you be real lucky this time! But be warned!' He turned to the other urchins. 'Anyone want to take a chance o' being cursed?' There were no further volunteers and so Tommo called over to Hawk, 'Put the lobster in the bag and come over!'

As Hawk approached the gang they started to back away from him. 'Don't run!' Tommo said. 'We got to lift the curse first!'

'What's you mean?' Boxey asked suspiciously, his voice slightly tremulous. 'You said we wasn't cursed if we be careful.' He seemed brighter than the others and suddenly asked, 'How come he's your brother and he be black?'

'That's what I means, we got to lift the curse!' Tommo replied.

'I were born same as him,' Hawk explained, pointing to Tommo. 'Same's me brother, but I got cursed by the horrible African lobster and now I's black, see!'

'What you just seen here be black magic and folk's not s'posed to see black magic,' Tommo said. 'So me brother, what's turned black and is now the black magician what's forced to pass on the curse, will wave the lobster over your heads and then the curse be lifted. Now, if you please, a circle. Hold hands and make a circle. I'll tell you when to close your eyes!'

The boys formed into a circle holding hands with Hawk in the centre. Hawk lifted a lobster out of the bag and held it high above his head.

'Close your eyes tight now!' Tommo instructed. 'If you peeks

527

you is cursed for life and you drowns all horrible out to sea but before that you turns black!'

Hawk started to recite:

> *Abracadabra, ho, ho, ho!*
> *Black as pitch, white as snow!*
> *Beware the black magician's curse*
> *Or things what's bad will soon be worse!*

Tommo waited for Hawk to place the lobster back into the bag. 'You can open your eyes, you be safe now,' Tommo instructed. 'Curse be lifted, but scarper quick and stay out of our way!' He then repeated Hawk's lines. 'Beware the black magician's curse, or things what's bad will soon be worse!'

'G'warn, clear off!' Hawk shouted, scowling fiercely. The urchins, terror etched on their dirty faces, turned and fled for their lives.

The two boys waited a few moments, most pleased with themselves. Then Hawk took up the wriggling bag of lobsters and they started to laugh. They continued laughing all the way up the hill to Mrs McKinney's fish shop.

'I reckons maybe Uncle Ikey be right,' Hawk said finally, then turned to Tommo and asked, 'Was you scared?'

'Yeah, shittin' meself!'

'Me too, but I reckon it's much better than getting your nose busted!'

'Blood' oath!' Tommo said happily.

Chapter Thirty-five

Towards the end of the seventh year of their lives, Tommo and Hawk disappeared on a perfectly calm winter's day somewhere on the slopes of Mount Wellington.

Hobart Town had wakened that morning to find that the first winter snow had fallen and crusted the summit of the great mountain. The day that followed was crisp, with winter sunshine bright and sharp as polished silver.

Mary had spent most of the day at the new Potato Factory buildings where the majority of her beer production was now taking place. The old mill was used increasingly as a bottle shop, managed by Jessamy Hawkins.

It was the daily custom of Tommo and Hawk to accompany Mary to the small cottage at Strickland Falls, which served both as an office and schoolroom, where she supervised their lessons.

However, on the day they disappeared the two boys had begged Mary to allow them to climb to the snowline. She had hesitated at first. It was a three-hour climb and the weather on the mountain had a habit of closing in even on a sunny day. But she had finally yielded to their beseeching, and at ten o'clock they took some bread and cheese and escaped their lessons to explore the snow at the summit before the warm sunshine should melt it.

Mary had cautioned them to be careful and to come home immediately wherever they were if the weather turned, and no later than an hour before sunset. Tommo and Hawk were as agile as mountain goats and had explored the mountain with Mary since they were toddlers. Furthermore, there was a log hut at the summit should the weather close in, and it contained a plentiful supply of wood left by the woodcutters who worked the slopes.

Despite the warm day it was always cold at the summit, and Mary had insisted they wear their opossum jackets which, though considered most unfashionable by the third raters, were much utilised by rural folk, shepherds, sealers, kangaroo hunters and woodcutters who worked the wilderness country. Mary had purchased these wonderfully soft and warm garments for the boys, and she kept them at the Potato Factory at Strickland Falls precisely because of the unpredictable moods of the mountain.

At four-thirty in the afternoon, an hour before sunset, like all mothers, Mary's ears were tuned for the homecoming calls of the two boys, although her expectation was pointless, because the roar of the falls would drown out the sounds of their approach. But they knew her routine, and her need to be back at the mill before the bells of St David's tolled for evensong.

Mary smiled to herself at the thought of the journey home with the two boys. It was the happiest part of the day for her, as she had them all to herself. She loved the walk through the woods and, as they approached the town, the smell of wood smoke and the sweep of the hazy hills across the great silver river spread below.

Tommo and Hawk would be scratched from crawling through brambles and so covered with dirt they might well need to be bathed even though it was not their tub night. Tommo would be running ahead and turning back and taking her hand, words tumbling out in fierce competition with Hawk to tell her of their grand adventure as they'd played in the first of the winter snow. Hawk would be carrying her basket, hopping and skipping beside her with his head full of serious questions or explanations of the things he'd seen.

They would arrive back at the old mill just as the working people of Hobart Town started to arrive to buy their beer to take home. It was a busy hour and Mary would help Jessamy with the customers until half past seven o'clock. Soon after, Ikey would arrive and Mary would make supper for them all. Then, when Ikey retired to work on the books, she would read to the boys. They seldom remained awake much beyond nine o'clock, when she locked up and washed her face and arms and retired to bed herself, but not before making Ikey a large mug of strong tea which he liked to take with milk and six teaspoons of caster sugar.

Though Mary worked exceedingly hard, she revelled in the calm of an ordered and uneventful life, and her ambition was in no way curtailed by the need to care for her boys. In fact they gave her a sense of purpose beyond the need to prove herself worthy in her own eyes, and on her own terms.

Even though Mr Emmett had been right and she had been socially ostracised because of her dark-skinned son, Mary had never been concerned about social acceptance. During her earlier life, when she had been known as Egyptian Mary, she had witnessed sufficient of the behaviour of the male members of the first raters not to wish to adopt their affectations and manners, and she did not expect people of the tradesmen class would be any better.

Indeed, Mary's fights with the wealthy beer barons and spirit distillers of Hobart Town had been possible because she knew these rich and important men for what they were, and had not been cowed by their bullying. Moreover, her opinion of these pompous tyrants' wives, formed during her days as a chambermaid, was not greatly in advance of what she thought of their husbands.

Though she loved and respected Mr Emmett, Mary did not covet his lifestyle nor wish to be included in his milieu as a first rater, even if such a lofty ascent had been possible. She saw him for what he was, a rare example of a kind and compassionate human being who was independent of any class, and she hoped one day to emulate his example.

But for now Mary devoted herself to Tommo and Hawk. She was certain that her luck in this new land had a purpose, that she would create a foundation stone upon which her sons could build and that something worthwhile and wonderful would emerge. In her imagination Mary could clearly see the little brewery she would create in its perfect woodland setting, an inseparable part of her magic mountain. While she was not by nature capable of so pompous a thought, the Potato Factory would be her monument to the ability of the human spirit to survive and prosper against all odds.

Mary thought lovingly of her two boys and smiled to herself. She now possessed a destiny, a continuity in her new land. Tommo X Solomon and Hawk X Solomon would be the source of her second generation.

Mary chuckled to herself as she always did when she thought of the X in the boy's names. When Ikey had appeared somewhat sheepishly at the government offices and declared himself to be the father of Tommo and Hawk, he had registered his so-called offspring with an additional single X common to both names. The clerk who had presided over the registration had evinced not the slightest interest in enquiring what the X stood for, and had written out a certificate of birth exactly as Ikey had indicated.

Later, when Mary had demanded to know what the X stood for, Ikey shrugged his shoulders. 'It has to be there, it be a proper part o' their names, my dear, a grand initial, an ancient Hebrew sign,' he lied. In fact, the initial X was simply Ikey's mind working in its usual convoluted way. He told himself it represented the X which Svensen of the *Sturmvogel* had tattooed through the name Tomahawk on Sperm Whale Sally's breast to cancel the rights of the *Merryweather*. The additional justification was that he'd split the name Tomahawk in half to give each boy his name, but their names could be re-combined with the X to make a whole. Thus, Tommo X Hawk = Tomahawk = Twins. But in reality their names had simply been conjured up that first morning when he'd presented them in the basket to Mary and the X was just a feeble joke he'd thought of on the spur of the moment when he had gone to register the birth of the two boys.

However, Mary deduced her own explanation for the singular initial. She, who was so very good at the business of numbers, concluded that the X is used as the unknown in mathematics, and that Tommo and Hawk were her two unknown factors. The letter X in calculations could be made to represent any number, and it was her duty to see that what it represented in her two sons was the sum of the very best she could do to make them men of whom she could be rightfully proud.

Mary smiled as she packed her basket in preparation for the boys' return. Then she bid the workmen goodnight, put on her warm coat, locked the cottage and walked over to the small bridge just below the falls, which she knew Tommo and Hawk must cross as they returned from the mountain.

Mary Abacus waited on the bridge and watched the water as it churned white at her feet. The thundering falls sent a fine mist into the air which created a rainbow in the late afternoon sunlight, and Mary could not imagine a more perfect moment. She was not to know that the magic mountain she loved so much had just swallowed up her precious children.

When the boys had not arrived by five o'clock she walked back to the office and found a lantern which had a good wick, and was well filled with the whale oil. Then she looked about and found half a loaf of bread, the remainder of the cheese she had given the boys and four apples. These she replaced in her basket together with several bandages and a bottle of iodine which she always kept on the premises. Then she took a small axe which hung behind the cottage door and this too she pushed, head first, into the basket. It was almost dark by the time Mary crossed the little bridge again, and set off along the path leading higher up the mountain.

There was only one path to the summit, though many hundreds of paths led from all over the mountain before converging on this main track, which was a forty-minute climb from the top. Mary determined that she would walk until the path which led from Strickland Falls intersected several others, a steady half-hour's walk up the mountain. The boys might have taken any of a dozen paths to arrive at this point, but she knew they must eventually turn into the one she now took for the journey home.

The trees became more dense as she climbed, and not more than twenty minutes after she had left it grew completely dark under the forest canopy. Mary stopped to light the lantern and then proceeded onwards. She had begun to call out, her voice echoing through the trees as she called their names.

Mary finally reached the intersection. It was getting cold so she gathered wood, a difficult task even with the help of the lantern, but she persisted until she had a large pile. She kept herself warm chopping the wood, stopping every minute or so to call out again. Finally she lit a fire and settled down to wait, hoping that if Tommo and Hawk were anywhere near they might smell the smoke or see the fire.

Though the night was cold it remained clear and no wind

beyond the usual breeze stirred the tops of the trees. Mary told herself that this might not be the case at the summit, and Tommo and Hawk might have been caught in a change of weather and taken refuge in the hut. They were young, but it was unlikely they would do anything foolish. If the summit was suddenly to mist over they would know to stay put until morning. But in her heart Mary was terrified. She imagined a rock slide set in motion by the weight of the snow. She saw them venturing to the edge of a bluff, perhaps the mighty organ pipes, and the snow giving way and sending them crashing downwards nearly a thousand feet. She imagined any of a dozen incidents and all of them became vivid and concluded in her mind.

After two hours Mary knew that she would have to come down. Once again she lit the lantern, which she had put out to save the oil during her vigil by the fire. Wherever Tommo and Hawk were they could not descend in the dark, and she knew that no search party would set out to find them until first light. Mary set off down the path again and arrived at Strickland Falls nearly an hour later. She was scratched about and bleeding, for travelling a bush path at night is harrowing and her descent had been perilous. She had fallen on several occasions, though fortunately she had not lost the lantern. It took her another forty minutes to get back to the mill where Ikey and Jessamy were waiting, both of them terribly anxious. They'd already been up to Strickland Falls, and found it locked and had themselves not long been home.

Ikey had never seen Mary cry, but now she sat at the kitchen table and wept as she slowly spilled out the story. She blamed herself for letting the boys go, though Jessamy reminded her that they had roamed the slopes since they were four years old and the mountain was, in every sense, their own backyard.

At midnight Ikey left Jessamy asleep in an old armchair and Mary seated at the kitchen table with her head in her arms. Although she was tired and distraught almost beyond thinking, the ever-practical Mary had devised a rescue plan. She would make her appearance at Peter Degraves' saw mills at seven o'clock the following morning, when the timber cutters set off to work the slopes. But first she would call at the Degraves home and ask him for permission to pay his men a day's salary to send up a search party for Tommo and Hawk. They would set off from Strickland Falls so that if the children had spent the night safely in the hut on the summit they would be met along the path, not more than an hour and a half after first light. At this point the search would be over and the men, already on the mountain, could return to their work.

Mary was not foolish enough to suppose that this permission would be easily granted, for while her past employer was by the standards of the time a good man, he was tough and she knew he would expect her to pay for the value of the timber not produced while his men carried out the search. The loss of Tommo and Hawk would not be seen by him as a matter of great importance. Mary was of course, perfectly willing to meet his demands. The cost of a day's work of a hundred timber cutters would exhaust her available liquid resources, and possibly put her in debt to the brewer, but she cared not in the least about this.

Having resolved what to do at first light, she fell into a fitful sleep at the kitchen table only to be wakened an hour before dawn by Ikey.

'Come, my dear, I have brought help!' he said, shaking her gently by the shoulder.

Gathered in the street outside the Potato Factory were more than a hundred people. A more motley collection of the hopeless and forlorn would have been difficult to find anywhere in the South Seas. None among them would ever voluntarily have put one foot on the lowest slopes of the great mountain.

They were the drunks and whores, gamblers, pimps, touts, publicans' cellarmen, barmaids, whalemen and jack tars as well as other assorted human scrapings from the Hobart waterfront. Ann Gower, now the owner of a waterfront bawdy house, had taken a donkey cart and loaded herself upon it together with a large tea urn, so that she, too, might help.

Mary took one look at the crowd and knew Ikey must have finally gone senile. Though she perceived a handful of jack tars young enough to be useful, if the vast majority of this scraggy lot set foot upon the mountain, even on a cloudless summer day, few would return with every limb intact or even their lives, and most would be incapable of reaching the first tree line.

'Whatever has possessed you, Ikey Solomon?' Mary cried.

'My dear, I had thought to find some stout lads who might be persuaded to take on the search, but it is a great compliment to you that many felt that they should themselves come!'

After the initial shock, the sight of Ikey's caring volunteers lifted Mary's courage enormously. She thanked them for their generosity of spirit, but pointed out that the mountain was a dangerous and foreign place for most of them, and that they would more easily lose their own lives than help to find Tommo and Hawk.

She told them of her plan to use the timber cutters who worked the mountain slopes for Mr Peter Degraves' saw mills. If he should lend his support as she hoped he might, the mountain would be extensively searched before the day was out.

In fact, Mary knew that the mountain could not be thoroughly searched in a week or a month, and if Tommo and Hawk had fallen down a precipice they might never be found.

'You have shown me a great honour,' Mary concluded, 'and I am most touched by your concern. I thank you from the bottom of me heart.'

People among the assembly shouted their encouragement and started to disperse when Ann Gower stood up in the cart. 'Oi!' she shouted, waving her arms to indicate that they should gather around. The crowd soon assembled about her, and waited for her to speak. 'You all knows who I is, and if ya don't, why not?' she bawled out. There was a ripple of laughter and she waited for it to die down. 'But Mary Abacus some 'ere knows only fer the decent beer she sells, but also knows 'er as a good woman. But she be more'n that, and I should know! Mary Abacus be the salt o' the earth, no better woman may be found on this island nor any ovver place I knows of!' Ann Gower paused and looked around her. 'Now we knows 'er brats what's lost ain't 'ers born, and we knows 'ow they come about. But that don't make no difference and even that one be black, that don't matter neiver! What do matter is that she loves 'em, and if we can't 'elp to find 'em because we not the sort to take to mountain climbin', we can pass the 'at around to pay for a few stout lads what knows the mountain and can make a search!'

She opened her handbag and took out ten shillings. 'Two shillin' be a good wage for a day for a timber cutter, so I now pays for five o' the buggers. Who's next?' Ann Gower pointed to Bridget from the Whale Fishery. 'Bridget O'Sullivan take orf ya bonnet and use it as an 'at, there's plenty 'ere what's mean as cat's piss, but they'll 'ave trouble denyin' a pretty girl like you!'

536

Very soon Bridget had collected a total of three pounds and sevenpence from the crowd. Ann Gower gave it to Mary, who knew well enough not to protest. It was a gesture of respect, and she accepted it for the generosity of spirit it represented.

Mary looked at the crowd with tears in her eyes. 'Thank you all,' she said simply. Turning to Ann Gower she smiled. 'You're a good woman, Ann Gower!'

Ann Gower drew back and looked askance at Mary. 'Don't ya go ruinin' me repitashin, Mary Abacus. I be a real bad woman, but a bloody good whore and ya knows it!' She turned to the crowd. 'C'mon, folks, it be sun-up soon, time to go 'ome to bed!'

Peter Degraves agreed readily to Mary's request but put only sixteen of his men to search the mountain, sensibly pointing out that the boys would only have covered a small section of the mountain to reach the summit and that sixteen men could cover this thoroughly. He accepted that she should pay them their daily wage though he did not ask her for compensation for the two days of sawmill profits he would lose because the men were taken away from their work.

'I'll write it off to good labour relations,' he laughed, Mary's earlier labour reforms at the Cascade Brewery had been maintained, and Degraves knew that he had been repaid a thousand times over by the loyalty and the honesty of the men who worked for him.

After two days the men had thoroughly searched the mountain and had not found the slightest sign of the two boys. Further searching was not practical. The mountain might hide their bodies for years if they had fallen down some deep ravine, but because it was assumed that Tommo and Hawk would have been in the area facing Hobart Town and near the top of the mountain, this was where the search was focused. Eventually Mary conceded that nothing more could be done, though she personally spent the next two weeks alone on the mountain still desperately searching for her children.

Once she found a trap set for wood pigeon typical of the kind the boys might make, and on a thornberry bush adjacent to it she discovered a tiny tuft of opossum fur. Her heart started to beat furiously. After two days of calling out the boys' names her voice had ceased to function, and now she searched grimly and silently, entering small ravines and squeezing through rock formations terrified that at any moment she might come across the broken bodies of her sons. She was badly cut and scratched about and when she returned at night her clothes were often ripped to shreds. She ate little and her eyes became sunken, and her anguished silence made people begin to think she had gone mad.

Ikey and Jessamy Hawkins tried to comfort her, though they, too, were distraught, and the men who worked at the Potato Factory walked about in silent concern when she appeared.

It was during these two weeks on the mountain that Mary slowly became convinced that Tommo and Hawk had been abducted. At first she told herself this notion was absurd. Who would do such a thing and for what purpose? There could be no possible value in the kidnapping of two small boys. The beer barons and spirit manufacturers who had cause to dislike her were a possible explanation but, she knew, a poor one. They would not damage their own reputation with the public by so gratuitous a revenge. Wild men? This seemed more likely but, if so, they would by now have demanded a ransom.

Yet the feeling persisted and by the end of the fortnight, without any logical reason, other than that the bodies of Tommo and Hawk had not been found, Mary was certain that they had been abducted. She stopped searching and started to evolve a plan.

For some months Mary had been working on a new ale. She had tested it on a number of her customers, who found it most pleasing to the palate. Mary now had acceptance of her bottled beer throughout the colony, and she was also shipping it to the new village of Melbourne on the mainland. She now decided to call her new beer Tomahawk. Upon the label she placed two arms, a black and a white, gripped in the manner of arm wrestling and directly under the inverted 'V' made by the two arms was a picture of the head of a Red Indian chief. Around the perimeter of the oval-shaped label were the words: * Pale Ale * The Potato Factory * prop. Miss Mary Abacus *

Directly under the Indian chief's head appeared the words: Fifty Pounds Reward! and under this the injunction: (see back). At the back of the bottle Mary placed a second label in the shape of a glass. It contained a crude sketch of two small boys, one black and the other white and the following words in the shape of a wine glass.

KIDNAPPING!!
FIFTY POUNDS REWARD!
For information leading to
the recovery of the two boys
answering to the names of
Tommo & Hawk Solomon
and who are identified in
person by Miss Mary Abacus,
or Mr Ikey Solomon as same.
Tommo be small with blue
eyes and fair hair. Hawk
be black of skin and
Negro appearance.
Both be 7 years
old.
NO
QUESTIONS BE
ASKED OF PERSONS
ASSISTING IN RECOVERY!

Mary hoped that one of two things might happen. That someone might have seen Hawk, a black boy and therefore a curious sight, in the company of Tommo, a white one. Or that the kidnappers might attempt to claim the reward. It was, after all, a fortune, three times the yearly salary of a labourer or farm worker, and would also prove a tremendous incentive to a bounty hunter.

It did not take long for the disappearance of Tommo and Hawk to be known throughout the entire colony, and it was shortly afterwards that Ikey received a letter from his son David in New Norfolk asking him if he would come to the river town on a matter of extreme urgency. Ikey was glad of the excuse to go. Hannah had not contacted him in more than a year, and she had forbidden him to visit her. Her de facto George Madden had greatly prospered in the barley and hops business and Ikey, who was more and more conscious of his mortality, was terrified that she was prepared to wait until he was dead, whereupon she could claim the entire contents of the safe in Whitechapel and eventually find a way to open it.

David had been in contact with Ikey on two previous occasions. At other times he had sent Ann and then, on the last occasion, young Sarah was despatched to visit him with the excuse that they cared greatly about his welfare and wished to see him cared for. Sarah, who had little recollection of Ikey's perfidious nature, decided to remain with him and now shared the cottage in Elizabeth Street. This suited Ikey very well. His daughter made no demands on him, and she washed, cooked, and generally looked after his domestic affairs.

On each of his visits, David appeared to be warm and friendly and acted as though their stormy past had been entirely forgiven. There was much talk of blood being thicker than water, and the suggestion that an eventual reconciliation seemed quite possible with Hannah. It was obvious to Ikey that the boy had a good business head on his shoulders and had learned well the duplicity of effective persuasion.

However, he had soon enough perceived the motive behind the visits of his son and two daughters. David had by now been in the employ of George Madden for some years and there was talk of a partnership. Not long after she had arrived, Sarah let slip that the offer was far from generous, and was inspired by a great deal of nagging from Hannah. Apparently George Madden didn't wish to share with her son any part of his burgeoning empire, but wanted to keep peace with the formidable Hannah, so he had made the partnership offer on the proviso that four thousand pounds was paid. It was more than someone of David's means could ever possibly hope to raise, though it was still a fair offer for a partnership in such a prosperous business enterprise.

Ikey felt certain the urgent request that he should visit New Norfolk was attached to the matter of the Whitechapel safe, so he was much encouraged by David's note. That Hannah's avaricious hand would be in it somewhere he had no doubt.

Ikey was met by David at the New Norfolk wharf and taken to his lodgings, a small cottage which he occupied with Ann. She was at her place of work but had cooked a mutton stew and left fresh curds for Ikey's supper, the supposition being that he would not take the afternoon ferry but would stay overnight.

David offered Ikey brandy but he asked instead for tea. Since the death of Sperm Whale Sally he no longer drank at all and his preferred drink in the taverns at night was ginger beer.

David was dressed in a good suit of clothes such as might have been worn by any young man of prospects in a solid community

such as New Norfolk. Predictably he misjudged Ikey by the fact
that the coat Mary had bought for him eight years before was now
ragged, and that his yellow pigskin boots, much soled and patched
on the uppers, were well past their prime. David, while attempting
to impress Ikey, had acquired the imperious tone of the successful
grain merchant, and now spoke in a somewhat patronising manner
to his father.

'The mater has put the affairs o' the family in my hands and it
is time we talked,' he said to Ikey after he had placed a mug of tea
before him.

'Oh yes, is your mother not well then?' Ikey asked, for he knew
Hannah would never give over the reins to any of their sons unless
she was on her death bed.

'In the very best o' health and much mellowed,' David said.
Not waiting for a response, he continued, 'As I says, she has left
things to me to clear up.'

'Things? What be these things, then?' Ikey asked.

'Well, I knows about the Whitechapel safe at home and I think
we should resolve the matter, don't you?'

Ikey looked curiously across at his son. He had grown into a
good-looking man, though already he was putting on weight, and
the gold watch chain he wore looped over a pronounced paunch.

'Does you all know?' Ikey asked.

'No, only my mother and I, and o' course Moses and John in
New South Wales.'

'Good, then your mother will agree to give me her half of the
number and I shall arrange to have it opened and she shall have
her share fifty-fifty, as was the original agreement!'

Ikey had long since come to the conclusion that he would give
Hannah her half share. He now intended to remain in Van
Diemen's Land, though not because he thought it a better place.
He knew himself to be a broken man and he was forbidden to
return to England. Should he move to another country, he would
not have the energy to start again, or even to become accustomed
to the life of a rich man in retirement.

While far from rich, he was no longer poor and life in Van
Diemen's Land had taken a not disagreeable turn for him. He had
grown happily accustomed to the presence of Tommo and Hawk
as well as Mary in his life, and the disappearance of the two boys
had both deeply shocked and saddened him. But he could never

agree to receiving only one-eighth part of the Whitechapel fortune, as Hannah had proposed, nor could he bring himself to trust her with his part of the combination.

There was a prolonged silence between the two men and then David finally cleared his throat. 'It be less than sensible to trust someone what's not a part o' the family, father. You have three sons, Moses and John in New South Wales and myself here. We are all business men and can be entrusted to do the task in a most sensible manner and at the same time get the most agreeable price in London for the merchandise.'

'Ha! Sensible for you will not, I daresay, turn out sensible for me, that I'll voucher!' Ikey said indignantly. 'Seven parts to you and one to me, that's what your mother thinks be sensible?' Ikey pointed to the gold chain draped across David's paunch. 'How much you pay for that fob?'

David looked down. 'Four pounds,' he replied, running his fingers along the chain.

'Ha! It not be worth a penny over two,' Ikey said. 'Sensible, is it? Negotiate a fair price, will you? Your lot wouldn't know a brass pisspot from the bloody holy grail, you wouldn't!'

'The holy what?' David asked.

'Nevermind, it ain't kosher anyway. Yes, fifty-fifty, but you gives me your half o' the combination or we ain't got no agreement, and that's telling you flat, my dear!' Ikey looked up into his son's face, expecting him to be intimidated.

Instead David smiled and said calmly, 'We can wait. You'll die soon, Ikey Solomon, but if you wants the money in your lifetime it's still only one-eighth to you and we gets your combination.'

At the mention of his death Ikey felt his innards tighten and then relax, and he thought, 'Oh Gawd, I'm gunna shit meself!' But he showed no outward sign of the dismay and was relieved when he felt his sphincter close and his bowels return to normal. 'Ha! I've smoked you, boy! I'll not die soon enough for you to buy the partnership you wants so badly with George Madden!'

David Solomon flushed, his face turning a deep crimson. He walked over to a drawer in the kitchen dresser and from it took a small package and handed it to Ikey.

'Open it, if you please!' David demanded.

The package was wrapped in brown paper and tied with string, the twine in a bow so that it came undone at a single tug. Ikey folded back the paper to find a second wrapping, this one composed of a scrap of white cloth. Ikey unfolded the cloth slowly, then gasped in horror and fainted dead away.

He recovered moments later to find David standing behind him shaking his shoulders vigorously. When he perceived Ikey to have come around he grabbed his ears and held his head tightly, so that he was forced to look directly in front of him and at the package which lay open on the table.

'That be your precious black child's forefinger!' David said. He released Ikey and came around to face him again. 'We got them both, Hawk and Tommo Solomon!' He had lost all pretence at politeness and shook his head and then spat on the floor. 'Jesus! How could you call them by our family name?'

Ikey looked directly down into his lap to avoid the sight of Hawk's severed finger. He was trembling violently and trying with little success to regain his composure. Ikey had seen much worse in his lifetime and there was no blood, the finger having long since been cut off. But the thought of it being Hawk's finger had shocked him more deeply than he could ever have imagined.

David took the parcel and in a most matter-of-fact manner rewrapped it and tied the string, then placed it back in front of Ikey. 'You have two days to give me your half o' the combination, Ikey Solomon, then we sends the second finger to Mary Abacus with a single instruction, a note what says '*Ask Ikey about this*'. If we don't hear from you in two more days, well, we'll send a third finger with the same note, then a fourth and then we'll start with a little white finger to match the black ones, does you get my drift, father?' David sneered.

'Mary knows nothing o' the safe and the numbers!' Ikey said at last, recovering his courage. 'But be warned, she has powerful friends in the government, she'll go directly to them and you'll be apprehended!'

David laughed. 'The whole bloody island knows about the kidnapped brats and the fifty pounds reward from the back o' her beer bottles. That were very clever, that was! But the finger could've come from anybody, we'll deny it come from us! The authorities well knows o' the quarrels between us. They'll not believe you, thinking it's spite. But *you'll* have to tell Mary what you knows,' David grinned, 'and you won't do that, will you, Ikey Solomon?' He took his watch from his pocket and clicked it open.

'It be half past three o'clock. The ferry for Hobart Town leaves at four o'clock.' David Solomon paused. 'Or perhaps you'd like to stay the night. Ann made you a mutton stew. Give us your answer in the morning?'

Ikey, shaking his head, rose from the table. 'I'll not be staying,' he said quietly, then he looked up at his son. 'I been a villain in my day. But I didn't do no harm what led to bloodshed, and them I stole from could always afford a little loss. I ain't saying what I done was right, but I've served my punishment and what's in that safe in England I've earned. Not one-eighth, but half and much more!' Ikey paused. 'But half will do, the other half be your mother's and she can share it any way she likes. But *you* didn't earn it, and let me tell you something for nothing, my boy! As for my name, the black Solomon and his brother make me proud of it for the first time in my life!'

David Solomon now shook with anger. 'What does ya mean, I hasn't earned it? You, ya bastard, you betrayed our mother so she were sent 'ere and Ann, Sarah, Mark and me, we were put in the bloody orphanage! We earned that money orright! Every fuckin' penny, ya miserable sod!' He stepped up to Ikey and tapped him on the chest. 'Two days, or ya gets the bloody boy what you're so fuckin' proud o' givin' yer name sent to Mary Abacus bit by fuckin' bit, and the white brat follows soon after!' David stepped back, the whites of his eyes showing, his hands now balled into a fist. He was breathing heavily and Ikey felt he was about to strike him, but for once he was not afraid.

Ikey shook his head. 'This was your mother's idea, wasn't it? It's not just the money, it be her revenge on Mary Abacus too, ain't that it?'

'She has a good right to it!' David said, dropping his hands to his side. 'That bitch tried to steal her husband and the affection o' her children!' He cleared his throat. 'You got two days, Ikey Solomon.' He picked the tiny parcel up and handed it to Ikey. 'Show this to your whore!' he shouted.

On the ferry home Ikey's mind was a whirl. David was right, he would not go to the authorities. With his record of family quarrels and vendettas they would never believe him and, besides, two urchins going missing was an everyday occurrence and hardly worth investigating. The mutilation he knew they would take more seriously, but it looked typically like the work of some desperate escaped convict or wild man, or even a sealer or kangaroo shooter who had heard about the reward. Moreover, it was a black hand. While they would not say so, Ikey knew they would attach much less importance to it than if it were white.

Having Hawk's finger in one of the pockets of his coat saddened Ikey most terribly. He could see Hawk's hands dancing in the air as he worked the silent language, his little black fingers so elegant and expressive. The thought that Hawk's dancing hands might soon be bloody stumps was almost more than he could bear. Yet Ikey could not bring himself to tell Mary of the money in the Whitechapel safe. He knew he must attempt to save the lives of Tommo and Hawk, but he was also convinced he would never see a penny of the money it had taken him a lifetime to earn if he gave Hannah his half of the combination. Ikey tried to convince himself that Mary would recover from the loss of her children. Even if she should never talk to him again, he was comfortable enough and sufficiently independent. 'Life goes on,' he repeated to himself several times. 'They were not really her children,' he told himself, though he knew Mary loved Tommo and Hawk as well as if they had been born her own. He, too, was greatly fond of the boys, but Ikey's entire life had been a matter of his own survival and the first rule was not to mourn the past but to move on. He refused, out of a lifetime of habit, to agonise over the matter. Although he might never bring himself to say so, Ikey knew himself to love Mary, but he saw no purpose in telling her about the safe in Whitechapel. He would need to invent something else to explain the package he carried. By the time the ferry had arrived back in Hobart Town, Ikey had cobbled together quite a different story.

The ferry had caught the outgoing tide on the lower reaches of the Derwent River and the trip back had taken slightly over two hours. It was just after half past six in the evening when Mary, helping Jessamy serve customers, saw Ikey arrive and motioned urgently for her to meet him at the rear of the mill.

She was already in the kitchen waiting, wiping her hands on her apron, when Ikey entered the doorway. It had been a month and two days since Tommo and Hawk disappeared. Mary ate almost nothing and was silent most of the time, talking only when she was required to do so and working until late into the night. The new Tomahawk beer had thankfully kept them all very busy, or they might not have been able to bear the thought of Mary's sorrow.

'What is it, Ikey?'

Ikey looked at Mary. 'Sit down, my dear.'

Mary saw the concern on his face. 'What is it?' she asked again and then pulled out a chair and sat down. 'It's bad, isn't it?'

Ikey nodded and drew himself up a chair, then told Mary the story of his visit to New Norfolk.

'So there it is, my dear, you get the boys back by signing the deeds to the Potato Factory over to David Solomon.'

Mary remained silent for almost a minute, then she looked up at Ikey, a terrible weariness showing in her beautiful green eyes. She nodded slowly and Ikey knew she would give up anything for her two boys. 'He were never a good lad, that David. Bright but of a mean spirit,' Mary said quietly, then she was silent again before adding a small voice, 'Show me.'

Ikey recoiled, his head jerking back. 'No, my dear, it will distress you!'

Mary looked up at him, her expression suddenly fierce. 'Show me! I want to see it for meself!'

Ikey removed the small parcel from the interior of his coat and placed it on the table in front of her. Mary's hands trembled as she picked at the bow and then removed the brown paper wrapping. Silent tears ran down her cheeks as she unfolded the grubby, white cloth so that she could barely see the finger. She started to weep, then to wail, choking at the same time, her head averted from the small dark object.

Ikey quickly rose from his chair to stand behind her and place his hands on her shoulders. 'Oh dear, oh dear! Oh my! Oh dear!' he babbled. He could think of nothing to say to comfort Mary.

After a while Mary reached into the pocket of her apron for a piece of rag, and wiped her eyes and blew her nose. Ikey reached over her to take up the parcel, but she saw his action and pushed his hand away. 'Leave it!' she commanded.

'But, my dear . . .'

Ikey stopped mid-sentence, for there was a surprised gasp from Mary and then she began to laugh, though in a hysterical manner, pointing at the finger.

'What is it, my dear?' Ikey cried, alarmed.

But Mary's hysterical laughter continued and finally Ikey

slapped her hard. She stopped and looked at him wild-eyed. 'It's not Hawk's finger!' she cried, then wept again.

'What do you mean?' Ikey cried out. He repeated himself several times, 'What do you mean? What do you mean?' before Mary stopped crying. Now she took deep gulps of air to calm herself.

'Whatever can you mean?' Ikey repeated urgently.

'It be the right forefinger,' she said, pointing to the object before her. 'Hawk had a long scar down that finger where I cut and sucked it when he had the snake bite. A long, clean scar, not to be missed!'

Ikey remembered the incident well. 'Are you sure it be the right and not the left?' he said.

'Left were once broken in a fight, it mended a wee bit crooked,' Mary said emphatically. She glanced at the finger on the table and gave a small shudder. 'Besides, that finger be too small, much too small, that be the finger of an Aboriginal child!'

'You mean this be a scam?' Ikey cried in amazement. 'They's seen the beer label and cooked it all up!' Ikey whistled to himself. 'Jesus, I never thought that whore Hannah had that much imagination!'

Mary looked at Ikey and then said fiercely, 'That finger still come from a little brat! That be wicked and cruel enough beyond imagining.' She paused and pointed at Ikey. 'They could have taken the Potato Factory, they could have had the bloody lot, if only it would o' brought back me boys!' She burst into tears again and then shouted, 'Ikey, I swear, I dunno how and I dunno where, but Hannah's going to pay for this!'

Chapter Thirty-six

It was four months after his visit to New Norfolk when Ikey, in the course of his nightly peregrinations, sensed he was being followed. He changed direction, cutting down the lane past New Market and quickening his pace, thinking to slip into the Hope & Anchor, the tavern at the end of the lane facing onto the safety of Macquarie Street. But then he heard his name called softly in a voice he was never likely to forget.

'You good pella, Ikey!'

'Billygonequeer?' Ikey called back in surprise.

'No, no, William Lanney!' Billygonequeer said urgently as he came out of the darkness not five feet from where Ikey stood.

Ikey listened to the voice from the shadows, amazed that Billygonequeer could have been so close without his hearing him. The two men embraced and as Ikey's hands clasped around Billy's shoulders, he felt the raised scar tissue across his back through the coarse canvas shirt.

'Blimey, I thought you be dead!' Ikey exclaimed, beaming at Billygonequeer's dark face. 'What's happened to you then, my dear?'

Billygonequeer, who now spoke quite passable English, explained to Ikey that under the name William Lanney he had become a whaleman for Captain Kelly on one of the local whaling ships which worked the bays and channels during the winter season.

548

'Ikey, listen,' Billygonequeer said finally. 'I come about the black kid on the beer bottle.'

Ikey's heart missed a beat. 'What's you know about that, Billygonequeer?'

'William Lanney! You gimme the name y'self!' Billygonequeer cried urgently. 'I still on the lam, man!'

Ikey listened carefully as Billygonequeer told him what he knew. He had been down south at the whaling station at Recherche Bay where they had been boiling down the catch. They had thereafter sailed up the D'Entrecasteaux Channel, but opposite Huon Island had hit a squall and done some damage to the mizzen mast and so had taken shelter in the Huon River. The wind being fair, they had sailed upriver to Port Huon, and put ashore for some minor repairs. Here, Billy had gone for a walk along the riverbank some way from the settlement when, to his surprise, he had met seven Aboriginals, five of them half castes and two of full blood.

The full bloods explained they came from the upper reaches of the Kermandie River to the south-west, which stretched to the high mountain. They talked for some time and then told him that several days previously they had been out hunting rat kangaroo when they saw a wild man who rode a horse, behind which he caused a black boy to run. Curious, they had crept closer. The boy was tied about the neck with a rope which was attached to the saddle. The wild man passed close to where they hid and they could see that the boy was not an Aboriginal, but quite different in appearance to their own people. Billygonequeer concluded by saying that, nearly three weeks later, he had heard some of the whalemen talking about the fifty pounds reward posted on the beer bottles and he'd asked one of them to read it aloud. Hearing Ikey's name, he had decided to tell him what he knew. 'You good pella, Ikey!' he said, laughing at himself, for he now spoke much better English.

'What sort of country be it, these mountains?' Ikey asked at last.

Billygonequeer shook his head. 'You can't go there, boss!' he protested vehemently. 'It black fella place, wild men convict and some timber getter, very bad country.'

'Can you go with troopers?'

Billygonequeer sniffed. 'Troopers can't go this place, wild men kill!'

'Will I see you again?' Ikey asked.

'Hobart Town very dangerous for me,' Billygonequeer said. 'Three day,' he pointed to the ground, 'same time, I see you here.'

At breakfast the following morning Ikey told Mary what had transpired.

'It's Hawk!' Mary cried. 'Oh, Ikey, I know it's him!'

'There were no mention by the blacks of a sighting of Tommo, so it may not be, my dear,' Ikey cautioned. 'Besides it be wild country, only escaped convicts and timber getters, the roughest and most dangerous o' men, all outside the law and with a price on their 'eads. You won't be able to pay any cove sufficient so he be mad enough to go into those mountains!'

Mary looked at Ikey. 'I knows mountains, I been all over Mount Wellington. I knows the way o' the bush, I'll go meself!'

Ikey was too shocked at first to react, but finally regained his voice. 'You're mad, Mary Abacus, this be wild country such as you've never seen. No trooper will venture there for fear o' death. There be no roads, not even paths, it be virgin timber, grown so close and tall it be dark in daylight!'

'And how does you know all this?' Mary said sullenly.

'You forget, my dear, I was in a road gang. I knows the way of timber, only this be much worse – no man what's not bred to the mountains can live there. Even the timber getters be o' the worst sort, Irish and most o' them villains or in concert with the wild men. If a woman should venture there, even if she should not perish soon from the climate and hardship she must endure, she would soon enough be used in such a way that she would die of other causes, if you knows what I mean!'

'I knows what you mean, Ikey Solomon,' Mary said grimly. 'But no wild man's going to treat my boy like an animal!'

In Mary's eyes was the look Ikey had come to know well, and he realised nothing would dissuade her. He inwardly cursed himself for telling her about the sighting. After all, there was no way of knowing if it was Hawk, or even if the natives had told the truth.

'Perhaps we could muster some troopers at Southport? You could talk to Mr Emmett?'

'I got more chance on my own, Ikey. A woman on her own be the best bait to hook a wild man!'

'Shit no! No, Mary, I cannot have you do this!' Ikey cried. He'd presumed, if not troopers, that Mary would take some sort of armed escort on such a perilous journey.

'They've taken my boy and turned him into an animal and tied a rope around his neck! I tell you, I'd sooner die than not go after the bastard what done that to Hawk!'

'You will die, Mary!' Ikey said softly.

'Then I die trying, that's all!' Mary said angrily. 'It be better than living ashamed!'

'I'll come with you!' Ikey said, suddenly making up his mind.

Mary, astonished, looked at Ikey and smiled, then her eyes filled with tears. 'If you were to come we would most surely guarantee to perish,' she said tenderly. 'But I thanks you, Ikey Solomon, from the bottom o' me heart!'

Ikey had to admit to himself that he was secretly delighted with this reply, for he already regretted his decision.

'You will need to make sure your affairs are all in order, my dear,' he said sadly.

The next day Mary's enquiries revealed that, in three days, a small trading ketch, the *Isle of Erin*, would be leaving on the morning tide for Port Huon, and then on to the tiny new hamlet of Franklin. Mary booked passage, even though it was a cargo boat, and there were no cabins except the one which belonged to the captain. She was advised to bring her own oilskins as she would have to remain on deck throughout the two-day journey, the ship having to lay up at night against the sudden squalls which so often blew up along the D'Entrecasteaux Channel.

Ikey urged her to wait until he had spoken to Billygonequeer again, but there was no other boat for four days and Mary would not delay a moment longer. She knew that if news of her impending journey leaked out she would be forbidden by the authorities to travel into such wild country, so she settled her affairs and Ikey was sworn to secrecy. Mary told Jessamy Hawkins and the men at the Potato Factory at both the Old Mill and at Strickland Falls that she was going to do some trading with the small settlements along the Huon River. She instructed that they send a dray loaded with six dozen cases of Tomahawk and Temperance beer, and four fifty-gallon barrels of her strongest dark ale, to the Old Wharf where the *Isle of Erin* was docked.

On the third morning, just before sunrise, Mary left Hobart Town not sure that she would ever return. She looked up at the great mountain which had swallowed her two sons and said a quiet farewell, for she was now convinced that her mountain had not murdered Hawk and Tommo. She sat on the deck of the *Isle of Erin* on a case of Tomahawk beer, her umbrella spread open and her hand clasping the Waterloo medal. 'Bring me luck, and send the green parakeets to find my sons for me,' she begged the mountain. The summit of Mount Wellington was covered in cloud and a light drizzle fell. Though it was late spring, and the almond blossoms already out, there was mist on the river as the barque lofted sail and slipped into the ebb of the outgoing tide.

The voyage proved slow though uneventful. By the time they reached the channel the day had turned to bright sunshine and the small, clumsy and overloaded ketch seemed to make unnecessarily heavy work of a light breeze. At nightfall, they hove onto the leeward side of Huon Island under a near full moon.

Mary slept fitfully, for the night was cold. She had brought two blankets, one for herself and one for Hawk, or one for each of her children, as she hoped she'd find them both. Mary also wore her warm coat, this being the most she thought she could carry on her back when she set out on her journey into the mountains. The blankets and a supply of hard tack biscuit and dried meat, matches, sugar and tea made up the remainder of her burden, except for the small axe she'd carried up the mountain on the night Hawk and Tommo disappeared. It was heavy, but she knew she would need to take it along. The blankets she would roll up and place across the top of a canvas bag she had constructed, which was not unlike a child's school satchel, though somewhat bigger. Mary also carried fifty pounds in notes which were hidden in the brass cylinder of her prisoner's purse and deposited up her cunny. In her handbag she carried sufficient money for any expenses she might incur and as well a pearl-handled, pepperbox pistol.

The pistol had been presented to her by Ikey, who had bought it from Ann Gower. Ikey was most particular that it be light enough for a woman to handle yet carried four chambers, could be ready loaded, and deadly if fired at close range. Not being in the least accustomed to the workings of firearms he had diligently written down the instructions on how it should be loaded and Mary practised until she was certain how it was done. Though she had never before fired a pistol, she was confident that she was capable of using it should the occasion arise.

The *Isle of Erin* arrived in the tiny settlement of Port Huon by mid-afternoon of the second day. Mary's beer was loaded onto a bullock cart to be transported to the Kermandie River settlement, the driver happy to take a case of beer instead of payment, thinking himself much the better off with such a bargain. Mary sat beside the driver as they made slow progress into the small settlement.

The town seemed to be entirely constructed of bark and mud. The streets, if streets they could be called, were ruts where the unwary traveller might sink his boot half way to the knee in the wet.

The buildings were a testament to colonial ingenuity. A framework of wood was raised, and bark was peeled from green eucalypt in strips six feet long and two feet wide. The strips were flattened on level ground by poles laid across them and allowed to dry. When dry and stiff they made excellent walls, as well as serving, if lightly strutted, as doors and windows. Brown, warm-coated stringy bark provided the roof cladding. All that was then required was a slabbed chimney built above a base of stone, and lined a further four feet with stone topped with turf to protect the walls from fire. The flue, also of bark, was then carried up on a framework of poles to a suitable height above the ridgepole. From the chimney-breast up, the flue was boxed on all sides and experience taught just where to place the chimney to avoid down draughts. Thus everything was made locally and, if care was taken in the construction, a comfortable home could be built in a very short time.

The surrounding countryside rose steeply from the river and clearings for the small holdings around the settlement were a testament to sheer hard work. The natural growth which had to be removed before the soil could be tilled was a staggering five hundred tonnes per hectare. Ring-barked trees two hundred feet high stood like dead sentinels, while from their trunks huge strips of bark whispered and flapped in the wind. On the ground below cows grazed in paddocks sown with English grasses, coxfoot and white york, which provided fodder and hay for the winter. The rich virgin soil was deep-loamed and full of nutrients; at milking time, milch cows came in from the runs with full udders.

But despite this appearance of a tranquil farming community, the rising ground and huge trees made each acre taken from the forest a triumph over the forces of nature. The small community clung to the banks of the Kermandie River, and the wild country stretching towards the Hartz Mountains was not yet penetrated by settlers.

These forbidding parts of the interior were mostly occupied by isolated communities of itinerant timber getters, many of Irish origin, who lived further upriver and were said to be half wild and dangerous and unlikely to welcome strangers in their midst.

All male convicts who arrived in the colony would spend some time at hard labour producing timber and from that time on, any misdemeanour would result in a further stint on a timber gang. So, almost by definition, the worst offenders learned the most about the skill of the sawing pit, splitting logs and getting timber. In addition, the Irish, many of whom lacked the basic skills to work in towns, and being usually among the most intractable of convicts and also Roman Catholics in an overwhelmingly Protestant community, found timber getting was the only lawful skill they possessed upon emancipation. For many, isolation became their only way of avoiding trouble.

They seldom ventured with their families into the nearby towns and their children were wild things. They would score the timber, each with his individual mark and the number of his agent, and float it downriver. Every few weeks one of their kind might venture quietly into the small settlement and collect what was owing to them all. He might stop at the tavern for a few drinks, though he would usually buy what he needed of brandy and rum to take back into the forest, and leave with no more than a grunt to the publican.

It was claimed that should the law be foolish enough to wander into a timber camp, and if the timber getters should first see the law and the law not see them, then the law would be unlikely to see the sunset on the river again. It was a brave set of troopers or special constables who ventured out from the police station at Southport to patrol the small, scattered and isolated communities who lived in the dense, dark forests. And those who did travelled on horseback, so that they could more easily cover the ground or avoid a surprise attack.

Though these backwoodsmen would come out of the forest in winter to work at the Recherche Bay whaling stations during the peak season, they still kept to themselves, but should they drink, they turned into the very devil himself. The money they made during this period was spent in provisioning at the general store which they took back into the forests for the summer months.

As well, in the summer, escaped convicts and wild men roamed the mountain country. Food was relatively easy to get in the form of small animals and the easily captured native hen. In the winter they came nearer to the towns to raid the small farms and take a sheep or even a calf or pig, and if the property were not well guarded, or the owner away, to rape any women or children they would find. These were men outside the law and, like the timber getters, they lived lonely and brutal lives deep in the forests and mountains. They left the timber getters alone unless they should find one on his own, when they would murder him for his boots or axe or some other possession.

The bullock driver took Mary directly to the front of the tavern to avoid the mud. From the moment they entered the outskirts of the little town dozens of urchins, all with black mud caked up to their knees, had followed the cart and rudely yelled questions at Mary. But now they stood around shyly as she alighted and, first jumping a small mud pool, walked onto the verandah of the public house. It was the largest building in town, though it too was built of bark, but featured at one end a wall of stone containing a great high chimney which promised a hearth in the interior of splendid proportions.

Mary bid the driver wait and entered the tavern. At first, the smoke, smell and noise overwhelmed her senses. But when her eyes became accustomed to the dark she saw it to be a large rectangular room with a crowded bar running the full length of one side. The only natural light entering the room was from three small windows set up on the wall opposite the bar, this so that they should not be easily broken if a fight broke out.

The hearth at one end was as grand in size as it promised to be from the outside, but its tall chimney had nevertheless been badly designed. Smoke filled the room so that, with the addition of half a hundred pipes and cigars, it was far past the point of comfort for both the eyes and the nose. The low ceiling was long since blackened by the constant fumes and added to the dingy appearance of the place.

Several card tables occupied the centre of the room and wooden benches were placed against the outside walls, and all were occupied by human forms who, from the noxious smell they emitted, had not washed in a year. Men stood everywhere drinking beer and rum, while the players at the card tables with neat stacks of coins at their side must have found it difficult to communicate the least instruction in such an awful din. Mary observed that there were no women to be seen, not even a barmaid behind the counter.

As she walked in, there was an instant lull in the hubbub as the rough men standing and sitting everywhere appraised her. Eyes red from smoke and drinking followed her as she moved over to the bar, and two men leaning upon it stepped aside to let her in.

'Is there a publican?' Mary asked.

This, for some reason, caused the men within the room to explode with laughter.

'Aye!' said a voice as soon as the laughter had died down. It came from a door set into the centre of the wall behind the bar and, at the same instant, a big, burly man with a completely flat nose and eyes stretched to slits with puffed-up scar tissue made his appearance. As he came closer Mary saw that his ears, too, had the cauliflower appearance of a rough goer. She smiled nervously as he approached her and thought him ideally suited to his surroundings.

'You must forgive the men, not too many o' the fair sex do come in 'ere, miss,' he said, drying his hands on his dirty apron. 'Gin is it?'

'Ginger beer,' Mary said.

The publican looked somewhat embarrassed. 'Don't 'ave much call for ginger beer 'ere, miss.'

'Best rum, half and half and half a tot,' Mary pointed to a clay pitcher, 'if that be water.'

'Aye,' the publican said and took down a bottle of rum from the shelf behind him and poured a half measure into a glass, topping it with water from the jug.

Mary's call for best rum seemed to amuse the men and a second wave of laughter filled the room.

'Now, now, we'll have none o' that!' the publican called sharply, whereupon the laughter died down abruptly.

'Mary Abacus, from the Potato Factory, maybe you've heard o' my beer?' Mary announced to the publican, her voice firm, not betraying the nervousness she felt within.

'By Jesus, yes!' the publican exclaimed, plainly astonished.

There was a murmur around the room and quite suddenly the mood changed. Mary sensed a new tone of respect from the drinkers.

'We don't get much o' yer stuff 'ere, Miss Abacus, though it be greatly liked when we does.' The publican stuck out his huge paw. 'Sam,' he said. 'Sam Goodhead.'

Mary fought back a smile at this inappropriate name. She said, 'I have some beer for sale. Would you be interested, Mr Goodhead?'

'Never get enough beer, miss. Always interested. Though o' course it depends on the price, don't it?'

Mary gave Sam Goodhead a description of the beer and told him the quantity and the price, which she'd set fairly low so that the beer would be seen as a bargain.

'I'll take the lot orf yer hands, Miss Abacus, 'appy to do business!'

'I shall need accommodation tonight. Does you have a safe room, Mr Goodhead?'

'Not 'ere I doesn't, but if you'd care to come 'ome to the missus, I daresay we can put some o' the brats together and find you a bed what's safe enough. We'd take it as a pleasure if you'd 'ave tea with us.'

The noise in the room gradually resumed its former level, though several men had left the tavern to inspect the beer on the bullock cart. When Sam Goodhead arrived with Mary the men were taunting the bullock driver, who now stood with his whip held aloft ready to strike at anyone who should attempt to lift a case of beer from the cart.

'Bring it 'round the back, mate,' the publican instructed. 'Two stout lads back there will 'elp you unload.' He turned to Mary. 'Them's well-coopered barrels if I say so meself,' he remarked.

'Keep them with my compliments, Mr Goodhead,' Mary said, then told the publican about the case of Tomahawk the bullock driver had taken as payment and that this should be deducted from the price and, further, that he should take a case of her new Tomahawk beer for his personal enjoyment with her compliments.

'We ain't 'ad this beer before, it be a new one then?' the publican said, shouldering a case of Tomahawk to take home with him. 'I shall look forward to it.'

Mrs Goodhead was an equal match for her husband in size and

to Mary's keen eye looked somewhat knocked about in life herself, with one eye permanently closed and some scarring on her face. It was not the custom to enquire into the background of someone recently met, as most people in the colony had a similar and unfortunate story to tell. But after several of Mary's Tomahawk beers both her host and hostess became most loquacious, obviously maintaining a good head for liquor and, except for warming to the prospect of discussion, not otherwise disconcerted by it. Though they spoke briefly of their time as convicts in New South Wales, this was only to establish more quickly Sam's true past vocation, which was, Mary was not surprised to hear, that of a professional fighter. His wife, Esmeralda, had also been a fighter of some renown, originally in Bristol and later in the colony of New South Wales.

Sam had risen and shortly returned carrying an old poster which he handed to Mary. 'Read it aloud, please, Miss Abacus,' he said, laughing.

Mary held the poster up and began to read.

> *Sam Goodhead hereby challenges*
> *to fight any man in the colony for*
> *a prize of Five Pounds plus travel*
> *expenses and two gallons of beer.*
> *My wife Esmeralda shall fight any*
> *woman in the country, bar none;*
> *and for a prize of Two Pounds, travel*
> *expenses and a bottle of English Gin.*
> *My dog will fight any dog of 45 lb*
> *or less for two shillings, plus a juicy*
> *butcher's bone! My cock shall fight*
> *any cock in the colony of any weight*
> *for a shilling and a lb of good corn!*
> * * * * *
> *Apply, Mr Sam Goodhead,*
> *Parramatta Post Office.*

Both Sam and Esmeralda Goodhead laughed uproariously as Mary concluded.

'Aye, it does ya good to 'ave it read out loud. Though we knows it orf by 'eart, we can't read neiver of us, so it's good to 'ave it read by someone else once in a while,' Sam declared happily.

This explained why the publican and his wife had not broached the subject of the label on the Tomahawk bottle, for they were by now on their sixth bottle.

Esmeralda finally rose and prepared supper, a meal of roast beef with potatoes and swedes and a most delicious pickled cabbage. She filled four plates for her children and sent them outside to eat, and then brought three more heaped helpings to the table where they had been drinking. It was a meal as good as any Mary had tasted, and much more than she could eat. She excused herself after having finished less than half the contents of the plate.

'Never you mind, love, the little 'uns'll polish that orf soon enough, or Sam 'ere!' Esmeralda laughed.

After tea Sam produced a clay pipe, and when he had it well stoked so that the room was fuggy with smoke, Mary addressed him quietly.

'I has a proposition to put to you, Sam,' she said, for they were now on Christian name terms.

'Put away, lass,' Sam Goodhead said, puffing contentedly on his pipe.

'It be in strictest confidence.'

Sam nodded. 'Aye, everythin' is. I'll not tell unless I can make a profit out of it,' he said with a wink.

'That be the point,' Mary said. 'If you stays stum, you makes a very big profit; if you talks, you owes me for the beer!'

'What's ya mean, lass?' Sam said, now most interested and leaning forward. Esmeralda, who was scouring a pot with her back to them, suddenly stopped scrubbing.

'I needs some advice and help, nothing more, 'cept I don't want any folks to know about it right off!'

'That's not so easy 'round 'ere.' Sam laughed. 'Scratch the 'ead of a pimple on yer arse and it's the talk o' the bleedin' town fer days. Your comin' 'ere today is already the news o' the month!'

'Year!' Esmeralda called.

'What is it then?' Sam Goodhead asked.

Mary told him that she needed someone who wouldn't talk about it to take her as far as it was possible to go up the Kermandie River and thereafter to give her, if possible, some directions which would take her to the high mountains. 'That's all, a boatman what will keep his gob shut and some directions possibly.'

Sam Goodhead whistled. 'And you'll give us what?'

'The whole consignment o' beer I brought,' Mary said.

Sam Goodhead sighed. 'I'm sorely tempted, lass.'

Esmeralda turned fom her pots. 'You'll do no such thing, Sam!' she shouted.

Sam Goodhead shrugged. 'If I did that, Mary, it be the same as killin' you. Ya can't take such a journey all alone. Ya can't even take a journey like that with a platoon o' troopers. I'm sorry, lass, it be suicide!'

Mary picked up an empty bottle of Tomahawk and read from the back label. Then she told them about the abduction of Tommo and Hawk and the news that Hawk, at least, had been captured by a wild man and had been seen by some Aboriginals in the region of the Hartz Mountains.

'Them blacks are a lyin', thievin' bunch. Most be now locked away, thank Gawd, but there still be a few 'round 'ere. Ya can't trust 'em though,' Sam said. His pipe had gone dead and he now set about scraping the spent tobacco from the top of the bowl and relighting what was left.

'Sam, I'm going anyway, all you can do is make it easier!' Mary cried.

Eventually she convinced Sam Goodhead that nothing would keep her from looking for Hawk.

'We've a lad works fer me at the pub, he 'as a boat and will keep 'is gob shut if I tells 'im,' the publican said. 'You'd best leave at first light, that way the town won't known yer gorn.' He puffed at his pipe. 'Though it won't take long before the bloody timber getters know!' He sighed. 'Gawd 'elp ya, Mary Abacus, yer a brave woman, and if I didn't know better, I'd say a very foolish one! If ya gets back alive I'll take yer beer as bonus. If ya doesn't, which be more than likely, we'll use the money fer a tombstone, though I'll vouch yer body won't be lyin' beneath it!'

Mary was surprised to see that Esmeralda was quietly weeping in the corner.

A heavy mist lay over the water as Mary stood on the shore waiting for a lad she knew only as Tom. She heard the slow splash of oars through the fog and soon the outline of a small, flat-bottomed boat appeared through the swirling vapour. Behind it was a second boat, a smaller dinghy, attached by a rope to the boat the boy was rowing. The boy shipped the oars and Mary pulled the boat onto the shore and stepped into it. The young lad standing midships took her canvas bag and stowed it in the bow, and held his hand out to steady her as she seated herself in the stern. Then, without saying a word, he pushed the boat back into deeper water, pulled it around with one oar until the boat pointed upstream, and began to row.

The Kermandie was a slow-flowing river, but rowing against the current with another skiff in tow was not an easy matter, and every half hour Tom beached the little boats and, his chest puffing violently, was forced to rest. About nine of the clock the mist lifted and the huge trees, which had appeared simply as shadowy outlines in the misted landscape, now showed clearly on either shore. Mary found herself locked into a narrow ribbon of water walled as surely and steeply by the giant eucalypts as if the trees had been sheer cliffs of solid rock. A flock of yellow-tailed black cockatoos flew over at one point, their tinny screeching the only sound they'd heard since leaving but for the lap of the oars in the water and once the flap of a flock of chestnut teal as they rose in alarm from the water. The sun was now well up and Mary worked herself out of her coat. They passed a black cormorant on a dead branch, its wings spread to the new sun, and soon after a white-faced heron stood on the shore, its long neck and sharp-beaked head moving in slow jerks, made curious by the slap of the oars. Though the trees on either side of the river still looked cold and dark, the glare from the water and the sun overhead made Mary feel uncomfortably hot. Tom's shirt was dark with sweat and his long, lank hair lay flat against his head. Mary saw beads of perspiration cutting thin streaks down his dirty neck.

The further they travelled the more dense the trees became. Giant prehistoric tree ferns, some of them forty feet high, grew at the water's edge, and occasionally they'd hear the splash of an unseen creature plop into the water from the riverbank. At one stage Mary, intimidated by her surroundings, whispered to Tom simply so that she might make some sort of human contact. But he held a finger to his lips. Once, about an hour out from the settlement, they heard the sound of an axe striking. Sharp, regular echoes seemed to bounce off the trees, though from somewhere much deeper into the forest. Mary was not sure whether the sound was frightening or comforting, but Tom shipped oars for a few moments and listened while the boat drifted backwards in the current. Then, Tom taking great care with his strokes, they moved on again.

After four hours with regular rests they came to a waterfall and Tom pulled the boats into shore.

'This be it, missus, we can't go further,' he shouted, his voice almost lost in the crash and tumble of water over rock.

Mary stepped onto the shore and Tom pulled the boat fully into the little pebbled beach, untied the smaller dinghy and dragged it also onto the safety of the riverbank. Then, straining mightily, he pulled the first dinghy into a clump of reeds and fern, piling the branches of dead trees over it until it was impossible to see. He placed three rocks close to each other, two together and one pointing to where the boat was hidden.

'I'll be back for the boat in ten days!' he shouted, pointing to the fern and reeds where it lay concealed.

Mary nodded and handed the lad a pound. He grinned, his work well rewarded. 'Thank 'ee, ma'am, Gawd bless 'ee now!' he shouted, touching the forelock of damp hair. Then he pushed the smaller dinghy back into the water. The tiny boat turned in the churning current at the foot of the falls, then the oars dug in and he steadied it, waved briefly and began to row away.

Mary watched as he disappeared around a bend in the river, rowing lazily in the firm current now driven faster by the falls. Then she rolled up her coat and strapped it with the blankets resting on top of her canvas bag, slipping her arms through its straps so that it sat firmly on her slim back. She stood for a moment and held the Waterloo medal in her hand, half praying that a pair of green rosellas might suddenly fly over as a sign, but nothing disturbed the bright blue cloudless sky overhead.

She had a map which Sam Goodhead had drawn, or perhaps obtained from elsewhere, and it showed a path leading directly from the waterfall in a direction due west. It took Mary some time to find the path, for it was much overgrown with bracken and fern. She soon stopped to take the axe from her pack, and her going was tediously slow. Though it was not past ten in the morning the forest was dark as though already deep into the afternoon, and as she travelled further into the giant trees she began to feel the weight of the journey on her mind.

For the first time Mary realised that she had no idea what she was doing or how she would find Hawk. Above her the trees towered two hundred feet into the air and the wind in the high canopy gave off the sound of endless waves beating against a lonely shore. At noon she stopped beside a small stream, ate a little of her biscuit and drank from the mountain water. The straps of her canvas bag had cut into her shoulders, she was already badly scratched about the hands and face, and her bonnet was saturated with perspiration.

At nightfall Mary was still within the forest and the track had become almost impossible to find, so she halted beside a small stream some twenty yards distance from the path, marking several trees with the blade of the axe so that she might find her way back in the morning. She ate a little more of the hard biscuit and some dried meat, lit a small fire and boiled tea in her billy. The night became bitterly cold but Mary could not take the chance of going to sleep with a fire. She doused the fire, wrapped herself in both blankets and still wearing her coat she fell into a fitful sleep. She was exhausted, and the night sounds did not unduly disturb her for they were no different to those she had heard so often on her own mountain.

Mary woke up with the sun cutting through the misted trees and lay for a moment, all her senses suddenly alert for she could hear a most familiar sound. It was friendly to her ear until a moment later she realised where she was. She'd heard the sawing of Peter Degraves' timber cutters a thousand times on the mountain, a cross-cut saw being worked in a sawing pit. But now she realised it was coming from close by. Had she continued on another five minutes along the path the previous night, she would have stumbled right into a timber getters' camp.

She folded the blankets and packed her bag and, with her heart beating fiercely, she drank from the stream and then regained the path. She crept along until she saw the camp ahead, four bark huts in a forest clearing. She could see several children playing and a pig tied to a stake and once a woman came out of one of the huts and yelled at the brats to come in and eat. And all through this Mary could hear the saw. Though she could not see the pit, she knew exactly what it would be like. The log would be placed longitudinally over the pit on wooden cross pieces, whereupon sawing lines would be drawn along it with chalk or charcoal. One man descended into the pit while the other stood on the log. The man in the pit pulled down to make the cutting stroke, the one above pulled the saw up clear of the wood and guided the cut along the line. It seemed such a normal and friendly occupation, and while she knew it was most strenuous work which built up bulging muscles if the body received sufficient nourishment, Mary had never before associated the sound with danger.

The path led directly to the clearing. Mary, hoping that the sound of the saw would cover her escape through the undergrowth, moved in a wide circle around the camp. She kept the sound of the saw in her ears so that she might find herself back on the path but on the other side of the timber getters' camp. Almost an hour later she regained the path with the sound of the cutting now well behind her.

But soon after Mary left the camp she had a sense of being watched. At first she told herself that her alarmed senses were a delayed reaction from having so nearly stumbled into the camp. But the feeling persisted and she could not be rid of it. Once she looked up to find a large, pitch-black, crow-like bird with burning ruby eyes looking at her. After the initial shock, she laughed quietly to herself. She was becoming frightened of shadows. At noon she stopped and moved off the path some distance and boiled a billy. She used only the driest, smallest twigs and built the fire against the trunk of a huge red gum so that any smoke she created would be sucked upwards against the trunk and dispersed unseen through the forest canopy.

It was then that she was attacked. From a hole in the tree she had disturbed a hive of wasps and they descended upon her in an angry storm. Mary had the presence of mind to grab her canvas bag and pluck the billy from the fire and run. She rushed headlong through the undergrowth, not caring about any sound she should make, the wasps stinging her furiously as she ran. She fell once and cut her arm and then got up and ran again until the wasps seemed no longer to torment her. Finally she stumbled to a halt and began to weep, her flesh covered in hundreds of stings so that she felt she could not possibly bear the pain.

She had stopped beside one of the numerous mossy banked streams that cut through the forest and in desperation threw down her canvas bag and ripped off her clothes. The wasps had penetrated through the material of her dress and her body and arms were covered in stings which hurt well beyond the lashes she had received on the *Destiny II*. Hysterical with the pain, Mary lay down naked in the stream. The icy water flowing over her body brought some relief, for her flesh soon grew numb. Her poor crippled hands were swollen to twice their normal size and her right hand was burned when she'd plucked the billy from the flames. Though her bonnet had protected her head and she had no stings in her hair, her neck and face were badly stung and her lips were so swollen that she could not open her mouth.

Mary was soon chilled to the bone and was forced to rise from the stream and cover herself with the blankets. As soon as she warmed again the terrible pain returned and she seemed close to losing her senses. Her body had grown quite stiff as though it were paralysed and she could not move, though she was shuddering violently as if in great shock. Then she lost consciousness. Several times she seemed to see the crow with its ruby eyes and long, sharp beak, as though it were seeking to pluck out her eyes. Then a dog-like creature sat and watched her from a short distance, its green eyes sharp as lights in the night, and sometimes she caught flashes of a dark face hovering above her. She tried to scream but no sound came from her lips which seemed, in her delirium, to cover her entire face, enveloping her nose and puffing up her eyes.

How long she remained in this state Mary had not the least idea, but when she awoke it was morning, though whether of the next day or several days after, she could not tell. Her body and face were covered in a sticky balm, as though the wasp stings had themselves suppurated, but miraculously the pain was gone, and the swelling had abated and did not hurt to the touch. Mary washed in the stream until the sticky substance was removed from her body, hands and face and then she dressed, distressed to find that her garments were torn in several places from her flight through the undergrowth.

Mary ate, and boiled the billy for tea, for she found herself very hungry. Then she packed her bag and prepared to leave, but suddenly she realised that she did not know where the path lay. She moved around for more than an hour without finding it and then knew that she had become completely lost. Sam Goodhead had cautioned her against leaving the track by more than a few feet. 'Fer if ya become lost in the forest ya will die as surely as if ya put a gun to yer own 'ead,' he had warned.

It was then Mary heard the screech of the green rosella, a sound she knew as well as the beat of her own heart, the curious 'kussik-kussik' call repeated and then a bell-like contact note; when alarmed, a shrill piping sound. Rosellas do not fly in flocks in the spring but in pairs, and now she heard them both as they chattered somewhere to her left. Mary, ever superstitious and with no better plan to follow, moved towards the sound.

Mary had been three days in the forest, for though she did not know it, she had lain all the next day and the night that followed beside the stream in the delirium caused from the wasp stings. Now, without questioning the curious circumstances that the sound of the two parrots never seemed far from her and that she never seemed to approach nearer or to see them, she responded to their call. Sometimes she would turn to take an easier way through the undergrowth and she would hear the shrill piping of alarm from the two birds. After a while she learned to correct her course to the sound of their calls.

Mary fervently believed that the great mountain had answered her call for help. Even in her most prosaic moments, Mary thought of the mountain as her friend and lover, which was why she did not question the call of the two birds and the fact that they never left her.

Late on the afternoon of the fourth day she suddenly came across the track again and soon after broke out from the trees. She had been climbing steadily all day and now she found herself in a small valley above the tree line, a dent in a mountain which rose steeply upwards. It was as though a sharp line had been drawn where the mountain broke out of the apron of trees and into the coarse tussock grass of the high mountain country. The track now led upwards and seemed quite well worn, there being no forest growth to obscure it.

Mary walked along the track a short distance but then, in the fading light decided to retreat into the forest for the night. It was some minutes after she had returned and moved a safe distance from the track when she realised that the 'kussik-kussik' calls of the two rosellas were no longer with her.

She rose again at dawn, her body stiff and sore, and boiled the billy for tea. She ate sparingly, not knowing how much longer she would be in the wilderness and conscious that if she should find Hawk she would need to share her supplies with him.

However, by now her hope of finding her son was greatly diminished. The forest had left her in despair and even though she had come safely through it, she now saw that a wild man might hide effectively from a thousand troopers and not be found in a lifetime. Her only hope was the notion that the monster who had captured her son rode on horseback, and horses do not find fodder in the forest but need grassland. He would be forced to live or spend time near some sort of pasture, and this meant open ground.

Mary climbed steadily all morning. The mountains, she discovered, were punctured with small, sharp valleys like indented cones, many of them turned to small blue lakes with grassy walls too steep to climb down into. She would often stop for breath and far below her she could see the endless stretch of green forest turned blue in the distance, and the glinting, wide stretch of the Huon River twenty or more miles away. The mountain, despite the sun, grew cold as she rose higher, and a sharp, icy wind whipped her skin.

On her first night she found a small box canyon which was protected from the wind and made her camp. It was perhaps a foolish place to spend the night, for there was no place to retreat, but her hand throbbed painfully where it had been burned by the billy and Mary was too spent of effort to care. Her greatest concern was to escape the cutting wind. Besides, the mountain, but for rock and grass and bracken fern, was bare of any acceptable hiding place.

Mary woke with the crack of a rock striking near her head, her nostrils filled with the musty smell of horse sweat. She turned to look upwards and saw a horse and rider not fifteen paces from where she lay.

Mary now sat up with the blankets still clasped about her neck to form a protective tent about her body, groping for the pistol which she had placed fully loaded under a rock near her side the night before. The folds of the blanket concealed her free hand as she found it, though her swollen hand made it difficult to grip firmly the small pistol.

The man on the horse did not make a sound but simply stared down at her. He was dressed almost entirely in kangaroo and opossum skins but for a trooper's high-topped white cap much battered and entirely blackened. His filthy beard fell almost to his waist and his unkempt hair hung wild and knotted to his shoulders. What remained of his face was dark with dirt and criss-crossed with scars and his nose was squashed flat, like a pig's snout, and from it a stream of yellow snot ran into his matted beard. A red tongue flicked from the dark hair of his face as though he was tasting the air or testing the nature of the wind, savouring her body smell.

It was then that she saw Hawk. Or perhaps it wasn't, except that the skeleton attached to the rope which led from the back of the horse was black in colour. Mary gasped. 'Hawk!' she cried. The skeleton raised both its hands but did not speak and now Mary saw that it was her son. His hands worked slowly and Mary tried to follow. Hawk's hands simply spelled, 'Mama'.

'Hawk! Mama's come!' Mary shouted and then looking up at the monster on horseback she screamed, 'He's my boy, my precious boy, give me him!'

The creature looked backwards and jerked violently at the rope so that Hawk was thrown to his knees. Then he slowly dismounted and, undoing the rope from the saddle, pulled it, bringing Hawk back to his feet. He then dragged him over to a large boulder and tied him to it. Turning, he drove his fist into the child's face. Hawk made no sound as he fell.

At the sight of Hawk knocked to the ground from the vicious blow, Mary began to weep. 'You bastard! You fucking bastard!' she moaned, repeating the words over and over again in her terrible distress.

The man moved slowly to tie the reins of his horse to the point of a sharp rock. He knew he had Mary trapped. The bluff rose behind and on either side of her, and he himself blocked her only chance of escape.

Now he advanced slowly towards Mary, who rose to her feet as he approached. He was no more than four feet from her when she raised the pistol behind the blanket, but the wild man, perhaps sensing danger, suddenly lunged forward and threw her to the ground. The pistol fell from Mary's swollen hand on to her coat, which she had the previous night spread on the ground, so its falling made little noise. Mary landed on her back, the pistol digging painfully into her ribs.

The monster, now on top of her, panting violently, tore open the blankets which still half covered her, then ripped the top of her dress exposing her breasts. He was not a tall man but wide and powerfully strong, and he now spread one thick hand around Mary's throat to pin her down. With his free hand he began to tear the skirt from her body.

He was slobbering at the mouth, his tongue darting in and out. Then his arm rose above his shoulder and he smashed the side of her face with the back of his hand. Releasing his grip on her throat, he got to his knees and quickly pulled down his greasy hide trousers to show a huge, jerking erection. Parting Mary's legs roughly, he tried to force an entry.

Mary, almost unconscious from the blow, did not scream but fought to keep her wits about her and willingly allowed her legs to open. The monster was grunting and puffing as he tried to penetrate, but Mary's prisoner's purse prevented his penis from entering her. She felt his fingers grope at her and then with a grunt he withdrew the brass cylinder and threw it aside. Then he jammed himself between her legs, again trying to force his way into her. Mary felt the sharp pain as he entered and at the same moment she pulled the trigger of the pistol she held against his stomach. She pulled back the hammer and pulled the trigger a second time.

A look of complete and uncomprehending surprise appeared on the wild man's face and then he gripped his stomach with both hands. Mary set the hammer back and pulled a third time, this shot moving upwards and entering his heart, shortly followed by another. The creature jerked once and then his body slumped over her. Instantly he voided from both his natural apertures.

The sound of the four shots echoed and reverberated through the small canyon as Mary lay terrified under the fallen monster, his member still jerking within her.

Screaming, she pushed at the dead man and after a few frantic moments was able to climb out from under him. She was covered in blood and guts, shit and vomit, both her breasts stained crimson with his blood, which also soaked what remained of her dress and petticoat.

Mary did not even think to pause but ran towards Hawk, who had regained his feet and now cowered against the rock. She grabbed him and clasped him to her and howled as though she herself were some primitive creature and then, at last, she wept and wept, holding her son in her arms.

Chapter Thirty-seven

In years to come Hawk would grow into a man who stood six feet eight inches tall and weighed two hundred and eighty pounds with no lard upon him. People would whisper as he passed that he had once cheated the gallows. As proof they would point to the thick collar of scar tissue about his neck.

'The rope could not break his neck,' they'd whisper, 'but it took his voice.'

This last part was an appropriate enough explanation. Hawk had been dragged behind the wild man's horse and the constant pulling and falling had destroyed his vocal cords. He would never speak again. So that the full trauma of his experience might be truly appreciated, it should be added that during the six months he was enslaved he had been repeatedly sodomised.

On the return journey a most fortunate circumstance befell the terrified couple. The timber getters had found Mary's trail and set out to find who had intruded into their domain. They came upon Mary and Hawk making their way down the mountain on the wild man's horse not two hours after she had killed him. Mary was wearing her blood-stained overcoat to cover her nakedness, and Hawk clutched one of the bloody blankets about his body.

Two of the timber getters continued up the mountain to inspect the corpse which Mary had covered with the remaining blanket, and the three others escorted Mary and Hawk safely down through the wilderness, allowing them to remain on the horse. The two men soon enough caught up with them and started to shout excitedly from some distance before they finally arrived.

'She's killed Mad Dog Mulray!' one of them cried. 'Shot 'im through the 'eart!' the other shouted so as not to be outdone by his partner. One of them carried over his shoulder a bundle made from the opossum skin coat the wild man had worn. The second one now wore a set of military pistols in his belt and was waving Mary's pepperbox pistol which, in her state of shock, she had entirely and most foolishly forgotten to retrieve.

There was much excitement among the three remaining men and the oldest, a man who had earlier most formally introduced himself to Mary as Hindmarsh, looked up at her admiringly. Then the lad threw the skin bundle to the ground and untied it. Inside was the severed head of the wild man.

Mary gasped, though she was too shocked to scream, or perhaps there was no screaming left in her. She instinctively grabbed Hawk and placed her hands over his eyes.

'You 'ave done us a great service, Mary Abacus,' Hindmarsh said at last. 'He were a divil, a monster creature, the anti-Christ hisself. He's murdered seven of our forest folk.' He touched the severed head with the toe of his boot and then turned to the lad who had placed it at his feet. 'Tie it up again, Saul.' Then he laughed. 'It will make a grand Christmas present on the gate post o' the police station in Southport!'

One of the young men now handed the prisoner's purse to Hindmarsh, who examined it briefly and then looked up at Mary.

'This be your'n miss?' he asked. It was obvious to Mary that he well knew the nature of the object he held in his hands.

Mary nodded. 'In it be fifty pounds, it were money offered for the recovery o' me son,' she explained. 'The reward like.' She placed her hand on Hawk's shoulder.

The men surrounding her were rough and ready and now they laughed and looked at each other, their expressions plainly bemused. 'The nigger be your son?' Hindmarsh asked surprised, looking first at Mary and then into Hawk's dark and frightened face.

'Yes, mine!' Mary cried fiercely.

Hawk jumped at the tone of Mary's voice and the blanket

slipped to his shoulders and now Hindmarsh and the others saw where the flesh was cut half an inch into the boy's neck to expose the bones. In other parts it was festered and suppurating and slabs of pink scar tissue had been laid down from earlier rope burns. 'Jaysus, Mary Mother o' Gawd!' Hindmarsh said. Then he handed the brass cylinder back to Mary.

'This is not ours to own,' he said.

'I be happy to pay it all, if you'll escort us back to the river where we has a boat,' Mary said.

'Yes we knows about that,' Hindmarsh said. 'It were not very well hid.' He smiled. 'We'll be after takin' you anyways, miss, you'll not be payin' us for *that* privilege!' He pointed to the horse and then the pistols in the young man's belt. ''Orse and pistols, they be payment more'n enough.' He looked at the four younger men so that they might pay keener attention to what he was about to say. 'We owes you, Mary Abacus. You be a legend from now among the timber getters, accepted as one of our own kind and welcome to return at any time you wishes, even though I daresay you be a bloody Protestant!' He paused and then added with a grin, 'And so we won't be after makin' you a saint though you comes a bloody sight nearer than most I've 'eard o' what comes from Rome!'

Hawk spent long periods on his own on the mountain. It was as though he was eternally searching for Tommo, trying to recapture the essence of his brother. He soon regained the flesh on his bones and his neck healed well as young flesh does. Mary changed the label on the back of her Tomahawk beer to contain only Tommo's name and description, though all else remained.

Tomahawk Ale was now most famous in the colony and also in Melbourne and Sydney and it seemed almost the entire colony knew of the disappearance of Tommo. Mary never admitted it, but she secretly believed that Tommo was dead, though Hawk did not. Despite being repeatedly questioned in hand language by Ikey upon his return, Hawk could remember next to nothing of the kidnapping. The shock of the experience had completely erased his memory of the incident, but for the fact that they had not been captured by the wild man but by men who knew their names and had been most friendly.

Hawk continued with his studies and was seldom without a

book in his hand. Always a serious child, he was now withdrawn and rarely smiled, though when he did, Mary would say, 'It's a smile that could brighten a dark room at midnight'. With the benefit of the hand language which Mary soon learned well, he was able to talk with her as well as Ikey and Jessamy, who had also learned the language. With others, provided they could read, he was able to write upon a slate which he carried on a string about his neck.

Ikey, fearing that Hawk's inability to talk might disadvantage him, spent more and more time with his adopted son. Hawk at ten was already working on the accounting books at the Potato Factory under Ikey's instructions. At thirteen he was most competent with a ledger and had developed a fair hand which Mary wished, when it matured, should be the most beautiful hand in the colony, and so she bought him the latest in handwriting manuals so that he might practise the perfection of his letters.

But Ikey feared that this was not enough and, without Mary's knowledge, he began to teach Hawk all the skills he knew. Hawk was too big in his frame to have ever been a pickpocket, but in all the other tricks of palming he became an expert. His large hands could conceal anything and there was not a card game he could not play or cheat at with great skill, though Ikey despaired of him for he would never cheat in a real game, but much preferred to win with his own wit and intellect. He taught Hawk how to 'christen' a watch, and how to recognise a forged banknote, of which there were a great many in circulation in Van Diemen's Land. Hawk also learned to lip read, even though his hearing was perfect. 'So you may read what a man says across a room or in a crowd,' Ikey explained. Conscious that he had been brought up by Mary to be honest in all his dealings, Hawk would sometimes ask Ikey why he should learn a certain skill.

'Bless you, my dear, it is not an honest world we live in and few can enjoy the luxury o' being entirely honest within it.' Ikey would cock his head to one side. 'Have you not noted that the expression most cherished by those who are rich is the term "the honest poor"? They take much time to extol this virtue in those who have nothing, whereas there is no expression in our language which talks o' "the honest rich"! Honesty, if it be truly earned, be, for the most part, the product o' poverty and occasionally, if it is practised by the rich, a characteristic of inherited wealth, though rare enough in even this circumstance!'

Ikey would warm to the subject. 'There is neither bread nor virtue in poverty but, because it be a necessity, for how else will the rich become rich if they do not have the poor to depend upon, it stands to reason that the rich must manufacture more poor if they are to grow more rich! The rich become rich by *taking* and the poor by *giving*. The rich take the labour o' the poor in return for a pittance calculated to make poor men near starve, so that they will fight each other for the privilege o' giving o' the labour the rich man depends upon!'

'But Mary be not like that, Ikey!' Hawk protested. 'There are none that starve who work at the Potato Factory!'

'Aye, Mary be different,' Ikey admitted. 'But you observe, she does not grow rich.'

'That be because she has no capital to buy the machinery she must have if she is to have a proper brewery!'

'Ha! Precisely and exactly and definitely and most certainly! My point precisely, my dear! If she should give the men less and not feed their brats . . . If she should employ children for tuppence a day and not men for a shilling, she might soon have the capital to expand.'

'I should not wish her to do that!' Hawk replied, his hands working furiously. 'Her conscience and mine would not allow it!'

'Conscience?' Ikey said, surprised, one eyebrow raised. 'That be a luxury you be most fortunate to afford, my dear! That be the single greatest gift and also the worst advantage Mary has given you.'

'Why then must I learn of these ways of yours?' Hawk asked.

'You mean the ways o' perfidy?'

Hawk nodded his head.

'The perfidious man be the normal you will come across in life. Everyone you will meet in business will seek advantage over you, my dear. So you must learn to recognise the cheat and the liar and unless you know the manner of his scam, the method of his ways o' doing you down, you will be beaten. If you knows how a man should cheat at cribbage you will call him early. To know the scam is to make sure it does not happen to you.' Ikey laughed. 'Ah, my dear Hawk, you do not have the character to be a liar and a cheat!' Ikey paused. 'My only wish is that I teach you enough o' the perfidy o' mankind to prevent you from being a fool.'

'You wish me to be hard but fair in my dealings?' Hawk asked with his hands.

'Aye, but also to remember the first rule o' doing business, my dear!'

Hawk had a peculiar way of raising his left eyebrow when he wished Ikey to explain further.

'Always leave a little salt on the bread!' Ikey explained.

Hawk's eyebrow arched again and Ikey wondered how best he should answer him. He found Hawk's demeanour most strange, for at thirteen the boy had developed an acute sense of fairness and a natural dignity, and already the men who worked at the Potato Factory deferred to him willingly and took their instruction from him without the slightest hint of malice. These were rough men, born to the notion that the possessor of a black skin was the most inferior man who walked upon the earth's surface, yet they seemed to love the boy and eagerly sought his smile.

Though the kidnapping greatly saddened him, and his love for Tommo had left some part of him permanently distraught, Hawk retained no bitterness from the terrible experience with Mad Dog Mulray. The men who worked for Mary seemed to sense this and respected him accordingly.

Ikey had been pushed into the street from the moment he could crawl about in the courts and alleys of the rookery, and only a minority of the children who had crawled in the filth with him had survived childhood. As soon as he could run from authority he was sent out to scavenge and pilfer what he could from the streets. He had learned from the very beginning that the means of life were desperately scarce and that they went to the toughest. Cunning, quick responses to opportunity and danger, freedom from scruples and courage were the ingredients of survival. The costermonger with his fly weights made a living while the drudging bricklayer went under. The prostitute on the corner fed her children while those of the bloody-fingered woman who stitched gunny sacks starved to death. In a few fortunate minutes a gang of urchins could rob a badly loaded dray and earn more from the goods than their parents could earn in a week of labouring.

Ikey accepted the terms of this society where only the strong survived. But on the first day his father had pushed him onto the streets to trade with a tray of oranges and lemons he had been confronted with a new conundrum, a contradiction to all he instinctively knew in the game of survival. A rabbi had stopped the small boy and enquired as to the cost of a lemon.

'That'll be a ha'penny to you, rabbi,' Ikey had answered cheerily.

'Vun lemon is vun half penny? For twelve, how much?'

'Sixpence o' course!' Ikey replied cheekily. The reb was a foreigner and even if he was a rabbi he must be treated with a certain English disdain.

'Ja, so, let me see, I take only vun lemon for vun halfpenny, or thirteen for six pennies?'

'No, sir, rabbi, that be wrong! Them lemons be twelve for a sixpence!' Ikey corrected.

The rabbi sighed. 'So, tell me, my boy. You like to sell twelve lemons or vun lemon?'

'Twelve o' course, stands to reason, don't it?'

'Then ve negotiate! You know vot is negotiate?'

Ikey shook his head. 'Does it mean you be tryin' to get the better o' me, sir?'

'Very goet! You are a schmart boyski. But no, negotiate, it means I must vin and you also, you must vin!' The rabbi spread his hands. 'You sell more lemons and also, I get more lemons!' He smiled. 'You understand, ja?'

'But you gets one lemon what you 'asn't paid for!' Ikey said, indignant at the thought that the rabbi was trying to bamboozle him.

'Alvays you leave a little salt on the bread, my boy. Vun lemon costs vun half penny, twelve lemons cost six pennies, then vun lemon you give to me, that is not a lemon for buyink, that is a lemon for negotiatink, that is the little salt alvays you leave on the bread, so ven I vant lemons, I come back and you sell alvays more lemons to the rabbi, ja?'

'I tell you what, rabbi, 'ow's about twelve lemons and an orange for a sixpence, what say you?'

The rabbi laughed. 'Already you learnink goet to negotiate,' he said as he took the orange which cost a farthing and the dozen lemons and paid Ikey the sixpence.

'Always leave a little salt on the bread' had become an important lesson in Ikey's life. From the beginning he had always paid slightly above the going price for the stolen merchandise brought to him and it had played a significant part in earning him the title Prince of Fences. The rabbi had been correct, his 'customers' stayed loyal and always returned to him. Ikey had come to believe that 'leaving a little salt' was the reason for his good fortune and the source of his continued good luck. Ikey, like most villains, was a superstitious man who believed that luck is maintained through peculiar rituals and consistent behaviour.

And so Ikey explained the theory of a little salt on the bread to Hawk, who seemed to like this lesson more than most and made Ikey write it out on a slip of paper for him so that he might copy it into his diary. Ikey quickly wrote: *Remember, always leave a little salt on the bread.*

It was about this time that an event occurred which would change forever the lives of future generations of both families who carried the name Solomon.

Like most great changes there was very little to herald its coming, for it emerged out of a simple puzzle which Ikey, in a moment of mischief and amusement, had composed to bemuse Hawk, although, as with most things concerning Ikey Solomon, it contained a hidden agenda.

Ikey was becoming increasingly rheumatic and found his nightly sojourn around the Wapping and waterfront areas especially difficult. On some nights, out of weariness of step, he would remain too long in one place, and therefore be unable to complete his rounds on time or even to arrive at the Whale Fishery. More and more he relied on Hawk to help him at the races and afterwards he went straight to bed so that he could rise at midnight to do his rounds. He also became more preoccupied with death and was a regular and conscientious member of the new Hobart synagogue.

Ikey also realised that if Hannah and David and his two sons in New South Wales were determined to wait until his death so that they might claim the entire contents of the Whitechapel safe, he was left with a most peculiar dilemma: how to convey his combination number without telling either Mary or Hawk about the safe until he was certain he was on his death bed. It was still his greatest hope that Hannah and David would relent and agree to a fifty-fifty share of the safe and that Hannah would entrust the opening of the safe to his youngest son Mark and to Hawk, who would each separately hold a half of the combination.

Ikey had several times made this proposal only to have it rejected by Hannah and David. They insisted on the eight-part split and grew increasingly confident that they would soon be in possession of the entire contents as Sarah would often express her genuine concern at Ikey's frailty when she visited her family in New Norfolk.

Hannah knew also that Ikey could not openly leave his half of the treasure to Mary or her nigger brat in his will for fear that the authorities might confiscate it. Nor could he write his combination into it because, as his wife, she had the right to attend the reading of the will so that, even if Ikey told Mary or Hawk his combination number, without the addition of her own they could do nothing.

David had once suggested, if only to spite them, that Ikey on his death bed might go to the authorities about the Whitechapel safe, so that they received nothing. Hannah knew this to be impossible given Ikey's nature. And in this she was right. Even if Ikey had not wished to leave his share of the treasure to Mary and Hawk, he could never bring himself to allow the laws of England to triumph over him, even though he should be dead. Rather a thousand times the perfidious Hannah and her odious sons than the greedy coffers of England.

Ikey would have liked to tell Mary about the safe and its contents but he dared not do so for fear she would immediately know that the incident where David had presented him with the severed finger of an Aboriginal child had been brought about, not by his son's demand for Mary's brewery, but because of Ikey's reluctance to trust them with his half of the combination to the Whitechapel safe.

Though it was not possible to prove, Mary strongly believed that Hannah and David were more than mere scheming opportunists when they set up the finger scam. She was convinced they had genuinely attempted to kidnap Tommo and Hawk and their plan had gone disastrously wrong. Though Ikey did not admit it, he, too, had always felt that David knew a great deal more than he had said.

But if Ikey did not have the courage to face Mary's wrath, he knew that before he died he must confess his guilt and tell her of the reward he was to give her as penance. To this end Ikey taught Hawk how to value jewellery and as much as he could about the characteristics of each precious stone and how they should be inspected for purity. He purchased a set of gold scales and a testing kit and drilled Hawk in the weighing of gold and silver and in the testing of both to see if they were genuine and of what quality, though Hawk often declared himself puzzled that Ikey should wish him to be so interested. One day, while Ikey was explaining the valuation of diamonds and carefully drawing the various cuts of the stones, Hawk signalled that he was impatient with the lesson and wished it to end.

'Please, my dear, you *must* pay attention!' Ikey had said in something of a panic. 'There is a fortune waiting for you in this knowledge!'

'Why?' Hawk signalled, his face sullen. 'I shall be a brewer. What has the cut of diamonds got to do with the brewing of ale?'

'If you are to get the machinery you will need, and own the land to grow your own hops as you must if you are to succeed, you will pay very close attention to what I say,' Ikey insisted.

Hawk was seldom impolite in his manners and though he knew Ikey to be a villain, he loved him, but now he had had enough. 'I grow weary of this stuff, Ikey. Mary says our great good fortune, our luck is in hard work and the making of good beer, that this is luck more than enough!'

Ikey looked at Hawk and then said quietly, 'Hawk, I shall give you a riddle and you *must* believe me, should you find the answer you may be halfway to owning a fortune which be a king's ransom!'

Hawk, who was very adroit at listening to his stomach, hearing with his eyes and seeing with his ears as Ikey had taught him, knew with absolute certainty that Ikey was no longer playing, or even attempting to teach him yet another tedious lesson. He indicated to Ikey that he was listening most carefully.

Ikey relaxed, regaining his composure. 'Ah, my dear, you 'ave done well, very well and exceedingly well and weller than most wells and better than most bests. I be most proud, you has the same affinity with numbers as Mary and perhaps you will become even better in time.' Ikey paused and appeared to be momentarily lost in thought, then he looked up at Hawk. 'Words can become numbers, just like the signs you now use to talk to me can become words. There are secret, silent numbers to be found in the most innocent words if you know how to decipher them. A code o' numbers to unlock a fortune!'

Hawk became immediately interested, for not only did he sense that Ikey had never been more serious, but that he was about to give him a riddle. There was nothing he loved more than solving one of his mentor's riddles. His eyebrow arched and his hands motioned Ikey to continue.

'Here is a riddle made to a poem to test you beyond all solving, my dear. But should you solve it, it be half o' the key to a great fortune.'

'And then shall I have the other half when I have solved this riddle?' Hawk asked wide-eyed.

Ikey shook his head. 'I cannot say, but without the answer to my riddle you have no hope. With it, there be a great chance that you will gain the fortune for Mary and yourself.'

'Will you give it to me then?' Hawk's hands shook with excitement as he made the words with his fingers.

Ikey cackled the way he had done when Hawk and Tommo were young and a new lesson was about to come from him, and he clapped his hands and rolled his eyes in secret congratulation at his own cleverness, just like old times, then he began to recite.

> *If perchance I should die*
> *And come to God's eternal rest*
> *Let me in plain pine coffin lie*
> *Hands clasped upon my breast.*
>
> *Let a minyan say kaddish for me*
> *in words ancient and profound*
> *In a chapel white, there safe it be*
> *'neath familiar English ground.*
>
> *On my flesh these words be writ:*
> *'To my one and only blue dove'*
> *To this cipher be one more to fit*
> *then add roses ringed to love.*

Hawk had never before been confronted with a riddle so elaborate or beautiful of rhyme and he fetched quill and paper and made Ikey write it down so that he knew every word was correct.

'Remember always,' Ikey chuckled as he read what he'd written, 'the answer is at arm's length and words can have two meanings!'

'Numbers from the words and words what has two meanings?' Hawk signalled, wanting to be sure he had it right.

'Aye, words what mean other things and numbers from words, if all is done properly you will be left with a three digit number! There be three more to come, six in all!' With this said, Ikey would co-operate no further.

Hawk worked for several weeks in what time he could spare on the riddle, but came no closer to solving it. Finally he had returned to Ikey, but he was evasive, other than to say, 'It be about London'.

This helped Hawk very little, for while Ikey had talked a great deal to the two boys about London when they'd been younger, he had only the knowledge of what he'd read about the great city and no more.

Finally, one evening when he and Mary were walking home from Strickland Falls after work, ashamed at his ineptitude, Hawk begged Mary to help him, telling her about the riddle and explaining what Ikey had said about it being half of a great treasure.

Hawk at fourteen was considered a grown man. He already towered above Mary and stood fully six feet. With his serious demeanour, many took him to be much older. He worked a full day with Mary at the Potato Factory and was reliable and hardworking, though Mary sometimes wished he were not quite so serious-minded for a young lad.

Hawk handed her the slip of paper with the poem and Mary, who had much on her mind, read it somewhat cursorily and was unable to venture an opinion so she simply said, 'It be a nice poem, lovey.' Though in truth she thought it somewhat maudlin and typical of Ikey's increasing preoccupation with his own demise.

'What's a minyan and kaddish?' Hawk signalled.

'It's Jewish religion, a minyan be ten men what's got to be present when a Jew dies and kaddish, that be the prayer they says at the funeral,' Mary replied.

'Ikey said it be about London and a treasure, a treasure in London,' Hawk repeated and then asked with his hands, walking backwards so that Mary could plainly see his fingers, 'Did he ever say anything about a treasure to you?'

Mary shook her head. 'Careful, you'll fall,' she cautioned, then with Hawk once again at her side added, 'Ikey be very tight-fisted about money, tight-mouthed too, tight everything!' She laughed. 'He often stored stolen goods in all sorts o' places when he was prince o' all of London's fences.' Mary stopped, her head to one side and seemed to be thinking. 'Maybe it be the number of a house where he's got something stashed?' Then she added ruefully, 'Well, it ain't much use to him now. He can't go back to find it and he won't trust any o' his sons not to tell Hannah, so he might as well . . .' She stopped suddenly in mid-sentence and pointed to Hawk and said softly, '. . . send you!'

Hawk looked startled at the idea. 'What do you mean?'

Mary did not answer for a moment, then she shrugged. 'I don't know, lovey, I'll think about it tonight. Make a copy o' this for me, will you?' She handed the poem back to Hawk.

Hawk nodded though he looked anxious. 'You'll tell me what you thinks, won't you? I be most anxious to be the one to work out the riddle.'

Mary laughed. 'Don't worry, lovey, it be more'n a mouthful, believe me. My stomach tells me Ikey be onto something what ain't no nursery rhyme.'

'A three digit number has to come out of all this,' Hawk said finally, folding the poem and placing it back in his pocket.

That night, after she had made Ikey his tea, Mary sat at the kitchen table with the poem and read it more carefully. The first incongruity which struck her were the words 'chapel white'. In the context of a Jewish funeral these seemed strangely Christian. Why would someone of the Jewish persuasion use them about his funeral?

'Chapel white?' she said aloud. She had passed the Duke Street synagogue a thousand times as a child and chapel to her was a word used by the Wesleyans and not at all appropriate to the ancient, gloomy building the Jews used as their church. Almost the moment she thought this the words transposed in her mind. 'Whitechapel!' she exclaimed triumphantly, clicking her fingers. Mary's nimble mind now began to sniff at the words in quite a different way. Long after her usual time for bed she had isolated a group of words which could have a double meaning or be fitted together: *safe*, *beneath*, *familiar* and finally, *ground*. She was too tired to continue and finally went to bed.

The next morning after breakfast, when Ikey had left to totter down to his cottage in Elizabeth Street to sleep, she gave the words to Hawk.

'Work with these, there may be something,' she said explaining the link between the words 'chapel' and 'white', into the word Whitechapel. Several days passed and one morning Hawk came into Mary's office at Strickland Falls and gave her his brilliant smile. Then he started to signal, his fingers working frantically.

'The safe in Whitechapel containing Ikey's fortune is within the house beneath the ground!'

'Huh?' Mary said, taken aback. 'What you mean, lovey?'

Hawk handed Mary a piece of paper and Mary saw that it was written somewhat as an equation. But first he had transcribed the lines:

> *In a chapel white, there safe it be*
> *'neath familiar English ground*

> *Safe = Safety + Iron box. 'Neath = under. Familiar = family.*
> *English = London. Ground = soil + below surface.*

Beneath these careful notations Hawk had written in his beautiful hand.

> *Translation: The treasure be in a safe below the ground in the family home in Whitechapel.*

'Good boy!' Mary beamed, delighted with her son's tenacity and careful analysis. But then she added, 'That be the second verse, what of the first and the third?'

Hawk signalled that he was convinced that the first verse was meant to deflect any suspicion of a hidden meaning and meant exactly what it said. Then he frowned. 'Last verse be most difficult, Mama.'

Mary set aside her barley mash register, a ledger in which she kept the temperature of the barley mash as it came out of the crusher. 'Here, let me see that poem again?' she asked.

Hawk produced the poem and Mary read the first and the last verse. She agreed that with the first verse Ikey had meant to mislead by the very fact that there was no ambiguity within it. But the last verse sounded very strange and she read it aloud.

> *On my flesh these words be writ:*
> *'To my one and only blue dove'*
> *To this cipher be one more to fit*
> *then add roses ringed to love.*

Mary pointed to the word 'cipher'. 'This verse is where the numbers be,' then added, 'but what numbers? Why does we need numbers?'

Hawk smiled and Mary was delighted at his sudden lightness of mood. 'Like the safe you bought, Mama, they be a combination!' he signalled.

'Oh my Gawd!' Mary cried. 'You're right, you're dead right!' Her heart started to beat so loudly that she could hear the thumping of it in her throat. 'If we can get the numbers from the verse then we've got the combination to the safe, the fortune!'

Hawk shook his head slowly.

'What you mean?' Mary cried, disappointment written on her face.

Hawk's fingers spoke. 'Half, we got half the combination.'

'Half?'

'Ikey said the poem only be half, three digits. Six is what's needed.'

Mary had in the past often wondered about Ikey's persistence with his family, for whom, with the exception of Sarah and perhaps Ann, she knew he had a general dislike, as well as a great loathing for Hannah and in recent years David. His periodical visits to New Norfolk, taken with their history with the Newmans and the debacle when he had come out of Port Arthur, had never made any sense. Ikey was a loner by nature and his pretence at being a diligent and caring family man had never convinced Mary in the least. She had often urged him, for his own peace of mind, to cut his ties completely, but he had always made the same reply: 'We have unfinished business, my dear.'

Now Mary knew what it was. Hannah had one half of the combination to the safe in their home in Whitechapel and would not part with it.

Mary urged Hawk to keep trying to isolate the numbers as she herself would, but admitted, 'Alas, I doesn't know nothing useful about the last verse, save that it should lead to three numbers, but if we should somehow find them then you must not tell Ikey!'

Mary realised that if she had half of the combination she had the means to avenge herself on Hannah Solomon. But she simply told Hawk of the probability that Hannah possessed the second set of numbers. Hawk looked disappointed. 'It don't matter, lovey. We will find a way. Trust Mama! It be most terrible important you stay stum! Ikey must not know, we tell him nothing, all right?'

584

Hawk nodded, his fingers working fast and his face took on a look of determination. 'I shall solve it or die!'

Mary grabbed him and kissed him. 'Life is too precious that you should die for money, lovey. If you has to die, then die for love!'

'Like you was prepared to do for me?' Hawk's fingers spoke and his eyes were serious.

Tears rolled down Mary's cheeks. 'You and Tommo, gladly,' she whispered.

'Mama, we shall find Tommo too!' Hawk's fingers said. 'And I shall never tell Ikey if we should find the numbers.'

Mary and Hawk became obsessed with solving the riddle of the last verse and were hardly able to wait for Ikey to go to his ledgers before they began each evening.

The third line in the last verse, 'To this cipher be one more to fit', seemed at first obvious to Mary. The second set of numbers, Hannah's set, were the *one more to fit*, which would give them the total combination. Hawk agreed that this might be so, but then logically the numbers must come from the first two lines in the last verse and, in particular, from the second line, 'To my one and only blue dove', as the first line of the last verse was simply a location of some sort and the final line, 'then add roses ringed to love', was an addition to whatever discovery or number they would make in the second line.

> *On my flesh these words be writ:* = **location**
> *'To my one and only blue dove'* = **key to numbers**
> *To this cipher be one more to fit* = **Hannah's combination**
> *then add roses ringed to love* = **additional information.**

It did not take them long to realise that the line 'On my flesh these words be writ' must represent a tattoo worn by Ikey, and while Mary had slept with Ikey perhaps a dozen times while they were joint owners of Egyptian Mary's she did not remember any such tattoo. However, she admitted to herself that the dreaded deed took place in the dark and that he might quite possibly have obtained the tattoo while a convict in Van Diemen's Land, in which case she would know nothing about it.

However, this did not overly concern them, they simply

assumed that the words were written on Ikey's flesh, as all the other information made sense, and worked on the second line for the numbers they were now convinced it contained.

Both Mary and Hawk were practised in leaps of logic and exceedingly good at numbers, and they soon worked out a logical way of converting the line 'To my one and only blue dove' into numbers. They took each letter and equated it with its number in the alphabet, for example the letter A = 1, B = 2, Z = 26, and so on. They gave each letter in the line its appropriate number and the total came to 276. If they reduced this number down to the next lowest it became 2 + 7 + 6 = 15 and if they reduced this further, it became 1 + 5 = 6. As they already knew the final result must have three digits the combination number could only be 276.

But they were both too logical of mind to believe this, for it made the final line 'then add roses ringed to love' redundant to the solution. Both knew Ikey's mind was too tidy for this and he would not simply add a gratuitous line to complete the rhyme. The final line must be one of great importance to the whole.

But they could go no further and after a few more weeks were forced to abandon their efforts, almost convincing themselves that the number must be 276. Finally Mary capitulated and gave Hawk permission to ask Ikey if the number was 276. Though she insisted he tell Ikey that he had reached this conclusion on his own, and if Ikey asked if she was involved to deny it. This way, Mary concluded, Ikey would tell the truth.

It was now six months since Ikey had posed the riddle and he was most impressed when Hawk told him he had solved it.

'I hope you are right, my dear!' Ikey said.

Hawk was ready to listen to his stomach, hear with his eyes and see with his ears. He handed Ikey a piece of paper with the numbers 276 written on it and Ikey laughed and shook his head slowly. 'No, my dear, you are quite wrong!'

Hawk, close to tears from frustration, bowed his head in bewilderment.

'I told you, the answer be at arm's length,' Ikey said, smiling. But again he would say no more.

At about this time a misfortune struck Mary, for she could not obtain sufficient hops from local sources to meet her needs and she was forced to buy expensive imported hops from Kent. This meant she must put up her beer prices, which was very much to her disadvantage, for times were still hard in the colony and competition most keen.

At first Mary believed it was the local brewers trying to make things difficult for her, but eventually she discovered it was yet another of Hannah's tricks. During this period when the supply of local hops had dried up, even though the season had been a good one, Ikey made yet another visit to New Norfolk and was depressed for days after his return. Mary then discovered that George Madden had cornered the entire market for the distribution of hops in the colony and it was he who would not sell to her. Mary was quick enough to realise that this decision was yet another pressure from Hannah for Ikey's half of the combination. Mary confronted Ikey with the reason for his visit and he admitted that this was what had happened, but again avoided the issue of the combination and explained that Hannah was still avenging herself on Mary for stealing the affection of her children and the love of her husband. Though he conceded that, under the circumstances, this was a somewhat bizarre explanation, he insisted it was true.

Mary, who was never easily beaten, determined that she would rent land and grow her own hops. She made the decision to use what few assets she had to send Hawk to England, to the county of Kent, so he could learn the most superior method of growing hops and return with all the varieties of seed he could obtain. She had only the money to pay his fare but if, when he returned, she could rent land with an agreement to buy it one day, she would never again be compromised by the likes of George Madden. Hawk was nearly fifteen years old and Mary had no hesitation in placing her trust in him, though she had a second reason for sending him to England.

Hawk still carried an absolute conviction in his heart that Tommo was alive.

'If Tommo were dead, Mama, I should know!' he would insist, and as he grew older the certainty that his brother was alive became even stronger. On several occasions he had 'spoken' to Mary about going to find him. Hawk now stood well over six feet and was enormously strong, and Mary knew that he was old enough to leave her. This single determination, to find his brother, was more powerful than anything else in his life. Hawk was all Mary had and loved and she thought that by sending him over to England for two years she would delay losing him.

Mary also had a plan which she revealed to Hawk on the morning of his departure. She handed him a brass key, a duplicate of one she had found some years before in Ikey's overcoat, which she knew to be the key to Ikey's Whitechapel home. She urged Hawk to use it to enter the house.

'We must determine whether a safe exists beneath the floor,' Mary said.

Hawk sighed and then signalled, 'But, Mama, we have come to a dead end, what is the use? We do not know Ikey's numbers, and if we did, it is only half the combination.'

Mary touched him on the sleeve. 'Ikey is not a young man and I believe he will give me his part of the combination if he thinks he is going to die. If there be a treasure he will do anything so as to avoid Hannah having it all, that much I know for certain.' She suddenly paused and announced dramatically, 'And I has the second half!' Mary relished the look of amazement which appeared on Hawk's face. 'That's right, I knows Hannah's combination, Ann give it to me when she were a little 'un in the orphanage! David Solomon were always writing it on his slate and working with it on the abacus. Ann told me it were a number their mother give them what they must never, never forget in case she should die! The number eight hundred and sixteen!'

Hawk signalled the numbers, '816?'

Mary nodded. 'Just you make sure there be a safe in that house, lovey.'

Ikey was terribly distraught at the news of Hawk's departure to England, for he was convinced he would not live long enough to see Hawk again.

Hawk was able to comfort him a little by promising to spend his last day helping Ikey at the Saturday races, even though he would rather have climbed the mountain and spent time with Mary. Hawk was by now doing most of the work at the races and he knew Ikey could not manage without him. This would be Ikey's last day as a bookmaker. Poor Ikey had given up his nocturnal wandering, unable to manage the walking. The races were his only remaining pleasure.

Hawk would take a sad memory away with him of this last day with Ikey. Late in the afternoon, while Hawk's back was turned, a drunken punter accosted Ikey, accusing him of cheating, and knocked him to the ground. Hawk arrived moments later and picked the drunk off Ikey's prostrate and squealing body, giving the man a cuff across the side of the head which sent him spinning to the ground. Hawk picked up the sobbing Ikey. The shoulder of his ancient coat and also the sleeve of his shirt had been torn in the struggle so that his thin white arm hung bare. It was then that Hawk saw the tattoo. It was of two blue doves surrounded by a garland of red roses, and in a ribbon across the top of the circle of roses was the legend, *To my one and only blue dove.*

Hawk took scant notice of this at the time, being more concerned for Ikey's welfare. Later, when he thought about it, he simply concluded that their guess had been correct and Ikey wore a tattoo with words from the poem. He told Mary of his findings and they congratulated each other on their perspicacity, but otherwise decided the information was of no additional help.

With Hawk away, Ikey seemed to fade and in the next year he progressively became an old man much dependent on his daughter Sarah, and on Mary, who was increasingly under pressure as local hops were being denied her and imported stock was not always available.

Ikey decided to relent, and acknowledged that one-eighth of his fortune was still sufficient to buy a large tract of land and give Mary the financial independence she desperately needed if she were to survive. He felt it was time to settle his moral debts before he died and though he was deeply humiliated that Hannah and David Solomon had finally beaten him, Ikey's love for Mary was such that he was prepared to compromise. But he decided not to tell Mary until he had the one-eighth portion safely deposited in her bank account.

Ikey proposed that one of Hannah's sons, he preferred it to be Mark, should take a ship to England with her combination to the safe, while he would instruct Hawk by letter of his combination and the whereabouts of the safe.

Hannah was adamant that David go. It delighted her to think that he was to be pitted against a fifteen-year-old nigger mute, and she felt sure David would not allow Hawk to win even an eighth of the value of the treasure. But she insisted that David leave immediately, that was in two days' time, when the *Midas*, a convict ship, was leaving Hobart bound for London.

Hannah's reason for this was so that Ikey's letter to Hawk could not arrive in London before David and thus allow Hawk to get to the safe first and have it removed, or worse, attempt to open it. Ikey argued that the safe could not be opened without the combination, even if it were given over to the Bank of England. Its removal would involve the demolition of a wall of the house and, as the safe was set in concrete, it would require a very large dock crane and a gang of men to lift it out of the ground. Nevertheless, Hannah was resolute that Ikey's letter must go on the same ship as David Solomon so that the two could meet and visit the Whitechapel house on the same day and simultaneously open the safe.

Ikey smelt a rat and thought David would bribe the captain to give him Ikey's letter, so he did not entrust it to the captain but gave it instead to the ship's chaplain whom he swore to secrecy and added further to the man of God's integrity with a nice little stipend for his ministry.

Chapter Thirty-eight

On a day of persistent drizzle, with swirling clouds obscuring the top of the great mountain, the *Midas* sailed from the river port bound for London. On board was Mr David Solomon, who had been carefully drilled in the description of each item in the safe and the value of the gem stones. Though Hannah was not as expert as Ikey in this she had a keen eye for appraisal and knew each precious stone individually. Also in his luggage was a set of scales for weighing gold and a new pistol of American design.

The voyage home to England was uneventful and the *Midas* berthed at Gravesend, where David immediately sent a letter by courier to Hawk at the hop farm where he worked asking him to come to London at once to meet him on board the *Midas*. On the same day Hawk received a message from the ship's chaplain that a letter awaited him from Mr Ikey Solomon which he was instructed to hand over to him personally on board.

When Hawk opened the letter Ikey was already dead. He had passed away not two weeks previously. His funeral had been a mixed affair, one of the first few to take place in the Hobart synagogue which had been open for five years. One hundred and eighty of the male Jews in Hobart Town attended Ikey's funeral and filled the tiny synagogue to overflowing. As well, standing outside, was a crowd which the polite society of Hobart found most undesirable. Publicans and whores, touts, con men, cock fight proprietors, sly grog merchants and most of the racing fraternity of Hobart Town stood outside the little synagogue.

The minyan of ten good men consisted of Hobart's most prominent Jews: Philip Levy, Samuel Moses, Jacob Frankel, Abraham Reuban, Judah Solomon, Isaac Feldman, Edward Magnus, Abraham Wolff, Isaac Marks and Philip Phillips. Ikey was buried in the Jewish cemetery according to the ancient rites and beliefs of his own people and though Mark and Moses attended, as only men are allowed to attend an orthodox funeral, Sarah stood outside the cemetery with Mary and both wept, while Hannah stood apart with Ann, dry-eyed and triumphant.

What transpired between Hawk and David is best revealed in the account David Solomon gave to his mother on his return to Van Diemen's Land. He told how the *dumb nigger* nodded in agreement when he asked if Ikey's letter contained his half of the combination to the Whitechapel safe. Then he proposed they both inspect and test the safe to ensure it had not been tampered with, and then remain present to observe while each worked his part of the combination. Finally, that the coin in the form of gold sovereigns be divided with one in eight going to Hawk, while the gold and silver ingots be weighed and that Hawk should receive one-eighth part of the total weight of each. The gem stones would be divided into lots of eight and then they would toss a coin to see who would have the first pick from each lot. To all this the *schwarzer* had silently agreed.

David then told of how they had set out in a carriage to the house in Whitechapel in the company of the shipwright from the *Midas* and his bag of tools. The shipwright had removed the heavy planking from the front door and then left. It was a miserably cold February day when the two men, each carrying a bull's eye lamp, entered the house, which had stood empty for over twenty years.

They moved along the dusty hallway, brushing aside cobwebs and going straight to the scullery, for both had a location plan, Hawk from Ikey and David from Hannah. David opened the closely fitted scullery door with a key given to him by his mother which had hung about her neck as long as he could remember.

The room contained no windows and the air within it was most stale, though surprisingly free of dust. While Hawk Solomon held the bull's eye lamp, David read the instructions which triggered the false nails in the floorboards, and carefully lifted each board until the door of the huge safe beneath was clearly exposed. David stooped down and tested the handle of the safe, giving it a firm pull. It was obviously locked. He rose and allowed Hawk to do the same.

David confessed that at this point his heart was pounding and his face must have shown his excitement, though he couldn't speak for the nigger, 'it being dark an' all'. His hands shook as he tried to hold the torch steady for Hawk as the black boy's numbers were the first part of the combination. Hawk had dialled quickly, his huge hands graceful to the touch and the numbers 690 appeared and then a distinct click sounded. Then Hawk rose and placed his torch on a shelf so that the room was dimly lit and then held David's torch directed at the wheels of the combination lock. David, his hands trembling, dialled 816 whereupon there was another click. For a moment all that could be heard was their rapid breathing, Hawk's steady and David's coming fast as though he were short of breath. Hawk tapped David on the shoulder and indicated that he should be the one to open the safe. David pulled, but nothing happened, the door remained shut.

'Oh Jesus!' David exclaimed.

Hawk pushed him aside and handed him back his bull's eye lamp, then he took the handle in both hands and pulled the safe open in a single jerk.

David would tell Hannah how he was not sure what might meet his eyes, perhaps small boxes and rotting canvas bags spilling over with gold and silver and precious jewels. But what they both witnessed was an empty safe, except for a single envelope sealed with red wax. It was addressed to 'The Solomon Family'.

Hawk, in his 'telling' of the same story to Mary, told how David was the first to react, dropping the lamp and commencing to hop from one foot to the other, wailing and moaning and tearing at his hair, while Hawk stood silent, his head bent, one hand covering his face though he continued to follow David by looking through his fingers.

Hawk told how he finally went down on one knee and reached into the empty safe to retrieve the envelope which he handed to David, whose hands were shaking so that he could barely break open the seal. Hawk had noticed a slight bulge in the envelope and now David removed from it a man's gold signet ring heavily crusted with diamonds and rubies. Then he withdrew the note and attempted to open its careful folds, but his fist had tightened around the ring and his remaining hand was shaking too violently to do so.

David, sobbing, handed the note to Hawk.

'Read it! Fer Chrissakes, read it!' he screamed at Hawk, forgetting that Hawk was a mute. Hawk slowly opened the note and held it up to David to read, without looking at it. In Ikey's handwriting were the words:

Remember, always leave a little salt on the bread.

'What can it mean?' David sobbed. 'Whatever can it mean?' Then he fell on his knees. 'We are done for! My family is destroyed!' he wailed. 'Ikey Solomon has beaten us all hands up!'

Later that evening, Hawk wrote a letter to Mary.

My Ever Dear Mama,

Today I have met David Solomon, the son of Mistress Hannah Solomon of New Norfolk, whom I know to be Ikey's estranged wife. With him we have visited the premises of Ikey's old residence in Petticoat Lane, Whitechapel, on an errand entrusted to me by Ikey in a letter received this day of which he tells me you are unaware and in which he begs me now to acquaint you of the contents, as he is not sure that he will remain alive in the many months for it to arrive in England. Ikey is ever the pessimist and I expect he is as well as ever.

However, I am happy to inform you that the letter instructed me to go with Master David Solomon, recently embarked from the ship, Midas, to the house in Whitechapel where Master Solomon had been acquainted by his mother as to the whereabouts of a certain safe hidden beneath the scullery floor.

Included in Ikey's letter was the combination number which I was to use upon the safe. Whereupon Master David, also bearing a number given to him by Mistress Solomon, would add his to make the complete combination, the two numbers to effect the opening of the safe.

Ikey's letter further instructed me to take a one-eighth share of the contents of the safe and then to return to Van Diemen's Land where I was to bring this portion to you. Though none of this is to be known by you. Alas, I cannot conceal it from you and I have not given Ikey my word that I would not tell you first in a letter, as he wishes me simply to arrive home as a surprise.

Ikey's letter also included the deeds of the house and instructed that I should sell the property and also return the money to you keeping a ten percentum for myself for expenses while I remain in England. A most generous offer which I shall accept with gratitude.

Alas, I regret to inform you that the safe when opened was empty, that is, save for a sealed envelope. When opened it contained an envelope addressed in printed writing to The Solomon Family, the note within contained only these words in Ikey's handwriting:

'Always remember to leave a little salt on the bread.'

You will recall it is a saying much favoured by Ikey.

And now to business which I trust will always remain only between you and I, dear Mama.

You will remember the two lines in the riddle poem:

'To this cipher be one more to fit
&
then add roses ringed to love'

By much speculation it came to me some months ago that 'To this cipher' meant not Hannah's part of the combination but only one number, and not three. *The lowest number when the number 276 is finally reduced is 2 + 7 + 6 = 15 and 1 + 5 = 6. I took the number for the line 'To my one and only blue dove' to be six.*

Then again, by working some weeks in my spare time on the conundrum I came one evening to the notion that the ring of roses seen surrounding Ikey's tattoo was in the shape of a zero, the cipher '0'. I now had two numbers, six and zero. But it was the final one which took me near to despair, until some weeks ago I chanced to read the final line in a different manner, 'then add roses ringed . . . to <u>love</u>'. The third number was, I concluded, contained in the reduction to a single number of the sum of the numbers made of the word, <u>love</u>!

These I soon worked out, which you will see from using the alphabet code are: 12 + 15 + 22 + 5 = 54. When reduced to the lowest possible number, that is 4 + 5 = 9. The third number was nine.

I now had three numbers, 6, 0, 9, and the final line tells me clearly that the ring of roses (the '0') is added to the word 'love' so the zero, I surmised, must come after the number nine.

I am pleased to inform you that I concluded the number must be 690. Using the numbers you had given me as being the combination held by Mistress Hannah, I had a sequence complete of 690816. This proved sufficient to open the safe some four weeks before I received Ikey's letter of instruction when David Solomon and I met on board.

I must inform you that Mr David Solomon has taken ship to return home with the sad news of the missing contents to the safe. This letter will be despatched in the care of the captain of the same vessel, the Mermaid, *bound for Hobart. You should expect great unexplained lamentation from Ikey and even perchance some effect to his heart, so you must tell him immediately! You should also anticipate considerable wrath should you meet up with Mistress Hannah, or she come upon Ikey. For with him Master David carries the note from Ikey and a magnificent gold signet ring encrusted with diamonds and rubies, so that Ikey could be true to the message written on the note. I feel sure Ikey will be most pleased at the notion.*

I am therefore delighted, my dear Mama, to acquaint you with the news that you are now a woman of most considerable means. The value of the gold and silver in sovereigns and in the form of ingots, and there be a great many precious stones besides, is in the region of one hundred thousand pounds. If you wish you shall have the land in the entire Huon Valley for the cultivation of hops.

I am now exceedingly happy to inform you that I have learned all we will need to know on the tilling, sowing, netting and havesting of hops and have, with my own hands, worked every part of the growing and harvesting process. I have also acquired fifty bags of the finest quality seed.

I now most eagerly and impatiently await your instructions to come home as I must set out upon my search for my brother Tommo.

I remain, your humble, loving and obedient son,

Hawk X Solomon.

P.S. I caution you to burn this letter at the conclusion of your having read it. I will include a bank draft for the value of Ikey's house made out in your name, to the Bank of Van Diemen's Land, though I shall find the ten percentum commission most useful. I shall bring you a new Sunday bonnet, some bright ribbon, which I do not suppose you will affect, a winter coat, two of the splendid crinoline gowns so popular with our young Queen Victoria and several pairs of good stout, English boots. H.X.S.

Hawk's letter crossed with one from Mary.

My darling Hawk,

I thank God every day that he has given you to me. Though I confess I also thank the great mountain as often. My news is both wonderful and sad; Ikey has passed away, though peacefully in his sleep. I wish you to come home at once. This letter is extremely short for there is a ship which leaves for England within the hour.

And now! Our Tommo is back!

This morning at eight of the clock there was a knock at the door and a boy in rags who looked not much more than eleven years old, skinny and of a dirty appearance stood as I opened it. His hair was fair and his eyes a most beautiful blue.

'Mama, I am home, will you take me back?' he asked.

I love you, Hawk Solomon, and we are all together again, Mary, Tommo and Hawk!

Your loving mother,
Mary Abacus.

THE
AUSTRALIAN
TRILOGY

PART II

TOMMO
& HAWK

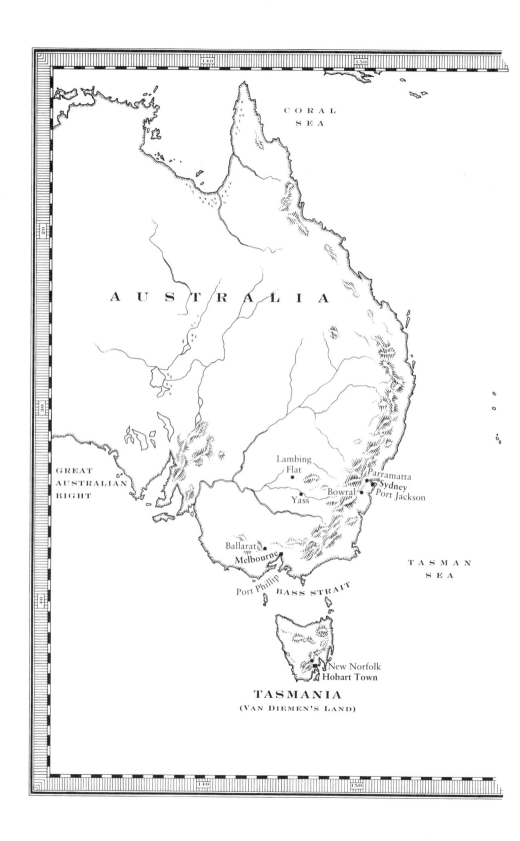

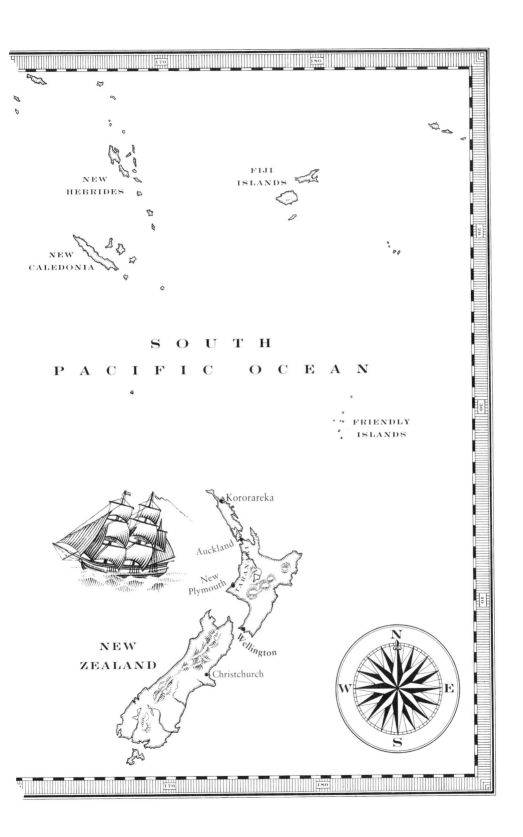

For Alex and Brenda Hamill

Acknowledgements

To Benita, my wife, who is first to read my work and who endured, mostly with good humour, the painful process involved in a partner writing a work of fiction.

Owen Denmeade, who helped in a thousand ways with small and large chores. Margaret Gee, who constantly combed my manuscript for errors of form and function and always improved upon it. Bruce Gee, who undertook the task of major researcher and never failed to find both the important facts and wonderful tidbits that give a novel both veracity and colour. Christine Gee, my indefatigable publicist.

Adrian Collette, Adam Courtenay, Tony Crosby, Alex Hamill, Alan Jacobs, Sylvia Manning, Lisa Mills, Essie Moses, Phyllis Pike, Roger Rigby, Sardine, Dr John Tooth, and Dr Brent Waters. Professor Terry Sturm at the University of Auckland, who read those sections dealing with the Maori Wars. The Tasmanian Museum and Art Gallery, The State Library of Tasmania, The Sydney Maritime Museum, and the inestimable State Library of New South Wales and in particular the staff of the Mitchell and Dixson Libraries for their unstinting and generous help. My abiding gratitude to the hundreds of past writers of books, newspapers, magazines and historical pamphlets from whom I learned both narrative form and fact and whose prior work made mine possible.

To my publishers, Bob Sessions and Julie Gibbs at Penguin Books Australia, who never flagged in their efforts to help me meet my deadline. Finally, my editor Clare Forster who, together with editor Laurie Critchley, worked long and hard to take my words and make them sing. What a joy it has been to work with you all.

I have a boy who cannot speak

and a boy who will not speak.

Both I love with all my heart

but do not know how to keep.

MARY ABACUS

BOOK ONE

Chapter One

TOMMO

Hobart Town
July 1856

It ain't long now before Hawk comes to fetch me, to scrape his brother off the floor of Brodie's sly grog shop.

Funny that, when you're mostly scared in life you feel things brave folk don't bother to feel. I know he's coming. I can hear his big footsteps coming down the hill two mile away. When you've been listening to fear as long as me, you can't never be fooled. Fear is always the little brat in you, ears pricked, heart thumpin', listening to what can't be heard, knowing what's gunna happen by the way your arsehole is puckering like a rabbit's nose. No matter what you learns in life, the fear in you never grows up.

That first fear, when you was seven and stolen from your family and took into the wilderness, that first big begetting of fear in your life becomes a part of every fear you has ever afterwards.

Fear builds up, like rust in a metal water pipe. Its beginning, its first trickle, is always about being alone. Not loneliness, but being alone and helpless, with no one what cares, no one what gives a fig, what will flick an eyelid if you lives or dies. You're a small creature alone what has no defences of its own and so is the natural prey to a world full o' hungry mongrels.

It don't matter if you grows to be big and strong, and cunning as a shithouse rat. It don't matter if you can defend yourself with fisticuffs or use an axe or knife like nobody's business. Fear don't

3

take notice of them things, it just don't grow up and start being brave. It stays with you, so you can't put faith in nothin' and nobody. If you can't trust, then it stands to reason you can't love, 'cause if you does, you'll become some mongrel's prey.

There is always someone watching you in the tall timbers. You learn to feel him like an itch under your skin. Like a chill breath on the back of your neck. You knows in your thumping heart it's a wild man comin' for you, a mongrel with harm in his heart. You can't see nothing, but he's lurking, creeping, minding his feet so his steps don't warn you. He's moving closer, one foot raised like a kangaroo dog, but you don't know where or which way to run. The wind roars in the treetops like waves crashing against the shore, killing the small sounds, the snap of myrtle thicket, the sudden flutter of a bird, all the things you depends on to catch him out.

You pull the air through your nose, sniff deep, testing for the sour smell of a grown man, but the early morning sun's sucked the perfume from the eucalypt, the sassafras and King Billy pine, filling the frosty air so you can't smell nothing behind the sweetness at the end of your nostrils.

You begin to tremble. You know what's coming. If he gets you he'll bugger you. Put his thumb and finger to his nose and snort his snot onto your back as he swives his cock into your arse. Then he'll hold you pinned, and whistle over to his mates to come. If you struggle, he'll pull back your head, twist and snap your scrawny neck like you was a new-born pup. Other mongrels comes over, charging through the undergrowth, brushing aside the fern, boots cracking twigs, urgently pulling down their breeches, tripping as their pants fall to their ankles, laughing. You stretched over a felled Huon log what has its bark ripped off, its lemon-yellow naked, just like you, your face kissing the damp, dark, musty earth.

'Eh you, dog shit!'

'Yes, boss?' Your teeth chattering.

'Ya ain't seen nothin' now, ya hear?'

'No, nothin', boss! I ain't seen nothin', no one!'

'Wha' are you then?'

'Dog shit, boss.'

'Louder! Say't loud, boy!'

'Dog shit!'

'Tha's better. You'll say naught t'no bugger, yer understand? Tell and we'll come agin, kill ya, cut yer froat ear t'ear!'

'Yes, boss.'

Then the crash of myrtle twigs as they melt into the trees, ghosts in the morning mist. You alone again in the forest. The bellbirds begin to call again, the sound of an axe striking deeper into the bush. You snivels a while, and try to wipe away the blood from your arse with a bunch of green leaves, then you scrapes the muck from your back and what's running down your legs with a strip of bark, ashamed. Nobody you can tell what cares. You shit bright red for a month after.

That's the all of it. It never changes, one fear begets another, but it's always the same fear. The same small brat in you facing the same mongrels. Once fear gets a hold of you, you can't trust no one no more, not even yourself, 'cause you know they be right – all you be is dog shit, and all they wants to do is bugger you so you never forgets what you is.

I got to drink down fast, get a few into me. Brother Hawk don't countenance me staying on no matter how much I plead at him to let me be. I'm not afraid of Hawk, just of Hawk coming. I'm afraid of Mary. Of Sunday dinner. Of meself.

'Mr Brodie, sir! Another snort o' acquadine!' I hold up me last shilling, won yesterday at euchre. Got to find a game today, but it ain't so easy on the Sabbath. 'Ere!' I twist the silver coin to catch the lamplight. 'I got the money, now quick, Mr Brodie, if you please!'

Brodie shuffles over, sniffing, stepping over bodies, spilling some of me precious tot. He grins toothless and puts the little glass down. 'There ya go, Tommo.' He grabs up me shilling in dirty woollen mittens what's got no fingers. Then he holds up sixpence change he has ready in his other hand. 'Shall I fetch t'other half then?' He twinkles the sixpence.

'Why not? I got to go soon. Bring it right off, will ya?' I nods.

Brodie smiles, a smarmy smile on his ugly gob, like he don't believe me and he makes a fuss of fumbling at the front of his waistcoat, pushing the sixpence back into a greasy pocket, his dirty fingers dancing like spider's legs over his pot belly.

The acquadine don't hit as hard as it should. Barely tickles me throat. Bastard's watered it down, doused the fire in it to make it last longer, though it's better than the Cape of Good Hope brandy he serves to most of his Sunday drunks. More like Cape of No Bloody Hope, all the good hope in it watered down to make a gallon of misery out of half a pint of trooper's joy.

Don't suppose I blames him, human nature being what it is. Fair enough, I reckon, the pubs are closed Sunday, so we're in his hands, ain't we? He's got us drunks all to himself. Brodie milking a few more pennies from the slops of Saturday night's barrel and charging us double for the privilege. Daresay I'd do the same. Can't feel too sorry for a Sunday drunk, can ya?

The sun should be well up by now, if it ain't raining outside. That be Hobart Town all right, sunshine, then rain, snow, hot, cold, calm and blow, all in the course of the same morning. Not that I mind, used to it, the wilderness be mostly rain and wind and bone-snapping cold. It could be nearly noon, though who'd know here in the oil lantern darkness. The shadows be the same now as if it be always midnight in the world.

I comes in early, not much past dawn, with the mist still hanging on the river. Birds just beginning t' chitter, currawong, kookaburra, green rosella calling and silver gulls wheeling. They be the early risers and the noisy buggers. Then come the little uns, scrub tit, scarlet robin, yellow wattlebird and blue wren, kipping in a bit, then starting to talk with the sun. Tide coming in, slapping, spiffing and spuming on Salamanca beach. I couldn't sleep no more, even though I were sozzled last night and should've been well able. But me restlessness is getting worse. Time to move on. Hawk knows I ain't gunna stay in Hobart Town now he's back from England. But he still talks of us joining Mary, of being a proper family again and doing brewery work up at Strickland Falls. 'It would be our fortune made, Tommo!' he reckons.

Ha bloody ha! A fortune in me hands would be poured down me throat, or lost at the dogs and horses. Can't make a copper penny stay long enough in me pocket to even gather warmth.

Hawk'll be here soon. Silent, bending double to get through the door, a great dark shadow hunched over, his head bumping against the rafters. Him so black the lamplight don't show nothing but the whites of his eyes, the silver sheen of the scar on his neck, and the shine on his nails where he holds his fingers to his nose. A nigger for me brother though I be as white as one o' Mary's best Sunday tablecloths. Hawk be twice my size too though we be born of the same mama. Different from the start, Mary reckons, from the day she set eyes on us, two mewlin' orphans in a basket. Even more different now. Hawk wouldn't be caught dead down here if it weren't for yours truly, even the stink's too bad for his well-raised nose.

But I don't smell nothin' no more. Don't take no notice. Not even of the farts from the drunks lying at me feet or curled up in the dark corners, snorting bubbles in their spew or seeing things terrifying what ain't there.

Reckon that'll happen to me soon enough. A few more years on the grog, then some mongrel like Brodie'll add too much acid to give a kick to his watered down spirits and that'll be the end of dear little Tommo. Over I topples, a nicely pickled feed o' flesh for the waiting worms. Or it'll be the horrors. I seen it happen to some younger than me, holding their ears and closing their eyes and screaming for the snakes to be took away. You'd think I'd be shitting meself. But I ain't. Truth be, I'm more scared of Hawk coming to fetch me to Mary's Sunday roast! More feared about sitting at her clean white tablecloth and chewing through a plate o' mutton with Mary's green eyes watching on me, so's I want to jump up and make for the door and keep running until I don't feel the disappointment in her eyes no more.

There be so much I've forgot in the seven years since I were snatched from Mary's tender care. Seven years I've been in the wilderness, but I never forgot Mary's white cloth spread on the kitchen table for Sunday dinner. She'd spread it like forgiveness, like whatever we done wrong in the past week was forgiven when we sat 'round her Sabbath table. Mary's white tablecloth religion was most accommodating of our weekly wickedness. You'd sit down a sinner and rise up with a full belly and a clear conscience, not a holy word spoken neither.

When I were left to mind Sam Slit's whisky still beside the river, cold, wet, starving, drunk and alone in a timber getter's bark hut, I'd recall into my mind Mary's kitchen of a winter's Sunday. The same wind churning the river and howling in the Huon pine. I was that wind, battering at Mary's kitchen door, rattling on the glazed windows of her cottage. And then, when it couldn't find no way to come into the warmth, howling its protest high up in the eaves. 'Wind off the Antarctic sea, the banshees howling be the widow ghosts o' dead sailors,' Ikey, picking his teeth with his pinkie nail, would say when it got particular furious outside.

Inside Mary's warm kitchen there were no need to heed the rain beating on the steamed-up window glass like a boy's tin drum. We was seated there at her Sunday table, snug as a bug in a rug. Mary at the head o' the table, Hawk and me at either side, and at the end, tucking in like there was no tomorrow, Ikey Solomon, what handed us over to Mary's care when we was born. It were Ikey what give us his name too though he weren't our papa nor Mary's husband neither. Ikey died before I found me way back, but he comes to me mind often. When we knew him, he was just Ikey. But before he got nabbed, he were the most high regarded villain in all of London Town. The Prince of Fences they called him, with a finger in every pie. I've heard say that he and Mary were in the brothel business together. But Mary be a ticket-of-leave now, and owner of The Potato Factory brewery, and she don't like much to dwell on the past.

So there we'd sit, a small, strange family. In front of us, on a big white oval plate with a picture of blue willow trees and two Chinamen on a little bridge, were a huge leg of hot roasted mutton. The very best butcher's hogget, with Mary standing over it, big fork in one hand, knife in t'other, carving onto each tin plate, then pouring on a rich, steaming river of gravy. Little pearl onions glistening and swimming in the bright brown gravy what covered the thick slices o' tender meat. Mary always putting the same on my plate as Hawk, her full knowing I could never eat all of it, that Hawk would polish off what I left, then eat Ikey's left-overs and then what meat was still on the bone. It were her way of feeding Hawk while not showing me up to be a runt.

And that's where I always supposed God would be on a howling winter's Sunday. He'd be seated at our kitchen table sharing our leg of mutton, with Mary's best sharp knife and fork in His almighty hands, His holy elbows on the snowy white tablecloth of forgiveness, fork stabbing at great chunks of meat, champing away like nobody's business. He, Him, the nabob of heaven, there with us 'stead of presiding over all the God business going on down at St David's church, where the true merinos, free settlers and lags what should've known better be praying and hymn-singing and freezing their bollocks and titties off. Them in church thinking they be earning extra points in heaven for going out in all the flurry and howl of a winter's blustering morning, and meanwhile God be sitting at our kitchen table all cosy-like, getting a good feed of Mary's best mutton and enjoying Hisself.

'Touch more gravy, God?'

'Don't mind if I do, Tommo, m'dear.'

God polite as you like while I pours Him more gravy, little

onions tumbling out of the jug. God ever so grateful to be out of the devil's breath weather what comes roaring and snorting down the mountain.

I'd lie there in the forest hut wrapped in me wet blanket, coughing and shivering, dreaming of Mary's Sunday kitchen. 'I'll come back, Mama,' I'd cry, teeth chattering fit to break. 'You just watch and see, little Tommo'll be back sure enough soon as I can find me way to Port Davey and stow away aboard a timber ketch.'

But now since I come back, me appetite's quite gone. Nothin' tastes good no more. Sundays were always me best days in them old days. Now they's bloody purgatory with me afraid to look into Mary's sad face. Me here drinking Brodie's sly grog, scared shitless because Hawk's gunna make me sit down to Sunday dinner with our own mama. How can I face Mary when I've forgot how to deal with kindness in me life? Hawk with his hands moving thirteen to the dozen, trying to make cheerful conversation, and me with me eyes on me plate, not wanting none of it 'cept to get up and run for me life.

Though Hawk can't talk no more with his voice, I can still hear him in my head. When he speaks with his hands I can hear him clear as a bell. All them years away and I never lost the sound of him. I promised meself when I were miserable that I were going back to my mama's Sunday dinner and to my brother's deep, sweet voice. Now it's gone. His voice what was always a comfort to me when I was away, always steady, unafraid, Hawk's beautiful blackie boomer voice is gone, rubbed away by the wild man's horse rope. Even then, in the wilderness, I had most strange feelings like something were trying to choke out Hawk's voice, but I tried to put it out of me head, for remembering was all I could hang onto.

Mary's told me what happened to Hawk when we was both kidnapped on the mountain and later became separated. A wild man took Hawk and starved him and led him behind his horse by a hide rope around his neck until his voice was rasped away. All he's got now is his necklace of scars. I've asked Hawk about this time, but he says with his hand language he can't remember anything except that we was took on the mountain by four men and afterwards nothing. I can't remember the early part either. I can remember how it were with Sam Slit, but I don't want to talk about it. Maybe one day we will.

I suppose I should count meself the luckiest cove in the world that I were spared the terrible thing done to make Hawk lose his voice. But I don't think meself lucky. Poor dumb Hawk, he's the lucky one. He didn't stay away long enough from Mary to learn to be afraid. Fear never took him and introduced him to the mongrels. He can still feel things. I've seen the tears brimming when he tries to ask what happened to me in the wilderness, his confusion when I shakes my head because I can't say for the bitterness inside of me.

I can see my brother's concern for me. But I don't feel it. Can't feel the love I know Hawk has for me. I could do before I was took. I could feel everything he were feeling, like we were two fingers on the same hand. Shit, now I don't feel nothing no more. Not for Hawk, not for Mary, not for meself. That's what the wilderness done to yours truly. It took all the feeling out of old Tommo and left only the fear of the mongrels what's always lurking in the tall timbers waiting to get you.

I calls for another shot. Brodie brings it, but before I can pretend to search for a sixpence I know I ain't got, a drunk on the floor begins to shout and jerk, taking a fit. Brodie curses and forgets to ask for me money. He goes over and kicks the poor sod in the head. Brodie knows his stuff – when a man's took to fitting, a kick in the head sometimes'll bring him to calm again. I suppose it be the shock. I can feel Hawk is close. Better drink up quick, Tommo.

Hawk says we got a purpose, him and me. Me, quick and nimble with a mouth full o' cheek. Him, strong and thoughtful and silent. It's a right rare combination what could work together, he says. Mary says we are her team to build up the brewery she started soon as she was freed. It's up to us now to gain folks' respect, be someone what our kind has never been before, what them merinos think the likes of us can never be.

'It's the world's best opportunity for the taking,' Hawk says. 'We'd soon be proper toffs, and your children, Tommo, they'd be true merinos!'

But old Tommo here knows that's crap. There's no purpose, no opportunity for the likes of me. You can't make nothing good out of nothing.

Take a look at me, will ya? Mary's little lamb is become a drunk, a useless scum what wakes up and needs a drink.

Somebody what can't think of nothing but a bottle to leach the anger and the hate out of his rotting guts. What's I gunna do? Wear a clean collar and learn clerking? Sit in a high chair with a green eyeshade, sharpened quill and blacking, working at profit and loss? Mary's precious little bookkeeper, Tommo X Solomon, beer baron in the making? Load o' rubbish, if you ask me!

I ain't clever but me hands, now, they's a different story. Dog-baiting and fist-fighting and timber-getting and burns from Sam Slit's whisky still, that's what's made 'em look bad. Every finger and knuckle looks broke or dog-bitten, and what's skin for other folk is scars for me, scar-tissue what can take most kinds of pain. They don't look much chop but they be good hands, even if I do say so meself.

That's the difference, see, they ain't like Mary's hands what are black and twisted and broken and I think most painful of movement. That's me one big secret, hands what looks battered but are sly as a fox.

Other broadsmen see me holding cards at cribbage or the Yankee game of poker what's catching on among the troopers and gold miners, and they thinks: 'Here's a go, little bugger can't do nothin' nasty with the flats using them poor sodding little mitts.' Ha!

What they sees is timber getters' hands, bashed in the sawpit, calloused on the axe handle, cut, broken, burnt. Hands what ain't capable of handling a deck or palming a card in broad daylight so that the most suspicious sharper can't see what's going on right in front of his very own eyes. No danger in them pathetic, scarred and sorrowful little paws. No sir, not them!

But that's where they be wrong! That's their biggest mistake! What Ikey taught us at cards, me hands took to natural, like they had a mind of their own.

Ikey himself were most complimentary about this. 'Most elegant and nimble, full o' guilefulness and most diabolical of purpose, flippers tailor-made by the devil himself to belong to a broadsman o' most superior talent. Congratulations, my dear.'

Ikey were right, me hands has a pure and natural ability for winning at cards by means of cheating. They's good enough kept on the straight, mind – they hold their own and more in any honest game, if such an event be possible. But they is most amazing on the cross. Sometimes they do things with a deck o' flats what can even astonish me. Never's the day they don't earn me grog enough to dampen down what's ugly and frightening and burnin' inside me. There's always some mouth who fancies himself at cards and who's got a silver sixpence to lose in a hurry. Or a trooper with the Queen's florin he wants to double or treble and who grows most confident when he watches Tommo's clumsy little hands busy at spreading the cards around the table.

That be me only asset, hands what are up to no good, good only for cheating at cards, fist-fighting, dog-baiting and being most fast and nimble when they are clasped around the handle of a small lopping axe, like the one I always carries on me belt in case of mongrels.

Them's me total credentials, me hands. Hawk says he'll learn me reading again, the trick of which I've long since forgotten. But I'm not so sure I can pick it up again. 'Look,' he says, 'you learned Ikey's hand language soon enough again. Reading is the same, you'll soon be schooled back to it again.' But reading be a thing of the head, and Ikey and Hawk's hand language be a thing of the hands. That's the big difference, me head's fucked but me hands ain't.

Nastiness is the only thing what I'm well schooled in now. Mary's nicely brought up little lad, Tommo, what even at seven years old had some book learning and writing, is now everything what's deemed bad. But Mary and Hawk expects that with a bit of plumping up, kindness and affection, what I am become will go away again. That the niceness is still inside me, only for a moment drowned out by me wilderness life, that with a bit of gentleness and love and a few gravy-soaked Sunday dinners under my belt, it'll all bob back to the surface, like a cormorant what's been fishing. And there I'll be, good as new, floating merrily down the river of happiness and contentment.

How the hell, I begs to know, does I do that? For seven sodding years I had the living daylights kicked out o' me by mongrels the like o' Sam bloody Slit! Now I'm supposed to pretend all is forgiven and the world ain't no longer a bad place. Can't them two see that ain't possible? That what's inside me is all screwed up for good?

A large hand come down on the back of me neck and squeezes. Not so it hurts but firm enough. Crikey, it be Hawk! I didn't see or feel him come in, so lost am I in me own stupid misery.

I grabs at the tot in front of me and tries to knock it back, but me head won't go back because Hawk's holding me neck and I spills most o' the precious liquid onto me blouse. 'Damn!' I twists away angry and looks up. Sure enough, Hawk's got his finger and thumb pinching at his nose, lamplight shining on his fingernails. I can't help but smile.

Hawk lifts me from the bench by me scrawny neck. He don't do it rough but he don't intend to have no protest from me neither. I could still twist and kick him in the bollocks, double him up, then head-butt him as he's coming down – I'll take on any cove what's up to a foot higher than me and bigger yet if I be drunk. Besides, I got me axe. But I don't, of course. I don't fight Hawk, who's like a band of iron around me neck. It ain't him what's making me angry, so I lets him steer me towards the door.

Brodie shouts I owe him sixpence.

Hawk lets go my neck, digs in his coat and flips him a shilling. Then he touches me lightly on the shoulder, directing me once more to the doorway. Brodie claps his mittened hands together but misses the spinning coin and curses as it clatters to the floor and two wretches, growling like a pair o' pit bitches, come alive and scramble for it at his feet, tits falling out. Brodie jumps aside dancing a jig, then kicks out wildly at the two soaks, screeching like a demented cocky-parrot.

Outside the sunlight be so bright I'm blinded and Hawk waits while I hold my hands up against my eyes and rubs. He can't say nothing to me 'til I can see proper, 'til me eyes adjust to the sunlight. So he stands and rests his big hand soft on my shoulder.

We stand outside with all the tiny lights flickering in front of my eyes, little stars and explosions floating in blackness. Hawk's hand on my shoulder feels safe. It feels good. Jesus! He's coming back to me, coming back into me heart! But then I thinks, maybe it's only Brodie's crook grog what's pumping through my veins giving me a drunk's false hope. So I rolls me shoulder and shrugs off his hand. No point him imagining what ain't true.

I can see clearly again and I note it's well past noon by the position of the sun. Hawk is standing waiting. Now he has his arms folded and clasped to his chest, looking down at his boots. His dark shadow cast in the dust is nearly twice the size of my own.

'Mary, is it?' I sneer. 'Commanding yours truly to Sunday bloody dinner?'

Hawk looks down sideways at me, his eyes narrowed, then he shakes his head slowly and spits to the side of his boots. 'Come,' he signals to me, 'our ship is leaving on the afternoon tide.'

Chapter Two

HAWK

Hobart Town
July 1856

Tommo's come back to us bad. The wild men have made him bad, taken his niceness and smashed it. His blue eyes are hard, the laughter in them gone.

'Tommo's come back to us damaged, Mama,' I say to Mary with my hands, the language I now use between us. 'He's lost himself somewhere.'

'Hush, you hear!' Mary says. She doesn't like what I'm saying. She looks at me accusingly. 'You're still good despite what you've suffered, so why not him?'

I shrug. 'It's not the same. I'm a nigger, niggers aren't supposed to have feelings.'

She leans forward across the table. 'Nonsense. Now you listen to me, Hawk, he'll come good. All he needs is a lot of loving.' She purses her lips. 'I'm not much good at mothering no more, a bit old for all that malarky, but now he's back, he'll get lots of good food and proper care. Least I can do!'

'Yes,' I say, trying to look more hopeful than I feel. 'He'll get that and more. I hope you're right, Mama. The wilderness took a lot from our Tommo.'

'Not more than it took from you!' Sudden tears well up in her eyes and Mary points to my neck, to the rope burns, the permanent scars that ring it in a band of silver tissue an inch wide against my

14

black skin. 'The wild man took your voice.' Her lips are pulled thin as she wipes her mouth with the back of her hand. 'Nothing could be as bad as that, now could it?'

She has never said anything about my voice before. Never spoken about it since it happened, since the day she found me in the mountains. Now I can see that it's more than she wanted to say, that she thinks it's come out wrong. So she thinks a moment, then smiles, brushing away the tears, trying to brush away the horror she's felt all these years at what was done to me.

'It were such a nice voice, Hawk. You was just a little un but your voice were already deep.' She smiles at me. 'Did you know that, son?'

I nod and she continues. 'Lovely it were, like a melody. Folk would listen when you talked, even when you were a sprat. The wild man took that, there's no making up for that.' She shrugs, eyebrows high, mouth twisted. 'You've come good. Tommo's got no lasting damage, a little to his hands but not like what happened to you, not like that.'

'It's inside, Mama.' I think about how Tommo's afraid. 'That's where he's broken, something's broken inside him.'

Mary looks strangely at me. She doesn't tolerate folks who feel sorry for themselves. When she speaks her voice is sharp again. 'Whatever it were what happened to Tommo, it were no worse than most of us gets in life. This poxy island be full of past suffering. Sadness be a part o' this place. Suffering beyond the wildest imaginings of them what's not like us. Tommo's still young, only just growed up, plenty o' time for him to settle down. Work will fix what ails him.'

She says all this quickly as if she has thought it all out. Mary mostly keeps things to herself. Thinks them out, then keeps them, holds them tight to use only when needed. Now I sense she's worried about my brother too. When you've lost your speech and must talk in hand language you learn to watch people more carefully. Ikey always said, 'Listen with your eyes, Hawk, it be your eyes what's your best ears,' and he was right.

I don't want to say it but I must. 'Mama, I don't think Tommo will want to work in the brewery.'

Mary draws back sharply. 'What's you saying? What's you talkin' about?'

It is late Sunday morning with a high blue sky over the

mountain and the winter's sun polishes the river like mirror glass. Mary's kitchen is bathed in sunlight. The window panes reflect bright squares that burn out the colour where they make a pattern on the dark brick floor. Specks of dust, turned to gold, dance in the shafts of light.

Tommo has gone down to Wapping to drink at Brodie's sly grog shop. Since he's been back he does a lot of walking on his own, learning Hobart Town that's grown and changed so much since we were kidnapped. He walks then stops off to play euchre or poker in a pub or grog shop, coming home late and drunk. Sad drunk. A fifteen-year-old who finds no cheer in the drinking he does.

Mary and I are sitting at the kitchen table, which is covered with a white cloth. On Sunday, Mary always spreads a white cloth on the kitchen table. Damask, she calls it. It's like her Sunday altar. We don't go to church. Mary doesn't believe in it and Ikey, the closest thing we had to a father, was a Jew. So was our real mother, or so he said. He used to tell Tommo and me that we were too.

Mary says she doesn't know anything about that. All she knows is our mother was Sperm Whale Sally, a whaleman's whore. She says Ikey made up a lot of things to suit, like the X he put in both our names. Ikey added it on the spur of the moment when the government man said it wasn't Christian to have only one name and demanded a second be given. So Ikey scratches his noggin and thinks a moment then says, 'Israel and Moses,' and the man says they aren't Christian either and he isn't going to write anything down until Ikey comes up with good Christian names for seconds.

'Tell you what,' says Ikey, 'I'll put X and then they can both choose a second name to their own liking when they've grown a bit.'

The government clerk thinks for a moment, scratching his head. 'Fair enough, all right then, X it be.' He can't immediately think of a reason why X is not Christian, it being a sort of cross and all, and he doesn't really care. So now it's Hawk X Solomon and Tommo X Solomon forever after.

'Can't trust the silly old bugger to get nothing right!' Mary said when she first told us she wasn't our real mother, nor Ikey our father, even though he gave us his name with the X added.

'Probably gave you his name then got nervous that maybe it weren't quite kosher, so he cancelled it by adding the X. Nothing would surprise me with him.' Mary snorts each time the story comes up but she's got a smile on her face too as she thinks of him. 'Ikey always did have a bet each way.'

Mary also told us that Tommo and I are twins, the same but different, the same mother but different fathers. A fluke of nature, she said, that happens sometimes with whores. Tommo came out with white skin and blue eyes, small as a tadpole, and I as black as the ace of spades and big as a bullfrog! It's very confusing to other folk, but not to Tommo and me. We're twins in the heart and in the head. Whether Jew or Mohammedan, twins are their own religion.

Anyway, Mary isn't much concerned with religion. 'Tell 'em you're Church of England,' she says when we're asked. 'Don't suppose it matters, do it? God ain't got no religion, now does he? As far as worshipping goes, it's best not to take sides.' She decided for all of us when she pointed to the mountain towering above us, 'Best off worshipping that!' She was not jesting either, for she loves the mountain. 'God lives in that mountain, right above the organ pipes!' she told us once. The organ pipes are the shafts of rocks that form a steep cliff to one side of the top of Mount Wellington.

When we were little, Tommo and I always skirted well clear of those pipes when we climbed the mountain, just in case Mary was right and we should bump into God.

'What would you say to God if we should meet Him up there?' I once asked Tommo.

Tommo thinks for a moment then says right off, 'I'd invite Him to Sunday dinner.'

'Why?' I asked.

'Because that's the most holy place we got, silly!'

He was right, too. Once when Mary spread her damask cloth we asked her why, and she said, 'It be our way of giving thanks to Him what keeps our bellies full. It be our altar cloth.'

'We belongs to the White Tablecloth Religion,' Tommo once told the curate at St David's who stopped us in the street and asked why we didn't come to Sunday School.

As for not going to church, Mary always says, 'If folk don't like it, well, that's just too bad now, ain't it? Knowing right from wrong is all what matters and I've yet to meet the preacher on this Gawd-forsaken island what does!'

There is little doubt Sunday is important to her, though, and a special occasion. Almost every time she spreads the cloth she says, 'One day I'm going to buy us some silver, some Sunday silver!' But I don't think she ever will. Such a gesture would be much too flash for Mary and we're still eating off the same tin plates and using the most ordinary cutlery you can buy.

Since I have come back from England with Ikey's stolen fortune, Mary could have a crystal chandelier in the kitchen if she wanted, and bone china and silver cutlery heavy enough to sprain your wrist. But Mary doesn't want people to think she's a free settler or a toff, or that she believes herself better than the rest of the lags. She isn't ashamed of who she is, a convict who has earned her ticket-of-leave and had her freedom granted after serving her sentence.

'It's who you is when folk knocks at the door of your heart what counts,' she always said when we were young. 'Hide the past and it gives them what's jealous of you the power to bring you undone.'

I remember her telling us always, 'Never give no one the power to shame you. Keep everything clear and in the open. Hiding from the past be the main business o' this cursed island, people trying to pretend they's better than other people, when they's dirt, the scrapings o' the barrel, just like what we is. Hannah Solomon be the prime example, putting on airs and graces, talking like a toff and trying to be a free settler, what she ain't and never can be.'

Hannah was Ikey's lawful wife, but all she did was try to do him harm. Now she and Ikey's children live with a cove named George Madden in New Norfolk. Mama once taught three of Ikey and Hannah's brats, David, Ann and Sarah, when Hannah was a prisoner seamstress in the Cotton Factory. 'They was bright too, those young uns,' Mary told me.

Mary doesn't care much for the free settlers here. 'Who'd come to this miserable place even if it were free, 'less they was third-rate to begin?' is what she says. But she is not being altogether truthful about her feelings. She'd not return to Blighty even if the governor granted her free passage. Mary loves this island, it is where she found the chance she was always looking for. Tasmania is what saved Mary and gave her back her character. She doesn't pine for the good old days like Ikey did.

'Blimey, what good old days was they, then?' she'd say sarcastically when Ikey got to reminiscing about London Town. 'For the likes of me they was shit!'

'And this ain't shit, my dear?' Ikey asks, sweeping his arm to include the whole island.

'Yes, but there be a difference,' Mary snaps back. 'There you was buried permanent in it, born in shit and drowned and died in it, no bleedin' hope o' rising above it. Here if you pushes 'ard enough you can get your 'ead up through the surface.'

'And when you does, my dear,' Ikey cackles, 'all you can see is arseholes!'

But Mary would not give in. 'Life's too bleedin' short to be frightened o' what's already been,' she'd say. 'Can't get yesterday back and change it, now can you?'

That is why Mary can't see what has gone wrong with Tommo. She won't ever look backwards. When we were put to bed as young uns she'd often say, 'Today is all we got, ain't it? I mean, who knows, tomorrow we could all be dead.' She'd take Tommo's hand and mine so that we were joined to her. 'Be honest, fair, listen, keep yer gob shut. Anyone can get through one day at a time. It's light and then it's dark and then it's bleedin' over, ain't it? Persistence, that's all what gets you there in the end. Believin' in yerself and persistence!'

Then, after she'd made this little speech, she'd let go our hands and tug at the chain about her neck and produce from her bosom the gold Waterloo medal Ikey gave her. She'd hold it tight in her fist. 'What's it say?' she'd demand.

'I shall never surrender!' Tommo and I would shout together, that being the legend written on the back of Mary's talisman.

'And don't you never forget it,' Mary would say. 'Persistence and character!'

That is everything Mary believes – never give up no matter how painful the journey. Overcome and persist. I know that in her heart she can't understand Tommo, how he's sorry for himself and won't forget the past now that things are good again. Drowning his sorrows in grog, not showing grit in his character, that's what she can't abide in my twin. I can sense she sees too much of Ikey in him. Not the Ikey of London Town, not the successful fence and forger much admired amongst thieves and villains and even accorded a grudging respect by policemen and magistrates; but the broken Ikey, the Ikey who was brought to his knees by hard convict labour and trained to obedience with the warder's whip.

Now I've told her Tommo doesn't want to take up her legacy

of persistence and character, to work at her beloved brewery. She looks down at the white damask cloth and begins to smooth it with both her poor broken hands. A little frown forms, her top lip covered by the bottom one, then she begins to speak quietly without looking at me, like she's thinking out loud.

'Course he'll want to work at the brewery! Tommo never were a lazy boy. He'll do his share. He'll come good,' she says, as though she's trying to convince herself, as though she secretly fears she might not be right about my brother.

'Mama, it's not that. He isn't ready to come back to us yet.'

But Mary will not look, doesn't want to see my hands, and continues. 'We'll buy all the new land in the Huon Valley we can get. We'll do it through Mr Emmett, so nosey parkers what can't mind their own business don't catch on. Surprise the buggers! We'll grow all the hops we need for the use o' the brewery and maybe some for the new colony of Victoria.' Mary lifts her chin and her eyes narrow. 'We'll not be caught short again because some bastard beer baron tries to put us out o' business. Not never again!' She grips the sides of the table, then she looks up and becomes aware of me again. 'Hawk, you'll not talk to no one about the money, Ikey's money, ever, you understand?'

I've been back from England three months and this is the first time Mary's talked about what we'll do with the fortune I took from his and Hannah's old Whitechapel home. Ikey's stolen treasure had lain there for years, hidden in an Austrian safe, for though Ikey and Hannah knew half its secret combination each, they never trusted each other enough to tell each other their half. Hannah believed she and her brats deserved the lot and sent her son David to claim it, but with a little luck and cunning, I got there first.

'You know I won't tell anyone, Mama,' I nod.

'Not even to Tommo, you hear!'

I look at her, shocked. There is nothing I have ever hidden from Tommo. 'Mama, Tommo's my twin!'

Mary gazes down at the table. 'Tommo's been away, we don't know where, he won't say!' She looks up, her eyes steady. 'You hear me, Hawk Solomon, don't you *never* tell your brother until I say!'

There is a part of Mary that's hard as granite, that won't brook any contradiction. Her mouth is drawn in a thin line, the skin seeming to barely conceal the hardness of the skull beneath. Mary has a look that can frighten me and now she's used it against Tommo, her dearest Tommo whom she loves with all her heart.

She lowers her eyes again. 'You know about growing hops, you learned it in England. That will be yours to concern yourself about. The Huon Valley, what we can buy of it, will be yours, Hawk. Tommo can work with me at Strickland Falls and prove himself, prove he may be trusted. He must learn what you already know about brewing. Catch up like, be an apprentice boy.'

I bang my fist on the table so she is forced to look up. 'Mama, Tommo won't, he won't come back, not yet!'

But she's too quick for me. She doesn't hear the half of it because her eyes are squinched tight closed and she can't see my hands speaking to her, though she's heard the smack of my fist and knows full well what I'm trying to say.

'The Potato Factory,' Mary says fiercely, her eyes still closed, like it's a holy catechism, 'comes first!' She opens her eyes and spreads her crippled hands against the white of the cloth, fingers splayed as wide as they'll go. Then it comes to her what she has just said and she adds, 'That be after you and Tommo, o' course.'

'Mama, we've got Ikey's stolen fortune, you don't ever need to work again if you don't wish!'

Mary is silent a moment, then she says, 'That be the whole problem. We has to make what's been stolen honest again.'

She can see that I don't understand her. She shrugs. 'All Ikey's money's been gained on the cross, not one penny comes from honest toil. It all comes from fencing, forging, laundering money, brothel-keeping and having his brats at the Academy of Light Fingers pickpocket for him. As for Hannah Solomon, hers comes from running scams in bawdy houses. All right, I put in me time in such places too, but I never cheated nor used poor kids what can't defend themselves. We has to put the money to decent use and make it clean.'

'But, Mama, *I* stole that fortune! *I* opened Ikey's safe using the combination we worked out from Ikey's riddle. We've no more call on that money than the Solomons have.'

'Hawk!' Mary shouts in protest. 'You know it's not the same. Ikey gave you the riddle that held his three numbers to the safe. He were as good as saying that if you be the clever one to crack the riddle what opens his half of the safe, then providing he could also find out Hannah's set of numbers, what were in it be ours, his to share with us!'

'Mama, Ikey didn't say anything of the sort! He didn't know you already knew Hannah's half of the combination! You never did tell him, did you? Ikey always thought it was just a clever riddle he'd given me to test my wits.'

Mary purses her lips. 'More fool him, then,' she says, but softly. 'He were a fool to underestimate the both of us, you in particular.'

'But even if I'd cracked Ikey's part of the riddle he knew it would give us only half title to the money.'

She smiles. 'If Ikey were alive he'd be proud, most proud that we beat the wicked cunning of that bitch, and her miserable brat, David Solomon! They were his natural family, but he saw them for what they were.'

She gazes at me fondly now. 'I were right to send you to England, to learn the growing of hops. Heaven knows we didn't have a penny to spare at the time, not for sending you, nor for purchasing land when you returned to do the growing. But I always knew it were the right thing to do,' she claps her hands suddenly, 'and look what happened, you returned with Ikey's fortune and the knowledge we needed. Now we can buy the whole Huon Valley if we wants!'

'Mama, perhaps we could argue that if Ikey hadn't died before the safe was opened, he would have left us the part of the fortune that was his to give. But half of what came out of that safe rightly belongs to Hannah Solomon! Ikey was willing she should have her share, he always said so. But Hannah demanded more, much more, and that's what stopped him giving her half in the first place – the thought that she wouldn't rest there! That, and the fact that he didn't trust her to do right by him, stopped them from dividing it fairly in the first place. They were both ruled by greed. But what was Hannah's wasn't Ikey's when he was alive! Nor is it for us to have now that he's dead!'

'Her half share be our compensation for the kidnapping of you and Tommo.'

'Mama, we can't prove she and David Solomon were behind the kidnapping!'

'Ha! And Hannah can't prove you opened Ikey's safe before David arrived in London either! That's two can't proves! We're quits then, ain't we?' Mary looks smug. 'Far as she's concerned, you were waiting in London with Ikey's half of the combination, and the two of you opened that safe together and found it empty.' Her expression turns grim. 'I *know* it were them,' she taps her chest with her finger, 'in me heart. I know it were David and Hannah Solomon what kidnapped my boys!' She points her finger at me, shaking it. 'All the bleedin' dosh in the world can't bring back your voice or undo what's been done to Tommo! They've *got* to be punished!'

Mary suddenly realises that she's shouting and looks around. She lowers her voice to almost a whisper even though there's no one about to hear us. 'Besides, if Ikey were alive and you'd brought him back the whole fortune from London, do you really think he would have divided it in half and given Hannah her share? Not bleedin' likely he would! I'll tell you something for nothing, he wouldn't 'ave given her a farthing! Not a brass razoo!' Mary folds her arms across her breasts. 'By keeping the lot we're only doing what Ikey would have wanted most!'

I shake my head slowly. 'Mama, we don't know that. It isn't a decent thing that we're doing.'

Mary's face reddens. She is suddenly furious. 'Don't talk to me about decent! Decent be what decent does. That bitch done nothing decent in her friggin' life! I ain't giving that whore nothing, you hear? Over my dead body! Not a bleedin' penny, you hear me? Me conscience be clear on the matter!'

I've never seen Mary so fierce and Ikey's words come back to me. 'Out of a clear blue sky, my dears, with not a cloud o' contention to be seen, not a fluffy puff o' ill humour on the far horizon, Mary can evoke a hurricane in minutes. She don't give a tinker's cuss for the consequences to herself of her malevolent tongue. Mary has a temper what can turn the sweetest harmony, the calmest waters into a raging storm at sea greater than that what wrecked the Spanish armada!'

There is nothing more I can say in the face of her anger. I shrug, but Mary's not finished yet.

'You think Hannah's going t' be happy with 'arf? She'll be off to the law in a flash if she knows we've got Ikey's money. Besides, who's to know what's hers and what were Ikey's?' She stabs a finger at me again. 'You going t' let her decide? Let Hannah Solomon tell you what's her fair share? Eh? You going to do that? You barmy or somethin'?'

What Mary says is logical. Hannah will never be satisfied until she has the lot, but Mary knows Hannah won't go to the law. When Ikey was sentenced to transportation for purchasing stolen goods, the Old Bailey ruled that whatever could be recovered of his stolen goods was the property of the Crown. Ikey always said that if we recovered any of the money we should never speak of it. 'The law has big ears, my dear. Ears what can gather taxes and fines like a dredger gathers mud! When it comes to money, stay stum, the less known all 'round the better, know what I mean?'

I remind Mary of this, knowing full well that she doesn't need reminding. 'Mama, you *know* Hannah won't go running to the magistrate. She won't want to draw attention to herself. Besides, she'd have done it before if she'd thought it an advantage to her. She already suspects we've got Ikey's money.'

Mary frowns, then shakes her head. 'Suspecting and knowing for certain ain't the same thing now, are they? Once Hannah and that son of hers knows for certain, they'd be after us. David Solomon wouldn't never let up. The humiliation of him knowing it were you what tricked him would be enough, he'd kill you!'

I shrug. 'Mama, you recall I left a ring in the safe with a little note that purported to be from Ikey: "*Remember, always leave a little salt on the bread.*" It seemed a good joke at the time. David still thinks Ikey outsmarted them. He thinks the fortune was taken when Ikey was still in England and that the note was intended for Hannah. As far as he knows, Ikey had the money and couldn't spend it before he died, so it must be here.'

'No!' Mary says. 'There's no proof of it.'

I shake my head. 'Listen, Mama, David *must* conclude that Ikey left the money to you. That would be a natural enough assumption, don't you think?'

'Assumption? Assumption ain't proof! That ain't knowing!' Mary snaps, still protesting.

'Ah, but if you buy the land in the Huon Valley he'll know soon enough, won't he?'

Mary thinks a moment then sighs. 'You be right.'

'But Mama, what if we tell them we wish to make peace? If we admit that Ikey left you *all* the money but that you wish out of the goodness of your heart to do the right and proper thing and give Hannah her half?'

Mary looks at me astonished. She's lost for words so I continue quickly. 'Mama, it would wipe away the wrongs done, and guarantee our safety. Ikey always said: "Mutual greed can make the worst o' enemies the best o' loving friends."'

Mary sighs and looks at me despairingly. 'Hawk, you is always trying to fix what can't be fixed between folk. This ain't a peace what can be bought. Them lot is filth, they won't abide by no goodwill, no conditions!'

'But don't you see, Mama? We'll make it so they *must*! We'll leave a sealed envelope with Mr Emmett. They know he's the governor's chief clerk as well as being your good friend and so can't be corrupted. We'll give him instructions that it's only to be opened if harm comes to any of us and they're involved. The note will tell the authorities about Hannah's possession of Ikey's money that rightly belongs to the Crown. Then we'll tell Hannah and David about the letter lodged with Mr Emmett.'

'Ha! Fat chance o' pulling that off! What about our money? The law would confiscate that, too!'

'What money?' I smile. 'We'll say Ikey left instructions before he died to give Hannah *all* his money, that when I came back from London I only acted as courier for a small commission. You were his executor, entitled to ten per cent that you're now perfectly prepared to rebate to the Crown.'

Mary shakes her head and tut-tuts. 'You've gone barmy, Hawk.' But I can see she's thinking. Frowning and drumming her fingers on the white tablecloth.

'Tell you what,' she says at last.

I shrug and spread my hands. 'What?'

'Get Tommo to stay put, to stay at 'ome with us and after he's been sober one year and worked with me in the brewery, we'll do it. We'll give Hannah a quarter share. That be more than what rightly belongs to her!'

She looks closely at me now, reading my consternation. 'And you still can't tell Tommo about Ikey's money neither. You hear me now, Hawk Solomon, you've got to stay stum!'

I shake my head. 'Mama, I must give Tommo a reason to stay! I *must* tell him. Helping to protect you from any harm might be the only way to convince him to stay. Please, Mama!'

'No, Hawk, he's not to be trusted yet!'

'Mama, Tommo would do nothing to harm us!'

Mary's lips are pursed. 'Be that as it may, you're not to tell about the money. Nor about David and Hannah hating us. Tommo ain't no fool, he'll want to know why.' Now Mary looks directly into my eyes. 'I'm worried he's going to run away from us. You'd not scarper too, go with him, would you, Hawk?'

My heart sinks. She must be able to see how distraught I am, how my throat aches with concern for her. Mary is counting on me and now, with Tommo returned, him also. She knows, though, that the brewery can get along without Tommo, but it will be harder without me.

'Mama, I can't leave my brother. I swore that if Tommo came back to us I'd never leave him again. If he goes, I must go too.'

I can feel the tears running down my black face now. I sniff, my hands working fast. 'Please, Mama! I beg you to understand. You must let me get the badness out of Tommo! Then we'll come back to you, I promise!'

Mary says nothing. Instead she pulls at the chain around her neck to bring up her Waterloo medal, which she clasps tightly in her fist. When Mary holds her good luck charm, it means she's not going to budge an inch. She will never surrender.

I feel defeated. Telling Tommo about Ikey's money was the last card in my deck, my only chance to make him stay. I was willing to compromise Tommo's peace of mind for the greater good, believing truly that he would be best off here at home with us. But now Mary forbids me this. She expects me to let Tommo go away on his own again. She's making me choose between my love for Tommo and for her. Mary, whom I love with all my heart. Mary, to whom Tommo and I owe our very life, who made us her own when Ikey brought us home in his tobacco basket, two brats of a whore died in childbirth, rats already eating the birth mess when he found us in the early morning sunshine.

I know what Mary has done for us, Tommo and I saw it often enough when we were small. Each morning at eight o'clock, after the Reverend Smiles had eaten lamb's kidneys and fresh eggs, with his napkin still tied about his neck, he'd take up his prayer book and come out to the churchyard beside the foundling home to bury the newborn dead. He would say what passes for a prayer for the unwanted infants left to perish in the churchyard or on the docks, under bridges and in ditches. In a hurry of words too fast for their meaning to be understood, he'd bury what the scavenger cats and dogs and the dock rats had not eaten. 'Dust to dust, ashes to ashes, rubbish to rubbish,' he might as well have said, for it makes no difference when there's nobody to mourn.

Tommo and I would have been in that graveyard if Ikey had not found us and Mary taken us in. They weren't man and wife, nor even living as such, but they became our mother and father. And Mary raised us up properly. She tutored us in reading and writing and sums until we were more advanced in these skills than other children and even most adults on the island. She loved us with a great fierceness, scolded us, bathed and bandaged our cuts and scratches, dried our tears and taught us how to be on our guard against a hostile world. Each night she held us tenderly. 'My boys,' she always said, kissing us on the cheek, 'my lovely little boys.' It was the last thing we heard every night.

Then when we were kidnapped, she went into the wilderness to look for us. She went on her own where no woman had ever been alone before, her life a hundred times endangered in the process. When she found me, she killed the wild man who'd captured me.

Now we are back together and all she asks of Tommo and me is that we stay and share in everything she's built with her own hands. That we stay and build her precious brewery now that Ikey's fortune makes it possible. That we become rich and happy and give her grandchildren to rock on her knee in her old age. But we will not. We cannot. Tommo's broken inside and needs to go away, and if I let him go alone, I know he'll never come back. Tommo doesn't think his life's worth a pinch of shit and it's up to me to help him see otherwise. If he'd never come back from the wilderness perhaps I could have eventually lived my life. But I grieved him every day he was away, and I always knew he wasn't dead. He was in my head first thing on wakening and last thing at night and a hundred times in between. Whatever should come to pass, I can never let Tommo go out of my life again.

The silence grows between Mary and me until it is almost unbearable. I sit at the table, looking out the window through my tears with nothing I can say. And Mary waits. Finally I cease blubbing.

'Tommo comin' 'ome for dinner then?' Mary asks at last. 'There's a nice leg o' mutton in the oven.' She says it quietly, then when I don't answer, she asks, 'Wapping, is he?'

I nod, grateful that she's left the topic of our conversation, but dreading she'll return to it.

'Drunk again, I suppose.'

She looks up to see my hands reply but I keep them in my lap and say nothing.

'Me old man were a drunkard,' she says quietly. 'How long's Tommo been drinking?'

'Since almost when he was taken into the wilderness. Six years, maybe more, he doesn't say exactly. The timber getter he was with ran a still.'

Mary sighs and shakes her head. 'Don't make sense. He can drink all the beer he wants here at 'ome!' She looks up and gives a bitter laugh, her eyes bright and wet. 'His mama owns a bleedin' brewery. Tomahawk's the best drop o' beer in Tasmania!'

'Mama, it's spirits he's taken to. He says it's the fire that's needed to kill the cold inside him.'

'Jesus!' Mary is suddenly angry. 'He even talks like a drunk! Drink don't drive away the demons, only character can do that!' Mary clucks her tongue. 'You can't make excuses for him, son. He'll promise you everything but he'll let you down, Hawk. Tommo'll break your heart before it's all over!' She stabs her finger at me. 'Mark me words, if Tommo don't stay, you won't cure him by being with him. Love never cured a drunkard! Hard work and watchin' over him like a hawk, that be the way, if there be a way at all.'

Watching over him like a hawk, that's funny, but Mary doesn't notice the pun. She leans over and touches my hand. 'Listen to your mama. If he stops here with us, at least we can both watch over him, keep an eye on him. We can see he don't come to no harm, maybe even bring him eventually to a cure.'

'Mama, Tommo's afraid. He's scared that if he stays he'll shame you, spoil things here.'

Mary looks aghast. 'Shame me? Me what's been the lowest of the low! Shame *me*? How do you propose he can do that? Tommo don't even begin to know what real shamin' be!'

'Tommo knows most folks think highly of you here in Hobart Town, Mama.'

'And you think I care? You think I'd put them miserable lot before my boys, before little Tommo?'

'Mama, it isn't what *you* think, it's what Tommo thinks.'

'Thinks?' Mary is growing furious. 'Drunks don't think anything but where their next drink be coming from. I know, I were practically one meself! Me old man were one! Christ! Don't tell me about drunks. I seen it, been it! I been broken like Tommo, let me tell you!

'See these?' She holds up her terrible hands. 'I got them broke by men, clerks looking for a job at bookkeeping. There was a job down the docks, see, East End. We waited, 'undreds of us, lined up to apply. All men, 'cept me. I gets the billet, out of all o' them I'm chosen and it's the happiest day of me life. I walks home, it's misty and you can't see nothin' down the wharfs. They's waiting for me, dozens of the bastards, waiting in the mist. "Woman taking our job," says they. "Clerking ain't for women, understand, bitch?"'

Mary begins to weep softly. 'They threw me down and raped me, then they held me and stamped on me 'ands 'til every finger were smashed and every bone were broke and more.' She places her hands into her lap below the table. 'That's how I become a tart. It were all I could do, me 'ands being useless and all. Then I were in a brothel and had a fight and run away and they sent the acid man after me, the slasher.' She turns her head slightly, showing the scar which disfigures her pretty face.

'I know how the bottle tempts you, numbs your pain when you's hurting. For a long time that were all I had, no hope for the future, nothin'.

'Then I hears on the grapevine that Ikey Solomon the fence be looking for a bookkeeper what'll keep their gob shut. I goes to Ikey and he gives me a job clerking, then later, running a bawdy house. Ikey were the one what first gave me a chance to come good, when nobody else would.'

Mary sniffs and jerks her chin upwards, knuckling the wet from her eyes. 'And that's what we'll give Tommo, a chance to come good. To make something of himself and forget what they done to him! To stop feelin' so bleedin' sorry for himself and get on with it! Begin a new life, just like I done. Believe me, there's not too many gets that chance given!'

'But Tommo is not strong like you were, Mama! He's not the same cheeky boy we loved, full of fight and vim.'

Mary's eyes soften at the memory of how Tommo was, then grow sad. 'He don't hardly say boo to a goose! He's been 'ome nine months and he ain't laughed proper once, just answers me polite-like, "Yes, Mama. No, Mama." He don't never meet me eyes.' The anger has now gone from her voice and she speaks barely above a whisper. She looks up, appealing to me. 'What's wrong with 'im? What's I done wrong to Tommo?'

'Nothing, Mama. I told you, Tommo loves you but he's shamed. Scared he's not good enough for us. He loves you, but it can't come out. It's stuck inside. He's forgotten how to bring it out.'

Mary's face grows hopeful now. 'Then we'll teach him! Me and you, Hawk! We'll show him how we both loves him. Show him there ain't nothing in the bottom of a bottle what can help him!' She jumps up and waves me away with the back of her hands. 'Go fetch him!' She's laughing. 'Garn, scarper, be gone with you!' She moves over to the hearth, wiping her hands on her pinny. 'I'll get the cabbage cooked, roast'll be ready in 'arf an hour. Tell him I done little onions and brown gravy too. Always liked a nice drop o' gravy, did our Tommo.'

Mary hasn't yet given up on the prospect of keeping Tommo or she doesn't want to face what we both know to be the truth, I don't know which. I smile sadly and shake my head, then I rise and go to where she's standing beside the hearth. Mary's head comes to not much above my waist. I'm fifteen years old, six feet and four inches tall and no beanpole. I stoop down to kiss her. It's not something I do often, and it's most clumsy.

Mary brings her hand up to her face and touches the place where I kissed her. A tear runs down her cheek and disappears into the notch between two fingers. Then she buries her head against my waist and clasps me tight.

'Don't leave me, Hawk. I loves you with all me heart. You won't leave your old mama, will you?'

I can feel my heart pushing up into my throat, filling my lungs so I can't breathe. Oh God! Mary is begging me. Mary, the hardest rock I know, is crumbling.

Suddenly I hate Tommo! Hate the ties that bind me to him. Hate him for spoiling all our lives. And I hate myself for my disloyalty to Mary. Mary is crying, sobs coming out of her breast so soft they're scarcely a whimper. And now I can't see her for my own tears. I am crying not because she's forced me to choose between her and Tommo, but because I love her so very much. I put her gently away from me.

'Mama, please, I beg you,' I try once more. 'Let me tell Tommo about Ikey's money. Perhaps he'll stay, if I tell him about the threat you face from Hannah and David. Perhaps that will be the difference to make him stay on.'

'No!' Mary shouts. 'No! No!' She bangs her fists hard against the kitchen wall, then turns to me again. 'You'll not dare tell him about the money!'

I can barely move my hands to talk for the pain in my chest. 'Then I must go with him, Mama,' I sign to her. 'I can't let him be parted from me again!'

Something snaps inside of her. I can see it, a dark thing that bursts out of her. I've seen Mary angry, her temper is well known, but I've never seen her like this. Her whole body begins to tremble. There is fire in her green eyes. Suddenly she charges at me, pushing me in the belly. She's screaming and hammering her fists against my chest. 'Go! Go! Go to hell, the both of you!'

These are words I've never heard from her and they break my heart. 'Mama, please?' I clasp her wrists. 'Mama! Mama!'

She pulls away, but I hold onto her wrists and she spits in my face. 'Lemme go, you black bastard!'

So I let go of her and cover my face, weeping. She's beating against me again. 'And don't you call me Mama! You both come from a whore's cunt, a nigger and a drunken runt, you ain't no part of me! You ain't no sons of Mary Abacus!'

I hold out my hands to her, pleading, sobbing.

Mary pulls back suddenly and grabs at the medal hanging from its chain around her neck and holds it in her fist in front of her furious face. 'I been on me own before! It ain't nothin' new!' Her skin is ashen and her voice grown cold. She is breathing hard, talking in short bursts, hissing out the words, her chest heaving. 'You hear me, Hawk! If you go with your brother the two of you will not be back! Not never again! Not to this house. You'll not get what's mine. I swear it!' She pauses a moment and shakes the fist holding the Waterloo medal. 'What's swore on this can't be took back, you hear me? Now fuck orf! Get out o' my 'ouse, pack your bag and get out! I don't want to see neither of you never again!'

I am weeping again, though it is not for Tommo and me that I cry, but for our mama. I know on the morrow or the day after, Mary will beg our forgiveness. She loves us with all her heart and mind and soul. But, like Tommo, what's happened in her life can't be banished despite what she's always said. All her own hurt comes flooding back when she's backed into a corner, and she knows only how to snarl and claw her way out to safety or perdition. She's the small brat who's never been loved. She's on her own and, to her own mind, when she's crossed, all she's got is herself to depend on.

In her heart of hearts I know Mary's lost hope in Tommo and doesn't think he'll ever come good. But she won't come out and say it, she *can't* say it of her own son. If she does, she'll be admitting she loves me more than him, when before we were taken it was always slightly the other way. When we were brats, Tommo always made Mary laugh, he was just about the only one who could. Mary has always blamed herself for not finding him, not rescuing him as she did me.

And now he's come back, she's once again lost what she wants most to love. To realise Tommo doesn't want her, has no place for her in his life, must be more than she can bear. And so she fights and orders us away.

She has made me choose between her and Tommo. Either I go with Tommo, for he will not stay here with me, or I lose him forever, and that I cannot do.

I rise slowly from the chair and without signalling another word to our beloved mama, I leave the kitchen, not sure if I shall ever return but knowing that I will ever love her.

Chapter Three

TOMMO

The Pacific Ocean
November 1856

We's been at sea for three and a half months, sailin' North on the Yankee whaling ship, *Nankin Maiden*, what be out of New Bedford, Massachusetts. The master is Captain Mordechai O'Hara, a fearsome pious man.

The *Nankin Maiden*'s an old ship, a barque, but a good un, one hundred and fifty feet from stem to stern with a beam of thirty foot, three hundred tons and well known these thirty years in the Antarctic, Southern Ocean and Pacific waters. She is after sperm whale and we was quickly told that the Yankee sperm whalers are the toughest there be on the seven seas. From the looks of it, there ain't many Yankees aboard 'cept for the three mates, the ship's carpenter, the cook, blacksmith, cooper, sail maker and, o' course, the master himself. That's only nine out of forty-two men. The rest is all volunteers, like Hawk and meself, rough men of every colour and shape from sea ports in the Indies and the Caribbean, Cape o' Good Hope and the islands of the Pacific Ocean. There is also a few Limeys, Irish and Dutchies, mostly picked up in Rio.

Though Hawk were brung up better than me, here he's treated as a nigger. There is four others, but they be true niggers, two from the Indies and two from the Cape. Hawk's bigger than all on board, except for one of the Maori and I am glad to have him about.

There be another black what's not counted a nigger, an

Aborigine from the Stoney Creek tribe, name o' Billy Lanney. Hawk says he must be one of the few Tasmanian natives what's not been shot as vermin or what died when they was took to be settled on Bruny Island. Lanney keeps to himself, though he is friendly enough when you talks to him.

Lanney is a small man, no bigger than meself, though his head seems larger than suits the body what carries it. Under his canvas breeches, what is rolled up for deck scrubbing and the like, he has sparrow legs, thin pin-like sticks. He's built narrow o' chest too, but he seems amazing strong for such a little fellow. He wears a beard of tiny curls, close to his face, and his hair is a thousand or more tight, springy curls clung to his head, though quite different looking to Hawk's. He has deep-set eyes and most pleasing white teeth when he smiles.

This bloody ship is owned by a Rhode Island syndicate, all of 'em Quakers what have vowed it a 'dry cask afloat', meaning that grog ain't permitted on board while she's at sea. The past three months and sixteen days have been the worst of me life. Not a drop of grog has passed my lips. Any breach of this rule is punished most cruel, as we witnessed a week out to sea with Billy Lanney the victim.

Lanney, a regular crew member much experienced in the whaling game, come back on board ship in Hobart Town and brung with him a quart bottle of Cape brandy. He knew he would be punished if it were found, but he didn't care. Sure enough it were found, by the first mate, Mr Crawlin Nestbyte. We were just three nights out to sea when he found Billy Lanney drunk as a lord, dancing a merry jig in the fo'c'sle and singing a bawdy ditty.

To my mind, the real tragedy of the whole affair is that only a quarter of the bottle were consumed before the first mate found out. The sentence would not have been a single stroke more had Billy drunk the lot, as I'd surely have done! In the presence of the lot of us, the rest of the precious brandy were poured overboard by the first mate, while me tongue stuck to the roof of me miserable mouth.

Nestbyte, like the master, is a Quaker and told us that the Lord in Heaven did not propose to show any mercy to the feckless black; nor should we expect any from the highest authority on earth. This authority turns out to be Captain O'Hara himself who, it seems, knows all about the will of God.

Five days later, at ten o'clock on Sunday morning, we be called on deck to hear Billy's sentence. The captain, in best black cloth suit and white lace bibby, stands on the fo'c'sle to address us. Billy Lanney is made to stand before him, his hands clasped to his front and his head bowed as though in prayer. Nestbyte stands beside him with one hand on Lanney's shoulder and the empty brandy bottle in his other hand.

'The Christ within us lives in you all, because something of God exists in every man,' O'Hara begins in a most reasonable voice. Then he says to Billy, 'Even in thee, an ignorant savage.' He turns to us and goes on, 'In thee also, in every man here, there is the inward light if he should take it into himself and illuminate his heart in Christ Jesus' name.' He brings his attention back to Billy. 'This inward light is a guide to us of good and evil, in thee and me. In thy case, Billy Lanney, I have sought to discover the Will of God by deliberation and by the illumination of that same light in me.' The captain pauses and stares towards the topmast in a sort o' holy-looking way. Then he fixes his eyes on Billy again. 'It has been made clear to me by divine revelation that thou art to be most severely punished. Evil exists in all of us and we have witnessed it now in thee. In bringing strong drink aboard we have seen clearly the spirit of Satan confronting the spirit of the Lord Jesus Himself. It is written that thou shalt take no strong drink and thou hast disobeyed, and so this evil must be punished. Billy Lanney, whaleman on the good vessel *Nankin Maiden*, in the name of Our Lord Jesus Christ our Saviour, I pronounce sentence of one hundred lashes.'

There is a gasp from the crew, for a hundred lashes with the knotted rope be severe punishment. The captain then picks up a book what he explains to us is the articles of the ship. I can't remember the exact words, but it more or less says that the *Nankin Maiden* be under the tender and loving care of the Lord Jesus and be therefore, according to the Holy Scriptures, 'an empty vessel, to be filled with the Spirit of the Lord'. The Captain is responsible for interpreting the word of God in all matters requiring discipline and for delivering punishments with his own hand in the name of Christ Jesus, Amen.

This means he can punish Billy any way he likes. When they strips Billy naked and ties him to the mizzen mast, his back be so scarred from past floggings that the rope at first can't cut through the flesh beneath. Billy don't take no leather strap to bite down upon, and all the way through the terrible beating he don't make no sound except a grunt as the wicked whip strikes him deep to flay the meat from his ribs and backbone.

When all's done, the captain stands bent over with his hands clasped upon his knees, sweat pouring off and him panting like a bitch on heat. O'Hara wears a gold signet ring on his right hand with a flat top the size of a shilling. Now a piece of Lanney's flesh is stuck upon it, so that it looks like it's set with a large ruby.

There is smiles of wonderment among the crew at the way Billy's taken his flogging. Some says that even if Billy be a black, never a braver man has put to sea, and all vows they would man a whaleboat with him any day o' the week. This is rare praise on board a vessel where it's every man for himself. The many languages the men gibber away in keeps 'em apart, and English is spoke only to give instructions, organise the whale hunt or give out punishment. But when the hunt is on, the six men who crew together in each of the four open whaleboats share a common destiny. They knows their lives to be in mortal danger and they stays close the better to survive. A crew member what's shown his mettle is not forgotten and Billy Lanney's courage under the captain's lash will hold him in good stead. This be even more true after what happens when he is cut loose from the mast.

When they cuts Billy down he stands unsteady, with the blood running down his open back to his scrawny bum and forming puddles o' crimson at his heels. Then he straightens, and faces out to sea, sniffing the air in great draughts. We watches silent, thinking that perhaps he's about to jump, when from deep within him comes the howl of the wild Tasman tiger dog, a long, mournful sound that I've heard a thousand times at night in the wilderness. Two Irishmen immediately crosses themselves and others is astonished, not knowing what to make of the strange noise so foreign to the human voice.

Then Billy turns slowly to Captain O'Hara and gives him a most gentlemanly bow, pointing to the master's white Quaker bibby which, with the rest of his blouse, is stained with Billy's blood and flecks o' skin. The black man gives a smile of tender sweetness and says, 'God bless thee, Cap'n, you be washed in the Blood of the Lamb and forgiven.' He says this in perfect English, which I ain't never heard from him.

O'Hara gasps and takes a step backwards. 'Blasphemy! Thou

hast blasphemed!' he yells, shaking his finger at Billy. 'A heathen savage hath taken the name of the Lord God in vain!' He orders Billy tied back to the mast and hands the blood-soaked lash to Mr Nestbyte, who gives him another fifty lashes.

When they cuts Billy down this time he don't howl like the tiger dog but stands at the ship's rails and looks out to sea, his hands fluttering as though he's trying to calm the waves. Then he turns to Nestbyte and points at him. 'Plurry big fish come get you, Boss!' He draws his finger slowly across his throat. 'Aarrrrk!' he says, like a man choking.

The crew moves back at this. Whalemen be superstitious by nature, but they knows this to be beyond mere fancy. Billy Lanney has put a curse on Nestbyte, right enough. Nestbyte turns away with a sick sort o' smile on his gob. 'Pagan nonsense!' he spits. 'God will punish you.'

Mary be right about religion. Them what's given themselves over to it, and what pronounce upon the rest of us in Christ's name, is more cruel than any other.

This is the first time since the age of eight years, when I were first made to tend Sam Slit's whisky still in the wilderness, that I've been without me daily drink. It's only today, fourteen weeks after I were took by Hawk from Brodie's sly grog shop, that I be feelin' the least bit better. The terrible sweats what come down upon me a day or two after I stopped drinking went away in two weeks and at about the same time, me gut settled down and me shit stiffened to normal. But the craving for strong spirits never stops. And yet, as I stands here on the cross-stays looking out for the whale, I be aware for the first time in many a year of the wind in me face, and the dancing of the white caps, like toy sailing boats stretched to the horizon.

The sky has clouded over since this morning when I climbed up the mainmast. What Hawk tells me in our lessons is cumulus cloud, now brooding against a grey horizon, has nudged aside the mare's tails what stretched across the horizon when me watch began. The sun, up above the gathering cloud, beats down warm on me back and it's excellent weather for a spotting of the whale.

Hawk and me ain't yet witnessed a hunt, though we've been among the blue whales twice. We did not give chase as they's too fast and strong to be harpooned. It is the sperm whale, the next largest in the sea, that we hopes to find.

I'm eating a bit more these days, though a whaler's daily ration ain't much good: hard biscuit what's a weevil's feast, a pound of salt beef or greasy pork or even horse, and two pound of plum duff on Tuesdays and Thursdays. This dreary lot is washed down with longlick, a mixture of tea, coffee and molasses, and three times each week a portion of lime juice for the scurvy. By decent folks' standards, the food is pig's swill, no man ashore 'cept a starving beggar would touch it. Hunger got me in the end, and I suppose the dead cockroaches in the molasses adds to its taste well enough!

Fancy dreamin' about eating possum stew again! It would be fair delicious right now, and the thought of a plump mutton bird split and flattened, then roasted on a fire of live coals, is enough to make me drool. I'd eat me own Sunday dinner as well as Hawk's at Mary's table, 'cept she don't want us there no more. But I can't think about that, and anyway I'd give up every morsel of food on earth for a single snort of Brodie's watered-down Cape brandy.

I'm a drinking man by nature, I know that now. From the very first taste of the hot whisky coming drop and trickle from the copper tubing of Sam Slit's still, I knew I'd found me true love. I did not come to drunkenness from despair, though I haven't said this to Hawk, what believes I am become a drunkard because of what happened to me in the wilderness. And without the whisky jug to fuel me through the bitter cold and rain of them days, the loneliness and the mongrels, I'd have surely died. But I sees it clear now – if I'd been born a prince, I'd still be a drunk. Now I'm just plain thirsty! Desperate for a drop!

I got a plan, though. I been collectin' raisins from the plum duff. On good days, there be as many as twenty a serve, and in not too many weeks I'll have a handy store. I'm gunna dry them and soak them, and then when I'm on galley duty, which is often enough, steal some of the yeast used for baking the skipper's bread to add to 'em. Sam Slit be of value to me at last! There were nothin' that bastard did not know about the fermenting of grog and I reckon a tolerable good brandy will come from these raisins yet. Yours truly shalt not be denied his grog by these God-gobbing Yankees.

Hawk is much pleased that his little brother eats more now. He is patient and tender to me when I sulks, dreaming of the drink. In our spare moments, he teaches me to read and write again from books and a slate he brought aboard with him.

Hawk is a fine teacher to me. When he hears something it remains in his noggin forever after. He can remember each and every word spoken by Captain O'Hara when he pronounced sentence on Billy Lanney. He's made me a copy of the captain's sermon on his slate as a means of me learning to write again, which is why I can now recall it word for word. Hawk reckons I must write to be educated and read so me mind might be alive to the world beyond the inside of a brandy bottle. The fact that I don't want to see nothin' but the insides o' that bottle don't worry him! Anyways, Hawk likes to teach me and I likes to learn from him. And on board ship I finds out something else – I can be a great help to him too, translating his hand language to the other men, though they's picking up a bit of it anyways.

Because Hawk is dumb, there's many reckon him deaf as well, and they shouts and hollers at him, so that I needs remind 'em he can hear as well as they. But being mute, he can't much talk to no one in his language save me, so we've asked to work together. To me great sadness, though, we ain't allowed to man a whaleboat together because I were declared too small to row with the strength of t'other men. I fights back on this, as I've rowed since childhood and also on the Gordon and the Franklin when I were in the wilderness. But the fourth mate, Mr Seb Rawlings, takes one look at yours truly and that be bloody that! 'No whaleboat for you, lad,' he says right off.

But with Hawk it were different. A week out to sea, Seb Rawlings set a whaleboat over the side with a crew including Hawk. This were to see if Hawk's amazing size and strength would serve him well with the harpoon.

All of us what watched from the deck could see that Hawk were quite steady in the boat with the twenty-five-pound harpoon held above his shoulder, even though the sea were less than calm. A barrel with a white circle painted on it were cast from the whaleboat with a light line attached, and allowed to drift away, bobbing up and down amongst the waves. Hawk were then told to aim the harpoon at the barrel while standing full upright in the bow.

At first the crew laughed as Hawk launched the harpoon and were thrown on his back again and again, and once even up-ended into the sea. But Hawk don't give up easy and with a little instruction, he soon improved.

By Hawk's fifth outing, we watched as he threw the harpoon a good distance. He were most accurate too, often spearing the dot painted on the barrel and never so much as missing by more than the few inches allowable for the hunting of the sperm whale. Mr Rawlings pronounced himself satisfied and Hawk were appointed a standby – what sees that the whaleboat's equipment be all ship-shape before launching and what can be called upon to crew if someone be ill or unable to take their place for some other reason.

It's a terrible disappointment to me that I can't hunt whale with me brother. Hawk ain't happy neither, and makes me say this for him to the mate. Hawk tells Rawlings of me previous life as a timber getter, where I gathered strength in me arms and back. But Rawlings only laughs. 'A whaleboat be no place for a boy of your size, lad. I would not have you on my conscience nor as a danger to the other crew.'

'Tell him I'll be responsible for you,' Hawk signals to me with his hands.

I translates once again and Rawlings smiles thinly at Hawk. 'Are you now the captain of my whaleboat?' I can see his patience is sore tried and he dismisses us with a backward wave of his hand. 'Go on now, be away with you!'

So here I is, Tommo the brave, standing on two wooden rungs at the top o' the mainmast on a two hour watch, searching for the spout of a whale but not allowed to join in the hunt. And me without a drink for one hundred and six days. If I does see a pod of whale, I've a good mind to look the other way. But that would be stupid. Two other men, one on each of the other masts, are also set to looking and the first to spot a whale receives a week's extra rations. It's food Hawk would relish, as he never seems to get enough to eat.

I'm forever worried about Hawk's hunger and have set about trying to satisfy it with fishing. As little lads, before we was took, Hawk and me were good fishermen, but he lost the skill of it when Mary put him to book-learning and clerking, and then sent him to England to learn about growing hops.

Hawk still talks o' London Town sometimes, though he sees it through different eyes to Ikey's. He were in Kent, studying the art of agriculture, with little money. He'd pen letters for the farm workers, many of 'em Irish, Tipperary men and the like, wanting to send word to their colleens or dear parents at home. For sixpence a letter, he'd write the most tender love letters, though he knows nothing of love or women. His letters be so sweet the eyes of his customers would fill with tears, and it got so that before a note were dispatched, it would be read to the whole gathering for their enjoyment. So successful did Hawk become with his flowery phrases that most of his Saturday afternoons were spent in this pursuit, and it made him sufficient coin to go up to London Town by train of a Sunday.

With sixpence for a cup o' tea and a sticky bun, and another for a pint of ale, Hawk would take the omnibus to the East End and Whitechapel, visiting all the places Ikey told us of. In our childhood dreams, London Town were a place o' palaces and broad streets where everyone were a toff and Ikey much respected, a prince amongst men! Alas, Hawk found the palaces and grand houses but these was outnumbered a thousand to one by the hovels of the poor and unfortunate what crawled like ants in every dark corner. Yet these was the very places Ikey meant when he'd spoke to us of the throbbing heart o' the great city.

'Ikey's corner of the world was mostly rags, poverty and drunkenness,' Hawk reckons. He tells of how often in winter it never grows light, the smog from the coal fires and factories closin' out the sun. When the weather got warmer the stench were unbearable and attacked his delicate nostrils long before the train pulled into Waterloo station. The fumes made his nose drip and his lungs wheeze, so that after a few hours he longed to be back in the fresh countryside. In winter, walking the streets in the cold, wet and dark, the terrible stench were gone, swallowed by the frost and snow. But this were a time o' despair for our big-hearted Hawk, when he'd see barefooted children wrapped in newspapers and rags, begging a penny and near to perishing. He'd take as many as he could to a pie shop and empty his pockets of all he possessed. It was common enough, he says, to find their little corpses under the bridges when they did not survive the cold of the night.

Hawk made many a visit to Petticoat and Rosemary Lanes and found them not much changed from Ikey's tales, though it were the same poverty witnessed everywhere. Sometimes he'd drink a pint of ale at the Pig 'n' Spit, the public house what was once owned by our true mother, Sperm Whale Sally, or as she were known then, Marybelle Firkin. Hawk tried to find Ikey's old coves, Sparrer Fart and Bob Marley, but to no avail. Some knew of Bob Marley, what they claimed had taken the boat for New York. All had heard of Ikey Solomon, though only some knew what had happened to him. Only one person remembered Sparrer Fart, and it were thought he'd been transported to Van Diemen's Land or New South Wales, not long after Ikey himself.

Hawk visited Ikey's Whitechapel home o' course, and though boarded up at the doors and windows, it were most impressive, a veritable mansion when compared to the rows of miserable houses for the poor what surrounded it, all stuck together with common walls.

Though Hawk talks often of the poverty he saw, he sometimes recalls London in spring, when the sky above Hyde Park were duck-egg blue, the sun warm to the back o' the neck and the larks singing high in the sky. Daffodils, crocus and bluebells were poking up everywhere in great patches through the green grass of the park; the squares fronting the big houses were ablaze with peach, pear and plum blossom, and the rich folks' window boxes filled with tulips.

Then he tells of lovers sitting hand in hand, and old people clapping to the beat as they listen to the military bands play their stirring marches in the parkland rotundas. He recalls the wonders and delights of Vauxhall Gardens and the pretty girls everywhere. But always his conversation turns back to the never-ending traffic, full of carriages, hacks and conveyances of every conceivable kind, where the tooting and whistling and whirring of rattles continues twenty-four hours, day and night, like a great living machine driven by some unknown hand.

'Tommo, London is every type of misery and despair though it is filled with delights beyond your imaginings,' he declares. 'But still, I missed the simplicity of Hobart Town, with folks stopping to greet you and pass the time of day.'

Hawk also remembers his constant hunger while he were in Blighty for he never got enough to eat. He's been near starvin' on the *Nankin Maiden* too and so I've started to fish for him. In exchange for me kangaroo skin coat, the blacksmith has provided me with a long braided line, sinker lead and various sized hooks. The Maori aboard have showed me how to make lures from cloth and wire, and I've got an arrangement with the cook whereby he keeps half what I catches and the remainder be fed to Hawk and me.

The bastard cheats us often, claiming more bone upon cleaning and filleting my catch than a fish could carry. But what we get adds greatly to our rations. Some days I catch even more than we can eat or the cook can cheat us of, and this is shared with the Maori and islander crew. Apart from them, the men aboard will not eat fish or shark freshly caught, much preferring salt beef.

We've become friends of sorts with these kanakas, this being a word from Hawaii what means 'man'. Our friendship with the Maori be especially strong and they welcome Hawk and me to be amongst them sometimes. Though their faces be every inch tattooed so that they appear to be primitive savages of great fierceness, they's a jolly lot and often laughing. They cannot say Hawk's name but call him Ork, what be good enough! Already I've some handy words of their language which Hawk also begins to understand. They show great delight when I make a word or string together a sentence in their tongue and are at great pains to correct me when I get it wrong.

And so my time when not on watch is well taken up, and not only with new learning at reading and writing. Billy Lanney has taken to showing us some of the many knots and hitches to be found in the seaman's trade. Splicing be the hardest, but I am learning to turn a neat splice, though Hawk with his big hands is making less progress. Sometimes I play cards in the fo'c'sle but it ain't the same without grog. It's fishing what is me most important daily task, almost more than gathering raisins. Fish ain't always plentiful and days may pass without me catching anything. I frets for Hawk when this happens. But though I don't never want to be parted from him again, I doubt that me love of Hawk is stronger than me love of grog!

It's near time for me to be called down from this bloody watch. Two hours spent standing on wooden rungs, me eyes peeled for whales, and the breeze stiffening and growing blustery in me face is most tiring work, and I'll be glad to be back on deck. But just as I'm thinking this, I sees a whale blow. At first I ain't sure, but then another whale breaks the surface and this time I sees the spouting clear.

'Thar she blows!' I yell at the top of my voice. 'Thar she blows!' I scream, pointing to starboard, my throat hoarse. Now I see them again, a pod of at least four, and big uns too. One begins to sound and I see its great fluke hit the water with an explosion like a small cannon fired against the wind.

What I've seen I takes to be sperm whale, though of course I'm no expert. But then the two men on the other masts see the pod as well. 'Sperm!' one shouts. 'Four of them! To starboard!' shouts the other. But the call is mine, the first sighting belongs to yours truly, Tommo X Solomon!

I am too excited to go down the mast straight away. Me heart is thumpin' in me chest and ears. I am needed below for it's every hand to the task when a pod be sighted, but me knees are gone to jelly and shaking beyond me control.

Below me on deck, there is a frenzy of activity, men running everywhere in great confusion. Our ship turns slowly to starboard, men adjusting the sails so that we might close the distance between the pod and ourselves.

The mates are shouting and waving their arms. The crew prepare to lower the whaleboats by means of the falls – a block-and-tackle arrangement which sets the boats to swaying in the breeze as they fall loose from their davits. Captain O'Hara on the bridge shouts, 'Where away!' for these be the words spoken when a hunt is on. From where I stand all is bedlam. I looks for Hawk but now the ship has turned, I cannot see the whaleboat on the starboard quarter which be his.

A whaleman has climbed into each of the three other whaleboats on the port side, making the harpoon and rope barrel ready and checking that the oars and all else be ship-shape and in their rightful place. The ship is making good progress in the stiff breeze, sailing towards our prey, which seem not to notice us.

Then the falls drop the whaleboats some two feet below the level of the main deck, and the remainder of the crews jump in. They takes their places at the thwarts with the oars and the steering oar shipped ready. At last the three boats are dropped into the ocean with a foamy splash.

As soon as the boats hit the water the five oarsmen in each, including the harpooner, begin to row at a frantic pace, with the mate at the steering oar. The hunt is on! The stiff breeze makes my eyes water as I scan the waves, trying to see the fourth whaleboat and if Hawk be in it.

But it's all hands on deck when a whale chase is on and I got t' get down where I'm needed. I scramble down the mast wishing I'd been chosen to man a whaleboat with me brother beside me. But at that same moment I has a second wish, and I pray that Hawk has not been chosen and that he be safe on the deck below me. He'll not be in the crew 'less someone be indisposed, and I tell myself there is nothin' to worry about. Then suddenly me heart is full of fear. I am back in the wilderness, caught in the tall timbers, and I can feel that *they* are near. Tommo has smelled the mongrels coming, but this time they be after my brother Hawk.

Chapter Four

HAWK

The Pacific Ocean
November 1856

I am seated in a quiet corner of the poop deck, my watch completed and two hours to myself. I am here because I can't bear being in the fo'c'sle, a hell-hole where those who are not on watch congregate for smoking, conversation and sleep.

It's worse than Brodie's sly grog shop, a cabin about sixteen feet wide and as many again from the bulkhead to the foredeck and so low that a person of my stature must bend almost double to walk. Around the fo'c'sle ladder are sea chests, greasy pans, pieces of rancid meat and soap kegs belonging to the crew. Along the walls a dozen small berths are piled high with evil-smelling bed linen, consisting of old foul weather clothes. The one small consolation is that few fleas, lice and bed bugs are to be found. This is not because of the lack of dirt and human ordure but because of the prevalence of cockroaches. The cockroach is a hunter of these vermin and eats them with relish, being particularly partial to the flea, which it will chase with an insane ferocity.

As you lie awake at night in the fo'c'sle with not a stitch of cover except a lather of perspiration, you can hear the cockroaches at work, their wings clicking away busily. All too often an army of them will climb up your arms and legs and scurry across your stomach in pursuit of some flea, or congregate to lick the sweat from your body. Though rats are more numerous on a whaleship than on any other vessel at sea, and it is common enough to see them gnawing at the calloused soles of some sleeping kanaka's feet, they are but a nuisance compared to these vermin.

The cockroaches are described in jest as being as big as rats and the rats as big as cats. If this is an exaggeration, it is not by so very much. There is a shanty I've heard the men sing:

And the rats, oh the rats,
be as big as dockside cats
And the roaches in the fo'c'sle
as big as Sally's flats.

Row, row, whaleman
Pull now at your oars,
We're sailing off to hunt our prey
wherever there be whaling
from 'round the Cape to Boston Bay
and down to the Azores!

Row, row, whaleman
Pull now on your oars,
The skipper's docked your pay away
with provisions from his stores
with . . . pro-vis-ions . . . from . . . his . . . stooooores!

In this weather the fo'c'sle is insufferably close. It is seldom cleaned and the dirt and stench are overpowering. But the men seem to prefer it to the clean breeze and sunshine on deck and there is always a game of cards going, the players' pipe smoke fugging the atmosphere so that the cards can scarcely be seen in the dim light cast by a whale-oil lamp. It is a place of much joshing and cursing, and every hour of the day it seems a fight is about to start. The knives come out at the slightest provocation. Yet it is the nearest a whaleman has to a home, and the men seldom come to blows.

It is mid-morning and a stiffening nor'easterly brings some relief from the heat. Tommo is on whale watch up the mainmast, a task which suits him well as there is still much of the solitary in him. He spoke once of how, in the wilderness, he would sometimes escape from his drunken master, Sam Slit, by climbing high up into the branches of a river gum. Slit, violent and angry, would fire a musket charged with birdshot to try to bring him down.

Tommo laughs at this memory. 'Them trees be too high for most of the shot to reach me and I be too well protected by the mighty branches.' I sometimes think of Tommo as a small child who climbs into the branches of a grog tree to escape his own miseries. I wonder how he shall become a man while still he seeks this escape.

But then I wonder, am I yet a man? How may I tell? How do we move from the state of childhood to manhood?

There must be a moment when we pass over into manhood. We are now sixteen, but it cannot simply be a time set by others when we are said to come of age. It is, I should imagine, a moment of the heart and of intelligence, or even, if there is such a thing, of the soul. But perhaps we can also lose our childhood too soon on account of suffering.

Tommo is an example of this. He has suffered too much and has been cheated out of his rightful share of childhood, its natural expectations and excitements. He has grown up too soon and thus is bitter and cynical.

But what of the others like him, the street urchins who hunt in feral packs around Hobart Town? Those brats who look at you with snotted noses and old, tired eyes, their only ability calculating the gain which might be made from your presence amongst them. Are they still children? Unlike Tommo, they are neither bitter nor cynical, for they expect nothing of life, only their certain death at the hands of others like them, or at the end of the hangman's rope. Perhaps the moment of manhood or womanhood is the moment when we give up hope for ourselves?

The feral children of Hobart Town are the flotsam on the tide of humanity. If the clergyman, judge, teacher and merchant – those four wise corners which frame our noble society – are to be believed, there is no hope to be held for any of them.

In the eyes of the clergyman, they are lost souls, doomed to a short life of no virtue and a pauper's grave. The judge believes it is his bounden duty to punish such delinquent brats for the sins they commit against their fellow man. To the teacher, they are simply the dull-minded infants who pay no heed in lessons and are quickly left behind. To the merchant, they are an easy source of stolen pennies, to be set upon by dogs when they beg for charity.

Yet if these pitiable slack-jawed children had been granted a childhood of love, decency and some useful learning, they might well have passed naturally into maturity and proved themselves as good as any other person. Even poor Tommo had the early benefit of love and teaching before we were kidnapped. Whilst I was fortunately returned to Mary quite soon thereafter, receiving her love and with it the opportunity to learn, Tommo spent his next seven years amongst some of the vilest of the human tribe. He has retained his intelligence, which was early formed, and is now only backward in its application. What he has lost is the ability to love and trust.

I fret for those lost children of Hobart Town and every other town, and I fret for my brother. I feel saddened and somehow responsible that I was saved, while my twin suffered. It's perhaps one reason why I am with him now, forsaking Mary. It is to care for Tommo and teach him what I know so that together we might turn back the clock and restore the love and trust he has lost.

At times, though, I wonder whether I am rescuing Tommo or he is rescuing me. Have I run away from Mary? Since rescuing me from the wild man, she wishes to know my whereabouts at every moment and seeks to direct my efforts at every turn. Mary loves me with all her heart but thinks me disadvantaged in two ways: I am only a black man and I have no voice to speak for myself. She sees herself as my protector and as my voice, and it would be ever thus had I remained with her in Hobart Town.

How then should I test myself? How then should I come to know my own character, whether I am good or bad, strong or weak? Do my dreams for the future exist only because I am a privileged creature and have no knowledge of the true nature of men? All these questions I think of on our voyage.

In the end, I confess that I have longed for an adventure such as this. When I heard that the *Nankin Maiden* was in port I was already well aware of Tommo's discontent. I believed that if only Tommo and I were on an American whaling ship which did not permit grog, then he would be safe, and we would both be embarked upon a grand adventure. When Mary bade us gone, I acted on this notion.

Perhaps whaling is in our blood? This is a question I also hope to answer. Our fathers were whalemen – Tommo's a giant Red Indian by the name of Tomahawk and mine an even bigger black man by the name of Black Boss Cape Town.

Ikey had told us how we were conceived as a result of that legendary night when the two harpooners wrestled for the singular favours of the giant whore, Sperm Whale Sally. Our mother was said to be imbued with the spirit of the whale, and those who coupled with her won good fortune for their vessel on the hunt. Yet only two men had succeeded in bedding her and sailing under the 'True Blue' flag which bestowed her blessing. These men were Tommo's father and mine. When the whaling season brought both their ships into port at the same time, each man was determined to claim her for his own. But in the end, neither man alone was strong enough for Sally and, to heal the rivalry between them, she gave herself to both. It is from this loving that twins were born, one white and the other black, one tiny and one huge, one Tommo and the other me.

When we were born and Ikey adopted us, he wrote to the Royal Society in London, hoping to gain some fame from this remarkable birth. They replied that while the fertilising of the one female egg by seed from two different males is most unusual, it was not unknown to happen among whores where numerous and near simultaneous couplings took place, and that it was not a matter of sufficient interest for their record books. Ikey always said that if our mother had been a duchess instead of a whore they'd have taken more notice and we'd be famous.

Knowing our birthright, it was only natural that I should choose a whaling ship for Tommo and me to sail on. All on board the *Nankin Maiden* have heard the legend of Sperm Whale Sally, and some old salts claim they know the two giant whalemen, though none has heard of, or seen, either for several years, and none knows we are their sons.

I am lost in these recollections when there is a shout from high above me. It is Tommo, high-pitched and much excited, shouting that he has seen a spout. 'Thar she blo-o-o-o-ows! Thar she blo-o-o-o-o-ows!' he bellows down at the top of his voice. Then the other two lookouts start shouting as they too see the whales.

For a few moments nothing appears to happen, then the whole ship springs to life, like a dozing animal suddenly surprised. My recent thoughts tumble into oblivion as I jump to my feet to play my part in the whale chase to come.

Seb Rawlings, the fourth mate, has not yet included me in the crew of the whaleboat he captains. Instead he has selected William

Lanney to serve as the fifth crewman along with four Maori whalemen led by Hammerhead Jack, an impressive giant of a man.

I am the 'stand-by' and must ensure that all the equipment needed in the boat for a whale hunt is kept in good working order and made ready. Now I climb in while it is still attached to the davits to make one last inspection before the crew is lowered into the sea.

I check everything thoroughly, though there is scarcely time. The fast launching of the whaleboats is of great concern to Captain O'Hara. Quickly I scan the two-thirds-inch manila rope in the aft barrel. Only yesterday I examined every inch of this line for fraying before folding it back myself, so I know all two hundred fathoms to be in good order. My secret mark is still upon it which means it has not been tampered with. Below me on deck I hear Hammerhead Jack lead his men in some sort of savage war cry, a ritual of theirs.

I check the splices to the two harpoons which will be attached to the line by means of short warps, and then look over the harpoons themselves. They are of the new double-barbed Temple iron which rotates ninety degrees within the flesh of the whale to form a T-shape which will not pull out. I examine the three lances and the five pulling oars, the steering oar and the paddles. I check that they are sound and that the rowlocks are well fixed. I make sure that the boat piggin is not holed, that three gallons of drinking water in a canvas bag are on board for the men, and that the two boat knives which are attached to marlin line are stowed. Finally I see that the small lug sail is in place with a spare roll of canvas. All is ship-shape. There are over forty articles in a whaleboat and I cannot inspect them all now, though I have done so as part of my watch on the previous day. I am climbing down from the davits in haste when I hear Billy Lanney beseeching Hammerhead Jack.

'I go crew, Jack! Me back be tickety-boo, number one!' Billy says in some anguish.

'Let me see your back then, Billy!' a voice demands from behind us. To my surprise it is not Rawlings' and I turn to see the first mate, Crawlin Nestbyte, standing in front of the little Aborigine.

Billy Lanney shakes his head vigorously. 'You no must see, boss! Rowing me can do! No plurry problems!' He swings his arms about like a windmill to show that they are not troubled by the wounds to his back.

As I drop onto the deck where the whaleboat crew are gathered, Hammerhead Jack grabs me by the shoulders and pushes me forward, smiling at Crawlin Nestbyte. 'Him, Ork, him good! He be crew, boss!'

Nestbyte hesitates. Hammerhead Jack releases me and, after removing Billy's hat which he drops to the deck, he grabs Billy's canvas blouse. He jerks it roughly over Billy's head and then lifts Billy bodily, spinning him around in the air and planting him down again so that his naked back is facing the first mate.

At the sight of Billy's back Nestbyte grins broadly. 'Ah, a spine well worthy of God's wrath!' he says happily, leaning forward to make a closer examination. ' "I am not mocked, sayeth the Lord," ' he pronounces proudly, and steps back well satisfied.

My horror at what I see must show clearly upon my face. Billy's back is a great yellow and purple suppuration with maggots among the deep furrows of his infected wounds.

Hammerhead Jack shakes his head in commiseration, jerking his thumb in Billy's direction. 'Him, Billy, brave man!' Then he clucks his tongue twice. 'Not come, boss, too much sick to row boat!' He says this firmly, stabbing a large finger at Crawlin Nestbyte's chest, and pointing to me. 'Ork, him come!'

Nestbyte does not much like Hammerhead Jack's demand, and anger clouds his expression. His fists bunch at his side. But then he seems to think better of it and his hands unclench. Though the first mate is by most standards a big man, the Maori is more than a head taller than he. Besides, there is not much time and the other boats to portside have already been launched.

'Watch thy tongue, kanaka bastard!' is all he says to Hammerhead Jack. Then he turns to me. 'Well, well, if it isn't Mr Rawlings' fine nigger pupil! High time to see if thou art a good nigger or a gutless one, eh? Mr Rawlings hath the tropical fever and Captain O'Hara is himself indisposed. It will be my privilege to break thee in . . . or break thee – which shall it be, I wonder?'

I smile, though I have a great desire to smash Nestbyte's teeth into the back of his throat. It is just my luck that both Rawlings and O'Hara are indisposed!

'Him good! Ork good nigger,' Hammerhead Jack says and laughs happily, not in the least concerned by the first mate's admonishment. He slaps me again on the back.

Hammerhead Jack is truly a huge man. He is taller by four

inches or more than I, and is also wider of girth and in the barrel of his chest. He has a long face and square jaw which are off-set by the height and flat surface of his protruding brow. This already extraordinary visage is framed by two great sweeps of hair which rise upwards and then hook down at the back. They are separated by an inch-wide scar which runs like a roadway from the front to the back of his skull, giving his hair the appearance of the claws of a carpenter's hammer, which is where Hammerhead Jack's name comes from.

At our first meeting Hammerhead Jack was much taken by the scar about my neck, pointing to his own scar and then running a finger around my neck, carefully tracing the silver ribbon of tissue. Then he shook my hand vigorously to indicate that we had in common a mutilation which, it was plain to see, he regarded as most handsome in appearance.

Our whaleboat is being lowered and we scramble overboard and into its bows as it passes the level of the top deck. Hammerhead Jack and myself are the last in, following the first mate.

The men working the falls lower us into the water with a great splash. Without thinking I take my place on the thwart, on the far side of the boat immediately behind Hammerhead Jack at the bow. He turns and gives me a great grin, pleased as Punch. 'Good Ork!' he says. The other three Maori laugh. 'Good Ork!' they shout, welcoming me to the crew and ignoring the scowling first mate who has taken up the sweep oar to steer us.

I would have felt more honoured if it had been Seb Rawlings who had chosen me. Mr Rawlings is no angel, a hard man, but he is fair in most things and respected by the men.

Nestbyte, on the other hand, is a proper bastard, a bully-boy who is much disliked for his harsh punishment of the smallest offences. It is said he is an expert with the blade and he carries an American bowie knife on his belt. If someone should so much as challenge him, he will pull it out and fight them.

'I'll take the bastard with me axe any day he wants,' Tommo boasts, but I have never seen my twin fighting with his axe and it is my earnest hope I never shall.

Sometimes the first mate is referred to as 'Creepy Crawlin' as he will frequently creep around the decks at night with a whale-oil lamp, hoping to find men at sodomy. When he catches two men at it, he has the permission of Captain O'Hara for a most heinous punishment. First the offenders are held down and a spoonful of ground Chinese chilli peppers is inserted up their arses. Their hands are then tied behind their backs and they are allowed to go for the night. If any should render them aid in their agony as the peppers burn their insides, they too will receive the same treatment. The following morning at muster the offenders are given fifty lashes, inflicted by the first mate's own hand. Then, with their backs open and bleeding, they are made to walk the main deck with huge bags of salt tied about their necks by a cord. The bags rest on their backs, leaking salt into their open wounds by means of small apertures. Their wounds aflame, they must walk until they drop from exhaustion. Nestbyte repeats this torture of chilli and floggings every day for a week, with the victims still required to complete a full watch each day.

After this, each offender is issued with a brass neck-plate bearing the inscription, 'A Son of Sodom' and under this the words, 'I am not worthy of God's redemption'. Those who have been caught are named Brass Bimbos by the rest of the whalemen, and there are half a dozen or more on board who wear this attachment. They do so without shame, as if it is a badge of honour, hard-earned – which, I suppose, is true enough!

Crawlin Nestbyte is a cruel braggart who talks endlessly of his exploits and derring-do with the whale. There is an old saying on a whaling vessel which goes thus:

> *That which the coward brags he will do,*
> *The whaleman true goes silent to!*

It must be said in fairness, though, that those men who have shared a boat with Nestbyte admit that he is not lacking in courage. He is known to be reckless and because of this no one who has previously voyaged on the *Nankin Maiden* will volunteer to his whaleboat, choosing any other by preference. While he takes delight in inflicting suffering on others, he is not afraid to take on a man his own size even without a knife. That is all that can be said in his favour. The crew are hard men who would turn like a pack of wild dogs on one of their own kind caught stealing or cheating. But they take little pleasure in witnessing Nestbyte's numerous cruelties to whalemen whom he believes have offended him or have been neglectful of their duties.

Though his Quaker mouth is full of God's words, his dark soul is in the possession of the devil himself. Nestbyte employs only two expletives, 'Bastard' and 'Damn', explaining to all that both words are not a blasphemy or foul language. The first is but the name for a child born out of wedlock and the second a shortening of the word damnation which is to be found frequently in the good book itself. If both words are innocent, then never was there a man who could inject more venom into them!

I have been out to sea only half a dozen times in a whaleboat, on practice runs while we were becalmed to learn the harpoon. Now the atmosphere is charged. I sincerely hope that I do not let my companions down, for I don't know what to expect. Seb Rawlings, on the last occasion he took me out, pronounced himself satisfied that I have the strength and skill to throw the harpoon. But as we rowed back to the ship he said, 'Ah yes, lad, but do ye have the courage to stand up to the whale and will ye use the lance correct?'

Do I have the courage? I now ask myself. Will I prove a coward? I cannot answer. I must wait for the moment to come, when I must throw a harpoon into a live whale and not a bobbing barrel, and use a lance at which I've had no practice. I am thankful that Hammerhead Jack is the harpooner in our crew, and I hope by watching to learn much from him.

Seated on our thwarts we are perilously close to the harpoon rope. This runs from the barrel at the stern, down the centre of the boat, to the crutch on the starboard bow where it is spliced to the two harpoons in front of where Hammerhead Jack is seated. When the rope is running to the whale it becomes sizzling hot. Should we suddenly be thrown against it, or move carelessly, it will in a moment cut inches deep into our thighs or slice our arms down to the bone, cooking the flesh it ravages.

We cannot see the other three whaleboats and our late start has caused some anxiety in Nestbyte. 'Row, row! Row, row!' he repeats urgently. 'It's first to the pod for us, or I'll see ye flogged and stretched to the mizzen! Row! Row! Row, ye cannibal bastards, row!' His voice grows ever angrier as he envisages us lagging behind the other boats.

I am not sure how much of this call is understood by Hammerhead Jack and the rest of the crew. Their faces show nothing beyond the strain of pulling at the oars and they do not quicken their stroke at the mate's admonishments. My arms ache and I wonder how much longer I can keep up.

The breeze seems to me to be stiffening and the seas beginning to rise. Nestbyte, who steers the boat from the stern sheets, counts the breeze insufficient to hoist the lugsail and we must perforce row on. As we come over the lip of a large wave, I can see there is new cloud boiling up from the horizon. A sniff of rain is in the air.

I have been told whalemen hunting in the Pacific Ocean are not concerned by a squall at sea. The Yankee whaleboat is well constructed from half-inch, white cedar clinker planking and difficult to capsize. If it should up-end, or be swamped, it will continue to float or even right itself. If the sea is moderately calm, it is no great hardship to clamber back in. But in the Southern Ocean around Cape Horn and towards the Antarctic it is an altogether different proposition. If a boat should be overturned by an errant wave, the crew will often freeze to death.

'Pacific whaling be a treat, lad,' Rawlings once confided at harpoon practice, 'with naught to bother about except for a mishap with the whale.' Then he grins. 'Mind,' he says, 'should the great fishy tail smash down upon you and you be thrown into the sea and not killed outright, with your boat smashed to smithereens, then naught awaits except drowning or being taken by the sharks who gather at the smell of harpoon blood and tear at anything that moves.'

Nestbyte hoists the lug sail and I am much relieved that we can ship our oars and turn to see where we might be going. The whaleboat takes smoothly to the waves and we are soon making good progress. It is pleasant not to hear the first mate's harsh voice urging us on. Hammerhead Jack calls for water. We are all streaming with sweat and the sun overhead is as hot as Hades.

'A mouthful each! No more, hear ye?' Nestbyte orders. The canvas bag is passed to Hammerhead Jack, who hoists it to his lips and takes a long drink. 'Enough! No more!' Nestbyte yells. 'If the hunt is long, ye'll beg me for it later!'

The big Maori hands the bag to me and I take a mouthful, then pass it back. 'That's enough! That's enough!' Nestbyte keeps saying before we've brought the mouthpiece to our lips.

The wind changes direction and the lug sail begins to flap. 'Man the oars!' Nestbyte shouts, though we have seen the change and already set to rowing.

'Backs! Put your backs into it, ye kanaka bastards!'

I begin to wonder if Nestbyte's constant yapping will ever stop. Then we rise over another wave and I damn near die of fright!

Not forty feet to port a sperm whale surfaces. The sea around us boils and our boat begins to rise and rise until we are fifteen feet above the highest waves. Nestbyte yells to ship our oars. With a thunderous roar of falling water, the giant fish surfaces from the depths. It is a bull, a monster, a creature a hundred times bigger than anything I have ever seen before. Its malevolent eye, which appears to gaze straight at me, is bigger than a pudding plate!

Suddenly we are drenched, as the spray from its spout pours down like a waterfall upon us. We are too close and I prepare myself to die in the moments left to me. Terrified, I glance at Hammerhead Jack to see what is to be done.

Hammerhead Jack is seated calm as you like, his hands gripping the edges of the thwart so that he might steady himself. He has his back to me but he must sense I seek him, for he turns his head and there is a grin upon his much-tattooed face. His head and shoulders stream with the spray from the whale's spouting. His lips appear to move but there is too much noise to hear what he is saying. I think it must be, 'Good Ork!'

We are suddenly plunged back to sea level as the wave caused by the whale's breaching rolls away and subsides beneath us. The boat begins to spin like a cork in the foaming water and Nestbyte works with frantic energy to steady it by means of the sweep. Then, the very moment the boat is more or less on an even keel, he yells at us to grab our paddles and to row towards the great creature.

Row towards? He must be mad! We are practically embracing the monster! Hammerhead Jack ships his paddle and the boat rocks as he goes to stand at the bow. I look up to see him take up one of the harpoons. He stands darkly silhouetted against the sky. It is him against the whale, St George and the dragon, Neptune and the sea monster. For a short moment I gain courage at his immense calm and resolve as we row towards our certain death.

We are no more than fifteen feet from the great fish and I can see a multitude of barnacles, scratches and scars upon its black carcass, deeply wrinkled aft of its flippers. Then Hammerhead Jack, with a shout, delivers the harpoon into its side. The harpoon's head is buried a full three feet into the whale's flesh.

He has aimed for the heart, just forward of the small dorsal hump not far from the whale's great head, which looks to me entirely composed of a nose with a whitish whorl at its end. At first the harpoon seems to penetrate cleanly, in the manner of a neat dart, but a moment later a huge gush of blood spurts from the side of the whale as though a pipe has burst. Then, just as quickly, the blood stops to a trickle.

Nestbyte screams to Hammerhead Jack, 'Another! Quick, the second! Damn thee, man, thou hast missed the vital part!'

But it is almost as though the whale itself has heard the first mate's shouts. Before the giant Maori can lift the second harpoon above his shoulder, the great beast raises its flukes and crashes them down against the surface of the sea. Rolling away from us, the whale sounds – diving down into the depths beneath us. There is another rush of water and then all hell breaks loose in front of my very eyes.

'Aft, come aft!' Nestbyte yells. He has already wound the manila rope around the samson post, putting a drag on the line which immediately begins to pay out and is soon screaming through the bow chocks. We are now being taken for a ride, towed by the mighty fish at breakneck speed, faster even than any good four-in-hand upon the macadam road to New Norfolk. Our whaleboat skims the waves and Nestbyte is still yelling at us. 'Come aft! In the name of Christ Jesus, *aft*, ye bastards!'

We rise from our thwarts and stumble over each other as we crowd to the rear of the boat, careful to avoid the zinging rope. We crouch in the stern so that our bow may rise high and stay clear of the waves, for should it follow the downward direction of the whale we will all be dragged under. The eldest of the Maori crew has taken up the piggin and is dousing the whale-rope with sea water to keep it from bursting into flame. But the moment he goes to take another scoop of water, the line starts to smoke again as it whirls about the samson post.

We now come across the other boats and wave to them desperately for help. But all three boats are attached to a smaller cow which sounds at that moment and they are too occupied to see us.

'Damn!' Nestbyte cries. 'We are alone with the monster! This old bull will prove too much for us!' He cups his hands to his mouth again and yells for one of the other boats to cut loose from the cow and come to our aid, but they are by now too distant to hear.

I am shaking like a wet dog in a cold wind, though whether from fear or excitement I cannot tell. The rope is paying out at a great rate from the barrel and, despite its turn about the samson post which is intended to slow the whale by adding our weight to its drag, we are tearing across the water at a great rate of knots.

I cannot believe the speed at which we move. It is as though the whale is a clipper fully rigged caught in a sudden gale, and we the float on a boy's fishing line suspended from its stern – a mere bobbing cork dragged helplessly through the angry seas. How can any creature in nature be possessed of such enormous power as is the whale!

The manila line within the barrel is not attached and should the whale take it all up in its dive, it will be free of us. Nearly the full two hundred fathoms of line have gone, and we begin to think we must soon lose our prey. My silent hope is that we do! Then the rope suddenly goes slack and we are at once becalmed. Thank God! I think. We are saved!

But it seems this is the very moment we've been waiting for. 'Pull in! All hands to the rope!' Nestbyte calls. We begin, hand over fist, to gather the rope back into the barrel.

It is the hardest of work and soon my hands are bleeding, but there is no respite. The task must be done quickly and we must be ready for the whale when he breaches. We pull at the rope until it is no longer slack and so we know it is attached to the whale lurking somewhere below us.

The very moment the rope is gathered, the Maori move back to their thwarts. I follow, scrambling to take up my oar behind Hammerhead Jack.

'We go!' he says happily to me. 'Whale come,' he makes an upward movement with his hands and then blows through his lips, 'Phiff!' which I take to mean that the whale will soon surface spouting again.

We have been occupied with the whale for two hours since the first harpoon and the sun is fierce upon our backs. I have heard how such fights may last six or more hours until, with the coming of the dark, the line must be cut and all is to no avail. I cannot imagine how we will sustain ourselves at our present pace if this old bull fights through the long afternoon.

Within fifteen minutes, the giant whale surfaces about a hundred yards away, and we must follow the rope now toward him. At almost the same moment we run into a squall, the rain belting down so fiercely we can see only a few feet ahead. The raindrops hit like bird shot but they are welcome enough for we have become heated pulling in the line. With the sheeting rain I am once again afraid of our proximity to the giant fish which we can no longer see.

Then, with the rain coming down and the sea misty, we come quite suddenly upon the whale. It is like coming upon a galleon through the fog, its huge shape looming unexpectedly in front of us. It would seem we have arrived midships as both the head and flukes of the Leviathan are lost to us in the pelting downpour. We take up the paddles again so as not to cause unnecessary noise.

Nestbyte looks for our line so that he can determine the whale's head from its tail, for when the old bull sounds again, its flukes could destroy us if we are too close to the tail-end. I can hear my heart beating in my chest as we paddle quietly towards the whale's head and heart so that Hammerhead Jack may make a good shot.

Then we see our line and, a moment later, our harpoon sticking out neat as a needle in a ball of tapestry wool. The old bull seems strangely oblivious of our presence.

Hammerhead Jack takes careful aim, as much as that is possible in the torrents splashing off the whale's back and cascading into the boat. He gives a shout and makes a mighty throw not five feet from the whale. Nestbyte wraps the line about the samson post and screams, 'Row, row! Row, row!' We are scarcely thirty feet away when the bull begins to roll to windward of us.

There is a sound like thunder as the whale's flukes smash down onto the waves, lifting the whaleboat clear into the air. I have no time to think of death as I grip the thwart, expecting to be thrown from the boat at any moment.

But by some miracle the whaleboat remains upright and comes down again with a mighty splash into a cauldron of roiling water. As the bull dives, its huge tail towers above us in the air and then with a great rushing of spray and sea, it sounds, and we spin madly in its foamy wash. We have barely time to make it aft as the whale dives only a few fathoms down before levelling out and surfacing a hundred yards away. Then we are off again, hanging on for dear life with the whaleboat bumping across the waves and the rain like sharp pellets peppering our faces as the whale tows us through the briny.

The wet rope seems to pay out even more quickly this time and the whine of it through the bow chocks pitches high above the wind from the squall about us. Despite the rain, we must still douse the rope as it smokes.

We are a hundred fathoms through the rope when the rain stops. All that may be heard is the bumping of the bows against the glassy waves and the high whining of the line. Then the rope goes slack. The whale has been lost to sight in the rain and now Nestbyte scans the sea to find him.

'Good shot!' Nestbyte says, plainly excited. 'We begin to have him!'

Again we begin pulling in the rope and the blisters which have formed on my hands are soon broken and bleeding. Whalemen who crew the boats constantly soak their hands in brine and piss to harden them, but mine have undergone no such preparation and the coarse manila rope has torn the flesh from my palms in bloody scraps of meat.

I recall now why Nestbyte is so well pleased that only half the line has been spent on our second ride across the waves. It means the whale has been struck well and is bleeding copiously from its spout. The blood will coagulate and prevent the whale from easily breathing. At the same time, the beast is weakened and will soon be forced to the surface to try and draw breath. But this does not mean the fight is done. A wounded whale can still move furiously fast upon the waves and can tow a boat beyond the reach of help.

With the line gathered a full sixty fathoms or so Nestbyte turns us to the south-east. 'Haul in the rope!' he screams. 'Put your backs into it, bastards!'

Hammerhead Jack sighs deeply and I look around to see him shaking his head woefully. Then, to my surprise, he says something in his native tongue and all but myself rest their oars.

'What means this?' Nestbyte asks in anger.

I am forced to ship my own oar as the giant Maori turns towards the first mate. He makes a tumbling motion in the air with his hands and points in the direction Nestbyte would have us row. I follow his direction but I can see nothing out of the ordinary.

Ignoring him, Nestbyte shouts, 'Take up the slack, ye bastards! Damn thee, Jack Kanaka! Pull!' I sense that his hot voice is not simply fuelled by anger at being challenged but also defiance, as though there is something else afoot which is beyond my ken. I wonder what it could be between the two men. 'Haul in the rope, bastard! Or it is the mizzen mast for thee!' Nestbyte threatens again. Hammerhead Jack shakes his head adamantly.

I search amongst the many whaling incidents I have heard of for an explanation. Ikey knew much of whaling from his nightly sojourns to the Whaler's Arms Hotel and would often regale Tommo and me with stories when we were young. And then I realise that Nestbyte has chosen to row us into the weather.

No whaleman will take a boat to the weather side of a big bull if it can be helped, for it is as close a thing to suicide as might be done in hunting a wounded whale. When a bull whale is struck and comes to the surface he always rolls windward, and if the whaleboat should be close enough to use a lance he will roll on top of it, killing all within. Even if the boat is further away, the wash from the bull's roll will almost certainly capsize it, spilling all into the sea. A mate must always approach a wounded whale from the leeward side.

But Nestbyte, who must know this well, will have none of it and insists we row weatherward. 'Ye'll all be flogged, ye kanaka bastards, I swear it in the name of Jesus!' he screams at Hammerhead Jack. 'Ye'll not get away with this disobedience! Haul in the rope, ye cannibal bastards!'

Hammerhead Jack shrugs his shoulders and spits over the side, then says something to the Maori crew. Reluctantly, they begin to take up the slack of the rope as Nestbyte, his face contorted with anger, steers us directly into the wind. The rope has begun to play out again, though not so rapidly; the whale, wherever he is, is moving sluggishly.

Nestbyte's calculation is proved accurate again for we see the whale breach three hundred yards from us about half an hour later. We sail towards the bull and as we close in on him we see that he is spouting, a spray of rosy water rising high into the sky from his great square nose.

'We have his chimney almost afire!' Nestbyte yells joyously, pointing to the bloody spray.

We have been going four hours and I am bone weary, my hands hurting beyond any pain I have felt since the wild man lassoed my throat behind his horse. If we must fight this beast much longer,

I am not sure I shall bear up. Death, should it come, no longer seems such a bad thing!

Hammerhead Jack's tattooed face is most serious, his lips pulled tight and his eyes narrowed. The others also appear unhappy. Nestbyte takes no notice, steering the boat directly towards the whale, which barely moves, its flukes slowly slapping the water. I am mindful of an angry man drumming his fingers on the table as he considers his next action. It is as though we are being forewarned that there is still much power in this beast, which must soon take vengeance on us or die itself.

All at once I am above my own miseries, aware only of the tension and the sense of death that prevails in the air about us, though whether it is ours or the old bull's, I cannot say. Judging from the expression on Hammerhead Jack's face I know that we are in mortal danger from this monarch of the deep. The sun, now out again, is warm enough, yet suddenly I am cold and a shiver passes down my spine.

We approach the bull from its windward side and from behind, keeping as quiet as possible so as not to alarm him. He seems unaware of our presence, his head facing away from our boat. He moves along slowly, spouting the rosy water we have seen at a distance. Under sail, we are well able to keep up with him, moving ever closer to the point where we might fasten. We are fifty yards away when Nestbyte pulls down the sail and instructs us to take up the paddles for a silent approach. We have only the three lances to make our kill, then we must ride it out or cut loose.

Now the whale turns on his side as though he is waiting for us, and all the while our boat draws closer and closer. Its left side is facing us, the side much favoured by the harpooner as it gives him a better chance to reach the aortic valve within the heart. The first mate turns the line in readiness about the samson post.

'Right up! We probe!'

Hammerhead Jack, who has taken up a lance, shakes his head vigorously. 'More blood! We wait some!' I take him to mean that the whale must lose more blood, that it is too soon to fasten.

'What have we here, a coward?' Nestbyte says.

I do not know how much of this Hammerhead Jack comprehends but he is plainly furious. We stop paddling and Nestbyte screams, 'Paddle, ye bastards! We must go close, ye damned cowards!'

For a moment it seems as if Hammerhead Jack will fight Nestbyte, for he has taken up the razor-sharp lance and they stand glaring. Each has his eyes locked to the other's in rage, Nestbyte with one hand on the bowie knife at the side of his belt.

'Coward!' Nestbyte taunts and spits over the side.

It is this single word which seems to defeat Hammerhead Jack and with a shrug he turns away. By now, we are but thirty yards away. I cannot believe what is unfolding before my eyes. Nestbyte has chosen to take us right up to the whale so that Hammerhead Jack might use the lance as a deep probing blade.

The lance is not a natural spear, but a razor-sharp two-sided blade, more like a surgeon's scalpel, spliced to a long wooden handle. It is best used once the whale is substantially weakened through loss of blood. Only then will a whaleboat fasten to the whale. The harpooner's task is to insert the lance and probe for a vital spot, seeking the heart or lungs or major artery to start the final massive haemorrhage.

Not only are we on the windward side, but rowing right up to a whale that, far from giving up the fight, is more dangerous now than ever before. It can only be concluded that Nestbyte has gone stark mad, for he is taking us right into the jaws of death!

'Ship paddles on the whale side!' Nestbyte commands. This is my side and I am sweating with fear.

'Stand off!' Nestbyte cries, meaning that I and the young Maori behind me should stop the boat from bumping the whale by means of our paddles held against its great carcass.

I have never touched a whale before, leastways one which may kill me for being so bold as to dare. My hands go out at one point when we go closer to the great sea beast and I feel its wet hide, soft to the touch under my palms.

Hammerhead Jack turns quietly to me and motions that I should take up a lance. I do so, but I am shaking like a leaf and he can see the fear in my eyes. 'Good Ork,' he says quietly.

He seems calm as he makes his inspection of the whale's flank. Then he indicates a place on its side and points to me and to the lance I am holding. Moving a foot or so away, he swiftly inserts his own lance, which seems to cut through the beast's flesh like a hot knife through lard.

Numbly, I follow suit. I am astonished at the ease with which the blade runs through the whale flesh. Hammerhead Jack twists and probes, churning the malevolent knife to find the blood pipe he seeks, grunting with the effort. I do the same, though I feel sick as my blade buries into the great beast's body, not knowing what it is I seek to find.

Suddenly a great arc of crimson, ten inches wide, sprays out from where I have made my cut, and both Hammerhead Jack and I are deluged in the sanguineous gush.

'Push away and stand off!' Nestbyte yells.

I am not certain how, in my bloody state, I find my oar, nor do I recall pushing away from the whale. But we are a full twenty feet away when the bull begins to roll towards us and his great flukes come up and smash down in a mighty explosion which rings my ears almost to deafness. He barely misses us as he prepares to dive. It is as though a mountain is falling on us and I am certain we shall be crushed to death.

Somehow the bull's huge bulk misses and we escape his crushing weight upon us. But with a roar of rushing water, a tidal wave overtakes us, and the boat goes over. I am under water yet can hear the scream of the line as it pays out. I struggle to free myself, knowing I have only moments to reach the surface before I must tangle in the line and be cut in half.

I come clear of the boat at last, gasping and taking great gulps of air. The water about me is stained red. A paddle floats past and I grab it. It sinks beneath my grasp and then I see that I am clutching a man's severed arm. I drop it from my frantic grasp and swim the few strokes towards the whaleboat, which has by some miracle righted itself. It is not yet moving, though the line is still paying out with a high-pitched whistle.

My terror spurring me on, I lift myself into the half-submerged boat. I rest a moment, sucking in the wondrous air, before looking about me. In the water around me other heads have surfaced and they swim towards the boat where I pull each aboard as best I can, three of the Maori and Nestbyte, but Hammerhead Jack is missing.

Then I see him twenty feet away. He is threshing the water with one arm, his head coming up and going down again in a foam of scarlet.

A moment more and I am sure my courage would have failed, but I am in the water before I know it and stroking out towards the wounded man.

'Leave him! Damn thee, nigger! Leave the bastard!' I hear

Nestbyte gasp from the boat, but I continue to swim. Tommo and I have been strong swimmers since childhood and in a few strokes I am upon Hammerhead Jack. I grab him about the chest and he has the good sense not to struggle or perhaps he has passed out, and I am able to pull him towards the boat.

As I reach the side, which is half-submerged in the water, a strong hand encircles my wrist and I grab back to make a better purchase. But at that very moment the line zings and stiffens, and the boat begins to move away. The whale, which has dived straight down, is now levelling off and pulling away again.

'Cut the rope! Cut the rope!' I am shouting, though only in my head of course.

'Leave him, nigger!' Nestbyte screams at me. 'Let go the damned cannibal!' Then he brings his boot up and, aiming it at Hammerhead Jack's head, kicks viciously downwards to separate him from me, or both of us from the boat, in order to chase his whale.

'Damn thee! The lance is perfect set, the whale is ours!' he screams.

I have my hand about the wrist of one of the Maori whalemen on board and my arm hooked through Hammerhead Jack's good arm and about his chest, my chin clasped to his neck. I will not let go, nor will the young Maori who is holding onto me. Blood drips onto my shoulder where Nestbyte has crushed Jack's right eye and nose with the heel of his boot. The water around us is stained crimson with the whale's blood, as well as that from the harpooner's severed arm socket.

I am hanging on for dear life as the whaleboat gains speed. Then I see the flash of a blade as Nestbyte brings his bowie knife down into the back of my hand. At the very same moment the whale finds a surge of strength and the boat's bow is pulled down and we jerk forward. The first mate, already off balance from his downward strike at me, loses his footing and with a cry of alarm is pitched over my head and into the churning sea. He is at once gone from sight.

How I am able to maintain my grip about the Maori's wrist and still hold on to Hammerhead Jack while the boat is moving I cannot say, for my palms are minced from hauling in the line. But somehow I do, and with the boat beginning to skim the waves, the two of us are finally pulled aboard. I reach for the boat knife so that I might cut the whale-rope and save Nestbyte. Before I can grab it, my arms are held by a Maori on either side of me, and I have not the strength remaining to resist.

The whaleboat is flying along and there is no turning back. Nestbyte will be drowned long before we can cut the line and return to search for him. Anyway, without oars, we have no way of rowing back to where he fell into the turbulent seas.

Nor do we have time to think about the whale. From a large artery at the junction of Hammerhead Jack's shoulder, blood is spouting to the beat of his heart.

I pull off my blouse, stained scarlet from the bull's blood now mixed with Jack's. What little I know of binding such a wound I have learnt only from a brief description in a book I once read about the Peninsular Wars. The wounds from a cannon shot cannot be much different to this one and though I am panicked, I try to recall the exact procedures advised. I cut and then tear some canvas into narrow strips and, taking twine from my pocket, cut a length and tie the pumping artery along with the smaller ones which are still bleeding.

Hammerhead Jack's arm has been torn clean out of his shoulder socket. This is fortunate as it means the socket hole is clean and the arteries protrude so the ties are easily made even though my trembling fingers are sticky with blood. Using the remainder of my blouse I make a pad to swab the socket hole and tie it as best I can to the unconscious man's shoulder by wrapping a strip around his chest.

I rinse my hand in the bloody water in the bottom of the boat and I see that my hand is bleeding from Nestbyte's knife wound. I look about me and see the weapon lying on the bottom of the boat where it must have fallen when Nestbyte did his fatal tumble. It is a handsome bowie knife, long-bladed with a fine ivory handle, the first mate's initials C. W. N. inlaid in copper. I put it in the stern, safe above the water.

I check the wrist of the Maori who hauled Jack and me into the boat, anxious to see if Nestbyte's blade penetrated through my own hand and injured him. But he shrugs and indicates a cut where the point of the bowie knife entered which has long since ceased to bleed.

'Good Ork!' he says.

It becomes clear to me what has befallen Hammerhead Jack.

When the whaleboat overturned and we were caught under it, the whale line kinked and took Hammerhead Jack's arm with it, tearing it from its socket as the whale sounded.

It can only be supposed that the giant Maori, in the split second left to him, kept his nerve and hooked his good arm about the thwart. By holding on, he knowingly sacrificed his captured arm, else he would have travelled downwards with the whale to be drowned.

Still unconscious, Hammerhead Jack is now held by the eldest of the Maori, his head resting on the man's lap. The older man sits in the stern, his legs and most of Hammerhead Jack's torso submerged in the water-filled boat. He weeps as he tenderly protects Hammerhead Jack's damaged eye with his cupped hand. His tears spill down his purple-patterned face, splashing onto the unconscious giant's chin. All the while he moans and wails in a strange manner which I take to be the savage way of sorrowing.

The two other Maori, both younger men, have begun bailing water out of the boat with the piggin. Thankfully, this is always attached to the whaleboat by means of a marlin line and so was not lost when we overturned. They too are sniffing and moaning but remain busy at their task. They work hard and our risk of sinking diminishes as this wild sea ride with the whale continues unabated.

It is then that I see what has become of Hammerhead Jack's right eye. It is a terrible mash of jellied orb held by a tangle of bloody veins and sinew, now resting on the lower part of his tattooed cheek.

I have no time to think, or the task will be beyond me. Using Nestbyte's bowie knife I cut the tangle of sinew high up so the eye and socket entrails fall into his blood-soaked lap. Then with my thumb, I push what's left back into the empty cavity. There is now little blood as I pull the bruised and swollen eyelid over the mess. Hammerhead Jack looks to me to be more dead than alive, so I hope not to have done him much more harm than he has already endured.

I bend down and carefully scoop the eye from his lap and am about to throw it into the sea when the old man grabs my wrist and then cups his hands to receive the tangled mess. He calls his companions from their bailing and they stand beside him as he begins to chant in a wild high-pitched voice, the two young Maori punctuating the oration with great belly grunts, deep as a big military drum. Then, when the chanting is finally done, the old man leans over the side and submerges his hands to just below the water so that Hammerhead Jack's eye floats away into the waves as the three of them sing a strange but beautiful melody, filled with harmonies and a sense of great tenderness.

The whale has been forced by its bleeding to surface quickly and now is some distance ahead of us pulling the boat at a steady rate of knots. The mast has been snapped off by the whale-rope when we overturned, and the lug sail lost along with the oars and paddles, so we are captured, prisoners in our own whaleboat, tethered to a great sea beast which may eventually stop or simply continue onwards until the rope runs out. Either way, we are as helpless as small children lost in a snow storm on Cradle Mountain.

We have not had a drop to drink for six hours and before then only a mouthful. My head is light and the horizon dances in front of my eyes. Our hats were lost when the boat capsized and the sun will surely addle our brains.

After what seems like more than an hour, the rope slackens; the old bull turns and, in an arc, heads back in our direction.

Now, I think, he has come at last to take his revenge. It is better so, more worthy that we should die this way than any other. We are done for anyway, there has been no sighting of the other boats or the ship and we are lost at sea. In an open whaleboat we will go through the night well enough, but we will not last long without water. Hammerhead Jack will be dead before the sun climbs to its zenith again and we who are left will not see too many sunsets after that. Better this quick death at the hands of a worthy foe than a slow and lingering one, lying cooked in the bottom of a whaleboat.

I think of my death, not in terms of my own demise, which is now certain. No, what worries me is the question of who will take care of Tommo. My thoughts go to him at this moment. Dear Tommo, who I think is slowly mending his ways – though he is winning too often at cards and the men are becoming suspicious. He has collected nearly twenty Yankee dollars and various rings, knives and scrimshaw as his winnings and he will even play for the raisins from their next ration of plum duff. I can only suppose he craves the sweetness for it is a most curious prize to win at cards.

I have told him his gambling must stop soon.

'If they catch you at cheating they will kill you, Tommo!' I plead.

'But I don't need to cheat with these duffers!' he protests, most indignantly. 'I swears it, Hawk! It is all done above board and on the square!'

I am unconvinced. But then again, it would be just like Tommo's luck to be killed at *not* cheating. What would our poor mama think?

No day has passed on our voyage that I do not think of Mary. What will become of her, on her own? I ache to talk to mama and I have written many pages of letters telling her of our adventures. But now she shall never receive them unless Tommo thinks to send them to her when he reaches port, and who knows what state he will be in then.

My heart is heavy for Mary and for Tommo as I prepare to meet my death. Not fifty yards from us, the great monster slows his approach and I see that his chimney is spouting thick black blood. We wait terrified – a dying whale is most dangerous until the final moment when he rolls over. The sperm whale has the largest brain of any creature in the universe and this old bull has no reason to spare us. As ninety feet and over seventy tons of malevolence bear down upon us, I can see from the sombre expressions on the Maori's faces that they too are aware of our approaching doom.

However, as we draw ever nearer, the creature seems unaware of our presence. We are now no more than thirty yards apart, with no means of controlling our path. The whale's giant mouth opens, blood falling like scarlet ribbons from his upper jaw, missing the great rows of teeth contained in the long, narrow lower jaw. This monster, should we come much closer, will crush our boat to tinder between those scrimshaw molars. Miraculously, the wind shifts direction a fraction and we drift a little further away again.

More than an hour passes in this way, as we drift in close proximity to death. The whale moves more and more slowly, his chimney frequently spouting blood and gore in a great scarlet spray. His flukes have grown lethargic, and they slap the surface, making no more sound than that of the wind snapping at bed-sheets on a backyard washline.

I think, after all, that our grand opponent is aware of our presence and, with none of his own kind around him, desires to be near us. This Prince of Fish does not wish to die alone. Ho, Great Fish! We will meet again at Neptune's tavern, for we will not be long behind you.

The sea about us is crimson, bubbling and seething for two hundred yards in the bull's wake. The blood pours from him like mud running down a mountain side after a storm. Sharks circle, snapping at the floating, bubbling gore, their fins cutting through the surface in ever increasing numbers.

Then, as the setting sun turns the western sky into a fiery blaze, and the sea grows so burnished the waves' reflections turn us into glowing red men, with a great roaring and sucking of water, the tormented beast rolls over, fin out. There is a sudden silence; the Prince of the Deep Waters is dead.

We are too tired for joy and must now pull the line in, a task which seems altogether too much for us. But we cannot risk drifting away in the dark and losing our line, for we count it safer to be tethered to the dead bull all night than drift helplessly at sea. If the *Nankin Maiden* comes a-looking in the morning, a dead whale will be easier to spot from the mainmast than a lone whaleboat lost at sea.

Though hope springs eternal, our rescue seems an unlikely event. With the three other boats having fastened onto the sperm cow, she was a certain capture. Captain O'Hara must tether her to the starboard of the ship, strip her of her blubber and boil it down for oil without delay. There is little chance that he will risk losing this valuable prize to come looking for us.

The supposition that an old bull sperm whale would prove too much for one boat to handle and the natural assumption following it, that we have perished under its flukes, is a most reasonable one. Our only hope is that we may be downwind from the ship so that sailing in search of us would not be an arduous task. It is to be hoped that the master places a great value on his first mate, Crawlin Nestbyte, for he would not search even to the bottom of a bucket of sea water for four kanakas and a nigger.

All the while the sharks have been gathering. They are now in their many hundreds, bumping their snouts against the belly of the whale and tearing upwards at his hide so that the old bull looks to be still alive but for the great fin sticking up into the air and the white patch now turned red on his underbelly. These jackals of the sea have the only true victory.

It is ended and, for what it is worth, we have won this bloody contest, even though the triumph of it will be short-lived before we die.

I sit upon a thwart, my hands dripping with fresh blood from hauling in the line, but I no longer care or feel the pain. It is almost dark, with only a sliver of the sun's brassy coin still showing above the horizon. I am weary beyond all endurance, yet there is something pestering at the back of my mind.

'Scratch around, look in the dark corners, clear the cobwebs, unlock the doors and open the windows, my dear,' I hear Ikey's voice say clearly to me. He would say this when I had lost track of an idea he had previously explained. 'If it is something you have thought or known before then it will still be there, stored in the old noggin box, to be retrieved when you should need it most. But when you look, my dear, do so in an orderly manner and all will be yours soon enough.'

So I go to thinking, letting this nightmare of a day pass once again through my mind and then, at last, I recall what it is that has been troubling me.

When I held Hammerhead Jack in the water and screamed to Nestbyte to cut the line, I swear I heard my own voice, not only in my imagination but out loud. Yet I know this cannot be. I have not uttered a single word since Mary rescued me from the wild man. I touch my throat, then swallow. It feels tender, raw, though this might equally be from lack of water during the long afternoon. Have my ears deceived me? I open my mouth to attempt to make a sound.

Chapter Five

TOMMO

The Pacific Ocean
November 1856

If I've spoken against the God-gobbers what owns this ship, or Captain O'Hara, the master, I now hopes desperately that Christian fidelity might save me brother's life.

It's near sunset and the other three boats returned to the ship two hours ago with a sperm cow in tow. They says they saw Nestbyte and his crew attached to a monstrous sperm bull what they at once judged too much of a handful for a single boat. The whale were ninety foot if it be an inch, with a ton to every foot. They was all made fast to the cow and none could let loose to follow Nestbyte and his Maori, though all felt sure that the first mate would be forced to cut the manila rope or that it would run out soon enough. They was sure that the giant sea creature would not find one whaleboat much of a drag upon himself and would easily out-run the two hundred fathoms of harpoon line.

But now it's close to dark and Hawk's whaleboat still ain't returned. Most now believes that the bull's got the better of them. It ain't unusual, though, for a whaleboat to stay out overnight if another hour might bring the kill and the moon be bright enough to see by. There is fresh water on board and a lantern-keg with a little ship's biscuit and salt beef, even clay pipes and a quid of tobacco for comfort in the dark hours. But all this I'm told as the very tag end of hope by the second mate, Tom Stubbs. If they hasn't returned by sunset it is likely that the crew, including me brother Hawk, be lost at sea or dead.

The men know Nestbyte is reckless. Many in the fo'c'sle reckons he has taken one too many chances, that his luck has finally run out. It's five months since the last taking of a whale and it's just such circumstances that make a man careless.

Seb Rawlings has come from his cabin where he were confined with the tropical fever. It be his boat what's missing and he feels to blame for not going out with his crew. He's shaking with the fever and his eyes is bright as agates, lips cracked and teeth chattering, but he seems to have his senses about him. He asks that I be allowed to take the watch from aloft, where I can look out for Hawk's boat. He says that as the light grows dim in the west, my young eyes might prove better than those of an older whaleman.

There's great to-do on the ship. The cow is thought to be some twenty tons and a good catch after such a long time without a sighting. She's already chained to the starboard side ready for flensing, when the blubber will be cut from her for boiling down in the try-pots. Her oil will be enough with what's already been took to fill half the ship's barrels. This is a most important event, for the first half of our cargo will pay the costs of the voyage and the second half will pay the whalemen and the owners. Whale oil burns clean, without smoke, and is used for lamps throughout the civilised world. It be a precious commodity. Not a drop of oil from this cow must be wasted to the sharks or spoilt by the weather, and the sooner the trying out is under way the better.

There's been no talk among the mates of going to look for Hawk's whaleboat, and the men is clearly against it. Only Billy Lanney and meself wants a search party and we holds no sway at all. Billy calls for a whaleboat to go, with him and me as crew. 'Shut yer gob!' several shouts at him. 'Abo bastard!' someone else growls.

The other kanakas and the niggers don't want a search neither. The islanders hates the Maori, and the four black men, though from different parts themselves, don't sees Hawk as one o' them. Nestbyte is hated by one and all and his loss thought a good riddance. Four kanakas and a dumb nigger ain't worth keeping the flensing and the try-pots waiting for. 'Let the cutting in begin!' they cry. None wants to see a drop of their precious booty wasted.

Unchaining the cow from the ship and anchoring her at sea while we searches for the missing whaleboat would let a full night pass with a thousand sharks tearing at her carcass. Meanwhile, getting all ready for the flensing to be done by dawn's light tomorrow would save much of her bulk from being destroyed. Already the water around the boat is full of these mongrels of the sea. If a man fell overboard he wouldn't last ten seconds before his flesh-picked bones would sink to the ocean-floor.

Whale blubber spoils fast in the tropics. After less than a day and a half in the sun, it turns rancid and its oil loses value. There be little loyalty on a whaling vessel greater than the promise of coin at the voyage end, and still less if the lost crew be niggers and kanakas, even if it does include me brother. Me old feelings of love for Hawk are starting to return, like blood coming back into a limb what's been deprived, and with him lost, I'm at me wit's end. It's Captain O'Hara what must make the decision to search, and me only hope is that he be a true Quaker, what's a religion of conscience, so it's said. Nestbyte's also a Quaker and the brother of O'Hara's wife. Perhaps this family tie, if nothing else, will make the master order a search.

But in me heart, I knows that feelings of family ain't as strong as feelings of greed. O'Hara is a New Englander and they is notorious penny-pinchers. It's conscience against greed and I ain't yet seen care for one's fellow man hold out against rapacity. As Ikey says, 'It ain't religion what makes the world go round, 'tis everlasting avarice, my dear.'

My mind is filled with anxiety as I climb up the mainmast to the highest of the watch stays. I stand on the cross-stays, holding fast to the masthead hoop. The sun's heat is weakening though the sky is not yet turned to saffron to make visibility difficult. It's fortunate that the hunt took place in a nor'easterly direction so that I need not face direct into the setting sun. It's good fortune, too, that it took place downwind from the *Nankin Maiden* so the sailing conditions be good. Tonight is a full moon and the earlier clouds have cleared. A sighting in the moonlight is by no means impossible.

I want to pray, but I'm not sure how. I ain't had much practice since the age of seven at bedtime, and then it were only to repeat at Mary's knee the words she give us to say.

Gentle Jesus, meek and mild
look upon this little child . . .

I forget how the rest goes.

The only God I knows is the one what comes to sit at Mary's table of a Sunday to escape from the cold and the wind moaning in the organ pipes on Mount Wellington. But I doesn't think our White Tablecloth God of the warm brown gravy and the roast mutton is the sort of cove to find a whaleboat what's a thousand miles out to sea and bring my brother back safe to me.

'I wonder if you'd mind very much going out and finding me twin brother, God?'

'And where might he be, son?'

'Whaling, Sir. His whaleboat be lost or took by a whale.' Then I adds for good measure, 'The master be a Quaker and very pious.'

'Whales, eh? Sperm, is it?'

'Yes, Sir,' I nods me head.

'Sperm whale be my particular pride and joy, Tommo. Biggest creature of all 'cept for the blue whale, what's just a bit too big for my liking, not quite perfect-made like the sperm. There be no other creature in the heavens, on the earth or in the waters like the sperm whale. Did you know that I gave that creature a brain five times the size of man's? The largest brain of any creature on earth? Did you know that, Tommo?'

'Yes, Sir, Hawk told me.'

'Well then, why d'you suppose I done that?'

'Dunno, Sir.'

'Well you see, Tommo, every creature's got its mongrels and the sperm whale, what don't do no harm to no one, has got *you* lot, the terrible-est bunch o' mongrels of all! Sometimes, if you've got sufficient brains, it is possible to win against the mongrels.'

'Yes, Sir. Thank you, Sir. It's just that I was hoping . . .'

'Pass the salt,' God asks and then adds, 'No day can be judged until night has fallen, Tommo.'

'Yes, Sir,' I says, not knowing what that last remark's supposed to mean. There is no arguing with the Almighty and I am more troubled than ever. I fears that God is on the side o' the whale and me brother forever lost. What God done for Jonah it don't seem likely he's gunna do for Hawk.

There is nothing to be seen out there 'cept an albatross what's been following us for two days, and the endless waves stretching to the horizon. A gold colour starts to spread in the sky and if a search don't begin before sundown it's unlikely to begin at all.

75

Old Tommo's on his own again, just when I were beginning to feel like a twin, knowing there be somebody else what's connected invisible-like to me. First I thinks Hawk a fool for wanting me back, wasting his life over yours truly. Then he become a nuisance, watching me, fetching me back home when I were drunk, looking sad-faced at me. Then, when he brung me aboard this ship, I think it better than staying with Mary, who made me feel so bad, like a naughty child. Later, I planned to jump ship as soon as we were in some port, piss off and leave Hawk to go home where he be needed by our mama. Yours truly would be alone again with his cards and a bottle, what suits me just fine! But now Hawk feels a part o' me again, creeping back into me heart and mind like when we was brats. Mind, I don't know how I'll feel when I gets me hands on a bottle again.

When I came down on deck this mornin' to find Hawk gone as crew in Seb Rawlings' whaleboat, with Crawlin Nestbyte in command, I were full o' fear. The feeling of the mongrels being near, what I had when I were aloft, come back so strong it took all me courage to stay on deck and not climb back up the mainmast, to hide up there, like the mast were a river gum and I back in the wilderness again.

All day I've felt Hawk be in danger and that's how I know our twinship is returning. It's like it were meself what's suffering. All day me hands hurt awful and I thinks at first they's becoming like Mary's. They is rough and battered from the years in the wilderness. But I know it's more than that, it's something bad to do with Hawk.

If by nightfall Hawk ain't returned, I'm gunna jump to me death from where I now stand. I ain't staying another day on this bloody ship without Hawk. If he dies I won't even have the black bottle to comfort me. Alone on this ship at sea, I'll be in a wilderness not much better than the last. Sooner or later I'll get in a row over the cards, or a brass bimbo will come for me in the dark and I'll use me axe on him, and that will be the end of yours truly too. It all be as certain as the sun coming up in the mornin'.

Suddenly I hear the rattling of chains and I look down to see men scrambling to the starboard. I can't believe me eyes! They's unchaining the cow from the side of the ship and two whaleboats has been lowered on the port side to tow her away and anchor her at sea. My heart thumps as I watch the men climb the rigging to unfurl the sails and the *Nankin Maiden* turns to catch the wind. The sun is setting in a blaze o' glory and the sky is afire as the search gets under way.

We sail for an hour and a half, and the moon is now well up. The sea is cast in bright moonlight and if I had with me one of Hawk's books I could read it as if it were daylight. It is then that I see the whale, a dark shape looming in the water to starboard.

'Whale-o! Whale-oooooo! To starboard!' I shouts. Me heart is beating so fast it must burst from me chest any moment and drop to the deck below. Then I see the whaleboat moored not fifty feet from the dead monster but I can't see nobody in it.

'Oh God! Please, God, Sir, let me brother be safe!' I looks upwards through the topmast to heaven. 'I promise I shall return to Mary if he's saved!' Then I think, 'Oh shit! Me and my big mouth, I should've waited until we got a bit closer!'

In the pouring silver of the night, I see a head raise up above the gunwale of the boat and then it stands up and I know it's me lovely twin brother and I begin to weep like a stupid little brat!

We lifts the whaleboat back on board and sets to towing the monster whale behind the ship. It's the biggest bloody whale killed in the history of the *Nankin Maiden* and Tom Stubbs reckons it be the biggest whale ever took by a single whaleboat. There is much cheering on deck, the whalemen having forgot that they was against the search. They's counting only their share of the oil, what now means profit for us all.

But I am only concerned to see me brother again. Hawk is the first to climb from the boat, and the Maori follow, carrying between them the limp weight o' Hammerhead Jack. It's clear they's been through a terrible ordeal. The boat is now empty, and we sees that Nestbyte is not among them.

Captain O'Hara ain't a happy man when he realises the first mate be missing. He's tall and frightening to behold, his eyes glowering from beneath midnight eyebrows, what meet across the bridge of his nose. As soon as they has lain Hammerhead Jack on the deck, he calls the four survivors to his cabin for an explanation. But o' course, none is possible. The four Maori got no English and, without Hammerhead Jack to talk for 'em, they is staying stum. Hawk, being dumb, can't say nothing without me. Finally O'Hara says he'll deal with the matter after we gets the cow, and gives orders to sail back to where she's waiting.

This is most lucky, for it gives me the chance to find out what happened. As we sails back, Hawk tells me the story of their hunt and I becomes afeared again.

'They won't believe ya, Hawk!' I says, after he explains how Nestbyte lost his balance and fell into the briny.

'Why?' Hawk says, moving his fingers slowly 'cause of the pain. 'It is nothing but the truth, Tommo.'

'It's a truth what will get you all hanged from the yard-arm!' I cry.

Hawk is wrung out. His hands is swollen to twice their size and is all red raw flesh. I've had me hands hurt from the pit dogs and the crosscut saw, and blistered once when Sam Slit's whisky still exploded, but never like this, never as terrible as this. He is nearly asleep as he speaks to me, his eyelids closing. Yet his great concern is not to tell me what happened nor that his hands be looked after, but that the skipper should give him medicine to care for Hammerhead Jack.

'He will die, Tommo,' he signals wearily to me. 'Then it will be my fault!'

'*You* will die!' I says. 'They will say you pushed Nestbyte if you tells it how it was. They won't believe you, Hawk!'

Hawk shakes his head. 'I am too weary to lie, Tommo. The truth will stand us in good stead.' He can't touch a finger to his palms without wincing with the pain and soon he gives up, too weary to use his hands or lift his arms to talk any longer.

I thinks to let him sleep awhile. I will hear him out again later, and talk a plan into him, once we is anchored alongside the cow.

It is nearly eight bells when we gets back to where we left her. In the bright moonlight there is so many sharks feeding on her that it be almost like watching a school of mackerel in the shallows of Salamanca beach. But the whalemen is much less worried now about losing bits of her bulk. The bull is good compensation, three-and-a-half times bigger in blubber than the cow. It's as though we has caught four whales.

We barely arrives when Captain O'Hara calls for Hawk and the three Maori. Seb Rawlings is also called from his sick bed, it being reckoned that they be his crew and perhaps he may get some sense from them. The fourth mate sends straight for me where I am working in the try-house to get ready for the flensing of the whales at first light. That I should be called upon be me deepest hope.

With me translating for Hawk I reckon we has a chance to beat the mongrels.

'Evenin', Cap'n, sir,' I says, removing me cap as I stands at the door of his cabin waiting permission to enter.

O'Hara grunts. 'Come in, boy!' he barks.

Hawk and the three Maori is standing in the small cabin and the captain is seated behind a table with Tom Stubbs besides him. Seb Rawlings is also seated, being too weak, I suppose, to be on his feet. With all of us in the cabin there's scarce an inch to move and I find meself squashed against the oldest of the Maori.

The captain turns to Stubbs. 'Thou mayst go, Mr Stubbs, there is much to be done. Mr Rawlings will remain as witness.' We push aside to let Tom Stubbs pass.

O'Hara points to me without looking up from the ship's log which lies open before him. 'Thou wilt speak to thy brother, and he will tell thee what happened and thou us.'

'Sir, me brother has already told me the whole of it. It will be much the shorter if I speaks and then you asks questions what I shall put to him.'

Captain O'Hara looks up sharply, thinking me to be too forward, but I keeps me head down and me hands clasped humble-like. 'The sign language be most tedious slow, sir. This will be the quicker.'

'Is this the lad who saw the pod this morning?' O'Hara asks Rawlings.

'He is the one, Captain,' Rawlings says. 'He is reliable enough and not too stupid.' He points to Hawk. 'They claim to be twins, though how this can be I cannot imagine!'

'Most curious,' the captain says, but there is no curiosity in his voice and I reckon he don't care if Hawk and me be twins or the first two of the three blind mice. 'Speak, boy!' he commands.

I tell of the placing of the two harpoons and how Nestbyte passed the other boats and shouted for help and then how, after being towed by the bull, they approached the whale from the weather side. I says nothing of the fight 'tween him and Hammerhead Jack. I tell how Nestbyte wished them to fasten to the whale while there were still much life in him, so's they might more quickly open a major blood flow, as the first mate did not think they could otherwise wear the bull down sufficient to take him with one boat.

'Mr Nestbyte did confide all this to them?' O'Hara questions.

'No, Cap'n, but it were clear enough to me brother.'

'Clear enough, was it? Your brother is an expert on the whale and whaling, and what actions to take in every circumstance?'

'No, Cap'n, but he didn't think Mr Nestbyte were going up to bid the whale the time o' day!' It were a stupid thing to say and I'm sorry the moment it come out of me big mouth.

'Hold thy tongue, boy!' O'Hara growls. 'I'll not take lip from such as thee!'

I drop my head. 'Yes, sir. Sorry, sir,' I says. Out of the corner of my eye I can see Hawk is trying to talk to me. I ignore him, not wishing at this moment to meet his eye, but Rawlings sees his movements, 'What's he saying, Tommo, what's your brother saying?' he stammers, all a-chittering and a-chattering o' teeth from the fever.

What Hawk's saying is that I should tell the story like he told it to me. He thinks the captain just wants to write it down for the record. Ho! I thinks. Hawk may be the smart one, but he don't know a mongrel when he sees one! Captain O'Hara here ain't just keeping his log, he's holding a trial. He wants revenge for his brother-in-law! I know this for sure. Old Tommo's nose for mongrels is working well.

'What does he say?' the captain demands to know.

'Yes, sir! He says that he's sorry for presuming to know what Mr Nestbyte was thinking about what to do with the whale. He says I must say only what happened and should otherwise shut me big mouth.' I doesn't look at Hawk as I says this, and I can only hope he's got the nous to keep his hands to hisself.

'Continue!' O'Hara commands, a bit happier.

So I tells how the whale rolled to windward and capsized the boat. How only the Maori and Hawk come up again, with Hawk rescuing Hammerhead Jack from the briny after he had lost his arm.

'Did Mr Nestbyte do anything when the whale rolled to windward?' Captain O'Hara asks.

It's not a question I can answer. So I turns to Hawk, who gives me a most despairing look, like I've done them in. He has no way now to tell the truth and must go along with my tale. He signals that Nestbyte shouted they should ship oars.

'He said that they should ship oars, Cap'n,' I reply.

'Aye, aye!' O'Hara says impatient. 'But did he *do* something?'

'Do something?' I look to Hawk, who says he does not recall anything. Meanwhile the others' eyes are near closed as they tries to sleep standing up.

'Me brother don't recall, sir.'

'Do something with this!' O'Hara shouts, taking up a bowie knife from under the table and thrusting it, blade forward, at Hawk.

The three Maori jolt awake in surprise and pull back, falling over each other. I am pushed against the cabin door, where I bump me shoulder.

'Ha! I have thee!' the captain exclaims. 'This is Mr Nestbyte's knife and there is blood on it! Human blood!' He stands up and with the tip of his forefinger indicates a dark stain on the blade and points to Hawk, 'Thou didst murder him and then threw him to the sharks!'

I am took completely by surprise. Hawk ain't said nothing about Nestbyte's knife. I look at Hawk and see that he is smiling and shaking his head. He alone has not flinched when the captain thrust the knife at him.

'Well? Answer me, man!' O'Hara barks.

'You were right, Tommo, he wants a victim,' Hawk says with his hands. 'Tell him the truth. I used it to cut the mess which was Hammerhead Jack's eye. The blood on the blade is Hammerhead Jack's and that on the handle is from my hands.'

I says all this and Hawk holds up his hands to show their cruel state.

'How came he to be in possession of Mr Nestbyte's knife?' O'Hara demands. 'A man doesn't leave his own knife lying around, leastways Mr Nestbyte didn't.' He stabs down upon the table with the bowie knife so that it judders as he releases it. 'Thou takes me for a fool, boy! There is a boat-knife for the purpose of cutting! Why did not Hawk use *that* knife?'

'Tell him that when the whale rolled, Nestbyte took out his knife to cut the line but we were thrown out before he could do so. He must have dropped the knife in the boat where I later discovered it,' Hawk signals to me.

It ain't Hawk's fault he's so bad at lying – he ain't had much practice like me. Besides, he's weary. First he says he didn't see Nestbyte do nothing when the bull rolled, now he says Nestbyte were busy cutting the whaling line with his bowie knife and loses it from his grasp as the boat turns over. So, I asks you, how could that be? The boat capsizes, and by some miracle Nestbyte's bowie knife grows hands of its own to cling to the bottom of the boat so it don't fall out with everything else?

But the captain is waiting for me to translate what Hawk's just told me so I has to invent an explanation quick. Billy Lanney has recently shown us how to tie the short-warp to the harpoon rope and so I says desperate, 'He took it off from his lanyard and give it to Hawk to fix the short-warp to the harpoon rope, Cap'n, the boat-knife being tied to a marlin line in the stern of the boat and the warp to be fixed in the bow. Me brother then pushed the knife into his belt on account that they had to quickly man the oars. He thought to return it later to the first mate.'

'This happened just before the whale rolled?' the skipper asks. He must think me a fool to fall into such a silly trap.

I talks to Hawk as though I were asking him the question with our sign language, but what I am saying is that I'll tell the skipper that the knots were done just before the second harpoon were used. It were then that Nestbyte noticed the splice were not right on the short-warp. It's a feeble enough explanation what I gives to the captain but it can't be proved wrong, and it makes some sort o' sense. But O'Hara ain't yet willing to give up.

'Then why, I ask thee, did the kanakas grow most alarmed when I showed the bowie knife?' he demands, his eyes narrowed.

'I cannot say, Cap'n. They be savages and I doesn't speak their lingo.' Then I ask, 'Perhaps they thought you was going to do them in on the spot, like? Why, sir,' I rubs me shoulder, 'I meself jumped when you thrust the knife at me brother.'

Despite his fever and the sweat glistening on his brow, Seb Rawlings half-smiles at my reply, and I sees he has no love for the skipper.

Captain O'Hara pulls the knife from the table and lays it down, then takes up the quill again and dips it into the ink well. All is quiet as he writes in the ship's log and we can plainly hear his quill scratching upon the paper.

At last he looks up, scowling. He points the quill accusingly at Hawk.

'I feel there is more to this business than thou hast admitted, Solomon. I warn thee, nigger, I will sniff out dishonesty! I shall pray to the Lord for guidance and then we shall see what we shall see. Thou mayst go, and thy damned cannibals with thee.' Then he turns to me, 'As for thee, boy, thou mayst be sure I shall find something to cool thy ardour and quell thy impudent tongue!'

We turns to go, the Maori shuffling out first, when Hawk signals frantically to me.

'Cap'n, sir!' I pipes up from the door of the cabin. 'Me brother pleads that he be allowed medicines for the injuries the harpooner got while most bravely killing the whale.'

'Hmmph! A nigger who cares about a kanaka! Miracles will never cease!' The captain turns to Seb Rawlings. 'We have here a nigger who cleverly turns Mr Nestbyte's whale kill to the credit of that damned savage, and turns himself just as neatly into a ship's surgeon! What think thou of that, Mr Rawlings?' He does not wait for the fourth mate to reply before looking at Hawk. 'But of course, I forget, thou hast already proved thyself most handy with a bowie knife!' He indicates Seb Rawlings with a flick of his head. 'Thou mayst issue a chit for medicine, though I think it much better for all if the savage should perish.'

O'Hara seems a little calmer, having rid himself of his spleen. He is well pleased with his crack about Hawk being a surgeon and with his last jibe about Hawk's supposed use of the bowie knife to kill Nestbyte. He twirls the quill in his fingers and muses aloud. 'The Lord's ways are indeed mysterious. I have the greatest need of a first mate on this ship and He hath taken my dear brother from me and allowed the devil to replace him with a cannibal savage, a useless kedger with one arm and one eye, who will draw from ship's rations and return me no profitable labour!'

He looks up at Seb Rawlings, his right eyebrow raised. 'Thou wilt charge the cost of the medicines to the kanaka's share of the lay, and he will be placed on half rations until he perishes or otherwise proves to be of some further worth to us!'

The captain is as good as his word and has found me a special punishment. I am working in the blubber room, where I must pitch up the pieces of blubber to be cut ready for the try-pots. These pieces is four foot long, and weighs nearly as much as me. Working them is usually a task for the biggest of the men. Two blubber-room workers in bare feet cuts the blubber with dangerous sharp spades and as a consequence of the deck pitching and rolling, one has had three toes sliced off and the other four, this being the badge of their trade. They is fierce men and don't like seeing the blubber they cut stack up. 'Git movin',' they snarls each time I forks another slab of blubber, 'we ain't got all bloody day!' I am soon knackered but there is no let-up. The deck is slippery with oil and whale blood and sometimes I near collapses under the weight of me blubber fork. 'Garn, move yer arse!' be the constant cry from the cutters.

Not one comes to me aid and some push me over when they see me loaded up so that I crash to the floor, falling on me face. Yours truly is a cause of great merriment to all in the try-works as I staggers to me feet covered in blood and oil. But it ain't the worst what's happened to me and I will not give in. No poxy bunch o' whalemen gets the better of Tommo X Solomon!

There be two hours to go and every forkful of whale blubber is stained with blood from me bleedin' nose. I feels a hand on my shoulder and I stops, expecting another shove. But it's Hawk, come to find me!

'I have been asleep and did not know of this,' he signals with his hands. They still be swollen to twice their size, yet he takes up me fork and begins to spear and lift the slabs o' blubber. Though the pain in his hands must be awful, it is as though he is shovelling straw into a hay-rick, such is his strength. One of the whalemen what has been amusing hisself at my expense now scoffs at me. Without turning, Hawk strikes him with the back of his huge hand, so that he flies across the try-deck and lands skidding in the whale oil.

It's the first time I've seen Hawk strike a man and it were like he was brushing away a fly. Then Hawk walks over to the whaleman, who is nursing a bloody nose, and with the fork pierces the greasy duck of his Norfolk breeches so that the tines fit under the man's belt. Hawk lifts him up and carries him across the room, depositing him on the blubber table in front o' the mincer. The mincer is a large man himself, dressed in a cassock made from the skin of a whale's penis, and he holds the blubber-room man down as though he's about to slice him to size for the try-pots, before letting him go again.

There is howls of laughter from the men watching. Hawk smiles his big white smile at the others in the blubber room and they ain't so stupid that they can't see that it carries a warning never to mock me again.

I am most shamed that me brother needs to defend me, though I be too tired to fight it. I tells meself that if it should ever come to an open fight, I'd even the score with me axe. But I know that Hawk's now a part o' me and that old Tommo is no longer alone in this world. And so I finishes me first watch in the blubber room.

The men is working 'round the clock to get the blubber into the try-pots so that it may be made into good oil, a most difficult task. The whale's tied by chains from its tail and head to the starboard side of the ship and the cutting platforms, hung from the ship's topside, is lowered to meet it. The cutting tackle is secured to the mainmast and also lowered so that the mates can begins the cutting in. With Crawlin Nestbyte dead and Seb Rawlings ill, two of the older, more experienced whalemen handles the cutting spades along with Tom Stubbs and Timbin Hollowtree, the third mate.

The men attaches the cutting tackle to the whale, using the blubber hook at its end. They cuts a long scarfing line about nine inches in width on either side o' the blubber hook. Then the hook is pulled upwards by the block-and-tackle and the mates frantically cuts the blubber to loosen it from the whale flesh. It's as though they is peeling a giant Spanish orange, though the blubber, if you can imagine it as orange skin, be about fifteen inches thick.

The power for the block-and-tackle is supplied by men working a windlass on deck, what is connected to ropes run down to it from the main top. The blubber peels off in a long, intact spiral what stretches from the whale right up to the topmast, pulling the whale's great carcass hard against the ship. The weight makes the vessel heel so that when the blanket of blubber is freed, the ship lurches violently back on her beam ends, as though buffeted by a stormy sea.

The long strips of blubber, what weighs as much as a ton, are then lowered by the tackle into the blubber room, where they's cut into slabs by the blubber-room men of the few toes. It is these self-same slabs of blubber which yours truly is required to lift and carry to the mincer. This cove cuts them into fine strips leaving only the skin attached so's the blubber now resembles the leaves of a book, known in whaleman lingo as bible leaves. These thin leaves, not much more than an inch thick, gives us the most oil. The bible leaves is placed into the bubbling try-pots and turned into oil, before being ladled into copper cooling-tanks and put into the cooper's casks.

If it all sounds simple enough, it seems to me a vision from the cavern of hell itself. At the cutting platform, not many inches from the surface of the water, the sharks is in a feeding frenzy, and the mates stabbing down at them with their cutting spades. This is no sport, for each shark killed means more blubber saved. A shark what's cut with the razor-sharp spade becomes the prey o' the other sharks, what's then distracted from the whale carcass as they turns to feed on their own kind.

Up on deck, the sails and rigging be completely clouded in black smoke while the deck is lit by the orange flames what keeps the oil hissing and bubbling in the try-pots. This fire ain't fed with wood for there ain't room enough on a whaler to carry timber. Instead the whale gives us the means to make its own oil. After the blubber is turned into oil, the skin and bits remaining, known as the fritters, is burned as fuel. The dense smoke makes it difficult to see. The men about the windlass be blackened by it, their faces like polished blackamoors' in the glare of the flames.

Every surface of the windlass and the decks, bulwarks, rails and try-works is covered in oil and slime from the whale. Inside the blubber room we is clothed in greasy duck and covered in oil, blood and blubber, as savage-looking a group of men as could be found on the face of the earth. The smell is beyond the ken of any landlubber. No abattoir or cesspool compares with the evil pong o' smoked blubber. This stink, once in the skin, can only be undone by weeks of scrubbing with lye. Us whalemen will be making our presence known to any what stands downwind for some time to come.

The *Nankin Maiden* pitches and rocks in the seas, like she's about to be engulfed in flames. And the rats is as many as ants at a picnic. They darts between our legs, feasting on the scraps 'til they's so bloated with blubber that they drags themselves along in the slime and may easily be kicked high over the ship's side as though they was footballs.

The final task is to take the precious spermaceti oil from the head of the whale. A hole is made in the whale's noggin and the spermaceti scooped out. This be a whitish, waxy liquid, what's five times more valuable than the best whale oil, and is used to make ointments and ladies' cosmetics. It makes the finest candles and incense what the Pope himself uses. The cow we took gives five barrels of this stuff and Hawk's large bull no less than twelve.

After me first watch I am too exhausted to feel shame that I would have collapsed had it not been for Hawk. But Billy Lanney comes up to me in the fo'c'sle and, patting me on the back, says in his peculiar lingo that I has done well. Such a job were for 'big pella' and the master be a 'plurry Kwaka Christmas sausage!' which I takes to mean, 'a bloody Quaker Christian savage!'

I crawls into me bunk and I has never slept more soundly in me life. I wouldn't have given a damn if the cockroaches had made merry over every inch of me body, though they was busy feasting elsewhere like the rats.

For two days and nights we works the try-pots and on my fourth watch, I am finally able to complete forking the heavy slabs of blubber without Hawk coming to my rescue. With a little help from his twin, yours truly has survived the ordeal what were meant to break him. Up yours, Captain O'Hara, sir!

At last we cuts the bloody remains of the whales loose and watches their blubber-stripped carcasses float away. The sharks still churn the water and tear ferocious at them, and ten thousand sea birds darts ever downwards for scraps. The top o' the whale carcasses look like giant rookeries with birds squabbling, wings flapping and beaks snapping for every available morsel o' flesh. In all the time we has been flensing the whales and boiling down their blubber, these birds has surrounded us with a screeching that has drowned out all other noise on deck and below, so that we must shout to be heard at more than a distance of three feet.

After the whales has floated far enough to the leeward away, so that they be two small dots on the horizon, I am amazed at the silence what surrounds us. It's like the great parties at the governor's mansion I has heard of, now finished and quiet, with every guest gone home again.

The first duty now, with the barrels stacked in the hold, is to wash down the decks and housing. This task is a tradition, a rite to bring successful hunts in the future. The men is knackered but they put great heart into the scrubbing of the decks, using absorbent cloths over their hands made from the tendons o' the whale.

Whale oil is most effective in removing stains of all kind and soon the vessel is ship-shape. But no amounts o' cleaning gets rid of the oily fish stink. Only the fo'c'sle, now lit by candles and whale-oil lamps, has a sweet smell. It don't take long though for the fo'c'sle to sink back to its former state, and who's to mind?

Hawk is more particular about cleanliness than yours truly. Cards and sly grog is seldom found in clean-smelling places, and pipe smoke and spittoons is as much a part of a game of flats as the Joker in the pack. A little dirt don't hurt no one.

Hammerhead Jack is still alive. He is weak and in great pain, yet he never cries out. Under Hawk's tender care he is slowly mending. Billy Lanney has had a hand in this too.

The medicines Hawk got from Seb Rawlings did nothing to keep the Maori's shoulder socket from festering. His face were swollen mightily and his eye socket leaked pus and gore, despite Hawk cleaning it each day, along with the terrible shoulder wound. For days, Hammerhead Jack were in a constant fever and delirium. His men was ever at his side, never leaving, and it were clear they believed he would die.

It were Billy Lanney, ever the curious one, what comes over one morning to take a look, shaking his woolly head and clicking his tongue. Two days later he be back, carrying a small tin filled with live maggots. These worms does not come from his own back, what is now well scabbed, but were procured most cleverly.

After Billy sees Hammerhead Jack, he asks me to catch a fish and give it him. That afternoon when I comes off watch, I catches a nice-sized tuna, about six pounds. This I gives to him and he gets the cook to lay it on top of a salt-pork barrel in his galley overnight. By morning all the maggots in the pork has crawled out to find the fresh fish and Billy scoops them up and brings them to Hammerhead Jack, who is still fevered and unconscious.

Billy carefully makes two poultices of live maggots and puts one on Hammerhead Jack's shoulder and the other on his eye socket. He binds the shoulder loosely so's the maggots stays inside and covers the eye socket from the light. By the following morning the pus has gone, and the wounds be quite clean.

Hammerhead Jack is now making a slow recovery with no fevers to plague him. Billy's maggots does the task better than the captain's medicines what was bought at great cost.

It is two days after the cleaning and scrubbing of the ship and we has changed our course. It is said we be headed for New Zealand waters, the talk on board being that O'Hara hopes to pick up another ship's officer there to replace Nestbyte. No doubt he plans to make more trouble for Hawk once we reaches port!

The crew be resting up from the trying out and cleaning o' the ship. The hold is well over two-thirds full with barrels, and there's a feeling of calm. On Hawk's warning, I has lost several card games in the fo'c'sle and am telling the story of the killing of the sperm bull to as many as I can.

All seems well and so it knocks me for six when Captain O'Hara sends Seb Rawlings and Tom Stubbs to arrest Hawk and the three Maori. He plans to try 'em for the murder of Crawlin Nestbyte.

I nearly panics but then takes heart, for the men's views has changed somewhat. Nestbyte is not missed and the fo'c'sle is a much calmer place for his death. I've been most careful to tell my cooked-up version of the hunt, making much of Hammerhead Jack's bravery and Hawk's courage in rescuing him when he were sinking in the briny in a foam of blood.

The crew already sees their bringing in a ninety-foot sperm whale as an awesome achievement, and Hawk, Hammerhead Jack and his Maori crew has become heroes of sorts. Although they's only a nigger and four kanakas, there is now a high regard for them, if for no other reason than each man on board will be more flush for their courage.

They has not forgotten, either, Hawk's backhanding of the cutter what scorned me. The man's name be Bob Jenkins and he's known to be a good fighter with a knife and unafraid with his fists. He's not small with it – fourteen stone and almost six foot, with good weight in his shoulders and nimble enough on his feet. News of Hawk's smashing him to the deck and then forking him up to the mincing man has spread throughout the ship. It has earned Hawk respect for his Herculean strength. The story grows more exaggerated daily. Jenkins is much shamed and vows he'll have his day.

When the master sends Rawling and Stubbs to fetch Nestbyte's crew and put them in chains, there is much unrest among the men. Hammerhead Jack is also brought into custody and on the Sabbath all is made to stand before the mainmast in front o' the entire crew.

Captain O'Hara is again dressed in his black Quaker suit with white lace bibby at his neck. Only his greasy stovepipe hat be the same as other days. He has in his left hand the Holy Bible which he holds against the pocket of his long coat. He looks 'round at us and begins to speak.

'We are gathered together here on the Sabbath and in the name of the Lord to witness that justice be done in the trial of the whaleboat crew under the command of the first officer of this ship. I have spent much time at prayer in the concern of the murder of Mr Nestbyte and have asked for higher guidance on the matter.' O'Hara frowns at the prisoners, what stand with their heads bowed before him. ' "I am not mocked, sayeth the Lord!" '

There is a groan from the crowd, for we has witnessed the Lord's word translated through the prayers of O'Hara before – and, o' course, through those of the recently deceased Nestbyte too. The Lord's instructions seldom turns out merciful to a whaleman. The crew be generally agreed that, if Christ Jesus were the skipper of a whaling vessel, there'd be none on board what would sign on with him, even though He could walk across the water to harpoon a whale.

'I have asked Mr Rawlings to speak on behalf of the prisoners,' Captain O'Hara now says, 'there being no one in their midst who can do so.'

'Me brother Hawk can, Cap'n, sir!' I shouts. 'If I may translate for him?'

The crew shouts their agreement. O'Hara has seen that the crew is of a contrary mood, and knows he's got to make his authority felt. 'We have heard sufficient of thy translations, boy!' he snaps. 'Thou and the nigger have not the sagacity to make a case for the defence!'

'Sir, I speaks only that me brother might speak. He is not without wit and is well learned at books. Has he not the right to defend hisself? May he be allowed to decide if Mr Rawlings be his defence or if he would speak for himself and the Maori?' I trembles at me boldness. But I must speak for Hawk, or die in the attempt.

'Oh, yes, thy brother we know already to be an expert at judging the whale after three months at sea, and he is a ship's surgeon too. Perhaps he is to be the judge and jury as well?' O'Hara says sarcastic.

'Cap'n, sir, it be one o' the rules of the sea that a seaman may speak in his own defence if he be accused.' I braves the mongrel once more, not knowing if what I says be true. But it becomes clear from the men's cheers that it is.

O'Hara's face grows red as I speaks and he begins to shake. 'Silence!' he roars. 'I am the captain of this ship and the law is mine to make while we are at sea! And make it I shall!' He draws breath. 'There is none amongst the kanakas who can speak English. Thy brother could accuse any of the crime and they could not defend themselves! Mr Rawlings will speak for all!' He turns and points to me. 'As for thee, boy, I will tolerate no damned sea lawyers on my ship! Another word from thee and it will see thee stretched to the mizzen mast. Thou art naught but a trouble-maker!'

The men is silent after this outburst. What shall become of Hawk? I despairs to meself. Then suddenly a weak voice is heard.

'Ork speak,' Hammerhead Jack croaks. He is being supported by the two younger Maori, for he is too weak to stand on his own feet. 'Him speak me!' He slowly raises his good arm and touches the two men on either side o' him, then points to the old man. 'Ork speak Maori all!'

O'Hara turns angrily to Seb Rawlings. 'What's he say? What's the savage say, Mr Rawlings?'

'He wants Hawk Solomon to speak on their behalf, Captain,' Seb Rawlings answers quietly, plainly gobsmacked. 'Perhaps, sir, it be best so done?'

O'Hara slaps the Bible to his knee. 'In the name of the Lord Jesus Christ, have I not made it abundantly clear how we shall proceed! Thou shalt defend them and I prosecute.' He holds the Bible above his shoulder so that all may see it. 'The Lord God Almighty will be the judge!'

There is much murmuring and shuffling of feet among the crew but nothing further can be said. It be clear to all that Hawk and the four Maori is doomed. Me stomach grows cold. The mongrels is winning.

'I shall read from the book of Jonah,' Captain O'Hara thunders, opening the Bible. ' "And God created great whales, and every creature that moveth, which the water brought forth abundantly."

'God hath himself given us this abundance. The sperm whale is God's gift to us if we should observe His ways and be true to His faith. This we see to be near His first pronouncement in the book of Genesis, chapter one, verse twenty-one.' Captain O'Hara raises his head to look over us, for he stands on a small platform surrounding the mainmast what makes him taller than any man standing 'cept for Hammerhead Jack and Hawk, what's at eye-level with him.

'It is here we see that Jesus Christ our Lord created a special dispensation for those who hunt the whale. The great fish is His gift to mankind from the abundance He hath brought forth from the waters. He gave not permission to the fisherman to hunt the skipjack or the mackerel, nor to the hunter to hunt the deer or the mountain lion. But to the whaleman He gave the greatest creature upon the face of the earth, for hath He not made man in His image?'

O'Hara pauses and looks about, holding the Bible aloft. 'If you need proof of this, I shall give it you!' He has the Bible marked with a bookmark made of whalebone and he flaps it open and begins to read. ' "And the Lord spake unto the fish and it vomited up Jonah onto dry land." ' The master looks up and says with deliberate quiet, 'The book of Jonah in the Old Testament, chapter ten, verse two!'

I thought that Quakers didn't sermonise but said their prayers silent amongst themselves, but O'Hara is just like a preacher in his pulpit.

'Thus spake the Lord God,' he continues, 'proving that He places God-fearing man above the whale, that He hath given them dominion over the whale, causing the whale to vomit up upon dry land that which hath been taken against the will of God, the creator of heaven and earth!'

Captain Mordechai O'Hara glares at us for some moments. It's as though he wants one of us to challenge his Bible learning. 'Would any amongst thee dispute the word of God?' he asks.

Only Hawk among us would be able to do so, for he read the Bible twice-over on his voyage to England, it being the only book on board other than the *Apothecary for a Ship's Surgeon*, what he read five times. But he has his back to me so I cannot translate for him.

'Now comes the case for the prosecution,' O'Hara announces. He looks up to the top gallant as though for inspiration from on high. 'It is plain for all to see that God favours His Christian children in the contest between whale and man, or why else would He command the whale to vomit the prophet Jonah back onto dry land?

'I have been the captain of a whale ship a full twenty years and in that time have lost many a whaleman to the sperm, but only this once a Christian man! At all other times they have been heathens,' he points to Hammerhead Jack, 'like this kanaka! Niggers, cannibals and savages, or Papists from the godless South American ports or the Portugee, or men from Dublin. If not them, then heathen from the East Indies and godless Limeys.'

O'Hara points again to Hammerhead Jack. 'The Lord hath clearly shown His direction in this when He took the arm and the eye of this hapless savage, intending him to drown – the arm which is used to throw the harpoon and the eye to aim it. God's message is abundantly clear. He took this heathen as the whale's sacrifice, knowing well that there is a Christian gentleman aboard!'

The master pauses. Well warmed-up to his mad notions, he looks about him, then points to Hawk. 'Thou rescued from the sea this heathen kanaka, and so did clearly transgress the will of God Almighty, Who had consigned him to his watery grave by removing his arm so that he could not swim!'

There is a grumbling among us what understands what the captain be saying, for many will be wounded in some future battle against the whale. Now we is being told that we won't be rescued 'less we is a Quaker Christian like our master. O'Hara takes no heed o' this muttering and mumbling from the men and continues to thunder at Hawk, shaking his finger at him.

'And then, when it behove God's servant, Mr Crawlin Nestbyte, to point out thy disobedience against the will of God, thou didst kill him with his own knife and throw him to the sharks!'

O'Hara speaks as though he himself has witnessed every part o' what took place. He snaps shut the Bible and with his free hand takes Nestbyte's bowie knife from his coat pocket, holding it high. 'This was the very knife used! The blood of human sacrifice is stained on the blade for all to see!'

There is a gasp from the crew, though most has long since lost the thread of O'Hara's reasoning.

'I rest my case,' Captain O'Hara says, most satisfied.

Seb Rawlings argues in Hawk and the Maori's defence. He tells Hawk's story as it were told that fateful night in the skipper's cabin, the version cooked up by yours truly. This he does most credibly, not missing much of the detail.

The men already knows the tale well and they nods in agreement as they hears it. Seb Rawlings be a plain speaker and it's clear they believes what he says to be true. They has all known danger while hunting the whale, and they knows the peril of bein' on his windward side. At the end of the mate's speech, the crew claps.

But their support has no effect on the captain. He steps forward. 'So be it,' he says, most abrupt. 'Now to the judgment of the Lord, who looks into all our hearts that He may find the truth!'

O'Hara drops to his knees on the deck and, clasping the Bible to his chest, raises his head towards the topmast and begins to pray, his lips moving silently. The men stands awkward, heads bowed, caps in hand, waiting, none daring to move, 'til a full five minutes later when O'Hara opens his eyes and rises, still holding the Bible to his chest.

' "I am not mocked, sayeth the Lord," ' he says in a deep, slow voice. Then he turns to Hawk. 'The Lord Jesus Christ hath spoken to me in a clear voice and I am commanded to say to thee: Thou, Hawk Solomon, and thou, Hammerhead Jack and your fellow kanakas, have received the sanction of the Lord Christ Jesus who hath sentenced each of thee to fifty lashes. Furthermore, from each of thee shall be confiscated that portion of the lay, the profit from the oil rendered from both whales most recent caught, when the final disbursement shall take place. This is the will of the Lord, till ye may be judged by temporal justice, the will of courts ashore.'

The men break into hubbub and O'Hara waits for them to quieten. The sentence is harsh, but those what stands before the mast of a whaling ship are brutal men. If they cares to give credit to a God at all, they counts His bounty by the number o' barrels contained in the hold. They praises Him if there be many and curses Him if there be few.

O'Hara now turns to the three mates. 'Mr Stubbs, Mr Hollowtree and Mr Rawlings, ye shall each administer fifty lashes upon the three Maori men and I shall fulfil my Christian duty by doing the same,' he points to Hammerhead Jack, 'to this damned kedger.' Then he pauses and looks over the heads of the men gathered about him. 'Bob Jenkins, where art thou? Come forward if you please,' he commands.

Jenkins, the blubber cutter what Hawk has forked to the mincer, steps out of the crowd.

'Yes sir, Cap'n,' he says, touching his cap.

'Thou shalt take the lash to the nigger!'

Jenkins grins widely. 'I shall do me very best, Cap'n.'

It be agreed that the mates shall go first, then Jenkins and finally the captain. The lashings is terrible and there is much yelling and groaning from the three Maori, what collapses to the deck sobbing when they is cut down. They are brave lads and the crew does not reckon them cowards for this. Fifty lashes with the knotted rope has been known to kill a man and there's very few like Billy Lanney, what be strong enough to accept such punishment in silence.

Then me brother's blouse is removed and he is tied to the mast. Jenkins steps forward, holding the bloody rope with a great grin upon his ugly gob. I vows that if ever we be ashore and I discovers where he is, I will take with me axe no less than three fingers from the very hand what holds the lash with such pleasure.

Jenkins flogs me brother, and Hawk jerks with each violent blow. Hawk makes no sound but, because he is dumb, the men don't see this as courage under the lash. Many winces though at the force Jenkins puts behind every blow. The blubber man grunts with each lash he places, and Hawk gets much the worst of the four beatings. My eyes smart with tears and I tremble with anger. The sod will pay for this.

At last it ends. They cut Hawk loose and he stands bleeding, though his head is not bowed. Slow tears squeeze from his eyes as he looks at me and sees that I too am weeping. Meanwhile, poor Hammerhead Jack is being lifted to his feet by the two mates, Tom Stubbs and Timbin Hollowtree. He is too weak to stand alone and when the Maori were beaten he was left to lie upon the deck. Now he struggles to rise with the support o' the two ship's officers. There is no fear in his eyes, though it's clear he has no strength left in his great body, and has lost much weight since the whale hunt. Through me tears I see that Hawk is talking to me with his hands and wants to address the captain.

I brush me eyes and step forward. 'Permission to speak, Cap'n, sir,' I says respectfully.

O'Hara stares at me. He has already taken the blood-soaked lash from Jenkins. 'What is it, boy?'

'Sir, me brother Hawk wishes to address you.'

'Hast thou not had enough then, nigger?' O'Hara scowls at Hawk.

Hawk speaks to me rapidly with his hands and I translates.

'Me brother wishes to accept the lashes on behalf of Hammerhead Jack.'

A murmur of shock passes through the crew and only then I realise what me lips have said. 'Hawk, no,' I protest, but he fixes me with such a look that I has no choice but to go on.

'The Maori is much weakened,' I hears meself say. 'He will die if he receives the knotted rope!'

'It is God's will that he should die!' O'Hara thunders. 'The Devil hath taken possession of thy soul, nigger! Thou hast once before disobeyed the Almighty in this matter, now, damn thee, thou wouldst do so again!' O'Hara is shaking all over, his fury risen to a pitch. The lash in his hands drips bright red onto his boot.

Now some of the crew what's been grumbling starts to shout. There is a growing anger amongst them for they realises that Captain O'Hara means to kill the giant Maori. Hammerhead Jack be only a savage but our good captain has gone beyond what even these port rats will stand. The islanders also have realised what is afoot and they too is growling, their fists held taut to their sides. Me heart begins to pound. The pack is turning on its master!

It is then that Seb Rawlings steps up to stand beside O'Hara. He has the captain's Bible and he raises it up. 'Silence!' he shouts. 'Be silent!' The men quietens down a bit. 'Silence there!' Rawlings shouts again, pointing to a small group o' Irishmen what still mutters angrily at the back o' the pack. 'Silence, you lot, or you'll have me to reckon with!' Finally all is quiet and he begins to speak.

'Captain O'Hara has already shown much of God's infinite mercy in dealing with this matter,' Rawlings says. 'I know him well enough to say that he will again put this matter to prayer so that God's will may be done.'

O'Hara jerks back in surprise at the fourth mate's words but he holds his tongue, allowing Rawlings to continue.

The fourth mate points to Hammerhead Jack. 'If God should intend this kanaka to die, He would have done so by means of natural causes abundantly available to him in the past few days. So, if the Lord God be our judge, as the captain has told us clear, and I be the defence, then I must ask Captain O'Hara to allow the Judge of Heaven to make a decision on this new request!

'I must most humbly ask, does God the Judge wish the kanaka to die at the hands of the prosecution? Or will He accept the plea for mercy from the defence? If He is the merciful judge, then I ask that He make the same judgment He made for the prophet

Abraham – that Hawk Solomon, like the ram caught in a thicket near Abraham's sacrifice of his son, be allowed as a substitute to the taking of a poor man's life.'

I am astonished at Seb Rawlings' learning. His knowledge o' the Bible is even more amazing for he does not seem religious and is the only one among the mates what ain't a Quaker. Captain O'Hara suddenly shakes himself, as though Rawlings has called him from some sort o' pious trance.

'So be it,' he growls. He hands the lash to Rawlings in return for the Bible and once more goes to his knees on the deck. We all holds our breath as we waits for the result o' his silent prayer. Finally, after three or four minutes has passed, he rises and turns slowly to Hawk.

'There is something of God in all of us – even in thee and the savage whom thou dost wish to spare the lash. The Lord hath spoken to me and thou shalt take unto thyself the kanaka's punishment.'

Hawk's back already bleeds freely from Jenkins' flogging, and the top o' his canvas breeches is soaked full to his knees with blood. But he is calm as they ties him again to the mainmast. The captain takes up the lash and begins lashing me brother.

I can't do nothing but watch as Hawk silently takes the savage blows. The mongrels is back, and beating me twin. You bastard, I sobs to meself. I'll get you too, whatever the cost! You, O'Hara, and you, Jenkins, both shall taste the edge of my axe! I swear it or I die!

O'Hara pants with the effort as he completes his gruesome task, Timbin Hollowtree counting each lash. Hawk's once-smooth ebony back is ripped to raw and broken flesh, the runnels of one lash running into the others. The captain's bibby is completely bloodstained, his dark coat wet to the front, and he has small scraps of red flesh caught up in his black beard. He strikes again and Hawk gives a soft moan.

At first I doesn't realise what I've heard. But another groan follows and yet a third, this time louder. I cannot believe my ears! Sobs catch in my throat. It is the first sound I've heard from Hawk's mouth since the day we was kidnapped.

Chapter Six

HAWK

The Pacific Ocean
January 1857

Tommo has spent all his gambling winnings on medicines for my back and for the Maori. This is mostly sulphur ointment and cheap enough ashore, though Tommo has been made to pay almost as much money as a whaleman would receive in wages after a successful two-year voyage. It is beyond all reckoning for the cost of medicines. Captain O'Hara has extorted this payment as further punishment and I have begged Tommo not to purchase the ointment, thinking we will heal as fast without it. But he will not hear of it.

'If I spends all I has it's in the best cause,' he replies and then grins. 'The lashes came hard, the winnings was easy.'

Our ship is sailing towards New Zealand waters from our position south of the Cook Islands. Captain O'Hara seeks a new first mate, or if not a first, then a new mate with experience, who has led a whaleboat crew.

There has been a robust migration of free settlers to the New Zealand shores, though not too many decent folk are among them. Even the missionaries are more concerned with buying up the land than preaching God's word. The Europeans are largely from New South Wales, including escaped convicts and a great many ex-convict deserters from ships. It is estimated that there are three thousand of the latter scattered throughout the islands of the

Pacific Ocean and half a thousand again in New Zealand. It's said that they have heard 'the wail of the wahine' and their bastard half-caste children may be seen on every island where there is a native tribe. This new generation is strong too, for they seem to be immune to the white man's diseases which now play havoc amongst the kanakas.

These new settlers have brought with them the European diseases of influenza, measles, small pox, venereal pox and consumption as well as other maladies. Measles has killed tens of thousands of islanders and as many again of the Maori. For every half-caste and white child born in New Zealand, ten Maori children have perished. This much I have learned from my reading.

It is amongst this motley crew that O'Hara hopes to find the man he needs. And so we sail to the whaling settlement of Kororareka in the Bay of Islands, a town long known as a centre of infamy and drunkenness, where at least three hundred whalemen reside.

The men are much excited about leave ashore, for they hope to encounter the 'dark, restless-eyed woman' as the Maori wahine is known amongst sailors. I cannot say that such a prospect does not excite me also, for I'm a man and so by nature weak of flesh. I have not yet taken a woman to my bed. I can only hope that the lighter, brown-skinned Maori will not see me as a nigger and despise me for the colour of my skin.

Six months have passed since we left Hobart Town and it will be good to feel land under our feet again. All the same, I would think O'Hara much better advised to sail on across the Tasman Sea to Australia, where he would more easily find a mate to suit his needs and meet our needs as well. Tommo and I intend to jump ship in Sydney or some other civilised port at the first opportunity.

We have grown weary of life at sea. Although it has provided me with a great adventure, this has been offset by a catastrophe and a brutal punishment which I did not deserve.

In truth, whaling is mostly an adventure to speak about at a later time, in the comfort of a warm parlour or in the company of men at an ale house. Mostly it is endless days of great tedium and repetition, with the hunting of the whale a rare interlude that we have encountered only once these six months.

We spent Christmas aboard the ship, a hot, sultry day with little wind. There was naught to mark it as a special day, save an hour-long sermon from the captain. Our rations were unchanged, salt beef and longlick, with not even a fish from Tommo to add to our repast, his efforts that day being unsuccessful and much curtailed by the captain's prayers.

For the Maori and islander crew, Christmas was a day as any other. But for me, it was a time of homesickness. Though Tommo and I are Jewish by birth, still Christmas was always observed in our family because of Mary, who made an occasion for yet another roast dinner. My thoughts turned time and again to our mama, home without her boys. I wondered if she had spread her white tablecloth out – probably not, she doesn't like to fuss over herself. Tommo was no comfort either that day. It being Christmas, the crew are merry enough and it is a grand opportunity for a game of cards in the fo'c'sle. Tommo does not share my sentiments, as there was no Christmas for him in the wilderness. When I came to sit with him at cards, the look he gave me made me feel more his keeper than his twin.

I am not yet fully convinced that Tommo has forsworn the demon grog. My hope is that his enforced abstinence may prove permanent and will rob him of the will to gamble, for grog and cards go hand in glove. With the one practised, the other must surely follow as night follows day.

The infamous settlement of Kororareka is just the place to test Tommo's resolve and I am ashamed to say I have great misgivings. I'm not at all sure that Tommo does not try to gull me with his claims that his need for ardent spirits has been quenched and that he will forsake gambling when we come ashore. He plays cards at every opportunity, now saying it is money for the medicine we need to cure our backs. He still wins too often for my comfort and each day I fear the men will flush him out in his use of relocation. But when I warn him he merely laughs.

'I ain't gunna relocate with *these* partners – they all be plough boys and dockside scum before they comes to whaling, half-wits and duffers! You insults me natural talents, Hawk, to say I relocate with them lot.'

Relocation was a favourite expression of Ikey Solomon's. In the beginning, Tommo's skill with cards came from Ikey's assiduous training. He taught us when we were small brats how to palm a card and a host of other nefarious tricks, each of which he would refer to as, 'One of life's little essentials, my dears.'

The idea of these 'little essentials' was that if a man should find himself in Timbuktu, broke and knowing nothing of the people, language or society, he could, through their use, earn himself a plate of food, a roof for the night and an ounce of shag. Ikey's 'little essentials' were a means of survival until the morning.

Ikey placed dexterity with a pack of cards as the topmost of these 'essentials' even before reading and writing. 'Every man on earth will gamble if he be given half a chance. The deck o' cards may be found from Bombay to Peking, Samarkand to Sydney, Cairo to the Cape o' Good Hope and London to New York. Like the roach, the flea and the bed bug, they are universally to be found wherever men congregate. The flats be a universal language, my dears, known to every level of society and transcending every tongue that man doth babble.

'There are rules to be learned by observation and, once mastered, to be broken. In any game o' chance, as much of the chance as possible must be removed. And success in any card game may be assured by placing a card where no card is thought to be. Relocation, my dears, that is it in a nutshell. And the most important requirement for relocation be dexterity, nerve, courage and a nimble mind.'

'Relocation? You mean cheating!' I once ventured when he talked of this.

'Cheating? Did I hear you say cheating, my dear?'

I nodded.

'Cheating be something what's done by them what's stupid and quickly found out. Cheating is in the dark, it looks over its shoulder, it pads on tender feet. It is a sneak, a dark thing. Cheating is not for the likes of you two, my precious little gentlemen. Relocation is the word, the word of princes and kings. Cheating is for beggars and vagabonds.'

'But is it not another name for cheating, then?' I asked again.

'Most certainly and decidedly not!' Ikey replied. 'Nimble minds, nimble fingers that never tremble and a look what betrays not the slightest beating of the heart go into relocation. All the skills of relocation depend on it taking place in the open, in the broadest daylight, completely kosher, cards seen by all who play with you.'

Ikey grabbed a pack of cards and shuffled it in a blur, spreading it with a great flourish across the table, with every card in its right place and right colour. One to nine, ten, Jack, King, Queen, Ace of Hearts, Spades, Diamonds, Clubs and Jokers at the very end.

'Now that ain't possible!' he crowed. 'If a man should shuffle a deck a million times, and then a million more, it ain't possible for the cards to come out in the right colour, correct sequence and nomination. It ain't possible, but you've just seen it done, my dears. Right in front o' your very eyes, shuffled and spread, fair and square! That be the noble art of relocation.'

He pushed the cards together again and, in a flash, shuffled and spread them into a fan shape once more.

'What's missing, gentlemen?'

'The ten of all suits!' Tommo shouted gleefully.

'Very good!' Ikey said, pushing the deck together again. He shuffled and spread, and there were all the tens, sitting back in their rightful place.

'Now you see it, now you don't. But you don't know you don't see it, until it turns up in a flush or a straight where it's least expected.' Ikey scooped the cards into a deck and without looking he said, 'A Jack, is it? Snap!' Down went a Jack. 'Fancy a nine of hearts and diamonds to make a much-needed pair? Snip! Snap! Or an ace to make the trump? Snap!' Tommo and I stared open-mouthed as he laid down one card after the other, not even looking at the deck in his hand. 'What a lovely coincidence, don't you think, my dears?'

Then Ikey pointed a long finger at us, his eyes rolling. 'Never an extravagance, you understand. A royal flush or four of a kind be a most dangerous boastification. They must come naturally, by means of chance and skill, but *never*, you understand, by relocation. Winning at the flats must not be come at with a drum-roll, but with the timpani of fingernails on a velvet pad. Modesty of purpose, my dears, that be the golden rule. The card you need when you need it and sometimes, if the pot be a small one, a restraint even with the restraint already shown.

'The great knack of winning,' he continued, 'is to look as if at any moment you might lose. Touch the forehead with the finger tips, rub a little, sniff, click your tongue – but not too much. Nothing bolsters the courage of a punter more, or deadens the brain more effectively, than a little acted clumsiness and a downcast expression.

'Cards, my precious little gentlemen, will buy you food and shelter, a good cigar and a little companionship wherever you be on this mortal coil. Learn the flats well and they will be your friends forever.' Again he rolled his eyes and spread his long fingers. 'But one more caution. Never practise relocation when it ain't necessary. Relocation is a compliment to be paid only to those who be your equals in the game you play.'

From that moment on, Tommo took to the flats like they were an extension of his fingers. Even as a brat, he always carried a deck. He'd constantly finger the cards in his pockets, calling for me to name one and then producing it blind as though by some sort of magic. His skill astounded me for my hands were clumsy and my mind elsewhere, in books.

When we were kidnapped on the mountain, Tommo had in his pockets a deck of new cards that Ikey had given him for helping at the races. He later told me that without them he could not have survived, for Ikey was right – the gambler is to be found in every man, whether nabob or wood cutter. Even the damage done to his hands didn't stop him.

Ikey had been most pleased with Tommo's talents as a little lad. There was only one other his age who could match him, he said, a boy in London by name of Sparrer Fart, also trained by Ikey in his Methodist Academy of Light Fingers.

'Sparrer Fart, if he should be here, would be too good even for you, Tommo, my dear. You must work harder to beat the Splendour of the Sparrer!'

And that, I think, is part of the trouble. Even in the wilderness, after losing all that you could call his life, Tommo took with him Ikey's challenge. Whenever it was bleak for him, which seems by all accounts to have been most of the time, he would seek the comfort of the cards. 'I'm gunna beat the Splendour of the Sparrer,' he would say to himself. This he has done. But his astonishing skill has brought with it a life that will destroy him.

Since Captain O'Hara's flogging, we have grown even closer to the Maori crew. Tommo, who is more clever than he knows, has begun to speak their language, and I to understand it. Hammerhead Jack confounds us all with the speed of his recovery and with Tommo feeding him fresh fish, he grows stronger every day. Tommo has been catching much tuna lately and Jack eats it raw, taken with a little salt and molasses which we save for him from our rations.

My back is healing well, though I never thought that I should learn to sleep on my stomach. As my wounds begin to bind, I often wake with a great itching to find a hundred cockroaches grazing upon the scabs like contented cows. At first, this disgusted me to the point of crying out. But Billy Lanney, who is an expert on matters of the lash, bade me be patient and led me to understand that these vile vermin do much good. Like the maggots in Hammerhead Jack's suppurating arm and eye, they keep the wounds clean.

We've learned that Hammerhead Jack is of the Ngati Haua tribe, though his hero is Hone Heke, leader of the Nga Puhi. Jack tells me that Hone Heke was the fiercest of warriors and also the first chief to sign the Treaty of Waitangi which recognised the sovereignty of Queen Victoria over the Land of the Long White Cloud, or Aotearoa as the Maori call their country. Though Hammerhead Jack is too low-born to be a chief himself, he is most intelligent and a natural leader of men.

Hammerhead Jack has taken to walking about the deck again and the whalemen, whoever they be, kanaka, white man or nigger, have a new respect for the one-armed giant. His missing right eye makes him most formidable in appearance, so that grown men stand aside as he passes by.

If Captain O'Hara should happen along, then Hammerhead Jack will grin his big white smile, and be as pleasant as can be imagined in his greeting. But his smile does not soothe the Quaker master, who growls and scowls and sometimes, if he is close by, spits over the ship's rails. Never does he return the Maori's salutations.

Tommo has asked the other Maori what they might do when we make landfall in New Zealand. They shrug and point to Hammerhead Jack. 'It is for him to say.' Although he is not *rangatira* or noble born, they see him as their leader. But, of course, Hammerhead Jack will be put ashore without further ado. Captain O'Hara has bled him dry of his share of whale oil entitlements and regards him as a useless kedger not to be tolerated on board a moment longer. What perhaps he does not understand is that he loses all three Maori when he throws Hammerhead Jack aside. He will lose a whaleboat crew of much valuable experience, aside from me.

Tommo has grown more excited by the day as he coaxes a

voice from my throat. At first I could make only a feeble grunt or two but he is wondrously patient and spends hours mouthing sounds he thinks I might produce, vowels in particular. I doubt he remembers that they are called vowels, but he offers these sounds as though by instinct. He works me until the pain in my throat is almost unbearable and then has me gargle with sea water. He insists I gargle every hour and when he is not on watch he attends to it himself.

Already I am making progress and hope in a week or so to say my first two words. These Tommo has decided upon as well as the following two. The first will be 'Tommo Solomon' and the next will complete the sentence, 'Tommo Solomon loves me!'

By the time we enter the harbour at Kororareka I am possessed of a voice that, while slow to form the words on my tongue, has a complete enough vocabulary of sounds. These sounds have grown familiar to my ear although my pronunciation is not always correct. The trouble is that while I hear the words as I have always done, my tongue can not yet form them clearly. But I am on my way and before long shall speak as a normal man, with perhaps a deep rasping that comes from a throat grown rusty in all the years I have been without a voice.

It is a strange sensation that I may now communicate without waiting for Tommo to cast his eyes in my direction first, and I am not yet accustomed to people looking upon me when I speak. It seems odd that their attention is not on Tommo, or Mary, as the case may be. I have grown so much a listener over the years that I doubt I shall ever be the main spokesman in any conversation.

Ikey would often say that I had been given a great gift in being without voice. 'Congratulations, my dear! You have been forcibly given the gift o' listening. That be very high up on the order as one of life's little essentials. Your ears be perfect tuned to savour the essence of every voice you hear. Mostly we drowns out listening with the need to hear our own voices. No man finds a voice sweeter to his ear than his own. But if you wants to know what's in a man's soul, listen to him, listen to his silences, they be louder than his words. Then listen to his speech, listen to what he's saying behind his voice. The conversation going on in a man's head be the one that tells you the most.'

By following Ikey's advice – though of course I had no option but to do so! – I have indeed learned a great deal about people. If the relocation of cards was Ikey's major gift to Tommo, then the skill of listening was his gift to me. Listening is my true language and I do not think I shall ever forsake it.

Kororareka is a settlement with nigh two thousand Europeans and numerous natives. The Maori to be found here are, for the most part, a poor-looking lot. They dress in flaxen mats or dirty blankets, though some who have prospered from port trade are in silk top hats and polished boots, with gold watches attached to chains looped across their large bellies.

A few quiet families are to be seen and children also, half-caste, Maori and European, many of them dirty and barefoot with snotty noses. It is a town well past its prime, though that itself was short-lived enough, I'm told.

Kororareka is a whaling town, possessed of five hotels, numerous grog shops, gambling hells and brothels. Drunkenness and lechery are everywhere to be observed, with the Maori man and his wahine consorts as bad as any whaleman. The dark alleys are filled with laughter and the grunts and groans of whalemen who have waited long enough to be serviced by the honey-skinned wahine at the cost of a silver shilling and a jigger or two of Bombay gin or sailor's rum.

It is in this very town that Hammerhead Jack's hero, Hone Heke, confronted the British some twelve years ago. Grown tired of British duplicity, he withdrew his allegiance to the Crown and showed his contempt for the symbol of British sovereignty by cutting down the flagstaff from which the Union Jack flew. He then sacked the town. Most Europeans contend that the reason for the chief's outrage was that the British had imposed onerous customs duties on Kororareka so as to encourage trading vessels to call at the new capital of Auckland instead. This meant that the local Maori were deprived of their earnings from the port's trade in flax and ship's spars, pigs and potatoes.

But Hammerhead Jack refutes this. Hone Heke, he says, had come to the conclusion that the Treaty of Waitangi was most treacherous to the Maori people, for it was an attempt by the settlers to steal their land.

From our conversations with the Maori on board, we have learned of some of their beliefs. Paramount among these, as far as we can understand, is that by swearing allegiance to Queen

Victoria and signing the Treaty of Waitangi, the Maori believed unequivocally that they had transferred merely the 'shadow of the land' to the British monarch, and that the substance remained their own.

'We cannot sell the land to the European, for it is not ours to sell,' explains Hammerhead Jack. 'One man, one chief, does not own the land. The land is owned by the Maori people and they would all have to come to one voice and one opinion if they were to give up forever their land.'

Hammerhead Jack waves his lone paw and makes a point too obvious to contest. 'Why would my people sell what is their *mana*, their spirit, their life force? Papatuanuku is our earth mother and we her children. Who would sell their mother? Land,' he explains, 'may only be gained by one tribe from another through war. Then it may be used by the victors, but it is still owned by the Maori. It keeps our *mana*, which is the same for all the tribes. The pakeha who wish to use the land may purchase its *shadow*, if the Maori tribe who control it agree. But though he may enjoy it and grow his crops upon it or graze his sheep over it, he may never own it! The *substance* must always belong to the Maori people, only the *shadow* of the land may be sold to the pakeha.'

It is a difficult concept for us who are not Maori, but it is Ikey again who helps me to comprehend the idea. For Ikey believed that property was also 'one of life's little essentials'. When telling me of the marvels of London, he would always explain how the English nobility are able to retain their fortunes and protect themselves against loss, even though they might spawn children who are drunkards and wastrels. The gentry build great terrace houses in the most salubrious parts of the city which may be leased for a period of a hundred years. If the purchaser of the lease wishes to vacate after only a few years he may re-sell what remains of the hundred-year period to another lessee, who may do the same again until the hundred years are up. Then the property reverts to the descendants of the nobleman who built it. They will then put it up for lease for another hundred years and, in this way, the aristocracy of England never lose the property they own, even if their sons prove profligate in the extreme and squander their inheritances.

I think upon this and decide that it is not so very different from the Maori selling the *shadow* of the land but retaining its *substance*. The British themselves have created a precedent and it would seem to me that those who own most of the land in Britain have their own kind of *mana*. They see themselves as the guardians of the spirit of their land, always maintaining the substance while leasing the shadow to any newcomer.

The great chief, Hone Heke, came to the conclusion that the *mana* of his land, its spirit and nourishment, had been stolen by Queen Victoria. The Maori people had become her slaves, for only the shadow has been given to them and the substance taken by the Europeans. Already twenty million acres of land have been purchased by the whites, who see this land as belonging to them for eternity. They see no cause for future redress to the Maori people, and what they have claimed, they will defend, if necessary, at the cost of Maori lives.

I am deeply saddened by this knowledge. If, as I have come to think, a good man must have a conscience, then the New Zealand Maori is much cheated by the rapacious white, who has shown no conscience whatsoever in his dealings with the land's original owners. Who amongst us is a good man, then?

As always, the church, which claims to be the custodian of the conscience of man through the salvation of Christ Jesus, is foremost among the greedy. It claims a large portion of the twenty million acres, some of which has been purchased at a cost of ten pounds for each four hundred acres, but most of which has been obtained for a few trinkets.

From the beginning, when in 1814 the Reverend Samuel Marsden, notorious chaplain of New South Wales, was instructed to establish the first missionary settlement in the Bay of Islands, Christ has become the major property owner in New Zealand. Jesus is now Hammerhead Jack's landlord.

There is no admission from the pulpit that the church owns only the *shadow* of the land. Instead these holy men give twice-on-Sunday praise to God that He has bequeathed them in perpetuity this new Land of Milk and Honey, this second Canaan, this green and pleasant paradise upon the earth.

It was this which caused Hone Heke to become disenchanted with the British since the signing of the Treaty of Waitangi. Queen Victoria, in return for dominion over Hona Heke's people, promised so much, but instead her rule has brought the Maori guns with which to kill each other in ever increasing numbers, disease, drunkenness, and a dependence on the white man amounting to virtual slavery. This is the real substance of her promises, so that the Maori are but a shadow of the mighty people they once were.

This is the New Zealand to which Hammerhead Jack returns, without one arm and one eye. A young whaleman who has been thus used by the white man is coming home for more of the same.

Since Hone Heke's vengeance destroyed the town, Kororareka has grown back in a most higgledy-piggledy manner and shows no promise of improving. The buildings, but for a very few, are rickety tin and timber affairs, with no sense of permanence about them. We are not anchored in the bay more than twelve hours before we learn that there is much foment among the Maori people. The great chiefs are once again on the warpath.

Our friendship with Hammerhead Jack is cut short when Captain O'Hara dismisses him from his service. It is a sad moment for Tommo and me. We have both grown most fond of the giant Maori, whose arm stump is not yet completely healed but which, he assures me, will soon enough be cured with the good medicine of his tribe.

Our friend will take with him only his few belongings, and a paper given him by O'Hara which shows how his lay has been fully and 'legally' used up with the provision of goods from the ship. Of course, there is no mention that these goods were, in every case, medicine to which he was freely entitled. The Maori is made to place his mark upon a duplicate and this is witnessed by Tom Stubbs. He will be rowed ashore on the morning tide.

I carefully explain to Hammerhead Jack in his own language that what has been done to him is unlawful and that he should complain to the colonial authorities, who may impound the ship while his case is heard.

But he scorns this. 'I am of the Ngati Haua. We do not go snivelling to the British! Their laws have robbed us of our *mana* and turned my people into drunkards.' He gives a bitter laugh. 'Look at me, Ork. Why should they take the word of a one-armed, half-blind Maori against the white captain of a whaling ship, who professes himself a Christian like Queen Victoria?'

I have long since known that Hammerhead Jack is not an ignorant savage and that he understands much more of the English language than he would admit to. I have also come to respect his understanding of the Maori situation with the pakeha intruder. He has often been surprisingly even-handed, admitting that much of what has happened to the Maori since the white man came is due to the wars they have waged amongst themselves, albeit with the use of the white man's gun.

'Our people must stand together against the white man or we are lost,' he has said often enough.

But I cannot convince him to pursue his case against O'Hara.

'If I complain against this madman O'Hara, then I am again a member of the British tribe.' Hammerhead Jack turns aside and spits his disgust. 'Accepting their justice and their ways in the past have not been good for my people. Why should I trust them to give me justice now?'

I search for words in my disbelief. 'You mean you will simply let this man go free, having beaten you and then robbed and cheated you?'

Hammerhead Jack throws back his head and laughs. 'With your new voice, will you complain for me, Ork?'

'Yes! Yes! I will go with you!' I insist. For a moment I feel almost confident that the law will prevail against the Yankee whaling captain.

'Don't be such a bloody stupid bastard, Hawk!' Tommo interrupts. 'It's bad enough a Maori complaining. What hope has a nigger got?'

I am at first hurt by my twin's outburst, but then I see the point and smile. 'You could do it, Tommo,' I reply, feeling brave. 'I will prepare an affidavit and tell you what to say. There would be no problems with the colour of *your* eyes and skin!'

'Me?' Tommo says, shocked. 'I trust them buggers less than Hammerhead Jack does! You can stuff yer affydavy up yer bum!'

Then, to my surprise, Hammerhead Jack, who gives no sign that he is listening, speaks to us in English. 'We do Maori way, Ork,' he says quietly.

The following morning with the six o'clock tide, Hammerhead Jack is lowered into a whaleboat carrying only a small canvas bag with his belongings. He waves his single arm at me as I stand much saddened by his departure. 'Ork good!' he shouts, then throws his head back and laughs. His laughter carries across the water and I am forced to laugh too.

'He be a good man,' Tommo says softly beside me. 'I hope we meets again.'

We are permitted to go ashore that afternoon. The whole crew has been granted shore leave, with the exception of the three remaining Maori, who are placed on watch by Captain O'Hara, under the supervision of Seb Rawlings. The skipper has refused them leave to go with Hammerhead Jack, though it is plain they wish to follow him. He says they must see out the voyage and guards them closely. O'Hara and the two other mates are also to go ashore, and a whaleboat will be beached for any who wish to return on board fifteen minutes before the midnight hour.

From the first of the morning light, Tommo has been anxious to go ashore. My heart is filled with trepidation that he will not be able to resist the first grog shop we come upon. There is nothing to do in this whaling town but drink and fornicate, and we have been told by the Maori that the pox is rampant among the wahine who frequent the grog dens, gin shops and brothels. 'You must not take these women!' Hammerhead Jack warns us. I am much afeared that Tommo will not be able to resist the temptation of hard liquor and so I conceal from him that I have money, hoping meanwhile that he has spent what coin he has won on medicine for our backs.

But, of course, I am deluding myself. The lack of money never vexes Tommo. He is a prime example of the value of Ikey's 'little essentials'. With a deck of cards and a space at the table Tommo can have cash in his hands in a matter of moments. Even if no card game is to be found, he will win the drink he needs by demonstrating his sleight of hand to the wonderment of all who watch. He can pluck a card from behind a whaleman's ear. He can make him shake the sleeve of his coat to watch the ace of spades he has nominated just a moment before fall from beyond the cuffs. He can even pluck one from the bosom of a doxy.

But Tommo surprises me when we come ashore. We visit many a grog shop and all five hotels and even a brothel, where we pass the time until the madam sees we are not customers and throws us out. Tommo asks me to buy two packs of cards, as he says his old ones are too well worn to be used on board and the others think he cheats by knowing every crease upon them. He picks two packs, one red and the other blue, both made by DeLarue & Sons, and asks me to hold them for him until we return to ship. And then it is onwards again. We enjoy the music and, at one hotel, the singing of six wahines who render love songs in a harmony to break any sailor's heart.

Tommo will not tarry long at any place but wants to see every hell-hole, grog den, gin palace, rum shop and hotel in this poxy whaling settlement. Card games are everywhere to be found. Men are going furiously at them in the one-shilling hells where they beckon him over and invite him to play. But Tommo shakes his head and grins. 'Too easy to take yer coin, lads!' It is as grand an exhibition of abstinence as ever I've seen and I am truly proud of Tommo.

In the course of the evening we meet every whaleman who has come ashore from the *Nankin Maiden*. At a hotel which is more salubrious, though only by comparison with the others, Captain O'Hara is to be seen seated in a private room leading from the main saloon. He is interviewing seamen to find a replacement for the late and unlamented Crawlin Nestbyte.

Several men sit on chairs outside this room with their knees held tightly together and their caps on their laps, in the manner of men anxious to make a good impression. They are a seedy looking lot, with raw faces and complexions which suggest that the rum bottle is a frequent gargle against the debilitating effects of inclement weather. O'Hara will be hard put to find a Christian gentleman among this scurvy assortment!

Tommo moves ever onwards from one hell-hole to another, but never a glass of spirits touches his lips nor a deck of cards his hands. His blue eyes dart everywhere and it is as though he is drinking in the sights and sounds he has missed for so long, that they are grog enough for him.

I am so proud of him, for he has been true to his word. I am already envisaging our happy return to Hobart Town and to our dear Mary, whose forgiveness I have begged for in a long letter telling of our adventures. This I posted as soon as we came ashore.

I am hard put to keep up with Tommo, for I am like a lumbering carthorse and he like a yearling with spirit. My back is not yet completely healed and hurts where my blouse sticks to it in the evening heat. After nine hours ashore I am anxious to return to the ship. I have not told Tommo that we have the means to pay for a doss house and a morning meal, eking out small coins for the ginger beer and sarsaparilla we are drinking. I fear he will have us up the whole night, visiting every nefarious establishment in town, though I believe we must nearly have done so already.

At last Tommo agrees to return to the ship. Before the midnight hour, we are back in the fo'c'sle, sober as two judges, with only the cockroaches and the snoring drunks who have made it back aboard to keep us company. Tommo has bought a bag of boiled sweets for the three Maori who have been forced to take the watch. He goes to give them their sweets. I can scarcely summon the energy I need to climb in to my bunk and am asleep on my stomach before the first cockroach climbs up my leg.

The following morning Tommo and I are summoned to Seb Rawlings' quarters and asked if we know the whereabouts of the three Maori. The watch, he says, has reported us as coming on board just before midnight, and being unusually sober as well.

He points to Tommo. 'You were observed talking to the three kanakas not much later.'

Tommo does not deny this, explaining about the bag of sweets, and I am quick to support him in this matter.

'I were back in the fo'c'sle not ten minutes past the hour, Mr Rawlings,' Tommo says.

'That is right,' I volunteer, though I have no way of knowing whether it is true.

'Besides your brother, who else saw you?' Rawlings asks Tommo.

Tommo shrugs. 'All who was aboard and not on watch were drunk and snoring in the fo'c'sle, Mr Rawlings. Only the night watch what saw us return in the whaleboat and the three kanakas would know we was aboard.' He shrugs again, 'As you already knows, Mr Rawlings, sir.'

Rawlings scratches his forehead with the tips of his fingers as though to smooth out the frown etched upon it. On a whaling ship there is not much that the crew do not know about the mates. It is known that the skipper remained ashore overnight and will spend tonight ashore as well. So too will Stubbs and Hollowtree. They have done Rawlings' duty watches while he was consumed with the fever and now, in return, he will remain on board and take their duties as well.

Rawlings is silent for some time. Then he says musingly, 'We have searched the ship, there is no whaleboat missing. They could only have escaped by monkeying down the anchor chain and swimming ashore!' He points to the town bathed in the early morning sun. 'It is a good two cables to the shore and this bay is well known for its sharks.'

It is not clear whether he says this in admiration or whether he thinks the Maori have likely been drowned or eaten for their trouble. At any rate, the three Maori lads have seemingly escaped the ship, and Seb Rawlings isn't happy. He has lost what remains of his whaleboat crew with only me, the new chum, remaining. Worst of all, he must explain this to O'Hara when he returns on board tomorrow morning.

'You two will be on watch today, and tonight you will be manacled to your bunks!' he barks.

'But why?' I ask. 'We have done naught!'

'You returned to the ship sober last night!' he retorts.

'Aye?' I say, my voice questioning.

'Six months at sea and you go ashore and return on board sober? I know you not to be religious. Do you take me for a fool, boy?'

'We are Temperance Union, Mr Rawlings, sir,' I attempt.

'Ha! You lie!' He points to Tommo but he is still looking at me. 'Your brother is a gambler and I have heard tell of how, when we were in Hobart Town, you were seen dragging him aboard from out of a notorious grog shop!'

'We were seen on shore last night by most of the crew, sir. They will vouch for us,' Tommo says.

'Christ Jesus!' Rawlings exclaims. 'No whaleman who ever lived returns from shore leave with a dry throat after six months at sea! They come back with sore heads and empty pockets, to a man!' He paces the tiny cabin and then turns abruptly. 'I shall know what you two have been up to, or I shall ask Captain O'Hara to strap you to the mizzen stays!'

Tommo meanwhile has his head bowed, but now he looks up slowly to meet the mate's angry eyes. 'We thought you was your own man, Mr Rawlings, but now we see that you is no different from the others.'

'Shut your gob, boy!' Rawlings shouts. 'You two were friends of the kanakas. I'll vouch you are all in this together!'

But Tommo, to my surprise, will not be quiet and now baits Rawlings still further. 'Oh, I see, guilty again is we? What will the Lord Jesus decide our punishment be this time, Mr Rawlings, sir?'

Seb Rawlings' face is close to apoplectic and he struggles to speak. 'Right! You will both be manacled and locked up below decks without rations until Captain O'Hara returns tomorrow morning!'

We have been alone in the dark with the rats and the cockroaches since yesterday morning. We have lost track of the time. Tommo, whose instincts are better than mine in such things, thinks it must be near to morning again.

We are in a dark hole amidships, a place where the harpoons and lances are kept under lock and key. No sound reaches us from outside and the only noises we hear other than our own voices are the creaking of ship's timbers, the squeaking and scurrying of rats, and the tic-tic-tic of cockroaches. We spend much time flicking off these last vermin as they clamber about our arms, legs and necks. This is a most difficult task with shackles and manacles on, and there is a rattle of chains each time we make the attempt.

The worst of it is the heat and our thirst, for we have had nothing past our lips but longlick, and that taken just before Seb Rawlings called us to see him yesterday morning. There is not sufficient room to lie down and we are forced to sit with our backs to the wall and our knees pulled up. My back is soon wet with blood and pus as I must lean against the wall, and my new-knit skin and the scabs covering my lashes break open again under the pressure. In all, it is a most uncomfortable situation, though we pass the hours at talk and I learn more of Tommo's lost time in the wilderness.

My twin has seen much in his seven years away. He never speaks as though he is sorry for himself, but is matter-of-fact and often humorous.

When I complain about our dark, cramped conditions, Tommo laughs and says, 'Ain't nothing compared to the cramped quarters known by Sam Slit when the timber getters turns on him.'

'Oh,' I say. 'So he finally got his come-uppance?'

Tommo has told me how Sam Slit would often give a drunken timber getter a pint of whisky from his still for the use of the man's half-caste Aboriginal woman or his little daughter. It was not so bad for the women, he said, who would get drunk anyway and not care what he did to them. But oh, how the little girls no more than ten or eleven years old would weep all the while and plead for mercy, to no avail. Sam Slit would have his way with them, then beat them unconscious, and rape them again and again. In the morning he would send them home to their huts in the forest, bruised and bleeding, with a flagon to soothe their daddies' hangovers.

'This time it were different,' Tommo recalls. 'This time he kidnapped a six-year-old half-caste called Gracie. Half-castes, particular if they be dark-skinned, be thought fair game at any age in the bloody wilderness. Ain't nobody what's going to make much of a fuss. But this time Slit picked the wrong sprat, for her daddy were a big fellow among the timber getters and not from a near settlement. He were most fond of his little black girlie. Slit took her without permission or in exchange, for he were drunk and liked the look o' this little urchin, and thinks he will square it with her papa later.

'But Slit, what's been drinking raw spirit, beats her and fucks her and kills her in the process.'

'Sam Slit was your master! Didn't you run to tell someone?' I ask, horrified by the story my twin is telling me. I cannot imagine he would stand by and let such a thing happen.

'Run to where? Tell who? This is the wilderness, ain't nobody to run to!' I can feel the bitterness in his voice. 'By wilderness laws what he done were normal enough. Besides, I weren't there, I were out setting possum traps and come back to find four timber getters at Slit's still.

'They has him slung on a long pole like an animal, tied wrists and ankles, and they are moving him out. He is moaning and groaning, but they've tied his mouth and his face is raw meat where they've beaten him. The little girl is slung over her daddy's shoulder like the two dead possums is slung over mine. I can see the dried blood around her mouth and nose where she's bled from inside.'

'Oh no, Tommo!' I exclaim. 'You need not say any more.'

Tommo is silent for a while then sniffs in the dark and I wonder if he is crying. He sniffs a second time and now I am sure he is. But a moment later he speaks. 'No, I'll tell you. After all, it's a story about cramped quarters.' He tries to laugh, but it comes out sad. Then he says, 'Besides, that little half-caste dying gave me the courage to come back to you and mama.'

Tommo draws a breath, then continues. 'I follows the men carrying Sam Slit most of the day, and that night they makes camp. I dunno how the little half-caste girl has come to be near Sam Slit's still, for these seem to be timber getters what are after Huon pine, for we has moved high up the Spring River, into the mountains where the big trees grow. I can only think they was on their way

116

somewhere and made camp near Slit's, which in itself is deep enough into the wilderness for the law not to venture. But now these cutters takes Slit much further in than I've gone before.

'We more or less follows the course o' the river all the next day and that night, I camps sufficient far away and downwind so I can make a small fire and cook me two possums. One I eat and the other I put into my tucker bag with some berries I gather during the day.

'On the second day, we follows the river again, climbing up past several waterfalls. We are much higher up in the mountains, and it's late in the afternoon when we comes to a clearing. It's here that the timber getters has their camp.

'It's about an acre cleared and to me surprise they has several bullocks, which I know is used for dragging timber, but I can't think how they could be brought to such a spot. There is pigs and goats and a host of chickens, a proper village, like, with meat drying and a smoke house for fish, and three sawpits dug with platforms in working order, and in two of them a Huon log half sawn.

'I've heard of the deep-pine people and seen some from time to time when they passed along the river on the way to Port Davey. But I has always thought them lone men – or two or three together at most – ticket-of-leavers, debunked convicts, mostly Irish, who cuts the Huon pine high up on the Spring or Davey, and floats it down the river.

'Now I sees there is about thirty people what lives here, six men and four women. Two or three families sharing land is not unusual closer to settlement, but I didn't know that it went on so deep into the high timber. The men's white, but the women half-caste, all with babes to their breasts, 'cept for one: an old, toothless hag, bent over with her paps exposed and hair to her waist, but with a baldness to one side of her head. The rest is brats of every size and shape, light and dark. Some wears a worn wool coat or a knitted jumper much holed, but most are in possum and kangaroo skin, barefoot and snot-nosed dirty.'

Tommo laughs in the dark. 'I has only come to cleanliness since returning to Hobart Town so I don't know why I should remark on the state o' the children. They was no more dirty than I were meself. Anyhow, I finds a sassafras tree what looks directly into the clearing and I climbs high into its branches, where I is well hid.

'As soon as the men comes into the clearing, the brats and women run towards them, laughing and smiling. But their expressions change when they see Gracie's body. The children fall silent, the women begin to keen. One what I takes to be her mama, a scrawny half-caste woman, falls to her knees, tearing at her hair. The women reach out, lifting her up and, taking the dead little girl from her papa's arms, they all goes inside a hut. Sam Slit is still alive, Gawd knows how after such a journey. I'd have thought they'd make him walk and save themselves the trouble, but they has carried him, trussed, all the way and I thinks him dead.

'But he's alive all right, and with his gag removed, he is screamin' and cussin' and beggin'. He is tied hand and foot, and left to sit in a small enclosure surrounded by the bark huts of the timber getters.

'The children gathers 'round him, at first fearful and then bolder. They pokes him with sticks or throws dust at him 'til it gets dark. The night is cold and I climbs down when the camp grows silent and makes a small burrow to sleep in, eating some o' the possum. I wakes at dawn and climbs back into the tree, where I am well tucked away by the time the sun comes into the glade.

'Sam Slit is still lying in the enclosure. The pigs grunt about him and the chickens scratch and schwark and dash away, wings flapping, with each of Sam's outbursts. He seems to have gained strength, and is back to his caterwauling, yet I ain't seen him get food or water.

'I thinks how small and pathetic he looks, though in truth, he were a big man with a huge belly and hands like soup plates – hands that more than once near killed me. But now he's just a piece o' dog shit in the dirt, like he called me, and I wonders how he could have held me afraid to run away so long.'

I break into Tommo's story. 'I too have wondered this,' I confess. 'You were familiar with the wilderness and grown quite independent, and certainly big enough to leave. Yet you remained with this terrible creature? Why, Tommo?'

I cannot see Tommo's face in the dark, but I can hear him breathing. He sniffs, but remains silent for some time, so that I think I have upset him. Then he says simply, 'Grog. I couldn't leave the grog. I'd leave but be back in two days. The craving were too much for me to bear.'

I am glad I cannot see Tommo's face, for I can hear in his voice that he is ashamed of this weakness. I know that, but for the darkness around us, he could never have said this.

'Tell me more of Sam Slit,' I prompt.

'Well, another full day passes, where the children taunts him and pokes him with sticks, and some of the older ones spits or kicks at him. As for the men and women – well, it be as though nobody knows he's there. They pass him all day without looking, even when he screams and begs 'em for water.

'I've eaten all of the two possums and think that I must scavenge about if I am to stay put. So next morning at first light I find a nearby stream with the mist rising upon the water. It's a good hour for yabbies which be plentiful and I catches a freshwater crayfish as well. But I ain't game to cook these and risk the smell o' smoke. Piners wake early and is ever alert for the smell of a fire if it does not come from their own cooking fires.

'It's not long past dawn when I finds a new tree. Now I am hidden again, high up in a tall gum, where I has a better view into the clearing.

'Then I realise something's happening. It's still early morning but other folk has come to the clearing, small groups o' twos or threes with their children. They has the same rough look and most are men, though some be women, white and half-caste. By midday there's fifty or sixty counting the children, and folks keep coming 'til early afternoon.

'I ain't taken any water with me when I climbed me tree at dawn, and I have eaten the yabbies raw what's made me thirsty. But at about ten o'clock, it rains for half an hour and I am able to get a drop. Sam Slit has his mouth open to the rain and is covered in mud as if he were an old sow. His eyes are now great blue bulges where the bruises have formed from his beating and he be altogether a sight for sore eyes, so to speak!

'After the rain a large amount of timber is brought, great logs what will burn for many hours, as well as kindling and smaller wedges to sets them alight. A big fire is laid. Then two sets of poles, crossed at the centre about six feet from the ground, is planted on either side of the fire pit which be about twelve foot long and five foot wide.

'About noon the fire is lit and soon after, I hears the bellow of a bullock and much shouting from the children. Though I can't see what's happening further out in the paddock, it ain't too hard to guess. They is slaughtering the bullock and will have a feast tonight. The two cross-stays will support the pole on which the bullock carcass will be hung.

'Now I sees that four men are took to working one of the sawpits. It be as if they is at some game, for each pair competes with the other at sawing and there is much laughter and close examination of the cut. Then, when the log is cut through, I see that they has sawn a perfect plank, not more than an inch thick, fifteen or so inches wide, and twelve or fifteen foot in length.'

Tommo pauses. 'I know something of sawing and the sawpit, and what they has done with a two-handed pit-saw be masterful. The beautiful pine, what looks the colour of churned butter, is perfect cut to an even thickness. It bounces springy on the shoulders of the two men what carries it, catching the afternoon light as though it was some bright blade itself.

'About two o'clock of the afternoon, the bullock, fully dressed, is carried to the fire. It's fixed on a pole what goes through its centre and extends through the neck and out its arse. It is carried by ten men, five on each end. The bullock is placed carefully between the cross-stays so that it's suspended above the glowing embers now burning red and free of flame. To either end of the poles are attached two handles so that the beast may be turned to the needs of its roasting.

'An hour later the air rising up to me is filled with the delicious smell of the roasting bullock and me stomach growls at the thought of the feast to come.

'Night comes quickly in the wilderness and by four o'clock the shadows is long. The fire is spluttering and sends up puffs of smoke when the fat, rich juices of the bullock drips upon it. The beast is beginning to get nice and brown, having been turned from time to time by two men on either side of the spit-pole.

'Sam Slit is still sitting in the dirt, no doubt made as hungry as me by the smell of roasting meat. His clothes is now caked with drying mud and his face is swollen with the bites of insects. The children has grown weary of taunting him and he is silent and alone. He's too weak or weary to wail and has rolled on his side in the dirt, perhaps asleep. The pigs, goats and chooks has taken to snuffling and scratching about him as though he were part o' the scenery.

'With the parakeets quiet at last and the currawong took to

calling the evening into coming, two men walks to a clearing directly under the tree where I'm hid. They carry long-handled spades and they beat away the bracken and the fern before they begin to dig a grave what I presumes to be the last resting place of the soon to be departed, Sam Slit.

'But after they's been digging a while, I see that the hole be much too small and I realise that it is for the little girl, who, I admits, I has quite forgot.

'Then I sees the coffin brought, and the men and women and all the children gathered 'round, now nearly a hundred in all. The coffin's been made from the pine plank I seen being cut and it is now placed within the hole. The folks all gather close and the little girl's papa speaks. He has the voice of a leader and it carries clear to where I sits high in the tree above the small grave. I remember what he says to this day.

' "We seem queer folk to others, though not to ourselves," he begins. "A people driven deep into the wilderness, though not by persecution, though God knows we have all seen enough of that, but by a need to be left alone. A need to be away from the Protestant and his shackles and his two hundred years of dominion over us.

' "We have no priest to bless us and our Latin catechism is all but forgotten. In God's eyes, we are His lost sheep, for we have not confessed our sins these many years. But we have ourselves and our freedom." He looks upwards as though he is lookin' for the Almighty and me heart nearly jumps out me mouth, for he is staring direct up at me in the tree and I'm sure I'll be found! But then he looks down again and continues talking. "Here in the wilderness no man and no law shall tell us what we shall or may do!" he says to all about him. "Nor where we shall go or what we shall be! And most of all, no man shall use his hands to take or use what be ours, hard won with the sweat of our brows or given as the seed of our loins!"

'He stops and looks about him, then turns his eyes to the small coffin. "We do not have much, but what we have is hard earned under a clean sky. It is honest bread. And most of what we have is our kin and our kith. If any of these be hurt or beaten or harmed, then we all be so hurt and beaten and harmed, and we must take into our own hands the means of justice required of decent men who live in the sight of a righteous and almighty God.

'Whomsoever harmeth one of my little children, harmeth me, thus sayeth the Lord.' "

'The little girl's daddy stops and looks around him again as though straight into the hearts of each of those what stands about the small grave. All is hushed, though the little girl's mama is heaving great, silent sobs.

' "Gracie were but six years old and she were harmed, she were broken, she were killed!" He points to the area near the fire and his voice thunders. "Damaged and broken and killed by yonder beast! He used her as meat for his fornication! He has the mark of the beast upon him and he must be returned to the beast. He will be sent to the devil, to Satan himself, to the very fires of hell where he will burn forever!" There is a long silence and then he says softly, "Amen."

'Throughout this sermon, the only other sound heard be the cry of a baby once and the night call of the mopoke. But now a fiddle plays the hymn "Abide with Me". The grave is quickly filled, with the soft, solid thud of earth clods hittin' the timber. None sings to accompany the lone fiddler, and the small community breaks up soon after. But they returns to the fire, where four of the women tend to the roasting of the bullock.

'What follows is a great feast, though not drunken as such affairs is known to be when wilderness folk comes together. There is now some hymn-singing and later songs of Ireland to which the fiddler plays a most melancholic strain. High up above, in the tree, I is starving hungry. I even envies the dogs what stand at the edge of the firelight, snarling and yapping over each bone tossed to them. Soon even the dogs has eaten their full. It is getting late and the smaller children has fallen asleep on their mothers' laps. What remains of the bullock is taken away and I thinks that I may soon be able to climb down from my tree as all takes their contented bellies off to sleep.

'But I am mistaken. As soon as it's quiet, the men what have seen to the remains of the bullock return. They carries a fresh pole on which the head of the bullock, still attached to the bloody hide, has been arranged. It is trussed in the same way as Sam Slit were trussed when he was took away from the still, hanging downwards and tied to the pole by its hoofs and forelegs. They places the bullock hide besides the fire, though not so close that it catches alight. All the men now stand in a semi-circle around it. The night is very still and several men light beeswax candles, cupping the flame in their hands, so that with the moonlight and the blazing fire, I can see every detail.

'Then, from the darkness beyond the perimeter of the fire and candlelight, I hears Sam Slit screaming. He's brought into the lighted circle, carried by three men. His ankles and wrists is bound as before, and his legs has been tied about his knees with strips of green hide, so that they remain straight and he can't kick. They places him besides the bullock skin, holding him to the ground.

'Suddenly I sees the old hag with the half-balded head and bare titties to her waist. She breaks though the semi-circle o' men and steps to where Sam Slit is whimpering and gasping. She has a basket over her arm as though she be out shopping, and she places it besides Sam and removes a knife. She stoops over Slit, who is bug-eyed with bruising and, as he begs for mercy, she cuts away his clothing until he lies naked upon his own dirty swaddling. I am looking directly down on him and can see his great hairy belly heaving in terror, with his fat worm lying slack against the inside of his thigh. The old woman cuts a length of twine and ties it tight at the base of Sam Slit's cock as he screams and pleads.

'Then she takes up a clay pot from her basket and dips her hand into it. Her fingers is coated in white stuff what I takes to be animal fat. She greases Sam all over. When this is finally done, she begins to work the fat 'tween his legs. To my astonishment, I sees Slit grow until his great purple knob stands hard against his belly-button while he howls like a dog against the pain of the cord, what cuts deep into the flesh of his erect prick. The only sound from the men what forms the circle is a clearing of a throat or someone turning to spit at his own feet.

'Then, as though knowing the exact moment, the old hag grabs up her knife and slices off Slit's stiff cock. She holds it up a moment for all to see, then throws it into the fire where it sizzles, the animal fat catching fire, turning the embers into sudden flames.

'There is a small spurt o' blood and a terrible screaming from Slit, but the cord acts as a tourniquet and the blood soon stops. The old woman now makes a loop of twine and slips it over Slit's knackers. Again she pulls tight, to Sam's yells o' pain. She grabs his balls in her hand and pulls hard so that the skin stretches a full six or eight inches, and her blade slices again. This time, the twine has held so tight that there is very little blood at all.

'Sam Slit is now jerking, screaming and sobbing, snot running from his nostrils. The old hag beckons with a bloody claw and four men takes Slit up, two by the legs and two by the arms. As they raises him from the bloody bundle of clothes I see that he has shit hisself.

'Six men, three on each side of the bullock hide, pull open the bloody skin. Then Sam Slit is lifted over their heads and placed within the hide. The wet rawhide closes 'round him as he jerks and struggles, but it is a snug enough fit – cramped quarters, you might say! With his arms and legs bound, he can't do nothing but beg for mercy. The old hag takes a stick and lifts Sam's dirty clothes and drops them into the fire, where they smoulders a while before being devoured.

'With her bare paps hanging to the surface of the bullock's skin and the ends of her stringy white hair tipped with Sam Slit's blood, the old hag begins sewing up the belly of the beast with an awl and twine. She's busy as a pox doctor, barely aware of the men standing 'round her, as though it be a job not in the least unusual. When she finishes sewing, she takes up the knife again and cuts the rawhide around Slit's face so that he can see and breathe but make no other movement. The old biddy now puts down the blade and takes up Sam's knackers. Forcing open his mouth with the handle of the knife, she pushes them into his mouth so that both his cheeks is blown out with the two horrible gob-stoppers.

'The bullock skin, filled with a different beast, is now lifted on its pole and placed across the roasting coals, each end fitted into the cross-stays.

'I watches from my tree as the well-basted Sam Slit is steamed and then roasted inside the bullock. His full gob prevents him from crying out, so that he bakes in the silent flames o' hell.

'The moon is at the centre of the sky when I climbs down from my tree. All is asleep among the dogs at the fire or gone off to their bark huts. I am stiff from sitting up there for so many hours but now, as me feet touch the ground, I want to run and jump, whoop and do cartwheels through the moonlit bracken!

'It's as though a great burden's been lifted from me soul. Seven years of fear and hatred are gone. When Sam Slit first took me I were no bigger than Gracie, and could not fight back but only scream and sob as he used me. Then, when I grew older, he got me on the grog, so I were too weak of character and spirit to run away.

But now, with the beast devoured in the flames of its own belly, I was free at last. I be no longer too ashamed to come home to you and Mary. For the first time, I got some hope that the mongrels upon the earth can be defeated by decent men.'

Tommo is silent for a spell. Then he says softly, 'But always I'm reminded that the small and the innocent is the ones what gets sacrificed. Even me freedom from Slit comes at a price. A child named Gracie died for it. I vowed in her name that, as long as I live, I ain't gunna let the mongrels win against the small and the weak, against those what cannot fight back.'

I sit, stunned, in the dark. The pain of my back has been forgotten as Tommo talks, and now we are both silent. Then Tommo speaks again, quoting the words of Gracie's papa.

' "We do not have much, but what we have is hard earned under a clean sky. It is honest bread. And most of what we have is our kin and our kith. If any of these be hurt or beaten or harmed, then we all be also hurt and beaten and harmed, and we must take into our own hands the means of justice required of decent men who live in the sight of a righteous and almighty God." '

This is a different twin from the one I thought I knew. Tommo has led me to believe that he is uncaring and cynical, hardened in the ways of the world, too damaged to care about his fellow man, concerned only with where and when he may find his next drink.

Now I perceive in him an anger, one which he will not always use judiciously, as witnessed by his answering back of Rawlings and our subsequent incarceration in this dark hole. But I tell myself it is a much better Tommo. There is much of my old twin come back, the smart-mouthed though always caring little boy, whom I knew and loved so well before we were parted. The years in the wilderness have not destroyed him completely, I am sure. His abstinence ashore last night has given me great heart, and I am filled with optimism for our future.

Tommo reaches out in the dark and clasps my arm in both his manacled hands. 'O'Hara and Jenkins hurt and beat you and the lads, my kith and kin!' He adds quietly, 'And so I've remembered the words of Gracie's daddy and I have kept me vow.'

Chapter Seven

TOMMO

*Kororareka
March 1857*

Staying sober that night were the most difficult task of me life. At every gin palace, grog shop, brothel and hotel, temptation stared me in the gob. Two minutes at a game o' cards in a one-shilling hell and I would've had a brandy in me trembling hand.

If Hawk had known that I stayed sober only to make sure of the whereabouts of Jenkins and O'Hara so that I might keep me vow of revenge, he would have been happy to see me gutter-rolling drunk. Being stranded on these God-forsaken shores, sitting in a gaol cell at Kororareka is a bloody high price to pay for what we done. But our revenge worked even better than I'd hoped, and we are well rid of the *Nankin Maiden*, though she still waits in the bay for her master to return from the surgeon's hospital.

Twice in two days we've been manacled and put in custody, first by Seb Rawlings and then by the local constabulary. We is to go before the district police magistrate when next he sits, though who knows when that might be. The other prisoners reckon that we'll be taken to Auckland.

Hawk is still furious that I acted against O'Hara without talking to him first. Now he sees how clearly I gulled him when we was ashore – he thought me show of temperance were from a new resolve to remain sober. I'll never get another drink in me lifetime if Hawk's got anything to do with it! I've even lost my raisin wine, the result o' nearly seven months of saving the raisins from me plum duff, and winning them from the rations of the crew when they lost to me at cards. I gave the cook five big mackerel for the yeast I needed to speed the fermentation.

Me ship-brewed grog were about a week off being ready when we was arrested and thrown into this foul nest. Now I won't never have the satisfaction of getting as full as a tick on board and thumbing me nose at Captain O'Hara and his pious Quaker owners with their bloody dry cask afloat. Never mind, I thinks to meself, our revenge on O'Hara and Jenkins be even sweeter than such a fine drop would've been.

We are sitting in this bloody cell where the vermin is as plentiful as on board ship. We has seen few rats and cockroaches but the fleas and lice are back and at night, the bed bugs, so that we is always scratchin'.

It is a good time to work with Hawk on his voice which comes along fine but is still very much on the rasp and low to the ear. I has to teach him to open his mouth and throw his voice wide. Honest, sometimes I dunno how me twin survived growin' up without me. Hawk has ideas what would make him the laughing stock o' men what know life for the misery it is. If those in authority ever knew his secret thoughts they'd arrest him for sedition. But, as I comes to think of this, perhaps they would not. He knows so little of the evil what lurks in men's hearts that those in power may well take him to be a harmless fool.

Since his voice is begun to recover, Hawk speaks much o' man's conscience and has the peculiar notion that men must form a brotherhood and act responsible, the each for the other.

'We have a new country, Tommo, why should we accept that we must follow old ways, old laws? Why must the poor be accepted as beyond redemption and not worth the smallest charity?' he asks.

'Because for the most part the poor be idjits!' I says.

'Only because they have no opportunity,' Hawk answers.

'Rubbish! Poor ain't an opportunity not given, it be how we looks at the world.'

He stares at me amazed. 'Bloody hell! You are right! *How we look at the world*. A way of looking at themselves and their own kind!'

It be the first time I've heard Hawk cuss with his new voice and

I laugh at the sound. 'When I were took by Sam Slit, I were just a seven-year-old brat, cheeky though, and bright, with an answer for all and a bit of a joker, wouldn't you say?'

'You were all that and more, Tommo,' Hawk chuckles softly.

'But when Sam Slit beat me and abused me I become a different boy. Soon I were like a kicked dog. When me master called I'd come, me eyes filled with fear for the beating I expected. But I would still come. What else could I do? I were a child and in the wilderness with a wild man. So I gets accustomed to it, tries to please him and be a good boy. Soon I don't remember that I were ever any other way!'

'That's what I mean!' Hawk exclaims. 'You were taught to expect naught but blows and curses. That is what you received and soon you thought the world no different.'

'That's right!' says I. 'That's why your brotherhood of men won't work. Men ain't kind to them as they don't have to be – not in this hard old world.'

'No, no, that's just it! We must change the conditions of the world. Men of conscience must stand together and change the conditions!'

'Ha, what a load o' codswallop!' I says. 'There be only two conditions what exists in this world, Hawk, strength and weakness. The strong shall destroy the weak, that's how it's always been, and I'll vouch that won't never change long as we live. Your fine ideas o' conscience won't change anything, neither.'

'But you said yourself in the dark that you took a vow to defend the weak, to look after your kith and kin. That is the *conscience* in you, Tommo!'

'Bull! That ain't conscience! The mongrels kicks you, and you finds a way to kick back, like we done to O'Hara and Jenkins. That be revenge and well took too!'

'Tommo, you went too far! You and the Maori, what you did that night was not right.'

I look at Hawk and shakes me head. 'What we did were no worse than what they did to Hammerhead Jack, and what O'Hara and Jenkins did to you and the other Maori!'

'We could have gone to the law!' Hawk says. 'We could have had the vessel impounded and our complaint heard.'

'The law! You heard what Hammerhead Jack said about British law, well he were damn right! Four Maori and a nigger against the Yankee captain of a whaling ship what's known for his Quaker piety! The case heard by some drunken district magistrate! For God's sake, Hawk!'

I think about how surprised Hawk were when we was taken out of the dark hole and brought to a crew muster before the mainmast. First up Hawk thinks it must be the crew count before we sail. I ain't sure the plan has worked so don't know what to expect. We stumble out of the darkness into the brilliant morning sunshine and our eyes is blinded for a time so that we needs be led by the bosun what's come to fetch us from the hold. The shouting of the crew alerts Hawk that there is something new afoot. As we pass, some of the men touch us on the sleeve and some grin and wish us well under their breaths.

Our eyes begin to get used to the bright light and I sees the three mates, Stubbs, Hollowtree and Rawlings, standing beside the mainmast. O'Hara ain't among 'em and Jenkins too is missing. Good! I thinks. The three mates are grim-faced and all has their arms clasped to their chests, watching Hawk and meself.

I am glad Hawk don't know what we've done, for he's a hopeless liar and might give the game away. As for yours truly, well, the wilderness taught me all I needs to know about lying. I'm all innocence in appearance, though not *too* innocent, that be just the same as looking guilty. Instead, like Hawk, I has confusion writ upon my gob, as if I be silent-saying to meself, 'What's goin' on then?'

Several of the men are pointing to the mainmast, a foot above the heads of the ship's officers. Hawk looks up and I follows his gaze. He gives a gasp and this is followed by me own, for what I see is not expected. Hawk's horror be genuine as he grabs at me with both his manacled hands. 'Look, the mast!' he shouts in his rusted voice.

There, nailed to the masthead, is the hand of Captain Mordechai O'Hara, chopped off at the wrist with his gold signet ring still on his third finger. This time it don't wear the ruby of Billy Lanney's flesh as it did the day of his beating. The captain's hand has been nailed stoutly to the mast with a three-inch copper nail, the fingers pointing to the heavens as though giving praise to the Almighty. A thin line of dried blood runs all the way from the mangled wrist to the base of the mast and gives the evil appearance of a hand stuck on the end of a rod. Beside it, like two pale sausages nailed likewise with cooper's barrel nails, are a forefinger and middle finger, what I knows belongs to Jenkins, for the ginger hair below the knuckles glints in the morning sun.

I gasps and grabs back at Hawk's arm, feigning shock and horror. But inside I be pleased as Punch, silently singing the praises of Hammerhead Jack's lads, what has done so well! 'Gawd bless the Maori! To hell with British justice, this one's for Gracie!' I says to meself.

Well, o' course, it's presumed we be guilty and the bosun now pulls us roughly by the manacles to stand in front of the three mates.

It is Stubbs what speaks first. 'What say you?' he shouts, looking at Hawk.

What can Hawk say? He knows nothing. He is still shaking from the shock and I hopes that they do not think it is because he is afraid. But with Stubbs' question he seems to realise what might be afoot. Hawk is ever the optimist, but he ain't stupid.

'Say?' Hawk says, removing his cap. 'I am deeply shocked at what I see!' He gestures with his manacled hands to O'Hara's hand and the two fingers nailed beside it. 'Who has done this terrible thing?'

The men have crowded forward, straining to hear Hawk's voice.

'You are in this!' Rawlings shouts, pointing to Hawk and then to me. 'You two are part of this!'

'Part? How? You know well enough we be locked midships all of last night and aboard ship yesterday at your instructions.' I cough lightly then add, 'Sir,' so as to show me disrespect, but not too much for I clumsily remove me cap from me head and hold it to me front. Hawk scowls at me. He's put two and two together. He knows I am up to my neck in it somehow, though how he still ain't sure. He knows Rawlings is a fair man at heart and does not wish to put him altogether on the captain's side. But Rawlings has little choice, he's got to take us to task as if he were O'Hara hisself. He is only the fourth mate, the most junior of the ship's officers, but he were in charge of the ship when the Maori escaped. And I doubts the other two, Stubbs and Hollowtree, will take the slightest share of the blame. Seb Rawlings is in big trouble and he must get to the bottom of this affair or be disgraced forever. No doubt there will be an official inquiry. Perhaps, I thinks, Rawlings can be pushed into saying or doing something foolish which might later be in our favour. Where the mongrels is concerned, yours truly is all for playing the crowd, and Rawlings is now on the side of the mongrels.

'You are in this, bastard!' he yells, spitting the words at me.

Now is the time to be humble. 'Mr Rawlings, sir, I begs your indulgence. As you know, the Maori took leave of the ship well after we returned the night before last. You yourself did muster us the morning following to ask if we did know their whereabouts. But, o' course, we did not,' I say innocently, and Hawk nods his head. We is now too deep into this affair for him not to go along with me and I sense that he knows what I'm up to with Rawlings. I continue, 'Then you locked me brother and me up 'til we be fetched but a few moments ago.' I turns towards the men. 'It is easy enough to ask the men if they seen Hawk and meself all the night ashore and also, if ever they did see us together with the Maori.'

There is a rumbling among the crew and some nods their heads. 'Aye, they be with us,' several call.

'Quiet!' calls Hollowtree, who ain't said a word until this moment.

'As a matter o' fact, sir, along with several of the men here, we was at the Whaler's Hotel at a late hour where we seen Captain O'Hara talking with some o' the locals there. I assures you, Mr Rawlings, sir, he were hale and hearty at the time we left to return to the ship!'

'Aye!' several of the men shout at once. 'That be God's truth! We'll swear to that!'

'Well then, what be this?' Stubbs shouts, holding aloft me kindling axe!

Hawk gazes at me in shock. It's a surprise to me too, but I quickly explains.

'Joshua Stokes, who were the watch, will be my witness that not ten minutes after me and Hawk come aboard from shore, I reported me axe stolen, sir. It were took from the fo'c'sle where I has me things and it were gone when we returned.'

Stokes steps forward. 'Aye, sir, that be right. The lad did address me on this matter!'

Stubbs steps two paces towards the mast and lifts the small axe and fits it to a deep cut within the wooden mast some four inches below Captain O'Hara's hand. The axe head sinks a full inch into the stout timber and fits snugly, so that Stubbs may leave it there. 'It were discovered here this morning at daybreak!' he says accusingly.

'Find who put it there and you has the man what stole it, sir!' I shrugs.

Now Hawk speaks beside me. 'I should be most grateful to have it returned to my brother, Mr Stubbs, sir!' he says in his gravelly voice. 'This is a ship full of villains as may be clearly seen,' he points to O'Hara's severed hand. 'I fear for Tommo's safety unless he may defend himself!'

The men falls to laughing uproariously so that the solemnity of the occasion is destroyed. There ain't a man on board what's sorry for the captain, nor for the blubber-room bully, Jenkins.

'Shut thy trap!' Stubbs shouts at Hawk and pulls me axe out from the mast. 'Thou and thy brother be in this up to your necks!'

'Which will soon enough feel the hangman's rope about them!' Rawlings adds. 'There is blood on the blade! Human blood!' He points at it and looks darkly at Hawk. 'This is the second time human blood has been found on a blade of your doing. Last time it was Nestbyte's knife. Now,' he brandishes the axe above his head, 'this!'

The men grows silent. I should learn to shut me big gob, but Rawlings is after me brother and it comes out without me thinking. ' "I am not mocked, sayeth the Lord!" ' I say for all to hear.

Well, Hawk and me is taken back to the dark hole, though it be plain to see the men ain't happy that this should happen. But this is a whaling ship and they ain't likely to mutiny over a spot of injustice, leastways for a sprat of a lad and a nigger. Most has been on board a full two years and the ship's hold is near full with oil. Besides, with O'Hara's hand lopped off, they probably think they will return to Massachusetts. There ain't a man among them what would sacrifice his share of the lay even if our lives be in certain danger.

As soon as we is back in the dark, Hawk ticks me off. He is fit to be tied, and I'm glad I cannot see his face and that his voice is not strong so that he must often rest as he shouts. But he grabs me arm with his manacled hands and shakes me 'til I thinks he will rip me shoulder out. My lip is bleeding from biting back the pain.

'Tommo, you are a damned fool! We are done for!'

'No! They got nothin' on us. We was locked in, snug as a bug in a bloody rug, here in this dark hole!' I protests.

'Your axe! They will say you gave it to the Maori! Don't you see, we are implicated!' Hawk yells again, his throat raw and hoarse. For a moment I wish he never got his voice back.

What he says is true enough, though. I did give me axe to the Maori when I told them where they might find Jenkins and O'Hara. But they agreed it should be thought they'd pinched it. I did not think they would return it.

'Tommo, my people will kill O'Hara,' Hammerhead Jack said to me several days before we reached New Zealand.

'No!' I tells him. 'We must cut off his hand!'

He pauses, thinking, then frowns. 'Why we not kill him?' he asks, puzzled.

'He's no warrior, he's a coward!' I says. 'He must live with the memory that he's a coward and a mongrel!'

'What is mong . . . ril?'

I don't try to explain, though perhaps I could have done for I has learnt a bit of the Maori tongue. Instead I says, 'Every time O'Hara lifts his arm, he's gunna remember that he cannot steal from a Maori, nor beat him when there is no just cause.'

'Nigger, too! He cannot beat Ork!'

'Yes! He must be punished for he is a mongrel!' I says again.

'Ha! Mongril!' Hammerhead Jack says. 'Mongril!' He sounds the word and seems to like the taste of it. Then he picks up me axe with his good hand. I were using it to gut a tuna when he comes upon me on the aft deck. He takes the axe head in his huge paw and tests the edge with his thumb, drawing a thin line of blood. He whistles in admiration, for I keeps it sharp as a barber's razor.

'Your hand has held this axe, Tommo,' he says in his own tongue. 'You must give it to us so a Maori hand may hold it when we find this mongril. This way we will share the pleasure of our *utu* with you and Ork!'

'You can have me axe, Hammerhead Jack!' I says, excited. 'But don't tell Hawk!'

Hammerhead Jack shakes his head and laughs loudly. 'Ork good! Not tell Ork!' he replies in English. He holds the axe in his hand as though weighing it. 'It has your *mana*, it will come back with this mongril's blood upon the blade, Tommo.'

I can't say I didn't know what would be done with my axe, but when Hammerhead Jack nailed O'Hara's hand and fingers to the mast, he did so without me knowing. It were an act of incredible bravery what I greatly admires. I can see it were done in order that Captain O'Hara would forever know that it were the Maori what had wreaked their vengeance upon him. Tommo's 'mongril' has been punished at last.

I also know that Hammerhead Jack returned me axe thinking that, because it were reported stolen, the blame for what had happened would be placed squarely at his feet. Hawk and I would be innocent even if we was under suspicion, the axe the final proof that the Maori alone were guilty.

Now, with Hawk shouting at me, I realise that Hammerhead Jack is a warrior and don't give a fig for the British coming after him. I'd be surprised if he'd gone after O'Hara himself, though. He is too intelligent, and still too weak to take on the captain or Jenkins with only one hand. One of the other Maori must have done it and now that they has escaped back to their people, the law would have trouble finding the culprits amongst the tribe.

Hammerhead Jack would know little of the law, caring only that me axe, me *mana*, be returned to me and that his beloved Ork be safe. It takes some hours to convince Hawk o' this, and he still ain't completely happy with yours truly. But I think he is slowly coming to the view that British law would never have helped us out in New Zealand.

'Besides,' I point out, 'when Hammerhead Jack said he did not trust in the law you said nothin'. I thought you knew the bastard would get away with it and I wouldn't have the opportunity to keep my vow.'

Hawk stays silent and I think perhaps I have him. Then he speaks quietly. 'I have it written down, Tommo. Every word O'Hara said to us, every syllable. Sooner or later he would have come to port in Hobart Town and, with Mary's help, I would have him in front of the governor and brought to trial!'

I've learned something new about me brother. He is patient and has a long memory. 'Will you do so now? Now that O'Hara has lost his hand?' I asks.

Hawk gives a short laugh. 'You may be damned sure of that! I shall make the law work for small men as well as those who have influence. If we do not force the judge or the magistrate to do his duty then we cannot complain that we are hard done by. Poor men should have fine lawyers too!'

'Ha! And how's your penniless beggar gunna find such a lawyer?'

'We will build a land where Mistress Justice is once again blind, the way she is supposed to be. Alas, she has long since seen her blindfold removed so that she now judges those who supplicate in front of her by the cut of their clothes, the base or haughty accent on their lips, and the depth of their purse.'

I shakes me head in the dark. He's got his voice back, all right. How on earth can I make this big nigger see that he tilts at windmills?

It is late in the afternoon when, with a rattle of keys, we is brought once again on deck and handed into the custody of two police constables. Though we asks why we are arrested, not a word is spoken. The men gather around and there is some protest, but finally all our worldly goods is thrown into a whaleboat and we is rowed ashore. The only words spoken is by one o' the four oarsmen what stand on the shore as we is led away. It is one o' the Irishmen. 'God bless ya, lads! Don't let the bastard British grind yer down, keep yer Irish up, yer hear now!' he shouts.

This morning the gaoler comes in to see us. It is the first time we've spoke though we has been here a week. He is a big man dressed in a uniform much the worse for wear, with most of his recent breakfast on its front. He looks like a walrus, with a ragged ginger moustache and no beard, and his whisky-pocked and bloated nose is like a polished plum planted in a hairy red nest. His cap sits askew on his head, with hair like the straw of an old scarecrow poking out. His eyes are dull as raisins and his ears large and bright scarlet where the light shines through them. This is a deep-drinking, thirsty man, if ever I seen one.

'Mornin', lads,' he says in a mournful tone.

'Mornin', Sergeant,' we replies, standing up with a clanking of chains.

'Nottingham's the name, but not the sheriff o' Robin Hood fame.' If this be a joke it comes out flat. 'Best stand to attention,' he says, and we brings our feet more or less together.

'Well then, lads, you're off to Auckland,' he goes on. 'Your vessel be there now, sailed two days since with your one-fisted skipper aboard.' He looks up at Hawk. 'You're a big fella, ain'tcha? Nearly as big as Hammerhead Jack.' He scratches his chin as though he's thinking. 'Now there's a big fella in more ways than one, what say you?'

'He's a big fellow, very tall,' we mumbles without much enthusiasm.

'Big trouble-maker, too! Can't say I'm glad he's back. Been in the wars, from all appearances. Whale got him, was it?'

Hawk nods.

'Dangerous big fellas, whales. But not as dangerous as big black fellas, eh? What do you know of the savage?'

'Who?' we both says.

'Hammerhead Jack,' he says. 'What know you of this hand-lopping affair?'

Hawk speaks to me with his hands, though he does not look at me as I read them. 'Watch him carefully.'

I nods me head as though I am listening to Nottingham and then reply in sign language, 'Drinking man!'

'What say you then of this affair?' the Sheriff o' Nottingham asks again.

'Nothing. We know nothing, sir,' I answers quickly.

He points a stubby finger at me. 'You the one with the axe?'

'Axe, sir?'

'You know! The weapon what did the dastardly deed!'

'I'm sure I don't know what you means, sir. Does you mean did I own the axe?'

'Aye, and use it!'

'Use it, no. It were stole from me and used elsewhere by persons unknown.'

Our gaoler spins around, amazing quick for such a stout cove, and sticks his same podgy finger into Hawk's chest. 'And you be the one who murdered the first mate, ain'tcha!'

'Oh,' I says, quick and cheeky. 'All settled then, is it? We be guilty, is that it?'

'Would be if I had me way. Take you out the back, string you up the nearest tree together with the big Maori and call it a damn good day's work! One of each kind of villain, black, white and brindle, couldn't be fairer than that now, could it? Shame you can't just do it, these days.'

'Well, I'm thankful for that,' Hawk sighs softly.

'Now it's down to Auckland, magistrates on the bench growing haemorrhoids, jury sitting on their arses twiddling their thumbs and, when all's said and done, probably the same verdict: hanged by the neck until you dies. Goin' to Auckland be just a waste o' time and taxpayers' money!'

'And Captain O'Hara, what about him, Sergeant Nottingham? Has you thought that he might be the real villain?' I points to Hawk. 'Ask me brother to show you his back!'

Nottingham dismisses this with a toss of his hand. 'Could be, could be. Quite possible. But it ain't, see. 'Cause it wouldn't be right. Wouldn't be the decent thing.'

'What do you mean by that?' Hawk asks.

'It's all about sides, ain't it? Sides and ingredients! Yankee whaling ship skipper, Christian Quaker gentleman. That be one side. Ingredients on that side be a lopped-off hand.' He stops and looks at us hard. 'Four Maori, a nigger and a white man what carries a razor-sharp axe about his person. Ingredients here be the bloody axe what done the deed. That be t'other side.'

'What about British justice in all of this?' Hawk asks.

'Justice don't come into trials. White jury, Christian folk, or professed to be. Yankee whaling ships what come regular into port be good for business and ain't to be discouraged under any circumstances. And like I said, Quaker Christian captain with a ship what's a dry cask afloat, so the crew drink the port dry at top prices when they comes to land. That's more commerce. This be the case for the plaintiff.'

Nottingham sniffs and grabs his nose with his forefinger and thumb, wiggling it vigorously. 'Maori and niggers known to be heathen savages what can't see reason, don't have no discipline, 'less both be brought about by means of a good flogging before the mast. That be the case for the defence. What say you then, gentlemen o' the jury, guilty or not guilty?'

Nottingham says all this in a steady drone. Now he pauses and looks down at his naked big toe poking out of his broken boot. He wriggles it as though he's surprised to find it there. Then he shakes his head slowly and squints up at us. 'I might be a gamblin' man, but I wouldn't venture threepence on your chances. You be pushing wet dung uphill with a broken stick, lads. Best confess and be done with it, eh?'

'You say you're a gamblin' man, sir?' I asks.

137

'Could be, could be,' he sniffs through his tangerine moustache. 'Depends, don't it now?'

'Play the flats, then?'

'Been known to play a hand or two from time to time. Fancy yerself, does you? Didn't your daddy tell you never to play cards with strangers?'

'With friends? You play with friends?' Hawk asks.

'Poker, is it? Or whist?' I butt in before he can answer Hawk.

'Play the odd game in town now and then,' Nottingham says, without answering my question.

'What, in them one-shilling hells, full o' chumps and whores? I'll wager there's not a decent game to be found in this whole town!' I laughs.

'Look, lads, you be in enough trouble, don't go looking for no more. This town's got a poker school what's too rich for your blood!'

'Aye,' Hawk says, 'most wisely spoken, Sergeant Nottingham. On the other hand, there could be a quid in it for you.'

Nottingham looks at Hawk shrewdly. 'Cost yer five sovs to sit in.'

I whistle. 'Five pounds!' I has no idea if Hawk's got this kind of money. I look at him, showing me surprise, but he signals she'll be right. 'That be a big game,' I says to the Sheriff o' Nottingham.

'Too big for me, and I suggests too big for the likes of you mangy lot.'

'If you can get my brother into the game, we'll go fifty-fifty, what say you?' Hawk challenges.

A greedy look comes into the gaoler's eyes. 'You've got five pounds to wager?'

'Could be, could be! Depends, don't it now?' Hawk mimics him cleverly.

'Fifty-fifty?'

Hawk nods.

'And if you lose?'

'No onus,' Hawk replies.

'If we loses, you gets our confession signed, sealed and delivered. Feather in yer cap and all,' I says.

I can hear Hawk's sharp intake o' breath at this offer.

'A feather in me cap, eh? A written confession?' Nottingham removes his cap to show a bald, shiny red pate, spotted with bright brown freckles like stars in the night sky. Then he punches the inside of the dirty, misshapen cap with his fist. The crown flaps loose and three dirty fingers wiggle through the gap. 'Even with a feather it ain't never going to be much of a cap.' He grins, showing gappy yellow teeth. 'There's no more promotion for Sergeant Nottingham, this be my final patch, my last station o' duty!'

'You mean, you'd rather have the money?' asks Hawk, coming straight out.

'What do you think?' Nottingham grins.

'Well,' says Hawk, 'what I think is that *you* think my brother and I will be condemned whether we are guilty or not, would that be correct?'

Nottingham smiles a secret little smile and shrugs. 'That's about it, lads. Ain't no jury in this land what's gunna condemn your Captain O'Hara for a bit o' Maori and nigger flogging.'

I am impressed at how quick Hawk's grasped the situation. Nottingham be a man what's condemned by his own habits, a drinker and a gambler, and a failure at both. Shit! I thinks suddenly, that's what Hawk sees for me! He sees Nottingham. He sees his desperation, his despair, in me future.

That's the difference 'tween Hawk and me. I sees a mongrel clear as daylight. Not a very important mongrel, mind, but one what can cause us harm and what's got power over us. Hawk sees a man what's on the bones of his arse, what's closer to prisoner than to policeman, trapped by what he is and where he be. A man what's dying same as the town around him, sinking into nothin'.

Hawk is a fair man, fair in his heart and mind. He don't understand that fair be not understood by such as Nottingham or even, matter of fact, by such as me. Fair don't come into the reckoning of poor folk. Hawk sees someone to be pitied and yours truly sees danger. Hawk be about to mess things up proper by trying to get Nottingham to let us escape for five pounds. Hawk don't understand how a gambler's mind works.

'This game o' poker, we're in, then?' I takes up the question again.

'Fifty-fifty?'

'Fifty-fifty, solemn oath,' I shoots back.

'Remind me what happens if you lose?'

I shrug. 'You ain't no worse off and we still be Auckland-bound. But if we wins, what then?' I asks.

This is the moment o' truth. I sense that even Hawk knows this. I try to keep the smile on me gob, hoping that I haven't struck too early, that me smile means it don't seem too important to know the answer if I've read him wrong.

Nottingham don't know for sure if we've got the five sovs, but he's got to figure we must have, or there's no point. Thank Gawd Hawk ain't shown it to him. Then I thinks, Christ Jesus! What if Hawk don't have it and he is bluffing? Nah, Hawk don't have the gall, he's got the money all right. Nottingham has to figure he has, too. So what's his options? He can take it by force – there be three constables as well as himself and we be in chains and manacles. Five pounds be a lot of money. Or, he can gamble there's more to come if I can win at poker. It's time for all Ikey's lessons to pay off.

'Sergeant Nottingham, sir, if you'd be so good as t' remove me manacles for five minutes, perhaps you'd care to witness the skill what's being brought to *our* side.'

Nottingham looks me up and down and I guess he figures there ain't all that much to me and that even he might make a show of capturing me should I try to scarper. Besides, the cell is locked behind him. We waits and he don't say nothing. If he says no, we're done like a dinner.

'Righto!' he says and, taking the keys from his belt, opens me manacles.

Well, it's all sporting stuff. Ace where no ace should be. Ace, King, Queen, Jack dealt straight off after Nottingham has himself shuffled the pack. 'Take a card please, Sergeant? Any card.' I offers the pack wrong-side up and he selects a card blind. 'Turn it over and put it down,' I points to the four picture cards already spread face up. He turns his card and puts down the Joker, amazement writ all over his rough gob. Then he smiles and I know we has won. Greed be the most dependable of all human characteristics.

'Righto, you can count me in,' he growls.

'Just a moment, Sergeant, what about *our* winnings?' Hawk asks.

'Fifty-fifty!' he says, indignant.

'Ah! Not what *you* win, what *we* win?'

Nottingham looks puzzled.

'If we are Auckland-bound,' Hawk continues, 'and if, as you say, the verdict is already decided?'

There is a long silence as Nottingham stands thinking, looking down at his broken boots. Then he slowly raises his head and looks squint-eyed at Hawk. 'You means, what price freedom?'

Hawk stays stum.

The gaoler seems to be thinking again, and then he says quietly, 'Fifty pounds.'

'Fifty pounds!' Fuck! I'm took completely by surprise. Fifty quid, I'll wager, be near six months' salary for a police sergeant! But Hawk don't even flick an eyelid.

'How big is the game?' he asks cool as you like.

'Five, six with him,' Nottingham points t' me.

'Can't do it,' Hawk says firmly. 'Five-pound stake for each player, that's only thirty-five pounds. If each isn't prepared to lose more than his buy-in, we can't make the fifty. Even if Tommo cleans them all out, which isn't likely. Let's say twenty pounds, which will be hard enough?'

Shit, Hawk's got twenty pounds on him, I thinks. If Nottingham accepts, he'll offer him the money right off so that we can scarper, never mind the poker game.

'There's some what will be willing to lose more than their stake,' the gaoler says. 'They don't muck around.' He pauses. 'You scared, is it? Sorry, lads, but I ain't sticking me neck out for less than half a hundred.'

Hawk shakes his head. 'Sergeant Nottingham, it isn't reasonable.'

Nottingham laughs, his fat stomach wobbling like a jelly. 'It ain't a reasonable world, son. It ain't *reasonable* that the jury should hang you in Auckland, but take my word they will. Fifty pounds, that be my first and last offer.'

'You're on!' I says suddenly. With twenty pounds I can build a proper scam. But Hawk's right, to take fifty pounds from a single five-pounds-in game is damned nigh impossible if they's good players. Even if I does a whole heap o' relocation I'll need two games to set it up.

'But it's got to be two nights, two games. Over two games we've maybe got a chance,' I says to the gaoler.

Nottingham looks doubtful. 'Two games? I don't know if these gentlemen will like that.'

'Tell you what they won't like? They won't like playing with a stranger for one game only!'

Nottingham accepts this. He's said himself he don't play cards with a stranger.

'Fifty-fifty if you should not make the fifty pounds for your freedom?' Nottingham says again.

We both nod. It is sheer bastardry, but what can we do? 'Fifty pounds in your hand and you let us scarper, right?' I want it from his lips once more.

He clears his throat like he's even nervous to think of it. 'Yes, but I'll have to come after you, mind. Do me duty.'

Hawk smiles. 'By going in the wrong direction, I sincerely hope?'

'Aye, I'll do that by and by,' Nottingham says, still shifty.

'Two games, right?' I persist, bringing them two back to the business at hand. 'Five pounds on the table to buy into each game. The second five held at the end of the first night as surety for the next – right?' I points to Hawk, 'Me brother to hold the second game buy-in, in trust overnight. Oh,' I adds, 'and two new packs o' cards, DeLarue & Sons, no other, one blue, one red, we breaks the seals at the table.'

Hawk looks at me and I shrugs. In for a penny, in for a pound. Worst what can happen is we are transported to Auckland and strung up. I'm making a book on Nottingham's greed. He's a gambler himself, he'll be itching to sit in on the second game and I hopes to make it possible. Nottingham's a mongrel, and mongrels has to pay.

'Right, two games,' the gaoler agrees. 'I think I can arrange that all right. But,' he points at Hawk, 'I don't think they're gunna let a known murderer hold the stakes overnight.'

I see Hawk scowl and his eyes grow hard at Nottingham's accusation that he can't be trusted.

'Safer than a bank,' I pipes up quickly. 'We ain't goin' nowhere, is we now?'

Nottingham laughs, relieving the tension. 'Righto, the nigger holds the buy-in and the wee lad gets new cards, DeLarue & Sons. By the by, what's the ante?'

'Let's say five shillings.'

'Five shillings?' Nottingham thinks for a moment then nods, 'Fair enough, lad.'

'With the right to raise it before each hand?'

The gaoler hesitates then says, 'We'll let the others decide, though I can't see they'll object.'

We leave it at that and Nottingham returns the Queen's

bracelets to me wrists. As soon as he's gone, Hawk asks me in strong lingo what exactly I think I'm doing.

'How much money has we got?' I ducks the question.

He hesitates. 'Twenty-five pounds,' he says.

I acts shocked. 'Shit, why didn't you say before? I thought I were gunna have to work with five! That I'd have to work a scam where we comes out square the first game so's we've got the deposit for the second. Twenty-five quid, eh? That's a king's bloody ransom! Now we can have a proper strategy.' I grin. 'With that much, the very best o' Ikey Solomon be possible.' I pretend to think for a moment.

'We'll lose fifteen right off! "Thicken the plot and sweeten the pot," as Ikey would say.'

'Lose? Fifteen pounds!' Hawk shouts, aghast. All these surprises is getting his voice up nice and strong.

I roll me eyes in the manner o' Ikey. 'Can't win in the first game, not kosher, my dears, not to be considered, quite out o' the question. Absolutely forbidden and not to be entered into!' I says, mimicking his voice. Hawk laughs despite himself, then grows serious again.

'What if we are taken to Auckland before there can be a second game and we've dropped fifteen pounds in the first?'

'Trust me,' I reply. 'Nottingham won't let that happen. He's a gambler what feels he's gunna get lucky!'

But I can't say I ain't worried. Any cove what plays regular in a five-pound buy-in is either cashed and most professional in his handling o' the flats, or apt to practise a little relocation hisself. Either way, such a cove don't much like losing to strangers and is likely to get violent.

'No grog!' Hawk says suddenly. 'Promise me, no brandy, no spirits!'

'Gamblin' can't be done without drinkin', Hawk!' I protest. 'Folks gets suspicious if you don't keep the tipple going.'

Hawk works his hands in the Ikey manner. 'Drink and think go together like boys, bishops and bedchambers – it has been known to happen but it is a most unholy alliance, my dears!' He can do Ikey even better than me.

I sigh and nod me head. At this rate, I ain't never gunna taste another drop.

The game takes place in the gaoler's office that very night, which leads me to think Nottingham ain't quite the innocent he seems. A high-stakes poker game don't come about this quick unless the players expect a pretty evening at someone else's expense. What, I asks meself, is Nottingham up to? It could mean two things. He's told the players we're easy fruit, ripe for the picking. But that be stupid 'cause he knows we ain't. So he's not going to shit on his own doorstep, is he? He's the one what has to live in this town. It might mean he's got a two-way bet – all the other players is in the game together against me, a case o' mutual benefit. Well, I thinks, there's no point in getting too clever at reading the bastard. I'll find out soon enough 'cause that's what the first game's for, ain't it?

Hawk is allowed in the room but he must be seated three feet behind me, and we is both shackled by the ankle to a chair leg.

It's a curious sort o' group, but no more strange, I suppose, than what's to be found in any sea port. Seated about the table is a Maori bloke, Hori Hura, what the whites rudely call the Hairy Horror. He is a merry fellow, what wobbles with laughter after every sentence. He can barely reach the card table for his big belly.

He is accompanied by Messrs Tate and Lyle. These last two are small, rough-looking gentlemen, though they wears good cloth-suits and clean linen with boots what have seen a shine. They is known as Maple and Syrup on account o' the fact that they's inseparable and their names is the same as what's on a Tate & Lyle maple syrup tin.

It turns out that both Tate and Lyle come to New Zealand as boys in 1844, transported on the *Mandarin* from Parkhurst Penitentiary on the Isle o' Wight, young felons to be apprenticed to settlers. But they soon ran away from their masters and took to living amongst the Maori to avoid the law.

This is how they met Hori Hura, himself only a young un. He is much taken with the pakeha boys, who soon learn Maori and teaches him English, including what Ikey would call a host of lively expressions fit to burn the ears off a church warden. They also teaches him the flats and now, for many years, they has become his partners in trading. Most curiously, there is no mention of what sort o' goods this trade be in. But they complains that much of their former customers is now took to Auckland, where they themselves wants to go. I reckons their 'trading' be of a gambling nature, with visiting sailors their patsy-mark. With so few ships now calling at Kororareka and most stopping off at Auckland, they thinks to move their shady operation to the larger port.

Maple and Syrup speak of their past with pride. Parkhurst boys is well known in Tasmania too. Such boys almost exclusively start out with a record as thieves. They is nurtured in vice and repeatedly convicted in the quarter-session courts of London Town until they finally appears at the Old Bailey. There they is given their free passage out to New South Wales or Van Diemen's Land or to New Zealand. Ikey told of how, when he first come to Van Diemen's Land, he would keep an eye on the Point Puer Reformatory near Port Arthur where the Parkhurst boys were transported, just in case the one and only Sparrer Fart did suddenly appear among 'em.

So, I says to meself, if these two bastards, Maple and Syrup, be on the straight and narrow as we're supposed to suppose, then our gaoler be the real Sheriff o' Nottingham, I be Robin Hood and Hawk, Maid Marian!

Then there is the Portugee, Captain de Silva, a small, dark man with a goatee beard and a most handsome moustache, waxed and curled high to almost touch his ear lobes. Nottingham introduces him to all, saying he has only come into harbour yesterday. When he went into the police station to post bond for his crew and pay his customs duty, he happened to enquire if there be a friendly game ashore.

The last of me erstwhile partners for the night is Mrs Barrett, what's in fact a man, thin as a rake, wearing a woman's dress and shawl, hose and boots. His grey hair is tied in a bun behind his neck and he has a long, black and very thin Jamaican cheroot in his mouth. His nose and cheeks is tattooed most unusual, an English rose on each cheek, one full blown, the other in bud, with the leaves and stems joined across his nose and his brow. It is a more friendly-looking tattoo than that of Hori Hura, who, like Hammerhead Jack and the other Maori aboard the *Nankin Maiden*, is covered in black squiggles and circles over every inch of his ugly gob.

Each player has brought along his preferred tipple. Hori Hura has rum, Maple and Syrup has Cape brandy, Captain de Silva drinks oporto wine and Mrs Barrett has Bombay gin. Me gut is howling like a dog at the moon with all these elixirs of heavenly transport placed before it. In their shining bottles they be so near to me yet so far from me reach. I has to concentrate all the harder

145

for not drinking than if I were swilling it down, on me road back to drunkenness as Hawk fears.

To rub salt into the wound, Nottingham explains to all assembled that, because I be a prisoner of Her Majesty, I cannot consume ardent spirits. This be a ploy suggested by Hawk so me abstinence ain't thought strange. So, here I am dealing the cards for stud poker with a mug o' stream water which I am obliged to sip, to the constant chaffing and the pretended commiseration of all what sits comfortable and comforted with their favourite tipple at their elbows.

'Now the flats be a game o' two characters,' Ikey would say. 'It is popular thought that if you know the man you know the game he'll play, but that, my dears, be purest codswallop. Cards bring out the best and worst in a person and often the opposite to what's expected. Timothy Timid can play like a lion and Terrible Tim like a lamb. The flats be the other person in each of us; find this second person and you've got your patsy-mark.'

It's soon apparent that Hori Hura, and Maple and Syrup be skilled enough but lack true intelligence. Of the other two, Captain de Silva, the Portugee captain is a careful player – highly skilled but one who ain't prepared to venture too much. Mrs Barrett appears to be the one to watch. Cunning as a rat, he strikes like a cobra. A very pretty player o' the flats indeed but a mite too hot-headed, and I think he is working a scam, which I will soon enough locate.

I loses slowly but steadily to each of them, dealing them good hands each time it is my turn. I'm losing less than I had hoped to Hori Hura and his Parkhurst boys who are, towards the end of the evening, a little too drunk and do not take all the opportunities me generosity affords them. Each ends the evening with their buy-in still intact and a bit more besides.

Captain de Silva wins three pounds. Mrs Barrett is the winner for the night with seven pounds – three taken from the captain in the final hand when only the two are left in the game and de Silva is forced to see Mrs Barrett by matching his last bet or dropping out. I be surprised when he chooses to drop out as I know he holds a better hand than Mrs Barrett.

This brings me to the whole point of the night. While I has managed to lose nigh upon fifteen pounds, I has also been able to substitute both packs with me own, which I have previously marked. I have took in with me the brand-new red and blue packs Hawk bought me on the night we went ashore from the *Nankin*

Maiden. These has been marked in Ikey's secret manner so it be almost impossible to discover. By the end of the night I has both decks substituted and I know every card on the table. This is why I know that if the Portugee captain had asked to see Mrs Barrett, he would have taken the pot. He's most cautious and this worries me some, for I also sees in him a hungry predator.

In all we are down fourteen pounds and sixteen shillings when the game finally comes to an end. With Mrs Barrett the big winner, local pride is intact and I has established that this fine lady-man is not in league with the other three locals, nor is he near as good as de Silva. I cannot be sure that he ain't in cahoots with Nottingham, but me final reading of him is that he cannot be relied on to win consistently. Nottingham would know this too.

As for the other three, they are clearly a syndicate, and Nottingham would, I reckon, be most reluctant to make a deal with them. Besides, he is all scowls at me loss and most hard put to show a brave face. I got to conclude that our gaoler has took us in good faith as a partner. But I still reckon there is something I has missed; something I has failed to speculate upon. 'Scratch around, look in the dark corners,' I hear Ikey saying to me. 'It will be there, stored in the old noggin box.'

Anyway, it be a neat enough evening's work and all are willing to put down their five-pound stake for the following night. It is decided, at Nottingham's suggestion, that we will play five-card draw tomorrow. Stud poker, the game we has been playing, is a great game for cheating if you knows what you're about. You has only to make sure you have the hole card you want and a good dealer can deliver the right card to make up a winning hand wherever he wishes to place it.

Poker is a game where cold decking is easily possible – that is, substituting a marked deck as I has done during the course of the game. It is a trickier business with five-card draw, though, and there is more chance to be discovered. I believe meself a good enough player with an unmarked deck and am confident I can hold me own with de Silva. If, in an emergency, I must substitute me own deck, I am a good enough mechanic to do it.

Hawk now asks Nottingham to put the two decks we has used tonight in the gaol-house safe. I has already removed me own marked cards and replaced the originals and so I am delighted when our gaoler refuses.

'We play with new cards tomorrow,' he says grandly. 'Captain de Silva has agreed that I should have the money from his winnings to purchase them.'

For my part, I am all brave smiles at my losses, just what might be expected from a good amateur what finds himself out of his depth but has too much pride and not enough sense to give it away.

'Better luck next time, eh lad!' they all says, patting me on the shoulder, pleased as Punch at the way things has gone.

Nottingham then collects the pot and makes Hawk give him five pounds so all can see we has the stakes for the next game. Hawk looks suitably long-faced when he hands over our five sovs and Nottingham is most unhappy that we have lost so badly but is trying not to show his anger to the other players.

Nottingham gives the thirty pounds to Hawk to keep and we is unchained from our chairs. 'See yer tomorrow night, lad. Could be yer night,' Syrup shouts as we is led back to our cells. We can hear them laughing all high and mighty.

When we is locked in again, Hawk sticks out his manacled hands. 'You said we'd lose fifteen pounds, we only lost fourteen pounds and sixteen shillings, where's the other four shillings?'

'Escape money!' I laughs, handing over the four shillings. 'I was keeping it for our expenses on the open road.'

'The open bottle, more like,' he says, a touch tetchy.

'That ain't fair, Hawk! Twice the Maori pushed his rum bottle to me when Nottingham weren't looking, "Help yerself, Tommo," he says.'

Hawk nods and grimaces. 'I wronged you, Tommo. I'm sorry. It's just my own misgivings over the whole affair. The fat Maori and those two villains from Parkhurst, Maple and Syrup, I think they are the most dangerous.'

'I know,' I says. 'But they is poor mechanics and cannot match the play. Their cheating is only for chumps what know no better.'

'We could ask that they be seated away from each other?'

'No, that would alert them that we're on to them. Besides, it'll make no difference. I'll take them slowly tomorrow night, driving the pot up only at the end when they be well out o' the game. And what does you think o' Captain de Silva and Mrs Barrett?'

'De Silva is kosher, I think, and I only caught Mrs Barrett relocating once.'

148

'He done it seven times. He's got an apron pocket behind his shawl,' I laughs. 'He's quite good but not too quick on the draw.'

'Seven times, eh?' Hawk exclaims. 'Not much help then, am I?'

'Course you is. Poker games can turn nasty at any moment, and having you behind me be a great comfort in a room full o' villains. They will think twice about coming at us.'

Hawk laughs. 'Big and clumsy, that's me. I don't know how I'd go at fisticuffs! Never tried it. Besides, our legs are shackled to the chair.' He pauses and then asks, 'How are we going, then?'

'I know their second natures now,' I reply. 'The Portugee captain worries me. I left him out o' my favours tonight. He is an outsider like us, and there ain't no need to gull him, so I lets him play his natural game to gauge his skill. I didn't observe him to be relocating even the once and it be astonishing that he managed to come out ahead in a game where I gives the others so much help.'

I turns to Hawk suddenly. 'Watch him tomorrow night. Forget the others. Watch if de Silva does anything different when he asks to see someone's hand. Watch him when he folds. Anything, you hear? Clears his throat, touches his nose or ear lobe, crosses his legs, wiggles his foot, sniffs, bites his nail, touches his eyebrow, runs his tongue over his lips. The smallest thing! Fingers his moustache, twirls it, taps his knee or the table, if he does anything before he makes his play. It just could be we've got a wild card in our midst.'

'What if he doesn't do anything?'

'Don't worry, he will. He can't help but show his excitement, though he fights with all his might not to show it. Look for his gesture. I promise it'll be there, it always is. Remember what Ikey said, "The flats be the other person in each of us." Outside de Silva be the calm one, inside he's got Mexican jumping beans in his stomach. Now listen well, Hawk. The lamplight be behind you and throws the shadow of all of us against the far wall where your head is the tallest in the outline. When you sees de Silva make whatever sign it is, clear your throat once, wait a moment, then lift *your* hand to your head as though to scratch your noggin, leaving one finger in the air. I'll see your sign in the shadow.'

Hawk grins and I know he is glad he has a part to play. There's hope for the lad yet, I thinks. A little corruption will do him the world o' good. Something to lighten up that heavy bloody conscience he's always carrying around.

As soon as his guests have gone, Nottingham is in to see us and loses no time in telling us of his extreme displeasure at me performance. He calls me a wee lad what couldn't win at a game o' marbles. He cannot trust me to win and demands that he take me place at the table and play with our stake. Of course we refuse, but after much argument and cussing from our friend, Hawk agrees to advance him our last five pounds against the fifty promised if we should win, an outcome which Nottingham seriously doubts. He jumps at the offer of having a stake in the game and leaves us a bit happier.

I has not told Hawk that I thought Nottingham would demand to sit in on the second game, nor how well this would suit us. But he has worked it out for himself. The lad is definitely progressing!

'That were well done!' I says to him after the gaoler has left.

'What was?'

'Bringing the bastard into the game!'

'What do you mean? We had no choice!' Hawk says. 'He was threatening to cancel the game tonight and we are down nearly fifteen quid!'

I spoke too soon. Hawk will ever be an innocent. Nottingham, as I expected, be just arrogant enough to believe he may save the situation if he should take me place at the table. As Ikey were fond o' saying, 'A compulsive gambler always feels at his luckiest when he watches someone else lose and very soon convinces himself that it will go different for him. This be just the perfect time to invite him into your game, my dears.'

'Right,' I says, trying not to laugh at Hawk. 'You done well.'

Hawk knows he's got the wrong end of the stick but not why. He shakes his head. 'What is it, Tommo?'

'You don't know, do you?' I laughs. 'Letting Nottingham into the game were a stroke o' genius.'

'It was? How so?' He is even more confused.

'Before the night be out I'll vouch we will halve our debt to him,' says I.

I lies awake the rest of the night, trying to work out what is going on. Finally I reckons there is only one way that everything fits. I knows I got to be careful not to imagine what isn't, nor see coincidence for someone's clever and deliberate ploy, what's easy enough to do when playing cards. By morning I realise there can be only one explanation. The Portugee whaling captain and Nottingham are in a scam together.

This seems most strange, and I don't wish to explain it to Hawk, for there is too much speculation involved and Hawk is one to work with the facts alone. But in me mind I see it clear as day. Nottingham was harping on a bit too much about playing himself. At first I'd thought his whingeing about me abilities with the cards were 'cause he be a compulsive gambler who thinks he can do better. Nottingham *wants* me to think this, but his real purpose is in fact to *lose*, so that he cannot be seen to be in league with de Silva. He will lose to me because it is a debt he can deduct from what we already owes him, and still we will be in debt to him. Now I feels sure that the reason de Silva has agreed to pay for new cards is that he will first mark 'em for himself.

Nottingham, I realises, has never believed I can win. Me skills with the flats he has seen as simply a young lad grown over-confident and showing off some trick. The gaoler just can't bring himself to believe that a 'wee lad' can take on the great de Silva and win. Tricks I may have, but five-card draw, he knows, is much more than sleight of hand.

How Nottingham knows of de Silva's skill, I don't know. But I swears the other four, what are also locals, ain't in the know, for they treats him too obviously as a stranger. I remember how very careful Nottingham were when making the introductions to say he were newly acquainted with the whaling captain, what he claimed had sailed into Kororareka only the previous day. If de Silva cleans up, Nottingham will say he thought the captain were just another patsy-mark off a whaling ship and, at the same time, point out that he too has been a victim of this cunning poker pirate.

Captain de Silva is certainly the best poker player of the five, and, I expects, also a master at relocation if it be necessary, though I have not observed him at this. Last night he lay low and watched the other players, so as to take greater advantage of them tonight. This is the sign of a very good poker player and a professional gambler. If he is playing with a marked deck this will not harm his confidence either.

By losing last night, I've shown Nottingham that he were right about me, that I does not possess the skill to win the fifty sovs required for our freedom. He thinks of me as the fool in the school, but still with a stake o' five pounds to lose in the second game and also what Hawk has loaned to him. Mrs Barrett, he knows, is the hasty type, what will think he is going through a lucky streak and so bring last night's winnings back to the table. Hori Hura, Maple and Syrup will argue to themselves that, if they can win when they is not entirely sober, there will be easy pickings to be had when their heads be clearer.

Nottingham, I feel sure, thinks that before the evening is out the Portugee captain will take all Hawk's money and Mrs Barrett's, the Hairy Horror's and the Parkhurst boys' as well – a clean sweep. I'd wager that the plan is to let Mrs Barrett lose all he made last night 'cept for his original stake and perhaps a trifle more. Then, before taking this also, de Silva will allow him to be last to fold from the game. A local player will have had a series o' good wins, so proving the game straight, despite the visiting captain surprising us all with his amazing skill.

I takes me hat off to Nottingham. It is well thought out. He has made only one mistake in all this. He knows that in the first game de Silva has played to hide his skill, but he don't know that the same is true of me. The fact that he has managed to get Hawk to stake him the five pounds to partake in the second game will only convince him of our callowness. Nottingham must feel himself a pretty clever fellow all 'round. He will still deliver Hawk and me to the law in Auckland without tarnishin' his name as a policeman, gaoler and servant o' the queen. What's more, he will do so at a profit to himself!

Me only concern therefore regards de Silva. Will he buy Nottingham's theory that I be just a brash lad? Or does he see me as his equal and therefore dangerous? If this be the case, he will be most wary and on his guard tonight. I decides to continue acting the amateur and show too much excitement when I chance to win. There is one last thing: if the new cards supplied by Nottingham be marked it will confirm that Nottingham and de Silva be in this together.

Well the first thing I gets right is that I has picked Nottingham for a compulsive gambler. In our game tonight, he loses his five-pound stake in the time it takes me to win ten pounds. I makes a right fuss each time I win a pound, as if I am a silly child what can't believe his good fortune. I even lend Nottingham five pounds against his promissory note.

Meanwhile Hawk, what through his years of being dumb has developed the habit of keen observation, soon sees a pattern

152

emerging in the Portugee captain. Each time de Silva holds a good hand or has relocated a card, he taps the tip of his left whisker. It be the tiniest gesture but it be there. Hawk clears his throat, pauses, then scratches his head and his finger rises above the shadow thrown across the wall in front of me. I soon gets the drift and refrains from calling de Silva whenever he has a strong hand.

Nottingham soon takes out another IOU from me and then another, 'til he owes me twenty pounds. I ain't yet certain that the decks are marked but know that if they are, Nottingham cannot read them and the marking method be de Silva's own. When Nottingham asks one last time for credit, I refuse and he is the first to be forced out of the game, amid much mockery.

I sense his fury, though I am still playing the lucky clown, with me tongue sticking out from the corner of me mouth like some country yokel. I win a little then lose it again and then win a little more, all the while holding me own. De Silva is winning slowly but surely at the expense of the four local lads and is gradually wearing down the weaker players. This is the ploy I would meself use in his position. My mission at present is simply to stay in the game and match me skill with the whaling captain, letting him slowly build his winnings at the expense of the others while I build me own.

Three hours into the game and all the locals is cleaned out. But the process o' taking their money has been played with much skill by de Silva and, if I may say so, yours truly. We raise 'em in small amounts to suck them in and so keep them in the game right to the end of their money. They has all committed considerable more pounds above their previous night's winnings and it is a pretty example of how to empty an opponent's pockets. I exclaims at each de Silva win so that the attention is taken away from me when I too win a hand. It is joyous clever poker, for each of the locals is made to believe that at any moment their luck will change for the better while they is being drained of every penny they possess.

I admires de Silva's patience and skill and he now has a large amount of gelt in front of him. Although I has been winning and losing steadily I am still only fifteen pounds ahead, so the remainder of the winnings sit in an untidy pile in front of the captain – by my reckoning, nearly fifty pounds. It is now only him and me as we continues to play. I am long since convinced the deck is on the straight and has not been shaved or marked. I'm playing against a very clever fellow, a master at the game o' five-card draw.

De Silva will challenge all me wits, but I am confident that me talents are sufficient to match his and perhaps a little more. I make sure that I seems no different in appearance and skill to the others, just fortunate to have lasted in the game as long as I have. I doesn't have the funds I will need to take him on if he should want to raise the stakes. But he plays me the same as them, raising me only small amounts.

Gradually, though, I starts to work up the stakes while sustaining some narrow losses to him, so that those what watches us groans and exclaims at me bad luck and grows excited as I win. I don't know if they see that I lose with a small bet and win with a larger one, for they's took to drowning their sorrows at their own losses. I reckon that if you asked them, they would say that it be only a matter of time before the whaling captain has me cooked as a plump bird, ready to be carved up and eaten for his dinner.

But I am playing well and have clawed back half of de Silva's winnings, though he is still much the favourite and has not yet lost his confidence. He is touching his whisker more frequently and Hawk is practically took to having a fit o' coughing. Any observer of his fingers would think the lice in his hair be biting most vicious tonight.

De Silva is just beginning to be of two minds about me. He is far from a fool and I know he will soon see that he is against a superior player, or at the least, a player to match his every skill. Then he will panic and try to end the game.

At last we reaches the stage where I feel that if de Silva gets one truly big hand he will grow impatient and risk everything. I can see that he has finally worked out what is happening. He is angry at me for winning or losing each time by only a very small difference in cards and so encouraging his ignorance of me true ability. He thinks he deserves to win, so soon he will make his big move when he holds an unbeatable hand.

It is now that I must cold-deck him. The moment has come, there will never be a better one, to substitute the deck concealed on me person for the one on the table. The deck be already stacked and awaiting its chance. Up to this point Hawk's signals have kept me out of trouble and I has proved the better player, but now I needs extra luck, a deck stacked for me and not for the captain.

It's my turn to deal and, using the stacked deck, I deal de Silva a truly high hand, a medium running flush. I can almost hear his inward sigh of relief. God Himself has dealt him a hand he knows cannot be beaten. So the Portugee captain raises the pot by five pounds and I does the same; he bets another five pounds, and I raises him again. He would teach me a lesson, and puts down another five. I does the same. Now he can do nothing but fold or keep raising me. His temper is rising. He cannot believe his hand can be beaten and he *must* punish me. He raises again. Soon I have but five pounds left on the table in front of me and de Silva ten. De Silva's eyes are shining, he has lost his reason and now thinks only of the kill. He wants the lot, and with it my humiliation. He raises me five pounds. I has no option but to fold or see him, and I slowly pushes me last fiver across to join the heap o' money in the centre.

The moment me money touches the pile, de Silva is unable to restrain himself. With a huge smile what shows off his six gold teeth, and some fast babble in what I takes for Portugese, he puts down his medium running flush. His hands shake with the thrill 'cause he thinks he has won the night.

I stays calm, though I admits me heart is pounding. I lay down a running flush as well. Mine is only one number higher than his, but it is enough. One tiny little number different and the pot is mine. The game is over, yours truly has taken the loot. Every bloody penny! De Silva groans and the other five players cannot believe what they has just seen. I look at him and point to the five pounds in front o' him. 'What says you, Captain, another hand?'

De Silva shakes his head and slumps in his chair. He can scarce believe what has happened. He has been made to wager everything on one card, and lost. The emotion I know to be always contained within him now bursts to the surface like a dam wall breached by flood water. His face crumples and he buries his head in his hands and starts to weep, his shoulders heaving.

It is Ikey what comes to me mind again. 'When you wager everything and lose, show nothing. When you wager everything and win, show even less. Cards played well be a game as cold as ice, my dears!'

I reaches over and scoops the pile o' money to me side o' the table, close to eighty pounds. I picks up his hand from the table and then me own and calmly shuffles the deck. With a little relocation, I replace it with the original, so that my own marked deck is returned to me. If Nottingham and de Silva has marked the deck and should examine it later, they will see that it remains what they bought.

Hawk and me are away, clean as a whistle! I hands the deck to our gaoler, who is gone purple from rage. Alas, poor Sheriff o' Nottingham, Robin Hood has slipped through your fingers once again! I smile at the other players and thank them most cordially for the two games. Then I nods towards Hawk, but says nothing. Finally I turn back to the gaoler. 'What says you, Sergeant Nottingham, a bit o' luck for the wee lad, eh?'

Nottingham turns away from me, unable to contain his anger or to meet me eye. I silently apologise to Ikey for this transgression of his laws o' behaviour. It is the biggest game I has ever played, and also the neatest win. I would have liked to play de Silva clean, for in the end I was sure I had the better of him.

Nottingham's promissory notes, plus the five-pound stake money Hawk gave him, takes care of twenty-five pounds of our freedom money and, while we still has to give him another twenty-five to make up the fifty, we have Hawk's original twenty-five pounds back plus close to thirty more. Our freedom has come to us at a great profit!

I lean back and give the gelt to Hawk, who I am proud to say don't smile. He folds the notes carefully and puts them into his pocket and slips the gold sovereigns into his purse. I turns back to the table and suddenly the old fear rises in me like swamp mist. Here, in the smoke-filled room of Kororareka gaol-house, I sniff the early morning scent of the wilderness, smell the wet damp earth under my nostrils as I lie over the skinned Huon log with my breeches down around me ankles. My heart is beating furious again. The mongrels are here in this room and they has us trapped.

I turn quickly to see that Maple and Syrup have come to stand on either side of Hawk. I look 'round. The Hairy Horror is standing beside the window holding his rum bottle by the neck, his great, ugly, tattooed phiz smiling drunkenly. His tiny eyes is hard as black agates and I know Hawk and me is in danger.

The huge Maori smashes the bottle against the window sill. The bottle is not more than half empty and a shower o' dark rum splashes into me face and over me blouse, so that me eyes sting and for a moment I can't see nothin'. I am too frightened even to lick at the rum and when me eyes clear I sees Hori Hura moving slowly towards Hawk with the jagged green bottle neck clutched in his enormous fist.

'You give back me money, nigger!' he growls.

Chapter Eight

HAWK

Kororareka
March 1857

I have just completed putting our winnings away when the two Parkhurst boys come to stand on either side of the chair to which I'm shackled. I am feeling most proud of Tommo, who has won us our freedom, and so I take little notice of Maple and Syrup. They are both small men, now somewhat tipsy, and I do not feel intimidated, though perhaps a trifle uneasy.

Nottingham seems most agitated by the events of the evening, and his complexion has gone from a rose to purple hue. This I cannot understand as he will soon be twenty-five pounds the richer. I suppose he is playing the bad loser. With the twenty pounds in markers that we have and the five-pound buy-in he owes us, he will no longer collect the full fifty.

I hear the sound of glass shattering and a shower of dark liquid hits Tommo in the face, splashing across his blouse as Hori Hura smashes his rum bottle against the window sill. He pushes the jagged neck and shoulder of the bottle towards me.

Maple and Syrup grab at my arms and of course my ankle is shackled to the chair leg. Nottingham is grinning evilly and behind him Mrs Barrett and Captain de Silva have backed away in alarm, their hands and backs flat against the opposite wall.

'Hawk!' Tommo yells as the two Parkhurst boys cling tighter to my arms and the huge Maori draws closer. 'The chair leg! Break it!'

I am not quite sure what happens next, for I have never fully tried my strength, other than to lift a firkin of beer ten times above my head as a joke for Mary's brewery workers, and to punish Jenkins when he tormented Tommo. But I stand up as much as my shackle-chain allows and jerk my arms free, sending the two villains flying backwards across the room. Then I lift the chair and with my free hand break off the leg. With the chain, and the chair leg attached to it, still about my ankle, I face the Hairy Horror. He hesitates a moment, giving me just enough time to swing the broken chair at him before the neck of jagged glass slashes towards my face. Hori Hura takes the blow on his shoulder, staggering sideways a single pace, and the glass misses me.

From deep inside of me comes a rage so cold and hard that everything in the room seems to slow down. I drop the chair, which appears to bounce on the floor, and I watch as my left fist takes an eternity to swing through the air and connect with the jaw of the fat man in front of me. He too moves backwards, and I hit him again with my right hand, the bones in his nose smashing beneath my bare knuckles. The broken bottle drops from his hand and he starts to fall. His eyes roll to white as the back of his head hits the stone floor. 'Get Maple and Syrup!' Tommo calls out, and I turn.

It is at that moment that I feel a terrible pain in my own head and all goes black.

We are back in our cell and I am manacled and shackled again. My head throbs mightily and my back, not fully healed, is wet with blood. I imagine it has torn open again, though I feel no real pain except for my head. Tommo too is much bruised about the face and has lost his blouse. His torso is black and blue and one eye a persimmon shiner, now completely closed. His lips are swollen so that he looks somewhat like a parrot fish. If he is any indication, the two of us must be a very sorry sight indeed.

'How's you feeling?' asks Tommo.

'Crook,' I croak. 'My head feels broken open.'

'That's because it is,' Tommo says. 'You've blood on yer back from yer head where they hit you with the chair, but it's stopped bleeding now.'

I suddenly remember and grab at my pocket where I have put our winnings.

'Don't bother yerself,' Tommo says bitterly. 'Bastards took the lot!'

'Nottingham? Where's Nottingham?'

'Buggered if I know. Ain't seen hide nor hair of the sod since last night.'

'What's the time?' I ask.

'Past dawn, though not much, the birds ain't been singing long.'

'What happened, did you see?'

Tommo tries to grin through his bruised lips. 'I never seen a better left and right thrown. Bam-bam! You pole-axed him!'

'Did I? What happened after that?'

Tommo tells me that when I turned around to hit Maple and Syrup, Nottingham picked up the broken chair and smashed it down on the back of my head so that it was dicky-birds and bursting stars as I joined Hori Hura on the floor.

'Meanwhile there I is, trying to break the leg off me bleedin' chair, same as what you done!' Tommo attempts a cheeky grin and shrugs. 'Mind, it must've been a much stronger chair 'cause the bloody leg don't budge. Then the two Parkhurst boys rush over and beats the living daylights out o' me. When they's given me face a good going over they topples the chair and puts the boot in while Nottingham just stands by and watches! One o' the bastards kicks me on the side o' the noggin and I'm history. Next thing I knows I wake up back in here behind bars.'

'Did you see who it was who took our winnings?'

'Nah, must have been after. I woke up and it were black as pitch in here. Me first thought were to find you. My ankles are tied though me hands are free and so I feels about and finds your head and me hand comes away full o' blood. Jesus, I thinks, they's killed you. But then you moans, so I knows you ain't dead – yet! I were shitting meself until enough light come to see you was gunna live!'

'Only just,' I groan. I lift my manacled hands to touch my head and realise that I am swathed in a sort of turban. I sniff the sour smell of rum and realise it is Tommo's blouse torn into strips. My brother has taken the shirt off his back to bandage my head.

The sun is well up and pushing through the little barred window high up in the wall of the cell. I think I shall die of thirst at any moment. Then there is a rattle of keys and the door swings open. The dark shape of Sergeant Nottingham stands there, the

daylight streaming into the cell behind his fat silhouette. Beyond
Nottingham is another man. As our eyes adjust, I see that he is a
constable, who carries two tin mugs and half a loaf of bread before
him on a small wooden tray. He puts this down at Nottingham's
feet and withdraws.

Tommo pulls himself over to the mugs using his arms. They
have used handcuffs to manacle his ankles. He reaches out for the
water but Nottingham's broken boot comes down on his hand.

'Not so fast, lad! Well, well, a touch thirsty then, is we?'

Tommo does not look up. 'Yes,' he sniffs.

'Yes, Sergeant Nottingham, sir!'

'Yes, sir,' Tommo says again.

Nottingham kicks at one of the mugs and it spills all of its
water as it rolls across the cell floor to rest at my feet. 'One to go,
lad. We must have proper manners now, show respect for our
betters! It's not "Yes!" It's "Yes, Sergeant Nottingham, sir!"'

Tommo is silent a moment. Then he snaps, 'You're a mongrel
bastard, Nottingham!'

Nottingham kicks the second mug over. 'Oops!' he says.
'Excuse I!'

'Where's our money, Sergeant Nottingham?' I ask.

'Oho! The nigger speaks! Money? What money?' He feigns
confusion.

'We struck a bargain – fifty pounds for our freedom.'

'Money? Freedom? I'm sure I don't know what on earth you're
on about, lad. Bribe, is it?' He throws back his head and chuckles.
'Oh, I see, a bribe, you're offering me a bribe? Fancy that! Fifty
pounds?' Nottingham clucks his tongue several times. 'Fraid I can't
give a known murderer freedom at the cost o' fifty pounds or even
a hundred. Matter o' duty and respect to my vocation.'

'Sir, I am not a murderer!' I rasp. 'Mr Nestbyte's death was an
accident which occurred while hunting the whale.'

'Nestbyte?' Nottingham frowns and touches the side of his
bulbous nose with the tip of his forefinger. 'Oh, yes! Yankee from
the whaler, wasn't it?' The gaoler shakes his head slowly. 'No, no,
no, lad. Not him! This be *another* murder altogether. A *second*
murder! I have arrested you for the murder of Hori Hura!'

He dusts his hands together and lifts his boot from Tommo's
hand, then kicks him in the ribs with the toe-cap. Tommo goes
rolling over but manages to bite back the pain.

'As for you, let's call it accessory before the fact! Aiding and abetting to the crime o' murder most foul.' Nottingham smiles expansively. 'The motive being attempted robbery, seventy-eight pounds took from five honourable gentlemen before you both were most bravely apprehended by yours truly with the help of Messrs Tate and Lyle. Attempted gaol-break valiantly prevented. Wouldn't be at all surprised if there's a commendation in it for me, and a medal from the governor presented to them two, for courage in the face of extreme danger.'

Nottingham farts loudly then pats his belly and burps, highly pleased with himself. 'This time the jury won't even be put to the trouble o' choosing between a heathen nigger and a Christian Quaker gentleman. This time there be five witnesses, all men of good repute, including a police officer.' He waves his hand airily and chuckles. 'The magistrate in Auckland will be delighted that he has been saved a long, tedious trial.'

I listen to Nottingham with growing consternation. The fat gaoler has tricked us out of our money and has me destined for the rope.

'It was self-defence, an accident, Sergeant Nottingham!' I cry. 'He was coming at me with a broken bottle, you saw it yourself!'

'Broken bottle? No sign of a broken bottle! No witnesses to a broken bottle! Nay, lad, that won't wash, won't wash at all!'

'You're a bastard, Nottingham!' Tommo spits again. 'I beat your scam and now you's robbed us of what's rightfully ours.'

Nottingham's mood changes quickly and he points angrily to Tommo. 'You're a brash young lad, Solomon. I'd bite my tongue if I were you. Evidence is clear enough – you and the nigger escaped from your cell and come across the five of us playing a nice friendly game o' cards in my charge office.' He changes back to his laconic self. 'No harm in a game o' cards, now is there? Tried to rob us, you did, demands our money or else. Threatens us with a chair leg! Ripped right off, it were. Hori Hura bravely leaps to our defence and is knocked to the floor and killed before the rest of us manages to overpower the two of you.' Nottingham pauses, shrugs and grins. 'Except for Captain de Silva, who has sailed away to whaling on the mornin' tide, there are four of us what will swear to the truth of this in front of the judge.'

I look at Nottingham, shaking my head. 'Six into eighty pounds is only thirteen pounds and six shillings each. If you'd taken our side you would have earned yourself almost twice, twenty-five pounds, even after you redeemed your promissory notes. It makes no sense.'

'Don't you tell me what makes sense, nigger! What don't make sense is that the likes of you should escape Jack Ketch! I shall take pleasure in watching you dangle from the beam.'

'You never did intend to let us escape, did you?' I say.

'Ya tried to work a double scam!' Tommo shouts. 'A doublecross! It were the Portugee captain what was meant to take the night with a running flush!'

Nottingham doesn't deny this, but sends a gob of spittle to the floor. 'You'll be going to Auckland tomorrow, took by boat, full manacles and shackles,' he says, then he stoops and picks up the half-loaf of bread. 'Maybe you'll have better manners when you be a little more hungry and thirsty, eh lads?' With this he clangs the heavy door shut, taking the bread with him.

We look at each other, waiting until the rattle of the keys dies away and we can hear Nottingham's footsteps departing.

'What on earth are we gunna do?' groans Tommo.

'We must try to get a message to Mary, have her call upon the governor so that he might intervene, talk to Governor Gore Browne over here.'

'It'll take too long for her to get here, we'll be dead by then.'

'*You* will not die, Tommo – only I perhaps,' I hasten to comfort him.

Tommo swallows. 'I wouldn't want to go on without you, Hawk.'

'Of course you would.' I try to remain cheerful. 'You could get drunk every day with nobody to nag you.'

Tommo falls silent for a while then begins to talk. 'More than once in the wilderness I wanted to give it away, toss it in, just walk out into the river and keep walking, but you were always there with me. I didn't know what had become of you, maybe the same as me, but I knew you was not dead, felt it in me bones. Long as I felt that, I could hang on.' He grins. 'I admits, I done it with the help o' Slit's whisky still. Without that,' he shrugs, 'I dunno.'

Then he says slowly, 'That were drinking with hope. The hope that one day we'd be together again. If the mongrels gets you now, strings you up, and leaves me here, that be drinking without hope. I'd sooner be dead, you and me together on the gallows, Tommo and Hawk together to the last breath.'

'Come here, Tommo,' I say.

Tommo crawls over to me.

'I can't hug you because I'm shackled, but you can hug me, little brother,' I say to him.

Tommo grabs my arm in both his hands and, putting his head against my shoulder, begins to weep softly. 'Oh God, I loves ya, Hawk!' he sobs. I can feel that he weeps not because of our predicament, but for all the years in the wilderness, all the loneliness. He cries for all the love in him that has dried up and shouldn't have.

'I love you too, Tommo,' I say. 'More than ever I can say!' And there we are, both of us bawling our eyes out.

It is Tommo who finally clears his throat to speak. 'Ya know what gives me the screaming shits most of all?'

'What?' I sniff.

'The fucking mongrels has won!'

'Only when the trap-door opens under our feet. We aren't dead yet,' I say, but there is not a great deal of conviction in my voice.

'Looks as though this time the Sheriff o' bloody Nottingham *did* get Robin Hood. What a turn-up for the books,' Tommo sighs.

I try to lighten the subject. 'Know what gives *me* the, er, shits?'

'What?' he asks.

'I never had a chance to know Maid Marian.'

'You still a virgin then? Well I never!' Tommo laughs.

I nod my head and grin, imitating Ikey. 'Absolutely and with certainty and not to be doubted, my dears, the wiles o' the fairer sex be most mystifying and bedding one what's not a whore is a most tricky set o' peregrinations and not always a journey o' the heart worth the sweat of one's brow!'

Tommo laughs again. 'It were the only nice part o' the wilderness, women wanting a taste o' liquor for a favour granted.'

I think to myself that I wouldn't wish it that way. Once perhaps, just to know what it feels like, but then I'd want something different. Not that I know anything about loving a woman. But I've seen how Mary looks at Mr Emmett and he at her. I don't think anything is going on between them – their different stations in life don't allow it – but the softness you can feel between those two, that's what I'd like to have.

Tommo interrupts my thoughts. 'You ain't missed a lot, swiving's a bit disappointing really. Well the sort of stuff I has done, anyway,' he laughs. 'Knee-tremblers, sort of. Breeches still on!'

I try to imagine what he's talking about. I think of these knee-tremblers and my size and I can see in my mind it isn't possible. Besides, I'm a nigger – I don't suppose any woman would have me unless I paid for it.

'Tommo, have you, er, been in love? You know, like in the library books?' I ask. I don't like to admit to him that I've read everything in Mrs Dean's Hobart Town Lending Library, including the romances!

'Nah,' he says, 'I reckon love only happens in them stories.'

'I hope not,' I says.

I must have sounded wistful because Tommo shakes his head. 'Christ Jesus, Hawk! What's wrong with ya? First you want men to have a bloody conscience, now you want a woman what loves you! And you want to love her back! You got about as much chance o' finding a woman to love as you got o' giving mongrels like Nottingham a conscience! Better keep on pullin' your pud, that way you'll meet a better class of woman than what would think to mix with the likes of us!'

I laugh. Tommo as always is the practical man. I can well imagine the dainty little lass that I'd like for my own, but I can't imagine anyone like her agreeing to marry me. Anyway, it's all pointless, isn't it? Nothing but divine intervention will save our lives now.

I think of our beloved mama and her life's motto, 'I shall never surrender.' I cheer up a bit at this thought. Perhaps I can delay the trial. I have read a little of the law, Mary always being anxious to know her rights, and the other brewers in Hobart Town ever threatening to force her out of business by means of the law. In their opinion, a woman has no right to be in brewing and moreover to be successful at it. Subpoenas, it seems, are a way of life with the pure merino brewers. Beer and barristers go together like a horse and cart.

'What's that noise?' Tommo asks abruptly. His ears are all the sharper for his time in the wilderness. 'It's people,' he answers himself, 'coming our way.' We fall silent, both listening. 'A mob . . . marching,' Tommo says, 'coming closer, here maybe.'

Then I hear it, faintly, I cannot tell from what direction. We wait and by and by the shouting and marching grows louder. 'What do you think it is?' I ask.

Tommo shrugs. 'Buggered if I knows.'

The noise escalates until we are sure it's a very large mob, heading towards the gaol. Strains of singing float toward us, mingled with shouting. Tommo listens intently, trying to make out the words. 'Shit! They're after us!' he cries.

Now I hear it for myself. '*Utu! Utu!*' Revenge! Revenge!

'Maori,' Tommo says quietly. 'Oh no, they's after you for killing the Hairy Horror!'

We listen as someone shouts for silence, and there's a hush as someone addresses the crowd. It's Nottingham. But his voice is quickly drowned out by a great roar of protest as a thunder of stones rain down on the corrugated iron roof. '*Utu! Utu! Utu!*' The chanting takes up again, though some of it is lost under the rain of rocks. We hear cheering and the sound of running and more rocks being thrown. Then we smell smoke. Fire!

'They's burning us down!' Tommo cries again. 'The bastards is burning us out!'

Suddenly there is a rattle of keys and the cell door is flung open. Four Maori push through the door with others crowding behind them. Beyond them, I can see nothing but smoke. There is no one to save us. They drag me out of the cell, cursing and shouting. I struggle as much as I can, but the manacles and shackles restrain me. Two of them, both big men, have me by the legs and two about the shoulders and then others rush to join them until a dozen hands are attached to me. I hear Tommo yelling behind me but there is no way I can turn around. 'Tommo, get out, don't fight!' I scream and then begin to cough from the smoke.

I am carried out to the front of the gaol and there is a terrible baying from the crowd which surges forward, shouting, '*Utu! Utu!*'

The crowd is now all around me. My abductors lift me high above their heads while others push and strike at the howling mob, beating them back as frantic hands try to claw at me. If my captors let me go I will be kicked and torn apart by the angry mob. The posse abducting me force their way through the roaring crowd, shouting threats and using their fists, until we reach a horse-drawn cart. I am thrown into it while several of the Maori leap aboard, sitting upon my body and at the same time shouting and kicking at the crowd who now surround the cart, holding on to it.

Soon we are clear of the main mob though others continue to run after us and some to hurl stones. A shower of rocks hits the cart and also one of the Maori who sits upon my chest. He gives a gasp and is knocked senseless, slumping forward.

I am sure my end is near, but my most immediate concern is for Tommo. If the crowd gets hold of him they will tear him to pieces. I begin to sob for my twin, whom I shall never see again.

By now we are pulling away from the town of Kororareka. As we travel up a small hill I can see a great billow of black smoke coming from the gaol-house. The road is deep-rutted and the cart bounces badly so that my blouse, stiffened with the dried blood of the previous night, grates against my back which is soon again soaked. Tommo's turbanned bandage is also leaking blood which I can feel running down my neck. I have not drunk water since the previous night and know without it I will soon faint from exhaustion in the day's heat.

'*Kahore o wai? Homai he wai moku,*' I croak. Have you any water? Please give me some water! I beg in Maori, though I must repeat myself several times to be heard above the rattle of the cart. A bottle of water is held to my mouth and I drink greedily as it rattles against my teeth, but it is too soon removed. I feel much recovered, though sick at heart when I think of Tommo at the hands of the mob.

For over a week I am transported on the back of that cart, with no word of explanation from my captors. They give me food and water, but they do not engage in conversation with me. Fatigue and injury have dulled my mind and I am a passive enough prisoner. We have long since left the road and taken paths that lead through forest glades or cut through the tu-tu grass that often towers high above the cart.

For seven days we pass no human settlement but, as the shadows begin to fall on our eighth day, we come to a village beside a small mountain stream. The others climb down from the cart and I am left to lie alone. Soon children with big brown eyes and serious expressions come to look at me. They are for the most part naked. Each time I move in my chains they scatter like startled chickens. But they soon enough return to stare silently at me again. I daresay they have not seen a nigger before and I am to them as curious a sight as an unknown species of wild beast.

It is not long since the Maori have forsaken cannibalism and there is often talk that it is still practised in remote regions where the pakeha are afraid to go. Perhaps this will be my unhappy end, to be eaten at a great feast. I am almost resigned. The law will not find me here, and even if it should, the courts would treat me no better than the Maori. After the authorities have broken my neck they would feed me to the worms, which I think is no better than the cannibal's cooking pot.

In days past, the Maori believed that to eat your enemy made you strong. The chief must inherit the strength of the chief and all the others he has killed in battle and to do so he must drink their blood and swallow their eyes so that the spirits of his victims add to his power, his *mana*. All this Hammerhead Jack told me in the long days we spent together at sea. When my friend's eye was destroyed by Nestbyte, he explained that it was no great tragedy for it was the right eye and not the left. The godhead of a chief, and the spirit of the Maori, lives in the left eye. Had his left eye been destroyed, he would not have wished to survive, for he would have lost his *mana*.

From what I have observed of the white settlers and their soldiers and policemen, the Maori people will need all their strength if they are not to be reduced to the status of beggars and drunkards in their own country. I have seen what has been done to the Aborigines in Van Diemen's Land and hope that the same will not happen to the Maori.

Perhaps it is better after all that I be eaten in an ancient ceremony than die in ignominy. I would much prefer a warrior's sharp teeth to slow consumption by maggots. Despite my misery I smile to myself. After all, what Tommo calls Mary's white tablecloth religion is based on a good Sunday roast!

I can hear God sitting at the table of the Maori chief.

'Did you say a nice leg o' pork, my dear?' God asks the chief of the cannibals.

'No, Sir,' says the chief. 'This be a nice leg o' *Hawk*!'

But then my humour changes. I am too sore and uncomfortable not to feel pity for myself. I think about my neck, how it seems to have an affinity for the rope. I lift my manacled hands to touch the band of silver tissue, the bright scar caused by the wild man when I was seven years old. It is now a well-defined track where the hangman will neatly fit the final loop of hemp to break my neck, that is if Nottingham and his Auckland jury should catch up with me. What a sorry end I shall have either way.

When I took Tommo from Brodie's sly grog shop I was bitterly saddened by Mary's anger and banishment. And yet I had thought we might have a great adventure together and return to our mama with Tommo sober and both of us much experienced in the world. Now, in the late afternoon, with the shadows falling in a strange village, I think of how little luck poor Tommo has had. How his mongrels have followed us and how, through no wrongdoing of our own, our young lives will soon end: him burned to death in the prison or torn to pieces by a mob of angry savages, and me eaten by same.

The children are clambering more boldly upon the cart and some reach out and touch me, then pull their hands away quickly as though I have burnt their fingers. I ask for water and try to smile but they are completely taken aback at the sound of my voice. They leap wildly from the cart and scatter, the smaller ones fleeing helter-skelter, their tiny feet shooting back puffs of dust as they run, yelling in terror as if followed by a wild, black beast.

And then a large voice rings out. 'Ork! Ork good!' And this is followed by a great laugh which resounds in the gathering dusk. It is none other than Hammerhead Jack!

My old friend soon has me ensconced in a large hut where a couple of plump older wahines minister to me. They cut away my blouse and gently remove the coarse linen from the broken wounds on my back, laughing every time I wince, as though it is a huge joke. They clap their hands whenever I find a word to use in their language.

The women make a poultice of leaves and sticky ointment which they apply tenderly to my skin, packing it in with black mud which is left to dry. Whatever the medicine is, my back is soon quite comfortable. Next they remove Tommo's turbanned bandage and shave the hair from the back of my head using the edge of a sharpened shell, which proves most effective. They laugh at my springy black curls, which one of the women gathers in her hand and cups to her thighs. After much cackling at this, they tend my head wound most caringly.

I drink what must be a gallon of water, and eat a large dish of yams and sweet potatoes with a little meat mixed in. Finally the kind women remove the poultices and bathe me, laughing all the more when I will not submit to the removal of my breeches. They carefully wrap a blanket around my shoulders.

It is well into the evening, with a three-quarter moon risen in a clear, clean starry heaven, when I am taken to the *marae*, the meeting place to attend a *hui*, a gathering of the men.

I am asked most politely to sit on a bright woven mat before the elders, the *runanga*, while the rest of the men are seated behind me. This, I surmise, is the *kawa* of the *marae* – good etiquette, which shows respect for me. Hammerhead Jack then addresses the gathering, speaking too quickly for me to understand everything he is saying. I soon realise, however, that he is telling of our voyage and the killing of the sperm whale. He points often to me, whereupon the elders facing me smile and those behind me murmur their approval.

My giant friend's arm socket is much improved and the skin, though tender in appearance, has no suppuration and is clean and healthy looking. The wound from his missing eye has healed up completely, the skin about the socket puckered like a Christmas prune. In the meantime, the left eye seems to have grown curiously larger and brighter in his huge head, and it is not so difficult to believe that his godhead lives there. This eye is most commanding. It opens wide and darts about as he talks, almost as though he is a cyclops.

Hammerhead Jack has the same air of authority about him as he did on board ship, while he still shows respect and pays obeisance to his chief. The chief is a man not much older than him, a tall solidly built *rangatira*, though somewhat smaller in stature than the whaleman. Finally, with a grand sweep of his good arm and a big smile, Hammerhead Jack points to me and says, 'Ork, good!' Then he bids me stand. After much poking out of his tongue and slapping of his thighs, he finally rubs noses with me.

Amidst cheering and clapping, the chief, whose name is Wiremu Tamihana, bids me sit again. He calls out and beckons to someone seated behind me. Presently a young Maori about my age comes to the front and, speaking in tolerably good English, translates the chief's speech of welcome to me. I later learn that Wiremu Tamihana speaks excellent English and has been well educated by missionaries but chooses not to use the invaders' tongue.

Chief Wiremu Tamihana first thanks me for saving Hammerhead Jack's life and says that his people are much honoured to have a brave man among them. He asks me to remove my blanket and show the lashes I have taken on behalf of his tribesman.

'Here is a man who has given his blood for the Maori people! Is he not our brother and welcome in the Ngati Haua tribe?' the young translator declares.

The chief tells me I am welcome to stay and that they will hide me from the pakeha policemen who might come looking. There is no mention of the death of Hori Hura and it is clear they do not see me as guilty of any crime against one of their own people.

The Maori chief ends by saying that his people cannot trust Queen Victoria, who has taken their *mana*, their land, their prestige, and their substance, from them and left them only the shadow. They have twenty muskets and ammunition and the men are well trained in the use of the *taiaha*, the fighting stick which, during earlier skirmishes against the pakeha, proved much superior to the British soldier's bayonet.

At this the men show their delight, stamping their feet and slapping their thighs to make a thunderous whacking noise which reverberates through the dark night. The chief then holds up his hand to silence them. 'We cannot fight the pakeha. We are one tribe only and too few. We must come together. All the Maori people must speak with one voice.'

Some of the men voice their consternation when he says this and I can see the elders are not of one accord on the matter. But Chief Tamihana does not wish to discuss it and, instead, invites me to talk.

I am still not well and have only a little voice left, so I ask the young Maori who speaks English to stand close. I speak slowly, using as many Maori words as I am able, and thank them for saving my life. I offer my service to the tribe, though I have no training in firearms and admit that, despite my size, I am no warrior. I have never killed a man.

'We will teach you, Ork!' Hammerhead Jack shouts jovially. 'It is much easier than killing a whale!'

This is followed by much laughter from the others and I begin to wonder whether my offer was wise. When the merriment lessens, I agree with their chief that the Maori people must speak as one voice. 'Many voices speaking at the same time can only be heard as a babble,' I say. 'The pakeha have the governor who can listen to their many voices and speak for them as one voice. Their unity is their strength.' I do not take this further, for the chief has already made his point.

'I can read and write and have some knowledge of how the white man thinks,' I say, thinking this a poor substitute for these warriors' experience, but it is all I have. 'I have studied the methods by which the soldiers of Queen Victoria fight and this may also be useful. To know the mind of the enemy is always of some advantage.'

'And how was the mind of the enemy, Captain O'Hara, when we chopped off his hand?' Hammerhead Jack asks gleefully. It is clear they all know the story, because there is another wave of laughter among the men.

'I am not sure that it was a wise thing to do,' I say, trying to force a smile.

Now the men are completely silent and I can see from the expression on Hammerhead Jack's face that he is confused.

Then the chief addresses me in English, to my surprise. 'Ork, do you know much of the missionary talk?'

'Some,' I say. 'But I am not of their faith.'

'Me neither, though I know some of their ways,' he says, as the lad now translates his words back into Maori for the elders. 'Does it not say an eye for an eye and a tooth for a tooth in the missionary's black book?' I nod. Indicating Hammerhead Jack, the chief continues, 'Well, my blood brother has lost his eye and not taken the white man's eye in return!' He points at the shoulder joint which once held the giant Maori's arm. 'And the pakeha has taken my brother's arm and we have *only* taken a hand in return. Why is this not wise?'

'The pakeha have laws which, when they are disobeyed, lead to severe punishment. We should not take the law into our own hands but must wait for a proper judgment,' I reply, though it sounds rather foolish even to me.

But the chief does not at once dismiss this. 'Ha!' he exclaims. 'Then which is the more important, the laws of Queen Victoria or the laws of the pakeha God?'

'In theory, the laws of God.' The chief can see that I am struggling with my reply and raises his hand.

'We are told that we must obey Queen Victoria, who is the most powerful pakeha. But we are also told that even she must obey the Christian God. Is that not true?'

'It is true, but . . .' I begin.

The chief stops me. 'So, the laws of the Christian God say we

171

must take an eye for an eye and an arm for an arm. When we take only a hand in return for an eye *and* an arm, and do not return the beating you took and the other Maori took to their backs, why will the pakeha whaling captain think we have acted badly?'

Tamihana pauses. 'I am told he is a Christian. Why, under the laws of his own God, should he not be grateful for losing only his hand?'

It is difficult to argue with the flow of his reasoning. I have read the Bible twice over, and there is much within it I have come to respect. To me, the stumbling block has always been that men piously preach God's laws on the Sabbath, but practise man's laws on the following six days. Any fool may see that the two are in direct contradiction – that in fact greed and corruption transcend charity and compassion in society.

'The Maori have much to fear from the pakeha laws but we cannot defeat them by ignoring them,' I venture. 'We must learn to use their own laws against them.'

'Ha!' The chief points to Hammerhead Jack. 'Like my brother, the pakeha laws have only one eye. The other is blind and cannot see the Maori people. The governor never does anything if a Maori is killed – only when a pakeha is killed!'

I shrug. 'The white man will not leave New Zealand. They will not go away. Queen Victoria has the Treaty of Waitangi, the paper which is signed by many of the Maori chiefs.'

'Then we must tear it from her hand! She has stolen our *mana*!' the chief replies.

'It is said that since the Maori people have learned to use the pakeha guns, they have killed more than twenty thousand of their own people and as many have died from the white man's diseases. There are now as many pakeha as Maori in New Zealand.' I know this from reading the *Colonial Times* back in Hobart Town.

The chief shows no surprise at my words, and sighs. 'You are right, Ork. We are allowed to kill each other as we please and Queen Victoria does nothing to stop us. Only if we kill the pakeha must we go to gaol. Is this not strange? Did she not swear at the Treaty that the Maori and the pakeha would be the same under her law? Or do you think Queen Victoria likes us to kill each other so the white man will soon become greater in number than the Maori?'

'What can I say? I am young and not wise.' I take a deep breath and gather my courage. 'But you are right, Chief Tamihana, you will only be strong when you speak with one voice. Now you are single tribes and can easily be divided. As long as tribe fights tribe and Maori hates Maori, the pakeha will always win. Believe me, I am on your side, Wiremu Tamihana. The pakeha do not win because their laws are more just or their God is more powerful, but because they all fight for one Queen.'

The chief nods. 'I will think upon this. I am the *ariki*, the descendant of the eldest son of the eldest son of each generation since the Maori came here from beyond the clouds and the bending of the earth line. I will talk to the ancestors.' Then he asks again, 'You think the Maori must have a leader, like Queen Victoria?'

The notion is, I can see, a new one for Tamihana, who frowns as he thinks about what I have said. 'It is not for me to say, Chief Tamihana. I do not know the Maori customs.' I search for further explanations. 'But one big tribe which fights together under one leader will win the war over many smaller ones which fight alone.'

'Ah! One tribe, one war! You are a good man, Ork.' The chief smiles.

'Ork good!' Hammerhead Jack cries, amidst much cheering.

I wait until the noise has died down. 'I would like to ask something for myself?' I say to the chief.

Chief Tamihana nods, granting me permission to make my request. I turn to Hammerhead Jack.

'My brother, Tommo? Can we find out what has happened to him?'

The men laugh anew and I look about me in distress. How can they laugh at this? Hammerhead Jack knows we are twins and very close. He grins broadly. 'Ho! The little axe man!' His single eye grows wide and shines bright, as though it has taken in the light from the missing other. 'Tommo is Maori also! He will join you in two days, Ork.' He holds up two fingers. 'We will welcome him when he comes. We have taken him another way to confuse the pakeha policeman. He is with the old man and the others who were together with us in the whaleboat.' Hammerhead Jack takes a step towards me and puts his huge single arm about my shoulder. 'Tommo good! Ork good!'

I try very hard to restrain myself, but all can see the bright tears that run down my cheeks and the stupid smile upon my black face. Though we are fugitives, for the moment Tommo and I have beaten the mongrels.

BOOK TWO

Chapter Nine

TOMMO

The Land of the Long White Cloud
June 1858

We has been gone nearly two years from Hobart Town and has lived among the Maori for over a year. We's playing it safe even though there was never any warrant for our arrest. From what we've heard the authorities believe that the Maori attacking the prison was seeking revenge for the death of Hori Hura. No doubt we's thought to be well and truly dead! The government troopers wasn't too keen to come in search of us even if we *was* still alive, for there be a growing dispute between the white settlers and the Maori people over possession o' the land. A bad quarrel is brewin' as the settlers becomes more greedy for Maori land, and the Maori chiefs more suspicious and unwilling to sell.

To send troopers in search of them what's killed two criminals, what was going to hang anyway, weren't deemed in the best interests o' the colony. Instead, the whole business has been quickly forgotten in the name of diplomacy. Sergeant Nottingham were given the boot and retired on a government pension. We hears he has become another drunk, cadging drinks in Kororareka's hotels. Maple and Syrup has absconded to Auckland, while Mrs Barrett ain't been seen since the night o' the card game, his whereabouts unknown. De Silva, o' course, sailed happily away.

What a rescue it were! Smoke and shouting everywhere and

I'm thinking it's all over for me and Hawk when he is carried out of the cell by four savages. Soon after, three blokes grab yours truly, and I expects we'll both be torn to pieces by the mob.

As they push me out of the cell, I sees Hawk through the smoke. He's being carried over the heads of his captors to the front of the gaol and I tries to follow him as they takes him towards the door. But them what's got a hold of me shoves me down a passageway towards the back of the gaol-house. In the corridor we come across Nottingham. He is on his hands and knees, with blood coming out his nose and mouth, coughing and wheezing from the smoke.

'Ya mongrel bastard, Nottingham!' I screams. 'Your scam failed, didn't it, you two-faced bludger!'

I suppose I should've saved me voice to pray for me life, but at that moment I hates the sod so much, I don't give a damn! Me brother's going to be killed 'cause of him and I only wish I had me axe so I could do the same to him. I hope the fire roasts the miserable pig like Sam Slit!

I can hear the crowd outside howling for blood. Strange, I ain't afraid for meself, only for Hawk. Without him there ain't no point anyways: might as well be back in the wilderness, or dead. I only hopes they make it quick. I don't want to die slow – hands clawing at me, feet kicking and stamping, me bones crunching under their sticks and stones. The mob is braying now. It's a weird sound. They must have Hawk, I reckons. I wish they'd kill me first, so I don't have to bear the pain o' hearing me brother bashed to death.

'May you rot in hell, Nottingham!' I screams as I'm bundled out the back door.

'Him mongril, Tommo,' shouts one of the Maori holding me about the shoulder, then laughs. I stares around in surprise. It is one of me mates from the *Nankin Maiden*! In me panic I haven't recognised him. What's happening here? I thinks. There's no one outside the back o' the gaol-house and them what's running me towards the bay are laughing like it's a huge joke.

Pretty soon we comes to a canoe well hidden on the beach, and we're off across the water and out to sea. We travels up the coast for several miles, then leave the canoe and head into the wilderness.

For over a week, we walks through mountains and valleys. Several times, we comes to a stream and we stops to bathe. It feels like we're goin' in circles and we does much of our walking in rivers to lose our footprints. Finally, towards the evening of the tenth day, we come to the *pa* of the Ngati Haua tribe and then into the village and there's Hawk sitting large as life with Hammerhead Jack.

Though me Maori friends has told me often enough along the way that Hawk would be all right, I were feared he could not make it through the mob unharmed. Hawk be just as happy to see yours truly as I am to see him and to me mortification, he lifts me high above the ground, swinging me up in his great arms as if I be some snot-nosed brat. But I can't wipe the grin off me stupid gob, as the tears roll down Hawk's cheeks. Hammerhead Jack roars with laughter and I can see he approves. 'We are safe from the mongrels here, Tommo!' Hawk tells me as he returns me to the ground.

And so we has been. But in the course of the year, I've learnt that life among the Maori can be as bloody difficult as life aboard ship. They has so many taboos, things they can and cannot do. They call this *tapu* and it is ruled over by the chief and the priests, the *tohunga*, what are the keepers of the tribe's history and lore. The *tohunga* are big men 'round these parts, second only to the chief himself.

Chief Wiremu Tamihana is not only the tribe's leader but also a kind of god. His *tapu* comes direct from the spirits and is the absolute law. All that the chief touches becomes *tapu* or, as white folk might say, holy.

We've only been in the village a couple of months when we sees how powerful this *tapu* be. Hawk and Chief Tamihana is sitting together, talking, with the chief smoking his pipe. By and by they takes a walk and the chief, not thinking, leaves his tinder-box behind. Four ordinary blokes happen by and, seein' the tinder-box, stops to light their pipes. But when they finds out whose tinder-box it be, they realise they has committed a terrible sacrilege by using it and they dies of fright. Truly, they dies! They is all stone dead, not twelve hours later, of the fear brought on by the *tapu*.

Tapu is most powerful in the chief, and he can get whatever he wants in the tribe just by saying it is his *backbone* or his *right arm* or some other part of his body. When the chief says this, he makes whatever it be sacred, so that no one else, includin' the owner, can go near it again. If a single drop of the chief's blood be spilled upon an object, then it is *tapu*, and can only belong to him.

In the common people, *tapu* is a more simple and practical thing. Say a man finds a piece of driftwood on the beach, he needs only cut a notch in it with his axe, and it becomes *tapu* and his property. What would Ikey thinks of this business, I wonders with a smile. A man can simply pull a single strip of flax across his doorway and no person can enter it until he returns to remove the *tapu*: a most efficient means o' protecting your property!

Of course for the white man, property be only owned by evidence of a government deed and protected by a gun. *Tapu* has often made it hard for the Maori to deal with the pakeha. Many white folks don't bother to learn the importance of their taboos and don't respect their rules. Living amongst the Maori, I has come to understand much about *tapu*, but I still makes mistakes. Hawk though has gone to much trouble to learn some of the complex *tapus* and laws o' the people. This has come in most handy in his dealings with the Ngati Haua tribe and many others. Me brother has become a big man among the natives.

Meself, I've had enough of adventures to last me a lifetime. I want us to move on, to find our way back to Australia. Being here ain't much different to being on the *Nankin Maiden* as Chief Tamihana don't allow grog in his villages, something what makes big brother Hawk happy, o' course! I am now almost two years dry, though not cured in the least of me desire for the fiery grape. Not a single day passes without me thirsting for a drop.

Hawk, meanwhile, is determined that we stay on in this dry place to repay our 'debt' to Hammerhead Jack.

'Debt! What's you mean, debt? We don't owe no debt! *You* saved *his* life!'

'You are wrong, Tommo,' Hawk says in his patient way what makes me want to kick him in the bollocks. 'I only helped him back into the whaleboat.'

'You saved him from the whale! And from being flogged to death!'

'Maybe,' he replies. 'But he saved both of us. Two lives! We owe him at least one, Tommo.'

'Me own, I suppose?' I says, sarcastic-like.

'No, Tommo, you needn't give up your life. But there is much we can do to help.'

Hawk reckons that a great injustice is being done to the native people by the white men. His conscience has got the better of him.

But the world be full o' mongrels and now, with as many settlers in New Zealand as there are Maori, they's taken over this place and claimed it for their own. What can Hawk do to change this? Nothing! But he won't listen. And now he tells me that war is coming.

'War!' I shouts. 'War between the pakeha and the Maori? And you wants us to be a part of it? On the side of the Maori?' I scream at him. 'What can *we* do, a nigger and a skinny runt? For Gawd's sake, let's scarper while we still can!'

'Tommo, we can't, not now!' he says, pleading.

'What? Why not? You gunna be a general in the army or something?'

'Adviser, no more,' Hawk answers calmly. 'The Maori must unite. The tribes must be brought together or they cannot prevail against the government troops and the settlers.'

'You know what?' I says, truly angry now.

'What?'

'You're gunna get us killed, that's what!'

'Listen, Tommo! The settlers, with the connivance of the government, are stealing Maori land. As long as the Maori are divided they have no hope of impressing the governor. They have no collective power to claim their rights under the treaty.'

'Where'd ya learn all this rubbish, Hawk? Nobody has no power to exert against no British government! You think *we's* got power to exert? You think the Aborigines in Tasmania, what's practically all perished at the hands o' the government, had power? You think Georgie Augustus Robinson, the government man what was meant to protect the Abos, was their true friend? All he done was herd Truganini and her people into nowhere so the whites could take their land! What treaty is ya talking about, mate?'

'Waitangi. The Treaty of Waitangi.'

'Waitangi? That piece o' shit-paper! The Maori may as well wipe their arses on it for all the good it will do 'em!'

'It says the Queen will guarantee the full, exclusive and undisturbed possession of their lands and estates, forests and fisheries and other properties they may collectively and individually possess, so long as it is their wish and desire to retain the same in their possession!' Hawk quotes all this right off, so that I want to punch his face in.

I shrug. 'The government's changed its mind, then, like it always does.'

'No, there's more!' says Hawk, his eyes gleaming. 'It is in the rest of the treaty that they are boxing clever now, thinking to evade their responsibility with misinterpretation!'

'Misinterpretation, is it now? Shit, Hawk, wake up!'

'Listen, this is what the New Zealand Company say,' and he takes to quoting again: ' "We have always had very serious doubts whether the Treaty of Waitangi made with naked savages by a consul invested with no plenipotentiary powers . . ."'

'What's pleni-po-tentiary mean?' I asks. Hawk and his big words!

'It means someone what has been given the full powers of the government, like an ambassador.' Hawk answers. 'Where was I? Oh yes . . . "invested with no plenipotentiary powers, without ratification by the Crown, could be treated by lawyers as anything but a praiseworthy device for amusing and pacifying savages for the moment."' Hawk stabs at the air with his finger. 'We *cannot* allow this to happen!'

'We? What's this "we"? Hawk, *we* is not Maori! *We* is supposed to be British, remember! Shit, *we* is supposed to be on the other bloody side, mate!'

'No, no, they are also British, the Maori!'

'British?' Now I'm curious. 'How come?'

Off he goes again and I think what a bloody bore he's gunna be if he ain't careful. ' "In consideration for consent to the Queen's government, the Queen will protect all the Maori people and give them all the rights and privileges of British subjects." ' Hawk looks at me steady. 'So you see, they are the same as the settlers in their entitlements, but their land be taken away from them with a clever ploy, a misrepresentation!'

'There ain't nothin' new in that! That's what governments do for a living, mis-bloody-represent!'

'Tommo, you must understand this thing! It is like we said on the ship, it's a matter of conscience, good men working for the common good of the common man!' He sees me doubtful face and adds, 'Not letting the mongrels win!'

I jerk my head and snort. 'The mongrels always win when they is the government!'

Hawk ignores me and if there were a tub nearby, I swear he'd have took to thumping it. 'The Maori do not possess the land individually like we do. Land is owned by the tribe, and if the individual should use it for his own, it is only by permission of all the tribe as represented by the chief. The tribe allows him to use the *shadow* of the land though the *substance*, the soil itself, belongs to all. It has been their way, their law, since time out of mind.'

'But it ain't our way, is it?' I insist.

'That's right,' says Hawk, 'but the British government understood this difference and recognised it. The treaty states that land can only be sold to the government with the full permission of *all* the tribe and its chief. Settlers may not buy land directly from any individual, only from the government. But the settlers are doing so, and the government is turning a blind eye.'

'There you are, what the eye don't see, the heart don't grieve over!' I claps my hands and laughs. 'Put down your spectacles, gentlemen, the little Queen in London Town owns all the aces in New Zealand! Can't expect her to see across the sea, now can we?'

'No, it's not right, Tommo!' Hawk shouts. 'It's deliberate cheating! It's Queen Victoria cheating her own subjects of what's rightfully theirs!'

'And so you wants to go to war against her? Ha! You must be mad!'

'The Maori people have a saying: "For women and land, men die."'

'And Tommo also has a saying: "We ain't got no women and we ain't got no land and so I'm telling you straight, we ain't gunna die for fuck-all o' nothing!"'

Hawk laughs despite himself. 'The Maori people *must* speak with one voice and Chief Tamihana wishes there to be a Maori king to bring all the tribes together. This he has almost accomplished. A new king will be announced in the next few months.'

'A king for them, a queen for us? You think *that* will solve the problem?'

'Tommo, Chief Tamihana has a most persuasive argument. He asks, "Is there not Queen Victoria of England, Nicholas of Russia, Louis Napoleon of France and Pomara of Tahiti – each a native monarch for their people? Each nation is separate, and I also must have a king for myself."'

'Sure, and *we* already has a queen. Why should we help him?'

Hawk looks hurt. 'Tommo, the Maori have always had their

wars, one tribe hating the other. That's the government's strength, to encourage one against the other, to divide and conquer! Since the musket was introduced to them, the Maori have killed more than twenty thousand of their own people! I can help Chief Tamihana to make peace amongst the tribes.' He is breathing heavy now. 'They have agreed to a king of their own but there is still much dissension between them on other matters. If they may be united then they will be a force to be reckoned with. Their wishes cannot then be ignored by the governor.' Hawk grins suddenly. 'For the first time in my life my colour is useful. I am neither white nor brown, I am as black as the ace of spades, so I have no axe to grind. I'm no threat to either side. This makes me the perfect go-between.'

'That's right, it'll be no different to always! Everybody hates the nigger, so now everyone can hate the black go-between! You be perfect for the job o' being hated,' I says.

'Please let me do this, Tommo! I have been given my voice back and I must use it well. What better way than to stand up for what's right and honest, eh? Chief Tamihana is a good fellow, he wants peace and unity. He has shown us great charity, you know this. He has not spared his hospitality and his people have treated us like their own kind. We have so much to be thankful for.'

'Hawk! We can't live with the Maori forever!' I brings my face close as possible to his. 'We's got to go home soon!'

Hawk's eyebrows shoot up in surprise. 'Home? To Mary? You are ready to go home?' He has this big smile on his gob.

Hawk has been writing to mama and she to him. Chief Tamihana has arranged for our mail to be collected from Auckland. Mama writes all her letters to 'Mr H. Abacus' as the authorities reckon Hawk Solomon's dead and he'd soon enough be a wanted man if he weren't. Hawk's explained the need for secrecy to mama by telling her that we deserted the *Nankin Maiden* – he ain't said nothing 'bout her boys going to prison and escaping, though!

Hawk read Mary's recent letter aloud to me. She is well and the brewery's going nicely. He misses her and longs to see her again, I know. But I ain't ready yet for more of our mama.

'We got to get to Australia,' I says now. 'There's more gold been discovered in New South Wales, Mrs Barrett said so in the bloody poker game. And where there's gold, there be card games.'

Hawk looks disappointed. 'And grog?'

'Yeah, but I reckon I'm cured,' I lie.

'After this, after Chief Tamihana has managed to bring all the tribes together with the new king, I promise we shall leave.'

'And who will be this Maori king? Wiremu Tamihana, is it?' There is an edge of bitterness to me voice. I don't like this business of a Maori king, I'll wager nothing good will come of it.

'No, no, he does not wish it for himself. His ancestors are not powerful enough. The tribes have chosen Chief Potatau te Wherowhero to be crowned next month.'

'King Potato!' I laughs. 'Queen Victoria versus King Potato! What a contest that will be! Her ancestors, William, George, Charles, James, Elizabeth and all the bloody Henrys,' I say, mixing up all me kings and queens. 'Them against King Potato, Onion, Leek, Taro, Cabbage, Carrot and Beetroot!'

Hawk don't smile at my little joke. 'The Maori's ancestors be just as important as England's kings and queens, Tommo. Just as noble. But you are right, it is an uneven match. The Maori's belief in the malignancy of their dead ancestors adds a host of terrors to the *real* evils which beset them. It will be difficult to convince them to make the accommodations necessary for uniting the tribes.'

As Hawk predicts, Potatau te Wherowhero is announced King of the Maori in August. In the months what follow, I grows to admire me brother for his patience in trying to bring the tribes to one mind. My respect also grows for Chief Tamihana, who is much put upon by the other chiefs and the *tohunga*, the priests, of the various tribes, but who always listens to all points of view. In the end most of the tribes in the North are united. All that dissent are a few small ones and the mighty leader of the Taranaki Maori, Chief Wiremu Kingi.

By now Hawk and I both speak the Maori tongue well, and Hawk's voice has a deepness and calmness what makes men listen. But there is one thing left that he must do to earn the authority he needs, and I am much puzzled when he comes to me one morning.

'Tommo,' says he, 'they wish to make me Maori.'

'Might as well,' I quip, thinking to meself it means nothing more than what's already happened.

'No! You don't understand, they wish to tattoo me, to give me *moko*.'

'What?' I cries. 'Your gob and all?'

'Tamihana says if I do this the other chiefs will listen to us the better. They will name me the Black Maori.'

I look at me twin brother and shake me head. 'Hawk, you promised soon as they got themselves a bloody king we could leave this place! How'd you be at home with all them purple whirls on yer face?'

Hawk thinks for a moment. 'It isn't much of a face, by my reckoning, so no harm will be done there. As to what folks would think at home? They think I'm just a nigger anyway. Marks on my face will just confirm their view that I am a primitive savage!'

Hawk is smiling, but I sees the hurt of all the years underneath, the humiliation at being thought a black bastard. He is now seven feet tall and, at seventeen years old, near full grown. He is taller even than Hammerhead Jack and his strength be enormous. What he says about his gob makes me sad. I'm not sure I knows what handsome is meant to be in a man, but when me brother smiles it makes other men feel the world is good. The wahine, I've noticed, looks upon him with desire, which brings me to another matter what's troubling me. The Maori laws are strict about women and Tamihana has barred us from being with the tribe's wahines. Yours truly has been a mite frustrated.

'Will they give you the right to take a wahine?' I asks Hawk now.

It seems he's thought of this too. 'I have asked for us both and it is yes!' He smiles shyly.

'No chance!' says I, most alarmed. 'I ain't gunna have me gob scratched with blue lines for no bloody woman!'

'The *tohunga* and the chief will make a special dispensation for you, Tommo. If I become Maori, as my twin you are also Maori, even without tattoos on your face.'

'Without the tattoos, but still with the wahine?' I laugh, but me heart misses a beat.

Hawk nods, grinning as well. But I still don't want him to do it. 'I can survive. Pulling the pud ain't so bad. Don't let them bugger up your face, Hawk.'

'Like I said, it's not much to bugger up!' Hawk laughs, and turns serious. 'I would think it a great honour, Tommo. I have much love and respect for the Maori race.'

'Don't do it, Hawk!' I shouts, angry now. 'You'll be sorry forever!'

'No! You don't understand, Tommo! These will be the marks of my conscience!'

'To hell with your conscience! You be stark, starin', ravin' mad!'

'Please, Tommo, I *must* do it, show that I am not afraid to be different, not afraid to fight for what's right and fair!'

'Your fight is gunna get us killed!' I shrug and look up at him despairingly. 'Nothing I say is gunna change your mind, is it?'

'No,' says he quietly. 'I love you, Tommo, but I don't seek your permission in this. I want only that you should understand.'

'I understand you're a bloody idjit!' I snort. But the anger is gone out of me voice and I gives up. 'Do what you like, it be none o' my business.'

Hawk grins. 'Thank you, Tommo. Perhaps I'll look the better for it!'

And that be the oddest thing. Hawk with all his Maori tattoos looks like a general. The blue swirls and markings are just visible on his black skin, but they seem to add to the strength of his face. Like I said, I don't know what handsome be, but Hawk is now a man what you is forced to look at with a lot of respect. He appears about five-and-twenty, and there is no mistaking him for a lad no more.

Life in the village is also gettin' better. There is a little wahine I've had me eye on for months, what looks at me the same. Most Maori women be too big for me, towering above, but this one be a perfect fit. After Hawk's tattooing, I talks to Chief Tamihana, and he gives the nod.

Maybe it comes natural with the Maori wahine, but it were never like this in the wilderness. My woman's name is Makareta and I am taken with her. She has a most beautiful disposition and laughs all the time. There ain't nothing she won't do for me and I be just as happy to care for her. I got no notion of what might be love, like Hawk sometimes goes on about, but whatever this be with Makareta, it will do me just fine.

We often goes walking together in the forest to gather koroi, the beautiful scarlet and black fruit what grows at the top o' these giant trees. I shimmies up their huge trunks, jumping like a monkey from branch to branch as I done so often in the wilderness, and Makareta laughs and claps her hands. She says I do it much better than the Maori lads. Other times we gather berries what's so delicious that half is always eaten by the time we gets home. I know something of the way o' the wilderness from me past, but Makareta teaches me more. She loves the birds and they are of a great variety here, carrying on, shrieking, chirping and calling out, so's you can hardly hear yourself speak. I know the wren, the fly-catcher, the robin and the bellbird, o' course. She teaches me to recognise the calls of the pio-pio, the thrush what be different to ours, the popokotea, the piwakawaka and the riroriro. This last one's a funny name for a bird, though riroriro be somewhat like the sound it makes, like some small steam-engine starting up.

Makareta knows all the forest plants. She were taught by her mother what knows much about herbs. She can name all the ferns, maybe a hundred or more, also the many parasites and climbing creepers, their huge coils and slender vines festooning the massive branches. She knows every detail of their bright leaves, blossoms and fruits, what's to eat, what's poison, what can be used to cast a spell or stop a pregnancy. I've always thought the wilderness a dangerous place, but now I marvels in the infinite variety and cunning o' mother nature and sees the beauty of the lichen, moss, fungi and vines. The graceful clematis is everywhere, its white blossoms the shining stars o' the forest firmament.

Makareta takes great joy in teaching me what she knows and, in turn, wants to know everything about me. But the things I should tell her about meself I'd rather she didn't know. So I shows her some card tricks and tells her about Mary. I even teaches her some o' the nursery rhymes, 'Three Blind Mice' and all the rest, as well as the songs Mary taught us when we were young uns. I tell her about climbing Mount Wellington and spearing yabbies and some of me and Hawk's boyhood adventures before we were took by the wild men. After that I don't say nothing and she soon knows not to ask, for she sees the look in me eyes.

I think Hawk is secret pleased about me and Makareta. He could have any wahine in the village, for he is now made *rangatira*, what best translates as a gentleman of high status among the Maori. But he has not yet taken a wahine for himself. I think even Chief Tamihana has took to wondering about him. He is always suggesting this wahine or that one, but Hawk laughs and says he will know when it's right and keeps busy with his work. There are some things about Hawk what's got nothing to do with our being twins.

After much fussing and shouting and to-ing and fro-ing, most of the objections of the other tribes are gradually sorted out. It takes many weeks, but at last the tribes agree to abide by the laws of the new Maori king. Our chief Tamihana is become known as the 'kingmaker' and 'peacemaker'. At last, I think, Hawk's work be done.

But Hawk is of a different mind. 'Not yet, Tommo. We have not yet got Chief Wiremu Kingi of the Taranaki to join the King Movement.'

'Then, after you's done that and all the tribes are united under your King Potato, *then* will you stop meddling?'

Hawk frowns. 'The pakeha and the government are most upset at the proclamation of a Maori king. Tamihana will need me at his side a little longer.' He looks at me appealing, 'Please understand, Tommo?'

And so we stays. I has been given the task of training five-and-fifty young Maori warriors in the art of the fighting axe, an art what's been invented by yours truly. It's one of me few talents. I've always been good with a hand axe, fast and accurate. Now I has worked out ways to fend off spears, knives and even bayonets with the axe handle. Chief Tamihana wants Hawk and me well instructed in the use of the *taiaha*, the Maori fighting stick, a weapon most formidable. In return, I'm to train his men with the fighting axe. This ain't difficult as the Maori are already skilled in using the hand axe for shaping their canoes and carving, and they quickly learns to use it as a weapon o' combat as well. Over many weeks I shows them how to throw it so the razor-sharp blade finds its target every time, but mostly we works on hand-to-hand techniques.

I calls me band o' merry men what I've trained, 'Tommo's Mongrel Killers'. The Maori can't pronounce this and so they has named us 'Tommo Te Mokiri', what I think sounds most pleasing to the ear.

It's no time at all before this new Maori king of ours has a flag, a magistrate, a surveyor, a council o' state, a police force and all the trappings. I be sure Hawk has had a hand in setting up all of this, though he denies it. The pakeha are not well pleased by these events and liken it to treason. There be a lot of hostility and some, even most, would march upon the new king to put a stop to such disloyalty to the queen of England.

Chief Tamihana, ever the moderate, says, 'The king on his piece, the queen on her piece, God over both and love binding them to each other.' I often thinks Chief Tamihana and Hawk both be idjits, birds of a useless, peaceful feather!

But Governor Gore Browne – a most pompous man, I gathers – thinks that the Maori will soon take to fighting among themselves. Hawk, who gets the newspaper from Auckland, reads the governor's opinion: ' "I trust that time and absolute indifference, a neglect on the part of the government, will teach the natives of the folly of proceedings undertaken only by the promptings of vanity and instigated by disappointed advisers." '

Hawk laughs, setting the paper aside. 'I think we, along with Tamihana, are the *disappointed advisers*, what say you, Tommo?'

'I say governors won't deal kindly with *disappointed advisers* what stands up to them. Like I said before, it's time to scarper, mate!'

In truth, I has grown more content with life among the Maori, what with Makareta and all. But I sniffs trouble brewing, and sure enough, me instincts be right. Six months after Patatau's crowned king, a row breaks out between the colonists and the Ati Awa people of the Taranaki, which is where the settlers most badly want to buy land. Chief Wiremu Kingi declares his tribal lands is not for sale at any price. He ain't, he says, going to sell even a blade of grass or sod of earth or handful of dust to Governor bloody Gore Browne. He knows that all the government will do is promptly sell it to the settlers!

It's bad news that the first chief to tell the governor to go to hell is not of the King Movement and some thinks this is why the government has chosen to go against him. Chief Wiremu Kingi, though he be most powerful, now stands alone against the pakeha government.

Our chief, Tamihana, thinks this an opportunity to influence the Taranaki chief. He offers Hawk's assistance and the tribes agree that the Black Maori should go to the Taranaki to help in the negotiations with the governor's men. He can help with translations between the two parties.

For once the governor is feeling the pinch. Only seven of six-and-twenty million acres o' land in the North Island has been purchased by the settlers. So Gore Browne ups and says, 'The Europeans covet these lands and are *determined* to enter in and

possess them, rightly if possible, if not, then by any means at all.'
No 'Excuse I' or 'By your leave' or 'Does you mind?' What a
mongrel bastard he turns out to be!

Well, Chief Wiremu Kingi ain't having a bar of it. He ain't
selling and that's bloody that! So Governor Gore Browne starts to
do a bit of re-interpreting of the Treaty o' Waitangi. He reckons
that if a Maori, what tills or uses a piece of land he has inherited,
desires to sell that land to the government, he can do so *without*
the permission of the chief and the tribe. He can even do it over the
chief's head, so to speak. It is the first time this be said official-like,
by the Crown itself, which means Gore Browne intends it to
become the law o' the land.

Soon enough the governor find a Maori turncoat by the name
of Te Teira, who offers to sell the governor some land at the mouth
of the Waitara. Quick as a flash, His Nibs agrees, provided a title
can be made out.

But, with Hawk cleaning it up for the governor's tender ears,
Wiremu Kingi sticks to his story. 'Listen, Governor! Notwithstanding
Te Teira's decision, I will not permit sale of the Waitara to the pakeha.
Waitara is in my hands. I will not give it up – never, never, never!
I have spoken.' And he storms off in a proper huff, like Hawk says
he should.

Things go from bad to worse when Mr Parris, the governor's
district land purchaser, decides that Turncoat Te Teira's title *is*
valid and the governor can buy his land at the mouth of the
Waitara any time Te Teira cares to name a price. Parris sends in his
surveyors to peg it, and a cove named Octavius Carrington marks
it out neat as you like. 'This is the Crown's land now!' he
announces, bold as brass to the applause o' the greedy settlers,
what soon hopes to purchase it for themselves.

'Oh no it is not!' says Wiremu Kingi. 'This is my land and my
people's land and my ancestors' land!' He then sends in the women
of the tribe to pull out the surveyors' pegs.

'There's trouble coming, big trouble!' I says to Hawk. 'Time to
back off, mate!'

'What?' says Hawk. 'Back off? Tommo, we've got right on our
side! Tamihana thinks all the Maori will be willing to come
together over this, and if he can persuade Wiremu Kingi to join the
King Movement, this would be the first time we are a united front.
The governor won't dare to go against all the tribes at once.'

'Just you watch him!' says I. Sure enough, ten days later the governor declares martial law and sends in the troops. 'So much for the king and the united tribes! Queen Victoria, it seems, don't give a fig about the Maori,' I says to me stupid brother with all his high hopes.

But Chief Wiremu Kingi is a man of his word and he don't frighten easy. He builds a *pa*, a Maori fort, on the disputed land. The governor sends in his troops and the two sides face each other. It be clear that the government has the better forces, with muskets and artillery at the ready.

'We're done for,' Hawk says bitterly. 'I blame myself. I didn't think the governor would go so obviously against the Maori. I have to persuade Wiremu Kingi not to fight or his people will be destroyed. This is a fight we cannot win.'

So Hawk sneaks off and, under cover of night, joins Wiremu Kingi in his *pa*. I am beside meself when I discovers him gone. Even when the game is up, me stupid brother won't save his own hide. I am all for going after him but Makareta begs me to stay. As she sees it, Hawk's gone to stop a fight and the chief will listen to the Black Maori. I hope she be right, and perhaps I have come to care for my wahine more than I thinks, 'cause I agree to stay with her, to wait and worry. The tribes of the King Movement are on the alert at the threat of war, and are watching the crisis most careful. Their informants be everywhere, so we hears all as it takes place.

With the government and Taranaki fighters facing each other, the governor sends an ultimatum to Chief Wiremu Kingi:

To the chief who obstructs the Queen's road,

You have presumed to build on Her Majesty's land, and to stop the free passage of persons coming and going. This is levying war against the Crown. Destroy the places you have built, ask my forgiveness and you shall receive it. If you refuse, the blood of your people will be on your own head. I shall order the men to open fire upon you if you not obey my order.

There ain't no road and there ain't no need for free passage. The land is not the queen's but is in dispute. Until this is resolved, it belongs to the Maori people, according to the treaty. But the governor's guns are pointed at Chief Wiremu Kingi's *pa* and Hawk, we hear, is desperate for the chief not to fight. Wiremu Kingi be no coward and it takes great persuasion. But at last he agrees and he leaves the *pa* swearing an oath of revenge as he watches the governor's troops destroy his fortifications.

In the six months what follow, Hawk tries to convince Chief Wiremu Kingi to meet with the governor. Ever the peacemaker, he argues that a forceful case may be made by the Maori, using the Treaty of Waitangi as evidence. They might yet save the day if they appeal to the colonial office in London or directly to Queen Victoria herself.

But Wiremu Kingi ain't in the mood to listen to Hawk's advice or any other. Instead he declares war against the pakeha. He explains his position in a most powerful letter to a chieftainess of his own blood:

> Peace will not be made, I will continue to fight and the pakeha will be exterminated by me, or by my younger brother Te Hapurona . . . It is well with your children and us, we die upon the land which you and your brothers left us . . . We are here eating the English bullets – My friends, my parents, this shall be my work forever. What though my people and I may die, we die for Aotearoa.

'Can we go now?' I beg Hawk when I hears of it. 'There's no more need for the Black Maori to stay. The war is declared and we has no part in it!'

As much as I care for Makareta, I'm afraid – afraid for my own skin, but more for me brother's. There is talk among the settlers of the Black Maori what be seven foot tall and speaks English well enough to trap the tongues of the governor's men. Hawk is thought to be a Maori of an extreme dark colour, for his tattoos are most correct and he is of the *rangatira* and so assumed to be high born. But his identity is a mystery. No one knows his true name and when he speaks to translate for any of the Maori chiefs or even for King Potatau himself, he's introduced only as the Black

Maori. King Potatau has decreed that it is *tapu* to talk of Hawk to the pakeha, so his secret be well kept.

And so the rumour has begun amongst the pakeha that the Black Maori is the true power behind the tribes. It is he what threatens to destroy them, a new general who will come silent in the night and murder their women and children while they sleep. Hawk reads aloud from the *Auckland Herald* to me:

Black is the colour of the devil and the Black Maori has all the appearance and characteristics of Satan himself! His hair is black and close grown to his head and is easily likened to the devil's cap. His nose is large and his eyes dark as pitch and evil in every malevolent glance. If he lacks a pointed beard, it is only that his cunning has caused it to be shaved from his chin. His ears cannot be so well disguised and are pointed like a goblin's. He speaks with a most acerbic tongue, enough to burn the ears of any gentleman and not to be tolerated in the presence of the fairer sex. If a child should perchance come upon him unexpectedly, it would ever after be in a state of dreadful fright, the image of the devil burned into its memory forever!

'Hawk, you know what they says of you! They think you a danger to them and they will try to get you. Let's go now while we still can!' I plead when I hears this.

But Hawk ain't gunna be swayed. 'Tommo, I must see this through or I am a coward. I have done everything I can to avert war but the pakeha will not relent and are determined they should have land in the Taranaki, land the Maori do not wish to sell. If Wiremu Kingi relents it will not end there. This is the beginning, not the end, of the settlers' true rapacity!' He stops, scratches his noggin, then adds, 'Besides, there is something else.'

'What? Ain't you done enough?'

'It is the way the Maori plan to fight, the organisation of the *pa*.'

'The *pa*? But it looks like a most excellent fortification.' The

Maori *pa* is a fort, usually built upon a hill with palisades o' logs, trenches, earth ramparts and underground chambers, as well as a river or some natural defence on one side. It is most difficult to attack and I don't know what Hawk could be on about.

'The *pa* is about defence. This is fine for tribal war, but in these battles, the Maori are often outnumbered by their British attackers, who also have superior arms and artillery.'

'But it has stood them well in the past. They talk of great battles won, of fighting the British troopers to a standstill from the *pa*.'

'Sometimes, yes,' Hawk agrees. 'But how well they remember the victories and how soon they forget the defeats. In the end, most attacks against the Maori *pa* were victorious for the British. The Maori are brave men who would willingly die for their land, but they are constantly under siege when they fight from a *pa*. If not beaten at arms, they can eventually be starved out.'

'But it be their way of protecting their women and children. How else should they fight?'

Hawk looks serious. 'I do not love war but have read much of it. Perhaps there is something to be learnt from the wars of England and their military procedure in battle.'

'You're gunna teach the Maori to wage war from books?' I ask. 'Hawk, they's warriors what come to it from generations! And you hates violence!'

'Sometimes there is no other way but to stand and fight. If we must do so, we might at least fight prepared with a knowledge of the enemy. The Maori do not have this. They have not designed the *pa* against the use of artillery. For their own wars, where they use spears and fighting sticks, it fares well. It may even be somewhat effective against the musket. But it is defenceless against an artillery piece which can pound away remorselessly for as long as the pakeha likes, day and night.'

'So what is they to do?'

'They must avoid pitched battles,' Hawk answers.

'You means they should run away?'

'Well, yes, in a manner of speaking.' Hawk clears his throat and I resigns meself to one o' his lectures. 'During the Peninsular War under the Duke of Wellington – you know, the general who led the British and won at Waterloo where Mary's medal comes from?'

'Yes, I know who you means,' I say impatient. 'Mount Wellington be named after him.'

'Well, the Spaniards, fighting in their own country which they knew well, devised a new way of fighting Napoleon Bonaparte's troops. They engaged in "little wars", guerrilla wars, as they called it.

'The idea is to strike by surprise and then withdraw so the enemy never knows when you'll strike or where you are. You ambush them, keep on the move, never fight a pitched battle. In this way, much smaller forces can oppose much larger ones. Artillery is rendered ineffective and the battles are waged with muskets and hand-to-hand combat.'

'Hand-to-hand fighting?' I'm thinking of me fighting axe.

'Yes, small fast units that can do a maximum of harm in a very short time. The Maori have shown that with their fighting stick, they can combat the British bayonet. If they can be persuaded to fight this way, I think they will prove most effective.'

'With a fighting axe, too!' I says, excited. 'It be an ideal weapon for this kind o' war!'

Hawk nods. 'Yes. But I don't know if I can make Wiremyu Kingi agree to my ideas. The Maori are stubborn in their ways of fighting. I worry that their ancestors, speaking through the *tohunga*, could forbid it.'

He scratches his brow. 'You see, the Maori do not like to leave their land to fight. They think that they must hold the ground itself, defend it under their feet. I must persuade them that they might win the war with these tactics. That they can take their fight onto the lands the settlers have stolen, then return in peace to the land they still hold.'

Hawk's eyes shine as he thinks of how all this might be done. 'If the Maori adopt these tactics, they should attack the settlers on their farms and drive them into the towns, make them afraid to venture back onto their land. Then the Europeans would be under siege with no crops to harvest or livestock to slaughter.

'The troops would have to come out after the Maori to regain vacated territory and they would be ambushed, never knowing where the enemy was going to strike next. There are not sufficient of them to protect the pakeha farmers, to guard every farm, as well as the army's lines of communication. The Maori irregulars will strike wherever the governor's forces are not to be found. This will not be a war the British can win with artillery, using accustomed fighting tactics.'

Suddenly I see that what Hawk says makes sense. The Maori know the land and can move fast and silent across it. Their great war canoes can creep up the coast, attack and be away again. They be proven at close fighting. By drawing the British into the mountains, they could easily ambush them. If the troops remain on the plains, they could attack them at night, coming down from the mountains, where they hold their women and children safe.

'You think if the Maori do this, they can win?'

Hawk shakes his head. 'No, in the end, they cannot win, because the pakeha are not willing to leave New Zealand and there are as many of them now as there are Maori.'

'So, whatever method o' war the Maori use, it be a waste o' time!' I sigh, shrugging me shoulders.

'No, not at all. That is the whole point, Tommo. The Maori *must* resist, or they lose everything. If they fight from the *pa*, they will soon be defeated and their land confiscated by the government and given to the white man.

'They must harass the settlers, chase them with their women and children off their farms and into the towns. If the British troops can never engage them in pitched battle, then the war can continue, until the settlers' lands fall into decay and cannot be ploughed or harvested, until all their livestock is killed or captured, and until the towns are brought to the edge of starvation. When this happens, the government will call a truce.' Hawk grins and spreads his hands. 'This time the Maori will have power on their side in the negotiations, and the government will have to listen with some humility. This time we will hold most of the aces.'

'Has you put this method of warfare to Wiremu Kingi?' I asks.

'I have done so, and he has said he will think on it.'

I grab Hawk by the arm. 'Then, Hawk, please! Ask Chief Tamihana if I can join you with the fifty-five fighting axes from our tribe, the Tommo Te Mokiri!'

'No, Tommo! It isn't possible!' Hawk throws up his hands in alarm. 'You must not endanger yourself! I am but an adviser, and will not myself fight.' His eyes grow wide. 'You could be killed!'

'Hawk, if you won't ask him, I will find a way to do it. Tamihana is well pleased with our skill with the fighting axe. If he lends some of his trained warriors to Wiremu Kingi, then the chief will surely want to join the King Movement! The Maori will be a united force like you want.'

I know Hawk's got to see the logic in this. After a while he says, 'I will ask Wiremu Kingi, but only if you do not fight with them.'

I laugh. I am no hero, but I'm never gunna get a better chance against the mongrels. I shakes me head. 'I trained 'em and I got to be with 'em when they fight. They will reckon me a coward otherwise!'

'Then I will not ask him,' Hawk says firmly.

'Hawk! I will find a way to fight, I swears it!'

'Tommo, if you get killed, why should I want to live?'

I look at him, furious now. 'Hawk Solomon, when you were in Wiremu Kingi's *pa* and the governor sent his ultimatum, tell me – if Chief Kingi had decided to fight, what would you have done? Run away?'

'I had resolved to fight,' Hawk says quietly.

'There! And did you think how I might feel? Here I am shitting meself that me twin is going to get killed!'

'Tommo! Tommo!' Hawk pleads, placing his hand on me shoulder. 'You don't understand. I don't want you to die for something I have done!'

'Well, we bloody near did in Kororareka gaol for something *I* done!'

Hawk sees I ain't giving in and changes tack. 'Right, Tommo! Let's go to Australia *now*! I will talk to Chief Tamihana. He knows nothing of my warfare plan. I will tell him it is time for us to leave. I'll say to him I can do no more for Wiremu Kingi and ask his help to get us onto a ship back to Australia.'

'Bull!' I says, jerking me shoulder away from his hand. 'You only want to go because of me!' I pauses and swallows hard. 'Of course I still wants to leave this damned place, sometime! But not as a coward and *not* because *you* wants to save me bloody useless life. And most of all, not so your stupid conscience be always troubled 'cause you ran away when you knows you should've stayed!'

I am shouting now and I wish I could punch his fancy tattooed gob! Smash his big white teeth in! 'Besides,' I yell, 'Makareta be expecting a baby!'

Chapter Ten

Hawk

The Land of the Long White Cloud
December 1859

Wiremu Kingi is set on war. He and his Ati Awa people have reached the end of their tether. The governor and his government will have no further discussions with the Maori, such is the white man's greed for land.

Once again I am sent by Chief Tamihana to persuade Wiremu Kingi to join the King Movement so that all the Maori on the North Island might speak with one voice. I try to convince the old chief of the advantages to be gained from waging guerrilla warfare as well.

'What know you of this war, Black Maori?' he asks. 'It is not the Maori way to leave their women and children. Have you yourself fought by these methods?'

I have to confess to him that I know of these tactics only through books.

'Ha! Books! Missionaries have books! What have books to do with making war?'

I explain to him that the British are fond of writing about their military tactics and methods of fighting. 'It is one of the ways in which they have conquered the world – they learn from history.'

This seems to impress the chief, but still he is obdurate. 'We have beaten the pakeha before. I shall build tunnels underground in our forts so that the big guns cannot harm us.'

I tell him that this is an excellent idea, but that a *pa* can only be defended for a limited time. 'If they cannot bring you out by means of muskets and artillery, they can starve you out, Chief Kingi.'

'That is true, it has happened before, but perhaps we will defeat them before it can be done?'

'It is possible that your fighters will be victorious once, or even twice, but the pakeha outnumber you in men and firepower. Sooner or later they will defeat you.'

At this remark the chief grows furious. 'Are you a coward to speak of defeat? We will kill all the pakeha. They cannot defeat us! This is our land, Maori land! Be gone. Come back only when you will talk of victory!'

I leave the *hui*, thinking that I have disappointed Tamihana. Expelled from Wiremu Kingi's presence and his tribe, I can do no good here. But it is late and I cannot travel until morning, so I prepare to rest.

Before I can close my eyes, a messenger, one of Kingi's warriors, enters my hut. 'Chief Kingi wishes to see you at once, Black Maori,' he says.

I wrap a blanket about me and go to the *marae* where the *rangatira* are still assembled. The old chief is silent a moment, then he points to me and barks, 'Black Maori, we have watched you now for many months. Why have you not taken a woman from our tribe? Is a Maori wahine not good enough for you? Answer, please!'

How can I tell him that I am a virgin? I have all the markings of the *rangatira* and though I have just turned nineteen, I look much older.

'I have had no time to look for a wahine,' I say, 'to find one who would take me willingly.'

'Willingly?' The Maori chief looks puzzled. 'I shall find you one!'

I thank him but say that I would like to choose her for myself.

His eyebrows shoot upwards at this. 'My choice is not good?'

'Your choice is most excellent, Chief, but it is a feeling I seek.' I put my hand to my heart. 'A feeling in here.'

Wiremu Kingi thinks this very funny, but after he has stopped chuckling he says, 'I have heard of this feeling, but it comes later, when a woman has been with you a long time and she has proved a worthy wife and given you many children.' He sighs as though he is talking to a young child. 'It is a good feeling to have for an old woman, who is a precious thing. How can you have such a feeling before you know what you are getting? When a wahine is still young and you have not tried her out?' Then, before I can answer, he adds, 'Perhaps she is barren, perhaps she cannot cook, or the milk in her breasts does not make your children strong. What if she is bad-tempered or lazy, cannot weave flax, or sings like a crow? What then of this feeling?'

'There is no Maori woman who sings like a crow,' I reply, smiling. How can I tell him that if I should love a woman, none of these things would matter to me? I shrug. 'It is something I cannot explain.'

Chief Wiremu Kingi looks at me shrewdly. 'Tell me, Black Maori, have you taken a woman to your bed?' The *rangatira*, who have been following our conversation with interest, wait tensely for my reply. I have never lied to the Maori but I think now is the time to do so. But Mary has trained me too well. 'No,' I say softly.

The assembled men howl with laughter and look at me in disbelief. Only Wiremu Kingi doesn't laugh. 'That is good, Black Maori. The Maori only die for two things, for women and for land. You will show us how to fight better for our land and I will show you how to choose a good woman to die for. A man cannot go to war without having known a woman! If you die now your ancestors would regard you with shame.'

'But . . . but . . .' I stammer.

'What is it?' The chief grows impatient.

'I am most honoured that you would choose a woman for me, Chief Kingi, but do I understand she is henceforth to be my wife . . . forever?'

This brings a fresh outburst of laughter and Wiremu Kingi shakes his head. 'There are a great many young widows in the tribe. I will choose one for you and she will bring her longing to your need. That will be marriage enough for the time being. She will not be your wife, Black Maori. We go to war and I would not have it that she be widowed twice over and so become bad *tapu*.' The chief waves me away. 'We will talk of your warfare after you have become a man.'

Some of the *rangatira* grin, but most nod their heads solemnly. I walk from the *hui* feeling small and ashamed, knowing all eyes are upon my back.

My heart is pounding as I try to think how it should be with a wahine. I have asked Tommo what it is like to make love, but his answers do not provide much enlightenment.

'Same as pullin' yerself off,' he offers. 'Only better and lots more happening upon yerself.'

'Like what?'

Tommo thinks for a moment. 'Softer, and her doing things back to ya.'

'What sort of things?'

Tommo looks a bit foolish. 'Kissing. Her tongue in your gob. You know, touching.'

'Tongue in my mouth, what for?'

Tommo grows impatient. 'It's nice, tongue in one soft place and cock in t'other.'

'Oh,' say I. Even though I have thought a thousand times about kissing, I have never imagined it as having anything to do with tongues. Soft, sweet lips touching my cheek or even sometimes my own lips, but I have never envisaged tongues anywhere but safely in their owners' mouths.

Watching me, Tommo suddenly gets a most mischievous look on his face. 'Not to mention sixty-nine.'

'Sixty-nine? What is sixty-nine?'

'Christ Jesus, Hawk! Didn't the blokes at the brewery teach ya nothing? Frenchies call it sixty-nine!' He grabs a twig and writes the two numbers in the dirt. 'Look! Can't ya see?'

I tilt my head to one side but all I can see are the numbers roughly marked. 'What's to see?'

Tommo looks plainly exasperated now. 'Your cock in her mouth and your tongue in her pussy!'

'Really?' I am taken completely by surprise and try to imagine such a thing happening. 'I am not at all sure I should like it,' I finally respond.

'Or just her doing it,' Tommo says.

'Just her?'

'Yes, sucking you, your cock in her mouth.'

'Oh,' is all I can think to say. This shocks me less than the idea of doing things to her with my tongue. 'What more should I know?' I ask softly, my heart pounding.

'Lots!' Tommo says. 'But I ain't telling you no more, you'll find out for yerself soon enough.'

We are both caught up in our own thoughts until Tommo breaks the silence.

'It's the softness,' he confides. 'Softness all over, and creaminess.' He has a faraway look in his eyes and a half-smile. It's a look I have not seen on his face before and it pleases me, for it contains none of the old bitterness. Perhaps it is the first sign of real happiness I have seen in him.

All the same, Tommo's description doesn't match the dreamy picture I've got in my imagination. My picture is a bit hazy, I suppose, and has the scent of roses about it, the rustle of crinoline dresses and someone very pretty standing on tip-toe so her ankles show. Her kiss is like a summer breeze touching my cheek.

And in my dreams, making love is something done politely, although I am not sure how. I know I would wish it to be most decent and allowing of every possible sensitivity. But exactly how to bring this about, I can't imagine. In my mind, it just happens and then is all over, beautiful and not spoken of, except with quiet looks.

Who would be the woman to let me love her so? As far as I can see, there are but two choices. At one end of the scale, there are the dockside whores, women damaged by life who would take a nigger the same as anyone else if he had the price. Then, at the other end of the scale, where I want to be, there is a prettiness pure as the driven snow. I don't rightly know what it would be like, loving all that purity, sort of like trying to touch a beautiful, perfumed ghost.

In the days following Chief Kingi's promise, I find myself looking at the Maori women, who are all most attractive. I can't help myself. I look at their lips. They have beautiful lips, soft and luscious, and I imagine them kissing me with their pink tongues inside my mouth and elsewhere too.

I try to put these thoughts from my mind. Nobody, I tell myself, is going to kiss a nigger that way, unless he pays extra for it with a whore. As Ikey always said, 'To brood over what you can't have be stupid, my dear.' On the other hand, he always added, 'But to believe you can't have something be even more stupid.' So I decide to keep the thought of it alive but tucked in the back of my mind, just in case Ikey is right.

It is my fourth sleepless night since my conversation with the chief, and the moon outside my hut is near full. The night is warm.

Thoughts of softness and creaminess keep drifting about in my head, although I am tired and it is late. There is an owl hooting somewhere and soft laughter coming from one of the groups around the fires. I think of Tommo and Makareta, and how gentle Tommo is with her, though he does not say much. I think too about Chief Kingi and how I hope to teach him guerrilla warfare from the books I've read. He, a great warrior afraid of nothing, learn from me, who is afraid of a pop gun. I must be mad!

I must have fallen asleep, for I feel a stroking of my body. Soft hands glide across my chest and my belly. I am in a dream, a beautiful dream. I move. 'Hush.' It is a woman's soft voice. 'Do not open your eyes, Black Maori.'

I do as I am bid and feel a touching on my lips. A wonderful softness from her mouth seems to go through my whole body. My heart starts to thump, I can hear it: boom, boom, boom. Her hand moves down across my belly and her lips seem to melt over mine, opening my mouth. How this is done I cannot say, but there it is, the creaminess, as her tongue moves into my mouth and at the same time, her hand reaches me where I have grown hard.

I have already removed my coat and blouse the better to sleep, but now her hand works at my breeches, as her other takes my palm and places it on her breast. My fingers are hungry for her softness, and her nipples soon grow firm from my touch. I now lie naked inside my blanket. My eyes are still closed and I dare not open them for fear that I am dreaming.

The woman speaks to me, her voice soft but clear. 'Oh Black Maori, I have wanted you so very long. I have eaten you with my eyes and I have tasted you in my heart a thousand times. I have moaned for you alone in my blanket and my mouth has cried out to hold your manhood. My breasts have grown hard from longing for you and I have brought pleasure to myself in your name.'

I am almost fainting with desire and her hands are everywhere at once. She places her lips upon mine and her tongue seems alive in my mouth. Then she draws back. 'Black Maori, open your eyes. I want you to see the woman who would make love to you.'

I open my eyes. Moonlight is flooding into the hut and throws a silver sheen across her skin. She is beautiful beyond belief, her breasts cast upwards and generous, and her stomach clean-curved as she sits on her heels beside me. Her thighs are strong, smooth and shining in the light, and I can see the curve of her buttocks and the narrowness of her waist. He dark hair falls across her shoulders, shadowing her eyes so I cannot see into them.

I open my mouth to speak, but she presses her finger to my lips. 'Hush, do not speak.'

Now she begins to kiss me across my chest and belly, moving lower and lower, and then her lips part and take me into her mouth. 'Oh, oh!' I cry. 'Oh!' I am in heaven. I fear I cannot last a moment longer as her soft lips stroke up and down, and each time seem to take in most of me. Then, when I am sure I shall die, she withdraws her lips from my trembling hardness. A moment later she is astride me. Her hand guides me so that I sink into a softness and a creaminess I have not imagined in my wildest dreams.

'Oh, God, oh, oh, oh!' I moan.

'Black Maori, you must wait for me,' she says, panting now, her voice urgent. 'Wait!' I don't know how she can believe I am in enough control to do anything. 'Wait, wait, I will tell you when,' she gasps. Her eyes are closed and her mouth half open, and I can see her white teeth and pink tongue.

I want to tell her I cannot wait a moment longer, but all I can do is moan as she moves up and down on top of me. Every part of her is pressed against me, her slender body caressing my skin. Now her lips are upon mine and her tongue is in my mouth. The softness and smoothness is everywhere and I must die for I cannot live another moment without release. Then she takes her lips from mine, and begins to moan. 'Now!' she says. 'Now, Black Maori! Hard, hard, I must feel your hardness! Now!'

With this permission I lift my body from under her and roll her over on her back, driving into her. Her legs clasp about me as she opens up so that my every inch is taken deep into her. I cannot stop the explosion inside me.

'More, more!' she screams, her nails raking my back. I feel nothing but the delight of her. 'Oh, oh, ohhhh!' she cries, and more and more of the same, which thrills my ear. She gives a loud and glorious moan and then a sigh. I drive the harder into her wetness as her voice dies to a whimper and her hips push back up into mine. Her arms come around me and she draws my head into her breasts. Then my explosion is over and, jerking wildly, the world collapses and me with it. I am emptied out and my youth has flown away.

We are gleaming sweat, panting together, our breath hot about our heads. I have never felt more a man, never more alive, more embraced by love and tenderness. I fear I shall not again in my life have another moment as beautiful as this.

'You are a warrior now, Black Maori,' the woman says at last. Pushing me gently away, she rises so that once again I see the length of her legs, the curve of her waist and the beauty of her glistening breasts. Her hair falls across her face as she kneels again. She brushes it away as she wraps the blanket about me and kisses me. 'Ah, you are beautiful,' she smiles. 'You are beautiful, and you waited.' Then she gathers up her own blanket and rising, wraps it about her and moves to the door.

'What is your name?' I call urgently, for I do not want her to leave.

She pauses at the door, the moon shining on her face. 'Hinetitama.' She laughs softly, then is gone in the moonlight.

'Will you come to me again?' I call, but there is no reply. I lie still, a great smile upon my face. 'Hinetitama,' I repeat. Flooded with happiness, I fall into a deep slumber.

In the morning I am summoned to the *marae* by Chief Kingi and the *rangatira*. When all are seated the chief addresses me, 'Five days ago, we talked to the boy but today it is to the man.' He grins. 'Did you dream well, Black Maori?'

I laugh. 'Better than I ever have, thank you, Chief Kingi.'

'That is good. Your ancestors will be most relieved.'

Laughter follows this reply, also applause, and then no more is said of it. The thing is done and I am welcomed. I feel as though something different has happened between these people and myself, something I cannot quite understand.

'We will talk of these small wars of yours,' Wiremu Kingi says. 'You will tell us all you know. Like the British, we too can learn from books, though blood is better!'

'Only when it does not belong to your side,' I reply.

'Ha! There is no shame in dying. If you have fought well it is an honour,' the chief replies.

I shrug. 'There is also no shame in living, if you have fought well.'

'Black Maori, keep your sharp tongue for the pakeha!' Wiremu Kingi rebukes me, but I can see from his eyes that he is not insulted.

'I have known a woman whom war has made a widow in your

tribe, and all I can say is that the dead must grieve greatly for their loss.' I hope that this compliment makes up for my forward manner.

The chief laughs suddenly. 'Well spoken, Black Maori. You are right, our strength is more in the living than the dead. Already the Maori have done too much dying in these battles. It is not only the dead who grieve their wahine, the tribe laments the barrenness that is then forced upon them. You will tell us more of this new way to fight the British.'

I spend the remainder of the morning outlining the principles of guerrilla warfare and listening as the *rangatira* discuss it among themselves. This is a most equitable process and Wiremu Kingi shows a great deal of patience. The *tohunga* argue fiercely that the ancestors will frown on a departure from the practice of fighting from a *pa*, but the chief is most persuasive. 'In addition to this new way of fighting, we will build a great *pa* in the mountains where our women and children will stay with sufficient warriors to defend them,' he declares.

'Perhaps the tribe should build many forts in the mountains so the women and children can keep moving?' I suggest. 'Food may be stored in secret caves, for I have been told there are many such places and few are known to the pakeha. We can control the mountain passes so that they cannot penetrate. Then we can attack them on their own ground, always where they least expect us. The mountains and the forests are where we will hide.'

'The Maori always hold the ground under their feet. We cannot defend ground which is not our own,' proclaims one of the *tohunga*, an old man who is much respected.

'Ha! It is all our ground!' the chief snorts. 'Our land, which the pakeha have stolen from us!'

But the old priest will not be dissuaded. He has been most persistent all morning and much involved with the thoughts of the ancestors in the matter of this new way of warring. He shakes his head as I further my argument.

'The *pa* was a strong place from which the ancestors defended their land, a fort built upon their ground and under their own feet. But since the pakeha have brought the musket here, more than twenty thousand Maori have been killed defending their forts. These are not Maori who have been killed by the pakeha. These are Maori who have been slain by their own kind – those who have used the white man's gun to kill their own people! These traitors, who know the *pa* well, have defeated it with the gun. The British have even more guns – huge ones that can tear down the palisades and tear up the ground. The Maori *pa* cannot always withstand the British system of war. We must have another system.'

There is much concern among the *rangatira* at this denigration of the *pa*. Chief Wiremu Kingi is patient though firm and in the end, he rules that we will try this new kind of warfare. He turns to his younger brother, War Chief Hapurona, who has a mighty reputation but who has said little during the discussion, leaving the task of reconciliation to his brother.

'What say you, Hapurona? How shall we fight?'

All are silent as War Chief Hapurona speaks. 'The Maori are quick to fight and slow to learn, but I do not agree that we must give up the system of the forts.' The men murmur their approval at this, and my heart sinks. 'There are times in war to attack and times to defend,' the war chief continues. 'With the pakeha we have always defended, and sometimes this has been right and sometimes it has been wrong. Black Maori is right, we must use both systems to be effective in this war.'

Wiremu Kingi turns to me and nods that I should reply. I have been so anxious to persuade him to embrace my new method of warfare that I have not seen the whole situation clearly as Hapurona has. 'War Chief Hapurona is our commander and what he says is right. It shames me that I have not understood this more clearly before,' I say, with my head bowed.

The old chief responds, 'You are not born a Maori, nor have you been a warrior, so you would not know the advantages of fighting a defensive action from a well-constructed *pa*.' He turns to Hapurona. 'Will you allow the Black Maori to be a general under you, to advise you in his ways?'

Hapurona walks over to me and places his hand on my shoulders. 'I shall prepare the feathers for a general's cloak.' He laughs. 'It is not often I must look up into another man's face. The women will need to gather many more baskets of feathers for the Black Maori.'

I tell Wiremu Kingi that I am greatly honoured but since I have not proved my courage in battle, I would be happy to be an adviser only.

The chief appears surprised at this. 'And if we should be defeated, who shall we blame? A mere adviser? Bah! We must have a general so that he is worthy of being put to death should he fail us – or of being honoured should we succeed.'

The *rangatira* laugh heartily at this and approve the appointment. Chief Wiremu Kingi then says, 'Black Maori, when you persuaded me not to fight the governor in the Waitara, that is something only a good war chief would do. You shall be a general for us, like those the British have, and we shall call you Black Hawk.'

And so I have been named General Black Hawk. I am a little afraid that I shall let the Maori down in this whole affair. Though they have agreed to fight small wars, they are by no means unanimous, and the *tohunga* led by the old priest are against it. I shall have to prove myself very soon with War Chief Hapurona, or I shall be greatly shamed and Chief Tamihana will be disgraced by me.

I return to my tribe to tell my chief of Wiremu Kingi's decision. Of course, I must also tell Tommo.

Tommo is not amused. 'Have you gone crazy?' he screams, banging his fist hard down on the table. 'General Black Hawk, is it? You think the pakeha don't already want your head on a plate? Listen, mate, they'll string you up by your balls outside Auckland Post Office while singing the flamin' Hallelujah Chorus!'

'But you said you wanted to come with me. You and your fighting axes, Tommo Te Mokiri!' I say.

'Yes, but that was when it were just me and you! Me, a regular soldier and you, an adviser, safe in the background. Nobody'd know nothin' about us being there. Then, when it's over, or if it goes badly, we can scarper, piss off, slip into the night!' He pauses and glares at me. 'Now you're a fucking general. The flamin' pakeha will see it as treason! Remember we're escaped prisoners. They're gunna have your guts for garters, mate, if they ever puts two and two together and gets four. Mine, too! But I got to be with you, Hawk – I'm not letting ya go on yer own.'

'Tommo, please wait here,' I beg. 'What if something goes wrong or we are captured? Makareta is with child. You would not wish her to be a widow.'

'Makareta already knows we got to go away,' Tommo snorts. 'I've told her I'll come back some day to fetch her and the child. I'm coming all right, but that don't mean you ain't an idjit!

Promise me when this is over, *if* we comes out alive, we're gunna get out of here.'

I nod my head.

'Promise, Hawk! Swear it on Makareta's baby!'

'I promise we'll go back to Hobart Town as soon as Wiremu Kingi's war is over.'

'No! I don't want to go back to Mary yet. We'll go to Sydney.'

'Sydney then, I promise!'

We are sitting in Tommo's hut and I am glad when Makareta comes over with some food. She will cool Tommo's anger. It's difficult to be angry with Makareta present. She has a mischievous grin, laughs often and loves Tommo with all her heart. She cannot help but touch him as though he is a part of her every desire. 'What will you name the baby?' I ask her, hoping to end the unfortunate subject of General Black Hawk.

'Icky,' Makareta smiles.

'Ikey,' Tommo corrects her.

I laugh. 'I'll wager he'll be the only Ikey Solomon who is Maori in the whole world or ever to come. But what if it is a girl, how shall you name her?'

Makareta frowns and looks downcast. 'I would want a son for Tommo. We have not thought of a name for a girl.'

I hesitate a moment, then venture, 'If it is a girl, may I suggest a name?'

'I know! You want to call her Mary, don'tcha?' says Tommo, now somewhat mollified.

'No, I had thought – Hinetitama?'

Makareta gasps and brings her hand to her breast. 'That is a name which may only be used for a Maori princess! It cannot be, Black Hawk! They will not allow it. Hinetitama is the daughter of Hineahuone, Woman Made From Earth, the first Maori woman. The mother of the earth called her daughter Hinetitama, the Dawn Maiden, because her cheeks were the same colour as the morning light.'

'That is beautiful, Makareta. If you should have a girl, I will ask Chief Tamihana if he will grant his permission to name her thus. I am *rangatira*, perhaps he will allow this honour through me.'

'He will not, Black Hawk. The *tohunga* and the ancestors would be angry. I do not want a *tapu* on my child!' She is most distressed, so I change the subject.

'It will be a boy,' I say quickly. 'There is a saying among the pakeha that a mother's beauty is stolen by a girl child in the womb, but if it is a son, the beauty remains.' I smile. 'And you, Makareta, are more beautiful than ever.'

Tommo sighs and rolls his eyes at this sentimental notion but I can see Makareta is pleased. Besides, her good manners do not allow her to show further disquiet. Her frown disappears and she laughs. 'You are right, Black Hawk. We will have Icky Slomon and save everyone much trouble.'

'Ikey,' Tommo repeats, 'I-key So-lo-mon!' He rolls his eyes, as though he has tried to teach her a hundred times and failed.

Makareta ignores him. 'Now you must eat,' she says, putting a large, steaming clay pot of fish and vegetables down in front of us.

'Ikey Solomon never saved anyone any trouble!' I laugh as I reach to fill my platter.

Tommo chuckles too. 'So, what's wrong with Mary?' he asks. 'It is our mama's name after all.'

'Nothing,' I say, 'Mary is a fine name, Tommo.'

'Well then,' says he, 'it's settled. Mary it is if we have a girl.'

But my thoughts have flown back to Hinetitama, and as soon as I return to the village of Chief Wiremu Kingi I try to find her. It is a large village of a thousand souls, perhaps more, but a widow of such beauty would, I feel sure, be well known.

My hopes are quickly dashed. All the wahine I ask about Hinetitama look anxious and shake their heads. 'We have no wahine of that name, General Black Hawk, not in this tribe,' they say. I come to believe it is a conspiracy, led by Chief Wiremu Kingi, to keep me from Hinetitama and, although I search widely, she is not to be found. I take to looking at every woman's face I pass. There are many who are great beauties, for the Maori are of the Polynesian race and perhaps the most handsome people on earth. Though many are comely, none could be mistaken for Hinetitama. I know from Makareta's explanation that the chief has honoured me with a princess, not just an ordinary wahine. But this makes it stranger still. A disappearing princess is surely an odd occurrence. Perhaps, after all, it was a dream? I have resolved, if ever an opportunity arises, to ask Wiremu Kingi if he will let me see her again. My heart is broken by her disappearance and I try hard to concentrate on matters of warfare instead.

I am now so engaged with the Maori and their struggle that I am too busy for thoughts of home and too occupied to yearn for our dear Mary. Christmas passes unnoticed amongst the tribes, although I send our greetings to mama.

I have not told Mary of my close involvement with the Maori fight against the pakeha, informing her simply of Tommo's recovery to health in Tamihana's village. If she suspects I dissemble, she says not a word. Nor does she refer to the bitter argument that preceded our leaving. Instead, she writes of the brewery and of the loving thoughts she holds for her two boys. I am anxious about how we shall ever get to see her again, but for now we prepare for guerrilla warfare against the settlers and my mind is much occupied with this.

In great secret, War Chief Hapurona and I plan our first attack against the settlers. But before we can carry it out, martial law is again declared in the Taranaki by Lieutenant-Colonel Murray, who is commander of the militia and the Taranaki Rifle Volunteers, a mounted corps armed with carbines, revolvers and swords. The pakeha soldiers do not wait for us to come against them but immediately attack, looting and burning several Maori villages without warning. The war has begun in earnest, for it is now clear from these actions that the settlers will use whatever force is needed to occupy Maori land.

'We must drive the pakeha from their farms into New Plymouth,' I cry, 'empty the whole countryside.' New Plymouth is a town of some two and a half thousand souls, which depends on the surrounding countryside for food or else must obtain it by sea. War Chief Hapurona agrees and small units that can move quickly over the terrain are sent out in a series of daring night-time raids. In each are two or three of Tommo's fighting axes from Chief Tamihana and they prove most effective. Tommo has lengthened the handle of the axe so that it may be used to fend off a bayonet or even in the manner of the *taiaha*, the Maori fighting stick. In these raids we do not kill the settlers, but simply force them from their farms with their women and children, thereafter burning and looting their homes and taking possession of their livestock.

Soon New Plymouth has become the only safe haven for all the pakeha in the district and the countryside is empty save for the Maori. The soldiers have fortified the town and created a citadel on the site of an old Maori *pa*, now known as Marsland Hill. From here they plan to defend New Plymouth against our attack. We are well pleased with this development, for we have no intention of attacking the town but only plan to contain the pakeha within it.

It is now that War Chief Hapurona and the old chief show their great skill as leaders. Hapurona commences to build a *pa* about nine miles from New Plymouth. He has studied the trenching systems the British have used to fortify the town, and he constructs his *pa* with a double row of palisades containing rifle pits and similar trenches. We also have underground passages to protect us from the British artillery.

The *pa* holds one hundred fighting men, whom Wiremu Kingi places under the command of War Chief Hapurona and his chief aide, a Maori war leader named Tamati Kapene. Though one hundred men is not much of a fighting force, we hope that it sends a direct challenge to the British militia to come out of New Plymouth and get us. We trust they will think this small force presents a great opportunity for a victory, and an easy one at that. 'They will think it is the old times when the Maori fight on the defensive,' Hapurona explains, 'and it will give them great heart. This is the way they *think* they know how to defeat us.'

After much debate, I persuade Wiremu Kingi to purchase a hundred double-barrelled shotguns. At first the *rangatira* and even the chief are in great doubt about the wisdom of this, thinking the new rifled muskets to be much the better weapons. They have long used shotguns to shoot duck and small game and have even fought with them before, but they have only a few in their armoury. It is my plan to use the shotgun as the main weapon of defence, to entice the British near and greet them with a hail of buckshot at close range.

Though I know little of guns, my argument is simple enough. A shotgun charged with buckshot is deadly when used close-up, which is the way fighting occurs in the *pa*. It has double the barrels and hence twice the fire power of a musket. The fact that the shot will pepper widely is to be recommended in close combat, and at ten or fifteen yards, it will kill more effectively than the *pu* – the musket – with its single lead ball.

As I point out to the war council: 'We will have the shotgun and the long-handled fighting axe as well as the *taiaha*, the spear, and the musket. All the enemy will have is the musket and the bayonet. At close range, when the British storm the *pa*, we will be the better armed.'

'Oh, so now General Black Hawk would be an expert on fighting in a *pa*. Do I not recall he was altogether against it not so long ago?' It is the voice of Hapurona's aide, Tamati Kapene, who from the beginning has opposed me in almost every endeavour. He is against guerrilla warfare and would return to the old methods if he had his way.

Tamati Kapene is in charge of organising the defence in the forts and though he is most talented, he is vainglorious for a man not more than twenty-five years of age – even I, at nineteen, can see this. As the son of a chief he has risen quickly and he is said to be a brave man. I do not contradict him but simply answer that we are no worse off with the shotgun and the axe, for we still retain all the traditional Maori weapons as well as the musket. 'We have added the shotgun and the axe without losing anything,' I point out.

My argument carries the day. But although in favour of the shotguns, War Chief Hapurona has decided that I shall remain an observer when the Maori fight in a *pa*, until I am well enough acquainted with the Maori fighting system.

Meanwhile my brother is also preparing for war. Tommo's men have not yet been tested in open warfare with the long-handled fighting axe, which the pakeha have come to call the tomahawk, after the American Indian weapon. This is, of course, a coincidence and not intended as a compliment to me and Tommo. However, it is not lost on the Maori warriors who think the pakeha must fear the new weapon to have named it in our honour. I explain the real origins of the axe's name to Hapurona, for of course the pakeha do not know about Tommo and still think of me only as the Black Maori. But he laughs. 'General Black Hawk, it is our luck that the men think it so. They will follow you and Tommo the better for it.' In Hapurona's *pa* there are fifteen axe fighters from the Tommo Te Mokiri and among them is my twin, so that I am secretly most afraid for his life.

We are still waiting for the British to come after us when Hammerhead Jack turns up. 'I have come to fight with my brothers,' he says simply. 'I have one eye and one arm, but one eye is sufficient to see the British. My one arm will use a fighting axe and my eye will see it find its mark between the two eyes of the British soldiers.'

I ask if Hammerhead Jack might be my aide and it is agreed.

Tommo is greatly pleased by this. He has spent much time teaching Hammerhead Jack the fighting axe, and knows him to be a formidable opponent who will do much more than his share in any fight. He is much reassured that he will be by my side in the event of close combat.

A few days later, in early March, we hear that the British have moved out of New Plymouth with a contingent of four hundred officers and men, as well as a naval detachment with artillery. Although they have only nine miles to go, they come with a long baggage train of wagons and carts.

I send out a small war party to reconnoitre and they report that the column is exceedingly well guarded by the 65th Regiment and that the navy is well equipped with heavy artillery. It is as though they expect to be attacked at any moment, for horsemen constantly patrol their flanks. This is not surprising as the surrounding country is wooded, scrubby terrain criss-crossed by ravines and gullies, with giant flax providing plenty of cover. Given their surveillance, it will be difficult to catch the British column by stealth. Moreover, there is little hope of cutting off their supplies. The Maori do not have much respect for the British regular who fights in the ordered and predictable manner of Waterloo and the Crimea, but I believe it will be a tough battle.

The British build a large redoubt overlooking the river and this becomes their base. War Chief Hapurona and Chief Wiremu Kingi decide our forces are too few, and their reconnaissance patrols too well armed, to attempt to ambush them. So, in the time-honoured manner of the Maori, we wait for the enemy to come to us. In the meantime, we send urgent word to Chief Tamihana and several other chiefs asking for their support against these superior odds. My chief, Tamihana, has already sent fifteen axe fighters with Tommo but he sends a dozen more, and encourages the Ngati Maniapoto, the Waikato and the South Taranaki tribes to also come to our aid. Though we are still greatly outnumbered, our overall strength is much increased by the time the British attack.

It is the seventeenth day of March 1860, a bright morning without so much as a cloud in the sky. A rain-storm last night has made the approach to our *pa* heavy going. At last Tommo and I are at war, though I very much doubt that I have the stomach for the killing of men. As the fighting gets under way, I quickly become accustomed to the crack of musket fire and the whine of bullets, even the swish of an artillery canister or the boom of cannon shot. We are mostly underground when the firing from the British lines is at its heaviest and we fire back at them whenever the occasion allows. The explosions produce much sound and light, but little harm seems to be done. Some of our palisades are damaged, and much mud and soil is kicked up from the cannon fire. Once, a roof catches alight, though this is quickly doused.

Tommo is most impatient. 'When will they come?' he asks repeatedly. Like me, he is a greenhorn, anxious not to make a fool of himself.

Towards afternoon, a shot from the British cuts the rope which holds our flag, a red banner, more there so that we should have a flag like the British than for the purposes of any loyalty. The Maori die for women and land, not for this piece of bunting which we name the Waitara flag so as to annoy the governor.

The flag flutters to the ground, close to the palisades outside the *pa*, and we do not think to retrieve it. Then, in the late afternoon during a lull in the firing, we are met with an amazing sight. The British, ever the heroes, have sent two horsemen to capture our fallen banner. Up gallop these two cavalrymen, bent on glory. Up come our muskets, bent on destruction. Bang, bang, bang! One of them is dead, while the other is medal-bound, for he has scooped up the red flag with his home-made lance, turned his horse in a shower of mud clods, and galloped away again, showing us his horse's arse. I daresay they will one day hang the flag in Westminster Abbey as one of their battle honours – telling their children of the bright bunting hard-won from the ferocious Maori in a noble war of the Empire. Meanwhile, the first man in this battle lies dead in the mud and we are happy that it is an English trooper and not a Maori warrior.

'Do we have another banner to throw into the mud?' shouts Hammerhead Jack to much laughter among the men.

At sunset the British decide to cease fighting for the day. They have been pumping shot and cannon fire into us since the early morning and have by now done considerable damage to the *pa*. It is too dangerous to repair our fortifications and there is some doubt in my mind that we can take another day of bombardment. We have seen from the firing that we are greatly outgunned and that the British still have much the superior numbers. At the war council, however, there is some elation at the day's events. We have not lost a single man, our food and water supply is intact and our men remain in high spirits.

Tamati Kapene is the first to speak after the general has summed up the day. He is full of bravado and looks meaningfully at me. 'We have proved the value of the *pa* to all who may have doubted it. The British guns cannot harm us, their artillery fire is like flies on our skin and their cannons are no more than noisy mosquitoes. If these pests should come tomorrow or the next day, we will brush them off with contempt!'

War Chief Hapurona, who has observed that his aide's remarks are directed at me, now speaks. 'What say you, Black Hawk? Have you now observed sufficient of *pa* fighting to see its value?'

Chief Wiremu Kingi watches me closely. I nod before speaking. 'I can now see well the virtue of the *pa* – it is a most excellent system of defence, a brilliant fortification, War Chief Hapurona.' Then I am silent.

'Ha!' Chief Kingi snorts. 'I think there is more, Black Hawk. Your eyes say there are more words waiting in your head!'

I hesitate a moment. 'With great respect, has it been observed what the British artillery and cannon have done to our trenches and palisades?'

'Nothing!' Tamati Kapene shouts. 'Our palisades stand firm, they will hold the battle through.'

'In four places, the cannon fire has filled in our trenches sufficient to allow both horses and foot soldiers to cross them without difficulty,' I say. 'In six places, the first row of posts is knocked down and the second palisade is also damaged. With a little more cannon and artillery fire, we will be breached. Tomorrow, towards afternoon if I am not mistaken, the British will be upon us with their guns and bayonets.'

Tamati Kapene points to me and yells, 'This man is wrong! If they come we have sufficient defences. They will pay with their lives.'

'And we with ours,' I reply quietly.

'Coward!' Hapurona's aide shouts, pointing straight at me.

A deep silence follows and I hear Hammerhead Jack whisper beside me, 'You cannot accept this insult.'

We are seated in a circle. Tamati Kapene is but an arm's length away and I know he is looking to challenge me. I have my eyes to the ground and I do not look up to meet his. Suddenly, it is as if I am back at the gaol in Kororareka with Maple and Syrup holding my arms and Hori Hura threatening me. I am not sure where the anger comes from, but it is there, slow and cool, rising from somewhere deep within me. My right arm shoots out and I grab Hapurona's aide by the throat. In a trice, my left hand joins it and at the same time I rise to my feet so that Tamati Kapene is jerked upwards. The aide is a big man, but he now seems slight enough, for I pull him higher and higher until his feet are well off the ground and his head above my own.

I can see the young Maori's eyes as they near pop from his head. His arms flail and his legs kick wildly. Then they stop, as though the strength has gone from them. My fingers tighten and there is still more pressure I can bring. I would not need it all to kill him.

'Put him down, Black Hawk,' Hapurona says in a low voice.

I drop his aide, who falls to the floor unconscious. It is only then that I feel the strain in my arms from lifting a human of more than two hundred pounds in weight and holding him in the air as a child would a rag doll.

'Sit, General Black Hawk,' Wiremu Kingi commands and I sink slowly back to the ground. The old chief signals for two warriors to drag Tamati Kapene out of the way. With the heat gone from me, I wonder if I should apologise. I make to open my mouth but Hammerhead Jack squeezes my shoulder.

'Ork good,' he whispers in English. 'No talk.'

'We will leave tonight, before the moon rises,' is all Hapurona says. 'Tell your men to be ready.'

'What's going on?' Tommo asks as I tell him to make his axe fighters ready to move out.

'Nothing,' I say. 'Tomorrow the small wars start in earnest.'

'About bleedin' time!' he replies.

Before we leave that night, Chief Kingi calls me to him. 'So, Black Hawk, we live to fight another day, eh? Is it always so with you, to run in the face of a fight? Soon they will no longer call you General Black Hawk but instead General Back Off!'

I am mortified by these words. 'Chief Kingi,' I stammer, 'to die foolishly does not make a man a hero.'

The old chief looks at me a moment. 'You are right, General Black Hawk. Tonight Tamati Kapene would have died foolishly at your hands and he would not have been a hero.'

'I am sorry, Chief,' I say.

His eyebrows shoot up. 'Sorry? You are sorry? I am not sorry, Black Hawk. The Maori are a stubborn people, sometimes even boastful. We are given to exaggerating our prowess at war. If you had *not* acted as you had, there would have been no small wars for you. Instead, I would have sent you back to Chief Tamihana like a dog with your tail between your legs. We would have stayed to fight the British and we would have been soundly beaten.'

'I am most grateful for your support, Chief, but I am told Tamati Kapene is a bold warrior, and I have humiliated him. I have yet to know if I myself will behave with boldness in this war.'

'He is bold and stupid! We have many like him. Sometimes the Maori give their lives too quickly!' The old man begins to laugh. 'We will soon enough see what you are made of, General. We go to a place called Waireka, where we shall build a *pa*, but in the meantime you will harass Colonel Murray and his regulars. It is good country for your kind of fighting and then we shall see what we shall see of this campaign.'

We leave the *pa* while the British slumber. Later I learn that at first light, the British pound the *pa* with artillery fire, thinking to take it in the early afternoon. When after three hours there is still no return fire, they keep firing, thinking it is a ruse to lure them closer. Then, towards noon, they send in the cavalry with swords drawn and find that the enemy has escaped from right under their superior British noses.

We have melted into the surrounding countryside and now it is my turn to fight. I have sent out raiding parties, for we have news that some of the pakeha have returned to their farms, believing that Murray will soon finish us off. I know I must quickly put a stop to this. Fear of the Maori's power to strike anywhere at any time is a most important aspect of our campaign.

Over the next week, my men raid the settler farms, and we come by many horses so that we now have several dozen fighters mounted on horseback, myself sometimes amongst them. Our attacks are designed only to instil fear, and to make a livelihood impossible by destroying property and stealing livestock. It is only against the army that we wage war.

We enjoy good success against Murray's regulars, harassing, ambushing and killing several of his troopers. Our small wars are proving most effective, for the Maori take to it easily and are well disciplined in action. The broken-wooded country provides our warriors with ideal cover, and our ambushes are swift and devised more to disconcert than to take many lives, though some of the British soldiers give up their lives stupidly.

I have convinced the Maori that to destroy a supply wagon or ammunition cart is more important than taking a trooper's life. Soldiers, I point out, fight on their stomachs and we are making it as difficult as possible for Murray to feed his troops. Already, much of their food must come by sea. As a result, we have captured or destroyed several wagons. Murray has only one trump card, the Taranaki Rifle Volunteer Company, and this he uses badly. We seek to avoid these sharpshooters at all cost, and I later learn that they are the first British volunteer force to engage an enemy in the field.

It is curious, and yet another measure of British arrogance, that Murray and his Imperial officers much underrate these men and do not give them credit for their knowledge. Nor do they allow them the opportunity to come out after us. I thank God for this, for the volunteers are able to match us in almost every respect. They are the sons of men from Cornwall and Devon, and nearly twenty years of Taranaki life has moulded them into expert bushmen, familiar with the forest tracks and the terrain, and thus able to meet us on level terms. Some are on horseback and, being more skilled riders than we, are able to move swiftly to harass us.

Chief Wiremu Kingi and War Chief Hapurona know well the families who form much of the hundred-strong Rifle Volunteer Company. The Atkinsons, Smiths, Hursthouses, Bayleys, Messengers and Northcrofts are all respected as good frontiersmen and as hard, brave men. We know we would be in for a good fight if we were to come up against them. But while we have only to contend with Murray's slow-moving and often badly led regulars from the 65th Regiment, we enjoy the upper hand.

We are now based at a strong *pa* at Waireka, only five miles from New Plymouth, and it is from here that I direct my patrols to look for any brave settlers who think it safe to return. Each patrol is only six men – three axe fighters, two shotguns and a musket. Tommo commands one of the raiding parties, for I cannot contain him any longer. He must, he says, lead his men by example.

Only ten days have passed since our confrontation with Murray, when Tommo's band comes across a well-defended homestead and, for the first time, encounters serious resistance. He tells me later that there are four muskets aimed at them from a well-secured position in the farmhouse. These rifled muskets are most accurate and Tommo's band is pinned down behind a small copse of rocks and scrub. One of his shotgun warriors is wounded, though only lightly. They are not close enough to use the shotguns, while the warrior with the musket is no sharpshooter and provides little enough firepower against the four settlers.

Tommo instructs his musket to keep firing at the farmhouse. The wounded man too is told to fire his shotgun as a diversion. Tommo takes the remaining shotgun warrior and the two axemen and they creep up to the rear of the farmhouse while the others draw the settlers' fire.

Tommo is hoping that the settlers will think they have wounded or killed the other four Maori. He has commanded the two Maori left behind to fire as rapidly as possible for about ten minutes, hoping that the enemy will retaliate with equal determination. His ploy works perfectly. Tommo and his men reach the homestead when both sides are firing with gusto, and the noise allows Tommo to break down a door at the back of the farmhouse and enter.

What follows is simple enough as Tommo's band takes the settlers completely by surprise. The house is filled with smoke from the muskets and when they reach the room from which the men are firing, Tommo and his men let go a blast from the shotgun, further filling the room with dense smoke. At the same time they rush in with their axes – Tommo in the lead. It is over in a moment, and four men soon lie dead at the hands of three axe fighters.

It is only then that Tommo discovers, to his horror, that two of them are mere lads of ten or eleven years old, though they stood bravely by their guns. Tommo is shocked and deeply ashamed. The three Maori with him swear that with all the smoke from the muskets and shotgun, it was impossible to see well enough to gauge the age of the four people in the room. Each of those four, they feel sure, would have killed them with an easy conscience had the surprise attack been the other way around. Nevertheless, Tommo believes that his fighting axes have spilt bad blood and he is anxious to go out again at the first opportunity to fight Murray's regulars. 'Give us a go against the British bayonets. I got no stomach for killing little boys,' he says sourly when he returns that night.

I try to comfort him and remind him that in the wilderness as a nine-year-old, he was deemed a man and could as easily have been killed by any timber getter. 'I know,' he says. 'But lads ten years old ain't yet mongrels in their hearts.'

Like Tommo, I am already sickened by this war. I fear Wiremu Kingi may be right and that I shall become General Back Off whenever I may find an opportunity to avoid bloodshed.

The British are enraged when they discover the killing of the two boys at first light the next day, even though it is quite clear that it was a terrible mistake. We fight only against the volunteer militia and the British military. Our enemies are those who have obtained Maori land without the permission of the whole tribe, or who fight to gain even more. Ours is a fight against greed, not against women and children. But the boys' deaths strike such terror that they cannot go unpunished and we wait for the soldiers to march against our *pa*.

We expect the British forces to attack us later that morning, but they do not issue forth from New Plymouth until one o'clock, a strange time to commence battle. We manage to keep them at bay, although their cannons and the artillery fire from their naval contingent keep us contained. For the first three hours it all seems to go in the usual way – the softening-up process by the British with us returning fire – and there is not much damage done except to a few palisades.

Then, to our enormous surprise, the British regulars from the 65th and the navy artillery contingent withdraw and set off to return to New Plymouth, leaving only the militia to hold us down. It is well before sunset and the volunteer militia, valiant and capable as they are, have only the old, slow-loading, smooth-bore muskets. As we will later learn, they have each been issued with only thirty rounds of ammunition to hold us for the night. Such is Colonel Murray's contempt for the Maori and disregard for the local volunteers.

For once the numbers are on our side and our weapons superior to theirs. There is great rejoicing in the *pa* and we send patrols out to harass the militia, intending to take them in a full frontal attack during the night when their muskets are least effective. They are not fools and retreat to a nearby farmhouse, where they construct a palisade. It is soon apparent that they cannot hold out against us. I am anxious to go in with a large force from the *pa* while daylight lasts, but this is an offensive under the control of War Chief Hapurona.

Hapurona decides to wait until nightfall. My fear is that these are settler militia who know the terrain and will use the cover of darkness to escape, as we did. It is here that I make a mistake of judgment which costs us dear.

So that they will not think to attempt escape, I use my men to harass the militia in the farmhouse and keep them pinned down. Unbeknownst to us, they have conceded that they must die in a night attack. With only thirty rounds of ammunition per man, they decide to use up all their firepower, hoping to intimidate my patrols before they perish, brave men all. For an hour they fire repeatedly as we wait for night to descend. Then Hapurona's warriors will go in with their shotguns and we with our fighting axes and spears against the settlers' swords and muskets.

A great many of Hapurona's warriors have assembled some distance outside the *pa*, ready to go against the enemy, when the navy suddenly re-appears. Later we learn that they have heard the gunfire and so have decided to disobey their orders to return to New Plymouth, choosing instead to march towards the sound of firing.

A terrible bloodbath ensues. We are trapped in near darkness between the militia and the *pa* by the naval artillery fire, and are cut to ribbons. Many of our warriors die before we are able to scatter into the night. What had seemed like a certain victory for the Maori before sunset, is by moonrise a dreadful defeat. The single initiative of a lone naval commander, who decided to disobey Murray's instructions, has saved the day for the British, at a great loss to the Maori.

If we had destroyed the volunteer militia here, it might well have made all the difference to the outcome of the war, for these volunteers are the most effective force the British possess. I am not blamed for pinning the militia down, so giving them cause to fire back sufficiently vigorously for the retreating navy to hear their guns. Nevertheless I blame myself.

During April, the British receive considerable reinforcements from Australia and many settlers return to their land, thinking the Maori defeated. The new forces, eager for action, lose no time in moving down the coastline, burning and pillaging our villages, hoping to starve us over the coming winter. We cannot meet them head-on for they are too well equipped with light artillery and grapeshot, and the most terrifying Congreve rockets. We must begin the old process of instilling fear in the settlers all over again. I send out patrols to burn every farm in those districts where we had not previously been and where the settlers have thought now to return. We carry off their cattle and horses and what food we can find, as the pakeha forces are doing to our people.

The governor, however, makes a great display of warning that we mean to kill all pakeha, including the missionaries. It must be obvious to him, though, that had we wished to do so, we could already have killed a score or more of the pakeha settlers. The Maori are upset by the governor's words, but I am not unduly concerned by them. I explain that it is the European way to build up hatred for the enemy. 'If the devil were to wage war with the angels of heaven, he would declare the enemy to be wicked and vengeful. It is in the very nature of warfare to make the enemy out to be monsters. Governor Gore Browne is only proving himself to be very good at it,' I advise the council.

'The ways of the pakeha are strange. Do not the enemy also deserve honour? Are they not also brave warriors?' War Chief Hapurona asks.

'It is called propaganda. They think it will aid their cause and will make their war seem righteous in the eyes of their own people.'

'War is only righteous when you defend your land, your women and your children. It is not righteous when you wish to steal another man's land,' Wiremu Kingi declares. 'We, the Maori, have fought each other for generations, hoping to take each other's land, make slaves of the other tribe's women and warriors of their children. But we did not call this a righteous war. We did not try to justify it as the British are doing!'

Murray promises to avenge the death of any white man killed, and the newspapers run lurid stories of those who have been tomahawked and scalped in the manner of the North American Red Indians! They have picked up the name of General Black Hawk, though they seem not to associate it with the Black Maori. They conclude that the Maori have recruited the famous Red Indian fighter, Chief Blackhawk, to teach them how to use the tomahawk on their pakeha victims. I am not sure such a man as

224

Chief Blackhawk even exists. Perhaps he is simply the invention of a newspaper reporter with a fevered imagination. Nevertheless, there is much speculation among the pakeha population that more North American Indians have arrived by ship, landing higher up the coastline. The paper reports a reliable rumour that there are more ships en route, with whole tribes of tomahawk-wielding Indians bound for New Zealand!

This in turn fuels further fears that a legion of Redskins, led by the legendary Chief Blackhawk, will soon attack New Plymouth on horseback, whooping their dreadful war cries as they scalp women and children.

Rumours aside, if we can keep the soldiers at bay until the winter, we may become strong enough to achieve an equitable truce in this war. The onset of winter works in our favour. The heavy rains make movement of the large British baggage trains near impossible, the roads turn into quagmires and the rivers are flooded. We are less hampered and our guerrillas roam the countryside until we have driven all the settlers back into New Plymouth.

By June we have recovered our strength somewhat and, working in difficult conditions, we construct two forts at Puke Te Kauere. I am forced to reconsider much of what I thought about fighting from a *pa*. I now realise the Maori have a genius for earthworks and fortification, and that we will need to meet the British head-to-head if ever they are to be brought to a truce. When this time comes, we shall need the forts to have some advantage in the proceedings.

The two forts at Puke Te Kauere are backed by heavy forest, the immense kahikatea trees. Wiremu Kingi takes Tommo and me into this primeval world of giant trees, ferns and damp. Tommo is at once at home.

'Ah,' he says, laughing, 'I knows this world of tall trees. If we was to fight in this I would become a general and we would surely win.'

Chief Kingi sighs. 'Not so long ago, much of my country was covered in great forests like this one. Now the pakeha have shaved us like a bald head, cutting down the trees which are older than our ancestors and have stood since time dreamed in darkness.' He turns away and spits to the ground. 'They cut them so that they might grow grass for their spotted cows. Once, there was the cry of birds in the morning, and the song of every kind of winged creature in the world filled the air. Now, where the pakeha have stolen the land, it has become silent and only the caw of the English crow is to be heard.'

He pauses and smiles sadly. 'If you listen with a Maori heart you may hear the earth trembling and weeping for the glory of the great trees. If the Maori do not hold onto their land, the pakeha will kill everything that is beautiful, so that they might make New Zealand like the faraway land of Queen Victoria, where there are no more tall trees to sweep the skies and brush the howling wind into whispers. The trees are the groves of life. Without them we are not ourselves, we are naked.'

I think of Tommo in the wilderness and our own sweet land of Tasmania, cousin to this one, where the giant gums grow as tall as the kahikatea. There, the timber getters harvest the Huon pine – and trees, a thousand or more years old, are bashed and beaten to the ground by the saw and the axe. I wonder how much longer they too will last upon this earth? Will our home become like New Zealand, a land shaved and broken by the plough of the white invader? Alas, we are of the same breed, and I cannot see how it will be any different. Perhaps, in our drier land, it will be even worse.

Looking at this forest, it is clear that we have placed the forts well, for no British column could think to gain access and attack us from the rear. To one side of the forts is a swamp. The water in some parts is well above waist height and it contains vast areas of sucking mud. To the other side is the heavily timbered country we can control. In the foreground, where the British will be forced to attack, lies thickly growing fern with abundant flax. It will make any approach, no matter how well organised, most hazardous.

We have built trenches and scarps twenty feet high and innumerable palisades. Both forts are a work of genius and give the defenders a great advantage against any assault by the British regulars.

After all is ready, we hold a final war council to discuss our tactics against the British. We have learned much of guerrilla warfare since the disastrous engagement at Waireka. With new regular forces coming from Australia, we do not expect that they will depart from conventional military tactics.

'These troops will not know New Zealand or the manner of the Maori,' War Chief Hapurona announces. 'Therefore we may fight them in our own way. What say you, Black Hawk?'

I am quick to agree, and point out that the terrain we occupy is not only easy to defend but also allows us to attack the enemy's flanks. Hammerhead Jack, an excellent tactician, has suggested to me that we also use the swamp to our advantage. Now I put these thoughts together. 'Should we not also come at them from outside the forts? They will think that, as always, we will only defend ourselves and so they will leave their flanks exposed. If we can attack them from our positions in the woods, from within the flax and out of the gullies, and you are holding them down from the forts, they will make for the ₃wamp, believing it to be good cover. That is where our axe fighters will take them.'

It is a bold plan and Hapurona is not sure we have sufficient men to both attack and defend. From their encampment less than a mile away, we know that the British have much the superior numbers. Finally it is decided that I should have command over the trenches outside the forts, and also have small roving bands with shotguns hidden in the forests, gullies and clumps of flax. Tommo and his axe fighters will be positioned in the swamp with their long-handled fighting axes, while others will wield fighting sticks to ward off the British bayonets. We have erected our flagpole in full view of the British camp. This time the flag is a black cross on a white field. We hope that they will once again seek to capture it.

We soon discover that Hapurona was right. The troops sent against us are plainly new regulars, greenhorns from Australia under British officers equally inexperienced at fighting our kind of war. The volunteer militia are nowhere to be seen and we are most grateful for this. I know that these local men are much too skilled to be drawn into attacking a position so well constructed and defended as our two forts.

After the disaster at Waireka, it is our turn for some luck. The British officers appear quite casual in their preparation and barely send out patrols to reconnoitre the terrain over which they must advance. It seems almost as though they expect some mild-mannered skirmish, a pleasant morning's outing for their men.

The British attack at daylight on the twenty-seventh of June, and are almost immediately in trouble. Our muskets start to pick them off from the trenches and the forts, and their advance is made most difficult by the heavily ferned terrain. The British think first to attack our flanking trenches and foolishly but valiantly charge with bayonets, but we simply retreat from the first line of defence, leaving them to face a second set of trenches beyond. Heavily loaded with equipment, they are exhausted, and now within reach of our double-barrelled shotguns. We begin to cut them to pieces with buckshot, so that they are soon forced to retreat. Not one trooper reaches us, though we shoot several at very close range. They turn to run with their entrails hanging to the ground and blood spurting from their mouths. They cannot even cry out, taking but a few faltering steps before they collapse and die. The British will later report that the storm of shot they ran into was worse than that of Balaclava.

As the soldiers withdraw, we come at them from the wooded flank and out of the gullies and flax, driving them towards the swamp where Tommo's men lie in wait. The black powder of the muskets creates a great deal of smoke, and we fight as though we are in a forest fire. It is Hammerhead Jack who directs this attack, for he seems to know every Maori position and when to employ it. It is he who is the true general and I will make this known to Hapurona lest I receive credit which I do not rightly deserve.

The retreating British regulars, thinking the swamp will provide cover and give them protection, are soon waist deep in water, and now Tommo's men attack with their fighting axes and *taiaha* sticks. It is slaughter of the most terrible kind and the cries of the dying are pitiful. Soon the corpses are so numerous that they float bumping against each other in the water, which has now turned the colour of blood. Those who manage to struggle back to higher ground are cut down by our warriors, who have emerged from the forts to attack the fleeing soldiers.

What remains of the attacking column is forced to retreat under cover of their artillery fire. The British have been routed and the Maori have established a new way of fighting.

I return to the *pa*, sickened at the sight of so much blood and death. Wiremu Kingi and Hapurona hail me as a hero, though I feel far from heroic. I have had enough. The Maori now know how to wage war differently and much experience has been gained. I can play no further useful part in their affairs. Tommo is right – it is time to leave.

Wiremu Kingi addresses me in front of the council of war. 'You have proved yourself, General Black Hawk, and your methods have changed the way the Maori will fight the British from now on. We owe you a great debt. Our ancestors will honour you as long as the Maori stand upon this land! Tonight we will celebrate our victory and you will be foremost among our many warriors.'

I know I should think this a great moment, but I am war-weary and most anxious to find Tommo, whose men have taken the brunt of the fighting in the swamp. The attentions of Chief Kingi and War Chief Hapurona and the other high-ranking warriors mean I am forced to remain with the war council until well after dark. In this time I am able to extol the virtues of Hammerhead Jack as a born leader of men, and I declare him a better general than ever I shall be.

I have already sent Hammerhead Jack to find my brother and expect them both to be waiting for me. Finally I am able to take my leave, and go to tell Tommo that our task with the Maori is complete, our debt repaid in full.

But Hammerhead Jack is waiting alone outside, and I see at once that something is wrong.

'What is it?' I ask in alarm. 'Where is Tommo? Where is my brother?'

'Ork, he has not returned from the swamp. Five of the axe fighters are not back, and he is among them.'

'Have you searched?' I start to shake him by the shoulder where his arm is missing. 'Have you sent men into the swamp to look for him?' My panic is growing rapidly.

'Ork, I have come out of the swamp to tell you. I have been in there myself with flax torches, and the others are still searching among the reeds.'

I notice for the first time that he is wet up to the waist. His breeches are covered in mud and he is shaking from the cold.

'The water is full of the bodies of the British and we have found three of our axe fighters dead,' Hammerhead Jack pauses, 'but not Tommo.'

'We must keep looking! I will come with you!' I turn to run out of the *pa* but Hammerhead Jack grabs my arm.

'Wait! It is full moon in an hour, we can see better then. You must eat first, you have not taken food today! You will have no strength, Ork. The swamp is freezing and treacherous with sucking mud. You will surely perish!'

'I must find Tommo!' I shout, tearing away from him. My heart is pounding and I think I will die of the fear that has taken hold of me. 'Oh God! Oh Mama! Ikey! Help me now!' I begin to run wildly towards the swamp.

Chapter Eleven

TOMMO

Puke Te Kauere
27 June 1860

I'm sitting up to me waist in a bloody swamp, near shitting meself. The redcoats are everywhere. There's smoke covering the battle so it's hard to see, but wherever there's a clear patch there's half a dozen British to be seen, loading, firing and panicking.

I had to open me big gob about the long-handled axe being better than the bayonet, but even after Waireka, I got me doubts. I've learnt a great deal from how the Maori handle a fighting stick, but it's different when a trooper with bad blood in his eyes is comin' straight at you – him with a reach o' six foot or more, and me with an axe what don't extend more than two foot. All of a sudden, it don't look too promising.

Ever since we took the farmhouse and them two young lads was killed, it ain't been the same for me. I've seen how the axe kills now. I've thought about that moment a thousand times. Could I have known they was lads before we struck them? The room were filled with smoke from their muskets and from the shotgun blast, so we couldn't see hardly nothin' at all when we entered. I know I axed someone, but who I couldn't tell. Just a neck and a bit of shoulder in the smoke and confusion. Our blood was up and running high 'cause we'd won the day. But when the smoke cleared, two young lads lay dead next to the two grown men. I don't reckon I'll ever get over that. So young and brave one minute, and then hacked meat at me feet. Oh Gawd! What would our poor mama think o' me?

We've been waiting here in the rushes for nigh three hours, having come into the swamp from the back. It's the middle o' winter and bloody cold! I'm thinking of Hawk in the trenches and worrying for him. But he says we're not to come out, we're not to fight in the open. Instead we must wait for the British to come to us. Let the swamp slow them down, then take 'em by surprise.

I know me lads, though. They can see the British be in a mess already on the higher ground and they'll want to go after 'em. I pass on the word, no one must move until I say. But these be young warriors, anxious to be blooded in battle. They won't like the idea of holding back, freezing their bollocks off while there's a hot fight going on.

How the hell does Hawk know the British will come? He's pretty new to the business of being a general. The lads have waited three months to have a second go at the British soldiers. They're spoiling for a fight. Me, I'm not so keen no more, not after Waireka and the farmhouse. When we comes back from that raid the *rangatira* called us heroes. Our attacks on the settlers be proof to them that we are of true value to them in this war. I'm not so sure. Waireka just about finished us off – Tommo Te Mokiri lost six good men that day. Now me boys are waiting for another chance to meet the British, and their turn will come soon enough if Hawk be right. He reckons the redcoats will run to the swamp for cover. I hope he's right. I can't hold me lads back much longer.

Suddenly it happens. I watch, hardly believing my own eyes, as the first soldier comes running towards the swamp. He's stumbling out of the smoke towards us, not charging with his bayonet, just running for cover, scared witless, fleeing the shotguns what's pumping hot. I pray the lads will wait, not take him at once in a rush and give the game away to the rest. I send out the word to let him come right up to us, right up to the bulrushes where we hide. The redcoat is splashing through the shallows, knees pumpin' high, trying to go faster, floosh, floosh, floosh. It's heavy going, 'cause his boots stick in the muddy, sucking bottom of the swamp, and he's panting and gasping, eyes popping.

Then they's all heading our way, coming thick and fast through the smoke. I can hear the Maori shotguns. Bah-bam! Bah-bam! It's a different sound from the muskets what sounds more like a ba-boom-whup. The shotguns are working fast and the redcoats are turning and making straight for the swamp. Any moment now there'll be ten or fifteen of them upon us and twice as many more behind. 'Hold it lads, not now, let them come in deeper, nearer, take yer time,' I orders under me breath.

My fear has left me, drummed out by the pounding of me blood. Next instant there's a face in front of me. It's black from gunpowder and almost comical-looking, the eyes red-rimmed and showing white eyelashes. The soldier's in up to his waist, with half of his musket under water. All he wants to do is get to the safety of the reeds and rushes. He's looking directly at me, but his eyes show no recognition of what they see. The axe in me hand seems to know its own way, and I feel the blade bite into the man's head, soft as butter. The poor sod don't have time to think, from the moment he sees me to the moment he's dead.

Now the British be everywhere around us. Some is trying desperately to fire, but most has come into the swamp with their muskets unloaded and not ready to use their bayonets. They're belted and booted, and their shako caps sit high and awkward upon their heads. They be weighed down with their packs and most clumsy-like. With us bare to the waist and carrying nothing but our light fighting axes, it ain't no contest. The men at the front are forced towards us, as others come in behind them, pushing them forward in their haste to gain what they think is the safety of the swamp.

Another redcoat comes at me now. He's seen his mate die and he's got his bayonet at the ready. 'Bastard!' he shouts, and tries to run me through. It's clumsy stuff in the water and I brush the bayonet aside, hitting him on the jaw with the butt end of the axe handle. His head goes back at the impact of the blow, baring his neck with the strap of his shako biting into it. It's clear and clean-shaven, and me blooded blade finds its mark. It is all too easy, and he don't even have time to cuss again before he's a gargle of frothy blood sinking into the water. His eyes look sort o' surprised, though his neck is almost cut through and he's already dead before his head hits the drink.

All around me there's screaming from the British, and shouting and grunting and whooping from the Maori lads. The strange thing is that the redcoats keep coming. They can see us clear as daylight now – well, maybe not *that* clear given all the smoke – but they must not know that trouble lies ahead. They're at the edge of the mud, not yet in the water, but they doesn't turn back. They just keep coming, shoving on those in front as they line up to die at the hands of the Maori axe fighters.

And then I hear the shotguns on the flanks driving them towards us. Bah-bam! Bah-bam! If they keep coming like this, we'll soon be too weary to kill them all. We're fighting in the water and the mud is heavy going, and there's too many o' the dumb bastards for one afternoon's killing!

From the corner of my eye, I see a soldier coming at one of my lads from behind. The Maori don't see him 'cause he's fighting another trooper with a big yellow moustache what's trying to stick him. 'Die, nigger!' shouts the moustache. The redcoat behind has his bayonet ready to run me lad through his back. I got no choice and my axe leaves my hand. It flies through the air and takes the trooper in the back of his head, splitting his skull, and lodging itself tight. The other man sees this and stops for one second, and that's enough for the Maori's axe to take him.

I starts moving towards him, shouting to the Maori lad to grab my axe. The trooper I've hit has sunk slowly into the swamp. He is dead, but he must be resting on his knees somehow, his head still showing above the water. My axe handle pokes up out of the crimson water still stuck in his skull. But in all the noise the lad I've saved don't hear me and moves forward to take on another redcoat.

In the back o' me mind I think I hear Hammerhead Jack shouting behind the smoke on the higher ground. There are bodies floating everywhere, troopers' jackets stained dark from the swamp water with little air pockets of brilliant scarlet bobbing above the surface, bright lilies in a blood-red stream.

A few wounded redcoats try to beat a retreat in the shallows, but they don't last long. The mud sucks at their boots, and most slip and fall to their knees. The Maori lads has stopped their whooping and has turned into a killing machine. The axe kills more surely than the musket and more swiftly than the bayonet – its aim in a good warrior's hands is always to the head or neck.

I'm wadin' towards my own axe, its handle now only six inches above the surface. The trooper's head has gone under. I hear a shot ring out and suddenly I'm knocked over. I'm down under the water, kicking out wildly, trying to catch me breath. Bloody hell! I've been hit. There is a terrible pain in my head and I tries to come to the surface, kicking and flailing my arms. The top of my head bumps against somethin' and I push against it. I try with all what's left in me to push me noggin past whatever's in me way but I can feel my strength failing. Then it's lights out for yours truly and I don't remember nothing no more.

When I come to, all is blackness and I can't open my eyes. Around me frogs is croaking and crickets chirping. I know I'm in water, suspended-like, not floating, though I'm not sure how my head comes to be above the surface. I am frozen stiff, so I can't tell whether me feet touch the bottom or whether I float upright. I try to force my eyes open but they's stuck closed. Perhaps, I think, they *are* open and I'm dead, or I've been blinded by the musket ball what hit me. Me head aches something terrible, but I have my senses about me. Only I can't move or see nothin'.

Slowly it comes to me. My eyes are stuck with blood, dried blood, my eyelashes glued together. In the distance I can hear singing. It's the singing what brings me back. The Maori is singing in the forts, singing their victory chants and shouting their fierce war cries. I must try to get my arm up, but it too seems stuck. How is my head held up out of the water? Why don't I sink? I try to work my eyes open again but cannot.

Then I hears me name. It's Hawk, shouting, 'Tommo! Tommo!' His voice is hoarse, as though he has been shouting a long time. I try to answer but nothing comes. Then I hear a swish of water as if someone passes nearby, and small waves lap against me head. Hawk is passing me! Calling for me and I can't say nothing! I can't lift my arm or kick or shout out or move me head. Inside, I'm screaming and, for the first time, I truly know how it must have been for Hawk when he were dumb.

An hour or more passes and then someone goes by again, calling out in a desperate voice. It is Hawk, still calling my name, though his voice be near gone.

Suddenly there is a bump as Hawk brushes into whatever is holding me. I hear a gasp and a great howl, like the cry of a hurt animal. Hawk pulls frantically at me, sobbing in big gasps as he lifts me from the water in his arms. 'Oh, Tommo! Oh, Tommo!' he bawls. 'Oh, Tommo, what have I done? I have killed you!'

He splashes out of the swamp and I hear others shout, then Hammerhead Jack's voice. I am laid down on firm ground and a head is put to me chest. It is Hammerhead Jack again. 'Tommo good!' he says. He starts laughin'. He can't stop and others join in. Then everything goes dark as I fall asleep or pass out.

When I awakes, I can see again. I'm lying beside a fire, wrapped in blankets, and my whole body aches as though it has been clubbed. But I ain't cold anymore, though my head still hurts fierce. Hawk is seated cross-legged beside me, his head on his chest and his hands in his lap. He is asleep. I am so tight-wrapped, I cannot move, though I can wiggle me toes and move me fingers. Best of all, I can see, but my throat's terrible sore from the cold and I doubt I can talk.

I look at Hawk sleeping and the tears run down me face. I dunno why, but I can't stop crying. Maybe it's relief 'cause I can see again. Maybe it's seeing Hawk. He has deep lines under his eyes and his mouth is pulled down from tiredness. Hawk and his stupid conscience got us into this bloody mess. Why can't he just be like other folk and not care, not give a bugger for naught, like his brother Tommo?

Then I think of Makareta and the baby what's due any day now. Maybe it's even come. God bless me soul, I could be a father already! Makareta were nearly a widow! With a shock, it hits me that I *do* care. I cares about the two young lads we axed, about Makareta, my unborn child, Hawk, even Mary! But, still and all, I don't know how *much* I care. Would I have done anything different if I'd known those two settlers were mere lads, even if one was pointing a loaded musket at me gut? Would I risk me life to save his? I don't think so. Hawk, he would. But not yours truly, that I doubts very much.

That's the thing about me brother – he don't measure how much he cares. If a man is kicking a dog he's gunna stop him, whether it be a flea-bitten mongrel not worth tuppence or a squatter's prize sheepdog. It don't bother the big bloke. Hawk just gallops to the rescue, bugles blowing, nostrils flaring, huffing full of indignation!

Hawk can't bear what's unfair in this world. I, on the other hand, knows everything's unfair. There ain't nothin' fair about this sodding world. The mongrels don't never go away. We has beaten the British but I know it's only *this* time. They'll be back.

The Maori cannot win. The pakeha wants their land and they'll get it, come hell or high water.

Hawk opens his eyes and sees me looking at him, sees me tears. 'Tommo?'

I smile.

'Tommo, speak to me!' He reaches out and shakes me. 'You all right?'

I nod.

'Can you speak?'

I open my mouth and a small croak comes out.

'Throat sore? But you can speak?' he asks, anxious. I nod again and he smiles. It's Hawk's real big smile, what can't be resisted. I smiles back, me gob nearly as wide.

It seems I owe me life to a dead British soldier, the redcoat I killed when I threw me axe, as a matter o' fact. When Hawk found me, my head were jammed in between the dead man's legs, the back o' me neck tight against his crotch, my axe still sticking out o' the floating corpse. The redcoat's knapsack kept him floating and my feet touching the bottom of the swamp kept him level in the water. His big British bum were the resistance I felt when I tried to come to the surface. It ain't a pretty thought, my head up a soldier's arse for ten hours.

In two days I have me voice back. There's a wound to the side of my head where a musket ball grazed me, taking some hair and a bit of me skull as well. I guess I'm lucky. I could've caught pneumonia in the freezing water. All them years in the wilderness must have toughened me up. And now I'm just a bit snotty and chesty and has a terrible headache. But I'm alive and grateful and, best of all, it's the end of the Maori wars for Hawk and me.

'Sydney! We is going to Australia!' It's the first thing I says to Hawk when me voice returns.

Hawk is too relieved at hearing me speak to object, and he nods his head. 'Enough of war and killing, Tommo. We cannot do any more here.'

I know Hawk'd rather head for Hobart Town, but I don't want to go back to Mary, not just yet. I'm not ready for the brewery or for mama and her green eyes looking at me – even though I know she wants us back and will do anything to accommodate us. In her last letter she underlined the word *anything* four times! She's talking about me – she'll have me back however much trouble I be.

She wants her precious boys home, she says. But I knows in me gut I'm not ready to see her again yet. We'll make our fortunes in New South Wales first, I'm certain o' that.

A gold rush be a gambler's paradise if you plays your cards right. For the man who can do a little relocation, there ain't no better place to be. I'm not intended for hard work of the digging kind. But with cards we can clean up. Then I'll return to New Zealand and bring back Makareta and me baby. Mary will have a grandchild and yours truly will be a respectable citizen, puffing his pipe and nodding his head and looking like he knows what he's doin' when he most probably don't.

I think about the grog. I ain't been near the black bottle for nigh on four years now. Perhaps I be cured of the drink at last. But I ain't been tested yet. Sometimes the craving still comes upon me awful. It gnaws at me gut, rips and snorts, and leaves me tongue hanging out panting for it! Other times it goes away for days at a time and I thinks it might be over. Perhaps having a woman and child to care for will help. I wants to get back to our village and see Makareta, to hear her soft, happy voice, to have her hold me tight in the dark and, if our baby be born and she be well enough, to make love to her again.

Now as I lies here and thinks of sweet Makareta, I realise how hard it will be to part from her and from all our Maori friends. They has been so good to me, Hammerhead Jack and the others on the whaling ship, with their axe revenge on Captain Mordechai O'Hara and our escape from the gaol at Kororareka. The one-eyed, one-armed giant is overjoyed at my recovery. This morning he comes to me and says, 'Always, Tommo, when we fall in the water, Ork comes to fetch us!' He throws back his ugly noggin and roars with laughter at his own joke.

But mostly I owes me thanks to Makareta, what loves me in every possible way. When I cries out in me sleep, she soothes me and holds me tight, or quietens me by letting me love her.

At last we take our leave from Chief Kingi and War Chief Hapurona, for I am strong enough for the journey back to our own tribe. There has been much praise heaped upon us and lots of feasting. Our fighting axes has killed more British than the muskets or shotguns and I am made *rangatira*. I am pleased for it means Makareta will have a higher status in the tribe of Chief Tamihana and when we're away, she'll be especially well cared for.

Chief Tamihana has grown in reputation among the Maori tribes, for though he is known as the kingmaker and peacemaker, he is also now known as a chief what is prepared to fight. His axe fighters has played a decisive role in the Ati Awa people's victory. Hawk, in particular, has been honoured for the work what he's done, and the honour is equally Tamihana's by rights and tradition.

In his farewell speech, Chief Wiremu Kingi says that we has both honoured the Maori people in battle. Hawk has proved he has the heart and *mana* of a Maori. There is nothing he cannot ask of the Ati Awa tribe save a chieftainship, what can only be bestowed by birth, though all says Black Hawk would make a very good Maori chief.

Hawk, as usual, don't ask for nothing. He just says it's been an honour to serve the old chief and his brother. Honour? I near loses me flamin' life and Hawk speaks of how privileged we be to serve! The chief says they want one of our ancestors to be included in the Maori tribe, to become an ancestor of the Ati Awa.

What ancestors? thinks I. Ikey Solomon be the only male what we knows, and he ain't either of our natural fathers. Ain't no good telling them about our true papas neither, 'cause we don't even know whether they be alive or dead. Maori can't have no female ancestors on their Council of the Dead, so we can't give them the fat old whore, Sperm Whale Sally, our true mother, or Mary, what I reckons might be of some use to them. More than them, we ain't got no ancestors to speak of. But to tell the Maori that would upset them something terrible.

'You must give the *tohunga* the name of your greatest ancestor and we will include him with our own, him you wish to sit beside the great ones. Will you tell us now who this shall be?' Chief Wiremu Kingi asks very solemn.

I can see Hawk don't quite know what to say. He can't insult the Ati Awa by giving no name, like we don't want our ancestor to be included in their tribal company. He scratches his head.

'There is one,' he answers, to my surprise.

The old chief turns to his *tohunga*. 'Black Hawk will give us this ancestor's name and he shall henceforth be in all your councils.'

The *tohunga* don't look too happy about this instruction. They don't seem to think it's a good idea, but they can't come out and say it, right there in front of us. Maybe later, among themselves, they will have the necessary arguments.

'Ikey Solomon,' Hawk says slowly.

'Icky Sloman!' all the *rangatira* repeat. 'Icky Sloman! Icky Sloman!'

'I-key So-lo-mon.' Hawk pronounces it carefully.

'We have it!' Chief Wiremu Kingi announces. 'Icky Slomon!'

I am hard put not to burst out laughing, but Hawk stays serious. 'I am most honoured,' he says, giving me a sharp look, 'and my brother is most honoured too that our venerable ancestor will commune with yours. Our ancestor's wisdom will always be available to the Ati Awa. On the affairs of the pakeha he is a great expert and will be happy to be on your side. I thank you deeply from my heart and on his behalf.'

'Tell us of this Icky Slomon,' War Chief Hapurona asks. 'To what tribe did he belong? What of *his* ancestors, what do you know of them?'

'A great deal!' replies Hawk. 'He belonged to the tribe of Israel and his greatest ancestor was a most wise king, King Solomon.'

'A king?' The old chief looks impressed. 'And this king, was he black like you?'

Hawk ain't gunna look at me in case he should laugh. 'No, he was like Tommo, like my brother, but it is said he took a black woman to his bed, the Queen of Sheba.'

'Ah, a white king and a black queen! So that is why you are black, General?' Hapurona nods towards me, understanding now how we come to be different, one from t'other. 'And Tommo is white.'

'Well, yes, it was not *quite* like that,' says Hawk, rubbing his chin.

But Hapurona don't hear, or don't want to. 'Then we are most honoured to accept the ancestor of a great king to sit with our ancestors,' he announces. I think he is glad we got a king, or someone what comes from a king, and is of the *rangatira*. Everyone, even the *tohunga*, now seems to agree that Ikey should be a Maori ancestor o' some prominence.

Hawk's turned two bastards born to a whaleman's whore on a beach into two noble princes. And there's old Ikey, peacefully dead in the graveyard in Hobart Town when, all of a sudden, without so much as a beg your pardon, he's whisked away in the middle o' some argument about who owes who tuppence ha'penny. Next thing he knows, he's sitting amongst a bunch of fierce cannibal savages what don't much care to be called 'my dears' and what thinks him more useful for the cooking pot than for his opinions on the art o' relocation.

I can hear Ikey in me mind as he expresses his alarm at being so abducted. 'Most strange and unusual, perplexing, astonishing, a whole sackful o' live rats and queernesses perpetrated upon a most properly dead and eternally slumbering soul, my dears!' Still and all, I reckon the Maori is probably more interestin' company than the dead of Hobart Town's cemetery.

Hammerhead Jack and the remaining of my troop of fighting axe men returns with us to Chief Tamihana's village. When we arrive at the *pa* of the Ngati Haua, we're greeted like heroes. We're escorted into the village and immediately taken to the *marae* for a ceremony to end the *tapu* what's been placed on us as warriors. This is conducted by the priests and makes us *noa*, that is to say, normal commonfolk once more.

Hammerhead Jack has told me that, not so long ago, warriors would feast on the carcasses of their enemies. This were known to be sacred food, *tapu* to any but themselves. In order for warriors to have the *tapu* lifted and become *noa* again, they was obliged to throw away the remains of the bodies what they'd been eating. Then the eldest female of the oldest hereditary stock, the *wahine ariki*, would eat the ear of the first enemy killed in battle. I, for one, be thankful customs has changed. I has already had me head up a dead redcoat's arse, but to have to eat him as well is asking too much o' yours truly.

Once we have been made *noa*, we gather at the *marae* for a great *hui* and there is much speechifying. I am made *rangatira*. Hawk receives a feathered hat and wears his black feathered general's cape for all to see.

Hammerhead Jack then tells the story of the battle so everyone might hear it first hand. He speaks of Hawk's wisdom and of my part in leading the fighting axe men. He tells of how I saved the young warrior's life, of how I were struck down and how I were rescued, giving it all in the most exact detail includin' how I killed the soldier and then got me head stuck up his arse. All assembled laughs heartily at this and one o' the elders points to the bandage on me noggin. 'Is that why you cover it?' he asks, to much merriment.

'So, Tommo!' says Chief Tamihana. 'Your new name shall be "The man whose face has seen the worst thing possible in battle."' I blush, for I thinks the chief is making merry again at my expense. But the Maori do not think this a joke and they nod sagely and clap at me new name. A warrior's name earned in battle be like being a knight o' the realm to the English. Then each of the axe warriors is named and honoured with a new song. Their names are took in by the *tohunga* and the dead is committed to their ancestors' care.

War Chief Hapurona and Chief Wiremu Kingi have sent a special envoy to Tamihana what now praises the tribe's warriors. The speech is long and boring and tells of the part each Ngati Haua warrior played in the Ati Awa's great victory. It is most flowery, but our *rangatira* takes in every word and I can see they be terrible proud of all us lads. Then we go to a great feast the women has prepared in our honour, with fifteen pigs slaughtered.

I am by now desperate to find Makareta, for I ain't been permitted to go to our hut. I had hoped to find her among the women what prepares the feast, but she ain't with them. Nor were she in the crowd what came out to greet us when we arrived. I can't leave the *hui* until I am given permission and it's very late at night before I can slip away.

I has only just left the edge of the great fire when I am met by Makareta's mother.

'Come quickly, Tommo. Makareta is birthing.'

'How is she? How long has she been in labour?'

'Since you came back, since sundown.'

'What! Why didn't you fetch me?' I cry.

Makareta's mother gives me a look. 'How may an old woman interrupt the affairs of men?' she says. 'Come, there is no time!'

Outside our hut, several women wait anxiously. 'The old women are with her,' says one as we approach.

'I got to see her.' I begins to shoulder my way to the door.

The women all draw back. 'It cannot be, it is bad *tapu* for the father to witness the birth,' Makareta's mother says sternly. 'You must wait, please.'

'Then tell me, how is she?'

But Makareta's mother goes into the hut without answering,

and one of the women brings me a drink of bush lime fruit. 'It is a difficult labour. She is not well,' she tells me, then asks if I want something to eat. I say no, and sit down to wait. From inside I can hear Makareta groaning and crying out. The sound tears at me very soul and I keep asking to go to her, but each time I am most sternly refused. My hands are tied. It would only frighten Makareta to see me, because of the *tapu*. Another hour passes and the feast is still going on, with a great deal of singin' and merrymakin'. I wish Hawk were here, but I know he can't be. Chief Tamihana will want him to stay at the feast all night.

Suddenly I feels them. The mongrels are here. I rise, not knowing what to do. I can feel them crawling under me skin and the hair at the back o' me neck stands on end. I swipe at my arms, trying to brush them off, and beat at my shoulders. Makareta's mother comes out of the hut, shakes her head, and starts to keen. It is the terrible, shrill sound of women mourning. The others takes it up immediately. They do not even look to where I am sitting, and it is as though I do not exist. Death has possessed their throats and there be no place for a man within their heads.

I push past them and run into the hut. One of the old women stands holding a small bundle what is squalling. Our baby! But Makareta is lying on a flaxen mat with much blood around her. She is breathing heavy and a rasping noise comes from her chest. Her lips is cracked and she is in a lather o' sweat, with tiny bubbles coming from her nostrils.

'Makareta?' I whispers, crouching down beside her. 'Makareta, it's Tommo! Tommo's come home.' There is no sound from her lips, only the rasping of her chest. I take up her hand and hold it in my own. 'Makareta, it's Tommo! Can you hear me? It's your Tommo, come home from the war!'

'She is dying,' the woman says. 'You have a daughter.'

I do not hear her at first. Then slowly it sinks in that she is talking to me as if Makareta be already gone. The pain in me heart starts to grow, not all at once but quick enough. It climbs up into me throat where it fills me 'til I know I'll choke with it. 'Oh God! Please don't let her die!' I hears meself say, though whether it be inside my head or out I don't know, for me fear and pain is blocking everything out.

I put my arms 'round Makareta, who is on fire to the touch. I bring her hand to my lips, and then crouches down and holds her in my arms. I rock her gently until my fear begins to fade, and I can breathe and speak once more. 'Please, Makareta, please don't die! I needs you! If you live I will stay here. I'll stay with you forever. Please don't die! Don't let the mongrels get ya, me darling!'

I feel Makareta's hand come up slow and touch mine. Her mouth moves painfully and she whispers once, 'Tommo!' She is too weak to say more, but I can see she is trying to speak. Her lips open, then close again, then open. She is trying hard to gather breath.

'What is it? I love you, Makareta!' I sob.

I feel her squeeze my hand again. There is no strength left and it is less than a child's hand putting pressure to mine. Then a tear falls from her left eye. Another follows from the right, rollin' ever so slow down her beautiful, sweet face. They roll across her cheeks and over her chin. In a whisper I can hardly hear, she says, 'Tommo, it is a girl. I am sorry.' Then she opens her eyes and looks at me, and I sees the love she feels. 'Tommo, will you forgive me?'

'Makareta! It doesn't matter! Please, please live, me darling!' I am sobbing, shrieking, unable to hold back any longer. 'Please?' I am now begging her. But she gives a small sigh, and the life goes from her.

I weep and weep. I do not hear the midwife leave with the infant. I cradle Makareta in me arms and rock her, as though if I should hold on tight enough she may live again. Everything is still. Outside the women are keening. It is like a pack o' dogs baying at the moon. The mongrels have won again. Me head aches something fierce. My tears are frozen to the back o' my eyes, like shards of glass. Tommo needs a drink! Yours truly needs the black bottle!

Chapter Twelve

HAWK

The Land of the Long White Cloud
July 1860

Tommo has gone. He left before dawn's light. I retire from Tamihana's feast at sunrise, too weary to think, and am immediately met by the old woman who is Makareta's mother.

'Makareta is dead!' she announces the moment I appear.

'Dead?' I cannot comprehend what I hear. 'Dead?' I repeat. Death through violence has been around me for so long that a death unrelated to war seems somehow impossible.

'She died in childbirth,' her mother adds.

Now I am suddenly alert and cry out in alarm. 'Tommo! Where is Tommo?' I should think first of dear Makareta, but it is concern for my twin which comes crowding into my head.

Makareta's mother shrugs. 'He is gone. I have not seen him.'

I try to gather my wits. Tommo gone? He cannot go without me. He is grieving, I feel sure, and cannot be far away.

'I shall send some young boys to find him,' I say to her. 'What of the child?'

'It is a girl. We have found her a wet nurse and taken her away. She is small but healthy.'

I nod, and the old woman sighs and moves away.

So Tommo has a daughter. But his child has cost him the woman he loves. Why must my brother always suffer such misfortune? The mongrels, as he calls them, seem to abound in his life.

244

I have not slept for nigh on twenty-four hours and think the same must be true for my twin. Perhaps he has gone into the forest and sleeps there. I send several young lads to find him, though God knows how they will do so if he is in among the tall trees.

'Do not wake him if he is asleep, but come back to tell me where he may be found,' I instruct them, and the lads run off, anxious to do my bidding. Weariness overcomes me. After I have slept a little I must attend to Makareta and ask the elders and the *tohunga* to arrange the funeral rites.

When I awake shortly before noon, the young lads are waiting outside my hut. 'Have you seen him?' I ask anxiously.

'We have searched everywhere, Black Hawk. He is not to be found. Some of the women who rise early say they saw him leave the village before daylight and take the path north.'

'The track to Auckland?' My heart sinks.

'It is the same.'

'Thank you,' I say. 'Let me know if you see or hear anything more.' They chorus that they will do as I ask.

Slowly my suspicions begin to grow. The demon black bottle. Tommo has been pushed over the edge. My brother is back in the wilderness and wishes to escape into the oblivion of grog.

I must speak to Chief Tamihana, but he is still asleep and I must wait. I pace outside his hut impatiently, then go to sit under a shady totara tree. But I am too anxious to remain seated and soon resume my restless vigil by his door. It is mid-afternoon before he emerges.

'Why do you disturb me from my slumber, Black Hawk?' Tamihana frowns slightly.

I apologise and explain what has happened. Then I beg leave to depart at once, explaining that I fear that Tommo has gone to Auckland.

'Why?' Tamihana asks. 'Why would he do such a thing? He is *rangatira* now. He will have a good life with us.'

'It is a matter of the heart,' I explain. 'My brother will grieve much over Makareta's death and will think not to show this to the Maori.'

'Why can he not grieve here? We will understand. We are not savages, Black Hawk.'

'With the pakeha it is sometimes different. They wish to drink spirits to forget their grief.'

'And Tommo has gone to obtain spirits so that he may forget?' I nod and Tamihana continues, 'We will send a message to our people, they will soon find him and bring him back.'

'No, I must go myself. He is of my blood.'

Chief Tamihana laughs at this. 'You, the man they want most, would walk straight into the enemy's camp? The pakeha will murder you. You cannot go, Black Hawk. I forbid it.'

'Tommo will not go to Kororareka, where they might recognise us,' I say.

'My friend, they know who you are everywhere! Kororareka, Auckland, even in Wellington they know of you! They know of the American Indian, Chief Blackhawk, who fights for the Maori.'

'But I do not look like an American Indian! The townsfolk will think me just another Maori. They do not know me by sight.'

'Ha! There are no Maori who are so black and stand so tall as you.'

'Nevertheless, I must go. I must find Tommo before he comes to harm.'

'Sit,' Tamihana now commands, indicating a bench.

I sit, and a woman brings us food and drink. The chief's food and mine are the same, but are served separately as it is *tapu* to eat from the same dish as Tamihana. 'Eat, Black Hawk,' he says. 'I wish to talk to you as a friend. It is most foolish to go to find your brother. You must stay here and I will send others to find Tommo and bring him back to us.'

It is then that I tell Chief Tamihana that Tommo and I have decided to leave New Zealand and, with his help, return to Australia.

He is silent a long while before he replies. 'A man cannot be held against his will, but we will miss you greatly, my friend. We have come to look upon you as a Maori. Your blood is our blood.' He pauses. 'You have brought great honour to our people, Black Hawk.'

I struggle to reply. 'I have only used what I knew, that is all.'

'No, beyond that,' Tamihana says. 'There is one thing you have taught us we shall always remember. Do you know what it is, Black Hawk?'

I shake my head.

'Do you not remember when you lifted War Chief Hapurona's aide by the neck, after he called you a coward?'

I look up, shocked that he knows of this. 'I am greatly ashamed to have done such a thing. He is a brave man.'

'A brave man perhaps, but also a foolish one!' Wiremu Tamihana replies. 'What he did was a thing of tradition. What you did changed this tradition forever.'

'I do not understand. What did I do? It was over in but a moment and I thank God I did not kill him.'

'Let me explain. If you had not spoken against staying in the *pa*, no one else would have. When Tamati Kapene called you a coward, he was following tradition. To talk of defeat is to be thought of forever as a coward and no Maori would have had the courage to do so. There is even a *tapu* against expressing such a thought.

'When you lifted Tamati into the air with your bare hands, you challenged the *tapu*. If you had killed him, as any Maori would have done, the *tapu* would have remained fixed. When you threw him to the floor and said not a single word, all who watched knew then that it is not cowardly to think about defeat and to live to fight another day. They knew that the *tapu* had broken itself.'

Wiremu Tamihana spreads his hands. 'The victory the Maori have enjoyed against the British in this last battle was because you helped defeat this great *tapu*, the strongest of them all. We are in your debt, General.'

I am astonished at these words. 'But it is to your people that my brother and I owe everything. When we first came, we were hunted by the law and you gave us your protection and shelter.'

Tamihana smiles. 'You will always be welcome among the Maori, my friend. But it is too soon for you to join our ancestors. If you go to find Tommo now, you will not last one day before the pakeha have your life. This time they will not wait to put you in gaol so that they might hang you later. They will shoot you like a dog.' He looks directly into my eyes. 'Please, give us seven days to find your brother. I shall send Hammerhead Jack by ketch. He will reach Auckland before Tommo.'

It takes three or four days to walk to Auckland. By boat, it will take Hammerhead Jack less than half this time. It is a sensible idea. 'If after this time there is no news, I must try to find him myself,' I reply.

Tamihana nods. 'We shall find Tommo and put him on a ship to Australia!'

I am horrified at this. 'He cannot go without me!'

'No, of course not,' reassures the chief. 'We shall take you to join him and smuggle you on board at night. We will find a captain who may need our friendship should he ever return to New Zealand.' Tamihana points to the dish of yam and pork. 'Now eat a little. All will be well, you shall see.'

I take some yam and wonder for a moment how Ikey is getting along with the Maori ancestors, who are said to feast on unlimited amounts of roasted pork every day!

Then I pluck up my courage once more. 'I have a great favour to ask you, Chief Tamihana. It concerns Tommo's woman and the name of their girl child.'

'Name? What can it matter what she is called? A girl's name is not important.'

'I understand and would not usually make such a request. But when we leave, and with the child's mother dead, I would wish for this girl to be well cared for. Her grandmother's hut is *tapu* and has been burnt down as is the tradition. The old woman too is *tapu*, having been associated with the dead mother, and might not live much longer. Last night you made Tommo *rangatira*. I would not wish for his daughter to be forgotten.'

Chief Tamihana dismisses this idea with a wave of his hand. 'She will come into my household,' he declares. 'We will care for her. The old woman cannot come but we will see she is fed until her *tapu* is lifted, then she can join the child again. You need not worry, the infant shall be brought up as nobility.' I thank Wiremu Tamihana profusely, but again he waves this away.

'What do you wish her to be named?' he continues. 'We shall give her a Maori name, or is it a pakeha name you want?'

'It is a Maori name, but it is not an unimportant one.'

'What is it?' Tamihana asks, curious now.

'Hinetitama,' I say, preparing for the scowl to come.

Chief Tamihana keeps his expression blank, but it is some time before he responds. 'Do you know that this is a name we can only give to a princess? How can I justify giving Tommo's girl child the name of the Dawn Maiden, daughter of Woman Made From Earth? In our belief, to call a commoner or even *rangatira* thus would be blasphemy – unless she were, in her own right, a princess.'

'I beg your forgiveness, Chief Tamihana. I did not wish to blaspheme against the ancestors.'

Now the chief looks at me hard. 'You knew this was not possible, Black Hawk, didn't you? Why then did you ask me?'

'It was a most foolish thing. I had no right,' I say, feeling myself suitably chastised.

'My friend, you are young, but you are not foolish. Is it because of the widow who came to you in the night?'

'You know?' My face grows warm.

Tamihana nods slowly, then explains. 'Wiremu Kingi asked me why you seemed reluctant to take a woman. If you were to be killed, he did not wish you transported to your ancestors still a virgin. I told him I wished the Maori woman you took to be from the Ngati Haua but he said that while he was responsible for you, she should be from the Ati Awa.' Tamihana laughs, then shrugs. 'Ever the peacemaker, I suggested that she be from another Maori tribe, so that we need not quarrel. To this, the old chief agreed. But we wanted to be sure that this woman from another tribe was no less worthy than our own wahine, so we asked for a certain princess who is the young widow of a great warrior. She was ready to enter life again, to be made *noa*.'

I try to conceal my anxiety at my next question. 'If I should wish to find her again, would you tell me how?'

Tamihana shakes his head. 'It is a matter best left alone. We shall find Tommo and then you will leave for Australia.'

I know I should not persist but cannot help myself – the thought of lying with the widow princess again clouds my judgment. 'My chief, I have a great yearning for Hinetitama in my heart. Will you help me?'

Tamihana thinks for a moment, his eyes cast down, then he raises them slowly to mine. 'I will make a bargain with you, Black Hawk. You have two choices: you may find Tommo and leave for Australia. Or you may have this woman and the children she will bring you and stay with us. You cannot have a Maori princess and leave the tribe. Will you forsake your brother for her? You must choose.'

I look to Wiremu Tamihana and hope the distress I feel does not show on my face. 'There is only one possible answer. It must be Tommo. Will you send Hammerhead Jack to find him before much harm comes to him?'

The chief nods slowly. 'He will leave within the hour, and he will be in Auckland long before Tommo arrives on foot.'

It is a day later when I am summoned to the *marae*. I arrive to find many of the *rangatira* and the *tohunga* already assembled. I have no notion of why Chief Tamihana has called this meeting, unless it is to tell them of my leaving.

I take my seat, hoping that at some point I may be allowed to ask for a good burial for Makareta. It is my wish she might be given some small honour in her death for the sake of her mother and Tommo. Despite my pleas, I have not been allowed to see Tommo's newborn child because of the *tapu* created by her mother's death and Tommo's presence at her birth.

'We are here today to discuss the business of a girl's name,' Chief Tamihana announces.

There is a murmur of surprise among the *rangatira* and the *tohunga*. I myself am in some shock. Tamihana pauses for a few moments before turning to speak directly to me.

'Black Hawk, we have heard that Chief Wiremu Kingi has taken one of your ancestors, Icky Slomon, to sit among their own ancestors. Is this so?'

I stand, though I am too nervous to look into the chief's face. 'It is true, Chief Tamihana. My brother and I have been greatly honoured by the Ati Awa, who have declared our ancestor Ikey Solomon to be worthy to sit among their ancestors.'

'And did you not explain that this Icky Slomon is of the tribe of Israel and directly descended from the great King Slomon himself?'

Chief Tamihana is missionary-taught and knows more of the Bible than I. He will most certainly be aware that King Solomon is an ancient King of Israel who can hardly be claimed as our direct ancestor.

I stammer slightly as I try to explain. 'Yes, I told Wiremu Kingi that King Solomon was a great and noble king of the tribe of Israel. It is also true that the name Solomon is given to the descendants of the great king.'

'You talked of the black queen, the Queen of Sheba, and of how King Solomon also took her and folded her into his blanket? And in this way, you explained how Tommo has come to be white while you are black? A white king and a black queen and ever after, the generations to come, both colours spawned?'

'That was the understanding of Chief Wiremu Kingi,' I reply, wondering at what point he will denounce this unlikely tale.

But instead Tamihana turns to the gathered assembly. 'As I have long suspected, both Tommo and Black Hawk are in their own right descended from a royal house. We of the Ngati Haua should recognise this along with our brothers from the Ati Awa.' Tamihana is playing along with my story of our lineage! He smiles at me. 'Black Hawk, we too would wish to honour your ancestors. It is only right that we should do so.'

I hear a general hum of approval amongst the *rangatira*. Finally Chief Wiremu Tamihana puts up his hand to signal silence and when the assembly is once again quiet, he makes his announcement.

'Two nights past, Tommo's wahine gave birth to a girl child. The mother has died in childbirth and there is only a grandmother to care for the newborn infant. Her paps are dry and so I have decided this child should come into my household.' He smiles. 'My women grow lazy and fat. They shall be happy to care for the infant.'

I can see that the elders are curious as to why Wiremu Tamihana would even speak of this women's business, and the chief responds.

'I talk of this because we have not hitherto acknowledged the true status of Black Hawk and his brother Tommo and must now do so in the naming of this girl child.' Tamihana gazes about him for several moments. 'I am *ariki* and have communed with the dead on this matter and the ancestors have found a way. They would like this child to be named Hinetitama.'

All this is so very neatly put by Tamihana that there is only a short discussion about it and this mainly by the *tohunga*, who search for a precedent in ceremony which they might use to help fulfil this request. Ten minutes later they nod their assent to the chief. Tommo's daughter is to be called Princess Hinetitama Te Solomon and her ancestral claim to this title is to be the great King Solomon of the tribe of Israel. The Ati Awa ancestors may have gained the services of Icky Slomon but the Ngati Haua have acquired a royal princess of impeccable lineage.

I am again overwhelmed by the kindness of this great chief, and my words cannot express the gratitude I feel for the honour he has bestowed on Tommo and me.

Chief Wiremu Tamihana then talks briefly of our wish to leave and explains that he will help us to gain passage on a boat to

Australia. This news is received with the greatest regret by all. Several of the *rangatira* make speeches asking me to reconsider. Even the *tohunga* are most cordial for once, and the oldest among them expresses the wish that Tommo and I remain within the tribe when we depart.

'We shall always consider you Maori, for no Maori warrior could have honoured us more,' Chief Tamihana concludes. 'Black Hawk, in the name of our ancestors we salute you and wish you a safe journey across the sea. Our spirit goes with you always.'

I am once more overcome with emotion. I have nothing but love for the Ngati Haua, who have shown Tommo and me such care. I fear we shall never repay the debt we owe them.

I stand to address the chief and the elders. 'Chief Tamihana and all of the Ngati Haua tribe, you have been my brothers in peace and in war. Your counsel and wisdom have turned me from a callow youth into a grown man and as long as I live I shall cherish you in my heart.

'I would like to commend to you the man who first brought us here, Hammerhead Jack. I know that I am less a man, with both eyes and both arms, than he is with only one of each. I shall honour his name and his tribe as long as I have voice to speak of them. I know that if my brother Tommo were here he would say the same.

'We have left behind a girl child, the Princess Hinetitama Te Solomon. She is proof to you all that we love and honour your tribe and I hope that we may return one day. I ask that you keep a place on the *marae*, for my brother and me, where we may sit with pride among the *rangatira* and the *tohunga*. I request most humbly that you keep our name and our lineage on the lips of your old women so that the Princess Hinetitama will learn of us and know that we left her with the people we loved.'

Much applause follows, until Tamihana holds up his hand for silence. 'Black Hawk, the women wait outside to sing and they have asked for a message to carry in your honour in some future song they wish to compose in your memory.'

I am close to tears and when the words come, they are the best I can manage. 'May you find peace and hold your land safe and secure for your children. Keep forever your pride in yourselves. I pray you do this in the name of your ancestors and your children yet unborn and their children.'

I bow to Chief Tamihana. 'I leave you knowing that whatever happens in my life, my spirit will always dwell among the great Maori people. Farewell, beloved friends. Until I return, I shall carry you in my heart always.'

We leave the *marae* and are soon surrounded by a great host of women who, except for the very foremost, are too close-packed to dance the *poi*. As we emerge they commence to sing a haunting lament and I am at once flooded with tears.

Chapter Thirteen

TOMMO

The Land of the Long White Cloud
July 1860

All I can think of is the black bottle. I doesn't think of Makareta or even our baby. It be too hard. I must remove Makareta from me head for I can't bear the sorrow. I got to drown it, kill it, make it go away before it takes a hold o' me. There is only one way I knows to do this, the black bottle. It's the Cape brandy for yours truly.

That's all I think of as I leave Tamihana's village. Even Hawk ain't in my mind. I can't think of anything or anyone what might stop me from getting a drink. My head hurts most terrible from the gun wound, and I don't care if I lives or dies. I think I'm goin' mad.

I pass several Maori on the road what greet me and seem to know who I am, but I don't care enough even to reply. I walk for hours before I even think about where I might be headed or what might happen to me if I'm recognised by a pakeha. I wears a blanket and sandals in the fashion of the Maori and would seem most odd to any white man what looks at me for more than a moment. It'd be stupid to go to a small town where I'd be recognised before I even gets a drink, and so I decides to push on to Auckland, where I can more easily disappear into a grog den or one-shilling hell.

I ain't felt the slightest hunger, me stomach craves only spirits, and there's a great gnawing at me guts. But by evening I knows I has to eat or I'll never reach me destination, the black bottle.

I stops in at a Maori village what I know ain't on the side o' the British as some 'round these parts are. It seems they don't know me, thank Christ. But I speak their language, obey their customs and wear their clothes and charms, and so they accept me. I ain't the first pakeha to take up the Maori style o' living and they are a generous-natured people. After feeding me they ask if I want a hut for the night. But I'm used to sleeping rough and now that I'm fed, I'm anxious to keep going. There is a clear sky for once and a bright moon, and no bitter cold wind blowing from the south.

On the morning of the second day I comes upon settlers twice. The first I sees is a lone man with a horse and dray, piled high with cabbages. The other is a man with his wife and family and all their worldly possessions packed on a bullock cart. I hides meself off the roadside as they pass by.

My head has cleared somewhat, and I realise that I can't enter Auckland dressed as a Maori and hope to sit down to a game o' cards. I should have bailed up the cove in the cabbage cart and swapped me clobber for his, though he were dressed as a farm labourer, a poor enough outfit for a man seekin' a game o' poker in the city.

Towards evening I spies a farmhouse set back from the road. The weather is fine but will soon enough close in, as it does most nights, and I need to find shelter. I'll watch the house and if the chance comes up, get inside and find me some pakeha clothes.

I follow a small stream up to the farmhouse and find a spot from where I can see the comings and goings of the farm folk. Sure enough, I soon see two lads bringing in half a dozen cows. For one terrible moment I thinks of the two lads we killed. I remember how me darling Makareta used to comfort me in the nights when I were sick at heart with meself. When I'd wake affrighted, having dreamt of the wilderness again. But I must put Makareta out o' me head. From now on, it's just Tommo on his own again. I looks more closely at the lads. One is near me size, dressed in rags, and the other's smaller, perhaps three years younger, nine or ten years old. The house is neat and well kept with a bit of a vegetable garden at the back. They looks like poor but respectable folk, probably church-goers, and if so the elder might have a change o' clothes for Sunday best what could fit.

I starts to make me plans. Cows need milking in the early

morning, requirin' all hands on deck. If there's a missus about then she'll be in the barn not long after dawn to see to the churning, and so the house will stand empty. The boys and the cows are followed by two border collies what might prove a nuisance. But dogs usually follow their masters and will no doubt be at the milking shed in the morning too for a dish o' milk or curds. The barn is upwind of the farmhouse and so they'll not scent me, and I reckon I can slip in from the back without being seen.

Shortly after I see the farmer coming in on a huge plough horse, the sort I've heard called Percherons. He's seated on its back without saddle or harness, a stout fellow, not too tall, though it be hard to judge with him sitting so high on the beast. Perhaps his Sunday best would suit me better than the lad's. Then a woman comes out the back o' the house and yells at the two lads to come in for tea. I reckons I has the family just about complete as there don't seem to be no farm labourers about.

I spends the remaining light exploring the creek, what I crosses so the dogs will not pick up me scent. The brook leads to a small river and 'round a bend I discover an eel weir and with it a nice fat eel in a basket-trap. I gather dry timber, what makes only a little smoke, and I cook the eel under the shade of a tree what will help hide any signs of a fire. With a full stomach I goes back and builds a snug hide, well concealed, from where I can easily see the farmhouse. I'm hardly inside it when the rain comes down and darkness falls.

Some squabbling tuis wakes me at dawn. This be most fortunate because next I sees the farmer's wife carrying two silver buckets towards the barn, the dogs yapping at her heels. Her two sons follow behind, and then the farmer himself comes out, scratching his bollocks and sneezing twice. I wait for another sneeze but it don't happen and I wonder if this be an omen or something. Gawd, I thinks, I'm becoming a flamin' Maori, looking for signs and portents in everything. I waits several minutes before removing me sandals and wading through the freezing water of the creek towards the house. A thin mist hangs low over the paddocks and the air smells of more rain to come as I creep towards the farmhouse.

The kitchen door be open, o' course, and there's a small fire on the hearth. I smell a stew and am half-tempted to help meself. But I press on into the main bedchamber, where I finds a large brass bed, a cupboard and a timber chest against the far wall. I am drawn to the chest and open it – only to find within it a wedding dress, careful folded away. Again I thinks o' Makareta, and that we might have been wed. Then I kills the thought quick and tell meself I has no interest in wedding dresses. I am about to close the lid on the chest and the picture it brings to me mind, when I thinks to look a little further. Beneath the wedding dress, to me great delight, is a suit of brown tweed, smelling of camphor. I pull it out and find it's an almost perfect fit. I can only guess it were the wedding suit of the farmer before his wife's cooking helped him to his present size. I thinks again o' the soup, what smells delicious, but I can't draw attention to meself by taking a bowl.

I place the wedding dress back as I found it, and close the chest. In the cupboard are three blouses hangin' upon a single peg. I takes the third what's hid behind the other two. It will do well enough, for it is made o' wool and has scarce been mended. Under the bed I finds a sturdy pair of well dubbined boots.

It will take until the Sabbath for the farmer to discover the loss of his boots and blouse, and months or years before he finds his wedding suit is missing. I am now possessed of a complete outfit. I am out the house in a flash with me booty under me arm and am halfway across the first paddock before I remembers a hat. Shit! I can't walk around with me head wound showing, and the Maori cap I wears won't look right with the pakeha clothes. I race back to the house.

In the small front parlour I find an old felt hat on the wall. It be too big for me and falls over me eyes but I am glad, as it will cover me wound without pressing down upon it. My heart is banging like a tom-tom as I flee across the paddock to me secret spot.

Long before the sun's climbed up in the sky, I'm back on the road in me new outfit. I has hid me sandals and Maori fighting axe in me blanket, and torn my old tattered blouse to make toe pads. These I stuff into me new boots so that they fits better. I does the same to the inside brim of my hat, leaving a small space so me wound can breathe and the lining don't rub against it. The suit fits well enough and, though the blouse is too big, I has it tucked in and bunched and knotted at the back.

I could hardly have done better for meself. The suit proclaims me a bumpkin well enough, but not one without resources.

A yokel come to the city to chance his luck or spend his butter-and-cheese earnings on matching his skill at cards. There is a soft drizzle to the day but the tweed's thick and will keep the damp out. I strap me blanket roll to me back and it's away to Auckland for old Tommo.

I know well what to do. Thanks to me wilderness years, nobody can play the idjit better. With my hat close-pulled over my eyes, I look like the original patsy-mark what makes a wharf gambler rub his hands with glee. It's a thorough disguise and in the dim light of a hell or tavern, I'll be nigh impossible to pick out as Tommo X Solomon. I am well through my nineteenth year and has grown a tolerable beard. Me face still makes me look young, all the better to gull some greedy bastard bent on fleecing me.

I'd be all set up for an adventure if it weren't for the craving in my belly, the pain in my head and the struggle not to remember anything. Instead, I knows I'm only gunna play long enough to secure a black bottle and then another and another 'til I can no longer remember my own name.

I will need a coin or two to match the stakes. Even a shilling'd do to enter a small game in an alley or tavern, and I think to sell me tinder box which, frankly, ain't worth much more. Two shillings will buy me a bottle o' Cape and I'll be damned if I can't turn one shilling into two in any game o' flats!

I'm less than an hour on the road when I realise my feet be in trouble. Since living with the Maori I ain't used to wearing boots. Now Farmer Moo-cow's boots be rubbing my heels most severe and I feel sure there be blisters forming the size o' me thumbnail. I stop and remove the boots and put me sandals back on, tying the boots together by their laces and slinging them 'round me neck – the way folks do in the wilderness when they's travelling some distance on foot to a wedding or funeral.

The next day I'm offered a lift on a settler's dray. At first I think to say no but realise this be more dangerous than agreeing. No white man'd willingly walk twenty mile when he can sit on his arse and spit on the heads o' any passing Maori.

If me new-found benefactor notices me Maori sandals he don't say nothing. In fact he proves somewhat a clod, a slow talking cove by the name o' Timmy Dankmarsh. He's a farmer and fisherman with six sprats – four boys, two girls – and his wife be with child again. I ask him to drop me off on the outskirts of Auckland, saying

I must visit a friend on a farm nearby. When he asks the name o' me friend, I says Jones quick enough – *Tom Jones* being the name of a most randy book Hawk taught me to read on board ship.

Mr Timmy Dankmarsh thinks about my friend's name for five minutes. 'Must be a new allotment. I doesn't know no Jones.' He thinks a few minutes more and shakes his head real slow. 'No, no Jones, I doesn't know him, that's certain.' Then he pauses again, so I swears I can hear him thinking. 'Not this side o' town anyways. No Jones this side o' town. Other side maybe, but not this side.'

'A trooper what's come with his family from New South Wales to settle,' I tries.

'Oh,' says Dankmarsh. 'Trooper, is it?' He thinks awhile then adds, 'Don't know no trooper fella lives that side.' But he don't say no more on the matter.

I walk the last two miles into Auckland and arrives as the one o'clock steam whistle sounds from the saw mill near the wharf. What a place! I had set me mind upon something different, perhaps like Hobart Town. I were expecting a proper town, with straight, well-paved, tree-lined streets, houses and cottages of a neat appearance of stone and brick, and shops with a good display of tempting merchandise.

This place ain't nothing of the sort! And it's the main port in New Zealand, the centre o' commercial life for the North Island! I can scarce believe my eyes. I comes across a main wharf what seems to be the centre o' the town. But the streets leading to it are mud tracks without a paving stone in sight and most with a trench dug to one side. I thought this were to channel the rainwater away, but later I hear it is to lay pipes for gas. I ain't never heard of a place what's got gaslights before paving stones.

The shops are mostly o' wood and brick, though dingy looking. Only one building o' grand design is to be seen. This be the Union Bank what's made of white stone, rising higher by three times than any other building. It has large columns from top to toe so it looks like one o' them Greek temples Hawk's told me about. I've never had no money in a bank, but I remember Ikey used to say that to own a bank and earn ten per cent on other folks' money is a most advantageous thing. On the other hand to deposit your own money and earn only two per cent is a terrible waste!

The town runs back from the water and up a steep hill, where the toffs live and where the troopers' barracks are. It's raining again, having stopped mid-morning, and the streets are muddy puddles, sprouting sudden wings o' wide brown water as the carts and sulkies go by. I has took to rolling up me breeches, and me feet are covered in red clay.

Now I see why that miserable sod, Nottingham, wanted us brought to trial here, for there ain't a shred o' kindness in any o' the faces around me. Still and all, every town has its bawdy houses and pubs and places what may usually be found with a little questioning. Muddied up to the calves, I walks along the waterfront hoping to find a suitable one-shilling hell. I see that other men has removed their boots, so I be no different to them. I enter a tavern, wipes me feet upon the mat at the door and puts on me boots. I don't even have the price of a glass of ale so must ask the publican straight out where a friendly card game may be had.

'Out!' yells the publican, pointing to the door. 'We don't have no truck with yer kind 'ere!'

Then I sees a grog shop in an alley, some ways up from the wharf, what's called the Scrimshaw Tavern. Two Maori whores stop me outside and make the usual offer. I tell 'em no, but politely and in their own language. Both laugh, showing me nice white teeth, and one says I can have it free if I want a knee-trembler behind the pub. The whores outside is good news. I got an instinct for places like the Scrimshaw, and I know at once things are beginning to go right.

I've seen two whaling ships moored in the bay and know there's a good chance o' finding some whalemen here. I'll strike up a conversation with them about finding a game instead of asking the owner. I hope there's none here what might recognise me ugly gob, but it's been well over three years since we was on the *Nankin Maiden*. Still I've no doubt that the tale of O'Hara's missing paw is by now a legend of the seven seas.

Inside, the Scrimshaw is crowded with whalemen, and I feel right at home. The tavern is a dark, smoke-filled cave what reeks o' rum and brandy, pipes and cigars, with a filthy floor, the daily sawdust barely covering the vomit. Here's a bloodhouse if ever I seen one and I be most delighted to have found it at last. I knows these men's lingo and it ain't long before I'm talking to an Irishman what works the try-pots on the *Cloudy Bay*, another whaling ship out o' New England.

'Tasmania, eh? Hobart Town? Bin there, know it well enough now, don't I?' he shouts when I tell him my home port. 'Got one o' your lot on board ship, a good man to be sure now. First class whaleman but always in trouble with the master. Likes a drink. Should be hereabouts soon enough, I would think.'

The Irishman offers to stand me an ale but I decline. Me lips are primed only for the taste o' spirits, for the sweet salvation of a bottle o' Cape brandy. A mug of beer ain't gunna do naught for what ails old Tommo. Besides, I has no way to pay him back.

'Suit yourself,' he says with a shrug, 'but I'll not buy you spirits, they be the ruination o' many a good man.'

'I ain't so sure I am a good man,' I says, then asks him if he knows of a poker game going. 'Later,' he says, 'around ten o'clock. Big game, five shillings to show, perhaps two pounds in the pot, you'll not be playing for a penny less, lad.'

'Oh,' says I. 'So you're not against the sport o' cards then, just ardent spirits?'

'Not at all, not at all,' the Irishman repeats. Bringing his frothy whiskers up from the mug he holds, he looks at me sternly. 'But they can't be mixed, now can they?'

'Cards and brandy? In my book they's part 'n' parcel o' the game o' poker,' I says, cheekily.

'Many's the ruination of the one by the other,' the Paddy says again, shaking his fat finger at me. 'Stay off the brandy, me lad!'

'This cove from Tasmania, decent bloke is he?' I asks, wanting to change the subject. I've grown tired of his 'many's the ruinations'.

'Aye, not too bad,' he says, then turns and walks away. But he spins around again and stabs a finger at me as if I might have forgotten so soon. 'I'll not buy you a drop, me boy, many's the ruination!'

I push my way through the crowd, feeling as out of place as a fart in church. I'm lookin' here and there, as though I be seeking my long lost cousin Jack. Without a drink in your hand it ain't easy to look like you belong. I've been away too long from the company o' white folk, I decide. When I first come in, it brought pleasant memories enough. But now I feels somewhat uneasy in all the noise and the smoke. I ain't the old Tommo no more, the bright lad fixing his mark with a smile, full o' malarky and bluff. Instead, I feel meself a stranger. My head hurts and me tongue's hangin' out, rusty for want o' small talk, even whaleman's talk what I thought would come easy to my lips. I can barely speak the queen's English no more, if ever I could! Suddenly I hear the Irishman's voice boom from across the room, 'Over 'ere, Tasmania, your nigger brother's come!'

I nearly drops dead from fright. Hawk has come for me! He's found me already and I ain't even had a drink! I look up towards the door expecting to see Hawk standing two feet above most o' the whalemen in the room. But I don't see nothing of the sort. Then me name is bein' yelled out for all to hear. 'Tommo!' I nearly shits me breeches. A thin black arm comes pushing through the throng followed by the grinning gob o' Billy Lanney.

'Where you bin, eh?' Lanney asks, clapping me on the shoulder. He's drunk, but not hopelessly so. I'm facing the man what brought a flagon o' good Cape brandy on board the *Nankin Maiden* from Hobart Town, and then took his flogging without ever once crying out. I'm glad to see him but don't know what'll happen next, not with his shoutin' me name out and all. But Billy is all smiles, patting me coat up and down as though he's trying to make certain that it's me. 'Plurry good, Tommo,' he announces finally. 'Plurry first class, eh?'

'Billy,' I hiss, 'I'm not Tommo, ya hear?'

'You, Tommo!' he says, patting me again.

'Johnny,' I hiss. 'My name's Johnny!'

'Nah, it ain't!' he shouts back. 'It's Tommo!'

What's a man to do? Should I scarper, get the hell out o' the place? I look 'round to see who's looking at us. But the Irishman is way across the room, and them what's close by ain't the least interested. No doubt we can't be heard above the chatter and din o' the pub.

I take Billy Lanney's hand. 'How's ya bin then, Billy?'

'You wan' a drink?' Billy asks. 'Brandy?'

I nearly faint at the thought. 'I'm skint,' I says, pulling out the lining of me trouser pockets. 'I can't buy you one back.'

'Ha, Tommo, me got plurry plenty, what'cha wan' eh?' He pulls out his purse and shows me half a dozen gold sovs and as many Yankee silver dollars.

'Cripes!' says I, and place my hand over his purse while I look about me. 'Not here, Billy, too many villains in a hole like this.'

Billy ignores me. 'What'cha wan' eh? You take, Tommo.' He

offers me his purse again. I close it and put it back into his jacket. Billy looks at me all solemn-like and puts his hand on me shoulder. 'Ya wan' a black bottle, eh, Tommo?'

It were always said he were a queer one, and when Crawlin Nestbyte went overboard, they all reckoned it were 'cause of Billy's prophecy. Now he's read me clear as a marked deck. He's seen right into my head, and spotted me cravin' for the black bottle. I'm tempted to answer yes, but I knows I'm gunna need three bottles, maybe more, and I ain't gunna steal from Billy. Billy follows the Aborigine way – if he's your mate, what's his is yours. He were most kind to me and Hawk when we come on board the *Nankin Maiden*. Some thought he were ten bob in the quid, but it ain't true. Billy's a proper gentleman and I ain't gunna sink to stealing from him, not now, not never. I ain't that kind o' drunk yet.

'Cards, Billy. I want t' play poker. Can you stake me?'

'Sure, sure.' Billy fumbles in his jacket and brings out his purse once again. He hands it to me. 'You take, Tommo.'

I take two gold sovs and an American silver dollar what be worth about five shillings. Then I put Billy's purse back in his whaleman's jacket. It's enough to get me into the big game and even to lose a couple of hands if I needs to set up some greedy bastard who thinks to take me.

I ask Billy what he's been up to, and he tells me his story, what be simple enough. After Hawk and me were took ashore under arrest, the *Nankin Maiden* sailed down from Kororareka to Auckland, where Captain O'Hara's stump were properly stitched up and took care of by the surgeon in the troopers' barracks. Then she sailed directly back to Nantucket, her hold being near filled. Billy gets paid his share when the boat reaches home port, and signs aboard the *Cloudy Bay*, what is bound for southern whaling grounds. But shortly after reaching Antarctic waters, the boat is damaged by an ice crush and must limp into Auckland harbour for repairs.

'This shit place, Tommo! No plurry good Aucklan', eh?' Billy shakes his head. 'Ya wan' a brandy, rum?'

I squeeze my eyes tight, but manage to shake my head. 'Billy, you're not to tell who I am.' I put a finger to my lips. 'I ain't supposed to be here, me name's not Tommo, ya hear?'

'Wha's ya name then, eh?' Billy asks, surprised.

I sigh. He sounds like he's three sheets to the wind but then again he always talks like this so I can't tell how drunk he truly is. I only hope he gets a handle on what I'm trying to tell him.

'Johnny Abacus. You calls me Johnny, right?'

Billy nods. 'Johnny, plurry good.' Then to me surprise he repeats perfect, 'Johnny Abacus.'

I laughs to meself. Billy, with his plurry this and plurry that, is easily mistook for being a bit slow, but he ain't nothin' of the sort. Billy's as good a man as you can have at your side and plenty smart with it.

It's nigh on ten o'clock when we is taken to an iron shed at the back o' the grog shop. Inside there's a table covered in green baize with three hurricane lamps hanging above to light it. Six chairs are set 'round the table and against the wall are two wooden benches. The room is warmed by a small pot-belly stove.

I takes a seat and when the owner asks what me poison is, I order milk.

'Milk!' he snorts. 'We don't sell no milk here, lad.'

The three other players what has come to sit at the table looks at each other, trying to hide their mirth.

'But I always drinks milk when we plays cards at 'ome,' I says, looking most disappointed. I pause. 'What be wrong with milk?'

The landlord sighs and looks to the ceiling. 'Nothing wrong with it, lad, but we ain't got none here.'

'Oh,' I says all innocent. 'Then I'll drink water. Does ya 'ave water, sir?'

He turns away in disgust. The other players all order Jamaican rum which, in a joint like this, is likely to have more than a drop o' water added, with a dash of tobacco juice to give it a kick.

Billy sits on the bench behind me with a mug o' brandy and seems happy enough. I has me hat pulled down low, and with me long hair and beard, there ain't too much of me gob to be seen. It's clear enough to the other players that they has a bumpkin on their hands. When they sees I got two sovs and a silver dollar in my possession, they'll know me for the best possible patsy-mark.

I wait long enough for them to give up staring, then starts up like Timmy Dankmarsh, the country clod what gave me a ride into town. 'Me pappy uh . . . er . . . he says, strong drink be the ruination o' . . .' I appear to be tryin' to remember what me pappy said, then gives up and shakes me head. I begins to giggle. 'He says it be the ruination o' something or other!' Then I take my hand out of my pocket and slaps down the two sovs and the silver dollar upon the green cloth. 'What's we gunna play then?' I ask, smiling cloddish-like again, not forgetting to leave me bottom lip hung open.

Suddenly I hears the scraping of the two remaining chairs. I look up from under the rim of me hat, and nearly falls off me chair. I feel the blood leave me face. If it ain't Maple and Syrup, them two bastards from the gaol-house at Kororareka what done Hawk and me in! It's the card-game all over again, and there's no way now I can make my escape. As if meeting Billy Lanney weren't coincidence enough for one night. Yours truly, I decide, is sailing very close to the wind!

The owner comes around and claims five shillings from all for the rent o' the premises and provision of the lookout. Gambling ain't allowed in Auckland. Billy ups from his bench, and pays it for me. 'Nigger yer banker then?' Syrup asks and the rest o' the table bursts into laughter.

'Aye!' I says slowly and grins. 'He can count better than me . . . and he don't use his fingers none.' I only wish my head didn't hurt so much – I'll need all me wits tonight.

The owner brings a new set o' cards and hands them all around for examination. I hold 'em up to the light. 'Why, they's all wrapped up!' I says. 'New, is they?' I lean back and hand the cards to Billy, 'Lookee there, Billy! Them's new cards an' all!'

Billy takes the cards and turns them around, shaking his head in wonderment. He hands them back to me. 'Plurry good, Johnny, eh?' he says.

Well, the game begins and I lose the first two hands by being purposeful stupid, but not so stupid that I look completely out o' me depth. Then I wins and acts most excited. The next hand I lose again – all this with my tongue at the corner of my mouth.

Maple and Syrup are the best o' the five players at the table and I lets them win from the others as well as me. But by the skin of me teeth I stays in the game. Finally it's just the two of them with the money piled up in front of where they sit and me.

It's the same as Kororareka all over again. They ain't learned nothing and I sets them up one at a time and cleans them both out with eight pounds snug in me pocket before midnight. After I've cleaned out Syrup, he asks if I'll take his marker. I look at him sorrowful-like, 'Mr Syrup, me pappy always said, neither a borrower nor lender be . . . for loan often loses both itself and a friend . . . and I wouldn't want to lose your friendship, Mr Syrup. Hee-hee.' Syrup gives a sickly sort o' smile and then there were only Maple left, holding a couple of sovs in change. I think he'll fold, call it quits, but he stays in the game and in two more hands, I've took the lot.

I reach down and unstrap my blanket roll so I can get to my axe quickly if needs be. My head hurts terrible but I've done the whole thing without any relocation of the cards. I ain't lost none o' me skill over the years! I pick up me roll like it's still strapped and put it under me arm.

'Thankee, gentlemen, much obliged.' I touch the brim of my hat to Maple and Syrup and bows, then does the same to the other three players what's now sitting on the benches. 'Come, Billy,' I says. 'Time fer some tucker.'

Suddenly Maple is standing in front o' me and Syrup to one side. 'I'm sure I seen you somewhere,' Maple says, pushing his finger into me chest.

'From Wanganui is you, then?' I says slow, but smiling like it's a nice surprise. 'Though I don't recall havin' seen ya.'

I can see he's trying to remember where he's met me before, but his head is rum-fogged and it ain't coming to him.

'I think you's cheated!' Maple accuses me now, and jabs my chest again, this time hard.

'Huh?' I says, open-mouthed. 'No, no! I'm a good Christian boy. Me pappy says . . .'

But I don't get no further, for Syrup has fastened on to me. 'Outside, you!' he says as Maple grabs my head under his arm.

'What's you mean?' I yells. 'I ain't done nothin' wrong!'

But both of them is dragging me away, back up to the pub and then through the front room of the Scrimshaw. 'Cheat! Cheatin' at the flats!' Maple yells to all what will listen. 'Him and the fuckin' black!'

When he hears this, Syrup cries out, 'Jesus Christ, now I remembers! Kororareka! The gaol, bloody Nottingham, you and the big nigger!'

'Billy, scarper!' I yell as Maple and Syrup throw me to the ground in the alley. There are whalemen tumbling out the door as fast as their feet'll carry them to witness the beating I'm gunna get. This is the moment I'm waiting for. I've hung onto me blanket roll

266

for dear life. I rise from me knees as they comes close, and Syrup takes a kick at me. I duck and his boot goes flying over my head so that he slips in the mud and falls on his arse.

'Why, you bastard!' he says, angry now. He gets quickly to his feet while the whalemen laugh at him.

'He's a crook, an escaped prisoner!' Maple shouts and takes a swing at me. This time, the blow grazes the side o' me poor old head and ear, knocking me down flat again. I can see Billy held tight by the landlord and one other bloke. I get back on me haunches and tear at the blanket. In a flash I has the fighting axe in my hands. Syrup swings a blow at me but I catch his wrist with the handle of my axe. Then I bring the flat head around and pat him polite-like to the chin and mouth. Suddenly there is teeth and blood flying everywhere. He drops to his knees, both hands held to his face. I slams him again to the side of the head with the flat of me axe, and he pitches face-first in the mud. He'll see dicky-birds for some time after, I reckons.

Maple roars and comes at me with his bowie knife, the eight inches of blade aimed straight at me gut. I swing the axe blade 'round and knock the knife from his hand, taking the top of his fingers with it. Then I reverse with the butt and strikes him in the face. I feel his nose and cheekbone crunch. It's all over in seconds and the crowd has drawn back, pushing against each other so that Maple and Syrup are alone in the mud at me feet, out cold, like a couple o' stunned mullets.

'That's for me brother, ya rotten scum!' I pant. With the handle of me axe I point to Billy Lanney. 'Let him go, he be a whaleman! Come on, Billy, let's get the hell out o' this shit hole!'

Several whalemen turns on the landlord and the other cove what's got Billy, and they lets him loose quick.

'He's a whaleman! Plurry good!' Billy shouts. 'Me, too!'

'And any of you what follows us,' I point with my axe handle to Maple and Syrup, 'you'll get the same as them, ya hear?' I pick up my blanket and sandals and begin to walk away. Then I stop and turn back to the crowd. 'And I didn't cheat! I wouldn't insult meself cheating with shore scum like them two Limey bastards!'

There's a cheer from the whalemen in the crowd at this. Then someone calls out, 'It be Tommo from the *Nankin Maiden*!' and there's a second cheer, this one louder. 'Go, Tommo, we'll see you clear!' another whaleman shouts.

'Plurry hell!' says Billy, coming to me side. Then under his breath, 'Tommo, we goes now, eh? Shit! Omegawd!' and he breaks into a trot.

'Don't run, Billy!' I grab his arm. 'Walk like you're not scared, then when we gets out o' sight, we'll run like the devil!'

We get to the end o' the alley and then take off, running as hard as we can away from the wharf. Soon we get to the outskirts of this miserable town. I stop, my axe and blanket and sandals feelin' bloody heavy by now, and farmer Moo-cow's shoes near killing me feet. Billy, who be fifteen years or more older than me, is well ahead. 'Stop, Billy!' I shouts. 'We ain't gettin' nowhere!'

Billy walks back to where I'm bent over, panting and dizzy, with my blanket and axe lying at my feet. There is something wrong. My head is now so painful from the running I am hard put not to cry out. The wound is bleeding, I think. I put me hand to me neck and my fingers come away bloody.

'Ya know what gives me the shits?' I says to Billy. 'I just won eight pounds at poker and I didn't even have time to buy a black bottle to drown me bloody sorrows!'

I dig into me pocket and takes out three pounds. 'Here's your stake and a bit more, Billy.' I add two sovs and ten shillings. 'And here's your share of the winnings.' I am left with just over three pounds and can buy enough gallons o' Cape brandy to keep me motherless for a week. 'Cept there ain't a grog shop left in this God-forsaken town I can go into without fear o' being arrested.

I hand him the money and am about to sit down to rest when I hears the sound of shouting coming towards us. They're after us! 'You leave me, Billy, go back to your ship! You ain't done nothing wrong. Garn, scarper, mate, 'fore it's too late!'

Billy shakes his head, 'No, Tommo, me stay.'

'Billy, piss off. *Please,* mate! You don't want no part o' this mess.'

'You me mate, eh, Tommo.'

'Billy, they're gunna kill me when they finds me. You too! Garn, git!'

Billy folds his hands across his chest. 'Nah, me stay. Tommo, you plurry bleedin' in ya head,' he says anxious.

It's dark and I'm facing him. Me wound is to the back of my head, hidden by my hat. How the hell can he tell I'm bleeding? It's his strange gift again. Now we hear the footsteps of them what's chasing us. I look about for some place to hide, but the rain has stopped and it's bright moonlight. There's nothing but road and flat fields on either side, not even a ditch.

I hear the call of a mopoke, followed by a plover. Me name's yelled out, shattering the night's calm. 'Tommo!' Then it hits me – the two bird calls is used among Tamihana's axe fighters to signal danger to each other. Hawk sent 'em to find me. I start to laugh. 'Bloody Hawk, he ain't never gunna let me have a drink,' I says out loud and then my head hurts even more, and I begin to sob. 'It's too hard to be a bleedin' drunk 'round here!'

Four Maori come around the corner. One of 'em can't be mistaken – he's near big as me brother with only one arm and hair what sweeps back like a hammer. I quickly rub away my tears.

'Tommo, it's me, Hammerhead Jack!' the one-armed giant shouts. 'Why do you run away? We are your brothers. We searched everywhere, we looked for two days. Did you kill those two pakeha?'

'Nah, just messed their faces a bit and took a couple o' fingers off one of them's pullin' hand.'

Hammerhead Jack laughs. 'We couldn't hang around to look – too many pakeha.'

'How'd ya know it were me what done it?' I asks.

Hammerhead Jack laughs again. 'Maori women in the alley saw it all. Every wahine in town is looking out for you, man! One went to find us, the other stayed to watch and follow if you left the grog shop.'

I look at my tweed suit. 'But how'd they know it were me?'

'Whores know everything. Your hair, Tommo, it's cut Maori and your smell, they smelled you. You smell like Maori now!'

'How's Maori smell?' I asks.

Hammerhead Jack smiles. 'On the whaling ship Maori smells no different, but in the village they smell different from the pakeha. It is the food. Besides, you spoke to them. How many pakeha do you think speak Maori?' He looks at Billy. 'Who's this?' Then he breaks into a broad smile. 'Billy Lanney!'

Billy steps forward and pats Hammerhead Jack on the chest. 'Plurry good, plurry good, Hammer Jack, eh?'

I laugh. 'He's had a few. Didn't stop him running faster than me, though.'

Hammerhead Jack claps Billy on the shoulder. 'Billy good!' he says, sort of absent-minded. Then he turns to me. 'We must get you out, Tommo. You can't stay here.'

'I know that,' says I. 'Can't get a drink here anyways!'

'We've got a boat waiting,' Hammerhead Jack points across the field on me left to the coastline, 'not too far from here.'

'What about Billy? Can't leave him here. Could we take him back to his ship so he's safe?' I asks.

'He can come,' Hammerhead Jack says.

So off we sets across the field what's wet from the earlier rain and sown with rye about ten inches grown, so that we leave a dark stain as a trail for all to follow. One of the Maori has picked up my axe and blanket and is carrying it under his arm. I'm feeling more and more dizzy in my head.

Soon enough we get to a path down a small cliff which leads onto a pebbly beach where several fishing boats are moored as well as a small ketch. The mooring is in a cove away from the main wharf, on the Maori part o' the waterfront. Several Maori lads comes out from the shadows to greets us, yawning and knuckling the sleep from their eyes. Hammerhead Jack says something quiet to one of them. Three of 'em pulls a dinghy down to the edge o' the water and Jack turns to Billy and tells him that two of the boys will row him back to the *Cloudy Bay*.

Billy comes over to me. Swaying a little, he pats me gently all over to say goodbye. 'Plurry hell, cheerio, top o' the mornin' squire, eh, Tommo!'

Despite the pain in me head, I laugh. 'Where'd you hear all that, Billy? That be proper toff's language.'

His footsteps zig-zag across the pebbled beach to the dinghy where the two Maori lads waits with their oars shipped. He climbs in, the lads steadying him. Two of the lads on the beach push the dinghy off into the harbour. Billy waves to me, then, with a great grin in the moonlight, he shouts, 'Ikey Solomon, he give me my name in Van Diemen's Land, he teach Billygonequeer speak English most good, my dears, omegawd plurry hell!'

Chapter Fourteen

HAWK

The Tasman Sea
July 1860

We are on board ship, bound for Sydney, and Tommo is in a bad way. When Hammerhead Jack took him in the Maori trading ketch from Auckland, they sailed to the Coromandel. It was here that I met him and we boarded the topsail schooner *Black Dog*, under the command of Captain Joshua Leuwin.

Of Tommo's voyage from Auckland he remembers little. Not long after he was taken aboard by Hammerhead Jack he fell into a delirium. His wound had turned bad on the outside and his head was aching beyond endurance. He was soon lost in a fever, murmuring gibberish.

Hammerhead Jack told me of their fearful voyage. The ketch was a decrepit old tub, one of the many derelict vessels replaced in Australia by steam. It was no doubt purchased by some errant Johnny strike-it-rich from Sydney who sailed it in fair weather across the Tasman to sell to the Maori, who can seldom afford a new vessel locally made.

A head wind blew most of the way from Auckland, so that sailing the small ketch with its heavy flaxen sails was most onerous. The wind blew ceaselessly in the wrong direction and the boat punched into the waves, which marched forward in unending grey-green lines flecked with foam. The vessel lurched up and down from trough to crest, constantly leaning at twenty-five degrees away

271

from the wind. The lee rail was often under water, a state of affairs which even for the hardiest man on board creates a great propensity for seasickness. Many lost the contents of their stomachs overboard, though the Maori are good rough-weather sailors.

To all this was added the crew's fear that Tommo's illness had been caused by the spirits of the dead. They knew he had run away from the tribe but had no notion of why, and thought that he must be in breach of some commandment. They believed he was being punished by the *atua* or ghost – the spirit of a dead kinsman which enters one's body and preys on some vital part. They would not approach him, nor touch anything he used, a dish or spoon or cup, for fear that he was *tapu*.

Even Hammerhead Jack, who has sailed the seven seas and seen the ways of the world, suggested bringing the priests, the *tohunga*, to our ship in the Coromandel. He proposed to delay our sailing several days so that they might come to cast out the evil spirit which dwelt in Tommo. He was of the most serious opinion that the spirit residing in my twin's head may have entered him through the arsehole of the dead soldier, whom Tommo had killed and then lain upon in the swamp.

Though I have become Maori in many ways, I politely declined Jack's kind offer, saying that I would nurse Tommo myself and seek further help when we reached Australia.

'Ha, pakeha medicine!' Hammerhead Jack snorted. 'Tommo spent much money on O'Hara's costly sulphur ointment, bought to heal our wounds, but what good did it do us? None!'

I acknowledged his point here. Superstition among the Maori produces some bad, but much good comes from it as well. By ascribing the protection of the dead to the chiefs, the tribes confer upon them an authority which they might not otherwise possess. This has created a remarkable sense of law and order within the community, and a respect for one another's property and rights.

It is a respect scarce seen in European societies, where greed among the wealthy together with crime and violence among the poor cause such great misery. In these societies, too, little punishment is meted by the law when the powerful cheat the weak, and the threat of prison or the rope seems not to deter those who would practise violence for gain. Alas, I fear we shall never learn to live differently. Most of those who have settled these lands of New Zealand and Australia have suffered in their mother countries of England, Scotland and Ireland. The Cornish tin miner, the Irish peasant and the Scottish clansman – all driven from their ancient lands by rapacious masters – now drive the Maori and the Aborigine from their lands. It is as though each man must have his turn against the fellow below him in the pecking order.

Somewhere, somehow, there must be some better system of justice which does not depend on superstition, religion or the rule of English law, for this last always favours the rich and powerful above the common herd. How this utopia might come about I cannot say, and who would help in this cause I do not know. As Ikey often opined, 'The poor be like mangy strays who fight in the dust over a dry bone but cannot think long enough to get together and raid the butcher shop, my dear. They may be relied upon to do as much to prevent an improvement to their circumstances as those who exploit their poverty and despair.' But perhaps Ikey may be proved wrong and some sort of brotherhood of those who are exploited could be formed against those who exploit them.

I confess myself too young and ignorant to know the answers, but the questions persist in my head and I shall not give up thinking upon their solutions.

I have dressed Tommo's head with sulphur ointment obtained from the skipper of the *Black Dog*, and have brought down his fever by placing poultices of vinegar upon his brow. Now, nine days out to sea, he is much improved, though he complains of headaches and constant nausea. His body has had a great shock and I can only hope that he will recover fully.

In my own passage to meet the *Black Dog* I was most fortunate. The Ngati Haua tribe owns several small coastal traders, in addition to the one which was taken by Hammerhead Jack. Included amongst these is a somewhat larger boat, a gaff ketch which is the sole property of Chief Tamihana himself. It is the vessel most prized for coastal trade, a carvel built in Tasmania and constructed of Huon pine, which is renowned for its strength and its resistance to woodworm and rot. Some of these boats, which were built forty years ago, are said to be still as good as when they left the shipwright's shed.

The equal of this ketch is seldom to be found in Maori hands and it was a great honour when Tamihana insisted I be taken in his vessel to meet my brother. We sailed in comfort to our destination and I was not once troubled with seasickness.

The *Black Dog*, on which we now sail, is of the best American design. Only ten years ago she worked as an opium clipper, making racing passages from Bombay to the Canton River. She has a long, low, narrow hull and the distinctive raked clipper bow. Her hull is curved back from the long bowsprit in a reverse curve to the waterline. She is painted black with a red strake and black masts. Never was such a fair ship more badly named. Though I confess myself romantic, should I own such a vessel with its great spread of billowing canvas, I would call her *Black Butterfly*.

Alas, there is little of the romantic about Captain Leuwin. He looks upon me with a most jaundiced eye and addresses me as though I am a nigger matelot. Of Tommo he has no opinion whatsoever and I do not believe he has said a word to him since we sailed. He has encouraged the four other Europeans aboard, the three mates and the bosun, a rough-looking lot, to act in the same truculent manner towards us. We are expected to sleep and eat with the crew and to draw the same rations. Luckily, because the voyage across the Tasman is a short one, these rations include some fruit and vegetables and, for the first three days, fresh meat.

I had greatly looked forward to talking with the officers aboard. It has been over three years since Tommo and I went to live with the Maori and there is much news to be caught up on and a thousand questions to ask. Instead I have made friends with the ship's hands, who are an odd assortment of Maori and Pacific folk from the Loyalty, Caroline and Marshall Islands. The *Black Dog* trades copra and cuts sandalwood for the Chinese market from all of these tropical ports, though our cargo at present is kauri timber from Arotorea destined for Sydney.

There is something strange going on amongst the men, which I cannot fathom. At the conclusion of each meal, Tommo and I are made to come on deck and remain there for an hour with one of the ship's officers standing beside the hatch to ensure we do not venture below decks. Even on the first three days, when Tommo was gravely ill and his mind wandering, Captain Leuwin insisted that I leave him below alone while I stood on deck. Despite all my protests, I would be kept on deck for an hour before being allowed back into the fo'c'sle to care for him. As soon as Tommo was conscious again, he was required to accompany me on every such occasion.

When I asked Leuwin why this was necessary, the captain

replied that the crew had work to do, adjusting and lashing timber which had shifted in the hold, and that it was too dangerous for us to remain below. I knew this to be untrue. The crew made me realise this, for they avoided my gaze whenever they spoke, and I knew they were afraid to tell me the truth, whatever it might be.

We are expected to reach Sydney tomorrow, where I shall be most grateful to disembark. With the heavy timber cargo it will have taken us a full ten days at sea to reach our port. There has been little of interest to break the boredom of our voyage beyond the daily noon sightings to determine our course and the twice daily streaming of the log to gauge our speed. Even though I have offered to help with duties on board, I have been refused. At least the voyage so far has been a smooth one, free of winter storms. The greatest blessing is that each day Tommo grows stronger, and his headaches have grown less severe, sometimes vanishing altogether for an hour or two.

I am not sure how Chief Tamihana persuaded Captain Leuwin, a man of immense ill humour and impatience, to remain an extra three days in harbour so that we might be taken aboard. He may have offered him money but I suspect he recalled some past favour that needed to be repaid. Whatever his method of persuasion, Leuwin does not feel obliged to be courteous towards his two passengers. He summons us on this last evening to the wheelhouse and says that, if the weather holds and the wind persists fair, we shall be coming into Sydney Harbour in the early part of the morning.

'You will please leave my ship immediately the gangplank is lowered. You will oblige me by not talking of me, nor making reference to your passage under my care. If I hear that you have spoken to anyone of this, I shall report you to the authorities. Do you understand me?'

'And what is it you shall say of us to them, Captain Leuwin?' I ask, curious to find out how much he knows of Tommo and me.

'Aye, there is always something,' he snorts. 'Chief Tamihana said naught about you two, not even giving your names.' The captain stabs a stubby finger at my belly. 'That can only mean there is much to conceal!'

'I will tell you anything you wish to know, Captain Leuwin,' I offer.

'No thank you very much. I shall mind my own business and thank you to mind yours.'

'But we have nothing to conceal from you,' I persist.

'Ha! What do you take me for? You introduce yourself as twins, you taller than a bloody lamp post and broad as a barn and him, no bigger than a sprat. You, black as the ace o' spades and him, white. You both call yourself Solomon, which is a Yid's name. What do you take me for? A black Hebrew and a blue-eyed one?'

I shrug. 'It is the truth.'

'Truth, is it? Well if that be the truth, then we'll have no more of the same. I'll thank you to shut your black gob and not to include any further truth about your voyage on the *Black Dog*.'

Tommo, whilst in his delirium, often cried out for Makareta. Now that he is well again, though, he has not once mentioned her death or even spoken her name. He responds only with a nod of his head when I tell him of his daughter and her adoption into the household of Tamihana. I try to recount the tactics employed by our mentor Tamihana to persuade the *tohunga* and the *rangatira* to accept the child's name as Hinetitama, thus elevating her to high status within the tribe. To my regret, he shows no interest. His mind is closed, wandering, and he is once again the sad Tommo who came back to us from the wilderness.

'But she is your daughter, Tommo!' I venture, gently as I can.

'Who?'

'Hinetitama!'

'Oh . . . yes,' he answers vaguely. 'Why did you not call her Mary?'

I despair. It is as if he has forgotten, or rather, he wishes to forget his life with Makareta. With her death, I fear that the whole passage of their time together has become another closed chapter in the secret life of Tommo Solomon, buried where he keeps all the woebegone thoughts of his past. For him, the mongrels have won again and I, who could do nothing to prevent what has happened, feel guilty that I have somehow failed him.

I leave Tommo in the fo'c'sle, and turn my mind to happier thoughts. Sitting on the deck, I unfold the crumpled letter which Hammerhead Jack brought me from Auckland. I have read it many times, but news from Mary always brings a smile to my face.

It is a glorious morning as we enter Port Jackson between two high sandstone cliffs. Small white beaches may be seen on either side of the harbour, and beyond them lie steep wooded slopes. I have heard it said that Sydney Cove is one of the most sheltered and treasured ports in the world and this does not surprise me, for it is a beautiful sight.

A good breeze carries us easily forward and soon enough we begin to see life on the harbour. Hundreds of small craft make their way on the water and some larger ones as well. Though sail predominates, steam ferries and tugs weave their way through the small craft which are carrying every assortment of goods.

Soon we see a dozen small sailing boats rigged for racing speeding towards us. These must be the provedore's agents I have heard tell of, the young butchers' clerks from various establishments, anxious to win the captain's business. Once the signal station on Flagstaff Hill has received the semaphore announcing a ship's entrance through the Heads, the clerks rush to the watermen to hire boats. It is generally accepted that the captain of a vessel will award the first provedore's agent on board the contract for the ship's meat and vegetables and other victualling requirements. But this does not prove true in our case. Captain Leuwin will not allow them on board the *Black Dog* and sends them packing with a string of curses. To my delight, these young clerks are not in the least retiring and return the captain's greetings in no uncertain manner, each vying with the other to hurl the most colourful insults at the *Black Dog*'s master by means of several hailing funnels.

Tommo is much amused by this. 'I think I like Sydney already,' he announces, and I am glad to see a faint spark of his old spirit.

Soon the city comes into view, spread back from Sydney Cove and what I shall later learn is Semicircular Quay and the Rocks. We are met by a steam tug and begin our final berthing.

At last we are in Australia. Sydney is like a gracious lady, of a size large enough to conceal Hobart Town in the pocket of her apron and barely reveal the burden. It has been many years since I have been in so large a city and, though excited, I am a little nervous too at the prospect of being among Europeans again, having grown so long used to our Maori friends. I miss their company, especially Tamihana's and Hammerhead Jack's.

Shortly after noon we tie up at a wooden wharf which extends outwards into the harbour, just east of Semicircular Quay. The gangplank barely hits the surface of the wharf when Captain Leuwin orders Tommo and me to disembark.

'Be off!' he commands.

I do not trouble to take offence, grateful only that we have arrived safely. So I bid him farewell and thank him politely for our passage. But he stands at the top of the gangplank, thin-lipped, arms crossed about his chest, and will not speak again or even nod, his small, obsidian eyes fixed to the centre of my belly.

Tommo pauses at the top of the gangplank and turns to the skipper for his own farewell. 'You're a right bastard, Leuwin. The pox on ya!' he calls, then spits over the ship's side.

The bosun, a big cove called Red O'Shea grabs Tommo by the throat. 'Git!' he says through clenched teeth, which are black and blunted with tobacco stain and rot. Then with his free hand he lifts Tommo by the belt. He is about to throw him over the ship's rail and onto the wharf, a dozen feet below.

I have both our canvas bags slung over my shoulder, the rope ties held in my left hand, when I reach him. I tap O'Shea hard to the side of the jaw with a right and he crumples at my feet like a rag doll.

'Come, Tommo!' I shout and proceed to walk quickly down the gangplank. Tommo follows hard on my heels, but halfway down he turns to face the captain again. 'You're still a right bastard, a mongrel, Leuwin!' he yells again, not in the least quelled by his recent fright.

I am now at the end of my patience. 'Tommo! Leave it! Come on, let's go!' I grab him by his scrawny neck and propel him down onto the wharf. With my hand closing gently around his neck, my fingers meeting my thumb at his Adam's apple, I realise how tiny my twin is, and how much I love him.

The skipper of the *Black Dog* has now recovered from the shock of seeing his bosun lying at his feet and shouts after us. 'You're scum! I'll have the law on you, you hear me!' He points to me. 'Be gone, you piece of nigger dog shit!' Then he spits down at us, though thankfully it does not carry to where we stand.

Tommo laughs as I let go his neck. 'He's not gunna call in the law!' he declares. 'The mongrel don't want no constables snoopin' around below decks. Does ya now, Leuwin?'

'Be gone, scum!' the skipper shouts down at us again, and then turns to attend to O'Shea, who is half-standing with his hands on his knees, shaking his head to clear it.

But Tommo is now completely recovered, I see, and won't let it alone. He shouts as loudly as he can, 'Hey, Leuwin!' The skipper looks down at Tommo. 'It's wahines you've got in the hold, ain't it? You're bringing Maori women to work as whores in Sydney, ain't ya?'

'What's the matter with you?' I yell at my brother. 'We're here hardly two minutes and you're already making trouble!'

Tommo shrugs. 'Ah, to hell with him. Me head hurts. Bugger you, Leuwin, ya miserable bastard!' he shouts back over his shoulder at the skipper of the *Black Dog* and we go on our way. 'And bugger you too, Hawk,' he mutters under his breath, with scant gratitude.

We walk in sulky silence around the Quay, past the Customs House to George Street, and then turn left, away from the harbour. Though most of the merchant premises are still closed for lunch, the street barrows and the pavement shopkeepers are open for business. One, heaped high with silver mackerel buried in a glint of chipped ice, catches my eye. Beside it, pigeons and gulls squabble and squawk, ever hopeful that a fish might tumble loose from the slopes of the snowy mountain above. They barely manage to hop and flutter beyond the path of our feet as we pass by, afraid they might lose their place in this feathered queue of wishful thinkers.

The city streets are a fine sight, with the grand clatter of carts and carriages and the slower creak of a bullock dray coming out of Lyons Auction House, carrying a billiard table and a grand piano. A coach and four turns smartly into Bridge Street and charges down the road as if enjoying sole ownership of it. Everywhere, shipwrights, coopers, sail makers and carpenters, mechanics and those folk who are now termed factory workers, hurry off to an afternoon filled with hammering and clattering, pulleys, pistons, belts and steam whistles.

We are now well away from where the *Black Dog* is moored on the east side of Sydney Cove, and I have determined that we are not being followed. Tommo has never said anything to me about there being wahine captives in the hold and I still don't know if he accused the captain only to make mischief. But if the skipper of the *Black Dog* should have these Maori women trussed up among the timber, he must feed them at least once each day. This would well explain why we were made to come above decks for an hour after the evening meal. It would also explain the reluctance of the crew to speak to us for fear of the captain's retribution should the secret come out.

I realise that Tommo has indeed spoken the truth and understand too why he has said naught of this to me. It is possible that, with his sharp ears, he heard the women below decks, probably when he came out of his delirium after those first two days at sea. Tommo would know that, had I been told of it, I would have felt compelled to rescue these women, thus jeopardising our safety. It would have been easy enough for the crew to feed us to the sharks on a moonless night. Tommo has all the while sought to save me from dangers, and although I would have hoped to help those poor women, I cannot remain angry with my twin for his actions a moment longer. Besides, I am much pleased to be here in Australia, with a high blue sky stretched above me and the smell of steak frying in a chophouse nearby. All I want is to enjoy the beginning of our new life here.

'Hooray, Tommo, we're back where we belong!' I cry, clapping him on the back. 'A cup of tea?' We have reached a barrow sporting a tea urn atop a small brazier with a sign upon it: *Cup T 2d. Milk/Sug. 1d ex.* Even this crude sign makes me feel at home and I clasp the steaming cup I have purchased with pleasure.

Tommo does not seem to share my pleasure and his attention is taken by the barrowman next door who is hawking hot potatoes cooked in their jackets. 'Taties, steamin' 'ot taties!' the hawker yells at passers-by as he juggles a hot spud from one hand to the other. Then he throws it up in the air, a feat accompanied by a whole lot of oohing and ouching, blowing on his hands and dramatic carry-on.

Tommo's hand shoots out and grabs the potato from the air. I think he must fancy it for lunch, and it is good news that his appetite is returned. But then he asks, 'Excuse me, mate, where's a good pub?' and hands the potato man back his spud which, I realise now, is stone-cold.

The barrowman puts down the potato and squints at Tommo. 'There be 'undreds o' public 'ouses in Sydney to choose from, matey.' Then he points down Bridge Street. 'The World Turned Upside Down ain't bad. They cleans the cellar pipes at sparrer's fart every mornin' and you'll get a nice drop of ale on tap in there.'

'What's the name again?' Tommo asks, not sure he's heard it correctly.

'The World Turned Upside Down. It's a queer name, that I admits, but good as they come,' the barrowman repeats.

'Brandy? Does they sell brandy?'

'Course. Bit early, ain't it?'

Tommo grins. 'Never too early, mate. Brandy be mother's milk!' Then he turns to me. 'So?' he asks defiantly, anticipating my disapproval. He shrugs and looks down at his Farmer Moo-cow boots, before meeting my eyes again. 'Hawk, me bleedin' head hurts! I need a *drink*, all right?'

'Don't, Tommo, please.'

His eyes screw up and he starts to whinge, then changes his mind. 'Just the one. I *promise*, just the one.' He grins at me, the old Tommo grin. 'T' wet me daughter's head, like! A merry christening!' Then he steps past me and crosses George Street, darting in and out of the carts and carriages and into Bridge Street, not once looking back to see if I should follow.

Oh Lord, whatever shall I do now? Tommo has walked away from me in search of brandy and I know that if I try to restrain him, he will never return. His head wound has changed him. He seems lacking in patience of any sort and his temper rises quickly. But with his beloved Makareta dead and his little daughter lost to him, I cannot deny that he has cause to drown his sorrows.

I feel sick at heart as I watch him shoulder his way through the crowd and disappear into The World Turned Upside Down hotel. In my pocket is half of the three pounds he won from Maple and Syrup in Auckland. This means Tommo has thirty shillings, more than enough to get him rolling drunk if he chooses. Strong drink has not passed his lips in four years, and it is my forlorn hope that he will soon topple over and be shown out, with a boot planted squarely to his backside. I still have his seaman's bag and axe, so he is safe enough from himself.

I can only await Tommo's return, which I hope will be in an hour or two. There is nothing else I can do, and I feel myself at a complete loss. Despite my anxiety I am starving hungry, for I did not breakfast this morning, being too taken up with our arrival through the Heads. I must eat first and then I shall commence my vigil in the street outside the pub.

I must also find a slop dealer. I have reluctantly agreed that the first of Tommo's poker winnings will be spent on seeing me suitably dressed. My whaler's clothes are in tatters and my boots split and worn. Tommo still wears Farmer Moo-cow's tweed suit and boots, which could prove a little warm as the winter sun is far stronger here. But of the two of us, he looks passably respectable while I appear the vagabond.

Already I have noticed the stares of passers-by, some of whom laugh as soon as they believe themselves beyond my hearing. I cannot blame them. I am now seven feet and one inch in height, and nearly two hundred and eighty pounds in weight. My black face wears the *moko* of the Maori. I am probably a most peculiar sight on a bright winter's day.

My course decided, I take another mouthful of the tea which I bought from the barrowman before Tommo left me. It is the first I have drunk with milk and sugar for many years, and it tastes strange. 'Is the milk fresh?' I ask the barrowman, who has been observing me with interest.

'Struth, mate! Milked the bleedin' cow meself this mornin',' he replies. 'Orf a ship, is ya? Whaleman?' I nod and he shakes his head and smiles. 'Takes three or four cups before yer's used to it with milk again. It's always the same with whalemen, first cuppa after they been at sea couple o' years, they always complains the bleedin' milk's sour.' He points at the blue enamel jug. 'That's practically fresh cream, that is. Matter o' fact I oughta charge more for it, Jersey cow an' all.'

I suddenly find this a most curious conversation. There is Tommo down the road wetting his daughter's head with the first of what no doubt will be many Cape brandies, and here am I, discussing the qualities of a barrowman's milk. 'I'll let you know about that when I have had the fourth cup,' I say, and put the mug down beside the urn. 'Can you recommend a chophouse, please?'

The barrowman winks, then jerks his head towards the potato man. 'Don't fancy one o' Lenny's spuds then? Don't blame ya. They's last year's crop, them taties, spent a long time in the cellar!'

Lenny scowls. 'You're right to think the milk's orf, mate. Alf's missus pisses in it to make it go further.'

But the first barrowman pretends he hasn't heard and rubs his beard, as though he is thinking deeply. 'Tell ya what, how d'ya fancy a pound o' corned beef, thin-sliced and curled over, steamin' 'ot with the mustard o' yer choice?'

I think sadly of Mary's delicious meals, but at least this sounds an improvement on the food we were served aboard the *Black Dog*. 'Corned beef will do me a treat.'

'Good on ya, mate, yiz not chose wrong. Mr Smith's above the

Cut, now there's an excellent eating-house and famous for mustard mixing. Can't miss it, right next door to the Rose of Australia, an excellent pub what the said gentleman and his missus also owns.'

Alf points back towards the direction from which Tommo and I have just come, explaining that the Argyle Cut is no more than a few minutes' walk that away. I hesitate, for it will mean losing sight of The World Turned Upside Down pub, and Alf grasps my dilemma in a second. 'Don't get yer knackers in a knot about the lad, mate. I reckon the little bloke'll still be there when ya gets back after yer feed, and more likely to come quietly besides. What'cha reckon, Len?' The barrowmen laugh uproariously together.

And so I put my fears aside and head up to the Cut, in the area known as the Rocks.

Alf the barrowman's recommendation proves an excellent one. At Mr Smith's eating-house I partake of one and a half pounds of corned beef, though I cannot yet stomach the spicy mustards, and I wrap up another half a pound in a bandanna for Tommo. With half a dozen nice-sized potatoes under my belt, and two set aside for Tommo, I have polished off a delicious meal. I wash it down with three cups of tea and, by the end, discover that the milk no longer tastes rancid.

I am feeling decidedly better and somewhat cheered. I reassure myself that the worst that can befall Tommo is another headache and a bout of vomiting, both of which he has experienced often enough over the past two weeks. I am about to go into the backyard to wash my face and hands when I hear a woman's voice cry out in a tone of amazement.

'Struth, will ya take a look at this!'

I look up from my plate to see a young lady staring straight at me. She is dressed to the nines, in a satin gown of palest blue, the bodice cut low to display a most ample bosom. She is powdered and rouged, with her golden hair swept up into a great knot on the top of her head. She wears no bonnet, but several gay ribbons of different colours are threaded through her curls. What appears to be a small stuffed black-and-white magpie perches at the very centre of her bun, as though upon a comfy nest. She is dressed as though she is stepping out to a ball, yet it is not too many hours past midday.

With this worldly creature staring at me, I am completely flummoxed. I quickly avert my eyes, and stare down into my empty tea mug. But I must act more manly! Collecting my scattered thoughts, I pick up my mug in both hands and pretend to drink quite casually from it. I gaze into the distance over its rim, so that she will think me not the least disturbed by her presence.

'Well, well, well!' the young lady says, standing with her hands on her hips. 'If yiz ain't the mostest nigger I've ever seen!' Then she floats over to where I sit and tilts her head, forcing me to look at her.

'Mind if I takes a pew, 'andsome?' Her lips, I notice, are ruby red.

I jump to my feet like a schoolboy and in my haste send my chair flying backwards. I grab the back of the nearest chair and pull it out for her. 'My, my, nice manners an' all,' she says smiling. 'Ta muchly.' As she sits, the silk of her gown pulls tight across, and I see that she has the nicest derrière to be imagined.

I retrieve my chair from where it lies, several feet from the table, and sit down. What I intend to say is, 'Would you allow me the pleasure of purchasing you a cup of tea, miss?' But what comes out is, 'Er, ah, tea, miss?'

'I don't mind if I do. Cuppa does ya the world, first thing, don't it now?'

I turn around and see the old woman who served me breakfast watching us. Too nervous to speak, I point to the empty mug and hold up two fingers. My mind is racing in circles, like a dog trying to scratch a flea bite on the tip of its tail. Once I penned love letters for other men to woo their sweethearts with, but now I am entirely lost for words.

'Cat got your tongue then?' my visitor asks. She looks me up and down, and I am suddenly conscious again of the fact that I am dressed in a whaleman's canvas breeches and jacket, all in rags and none too clean. But if she notices my ragged state, she does not show it. Instead, she reaches over the table and puts her hand over mine. It is small and feels cool and clean. My heart jumps into my mouth.

'We could begin by introducin' ourselves. What's ya name?' she asks me.

My breathing has stopped and I must swallow before answering, 'Hawk . . . Hawk Solomon.' My throat, with my heart still sitting in my mouth, feels as though the silver band of scars about it has been suddenly pulled tight.

'Garn then, Hawk, give us a smile?' she teases.

I smile and she brings her hand up over her mouth and giggles. I see how very young and pretty she is.

'Why do you laugh, miss?' I ask.

'You has such a stern face, but when ya smile, yiz beautiful!'

I try to keep my face straight, but I am forced to laugh. 'Men can't be thought beautiful,' I protest.

'Most ain't, but you is!' She points a finger at my face and makes a little circle in the air. 'Them whirls on yer face, you look like the prince o' the cannibals!' She laughs again and claps her hands. Then she tilts back her head and says suddenly, 'Do you think I'm beautiful?'

She has put me at my ease and now I look closely at her, noting her every feature. She is not beautiful but very pretty, with a small nose, big blue eyes and a mouth perhaps a trifle too big but which already I long to kiss. She returns my gaze with complete candour, not the least show of modesty in her scrutiny of me. There appears to be something resembling boot-blacking over her eyelids and she has darkened her lashes so that the colour of her eyes is intense. Her gaze is too direct for me to return and I am painfully aware of her abundant breasts at which I try not to stare. 'Yes,' I declare after a few moments. 'You are very beautiful.'

'Bull!' she exclaims. 'I'm pretty if I works bloody 'ard at it, but I ain't beautiful.'

I am not sure what I'm expected to say next, but she speaks before I am able to gather my thoughts.

'You could ask me name! A girl's not supposed to introduce herself, it ain't polite now, is it?' At this moment, the old lady shuffles up to bring our tea. 'Mornin', Ma Smith,' my companion says without looking up.

'Morning,' the old woman replies, and it is clear from her voice she does not approve of what's going on. She places down a tin tray on which sits a china teapot, two cracked cups, a milk jug and a sugar bowl with a piece the size of my thumbnail missing from the side. Then she sniffs and leaves.

The young lady arches one eyebrow at me. 'Stupid old cow,' she whispers, then giggles. 'Garn then, Hawk, introduce us. I can't hardly wait to make yer acquaintance proper.'

I'm not too sure how I should go about this. So I rise from my chair and do a little bow. 'I'd take it most kindly if you'd allow me to make your acquaintance, miss,' I say politely, once again aware of my poor rags. I feel a little foolish acting as though I'm dressed in a black tail coat and silk hat, when I look like a drayman's boy.

'Well, it's about bloody time, sir! I thought yiz was never goin' to ask! Maggie Pye,' she says, sticking out her dainty hand. 'Pleased to meetcha, Hawk Solomon.'

'Likewise, Maggie Pye,' I answer. Somehow she has taken my shyness from me. Then she leans over, and with her bosom practically popping out of the top of her gown, so help me, she stretches up and kisses me on the cheek. 'We'll be friends, Hawk,' she says. 'Good friends. What 'elps each other through thick an' thin.'

My heart leaps and bounces back up into my throat. It is as though my dream has come to life. A dainty, pretty girl is kissing me softly on the cheek. My shyness returns in a flood of embarrassment, and I blurt out the first thing that comes into my head. 'But how could a pretty miss like you kiss a nigger?'

Maggie Pye draws back and looks at me in mock-surprise. 'Well I never! You ain't a nigger, is ya?' She reaches over and picks up the teapot and begins to pour. 'I'm a whore and you're a nigger – there's a couple o' known facts we don't need to quarrel about no more. Now we can get on with what we don't yet know about one another but 'opes to find out.'

'I'd never have believed you to be a . . . one of them,' I stammer, unable to bring myself to say the word.

'A whore?' Maggie replies. 'Jesus, Hawk, where's ya been all ya life, under a flamin' toadstool? It's two o'clock in the afternoon, an' me dressed like this. Who does ya think I am, Cinder-bleedin'-ella?'

Since I've come in, the eating-house has begun to fill up with clerks and shop assistants, chatting and making a racket. Some have a pint of ale in front of them, which they've brought in from the tavern next door. From the sound of them, it isn't the first they've had today. A few have turned to watch this exchange between Maggie and myself, and I hope none has heard me.

'I beg your pardon, Maggie Pye,' I say. 'I should never have said what I did.'

'What ever do ya mean?'

'I should never have let it seem as though I should feel differently about you because of what you might be.'

Maggie sighs and puts her elbows on the table, resting her chin on her cupped hands. 'Look, ya silly, long-winded bugger, it don't matter what I am. It's *who* I am in me 'eart what matters, don't it?' She reaches out and touches my hand again, giving me a crooked smile. 'Besides, I ain't a common whore. I'm Maggie Pye! Just like you ain't a common nigger, you're Hawk Solomon! Now ain't that worth celebratin'?'

I don't dare ask her what she means by all this and she explains no further. But I can hear Ikey's voice as plainly as if he were next to me. 'Whores, my dear, don't come with soft hearts. Whores only has charms when their patsy-mark's got silver. They're hard as granite and not to be trusted under any circumstances whatsoever! A good whore be one what's robbed you of every penny you possess while you was sleeping but what ain't took your breeches as well!'

But then I think of Mary. Our own dear mama was once a whore – as was Sperm Whale Sally, without whom I would not be here to meet Maggie Pye! I decide that Ikey, who never had much luck with the fairer sex, might just this once be wrong in his advice.

'I think I understand what you mean,' I say to Maggie.

'Nah, ya don't, but ya will soon enough.' She points to my cup. 'You ain't drunk none o' ya tea.'

'Nor have you,' I say, grinning.

'Why's that, then? I love me tea. Maybe we's in love, Hawk?' Maggie tilts her head up at me again. 'Have you ever been in love?'

She asks this with such a serious demeanour that I don't know what to think. I have secretly counted myself in love with Hinetitama, but that now seems like being in love with a beautiful ghost who was half made of moonlight. I can hardly count such pinings as love, can I? At any rate, it isn't what I think Maggie would call love. Her notion of love, I'm guessing, would be loud and alive, with lots of laughter and sweetness in it. 'No,' I say slowly. 'No, I haven't.'

'Me neither,' she says wistfully. 'Many's the time I've thought I were, but it always turns out the same. Men just wants to fuck ya and women just wants to love ya, and the two things don't mix, do they?' She seems to think for a moment, then adds quietly, 'Well anyhow, if yiz a whore they don't.'

I've never before talked to a woman like this. But then I don't suppose I've ever really talked to a woman at all, except Mary. That one night in Wiremu Kingi's village when the moon was full and my manhood was taken or given, I didn't do much talking. Maggie, who's watching me carefully, can see that I am completely out of my depth.

'You'll need to visit the slop-shop,' she announces now. 'I can't be seen with you lookin' like Robinson bleedin' Crusoe, now can I?'

'Surely you mean Man Friday?' I retort, pleased I've still got some wits about me.

'That's clever an' all!' she laughs. 'O' course, I've always been of the opinion that Robinson Crusoe and Man Friday were up to a bit o' hanky-panky theirselves.' She grins wickedly. 'I mean, what else could ya do all alone on a bleedin' desert island?'

Most of what Maggie says seems to end in a question. Happily, I am slowly coming to realise that she doesn't expect an answer from me each time.

'Tommo will need to win at cards before I can hope for new clothes,' I say. 'And no slop-shop will have my size. It's a dealer I need.'

'Tommo? Who's Tommo, then?' she asks.

'Tommo's my twin,' I reply, realising that I haven't thought of Tommo in quite a while and that I must be getting back to Bridge Street to find him.

'There's two of ya?' Maggie exclaims in astonishment. She points a finger at me. 'Ya means to tell me there's two niggers your size in town?' She throws back her pretty head and laughs. 'Crikey! And they say there ain't no Gawd in heaven!'

I explain about Tommo and Maggie's face is a study in disappointment when I tell her that he is as little and as pale as she, and a gambling man.

'There's trouble!' she comments. 'Only one thing makes more trouble than men and whores and that's men and cards. Even worse if it's little men and cards!'

'Don't I know it!' I say, looking heavenwards.

'You a gamblin' man too, Hawk?'

I shake my head.

'More I hear, the better it gets. Does ya fart in bed?'

I'm shocked, but I also have to laugh. 'Only in the fo'c'sle to kill the stink,' I reply, using one of Tommo's jokes for my own, amazed at my own boldness. I'm glad I'm black, otherwise my face would surely show as scarlet as a trooper's jacket.

Maggie grins. 'You'll keep,' she says, and takes a small mirror from her purse. Pouting her lips, she examines herself carefully in it. Then she wets the tip of her forefinger on her pink tongue and runs it across her right eyebrow, before doing the same with the other. 'Don't I look a fright!' she says, pulling a wry face.

'Why, you look perfect, Maggie Pye,' I say, trying my hand at being gallant, for Maggie Pye is much to my liking and I wish her to like me too. But then I am troubled by a nasty thought. What if she only likes me as a customer?

Maggie puts back the tiny mirror and smooths her hair with both hands, finally touching the tips of the magpie's wings. 'Time for me to attend to business, Hawk,' she smiles, glancing up at me. To my surprise, she seems a trifle shy. A silence which seems to last forever stretches between us, and then I clear my throat and manage to blurt out, 'Will I see you again, Maggie Pye?'

'Christ, I thought ya were never goin' to ask!' she replies, her face lighting up. 'Hero o' Waterloo, six o'clock t'night.'

I move to get up from my chair. 'No, don't,' she instructs. 'If ya gets up, 'ow's I gunna kiss ya?' She rises from her chair and at her full height she's only three inches taller than I am when seated. 'Six o'clock, don't be late, Maggie don't like to wait even if she's late herself, what's more than likely, life being what it is, if you knows what I means?' It all tumbles out in one breath. She gives me a kiss on the forehead. 'Ta-ta then!' she says loudly and turns and walks out, her derrière moving like it has a life of its own.

As she saunters out, catcalls and whistles rise from the clerks and shop assistants and I am all at once angry. I rise from my seat. 'Be silent!' I shout, and bang the table with my fist so hard that the two cups of tea jump up and spill over, dribbling liquid to the floor. I see that Maggie's left a florin beside her tea cup.

As the sound of my protest dies away, the room is so quiet you could hear a pin drop. Everyone has their eyes downcast, staring at their cup or plate or beer mug to avoid my gaze.

Maggie Pye whirls around at the door and puts her hands on her hips. 'You low bastards couldn't afford to pay for what the nigger's goin' to get for free!' she announces. She blows me a kiss. 'Hawk Solomon, welcome to Sydney!'

I have never felt so embarrassed in my whole life. The tea drips onto the floor and onto my boots while the clerks and shopkeepers all look up at me with their stupid grins.

Maggie swishes out of the door like a princess. I pick up her florin, and walk over to where Ma Smith is seated beside the kitchen door and pay her. 'Thank you, ma'am, the brisket was excellent and the potatoes amongst the best I've tasted,' I say softly.

'Humph!' she snorts, handing me my change. 'You'd do well to stay away from that one!' Her lips are stretched so thin I think they must snap. 'She'll take every penny you've got and more!' She looks up at me with her rheumy, red-rimmed eyes and cackles, 'Why d'ya think she's called Maggie Pye, eh? 'Cause she collects bright little valuables for her nest, that's why!'

I laugh and look down at my tattered coat and blouse, my breeches, frayed and torn at the knees, and my poor old boots. 'Thank you, ma'am, I'll take care that she doesn't diddle me out of my riches!' I bow slightly to the old crone and take my leave.

I'm feeling good as I walk out the door with all eyes upon me. It isn't natural for me to enjoy such attention and yet I do! Then the men commence to whistle and clap and laugh. 'Welcome to Sydney, Hawk Solomon!' someone shouts and I can't help grinning. I feel light-headed and wonder if at last this might be love. It seems not such a bad idea. Maggie Pye and Hawk, birds of a feather!

Chapter Fifteen

Tommo

Sydney
July 1860

When Hawk asks me if I wants a cup o' tea that first morning it's the last straw. With me head hurtin' from the musket ball more than I'm willing to admit, I can think of only one way to kill the pain. I'm thirstin' for the black bottle, for half a pint of the most glorious grape, me Cape brandy, not a cup of friggin' tea!

Well, I've waited long enough for it, haven't I? Four bloody years! My tongue is hangin' out so far that my boots are fair tripping over it. So the moment I gets the chance I tells Hawk I'm off.

I walks down Bridge Street not even lookin' back to see if Hawk is following. If he tries to stop me, I swear I'll leave the bastard forever. But he lets me be and I stroll into The World Turned Upside Down pub. It's full with lunch-time drinkers from the docks and the markets. With me sore head, I'm in no humour to be among the yakking, 'baccy-smoking, beer-swilling mob. So I make me way into the saloon bar, what's nice and quiet, with only a couple of well-dressed coves having a bit of a natter in the corner.

I walk to the bar and gives the bell a good thump. Soon enough the barmaid comes through from the main bar. She ain't what you'd call young nor pretty and seems none too happy at the sight of me neither. 'Be 'appier next door, I should think?' she sniffs, indicating the main bar with a nod of her head.

'I'm fine right here, thank you, miss,' says I, then turns to the two men in the corner. 'Providin' these gentlemen don't mind?' A little bloke no bigger than me and a bit of a toff, though with the look of a weasel about him, nods friendly enough. The fat cove what's with him don't twitch an eyelid. 'Looks like I'll be stayin',' says I.

'Suit yerself,' says the snooty barmaid. 'What'cha want?'

'Brandy. A daffy o' Cape, thank you, miss.'

'A daffy?' she asks, one eyebrow raised most high and mighty.

'Fer goodness' sake, Doreen! Give the gent a nobbler of brandy and stop making trouble.' It's the little weasel bloke what speaks.

'Much obliged,' I says to him. 'Nobbler, is it?'

Doreen turns on her heel and she's about to vanish into the main bar when I shouts after her, 'Nobbler of *Cape*, miss!'

She soon puts down a glass in front o' me. I pick it up and sniff, waiting for the smell o' the precious ambrosia to hit me nostrils. I sniff and then I sniff again. 'This ain't Cape,' I says, looking straight at her.

She shrugs her shoulders. 'It be better than Cape.'

'Thanks, miss, but it's Cape I asked for and Cape I'll have! You know, brandy what comes from the Cape o' Good Hope!' Me head feels like it's gunna explode and I push the brandy away. Next moment the little bloke's besides me. He picks up the glass and sniffs at it.

'This ain't brandy!' he exclaims and pours the glass o' spirits into the brass spittoon beside the door. 'Now get this gentleman a Cape brandy, or I'll call Mr Hodges!'

'It ain't right!' Doreen cries. 'I tries to keep the saloon bar nice for the better class o' person like you and ye friends.' She sniffs and looks directly at me. 'Mr Hodges don't like it when the hobbledehoys comes in the saloon bar!'

Christ Jesus, I thinks, what is this? Ain't I ever gunna get a drink? If I had my axe with me I'd know exactly what to do with Doreen's saloon bar.

Anyway off she flounces and the little cove pats me on the shoulder. 'You'll get your brandy now, matey.' Then he sticks out his hand. 'Art Sparrow.' I take his hand a bit reluctant-like, for I don't want no company. I catch sight of the ring he's wearin' what sports a diamond the size o' me pinkie nail. Then he withdraws his hand and there, 'tween forefinger and next, is a small white card. 'My card,' he smiles, bowing his head.

It's a neat piece o' palming, not difficult mind, but nicely done. I take the card and read it, thankful that Hawk made me take up learnin' again at sea. It's very fancy lookin'.

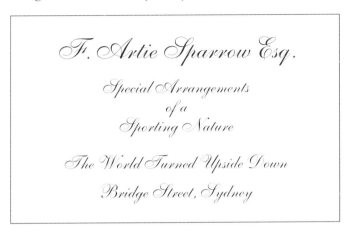

F. Artie Sparrow Esq.

Special Arrangements
of a
Sporting Nature

The World Turned Upside Down

Bridge Street, Sydney

I dunno what makes me do what I do next, but I hold his card up, close me hand over it, and then open it again. Where his card was, I now holds the ace o' spades.

'Well I never!' he exclaims. 'Use the flats, then, does you?'

'Some,' I reply.

He glances down at the playing card then he sticks out his hand again. 'How do you do, Mr Ace O' Spades?'

I don't feel much like smiling but it's clever enough said, so I oblige. 'Pleased to meetcha, Mr Art Sparrow,' I says, though me greatest pleasure would be for him to go away and leave me in peace.

'My friends calls me Mr Sparrow, and me enemies . . .' he pauses a moment and points to his card. 'Well, I'll leave that to yer imagination!' I looks at his name on the card again, F. Artie Sparrow. 'Frederick Arthur Sparrow,' the little cove says. 'I most sincerely hopes we can be friends and you'll call me Mr Sparrow?'

'Thank you, Mr Sparrow,' I says, though it's hard now not to think of him as Fartie Sparrow. I know a mag artist when I see one. But I think it best to humour him a while. Otherwise, he might see that Doreen here, or even Mr Hodges, sends me on me way without a drink.

'I ain't given you my proper name yet, Mr Sparrow,' I says.

He throws up his hands in alarm. 'No, no, don't! Leave it be, my dear. Ace O' Spades is a grand name for a young Irishman who plays the flats.' He cocks his head. 'That is, if you can play sufficient well to earn it as ye handle?'

Before I can tell him I ain't Irish, Doreen brings in my brandy and I goes to pay her.

'No, no, my dear – my stand,' Mr Sparrow insists. 'Make that two more. We have to celebrate Mr Ace O' Spades arrival in Sydney!'

'Cape again?' Doreen asks him.

Mr Sparrow grins. 'Now don't you be cheeky, my dear. It's finest cognac for me and rum for Fat Fred over there as you know well enough.' He nods to the corner. 'Bring your poison, Mr Ace O' Spades, and come over and meet Mr Fred. Perhaps you fancy a hand or two of poker? What say we play fer drinks, eh?'

'Much obliged, Mr Sparrow, but if you don't mind I won't today.' I points to the brandy in front o' me. 'I come in here to get a few drinks in me, and that is what I intends to do.'

'A misfortune or a celebration, my dear?' he asks, not in the least put down by me knocking back his offer. 'Celebration or misfortune, which is it then?' he repeats.

My head is aching so much I can't hardly remember why it is I wants to get drunk. Is it to mourn me beloved Makareta or am I wetting the head of me new baby daughter? I don't even know where the poor little mite is. Perhaps it's about coming to Australia, or perhaps none o' them things?

'Sort o' both, I suppose,' I replies. 'I'm best left on me own at the moment.'

Doreen brings Mr Sparrow's brandy and takes the other tipple over to Fat Fred. He's a hugely fat man with a very red face what has several spare cheeks and a spirit drinker's knobbly nose. I reckon he's about forty years of age and Mr Sparrow near enough the same. Fat Fred has his elbows on the small table in front o' him and his chins cupped in his hands, so that the flesh spills out the side most handsome. When Doreen puts down his rum, he makes no sign he's seen her, his piggy-eyed expression of darkest gloom unchanged.

'Cheerio, then!' Mr Sparrow throws back his head and swallows his drink in one go. With nary a glance in his direction, Fat Fred in the corner does the same, to the exact second, so that they bang down their empty glasses with a single sound.

Meanwhile all I has done is lift me glass and bring it close under me nose. The sharp fumes rises to my nostrils like an ancient memory. I close my eyes a moment. Then I takes a sip and damn near faints. The Cape hits me like a red hot poker down me throat. 'Bloody hell!' I gasp.

'What's the matter, lad?' Mr Sparrow asks most concerned, thumping me back as I choke and splutter. 'Doreen!' he cries. 'What's she done to yer brandy then?'

My eyes is watering and I can't hardly speak. 'Nothing's been done!' I croak. 'It's bloody delicious! But it's been a long time between drinks.'

'Oh dearie me!' he laughs. 'Whaleman, are yer?'

'I was.' I knuckle the tears from me eyes. The brandy is warming my stomach something wonderful.

'Harrington Arms be the pub for whalemen,' says Doreen, who's popped up from nowhere. 'T'ain't far from 'ere!'

'Right,' I say, taking another small sip. 'But I ain't a whaleman no more and intends to be a gentleman, if that be all right with you then, miss?' All it takes is a single sip o' the glorious grape and Tommo is back to his old self.

'*Course* you aren't a whaleman no more, it's plain for all to see you're a gentleman,' Mr Sparrow glowers at Doreen.

'It is, is it?' I grins. 'Could've fooled me!'

Doreen gives a 'Hmmph!' and stamps off again.

Mr Sparrow smiles. 'I like a man with a nasty sense of humour. And it's good to see you enjoy your brandy!'

I take another sip o' the blessed Cape. 'I'll be fine now, thanks. It's been a pleasure to meet you, Mr Sparrow, but I'd best keep to meself.'

Mr Sparrow looks at me with sympathy. 'Naturally, after all yer time at sea, you'll want to fully savour yer drink.' Suddenly his voice grows hard. 'But may I remind you, sir, it's your turn to stand a round.' He's smiling, but this time it's different and I sees the weasel again. 'Wouldn't do to neglect your stand, now would it?'

'Oh, of course, I begs your pardon, Mr Sparrow.' I dig in me breeches for coin.

'No 'arm done, Mr Ace O' Spades, it's not yours to know the local form. Tell yer what? I can see you want to be on yer own, so we'll spread the flats once each. You win and there's no need to shout me and Fat Fred and we'll leave you well alone. Can't be fairer than that now, can I?'

Mr Sparrow says he'll shuffle and then select five cards what he'll show. Then I'm to do the same, and if mine beats his, I win. Well, Tommo don't like to say no to such an offer. So Mr Sparrow picks up the cards and examines them most careful. I ain't shaved them none and they be in most excellent condition. He shuffles the deck a few times to get the feel and I'm interested to see how he does the relocation. He's very good, as I knew he'd be, and there's a pretty blur of the broads as he spreads them in a straight line across the bar counter. Then he picks five cards and turns up each in turn. Three queens and a pair of tens, a full house – the perfect poker hand.

'Nice.' I keep me voice steady. In fact it be most skilled and I can't understand why he's done it. A cardsharp as good as him don't play boastful with a stranger. I can see he thinks I'm a whaleman paid off in Sydney – a slip of a lad with a pocket full o' brass what a few games o' poker will soon empty. But why the big trick? That would do nothing but scare away a patsy-mark. It don't make no sense whatsoever.

Mr Sparrow takes a cigar from the inside pocket of his coat, bites the end off and sets about lighting it. He looks even more the weasel with his sharp little teeth bared, some missing to either side, and gold in three of 'em. I wait 'til he's got it going and the air about is filled with the rich smell o' tobacco smoke. Then I takes up the cards and shuffles, laying them down in a perfect circle with one card placed in the dead centre the way Ikey taught us. It's a trick, no more, and not to be used in any card game. But it takes hundreds of hours of practice to get it right, and few can do it well.

'Hmm!' says Mr Sparrow, chewing at his cigar. 'Card tricks, eh?'

I selects a card from the very top o' the circle and the next from the very bottom, leaving two gaps exactly opposite each other. I does the same to the left and the right so that the circle, but for the four matching gaps facing each other, remains perfect. Now I has four cards placed face down in front o' me on the bar. In a manner most casual, I turns them face up. King, then another king, then a third, then a ten. I reach out and take the card from the centre o' the circle and places it face up to show another ten. Three Kings and two tens. My full house beats his!

'I'll be damned!' says Mr Sparrow. 'If I hadn't seen it with my own eyes, I'd not have believed it!'

'I'd be much obliged if you'd let me be now, Mr Sparrow,' I says, upping me glass and drinking down what's left of my brandy. I do this so he can't see the big smile on me gob!

But Mr Sparrow's still staring at the five cards I've laid out on the bar. 'Ace O' Spades, there be only one man in the world what I've known can do that, and he's long dead.'

'Ikey Solomon?' I says. The cigar drops from Mr Sparrow's lips onto the floor. I lean down and pick it up. Then I put it carefully on the counter with the lighted part over the edge. 'You'd be Sparrer Fart, then, I presume?' I say, cool as you like.

'How the devil –' he exclaims. 'Who are *you*, then?'

'Tommo X Solomon, at ya service!' I says, sticking out me paw. 'Ikey said I couldn't never beat ya, but I bloody well just did!'

Mr Sparrow, alias the one and only Sparrer Fart, is too astonished to take offence.

'Yer Ikey's boy! Ikey Solomon! Prince o' London's Fences, sent to Van Diemen's Land?'

'One and the same,' says I. 'And you be Sparrer Fart, what Ikey considered the best pickpocket of all the lads he ever trained and a master o' the flats when you was ten years old.'

'I was, too!' Mr Sparrow muses. 'Thought I still was, until a few moments ago!' He looks me all over like he's looking at me for the first time. 'Glory be! Ikey's lad, eh? This is a most momentous occasion!'

I sighs. Me and my big mouth. I just never learns to keep me cleverness to meself. There's no hope of getting rid of Mr Sparrow now he knows who I am.

Mr Sparrow is banging the bell and the lovely Doreen appears once more. ''Ere, same again,' he calls to her.

I raise my hand to object. 'Mr Sparrow, please, we made a deal. I won, now I wish to drink me fill on me own!'

Mr Sparrow stops and gazes at me a long time. A tear escapes from one of his little red weasel eyes and runs down his cheek and across his small, sharp face.

'Son,' he chokes, 'I've waited thirty years for this moment. Ikey Solomon were the closest thing to a pater I ever 'ad. He give me a family – all the likely lads from the Academy o' Light Fingers. Ikey was our beloved kinsman. He found me when I were nothing but a starvin' guttersnipe. He taught me the most noble art o' tooling until I were the best pickpocket in London. He give me book-learnin' and writin' and taught me cribbage so that handlin' the flats became me second nature.

'Ikey Solomon gave me everything I am become, son. When Mr Dickens picked me character for the Artful Dodger in that book of his, *Oliver Twist*, I were the very finest example of the genius of Ikey Solomon.' Sparrer Fart pauses. 'Now I meets you, Tommo Solomon, alias Mr Ace O' Spades, Ikey's lad!' Another tear escapes. 'And you tells me t' piss orf? I'm 'urt, 'umiliated to the uttermost!'

Fat Fred lets loose a gentle snore.

From the way he's talking, it's like Sparrer Fart's once more the little ragamuffin what Ikey found starving in Rosemary Lane. I don't know what rightly to say to his outburst. I know I'm being had, but also that some o' his declaration is genuine enough.

Ikey would always tell us, 'A good scam be from the heart as well as the head, my dears. Always find yourself something what you can say with a sense o' conviction, what makes you sad or happy or angry, then work it in like butter and flour. The result be most soulful and is as effective on your patsy-mark as mother love.'

Now Mr Sparrow has gave me a proper lesson in doin' this right. For a moment, I thinks I must cry for the memory of Ikey, which be most funny, for as far as I know ain't nobody much ever cried over the memory of Ikey Solomon. Mary might have shed a few tears what quickly dried, and so might me soft brother, but nobody else. It all goes to show the skill o' Sparrer Fart.

'You're right, Mr Sparrow, I've been most hard-hearted,' I says, even half-meaning it.

'No, no, lad!' He takes me by the arm. 'Tell you what? We'll 'ave a couple o' nobblers. My stand. Me and Fat Fred will nurse our drinks on our own, and leave yer free to take up the slack on your grief or celebration or bit o' both. Then afterwards, I want you to accompany us on a proper adventure. Put money in your pocket too. What do you say, eh, lad?'

'Adventure? What sort of adventure? Can't be better than getting shickered after four years!'

'Much better, a thousand times better, I promise. It'll fix whatever ails yer.' He bangs the bell and orders two nobblers each for us. I hasn't even touched the last one Doreen brought.

'But I ain't said yes, Mr Sparrow,' I protest.

He ignores me and retires to the corner as promised. He gives Fat Fred a shake and they talk quietly between themselves while I stand at the bar and tackle the three Cape brandies in front o' me. By the time I've finished the second, me head is spinning. It ain't sore any more but the saloon bar looks as wavy as if I were still aboard the *Black Dog*. I drink the third, spillin' some of the precious liquid on the front of me jacket. Then I take up the fourth.

All I remember after that is Mr Sparrow's voice murmuring. 'Steady now, take it easy, Tommo, there's a good lad.' Then he's talking to someone, what could be Fat Fred. 'We'll take him upstairs,' I hear him say. Then I don't remember nothing.

I wake up in a dark room and I'm lying on a proper bed with a blanket covering me. Me head hurts, but not too bad. I has a strange recollection of being waked from time to time and made to drink gallons of water, or so it seemed in me dreams. Now I'm busting for a piss. I lie a moment, listening for sounds, and see a thin strip of light coming in from the drapes. It's daylight and I can hear street sounds, but they is some distance below me.

I gets up and sees that me boots has been took off, along with me trousers and jacket. All I'm wearing is Farmer Moo-cow's woollen blouse. I walk softly over to the door and tries the knob, but it's locked. Then I goes to the window and pulls the drapes open. I'm looking down into a narrow lane, more a cutting between buildings than a passageway, barely wide enough to walk through. Two stray dogs are sniffing each other's arses, turning 'round and 'round, and bumping into the walls on either side. There's no sign of anyone else. I try to open the window, thinking I might piss out of it into the lane below, but it won't budge. What am I to do? Then I see a small washstand with a basin atop. I ain't tall enough to piss straight into it, so I put it on the floor and passes water for maybe ten minutes or more o' blessed relief.

I'm a new man when I lift the basin back up onto the washstand. Then I starts thinking about me predicament. Has I been kidnapped? How did I get here? Slowly, my memories of the pub comes back to me. Four brandies! Once I could've took ten and walked home. Hell, what time is it? Is it morning? Afternoon, I thinks, from the look of the lane. Is it today still or tomorrow? Where's Hawk? He'll be goin' spare!

I walk to the door and bang upon it with me fist. 'Anyone there?' I shouts. It don't take a moment before I hear the rattle of a key and the door is opened. Two lads, no more than ten or eleven years old, stand looking in at me.

'Afternoon, squire,' says one of 'em, cheeky-like.

'Where am I? What's the time?' I demand.

'It be just after noon, the post office clock just gorn not more 'n ten minute since, squire.'

'Don't call me squire! Who brung me here?' I ask.

'You was shickered, guv. Mr Sparrow said we should mind yiz. Been 'ere all bleedin' day, we 'as.' He jerks his thumb at the second boy. 'Him an' me, we's had no sleep and nothin' to eat all day, neither.'

'Where is he – Mr Sparrow? Can ya fetch him?'

'If you'll let us lock you back in? Strict instructions, we's got.'

'Where's me togs?' I ask.

'Dunno. Fat Fred took 'em this mornin'.'

They close the door and I hear the key turn in the lock.

Before long there are voices outside and soon enough in comes Mr Sparrow, carrying a brown paper parcel tied with twine.

'How are we feeling, Tommo? How's your poor noggin?' He smiles, then reaches into the pocket of his breeches and hands me a small flask. 'Hair of the dog, lad. One sip only, mind. We got business t'night.'

'I've got to find me brother now, Mr Sparrow.' But I reach for the flask and take a long swig.

'Now, now! Steady on, we've got a long afternoon and night ahead, lad.'

I hand Mr Sparrow back the flask. 'Where's me clothes? I've got to go and find me brother.'

'The nigger?' he says straight away.

'Aye, Hawk Solomon, me twin. He'll be out lookin' for me.'

'Twin? Him? You and he be twins? T'ain't possible – he's pitch-black, a giant!' Mr Sparrow grins his weasel grin. 'Ikey knock up a black gin then, did he? Dirty old bugger!' Then he looks puzzled. 'But then that don't explain you, does it?'

'I'll tell you how it come about some other time,' I says, impatient. 'You've made Hawk's acquaintance then, has ya?'

'I ain't, but I heard he's been downstairs asking for yer.'

'Didn't that bloomin' Doreen tell him she'd seen me?'

'Doreen only sees what she's told to see. She's blind as a bat when she needs to be.' Mr Sparrow smiles. 'But don't you fuss none, Tommo, we've had 'arf a dozen of my lads following your brother. I daresay it ain't too easy to lose a seven-foot nigger. How's your head, then?' He grins again. 'We gave you plenty o' water on the hour.'

'Me head's fine, where's me clothes?'

'Be here soon, a new set for you.'

'What's you mean?' I cries. 'Where's me own clobber? Ya took me flamin' clothes!'

'Not took, replaced. You can't be seen to be the country bumpkin where we're going tonight, Mr Ace O' Spades. I even took yer shoe size when you were asleep. Yer precisely the same size as me.' Mr Sparrow hands me the parcel under his arm. 'They be my third best set o' crabshells.'

I'm still holding this parcel when a lad comes to the door with another large paper package, his head and cabbage-tree hat barely peeking out above it. 'From Hordern's Drapery, Mr Sparrow,' he announces.

It seems Sparrer Fart is King of the Sydney lads. Apart from the two what were guarding the door, there's three more on the landing, and now this one's appeared. Not to mention the half dozen what's following Hawk.

'Help yourself, Tommo,' Mr Sparrow says proudly, putting the parcel on the bed. 'Best there is, short o' tailor-made!' Inside the parcel is a good worsted suit of clothes, three new blouses, a waistcoat and a fancy neckerchief of the kind toffs wear. There's even a hat of a sort I've never seen before.

Mr Sparrow picks it up, removes his own headgear and places the new one on his head at a rakish angle. 'Latest fashion, all the rage in London, most suitable and becoming for a young man about town like yerself.'

'Look, Mr Sparrow, I don't know what you're doing, but I don't want no part of it 'til you explains everything. What the hell's goin' on? All I wants is me own gear back so's I can get out of here and find me brother!'

'Steady on, lad,' Mr Sparrow soothes. 'You get dressed and I'll tell yer all about the grand adventure I've got planned for us tonight.'

'Oh, an adventure this very night, is it? No doubt a thousand times better than getting pissed, is it? I told ya already, I'm off!' I picks up a blouse and starts to undo the buttons when two young lads bring in a jug of hot water, steam coming out the top.

'Pour it in the basin,' Mr Sparrow instructs.

'What's that for?' I asks, suspicious. The lad hesitates and looks at Mr Sparrow.

'Don't suppose a wash be out the question, seeing you're near naked but for your woollen blouse?' Mr Sparrow says. 'Bit of a scrub up do yer the world o' good, plenty o' hot water and a clean towel, what do you say?'

I hesitate. Truth is, I fancies a bath. Hawk's put me in the habit o' cleanliness and I hasn't had a wash for longer than I cares to remember. But what's I gunna do? There in that basin is my own piss! It must stink something awful. 'Much obliged, Mr Sparrow,' I says, and turn to the lad holding the jug. 'Leave it here.' I set the new blouse aside and, rising from the bed, takes me time getting me old blouse off. Then I pick up the jug and walk over to the washstand. I pour the water into it and bend over as if to wash me face. Then I pause and sniff. I pull me head back in alarm.

'What the hell . . .' I exclaim. 'It stinks!' I point into the basin, then I looks 'round angry at the two lads. 'What's you brats playin' at?'

'What's wrong, Tommo?' Mr Sparrow asks.

I point to the empty jug. 'Some dirty little bugger's pissed in me jug of hot water!'

Mr Sparrow throws a conniption on the spot. He sends for another basin and jug of hot water, and soundly boxes the ears of the two boys, what jumps up and down, whining their innocence. Then, when me clean water arrives, he tells all the lads to scarper, so that we's on our own. He laughs quiet at me. 'I like a nimble mind. Piss in the basin, did yer?'

I grin in reply. He's a man after my own heart, I reckons. I bathe and dress and Mr Sparrow tells me about his plans for tonight. It seems that, amongst other things, he runs a regular game o' cards. It's mostly for rich toffs what wants to taste the entertainments of Sydney. 'Not just cards – women, grog, a prize fight if we can arrange it. Delights of the Night, I calls it,' he says. He explains that Fat Fred is the manager of several prize fighters. 'Nothing like a prize fight to bring out the nabobs and open their purses, Tommo.' But while the gambling on the fights be a good earner when there's a big purse on, poker's the mainstay. Seems everybody's up for a game o' flats – merchants, squatters, barristers and judges, graziers, men rich from the goldfields, even the celestials what has learned to play poker out in the diggings.

'The Chinese from the goldfields?'

'Aye, they be very keen gamblers.'

'And they comes to yer poker games with the landed gentry?'

'No, once a month we play down in Chinatown and the landed gentry come to them. Very exotic it is, too. There be other attractions in Chinatown as well as a good game of poker. Matter o' fact, that be where we're going tonight,' Mr Sparrow smiles.

'We? I ain't said I'm coming!' I'm sitting on the edge of the bed lacing up Mr Sparrow's spare boots. They fit a treat and I has to admit I likes the feel of boots with hose again.

'Stand up and let's look at you, Tommo. Breeches fit, I can see that. Shoes?' I nod. 'Put the jacket on.' I does as he asks. 'Not bad, not too bad at all, a little bit o' fattening up and the fit'll be perfect.'

Suddenly Mr Sparrow takes a step forward and grabs me by the lapels of me jacket. He pulls me close. 'Look, Tommo, don't be a fool!' His voice is hard and he looks most weasel-like. 'If you're as good as I thinks, and if you're trained by Ikey Solomon, you'll clear a fiver tonight. You'll win a lot more, but the rest is mine until you're tested, then we'll split a bit more even. That's me best offer! Take it or leave it! Now make up yer mind, son!'

'A fiver, you say?'

'I'll guarantee it.'

'You're on.'

'You'll not regret it, my dear Ace O' Spades,' says Mr Sparrow, very pleased with himself. He points to the bed. 'Sit down. There's more to tell.'

In me new togs I feel my confidence return, and I like the sound of this adventure more and more. I sit back and Mr Sparrow starts to fill me in on the detail. 'Now, you don't know me from a bar o' soap, yer hear? That's the first thing you has to get into your noggin – we're strangers. You've just arrived from Tasmania and is looking for a game o' cards. You've got a quid or two – family has a sheep run and a good stand o' timber – but you're a bit of a cornstalk. This way, no one will get suspicious if yer can't answer their questions, seeing as you're from Tasmania an' all.'

'Well thanks very much,' says I. 'Wait 'til you meet Hawk. He's from Tasmania too.'

Mr Sparrow looks at me hard, not liking me little bit o' fun. 'Now listen, lad, we play straight unless we're losing bad. If I light me cigar and blow a single smoke ring, you may consider relocating your cards, but not a moment before, you understand?' I nod and he continues. 'The Chinese don't usually take to the flats, they's got their own ways o' gambling, but this lot's learnt in the goldfields. Don't make the mistake o' thinking them new chums to the game, though. If they think you're relocating, they'll have a knife in your belly soon as look at yer. I mean it, Tommo, no cheatin' unless I say. And yer name is Ace O' Spades. Incognito be well accepted around here. The chief justice himself be known as Tom Jones, and the attorney general as William Pitt.' He leans back and cups his hands about his raised knee. 'By the way, we've got a partner in this endeavour, Mr Tang Wing Hung. He arranges the game and the entertainment after and takes his cut.'

'From me fiver or from what I earns for you?'

'It don't work that way. What we earns in cash, we keeps. The celestials are back from the goldfields and they've got a lot o' gold dust. They'll play with coins or notes at first, but if they loses what they've got, and it's your job to see they do, most won't quit, they'll just think to change their luck by bringing out their gold.

'It's Mr Tang Wing Hung's pleasure to cash their gold nuggets or dust for currency at special rates, no doubt most onerous, it's not my concern. That's his profit and not to be questioned or shared with us.'

'I'll have to tell Hawk where I is,' I says. 'He'll be fretting that something's happened to me.'

'No, Tommo. This Chinese game be most private organised. There'll be some big wigs there what can't be seen in Chinatown. I can't take no chances of you tellin' anyone. There's reputations at risk. If the nabobs are seen to gamble with the celestials, heads will roll! You stay stum, not a dicky-bird to no one, you swear?' I nod and he says, 'Can you write?'

'A little. Me hand is very poor, though.'

'That don't matter, long as yer brother knows it well.'

'Well enough. He taught me.'

'Good! Then write yer beloved brother a note in yer own hand, telling him you're safe and you'll see 'im in the morning. One o' the lads will deliver it, I promise yer.'

After a moment I agree and he sends one of the ever-present lads standing outside the door to fetch pen, blacking and paper.

'Just one thing more, Mr Sparrow, to settle me mind. Why'd ya do that relocation this morning? That full house be a trick what a man of your skill with the flats would never reveal to someone he don't know. If you was thinking me a whaleman just paid out, ya would've scared me away with your tricks!'

'You insult me, my dear. I don't play with such bowyangs. Not my style, not my style at all.'

'So, why did ya waste yer talent on me? Easy to see I ain't no true merino!'

'I admit, when you walked in wearing those old togs, you had me fooled. But when I come over and took up the glass o' bad brandy Doreen gives yer, I take a gander at your right hand, and I see the calloused edge to yer thumb and forefinger. That comes from only one thing, my dear, playing with the flats, practising yer skill. It takes thousands and thousands of hours to build up that ridge o' skin and don't I know it! I saw at once you were no whaleman but a broadsman. I had to brave the next step, get you to show me yer form, see if you'd back off or not.'

'But what if I couldn't match your very superior piece o' relocation?'

'Matter o' fact, I was pretty certain you couldn't. But as the great Ikey Solomon would say, "Never take nothing for granted, my dears. The day you lose is the day you think you can't be beat. Sooner or later there's someone comes along what's younger and better than you. If you're ready for him, then you can delay the fall, make a deal, a partnership. But if you're not ready, then he will gobble you up." '

'And you supposed it could be me? That I could be the one what's younger and better?' I ask, amazed.

Mr Sparrow holds up his right hand, and with the forefinger of his left traces the calloused ridge on his thumb and forefinger. 'See that? It took me near thirty years to build and I'm getting older and slower, lad. It's rare to see a ridge what even comes close. I had to find out if you'd the nerve, the speed and the mind to match. If you were worth the training. I didn't think you'd best me. No, I thought when you saw what I could do, you'd want to learn from me.'

'And now?'

Mr Sparrow laughs. 'I can still teach you a trick or two, Mr Ace O' Spades! There's other things you'll need to know if you don't want to be found floating in Sydney Harbour with yer throat cut. We begin tonight with the celestials. I hope to make Ikey Solomon, may he rest in peace, most proud of the both of us. Proud of me fer listening down the years and you fer agreeing we be partners.'

'Ikey would've liked that,' I say. I thinks of him, stranded amongst the Maori ancestors, nothing to eat but roast pork three times a day. Old Ikey must be wondering what he done wrong to me and Hawk for us to put him into such a terrible predicament. 'I don't think Ikey's playing much cribbage where he is,' I confides to Mr Sparrow.

But wherever he is, I thinks, to meself, I hope Ikey's proud o' me for beating the Splendour of the Sparrer!

BOOK THREE

Chapter Sixteen

Hawk

Sydney
September 1860

Sydney is thriving. The houses of the wealthy merchants are most elegant, with not a lick of paint spared, and every brass doorknob highly polished. Many of them sit in pleasant gardens filled with native and English plants of all description, some even sporting fountains in this city short of water. The government and commercial buildings and the churches which, for the most part, are made of the local sandstone, are handsome and well maintained.

The streets are paved and have footpaths. Those running up from Semicircular Quay and across the length of the city are wide, though many a cross street is no more than a narrow lane. Hyde Park, a long strip of dust quite unlike its London namesake, is a popular area for promenading and recreation, a few minutes' brisk walk or a twopenny omnibus ride from the centre of town.

Only the Rocks, below the Argyle Cut, remind the curious of what the earlier convict settlement must have been like. It is a chaotic arrangement of mean huts, wooden skillings, slaughter yards, knackeries, cow pens, leather tanners, open sewers, broken fences, rutted streets, one-shilling hells and taverns, all crawling with rats and mangy cats. A hundred yards up from this sprawl, in George Street, the places where people go to drink are known as public houses or pubs, but here in the Rocks, such places are often called taverns, after the age-old tradition of the sea. Sailors drink at taverns when they come ashore and shall do so evermore. In the Rocks, these notorious bloodhouses carry names such as the Black Dog, which is also the name of Leuwin's schooner, though if there is a connection none I asked knew of it. Here one may also find the Brown Bear, the Whalers' Arms, the Hit or Miss, the Lord Nelson, the Mermaid, the Erin Go Bragh, the Cat and Fiddle, the Jolly Sailor, the Rose of Australia, the Hero of Waterloo, the Sheer Hulk, the Labour in Vain, the Sailors' Return and the Help Me Through the World. Tommo, alas, has become a steady visitor to The World Turned Upside Down in Bridge Street.

If the advantageous effects of the gold strikes may be seen in the upper reaches of George, Pitt and Macquarie Streets, and in the handsome houses of the well-to-do, here at the Rocks the discovery of gold has had quite the opposite effect. A great many working men have left good jobs to seek their fortunes at the diggings at Lambing Flat and Braidwood, amongst others. Most of these hard-luck fossickers find nothing but hard luck, and their women and children are left here without any livelihoods, so that misery, desperation and destitution are everywhere to be seen.

Many a respectable mother has been forced to resort to the 'purse between her legs' to feed her starving children. Some have forsaken their young and for a silver shilling are available in the Argyle Cut for a quick knee-trembler. The streets near the Semicircular Quay are over-run by tiny, barefoot urchins in tatters, begging for halfpennies. Others, boys and girls not much beyond the age of seven or eight, become child prostitutes and catamites to the sailors and many a so-called upstanding citizen. Most of these wild children die young. But if a boy should survive long enough to become one of the 'Sydney lads', he will be as tough a young specimen as you may find pound-for-pound anywhere in the world.

Here in the Rocks, the roads and the footpaths are so filthy and in such bad repair that no respectable person would venture down them. This matters little enough to the people who dwell here. They know themselves to be the flotsam of the human race, driven by poverty and despair to this dirty corner of the city. Some say that they are a tribe of their own but I don't think this is true: drink and poverty do nothing to unite a community. For those already in the clutches of the demon drink, the Rocks is the end of their journey and for those unfortunate enough to be born here, it is the beginning of a hard life.

There is also a Chinatown bordering the Rocks where large numbers of orientals reside, many of them on their way to and from the goldfields. These 'celestials' are treated with a contempt only surpassed by the treatment meted out to the 'niggers' or blacks as the Aborigines are called. I have noted that the Aborigines are also referred to in the *Sydney Morning Herald* as 'Sable Australians'. But this I believe merely reflects polite society's need to disguise the contempt it feels for the native Australian.

Those who live in the Rocks, even the poor whites whose existences are meagre, do not bother to hide their feelings towards the niggers of this squalid place. These poor blacks, who almost without exception dress in discarded rags, are mostly drunk from morning 'til night. Their women, known in the local parlance as 'gins', fight each other when intoxicated, with a screaming and caterwauling that would wake the dead. The men sit bleary-eyed in the dirt, their mangy kangaroo dogs panting beside them and their black bottles and clay pipes close to hand, taking no notice of the women's battles. Naked, snot-nosed children, with bloated bellies and flies clustering around their dark eyes, scream and dance in agitation as their mothers roll and claw at each other in the dust.

The gin-fight is so common a spectacle here that the regular denizens of the Rocks pause only a few moments in their passage to watch. It is the visiting sailors who are most amazed by these scenes, often betting on one or another of the women and then, at the end, tossing them a few coins so that they may drown their sorrows at the back door of the nearest tavern, for they are not permitted within.

I am black myself and know that men call me a nigger. Yet my lot is nowhere near as difficult as that of the Aborigines, who have suffered so much since the coming of the white man to Australia.

The corruption of the Aboriginal nature which has been brought about with grog is tragic. Each time I see one of their kind near dead from the drink, or one of their gins offering herself to a passing sailor for sixpence, I think sadly of our friend Billy Lanney from the *Nankin Maiden*. I know him to be a brave, generous and true-spirited man, who faithfully stood by Tommo in Auckland. I also now know him to be the much-loved Billygonequeer of whom Ikey spoke. Yet he too is the lesser man for the drink. But which man is not, black or white? I cannot let myself pass judgment on Billy, nor the sad people I see here, for my own brother is just as much a wretch when he takes solace in his grog-wilderness. Who then can blame the Aborigines for their plight?

While the Aborigines are abandoned to their fate, efforts are afoot to save the white man from the temptation of the bottle. All over town this past week, I have seen posters telling of a lecture to be given by the Reverend Hannibal Peegsnit at the Congregational Church in Pitt Street this afternoon. His topic is most clearly announced:

WHERE GOD CAN NO LONGER REACH!

The death and disaster,
terrors and tribulations,
caused by
the pernicious celestial poppy.

The Reverend Peegsnit's special mission is to the drunks and especially the opium addicts of Sydney. And no story is dearer to his heart than that of his own salvation, which has become a tale all too well known in Sydney.

Peegsnit was educated at Oxford and came to New South Wales as an Anglican cleric. He soon took to the black bottle and sank to the depths of depravity. Cast out by his own synod, he became a dipsomaniac, visited in his delirium by serpents and hobgoblins – rats gnawing at his fingers, toes and nose, and monkeys jabbering into his terrified face, showing their tiny jagged teeth and sharp little claws.

Peegsnit's personal epiphany occurred when he lay drunk in the gutter outside the Town Hall on St Crispin's Day. Christ appeared to him, immediately banishing the simian creatures and assorted pestilences that plagued him, so that his mind was at once restored fully unto him. Then the Lord took his trembling hand and charged him henceforth to administer to drunkards. His Redeemer also warned him specifically of the pernicious influence of the Celestial Empire and 'the smoke of the scarlet flower,

Papaver somniferum, on this Christian colony'. It was miraculous indeed that the Lord Jesus remembered the Latin in his warning against the opium poppy.

And so the Reverend Peegsnit asked to be returned to the bosom of the Anglican Church. But the Bishop of Sydney, the Very Reverend John Casper, was not convinced of the redemption of their prodigal son and refused. Denied the reversed collar by the Episcopalians, Peegsnit became a preacher in the Congregational Church.

The Reverend Peegsnit teaches that God's hands are always stretched out to sinners and especially to drunkards, no matter how wretched. But, he insists, there is one exception to Christ's ever-present promise of salvation: the opium smoker. I am curious about this man and his popularity, especially among the women of Sydney who see their husbands drunk most nights, and so have come to hear his lecture. When I enter the packed church, Peegsnit is already in full flow.

'We must stop this pernicious oriental influence before it destroys the noble British character!' he thunders, and expounds on his topic at length.

I settle myself comfortably against the back wall, for it is standing room only, and observe a sea of rapt faces drinking in the reverend's every word. I listen too but find myself wondering about this noble British character of which he so eloquently speaks. It was the English who created the opium trade. Even as the good reverend speaks, British merchants are buying the paste in India and sailing their fast clipper ships to the mouth of the Canton River. There, in the safe harbour of the island of Hong Kong, they exchange the opium for tea leaf which they bring to Britain for export to the colonies. Any Chinese addiction to opium, then, is a direct result of this noble British character and trade!

What's more, the colony of New South Wales is a chief beneficiary of the opium trade. The government here gains a tax of ten shillings per pound on its import and places no limit on the amount which may be brought in, despite the fact that the authorities are well able to gauge the amount needed for medicinal purposes. For those in pain, opium is a great blessing and it is called the 'Angel's Kiss' by those whose suffering it alleviates. But it is also called the 'Devil's Smoke' by those poor souls who are addicted to it.

While I am engaged in these thoughts, the Reverend Peegsnit has, through his fearful oratory, roused his audience to sobbing and strange excitement. Much of his passion focuses on the race whom *he* holds responsible for the corruption of our society. There is no doubting who they are – in his mind at least.

'The yellow-skinned, slant-eyed Mongolian presents our precious offspring, our sweet daughters and robust sons, with a pipe and a substance which allows them to indulge in an evil clothed in its most hideous form, until the nerves begin to wince and the frame to totter from excessive stimulation!'

Peegsnit thumps the Bible on the lectern. 'The Devil's Smoke renders them shameless and they are overtaken by an immorality which utterly beggars description. These are our beloved sons and daughters who, through opium, impair their mental, moral and physical systems beyond salvation and bring upon themselves the greatest of all vices.' He stops for breath and looks about him. 'The vice of *indolence*!' Peegsnit pauses again for effect, then repeats himself, thumping the Bible with an indignant fist. 'The vice of indolence! Once this is acquired, indecency and immorality follow closely in its train!'

Like the others, I feel myself affected by the Reverend Peegsnit's oratory. Once again, however, I am forced to consider that if indolence is the most heinous of opium's consequences, then half of Sydney's population must already be addicted and beyond recovery, for indolence is an affliction I have observed everywhere about me in 'European' Sydney. In contrast to this, the Chinese seem to be very hardworking. How is it, I now ask myself, that they are not also afflicted, if idleness is caused by opium? An article in the *Sydney Morning Herald* just the other day reported that out of every one hundred Chinamen in the colony, sixty-two are primary producers of wealth. Of every one hundred Europeans, however, only twenty are thus self-employed.

The thump of the Bible hitting the lectern startles me back to attention. Peegsnit's lecture has concluded with a bang, and with much relief I walk outside into the sunny day. It is several weeks since Tommo and I arrived in Sydney and, sadly, I already have reason to be preoccupied with the subject of opium and its effects. My little brother has taken up the pipe, and I am in two minds as to what I can do. Tommo is happy enough as a professional gambler in partnership with Mr Sparrow, and I cannot help but

314

feel buoyed that some of Ikey has come back into our lives in this way. It is sentimental of me, I know, especially as I have some misgivings about Mr Sparrow's intentions as concerns my twin.

I have been warned that Mr Sparrow is a hard, even dangerous man, and that Tommo will not in the end benefit from the association. But he has taught Tommo much about gambling with the rich, and how to conduct himself in an acceptable manner with such people. This means that at least he is not forced to play with rough sorts in rough situations. These days Tommo is quite the dandy and he bathes and changes his linen twice a week. While he still craves the brandy bottle, Mr Sparrow watches him carefully, with one of his lads always on duty to see that Tommo does not drink during the day. At night, at the card table, he is permitted to imbibe, but only at a level which does not damage his concentration – and this only so he is seen to do his fair share of drinking with the other players.

As Tommo points out to me, no punter will play cards with him unless he is prepared to go along with the grog shout. It seems nothing is done here in Sydney without the 'nobbler' – the name used for a portion of spirits. Every merchant keeps a black bottle in his desk drawer to aid in his business with customers.

Drinking is seen by many as the mark of a man, and is certainly more prevalent than any sign of religion. Within two miles of Semicircular Quay, there are six churches and hundreds of public houses. The clergy may denounce the drinking habits of the citizens at every opportunity, but very few heed their call to higher things. People seem to live only for the present, not the afterlife or the past, for not far away are memories of the rattle of leg irons.

I am so taken up with thoughts of Tommo that I am almost run down by a carriage as I cross the street away from Peegsnit's church. I can think of no other place where the streets are in such a state of confusion. This includes London which, at the time of my visit, was said to be the most congested city in the civilised world. Here in Sydney, wheels are all-important. Those who in any other society could not imagine a means of locomotion beyond placing one foot in front of the other, here demand to be transported to their destinations. Such transport is provided by as motley a collection of doddering old horses as you can imagine. Most of these poor nags are long past their appointed hour with the knacker's yard. Every day I see some poor beast, its ribs sticking out like tent poles, collapsed on the street, with its owner kicking and lashing it in a vain attempt to raise it from the dead.

Carriages consist of contraptions of every sort, many of them most peculiar in construction, the work of some backyard mechanic. Even dogs are used to draw carts piled high with newspapers. These are led by news boys who dodge in and out of the traffic on the way to their accustomed corners. I feel sure that if cats or rats could be trained to the task, they too would soon enough be put into harness. There is even the story of a retired ship's captain who harnessed his African ostrich to a milk cart and caused the traffic to come to a tangled standstill as the bird panicked and rushed headlong up George Street on its way to Parramatta.

The streets here resound with the curses of cab drivers and cart men, who turn the air blue with their invective. Coach horns and rattles blast away and the drivers of bullock drays will even take their whips to other vehicles on the road. Every few minutes some form of accident occurs with its attendant altercation.

There is talk of a horse-drawn tram commencing next year which will run on tracks from Semicircular Quay down Pitt Street to Redfern Station. Today's *Sydney Morning Herald* speculates that once this is established, no Sydneysider with three pennies to jingle in his pocket will have to walk anywhere, bringing about the total collapse of the bootmaker's trade. It is claimed that the entire mile and three quarters of the journey will take no more than ten minutes.

The Sydney lads are as wild as the Sydney traffic. I have grown up with the wild youth of Hobart Town who, in concert, may become a dangerous mob but who, individually, lack wiles and nerve. The lads of Sydney are a different kettle of fish altogether. There seem to be two types of physiognomy amongst them. One lot are slim, dark-eyed, olive-complexioned, the other are carrot-topped and blue-eyed, with much accumulated dirt obscuring their freckles. The Sydney lad's hair – whether ginger or dark – is shiny with grease and falls across his brow, so that he is constantly brushing it away from his eyes. A cabbage-tree hat clings precariously to the back of his head, and from this a snip of black ribbon dangles like a rat's tail. The knees of his breeches and the elbows of his jacket are always covered in grease. If he is younger than ten years of age, he is likely to be barefoot. If older, he wears scuffed boots with no hose.

All are up to no good. The Sydney lad is insolent to everyone, particularly servant girls, police officers and new chums. He pushes and shoves his way along the street, not caring a whit for the small child, dainty female or elderly. He fears no one in authority and has no regard for any man, unless a cricketing hero or a challenger at chuck penny.

The Sydney lad is no coward and, at the least excuse, he will remove his cabbage-tree hat and greasy jacket, wipe the snot from under his nose with the back of his hand and 'have a go'. He will often take on someone older and bigger than himself, with a cussing and swearing that would take the paint off the Queen's mailbox. Should he have a halfpenny to spend, the lad will buy a thin black Mexican cheroot. This he will light immediately upon meeting an acquaintance and then, after taking a single puff and blowing out the smoke in a lofty manner, he will extinguish it so that it may be saved for his next assignation.

Sydney lads call all their female friends after the ships in which they arrived, hence Susie Blue Wren, Mary York Town, Jenny Memphis, Mary Armageddon. And they refer to all policemen as Israelites after a ship named the *Exodus* which brought a large consignment of English constables to the colony.

At the age of ten, the Sydney lad is out in the world on his own. By this time, he believes himself master of his own destiny and a man in all respects, earning good wages by some clandestine means or other, which does not involve manual work. By the age of twelve or thirteen, long before he has the slightest blooming of manly hair upon his grimy cheeks, he has tasted most of the joys and sorrows of existence. Mr Charles Dickens, the English writer, has much lauded the genuine cockney lad, but for shrewdness, effrontery, truculence and the affectations of manhood, the cockney lad pales beside the young gamins of Sydney.

Much of what I know of the Sydney lad, I have learnt from my brother. Tommo already knows many of these lads in their cabbage-tree hats. It seems that Mr Sparrow commands the nastiest of these scoundrels, which he addicts to grog early. They cannot be good company for Tommo, but of far greater concern to me is Tommo's wounded head and his increasing reliance on the Angel's Kiss, the dreaded celestial poppy.

Tommo insists he takes opium only to alleviate the pain of his injury, which certainly remains a serious condition. But I am much afraid that the Angel's Kiss will eventually turn into the Devil's Smoke and he will become addicted. He has been using the opium pipe since the first night we arrived.

I waited all afternoon for him outside The World Turned Upside Down that day, and then made urgent enquiries at the bar when he failed to emerge. But all who worked there claimed not to have seen him. Naturally, I was distraught and even close to panic. I searched the Rocks half the night and then went up to Hyde Park to see if he was there, perhaps lying under the gum trees with the other drunks. I missed my meeting with Maggie Pye, although I left a note explaining my predicament, hoping she would not be angry and that we might, with luck, meet again. I spent a most miserable night looking for Tommo, only abandoning my search when the currawongs called at dawn.

Hoping that Tommo might find me in the Rocks once he'd recovered, I went back there to look for accommodation. I soon found a decent enough room with two mattresses and after paying the landlady ten shillings for the first week's rent, I left our belongings with her and went straight to the public bath house. There I paid a penny for soap and another for the hire of a razor, and shaved for the first time in a fortnight. I also gave myself a good scrubbing, and washed my clothes, wringing them out as best I could before returning them to my body damp. I spent a penny more on two loaves of bread and went to sit in the sun, watching the boats on the magnificent harbour as I breakfasted. I meant only to stay until my clothes were dry but I must have fallen asleep. I woke to hear two chimes of the post office clock and realised with a renewed burst of anxiety that it was past noon. As the last chime faded to silence, I felt a small hand on my shoulder. My heart leapt and I swung around, hoping to find Tommo. Instead a scruffy lad with a cheeky grin stood before me.

'Yer name Solomon? Hawk Solomon?' he demanded.

'Why do you wish to know?' I replied, looking as stern as I could.

'Ere,' he thrust a piece of folded paper at me. It was a note in Tommo's unpractised hand, telling me that he was well. I was to meet him outside the same pub in Bridge Street at seven o'clock the following morning. Not content with so little information, I looked up to question the lad further, only to discover that he had disappeared.

I was furious with my errant twin. A night wasted in worrying. It was then that I resolved to visit the Hero of Waterloo, where Maggie Pye and I had agreed to meet. Maybe I could make enquiries and perhaps find my new friend again.

The pub, when I arrived, was crammed with customers and my heart, which had taken to thumping faster as I drew near, sank as I scanned the crowd. Suddenly, in the far corner, I caught a flash of black and white as Maggie's magpie bobbed cheekily up and down. I quickly made my way through the crowd, then I stopped short. Maggie was talking to someone – a customer perhaps? She looked up and our eyes met. With a big grin and a look of welcome, she waved me over.

I smiled and pushed my way through the crowd to her. 'I'd not have spotted you if it wasn't for the bird.'

'Me trademark,' she replied sweetly. Then she climbed up onto a nearby bench and promptly kissed me on the lips, a soft, welcoming kiss which made my knees tremble. 'Yiz better not be late again, Hawk, but I'll forgive ya this once! Now come and meet me friend. Mr Isaacs, this be Hawk Solomon what I told yiz about.'

Looking down, I saw a small, round man, neatly dressed, who was about fifty years old. His head was so bald and polished that his pate reflected the glow from the gaslight on the wall. He had a tape measure about his neck and held out a plump, well-manicured hand. 'Pleased to make your acquaintance, Mr Solomon,' he said.

'Mr Isaacs owns the slop-shop in Pitt Street. He's a tailor, do you up a treat,' Maggie explained.

'How do you do, sir?' I extended my hand.

'Hawk Solomon. Your name is Solomon? But surely you ain't a Jew?' The little man looked puzzled.

'I was christened a Jew,' I explained.

'Ha! Not possible! Jews ain't christened!'

I laughed. 'Pardon me, it's a figure of speech. My brother Tommo and I were born to a Jewish mother, who died, then we were given the name Solomon by Mr Ikey Solomon, who was our father of sorts.'

The little man sniffed in disbelief. 'Well, he must have been colour-blind, if you'll forgive me saying. A schwartzer for a Jew, I ain't heard of that before!' As he talked, he measured me. Like

Maggie when she kissed me, he stood on the bench to get the width of my shoulders, my neck and the measurement under my armpits, making me feel most foolish all the while.

'We wants the best, Mr Isaacs,' Maggie instructed.

'Maggie, it will have to wait.' I thought of the few coins left in my pocket. 'Mr Isaacs, I'm afraid I can't afford new clothes.'

'Who said anything about money?' Maggie grinned. 'Did I say anything about money, Barney?' She didn't wait for his reply but turned back to me. 'I have a long-standing arrangement with Mr Isaacs, Hawk, and none of it your business, sweetheart.'

Barney Isaacs had hopped down from the bench and, at Maggie's words, he shook his head forlornly.

'What?' Maggie had one eyebrow raised and her hands upon her hips.

'I can't oblige you, my dear,' Barney said, his face serious. 'Can't do it.'

'Why ever not?' Maggie demanded to know.

'Too much cloth and stitching, my dear. Mr Solomon 'ere be the biggest man I've ever been called upon for to fashion up a set o' gentleman's apparel.' The little man looked up from under his eyebrows at her. 'Couldn't honestly see meself doing it for less than . . .' he shrugged and spread his hands, 'three?'

'Three!' Maggie screamed. 'You dirty bugger! Christ, you've already had a down-payment an' all!'

'But he's a giant!' the little tailor protested. 'Biggest man ever I seen!'

Maggie took two steps forward so that her pretty face was right up to his. 'You tryin' t' cheat me? You got the wrong whore, Barney Isaacs! What if I says no, eh? Or I gets the nigger 'ere to wring your bloody neck? Or I even does it meself? How you gunna give me back what you already spent, answer me that?'

The tailor shrugged again. 'We could come to another arrangement – maybe a silk shawl, embroidered, from China? Or a new coat? What do you say, me dear? A nice warm coat for the winter, best worsted?'

'Maggie,' I interrupted, 'what's going on? I told you I can't pay. Send him away!'

Maggie turned on me suddenly. 'Oh, fer Chrissakes, will ya shut yer gob. This is between his nibs 'ere and me! He's tryin' to rook me!'

'Tell you what,' Barney added as though he hadn't heard anything. 'Make it three, and I'll toss in the blouse and hose?'

I had heard enough. I was halfway out of the pub when Maggie called out, 'Oi, where's ya goin', Hawk?'

'I don't need your charity, Maggie, especially not that sort!' I replied, angry now that I began to understand her method of payment.

Maggie sighed. 'Ah, Hawk, stop being so prim and bloody proper! Lemme sort this bastard out and then I'll explain everythin' to ya!'

She moved purposefully towards the tailor, who retreated until he bumped against the bar, holding his hands up to his chest to protect himself.

'Give him one, Maggie,' someone shouted. 'Kick him in the bollocks!'

'Maggie, come on now, he's seven foot tall and broad as a ship's mast,' Barney yelled. 'I swear it'll take twice the cloth and sewing and I'm only asking half again. Be reasonable, it's a most fair offer!'

Maggie stopped suddenly and tapped the little man on the chest with her finger. 'Righto,' she said. 'I admits he's a big bastard. I ain't goin' to fight ya and I ain't goin' to pay ya three either.' She took a step backwards and looked him directly in the eye. 'You've already had one fuck – that's fer the jacket. You'll get one more for the blouse and the hose and I'll go down on ya for the weskit. Two and a half, that's me final offer!'

Barney nodded eagerly, then pointed to my broken boots. 'Tell ya what, Maggie, the lad's going to need a new pair o' boots. What do you say, my dear, the other half and I throws in a pair?'

'Too late, ya bastard!' Maggie cried, clapping her hands happily. 'I already has an arrangement with the I-talian in Bligh Street, what's bootmaker to the governor!'

The tailor shrugged and departed and Maggie and I went to sit in a corner. She ordered a large gin and asked if I wanted something to drink. I declined and sat silently.

'What's the matter?' Maggie touched my arm. 'Cat got yer tongue?'

'Maggie, I don't want any charity, and I don't want you to keep me. I've always made my own way and always will. If we become friends or more, then it should be I who keeps you. I mean, once

I'm back on my feet. I don't want you to do it to that man, do you hear me?'

Maggie leant over and kissed me. 'Hawk, that be the nicest thing what's ever been said to me. Lotsa men wants to fuck me, but ain't never been one what wanted to keep me.' She smiled. 'I don't blame them neither. I'm a whore, an expensive whore, but still a whore. But when all's said and done, darlin', Barney be a regular, and I always takes me just reward in kind with him.'

'Maggie, I don't want you to do that for me!'

'You'll be the same, Hawk. You'll see, once you've put yer big black snake into me, you'll want it regular too. Need comes first, then greed! First the free fuck, then the free dinner!'

'Maggie! Don't talk like that. It isn't nice,' I protested.

'Talk like what?' she tilted her head at me.

'Talk dirty like that!'

'What's you mean?' she asked, genuinely astonished. 'I'm a whore! Dirty? Talk dirty? Have I said anything what hasn't already crossed yer mind, Hawk Solomon?'

'Well yes, you have. It had not crossed my mind to . . . er . . .'

'Fuck me?'

'Well yes, that I admit. But not then to live off you.'

'Oh, what's you plan to do, then? Fuck me and piss off?'

'Maggie, I don't feel that way about you!'

'Yeah, o' course you don't – now. But after you've had it, that's when you can't get away fast enough. Take me word for it, darlin', and don't get too fussed. It's what I expects. You pays yer money, has your way and then ya buggers off!'

'Some might do that!' I protested. 'But not I! We will be more than that to one another. You said yesterday we could be friends. Good friends who help each other through thick and thin, that's what you said.'

'Hawk, it's me standard patter! I says that to all the punters. Men enjoy a lasting arrangement – providing it don't last much beyond when they get their breeches back on.'

Maggie made me feel like a schoolboy. In such matters I suppose I am. 'Maggie, I don't understand all this. I don't understand why you would do what you plan to do just to get me a suit of clothes. It makes no sense if I'm just some bludger like the rest of your, er . . .'

'Customers?'

'Yes, customers. I admit I desire you, Maggie. You're beautiful and I can't help what's in my nature. But I am no bludger and I would never exploit you!'

'Why not? What's ya goin' to do instead, pull yerself off?'

'Maggie, stop it!' I was suddenly angry. 'You don't have to speak like that! And you don't have to do it with that tailor fellow for my sake.' I looked down at my ragged apparel. 'I can get my own clothes, thank you! It will take a bit longer, that's all.'

'That's just it, see, I don't want t' wait.'

'Oh?'

Maggie grabbed my hand. 'Hawk, listen to me. There's a big prize fight Friday night and I wants yiz on me arm an' all! I wants a seven-foot beautiful black nigger on me arm.' She grinned up at me. 'I admits, it's t' show off! Me screwin' Barney ain't no charity to you, it's well worth it to me!'

'Oh Christ, Maggie, what's a man getting himself into?' I said, rolling my eyes heavenwards.

Maggie laughed. 'With a bit o' luck and a fair wind, you're getting yerself into the warmest little bed a man ever sailed into.'

I blushed and didn't know what more to say, so changed the subject instead. 'You like the fights then, do you Maggie?'

'Loves 'em, darlin'. All the crinoline cruisers will be there, the toffs, squatters, strike-it-rich-Johnnies, but I wants the best on me own arm.'

'Crinoline cruisers?'

'Whores, stupid!'

'Maggie, you don't have to buy me clothes and take me to your bed to have my company. I'll come to the prize fight with you anyway,' I said, though I knew full well that I secretly desired to make love to her more than anything in the world.

Maggie looked at me, her blue eyes blazing. 'You mean ya doesn't want me, is that it? You're too 'igh and fuckin' mighty t' be with a slut?' She was furious. 'Well fuck *you*, Hawk!' Throwing what was left of her glass of gin into my face, she stormed out of the pub.

The drinkers standing near were suddenly quiet. Then I heard one say, 'Go get her, mate! Beat the living daylights out of her!' This brought me to my senses, and I wiped the gin from my face. The fellow who addressed me was the same bloke who wanted Maggie to go for Barney Isaacs. He was a big fellow but I barely noticed this as I grabbed him around the throat. Lifting him off the ground, I threw him halfway across the pub, where he knocked over several stools before landing against the wall with his eyes glazed and tongue lolling. 'Watch your dirty mouth!' I growled, as I went out after Maggie.

I caught up with her halfway down the street, as she strode towards the Argyle Cut. 'Maggie, wait! Maggie, please! I didn't mean what you think!'

'Bugger off, Hawk!' she cried.

'Please, Maggie, listen to me?' I put my hand on her shoulder.

'Don't touch me, ya bastard!' She shrugged my hand away and started to beat her fists against my chest. How sweet and clean she smelt as she hit me, the magpie jumping up and down in its nest as if it were about to fly away, wanting no part of her temper tantrum.

I began to laugh at this, then I held her tight. 'I care about you, Maggie!' I said, surprised at my own words but also liking the bold sound of them.

'Leggo o' me, ya shit!' Maggie yelled, then started to weep against my chest. I stroked her hair carefully so as not to disturb the magpie. After a little while she pulled away. 'Bet I look a proper mess, don't I?' She sniffed and, taking a small handkerchief from her handbag, wiped her big blue eyes.

'By Christ, no. You're beautiful.' I held her by the shoulders and looked down at her.

She laughed and then began to sob again. 'Oh, oh, ya bastard! Ain't nobody said that ever before!' she bawled. 'It ain't true, you silly bastard, but I loves ya for it.' She sniffed and laughed and cried a bit, then laughed again and finally dried her eyes. Then she tilted her head and asked, 'Friends?'

'Friends,' I repeated solemnly.

And that's what we've been ever since – friends. Almost every afternoon we have a drink or a chat at the Hero of Waterloo, with no more said of me sharing her bed. Thinking of Maggie has nearly driven my worries about Tommo from my mind, and I am smiling as I enter the bar to meet her again.

Today Maggie is scrubbed of all her paint and dressed in a grey gown and black shawl, neat and clean. By contrast to her appearance most afternoons, she looks decidedly modest, and might easily be mistaken for a servant girl on her day off, except for her hair, which still sports the magpie sitting in its nest.

'Don't you look fine,' she says with a grin, after greeting me with her usual kiss. 'Has you eaten?'

I shake my head.

'Ya must be starvin', darlin'! Come on!' She leads me out of the pub and we stroll down to a chophouse just the other side of the Cut. I have never been here with Maggie before, though they all seem to know her and greet her most cordially. A young lass wearing a mob cap and an apron comes up and Maggie gives her a hug.

'This be Florence. Flo, this be Hawk.' Maggie's got a smile like the proverbial Cheshire cat. 'What's ya think, eh?' she says to Florence.

Florence looks up at me and brings the tips of her fingers to her lips and giggles. 'Crikey, Mags, you gorn an' done it proper this time, ain'tcha?' she says.

'You betcha!' Maggie exclaims. 'One hundred per cent black magic! I told you so, didn't I?'

Flo giggles again and runs off.

I follow Maggie to a table and Florence soon reappears with a loaf of bread and two large soup plates, spoons and a ladle. She sets our places, trying all the time not to laugh.

'Don't be stingy now, Flo, Mr Black Magic 'ere takes a whole heap o' feedin',' Maggie instructs and then laughs. 'And, by crikey, he's gunna need all the strength he's got!'

'Is Florence your friend then, Maggie?' I ask.

'More like me little sister. Stopped her from cruisin' when she were twelve, and saw that she and her folks got work 'ere instead. Tom, the grocer's son, is gunna marry 'er.'

Just then Florence returns carrying a large pot of stew which she places on the table. 'Me papa reckons if the nigger can eat it all, it's 'arf price on yer tab, Maggie,' Flo winks. She looks at me, wiping her hands on her apron. 'He wants to know how tall ya is, Mr Hawk?'

'Seven feet and one inch, last time I was measured,' I reply. 'It isn't always convenient.'

'And it's all in proportion!' Maggie laughs, happily. 'The parts what can't be shown to an innocent little girl like you be just as big, I'll betcha!'

Flo's eyes grow large with surprise and she runs from the room back into the kitchen, where we can hear her laughing fit to burst.

'Maggie! You must be careful!' I admonish her, thinking how lucky I am to be black so that she can't see my own embarrassment. But still, I love being with her! Here I am in the middle of this noisy chophouse with a pot of stew in front of me and suddenly I realise that I love Maggie Pye. I sit stock still.

'C'mon, darlin', eat yer tucker! I got big plans for you after this, what will have yiz grinnin' like a butcher's dog!' Maggie leans over and, with the back of her hand, strokes the side of my cheek. It is so lovely I want to cry.

But even in love, I am ravenous and Maggie keeps filling my plate from the pot of mutton stew, which I must say is delicious. Soon enough, the pot is empty and I'm full as the governor's prize pig.

'Come, Hawk,' Maggie says, finally. 'I lives upstairs. Time to make yiz a nice cuppa tea!'

I follow Maggie upstairs to her home. She has two rooms and when she opens the door on her landing, I am almost forced to crawl into a small kitchen with a hearth. Even when I am seated at her small table, the ceiling is not much higher than my head. But Maggie can stand up straight and, as I look around, I see that her home is as neat as a pin. Everything is scrubbed clean, with pots and pans hanging from the wall and a flower pot on the window sill. A grey striped tabby, which she tells me is called Sardine, hops off the window sill and comes a-meowing the moment it sees her. Maggie feeds the cat with a scrap of stew meat she has brought from downstairs. Then she puts the kettle on the hob and lights a set of twigs and a bit of coal she's obviously made up earlier.

Now I'm starting to feel nervous. I don't know what's going to happen after the cup of tea, or what Maggie has planned, and I don't know how to behave. I'm not willing to tell her that I am almost a virgin, either. I well remember what happened that wonderful night with Hinetitama. But it may be nothing like whatever might happen with Maggie, should she decide to take me to her bed chamber.

Besides, Maggie has often made jokes about having her way with me, and I am not sure she isn't just joking.

I know what I would like to happen, but I'm not sure how to proceed even supposing Maggie wants to. I would like to treat her like a proper lady and not a tart, but is that what she'd expect? It's impossible for me to think of Maggie as a tart. She says she is one, but I can hear the sadness and longing for something else in her voice.

Suddenly I have a picture of Mary tucking Tommo and me into bed when we were little uns. 'I loves you, Mama,' Tommo says. Mary looks at the two of us and a tear rolls down her cheek. 'That's all I've ever dreamed of, Tommo,' she says softly and then kisses us. 'Just remember, all a woman ever wants is to be truly loved.'

'Are you truly loved by Ikey?' I ask. Mary smiles but doesn't say anything.

'Course not!' Tommo exclaims. 'Mama loves Mr Emmett!'

'Hush, Tommo! Don't you ever say that. Mr Emmett be a married man!' Mary admonishes him, but we both see that she's gone beetroot in the face.

Well, I now say to myself, I truly love Maggie. I know this is stupid, and that I barely know her. Yet I feel something which I suppose will some day prove foolish and young but now seems certain. If folks knew of it they'd probably laugh. Other men would no doubt wink at each other, thinking that only a callow youth could fall for a whore. Despite all this, Maggie makes my head spin. She makes my heart so happy that I don't even think of Tommo when she's near. Maggie claims me completely and I am besotted. She fills my being and even if I should try to cast her out of my thoughts I cannot.

How should I behave, then? 'Hawk, you are a gentleman.' Mary's words, which she has said so often to me, come into my head. 'Not a toff, not thinking yourself special, or putting on airs, pretending you be a true merino, which you ain't, but a true gentleman.' I have always tried to live up to my mama's words – Mary, who has seen and been everything but who wants me to be a gentleman. I sense there is something of Mary in Maggie, and perhaps it is this in her which I so dearly love already.

Then I have a shameful thought. Can a gentleman, even mama's sort of gentleman, love such a woman as Maggie? Hinetitama was different, a Maori princess, a ghost in the night. Maggie is so rudely alive, so loud and truthful and coarse. If Hinetitama were the shadow cast by the moon, Maggie is the blazing sunlight, every inch afire. Yet underneath, I sense, she is sad and wistful.

Perhaps I imagine all of this, I think now. Perhaps I should concede to Ikey's theory that there's no such thing as a good whore. What I do admit is that Maggie is altogether too much for me and I don't know what to do next. I feel like a bunny that should bolt down its burrow while there is still time!

Maggie has put the kettle on the hob and brings me a cup of tea. The cup is dainty and my big clumsy fingers can hardly grasp the handle. The tea is of the best quality and she has served it black with a slice of lemon. It is not sweetened, which I am unused to, but I find that it soon cleans my palate of the fatty mutton stew.

'Would you like a bottle of ale?' she asks. I am surprised at her voice, for it is suddenly shy and softer in tone. It is as though here in her home, she can be a different woman. 'Fetch you one from the pub on the corner, won't take a minute?' she volunteers.

I shake my head gently and she comes over and sits on my lap. A woman has never sat on my lap before and I am immediately overcome by the consequences. A terrible boldness grows between my thighs, as Maggie holds me tightly and kisses me all over my face and neck. I feel her sweet lips touch mine, demanding I should open them. And then, her tongue is inside my mouth! My whole body is aflame, and I find my arms encircling Maggie, drawing her ever in towards me. We kiss, she like an angel and I most clumsily. I think I must burst through the fabric of my breeches. She must, I am sure, feel the hardness under her buttocks, and she squirms about on my lap until I think I shall faint with the pain and the ecstasy of it.

I am beyond thinking when Maggie stops kissing me. Drawing back, she looks into my eyes. 'Come, darlin', into Maggie's nest.' She rises and takes my hand. I am afraid to stand up for the straining in my breeches, and am most grateful that the ceiling means I must remain stooped over as she leads me through into the other room. Here the ceiling is a little higher but not by much, and I am amazed at what meets my eyes.

I have never seen a whore's bedroom before, but this is unlike anything I have heard described by my companions at sea. Maggie has created a veritable Aladdin's cave in her tiny attic room.

The first thing that comes to mind is the 'palace o' purest pleasure' which Ikey and Mary once possessed in London. It was, Ikey told me, filled with Persian carpets, silks, brocades and erotic statuary, so that it resembled nothing so much as a maharaja's harem. But Maggie's boudoir has not entirely been taken over by the notion of titillation. There is a certain warm homeliness here as well. The room is very pretty, with lots of shiny bits, satin cushions and brocade curtains and a carpet, all in red. But there are white lace half-curtains to the single attic window, just like Mary's at home. It is the bed, though, which commands my attention and which I now observe with a mixture of purest terror and delightful anticipation.

Maggie's bed nearly fills the room and I cannot imagine how it could have been brought up here, unless it arrived in pieces and was built in the room. It is a large four-poster of the best cedar, resplendent with a red canopy, silk tassels hanging from each corner. There are no blankets, only red silk sheets and cushions to match. Lying at the centre, propped up against one of the cushions, is a golliwog doll with his round black rag face, red jacket and striped pants.

Maggie scoops the rag doll up into her arms. 'See, Hawk, I always were partial to darkies! Many's the night I've slept with him in me arms.' She holds the golliwog up so that its face is looking into hers. 'Ain't no secrets between us, is there, Golly? We've been lovers a long time now, hasn't we?' She shakes the doll's head so it appears he is agreeing. 'You can watch us, you're a good boy,' she says to him and props the doll against the bottom of the bed.

Maggie turns and smiles at me. 'Truth is, when I holds Golly in me arms and pleasures meself, he's the best fuck I've had all day.'

I'm shocked at this admission, which somehow seems more coarse said in this pretty room. But I'm also excited at the vision it brings to mind. I can see Maggie's slim little body naked as she hugs her little black Golly to her lovely breasts, her urgent finger stroking her pretty pussy as she arches in pleasure.

Maggie has removed her shoes but she is still dressed when she jumps onto the bed. She crosses her legs beneath her and pats the mattress. 'Come sit, Hawk,' she smiles.

I am still half-stooped over and I sit on the bed beside her, hoping she won't see my erection, though I don't know how she can miss it. It feels like a tent pole sticking up beyond my nose, a great tent of lust rising from my groin.

'Maggie, I haven't had, er, much experience of women,' I

stammer. 'You know, making love to them,' I say, deciding I should come clean before she finds me out for the duffer I am.

Maggie laughs and stretches up to kiss me on the cheek. 'I ain't had much experience of loving neither, Hawk.'

'What do you mean?' I am surprised.

'I'm a whore, darlin', not a cheap whore, but a whore. I've been fucked 'undreds o' times, thousands, but ain't nobody's never made love to me.' She kisses me again and asks softly, 'You going to make love to me, Hawk?'

Maggie has the end of my belt and now she pulls against the buckle to loosen it. Then she turns me around and draws my blouse up over my head so I'm sitting with only my much-loosened breeches on. She throws my blouse on the floor beside the bed, and then suddenly yells, 'Oh me Gawd!'

'What? What is it?' I try to rise from the bed but Maggie has grabbed me by the shoulders from behind and has buried her head against my shoulder. She turns my head to look at her.

'Who done that?' she asks.

'What?' I ask, still mystified.

'Yer back! Who done that to yer back, Hawk?' A tear rolls down her cheek.

'It was a flogging on a whale ship, but it was long ago,' I tell her, not wishing to distract her from other things. She is stroking my back and kissing the scars which run like old wickerwork from my neck to my waist. I confess it is a wonderful feeling, Maggie caressing and kissing my back. I want to throw her on the bed and rip her dress off and make love to her. But I don't have the courage.

'Lie down, darlin',' Maggie says. The bed is big but not long enough, and my feet stretch several inches over the end.

'That's right,' Maggie says. 'Now lift yer bum.' Leaning over me, she grabs my breeches on either side of my waist and pulls them down. They get stuck on my stiff cock and I think I must die of shame. But Maggie laughs and takes hold of me. She pushes downwards, and pulls with her free hand, and down go my trousers. I have closed my eyes at her touch, praying to whatever gods there be. Now she pulls my breeches over my ankles and I am naked. 'Oh, Jesus, yiz beautiful, Hawk!' I hear her say. Then there is silence but for the rustle of a garment, and I must open my eyes to look.

Maggie has loosened her gown and it has fallen to her waist.

Slowly, she pushes it down further still, until it pools at her feet and she steps out of it. She stands naked with only the magpie still perched on its nest of hair. 'Oh, Maggie,' I venture to say, my voice trembling. 'You are beautiful!'

'Nah. Only cute,' she says, stroking her lovely breasts and then running her hands down the curve of her slim waist and over her thighs. She touches her breasts again, pushing them upwards so the two little nipples look like rose buds. I ache to do the same, to touch and then lick them. I take a quick peek at the neat, little upside-down triangle of fur between her legs but I'm not brave enough to let my eyes linger.

'My, my, Hawk, that be a Maypole worthy of a dance or two,' she giggles, climbing onto the bed so that she is leaning over me. I hope she will kiss me again, lie on me and kiss me, but if she does I don't know how I shall hold out. I feel her lips on my chest and then my stomach, soft little kisses like a butterfly's wings touching against my skin. Then her hands reach out for my cock which lies hard against my stomach. She lifts it and her mouth closes over it. With her hands and with her lips, Maggie begins to stroke up and down.

'Maggie!' I gasp. 'Oh God, Maggie!'

'Shhh!' she murmurs. 'Hold on, Hawk!'

Just as I think I'm gone, she stops. 'A-ah, not yet, darlin', it's Maggie's turn. I wants some black magic! Show me yer tongue.'

Mystified, I do as I'm told and stick out my tongue. Maggie's leaning over me, and she and the magpie are having a gander down into my gob.

'Further!'

I stick it out completely, feeling foolish.

'Now wiggle the tip, up and down and sideways.'

I laugh, but do as Maggie says.

'That's good. Now put it deep into my pussy, darlin', right here.' She rolls over and lies on her back, guiding my hand to the triangle between her legs. I'm completely confounded. Tommo has told me about sixty-nine, but this is thirty-four and a half, a sum I don't know how to do!

Maggie grabs me by the hair and pulls my head towards her so I have no choice but to go down between her beautiful legs, not knowing what to expect. Well it doesn't take a moment to see why my tongue is needed, the way she begins to pant. I caress her with my tongue for all I am worth, not knowing if I am doing it right, but anxious to please.

'Gentle, Hawk. Talk to me pussy with yer tongue, talk soft, rub nice and slow and . . . oh yes, oh, oh!' I'm amazed at how soon I get the hang of it and how nice it is, Maggie's taste on my tongue.

I put my hands under her bottom and lift her gently to my mouth so that her back is arched and more of her is open to me. Soon her legs are gripped about my neck as I eat from her delectable dish, exploring her hidden places. She begins to moan and whimper as my long tongue moves and flicks over her. Then I find a little button, a sweet, hard little button which I begin to stroke with the very tip of my tongue. Maggie gasps, 'Hawk! Oh Hawk, yes, yes . . . ya bastard, yiz got me! Oh, oh! I'm coming home, darlin'! Oh Jesus! Ooooh . . .' Her hips grind frantically into my face and my tongue darts and moves deeply inside her, as she moans loudly and spills a great sweetness into my mouth, all the while whimpering and sobbing. Then she collapses back into my hands and I lower her gently to the bed, where she rolls away onto her side still moaning with pleasure.

My darling Maggie. I spoon her with my body, her back against my stomach, my hard cock resting between her legs and my arms about her so that my hand cradles her left breast. I rock her like she's a little girl, kissing the back of her neck where her hair is damp with heat.

Maggie rests a while, breathing hard. I can feel her heart beating under my palm. Then as we lie spooned together, her hand takes me by the stem and guides me deeply into her. She takes every inch of me as she moves her beautiful derrière against me, pulling the whole of me into her, then out again to the very tip, then sucking me slowly in again until I think I must die of ecstasy. It is all done slowly and firmly and tightly. She is panting again and I am too, as she leads me into a state of bliss I have never known before, not even on that night with Hinetitama.

Then she pulls away from me and turns to lie on her back. She takes up my glistening branch and feeds it slowly back into her softness, her hand holding my throbbing stem. I can hardly bear the pleasure of it. 'Me breasts, darlin', kiss Maggie's tits,' she says. I put my lips over her right breast, rolling her nipple on my tongue. In a moment it grows hard and her breast seems to swell and stiffen under my tender kissing. 'The other, kiss the other please, darlin',' she urges and I can feel her starting to pump against me as her legs wrap about my waist. I am trying to remember every second of it, in case this should never happen to me again. I want to touch and suck and stroke and make love to every part of her glorious body.

Maggie is now surging against me. It is magical what her pussy can do, and a miracle I have lasted this long. 'Now!' she says abruptly. 'Now, Hawk! Hard! Hard!'

I lift my head from her breast, and put both my hands on her shoulders. Arching my back and neck, I drive downwards so strongly that I fear she must surely split open or the bed must break. My body is drenched with sweat – it runs down my neck and chest, and into my eyes. I have become a wild animal possessed of some instinct which cannot be contained. Maggie is thrashing under me, crying out, and I cannot think but to ride her up and down, my urgent shaft driving with all my force. I am about to burst asunder when Maggie cries out, 'Take me, Hawk. Take my pussy. Fuck Maggie. Fuck me!'

I explode into her, thinking I must surely die, and that if I should, how happy I would be. Maggie cries out, panting and gasping, and I am laughing and crying, so pleased to have made her so happy. It seems to me that I have discovered something two people may do together which allows both to touch the face of a loving God.

And then I see it looking at me! Maggie has lifted her head and reached out her arms to me and I see her damned magpie still on its nest. Though her pretty curls fall every which way from their former neatness, somehow that blasted bird remains undisturbed. It looks at me with its hard, bright eyes, and I shudder.

'Maggie! That bloody bird is still upon your head!'

'Of course. Where else should it be? I told you it's me trademark, goes everywhere with me, Maggie Pye's magpie.'

I try to laugh, yet I don't like it one bit. 'But it's seen everything, you and me, us making love!'

'Hawk! That bird's seen more fucks than you've had hot breakfasts!' She laughs. 'It's a magpie, not a stickybeak!' She stretches out and grins wickedly. 'Don't worry, lovey, it's too busy on its own nest to be bothered with you on yours!' She points to the bottom of the bed to where the golliwog lies sprawled. 'He's the one what's got the dirty mind!'

'Maggie, is that all it was, you and me, just another trick, like another hot breakfast?' I am hurt, even angry, though I know I have no right to be. Maggie has been most generous. Why should I think I hold a special place in her affections?

Maggie looks at me and, for an instant, I think she is going to cry. Then she sniffs and brushes the underside of her nose with her forefinger. 'Hawk, I'm a whore. That's all I am, all I'll ever be. You hear me? Maggie Pye is Maggie Pye and don't you forget.'

Chapter Seventeen

TOMMO

The Rocks
March 1861

Two things happen at the Rocks on the Sabbath what always tells me it be Sunday, even when I has the worst head after a heavy night. The first be the church bells, o' course. They don't only call folks to worship but also, from the crack o' dawn onwards, they toll for the week's dead. One peal for a child, two for a woman and three for a man. Though I dunno why a man gets three and a child one. I reckons there ain't nothing what makes you any better than anyone when you've snuffed it.

The second thing 'bout Sunday is the delicious smell of roasting meat. It be the only time in the week when the Rocks don't smell of the shit what comes from the houses of the wealthy who lives above us in the big houses on the cliffs above the Argyle Cut. Us lot, what live at the bottom of the cliffs below them, receives gratis and free of charge the sewage, what runs over the cliffs into our streets and homes. There's talk of building sewage pipes to go out to sea but it ain't happened yet. Maggie Pye, Hawk's sweetheart, says she can't wait for them pipes to go into the briny, so's when the rich eat a fine fish, they'll find it stuffed full of their own shit! In the meantime, when the church bells toll, it is mostly for the poor.

Still, some folks here below at the Rocks like to keep up a bit o' decency. If they save a spare florin by the week's end, they'll have a proper Sunday roast. Few if any goes to church, knowing themselves to be of no consequence to God. Instead, while the rich kneel at prayer, the poor partake of the ancient ritual of the Sunday roast. The cottages and skillings here don't have no stoves nor colonial ovens, only open hearths. So the women buy a joint o' meat at the butcher shop and take it to Berry's Bakery, what on a Sunday turn their ovens over to meat-roasting.

Comin' home from me cards one Sunday morning, I happen to pass the bakery and I see women standing in a long line outside – each holding a baking dish with a piece of meat and lots o' taties. Some even has Yorkshire pud. They all be waiting to cook their roast, though it's no more than ten o'clock in the morning.

I stop to have a gander. Inside the bakehouse stand two tables what run the length o' the room and on these you can see two great rows of dishes with more than a hundred baked dinners in the making. Two bakers push the dishes deep into the oven with long poles. The women bring their roast in no later than eleven o'clock and call for them at one. Each woman is charged threepence and given a tin disc with a number on it. Another disc, what's got the same number, is stuck into the roasting joint.

Many's the fight to be seen when the time comes to collect the tucker. Some of the women has gone down to the pub to wait, supped a few drinks and lost their number discs meanwhile. Others remember their particular joint as bein' a much nicer cut o' meat than what they gets back. Often there's a bit of a set-to amongst the women, and the bakers are called on to sort it out. Then they make the offenders wait 'til last, in case they are just chancing their arm, hoping to steal another's dinner.

Mostly, though, waiting for the roast is a friendly time, with poor folk catching up on a bit o' gossip. And later every street and lane smells of mutton, pork and roast beef as the women hurries home to their families so's the joints still be steaming hot for their triumphant arrival.

After I sees this, I tell Hawk about it. What a damn fool idea that were. A do-good expression comes upon his gob, like God's touched him on the nose or something. 'Righto, Tommo,' says he, 'the first quid you win at cards on a Saturday night goes to the butcher and the grocer for meat and potatoes. We're going to feed the urchins with Sunday roasts!' I'm none too happy about this. Sometimes the first pound is hard-earned and then, quick as a flash it's purloined by Hawk, and I has to begin grafting and relocating 'til I've earned it back again. Knowing that if I don't take a quid right off them brats will go hungry is a bother I don't need at the card table. Hawk don't mind reminding me o' my responsibility neither. 'Don't forget my urchins, Tommo!' he always says before a Saturday game.

Hawk's bought ten roasting dishes and every Sunday, he's up at dawn peeling spuds. By seven o'clock he's at the butcher's, haggling like a fishwife over the size and quality of the meat, demanding with that big, scary smile of his that a portion o' cracklin' and basting lard be thrown in for free. By half-nine he's in line outside the bakehouse along with twenty or so dirty little ragamuffins, each pair holdin' a dish, with meat and potatoes set out pretty as a picture.

There's our Hawk, mother of the unloved and unwanted, standing two and a half foot taller than all the old biddies in line. They're teasing him about the size of his brood and what's in his breeches – all of 'em havin' a grand old cackle like people do when they's expectin' a good feed. Soon as it be ready, there's Hawk and Maggie Pye down by Semicircular Quay, carving meat for fifty or more little brats, what guzzles on the proceeds of me toils like a pack o' starvin' dock rats.

Mr Sparrow were anxious that we finds ourselves better lodgings as soon as we was able, in a more respectable part o' town, but Hawk would have none of it. He seems to want to stay here and look after his urchins – and me. All he agreed was that we should get better rooms, nearer the Argyle Cut, which is where we be now. Hawk loves his brats and they loves him, following him 'round like he's the Pied Piper, a ragged army of starvin' kids what he tries to feed best he can. Every chophouse knows him for he goes knocking on doors to beg for leftover scraps for his ragamuffins. In the evenings, down by the ferryman's wharf, he can be heard telling them tales o' derring-do. They listen enchanted and for a short time seem to forget the hunger gnawing at their bloated bellies.

Today, though, it's gunna be Flo what feeds them their Sunday tucker, for Hawk, Maggie and me are goin' up the Parramatta River to a prize fight. In the evening Mr Sparrow has arranged a game o' stud poker at the Woolpack Hotel. 'Some of the Irish gentlemen,' he cocks an eyebrow, 'if there be such a commodity, fancy their luck at the card table. I count on you to oblige them and to win 'andsomely.' He sticks a bony finger in me chest. 'So mind you do, lad.' I confess, there ain't much left what I likes about Mr Sparrow.

I ain't all that happy about Hawk and Maggie Pye being sweethearts neither. After all, she is a whore, or as the sporting gentlemen o' Sydney would call her, a crinoline cruiser. This is the name for a somewhat higher class o' slag, but still a slag. Crinoline cruisers hang about sporting occasions where respectable women ain't found, like dog fights, bare-knuckle bouts, cockfights, card games, and the horse races at Homebush.

I has to admit though that Hawk seems a happy man these days. He and Maggie has been together more than six months now. When I warn him about catching the pox from her, he nods, with a serious sort o' look on his face, but I know he ain't gunna take no notice of me. He's talking about takin' Maggie back to meet Mary, for Gawd's sake! In fact, the two of them women ain't so unlike. Maggie's bright but also has a terrible quick temper like Mary, and a tongue to put many a tar to shame. But she's witty with it and good company.

Maggie likes her gin, though I be the last to judge her for that. After all, grog comes with the job for us both. Gin and women is often an ugly combination, though, and it don't seem likely to lead to connubial bliss. But Hawk, so sensible and solemn, won't hear no ill spoken of Maggie Pye and thinks the world of her. I tell him not to mention the prospects we has in Tasmania, for he is a man of potential wealth. He promises he won't, and I know it be most important to him that Maggie loves him for hisself. I just hope she ain't a gold digger looking for a life of ease at Hawk's expense. I'm gunna keep a good eye on that Maggie Pye!

As for yours truly, I can't say I fancy any of the women around here. Me darlin' Makareta has spoiled me for the average tart, I reckon, though I don't let me thoughts dwell on her much these days. Nor me daughter, Hinetitama, neither. My new mistress, the opium pipe, be a great help in that regard. It takes away much of me desire for female company too. It's a blessing that it does, for good women be thin on the ground in these parts o' the colony.

Any respectable girl what reaches the age of sixteen gets herself married quick smart. If you sees a younger girl on the arm of a man, you can safely guess she be a slut in apprentice, or one what's been on the game for a few years already.

The Rocks don't hold much hope for the bloke what seeks a lady's companionship. Instead, the Botanical Gardens is where the fashionables of Sydney's fair sex may be found. This be where young toffs go to meet the members of the opposite sex. For a laugh I go up there meself one day. Hawk tells me they ain't really Botanical Gardens – not like the Kew Gardens of London, what's a grand creation with exotic trees and shrubs o' great variety, growing in a green and watered landscape. What we has in Sydney is two rows of stiff gum trees in a long avenue leading into a wasteland of dusty ground. When it's dry, the slightest breeze blows up clouds o' sand and dirt.

But if you go up to these scrawny old Gardens today, you'll see many gay parasols surrounded by young coves dressed in their Sunday best. The female specimens beneath these bright sunshades only show themselves if you can push through their admirers for a closer look. Most has long since passed the summer of their life and make much use of powder and lip rouge and extravagant bonnets. They is expensively attired and bejewelled, their gold trinkets no doubt the gifts of admirers who've failed to make the final journey to the four-poster bed.

At Semicircular Quay, the boats from Europe are always met by scores o' young swells hoping to find, for the purpose of marriage, any single female within five years of their age. At card games and the like, I has heard many a bachelor say that there ain't much choice among Sydney's unmarried ladies. The demand is great, the supply small, and Europe a long way away, so that the poor specimens what does exist are quickly snapped up by the sons o' the goldocracy.

But like I said, I ain't much worried by all this. I'm busy with me cards, me pipe, and when I can get it, me bottle. The life I've taken up with Mr Sparrow don't let me drink during the daylight hours and only a little during my card games at night. Still, I usually glug down the better part of a black bottle before dawn. But I always keep my senses about me, 'specially now I has a new way to ease me pain.

I found the Angel's Kiss the very first night I played cards for Mr Sparrow, in a gambling den owned by Mr Tang Wing Hung. He's an important man among the Chinese what comes to Sydney from the gold diggings. He's tall for a Mongolian, six foot, and thin as a rake. He don't say much but Mr Sparrow reckons there ain't much business among the Chinese what he don't control, and says his bony yellow fingers may be found in many a pie concocted by a Sydney broker or merchant.

That first night in Chinatown, I did exactly what Mr Sparrow told me. I acted the country bumpkin, a wealthy settler's son from Tasmania, innocent of the ways of the world. There were no need for Mr Sparrow to blow a smoke ring so that I might resort to 'other' methods of winning – me skill proved sufficient. I cleaned up a pretty penny and earned five pounds.

By dawn's light, when the game finally came to an end, me head was so painful I couldn't bear it. When he heard about this, Mr Sparrow talked to Tang Wing Hung and I was took into a small room and given the opium pipe. The pain lifted at once and I came away most grateful to the Angel's Kiss.

Hawk is most worried about me new medicine, but I has assured him I use it sparingly and only when me head hurts. The black bottle is still old Tommo's first love!

I am now a solid member of Mr Sparrow's sporting fraternity and Hawk and me is well set up. I earn a fair bit from me card games most nights – though not always so much as five pounds. Mr Sparrow is talkin' of a partnership, now that I've learnt much about what he calls 'the predilections o' sporting gentlemen'. Mr Sparrow dabbles in sports of all kinds: horse races, dog races, cockfights, dog fights, gambling and o' course women and opium. He promises that I shall be a part of all this if I play me cards right.

In all these months I ain't found a broadsman what can better me and it's grand to have a quid or two. After me first night at the game in Chinatown, I were very glad to see Hawk's smiling phiz outside the pub, as me note had asked. Hawk takes three pounds of the five I've earned. We goes off to a tailor in Pitt Street, by the name of Barney Isaacs. There Hawk pays for a suit o' clothes, two blouses, and two pairs of hose what he's had measured up for himself. He said somethin' about paying his own way, what's a bit of a laugh as it's my earnings what's paying for it! But I don't begrudge him none. As soon as his clobber were made up and boots bought from the Italian bootmaker in Bligh Street, Hawk gets a position as clerk at Tucker & Co. in George Street.

Hawk got the job 'cause of his experience in Mary's brewery and his knowledge of hops and beer. Captain James Tucker, the brother of the founder, William Tucker, is a wine and spirit merchant. Even though Hawk knows little of this side of the liquor trade, Captain Tucker seems pleased to have me brother in his employ. He were once a ship's captain himself and likes the fact that Hawk has been to sea. My twin has proved a careful bookkeeper and is always happy to help out, loading the drays and stacking shelves when times is busy in the warehouse. This counts for a great deal with Captain Tucker, what ain't a man to stand on ceremony and will himself roll up his sleeves when needed.

And so we've made our lives in Sydney. Hawk is still my keeper though I don't see that much of him – only at breakfast when I returns from a game, not always sober, and then again at supper. He puts me to bed after a breakfast of eggs and bacon or fish, and gives me a good dose o' Seidlitz powders so that when I get up on his return from work, I ain't got too much of a hangover. Often when it's just the two of us, he reads to me from newspapers and books. He gets me to do the same, so that I be ever improving, catching up on what I lost all those years in the wilderness.

This morning I ain't retiring to bed though, for we are on a family jaunt, making our journey up the river. The prize fight be organised by none other than Fat Fred, Mr Sparrow's henchman and the colony's principal procurer o' prize fights.

Mr Sparrow and Fat Fred can always depend on a big crowd as they are the only proper prize-fight promoters in the colony. Prize fights is against the law and most comes about as a result of a direct challenge from one recognised fighter to another. Then a venue is hastily arranged behind a pub or sly grog shop. When news of the fight spreads by mouth from pub to pub, the bookmakers and amateur oddsmen turn up and the betting begins, the odds changing constantly during the progress o' the contest. Often the ring is simply marked out with stones on the grass and the crowd what gathers around the fight surges backwards and forwards into the ring as the fighters advance and retreat.

Mr Sparrow, however, will tolerate no such higgledy-piggledy set-ups. He 'licenses' – some would say owns – all the bookmakers at his fights and rakes in a percentage from each, closing the betting after the start of the bout. At other fights it ain't unusual, if a favourite looks like he'll be beat, for some of the crowd to storm the ring and declare the fight 'no contest' so's to get their bets back. But Fat Fred has the rings well guarded by ex-pugs and bothermen what are prepared to spill considerable claret if a member o' the crowd comes too close.

A prize fight what's organised by Fat Fred be a most popular event, and despite today's fight being writ up for weeks beforehand in *Bell's Life in Sydney*, the police don't seem to know of it.

Maggie is much excited at the prospect of the fight and an outing in the country. She has packed a large basket of cold mutton, roast taties, a fresh baked loaf, three bottles of the best beer and some other tidbits from Flo's mum, what is a most excellent cook. Even if the fight be stopped by the Parramatta traps, Maggie promises we shall have us a lovely picnic.

Maggie never works the fights, even though they be a rich fishing ground for Sydney's tarts. Instead, she dresses up in her finest black crinoline with a black-and-white silk bonnet, her 'magpie' colours as she calls them. She takes a great deal o' pleasure from being seen on Hawk's arm at these events. Maggie Pye's become a right dolly bird, cocking a snook at the other girls as they shows their tits in their gaudy silks and wiggles their hips, trolling for a gold fish – what in their lingo means searchin' out a rich bloke!

We are all set to go upriver to Parramatta Town aboard one of the little Billy steamers leaving from the Quay. Maggie has persuaded us not to take the railway what has recently reached Parramatta Town but is still somewhat a novelty. Hawk reckons it'll be nice to be out on the water again and I don't give a bugger which way we goes.

Our steamer seems decked out as though for a festive voyage. She's brightly coloured with a copper funnel and a wide-rimmed chimney, and her shade awnings are of a bright purple and ochre. We're in for a merry time, the boat being full o' folk what's goin' to the fight, though we're calling it a picnic so's to fool any copper who's aboard in disguise.

Just as we're about to cast off, a great noise is heard from the wharf and we see a small tribe of blacks running towards the steamer. They comes on board panting, laughing and cussing, carrying and dragging small children. Several are pulling chains o' kangaroo dogs behind them. They are nearly all drunk and some of the passengers shout to the crew to 'off-load the niggers'. The newcomers climb up the ship's ropes and stumble about the decks.

We is hardly clear of the wharf when some of the black women take off their blankets and start fighting. They's cussing and screaming, rolling, kicking and punching, their blood and snot all over the deck. The kangaroo dogs are barking and the little black urchins are howling their heads off.

To the cheering and yoicking of the rougher folk amongst the white passengers, the women sets to hurting each other. They's pulling out tufts o' hair and one of 'em, a fat gin with breasts hanging to her waist, bites a large piece off her opponent's ear and dances about, holding it aloft for all to see. Meanwhile their husbands go 'round with their hats and begs tuppences off the spectators.

Some of the passengers reckon it's all a grand lead-up to the prize fight this afternoon. But Hawk puts a stop to it. He takes ten shillings from his purse and gives it to the bloke what looks to be their leader, asking that the women stop their scratching and caterwauling. There is some protest from the whites when they see what he is doing, but Hawk ignores them. One fat rowdy shouts, 'Garn then, nigger, leave it off! Let's have a bit o' sport from the black bastards!'

Hawk stops and walks over to this cove. 'What say you and I have a bit of sport, then?' he suggests, and a sick smile grows upon the bloke's phiz.

'Begs your pardon,' he says backing away, as the rest of his mates laugh at him.

The Aboriginal chief carries a large stuffed snakeskin coiled about his neck and seems most impressed with Hawk, what's as black as he is, twice as wide and two foot taller. Hawk ain't afraid to stand up to the white devils neither as they can see. Grabbing a big stick from one of the other men, the Aborigine beats the women over their heads and backs, shouting at 'em in their tongue, 'til they stop fighting and stumbles away to lick their wounds. The chief signals that he wants Hawk to take back his money and, for the sake o' peace, Hawk finally accepts it.

After this, the journey is pleasant enough. I look about the little steamer with interest as we make our way towards Parramatta. Dozens of live ducks, tied by their bright yellow feet, has been thrown upon several trusses of hay. Aft, four pigs grunt and snuffle amongst a pile o' cabbage leaves, and a donkey and two nanny goats are secured by their hind legs to the railings. In one corner I counts twenty wicker baskets of fish, some still alive, bars o' silver in the sunlight.

On either side o' the river the land slopes gently upwards, green from the recent summer rains. The gum trees what grew here not so long ago have all been rooted out and many a stump lies with its tangled roots sprouting like Medusa's head out of a great ball o' red clay. Along the river bank, poplar and willow has taken their place and the hand of civilisation is everywhere to be seen. Farmers have cleared the bush and tilled the land to beyond the horizon. Each farm is much like the one beside it, a homestead sat upon a farmyard square, the borders made up of a windbreak of fruit trees. These be lemons and oranges for the most part, though here and there I sees some quince and pomegranate. In every vegetable garden is cabbages, what must fetch a good price at market to judge by their numbers. Everywhere, there are rows o' green cabbages, each in its own nest of leaves. Sometimes there's a rose garden, what makes a circular patch of flowers at the very centre of the vegetable garden, and Maggie thinks this most romantic.

When we reach Parramatta Town, several of the passengers get off, including the Aborigine tribe. Yowling brats is taken by one arm and dragged off the boat by cursing gins, some still bleeding from their wounds. The old chief strikes willy-nilly at the brats and the dogs and the motley mob tumble together down the gangplank.

The rest of us continue two or three bends upriver, some four miles southwest beyond the town. Here we pulls into shore and the steamer moors beside a crude wharf made up of a few slippery logs.

The skipper announces that the Billy steamer can't go no further as the river ahead is silted up. We has to walk from here. The countryside about us is heavily timbered, scrubby terrain. The captain points to a small hill what has been cleared of trees, atop of which sit two fair-sized buildings – neither showing no sign of life. He explains these be a school and a church for the Irish navvies what's building the railway west to the Blue Mountains. Their camp lies beyond the hill, and cannot be seen from the river.

We're told to walk around the hill to the Katoomba Road, turning right to A'Beckett's Bridge and the Vauxhall Inn half a mile or so away. There we is to turn left into Dog Trap Road, what we're to follow beyond the Irish camp. And so we sets out with two or three dozen others to find the location of the prize fight.

Hawk and me is dressed in coats and collars and Maggie turned out in all her finery. We ain't dressed for a hike and are most uncomfortable trudging along. Soon our coats are placed on top o' Maggie's basket what Hawk carries, and our collar studs loosened. To our surprise, Maggie – never the sensible one – has brung old boots to wear until we gets to the ring. It's wet and muddy underfoot and by the time we reach the road the hem of her dress is soaked all the same.

The road when we gets to it is busy with folks walking from Parramatta Town railway station. Added to those of us on foot are the hacks, sulkies, drags, carriages and carts all headin' for the fight. A coach filled to the gunnels with merry punters passes us by. The coves inside laugh and joke at us what walks, and many an insult is hurled back in return.

It is only when we reach Dog Trap Road that we see the true size of the crowd. It be so full o' punters that we must walk at snail's pace. Mr Sparrow and Fat Fred has chosen their venue with a good knowledge of the district. The Irish are all around here and these merry punters pours out of their shacks to join the Sydney and Parramatta Town throng. There never were a keener sportsman than an Irishman with a dram or two o' whiskey in his belly and a week's wages in his pocket.

The navvies' camp on Dog Trap Road is a miserable sort o' place, with huts made mostly of slab and bark. Mangy dogs, snotty children and hard-faced women comes out to stare at us. Many of the smaller brats are naked and much in need of a wash. These are the people brought in by the government to meet the labour shortage what's been caused by the colony's men flocking to the goldfields. Some folks now reckon the bog Irish, as they's known, is lower than all but the Aborigines, but I wonder who they be to judge!

Dog Trap Road is rutted and rocky and the many conveyances what have thundered down the Katoomba Road are having trouble travelling along it. They hinder our progress and gets a fair amount o' curry from the mob on foot. The road ends suddenly, well short o' the spot where the fight will take place. The various vehicles can go no further, and the toffs and sporting gentlemen will need to huff and puff a good quarter of a mile through thick scrub.

The place Fat Fred and Mr Sparrow has picked for their fight is an inspiration. It turns out to be a sort o' treeless hollow, what Hawk calls a natural amphitheatre. The prize ring lies at the centre and there is room all about for several thousand folk to look down upon it. Fat Fred has built a roped enclosure directly about the four sides of the ring for the swells. It must have took a good many hours to get the place ready for the sporting gentlemen. Compliments of three red tickets given to me by me lord and master Mr Sparrow, Hawk, Maggie and meself is numbered among 'em.

As we make our way to the enclosure, Hawk with Maggie on one arm and the basket on the other becomes the focus of the crowd's attention.

'Who's the nigger on stilts?' someone calls out.

'It's two niggers, one atop the other, dressed in a suit!' some wit replies.

'No, it's Red Riding Hood and the big bad wolf!' cries another.

'Look, he's got his dinner on her bonnet, the last o' the four 'n' twenty blackbirds!' offers the first, all to the merriment of the crowd.

Hawk smiles but I know all this attention don't sit well with him. Still, the crowd is friendly enough. Hawk stands two foot taller than most, a black giant with Maori markings on his phiz and a young tart on his arm with a magpie nested in her hat. We must make a funny old sight as we join the fat sportsmen what's paid good money to be here.

Maggie has her pretty nose in the air and wears a big smile. She knows she's watched by folks on every side of the enclosure and acts every inch the respectable woman. All the other working girls in their ribbons and bows is here to troll for sporting gents what might take a girl to one of the inns along the Parramatta Road for a glass and an hour or two o' dalliance. Today Maggie ain't working. When a gentleman sportsman tries to catch her eye, she ignores him, giving a superior sniff. I laughs, thinking to meself that her just being at a prize fight tells all there is to know about her. She's happy though, and as we take our seat, she flashes me a smile.

The ring is twenty-four foot square, roped in two spans and raised two foot from the ground so all can see. It's hard to believe the Parramatta traps could miss an occasion of this size, and I chuckles when I recalls Mr Sparrow saying how two of the three troopers responsible for law and order in town found an urgent need to visit Newcastle this very day. The one left in charge has had a severe attack of the trots and may not move further abroad than the shit-pit in the backyard.

Much of the excitement about today's fight is because it be between two heavies – most fighters being in the range of eight and nine stone, little fellas like meself. But today, Ben Dunn, the Sydney heavy, takes on a Welsh miner by the name of Thomas Thomas. The Welshman is but a week in the country, though *Bell's Life in Sydney* declares him a serious contender. He has eight fights to his credit and all of them won against well-known English opponents.

The betting is heavy on Dunn, for his form is well known. Among the heavies, there ain't no boxer in the colony that he ain't defeated, and several more than once. But some in the crowd reckon that the local heavies be soft, backwater fighters, and that Dunn has yet to face a real opponent. They think a bloke from the old country will give the currency lad a lesson in the art o' fisticuffs. Today's fight will prove them right or no.

The two fighters are called to the ring at three with the noonday heat now gone but with plenty o' daylight left. Mr Sparrow is ever present, clasping mawleys and spouting opinions, ever the jovial host. He is as busy with the nabobs and toffs as a one-legged man in a kicking contest and has no time to greet the nigger, the tart and the cardsharp.

Fat Fred is the referee and announcer and stands in the ring in a lather o' sweat. He holds a hailing funnel and constantly wipes his gob with a large, red, miner's bandanna. We all stand as the fighters enter the ring.

Maggie is on her feet at once, hopping from one leg to another. She's on tippy-toes with excitement, having given up all show o' respectable womanhood. Her bet of five pounds is on the Welshman, what's at long odds and I reckon a risky gamble. He is only a week off the ship and must be out of condition after the two-month voyage.

The two men is stripped to the waist and wear spiked boots to hold their grip in the ring. The fight is at catch weight so their weights ain't announced. The Welshman is much bigger than Dunn, what ain't large for a heavy, being estimated at around thirteen stone with no lard on any part o' him. This can't be said of his opponent what looks a stone and a half heavier and carries quite a belt o' fat about his waist. His titties wobble as he jumps about the ring to warm up.

'It don't look good for your man, Maggie,' I says. 'Ben Dunn be much the better lookin' specimen.'

'It's the heavies, Tommo. Speed don't count. Reach and power is what does it. The Welshman's got three or four inches on Dunn and he's a miner, ain't he?' She points to Thomas. 'Look at 'is arms – they can pump all afternoon!'

I has a quid on Dunn but there's something to what Maggie says. 'Nah, he'll not be able to take it in the bread basket,' I says hopefully, patting me stomach. 'Look at Ben Dunn, every inch the wild colonial boy!'

'Wild! Jesus, Tommo, he be about as wild as a nun's confession!'

'What d'ya mean?'

'Can't get it up for the girlies!'

I look quickly at Hawk to see how he takes this but in the middle of all the excitement he's sitting reading a book. He ain't taking no notice o' nothing 'til the fight proper begins.

'You'd know about that, o' course,' I says now, sarcastic-like.

Maggie ain't the least offended. 'Oath I'd know!' she agrees. 'I went to Johnny Sullivan's Sparring Rooms in Pitt Street. You know Johnny, the Champion of the Light Weights, we's good mates . . .'

'Mates? Ha, ha!' I laughs. 'Come off it, Maggie, yer talking to old Tommo here!'

Maggie stares at me hard. 'You know what's your problem, Tommo Solomon? You've got a dirty mind! Mates! That's all. Johnny and me grew up together, in the same bloody gutter. We're mates, and always will be!'

I takes another glimpse over at Hawk, to see if he's heard Maggie tellin' me off, but his eyes is fixed on his book. 'Sorry, Maggie,' says I.

'No need,' Maggie replies. 'If Johnny wants it from me, he can 'ave it for free any day 'cept Sunday when it belongs only to Hawk. Johnny's a champ o' more than fisticuffs!'

'So, what about him?' I asks, pointing to Dunn what's standing in the middle of the ring, throwing punches in the air and snuffling like a prime porker. 'What's he got to do with yer mate Sullivan?'

'Oh yeah, him. Well, he were working out at Johnny's rooms

last summer, see, and I hears about it. At the time, he were my hero and I figures I'll drop by – see 'im in the flesh so t' speak. It ain't unusual for a tart to be seen 'anging around a prize-fighter. The cove at the door what knows I know Johnny says he ain't there. But I tell him I've come to see, you know, Ben Dunn, so he lets me in.'

Maggie stops and sniffs, as though she's about to tell what she'd rather not. 'I goes in and there's a few fighters sparrin' and workin' at the bag and so I sits at the back o' the room. Ben Dunn's in the ring, sparring with a big hairy bugger, a fighter what I've never seen before. Then after a while he climbs down from the ring and goes into the changing room.'

Maggie gives a little smile. 'It were stupid an' all, but you know me, nothing ventured, nothing gained, so I walks in behind him.

'"Hello," says I.

'He turns about. "Who are you?" he asks.

'"Maggie. Maggie Pye," I says smiling. "I'm one o' ya greatest admirers, Mr Dunn."

'"You a whore?" he asks.

'I'm in me glad rags, showing everything I've got, ribbons and bows, and tits near poppin' out. "Well, I ain't the governor's wife," I says cheeky, giving him another flash of me pearly whites.

'"How much?" he wants t' know.

'"This ain't a business visit, Mr Dunn. It's just that I admires ya very much and wanted to tell ya in person!"

'But Dunn's got a look in his eyes what I've seen often enough when a man's goin' to do something bad, and suddenly I'm frightened. He spits on 'is hands and rubs them together. By now I'm walkin' backwards towards the door. Quick as a flash he's moved 'round me and stands blocking the doorway.

'"Not so fast, Maggie Pye!" he says, smiling, but it ain't the right sort o' smile and believe you me, I knows every kind o' smile a man can give. "If you're not to be paid and you're here on a social visit, then you wouldn't mind obliging . . ." He wiggles his hips and thrusts 'em forward to show what he means, holding his hands out like he's hangin' onto me hips.

'"It ain't convenient. I don't do knee-tremblers, I ain't that sort o' whore!" I says. "Lemme go, please!" I try to push him aside so I can pass by.

'But he sticks his arm across the doorway and looks over his shoulder. "Lads!" he shouts. "Come 'n' get yer Christmas box!"'

Maggie looks up at me. 'Don't need to tell yiz the rest, do I? They rapes me, all ten of the bastards!' She is quite matter o' fact as she speaks, though her voice is soft. She points to the ring where Ben Dunn is still snuffling and punching the air, glaring at the Welshman. 'All 'cept him, your wild colonial boy. He's sittin' on a bench against the wall with his dick in his hand!'

'The mongrels – they's always there waiting,' I whispers to meself.

'What's you say?' asks Maggie.

'Nothing. He's a mongrel, Maggie. I put a quid on him but I hopes he gets the daylights knocked out o' him by the Welshman!'

Maggie laughs. 'Thank you, Tommo. But I ain't finished yet. You know what he says? After them what's raped me has scarpered, when I'm trying to put me torn dress in order?'

I shake me head. 'Please Maggie, you've told enough.'

But she goes on. 'He says, "Maggie, if you wants tickets to me next fight, come see me again."

'"Fuck off," I tells him. "I might be beaten, but I ain't broke."

'"What did you say, girlie?" he asks and grabs me nose between his finger and thumb and twists it. His 'arf hard cock's still hanging out o' his pants.'

Maggie shrugs and grins. 'I know I should've kept me gob shut. I can either cry or lose me temper, so o' course I gets it wrong, don't I? I lose me temper.

' "Fuck off, arsehole, I wouldn't shit in your mouth 'case I got bit by somethin' poisonous!" I screams at him, scratching at his face. I feel the first haymaker to the side of me head and down I goes. I know well enough to stay down, and so I plays possum and he kicks me 'til he thinks I'm out to it.

'Then the big hairy bloke comes back in and Dunn fucks him from behind, right there beside me, the two of 'em grunting away while the blood runs down me head. It's been a long time since I've took a worse beating.'

Maggie sighs. 'I must've eventually passed out because Johnny Sullivan finds me an hour later. He's scared every bone in me body is broke. But it turns out that only most of me ribs are busted and two teeth at the back is missing. The rest is only bruises and blood, though I couldn't walk for two weeks nor earn a penny for nigh on a month. It were Johnny what looked after me.'

I wonder if Hawk's heard any of this sorry tale. Maggie has

kept her voice low and there's a lot o' noise from the crowd anyway. Sure enough, me twin's still happily reading his book, as though he's sitting in some quiet library and not among five thousand screamin' punters. When Hawk carks it I'm gunna put a book in his hands and half a dozen more in his coffin, 'case it's a long journey to heaven!

Well, the fight begins and it's all bluff in the first round. The two heavies walks 'round each other, sniffing and snorting, and Dunn lands a good blow to Thomas's chest. This is returned a minute later, to the side of Dunn's head. Then Dunn grabs Thomas and throws him to the ground. End of round one.

Round two is more of the same but this time the Welshman catches Dunn a tremendous blow on the chin and the local boy goes down. He's back up on his feet quick-smart. A knockdown means the round be over. It looks as though Maggie's picked the right bloke.

During round three, Dunn spends most of the time staying out o' the way. Still he manages to hit the Welshman two good blows to the stomach, and Thomas grabs him and pulls him down.

By round five, Dunn can see the Welshman is tiring so he steps up the pace. In return for three weak blows to the shoulders, he manages half a dozen of his own into his opponent's bread basket. Suddenly Thomas clutches at his stomach and Dunn unleashes a big uppercut, what knocks the Welshman sprawling to the canvas. It's clear to all that he won't get up, and his ring man throws in the sponge.

The fight's all over in five rounds. It's taken less than an hour, and the punters ain't happy. They boos and hisses, the toffs included. Many has come a great way and they wants more for their money. The booing gets louder and many around us shout that the fight's been fixed.

I puts an arm around Maggie. 'Bad luck, love, the good uns seldom win in this world.'

At this minute, Ben Dunn comes to the ropes near us and signals to Fat Fred. They talk a moment together, and then Fat Fred nods. Signalling to his minders to lift him into the ring, he grabs a hailing funnel and calls for quiet.

'Gentlemen and, er, ladies! Your attention, please!' He keeps at it 'til the crowd shuts up. 'Mr Ben Dunn, heavyweight champion of the colony, is aware of yer disappointment at the duration of today's bout and he agrees to fight anyone here for his purse won from Thomas Thomas of one hundred pounds. The contender puts only five pounds down as a sign o' good will, winner takes all!' Fat Fred pauses, looking over the heads of the crowd and then, as though he feels he should add somethin' to his offer, shouts, 'The winner gets the title as well!'

The crowd bursts into laughter and more jeering. It's a joke of course. No man unless he be drunk or a fool will pay five pounds to have his head knocked off.

'Is there not an Irishman among you who's game enough?' Fat Fred taunts. I imagine there be plenty of Irishmen game enough but none big enough, them poor bastards being starved by the English for generations and this lot being the poorest physical specimens of them all.

'Have we got five pounds, Tommo?' Hawk asks suddenly.

'Sure, it's me stake for tonight's poker game,' I replies.

'Give it here,' he says, putting out his hand.

'Hawk, are you mad? You're not gunna . . . ?' I point to Ben Dunn what's dancing about the ring.

'Come on, Tommo,' he says impatient. 'Pass it over!' I hands him the fiver and he walks up to the ring and holds it out to Fat Fred.

It be the first and probably last time I sees Fat Fred smile, as he takes the money and holds it up. Over the hailing funnel he announces, 'Gentlemen and punters, we have a contender!'

There's a roar from the crowd as Hawk lifts himself into the ring. Maggie is sobbing and laughing and jumping up and down and biting her little clenched fist. She digs in her handbag and holds up a pound note. 'Who'll give me ten to one odds the nigger wins!' she shouts. The punters rush to the enclosure to take up Maggie's odds.

'Maggie, don't be a fool!' I yell as I climbs into the ring to be beside Hawk. Mr Sparrow follows me and we stands beside Hawk as he undoes the buttons on his blouse. He pulls it off and hands it to me, and the crowd sees him proper for the first time. He stands a foot above the heavyweight, and is six inches broader at the shoulder and six inches narrower at the waist. There ain't an ounce o' fat on his shiny black torso what's all power and muscle.

As for me, I'm plain terrified. He's gunna get the hiding of his life from the Sydney bruiser what's had more than fifty fights, with only four lost. Hawk knows nothing o' fighting with his fists and his size'll only make it easier for Dunn to hit him.

The fight begins, with Fat Fred the referee. Just as I expected, the champion of the colony hits me twin at will. I scream at Hawk to grab Dunn and bring him down so that the round may end. But Hawk don't hear me or don't care to listen, and they fight for fifteen minutes, though he barely lands a blow.

Dunn has a grin on his face as he smashes blow after blow into Hawk's body and head. Soon Hawk's left eye is closed and claret streams from his nose. But me brother won't go down. Nearly half an hour has passed and the crowd, what admires his bravery, is beginnin' to yell for the nigger.

Dunn ain't used to staying on his feet this long without a rest and he begins to slow somewhat. I reckon there's less strength to his punches but still he's making mincemeat out o' Hawk.

'Go down, take a rest!' I shout at him. But Hawk stands defenceless in the ring and won't move. I can't bear it no more and I look for the sponge to throw it into the air. 'Where's the bloody sponge?' I scream at Mr Sparrow. 'We got to end it now!'

Then I see Hawk starting to move around his opponent. It's like he's slowly come to life. Suddenly his arm shoots out and he hits Dunn on the nose. The champion's face seems to cave in as he drops to his knees, a look of utmost surprise on his gob. It's thirty-five minutes after the start of the fight and round one is ended. The mob howls with delight.

Hawk comes to his corner. 'We're gunna stop it, ya hear!' I yells at him. 'He's killin' ya!'

'Have you had enough, lad?' Mr Sparrow asks.

'Course he has!' I scream. 'We're stopping now! Where's the bloody sponge?'

Hawk is panting and don't say nothing. There's blood in his mouth and a steady flow from his nose and I still can't find the sponge. I takes up his shirt and, dipping it in the bucket o' water, washes his face. Then I squeeze water into his mouth for him to rinse. He spits out the water into the bucket and his breathing starts t' come back. Dunn has also tottered to his corner and sits there, glowering.

'It's all over, Hawk,' I says, patting his huge shoulder. 'You've fought good, mate, but ya can't go back in there for more!'

Hawk looks at me through his one eye. 'I must, Tommo, or the mongrels win. Tell Maggie the next round is for her,' he pants. 'I cannot last beyond it.' I shake me head at his stubbornness, for my body aches with his, and I know how bad he hurts. Sometimes, being Hawk's twin be a most painful affair.

The second round is called five minutes later and it's as though Hawk has it all figured out in his head. Dunn is recovered but is very cautious. Hawk walks around him, always stayin' on the western side of the ring – he won't let Dunn out of the eastern half. Then I realise what he's doing! Hawk's making Dunn face into the sun, what leaves him half-blind. He sets about him now. There ain't much polish to Hawk's punches, but they comes straight and hard. Each blow seems like it must break something inside the champion.

Dunn hits Hawk several times, but the strength seems to have left him. Hawk just walks through the champion's punches and keeps coming, sometimes hitting Dunn twice in as many seconds. The smack of his enormous fists into the flesh of the other fighter makes the ringside crowd wince and moan.

Dunn tries to pull Hawk down but Hawk's too strong and throws him off. Then, with the Sydney fighter slightly off-balance and his arms spread wide, Hawk hits him on the chin with a clean right-cross. It starts from way back and is so well timed and so hard that it lifts the heavyweight champion of the colony off his feet and, some will later swear, three feet into the air. Dunn's out cold before he hits the deck. His corner can't do nothin' but throw in the sponge. The fight is over. Dunn won't be rising to his feet again 'til well after sunset.

'Well now, my dear Ace O' Spades!' Mr Sparrow says to me, taking the missing sponge out o' his coat pocket. 'I think we've found ourselves a true champion!'

Fat Fred is laughing, and I don't reckon nobody in the history of the world has ever seen Fat Fred laugh. He grabs the hailing funnel and holds Hawk's arm up. 'Ladies and gentlemen, in a winner-takes-all contest, I give you Hawk Solomon, the new Heavyweight Champion of the Colony o' New South Wales!'

'And future champion of the whole bleedin' world!' Mr Sparrow shouts beside me.

I rushes up to Hawk and hugs him about the waist. Then I sees Maggie climbing up into the ring, crying and laughing as she too rushes into me brother's arms. 'Hawk, I loves ya! I loves ya,' she sobs.

The crowd is yelling and trying to reach the ring to shake Hawk's hand. The minders kick at them wildly. It's all they can do to keep them at bay, for the mob is determined to carry Hawk off on its shoulders. The din is something terrible but I still hears what Hawk says to Maggie.

'Maggie,' he pants. 'Please, Maggie, next time stay away from Johnny Sullivan's Sparring Rooms!'

Chapter Eighteen

HAWK

The Rocks
May 1861

Life has become most tedious for me of late. Everywhere I go I am followed by the Sydney lads who see me as their hero. In fact, when one recalls that prize-fighting is against the law, it seems strange that there is hardly a soul in Sydney who doesn't know of my fight with Ben Dunn.

Merchants lift their hats as I pass and many a toff bids me good day. I have become a curiosity, well nigh a fairground exhibit, and I find it exceedingly uncomfortable being the subject of confabulation in every tavern. Every man now claims to know me. Only today I heard that the cove who insulted my Maggie in the Hero of Waterloo, whom I threw across the room, now boasts of our fight. He is enjoying a low fame accordingly.

Even *Bell's Life in Sydney* has waxed lyrical about my native abilities as a bare-knuckle fighter. It predicts that, with training, I could be a future champion of the world. This is quite ridiculous, of course, and I am amazed that grown men talk everywhere of such a nonsensical possibility. I am big and clumsy and know nothing of the art of fisticuffs. Moreover, things do not sit well with myself and Mr Sparrow, who would arrange my life for me since that day at Parramatta.

After the fight with Ben Dunn, Mr Sparrow and Fat Fred were most anxious that I should fight again and that they should handle my career in this regard. I was then, and still am, most anxious not to enter the ring ever again. I have been stared at almost all my life for my size and blackness. To further encourage folks' attention is more than I can bear.

Only amongst the Maori did I feel comfortable about my size. Here it is a wretched nuisance. The average male in the colony is about five foot and three inches tall. Ben Dunn the heavyweight is considered a near giant at five foot and eleven inches. If he is a giant, then I am a freak of nature.

Fat Fred says I would make a fortune ten times over should I become a fighter. But I can see little sense in being knocked about for the sake of a few pounds. What's more I feel fairly certain that a great deal of money would end up in Fat Fred and Mr Sparrow's own pockets. As Ikey would say, 'If you cannot turn a man with words and you agrees to fight him and should win, you will have lost anyhow. The hero dies young on some soon forgotten battlefield, but a good coward dies in bed with his own bugs to bite him.' But Ikey's continued influence in our lives, in the form of Mr Sparrow, has caused me much aggravation of late. Perhaps there was more to Ikey than his gems of wisdom which I now recall.

I was bruised for a fortnight or more after fighting Dunn. I think he broke a number of my ribs, for I coughed up blood for several days after, and my sides and kidneys were particularly painful. My teeth seemed to rattle in my head and my nose was twice its usual size. My fists, which have never been cured in brine, were so sore that I could not hold a pen for four days. While my employer, Captain James Tucker, was most understanding, it is not my intention to let him down again. With Tucker & Co. I feel myself achieving something, whereas I fail to see that my striking down of another man, or he of me, offers any valuable lessons in life's progress.

'Oh,' said Mr Sparrow when I told him that the purse did not merit the punishment I received from Ben Dunn and that I did not wish to enter the prize ring, 'that was only because you lacked the skill to avoid such blows. We will teach you the art o' fisticuffs so that you will take little punishment – at most a few rib-ticklers and pats to the jaw from the most belligerent pug. It's Johnny Sullivan's Sparring Rooms for you, lad. We'll soon have you ready to take on your first customer!'

Fat Fred nods most solemnly at this advice. I wonder how much punishment he himself has taken, other than the dozen meat pies and Cornish pasties I witnessed him eat after my fight with Ben Dunn. As for Johnny Sullivan, it was Maggie's visit to his sparring rooms which caused the whole furore in the first place!

Tommo, I know, is under some pressure from Mr Sparrow to persuade me to fight again but he will not speak on their behalf. I receive more than enough persuasion from Maggie, who wishes me to fight, thinking only of the excitement and believing me invincible, bless her bright eyes.

'You will be a hero, and me on yer arm!' she laughs happily.

'More likely a lamb led to the slaughter and you ashamed of me,' I reply.

'No, no!' she protests. 'I has it on the best authority you will be the champion o' the whole world!'

It is useless to try to put reason into her magpie head. Maggie has become quite famous after the fight at Parramatta, as well making a large amount of cash from my win against Dunn. She collected nearly fifty pounds in total from those who honoured their bets. A great many made themselves scarce, melting into the jubilant crowd as soon as she climbed into the ring to be with me after the fight. Thank God I was fortunate enough to win. At ten to one odds to all takers, had I lost, Maggie would have been on her back ten hours a day for the next ten years paying off her debts.

She has spent some of her winnings on a new outfit from Farmer's in Pitt Street. A great deal more went on a spectacular bonnet from Mr Israel Myer's emporium in George Street. She has had this hat fitted with a newly stuffed magpie, which sits resplendent amongst ribbons, bows and artificial flowers of every colour of the rainbow. But much the better part of her winnings was spent on me. She paid to have a solid eighteen carat-gold ring made for me, of the signet style. On the face is a magpie and inside is inscribed *Maggie Pye loves Hawk Solomon, Champion of the World*. It is the most beautiful gift I have ever received and I shall cherish it all the days of my life.

Maggie, who can scarcely read or write, does not see why I should wish to work eight hours a day at Tucker & Co. when I could earn fifty times my weekly wage with one fight. Of course she doesn't know about Mary and the brewery and how it is in my best interest to learn all I can of the liquor business before we return to Hobart Town. But although I haven't told her of my plans, I find myself hoping she may even accompany Tommo and me.

Meanwhile, Maggie weeps in my arms and begs me to take up prize-fighting. I'm afraid it will come between us if I cannot resolve the matter soon. Now, seven weeks after the fight, she plain refuses to make love to me and bursts into copious tears.

We have fed the brats their Sunday roast and have gone up to her rooms where it is our custom, after taking a meal downstairs, to make love. But she pushes me away when I would take her in my arms.

'No!' she says, her mouth turned down.

I have learned something of women and so ask her gently if it is her time of the month.

'No!' she says again, and a tear runs down her pretty cheek.

'Maggie, what is it? What have I done?'

'The girls mock me!' she wails.

'About me?'

She nods, unable to speak.

'Why? Because I'm big? A nigger? What is it, Maggie?'

'They say you're a coward!' Maggie wails. She flings herself onto the bed and begins to howl in earnest.

'A coward? How so?' I ask.

Maggie's eyes glisten with tears and she catches a sob in her throat. ''Cause you won't fight!' Then she buries her face in her arms and sobs fit to break a man's heart.

I sit down on the side of the bed and put my hand on her shoulder, but she shakes it off. 'Maggie, beating another man senseless won't make a man a hero. You should know that!'

Maggie sniffs. 'It be 'umiliating. The girls say you're a big black cock with a chicken's heart! Oh, oh, *oh*!' she cries, burying her head in a red satin cushion.

'A big black cock with a chicken's heart, eh?' I laugh. 'That is amusing. Maggie! Maggie! Come along sweetheart, you know better than that! It's obvious, isn't it? Mr Sparrow and Fat Fred have put this about. They've put all the tarts up to it, trying to get me to fight!'

'Johnny Sullivan says it, too!' she replies, looking up quickly.

'Maggie, surely you haven't been hanging about Johnny Sullivan's Sparring Rooms again?'

'Only the once, to see the Lightning Bolt, the heavyweight champion of all Ireland what's been landed a week from Belfast.'

'And that's when Johnny Sullivan called me a coward?' I shake her softly again. 'Look at me, Maggie!'

Maggie lifts her head from the pillow, then props herself on one elbow. 'Well no, he never said you were a coward.'

'What, then?'

'He says he could train you up to beat the Bolt, but he don't know if you've got what it takes.'

'What's that, then?'

'Internal fort-e-tood, he called it!' Maggie gazes up at me, her big blue eyes still wet with tears. 'Oh Hawk, you has got it, hasn't ya?'

I am forced to laugh again. '"Internal fortitude", I think, comes straight from the vocabulary of our friend Mr Sparrow, and not from the likes of Johnny Sullivan.' I look at Maggie, thinking how much I love her.

'Maggie, I'm no coward, but I'm no animal, either. Beating a man with your bare fists until he is half-dead, what does that make you?'

'Rich!' Maggie yells, jumping up on the bed and grabbing me around the neck. 'Stinkin' bloody rich! Oh, Hawk, you could take me to England to meet Queen Vic, or Lola Montez!'

I stifle a laugh. 'A hundred pounds to be beaten senseless? That's not rich, that's plain foolish! Anyway, what if I should lose? I'd be beaten stupid with nothing in my pocket!'

'No! Not a hundred pound! Johnny says there's *five hundred* pounds to be won. He reckons there's plenty o' folks what'll cover your stake, what's half of the prize money, with all the Papists betting on the Irishman and all the Protestants on you!'

'Maggie, I'm a Jew!'

'Them too,' Maggie answers, quick as a flash. 'Mr Israel Myer and them lot in George Street, they'll back ya.'

'To the tune of two hundred and fifty pounds, eh? That's a lot of money, Maggie. A lot of gelt to wager on a bloke who's had just one lucky fight!'

'Johnny says yiz a natural!' She pauses then adds, 'If ya has the internal . . .'

'Internal fortitude?'

'Yeah, that. He says you're fast for a big bloke and ya uses your noggin. He says your ploy with the sunset in Dunn's eyes were a stroke o' genius.'

'That comes straight from *Bell's Life in Sydney*. I read it to you myself, Maggie!'

'No, it's the truth, Johnny said it too.'

'The only sunset I'm likely to see against the Irishman is the sunset of my life,' I say. 'Mr Lightning Bolt is not only the Irish champion but the English as well. If you leave out the Americas that makes him practically the world champion.' I shrug. 'Maggie, can't you see? He's come out here to clean up the locals, to fight Ben Dunn and the like and take home a pretty penny, because the stupid colonials think their man can win!'

'That's right! That's what Johnny said, and Barney Isaacs . . .'

'And, no doubt, Mr Sparrow!' I interject.

'I dunno about him.'

'Maggie, you know there isn't a sporting venture goes on in the colony that he and Fat Fred don't have a finger in.'

'No, listen, Hawk, listen to me! It ain't like that,' she pleads, then jumps off the bed so she's standing up and has her face close to mine. 'The Irishman's gunna fight all comers. Ben Dunn and Fred Woods, Jack Robbins o' Victoria, Jimmy Shanks o' Queensland and whatsisname, you know, that bloke in South Australia what beat Jericho Joe, the darkie? 'Scusin' me. They's all coming here to fight him. The punters, them what's Church of England, will bet on the locals. And o' course the Tipperary men will bet on their man and be most chuffed at the sight of their own Catholic champion from the Emerald Isle beating the livin' daylights out o' the local proddie lads.'

'But wait a minute. Maggie, aren't you Irish too?'

'Yeah, I am an' all, a fat lot o' good it's done me!' she shoots back. Then without drawing breath she continues, 'When the Bolt's cleaned up, like, and thinks he's fancy-free, that's it, ain't it?'

'That's what?'

'That's when *we* challenges the bugger to fight for a prize of five hundred pounds. That's more than he's made beating the living daylights out o' the local lads. It's five hundred pounds to win against someone what's had only one fight. He can't say no!'

'So all the smart money bets on the Irishman and I get my brains boxed!'

Maggie draws back. 'Maybe Johnny's right, you are scared.'

'Damn right I'm scared!' I snort.

'Well if all the smart punters are gunna bet on the Irishman, how come there's some like Johnny what's willing to wager on you? Answer me that, Hawk Solomon?'

'Maggie, it's called a sting.'

'A sting?'

I explain. 'See, Mr Sparrow has most likely arranged a consortium of sporting gentlemen who are well known to the punters, a few toffs, merchants, squatters, to put the word about that I can take the Irishman.' I pause. 'By the way, where do they plan to hold this fight?'

'Johnny reckons one of the gold diggings, they can't say exactly where as yet, 'cause of the police.'

'Yes, the goldfields makes sense, somewhere where there's lots of money and stupidity, all of it available at short notice. It's perfect for a sting. What are the chances that the only bookmakers allowed to take bets are in the employ of Mr Sparrow and Fat Fred? The odds given on the Lightning Bolt would be,' I think for a moment, remembering what I've heard around the pubs, 'four to five on – short odds, so as to discourage your ordinary punter and to make sure the Irish don't win too much. Then on me it's ten to one!'

Maggie looks a little puzzled by all of this, but I continue. 'If I'm not mistaken, there will be a great deal of secret hullabaloo stirred up about me. You know, whispers into hot ears in pubs about my secret training – how I'm punching tall trees to the ground. An incident is reported where some man swears he's seen me lift a dray cart single-handed to rescue a child in Pitt Street and then wander away into the crowd so I can't be given the credit. I've been spotted pulling a four-in-hand drag down the street and all for a wager of a sovereign. It's said I can arm-wrestle six men, two at a time, all in a row. A punch thrown in training near kills my sparring opponent who, as a consequence, lies unconscious for a week.

'There'll even be a tale that when I was a brat some Irishman, believing me to be the very devil, put me in a sugar bag, tied the top, said a brace of Hail Marys and threw me into the river to drown. And to back all this up, there'll be the famous Parramatta fight, which by now will have me lifting Ben Dunn ten feet off the ground with a single punch that lands fifteen feet outside the ring!'

Maggie giggles. 'I've already heard some o' that sort o' thing!'

I chuckle too at my imaginings and at Maggie's smile. 'Well, anyway, enough of that nonsense. But what will happen is that all the miners and the little punters will be taken in by such stories and will bet heavily on me as a result. And there you have it: the sting is in.' I take Maggie into my arms so her head is tucked snug into the crook of my neck. It feels wonderful. 'Will you be there, Maggie Pye, to sweep up all the broken feathers of the dead Hawk and to watch the Sparrow fly away, with his fortune made?'

Maggie struggles away from me. 'Hawk, yiz wrong! It ain't like that at all! I trust Johnny Sullivan. We was brats together, he wouldn't do no wrong by me!'

'Not by you, my darling, by me, the big, stupid nigger.'

'But he knows I loves ya!' Maggie protests, most perplexed.

'Of course!' I say. 'Who better?'

'Who better what?' she asks.

'Who better to help set up the sting?' I say gently.

'You know somethin', Hawk Solomon, I'm glad I ain't got no brains. There's five hundred pounds going beggin' and you're full o' bullshit about a bee sting! Listen t' me, ya stupid bastard! I thinks ya can win!' She looks about her room, her precious home, and waves her arms to include everything in it. 'See this, it's took me four years on me back to get this. Four years to sleep in a decent blanket what's got no bugs and fleas, in a room where you don't wake up with rats running over yiz! It cost me two 'undred pound to make this place beautiful.'

'Maggie, two hundred pounds! Why, you could own your own house for a hundred.'

Maggie clicks her tongue at me. 'I ain't completely daft, ya know! I do, don't I? I owns this building and the chophouse below. How else d'you reckon I got jobs fer Flo and her folks?' She bounces on the bed. 'This bed once belonged to William Charles bleedin' Wentworth, or at least his fam'ly, one of his sisters. Now it's mine.' She knocks on the headboard with her fist. 'Pure cedar, that is!' She smiles at me and I am taken by the lovingness of her expression. 'I'd sell it all tomorrow and put every penny I gets fer it on yiz beating the Lightning Bolt. I means it, Hawk, every sodding penny!'

I hug her tight. 'Maggie, Maggie, you haven't even seen the Irishman fight. You'd bet on me without even seeing his form?'

Maggie grins. 'I seen *your* form, Hawk, and not only against Ben Dunn!' And she begins to pluck at the buttons of my blouse.

Later, when we're lying there together, I am reminded again of how big I am and how careful I must be holding her. But Maggie seems happy enough, content to be loved and in my arms. I know little of the fairer sex, but what I'm learning is that they need to be held and cherished, stroked and kissed long after you are empty of passion. This is when kissing has no other purpose but to tell them you love them. I have discovered that in the business of passion, a man's arms are just as important as what's between his legs.

'Hawk,' Maggie says suddenly, 'the Irish didn't really put you in a sugar bag and throw you in the river, did they?'

'No more than I pulled a four-in-hand dray quicker than a team of four thoroughbreds,' I laugh.

Maggie laughs too. She has a lovely laugh – a sort of tinkle, like a silver bell ringing. It's the kind of laugh you'd expect from the governor's wife, a toffy-nosed tinkle, soft as a sunlit morning.

'Hawk, how does ya know? I mean, that it be a sting an' all?' Maggie asks.

'Maggie, I took on Ben Dunn because I overheard you and Tommo talking. I was so furious at what he'd done to you, I don't believe he could have brought me down no matter what he did. He'd have had to kill me standing upright.'

Maggie kisses me, her lips soft against the silver scar around my neck. 'Ain't nobody done that for me nor will again. I ain't worth it, but I loves ya, Hawk Solomon.'

I smile, and my heart is full of love for her, but I cannot tell her I love her. Not yet. 'If I come up against the Irishman I won't hate him, I won't feel anything. It'll just be one man against the other. The difference is that he's an experienced pugilist and a champion, and I'm just a big nigger with clumsy feet and fists.'

'But what about yer noggin? Johnny said you thinks real good.'

I grin. 'It doesn't need Ikey's brain to work out that a fast noggin and a slow body is not as good as a fast body and a slower brain!'

'But Johnny said, fer a big un you moves fast and ain't clumsy!'

'As fast as an elephant dancing the Irish jig!' I laugh. 'It would be no contest, Maggie. I'd get my teeth knocked through the back of my throat, and the little people would lose their shirts. Only Mr Sparrow, Fat Fred and various sportsmen, toffs and swells, including your precious Johnny Sullivan, would benefit.'

Maggie is silent a while and then announces, 'Hawk, I've changed me mind. Them bastards can't have ya, not even for five hundred pounds.'

But a mischievous thought has crossed my mind, an idea quite out of character. Perhaps Tommo and Maggie have encouraged in me a daring I never thought to have. 'Hold still a minute, Maggie. As Ikey would say, "My dears, one good scam deserves another!"

I think we should talk to Tommo. On these sorts of matters he is much smarter than I am. After all, he's beaten Mr Sparrow at cards, which Ikey said was not mortally possible.'

Maggie looks perplexed but shrugs, and returns to her nap, leaving me to ponder. Should I raise with my twin the possibility of a sting within a sting? And do Tommo and I want to get into another scrape? What would our dear Mary think? Since we've been back in Australia, I have written to her every week, telling her of our various doings. I have given much thought to our homecoming and how Tommo and I would fare in Hobart Town.

Though he denies it, my brother is in the grip of opium. It is no longer the Angel's Kiss and I can feel the hot breath of Tommo's devils from the wilderness closing in again. I am beginning to think it could be time to leave Sydney, for there is no opium that I know of to be had in Hobart Town.

But Tommo, still struggling with his demons, says he is not yet ready to return home. Nor, I confess, am I. There's Maggie Pye to think of, for a start. I'm not sure she'd like Hobart Town. I would also like to try my hand at shopkeeping – a venture that is of my own doing, not Mary's – something which would allow me to feed the many hungry children who roam the streets in every place I've been. And I can see my little bower bird Maggie Pye doing very well in such an enterprise! If we could acquire the capital, we could open a shop, perhaps in the goldfields. I have kept all the one hundred pounds I won from the Dunn fight for this very purpose – though not without some argument from Mr Sparrow. When the money was handed over, he demanded sixty per cent of the purse.

'Wait on!' I said. 'Fair go! Sixty per cent, for what?'

'Expenses, my dear. You were fighting at my venue, engaged in fisticuffs with my fighter,' he replied imperiously.

'No fear,' I said, amazed at his audacity. 'You had a near riot on your hands because the Welshman couldn't fight. Though it was unintentional, I saved the day and saved your hide.'

'But this is the agreement I have with your brother. It's what Tommo gives me from his poker winnings as my commission.'

'Sixty per cent?'

'Aye, there are a lot of expenses to this game!'

'None ventured on my behalf, Mr Sparrow. I have no agreement with you and you'll receive no commission from me!' I stood my ground.

'I see,' replied Mr Sparrow. 'In that case you can go to hell and your brother with yer!'

'What about the future champion o' the world you was so keen on an hour ago?' Tommo mocked.

'Business is business!' Mr Sparrow sighed. 'Didn't Ikey Solomon teach you nothing?' Then his mood grew darker. 'You know what, Ace O' Spades? You're getting too big for yer boots!' He pointed to Tommo's feet. '*My* boots! The nigger don't take care of you, lad. I does! You'd best remember that! You'd 'ave been nothing, a starving bloody drunk, without me and Fat Fred here!'

'And I'd be a lot less than nothin' without him, Mr Sparrow,' Tommo pointed to me. 'You gets sixty per cent of me card games, me twin gets one hundred per cent of me life!'

'We'll see how you go without me,' Mr Sparrow sneered. 'There's not a card game in this colony you'll be part of, son!' He flounced off and Tommo waved him away with a backward flick of his fingers. 'Toodle-oo, then.'

'We'll talk again, my boy,' Mr Sparrow murmured to me on his way past, wagging his finger. He didn't say anything further to Tommo but spat to the side of his boots.

Not five minutes later he came and apologised to us both, all smiles. Straight away I wondered what he was up to.

'It be the excitement of the fight, boys. Me nerves were on edge in case the police arrived and stopped it,' he explained. 'I lost my temper. You see, it cost me a pretty penny to stage. What I asked you for be the commission Ben Dunn would've also had to pay.'

'Shall I go and ask Ben Dunn, then?' I replied, not willing to accept Mr Sparrow's smarmy apology.

'No point,' he cackled. 'You took all the gelt!' He brought out a Cuban cigar, bit the end in his yellow teeth and fussed about, lighting it up. Then, through a puff of smoke, he remarked, 'What a fight, eh? Worth losin' my commission just to see it, lad.'

But Mr Sparrow's eyes narrowed as he said this and I could see by the way he chewed his cigar he didn't like losing his commission one bit. I realised he was the type to sweep insults under the carpet in order to tidy up, but that he would come back to the dirt at a later time, never minding who got brushed aside then. I felt certain I had not heard the last of this business. I knew Mr Sparrow still intended to get the sixty per cent of my prize money, with a great deal of interest added, before he was through with me and Tommo.

But on the surface Mr Sparrow was all smiles and forgiveness. He wanted Tommo to sit back in on the poker game that night too. 'Plenty o' rich pickings, lad. The gold finders pay in kind, nuggets and dust. It'll be a most profitable enterprise!' I thought of Ikey, who would never have lost his temper and then come crawling back. Mr Sparrow is not a patch on his old teacher.

'I'll come, but only for an extra ten per cent of the action,' said Tommo, cocky as hell. 'From now on we shares fifty-fifty, including tonight. What's you say, Mr Sparrow?'

'Oh no, Tommo, I can't agree to that, lad,' Mr Sparrow murmured, nice as pie. 'I'm in business with Mr Tang Wing Hung and must first discuss everything with him.' He took a puff of his cigar and exhaled. 'You do understand me, don't you?'

I saw at once what he was getting at and my heart sank. More and more, Tommo had been visiting Tang Wing Hung's opium den before going to his poker game. Now I knew that Mr Sparrow had Tommo in his tiny claws. One word from him and the opium pipe would be withheld from poor Tommo. I closed my eyes and held my breath, ardently hoping that Tommo wouldn't give in to the threat hanging in the air. It wouldn't be the worst thing that could happen, should Tommo be denied the pipe. I would be with him, and would stay at his side however long it might take to rid him of his new addiction.

Tommo grinned foolishly. 'Sorry, Mr Sparrow,' he said quietly. 'I begs your pardon. Sixty-forty as always and no harm done, eh?'

'Ah,' smiled Mr Sparrow, 'that's much better, Tommo. I only wish yer brother could see it as commonsensical. A little co-operation and all's well with the world, ain't that so?'

I wanted to weep. For the first time, I saw how weakened Tommo was by his need for opium, for it had him grovelling to this overblown gnat. I could still taste the blood in my mouth from the fight, but I was almost overwhelmed by fresh rage. I wanted to crush Mr Sparrow and, for the moment, Tommo with him. I had an urge to wring Mr Sparrow's scrawny, miserable neck with my bare hands, and to put Tommo out of his misery too. I knew then that my brother had succumbed to his old despair, even though I would have done anything to prevent this.

'Tommo, tell him to go to buggery! We don't need him!' I pleaded quietly.

But Tommo looked down at his boots and stayed silent. I felt deeply ashamed for my twin. How was it that I wanted to kill him and love him and hold him and protect him all in the one moment?

'Tommo! Tell the bastard *no*, Tommo!' I yelled, the words coming from deep inside.

Tommo looked at me and I could see he was crying. 'I can't, Hawk, the mongrel's got me!' he wept, burying his head in his hands.

I turned to Mr Sparrow and grabbed him by the coat front, picking him up off his feet. 'Leave us! Before I lose my temper, you bastard!' Then I threw him to the ground.

Mr Sparrow lay at my feet cringing. He covered his face with his hands, thinking I would kick him. Now it was not the great Mr Sparrow, a sportsman game as a fighting cock, but Sparrer Fart, little brat who was terrified. I leant down and took him by the collar, lifting him back up to his feet. He came no higher than my elbow and I could feel his whole body trembling.

'Please, Hawk,' he grovelled, 'don't hurt me!' He closed his eyes, expecting the blow to come. 'I'll give him fifty-fifty, whatever you wants.'

I let him go, disgusted. 'If any grief comes to Tommo, any harm, I'll come for you!' I growled. 'I'll see you pay, no matter what it takes!'

And so here is Sparrer Fart once again in our lives, become 'Mr Sparrow' as if no longer Ikey's little pupil. He's got Tommo in his clutches, and now he wants me. The sting is his revenge on our getting the better of him. He is using Johnny Sullivan, who is using Maggie, the innocent party in all this. I am pretty certain Mr Sparrow's vengeful mind is pitting me against the visiting Irish fighter so I can get my brains knocked out and he can clean up at my expense.

Ikey would see my idea of beating Mr Sparrow at his own game as an excellent way to get even, with a bit of solid business added. I feel in my bones that I am right and that it is not some crazed idea I have constructed out of my overheated imagination. How I have grown to despise Mr Sparrow. If he has learned his ways from Ikey, then I must think carefully about what this means for Tommo and me, Ikey's sons.

Sunday is usually Tommo's night off. On the Sabbath, the toffs, merchants and senior government officials, who enjoy the sportsman's life on all other nights of the week, generally settle down to Sunday roast with their respectable families. This is their time to pat the heads of their offspring and to grunt while their wives attempt polite conversation. They must also be seen at the evening service, for many will have missed the morning one because they were sleeping off hangovers gained from a night of gambling and carousing with the likes of Tommo and the ever-present Mr Sparrow.

I know Tommo will have risen at about five this afternoon. He will have gone to visit Tang Wing Hung's opium den, and will be returning shortly to have his evening meal with Maggie and me downstairs at the chophouse run by Flo's father. I will ask his opinion of my plan then, for Tommo has lost none of his wits.

This is the curious thing about opium. Whereas brandy will cloud the brain, the same is not true of opium which is said by some to promote great clarity of thought. Caleb Soul, my friend and colleague at Tucker & Co., is of this opinion. A pharmacist by profession, he speaks of opium's powers to promote intellectual thought and cites for example the work of Lord Byron, Percy Bysshe Shelley and de Quincy amongst other English luminaries.

This is still no reason to embrace opium, nor will I for one moment condone its use for anything other than alleviating pain. These days, Tommo cannot live without the Devil's Smoke, and it is my sad opinion that he could not give up the celestial poppy even if he most sincerely desired to.

Nonetheless, Tommo is in fine form when we meet for dinner, smiling and sipping quietly at a glass of his favourite Cape brandy. Though it tears at my very soul, I have accepted that he must drink. Accordingly, I have offered him the very best brandy imported by Tucker & Co. He will have none of it, preferring the rough Cape grape to all else. I have noticed that after taking opium he drinks less, though this only in degree.

'So,' Tommo says, when I raise the subject of Mr Sparrow's sting, 'have you decided to fight then, Hawk?'

I nod. 'Only this once, and only if we can think up a way for me to win and the money to be made is, as Maggie says, five hundred pounds.'

'Maggie's right,' Tommo says. 'Mr Sparrow is most confident of the winnings to be had. With the Protestants and the Jews against the Catholics, it be a holy war of sorts, he says. What a strange thing! Here we is, brought up with no religion to speak of, and you's gunna be promoted as a Jew.' Tommo chuckles. 'I reckon Ikey would have a good laugh at that! But Hawk, tell me. Why d'ya want to do it?'

'The gelt,' I say.

Tommo grins and shakes his head. 'Pull the other one, Hawk!'

I look at Maggie, who appears to be most interested in her bowl of Irish stew. 'It's true, I want the money – the reason being I want us to open a shop. You and Maggie and me. We could make a tidy sum from this fight – enough to set us up with a shop, perhaps at the goldfields where I've heard there's a fortune to be made.'

'Come on, Hawk! You're talkin' to me, Tommo, your twin! It ain't in your nature! Since when would you take up fisticuffs to earn money?'

'What's wrong with that?' Maggie asks sharply. 'Ain't nothin' wrong for a man to earn an honest crust at prize-fightin'!'

'Like I said, it just ain't in Hawk's nature, Maggie,' Tommo sighs. 'You've seen him with the brats. He'd rather give it to others than keep it for hisself! Besides, he's gunna take a terrible hiding in that fight.'

'No he ain't!' Maggie replies, looking furiously at Tommo.

'You can't win!' he says to me. 'This bloke's the champion of Ireland *and* England, for Gawd's sake!'

'*Hawk* could be the champion o' the world,' Maggie protests.

I cut across them both. 'You're right, Tommo, it's not just about the money. Though it's true, I'd like us to open a shop. In the end, though, it's not that.' I pause, not sure that even Tommo will understand what I'm going to say next. I take a deep breath. 'It's about getting Ikey out of our souls!'

'What? What about Ikey? What's all this got to do with him?'

'To my mind, everything!' I lean forward across the table. 'Don't you see, Ikey lies at the heart of our troubles!'

'Hawk, you're talkin' nonsense! What's you mean, Ikey's the reason for our problems? He's our father! Without Ikey's voice in me head, I'd never have come out o' the wilderness!'

'Without Ikey, you'd probably never have been taken there in the first place, Tommo!'

Maggie rises from her chair and picks up her bowl of stew. 'If you two are gunna fight I'm goin' into the kitchen,' she says, marching off.

We ignore her and I continue. 'Tommo, it all started with Ikey's greed over what was in the safe at Whitechapel – not wanting to share his half with Hannah and his children.'

'What the hell is you talkin' about, Hawk? What safe?'

In my excitement I've forgotten that Tommo knows nothing of the safe full of stolen treasure, which Ikey and Hannah had left buried under the pantry floor of their Whitechapel house. I'd also forgotten my oath of secrecy to Mary, though I suddenly recall her every sharp word as if it were yesterday. *'Hawk, you'll not talk to no one about the money, Ikey's money, ever, you understand? Not even to Tommo, you hear!'*

I look up at Tommo. He *has* to know. My loyalty to my twin is greater than to Mary. And so I tell him the whole story of how Mama and I conspired to win Ikey's fortune for ourselves. How, while in England to learn about hop-growing, I found the safe and secretly emptied it of its contents, stealing the fortune from under Hannah and David's nose, and leaving only a ring and a note which said: *Remember, always leave a little salt on the bread.*

Tommo bursts out laughing, 'That were clever to use Ikey's favourite saying!'

I recall how David had fallen defeated to his knees, clutching the ring in his fist.

'Whatever can it mean? We are done for! My family is destroyed!' he had wailed. 'Ikey Solomon has beaten us all!'

'But it was Mary and I who'd beaten Hannah and David and the rest of Ikey's family. It was Mary's revenge for our kidnapping,' I confide to my astonished twin.

'Why'd ya never tell me this before?' he asks.

'Tommo, forgive me, but Mama made me swear I wouldn't tell you. When you came back from the wilderness and,' I pause, 'all was, well, not right between you two, she felt she could not trust you with the secret of Ikey's money, and so she asked that I keep it a secret. I didn't want to, but in the end I agreed. I'm sorry, Tommo.'

'Never mind, Hawk. You done the right thing. You didn't know how I'd be.' He smiles. 'I didn't know how I'd be meself. How rich is Mary?'

'Very!'

'All from Ikey's safe?'

'No, not all. She's done well for herself, as you know. But still the larger portion by far is Ikey's money from the safe. So now you know what happened, Tommo. It was greed that led to our kidnapping.'

I swallow. 'The same greed that made Mary take all of Ikey's money and then throw us out of our own home. While David Solomon will never know what truly happened to Ikey and Hannah's fortune, I fear he may have concluded that Mary now has all his parents' hidden wealth. That's still the same greed working to destroy us. Even Mr Sparrow putting in the sting is more of Ikey's greed at work – Ikey, who taught him all he knows!

'It's like a curse working over and over again, from which we must somehow escape.'

I want desperately for my brother to understand, but Tommo isn't listening. 'You sure us bein' kidnapped were David and Hannah's work?' he asks abruptly.

'I can't prove it, but who else would do such a thing? Mama wasn't rich at the time, and there was no cause for anyone else to kidnap us.'

'But what happened to us, Hawk? How were we parted? Can you remember? I can't. I've tried a thousand times! I don't have no memory of what happened after we was took on the mountain.'

'I didn't either – at least not until I got my voice back,' I say to him. 'Since then it seems to have slowly come back to me, bit by bit, like pieces in a child's kaleidoscope. Of course, I don't know what happened to you after the wild man took me away into the mountains.'

Tommo leans forward across the table. 'Tell me, Hawk.' His voice is urgent and his eyes bright with hope. 'Maybe I'll get better if you tell me!'

I close my eyes and slowly draw back the past. Then I begin to tell my sorry tale.

'We were climbing down the mountain where we'd been to see the snowline when four men grabbed us. They blindfolded and gagged us, and stuffed us into hessian bags, after binding our feet and hands. Then they lifted us onto some sort of stretcher.

'They must have struck out across the mountains to a road where they had a cart waiting. All I remember is that when they take us out of the bags, we're both crying. They take off my gag and give me some water and a crust of bread. Then we're both put back into our separate bags and onto a horse cart. I must have slept some, because the next thing I remember is hearing a voice shout, "Stand to!" and the cart coming to a halt. Then there are four rapid shots and a man screaming and crying out for mercy. Then another shot, then silence.

'Soon enough a hand opens the bag and I'm pulled out by my hair. When the gag and blindfold are taken off, I can't see anything for a while. Gradually I make out a man holding me. Beside the cart lie three of our captors dead, and another further away a bit. All look like they are sleeping – all except one who lies on his back with his arms and legs sprawled and blood coming out his mouth. Already, there are ants around him. I begin to cry again and look about for you, but you're still hidden in your sack and I can't reach you. Then the man who shot them comes over and hits me on the side of my head. "Nigger!" he spits. Just the one word. "Nigger!"

'He is dressed entirely in kangaroo and possum skins but for a trooper's high-topped white cap, and he is filthy. His beard falls almost to his waist and his hair is wild and knotted on his shoulders. What can be seen of his face is dark with dirt, the skin weathered and criss-crossed with scars. His nose is flattened like a pig's snout and from it a stream of yellow snot trails down to broken and lopsided lips. His tongue constantly darts out, licking the snot. He is barefoot too, with the soles of his feet cracked and the long toenails all broken.'

'A wild man,' Tommo says, and I nod.

'Then I realise there is another man, mounted on his horse. He is dressed in skins and ragged breeches and boots, ancient and cracked. He too has a ragged beard and his dirty face is deep-burned to a copper colour.'

'Was he bald?' Tommo questions me.

'I think not . . .' I think hard for a moment. 'No, he wore a hat, a bushman's hat. I remember, he took it off to hide whatever it was he'd taken from the dead men's pockets in it. He had dark hair and a deep scar across his left eyebrow, running into his hairline.'

'Well, it weren't Sam Slit,' Tommo says. 'Sam were bald and no scar.'

'It's most likely this bastard sold you to Slit, because he takes the cart and horses and you. You are still wriggling in your bag when the wild man takes me away.

'The wild man puts a rope about my neck and ties me behind his horse. I can't walk because my ankles have been tied and have lost all circulation. So he drags me along by my neck, me in the dirt and him not looking back. I'm screaming your name, blubbing and choking from the noose about my neck, stones cutting into me. I just want to get back to you.'

It is the first time I've spoken aloud about what befell us and now I begin to weep. Tommo reaches out and puts his hand on my shoulder. 'Hawk,' he says. 'Oh Hawk!' Then I see he too is weeping.

I am grateful it is Sunday night and well past dinner-time by now, so that the chophouse is empty. Tommo and I sit and have a good old cry over the past. I can hear the clatter of dishes and laughter in the kitchen as Maggie makes some joke. After a while, we're all right again.

'Can you remember the rest, when Mary come to find you?' Tommo asks, once our tears have dried.

I nod. This is the darkest of my memories and has only returned to me recently.

'Can you tell me?' Tommo gazes at me. 'Or don't you want to?'

'I do remember, and I will tell you,' I say gently. 'But first, you. Do you not remember anything of what happened when we were parted?'

'There must be something. Something what I remembers.' Tommo gives a bitter little laugh. 'Though I dunno why I want to. It were all so bloody awful.' He seems to be thinking and he looks up to the ceiling as he speaks, his blue eyes glistening with tears again, his voice unsteady.

'I remember going up the mountain, you and me, the first snow, racing up to the snowline.' Tommo smiles through his tears. 'Me winning, 'cause I were smaller and faster and you a bit clumsy on the rock and shale. Then coming down again, to return to Strickland Falls, to Mama.' Tommo stares straight at me for a moment, his expression so very sad, like a little boy who doesn't understand what he's done wrong.

'And then Slit. Slit and the sweet, sticky smell of the whisky still and the wilderness all about, stretching forever, darker and darker. It be as though I blinked me eyes, and everything changed. One moment I were playing with you on the mountain and the next I were with Slit in the wilderness – Slit beating the daylights out o' me most days!'

'Tommo, poor Tommo, let's not speak of it any more,' I say,

trying to comfort him. 'I'll tell you how Mary found me some other time, eh?'

'No, tell me now,' Tommo presses me. 'That silver scar 'round your neck, it haunts me. I needs to know!'

I close my eyes tightly and feel warm tears run down my cheeks. 'Every day the wild man led me behind his horse through the high mountains with the rough rope pulling tight around my neck, so that it bled and festered constantly. This went on for months until my neck was worn almost through. At night he'd tie me up, beat me, the rope still around my neck tied to a tree. I couldn't move away from his blows or I would choke myself. I hoped I would die. He was a monster worse than any in the books Mama read to us. Finally I lost my voice.'

Tommo is in tears again. 'I could feel it!' he sobs. 'In the wilderness with Slit, I could *feel* your pain, I swear it! When did you lose your voice?'

'Towards the end, just before Mama came. I don't know, five months, maybe a bit more. Why, Tommo?'

'I remember how Slit beat me for weeks 'cause I couldn't answer him. Me throat were closed up, shut tight. I knew I could talk, but then again I couldn't. It were our twinship, I s'pose.'

We both pause. 'But how did Mary rescue you?' Tommo urges.

'Well, we're climbing up a mountain one day – it's early morning and very cold. I was never warm in all that time, not once. I don't know where we're going, but the wild man keeps stopping and looking up at the track, a narrow path which seems to me all stones. He's sniffing, testing the air, his tongue darting out like he's tasting it. He sucks his finger and holds it in the air above his head, testing the wind. Then up we go, climbing the mountain. Suddenly he stops and turns his horse and we descend into a small box canyon.

'And then I see Mary. She is sitting up holding a blanket to her neck, and I realise that she has seen the monster and is filled with terror. Next she spies me, standing behind the horse with the rope around my neck.

'"Hawk!"she screams.

'But I've got no voice and cannot answer her. I just stand trembling in the bitter, cold morning. I raise my hands to confirm it is me, to tell her that I've heard her. I speak to her in the sign language that Ikey's taught us, and which Mary knows also.

'"Mama!" I say.

'"Hawk! Mama's come!" she screams. Then she looks up at the monster. "He's my boy, my precious boy, give me him!"

'The monster jerks at the rope so that I am thrown to my knees. Loosening the rope from the saddle, he drags me to a rock and ties me to it. And then he drives his first into my face and I fall to the ground.

'Mama is still yelling at him, "You bastard! You fucking bastard!"

'I look up in my daze to see the monster, his tongue darting in and out and licking at his snot, ties his horse to another boulder and walks towards Mama. He's got her trapped, blocking her escape. He throws her to the ground and leaps on top of her, pulling his breeches down. He's grunting and puffing and tearing at her clothes and skirt, one hand around her throat. Then I hear the shot, and three more, and the wild man slumps down over Mama, vomiting and shitting himself. She's shot him.

'Mary is covered in guts, shit, blood and vomit but she pushes him aside, drops her pistol and comes running towards me, arms outstretched. She grabs me and howls like some primitive creature. Then she weeps and weeps, and I with her.'

I am exhausted at this telling and Tommo is once again reduced to sobs. 'Tommo,' I say, clasping my hand to his shoulder, 'Mama found me, but she never gave up looking for you. Not one day passed that she didn't try to find you! She offered a king's ransom if anyone should report your whereabouts. She put your likeness and description on the back label of every bottle of Tomahawk beer she sold. She questioned me for years about what happened and where you might be – all the time you were away.

'"Think, Hawk!" She'd shake me by the shoulders. "Think, darling! The man what took Tommo, what did he look like? Can you remember anything, darling, the smallest thing?" But of course I couldn't. Not then.'

I grip Tommo's shoulder hard. 'It's all so clear now. I can see him, the man with a scar across his eyebrow. The scar went deep into his hairline, as if it had been done with an axe. Black eyes, dead like lumps of coal, another scar across his mouth, intersecting his bottom lip. That's who took you.'

'It weren't Slit,' Tommo mutters, and stares into the distance for a long time. 'So why must we get Ikey out of our souls?' he asks at last.

'Don't you see? Ikey's greed is at the root of all this misery. It wasn't his fault – he wasn't evil. But life was hard and that's how he survived. He had to be greedy just to live. That greed is still with us, it haunts us, Tommo!'

'But we're of Ikey's making!' Tommo says, wonderingly. 'He taught us everything, all we needed to know to survive.'

'We're of Mary's making too, Tommo. It was Mary who brought us up, who gave us decency and love.'

'But I loved Ikey,' Tommo says sadly, as if I'm taking away one of his few pleasant memories. 'Without him in me mind I couldn't have survived – not in the wilderness nor out of it, for that matter.'

'Me neither! There was much good in Ikey, Tommo! But we must also put his greed behind us! Ikey's greed lives on in Mr Sparrow, in the opium pipe he feeds you. It's going to kill you, Tommo!'

Tommo looks down, examining his nails. 'So now you wants to fight the Lightning Bolt, what'll beat you to a pulp, so's you can defeat Mr Sparrow and rescue yours truly. Is that it?' He speaks quietly, but is plainly angry.

I nod, knowing that I must step carefully here. But I can control my own anger no longer. 'He has turned you into his slave! He can't be allowed to do that. The mongrels *can't* keep on winning. Somebody must stop them!'

'Ho! That's my saying, Hawk, and it ain't got me nowhere. You *can't* win, Hawk. You can't win against the Irishman, and you got even less chance against Mr Sparrow!'

'Tommo, listen to me. I loved Ikey too but we must be rid of this curse once and for all.'

'How? By getting thrashed by an Irishman? That's precisely what Mr Sparrow wants, to see you killed and him get rich at your expense.'

'Tommo, you've got to think up a way I can win the fight! I *must* win. For all our sakes.'

I don't tell my brother the last reason behind my determination to take on Mr Sparrow and succeed. I have received another letter from Mary, in which she tells me all that has happened. The more I think of it, the more I know the time has come. If we are to make lives of our own, if my dream of a shop is to come to pass, Tommo and I must first make our peace with Mary. The time has come for Tommo, Maggie and me to prepare to go home.

The Potato Factory Brewery

'The Cascades'

Hobart Town

Tasmania

May 8 1861

My dearest Hawk and Tommo,

I count each day you are away as though it be a year. Every morning when I rise, I go out into the yard and look up at the mountain. I have it perfect timed so I see a flock of green rosellas as they fly each day from the mountain across the Derwent River to some place too far for the eye to follow. How they screech and carry on as they pass overhead!

These emerald green parakeets have always been the birds of my good fortune. The very first morning I arrived in Van Diemen's Land, a flock flew over the ship's high mast and I knew then that I would survive. I clasped my Waterloo medal and swore that I would begin a new life and that the green birds would be my talisman.

This morning I waited for them to fly over, preparing to call out, 'Bring back my boys!' like I always do. They came, just as they do every day, but this time to my astonishment, they wheeled and came to rest in my garden – some on the peach tree what's in blossom and some on the washing line – screeching their hearts out.

'It's a sign!' I yell. 'A sign!' I clap my hands and with that sound they's gone, up and away, taking the same route as always.

This be the first time they've wheeled and stopped and I found myself crying, though for joy or sorrow I cannot say. Is it a warning? I fear for my boys – that one of you might be harmed. Or should I fear for myself?

David and Hannah have bought up the entire hops crop on the island this year – and our own planting has failed. There is word that David will start his own brewery soon and he vows to take away my business. Buying hops from the mainland makes my Tomahawk Pilsener and my Temperance Ale most expensive to brew and if I pass the cost on to my customers I fear it may lose me many a working man's custom.

Still, I shall manage, though I feel I haven't the heart if my boys don't soon return. Were you and Tommo here, we could buy land further up the Huon Valley where hop-growing is more reliable. I have also thought we might open a brewery in Melbourne or Ballarat to supply the diggings, and that you and Tommo could undertake this task in a year or two after you are once again acquainted with what is required.

David Solomon meanwhile spreads vicious rumours, ably aided by Hannah, that I have long been Mr Emmett's mistress and so have gained favours and concessions from the government. 'How else,' he asks, 'can a woman prosper over a man in the brewing business?'

This has caused me the greatest distress for, excepting my love for my two boys, I treasure Mr Emmett's friendship above all else. He has retired from the government and so David is now able to talk openly without fear of reprisal. There are plenty here too who are willing to believe him, even though I am innocent.

To make matters worse, Mrs Emmett has died recently and already there are those who say it was brought about by grief at the knowledge of our alleged association. I cannot protest, for to do so would give credence to this wicked accusation. Nor can I go to my dear friend and offer him comfort, for fear that it will be seen to confirm their gossip. Though I don't give a fig for their good opinion, I would not wish to cause Mr Emmett the least embarrassment.

I admit I did not care for Mrs Emmett one little bit. I find it hard to credit that a man so noble of spirit could have loved a woman so determined to look down her long and imperious nose at those she thought inferior, such as myself.

I hope and pray that dear Mr Emmett will forgive my not attending the funeral service but I am grown too old to turn hypocrite now. I did send flowers out of the respect I hold for him. I took to the mountain and picked wildflowers and made a wreath twined with the honeysuckle that grows there. I'll venture it was the only one of its kind among the pompous floral tributes on her grave.

My dearest boys, I think of you a hundred times each day and my heart aches with longing for your return. How I wish to hold you each by the hand as when you were young and tell you how your mama loves you.

Please write to me soon, I long for news that you are well.

Your loving mama,

Mary Abacus.

Chapter Nineteen

TOMMO

The Rocks
May 1861

When Hawk tells me he's going to fight the Irish champion, I'm most terrible worried. Hawk don't have the nature of a true fighter – he's a man of peace. If he takes on the Lightning Bolt, he won't be fighting the true object of his anger. In his mind, he'll be entering the twenty-four-foot ring against Mr Sparrow, and that ain't enough.

Hawk knows this himself. And yet he says I got t' help him win. He wants me to come up with a plan what will undo Mr Sparrow and his sidekick, Fat Fred. Somehow we also has to raise the money for the stakes – two hundred and fifty pounds in a prize of five hundred pounds, winner takes all – so that we won't have to forfeit any of what we makes to Mr Sparrow or his gang.

So far me plan is this. I'm gunna go to Mr Sparrow and tell him I have persuaded my brother to fight the Irishman. This will keep me in his good books as I depends on him for me living at cards and o' course for the favours of Mr Tang Wing Hung. If only it were possible to play in a Sydney card game what the bastard don't control, then I'd soon enough have the stakes for Hawk's fight with some to spare!

But how am I to tell Mr Sparrow that Hawk don't require Fat Fred as a manager and trainer, nor Johnny Sullivan's Sparring Rooms for training? It's gunna be awkward enough explaining that Hawk plans to raise the stake money himself, without me master's friendly involvement. I'll have to tell him flat that Hawk ain't yet buried the hatchet over Mr Sparrow demanding sixty per cent of his prize money from the Ben Dunn fight. Mr Sparrow will be miffed but, in the end, he'll accept Hawk's terms, knowing that me twin has little chance o' winning. Besides, the true profit for Mr Sparrow is in the betting ring, what he controls. And such a deal will make him a cleanskin. He may now promote the fight and fix the betting ring to his advantage. When Hawk, after much huffing and puffing, loses to the Irishman, Mr Sparrow can't be accused of arranging the outcome.

Maybe I'll say that the stakes for Hawk's side of the prize is being raised in secret by Captain James Tucker – Hawk's employer, what's known to be a sporting gent with the horses. This ain't something Mr Sparrow could go sniffing out the truth about, as it ain't proper for a gentleman of Captain Tucker's standing and a member of the Union Club to have an interest in an illegal fist fight.

I'm also gunna have to tell Mr Sparrow that I won't be keeping him advised of Hawk's progress. What worries me is that he'll withdraw me supplies of the Angel's Kiss. But I'll tell him that Hawk won't fight if he does this, and I reckon he'll give in to his own greed. There's big money to be made from this fight and nobody knows it better than Sparrer Fart.

That's as much as I've got planned at present and there's two questions still facin' me. How does we raise the stake? And how can I make Hawk a certain winner? What Mr Sparrow wants above all else is that Hawk gets beaten near to death. He reckons he's been cheated and humiliated by me twin. He wants his revenge, and he wants it at a profit. I ain't even begun to come up with a certain double-sting.

I think about this problem for several days on end but naught comes to mind. Me head wound, the pain of which never quite leaves me 'cept with opium, starts hurting something awful. And then the answer hits me like a flamin' bolt out o' the blue!

Mary! Our own mama!

Hawk has told me of Ikey's stolen fortune what's now in Mary's possession. If I could do a deal with Mary and get me hands on some of that money, I could offer the Irishman twice his winnings to *lose* the fight. For a sum of a thousand pounds, he'd surely do it. We'd set up what looks like a grand fight to the punters – a fight in which both men shows good scientific points and there's much ballyhoo in the ring – an excellent circus all 'round. We'd lodge the money in a trust account in England to be paid to the Irishman in the event of a deal well done. And if I was to offer him some cash up front, so that he could bet against himself at good odds, he'd be even further tempted. He'll take our bribe, let Hawk win, and go home happy enough besides!

The Bolt ain't a young man and he's well past his prime, though he'd still thrash our Hawk – no matter how strong me brother be. And he wants that prize purse bad. *Bell's Life in Sydney* reckons the Bolt's come to the colonies to get his snout into the money trough one last time. The Irishman talks o' retiring from the game and opening a pub in Galway, inviting all from the colonies to visit him. This be the ambition of just about every prize fighter what ever lived!

I've already seen the Bolt twice at the card table in Chinatown and has come to know a little about him. He's a fair enough player, game enough to win the occasional pot. He be just the sort to lose in the company of a player such as yours truly – and stupid enough to believe his loss has come about through bad luck on the night. On both nights Mr Sparrow told me to let him win enough to pay his grog bill and a bit more. I've also heard him boast that he ain't once had to pay for the pleasures of the sweet colonial lassies what visit his rooms above Mr Hulle's Shipman's Hotel at Brickfield Hill. Maggie says she'd bet London to a brick these girls works for Mr Sparrow, for the Bolt ain't no charmer to get it for free. What this means is that Mr Sparrow's softening him up. He plans to own all or a good part of all the Irish fister before he takes on me brother.

The Bolt's well-loved by the Tipperary men and they follows him wherever he goes. On Saturdays, the Irish navvies come in their hordes to drink all day in the Shipman's Hotel – just to catch a glimpse of the champion o' the Emerald Isle and conqueror o' the English bulldog. Some has even painted a large banner sporting a crude likeness of the Bolt standing with one foot upon the stomach of a bulldog, lying on its back with its legs in the air. The dog's tongue, what has the stripes of the Union Jack painted upon it, lolls out o' the corner of its mouth. Blood spouts like a fountain from its nostrils and falls into a glass held waist high by the champion, who's smacking his lips. This banner they raise on poles and carry about as proud as you like, with three men to the front, one beating a drum and the other two playing the cornet and fife, and any number of Irishmen marching behind.

If anyone mocks the Bolt, he's at once challenged to a fight by each and every Tipperary man within hearing. The Shipman's Hotel has become a dangerous place because of these shenanigans. The townfolks keeps well away from the drunken men what mills about the station at Strawberry Hills, waiting for the late Sunday night train home to Parramatta Town.

Imagine the hullaballoo when we declares Hawk's fight with the Irish champion! 'Hawk, the Black Jew, fights the blessed son of Erin who was baptised in the holy waters of the Shannon River.' What a banner that will be!

Now that I've worked out the sting I must get Maggie Pye's help to put it in place. Of course, it ain't worth a pinch o' shit 'less I get Mary's money to bribe the Irishman with. Without saying nothin' to Hawk, I writes to Mary in me best hand, what Hawk'd be proud of if he could see it!

Sydney

May 25, 1862

Our dearest Mama,

Hawk and me be in a spot of bother. Please come to Sydney and bring five hundred pounds. You can leave a message for me at the Hero of Waterloo in The Rocks.

Your obedient son

Tommo X Solomon.

I dunno if that'll do the trick – but I hopes so. I feel bad about keeping the sting a secret from Hawk but I tells meself it ain't worth bothering him with 'til I know if it might work. As Ikey says, 'First get the most important agreement, my dears, then use it to obtain any others you may need. It be most difficult to persuade a partner when you has nothing o' substance held up to advantage.' And so I'll wait 'til Mary agrees before I tell Hawk she's coming to Sydney.

In the meantime I try to come up with a way for Hawk to beat the Bolt if Mary won't give us the bribe and we has to do it kosher. Something comes to me in Tang Wing Hung's opium den in Chinatown, though it's still mostly chancy.

Mr Tang Wing Hung has a place what's entirely for opium-smoking two doors down from his eating house. Those of 'respectable' European background goes to a private room at the eating-house and escapes through a hidden doorway into the alley behind. A signal is given from two doors down and the opium den is opened.

Mr Tang Wing Hung's opium den is no filthy hovel inhabited by creatures half-alive what slither and crawl about in a dark and fetid atmosphere. His room is a grand place, with six couches in maroon brocade what has dragons leaping and twisting, and exotic flowers about the place. The couches has curtains drawn about them for privacy. The customer never gives his true name even if he be the governor himself and known to all. Only Europeans what can afford Mr Tang Wing Hung's price may enter.

I am greeted by an ancient celestial with a pure white pigtail. He wears an oriental cap upon his head and a gown o' silk down to his ankles. His long pointed beard flows to his waist and his moustache droops downwards to disappear into the fall o' his snowy beard. His yellow skin is creased like crumpled butcher's paper and his narrow eyes show barely a glint of light.

This is Ho Kwong Choi, what's always silent and always ready to prepare the opium pipes. The pipe be a piece o' bamboo cane about one inch and a half in diameter, and two foot in length. The bowl is fixed about a third of the way down from its end. It's broad and flat at the top, with a small hole in the centre where the opium paste sits.

All is quiet here. Outside there's the call of children playing, a hawker's cry, or the busy rattle of a hackney in some nearby street. But these are dull and seem far away. A small bowl o' paste is placed on a lacquer table beside me couch. Next to it is a lamp, its glass like an upside down bell, the shape of an Easter lily, so that the opening is pointed uppermost with the flame licking at its centre. I watch as Ho Kwong Choi dips a long steel needle into the bowl and quickly winds up a small amount o' paste what's somewhat like treacle on its end. This he holds over the flame until the precious pearl of opium begins to bubble.

Then he places the smouldering opium into the bowl of me pipe and I pull the glorious smoke into me lungs, letting it float in dragon trails through me mouth and nostrils. Each pearl o' perfection allows only three or four puffs before Ho Kwong Choi must roast another. He does this for near on an hour until I feels like I'm in heaven.

I'm here enjoying me smoke when the peace of the den is suddenly shattered. The door is battered open and six lads, much the worse for grog, charge into the room. There are three of us within, not counting Ho Kwong Choi, all drawn deep into ourselves from our smoke dreams what are now broken by these louts. They pulls out truncheons from their belts and one wields a rattle what makes a fearful racket. Then they sees Ho Kwong Choi as he comes from behind a curtain into the centre of the room. They storm towards the old Mongolian what stands alone and defenceless. I'm in a cloud o' confusion, not capable even o' standing up.

I ain't sure if what I sees is part of my opium dream or real but the old man seems to grow into some sort o' peculiar human spider, his arms and legs flashing through the air with grunts and hisses. He don't make no noise apart from a grunt or two when he delivers a few chops with the side of his palms to one of the fellows. Another he holds in such a way that his eyes roll back in his head and his knees buckle as he drops to the floor. In a few moments, all six lads is out cold or trying to stagger up. Ho Kwong Choi stands calm among them.

Four of the blokes slowly rise. They drag their two unconscious mates behind 'em, and the frail old man bows politely as they stumble out the door.

I am amazed at what I've seen. If I can get Ho Kwong Choi to teach Hawk, perhaps me brother might bring some o' the venerable Mongolian's skills to bear on the Irishman. This be our only hope for Hawk to win if Mary don't agree to pay for the fix.

It is also the plan I tells Hawk about.

'Within the rules of bare-knuckle fighting, is such a method permitted?' he wants to know.

'I'll lay a bet that such a thing ain't never been seen in a fight before!' says I. 'You can't forbid what's unknown now, can ya?'

'You mean it will come as a complete surprise?'

I nod.

'I must see this Mongolian method only as a part of my success. The other part must be competence in the true business of fist-fighting.'

'You be right in that,' I agree. 'At best we got three months to teach you the fighter's trade.'

'Three months? Can we do it?' Hawk asks.

'It's all we've got. That be the time it will take the Irishman to fight with all the big men coming here from around the country, includin' Ben Dunn. So you'd best start training, Hawk!'

'Yes, so I see! I told Maggie that we would not work from Jimmy Sullivan's Sparring Rooms and she is most concerned, thinking him the best trainer in the colony,' Hawk says.

'Hawk, your training's got to be a mystery, taking place in a hideaway so that we can build a frenzy o' rumour and speculation about your form. We has to make the punters think that you can win,' I says to him. 'That's what Mr Sparrow wants and that's what we wants also. Only difference is that he must be made to think you *can't* win, and we knows you can!'

'That should not be too difficult. Mr Sparrow already thinks I can't win. He just wants me punished.'

'Yes, but he's got to be absolutely certain you can't win.'

'How are you going to do that?'

'I dunno,' I says. 'I'll think o' something. The most important thing Mr Sparrow wants right now is to build up the expectations among the punters that you *can* win. I'm gunna make that very difficult for him!'

'How so?'

'Well, we're in secret training, ain't we? I ain't telling him nothing. So he's got no news coming out of your camp.' I spreads me hands. 'How's he gunna get the stuff to feed the punters about your prowess?'

'Make it up?' Hawk offers.

'Nah, that won't wash. The sportsmen will catch on that it's all bull. He's got to have a reliable source.'

'You got any ideas?'

'Yes. Maggie!'

'Maggie? That's ridiculous, everyone knows she's my sweetheart!'

'That's right,' says I. 'Here's the shot. Maggie goes to Mr

Sparrow and offers to help him for five quid a week, pay on results end of each week. That way he won't think it's a scam and he'll still think he's in control.'

'And what exactly does Maggie do for him?'

'She starts rumours in the pubs about yer secret training. But she does this most reluctant, only letting a few stories slip out after a few drinks – never meaning to say nothing. Know what I mean?'

'That's fine, but how do we know that's what Mr Sparrow will want her to do? Why should he trust her?'

'She's a whore. He'd trust a whore to see an opportunity and make something out of it. It's how Mr Sparrow thinks hisself.'

'What if he doesn't?'

'Hawk, you got t' learn to think like a confidence man! It's obvious, ain't it? Maggie's on the inside. She knows what's happening in your training. She agrees to spy on us and he tells her what rumours she must spread when she's in the pub.'

'And the punters will trust her?'

'That's right! She's known to be your woman, but she's a woman all the same, what can't never keep a secret.'

'Tommo, are you sure that's how it will work?'

'It'll work better than that! Don'tcha see, Hawk? Maggie will tell Mr Sparrow how things is going real bad for you. You know – you ain't learning nothing, you've took sick, you won't work at training, you've broke two fingers on your right hand, that sort o' thing. That way, we build his confidence that you can't win.'

'And he gets Maggie to spread the *opposite* information! He'll ask her to drop little tidbits about my awesome prowess!' Hawk chuckles. 'And then close to the fight, Mr Sparrow offers very good odds against me winning?'

'You've got the idea!' I says, patting him on the arm. 'The excitement's been building for weeks and Mr Sparrow dangles great odds. All the punter fish, takes them hook, line and sinker, 'cept the Parramatta Irish.'

Hawk laughs. 'Tommo, I hope to hell you're right.' Then he looks concerned. 'But if Maggie agrees to co-operate, there'll be no harm come to her, will there? I mean, if we win the fight?'

'Can't see any likelihood of harm. If we wins it'll cost Mr Sparrow every penny he's ever owned. He'll be ruined and there's plenty waiting to see it happen so's they can put the boot in! Then he'll have no friends to protect him anymore.'

'Well, we must ask Maggie about all this herself,' Hawk says. 'If she's one bit worried, you're not to push her, Tommo!'

'You're on,' I says. But to meself I'm hoping our Mary comes in to save us. This whole ploy's too bloody risky for yours truly! I thinks what Ikey would say in such a situation and I can hear him clear as a bell. 'Never let no wrongs and rights creep into a deal, my dears. Who's wrong, who's right, that ain't the answer to the question. It's who profits at the end of the day!'

Now we's embarked on a scheme what's all about wrongs and rights and the money question only comes after. By Ikey's rules we've got it arse about face. I don't like it. I don't like it one bit.

On Sunday, after Hawk and Maggie has fed the wild brats their roast dinner down the Quay, I gets up from me bed to join them at the chophouse. I has a hangover to end all hangovers. Maggie tries to get me to eat a bowl of Irish stew but the thought of it damn near makes me puke. Hawk eats my tucker as well as his, and we puts the whole plan to Maggie. It don't take her long to agree.

'It'll give us another fifty pounds towards the stake too!' she says. 'All the better coming from his nibs, Mr Sparrow.'

'Maggie, it could be dangerous. He's a rough un underneath,' I warns.

'So's I, Tommo,' grins Maggie, 'and not too far underneath, neither! If Mr Sparrow buys it, we'll use the folk what live here in the Rocks. They's always in the pubs and will warm to the task o' spreading news from a most reliable source.'

'What reliable source will that be?' Hawk teases.

'Me, o' course!' Maggie laughs. 'Maggie the Mouth! What with women being notorious for gossip and me being well acquainted with fighters and their form, I'm a perfect choice!'

'Folks 'round here be most respectful of you, Hawk. They'll be 'appy to spread news about their hero!'

'Maggie, Tommo and I are only supposing how Mr Sparrow will react. Perhaps he'll not trust you after all?'

'He will,' Maggie says. 'He'd expect a whore to change sides for profit, just like he would himself.'

'The punters, will they not suspect Maggie?' Hawk now asks me again.

I sigh. 'You know what yer problem is, Hawk? You always think men is mostly intelligent when the truth is they's mostly stupid. 'Course they knows Maggie's your doxy! That be why they'll question her! She'll pretend to know nothing, naturally, bein' the very picture o' female innocence. But, ah, wait! With her tongue loosened by a shout or two o' Bombay gin, she'll tell 'em just a little. With each drink, she'll tell 'em a little more. Until, by the end o' the evening, the dullest dunderhead in the pub will feel sure he's heard it from the horse's mouth. Men's always willing to think women is stupid and can't keep a secret.'

'Tommo's right!' Maggie says, smiling at us both. 'There ain't a man in the world what don't underestimate the intelligence of a woman. Two o' them's sitting right here in front o' me!'

We laugh. 'Maggie, we never doubted you for a minute,' says I.

'And my trainer, who will he be if not Johnny Sullivan?' Hawk asks.

'That's it!' Maggie exclaims, clapping her hands. 'That's who I'll get to front Mr Sparrow for me! Good old Johnny Sullivan will tell him Maggie Pye requires an urgent and confidential with Mr Sparrer Fart, Esquire.'

'Perfect,' says I. 'As to trainers, there be two of 'em. We've got the services of an Aborigine and a Maori, both top-notch fighters in their time.' Hawk and Maggie look startled at this news, but I continue. 'Just imagine the talk when it comes out that the Black Jew has an Abo and a Maori to train him! It'll set a thousand tongues to wagging.'

Hawk looks bewildered. 'Tongues to wagging, as may be, but will they get my fists to fighting? Who are these two men?'

'Bungarrabbee Jack and Johnny Heki. The Abo were a lightweight and the Maori a heavy. Both copped a lot o' punishment from white men and they's most anxious to help you out against the Bolt, Hawk.'

'And the old Chinaman, have you asked him?'

'He's said he'll train you on the sly on Sunday mornings when his opium customers are all at church with their wives. As long as Tang Wing Hung don't get wind of it, we'll be right.'

'I've seen him,' Maggie chimes in. 'Funny old bugger, looks like he's come straight out o' me nightmares.'

'Can he speak English?' Hawk asks.

'Not much, but his sort of fighting is show more than tell!'

Maggie's got to go. She kisses Hawk goodbye, then me, her lips soft on the side o' my cheek.

I waits for Hawk to ask the final question, the biggest of them all, and now he does.

'We have the one hundred pounds from the Dunn fight,' Hawk says slowly. 'That will do for a down payment but how will we obtain the rest – the other hundred and fifty pounds?'

'If Mr Sparrow pays Maggie a fiver a week to be his informer, that's another fifty or so. She reckons she can also get a loan of another hundred pounds on her property if she throws in the chophouse. With your money, that's all we need!'

'No!' says Hawk, shaking his head. 'Maggie must not get a loan on her property for my sake!'

'Hawk, she loves ya! She *wants* to give you the money.'

'No, Tommo!' Hawk bangs his fist on the table.

'She thinks you'll win. It's only a loan. Besides, she'll be bitter disappointed if you don't let her. She'll think you don't love her!' I jokes.

'It's because I *do* that I don't want her to risk her money!' Hawk shouts at me.

'Oh!' says I, me eyes wide open in surprise, 'loves her, does ya? Loves Maggie Pye?'

Hawk's eyes drop to his hands what rest in his lap, his hands what used to do all his talking. Then he looks up slowly and asks quietly, 'What if I do?'

'Nothin',' I shrugs. 'Me brother loves a whore, that's all. Nothin' wrong with that, I suppose.' I raises an eyebrow. 'After all, our mama were a whore, weren't she!' I don't know whether what I'm saying is good or bad, comforting to him or an insult, it's all mixed up in me head. But I'm shocked more than I can say.

I likes Maggie, it's true, but always in the back o' me mind is the thought that she's a gold digger. If ever she hears of Hawk's prospects at home she'll dig her claws in, she'll suck him dry.

'You hasn't told Maggie about Mary and the brewery, has ya?' I asks.

Hawk looks up at me and I see a tear run down his cheek. 'I haven't told her anything, Tommo. She doesn't know that I love her, nor does she know about Mary's brewery!'

'Hawk, you remembers what Ikey says about whores, don't you? Once a whore, always a whore. There ain't no good ones, no matter what.'

'Ikey!' Hawk yells, banging his fist down on the table. 'Ikey's dead, why must we always kowtow to Ikey Solomon?'

'Because he were a first-class villain what got most things right,' I says. 'Ikey knew more whores than you've had hot dinners!'

Hawk clenches his fists for a moment, then sighs. 'Look at me, Tommo. I'm a nigger. You know what white people think of a big nigger? They think I'm going to rape their wives or harm their children. They think I must be stupid or inferior and when they find out I'm not, they like it even less. Now here's a white woman who loves me for myself!'

'Hawk, if women knew about Mary's money they'd be linin' up for ya.'

'That may be, but it's not enough. I want someone to love *me*, someone I can love back!'

'And so you think only a whore could love you for yourself, is that it?'

'I think this one loves me, Tommo!'

'But you won't let her help you?'

Hawk glares at me. 'Do you know what it took for Maggie to buy her home and the eatery? Most of the brats she grew up with are dead from violence or drink or opium. She's survived, to get her own place, own a small business, make things nice. That was done the hard way, but she did it!'

'The hard way? She done it on her back!'

'How else *could* she do it? Our society doesn't educate Maggie's kind. How many parlour or kitchen maids do you know who own their own rooms and business? None, that's how many! Whoring was Maggie's only way out of the gutter.'

'So why don't she stop, now she's a person o' property? She's still a whore, ain't she?' says I.

Hawk shrugs. 'Maggie has the right to choose how she lives, Tommo. This is a good time for a young and pretty woman like her, providing she doesn't go to her ruin on gin or the poppy. The gold diggings has made many a poor cove rich and generous and many a rich man very indulgent. Maggie's taking advantage while she can, knowing it won't last forever. I understand this of someone who's had her difficulties in life. She wants to give up one day, though.'

'What then? After she's done her share o' gold digging, she'll retire the magpie off her hat and marry a squatter, or even become Mrs Hawk Solomon?'

'I haven't asked her, Tommo. I don't expect she would if I did.'

'Hawk, ask her. Garn, ask her to marry you!'

There's a method in me madness here. If Maggie hears the true story of Hawk and me before he asks her, we'll never know if she's said yes because of the money. If she says yes before she finds out, that be quite another matter.

'I can't,' Hawk says in a low voice.

'Why not? You just said you loves her.'

'It isn't possible right now.'

'Why? Because of me? What's you trying to say, Hawk? You won't marry Maggie because of me?'

Hawk folds his arms across his chest. 'Tommo, when you came back from the wilderness I swore I'd never leave you again, that we'd be together no matter what. If I married, I'd need to settle down and that would mean returning to Tasmania for good. No more adventures, not even a shop in the goldfields. It would break Mary's heart all over again if I were to stay away once I married.'

I look at my brother and think how much I love him. 'You know what your problem is, Hawk?'

'Yes, you just told me. I think men are mostly intelligent when they're mostly not.'

'And you are the stupidest of 'em all! You try to please everyone when it can't be done.'

Hawk smiles. 'Tommo, I *won't* leave you.'

'You're talking rubbish, Hawk! Ask her! Ask Maggie to marry you! If she says she will, then I'll go back to Hobart Town with you both!' I stares at him, furious.

Hawk stretches out his hand to me. 'Tommo, will you?'

I realise what I've just said, and stops short. 'You cunning bastard.' I grin. 'But I'll go back on me own terms, understand? I'll give it one more go, one year in the brewery. But if it's no good with mama, that's it. I'm off, and you stays with Maggie, that's the deal!'

The whole thing's bloody stupid. Hawk's fighting the Irishman to get even with Mr Sparrow for what he believes he's done to me. He thinks this will get the bad bit of Ikey's inheritance out of our lives. But Mr Sparrow didn't put the opium pipe in me mouth and Ikey didn't give me a thirst for brandy. Yet Hawk believes that what's happened to me is evil what started with Ikey and got carried on by Mr Sparrow. If he destroys Mr Sparrow, he thinks that somehow I'll be safe, that the bad stuff in me life will all somehow go away.

I want to tell Hawk here and now that I don't *want* him to fight the Irishman. Mr Sparrow *does* own me, Tang Wing Hung's opium owns me and the poppy is stronger than me love for him, stronger than anything. I'll go back to Mary like I promised, but it won't last, even if I can get opium in Hobart Town. I can't be trusted to do the right thing, not even by meself.

I wants Hawk to marry Maggie Pye so he'll leave me alone. Yours truly never was no good, never will be. But I knows Hawk. Once he gets an idea there ain't no shaking it loose. Deep inside me, I knows Hawk has to fight the Irishman, has to try to destroy Mr Sparrow. It's like a sign that all ain't lost with his twin, that I can yet be saved. If he don't go through with the fight, he'll never be able to live with himself, thinking forever that he's let me down. Why has I got to have such a big, dumb, stupid, wonderful nigger bastard for my twin?

'Tommo,' Hawk says, 'thank you for agreeing to come home. But you are not ready to go back to the brewery and nor am I. If we win the fight, we'll go to the goldfields – you to gamble and me to open a Johnny-all-sorts. Caleb Soul from Tucker & Co. says to be a shopkeeper at the diggings is where all the real gold is. I've always fancied being a shopkeeper. We could do it on our own – not with Mary's money and not with Ikey's. You and me, Tommo!'

'And what about Maggie?'

'Maggie wants to come with us.'

'Oh, *I* see, Hawk the shopkeeper, Tommo the gambler and Maggie the whore!'

'No, Tommo. As I said, Maggie wants to give up the game.'

'She does, eh? What about the chophouse?'

'Flo's family will take care of it. Maggie thinks maybe she could open an eating-house at the diggings. Caleb Soul says miners will pay good money for a simple meal.'

'Christ Jesus, Hawk, how long's it been since Maggie done a day's work o' that sort? She's like me, a creature o' the night. Can she cook?'

'Flo's mother will teach her.'

Hawk must be in love to be thinking such foolish things.

Maggie a respectable woman, cooking dinners! He's a dreamer, that's all, and always will be. 'Hawk, we ain't even got the stake for the fight yet, and then, if we gets it, we still has to win it! You could lose your bloody shirt. Mine too!'

Hawk laughs. 'You're right, Tommo, but we could also make a go of it together, what do you say?'

I am silent a while. 'What do you say, Tommo?' Hawk asks again.

'You forgets one thing,' I says softly. 'Me head.'

Hawk sighs. 'Tommo, there is opium at the diggings. The place is swarming with celestials. The Angel's Kiss will be there for you.'

I don't say nothing. What Hawk doesn't know is that Mr Tang Wing Hung controls all the opium in the New South Wales diggings. If Mr Sparrow has a word to the Chinaman, that's the end o' yours truly. Without me pipe, I'll die. I know it.

'Now,' says Hawk, full of hope, 'let's think how we might find the remainder of the stake money.'

Well, if he wants to go on with it, I've got to help him. I've already thought of how we might get the money ourselves without Mary's help. But it's not certain that we will and, if we do, it will only be enough to make the stake. Hawk will have to win for real.

'Do you think Caleb Soul would let me go with him next time he travels to the goldfields?' I asks.

'Why?' says Hawk.

'I think I could win the difference at cards, playing on the diggings. There's plenty o' patsy-marks waiting to be fleeced there, so they say.'

'Would Mr Sparrow let you go?' Hawk wonders.

I shrug. 'He'll have no choice. Come the time, I'll just scarper and be back soon enough. He needs me at the card table, so it'll be all right.'

'And the poppy for your head?' Hawk asks slowly, like it hurts him, but he knows I've got to have it.

'As you say, there's opium to be found there. Or else I could try and take some with me.'

'Maybe you'd be safer that way,' says Hawk. 'Caleb Soul worked as a chemist when he were in the old country. He'll know how to get opium for medical supplies – he sometimes helps out in the dispensary at the hospital in Macquarie Street.' Hawk thinks for a moment and smiles. 'Tell you what, Tommo. I'll come with you. I feel sure Captain Tucker will allow me the leave.'

'That's it, ain't it?' says I. 'I'll tell Mr Sparrow we's going to the diggings at Lambing Flat to drum up interest in the fight! That be where he wants to hold it anyhow, or somewhere near. The place is full of Irishmen. I'll tell him it's a chance for the fossickers to see ya for themselves. That'll suit his plans. It'll encourage the proddie miners to bet big on you, come the day o' the fight. How long will it take to get there and back?'

'About a week and the same back if we take the two-horse trap. Then you'll need at least three or four days there to get the lay of the land and set up a game. Three weeks in all, near enough,' Hawk replies.

'How soon can we go?'

'There isn't much work at Tucker's this time of year. Captain Tucker might even let me go with Caleb when he makes his next trip. That's only a couple of weeks away.'

I'm worried, o' course, that Mary might come to Sydney while we's away. It's over a week since I've written to her, but there ain't nothing I can say to Hawk. I went to the Hero last night to see if there were a message from her, but so far nothing's come. Perhaps she won't help. If she don't come to Sydney or send the money, Hawk and me must be off to Lambing Flat and get back to Sydney in time for him to train with Bungarrabbee Jack, Johnny Heki and Ho Kwong Choi. We'll need another thirty pounds to pay for them lot, plus premises for training.

Next day, Hawk tells me that Captain Tucker said that he may go with Caleb Soul and he's given me the nod to go as well. As the time draws near and there's still no news from Mary, I decides I has no choice. I has to tell Maggie what's happening.

I've thought a lot about her and Hawk and if he should marry her. I reckon that if she's a gold digger and not truly in love with me twin, it'd be better to flush her out now, rather than be sorry later.

I makes a time mid-afternoon to see Maggie at her chophouse, The Cut Below – there being another chophouse above the Argyle Cut called The Cut Above.

Hawk gets home from work at six o'clock, what gives me enough time to see Maggie and be back in me bed for him to wake me up later. Like me, Maggie don't start work 'til late at night. We meet at three, with the sun still shining bright as a new silver shillin' on the harbour.

'Gawd!' she says, coming into the eatery where I'm already waiting. 'I ain't seen a Tuesday arvo this bright since I were a brat begging ha'pennies in Hyde Park. You hungry, Tommo?'

'Nah, Hawk'll cook me something when he comes home from work. If I don't eat he'll fret. By the way, I don't want him to know we're meeting.'

'Oh?' Maggie says, suspicious.

'I'll explain soon enough.'

Maggie pulls back a chair and sits down opposite me at the small table. 'Yer know something, Tommo, yer brother's too bloody good fer the likes o' you.' She stabs a finger at me. 'Ya knows that, don'tcha? He's too bloody good fer me too – fer the both of us.'

Maggie smiles to herself as though she is remembering. 'The bleedin' Virgin must 'ave smiled on me the day we met at Mr Smith's eating house. Jesus, he were beautiful! Sitting there, diggin' into his grub like it were the first tucker he'd had in a week. Him in rags and split boots and no hose! But bloody beautiful with all them lovely circle marks on his face, like a savage what wants to eat you up! "Crikey! That's for me," I says to meself, "and it'll not cost the nigger a penny. Stay as long as he bloomin' likes!"' Maggie giggles. '"See if I care if he eats me up!" That's what I said.'

I laugh with her. 'You done Hawk the world o' good, Maggie.'

'Yeah, maybe,' says she. 'But it won't last.' Her pretty mouth turns sad and her eyes are downcast. She's a lovely little bird, all right, that I can see.

'Hawk be most fond of you, Maggie. Why d'ya reckon it ain't gunna go on? You ain't planning to leave him, is ya?' I asks, against me own self.

'Nah, I loves him with all me heart, Tommo. But sooner or later I'm gunna do somethin' stupid, chase him away, say somethin' he can't forgive.' She looks at me fit to break my heart. 'We's the same, Tommo, you and me. Hawk ain't like us, that's all. What's bad in us ain't in him. Two of a kind, whores the both of us.'

I nod. Suddenly a picture of Maggie in her bed chamber comes into me mind, and I wonders what her punters see. Then I put it quickly to the back of me mind. She's Hawk's woman, I remind meself. I clear me throat. 'Hawk don't give up easy, Maggie. He's stuck with me come what may. If you do something to hurt him, he's got a lot o' forgiveness in his heart. I should know!'

She sniffs. 'That's different, you're his twin.' For a moment I think she's gunna cry and then what'll I do? 'Anyways he's still a man,' she says, smiling brightly now, her eyes wet. 'Sure you don't want ter eat somethin'? Tea? Nice cuppa tea?' She touches me arm. 'Do you the world. Flo, bring us a nice cuppa, will ya, darlin'?' she calls out loud. 'A pot, two cups!' Then she turns to look at me. 'So, why's you robbin' me of me well-earned sleep, if I might ask? Why's we here without Hawk knowin'?'

'Maggie, have you seen Mr Sparrow yet?'

'T'morrer. Johnny's set it up, t'morrer, six o'clock at his place.'

'Do you think he'll fall for it?'

'Sure, why not? I'm a whore, ain't I?'

'Maggie, what does you really think Hawk's chances are of beating the Bolt?'

Maggie looks at me suspicious. 'What's you saying, Tommo?'

'I mean, you know about prize-fighters and their form. Do you think me brother can take the Bolt?'

Maggie looks at me strangely. 'Tommo, what's this nonsense?'

'Hawk's gunna take a fair walloping. He's gunna be thrashed!'

It's like I've smacked her gob with the back o' me hand. 'No, he ain't! No, he bloody well ain't! Jesus, what's you gettin' at, Tommo?'

I reaches over and grabs her by the arm. 'It's true, Maggie, the Irishman's gunna be too good for Hawk.'

'No! No!' Maggie shakes her head. 'You're wrong, Tommo. Look what Hawk done to Ben Dunn!'

'Maggie, the Irishman could take on Ben Dunn with one hand tied behind his back. Why do you think he's come out here? Let me tell ya, he's come out here to take up a collection for his old age. There ain't a heavy in the colonies what can match him blow for blow, even go five rounds if he's serious!'

'Bull!' Maggie shouts.

Flo brings the tea and hurries away, leaving a plate o' scones and jam.

'Maggie,' I urges, 'you says you loves Hawk. Do you want to see him killed? Be sensible. You know him – he'll keep fighting 'til he's mincemeat!'

Maggie's hands are shaking as she pours the tea. 'Tommo, I've been around the fights a good while, ever since I was a brat. First cove what screwed me when I were ten years old were a fighter – only a featherweight, thank Gawd! I know form when I sees it. Hawk be a champion. Maybe the world champion. The blow what knocked out Ben Dunn lifted him three foot into the flamin' air!'

'Maggie, I know, I saw it. In New Zealand he killed a Maori in a card game with just such a blow.'

'Well then, what's this talk o' him being made mincemeat?'

'Hawk were angry then, just like he were angry with what Ben Dunn done to you. When Hawk's angry 'cause he thinks something's unfair or evil, he can't be stopped, the devil hisself couldn't do it. But that ain't the case here. Hawk ain't angry at the Irishman, he's got no reason to hurt *him*.'

'Yes he has – Mr Sparrow, he's reason enough!'

'It ain't the same thing. Hawk won't see that beating the livin' daylights out o' the Bolt be the same as beating Mr Sparrow. He'll want t' win, sure enough. But without his terrible anger, he's got no chance to beat him! Hawk is a gentle soul at heart. He ain't naturally mean, and he ain't got the skills in the ring. Put together, that's a recipe for disaster.'

'He can learn to be mean,' Maggie says stubbornly. But her eyes show she sees some sense in what I've just said. 'Johnny Sullivan could teach him.'

'Johnny Sullivan be in cahoots with Mr Sparrow and Fat Fred. He can't train Hawk, not for a fair fight anyhow, you know that.'

'He's me mate, and I know him to be his own man. He'd listen to me I know, he'd change sides,' Maggie protests.

'He's a poppy head. I've seen him at Tang Wing Hung's. He'd be in the pay o' Fat Fred, and that's the same as being owned by Mr Sparrow.'

'Tommo, what's you saying? Are we gunna stop Hawk fighting the Bolt? Throw up the sponge before we even gets in the ring, forget the sting?'

'Nah, nothin' like that.'

'What then?'

'We got to *fix* the fight, get the Irishman to lay down.'

Maggie bursts into laughter. 'And how's you gunna do that? Jesus, Tommo!'

And that's when I tells her the lot, all that Hawk's asked me not to. I tells her about Mary and us, and about the brewery. And I tells her about me idea for Mary to give us the money to bribe the

Irishman. Maggie listens, never taking her eyes off me own and then, to me surprise, she begins to blub softly.

'What's the matter?' I asks.

'I told yiz, didn't I,' she sobs. 'I, I . . . thought it'd be something wrong what *I'd* do, but it ain't me, it's him!'

'What d'ya mean, Maggie?' I says, confused. 'Nothing's wrong with Hawk!'

She sniffs, trying hard to stem the tears, knuckling them away from her eyes. 'Yes there is! He's *rich*, the bastard! That changes everything!' She gulps, then hiccups. 'Oh shit, shit, shit!' she howls.

'Oh, Maggie . . .' I puts me hand on her arm and tries to comfort her but I never was too good at that sort o' thing, even with me poor Makareta. Now I can see Maggie ain't no gold digger, she loves Hawk any which way. I can't tell her Hawk loves her if he ain't told her hisself – it ain't my place to tell her. But to me surprise I wants to. I sit helpless 'til eventually she calms down.

'Gawd, I must look bloody awful,' she says, blowing her nose. 'So what do you want me to do now, Tommo? Why did ya come here? Does I still see Mr Sparrow?'

'Nothing changes with Mr Sparrow. We've still got to get the punters betting on Hawk and I can't be sure Mary's gunna come good with the money. Hawk and me is going to Lambing Flat so's I can try to win the money at cards.'

'You think you can win what you needs to bribe the Irishman at the gold diggings?' She looks at me astonished.

'No, 'course not. If I'm real lucky, with a bit o' relocation, I may win the the rest of the stake and training money for Johnny Heki and Bungarrabbee Jack.'

'Poppy money, more like,' Maggie snaps. 'Ya mean Hawk'll have to fight straight if yer mama don't come good?'

I shrug. 'Well, yes, that's about it.'

Maggie smiles. 'Well, you forgot me one hundred pounds what I'd put in from the loan on this dump.'

I swallows hard. 'Maggie, Hawk won't take it from ya.'

'Ha! See, I told yiz! Rich man don't want to owe no favours to a whore, that's how it is!'

'Maggie, that ain't fair!' I protest. 'That ain't it at all. Hawk knows he might lose!'

Maggie shrugs. 'So? I been broke before, but I ain't never loved someone like I loves him.'

I've got no answer to this one, so I try to change the subject. 'Maggie, will you meet Mary? Look after her if she comes to Sydney when we're away?' I asks.

Maggie's eyes grow large. 'She's coming here? Oh, Jesus no!' She brings both her palms up to cover her mouth. 'I couldn't!' She shakes her head. 'Her, a rich lady, finding out her nice boy has been beddin' a whore what says she loves him! Ooh, can't ya just see it! Her dumpin' a bucket o' shit over me! No, Tommo! Anything else, not that!'

'Maggie, please, Mary ain't like that at all! If you love Hawk, you'll do it,' I begs.

Maggie begins to cry. 'Damn ya, Tommo!' she howls. 'He don't need his mama's money. Hawk could win on his own, I know it!'

Chapter Twenty

HAWK

New South Wales
June 1861

Tommo and I are on the road to Lambing Flat. We have been most fortunate, for we have been given permission by Captain Tucker to accompany Caleb Soul in the Tucker & Co. trap to the goldfields. With the right introductions from Caleb, who knows everyone of importance in the diggings, Tommo will be able to arrange a card game quickly. Our hope is to be back in Sydney in no more than three weeks.

Once I had told him about Tommo's terrible pains from his head wound, Caleb Soul kindly procured opium for my brother to take on our journey. I know that he will not talk to anyone of Tommo's addiction. I also hope Caleb will introduce Tommo to some of the big gamblers here and I do not want his reputation tarnished, so I ask Tommo to employ no relocation in his card games.

Tommo is, of course, most indignant that I would even think that he might use such tactics when playing with a bunch of miners.

'Tommo,' I warn, 'there are men here from all around the world. If there are not one or two cardsharps among them, I would be tremendously surprised.'

'And if there is, you still want me to play kosher?'

'If they're not on the straight then you must make up your own mind. It's just that I do not wish Caleb's good name hurt.'

Caleb Soul is of a sanguine disposition, a man who is most

402

interested in sports. He doesn't know yet that I intend to challenge the Irish champion – unless the rumours already circulating in the Rocks have reached his ears. However, I shall tell him of my intentions further down the road and thus explain why we need introductions to a card game where the betting is high enough to earn us some of the stake money.

I must confess, I am full of dreams about the diggings, though I have no desire to search for gold. It seems to me that the true rewards are to be obtained by supplying the men with their needs. If we should win the fight against the Irishman, I have in mind to open a Johnny-all-sorts store, with Maggie and Tommo alongside me. How happy we should be!

Winning the fight is essential to my dreams for the future, although I do not like my chances against the Irishman. But, I tell myself, for all of our sakes, I must win. If Ho Kwong Choi can teach me the Oriental fighting art and if I can absorb sufficient of my opponent's blows long enough to keep me in the fight, I hope that my endurance will see me through. I need to learn enough skills to soften or side-step some of the Irishman's harder blows, until he tires and I can get a decent crack at him.

I am well aware that I won over Ben Dunn because he had already gone five rounds with the Welshman, while I came fresh to the fray. He is demanding a return bout so that he may regain his title. As he puts it, 'I will break every bone in the nigger's overgrown carcass!' For my part, I believe that the title belongs rightly to him and have said so publicly. But he demands an opportunity to earn both his title and his revenge honestly, and will not hear of taking the champion's belt. This I have returned to its makers, J.J. Cohen of George Street, asking them not to engrave my name upon it, but to keep it until Ben Dunn chooses to claim it.

I know that the Bolt, who is vastly more experienced than both Dunn and I, will come well rested to the ring. With the encouragement of the Parramatta Irish ringing in his ears, he will be keen to make a fool of me.

Tommo reports that the Bolt drinks deeply of Irish whiskey, each dram chased down with a pint of beer. He spends most of his nights at cards and thereafter with various of the women procured for him by Mr Sparrow. He has a drinking toast which he often recites to the amusement of all.

Your doctors may boast of their lotions
And ladies may talk of their tea,
But I envy them none of their potions –
It's a pint of best Irish for me.

A doctor may sneer if he pleases,
But the recipe for keeping me frisky
Is the physic that cures all diseases
A bottle of good Irish whiskey.

So to Colleen, Bridget and Mandy,
You may prefer brandy or gin,
But to make a good Irishman randy –
Pour a pint of good whiskey in him!

Maggie keeps a close eye on all the Bolt's doings at the same time as she prepares to talk up mine. Mr Sparrow has accepted her as his informer and she is already busy in the pubs laying the groundwork for tales of my prowess. I fear she herself may even begin to believe the outrageous stories she concocts in bed of a Sunday.

Her favourite is the story of my Zulu ancestry. It seems I am the true grandson of one of the greatest fighting generals of Africa, the mighty warrior Dingane – or so the legend goes! Now that I have decided on prize-fighting, to hear Maggie tell it, my natural instincts have come to the fore, and those who would enter the ring to spar with me should tremble in their boots. I can fight two at a time and such is my speed and ferocity that they seldom last two minutes before crashing to the ground, spitting out teeth as they fall.

In truth, I cannot hope to learn even the most basic rules of fist-fighting in the few months available to me. How will I defend myself against an opponent who is a wily old campaigner, seasoned in every dirty trick of the trade? While I listen with interest to news of the Bolt's slapdash training, I know also that he has more than sixty bouts against his name, some of them against the best prize-fighters in the British Isles and Ireland. Even if he is past his prime, for a purse of five hundred pounds he will be sure to give himself a good margin of safety when he enters the ring.

Stamina will be my only chance of success. My legs are often enough described as tree trunks. I hope they will see me through as many rounds as are needed. My strength and endurance must help me to survive in the boxing ring long enough to win.

With this in mind I have developed my own training schedule, quite apart from what I shall be taught by Bungarrabbee Jack and Johnny Heki when I return to Sydney. At Tucker & Co., much of the liquor is stored in a great loft and pulled up by pulley, with fifty gallon barrels of rum and whisky being hoisted by three average-sized men on the rope. Each afternoon, I lever the large casks up to the loft, working the pulley singlehanded, to strengthen my arms. Then I run up the inside stairs to this same loft, carrying two ten-gallon firkins of port each time, one on either shoulder. Every day I spend longer at these exercises.

Captain Tucker knows that I plan to fight the Irishman and has announced himself my keen supporter. He has even employed the services of a physician, Doctor Nathaniel Postlethwaite, to check my weekly progress and allows me to train secretly in the loft.

The road to Bowral and beyond, on which we now travel, is in very poor repair. Since the discovery of gold it has seen much more traffic than was ever intended by its original builders. We pass hundreds of men who are making the journey on foot. Most carry only a swag, although some are equipped with a pick and shovel as well. Moreover, I count fifty-seven drays and carts before we reach Mittagong. These are heavily laden with tents, sluicing rockers, mining tools, bags of flour and sugar, large tins of tea and all sorts of stores and utensils. The drays contain as many as eight men and there are seldom fewer than four aboard a cart. Most men bear firearms, having read in the newspapers that bushrangers abound in these regions. With their equipment, the men of each dray may set up a camp, from where they hope to earn an easy fortune from the generous earth.

Some of these gold getters look eager and impatient to arrive while others are thoughtful, or wear a dogged, abstracted air. A few men smile sheepishly as we pass, as if half-ashamed of their errand. These men tend to be of the syndicates with cash behind them. Their equipment is new, and their firearms look unused, the butts glossy with varnish. Their horses too are stout, and wear harnesses fresh from the saddler's hands. But as Caleb Soul observes, these smartly turned out men are no more likely to find luck than the humblest man they pass on foot.

Some of those on foot are still in their city clothes. They are clearly clerks and shop assistants, their coats over their arms and their once-white shirts grimy with the dust and dirt of the open road. It's as if in the middle of adding a column of figures, or while selling a customer an ounce of shag tobacco or a set of suspenders, they have cast aside the task at hand and set off to seek their fortunes down the Parramatta Road.

Others are working men, wearing trousers tied with a lace below the knee. They already seem hardened to the pick. No doubt they too dream of finding enough gold never to have to return to their previous station in life.

Several push wheelbarrows loaded with all their possessions and such miner's tools as they can afford. Those who have already adopted the clothes of the miner wear gay-coloured woollen shirts and comforters and Californian sombreros of every hue and shape.

All these men have one thing in common. In every head resides a dream of riches, of castles in the air with flags flying from the turrets. Alas, most will return to their homes poorer than when they left, to find their wives bitter and their children starving. All this I'm told by Caleb Soul, who has observed every aspect of life on the goldfields and has not yet been tempted to give up his job at Tucker & Co. for it.

In fact, as he reveals to us, Caleb has quite a different ambition. He hopes one day to return to the art of pills and potions, to work as a pharmacist as he was trained to do. 'Liquor makes 'em sick and my pills and potions will make 'em well again!' He'll work at selling grog to the goldfields until he has sufficient to start in the chemist business. He laughs. 'It's the same business but at different ends, so to speak!'

Caleb now suggests, though perhaps only half seriously, that we should both come in with him in the chemist business, as he knows a great deal about medicines and selling, but very little of keeping books. 'Hawk, you will be the bookkeeper. I hear naught but good things about your penmanship and accuracy. Captain Tucker says your ledgers are a veritable work of art.'

'And me?' jokes Tommo. 'What a partner I would make! Good for nothing but cards. I'm most grateful you got the poppy paste for me, Caleb, but that's about all I ever wants to know about chemicals.'

It seems as good an opportunity as any, and so I tell our friend of my decision to turn prize-fighter and the real reason for our journey. Caleb greets my announcement with enthusiasm, and my fight becomes the focus of many a discussion.

We move southwest on the road to Lambing Flat along with a vast troop of men. There are almost as many men returning from the diggings as there are going to them. Their clothes are tattered and they appear half-starved. They are sullen and withdrawn and seldom respond to our greetings. Occasionally one will shake his head and spit at the ground as he passes those headed for the diggings. Mostly they stumble on unseeing, too disillusioned to care about the many fools who follow in their footsteps. Still, I notice that not one of our gold-seeking compatriots turns back at the dismal sight of these broken men.

After six and a half days on the road, we are well past Goulburn and have entered gold country. We hope to arrive at Lambing Flat shortly past noon. In the morning, we travelled through forested countryside, but it is now as if we have taken a journey to the moon. Dirt mounds and holes abound and not a single tree can be seen. What was once a wilderness of green and living stems has been chopped down to become hoists, crude shaft-heads, sluices, cradles, cabins, rough fences – dry sticks doing service to man's greed for gold. It rained last night and the dust has settled which, from all accounts, is something to be most thankful for. I am amazed to discover that a town, albeit constructed mostly of shanties of canvas, has risen so quickly on what must have been a wild and sylvan landscape not so long ago.

There must be ten thousand tents here, some with crude huts adjoined to them, most with bark chimneys of every sort sticking out from the canvas. Some even have small yards with fences and chicken coops, while others are not much more than bark and flour bag humpies. A few shanties have walls of no more than three feet, made from stones piled up together with a pole at each corner, and a canvas roof. We pass a wattle and daub cottage with a single glass window set somewhat askew in the wall, the most solid residence to be seen.

For every tent or shelter, there appears to be a hundred holes in the ground. If you were to look down from one of the rolling hills which frame the valley, and which themselves are almost as pocked, punctured and scraped raw as the flat ground below, it might seem as though some ragged alien army is camped here.

The town itself is chock-a-block with miners in woollen shirts and Californian sombreros, these items of headwear being almost as numerous as the ubiquitous cabbage-tree hat. Visitors and newcomers are easily recognised, dressed as they are in their grey or black city clothes, looking as drab as a convocation of curates.

The main street – if the largest of Lambing Flat's bumpy thoroughfares may be so called – was churned to mud early in the day. Now the noon sun has baked it dry, and it is so rutted and crowded that we cannot proceed any further. Caleb Soul pulls up beside a large tent.

'We'll stay around here,' he announces. 'Find a spot to pitch our tent nearby. The tucker here is good and the helpings plentiful. It's only mutton and damper mostly, Hawk, but I know you'll fancy their bread pudding with plenty o' plump raisins. They also make an Afghani curry which is delicious taken with rice.'

'How do we reach the centre of town?' Tommo asks.

'Not sure there is such a place, lad,' Caleb Soul laughs. Then, understanding why Tommo asks, he adds, 'Tommo, you must allow me to find out about a card game for you. Don't do it yourself, or it will be immediately concluded that you are a cardsharp. A mining camp may look like mayhem, but it has its own rough kind of order that must be observed.'

Tommo has grown to respect Caleb Soul during the course of the journey and nods at this advice.

'Why don't you accompany me on my rounds tomorrow and get the feel of life at the diggings?' Caleb suggests.

He takes out his hunter watch and clicks it open. 'I will meet you back here for dinner at six o'clock. In the meantime, perhaps you lads could pitch the tent and tether the horses. I'll arrange for hay to be brought, as there's no green grass anywhere about! It will be a little cramped for the three of us in the tent, but we shall manage well enough if you can bear my snoring.'

He moves away, then turns back to us. 'Oh, mind you don't pay more than two shillings a night rent to the cove on whose claim we stay. Explain to him why we're here or he'll become suspicious.' He grins. 'Everyone in the diggings is suspicious of everyone else, and doubly suspicious of a couple of faces they don't readily recognise.'

'Such as a seven foot nigger and a little dandy?' I ask.

Caleb Soul laughs uproariously on his way as Tommo punches me hard in the stomach.

We soon find a cove nearby who agrees we may put up our tent on his claim and after some argument agrees to a rent of three shillings. I am about to pay him when Tommo stops me.

'Wait on,' he says to the man. 'Show us your claim licence, then.'

'What licence would that be?' replies the man cockily.

Tommo points to a board nailed to a small post which has a figure written upon it. 'The licence what shows that number.'

'Oh,' he says, '*that* licence. Me mate what's working another claim has it in his pocket. I'll show it to you at sunset.'

'Right, I see,' retorts Tommo. 'That must be the mate what struck it rich in the claim what he staked out the other side of sunset? Garn, piss orf, will ya!'

The man grins. 'It were worth a try. Couldn't lend me a shilling, could ya?'

'Bugger off,' says Tommo, 'before me brother belts ya one.'

So we wander on until we come across a woman outside a bark shanty. She's feeding a cat scraps from a tin plate and it's questionable who looks mangier, the cat or the woman. For two shillings she agrees we may pitch our tent and, for another, we may tether the horses to a stump on her claim. She goes in to fetch her claim licence and asks upon her return if we'd like a cup of tea. 'It's bush tea but not too bad if you closes your eyes and holds yer nose!'

We laugh but refuse politely. Our bones ache from sitting too long in the trap and we are both eager to stretch our legs and look around. 'There'll be a cuppa here when you gets back, then,' she says. 'No sugar though, run out weeks ago.'

We set off and find what we take to be the centre of the town, though as Caleb has said it's hard to think of it as such. It's a hodge-podge of shacks and holes and people – many more people than I had ever supposed.

Caleb Soul has told us that Lambing Flat, known to all as the poor man's diggings, is the most profitable market for Tucker & Co. outside of Sydney. As he explained, almost every man who is prepared to work hard and who owns a pick and shovel can make a wage here and some, occasionally, make much more. 'In the grog business,' he observed, 'a lot of men with a little money in their pockets is much more advantageous than a few men with a lot. There are over fifteen thousand souls in this district, nearly all of 'em drinkers.'

Caleb does not have a very high opinion of the folks to be found here. He says Lambing Flat contains the human dregs from all the other diggings where fossicking for gold is more hazardous. Here, the easiest gold can be found at three feet or less, and the very hardest from sixty to eighty feet. Every soul in these diggings can make a go of his claim if he is willing to put in a good day's work.

Unfortunately, many are not prepared to make the effort. While the Chinaman is not afraid to bend his back and does not expect to come by his wealth easily, his European counterpart is not so fond of small earnings and hard work in the hot sun. Every day he looks to strike it big and will take up a new claim with great expectations. He works it for a few weeks, grows impatient at the small pickings and abandons the site for what he believes is a more propitious one elsewhere – whereupon the Chinaman, who seldom starts a claim from scratch, moves in to rework the ground the European has abandoned. When the European is again disappointed and returns to his old quarters, he finds the Chinaman has worked it at a nice profit to himself, and so he demands it back!

Their hard work has made the Chinese the subject of the white man's resentment and hatred. The *Miner's Gazette* scurrilously describes them as 'filthy, immoral, treacherous and quarrelsome, heathen celestials, who waste water, steal gold, ruin good digging ground, spread leprosy, and practise secret vices on the bodies of white women and white boys.' It is firmly believed by many that the Chinese rape white women and children at every turn, without an ounce of evidence to support it – although some men will swear blind they've seen them.

Caleb Soul takes umbrage at this. 'It is often enough said that the Chinese are lesser beings than the white folk, but I count them a better breed than most of the European rabble at Lambing Flat. This particular diggings has the worst class of men of any goldfield I've seen. It's crawling with adventurers of the lowest type,' he confided to us before we arrived.

'I had hoped for the worst class of man with a pocketful of

gold to lose at the card table,' Tommo had replied. 'Poor men with a little to spend may be good for your trade, Caleb, but for mine they be a disaster!'

Caleb Soul laughed at this. 'There are sufficient here who've struck it rich to fill your pockets ten times over, lad. Some of these men did not once have five pounds, and are now worth thousands. Poor men who grow rich overnight are careless with their money.'

At my suggestion, Tommo and I go into one of the general stores, to see what the trading is like here. The shop we enter is a tent like any other, but a bit larger and squarer, with a flag flying from the tent pole to denote that it is a shopkeeper's establishment.

I am unprepared for the scene that meets us within. Laid out before us is a collection of every known object used by man in the course of living. How such an accumulation of contradictory merchandise may be gathered in a lifetime defies the imagination. Yet the storekeeper has obviously managed to bring them all together here, to one of the remotest regions of New South Wales, from all corners of the globe. From sugar candy to potted anchovies, East India pickles to bottles of Bass's pale English ale, slippers to stays, babies' booties to picks and shovels, every form of mining equipment, household essential, foodstuff and frippery is here. A pair of herrings hangs over a bag of sugar. Nearby lie raisins, dried sausages, saddles, harnesses, ribbons and bonnets. Cheeses in the round and loaves of bread are stacked on the floor next to bars of yellow soap. Tins of every conceivable type of vegetable, fish and meat, and even a crate of champagne, line one side of the tent. All this I see in my first casual observation. A closer inspection would reveal a thousand more of these et ceteras, I'm sure.

The shop is crowded with men swearing and guffawing, children bawling and squealing, and women wagging their tongues – their shrill voices rising above the buzz. Banter, blubbing, brouhaha, laughter and earnest talk fill the tent.

In one corner stands the storekeeper. He seems undismayed by the cacophony around him and is buying gold from a miner, no doubt using every trick known to cheat a free fraction of an ounce from the precious hoard for himself. The storekeeper has put a priority on dealing with the miner and ignores the crowd waiting to be served. Not wishing to buy anything, we take our leave.

Tommo and I visit several of these stores in the course of the afternoon. They all have a great variety of merchandise, much of which I would never have thought necessary at a gold diggings. One shop has a tailor's dummy on which is displayed a dress purported to replicate Queen Victoria's wedding gown. It is of a cream-coloured taffeta silk and glorious to behold, with many pearls stitched to it, though I don't suppose these are real as in the original. It is a trifle dusty and soiled in places where curious fingers have plucked at the material, but still it wears a price of fifty pounds. A notice is pinned to the frock.

HRH Prince Albert's wedding clothes
are also available upon enquiry.
Alterations made within the week.

I am much bemused by all I observe and wonder how as shopowner I should ever know what to order beyond those things normal to every store. I purchase a pound of tea and the same of sugar for our new landlady and am shocked at the price! I perceive at once how a shopkeeper's fortune is so readily made. The profit is upwards of four hundred per cent on each item.

Tommo and I return to our landlady's shack and I give her the tea and sugar. She fumbles at the hem of her petticoat to find a small knot. 'I must return your rent, then,' she says. We refuse as gently as we can, whereupon she brings her soiled pinny to her eyes and, sobbing, rushes into her miserable little shack.

We walk down to the creek and have a wash. The water is muddy and cold. What appears to have once been a wide river is now the merest trickle – the miners have used up the water for sluicing in their long toms, cradles and panning dishes.

Tommo points to several tree stumps rooted out and tossed upon the scarred banks. 'That's wattle,' he observes. 'It would have looked a treat flowerin' here once. Now it's nothing but mud and gravel.'

As the sun sets, it grows cold and I realise I am famished. I have not eaten anything other than two cold chops and a pannikin of tea at dawn. My twin, however, shows no sign of hunger. He sips from a black bottle he carries with him, one of several I have bought for him from Tucker & Co. Tommo has grown fidgety and his eyes take on a vacant look I have come to know when he craves opium. On the road to Lambing Flat, Tommo would simply take himself away from our camp and return in an hour or so. Now he will probably go quietly to the tent and light his little lamp, seeking salvation from his poppy pipe. When I suggest it is time for dinner he shows no interest.

'Bring me something,' he says absently.

'Will you be in the tent?' I ask but he is already walking away from me. 'I'll see you in an hour, then!' I shout, and he lifts his arm to acknowledge he's heard me. As he goes he rubs the tops of his arms as though his skin has a terrible itch upon it. His head is bowed and he has acquired a sort of shuffle, and looks weary of life.

There is a lump in my throat as I watch him depart. He is so small that his shoulder can snuggle under my armpit and so fragile in appearance that it seems as if he might blow away. In the past few nights, I have become aware as never before that Tommo cannot live without the dreaded Chinese drug.

I ache with the pain of knowing this, and my eyes blur at the sadness in him. I would give anything that my brother might be cured. I resolve again to do whatever it might take to win against the Irishman so that I can destroy Mr Sparrow and his vile greed. Surely then Tommo will escape the grasp of this evil addiction. Poor Tommo, I love him so very much and yet can do so little to help him. The more I try the more I seem to fail.

I think of Maggie, my heart's delight, who makes me laugh and who loves me. How very much I would like to take the magpie from its nest and place a bridal veil in its place. I sniff back my tears and chuckle at this thought – the white lace of purity and chastity for my Maggie Pye! It seems ridiculous, yet there is a purity and openness in her loving heart which I have not observed in anyone else. It is as though, having faced the worst in life, she has come through the flames and the dross has been burnt off, leaving only the pure gold remaining. But sometimes I think I must be deluding myself – that whatever virtue I ascribe to her, Maggie is still a whore. '*And once a whore, my dears? Always a whore.*' I beat back Ikey's words from my memory.

I love Maggie and wish to be with her all the days of my life. But not at a cost to Tommo. I shall never leave Tommo as long as he needs me. For the seven years he was lost in the wilderness, even Mary believed him dead. But never I. Every day at the moment of waking, I could feel him alive, the pulse of him within me. I could hear him breathing in the silence of my own breath and, when feeling my heart beat under my palm, I could feel two beats for every one – two hearts, his and mine.

It's just gone six when I reach the large tent where Caleb left us this afternoon. My friend is waiting for me in a long line of men. He indicates for me to join him, turning to those in the queue who grumble. 'He's the heavyweight champion of the colony. Would any of you lads care to have a go? Anyone game?' He points to one of the complainants. 'You, sir?'

The crowd laughs, and a chorus of voices bids me keep my place, though I worry it is not fair. Some wag shouts, 'Will he pay double for the size o' the supper he eats, 'cause he ain't gettin' mine!'

'What's yer name, then?' someone else asks. 'Yer fighting name?'

I think for a moment. Hawk Solomon does not sound too exotic to the ear. 'Black Hawk,' I say on impulse, remembering my Maori name.

Caleb Soul looks delighted. 'Black Hawk, heavyweight champion of the colony!' he shouts so all may hear.

This is repeated by several of the men around me, and passed up and down the line. 'Who's you fighting next?' someone asks.

'The Lightning Bolt! The Irish and English heavyweight champion!' Caleb Soul answers for me again.

'Jaysus!' a voice nearby exclaims. 'You be the blighter what knocked Ben Dunn out the ring. Right over the bleedin' ropes into the lap of a whore! I read it in the *Gazette*.'

'Not quite,' I reply, surprised at how quickly the story has spread and grown. 'I was lucky to hit him at all.'

'Yes, with a sledgehammer!' Caleb Soul laughs and holds up my arm. 'Take off your jacket. Make a fist now, champ!'

I feel most foolish, but realise it is all for the good of the coming fight, so I remove my coat.

'Roll up your sleeve, let the lads see,' Caleb instructs.

I think to refuse but he's a decent sort and means well. I pull up my sleeve and clench my fist, bending my arm at the elbow. 'Holy Jeremiah!' someone shouts and all around us laugh and exclaim.

I am most relieved when at this moment a man comes to the

entrance of the tent holding a large metal triangle which he beats with a bar. 'Tucker's up!' he shouts over the clanging. 'Pay at the door! Them what's weekly, show yer grub cards!'

'That was a good start, lad,' Caleb says as we move forward. 'News of your arrival will be all over the diggings by morning. Shouldn't be too hard to get a card game going for Tommo!' He looks concerned. 'He is coming to eat, ain't he?'

'I'll take him something, for his appetite is poor.'

'He should eat more,' Caleb worries. He has said the same thing to Tommo himself, every night on the road, with Tommo always replying with a little poem of his own.

> *I eats like a sparrow*
> *And drinks like a fish,*
> *Brandy's me water,*
> *Thin air's me tasty dish!*

Inside the tent I take my mind off my little brother, knowing that worrying will achieve nothing. Caleb points out two of the gold commissioners among those around us as well as several bankers, squatters and swells who have come to see the rush. The room is mostly occupied by diggers, sweat-stained and dirty. Shopkeepers, bullies and loafers are there too. The diggings is a great leveller of men and all mix happily enough together.

The kitchen is on the other side of a wall of logs. It is built like a cabin, with a porthole set at waist height through which the various comestibles are pushed. The cooks within scream out to the waiters as each plate comes through – 'Irish stew!' 'Liver and bacon!' 'Roast mutton!' This mingles with the clatter of plates, the rattle of knives and forks, and the sounds of hungry men demanding to be served. All over the tent plates are held aloft and voices are raised to the waiters requesting a return, which Caleb explains is a second helping.

I eat everything that is placed before me, leaving nothing for Tommo. As soon as my plate is wiped clean, I too hold it up and yell for roast mutton, this being the easiest food to carry away with me. Just as the waiter places my second helping down, a fellow at the next table takes the plate.

'Oi, that's not yours!' says the waiter.

'Is now!' retorts the cove.

'It is not,' the waiter reiterates and goes to grab it back. The cove smashes him in the face and down he goes. Two miners next to the plate-snatcher also jump up and kick at the waiter, one hitting him in the head. Another ruffian leaps from the next table and lashes out at the fallen man's ribs. Several more rush to the fray.

I rise from my seat. 'Stop it!' I yell, pulling some of the ruffians away, but more come, kicking and stamping on the poor wretch with evil satisfaction. The man on the floor is now in a state of insensibility, his features battered beyond recognition. Another heavy boot lands toe-first into his face and several teeth depart from his jaw.

I am still trying to pull people away, and now grow furious. With a roar, I land my fist into one villain's face and then again into a second man. Both drop to the ground but are immediately replaced by others. I hit them too. Five more men come running. I grab the first by his belt and neck and, lifting him above my head, throw him at the other four, sending them all sprawling. In the process, several tables and the people seated at them go flying.

It is all over and a deathly quiet falls over the room as I pick up the little waiter and carry him in my arms to the porthole. The other diners gasp as they see what has been done to him. He is taken by hands I cannot see and I walk back to Caleb Soul, stepping over the five ruffians who are either unconscious or playing possum.

'I think we should leave, don't you?' I say, panting slightly from the fight.

We turn to walk out when, almost as one, the men in the tent stand and begin to clap.

'Good on ya!' someone shouts.

'Well done, lad!' yells another.

'Hooray!'

A small door set into the log wall opens. 'Mr Black Hawk! Mr Black Hawk!' It is the chef, whom Caleb has told me is also the proprietor. He is hurrying towards us from the kitchen.

'Here's trouble,' I mutter to Caleb, thinking the man must want me to pay for the broken crockery.

But as the owner comes up, I see he is carrying a plate piled high with mutton and potatoes. 'You've not had your returns!' He proffers the plate. 'Here, lad, eat up!'

416

'I think we'd best leave, Felix,' Caleb Soul says. 'We've caused enough trouble for one night.'

'Trouble? No trouble at all, mate! I've been hoping something might happen to them bunch of bully-boys.'

'Is the waiter all right?' I ask.

'Not good, lad, not good at all. But we've sent a boy for Doctor Bullmore. Let's hope he ain't too drunk to attend.' Felix holds the plate of food out for me to take. 'Bring back the plate tomorrow, will ya, lad. You're welcome to come back anytime. Your grub's on the house.'

We walk out into the night. It is near freezing cold, with a full moon, fuzzy at the edges. I think there'll be a heavy frost in the morning, though the stars are amazingly bright. I wonder at the grandness of nature and the depravity of mankind. Why is it we reduce everything to greed and hate and try to settle all with our fists?

Caleb Soul chuckles quietly beside me.

'What's the joke?' I ask.

'By Jesus, if the mob didn't know before, they'll certainly know Black Hawk is in town by breakfast tomorrow! If we'd paid those ruffians, they couldn't have done any better for us.'

When we get to our tent, I can see no light from inside and I wonder if Tommo is asleep. But he is not there and I can only think he has gone some place else to smoke his opium.

The landlady's cat comes up and I feed it a slice of mutton. Then the woman herself appears, rubbing her eyes. 'Too late fer tea. No fire, I'm sorry, lads.'

It is bright moonlight and she can see the plate of meat and potatoes I hold. Her eyes grow big. I take two slices of mutton and a large potato as Tommo's share and hand the rest of the plate to her. She snatches it and scuttles back into her bark hut. 'Gawd bless yer! Gawd bless yer!' she murmurs as she goes. The tabby follows her back into the hut, no doubt thinking to get himself another share, though I don't like his chances.

It is not much past seven o'clock and I take some of the hay Caleb has ordered to the horses. Caleb joins me and we sit in the trap, while he smokes a pipe.

Since Caleb has learnt of my plan to fight the Lightning Bolt, he has become my most ardent supporter. He knows that we are on this trip in the hope that Tommo will raise the money for our stake at a card game or two, and that promoting the match will bring the punters to Tommo's table. My brother has arranged with Mr Sparrow that we be allowed to drum up interest in the fight – though this is normally his and Fat Fred's domain. He readily agreed – no doubt thinking it a sign of how vainglorious I have become. Caleb does not like to see anything approached in an ad hoc manner, even gambling, and he now turns his mind to how best to stir up interest in the fight before Tommo sets up a game.

'There's a cove who does printing in Yass. We'll have handbills printed!' he says eagerly, then leans back. 'I can see it now.' He enthusiastically describes it for me.

PRIZE FIGHT!
HEAVYWEIGHT CHAMPIONSHIP!

BLACK HAWK,
heavyweight champion
of the Colony of New South Wales, to fight
THE LIGHTNING BOLT,
champion of all Ireland and Great Britain!

Time and location soon to be announced.

Caleb looks well pleased with himself and takes a puff from his pipe. 'That ought to get the tongues wagging. I'll take the trap into Yass tomorrow, get the handbills done and announce that you'll meet the punters on Sunday morning at ten o'clock outside the George Hotel.' Caleb knocks his pipe out against the heel of his boot. 'I'll leave before dawn. I'd better get some sleep.'

I clear my throat. 'Caleb, it is most kind of you to help us, but Tommo is in charge of all the plans. I'd be most obliged if you would discuss it first with him.'

Even in the moonlight I see the look of disappointment that crosses Caleb Soul's face.

'I feel sure Tommo will agree with your idea, Caleb,' I say

quickly. 'And it will help us find punters for Tommo's cardgames as well, that is, if you see fit to take the handbills on as a project. It's just that I don't like to do things without my brother being involved.'

Caleb is silent for a moment. 'Quite right, Hawk. I didn't mean to interfere,' he says at last.

'Caleb, please, we are most grateful that you should care enough to assist us.'

My friend seems suitably mollified. 'I'll wake you in the morning, see what Tommo thinks, eh?' He climbs down from the trap and disappears into the interior of the tent.

There is no wood for a fire so I take my blanket from the carriage and wrap it around me. I sit on a tree stump, waiting for Tommo to come home. The cat appears again to keep me company, purring and brushing against my leg.

By nine o'clock, it is eerily quiet. As we have seen, the river has run near dry and its banks have been churned to clay, and so there are none of those sounds of the night which are usually heard near a stream. No crickets hum or frogs croak. I hear no hoot of an owl nor the throaty hiss and rattle of the opossum.

The miners, who work from dawn to dusk, are asleep only moments after they eat. The diggings are brutally hard work, and men spend most of their days up to their knees in mud and water. Bouts of dysentery caused by the poor water are common, along with a terrible eye condition known as sandy blight. Because their tents are roughly made – usually just a single tarpaulin held aloft by wattle poles – the miners often sleep in wet blankets, even in the freezing cold of winter. Some do not even trouble to remove their muddy boots, and footrot is a complaint common to all.

Though Caleb Soul assures me there is gambling and drinking aplenty in the grog shanties, brothels, eating tents and pubs, there is absolute quiet where we have pitched our tent. I go to fetch another blanket. I can do nothing to find Tommo, who could be anywhere – the diggings stretch five miles in any direction. The full moon's silver light spreads over the desolate landscape. As ten o'clock draws near, an idea comes to my anxious mind.

I go to the tent and waken Caleb. He sits up quickly.

'What is it?' he asks groggily.

'Caleb, how much opium did you give Tommo for this trip?'

Caleb Soul scratches his head. 'A few ounces – all I could obtain.'

'How long would that last?'

'Depends. For severe pain, a few days.'

'And for smoking? In an opium pipe?' I try to pull the answer from him.

'I can't rightly say, I have never smoked it.'

I think back on Tommo's state of agitation when he left me today. It can mean only one thing. Tommo did *not* have a sufficient supply of opium. The craving has come upon him and I would guess he has gone to the Chinese encampment to try to get more. I decide I cannot wait here any longer and must go after him. I have a strong feeling my twin is in danger.

I go to the trap and from among Tommo's things, I take his fighting axe. He has not used it since we have been in Sydney but still keeps it razor sharp. I push the axe into my belt and pull my two blankets over me. Then I set out in the bright moonlight towards the celestial encampment, which is about a mile to the north of the diggings and somewhat clear of the European settlement.

A heavy frost has fallen. The ground clunks under my boots and, though I now have both blankets wrapped about me, a chill seeps into my bones. I walk over a short rise and come upon the camp of the Mongolians. All lies perfectly still in the moonlight. Two Chinamen, about thirty feet away, guard the camp. They huddle in their blankets near a small brazier to keep warm. As soon as they see me, they leap to their feet, their blankets dropping from them as they flee, yelling strange imprecations at the top of their voices.

Soon there are people everywhere as they rush from their tents and humpies while I stand quite still, not knowing what to do next.

'Ho!' I say. 'Ho, there!' I lift my arm out from under the blanket. 'Don't panic!' I shout. 'I mean no harm.' It dawns on me how I must appear. I am just over seven foot tall, and the blankets drape about my shoulders like a ghost's cloak. My face is clearly visible in the moonlight, black with strange signs carved upon it. I must look like a monster!

Some of the Chinese have stopped a little distance from me – no doubt thinking themselves safe with plenty of time to run should this ghost devil suddenly advance upon them. I remove the blankets so they might see me standing like a human. 'Friend!' I shout. 'I am a friend of the Chinaman!' Nevertheless, some at the back of the throng start to run, perhaps seeing Tommo's axe stuck into my belt. But some of the braver souls hold their ground.

'Friend of the Chinaman!' I shout again. In the earlier panic, an old man has fallen on the path near me and no one has dared go to his rescue. I carry this ancient Mongolian back to where my blankets are and I cover him with one of these. 'Friend of the Chinaman!' I repeat as I rise.

One man breaks from the group and walks towards me, to the shouts of warning from those watching. He stops perhaps ten feet away and brings his hands together to his chest, bowing deeply. I can see that his knees are shaking.

'Friend?' he says, trying to smile.

'Aye, friend!' I assure him, smiling. He moves forward to shake my hand and in an instant I am thrown onto my back, my head hitting the ground hard.

It is some moments before I recover, to find six men sitting upon me and a dozen more crowded around. I think that maybe they will kill me. Curiously, I am not afraid and through my mind flashes an imagined bill poster:

GIANT NIGGER JEW KILLED

BY MONGOLIAN HORDES!

I start to laugh. After what Tommo and I have been through, this is a stupid way to die.

To my surprise the celestials crowded about me also begin to laugh. I get up and dust down my breeches – looking for the Chinaman who has thrown me to the ground. I pat him on the back and grin. 'Good! Very good!' Then I lift him into the air above my head and twirl him around, before putting him down again. This time we shake hands like gentlemen.

'Friend,' says he.

'Friend,' say I.

It is too cold to stand around and slowly the crowd disperses, but for four whom I take to be the leaders.

Now I find myself in difficulty. How shall I tell them I am looking for Tommo?

'Do any here speak English?' I ask. 'English, speak English?'

It is soon apparent that none do, even my new-found friend. One of them hands me a black bottle. I do not as a rule drink spirits but now I take a deep swig. I cough as the brandy burns down my throat and warms my stomach, and hand it back with a smile. My hosts smile too. They give me back my blanket, the one I used to cover the old man. Still, I have no way of asking them how he is.

Then, from nowhere, a woman is pushed towards me. I can see she is European but cannot judge her age. She is wrapped in a torn blanket, and her eyes are sunk deep into her skull so that I cannot see them but for bright pinpricks within dark sockets. Her skin is drawn yellow and taut, and her nose is half eaten away. Her lips draw back in a snarl to show black, rotting teeth.

One of the Chinese prods her and jabbers something. 'Inlish!' he says to me.

'Do you speak English?' I ask the woman. 'What's your name?'

'Sally, sir,' she answers in no more than a whisper. Her face may be that of an old crone's but her voice is a young girl's.

'How old are you, Sally?'

'Twenty, I thinks, sir.'

I have heard how young women are caught up in the craving for the Devil's Smoke and how they come to the Mongolians for opium and then cannot leave, paying for the poppy with their bodies until they die in some wretched hovel.

I know full well that there are lots of Sallys, but this is the first of them I've seen. She is clearly beyond all hope of recovering from the addiction. I know I am speaking to someone who will soon be dead and that she seeks no salvation from me beyond the price of her next pipe.

I feel desperately sorry for the poor creature, but I am also relieved. Possibly she knows where Tommo is.

'I am looking for my brother who seeks to buy opium. Have you seen him, Sally?' I say gently.

'There's no nigger here, sir.'

'No, he is not black. A small man, not taller than you, fair hair and blue eyes.'

'I dunno, sir. I can't rightly say,' Sally shrugs.

'Can't say what? You have not seen him?'

'Sir, I needs two shillings to eat,' she whispers.

I take a florin from my pocket and hand it to her. Sally's hand comes out to grasp it, but the moment she takes the coin the Chinaman standing beside her strikes at her wrist and the florin goes flying. He picks it up and hands it back to me. Sally cowers and whimpers.

'I'll give it to you later,' I assure her. 'Have you seen my brother?'

'There's someone like what you said,' she replies. She is shivering, rubbing her arms, just as I've seen Tommo do.

'Can you take me to him please?'

She looks at the men around her as though to ask permission. So I point to her, then to myself, and then back to Sally. The Chinamen laugh. They must believe I want to sleep with her. They nod their heads, and I bow to each respectfully. Now I take Sally by the bony shoulder and she leads me through a maze of tents until we come to a miserable hut made of bark slabs and hessian sacks. She parts the sackcloth and I must stoop to enter a smallish room, the floor of which is covered in filthy rags. In the light of three wax candles placed on an upturned log, I see two naked females lying on the floor. Their carcasses are stripped so bare of flesh that I can see their veins through their translucent skins. Between them lies Tommo, also naked. One of the wretches is holding a pipe to his mouth. Though his eyes are closed, his lips make a soft sucking noise, like that of a newborn pup. White smoke curls slowly upwards from his nostrils.

'That him?' Sally asks, her voice now bolder than before.

I nod, unable to speak.

'Give us the money, then!' She holds out her claw and I give her the florin. 'More!' she demands. I am too shocked to resist and hand her a pound note, not caring.

As she takes the money, a bundle of rags and hair and ancient skin scuttles from a dark corner to snatch the note from Sally's hand. It is a Chinaman, or perhaps a woman, I cannot tell. It hands Sally a pipe and a small wad of opium and as quickly as it appeared, vanishes back into the darkness beyond the candlelight.

Sally unclasps her ragged blanket and I see that she too is naked. She does not look at me but sinks to her knees beside the candles. She begins to work a small dob of opium around the point of what looks like a steel knitting needle, then she holds it to the candle flame.

423

'Tommo!' I call.

Both hags look up at me but say nothing. Tommo does not respond. 'Tommo!' I say again, this time more gently, bending down over him. Pushing one of the wretches away, I kneel beside my twin and shake him. My brother is as limp as a rag doll.

'He dreams,' says one or other of the hags. 'He'll not wake in an hour or even two.' She reaches across and touches me on the shoulder. 'You want me? Two shillings!'

'Where are his clothes!' I say through clenched teeth. She shrugs and points. I rise and move into the corner she indicates, and now I see the creature there, toothless, its mouth open with fear. It holds out Tommo's clothes in its claws. I take them and search through the pockets for his purse. It is missing. I grab the creature and hold my hand out, but it does nothing in response. Then I see it has been squatting upon a small lacquer box, about twelve inches square.

I take up the box and force open the lid. Inside is Tommo's purse. The rest of the space is filled with small parcels of opium tied in bamboo leaves. I scoop up two handfuls of the opium parcels and put them in my pocket, dropping some money into the now half-empty box in exchange.

Meanwhile Sally has fixed her pipe and is on her haunches pulling at it. The two wretches have the other pipe, which is spent, and now they pester Sally until she hands them the wad. They have forgotten I am here and can think of nothing but their craving.

I wrap poor Tommo, still unconscious, in both blankets. His clothes I stuff inside my shirt, stained and stiff with blood from the fight at the eating tent. I tie the laces of his boots together and hang them around my neck. Then I pick up my twin, horrified at how light he is. I push aside the hessian-sack door and carry him out into the night.

The moon is at its zenith and it is almost as clear as day as I begin to walk out of the camp. By some miracle I am not lost in the maze and soon find my way back from whence I came. To my surprise, the four Chinese are still standing beside the brazier and they rise as I approach. I put Tommo down, though he is light enough, and shake their hands. They now know why I have come and nod their heads in sympathy.

'Me, Wong Ka Leung,' says the Mongolian who threw me to the ground.

'Me, Hawk Solomon,' I say.

'Friend!' they all chorus.

It is not these men's fault, I realise, that Tommo suffers so. It is the fault of greed.

'Goodbye, Wong Ka Leung,' I say and shake his hand solemnly again. We both bow deeply to one another.

I pick up Tommo and sling him across my shoulders, walking over the small rise. As soon as I am out of sight, and beyond the hearing of the Mongolians, I burst into tears. Tommo breathes deeply, then sighs against my back. I think of Mary and all her hopes, of her love for me, for Tommo, for both of us – her two precious boys! 'Oh Mama, whatever shall become of us?' I sob.

Chapter Twenty-one

TOMMO

Lambing Flat
30 June 1861

It is early Sunday morning and we've been in the goldfields just over a week. I've slept badly and am up early, wandering through the diggings. The day's very still and several of the miners I pass reckons there might be snow in the air.

The Sabbath be the one day of the week the authorities don't allow work at the diggings, what's very funny when you thinks about it, 'cause the miners use this day to get themselves drunk as lords. Then o' course they fights and carouses for as long as they can. Sunday be the most *unholy* day of the week!

Just last Sunday a priest come up from Melbourne to hear confession and say mass for the Irish. They was given plenty o' warning of the good father's arrival and a church and confessional was specially erected out of canvas, but not a single bloke presented himself for the absolving of sins and the taking of the wafer and wine. Some wag reckons that the Pope, upon hearing of this shameful event, will rename Lambing Flat 'Sod 'em and T'morrer'. The 'sod 'em' is for not attending mass and 't'morrer', the day after the Sabbath, is when they'll all be excommunicated and condemned to hell.

Caleb Soul returned from Yass earlier in the week and brought with him the handbills announcing a meeting for the punters to see Black Hawk. The venue is the Great Eastern Hotel, as it's one of

426

the few proper buildings of Lambing Flat. It's away from the diggings and the river, and is a favourite meeting place among the miners.

Caleb has arranged a rough timber platform for Hawk to stand on. Thank God, though cold, it's a day o' bright sunshine, otherwise my brother might be a little chilly! He's to strip to the waist and wear a bright red cummerbund so that all may see he's in the very best physical condition. To show his strength, he'll challenge anyone in the crowd to arm-wrestling, taking a new opponent every ten minutes. Hawk don't much like the idea, saying it be boastful, but Caleb and me told him that were the whole idea! Anyhow, he's agreed to do it.

We has put up the handbills everywhere – in the grog shanties, brothels and pubs as well as the chophouses and about the miners' fires where they cooks their meat and damper.

Already there's a strong rivalry among the men, with the Irish going for their own man, the Lightning Bolt, and t'others going for Hawk. Hawk's become somewhat of a hero after giving the ruffians a walloping the night they attacked the waiter. Turned out they was Irish and now all the Irish has made the 'Nigger' their sworn enemy. As Caleb Soul says, 'It could not be a better situation if we tried.'

Since that night, there's been some muttering about the Irish boyos taking revenge. Hawk's been warned to have a few stout men with him when he presents himself this morning. I'm a bit worried for him, but Hawk insists we goes ahead as planned. 'I can't scuttle away like a cockroach on the *Nankin Maiden* when they make the slightest threat! I must face this if I'm to face the Bolt!'

This morning's turnout promises to be a big un. The Miners' League, what has been formed to protest against the presence of the Chinese at the diggings, will be there. The League has as many as two thousand men in their membership along with a brass band, for they likes a bit of a march. I've heard how it's made up of different chapters, each with a banner showing the diggings they hail from. There's Blackbutt Gully, Tipperary Hill, Possum Creek, and the like.

They'll be marching behind their leaders and carrying their bright banners with pride, so the whole thing'll look like a bleedin' carnival. Caleb has even paid 'em to play a tune or two at Hawk's appearance!

427

One of the leaders of the Miners' League, Mr Cameron, told Caleb that if the payment were a subscription fee for the three of us to join, they'd play the whole morning for naught. But we has refused, being most wary o' those who are against the Chinese, what we thinks has done nothing wrong other than to be a different colour.

A special correspondent from the *Sydney Morning Herald* has come out here incognito to report on the Miners' League and their battle against the celestials. He's said to lurk about the diggings, making up scurrilous lies about the miners. Caleb reckons we should recruit him to our cause but we don't know who he is! Still, if we could encourage the special to add a few lines about Hawk and his fight, that would stir the possum nicely.

The special's pen has already struck some hard blows against the diggers, telling his readers that the Chinese ain't done nothing to the miners and is a most peaceful group. The special also points out that the rough element in the diggings is the real culprits behind the uproar. They make trouble with the Chinese and then steals their claims. Hawk reckons this a very fair point of view, but the mob don't like it one bit.

Meantime I has had meself two card games thanks to Caleb's introductions. The first were with the various shopkeepers, what's among the richest folk in the diggings, and the second were with the sly grog shop owners and publicans, what's not short of a bob either. Yours truly won at both!

Me winnings were ten pounds each time. Twenty pounds is bloody good wages but it falls far short of our ambition. These blokes ain't true gamblers and is too timid with their wagers. We still need another eighty pounds towards the stake – and that don't even begin to cover the cost o' Hawk's training. I got to get one really big game if I'm to have any hope of making this.

Tonight I've a game with the Irish. It ain't one set up by Caleb who has warned me against playing poker with these boyos. 'Tommo, there will not be an honest cove in the game and all of them broadsmen,' he warns. I can hardly tell him that I won't be adding even one per cent of honesty to the game meself! I'd rather take me chances and pit me own talent against villains than play with the duffers what he's lined up.

With only two games played, the word about Tommo is already out among the respectable folk and they's all gun shy, even though I didn't cheat once! At least the rough mob play for big stakes. Besides, I got no choice. We must leave on Tuesday morning to return to Sydney, so this is me last chance.

I first come across this mob I'm gunna play with while passing out handbills at a place called Possum Creek. They's not working a claim and they don't look like they intends to neither. They all sit outside a bark hut playing the flats. I put down a handbill and stop to watch them a while. They's playing whist and one of the players what's thrown his hand in picks up the poster.

'What's it say?' he asks, holding it upside down.

I read the handbill out to them and they all stops to listen.

'By Jaysus, that be clever an' all,' says one o' them. 'The Irishman cannot be beat!'

'Oh? Who says?' I asks.

'I says,' he replies. 'You work for the nigger, then, does yer?'

'Aye,' I replies. 'I helps Mr Caleb.'

Still seated, he grabs me by the shirt front so I'm standing up against him. I'm looking into his foul, grinning mouth of broke teeth. 'That black bastard be askin' fer a hidin', and my oath, he'll be gettin' one at the hands o' the Irish champ!' He shakes me. 'I'm inclined to give you a taste o' what he's in fer! How'd yer like that, eh?'

'Not much,' I admits. 'But I tell you what! If the Irish fight as poorly as they cheats at flats, your man ain't gunna win.'

'What's yer mean?' he growls.

I take out an ace of hearts from his sleeve and a Jack of the same from behind his collar and throws them down in front of his mates.

'Why, ya right bastard, Micky!' they chorus.

'Dunno why you bothered. Whose deck is that?' I point to the cards on the table. All eyes turn to another of the Irishmen. 'Well, it's shaved, ain't it?' I says.

It's a guess o' course. I can't tell from where I'm standing. But the moment I says it I see the sly look in the eye of the one they're all looking at, and I know straight away I be right.

'What's goin' on, then?' one o' the ruffians shouts, throwing his cards down and rising from the bark table to glare at his mate.

'Righto,' I says, me heart in me mouth. 'That's two of yer what's cheating. How about the other three, eh?' Each man looks at the other narrow-eyed. 'Tell ya what,' I suggests, 'let me sit in

429

on yer game. I'll play ya all together, the lot of you against me! What say you, a shilling a point? But if I catches any of ya cheating, ya drops out of the game. If you catches me, I'll double any winnings on the table and it all be yours. Are you game, then, gentlemen?'

Me suggestion's just silly enough, and them's just stupid enough to accept. An hour later, three of them's been tossed out of the game. The other two I clean out too. They look fit to kill when I rise from the table, scooping the pool. Then I hand 'em back their money! 'Sorry gentlemen, but the nigger lover don't play with amateurs.'

The one what grabbed me in the first place has grown very red in the face. He balls his fist. 'Mind yer mouth, laddy,' he growls.

I pretend I ain't scared. 'Know a big game, then? High stakes?' I asks. 'Among yer mates? Someone maybe ya don't like, someone what owes ya? Or perhaps you wants revenge, eh? Tell ya what, gentlemen. If you has the nous to set up a big game, high stakes, I'll cut ya in on ten per cent. But it's got to be real big. How's that, then?'

'Twenty,' says one of 'em.

'Fifteen,' says I.

They agree and we shake on it. I share me black bottle with them and then goes off, telling them they can contact me by leaving a message at the Great Eastern. As I leave I yell, 'Oh, and gentlemen, take me advice, put yer winnings on Black Hawk!'

'Bullshit!' one of 'em shouts, but this time they laughs. 'See ya right soon, Tommo!' another yells after me.

Well, since then they've found me a game with the Callaghan mob, where the stakes are ten pounds in. It's to be held in the Great Eastern Hotel, starting ten o'clock tomorrow night.

Me and Jonah Callaghan, what's leader of the mob, made the booking. Him and me went to see the proprietor of the Great Eastern, Mr Makepeace Chubb. He's a little cove, fat, bald and always with a coating of shiny sweat to his florid face. We inspect a room upstairs, to the back of the hotel. Each of us pays the publican a pound for the arrangements, and then we arrange for him to get in two brand new decks o' cards.

'I've got 'em on sale here,' he volunteers.

'Give us a look then?' Callaghan asks.

The publican returns with two packs of Mermaid Brand.

'What's this shite?' Callaghan growls.

'He's right,' I says to Chubb. 'They has to be DeLarue & Sons.'

'Oh,' says Chubb. 'That serious, is it? I'll have to get 'em in. Jeremiah Neep has them in stock as I recall.'

'We'll be in on Sundee mornin' ter inspect them,' Jonah warns. 'Have pen and ink ready, much obliged.' Though Jonah Callaghan's words seem mild enough, the way he says them ain't at all pleasant.

So ten o'clock this morning, accompanied by Jonah Callaghan, I goes to the Great Eastern. Makepeace Chubb is busy out the back and we sends a message we wants to see the flats. A few minutes later, he comes huffing and puffing to the bar, and puts two packs down on the counter in front of us.

'Where's pen and quill?' Callaghan demands.

The publican sighs and leaves to fetch same.

I orders two nobblers of Cape brandy and when they comes, I push one in front o' the Irishman and invite him to inspect the decks. He looks down at the brandy in front of him. 'What's this shite?' Before I can open me mouth he pushes the drink over to me. He throws his head back and shouts to the barman, 'Oi, you! Irish!'

'Suit yerself. Only trying to be friendly,' I says, a trifle miffed.

'Yeah, well don't waste yer breath,' he replies. 'Two! With a pint o' best to go with it!' He knocks one nobbler o' whiskey back, chases it with half the beer, then the other Irish whiskey follows and the remainder of the beer. All of this is done straight off, no pause between. Good, I thinks, he'll be drinkin' whiskey and beer all night at the game. It's got to catch up with him unless he be made of cast iron.

Callaghan wipes his mouth with the back of his hand. He then picks up a deck and examines it closely, picking gently at the seals with his fingernail to make sure they's tight closed. He does the same to the second pack of DeLarue. Satisfied, he dips the quill into the ink pot and makes his mark across the seals. I does the same, spending even a little more time at examination before I signs.

We call for the publican and makes him sign across the front of each pack. Then we follow him out the back and into his office, where he has a small safe for miners to keep their gold in. He fiddles with the combination, groaning as he stoops down low with his back to us. With the safe open, he steps aside so that we can see it's empty, 'case we've got any ideas. He puts the two decks into the safe and closes the door, scrambling the combination once again. 'There,' he says, puffing, 'all safe and sound, lads.'

'You'll be sure to see there's plenty o' firewood and the hearth be well lit and the room warm?' I asks. 'We'll be playing in our shirt sleeves rolled up to here.' I indicate the top o' me arm. 'No hats to be worn either.'

'Eh? What's this, then?' Callaghan scowls.

'Just helps to know there ain't no handy sleeve or hat about. I've known cards what had a natural affinity with sleeves and hats. Hand goes under a hat to scratch a louse. Never know what it might find lurking! Could be the king or queen herself. Or an ace may pop out of a coat sleeve, know what I mean?'

Jonah turns and stabs a hard finger in me chest. 'Think we's gunna cheat ya, does ya?'

'It's been known to happen,' says I. 'But I'll find you out if you does.'

'Like hell yer will!'

'Steady on now, lads,' says Makepeace. 'There'll be no cards played in this house if yiz going to fight. A drink on the house with my compliments will settle youse down! Cape and Irish with a chaser, if I remember rightly.'

We follows him through to the bar and he pours the drinks. 'On the house!' he repeats, looking a bit pained. 'Oh yes, and the house takes ten per cent, lads.'

'What?' Callaghan grumbles.

Makepeace shrugs, safe behind his bar. 'As you wish, take it or leave it.'

'It'll be fine,' I says.

'Bloody hell it will!' Jonah growls. 'Fine is it? It'll be just fine for you to pay it, laddy.'

'Oh, and another five pounds to cover breakages. Returnable o' course, if nothing's damaged!' Makepeace adds.

After each of us puts down our share, Callaghan and me walks out into the bright, crisp sunlight and I sticks out me hand. 'See ya t'morrer, then.' He ignores me, spitting to the side o' his boots as he walks away. 'Charming!' I exclaims. 'Real nice to know ya, Callaghan!'

'Fuck off!' he says, not looking back.

Well, I thinks to meself, everything's going just right and dandy for yours truly. Now I'll go and see how Hawk's faring.

Hawk still worries about me too much, I reckon. When I tells him about me game coming up, he looks most worried. 'Tommo, Caleb Soul says these men are dangerous. They don't dig for gold but live by robbing others of their dust. Two of the brutes I subdued in Felix's eating-house were from their gang, or so I was told.'

I shrugs. 'Cards is funny. If you win against a villain and they think it's kosher, or they can't work out how you done it, you got their respect. It's sort of honour among thieves.'

'Do these men know this?' Hawks asks. 'I'd best come with you to make sure.'

'Hawk, let me go on me own!'

'What if something happens?'

'If you comes with me, o' course something *will* happen!' says I. 'This time you've got to stay a mile away. Them Callaghans don't know I'm yer brother, only that I works for Caleb.'

'What about today, then? They'll see you with me, won't they?'

'Caleb can handle the show with you. He'll love to spruik it. I'll just be in the crowd watching. Cheering you on, Hawk!' I can see Hawk ain't happy about letting me go alone to the game, but he knows that it's our best chance to raise the gelt.

'Tommo, be careful, won't you?'

'Course I will, big brother,' I say.

It's near noon, and already there's a big crowd outside the Great Eastern Hotel waiting to see Hawk, a brisk trade going on at the bar. It's about time for Hawk to meet the punters. He walks out and I can see his head sticking up nearly two foot above the crowd. His black shoulders, scarred from O'Hara's knotted rope, shine ebony in the sunlight. He turns and smiles, showing a row of gleaming white teeth. They be most unusual at our age when most men's teeth is yellow from tobacco-chewing and pipe-smoking. Hawk's Maori tattoos give him the look of a black prince or warrior.

As he wades through the crowd, I admire his huge shoulders and narrow waist. His legs is like tree trunks, but he is trim at the ankle and can move surprisingly quick for such a big fellow. He's bulging with muscle everywhere – a result of all his work hoisting barrels at Tucker & Co. And his stomach's like a washboard. I can't believe the Irishman won't tremble when he sees him in the ring.

Hawk climbs the platform to cheers and boos from the crowd. I can tell from their murmurs that they's struck with his massive size. Just as I walks up to join the mob, the Miners' League marches in and their band strikes up. I reckon there must be more than two thousand of 'em all up. They play a marching tune with cries of 'Roll up! Roll up!' from those behind the banners. It is a grand sight and everyone claps as they comes to a halt. A single drum marks time and at the command of each section leader, each group falls out.

Meanwhile Hawk stands on the platform like a black general surveying his troops. With blokes from the Miners' League joining it, the crowd is huge. Caleb Soul has got up on the platform beside Hawk. He brings a hailing funnel to his mouth and calls for silence. When at last the mob settles down, he nods to someone at the foot of the platform. There's the roll of a kettledrum.

'Diggers and gentlemen!' he proclaims. 'I give you the next world champion in the division of heavyweight – the inestimable, pugilistic, ferocious and *undefeated* Black Hawk, champion of the colony of New South Wales!'

The crowd cheers and then a voice near the platform calls out, 'Garn, tell us how many fights 'e's 'ad!'

'Only recently discovered, the Black Hawk has beaten the redoubtable and famous heavyweight, Ben Dunn!' Caleb bellows over the crowd's laughter, not missing a beat.

'Who?' shouts the same wag, to more laughter.

'You, sir,' says Caleb, pointing to the man, 'step up and let's see your form. Up here, lad!' he indicates the platform. A small man, not much bigger than me, climbs up, with Caleb lending him a hand.

'What's your name?' Caleb asks.

'Pat Malone.' The little cove grins.

'How about you arm-wrestle Black Hawk, Pat Malone? Five pounds to you if you win!' Caleb says.

The little cove don't back down. 'Can I stand up and use both arms?' he asks, quick as a flash. Caleb looks at Hawk, who nods. I ain't so sure it's a good idea. Though small, the man's a miner, hardened to manual work. With the use o' both his arms and his body-weight he won't be easy to beat.

The crowd grows quiet as Hawk sits at the arm-wrestling table. The miner takes up his position, his legs wide apart, and grasps Hawk's hand in both of his. Caleb holds up his bandanna. 'Take the strain!' The bandanna drops. 'Go!'

The little cove is no shirker and he keeps Hawk's hand vertical. Then me brother's arm starts to go down, and the crowd begins to shout their encouragement.

The miner is gaining on him and the mob thinks he's gunna win, so they shouts him on. Hawk's knuckles is about to touch the deck when he gives a great grunt and swings his arm up. He pushes the little bloke backwards so hard that the miner loses his balance and goes flying off the edge of the platform, into the crowd. It's an amazing feat of strength.

Hawk rises quickly to see if Pat Malone's been hurt. He pulls him gently back onto the platform. The little miner seems no worse for his fall, and Hawk lifts his challenger's arm as if declaring him the real winner. Then me big brother lifts Mr Malone high above his head and the crowd cheers at this show o' sportsmanship. He puts the miner down and they shakes hands like the best o' friends.

Caleb holds up a five-pound banknote for all to see. 'Five pounds to Pat Malone for having a go!' he shouts. 'Let's have three cheers for the miners, lads!' The crowd is completely won over.

'Shit, that's another fiver I has to win,' I mutters to meself, but Caleb has done good. The band strikes up a rousing song.

Caleb now announces that Hawk will talk. 'Hear from the champion himself!' He hands the hailing funnel to Hawk. The crowd draw closer so that they hears his every word.

'Gentlemen! I thank you for your time. It's grand to be among so many friends.' There's more cheers and boos. 'Let me tell you about the Irishman, the Lightning Bolt.'

The fighter's fellow countrymen raise a great swell o' noise at his name and Hawk waits 'til they has quieted down. 'My worthy opponent is better known as the Bolt, because he can take a great hammering to the head and yet remain true to his metal.' The Irish like this remark and I can see they'll store it up to repeat a thousand times. 'He is the champion of Ireland and Britain and there is much speculation that he cannot be beaten by anyone in this colony or any other in the Empire! He is a most formidable adversary.'

Hawk points to Pat Malone, what's sitting on the edge of the platform. 'It is quite true, as my little friend here says, that I lack experience in the prize ring and my stamina has yet to be tested. Some say it was a lucky punch that knocked out Ben Dunn.' Hawk pauses a moment. 'Ben Dunn himself has been heard to espouse this theory!'

A roar of laughter goes up from the crowd and I can see they is warming to my twin. He waits for it to die down before continuing. 'I admit, Mr Dunn was most tired, having just fought five rounds. But those who speculate on these things and know better than I say that the Irishman will take Ben Dunn with one arm tied behind his back and a glass of good Irish whiskey in the other.'

The Irish in the crowd cheers wildly. 'So, if you are an Irishman I will reluctantly accept that your wagers will not be placed on me. If, on the other hand, you are an Englishman, you may well be in two minds, not wishing the Irishman to win, but not too sure of the big nigger, either!'

Most know what Hawk says is true and they admires him for it. Hawk takes the hailing funnel from his mouth and smiles, 'til the laughter and clapping settles. 'But if you are an *Australian*, then you will know we are a new breed of men and not given to easy surrender!'

The crowd rises to a new peak of excitement at this and it takes some time to calm down again. 'In my favour, I have my size and, if you will allow me to say so, a great determination to win. I trust you to make up your own minds about me and not to be swayed overly much by the bookmakers' odds! I thank you for hearing me out. May your efforts reward you with gold aplenty!'

Thunderous applause and cheering follows as me brother ends, and the band strikes up 'The Wild Colonial Boy'. There's men about me what has tears in their eyes. It's a brilliant piece o' work. Hawk's pulled off what no amount of vainglorious bragging could do, for these ordinary blokes knows sincerity and the honest truth when they hears it.

Hawk arm-wrestles half a dozen or so miners, one directly after t'other, with no rest in between. He beats all six. But the seventh, a big man, wins 'cause Hawk is knackered. These are men what works hard with picks and shovels and ain't no milksops. 'Luck of the Irish!' Caleb shouts, as he hands over five quid. He thanks the crowd once more and the show is over. Now it is left to me to do the rest with Jonah Callaghan's mob.

The meeting of the Miners' League is to take place at two. The

436

men has been drinking steadily all morning and many is starting to fall about. Hawk wants me to rest in our tent for he sees how tired I am after my bad night's sleep. I don't say no. Sleeping during the day comes natural to me!

I stops at the butcher's on me way and buys two pounds o' chops and a quarter o' chopped liver. When I gets back to the tent I calls out to Lucy, our landlady. She be a widow what tries to make a living as a washerwoman. If she has a surname, she ain't giving it to us. 'Just Lucy,' she replied when we asked. 'Me husband were a right bastard when he was alive. I don't see I has to carry the burden o' his name now 'e's dead, does I?'

So our private name for her is Just Lucy. 'Lucy, I brought something for the moggy!' I shouts as soon as I gets back. She's out of her bark hut quick smart, carrying the mangy cat what seems to be her only company. 'Mornin', Tommo.' She squints up at the pale sun. 'Or is it afternoon? It's me day orf, no washing on the Sabbath, so I's kipped in a bit.'

'Here, chopped liver and chops for the tabby.' I hand her the meat and she lets the cat jump from her arms. She unwraps it careful, like it were a late Christmas present.

'Cat can't eat six chops, Tommo!' she says soft.

'Sorry Lucy, I doesn't know much about cats. You'll have to find some other use for them chops.' Just Lucy don't like charity. Since the tea and sugar Hawk bought her, she's been trying to do our washing and cooking.

'Yer a good boy, Tommo.'

'Nah, I just likes cats! They don't give a bugger for no one, like me!'

'A likely story! How'd ya go with the packs of cards at the hotel, Tommo?' she asks, dropping a lump of the chopped liver at her feet for the cat.

'Perfect, Lucy. Matter o' fact, couldn't have done better meself.' I take out a pound and hand it to her. 'It's what I promised if it worked, so this ain't charity.'

'Ten shillings you promised, Tommo!'

'Ten shillings a pack!' I says.

Just Lucy shakes her head but takes the money and puts it in her pocket. I see her eyes getting a bit wet.

'No, no, don't cry, Lucy!' I says in alarm. 'It's yours well earned. How long did ya have to wait in Jeremiah Neep's shop?'

'All Saturday afternoon, almost. About five o'clock, in comes a young lad and asks for two packs o' DeLarue cards.

'"DeLarue, eh?" Mr Neep says. "Where's you from, lad?"

'"Great Eastern Hotel," the boy says. "Mr Chubb sent me, sir."

'"Must be an important game. Sold a couple o' the self-same packs yesterday. Don't get much call for DeLarue, too expensive, they is."

'"Dunno how come, sir," says the boy. "Mr Chubb just said they must be *them* cards, no other."

'I'm standing like you's told me, right next to the shelf where the playing cards is kept. I puts yer two decks where you said, on the top. Then Mr Neep comes over. "Here we are, then. Right on the top they is, the last two." He takes yer two packs and wraps them up proper and gives them to the lad, what pays 'im ten shillings. He sends the boy away with a bright red sucker from a jar.'

'And Mr Neep ain't suspicious, you standing in the shop all afternoon?'

'Nah,' says Just Lucy. 'He be a decent man. I asks him if I can stay there so as to ask customers if they wants their washing done.' She grins. 'I got two new customers out of it, too! Took Mr Neep's dust coat 'ome to wash, for his kindness, like!'

'Well it were nicely done, Lucy.'

Just Lucy looks at me. 'Tommo, why'd ya give Jeremiah Neep back the two packs o' cards you bought yesterday, them brand new and not ever been opened?'

I points to the moggy what's busy eating the liver. 'Cat's got me tongue, Lucy,' I says, laughing.

'Oh, sorry, always were a bit of a stickybeak. Too curious for me own good.'

'It ain't that, Lucy. What you don't know you can't be hurt by if someone should come asking questions.'

'You mean I didn't never go into Mr Neep's shop, 'cept to find new customers for washing?'

'That's right, Lucy. That's the bonus earned for keeping your gob shut.'

'Happy to oblige, Tommo. Fancy a nice chop fer ya tea?'

'Maybe when I wakes up. Got to get a few winks.'

'I'll see yer not disturbed,' she promises.

Well, I does get disturbed. About three o'clock Just Lucy herself sticks her head in and shouts, 'Tommo, it's the miners, they's marching on the Chinamen's camp!'

I dunno how, but I know straight away that Hawk's there and he ain't marching with the miners. I runs to the trap and fetches me fighting axe. 'Be careful, Tommo!' she shouts after me as I trot down the path to the celestial encampment.

It be a good mile or so to the Mongolians and I'm half running. As I draws near, I hears the mob shouting and the band playing, and some musket fire in the background. Smoke billows up on the horizon. The running has made me head ache real bad and it's near time for me smoke. But all I can think of is that Hawk's in danger. I can feel it in me gut and in the back of me throat.

I get to the camp to find half of it already destroyed, tents and huts up in flames, people's belongings strewn on the ground. Two Chinamen lies face down with several miners kicking at them, though I soon enough realise they're dead. I run towards the noise and suddenly I'm in the middle of the fray. Men on horseback are firing pistols into the air and running down celestials, what are fleeing in every direction, screaming for fear.

Two horsemen corner an old Chinaman with a scraggly beard. A mob of ten or so men runs over and drags him to the ground. They're yelling and laughing like wild things. Four men roll the Mongolian onto his stomach and two of 'em holds him down by sitting on his legs. The other two plants their boots on him, on each shoulder and each wrist. Then they both grabs a hold of the Chinaman's pigtail and, to the count of 'One, two, three!', they rips it out of the back of his head. The men all cheer as one holds it aloft, bright drops o' blood dripping steady onto his dusty boots. Then they begin to kick the old man to death.

I keep running, looking for Hawk, and pass several more dead Chinamen. All is lying on their stomachs with crimson patches to the backs of their heads, the blood still running down their necks and shoulders. One what I thinks is dead gets up and starts to stagger away, holding both his hands to his gut. But he gets only a few feet before he collapses again. Someone has sliced his gut open and his intestines spill out as he falls.

In the smoke, white miners shout excitedly as they comes across stuff they wants in the Mongolian tents. Some carries armloads of loot, piled up to their chins – lamps and picks and lacquer boxes and every manner o' thing you can imagine. One has a sack of rice over his shoulder. It leaks out the bottom, where some wag has stabbed into it, so that he leaves a white trail as he dashes this way and that. Up ahead I sees a mob of about fifty miners, shouting and throwing their fists in the air. I run through the smoke towards them.

I am exhausted by the time I get to the circle o' rioters. As I draws near, I sees Hawk standing right in the centre. Oh, shit! I force me way through the yelling miners, pushing them away with the handle of me axe 'til I gets to the inside.

There stands Hawk, with a white woman what's holding a Chink's baby. Four other Chinamen stand close beside him, three younger men and an older bloke. They's whimpering and shaking from head to foot – all 'cept for the old bloke, who stands calm to Hawk's back. Hawk is holding a pickaxe handle. Most amazing of all, he's calm and smiling!

'Come on, then,' he cries. 'Who's willing to die first? I'll take ten of you before you take us!'

I push through the last o' the crowd to join him.

'Tommo!' Hawk shouts. He reaches out and grabs the axe from me. 'Now it's fifteen! Fifteen men will die before you harm these people! Who will it be among you, gentlemen?' He points with the axe. 'You holding the pigtail, like to be scalped?' He hands the pick handle to me and whispers, 'Cover the side.' Then he raises the fighting axe and takes a step towards the cove with the pigtail. The mob tumbles backwards, falling over each other in their haste to get out of his way. The bloke with the pigtail drops it and runs.

Just then a man on horseback rides up, raises his pistol and fires at Hawk. His horse shies as the mob runs towards him and the bullet misses, hitting the ground. I use the pickaxe handle like a Maori fighting stick and a second later the bastard is on the ground, with all his teeth smashed and his nose missing. The pistol has gone flying as he falls and quickly I rush to pick it up. The horse gallops away, whinnying, and the cove with his face missing gets up and runs blindly into a hut what's burning fiercely. Soon his clothes are alight and he's screaming blue murder.

Hawk is moving forward with the axe and me with the pistol. The woman and her brat and the four Mongolians keep close. There's smoke everywhere and not a tent or hut left standing. All around us, the miners say and do nothing as we make our way out o' the burning camp, passing dead men lying in the dust. In the distance, we hears the band playing 'Cheer, Boys, Cheer!'

The woman holding the Chink baby begins to sob. One of the Mongolians takes the child in his arms and lays its head against his shoulder. He puts his arm 'round the woman as we walks towards the Yass Road, with no one daring to follow.

When we reach the road, Hawk stops beside the stump of what was once a big river gum. It's been burnt and blackened but stands solid beside the track. 'Tommo, go get the trap and meet us back here. Whistle when you get back – we'll be lying low nearby.'

I hand him the pistol. ''Ere, gimme back me axe. I don't care for this thing. Reminds me of Sam Slit.' Hawk takes the pistol and gives my axe back. In my hands, the pistol felt big and clumsy and I doubt I could've fired it. In his fist, it looks like a child's toy.

Almost an hour later I'm back with Caleb's trap. It's turned dark and I whistles for me twin. Soon enough Hawk, at first a huge dark shadow, appears. He calls to the others.

'Tommo, I want you to take them into Yass. They'll be safe enough there. Then head back here as soon as you're able. It's a hard pull for the horses with six people but they'll make it well enough.'

'No sir!' I says. 'It's twelve hours to Yass and I've got a game o' cards to play tomorrow with the bloody Callaghan mob! I'll never make it back in time. Betcha boots they was in the front of the Miners' League this arvo!'

'Tommo!' Hawk exclaims, looking cranky. 'I'm the weight of two men. I can't go! It's too much to ask the horses to pull!'

'They're game enough. Good nags them two. Take it slow.' I fold me arms. 'I ain't doing it! I ain't gunna let them Callaghan bastards off the hook.'

'It isn't *safe* to play cards with them!' Hawk yells at me.

'It's safer than rescuing Chinks!' I yells back.

Hawk tries to argue some more. I shrug. 'I ain't had me stuff. I'll be useless in an hour.' Hawk stops, knowing he can't win. In fact, I had a pipe o' poppy when I returned to get Caleb's trap but I ain't gunna tell him that. Hawk calls to the Mongolians to climb into the trap. The woman and her baby, the old man and the smallest of the remaining men gets in the front. The other two stands on the back platform, what Caleb uses to carry a couple o' cases of sample liquor. Hawk climbs in and takes up the reins and I can see it is a tight squeeze. The woman ain't said a word all along and now she's feeding her brat by a tit what don't look too promising a source if you ask me. The baby's little mouth is working overtime.

One of the Chinamen steps down from the back platform. He comes over to me and bows low. It's the man what earlier took the woman's baby and put his arm about her. He looks up at me in the moonlight and smiles. 'Me, Wong Ka Leung!' He sticks out his hand and shakes mine up and down several times. 'Very good, sir.' He bows again, then climbs onto the back of the trap.

'I'll be back Tuesday!' Hawk calls.

'Yeah, see ya,' I says. He hasn't once mentioned the camp or what's happened, just gone about the business of doing what needs to be done.

I watch them move off. I'm about to turn and walk back to Lambing Flat when I sees him rein in the horses.

'Tommo!'

'Yeah, what?' I shouts back.

'I love you!' Then he's off in a clatter of wheels and hoofs down the rocky road.

Jesus! I thinks. Four useless bloody Chinks, a wore-out white whore with a half-caste Chinky brat, and me twin risks his life to save them! When is that big nigger gunna grow up some?

I begin to walk back to the camp and the card game. It's bloody cold.

Chapter Twenty-two

HAWK

Lambing Flat
1 July 1861

I return to Lambing Flat from Yass shortly before noon on Tuesday, having travelled through the night. As soon as I arrive, our landlady, Just Lucy, tells me that Tommo is still at the Great Eastern Hotel. Just Lucy enquired after him at ten o'clock this morning as soon as the bar opened for business. The barman said that Tommo and the lads were still upstairs. Some of the lads had ordered kidneys and hard-boiled eggs at dawn, but Tommo and Callaghan played on at stud poker.

This is somewhat alarming news. I unharness the horses and Just Lucy gives them a feed of hay. Meanwhile, I take myself off to the hotel to see Mr Makepeace Chubb. The publican is in a regular sweat when I find him. For the past eight hours, two of the Callaghan mob have been stationed in the passage outside the upstairs room where the game is taking place. They will not allow anyone to enter. The publican is afraid they are holding Tommo captive. Since midnight, several bottles of Irish whiskey have been ordered, but no Cape brandy, which he knows Tommo drinks. All the bottles must be left halfway up the stairs, where they are collected by the two ruffians guarding the door.

'Should we not call the troopers?' I ask, concerned.

'You won't find them, lad,' says Makepeace Chubb. 'They're all busy investigating the miners' riots on the Chinese encampment.

'Besides, I hasn't got a gambling permit and if the traps find out, I'll lose my liquor licence,' he adds. 'They'll put your little mate in gaol too, with his winnings in the pocket of some good officer.'

I thank him and return hastily to our camp. The road leading from the hotel is strewn with sleeping drunks. Others sit with vacant expressions, mumbling or shouting insults, each nursing a black bottle and often covered in their own vomit.

Back at Just Lucy's, I take the pistol gained on Sunday from the horseman in the Chinese camp. I reload it and place it inside my blouse where it cannot be seen. Next I find Tommo's fighting axe. It's where he usually keeps it, wrapped in an oil cloth in his blanket roll, together with his opium pipe and lamp. How I wish I could smash these last two objects and his addiction with them.

I take some comfort from knowing that Tommo does not have his axe with him. He is deadly with this weapon and could easily take four or five men at once with it. But under the circumstances, he is much better without it. On consideration I too decide to leave the axe where it is, telling myself the Callaghan mob would not kill him on the hotel premises. Tommo is safe enough while he remains at the Great Eastern.

And so I return to the pub and ask Chubb to direct me to the upstairs room. He takes me as far as the base of the stairway and points upwards before he tiptoes away. The short, narrow stairway is made of timber and without the benefit of a carpet, so there is no possibility of a stealthy approach. Instead, I prepare to bolt up the steps, hoping to take Callaghan's two guards by surprise.

I pull a large breath of air into my lungs and, taking the stairs three steps at a time, reach the top only moments before the two villains get there themselves. I knock them both to the ground and they go sprawling, their knives clattering from their hands. Picking up the knives, I kick one villain in the ribs and the other in the small of the back, hurling their weapons down to the floor below. Then I charge the door. The lock cracks from the door frame and it flies open.

Three of the Callaghan mob lie asleep on the floor while Jonah Callaghan and Tommo sit at the card table. Tommo has his back to the door and another member of the mob stands beside him holding a bowie knife. I smash my fist into his jugular as he turns his head at my sudden appearance. He staggers backwards, cracking his skull hard on the wall behind him, then slides to his knees and plunges forward onto his face.

A loud explosion fills the room. Jonah Callaghan has fired a pistol which is still pointing at me, though the bullet has missed. His hand waves drunkenly and he squints to aim a second time, just as Tommo pushes hard at the table. Its edge shoves into Jonah Callaghan's guts, spilling his chair backwards. He falls, knocking the back of his head against the floor. Somehow he still holds the pistol, which goes off again, the bullet passing through the ceiling. Tommo jumps from his chair and stamps on Callaghan's wrist, then kicks him hard in the jaw.

The three who were sleeping on the floor are now awake, but still drunk. They come to their feet dazed and unsteady. I pull my pistol and point it at them. Meekly, they put their hands upon their heads.

Tommo has now got hold of Callaghan's pistol. 'There are two at the door, mark them!' I shout to him.

'They's scarpered,' he replies. 'Bastards!'

I make the three men face the wall and put their hands flat against it. Tommo takes the bowie knives from their belts and as he does this, I see that each has a pair of Chinese pigtails hanging from his belt. No doubt Jonah Callaghan and the other cove who lies unconscious also have these gory trophies, ripped straight out from their victims' skulls.

'Tommo,' I say, 'take only what winnings are yours – leave what's rightfully theirs.'

Tommo seems remarkably sober though his eyes are bloodshot and his face pale from fatigue. 'It's all bloody ours!' he snorts. 'Callaghan took me winnings and made me play for them a second time at gunpoint.'

'Well if it's rightly yours, put it into my pockets. Take the cards as well. Call the publican and tell him to bring some rope so we can tie this lot up.'

Tommo is soon stuffing my coat pockets. To my surprise the loot feels very heavy. Then I realise he's stashing small bags of gold dust and nuggets. These are followed by a fistful of banknotes and gold sovereigns until both my coat pockets bulge. 'I've took the cards too,' he says, and goes off to call Chubb.

Puffing for breath as usual, the proprietor of the Great Eastern Hotel arrives with three of his men. He walks cautiously into the room, which is a sorry sight – the table upturned and the hearth strewn with broken whiskey bottles and plates, chop bones, eggshells, spent tobacco and Mexican cheroot butts.

Chubb takes in the scene and wipes his red face with a bandanna from his back pocket. 'It'll cost a pretty penny to set this straight. Lock's broke too,' he complains.

From downstairs, others have come to the doorway to peer at the disturbance. 'Leave it off, all of you downstairs, you've got work to do,' Chubb snarls at them, then he closes the door.

'Mr Chubb, I want you to call a trooper to place these men under arrest. But first tie their hands.' I point to the pigtails hanging from their belts. 'There is plenty of evidence to suggest that these men are implicated in the murder of several Chinese in Sunday's riots.'

Chubb frowns. 'What about the card game? I'll lose my licence, lad. Besides, miners drink here. They won't like it if I gets their mates arrested for a bit of rough and tumble with the celestials.'

'What card game?' I say. 'Do you see any cards? It's clear these villains have been drinking and have smashed up the room. You've broken down the door, very brave too, and made an arrest in the interests of law and order.'

Tommo laughs at this. 'Wouldn't be surprised if you doesn't get a medal for this, Mr Chubb. Anyways these men ain't miners, nor mates of them neither. They're thugs and standover men, Callaghan's mob – they'll get no sympathy from the miners.'

'Aye, I get your drift,' the publican says with a sly grin. 'They can be the troopers' scapegoats for causing the riots.'

One of the men with Chubb begins to tie up the villains, who are still standing facing the wall. Not a word is spoken as their hands are secured behind their backs. Then the same is done to the two lying on the floor, and their ankles bound for good measure. I think Tommo's boot must have broken Jonah Callaghan's jaw, for it has a peculiar lopsided look and blood runs from the corner of his mouth into his beard. The cove I punched in the throat is now making rasping sounds. I'm most relieved I have not injured him fatally. It is good, however, that neither man will be able to tell tales of what has happened for some time.

The publican is examining the table and the chair. 'Both broken,' he says mournfully, and he waves his hand vaguely about the room. 'Lot o' damage done over all, ain't there? A lot of repairs will be needed.'

There is probably not much that couldn't be fixed by a maid

with a bucket and a mop, or a carpenter for a pound's worth of work. But I know what he is getting at.

'How much for the repairs?' I sigh.

Chubb looks around again, pursing his lips. 'Four quid would clear it nicely, I should think.'

I nod. 'What about my ten per cent, lad?' Chubb asks my twin.

'What ten per cent be that, Mr Chubb?' Tommo asks politely.

'The house takes ten per cent o' the winnings of the card game.'

'Card game?' Tommo queries ingenuously, scratching his brow. 'I thought you just agreed there were no card game, only villains what's murdered Mongolians. A respectable pub owner like you wouldn't take a chance on losing his licence for gamblin', now would he?'

Chubb looks down at his boots and shakes his head slowly. 'Aye,' he says, 'I can well see yer point.'

I hand the publican my pistol and Tommo gives his to the man who has supervised the tying up. The three Irishmen now sit facing the far wall.

'You'll be wanting to send a lad to fetch a trooper?' Tommo suggests to Chubb. 'Citizen's arrest – your name in the *Sydney Morning Herald* for sure.'

'"Brave Publican Arrests Irish Murder Gang!"' I quip.

'Single-handed!' Tommo adds.

I pull out a handful of Tommo's winnings and select a five pound note, issued by the Oriental Bank, and push it into the publican's vest pocket. 'For the repairs, and a bit extra to buy the lads a drink. We're off to Sydney within the hour and I'm sure we'll not be needed at the enquiry. After all, you've captured the Callaghan mob all by yourself, isn't that so?' I pluck three more pounds from the bundle in my hand and give one to each of the hotel employees.

'Much obliged,' two of them say and take the money shyly. The third, who still holds the other pistol, grins. 'I'm gunna bet it on you beating the Lightning Bolt, Mr Hawk. In the meantime, we ain't seen you two, that I'll guarantee. Blind as a bat we is, eh, lads?' The others nod their heads.

'I'll thank you to call the police after we're gone. Give us ten, perhaps fifteen minutes,' I say to Chubb. He wipes his face again with the rag and smiles greasily. 'Another fiver would seal my lips, and a sov more to each o' the lads would settle 'em down nicely.'

'It ain't necessary,' the man with the pistol protests, 'not fer our part.'

Chubb glares at him. I dig in my pocket and give a pound to each of the men. 'That's so your men will not feel inclined to falsely report that a card game has taken place and so get their master into trouble with the police,' I say to Chubb.

'Much obliged to ya, Mr Chubb,' Tommo says. 'We'll be off, then.'

'Never trust a nigger!' I hear Chubb mutter as we leave.

When we return to our camp, we find that Caleb Soul has harnessed the horses again to the trap. 'I'm anxious to get going, lads. It's chaos all about – we must get back to Sydney.' He points to the horses. 'They're good for a stint before they're done for the day. Hawk, you don't seem to have pushed them too hard.'

I nod, for I'd taken them slowly knowing Caleb would be keen to leave upon my return.

'We'll camp a few miles out,' Caleb says, 'and let them graze the night. I've purchased provisions for the road.'

I think what a good man Caleb Soul is. He has already pulled down the tent and packed our belongings. Tommo and I do not have much gear – a blanket roll, a shirt or two, shaving tackle and the like – but Caleb has carefully loaded it all, ready to leave. Tommo goes quickly to the trap and takes out his blanket roll to check to see his fighting axe, opium pipe and poppy lamp are there. Poor Tommo, all that is precious to him is destructive.

We take our farewell from Just Lucy and Tommo gives her a fiver. She waves us goodbye, blubbing all the while. I note that her moggy is nowhere to be seen. It's most likely asleep in some sheltered spot, catching the best of the afternoon sunshine. Cats don't give a damn for farewells, even though this one's been fed like a king since we've been here.

As soon as we're on the road, I ask Caleb's forgiveness for using the Tucker & Co. trap to help get Wong Ka Leung and his family to Yass. But he is most kind, saying we are heroes for it. This I cannot agree with. Tommo is a hero, yes, for he fought a hostile mob to be at my side. But as for me, it was simply a debt repaid. Wong Ka Leung, or Ah Wong as he's said I may call him, helped me with Tommo. I owed him a good turn.

'What a day – look at that blue sky!' Tommo smiles as we

move along. I am only grateful that he is able to see this glorious day and is not dead in a pool of blood in that stinking hotel. I know now that, in his drunken fury, Jonah Callaghan would have killed my twin without thinking twice about the consequences.

The brilliant blue sky reminds me of Maggie's eyes. We have only been away for just over two weeks but oh, how I long to return to her. She has found a place in my heart so that I think of her a hundred times each day. I do not think I could bear to be parted from her again. Every morning and every night I take off Maggie's magpie ring and read the inscription: *Maggie Pye loves Hawk Solomon, Champion of the World*. Then I kiss it and put it back on my finger. Soon enough I spy a magpie carolling away, high up on a dead branch of a gum tree, as we pass by. 'Maggie, I'm coming home!' I say silently to the bird. 'Tommo's got our stake and all's well, my darling.'

We have not been on the road long when Tommo takes to shivering. He complains to me in a whisper that his head wound is giving him merry hell. After a while, he drops into a fitful sleep, moaning and waking and falling asleep again. Though he is exhausted, I can see he is also in pain and will soon need his pipe. As he sleeps, I wipe the sweat from his face, though the air is cold.

'He's been up all night,' I explain to Caleb.

'Poor lad,' Caleb says. 'I know a nice place with a running stream. We'll camp there for the night. Not too far to go now – it will give Tommo a chance to recover.'

He asks me how the card game went, and I tell him more or less what happened. He cannot resist reminding me that he had warned Tommo against playing cards with Callaghan and his mob.

'They could've killed him,' Caleb says, nodding his head at Tommo's slumbering form. 'And most likely got away with it, leaving his body in the Chinese encampment. He would have been just another corpse – the lone white man to die in the riots.'

'What happened to the man who was burnt, a white man?' I ask, thinking of the horseman Tommo clobbered.

'He lives, though he's badly burned all over. There's some justice, though God knows it's little enough,' Caleb observes.

'Well, we were lucky. We got away, and got our stake to boot.' I take a small bag of gold dust from my pocket. 'Would you know its worth?'

Caleb switches the reins into one hand and judges the weight of the bag in his palm. 'I'll put it on the scales when we stop for the night, but I'd judge it at fifty pounds, give or take.' He hands the bag back to me.

'Well, Tommo's won six of them and three small nuggets as well. There's also some banknotes and gold sovs which I haven't counted yet.'

'Exactly the same size bags?' he asks.

'Yes,' I reply.

Caleb nods. 'Well, there's no doubt where Callaghan got these from. They're Chinese, see, made from rice sacks.'

I look at the small bag and see it has been neatly stitched with a drawstring pulling it tight.

'Open it, you'll see it's lined with silk. Gold doesn't stick to silk,' Caleb says.

I work the drawstring open and see that he is right. The gold dust gleams in the afternoon light. 'What are we to do now?' I ask, concerned.

'Nothing, lad. The true owners are dead or fled. Callaghan's mob looted it, but Tommo won it fair and square.'

I suspect that Tommo won the loot thanks to a couple of marked decks but I refrain from saying so to Caleb. Privately I resolve to give one bag to Ah Wong when we meet as arranged in Sydney.

'You must let me pay for all your expenses. We have enough,' I say to Caleb, holding up the bag again.

'I'll take a pinch tonight when we weigh it. It will pay for the handbills.'

'Yes, and what about the ten pounds you paid to Pat Malone and the Irishman who beat me?'

Caleb chuckles. 'Righto, seeing you're so flush, I'll accept.' I pay him what's due and he jams the notes into his vest pocket with his thumb.

'There is much more we owe you, Caleb, I've kept a record.'

'No, no, Hawk, no more,' Caleb smiles. 'It's been a long time since I enjoyed such company. I'm in your debt for the good fellowship you've provided me on my last trip to the diggings.'

'This is your last trip?'

'Aye. It ain't been bad work and the recompense is fair, but it's a hard life too. For a start, I have to drink too much with the customers.'

'But I've never you seen intoxicated!' I exclaim.

'Not ever quite sober either.' He jigs the reins and the horses move a little faster. 'It's time for me to take out my pills and potions, time to settle down, have a family. I've put a fair bit away, and pharmacy is what I really want to do.'

I think on this. If Caleb is correct I calculate that Tommo has won about four hundred pounds, most of it in gold.

'Caleb, you asked Tommo and me once –' I hesitate '– if we'd be partners with you in your pharmaceutical company?'

'I did.' He looks at me. 'I'd be proud to have you in with me, Hawk. Your brother too, though I don't know quite what he'd do.'

'What would such a partnership cost?'

'I thought you wished to try your hand at being a shopkeeper at the diggings?'

'Caleb, like you, I think it's time to settle and have a family. But now I see that the goldfields are no place for a woman and children.'

'You're not wrong,' he says. 'Then you'd consider coming in with me?'

I clear my throat. 'Caleb, I haven't been entirely forthcoming with you. Tommo and I must go back to Tasmania for a while – perhaps even longer than a while. I'd like to be your partner and maybe work with you later, but I would be joining you as a silent partner for the present. There's the fight and then there's my duties in Hobart Town . . .'

'Your lass? She's down there, is she?'

'No, she's from Sydney, but I'll have to present her to our mama. I must have her blessing.'

'Quite right,' Caleb murmurs. We don't speak again for fifteen minutes, then Caleb says, 'Hawk, I'd rather our partnership was fifty-fifty, with us both putting in equal amounts of capital and working together. But if you want a one-third share as a silent partner for now – with this to be revised to a half share should you come as a working partner within two years – it will cost you a hundred and fifty pounds.'

'Will you measure it out on the scales in gold dust tonight?' I ask. 'Plus, of course my share of the legal expenses – including the cost of drawing up the papers for Tommo and me.'

Caleb Soul leans over and offers his hand. 'You'll not regret it, Hawk. Two things are certain in this life. People will always need grog and they'll always need potions.'

So my course is set. I have resolved to marry Maggie and

I must somehow persuade Tommo to return to Hobart Town with me. Mary's last letter was most unhappy – she misses us terribly and I know she fears she may never see her boys again. I sink back into silence, much preoccupied by how I shall bring together all my loved ones at last.

Our friend is true to his word and we camp by a pleasant stream late in the afternoon. I help him set up the tent while Tommo goes away to attend to his pipe. Later that evening, Caleb brings out his gold scales and, after considerable reckoning, he declares that we have, at the very least, five hundred pounds! When I ask him to accept a little more for the trouble he has taken on our behalf he adamantly refuses, requesting only that he might help with the preparations for the fight. This I readily agree to.

A week later we are back in Sydney, where Maggie receives me with joy and tears. I too am overcome. Oh dear, how very much I love her and, from her joyous reception, it seems she loves me too.

'Oh, Hawk, ya lovely bastard, I loves ya!' she says, jumping into my arms.

'Maggie, what would you say to giving up your work?' I ask her after we've made love.

'What's ya mean?' she asks, horrified. 'Become respectable-like?'

'Well, yes, sort of.' I cannot quite imagine Maggie completely respectable.

'Jesus, Hawk! What's you on about? Respectable? Is you ashamed o' me?' Her lips begin to tremble, but then she gains control and her big blue eyes come to fire. 'You bastard! You nigger bastard!'

I hold her tight against my chest as she yells at me in anger. 'Lemme go, you black shit! Lemme go!'

'Maggie, Maggie! Hush! I'm asking you to marry me! To have my children.'

Maggie goes totally still in my arms and I release her.

'Brats?' she asks.

'Aye!'

'Me own brats? Oh Jesus!' Maggie begins to sob.

I don't know what to do. I thought to see her anger or scorn, but not these tears. I pat her on the back. 'You'd like to have children, then?' I query, anxious that I may have said completely the wrong thing.

Her head buried in a pillow, Maggie nods. Then her sobs begin afresh. 'Brats,' she howls, 'oh, shit! Oh, oh, oh!'

I continue patting her and then begin to stroke her back and thighs. My hand wanders over her tight, sweet derrière to the inside of her legs, and I let my finger slide into her warm and creamy place. Maggie opens up to receive me, and I push her gently onto her back and enter her. Her sobs turn to whimpers and moans, and I think how beautiful she is and how much I love her. 'Oh, Hawk,' she cries, wrapping her legs tight about me. 'Oh darling, Maggie's coming! Oh, Jesus! You bastard, you lovely bastard! Brats! Me own!'

Afterwards, she sits up almost immediately. 'You wants me to marry you? Be respectable-like?' she wonders. 'I ain't never been respectable. Don't suppose I've got the knack.'

'You'll get the hang of it soon enough,' I laugh.

Maggie makes a pair of dainty fists and knuckles away another rush of tears. She's sitting cross-legged on the bed, her blue eyes red-rimmed from crying, but her pretty mouth is set firm. 'On your wages? No bloody fear, mate! Respectable takes money. I ain't gunna be respectable washin' the bleedin' floor, scrubbin' pots 'n' pans. I'm a respectable whore, not a bleedin' respectable scullery maid!' She looks at me fiercely. 'You can shove yer respectable up yer arse, Hawk Solomon! I'll work and keep ya 'til you makes somethin' out o' your life!' She stops and thinks for a moment. 'And not out o' fisticuffs neither, I ain't marrying a prize-fighter. O' course, you can fight this once against the Bolt!'

'Then you'll marry me? Oh, Maggie!' I go to embrace her but she pushes me away.

'Only if I stays what I am 'til we can afford better. I ain't gunna scrub no floor for no one! I loves ya, Hawk, with all me heart, but I ain't gunna go down on me knees for no bastard!'

'Maggie, it doesn't matter to me what you are. I love you with all my heart too.'

'Yeah,' she says, 'it don't matter to *you*. I know that now. I didn't never think it could 'appen to me. Oh sweet Mary, Mother o' Jesus, I loves ya, Hawk Solomon!'

I hold her for a while. 'Maggie,' I say eventually, 'now you must meet our mama.'

Maggie draws back. 'But she don't like me!'

'Of course she will. Mary will love you, you'll see!' Then I see

Maggie has brought her hand to her lips and wears a look of consternation. I hear again her last words in my mind. '*What* did you say?' I ask slowly, my heart pounding.

'I said what if she don't like me?'

'Maggie! That's not what you said!' I frown.

'Orright,' Maggie says tremulously. 'I'll tell ya the whole story. Tommo think yiz gunna get beat. Hurt bad. He asked your mama to come up here!'

'What, here? To Sydney?'

Maggie nods and sniffs. 'We needed her help!'

'What for?'

'Oh, Hawk, don't ya see? There's only one way yiz can win. The Bolt's got to take a dive, least that's what Tommo thinks!'

'And you? Do *you* think that?' I ask her. Maggie drops her eyes but says nothing, her fingers playing with the corner of the pillow. I grasp her by the shoulders. 'Answer me! Is that what you think, Maggie?'

'Leggo, yiz hurting me!' she cries, but I continue to hold her. 'Please! Yiz bruisin' me, Hawk!'

I cannot bear the idea of hurting Maggie and all the anger goes out of me. I sigh. 'I can't possibly win no matter how much training I do, so Tommo's going to fix the fight! Is that it?'

Maggie's eyes grow big. 'Hawk, yiz the bravest man I've ever known. It's just . . .'

'Just what?'

'Well, Tommo says you can't learn enough technique in time to fight the Bolt, no matter what. I know prize-fighters and I thought you could win but he's made me believe you're gunna get hurt.' She tilts her head at me. 'Oh, Hawk, I don't want them to hurt you! The Irishman will be too crafty and cunning. You don't have the skill to take him on! You said so yerself, remember?'

'Yes, but I've changed my mind.'

'That don't change nothing!' Maggie exclaims. 'Think the Irishman's gunna shit his pants 'cause you've changed your bleedin' mind?'

'You're wrong. It changes everything,' I say. 'We're going to set it up so that Mr Sparrow lays down all his money against me, and then I'll take on the Lightning Bolt fair and square and win – even if I get killed in the process.'

'But why?' Maggie pleads. 'I can take care o' yiz. And you'll soon get on in yer job, get a raise! We don't need to do this bloody fight!'

'Maggie, you forget what Mr Sparrow's done to Tommo! He's a mongrel. You can't let the mongrels win.'

'Oh bull!' Maggie exclaims. 'What's been done to Tommo he's done t' himself! There's always a Mr Sparrow. Get this one and another'll take his place soon enough. World's full o' bastards what you calls mongrels – always has been, always will be!'

'It's more than that, Maggie. It's what happened to Tommo and me when we were brats. Mr Sparrow's a part of that. It's time to change our fates.'

'I dunno what yiz talkin' about, I'm sure,' Maggie sniffs.

'Yes, well, be that as it may, Tommo's got to answer for himself, and so do I. Part of the answering is believing the mongrels don't always win. You can't just give in to evil, you have to fight it! If you don't, it destroys you. If I have to fight the Irishman to beat Mr Sparrow, then I shall. And I mean to win.'

'But you *will* win!' Maggie insists. 'That's it, ain't it? We bribe the Irishman to take a dive, and Mr Sparrow loses all his loot on the betting ring. Abra-bleedin'-cadabra! You've won!'

I sigh. 'Maggie, you have not heard a thing I've said. I can't win by cheating!'

'Shit, why not? What's wrong with cheating, all of a sudden? What's Tommo been doing these past weeks to raise your stakes if it ain't cheatin'?' Maggie asks.

'That's different! To bribe the Irishman to lose is to be just like Mr Sparrow. All the things that have destroyed us – me, Tommo, even you – are the result of good men standing by and watching, while mongrels like him corrupt the human soul!'

Maggie shrugs. 'Well, I shouldn't worry about it too much. Nobody's gunna bribe nobody. She ain't got the money.'

'She? Who hasn't?'

'Mary bloody Abacus!'

'Maggie, you've met our mama, then?'

Maggie sticks out her chin. 'Yes I has. Tight as a squid's bum, that one! I don't mean t' insult yer mama, Hawk, but Tommo said she'd be willin' t' pay the bribe.' Maggie pauses, then meets my eye. 'Well, it ain't so.'

'Maggie, what has Tommo told you about Mary?'

'He told me she were rich.'

'Oh Lord. And then?'

'I started t' cry, 'cause if she were and you also, then you wouldn't love me when ya went back to Hobart Town. Rich blokes fuck whores, but they don't marry 'em. But now I knows different. She told me she ain't got no money.' Maggie looks at me, still near to tears. 'She *don't* like me, Hawk. She said I were a whore!'

'Well, you are, aren't you?' I say, cuddling her. 'You say so yourself!'

'Yes, but the way she said it, it were different.' Tears begin to roll down Maggie's cheeks. 'At least she can't think me a gold digger if she ain't got no money to give ya.'

I can see in my mind what's happened. Mary's arrived dressed in a simple black dress, hair brushed tight under a dark bonnet, looking plain as a crow, hoping to seem a respectable working class woman. She's taken one look at Maggie and made up her mind in an instant. So she cried poverty, thinking to send the little gold digger away.

I sigh at these thoughts. 'Maggie, you aren't marrying Mary Abacus. You're marrying me, Hawk X Solomon!'

'I suppose,' she says doubtfully. 'But I'm glad she ain't rich after all. I can look after ya, Hawk, honest. I'll work harder. We'll save a bit, we've got me rooms and we won't starve.'

'How long has Mary been in Sydney? Does Tommo know she's here?'

'Tommo knows. She's at the Hero of Waterloo. She only came in last night. Mr Harris sent a lad to tell me. I got her a nice room, paid a week's advance meself, full board.' Maggie looks accusingly at me. 'She didn't even say ta!'

'I'm sorry, Maggie. Mary's pretty plain-spoken, that I'll admit, but she is not usually rude. She's a good woman, Maggie, you'll see. Did she truly call you a whore?'

'Good as! It were the way she looked at me. I wore my best outfit too and me new magpie hat from Mr Myer's Emporium. It were me red silk gown, what I bought from Farmer's after the Ben Dunn fight. I wanted to do ya proud, Hawk, so your mama'd think I were pretty enough for yiz! I even wore one o' them Chinee silk shawls what Barney Moses give me, so she wouldn't see me tits.'

I close my eyes. I can just imagine the set of Mary's thin lips when she first set eyes on my darling Maggie in all her finery. As to what she'll have to say to me when we meet, I am loath to think!

Chapter Twenty-three

TOMMO

The Rocks
July 1861

Hawk's flaming mad about our plan to bribe the Bolt. He says I've lost me marbles. He even threatened to get Caleb Soul to take charge of our side of the arrangements. I tried to tell him I didn't think he could win no matter what, 'cause he don't have the experience to fight a pug like the Bolt.

And Ho Kwong Choi's turned out to be no help to us. On me first visit to Tang Wing Hung's opium den, after we gets back from Lambing Flat, old Ho tells me he can't help us none. He said he couldn't remember nothing what could be useful to Hawk. But I reckons it's a set-up – he spoke to Mr Tang Wing Hung after all, what told Mr Sparrow, what warned the old man not to help Hawk.

I should've saved me breath, tryin' to persuade Hawk to my way o' thinking. Hawk's a stubborn bugger and once he's made up his mind he don't change it too often. He reckons if we win by cheating, we ain't beaten greed, greed's beaten us. And if it ain't a straight victory over the Bolt, then we'll still be in Mr Sparrow's power – and he'll have won after all. As usual he's done a measure of practical thinking about the whole set-up too. What he's come up with isn't half bad, even if it won't be of any use in the end.

Hawk points out that the Bolt has now fought and won against most of the champions of the various states. He's already beat Ben

Dunn as well as Fred Woods and Jimmy Shanks, and all of them stopped well short of twenty rounds. Ben Dunn did best, lasting nineteen rounds before his corner threw in the sponge. *Bell's Life in Sydney* reckons the local champs have given the Lightning Bolt no trouble whatsoever – his ringcraft and cunning had them well and truly beat.

'The Bolt boasts that he hasn't done a lick of training and that against Jimmy Shanks he took a bottle of Irish whiskey into the ring to drink between rounds!' Hawk looks at me most earnest. 'Don't you see, Tommo? He's well cashed from the bouts and from betting on himself. He's ready to return home after one last easy fight. Maybe I can't match his cunning but I've got height and reach and strength. I reckon I can outlast him, wear him down 'til his legs give in.' Hawk smiles. 'The Bolt hasn't yet had an opponent who could do that. All of them have been old pugs, not one of them a day younger than thirty-five, and not trained for stamina.'

'Hawk, it won't come to that,' I argues. 'Bare-knuckle fighting's a dirty business. There ain't no rules for sportsmen! It's a free-for-all in the clinches. He'll stamp on your insteps, knee you in the bollocks and head butt you as he pulls you in. It ain't about stamina or about outlasting him. It ain't even about punching. It's about fighting cunning!'

But Hawk won't listen to none of what I tells him and so I've done me best to see he gets the right training. Most of the past two weeks I've been waking early so I can watch him spar before I goes for me smoke and night of poker. It ain't left me much time for Mary, what's been in Sydney since we got back from Lambing Flat. She's still at the Hero o' Waterloo and after telling me she ain't gunna get involved none 'til she's seen for herself what's goin' on, we've barely spoke – what suits me just fine, thank you very much.

Since he started training proper, Hawk's built his strength up and has shown himself a quick learner. Bungarrabbee Jack and Johnny Heki, the Aborigine and Maori blokes what's training him, are old-timers and knows all the dirty stuff what's likely to come his way.

Johnny Heki loves Hawk like a brother and they chatters away together in the Maori tongue for hours. Hawk has Maori tattoos of a very high order and so is much respected by Johnny, who imagines me brother is fighting for his people's honour. In a way that's true. I reckon Hawk's fighting for all of us what's been wronged – all what's been taken advantage of, as he sees it.

Johnny tells Hawk how the dirty fighting's done in the clinches, when the referee's to the back of you so he can't see what's going on below the belt. He shows Hawk how to stand with his feet wide-spaced, so that he can lean against his opponent and still keep him from getting too close. Johnny Heki and Bungarrabbee Jack reckons the Bolt will try to draw Hawk in, and that's where Hawk can do his best work. They teaches him how to use his knee in a groin and grab his opponent's bollocks. But it's not the kind o' fighting me brother takes to, it's too low-down and dirty for him.

Instead, Hawk must learn to avoid having these things done to him. So his trainers show him how to rest his head on his opponent's shoulder when he's pulled close to prevent a head butt. Hawk must keep his head above his opponent's shoulder at all times, 'cause if the canny Irishman can lower it to his chest, he'll surely poke his fingers into Hawk's eyes or get two fingers up his nostrils, tearing his nose so bad the fight must be stopped for the blood what's pouring out. Everything, Hawk's coaches explain, happens in the clinch, in the hugabug. So Hawk must use his reach and strength to avoid the clinch.

Both blokes teach Hawk how to defend himself from body blows and, in particular, from blows below the belt. They reckons Hawk can only learn one good combination punch in the time they've got, so they teaches him how to lead with a left and follow through with a right. Bungarrabbee Jack calls this the 'one-spot, two-shot, left-right, bang-bang!' He makes Hawk practise this combination over and over again 'til he can do it without thinking. Hawk's left can drive a man back several paces and the right hook what follows up and under the heart will lift his opponent's feet off the ground. The Aborigine slaps his palms together as though he is dusting them, 'Ten times, boss! One-spot, two-shot, left-right, bang-bang! Ten times one fight, all over – sleepy time!' Bungarrabbee Jack reckons if Hawk can land a good left and a right under the heart ten times during the fight he'll stop any man on the planet.

They also school him to keep hitting under his opponent's heart, what's much better than trying to hit him in his head, where Hawk could easily break his hand and leave himself defenceless.

459

'Same spot, boss!' Bungarrabbee Jack keeps repeating, as he drives his fist under Hawk's heart. 'Keep hittin' him same spot! Time come he can't stand no more. Same spot, eh!'

Then, just a few days ago, things really began to look up. Hawk were hauling barrels up to the wine loft as part of his training, when a boy apprentice comes to say there be a Chinaman at the gate. He hands Hawk a scrap o' paper what the man has given him. Hawk sees that the note is in his own handwriting and has his name and the Tucker & Co. address. It's the note he gave Wong Ka Leung – or Ah Wong as he calls him – when he left him in Yass after they'd fled from Lambing Flat.

Hawk goes immediately to the gate to greet the Chinaman. Me big brother is most anxious that Ah Wong should get one o' the bags o' gold I won from Callaghan. Yours truly argues against it. After all, I won it fair and square – it ain't the celestials' no more – and Hawk's done enough by rescuing Ah Wong and his family.

But Hawk as usual sees it quite the opposite. 'We've profited, but he's lost everything! He can't go back to Lambing Flat. He's skint, poor bastard, with a wife and child to support, and we're rich. It isn't fair he should suffer more while we benefit from his misfortune.'

'So what about the other five bags o' gold? They must've been took from the Mongolians too?' I says, just to make trouble.

Hawk sighs. 'There's an old Chinese proverb, Tommo. "Every journey of a thousand miles begins with one step." We don't know the others who lost their gold, but we do know Ah Wong. He is our first step to making things right.' Where Hawk's learnt a Chinese proverb I'm buggered if I know. Them books he reads go straight into his head and he don't seem to forget nothin'. Stuff comes out when you least expects it.

So Hawk goes to the gate to welcome Ah Wong, and gives him money for food and arranges to meet him later that night in Chinatown, at the scrag end o' the Rocks.

When Hawk gets there he finds Ah Wong and his family sharing a filthy cellar room with eleven other men. The property belongs to an importing merchant what has a godown on the wharf. All these men works eighteen hours a day just for food and a corner of the room.

Ever the bloomin' mother, Hawk takes one look and immediately buys food, clothes and blankets as well as all sorts of oriental paraphernalia, like chopsticks, cooking woks and bamboo baskets. He buys a bolt o' black cotton for clothes, boots for their feet and everything what's needed to set up Ah Wong and his family. Then he rents them a room what's only for them. After all this, when they's safely moved into their new home, he gives Ah Wong the bag o' gold to get him started out in life again.

Two days later an uncle of Ah Wong's family turns up at Tucker & Co. to see Hawk. He can't speak no English, so it's all busy hands and sign language between the two of 'em. Hawk can't make head nor tail of what the old man's on about. Suddenly the Chinaman takes a step forward and brings the fingers of his right hand up into the top of Hawk's throat and presses. Hawk feels the strength leak out of him and he sinks to his knees.

So now, with Ah Wong's uncle teaching Hawk the ancient celestial arts, we has our replacement for Ho Kwong Choi. And this time Tang Wing Hung and Mr Sparrow don't know nothin' about it. I begins to feel that perhaps Hawk *can* win the fight against the Bolt. It ain't much of a chance, but it's better than a kick in the arse.

Meanwhile Maggie's been going all out in the pubs and sporting houses. Anywhere people might listen she's letting drop her rumours, where they spreads and spreads. Her latest story is that Hawk's been running a hundred yards with a grown bullock across his shoulders, not even puffing at the end. Some o' the likely lads even swears they's seen it with their own eyes.

Most of the stories we come up with are so wild and ridiculous, you'd reckon people'd die laughing. But the punters lap 'em up and clamour for more! There's even tales what we didn't invent spinning about, each one stranger than the next. Mr Sparrow is delighted. He offers most attractive odds on Hawk while keeping them short on the Bolt.

The smart punters ain't took in by the brouhaha, of course. *Bell's Life in Sydney* still rates Hawk as no chance against the Irishman. They ain't seen Hawk spar and so they concludes 'he is hiding the defects he plainly suffers as a fighter'. They reckons that he ain't game to be named for the mismatch they feel sure this prize fight will be and, given all o' this, rates me brother at forty to one.

The views of *Bell's Life in Sydney* don't seem to matter, to the little punters anyways. The average bloke is all for Hawk and Mr Sparrow's booking shop is taking a king's ransom in bets what favour him. Fat Fred is now claiming to be Irish and has opened another booking shop in Parramatta Town, where the Irish bets their weekly wages on their own champion, the Bolt. Meantime Mr Sparrow has his betting agents in all the goldfields surrounding the district o' Yass and forty miles beyond the Victorian border, where they's doing a roaring trade.

The Irishman is still taking on the local fighters to the tune of one a week. And each time he wins against the champions of the various colonies there's trouble. Extra police is called out to control the Irish mob what comes from all about to celebrate. When the story come out about the Bolt drinking whiskey between rounds, Tucker and Co. trebled their regular sales of the liquor. That were on top o' sales what were already doubled since the Irishman arrived in the colonies, and still the pubs has been drunk dry by midnight. The Bolt is the darlin' of the publicans, what has named a new drink for him: 'Irish Sunrise'. It's Irish whiskey and crème de menthe in equal measure took straight. 'The gold of the whiskey and the green of the crème de menthe be heaven's golden light upon the green and pleasant land of Erin', so I hears. I don't know how much golden light a bloke'd enjoy in the gutter after a dozen of 'em.

Maggie's been reporting back on all her doings to Mr Sparrow. She tells him most convincing that Hawk is at the point o' complete despair. 'He ain't got the nature to be a fighter,' she confides to me master. If our Maggie's to be believed, Hawk hates to go into the ring for sparring and the two broken-down pugs what's training him can hit him almost at will, for he's too slow to parry their blows.

Twice she has gone to Mr Sparrow seeming at the end of her tether. 'Hawk wants t' give it away,' she wails the first time. 'He don't lack the courage, mind, it's just he can't learn the craft of it. He's strong as a bull but just as clumsy. The Abo, what's 'arf his size, can put him down any time he likes and the Maori sits him on his arse a dozen times each sparring. He's took to speaking to no one and he seems most down in spirits.' Maggie brings tears to her eyes. 'He don't even want to take me to bed no more!' she howls. 'Mr Sparrow, honest, I don't think he's gunna hold up. What shall I do?'

Maggie reckons that's when Mr Sparrow started to tremble. 'You keep him in the fight, Maggie, you hear!' he shouts. He fumbles in his purse. 'Ere!' He hands her another pound. 'I don't care what it takes! You keep him matched up!'

The second time Maggie goes to him with the same story 'bout how Hawk wants to quit, Mr Sparrow don't even waste time trying to bribe her. 'You keep him in!' he screams.

'Don't know that I can, Mr Sparrow, he's that forlorn,' Maggie says, her blue eyes wide and misty. 'He don't listen t' me no more!'

Mr Sparrow speaks very low and calm now. 'Maggie, you keep the nigger in the fight. Don't let me down now. You know I hold yer responsible!'

'I'll try, Mr Sparrow, but I can't work no miracles, now can I?'

'Maggie, let me tell yer something.'

'Yes, Mr Sparrow?'

'If the schwartzer goes, *you* go. Know what I means?'

'No, Mr Sparrow.'

'Then I'll leave you to think about it, girlie.' Mr Sparrow points his bony finger with its big diamond ring at her, before bringing it back and drawing it across his throat. 'It ain't no idle threat, neither,' he warns.

Maggie gets a real fright at this. 'I ain't done nuffink! I only done what you asked, Mr Sparrow! It ain't fair!'

'*Life* ain't fair, Maggie. That's my last word. Keep him in, or you're done like a dinner!'

Poor old Maggie, she ain't having a great time of it. She don't say much but I'd guess Hawk ain't doing his duty by her in the bed chamber. He's plain exhausted by the time he's finished with his sparring and lugging o' barrels. He's still trying to do some clerking, even though Captain Tucker says it ain't necessary 'til after the fight. But Hawk's dead proud of his books and he don't want someone else messing up his ledgers, all marked up in his own beautiful hand.

On Sunday, when he and Maggie are together, Hawk can hardly get himself out o' bed to buy the roasts and take them to the bakery for the orphan brats at the Quay. He keeps falling asleep while he's waiting in the line, much to the amusement o' the housewives. Maggie's took to carving the roast herself, in case Hawk cuts himself.

Sunday be Maggie's only day off and she treasures it, for it's the only time she gets t' see Hawk properly. When they're through feeding the brats, they usually goes to The Cut Below. There they has themselves a late dinner before popping upstairs. But these days I reckon Hawk'd be asleep before he gets to the bedroom.

And now, to add to Hawk's load, our mama's decided me and him should have our Sunday roast dinner with *her* every week. Mary has arranged with the publican, Mr Harris, for a special room to be made into a dining room for her on Sundays at the Hero o' Waterloo. She's even bought a snowy white tablecloth like the one from home, so's we can have our white tablecloth Sunday dinners again, or so she hopes.

This Sunday'll be the first of the new set-up but Mary ain't invited Maggie and Hawk says he ain't coming if she don't. The two of them, Mary and Hawk, are standing toe-to-toe and I can see Mary ain't gunna give in despite the fact her boy's towering over her.

'She's a slut!' Mary snaps at him.

'Mama, don't speak like that. I *love* Maggie.'

'Humph!' Mary snorts. 'Love! My son loves a whore!'

Quick as a flash Hawk replies, 'You were a whore, Mama, and I love *you*!'

I ain't never seen Mary so taken aback. Her jaw drops and she sits down with a bang, then begins to weep. But deep down she ain't upset – she's pleased at what he said in a funny kind o' way, pleased he loves her. Mary is still Mary, though, and underneath she's made of steel. Soon as she stops crying, she says, 'Hawk, don't throw your life away. Come home, lovey, you and Tommo. There's many a fine young lass in Tasmania what would be proud to call herself Mrs Hawk Solomon. Mrs Tommo Solomon too, I've no doubt! The both of you be most eligible young men.'

Hawk says firmly, 'Mama, I don't want any of those fine young lasses. I want Maggie!'

'And she wants your money!' Mary retorts. 'Mark my words, I know her sort. She'll bleed you dry then leave you for some pimp with a celluloid collar and a set o' gold teeth! That one ain't done a day's honest graft in her life.'

'Mama, she ain't like that,' I says in Maggie's defence.

'Oh, what would you know!' she snaps at me.

'That's not fair!' Hawk says. 'Tommo had his doubts about Maggie too, Mama.'

'It's true, Mama, but I've changed me mind. She's a wonderful girl!' I blush at meself when I says this, but it's true, I reckon.

As soon as she sees she can't win this one, Mary changes tack and smiles up at Hawk. 'Please, Hawk, just this one Sunday, just the three of us, Tommo and you and Mama, like old times? Look, I've even brought me big gravy boat from 'ome.'

'Is God coming too?' I asks, trying to lighten the mood.

But neither takes any notice of me quip. Hawk shakes his head slowly. 'No, Mama, Maggie's my betrothed. If you won't have her at your table, then you won't have me. Maggie comes on Sunday or I won't!'

Hawk is laying down the law and Mary can see he ain't messing about. Still, she tries again. 'Oh Hawk, I've missed me boys something terrible. It ain't been easy on me own, with David and Hannah bloody Solomon on me back all the time. My arthritis is playing up something terrible. I don't suppose I've too long left, and I ain't seen much of you these last couple o' weeks.'

She looks at both of us with pleading eyes. 'All I want is for me two boys to be home again. I don't ask nothing more. I've got the brewery built to give you something in your life what's your own. I done it for the both of you. I've had a hard life, and you two boys has been the only joy in it. Come home, I beg you! I'm beggin' you on me knees.'

Mary strings all these reasons together, like if she can find enough of them we'll be convinced. But she don't go down on her knees like she says. I don't reckon Mary would go down on her knees for the Almighty Himself. She might make Him Sunday dinner, second helpings and all, but that's about as far as she'd go. In me head, I hears her putting Him in His place.

'Help yourself, Gawd, plenty o' mutton left, gravy and onions. Here, have another tater. Bleedin' cold up the mountain, ain't it? Soon be warm in here, that's a red-gum log in the hearth since mornin'. Soon warm the cockles of your heart.'

Then God says we ought to give thanks for our blessings before we tucks in.

'Hang about!' says Mary. 'Thanks to who? Who done all the bleedin' cooking then?'

'Well, *you* did, my dear,' the Almighty says. 'And very nice too. Nobody does them little onions in gravy like you.'

'Well then,' says Mary with one of her sniffs, wiping her hands on her pinny. 'Anyone going to give blessings 'round here can bleeding well thank me. And I don't need no thanks neither, thank you very much! Go on, tuck in and don't be so high and mighty!'

'Quite right, m'dear,' says the Father of Heaven. 'Couldn't have put it better myself. Would another slice o' mutton be out o' the question, do you think? Splendid! Pass the gravy please, Tommo.'

Afterwards God always says thank you most polite to Mary, in case He don't get invited back.

Now here's Mary, who ain't afraid of God Himself, saying she'll go down on her knees for us to come back. She won't, but even for her to say it is quite something, for she's the proudest person I've ever known.

'Mama, I love you, we both love you,' Hawk says softly, glancing at me. 'But I will not come home without Tommo and Maggie, and I will not come on Sunday without her either.'

Mary sighs. 'All right, then. I'll set the table for four. Don't be late. I've spoke to the cook, leg o' mutton be ready one o'clock sharp!' Then she manages a smile. 'Where d'you reckon I'll get them little onions around here?'

Mary may have given in but our first family Sunday dinner looks like it ain't gunna be the most pleasant gathering ever. We're all in the saloon bar of the Hero. God's definitely missing, Mary's looking down her nose at Maggie and Maggie's scared to death about the whole thing. It all starts to come apart while we're still having our drinks before dinner. Mary's having a lemonade and Hawk a beer, me a Cape brandy and Maggie a double o' gin for Dutch courage. I've come to realise that Maggie ain't in fact a big drinker. She can nurse a single gin an hour or two and often she'll make it look like she's tippling by arranging with the bar for them to give her plain water instead.

Maggie's wearing a plain black dress made of what she calls bombasine, buttoned up to the neck. All the same, it's fitted tight to the waist and shows off what's hers to show up top. It's her hat what's the problem though. She's wearing a black bonnet – 'cept it's been fitted with a birdcage, like they sells down at the markets to keep your songbird or canary in. Maggie's got a young magpie in hers, and it's chirping and jumping and bumping against the wires, shitting everywhere. It clearly ain't too happy about it all.

Hawk, o' course, don't notice anything's wrong. He probably thinks his little magpie is very clever, but Maggie should've known better than to wear this trumped-up bonnet today of all days. It's all show, I reckons – she's frightened and this be her way of pretending she ain't. Maggie don't take no lip from no one but I reckon she were expecting a heap from Mary. She's done the magpie deliberate so's to get it all over with.

Now Maggie don't know it, but Mary has a special love for birds. She just about worships them green parakeets, and she can't abide birds being kept in cages. She once spent time in the dungeons of Newgate Gaol in a cage of whores, and she reckons that's exactly what a birdcage must be like for a little winged creature what's born to fly free.

'Stupid girl!' I hear Mary muttering under her breath when Maggie's back is turned. But she don't say no more and we goes into the dining room. Mary's already been into the pub kitchen to make sure the cook's done the leg o' mutton to her liking. Now she says that she don't trust him with the gravy and must make it herself. 'Them little pearly onions must be cooked just right – simmered in gravy made with the dripping from the roasting dish – just the way my boys like them.'

While she's away seeing to the gravy, Maggie downs another double o' gin. Hawk don't say nothing and I ain't game! By the time Mary returns, with the cook carrying in a monster leg of mutton and her behind him with a large gravy boat, Maggie's three sheets to the wind. During the dinner she giggles and snorts and whispers into Hawk's ear, making a terrible mess of her plate. There are drops of gravy splashed all over Mary's white tablecloth. Mama's forehead is as furrowed as a new-ploughed hill paddock and things definitely ain't going too good.

'Oops! *Pardonnez-moi!*' Maggie giggles in the Frenchy lingo as she spears at one o' the little gravy onions and it shoots off into Mary's lap. Mary stays stum and picks up the onion and puts it to the side of her plate. She's wearing white gloves to conceal her poor hands and now the finger and thumb's got a big, brown blotch on the tips.

But Maggie don't quieten down even at this. She's got the giggles again and stabs at the next onion on her plate. This time the whole plate wobbles, spilling more gravy. Two sprouts roll off and half a dozen little onions merrily follows across the tablecloth.

'Shit!' says Maggie, not speaking the French no more.

Hawk too is now scowling. Perhaps it's 'cause I'm anxious for him and Maggie but I'm pissing meself with laughter inside, and trying not to show it. A shame God ain't been invited. He'd get an almighty laugh from what's happening.

Maggie becomes aware there's silence all about her. 'What's wrong with yiz all?' she asks suddenly, jamming the handles of her knife and fork down on the table. 'It ain't my fault them stupid little onions ain't growed up yet! How's I supposed to eat them, the slippery little fuckers?'

I can't hold me laughter in no more and I bursts out and Maggie with me. She's shakin' her head up and down and the bloody magpie is chirping and fluttering and there's feathers floating down onto the table. Then the door to the cage flies open and out jumps the little magpie, straight into the gravy boat, landing in gravy up to its neck.

Out steps the birdy into the middle of the table and shakes itself like birds do after a bath. There's bloody gravy everywhere and Mary's face is spotted – it looks like she's got a bad case o' brown chickenpox! The bird tries to fly away, but it must have got gravy in its eyes or something, 'cause it's banging into everything. Maggie says, 'Oops! *Pardonnez-moi!*' again then gets the hiccups. We both goes after the flamin' magpie but we's laughing so much, we falls over each other, and the bird escapes our clutches. It's still flying about, leaving splotches o' gravy on the walls and everywhere. Finally I catches it, opens the window, and lets it go. Off it flies, dropping globs o' Mary's best gravy as it leaves. Maggie runs to the open window and yells after it, 'Come back, ya forgot the bloody onions!'

Then she turns and sees Hawk's face and her bottom lip begins to tremble. She reaches up and pulls off the bonnet with its empty cage and throws it to the floor. 'Oh, oh, oh!' she sobs and slides down, with her back against the wall. She starts to howl, her head between her knees.

Mary bangs her fist against the table so that everything rattles. 'She's a whore!' she screams at Hawk. Our mama ain't wiped the gravy from her face and it's gone pale with rage. The scar down her cheek be bright purple, and her beautiful green eyes is on fire.

There follows complete silence, 'cept for Maggie's crying. Slowly, Hawk gets up and walks over to Maggie. He takes her gently under her arms and lifts her to her feet. Then he swings her up so that she's got her arms about his neck and is sobbing into his chest. He turns to Mary. 'Perhaps she is, Mama,' he says quietly, 'but she's mine and I love her.' He carries Maggie out of the room, out of the pub, and down the street towards the Argyle Cut as I watches from the window.

Back in the room, Mary's still sitting like she's got the headmaster's cane stuck down the back of her black dress. I can't see her expression 'cause she's got her back turned to me.

'Mama,' I says, trembling in me boots as I does so, 'Maggie's a nice girl, truly. She don't drink much as a rule. She were scared, that's all, and took a drop too much.' I go to sit in my chair, though I feels like running away – scarpering out o' there like Hawk and Maggie. I looks up to meet Mary's eyes and, to me surprise, she's smiling!

'Hawk's got himself a good un, Tommo. Lots o' gumption, that Maggie, ain't scared o' life like most. Bit narrow in the hips though. Birthing won't be no picnic, but we'll get a good midwife to attend.' Mary's laughing now. 'Mr Harris says she's got a good head on her shoulders, owns her own chophouse and the building it's in.' She's laughing while she wipes the gravy from her face. 'A bit headstrong, mind, she'll need a bit o' straightening out, but I reckon she'll get there.'

'Mama, Maggie ain't easy to push around,' I say, starting to like Mary for the first time.

'Hmmph! I daresay we'll learn to live with her and her with us.' Mary dabs the napkin to her lips then folds it carefully and puts it on the table. Her eyes fill with tears as she looks at me. 'Tommo, please come back to Mama? Come home, lovey?'

'Mama, I ain't no good for you!'

'Oh no!' she protests. 'You're good enough for the likes o' me, son. I weren't an angel myself!' Her eyes glisten with tears though she tries to smile. 'Ha! Fancy me, Mary bleedin' Abacus, calling Hawk's Maggie a whore. Me what's been the very same. That's funny, that is, me the respectable one!' Then she stops and clears her throat.

'I know about the opium, Tommo,' she says, very quiet.

I'm shocked. 'Who told ya?' I asks, tryin' to look like I don't feel guilty.

'Hawk. He made it a condition.'

'Condition?'

'Well, a condition if you were going to come back. Him too. If ever you was to come back, I'd have to accept that you're . . .' she thinks a moment, trying to find another way to say it, but Mary can't not call a spade a bloody shovel, 'addicted to the poppy.' Then she adds quickly, 'He told me about your wound, I mean, how it gives you great pain and you need the opium.'

'Mama, I *told* you I was no good,' I says. 'But Hawk ain't got no right to be telling you about the opium!'

Mary sighs. 'Tommo, he *had* to tell me. He won't come back 'less you do, he's said that to me, time and again since I been here. He's told me that if you two was ever to come back it would have to be on your terms, you'd have to agree and me too.' Mary smoothes the tablecloth in front of her with both hands. 'Well I do, I agree.' She looks into me eyes.

'Mama, how long would it last? I can't work in the brewery, I ain't the type. I'm a gambler, cards is me life.'

Mary reaches over and pats me hand, then leaves her hand covering mine. I look at them together, mine all mangled from the wilderness, hers from the bad things what happened at the docks.

'Tommo, I ain't goin' to judge you,' she says, giving a bitter little laugh. 'Me, judge? I ain't got no bleedin' right, have I? I was addicted meself to the stuff once. Opium and a few other things what I don't care to talk about.' Her voice is very soft now. 'I love you for what you is, Tommo Solomon. What I done after you come back from the wilderness were wrong and I beg your forgiveness! But I never stopped loving you.' The tears are rolling down her cheek and I feel a lump in me own throat. 'Never for one moment, through all the dark years, did I ever stop loving you. "Tommo'll come back," I'd say to myself every morning as I woke and every night before I closed my eyes. And wherever you was, I'd always say, "Good night, Tommo. Mary loves you, darling."'

'Oh Mama!' I bursts into tears. I can't help it, it's like a dam in me's just burst and I can't hold back the flood. All the loneliness of the wilderness comes back – the cold, the beatings, what the timber getters done to me when I were a little brat. I blubs and blubs and Mary rises from her chair and comes t' hold me. Then she starts to cry and the pair of us is howling and hugging and I'm seven years old again and Mary's got me in her lap and I'm safe, Tommo's safe again.

Mary orders a bottle of Cape brandy for me and I has a drink as she begins to talk. It's like it's all been bottled up in her as well. We already knows from her letters that things were bad 'tween her and David and Hannah. But now Mary pours it all out like she wants me to hear it straight.

It seems old man Madden, what's now married Hannah, is stricken with the gout and crippled with arthritis, so he spends all his days in bed or in a bath chair. Hannah and David has took over his timber and wheat-milling business, with David proving a sharp businessman. It ain't long before he and Hannah sees their chance to make things difficult for mama by making it hard for her to get her supply o' brewing hops.

New Norfolk, where David and Hannah lives, be the best climate for the growing of hops and they buy up land and plant hops. They also purchase in advance, at guaranteed prices per bushel, the crops of all the other hop growers. They even gain control of all hops imported from New South Wales and Victoria. Soon Hannah and David have got a monopoly and Mary can't get her hops from nowhere 'less she imports 'em from England and sometimes from Cape Town, what's both unreliable and expensive.

Then David does nearly the same thing with Mary's supply o' glass by buying into the Tasmanian Bottle Co. Now Mama can only obtain her bottles from Melbourne, what adds greatly to their cost. He's even building his own brewery in Launceston to compete with her.

Mary tells me all this and shrugs. 'I've only got one pair of hands and none what I can trust or ask for advice 'cept Mr Emmett. I need my boys to come home. Hawk tells me you got a quick mind, Tommo.'

Well, o' course I'm pleased by this as well as worried for her. 'But Hawk says Mr Emmett's always helped you lots, Mama? Can't he keep an eye on David and Hannah? See what they's up to?'

'He did help me a great deal, it's true. But with the death of his wife, Gawd rest her pernicious soul, he's retired, so he can't no more,' Mary replies.

I knows Mary has a soft spot for Mr Emmett, what's always helped her from the very beginning when she were in the Female Factory. Whenever she was with him she were like a young girl, giggling and flirting. Even as brats, we knew that, beside us, Mary's only great love were for Mr Emmett. She cared for Ikey too, but that were different. For days before she was going to see Mr Emmett she'd be in a regular dither, burning the porridge and dropping things. And her what's always rushing around would take t' standing about and daydreamin' with half a smile on her face, her head tilted to one side.

What with Mr Emmett being a true merino and a married man, and Mary thinking herself a common ticket-of-leave, there weren't much chance o' their friendship turning into something more. But now Mary's wealthy and Mr Emmett a widower on a government pension, so perhaps it ain't impossible after all.

'Mama, what about Mr Emmett and you?' I asks, screwing up me courage.

Mary goes quite scarlet. 'Tommo, mind your tongue!' she gasps, like I've just used a dirty word in front o' the vicar.

I laugh at her embarrassment. 'Well, you loves him, don't you?'

'Mind your own business!' Mary retorts, but she won't meet my eye.

'Why don't *you* ask Mr Emmett? No harm in asking, is there? Him alone and you alone, two lonely people. It don't make no sense not to!'

'You think *I* should ask *him?*' Mary ain't too sure she's heard me right. 'Propose to Mr Emmett? Me?'

'Aye.'

'Don't talk nonsense, Tommo. Mr Emmett's a gentleman and me common as muck! Chalk and cheese! It ain't possible for them two things to get together. The whole bleedin' island would sink under the shame of it!'

'Mama, Hawk says there ain't no one person better than another. It's how we lives what matters, not how we's born.'

'Hawk's right too, but try telling that to the governor's wife, what calls me *Miss* Abacus like some reptile hissing it out. The nabobs don't marry the thingumabobs in this world, Tommo!'

'All right, well at least put Mr Emmett on your board of directors. Hawk reckons ya should, least that's what he said to me. Ain't no harm in that, is there? It'll keep his wise head working, Hawk says.'

'Hawk said that?' Mary looks pleased and I can see she thinks it a fine idea.

Never in me life have I talked like this with Mary. When I comes out o' the wilderness, she thought me a bit of an idjit. She'd talk to Hawk about the brewery and the business but never to me. Now she's treating yours truly like she wants my opinion, and I must say I likes it!

'Perhaps, perhaps,' she says, folding and unfolding her napkin again. 'Anyways, that's quite enough nonsense about Mr Emmett!' She throws her napkin aside. With the finger of her glove she picks at a spot o' dried gravy on her bodice. 'Now listen, Tommo, I wants to talk to you about Hawk and the Irishman. The more I sees, the less I like of this fight. We must stop it at once, at all costs. How does we do it, Tommo?'

'Mama, we can't! Hawk's got it into his noggin that this be a fight between good and evil. He reckons the evil began with Ikey and carried through to Mr Sparrow, what's got me under his thumb now.'

'That Sparrer's bad news and no mistake. But Hawk blames *Ikey* for all this?' Mary asks, surprised.

'Not Ikey hisself. Hawk loved Ikey, we all did. It be what happened to us because of Ikey's greed. That's what Hawk says he's fighting.'

'Oh me Gawd!' Mary thinks a while. 'Ikey were not the only one who were greedy. Hannah were even worse and now David.' She pauses, then says softly, 'Even me.'

'That's just it! Like Hawk says, it's a canker, it festers and turns everything rotten. Greed destroys everyone it touches!'

Mary's lips are pursed as she listens. 'Tommo, let's not forget the hard things what happened to Ikey too. He were a creature of the times, a survivor. To be a poor Jew in London when Ikey were a child was to be treated as dirt – lower than dirt! The lowest villain there was would think himself better than a Jew and spit on him. That ain't no way to treat another human being, but Ikey survived all that and he beat all who would destroy him.' Mary looks at me. 'Don't forget how much he gave me and you boys. Ikey were a truly remarkable man, Tommo.'

'Mama, I've told Hawk that. It's not Ikey what's the problem. If it weren't for Ikey I couldn't have survived the wilderness. But Hawk says, if it weren't for Ikey we wouldn't have been took by the wild men in the first place. If Ikey *had* shared his fortune with David and Hannah, we wouldn't have been kidnapped and there wouldn't have been no wilderness for me and for Hawk.'

'It weren't quite as simple as that,' Mary protests, though I can see from her expression that this line o' thinking ain't entirely new to her. 'It were Hannah wanting more than she were entitled to! It were *her* greed more than anything!'

'Mama, how is we to know what Hannah really deserved?

Who knows what went on 'tween her and Ikey?' I shrug. 'I'm just tellin' ya what Hawk thinks. When Hawk gets an idea in his head nothing's gunna shake it out. He thinks Mr Sparrow's another example o' greed destroying everything it touches. And he's got a point. Mr Sparrow turns everyone what works for him into addicts and drunkards, and when they's no further use, he throws them out onto the street to die.

'Now, with the fight, Mr Sparrow thinks to take all the little punters to the cleaners. He's tempting 'em to bet every cent they has with his odds, when he *knows* Hawk can't win. For him, Hawk losing to the Irishman be a certainty. If he thinks Hawk's got a chance, he'll do something to stop him. Hawk says it's always the little people what gets preyed upon.' I draws breath. 'He says *somebody*'s got to stand up for the poor and that if we expects it to be somebody other than ourselves, it ain't never gunna never happen. The villains will win again!'

Mary sighs and remains quiet a long time. 'We could still bribe the Irishman to lose? Hawk don't have to know. The poor *will* get their winnings, Sparrer Fart – or your Mr Sparrow as he now calls himself – *will* be ruined and Hawk won't be hurt too bad in the meantime!'

'Well,' I says, 'there's a lot o' "wills" in there, 'cept the one you ain't thought about at all. You *will* lose Hawk forever if he finds out. I sees that now. I were wrong even to think of it in the first place, Mama. Completely wrong! Wrong to ask you to come and wrong to ask you for the money to make the bribe.'

'I'm glad you did, Tommo. It's given me a chance to see you and Hawk again. And to help you, if I may.'

'Mama, if Hawk thinks you and me and Maggie don't believe in him, he would never get over it. He knows he's gunna need a miracle to win, but our Hawk believes in miracles!

'Matter o' fact, he works so hard at his training that I'm beginning to believe in 'em meself. He soaks his hands in brine every day and they be hard as mallets. He's training with Bungarrabbee Jack and Johnny Heki and Ah Wong's uncle, too. They's all saying that if Hawk can just stay on his feet long enough and keep out o' the clinches, he might win the fight.'

I can see Mary ain't convinced by this so I goes on. 'Best thing we can do is believe in Hawk – and hope,' I says. 'Hawk be the bravest man I've ever seen and he's awful strong, Mama.'

'I'm coming with you to the fight,' Mary says suddenly. 'If me boy's gunna be hurt, he'll need his mama.' Mary looks defiant at me, thinking I'm gunna object. 'And I want Hawk to know I does believe in him, with all me heart and soul.' She grabs her handbag from the floor beside her chair. 'Tommo, I want you to put five hundred pounds on our Hawk to win. Mind, you put the bet with our Mr Sparrow so it costs him dear and he knows it when the time comes. We want him to know the true price of underestimating the underdog, eh, Tommo?'

Mary snaps open her bag and digs into it. She brings out a roll of banknotes as thick as me forearm and slaps it down on the table in front of me. 'Now take me to Maggie. I'd best make things right with her and start making plans for the wedding and all. You'll be Hawk's best man and I'll ask Mr Emmett to give Maggie away! Let's be off!'

Chapter Twenty-four

TOMMO

New South Wales
August 1861

I walk around with Mary's five hundred quid stuffed inside me coat for near on two weeks before I figures what to do with it. I can't just do what she reckons and put the whole lot on Hawk. Mr Sparrow would smell a rat straight away! A hundred quid placed on the Irishman by a squatter or a big merchant would be all right. But if five hundred or even one hundred were put on Hawk, all the sporting gents'd want to know what rich fool made such a stupid bet! Or else they'd want to know what was going on with Hawk, in case they too should be stickin' their money on him. Either way, it wouldn't be wise to plonk the whole lot down on me twin at once. Finally I decides to get Caleb Soul and a few of his mates to dole it out for us in smaller bets of twenty quid or so. Even this be a big bet on Hawk and in the days what follow it causes noise enough.

The fight's just a week away but we must leave Sydney today to be sure o' making it. Its location's a secret so's the law can't prevent it, but we has to go to Yass, where we'll find out where it's at. Mary's hired a coach-and-four for all of us, with full provisions for the six days' journey. One thing's certain, the fight ain't gunna be at Lambing Flat. Since the riot there, the diggings have been crawlin' with about two hundred military men, marines and police.

We sets out on our journey and I reckon Mary and Maggie, what's made their peace together, would be enjoying themselves if it weren't for the flies. We've had a bout of warm weather and the flies are swarming *everywhere*. We take to startin' out early, to try and avoid 'em, but the moment the sun comes up, the little black flies comes to life again and they keeps up with us all day. They stick to the horses so that scarcely a patch o' horse hair can be seen beneath them. They gets in our eyes and noses and mouths. Luckily Caleb Soul, in his trap behind us, has brought along netting what Maggie makes into veils and attaches to our bonnets and hats, giving us all a most mysterious appearance!

But if the flies is bad, the blowflies is worse. They get into the woollen blankets by day and spoil 'em. They lay their larvae and in a matter of hours the blankets is covered in patches a foot square with maggots, what are at once fried by the sun and stick to the blankets. Again, Caleb saves the day by wrapping the blankets up in lengths of oilskin before sunrise and protecting them against the blowflies.

At first Maggie and Mary stay in roadside inns overnight, with us camped nearby. But soon they's complaining about the bed bugs and the noisy drunks, both of which be plentiful! They decides to camp with us, rough though it be.

The road is full o' people what's heard about the fight. Many reckons they'll go to see it and seek their fortunes in the diggings afterwards. Some have been walking for weeks to get to Yass. Lots of 'em cheer heartily when they sees Hawk. They run beside our coach to wish us well, stretching out their hands so that Hawk might touch 'em for luck.

I can see Mary is thrilled to see all the fuss being made over her boy by the passers-by. But every now and then I catch her watching Hawk with an anxious, loving sort o' look, as if she's seeing terrible things happen to him at the hands of the English and Irish double champion. Some of the travellers around us ain't so pleasant, with a band of rough Tipperary men jeering insults at Hawk and his team, Bungarrabbee Jack and Johnny Heki, sitting atop the coach with Ah Wong and his uncle, Ah Sing. But Mary brushes off the insults and is back quick enough to her staunch old self, declaring that o' course Hawk will win!

Mary and Maggie is having a grand time together as we trundles along, which pleases Hawk very much, and me too!

Maggie makes Mary laugh such as we ain't never heard. The two of 'em gossips from morning 'til night, swapping whispered stories about their work on the streets – at least that's what I gathers from the way they huddles together, and then bursts into giggles, like two naughty little girls! Maggie's even told Mary the rudiments o' bare-knuckle fighting so that she can follow the bout.

When we arrives in Yass our carriage is mobbed by every sort of human being you could imagine – women, young and old, men from the city, men from the diggings, men of all nations! There's as much booing as cheering around us. Our carriage can hardly move an inch down the street for men hanging off the harnesses of the horses. It's said that our welcome be every bit as big as that of the Irish champion.

The Bolt arrived the previous day and is now settled in at the Golden Nugget Inn. He's taken three rooms for himself and his six doxies, what I reckons be mostly for the look o' things.

With his doxies on his arms, the Bolt is already a great favourite with the crowd. We hear that last night in the pub, he challenged everyone there to down one drink to his two. He were the last man still standing at dawn, waving a whiskey bottle and singing *Mother Macree* and *Danny Boy* to the cockerels! They reckon he drank four bottles of Irish whiskey in all, followed by any number of beer chasers. The publican's made a fortune in drinks and out o' sheer gratitude has sent his wife to stay with a relative and given the Bolt their very own bed chamber for his visit.

We're staying with the manager of the Oriental Bank, a mate of Caleb's. Mary and Maggie will stay in the house with him and his wife. We'll camp behind the bank in the yard, what has a high wall to protect us from them what wish us well and them what wish us dead!

By nightfall several thousand visitors are in town. The diggings for a hundred miles around be just about empty o' manpower. The celestials has made their own camp a couple o' miles out, so as to avoid harassment by the drunken revellers. Ah Wong and Ah Sing has gone to join them and will make their own way to the fight.

At eight o'clock at night, a young boy arrives with a message from my employer. 'Mr Sparrow sends his compliments!' he says brightly and I brood darkly for a moment on what Mr Sparrow's idea of a compliment might be. 'The bout will take place at Black Billy Creek, about five mile out o' town on the road to Lambing

Flat, noon tomorrer! Fighters to be there an hour before!' he tells us. Mr Sparrow must be bloody confident of the Bolt to make his man fight in the midday sun.

After that news, we all tries to settle in for a good night's sleep. But all night long, folks is arriving by whatever means possible, and making a lot o' noise about it too. It's hard to get a wink what with all the hullabaloo. Hawk seems calm enough and sleeps soundly all night. I've learned a long time ago that whenever Hawk's gunna face some manner o' danger, he draws into hisself. In the Maori wars, when every other bloke were shouting, singing and doing the *haka* to get a bit o' courage, Hawk'd be away on his own, sitting very still and silent. He be at his most powerful then and so it is on the morning of the fight. He ain't even got eyes for Maggie.

'What's up with 'im then?' she pouts as we climbs into the coach at nine o'clock to go to Black Billy Creek.

'He's gettin' ready to fight,' I comforts her. 'To win!'

'Ooh, I hopes 'e does!' says Maggie, smiling and squeezing her arms with anticipation. 'Then he might be ready to go a few rounds in the bed chamber again!'

'Maggie!' I look 'round to see if Mary's heard. But she just gives Maggie a little smile and I reckon I sees a wink there too!

The road is rocky and rutted, with a vast army o' men walking along, and others on horseback or in carriages, traps and drays. We even pass a one-legged man what's being pushed in a wheelbarrow. It takes us nearly two hours to cover the five-mile distance.

Mr Sparrow has a genius for picking locations, I'll give him that much. This one's right near a billabong and is like a natural amphitheatre in a sort o' half-moon shape. Several thousand men can be seated on the slope with the prize ring built below. There's plenty of water for the horses and men, though already the banks o' the billabong are knee-high deep in black mud and several men are trying to pull a mare out what's got herself stuck.

Rumour has it that Mr Sparrow's arranged for all the local traps to be called to Lambing Flat to meet with all the militia, navy and police forces what's gathered there. What a piece of timing! Even though he's our sworn enemy, I still can't help admirin' the way he operates. Me boss has his very own police, the fight stewards what wears red armbands and carries truncheons, and they ain't reluctant to use 'em either. It's their job to keep the drunks under control and break up any fights between the two sides. But the atmosphere here is mostly one o' goodwill, with lots o' loud singing and good-natured chaffing from both sides.

The crinoline cruisers are all here, parading about in their finery. Some be from Melbourne and others Maggie knows from Sydney. The rougher sorts from the brothels in the diggings is also trawling for business, and many an insult is traded between the city whores and the gold dust girls.

Mary's the subject of much curiosity as she walks in. She's dressed in a respectable black gown, with a black veil over her face, looking like a good Christian lady on her way to church! She sits herself down on the small stool she's brung with her, as prim as someone's maiden aunt what's turned up at the wrong place but won't admit it.

Maggie, seated beside her, is the only other woman in the ring enclosure. While Mary sits stiff as a musketeer's ramrod in her black dress, Maggie's as bright as a butterfly, in a blue silk gown what's displaying all the necessary. She wears a matching blue bonnet with her magpie roosting atop – a stuffed one this time. Maggie's nigh impossible to contain and keeps jumping up from her seat while we waits for the fight to begin, chirping like a bloody budgerigar.

From where I stands in the ring, I can sense both women's fears. Mary's silent and thoughtful, like Hawk, and Maggie's a regular chatterbox – but both are worried. Caleb Soul is with them and seems to be tryin' to keep 'em occupied.

Bungarrabbee Jack and Johnny Heki are with me in the ring. Johnny Heki is massaging Hawk's shoulders and torso with eucalyptus oil, and the Aborigine has a branch o' coolibah leaves what he's using to swish the flies away. Our corner is the red one, shown by a red bandanna tied to the ring post. There's a green one tied to the ring post where the Lightning Bolt will sit. Hawk also wears a sash of red to hold up his knee breeches – no doubt the Bolt will be wearing one of the best Irish green.

It's nearly half-past eleven, but the Bolt ain't yet arrived. Bloody cheek, I reckons – we've been sweating in the ring for half an hour. It could be a tactic o' course to make us anxious. Finally at ten to twelve, just before the bout is meant to start, the Irishman makes his way to the ring from a tent, followed by our dear friends, Mr Sparrow and Fat Fred. The crowd is on its feet and roaring.

The Bolt's gained nearly twenty pounds o' lard since arriving in the colonies. He's most flabby 'round the waist, his gut sticking out further than his great barrel chest. His knee breeches show the bottom part of his legs, the calves still thick, and the skin scarred from a hundred fights. Scar tissue what's built up on his shins shines pink in the bright afternoon sunlight. His nose has been broke beyond ever looking natural again, and his ears are half the normal size, bunched up like cauliflowers. His head's fresh-shaved and gleaming and his broad smile glints with gold teeth.

The Irish champion climbs up the crude steps and slips between the ropes and into the ring. He's followed by Fat Fred, what lumbers up behind. He's much too fat to fit through the ropes, and the Bolt has to come back and hold 'em apart for Fred to climb through. Once in, Fat Fred takes up the hailing funnel what a fight steward's given him. With Fat Fred as the referee, I wonder, what chance have we got? But I keep my thoughts to meself.

Mr Sparrow's perched high on a special timber seat built up so he can see clearly how the fight progresses. He don't acknowledge Hawk or me, though he smiles when the Bolt nods in his direction.

The crowd hushes. Only the melancholy sound of a crow cawing can be heard as Fat Fred starts his announcement.

'Gentlemen, sportsmen and punters, I welcome you on this grand occasion. Today is a tournament, the greatest bare-knuckle fight yet fought in the colony of New South Wales. Two truly great behemoths contesting for a purse o' five hundred pounds – *winner takes all!*'

The crowd gives a good cheer, after which Fat Fred declares, 'This be the biggest purse in the history of the colony!' There is further clapping and yelling and Fat Fred waits for it to die down before gesturing to the Bolt, what's holding up his arms and waving to the largest group of his supporters on the centre of the hill. 'In the green corner, we have the champion o' Great Britain and Ireland! Undefeated in the colonies, the most remarkable pugilist in the known, civilised world – the one and only, *Lightning Bolt!*'

The Bolt jumps up and down as the crowd roars. Then he

catches sight o' Mary and Maggie and he blows a kiss at Maggie. Maggie lifts her veil at this and the Bolt blows her another kiss before wiggling his hips and thrusting them at her. Hawk's kept his eyes well down so far but at the very moment the Irish fighter does this, he looks up and sees it. His whole body stiffens and he begins to rise, taking the three of us to restrain him. Maggie makes matters worse by giving the Bolt a knowing tap of her finger against her nose, as if to egg him on.

Hawk don't see this, as he's too busy staring at the Bolt, what gives another big thrust of his hips in Maggie's direction. Johnny Heki has his arms about Hawk's neck trying to hold him down, with Bungarrabbee Jack hanging on as well, but Hawk's too strong for them both and brushes them aside. He rushes towards the Irishman.

'Hawk! Come back!' I yells, but he hears nothing. Reaching the Bolt, he grabs him by the neck. He's holding him at arm's length and has started to squeeze. The Irishman's trying to tear Hawk's arms away but he ain't got a chance and his eyes is beginning to pop. Then Hawk throws him to the ground and the Bolt goes sprawlin'. Me brother bends down now and says something to him, though I don't hear what. Then he walks calmly back to his corner. Mary's pulled up her veil the better to see all this, and has a huge smile on her face, what she tries to hide behind her glove.

The Irish fighter rises to his feet. He ain't hurt, but he's angry. If half a dozen ring stewards hadn't jumped into the ring to hold him back, the fight would've started then and there.

Back in our corner, Hawk's sitting down again but his nostrils are flared and his breathing's a bit fast.

'Calm, be calm,' I says. 'If ya fights him with temper he'll get the better of ya.'

He nods, and takes a few deep gulps of air.

Meanwhile the stewards have pulled the Bolt over into the green corner and his seconds have made him be seated. Fights are breaking out all over the hill and the crowd is screamin' and roarin', each side wanting blood.

Up gets Fat Fred, sweating lots and keen to get the preliminaries over with. 'Gentlemen, sportsmen and punters, in the red corner, we have the Black Hawk, New South Wales champion and challenger for the British and Irish title! May the best man win!' Before we knows it, the two men are facing each other alone in the centre. The fight against the mongrels has begun.

My heart is in my mouth as I watch Hawk prepare to meet the Irish fighter. The Bolt's also reined in his temper and smiles as he approaches Hawk. Like true pugs, they spends the next few minutes walking about each other, sizing each other up.

The Bolt takes the first move, a good kick at Hawk's ankle. But he misses and in that moment Hawk's left goes in hard, followed by the right. The one-spot, left-right, bang-bang is seated right under the Bolt's heart and it's plain to see Hawk's hurt him.

The Irishman draws back and circles 'round. Closing in, he plants a punch in Hawk's belly. You can hear the smack of his enormous fist as he puts the full weight behind it. He has hit Hawk a blow what would put most fighters to the ground or, if not, leave 'em clutching their bellies, so that they's opened up to the uppercut. But Hawk don't even flinch. Now the Bolt realises he's gunna need every trick in the book to win against this opponent.

He rushes Hawk, lashing out his leg. Over goes Hawk with a mighty thud. In an amazing exhibition of the fighter's craft, the Bolt manages to head butt Hawk at the same time and my twin lies dazed on the ground, his eyebrow split wide open.

Fat Fred begins to count, but Hawk is up by the count o' five, though dripping blood from the cut to his eye. The first round is ended after seven minutes.

The second round be a longer affair, as the Bolt's much more careful in his approach. Hawk manages to hit him several times, though mostly on the arms. Twice the Bolt lands good blows to me twin's ribs and stomach. The round has gone nearly fifteen minutes and I can see the Irishman's getting tired. Hawk's watching him most careful, expecting to be rushed and sure enough, in comes the Irishman. He grabs at Hawk, ready to deliver his head butt. This time Hawk's ready and in goes his fist – one-spot, two-shot, left-right, bang-bang – straight under the Tipperary man's heart again. The Bolt goes down like a sack o' potatoes but manages to rise unsteady to his feet at the count of nine. Fat Fred quickly brings the round to an end.

The next fifteen rounds goes along much the same lines. I keep me eyes fixed on me twin – not looking at Mary, Maggie, Mr Sparrow, or the crowd – as if by doing this I can somehow help him. The Irishman uses all his dirty tricks against Hawk, butting and gouging. Twice he knees Hawk in the groin as they go down. He is awful cunning and always has his back to Fat Fred so his actions can't be seen. Fat Fred ain't too eager to look neither. The Bolt's having a grand old time at Hawk's expense. Several of the toffs and sportsmen in the enclosure complain about the dirty play, shouting 'Fair go!' and 'Steady on!' but nothin' happens about it. I complains twice too, but Fat Fred waves me away. 'All in the game, lad. All in the game o' fisticuffs!' he says, smiling.

Hawk's shins are cut deep by the raking of the Bolt's spiked boots and his left knee is much swollen where the Irish champion's stamped upon it as he's pulled me brother to the ground. In round twelve the Irishman suddenly bites Hawk's ear and Fat Fred is forced to stop the bout. The Bolt is all innocence and points at the corner post, what has some blood on it where he's pushed Hawk's head against it. 'The post done it, I swear!' he protests.

Fat Fred accepts his explanation straight off and orders the fight to go on. Part of Hawk's ear has been completely torn away and we has great trouble stemming all the blood, though a doctor stitches it up with horsehair.

All the cloth rags we got is now soaked in blood. Between rounds Johnny Heki fetches buckets o' water and rinsing cloths. But, by the end of each round, Hawk's shoulders and chest is smeared crimson from the claret leaking from his ear and the cut to his eyebrow.

The Bolt don't seem damaged almost at all, though he's huffin' and puffin' and starting to wear out. In round twenty he manages to get Hawk into a clinch and he brings his head down to break me brother's nose with a mighty crunch. Now the whole crowd can see that the Irishman's fighting dirty and as the blood gushes from Hawk's nose, a huge cry o' protest goes up. It's the second time Hawk goes down himself to end the round and his bleeding's getting worse.

But the Irish pug ain't finished with him yet and, in the very next round, he tries the same routine again. This time Hawk's ready for him. His hand comes up under his chin and I see him make one of the Chinee grips what Ah Sing's taught him. A moment later the Bolt's eyes roll up and he goes limp. Hawk lets go of him so quick that nobody sees what's happened. The Bolt begins to topple, his eyes wide open in surprise. It's like a mighty mountain crumbling. Now Hawk sees the spot clear and it's the one-spot, two-shot, left-right, bang-bang as the Bolt goes down. I can see the fear in the Irishman's eyes.

To me surprise the Bolt gets up again at the count o' six and in the very next round, gives Hawk a few more of his rotten tricks. He uses every pug trick in the book, gouging Hawk's left eye and biting his lip so that it bleeds into his mouth. He's torn Hawk's ear again and I can see me twin's losing too much blood. In every clinch what follows, the Bolt makes sure to tweak his nose hard to make it bleed the more. Hawk's knee is paining him too and the Irishman bangs his kneecap into Hawk's swollen cartilage at every chance. As a result, Hawk's knee has blown up like a balloon and he's dragging his leg behind him.

Now the Bolt's starting to hit Hawk more easily. If he weren't near exhausted himself he'd quickly finish me brother off. Only Hawk's top physical condition keeps him going. The Irishman goes into a clinch and brings his hand up to hook into Hawk's nostril with two fingers. But he's a slow learner, the Bolt, and Hawk's hand comes up under his throat with another Chinee grip. The Irish fighter's eyes roll up, his arms fall to his side and he tumbles backwards like a sack o' spuds thrown from a dray. I think Hawk's killed him! Even those standin' close by don't see what's happened, and they shouts at him to get up and get on with it. Most o' the crowd now favours Hawk, for they sees how the Bolt be fouling him cruel at every chance.

The Bolt stirs and gets himself on all fours but can't rise any further. His seconds rush to help him to his corner, where he stays for nearly ten minutes before the next round is called. Fat Fred's given the Irishman as much time as he can to recover – only the crowd's jeers to get on with it makes him announce the next bout. From the way the Bolt rubs at his throat, it's clear he ain't gunna risk fouling Hawk again for fear of another o' these secret manoeuvres. Even so, I fears Hawk has left his run too late. At the end o' round twenty-six, I'm weeping for him. He's hurt bad and bleeding everywhere. He can barely speak through his busted mouth. His nose is broke and spurting blood, one eye's been bashed and has closed up, his ear's almost ripped off, and the deep gash on his forehead's pulled open even more.

'Hawk, you has to stop,' I urges.

He shakes his head as I sponge the blood away. 'No. He's slowing down, tiring. He can't last much longer,' he gasps.

'You neither!' I cries. 'Let me throw in the sponge.'

Hawk looks at me through his one good eye. 'No, Tommo. If we throw in the towel, Mr Sparrow wins. We'll not get a second chance at the mongrels.' Hawk ain't forgotten why he's here. He tries to smile and nods his head towards the green corner. 'Besides, he mocked my Maggie!'

For the first time I realise that Hawk will truly die in the attempt rather than give in. If this be an example o' good versus evil, good seems to be getting much the worse of the deal as bloody usual. Fat Fred signals the fight to continue and Hawk rises wearily, dragging his bad leg.

Now we see the game change. Hawk begins to stalk the Bolt what's mostly trying to stay out of harm's way. His flab and lack o' fitness has finally caught up with him and he's all scarlet, puffin' like a steam engine. Hawk's waiting for the opportunity he knows must come to him. Still, the Irishman is cunning. Whenever Hawk comes too close he pulls him in and holds him tight, then drops to the deck to end the round.

Hawk follows him doggedly and, in the next three rounds, finds him time and again with the one-spot, two-shot, left-right, bang-bang! Now he's brushing off the Irish fighter's feeble punches like they was flies. The Bolt is on the run.

Hawk is stalking his prey like a lion. He moves forward but slips on his own blood. He grabs wildly at the ropes to keep his balance but as he does so, the Irishman kicks out viciously, landing his boot hard and deep into Hawk's crotch. Hawk gives a gasp and collapses in agony on the deck. Fat Fred counts to nine before Hawk somehow manages to rise onto one knee, his hands cupped to his bollocks. He can't stand up. It *must* end. I pick up the sponge and Hawk sees me. 'NO!' he screams. 'NO, TOMMO!'

We drag Hawk back to his corner. Fat Fred comes across and I starts shouting at him like a mad man. 'Foul! It were a foul, ya mongrel!'

'One more word from you, lad, and you're out of the ring!' Fat Fred hisses at me. 'Understand? That were no foul, his foot slipped. It were an accident, no more.'

'An accident! Listen to the crowd, they bloody seen it. Everybody seen it 'cept you, ya fat, useless bastard!'

Fred looks at me hard and points a sausage finger in me face. 'You'll keep, son. You'll keep.' He turns to Hawk, what's retching with the pain. 'Now, does you fight on or does you quit?'

Hawk spits out more blood and gasps through his broken mouth, 'I shall never surrender.' It's the words from Mary's medal! 'We fight!' he says.

I hold back a big sob. 'Aye, we fight on,' I says to Fat Fred.

'You sure?' he asks. I can see he's hoping the fight will end now and suddenly me temper gets up. 'Tell the Bolt me brother ain't *begun* to fight yet! Tell him we're coming for him! Coming for all o' you mongrels!'

Fat Fred moves closer. 'We'll give you a thousand pounds if you throw in the sponge,' he whispers. 'You get five hundred, Tommo, and your brother gets another five hundred. You'll get a thousand between you. I swear it upon my mother's grave,' he whispers.

'Fuck you!' I snarls.

'Righto!' he shouts, straightening up. 'Yer man's rested enough, it's back in the fight!'

But Hawk ain't in no condition to go back just yet and needs another few minutes. The Bolt's been given ten minutes for much lesser wounds. 'Fair go!' I cries, hating the fact I has to ask him for mercy.

'Fuck *you*, son,' says Fat Fred and goes to the centre o' the ring.

Meanwhile the crowd's getting ugly – they can see what's going on. Fat Fred signals the fighters to come out o' their corners and Hawk, plainly half-dead, rises slowly. 'I need two more!' he says, as though to himself. 'Two!' he mumbles, holding up two fingers and looking at Bungarrabbee Jack.

'Two, boss! You get 'em!' the Aborigine shouts gleefully.

It is round thirty, over five hours since the fight began. I wants to blub at the sight o' me brother as he drags himself towards his opponent, barely able to stand upright. I'm sure Mary and Maggie would both be crying, though I ain't been able to look at 'em.

The Bolt hits Hawk with every punch he has at his command. Even so Hawk only goes down three times and each time to a foul what the crowd insists Fat Fred call. The stewards are looking worried – they knows they could have a riot on their hands. While Hawk can't last much longer, the real power is gone from the

Irishman's blows and he's struggling. He'd hoped to finish Hawk off long before now and it ain't worked! When Hawk comes at him now he's dead scared and ready to run, if only his weary legs would carry him. Hawk manages to get in a one-spot, two-shot, left-right, bang-bang.

In his weakened state, the Bolt can't stay more than two minutes at a time for the next two rounds. He drops willingly to the ground after Hawk taps him, so as to rest a moment and regain his breath. Then I sees why. The patch under his heart is become a horrible purple bruise. At the same moment, Bungarrabbee Jack starts dancing beside me.

'One more, boss! *One*!' he is shouting at Hawk. 'One-spot, two-shot, left-right, bang-bang – *sleeeepy time*!' Bungarrabbee Jack is boxing the air, most excited. He's seating his left and then his right into an imaginary opponent like he wants Hawk to do.

'Open him!' I'm not sure if Hawk can even hear Johnny Heki. 'Now's the time! Hit him to the head to open him up!' Johnny Heki shouts at Hawk in Maori. Never before has I heard Johnny tell Hawk to hit to the head, so I knows something's up.

Then I sees it happen. Hawk's great fist slams into the Irishman's face, right into the flattened nose, crashing into his mouth and jaw. The Bolt's face appears to collapse under the impact. Bits o' gold teeth go flying and I hears the crack o' bone as the Irishman's jaw breaks – or perhaps it's Hawk's hand?

The Bolt begins to reel backwards and Hawk comes in again. Wham! Wham! Left! Right! Bang! Bang! The Bolt is lifted clear off the ground and bounces hard against the rope. Hawk grimaces in pain and I know his hand be broke.

Somehow the Bolt is still on his feet. But his knees begin to buckle as Hawk hits him again with a left, followed by a right, plumb on the deep purple spot under his heart. I can hear Hawk's howl o' sheer pain as his broken fist smashes into the Bolt with all the force he has left. The Lightning Bolt sails over the ropes and, after knocking several toffs over on the way, lands at Maggie's dainty feet. There he lies still. They be the two hardest blows I've ever seen struck.

'Ho! That bugger never fight again in this life, Tommo,' Johnny Heki says with deep satisfaction.

'Bloody beauty, eh!' Bungarrabbee Jack says, dancing about in delight. 'It work! It work!'

Maggie leaps over the unconscious loser and climbs into the ring, her petticoats flying. She is sobbing and laughing at once as she clasps her arms 'round Hawk's waist and buries her face in his bloody torso. 'Oh, oh, I loves you, Hawk Solomon! More than me own life!' she howls, her birdy bonnet falling to the deck as she hugs and kisses him all over. With the last of his strength, Hawk picks her up and holds her in his arms and the crowd erupts. They has a champion they will never forget as long as they lives. Even the Irishmen are crying, though it may well be for the money they's lost on their fallen hero.

Mary's standing with her gloved hands pressed to her face, looking down at the Bolt, what lies out to it. Then she looks up and gives me a watery smile as her eyes turn to Hawk and Maggie. She turns her face towards me and blows me a kiss.

'I love you, Tommo,' she calls out.

'I loves you too, Mama,' I calls back, me voice catching.

And now I realise it all be over. We has won. We's beaten the mongrels. And I am very, very tired.

Suddenly the hair on the back of me neck prickles. I glance up to see that Mr Sparrow has disappeared from his perch in the fading sun. My heart's hammering as I searches the crowd, hoping to see him. I turn towards the billabong, now dark against the surrounding bush. A currawong calls from the clump o' coolibah trees. And then I sees him. He hops into a carriage what moves away into the night at a fast pace.

'Wherever ya runs, I'll find ya,' I vows. 'This time Tommo ain't gunna let ya win, ya mongrel.'

BOOK FOUR

Chapter Twenty-five

HAWK

The Rocks
September 1861

Since returning to Sydney after the fight with Ben Bolt nearly three weeks ago, I find myself a hero beyond any possible reckoning. *Bell's Life in Sydney* has proclaimed the event to be one of the great fights in history. It must also have been one of the greatest hidings in history for I am somewhat of a mess. The surgeon has straightened my nose and stitched my lip, ear and the wound above my eyebrow – but I still look like a golliwog that's been run over by a cart.

Despite my appearance, people carry on as though I am an object of exquisite beauty. Maggie, Mary, Tommo and I have even been invited to a garden party held by His Excellency the Governor. The whore, the gambler and the nigger are now the toast of the town! Suddenly Maggie is called Miss Pye by shopkeepers and merchants who would have spurned her not so long ago. Their womenfolk still refuse to have anything to do with her, for she is well known as a whore, and we learn later that numerous members of Sydney society have refused the governor's invitation.

But Maggie is puffed up with pride for me, and takes no notice of such snubs. She parades down the street with her head held at a jaunty angle, her magpie perched high atop her pretty hair, and men doff their hats as she passes by. The Sydney lads think her almost as much a hero as they do me. I shall be most glad to return to Hobart Town where Mary thinks we should have the wedding – well away from all this fuss and bother.

Maggie and I are officially betrothed, our forthcoming marriage announced in the *Sydney Morning Herald*, and Maggie has given up working since Mary's come to town. She tells me of her decision to stop work the night after the fight, when we make the most tender and considerate love, and she uses her mouth gently so as not to hurt my many wounds and bruises. She kisses my face everywhere except the places that the surgeon has stitched.

'Hawk, yours be the only body I shall ever again give me love to. No other man will lay a finger on me again, even if you should die before me,' she says, looking solemnly at me with her big blue eyes. 'I swears this on me life, may Gawd strike me dead this moment if I don't tell the truth.'

Now she no longer sleeps all day and by mid-morning is out and about with Mary, shopping and fussing about the wedding details, or having afternoon tiffin in all the best tea rooms in town. The only thing she hasn't forsaken is the magpie in her bonnet. And when she doesn't wear a bonnet, the bird still nests in her hair.

David Jones' and Farmer's, the two great emporiums, are now well accustomed to Mary and Maggie's visits, and our mama has been on a shopping spree the likes of which she's never indulged in before. The Belgian lace and the ribbon and satin cloth for the wedding gown have all been purchased here and the various department managers fawn over the two of them as though they are the grandest of gentlefolk.

On one occasion, Mr David Jones himself came down from his office to serve them and sent his compliments to the champion. He even donated five yards of the best French grosgrain ribbon with his good wishes. 'A small nuptial contribution, with my compliments,' he said fussing, 'to remember a great occasion.' He smiled when Mary shook his hand before leaving. 'Delighted I'm sure,' he beamed. 'Such a nice lady,' Mr Jones now tells all around him.

Barney Isaacs, who made my first set of clothes at Maggie's behest, now begs to make the wedding gown for the cost of the workmanship alone – provided, of course, that he can display the grand creation in his George Street window.

While Maggie and Mary spend their days together, we all meet as night falls. Tommo, naturally enough, is not working, for all Mr Sparrow's card games have come to a halt. But he remains a creature of the night and persists in his habit of sleeping all day, seeming to find games enough on his own. Because I have lost so much time with the fight, I have a great deal of bookkeeping to catch up at Tucker & Co. At six o'clock every afternoon when I finish work, we meet at the Hero of Waterloo to have supper together and to hear all the gossip from the two women. It comes mostly from Maggie, as Mary seems to enjoy the retelling as much as Tommo and I. Maggie is like a small child in her excitement, chirping, like the magpie she is, at every new experience and making an event or grand joke out of everything that's happened in the course of the day. It seems my great affection for her only increases every day, and I have come to love her with my very life.

How very much things have changed since Tommo and I arrived from New Zealand on the *Black Dog*. On that same day I met Maggie in Mr Smith's eating-house after I'd had my fill of his best corned beef. I recall with a smile to myself how I came here in my whaleman's rags and split boots with Maggie leaving a florin on the table to pay for my breakfast. I have much to thank her for besides the special love she has brought into my life.

While Maggie and I are not exactly the cream of society, the *Sydney Morning Herald* is all a-twitter about the bride and groom to be. It has suggested a wedding in the Botanical Gardens so that the general population may turn out to support the champion of the world among the spring blooms. The *Herald* has even reported that the military band from the New South Wales Regiment would be pleased to attend, with Sydney's mayor, Councillor John Sutherland, handing us the key to the city at a reception in the Town Hall.

Meanwhile this same newspaper has been raging on about Mr Sparrow and Fat Fred. The editor has put on a 'special' who has lost no time digging out unsavoury facts about boxing's two worst scoundrels, as he terms them! Not a single penny has been paid out to the punters who backed me. Everyone is holding onto their betting tickets which entitle them to their winnings, but to no joy. Mr Sparrow is holed up with Fat Fred in his rooms above The World Turned Upside Down and will say nothing to the newspapers except that he is 'consolidating his assets so he can pay'.

'Assets!' snorts Mary. 'I'll bet me own gravestone he declares himself skint! I know his sort. Ikey were of the same mould. What he's got, and it be plenty you may be sure, he's got stashed. There'll be no bank account with money lying about in it. He lives in rented rooms above the pub and if he owns property it will not be in his name. The Sparrows of this world travel light. They keep their fortunes portable – of the kind that can be carried away in a saddlebag on a dark night or slipped aboard ship in a suitcase.' Mary pauses. 'Blimey, I should know one when I sees one! I lived with Ikey for Lord knows how many Gawd-forsaken years. We'll have to be on our guard or our Mr Sparrow will vanish.'

There's little chance of that. Mr Sparrow and Fat Fred owe the townfolk here a fortune. There's not a single street corner, a single laneway, where eyes are not searching for them and tongues telling tales. Every kitchen maid and barman, matelot and mechanic, hackney driver and barrowman is on the lookout should they make any move to leave the pub.

Bell's Life in Sydney and the *Sydney Morning Herald* have both leapt to the defence of the thousands of small punters who put their money on me. It is estimated that two thousand or so punters in the gold diggings alone have placed bets, and in Sydney nearly twice as many again. These are all small gamblers who placed their money on a local hero, much against the advice of the so-called experts, and won. That they should now bear the brunt of Mr Sparrow's outrageous efforts to defraud the public is terribly unfair.

The press also declare Mr Sparrow and Fat Fred ruined for life and vow they will keep a watch on these scoundrels. If Mr Sparrow doesn't meet his obligations, declares the *Herald*, then he must not be allowed to operate in any part of the sporting business again. A front page headline shouts:

F. ARTIE SPARROW BANNED FOR LIFE!

The *Herald* is particularly keen on this idea but points out that, because prize-fighting is illegal and gambling equally so, Mr Sparrow may get away with his monstrous confidence trick. They ask that, at the very least, he should give the money he has taken to the Orphanage Fund.

At Mary's white tablecloth dinner on Sunday I propose a toast. 'We have ruined Mr Sparrow and so defeated one of the world's worst mongrels. He will never again live off the profits of greed and corruption.' I lift my glass.

'Oi, I ain't drinkin' to that!' Maggie exclaims. 'It's the poor folk what's suffered again, not Mr bleedin' Sparrow. That bastard's still rollin' in it. What about all the money he took in the betting shops? Yiz told me yerself. The newspapers reckon it were nigh on twenty thousand pounds.'

'But he is ruined, Maggie,' I protest. 'Mr Sparrow and Fat Fred must find near one hundred thousand pounds to meet their creditors. The loss of folks' gambling punts is a small price to pay.'

'Small price! Hawk Solomon, what's yiz talkin' about? Many of the folk here in the Rocks bet a week's pay – hoping to win a month or more's wages. They's skint! Their brats don't have no food. Those that can get credit won't even be able to pay it back for months! No nice Sunday dinners for them and the rest is starving.'

'We's dropped five hundred pounds ourselves,' Tommo reminds her.

'But we're still eatin' our Sunday roast dinner, ain't we?' Maggie says sharply.

'Everybody's lost. Even Mr Tang Wing Hung,' Tommo sighs, thinking of his opium no doubt.

'Tang Wing Hung? But he's Mr Sparrow's partner, surely he's not been touched?' Maggie exclaims.

'Oh, he's been touched, all right,' Tommo says. 'Ah Wong told me about it, so's I knew who I were dealin' with. Seems Tang Wing Hung's the head of some sort o' Chinese secret society, called a triad, what's thousands of years old. Most of Sydney's celestials come from the same place in North Shanghai and they owes this triad for all sorts o' favours. In Sydney, Tang Wing Hung's the head bloke, the Dragon Master, as they calls it. All the fellows here has got to pay him a percentage of their profits, including what they makes gambling. In return, he's s'posed to look after them, if you knows what I mean.'

Tommo pauses and puts up his finger. 'Now, from what I can make out, Mr Tang Wing Hung went and told all the celestials they should bet on Hawk. If Hawk had lost, like he were supposed to, then Tang Wing Hung would've shrugged his shoulders and said he made a mistake. He'd have probably told 'em he'd lost his money too.'

'But now they's won and Mr Sparrow won't pay. So Tang Wing Hung must get their money for them somehow – even pay it himself out of his own pocket – or he'll lose face. It ain't done for the head of a Chinese triad to lose face. Ah Wong says it be at least a hundred years of shame brought down upon his head!'

'Tommo, can we see this Mr Tang, er, whatchimacallit?' Mary asks.

'Tang Wing Hung, Mama,' Tommo corrects. 'He's a big nob so you has to use all three names.'

'Blimey, it ain't 'arf a mouthful!' Mary exclaims. 'Will he talk to us? I mean, him being Mr Sparrow's partner and all?'

'I dunno, Mama,' Tommo shrugs. 'What's you have in mind?'

'Well it seems to me,' says Mary, 'that Chinatown and the Rocks be the same kind o' neighbourhood.'

'Not if the folks in the Rocks can help it,' Maggie interrupts. 'They hates them Mongolians.'

'Yes, I know, I've noticed,' Mary nods. 'But what if they has sudden cause to like them?'

'Mama!' I exclaim. 'However do you hope to bring that about? Folk here believe our Chinese friends caused the cholera that broke out two years ago. They blame them for spreading leprosy and every imaginable type of disease, despite the lack of evidence that it is so. And they reckon the Chinese are taking white men's jobs. They aren't going to suddenly take to the celestials and claim them as good neighbours.'

But Mary is adamant. 'I'd still like to speak with Tang Wing Hung, if it can be done,' she insists.

Through Tommo we are granted an appointment with the rich Chinaman the very next day. I must confess I am curious to meet the man who people say rules the life of every celestial in New South Wales.

We go to Tang Wing Hung's chophouse in Chinatown and are shown into a private room at the back. It is decorated in the Chinese tradition with opulent silks and painted lacquer furnishings showing cherry blossoms, dragons, colourful birds and peacocks. Tang Wing Hung sits on a couch of his own while we share two others of the same size. I take up almost all of one of them and Maggie must squeeze in beside me. I can feel her warm thigh, comforting against my own.

A servant brings jasmine tea which he pours into beautiful little bowls. We all watch as Tommo takes his up, sips at it politely and then puts it down. I then do the same and find that it tastes pleasant enough and refreshes the mouth.

A plate of little dumplings is brought to the table and chopsticks put about. Another plate arrives, this time bearing biscuits which look like small sea shells. The little dumplings smell delicious but we are not accustomed to using chopsticks and dare not try them. So we sit not knowing what to do.

'Them dumplings are most delicate to look at,' Mary breaks the silence at last.

The tall Chinaman smiles. 'This is dim sum – it means "touch the heart". You try, please!'

'Can't use them chopsticks,' Mary replies, forthright as ever.

Tang Wing Hung leans over and picks up a little dumpling between his fingers. He dips it into a small bowl of dark liquid. 'This soy sauce,' he says. He pops the dumpling into his mouth. 'You try, please.'

Mary takes one of the little balls and, as our host has done, dips it into the bowl of sauce. We all wait as she pops it into her mouth. 'Delicious!' she declares.

Tang Wing Hung looks at Tommo, Maggie and me, indicating the dumplings. 'Please,' he insists.

To my surprise, Tommo and Maggie pick up their chopsticks and, taking up one of the dumplings each, dip them into the sauce and bring them up to their mouths with ease. I know I could never use the delicate sticks as they have, and so I reach over and pick up one of the little shell-like biscuits. Just as I am about to put it into my mouth, it smashes to crumbs between my fingers and a piece of paper flutters to the carpet.

I am most embarrassed. Tang Wing Hung rises and stoops to pick up the paper.

'This is fortune cookie,' he explains. 'An American invention, but Chinese recipe. Very popular – mostly we have after food!' He looks at the slip of paper. 'You be very lucky, Mr Hawk. *True love will come to you!*' he reads. Then he glances at Maggie and smiles, 'I think this fortune cookie already too late, eh?'

Then Tang Wing Hung takes a cookie himself, putting his thumb and forefinger to each end and bringing it up to his mouth. He pulls his head back the moment he bites at it and the cookie falls apart in his fingers, its crumbs clinging to his mouth. He retains only the slip of paper between his lips.

'*"Today a fortunate opportunity will present itself."*' He smiles at Mary. 'Perhaps we both get good fortune?' Then he calls the servant to take the plate of cookies away. Bowing, the man leaves but reappears soon enough with a plate of good English wheaten biscuits. 'You like better, I think,' Tang Wing Hung explains to me.

Turning to Mary, he asks seriously, 'Why you come to this humble place to see me? I not worthy, madam.'

'I am grateful that you would see us, sir,' Mary replies. She does not tell him that she knows of his predicament as Dragon Master of the triad. Instead she speaks about the bad blood that exists between the folk of Chinatown and the Rocks, and how both the poor celestials and the poor white folk have lost because they bet on me.

She looks up, appealing to Tang Wing Hung, her green eyes full of sincerity. 'Poor folk may have a different colour, but they have the same needs,' she pronounces. 'They are always trying to find enough money to feed and clothe their children. It is the same with Joe Chinaman as it is with Joe English. Now both have won by betting on my son. They are owed a small fortune and they stands never to be paid.'

'It is sad,' Tang Wing Hung shrugs, 'but what can I do?'

'Yiz can join us t' put the squeeze on Mr Sparrow!' Maggie blurts out.

Tang Wing Hung is somewhat taken aback by her outburst. 'How can I do this? A Chinese man cannot threaten a white man!'

'Ah,' says Mary, 'but white men and Chinese men can come together to fight a common enemy. Your people are owed how much in bets? Two thousand? Three thousand?'

Tang Wing Hung appears to be in deep thought for a moment. 'Hmmm . . . perhaps three thousand pounds,' he replies at last.

'Right! And we reckons the folk in the Rocks and us are owed about the same – if we don't take what we've won and only what we've bet.'

'You bet how much?' Mr Tang Wing Hung asks.

'Five hundred pounds!' Maggie answers, unable to contain herself any longer.

Mary frowns. I can see she is a trifle annoyed at Maggie. I know she feels that some things are best left unsaid but I don't know if my Maggie will ever learn this.

'Five hundred pounds! You very brave!' Tang Wing Hung

exclaims, clapping his hands and affecting an expression of astonishment.

'No,' replies Mary. 'I have a very brave son.'

Tang Wing Hung nods and smiles. 'Too brave, perhaps.'

Mary ignores this. 'It were reported in the newspaper that Mr Sparrow took about twenty thousand pounds in bets and now owes one hundred thousand. Well, if he pays us – that be the folks in the Rocks and your folks here in Chinatown – back what we bet, that's only six thousand. We know he can pay us all from what he took all up.'

'There were other expenses,' Tang Wing Hung points out. 'To set up such a fight costs much money.'

Mary smiles. 'Mr Tang Wing Hung, I weren't born yesterday. I know what it takes in bribery and corruption and "miscellaneous expenses". That ain't my concern – though I'm sure he's got plenty.'

Tang Wing Hung brings the tips of the fingers of both hands together and touches the end of his chin. His lips pout slightly as he thinks. 'Madam, why I do this? I can make Mr Sparrow pay only the Chinese people – only three thousand pounds, much easier for him.'

'And a bleedin' sight more expensive for you!' Mary snaps. 'What do you think the white folk are going to feel about the Chinese folk then? They know you're Mr Sparrow's partner, or if they don't they'll soon enough be told by the newspapers. Imagine, if all the celestials get paid and none o' the Europeans. What you think's going to happen then?'

Tang Wing Hung laughs. 'You think clever like a Chinaman, missus.'

'Well, I'm plain-spoken by nature, Mr Tang Wing Hung.' Mary smiles. 'If we work together and the white folk of the Rocks know they got paid because the Chinese helped, everyone'll feel better all 'round.'

Tang Wing Hung rises, bowing very slightly. 'It's good plan – but what do you ask of me?'

'You must tell Mr Sparrow that you have bought all the betting tickets belonging to your own people and also all those belonging to the folks in the Rocks. Now you want full payment. Six thousand pounds in the next forty-eight hours.'

'And if he will not?'

'Then you will kill him!' Mary says.

'I cannot!'

'You don't have to do it, just say it!' Mary explains. She pauses and plays the ace in her hand. 'If the head of a Chinese triad should threaten Mr Sparrow, then he will believe he will die – and it ain't no use reporting nothing!'

Tang Wing Hung draws back in surprise. 'Where you hear about triad? I am businessman, madam.'

'It don't much matter to me what you calls yourself, Mr Tang Wing Hung. You're the boss of the Mongolians, ain't you?'

'I have a little influence maybe. Most Chinese come from same place as me, they know me.' Tang Wing Hung shrugs.

'So where does that leave us, then?' Mary asks bluntly enough.

Tang Wing Hung pauses. 'I will do it,' he says at last.

Mary smiles and so do the rest of us.

The Dragon Master raises a forefinger. 'But I do it because the Chinese owe your sons.' He gives a little nod to me and then to Tommo. 'For Lambing Flat when they help my people. They are brave men and so we will do this thing.'

Out of the corner of my eye I see Tommo squirm in his chair a little at Tang Wing Hung's thanks, but I do not look at him. We had been worried that Tommo might be banned from Tang Wing Hung's opium den on our return from the fight, the Chinaman being in cahoots with Mr Sparrow. Now I understand why this was not so. It seems the story of how Tommo and I rescued Ah Wong and his family is known among the Chinese of Sydney.

Tang Wing Hung pauses, then returns to the subject at hand. 'Not six thousand pounds, ten thousand pounds. We will demand ten!' He claps his hands and then bows to Mary, deeper this time. 'What is left we share.' Tang Wing Hung works a large gold ring from his finger. 'Here, you take.' He hands the heavy gold ring to Mary. 'It is a gift given to me by Mr Sparrow. Give it to him. Tell him it is returned – our partnership is broken forever. Tell him he must pay or he will die.' He grins. 'Mr Sparrow will understand.'

'But will you not tell him yourself?' Maggie asks.

Tang Wing Hung sighs. 'I cannot be seen to go near Mr Sparrow. There may be those who think I am still in business with him. No, no, you must go in my place.'

'I will then.' Mary puts the gold ring into her purse. 'It's been very nice doin' business with you, Mr Tang Wing Hung.' She pauses, thinking. 'But I need one more thing. I need a letter from you to Mr Sparrow to put the wind up him.'

'No, no, you do not understand. No letter. I cannot make threat to him!'

Mary laughs. 'You don't have to. All I wants is a letter written in Chinese. You can make it one of them poems by that bloke Confucius that Hawk's always quoting. Anything you like, so long as it's written in Chinese letters and sealed with wax and a chop – any chop. Then on the envelope you must put Mr Sparrow's name in Chinese *and* English.'

Tang Wing Hung smiles and bows his head. 'Very clever. Mr Sparrow, he cannot read Chinese, and he will think this message a threat? Very clever! You give him ring and letter!' He claps his hands and the servant appears. He speaks to him in rapid Chinese and the man nods and is gone.

'You will have such a letter in half an hour. And I will make sure no Chinaman tell him what it means. You wait here, please. Drink tea? I must go now, thank you very much.'

Mary has managed Tang Wing Hung wonderfully. She has shown him how to avoid losing face in front of his own people and convinced him to serve our purpose as well. And it will not cost him a penny other than the gold ring. I am most proud of our mama.

'How do we know the bludger will come good, give us our share of the brass if Mr Sparrow pays?' Maggie asks as we make our way back to the Hero, where Mary has promised to buy us supper.

'Face,' Tommo says. 'He'll lose face if he don't.'

Mary sniffs. 'I don't know about face, but I know about business and so does our Mr Tang Wing Hung. We've just got Mr Dragon Master off the hook. We've made him look like the hero of Sydney's Chinese and he'll make a tidy profit to boot.'

Mary has clearly taken charge as the general of our campaign and means to see that the folks in the Rocks and Chinatown get their bets returned in full. Over the next two days, she sends Maggie around to all the pubs to ask the publicans to chalk up the amounts their customers show them on their old betting tickets. Soon we know that we'll have more than sufficient to cover the money bet.

Mary decides that the best way to get to Mr Sparrow is to see him herself. 'It's our best bet,' she announces. 'A woman's hard to deny and thought to be harmless. If I says I've been sent from Mr Tang Wing Hung and have proof,' she holds up the gold ring, 'Sparrer can't refuse me.'

'May I come too, Mama?' Maggie begs.

Mary smiles and nods. She's pleased when Maggie calls her mama. 'I want to see Mr Sparrow's ratty little phiz when he sees it's us what's got him well and truly nailed!'

'When will you go?' Tommo asks. 'Now?'

'No, first we must scare him somewhat, I think!' Mary turns to Maggie. 'Do you think you can get folks here to march on the pub and shout a bit? Make our Mr Sparrow fear for his miserable carcass? It'd be a way of softenin' him up.'

'Daresay I can,' Maggie says. 'The pleasure would be all mine!' She giggles with anticipation.

But both she and Mary draw the line when I say I'll go with her. Mary shakes her head, 'No, son, you and Tommo must stay well clear! If this business should end badly, the magistrate mustn't see it as an act of vengeance, with us taking the law into our own hands. Maggie be the ideal person to spread the word and she's happy to do it.'

'Happy ain't the word!' Maggie exclaims. 'I'd count it a great privilege to give them two mongrels a fright!'

Our mama has thought of every detail. 'Pick four strong leaders, men what won't lose their heads and start a riot,' she instructs Maggie. 'No stones or clubs, mind you – just drums, bull-horns and bugles. They're to make a lot of noise. Remember, this be a protest, an orderly but very noisy protest. The *Sydney Morning Herald* must describe it as an outcry by common folk what's been cheated out of what's rightly due them by a pair o' scoundrels.'

Mary now turns to me. 'See that the police are informed of the march so they're on hand when the mob arrives at The World Turned Upside Down. We don't want any in the crowd to get no fancy ideas of storming young Sparrer Fart's lodgings.'

Maggie is delighted with the task she's been given. That very night, she visits the Hero of Waterloo, the Rose and Crown and half a dozen other public houses. By the time she returns home, the march against Mr Sparrow is all set.

'Folk are only too happy to make their feelings known,' she tells me.

The protest is to take place the following afternoon when the men come home from work.

'We'll put some real fear into them upstairs. Make the little shyster and his fat mate think the mob's come to get 'em!' Mary laughs when she hears Maggie's news. I can't help feeling she is enjoying the whole campaign.

By the following afternoon the news has spread throughout the Rocks and three or four hundred men march on The World Turned Upside Down. Here they are met by three constables who tell them that Mr Sparrow and Fat Fred are not in residence in the rooms upstairs. Nevertheless the crowd makes a great deal of noise, banging on drums and blasting on bugles. Towards the end a rock is thrown which breaks one of the upstairs windows. But the protest is, in fact, quite orderly. Maggie has picked her leaders well – there's noise and threats enough hurled at the windows to frighten Mr Sparrow and Fat Fred, who we know are in residence no matter what the policemen say.

Mary and Maggie have Tang Wing Hung's ring and sealed letter with its beautiful Chinese characters and F. Artie Sparrow Esq. written on the envelope. As the protesters slowly drift away, they prepare to confront the villains.

Tommo and I wait downstairs in the saloon bar of the pub which has just this minute opened its doors once again. Tommo insists on wearing his axe in a shoulder holster under his jacket. These days the barmaid, Doreen, welcomes him like he's an honoured guest, bringing him a Cape brandy without his even asking. I order a glass of best ale and she does a sort of curtsy. 'Honoured ter serve ya, Mr Black Hawk,' she says, all smiles. Mr Sparrow has clearly lost the sympathy of the staff here as well.

At first the three Sydney lads guarding Mr Sparrow's staircase won't allow Maggie and Mary into the corridor that leads upstairs. Maggie kicks up a bit of a fuss and one of them goes leaping up the stairs. Soon he returns with a hulking lad in tow. This one has a runny nose and an ugly, festering scar down the length of his cheek. The newcomer sniffs and folds his arms across his chest.

'What's yiz want?' he says to Mary, as Tommo and I wait at the ready in the saloon.

'How'd you get yours?' Mary asks.

'Me what?'

Mary runs her finger down the red line on her own face. 'Your scar. Were you cut by a villain too, acid thrown in after?'

The boy looks impressed. 'Nah, just a fight. Weren't nothin' much.' He begins to pick absently at the weeping scab.

'Don't pick at it, lad. Give it a chance to heal itself, won't show so bad then,' Mary advises gently.

'Don't much care if it do, missus,' the lad grunts.

'Hey, I knows ya!' Maggie exclaims, pointing at him. 'Johnny Terrible! Yiz got a brother and sister, both little uns, twins ain't they?'

Johnny Terrible nods.

'They comes to our roast dinner on Sunday. One of 'em, the little girl – Alice ain't it? – once gimme sixpence for her dinner though we never asked. She said ya told her t' give it t' me!'

Johnny Terrible gives a little half-smile, and Maggie can tell he's pleased to be recognised. 'Want ter see Mr Sparrer, does yer?' he now asks.

'The very same,' Maggie grins.

'What fer?'

'Business that's to his benefit. Tang Wing Hung's sent us,' Mary says.

Johnny Terrible gives a deep sniff and wipes his hand under his nose. 'Tang Wing Hung? What proof's ya got yiz from him?'

Mary shows him the ring and holds up the letter with the Chinese characters. The boy takes the ring and looks at it.

'See what it says inside,' Maggie urges, then recites from memory, '"To Tang Wing Hung in sincere friendship, F. Artie Sparrow".'

'He won't see yiz anyway. He's in the wardrobe,' Johnny Terrible says, handing Mary back the ring.

'In the wardrobe? What's you mean?' Maggie asks.

'It be the riots, he's gorn panicky.'

'Does he often go into the wardrobe?' Mary enquires.

'He's took it up since the fight. Spent four days in there when he got back from Yass!'

'What about Fat Fred?' Maggie asks.

'He's drunk, shickered. Drinks a gallon of Portugee port 'fore noon each day, cryin' all the while that it weren't his fault, and that he only done what he were told. He'll be no good ter ya, Miss Pye.'

'Call me Maggie, darlin',' Maggie smiles.

506

'Well then, we'll just have to see Mr Sparrow in his wardrobe,' says Mary.

'Easier said than done, missus.' Johnny Terrible snorts deeply and makes a loud noise sucking the phlegm down his throat. 'He's got the lock put wrong way round so he's got the key on the inside. Locks hisself in.'

'Can he hear ya when ya talks?' Maggie asks.

'Depends if he wants ter. Don't rate yer chances. Sometimes he hears but he don't talk to no one 'cept me. Reckon I'm the only one what can figure out what he's sayin'. But yiz can try.' Johnny Terrible brings two fingers to his lips and gives a sharp whistle. Three scruffy heads pop around the top of the banister. 'Take the ladies to see Mr Sparrow,' he orders.

'Ta, muchly,' Maggie says, giving Johnny Terrible a kiss on his dirty face. The three Sydney lads on guard laugh. 'Shut yer gobs!' Johnny Terrible snarls and they are immediately quiet.

'Extra 'elping comin' to ya little brother and sister on Sunday, Johnny,' Maggie promises. 'Come down yerself and I'll put some iodine on yer cut, do ya the world.'

They are halfway up the stairs when Johnny Terrible shouts, 'Eh, Maggie, is it true yiz gunna marry the nigger?'

Maggie turns and looks down at him. 'What if I am? What's it to you, Johnny Terrible?'

'Nuffink,' he sniffs. 'I think yiz done good. He be a great champion, the strongest man in the world.'

'You don't want t' believe all ya hears,' Maggie retorts. 'I can beat him up anytime I likes!'

What follows we hear from Maggie and Mary once we're back at the Hero of Waterloo. The two young lads make a great fuss of unlocking the stout door that leads to Mr Sparrow's lodgings, then ushers them into a parlour fitted with a red and blue carpet of Chinese design that covers most of the floor.

The room has two tall windows facing onto the street – one of them with a broken pane. The windows are draped with maroon velvet curtains, somewhat dusty, with tassels tied at the centre. It's clear that the drapes haven't been drawn in a long time. Indeed the windows seem the only source of light in the room as there are no gas lights and only two empty lantern brackets on the wall. Against the wall opposite the windows is a large, double-winged cedar wardrobe. But what first catches Maggie and Mary's eye is a long, horsehair leather settee, badly scuffed and worn in several places, that sits in the centre of the carpet.

Laid out upon its leather upholstery, so that in some places its worn springs nearly touch the ground from the weight of him, lies Fat Fred. He is heaving and snorting, his great belly making rumbling noises like a small volcano preparing to blast its contents out into the firmament. Six boys aged between ten and twelve all sit cross-legged on the carpet before him, playing cribbage. They jump up when the two women enter.

Mary and Maggie can't tear their eyes away from the supine form of Fat Fred. Though it seems hardly possible, the man has grown even fatter in the weeks since the fight. Little bubbles of snot come out of his nostrils. He wears only a pair of black Chinese silk trousers which are very dirty, and his huge, hairy stomach dominates the room.

Fat Fred's stomach has, as they tell it, become a creature in its own right. It resembles nothing so much as a live container in which secret and dangerous chemical concoctions are being mixed with other equally dangerous substances – causing an amazing series of oleaginous gurgles, sighs, splats and small muffled explosions.

Every few minutes the pressure within this amazing container builds up, resulting in an alarming tautness. Then the entire stomach holds dead still, but only for a moment as though it has reached a point where it might at any second split wide apart. At this point, it lets go a truly resounding fart so that the great belly wobbles and reverberates like jelly.

Each eruption of gas makes the lads snigger behind cupped hands. They seem to know the precise moment it will come. Eventually Maggie too takes to giggling. Soon they are all having a merry laugh, and even Mary joins in, though her finger and thumb remain firmly pegged to her nose.

With this intestinal factory commanding all their attention, it is some time before Mary and Maggie become aware of a series of soft and urgent whimperings emanating from the wardrobe. Later they realise it is Mr Sparrow asking, in his peculiar new way, who has come into the room.

Just then, as Fat Fred lets go another of his great and glorious farts, Johnny Terrible walks in.

'Play him, Johnny, garn, show the ladies!' one of the lads shouts. 'He's ready tuned, he's bin doing lots o' them big ones.'

'Yeah, garn, Johnny!' the others chorus. Whereupon a boy of about eleven rushes to pull up a Windsor chair, which he places in front of Fat Fred, as if before a pianoforte.

Johnny Terrible's face doesn't move a muscle. He walks over and sits down, laying his hands upon the enormous stomach as though upon a truly great instrument. He appears to be lost in thought as though considering a repertoire in his head. And then, to the astonishment of Maggie and Mary, he draws a great breath and, with a flourish, commences to push his fingers down into Fat Fred's belly.

Sometimes he plays hard, sometimes soft, his fingers darting to various parts of the great expanse. Each time he prods or pats the monstrous organ, Fat Fred lets out a fart of a different timbre, tone and length of duration – a sort of musical note. Some are short and sharp, others prolonged. Some are deep-toned, others high and squeaky. Johnny Terrible uses his fists for some notes, his thumbs for others, and his prodding fingers go deep into the hairy flesh for yet more flatulent harmonies. His hands flash and plunge in a truly virtuoso performance – his head bouncing as he performs.

'Can you hear it?' one of the boys shouts over the din. 'Can you hear it, missus? "Gawd Save the Queen", he's playing, "Gawd Save the bleedin' Queen"!' Indeed, after some concentration, it becomes apparent that this is precisely what Johnny Terrible is playing on Fat Fred's abdomen. It is a strange and discordant key, but the notes are accurate enough. A most positive and sustained trombone effect is created to honour the final strains of the anthem to Queen Victoria.

At the end Johnny Terrible rises from his chair to the claps and cheers of his companions. He does not smile as he bows to Mary and Maggie. It is as if he regards himself a true concert artist, and is merely receiving the accolades due him from an appreciative audience.

Then he turns to the boys in the room. 'Orright then, bugger off the lot of yiz! The miss and the missus here got business with Mr Sparrow!'

The six lads in the room troop out obediently. Johnny Terrible moves the chair from beside Fat Fred and carries it to one side of the wardrobe door. Then he fetches a second and places it to the other side of the door, before asking Mary and Maggie to be seated.

'I'll act as yer translator, Maggie,' he says.

'What's wrong? Can't he talk for himself?' Mary asks bluntly.

'He can, but he won't. I'll have to tell yiz what he's sayin'. It's his code what only I understands.' He nods his head for Mary or Maggie to begin. Mary nods to Maggie.

'Hullo, Mr Sparrow, it's Maggie Pye here, come to visit yiz! How's ya going, then?' Maggie waits for a response from inside the wardrobe. There is complete silence for a minute, then a few high-pitched whimpers are heard.

'He wants ter know what yer wants?' Johnny Terrible interprets.

Mary takes over now. 'Now listen 'ere, Sparrer Fart, it's Mary Abacus. You might remember me from London! I come with a letter of demand from Tang Wing Hung for ten thousand pounds.' Mary is shouting to make sure Mr Sparrow can hear every word through the oak panelling. But no sound, not even a whimper, is heard.

'It be Tang Wing Hung what's bought up all the celestials' betting tickets from the fight and some from other folks as well,' Maggie explains. But still there is no reply from inside the wardrobe.

Maggie looks at Johnny Terrible as if to ask if she should speak again. He nods and she says, 'Mr Sparrow, listen t' me! Yiz got two days, today, tomorrer and the next mornin' only – that be Friday mornin'! Forty-eight hours from now yiz got to come up with the readies, ten thousand quid! If ya don't, well Tang Wing Hung ain't gunna like it. He don't want to be no business partners with you no more. He says to tell yiz! You know what that means don'tcha?'

There is silence again and then a few muffled sounds which are followed by several knocks to the interior panelling. 'He says how does he know yiz from Mr Tang Wing Hung?' Johnny pronounces.

'I have proof. Mr Tang Wing Hung's ring that you gave him and a letter wrote in Chinese!' Mary takes a deep breath, adding, 'It be a death threat from the triad.'

There is the sound of a key turning and the door of the wardrobe opens a crack. Mr Sparrow's little hand with the diamond ring on its pinky comes out, the fingers twitching like spider's legs.

'Give him the letter an' the ring,' Johnny Terrible instructs.

Mary hands Mr Sparrow the letter first and it's snapped up and taken inside the wardrobe. A moment later the hand reappears in a cupped position and she drops the ring into it. Then there's the sound of the lock turning again.

'How can he see in there?' Maggie asks.

'He's got a bull lamp.'

Just then, the whimpering begins again. It's fast and high, and makes no sense to the two women. Finally, there are several knocks on the panelling.

'He wants seven days ter pay,' says Johnny.

'Forty-eight hours!' Mary shouts. 'That's all and not a minute more! It's what Mr Tang Wing Hung says – after forty-eight hours, your life won't be safe a moment longer.' She turns to Johnny Terrible. 'You be me witness, Johnny Terrible, that I delivered Tang Wing Hung's letter to Mr F. Artie Sparrow Esquire. I don't want his death to come as a surprise!' She takes out her purse and hands Johnny Terrible half a sovereign. He takes it, bites it to ascertain it's gold, then flips it in the air, grabs it and puts it into his pocket. He nods silently to Mary's request.

Another of Fat Fred's enormous farts resounds from the centre of the room, as if signalling that the interview with Mr Sparrow is over. Johnny leads them to the door. 'Yiz'll have ter go now,' he says. 'The Chinaman's comin' soon.'

'What Chinaman?' Maggie asks in alarm.

'The old bloke, Ho Kwong Choi. He comes ter give Mr Sparrer his pipe.'

'Opium?' Mary asks, surprised.

Johnny Terrible shrugs, his face blank as ever. 'Yiz got ter go now,' he repeats.

Mary walks quickly back across the room and leans close to the wardrobe door. 'Oh, and Tang Wing Hung says after forty-eight hours no more opium, ya hear? Your supply'll be cut off unless o' course you pays up! Don't make much difference I suppose – except, instead of dying happy, you'll die miserable with the shakes and pains!'

Mary and Maggie follow Johnny Terrible down the stairs to where the three boys are still standing guard. 'You was most harmonious on the stomach piano!' Maggie says giggling. 'Come Sunday to Semicircular Quay and I'll fix yer cheek. That wound could turn nasty on ya. Iodine's what's called for. Burns like buggery, but it'll fix yer cheek, 'andsome!'

Tommo and I roll with laughter when Mary and Maggie retell their story of the interview with Mr Sparrow. All of us imagine him crouching in the dark, hugging his bony knees. Maggie recounts the most of it and she tells it well. Even Mary is taken with a fit of laughter but then she stops.

'Maggie, that Johnny Terrible, he were sociable enough and done what we asked and all, but did ya see his eyes?' she asks abruptly.

'Eyes? Can't say I noticed. Brown, ain't they?'

'Yes, and dead. No light in them, no expression.' Mary shivers suddenly. 'I seen eyes like that before, on a man in the East End o' London named Bob Marley!' She runs her crooked finger down the scar on the side of her cheek. 'It were him what cut me and marked me with the acid. One moment funny and most clever and sociable, the next gone cruel and crazy. But his eyes were always the same, just like that Johnny Terrible today – dead eyes!'

I shudder, for Ikey had once told Tommo and me about Bob Marley, who would only work for gold sovereigns counted into his hand before a job. 'Always in advance and then always done what was asked of him, no matter what.'

Ikey had admired Bob Marley greatly. 'A true professional, my dears, only once half-nabbed by the constabulary and then got off with a marvellous alibi he'd worked out beforehand! Twenty-five years a thief and no form whatsoever, remarkable!'

But even as youngsters, we could tell that Bob Marley was also the only man who scared Ikey Solomon. 'When you can't reach a clever man with your wit or soften him with your tongue, then know him to be most dangerous!' I recall him saying.

Maggie, however, laughs at Mary's fears. 'Johnny Terrible? Nah! He's just a bad lad brought up rough. Thousands like him, proper hooligan. Ain't no real harm in him – he'll steal, fight, be cheeky, rob old ladies. I grown up with his sort. They only murders if they 'as to!'

Maggie now tells Tommo and me how Johnny Terrible played 'God Save the Queen' on Fat Fred's stomach. We are soon roaring with laughter again as Maggie imitates with her lips the noises that came from Fat Fred.

Suddenly I think that we've never been so happy since we were brats. Maggie's made us a family again. Mary's come alive – it's something more than just being happy to be with her boys. She's grown most fond of my Maggie, and it's as if she's found, in our upcoming nuptials, new hope and meaning in the future.

I smile at this, then return to the conversation around me, hearing with surprise of Mr Sparrow's addiction to opium. But Tommo just says quietly, 'That's how the bastard knows it can enslave others to his will.'

Mary reaches over and takes his hand in hers, patting it. 'You'll be all right, my boy,' she says, 'you'll be all right.'

Chapter Twenty-six

TOMMO

The Rocks
September 1861

I'm back in New Zealand, walking in the forest with Makareta, when a great noise brings me awake. At first I thinks it's part o' me dream, and a pakeha settler's fired his musket at us again, but then I realise I'm back in Sydney, me beloved Makareta's dead and it's someone at the door. The sun is streamin' in and it's too early in the day for me to be up, especially after me celebrations of the night before. Yesterday, Mary and Maggie put the squeeze on Mr Sparrow, what I now knows needs the Devil's Smoke as much as yours truly. I had a good night with the flats after that, and an extra bottle of the Cape besides, and I ain't too pleased about being waked up early.

I opens the door and sees Mary there. She is none too happy neither. Seems she were meant to meet Maggie this afternoon, but Maggie never showed. Normally, them two's together from early morning, but today, Maggie had some other business to see to. She and Mary were to meet at noon – when they were gunna look for a canteen of sterling silver, Mary's wedding present to Maggie and Hawk. Only Maggie don't get to the Hero on time. At first, Mary ain't too concerned. She's scolded Maggie plenty o' times about being late, but it's never done no good – Maggie simply don't have no sense of time.

But by two o'clock Mary's a little worried, so she walks down through the Argyle Cut to Maggie's rooms above the chophouse. There's no answer to her knocks on Maggie's door and so she goes downstairs to the Cut Below. Flo tells her that Maggie were in for a cup of tea and a fresh bread roll at about nine this morning, as is her habit now that she's up and about in the daytime.

'How were she?' Mary asks.

'She's always the same. Whether she be up all night or just woke up, she's ever cheerful.' Flo smiles. 'This mornin' she said she was gunna let me have a borrow of her wedding dress when I gets married.'

'And then she left?'

'Yes – no, hang on. Me papa come through from the kitchen and brung her a letter what he said were left earlier by a lad. I remembers 'cause the brat wouldn't say nothing 'bout who it were from – just gave him the letter and scarpered.'

'A letter? What sort o' letter?' Mary asks.

'Dunno. It were in an envelope, sealed with red wax on the back. I remember me dad handin' it to her with the blob of red wax uppermost. Then when Maggie turns it I sees the writing on the front's a bit scratchy and untidy-like, not nice like Hawk's.'

'Did she read it?'

'Nah, Maggie don't read too well. She can make out what's on the page but it ain't easy. She has ter take her time, like. So she laughs and says she'll read it later. Then she kissed me like she always does. "Be a good girl then, Flo, but if yiz can't, for 'eavens sake be careful!" She always says the same when she's leaving, ever since I were a little brat.' Now Flo looks anxious. 'Is somethin' wrong, Mrs Abacus?'

'No, girlie, she's late to meet me, that's all. So I thought I'd come down and fetch her,' Mary tells her.

'She's always late,' Flo points out hopefully.

'Blimey, don't I know and all,' mutters Mary and goes to take her leave. Then she stops. 'Did she wear a bonnet, like she were going out?'

'She had the magpie nested in her hair what she often wears instead of a bonnet,' Flo answers.

Mary goes back to the Hero and waits another hour. By now it's three o'clock and even Maggie ain't ever this late. So Mary has come down to where Hawk and I has our lodgings and woken me up. I don't waste any time and get dressed in a minute.

'Shall we fetch Hawk?' Mary asks as we leaves the house.

'Nah, we'll check the pubs first. Maggie said she were gunna thank the boys what led the march on the pub. Hawk give her money to buy them all a drink.'

'Maggie don't drink during the day, well, not with me she don't,' Mary says doubtfully. 'I has the habit of trying a different brand of ale or beer in Sydney every day 'case I comes across a blend I likes. She's never once joined me – always asks for sarsaparilla and a slice of lemon.'

'Maggie be unpredictable, Mama,' I says to comfort her. 'Never know for certain what she'll do next. We'll go ask around first before we tells Hawk. She'll turn up, you'll see. She probably took a gin or two too much and fell asleep.'

But Mary ain't convinced. 'She was that excited about the canteen o' silver, she'd not have got drunk!' she insists. Finally she agrees we should check the various pubs around the Rocks. Two hours and eighteen pubs later, we finds out that none o' the publicans – what all know Maggie well – have seen her today. It's nearly six o'clock by the time we gets to the Rose and Crown where the owner, Daniel 'Pinchgut' Lewis, tells us that Maggie were meant to have a drink with the lads here at eleven o'clock but never showed.

'Can't think what's happened,' he frowns. 'Maggie's always late, but she turns up in the end.' He chuckles. 'Matter o' fact it be good for business, Maggie always being late. Folk'll wait for her, guessing at her excuses, what be that marvellous inventive that it's worth the waiting no matter how late she be. And o' course they keeps buying drinks in the meanwhile!'

It's now well past six o'clock. Weary of soul and terrible worried, we hurries back to the Hero of Waterloo where we'll meet Hawk. We still holds out hope of finding Maggie there but it ain't much of a hope.

We hasn't yet reached the Hero when suddenly I stops. Mary can see that I be shivering with me arms clasped about me chest, rubbing and scratching the tops, near the shoulders, like I'm cold and itchy.

'Mama,' I says, 'I'll be just the half hour then I'll be back. Tell Hawk not to do nothing 'til I returns.' I looks pleadingly at Mary. 'Half an hour won't make no difference if Maggie ain't there.'

Mary nods. She's never seen me before when the craving for

the poppy has took me, but she knows at once what it is. 'We'll wait for you, Tommo. Mind you come back quick now.' She's fighting to keep back her tears.

'I loves you, Mama,' I says, reaching for her hands.

'I love you too, Tommo, with all me heart,' she says, squeezing mine.

The sun is setting and there be a golden blaze across the harbour. The water has turned a deep red. As I starts to walk away, Mary calls after me and I stops and turns. 'What, Mama?'

'Tommo, you were the sweetest little boy,' Mary says, then smiles. 'You still is.'

Chinatown be only a few minutes walk from where I left Mary. I feel such a weak bastard, having to get me fix of Devil's Smoke. But in the past few weeks the pain in me head has been near constant. By nightfall I can't bear it no longer and am just waitin' for Ho Kwong Choi's pipe of blissful relief.

Hawk has often found me moaning with me head in me hands. He knows me wound's getting worse, for he hears me cry out in me sleep as I thrash about having nightmares of the most frightening kind. He's always asking about me head and when I tells him not to worry, gets angry.

'Tommo, you lie, *I* can feel it,' he says, touching his hands to the exact spot where the pain be.

But I says nothing. He is so happy with Maggie and if he knows how bad it is for me I fear it would spoil his happiness. I meself am happy for them. I have grown terrible fond o' Maggie meself and thinks what pretty children they shall have.

But my own pain has grown such that I has even lost at cards once or twice. This has mostly been in the early hours when me afternoon pipe has worn off and I am quite beside meself with the ache in me noggin. These days I've took to visiting Tang Wing Hung's opium den in the mornings before I returns home, as well as in the evenings. Without the relief of the poppy I'd go quite mad.

Sometimes a dizziness takes hold of me and I cannot see and must sit down in a hurry. I tell all this to Ho Kwong Choi, who nods and clucks his tongue as he prepares the paste for me pipe. It be stupid, I know, telling me troubles to a Chinaman what can hardly speak English, but he has looked into my dreams and heard me cry out. Sometimes, when I wake after a pipe, I find he has put a cool cloth to me head. He has seen poor bastards like me before and much worse, I reckon. He's a mate, in a way, but still I can't read the diamond pricks of light in them eyes what's cut like slivers in his paper-creased face.

Now, as I gets to the opium den, Ho Kwong Choi comes forward, his hands clasped together and his head bowed in greeting. I bow to him too.

'Ho Kwong Choi, you got to be quick tonight, then I come back later, maybe eleven o'clock, you savvy?'

He nods his head and shows me to a couch before shuffling away. He seems most solemn tonight. Me head is nearly took off by the pain as he prepares the pearl at the end of the needle, roasting it in the flame, before handing me the opium pipe. After the fourth or fifth puff, I starts to feel a bit better. By the time the pain is took away, not much more than fifteen minutes has passed. Soon I'm feeling bright enough, though slightly light of head.

Ho Kwong Choi brings me jasmine tea after my pipe and stands there waiting and watching as I sips it as fast as I can. Suddenly he says, 'Tommo, you go Mr Sparrow.'

'What?' I asks.

'Quick, quick!' He takes the bowl of tea from my hands. 'Now!' He is shaking slightly. 'Hurry up!'

'What is it, Ho Kwong Choi?' I grip him by the shoulders, even though he could kill me in an instant if he wished.

'Missy Maggie! She with Mr Sparrow!' He trembles under me hands. 'You go now, hurry, hurry!'

Still light-headed, I run from the opium den out into the back lane and then all the way to our lodgings, where I tear me blanket roll apart. I rip off the oil cloth what keeps my axe from rusting. Frantic, I take off the leather sheath that protects the head. I test the blade on my thumb and a tiny drop o' blood appears. It is razor sharp. I put the axe back in its holster what fits under me jacket and then I starts to run towards Bridge Street.

By the time I get to The World Turned Upside Down I'm panting and has to catch me breath for a few minutes on the pavement opposite the pub. A watchman what's sitting there with a lantern beside him sees me and shouts, 'Move on, mate, I don't want no trouble.'

I duck across the street towards the pub, only I does it a little higher up so the watchman can't see me. I dodge between two hackneys and a toff what's drunk and driving his own sulky, lashing at the poor nag. The gaslight here is dim, so I'm in the shadows as I cross. I stay in the darkness as I make my way towards the hotel – waiting for the right moment, before nipping into the dark alley what runs alongside it. There's a door here what leads straight up to Mr Sparrow's lodging. I've used it often enough in the past, when I come to see him. This time though I'm gunna have to break it down with my axe, I thinks.

I put my hand to the door to find where the weakest spot in the panelling might be, and to me surprise it swings open. I push it a little further and peers into the dark passage. I can hear the faint sound of the drinkers in the public bar through the wall beside the staircase at the end. There's no light in the passageway and I can't see a thing. Odd there's none of Mr Sparrow's lads about neither. Is it a trap, I wonder? If some of his more vicious lads be hiding in the dark, I'd have no chance to defend meself if an arm with a knife were to suddenly appear.

I take out my axe as quietly as I can, and move forward slowly towards the dark stairway. My heart is boomin' like a drum and I'm terrified I'll be jumped any moment.

One hand on the banister, the other holding my fighting axe at the ready, I feel my way carefully upwards. The steps are wooden boards and creak at every step I take. I be certain Mr Sparrow's boys are hidden in the blackness of the landing, watching for me, waiting to cut me down.

At last I get to the top of the stairs and I wait a full minute to steady meself before slowly going along the passage. My heart's thumping in my throat as if to jump clean out of me mouth. I has my back pressed to the wall and I hold my axe with both hands in front o' me face.

My shoulder touches the frame of the first door but I know it ain't the one I need and I pass across it. I reach the second door frame, what I knows to be the parlour door of Mr Sparrow's rooms. I decide it's the third door I want, and so I pass across the second also, quietly testing the door handle, what's locked.

When I reach the third door, I try the handle and it turns easily in my hand. Taking a deep breath, I push it open. It creaks like the timbers on a ship at sea and I near faints with fright. I wait for the count o' ten, but there's still no noise from within. I go through and am in Mr Sparrow's parlour.

I take two steps further and stand on the Chinee silk carpet looking about me. The curtains be open and one window pane is broken. There's a faint light coming in from the gaslight 'cross the road and, compared to the dark passage, the parlour seems quite light. A dreadful smell of shit hangs in the air.

Then I see the settee, a dark shape in the centre of the room. On it lies a huge form, what from its size looks like Fat Fred though it is too dim to be sure. I stand still, listening – but the noise from the street below is too loud for me to hear the rise and fall o' someone's breath.

I move closer to the couch. Swallowing, I put out a hand and touch naked flesh, hairy and cold. It is a huge body lying on its stomach, and I am touching its back. It's a warm evening yet the flesh is stone cold and dead still. It can be no other than Fat Fred – and he's carked it.

I'm sure I'm alone in the room, but I need light to find out what's happened. I look about, then run me hand across the walls to see if I can find a light fixture. On the far wall, what be in almost complete darkness, I touch a wardrobe. It be the one Mary and Maggie talked to Mr Sparrow through, I'm sure. Finally I comes upon two lamp brackets but with no lantern hanging from them.

Then I remember the night watchman across the street. I hurries downstairs again and, crossing to where he's sitting, and offer him half a sov for his hurricane lantern. It's five times what it's worth and he all but falls over himself handing it to me. This time, I climb the stairs as quick as I can. I go back into the parlour and turn the lamp wick up.

Fat Fred's monstrous carcass is lying on the couch with his great arse up in the air. He is dead and no mistake. The very moment folks die they shits themselves and I sees shit all over the back of Fat Fred's huge thighs, which is where the terrible stench comes from. His enormous stomach is sunk into the lounge so that the bottom of the springs touch the carpet beneath.

Then I see them. Lying on the carpet beside the couch are three black-and-white magpie feathers. Just three feathers. A grief takes hold o' me heart such as I've never felt before, not even at me darlin' Makareta's death.

The mongrels have come, and this time I heard no warning. I feel a most terrible pain as though I've been stabbed. I starts to moan like an animal, moving frantically 'round the room, searching for Maggie Pye. That Hawk's darling Maggie should come to grief at the hands of these bastards be too cruel a fate for anyone to bear. Then I see the wardrobe and suddenly I know what I must find inside it.

I rush towards it and see there are no knobs or handles on the door. It's been locked from the outside.

'Ya bastard, ya fucking mongrel bastard!' I scream and kick the door. Taking up my axe, I smash a large hole in the panelling around the lock. I cut the frame above and below the lock so that the door is free and open it. I can see the faint outlines of a body on the wardrobe floor and now I pick up the lamp and shine it into the dark interior.

Inside, trussed and gagged so that it be impossible for him to cry out or move an inch, is Johnny Terrible, one eye looking directly up at me. Such is my grief and fury that I immediately swings my axe to take his throat, before it hits me that he ain't the villain. I turn me wrist and the blade grazes his scalp, sticking into the wood at the back of his head.

With a grunt, I jerk the blade out. I've already cut free the centre frame of the wardrobe and now I fling open the second door. Johnny Terrible lies huddled at me feet. His legs have been bent backwards so that his boot heels are tucked into his bum and a rope has been lashed around the tops of his thighs and ankles. His hands are also tied behind his back and more rope coiled about his chest and arms. Even his head has been tied so it cannot move. His gag has been pulled so tight that the cloth fills his gob and cuts his mouth.

Johnny's face has been badly smashed. His nose is broken and caked with blood what has made a dark stain on the front of his blouse. One eye is completely closed and the scar to his cheek is tattered and raw, newly opened and filled with pus and blood.

I pull him out of the wardrobe by the ropes around his wrists and see that his hands have gone a deep blue from the tightness of the cord about them. He falls face down upon the carpet.

I cut the various ropes away with my axe blade. But though Johnny's free, he can't move. Bending down, I pulls his legs to straighten 'em and he screams at the pain. I does the same with his arms and then begin to rub his wrists until his fingers start to twitch. I have left his ankles loosely tied so he cannot jump up but must remain where I have dragged him, and I sit him up with his back to the wall.

Apart from his groans and screams as I pull his legs straight, Johnny ain't said a word. But now he begins to sob, though almost silently, the tears running down his face and splashing onto his blouse what's covered in blood.

I hold the three feathers right up to his eyes.

'Where's Maggie?' I says, with cold anger in me voice.

He tries to speak but his throat must be too parched. I take the lantern and goes into Mr Sparrow's bedroom, the same where he took me the first day we met. I grab the jug from the washstand what's half full and, going back, pours the water over Johnny Terrible's head and into his mouth, so that he nearly chokes.

'Where's Maggie?' I says again.

Johnny still can't speak but raises his hand slowly and points to Fat Fred.

'No! Damn ya! *Maggie! Where's Maggie Pye?*'

He points again to the dead man and a rasping noise come out of his throat. 'Unn . . .'

I clocks him hard on the cheek and me hand comes away messed with pus and blood. 'Where?' I yells.

'Unn . . . unnerneath!'

'Underneath?'

Johnny Terrible nods his head, but it ain't possible for anyone to fit underneath that couch.

Suddenly I go cold. I walk over to Fat Fred and shine the lantern light over his huge form. And then I see it. The tips of the fingers of a small female hand sticking out from under his shoulder.

Maggie lies underneath this mountain o' dead human flesh.

I scream and grab the dead man's arms. I pull and pull at him, but Fat Fred's body will not budge. 'Help me!' I scream to Johnny Terrible. He tries to get up but can't. 'Help me, ya bastard, help me!' I keep pulling at Fat Fred's arm, and I begin to blub. If Hawk were here he'd lift him off in an instant and Maggie'd be free!

'It's no good, Tommo!' Johnny Terrible's voice rasps. 'She's dead!' I am frozen in me grief, listening to him. 'Mr Sparrow done it . . . with the lads . . . before they scarpered.'

'What happened?' I whisper.

'They thought it be a great lark . . . yer know,' Johnny

swallows, 'Fat Fred and Maggie.' He swallows again and his voice grows firmer. 'Mr Sparrow sent a note to Maggie tellin' her to come an' get the money what he owed ter Mr Tang Wing Hung. But he never meant fer her to 'ave it. Instead he told the lads to grab her soon as she got 'ere. Then they gags her and ties her to the couch with her legs spread ready. Fat Fred, what's only half drunk, climbs on top and fucks her.'

Johnny's hoarse voice chokes. 'Suddenly Fred raises his head . . . and . . . he gives a groan and grabs his chest. All the lads are clapping, thinking Fat Fred's had his pleasure. But he 'asn't, it's his fuckin' heart!' He takes a breath and forces the words out. 'Fred gasps and gurgles and falls over Maggie, so she can't breathe none. And all the time the lads just thinks it's Fat Fred enjoying hisself!'

Johnny Terrible's voice trails away and he just looks at me as the tears run down me cheeks. 'Then . . . when they finds out Fat Fred's took dead . . . they all scarpers. Mr Sparrow leaves with a big bag o' stuff, thousands and thousands worth, and him disguised like one o' the Sydney lads.'

'The fucking mongrel! Where is he?' I sob, hitting my hand to my pounding head in anger.

Johnny Terrible points to his mouth and begs in a croaking voice, 'Water.'

I splash what's left in the jug over his gob.

'Where is he?' I yell again, shaking with pain and rage.

'I'll tell ya. What's the time?' he asks.

I take my hunter from me pocket. 'A quarter to eight.'

'Tide turns at nine o'clock. He's on the *Morning Song* – a trading vessel, kanaka crew. She's bound for the Fiji Islands, sails with the tide tonight.'

'Tonight? Christ Jesus! Where's she moored?'

'Anchored midstream, in the harbour two hundred yards or so from Kellett's Wharf.'

'Are you sure?' I shout. 'How'd ya know he's there for sure?' I shove his leg with me boot in a wave of fury.

'I done the arrangements meself, paid the master one 'undred quid, the same to be paid again by Mr Sparrow when he comes aboard safe,' he replies sadly. 'Tang Wing Hung sent a message with Ho Kwong Choi this morning when he come to give Mr Sparrow his pipe. He said if he paid the ten thousand what he owed, he were free to scarper.' Johnny Terrible shrugs his shoulders, wincing as he does so. 'Mr Sparrow gave the old Chinaman diamonds and emeralds and other valuables and he went!'

'Why'd he not take you, then?' I snarl. 'You're his bleedin' right-hand man.'

To me surprise the tears run down Johnny's cheeks. 'I tried to save Maggie when Mr Sparrow wanted his revenge on her – for scheming with you lot against him. "Let me just beat her up bad, cut 'er tits, that be all that's needed," I offers him.' Johnny Terrible is now sobbing. 'But he said I'd changed sides on 'im – and that he couldn't trust me no more, and he set the lads on me and had 'em tie me up.' He wipes the snot from his bleeding nose.

'He were like a father to me, he were – the only one I ever had.' Johnny puts his head between his knees and sobs. 'I dunno why I didn't do what he said. She were only a fuckin' whore. Why should I care anyway?' He looks up at me puzzled. 'She were the first woman what's ever kissed me, and she said she'd fix me face up fer me!' Now he begins to howl like a little boy. Despite me pain and grief, I can't help feelin' sorry for the lad. He were only a pawn what the mongrel's used, and he saw the good in Maggie too.

'Johnny, I got t' go!' I says, though I want to howl meself. The fucking mongrels have taken Maggie and destroyed my brother's life. I would gladly die if only it would bring Maggie back for him. Sweet Maggie Pye, who Hawk loved so much. I feel despair overtake me.

Then Johnny Terrible speaks up. 'Mr Sparrow never did love me, I know it now, never at all!' he blubs. He swallows his tears. 'Mr Sparrow ain't got no heart, that's what!'

'Mongrels don't have a heart, that's why they's mongrels,' I hears meself say. And I start to get ready to go. I have but seventy minutes before the tide turns.

I put the axe back in me shoulder holster and, giving the lamp to Johnny, turn to leave. I'm already at the door to the passage when I hear him say, 'Tommo, they'll be watching out fer trouble 'til they sail. Don't take a row boat. Can yiz swim?'

'Aye,' I replies, I'd swim the seven seas to get the mongrel what killed Maggie. And there ain't a single doubt in me head that I'm gunna. Mr F. Artie Sparrow be as good as dead already – he just don't know it yet.

Suddenly, I remembers something what Mary told Hawk

before he left for London, and what later he told me. 'Life is too precious that you should die for money. If you has to die, then die for love!' Up to now, it's always been Hawk what took on the mongrels. This time the fight's all mine. Old Tommo must be his brother's champion.

'Johnny, soon as you can walk, fetch Hawk. He's at the Hero o' Waterloo. Tell him everything what's happened. And tell him Mary must not be with him when he comes to fetch Maggie.' I swallow a sob.

'Tell Hawk everything and Mary can't come,' Johnny Terrible repeats.

I'm halfway down the passageway when I turn back.

'Johnny?'

'Yes, Tommo?'

'Tell my mama I love her – and tell me brother I loves him too. Tell Hawk I wish him a long life and ask him to look after me daughter.' I hand Johnny the three magpie feathers what I've held clasped, bidding Maggie a silent farewell. 'Tell him that by the time he gets these, I'll have took care o' the mongrel for him, and tell him now I finally knows what's worth dying for.'

'Righto, Tommo.'

I don't suppose Johnny Terrible will remember all that, but then I don't suppose it matters. Hawk knows yours truly loved him.

PART III

SOLOMON'S SONG

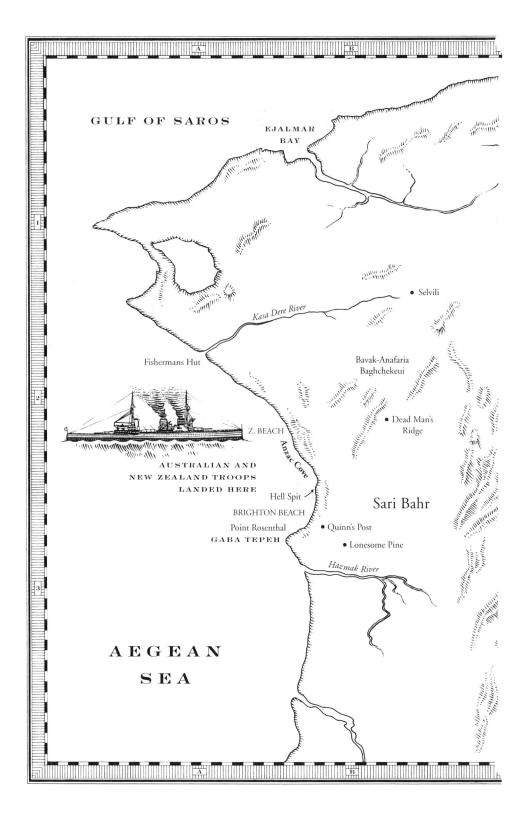

GULF OF SAROS

EJALMAR
BAY

• Selvili

Kasa Dere River

Fishermans Hut

Bavak-Anafaria
Baghchekeui

Z. BEACH

• Dead Man's
Ridge

Anzac Cove

AUSTRALIAN AND
NEW ZEALAND TROOPS
LANDED HERE

Sari Bahr

Hell Spit

BRIGHTON BEACH
Point Rosenthal
GABA TEPEH

• Quinn's Post
• Lonesome Pine

Hazmak River

AEGEAN
SEA

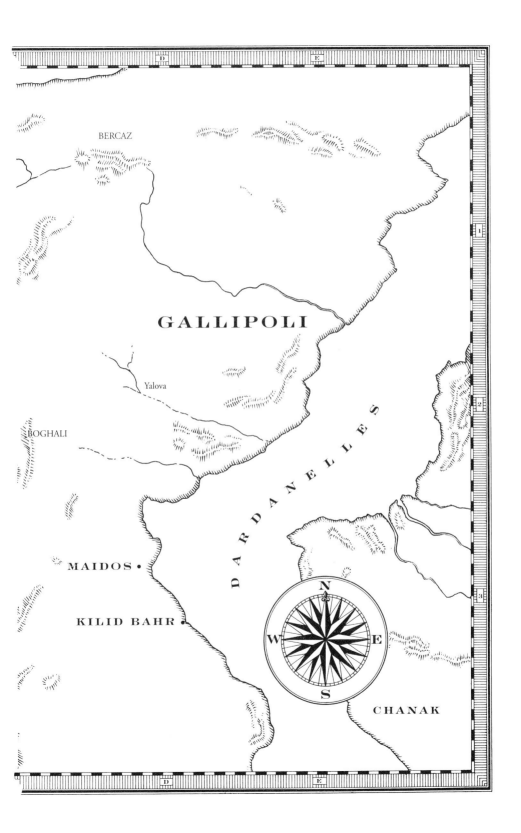

For my grandsons
Ben and Jake Courtenay

Acknowledgements

One of the advantages of being older is that one has had the good fortune to meet a lot of people who are experts on a great many topics. I never cease to be amazed and gratified by friends and acquaintances who so willingly part with their hard-earned knowledge.

Quite often a younger person, having read one or another of my books, says to me, 'How do you know all those things, Bryce?' Well, of course, I don't. My friends do. Authors steal stuff, most of us have 'news-stand' minds, we accommodate knowledge for very short periods.

Here now are some of the generous people from whom I 'borrowed' information and who allowed me to appropriate the wisdom I don't have. I have also included at the end of the book a bibliography of those writers without whose books it would have been impossible to write this one (see A Note on Sources).

To Margaret Gee, my line editor, proofreader, confidante and often fearless critic, my heartfelt thanks for being at my shoulder when I needed help and quiet as a mouse when I didn't.

To Benita Courtenay, who reads each chapter while it is still warm from my desktop printer and is never afraid to comment usefully, I am, as always, grateful to you.

My admiration and gratitude go to two great professionals, Bruce Gee, who is best described as a polymath, and John Arnold, Deputy Director, National Key Centre for Australian Studies, Monash University, who, assisted by David Green and Robin Lucas, became the mainstay of my research.

It has always been my contention that the historical facts in a work of fiction must be accurate and that readers should be able to rely on them to obtain a knowledge of the times in which the narrative takes place. In this regard Bruce and John and my editor Kay Ronai have done me proud.

I have a special debt of gratitude to Bill Fogarty, Senior Curator – Photographs, Sound and Film at the Australian War Memorial. Bill was with me at Gallipoli and together we covered the battlegrounds where, in a true sense, Australia forged many of those unique elements which make us who we are as a nation today. For the many bottles of cheap and utterly atrocious local red wine shared as we pondered over maps and explanations, for reading and correcting the military detail in this book and for the willingness to help at high speed, I shall be forever grateful to you, Bill, and also to those of your colleagues who worked with you.

There may be some who will disagree with my perspective of Gallipoli and France, but I would be very surprised if Bill Fogarty, Ashley Ekins, Historian, Official History Unit, and Graeme Beveridge, Education Unit, all of the Australian War Memorial, who supplied material and painstakingly detailed my narrative, have got any of the hard facts wrong.

And now for those who helped in a hundred different ways: John Waller, Managing Director of Boronia Travel Centre in Melbourne, who generously allowed me at the last minute to accompany his official tour to Gallipoli. Essie Moses, of Woollahra Library, who never fails me in matters Jewish and others. Owen Denmeade, Dr Irwin Light, Christine Lenton, Sylvia Manning, Sardine, Ethna Gallagher, Alex and Brenda Hamill, Tony Crosby, Danny Persky, Cheryl Bockman, John Robson, Robbee Spadafora for help with jacket designs, Alan Jacobs of Consensus Research, Harry Griffiths for further material and for the good companionship on the Gallipoli tour. To Peter Darnell, who generously allowed me the use of personal family papers and letters concerning his granduncle, Major Aubrey Darnell, who was killed in France in 1918. ETT Imprint, for their kind permission to reproduce Mary Gilmore's poem 'Gallipoli' from *Selected Poems* (Sydney, 1999). Wilfred Owen's poem 'Arms and the Boy' from *War Poems and Others* (Random House) was first published by Chatto & Windus. The epigraph to Chapter Seventeen is Rudyard Kipling's 'Common Form', from 'Epitaphs of the War, 1914–18'. The poem 'Gallipoli' on page 573 is by W. S. Pakenham-Walsh, 1916.

Then there are the Mitchell Library, State Library of New South Wales, and the State Library of Victoria, two of the most splendid, resourceful and co-operative institutions in the land, without which this book could not possibly have been contemplated. I thank you for your scholarship, dedication and the many examples of the best possible library practice.

My thanks to my old friends Sir William and Lady Dulcie Keys, who will launch *Solomon's Song* and, I know, will do so with great aplomb.

ACKNOWLEDGEMENTS

At Penguin Books I thank the staff who support me so generously and those backroom people who quietly make things happen, in particular my gratitude to Ali Watts, Senior Editor, Beverley Waldron, Production Manager, Leonie Stott, Design Manager, and her people in the Design Studio, Ellie Exarchos, text designer, and Nikki Townsend, jacket designer, you were all inspired.

To Peter Field, Peter Blake and Gabrielle Coyne who are responsible for the marketing and publicity, I know of no publishing house that does it better.

Then there are the Penguins who boss me around, my publishers, Bob Sessions, Julie Gibbs and Clare Forster, with Clare in the hot seat responsible for this book, you have all been patient, supporting and, as always, a delight with whom to work. Clare, I simply couldn't hope for a better working publisher.

As always, the best is left for last, my editor Kay Ronai. Kay, will you please edit my next book with me? You are simply the best. Absaloodle!

BRYCE COURTENAY

ARMS AND THE BOY

Let the boy try along this bayonet-blade
How cold steel is, and keen with hunger of blood;
Blue with all malice, like a madman's flash;
And thinly drawn with famishing for flesh.

Lend him to stroke these blind, blunt bullet-leads
Which long to nuzzle in the hearts of lads,
Or give him cartridges of fine zinc teeth,
Sharp with the sharpness of grief and death.

For his teeth seem for laughing round an apple.
There lurk no claws behind his fingers supple;
And God will grow no talons at his heels,
Nor antlers through the thickness of his curls.

– Wilfred Owen, 1918

BOOK ONE

Chapter One

What Happened to Tommo

Sydney 1861

On a dull early morning with the cumulus clouds over the Heads threatening rain, roiling and climbing, changing patterns and darkening at the centres, the incoming tide washes a body onto Camp Cove, a small inner-harbour beach within Port Jackson which is becoming increasingly known as Sydney Harbour.

Paddy Doyle, the shipping telegraph operator stationed at South Head, out with his dog hears its persistent and, what seems to his ear, urgent barking coming from the beach below him. He makes his way down the pathway onto the small jetty to see his black mongrel yapping beside what, even at a distance, is plainly a human body lying high up on the wet sand.

Doyle, a stout man not given to exertion, hesitates a moment, then jumps the eighteen inches from the jetty onto the sand and breaks into a clumsy trot, the sand squeaking and giving way under his boots. Commonsense tells him no amount of hurrying will make a difference, but death has a haste that ignores the good sense of walking slowly on a sultry morning. He is puffing heavily by the time he arrives at the wet bundle of wool and limbs from which trail several long ribbons of translucent iodine-coloured seaweed.

Immediately he sees that those parts of the body not protected by clothing are badly decomposed and much pecked about by gulls, crabs, sea lice and other scavengers of the deep. But not until he comes right up to it does he realise the body is missing a head.

The neck of the dead man protrudes from a dark woollen coat, a grotesque stump, ragged at the edges, torn about by the popping mouths of countless small fish. It is an aperture made less grisly by the cleansing effect of the salt water but more macabre by its bloodless appearance. It looks like the gape of some prehensile sea plant designed to trap and feed on small fish and tiny molluscs rather than something made of human flesh and blood.

Paddy, an ex-convict, brought to New South Wales on the barque, *Eden*, the last transport of convicts to Sydney in November 1840, thinks of himself as a hard man. But twenty years of half-decent living have increased the size of his girth and heightened his sensibilities and he vomits into the sand.

After a fair endurance of spitting and gagging he rinses his mouth in the salt wash and stands erect again, kicking the sand with the toe of his right boot to cover the mess he's made at his feet.

The sun has broken through a break in the clouds and almost immediately blowflies buzz around the corpse. A sickly stench starts to rise from the body, but with his belly emptied of his breakfast gruel, Doyle is now better able to withstand the smell and he squats down to make a more thorough examination.

A narrow leather thong around the base of the headless neck cuts deep into the swollen flesh and disappears inside the neck of a woollen vest. Doyle, reverting to his darker instincts, tugs tentatively at the cord. At first there is some resistance, then a small malachite amulet, a Maori Tiki, is revealed.

Doyle, like all past convicts, is deeply superstitious and is alarmed by the presence of an amulet known to ward off evil spirits and put a curse on those who harm its wearer. He hurriedly tucks it back under the wet vest, afraid now even to have touched it. Without thinking, he rubs the palm of the offending hand in the wet sand to cleanse it, then crossing himself he mutters, 'Hail Mary, Mother of God, protect me.'

The body is that of a white male of unusually small stature. The fingers of both his hands are clenched to form puffy, clublike fists. Whether from the sudden heat of the sun or the drying out of the corpse, the right hand begins to open and Doyle observes that the nails have continued to grow after death and are deeply embedded into the fleshy upper part of the dead man's palm. As the fingers unlock and open there is no sign of blood oozing from the fissures the nails have made. Each finger now wears a hooked talon with the finger pads puckered and raised from the immersion in sea water, so that the skin surface seems to be covered by nests of tiny white worms.

The nails are smooth and clean with no cuts or scars nor is there any permanently ingrained dirt etched into the lines on the palms to indicate a man accustomed to physical work. The skin on his arms is bluish-white from the sea water, but shows no signs of having ever been exposed to the sun. 'Some sort of toff,' Doyle thinks, 'no doubt up to no good and come to a sticky and untimely end, good riddance. Still an' all, choppin' off his 'ead's goin' a bit bloody far!'

Later, when he has pulled off his boots and placed them on the stone steps of his hut to dry and dusted the sand from his feet, he telegraphs Sydney to report the headless corpse. Then, in what Paddy thinks is an amusing appendage to his message, he taps out, *Best get a move on it don't take long for them blowflies to lay their maggot eggs.*

Two hours later, with the threatening clouds now well out to sea and the sun hot as hades in a clear blue sky, a steam pinnace from the police mooring at Circular Quay with two police constables aboard puffs up to the Camp Cove jetty to claim the body for the Pyrmont morgue.

While searching the corpse, the morgue attendant, observed closely by Senior Detective Darcy O'Reilly of the Darlinghurst Police Station, discovers a small leather wallet inside the jacket. It contains four pounds and several personal calling cards which identify the headless man as Tommo X Solomon.

Detective O'Reilly immediately sends a constable to Tucker & Co. to inform Hawk Solomon that he is required at the city morgue to identify what may be the remains of his brother.

Hawk, at Mary's instigation, had reported Tommo missing in case any of Mr Sparrow's lads might have seen him entering his lodgings on the night of Maggie's death and declared his presence to the police.

A further search of the victim's clothing reveals a deck of DeLarue cards, the kind generally used by professional gamblers of a superior status. Finally, a gold hunter watch, with the ace of spades enamelled on its outer lid and a sovereign hanging from its fob chain, is discovered in a buttoned-down pocket of his weskit. It has stopped at twenty minutes past ten o'clock. Senior Detective O'Reilly writes this down as the presumed time of death and then pockets the watch. The corpse is left clothed for the pathologist to examine and is lifted onto the zinc dissecting table in preparation for the autopsy by the Chief Government Medical Officer, William McCrea M.D., who will closely examine the clothes before removal, noting any tears or stains that may help to define the method of death.

Conscious of the corpse's advanced state of decomposition Dr McCrea loses no time presenting his findings to the coroner, Mr Manning Turnbull Noyes, known in the magistrates courts as M. T. Noyes and by the hoi polloi as 'Empty Noise'.

The hearing and its immediate aftermath is best summed up by the following day's *Sydney Morning Herald* report on the murder by its popular senior crime reporter, Samuel Cook. Although Mr Cook's name is not used in the paper his style is easily recognised by his many readers who know him for his fearless reportage. He enjoys their respect for his ability to ask awkward questions which have a habit of greatly embarrassing nobs and government officials of every rank. Cook has even been known to take on the governor when a wealthy merchant of dubious reputation was included in the Queen's Honours List. There are some who believe he wouldn't back down to the young Queen Victoria herself.

Samuel Cook is the scourge of the police force, in particular of Senior Detective Darcy O'Reilly. And while every magistrate in New South Wales, given half a chance to nobble him, would cheerfully sentence the *Sydney Morning Herald* reporter to a ten-year stretch in Darlinghurst, it is Noyes who would call in the hangman. Like O'Reilly, M. T. Noyes is a special target for his remorseless and acerbic pen.

HEADLESS BODY WASHED UP ON CAMP COVE BEACH

A special report.

The headless body of a white man thought to be that of Mr Tommo X Solomon was discovered yesterday washed up on the beach by Mr Paddy Doyle stationed at the Camp Cove telegraph office.

Mr Doyle reported that he

6

had initially been alerted by the unusual barking of his dog and had walked down to the beach to investigate, thinking perhaps a seal had come ashore on the rocks at the far side of the beach as they occasionally do at this time of the year.

Upon discovering the murder victim Mr Doyle lost no time alerting the authorities and the body, sans head, was recovered by the police some hours later and taken to the city morgue at Pyrmont.

The investigation into the murder is under the direction of Senior Detective Darcy O'Reilly of Darlinghurst Police Station.

Dr William McCrea M.D., Chief Government Medical Officer, successfully applied to the magistrates court at Darlinghurst to submit his findings immediately to the coroner, Mr M. T. Noyes, citing the humid and inclement weather and the decomposed nature of the corpse. Permission was granted by the stipendiary magistrate and the inquest was held late yesterday afternoon.

In his coroner's report Mr Noyes stated that the head of the deceased had been removed by an instrument thought to be an axe with the blade prepared to a razor-sharp edge.

Senior Detective O'Reilly stated in evidence that, as the victim had not been robbed of his wallet, or his gold watch and chain, he appeared to be the victim of an execution-style murder.

The coroner, well known for his acerbic wit, remarked that in his experience on the bench he had not yet heard of a suicide where the deceased had entirely removed his own head with an axe. He hoped the senior detective might in future restrict himself to any information which might be useful to the constabulary in their efforts to solve the case.

The senior detective then stated that the murder may have taken place on board a ship at sea. However, the more likely conclusion was that the head had been removed from the body and the body taken outside the Sydney Heads and dumped at sea.

'I would be most surprised if the head isn't buried deep somewhere ashore, Detective O'Reilly,' Mr Noyes opined.

The detective sighed audibly. 'Yes, your honour, we are most grateful for your opinion,' though what he really thought of the coroner's gratuitous insight this correspondent dares not even suppose.

The coroner made a finding of murder by person or persons unknown and the court was adjourned.

Asked outside the court who he thought might have done such a grisly execution Senior Detective O'Reilly stated, 'Decapitation is not a common method of murder, but is known to be used among the celestials. Though I have not heard of it used against a white man before.'

When it was pointed out that the victim, Mr Tommo Solomon, was a user of the opium poppy and well known in Chinatown, he refused to speculate further on the matter.

'Our enquiry will determine soon enough what we need to know,' he stated.

'Did you know that the murder victim was a partner in a gaming syndicate run by the well-known "sportsman" Mr F. Artie Sparrow?' he was then asked.

'No,' came the prompt and surprising reply.

'Did you know he was a member of a regular illegal card game that was known to take place in Chinatown on the premises of Tang Wing Hung the Chinaman importer?'

Not entirely surprising, his answer was 'No' again.

Your correspondent then asked if the murder of Mr Solomon might be linked with the deaths on the premises of Mr Sparrow's lodging of the boxing promoter known as Fat Fred and the prostitute Maggie Pye, the latter suffocating under the weight of the dead body of the former.

Senior Detective O'Reilly replied that the coroner's report on the state of decomposition of the victim's body supported the theory that Mr Tommo Solomon might have been murdered at around the same time, but that it would be foolish to link the two incidents.

He stressed that the coroner's findings of the two previous deaths had been that Fat Fred, while involved in sexual intercourse, had died of a sudden and massive heart seizure and Miss Pye of asphyxia while trapped beneath his body.

'We have no reason to suspect foul play.' Senior Detective O'Reilly added, 'We are hoping that Mr Sparrow will help the police with our enquiries but, as of this time, we have been unable to locate him. I ask anyone who knows of his present where-abouts to come forward.'

The good detective was then asked if he thought it a mere coincidence that the murdered man was the twin brother of the professional pugilist Hawk Solomon who, in turn, was betrothed to the murdered prostitute, Maggie Pye?

'All coincidences will be carefully examined,' O'Reilly replied loftily.

Your correspondent then asked if Senior Detective O'Reilly was aware that Mr Sparrow was also known to owe Mr Tang Wing Hung and Miss Mary Abacus, the mother of the adopted twins Tommo and Hawk Solomon, a considerable sum of money, this being their winnings from bets made on the prize fight between Mr Hawk Solomon and the Irish pugilist who goes under the sobriquet, The Lightning Bolt?

Senior Detective O'Reilly declined to comment, but pointed out gratuitously that both barefist boxing and wagering on such contests are illegal in the colony of New South Wales and that no such claim, if true, would stand up in court.

'Did this not then suggest a reason why Mr Sparrow might have "gone missing" and wasn't it worthwhile following up the evidence of the lad known as Johnny Terrible, who stated that Mr Sparrow had sent a note to Maggie Pye suggesting she be the emissary between himself, Tang Wing Hung and Miss Mary Abacus?'

'Sir, you are fully aware that the particular note found on the premises belonging to Maggie Pye was tabled and read out in court. It simply contained the words, *Come and see me, my dear*, and was signed by Mr Sparrow.'

'And the evidence of the boy, Johnny Terrible?'

'The magistrate chose not to take into consideration the boy's evidence as he has been in trouble before and is known to lie under oath.'

Senior Detective O'Reilly then looked at your corre-spondent with an expression suggesting some bemusement. 'I find myself surprised at your questions, sir. Given the known occupation of the deceased woman, the magistrate, I believe, has correctly con-cluded that she was acquired by Mr Sparrow for the pur-poses usually associated with women of her profession. The note received by Maggie Pye can possess no other explanation,' he concluded.

Your correspondent then countered with the suggestion that it was common knowledge that Mr Sparrow was not known to favour the fairer sex and that his preferences lay, to put it in the kindest terms, 'elsewhere'. Furthermore, it was a well-known joke among the Sydney lads employed by Mr Sparrow that Fat Fred was usually incapable of dalliance of any sort and that drink rendered him impotent.

Senior Detective O'Reilly then said, 'You are raking over old coals, sir,' and declined to answer any more questions from your correspondent.

Miss Mary Abacus and Mr Hawk Solomon, who had earlier visited the morgue to identify the body and later also attended the coroner's hearing, declined to be interviewed by this correspondent, pleading that they be allowed the right to mourn the loss of a beloved son and brother.

Hawk stops off first at the Hero of Waterloo where Mary has her temporary lodgings, and together they go to the Pyrmont morgue to identify Tommo's corpse. Here they are made to place a tincture of camphor oil to their nostrils to kill the unmistakeable odour of decaying flesh before they are taken into the morgue's coldroom to examine the corpse which has been stripped of its clothing but, at the suggestion of Senior Detective O'Reilly, the Tiki remains with its leather thong about the tattered and truncated neck.

A square of canvas has been neatly arranged over the top of the neck to conceal the absence of a head, though the Maori amulet can be clearly seen resting on the exposed chest three inches below the base of the neck. A second square of canvas in the form of a loincloth covers the private parts. Mary scarcely pauses to examine the body before confirming to Senior Detective O'Reilly that it is her adopted son, Tommo.

She notices O'Reilly's bemused and doubtful countenance at so quick an identification of a corpse, which, after all, lacks a head, the most common method of recognition. She points to a large mole high up on the left shoulder. 'Born with it, big as sixpence, can't mistake it, looks like a map of Tasmania,' she states. Remembering her grief, her voice quavers slightly and she touches the corner of the small lace handkerchief to her right eye and then her left and returns it, perhaps a little too hastily, to cover her nose, for the stench rising from the body has even defeated the efficacy of the camphor oil.

Hawk is hard put to contain his surprise for, almost at once, they have both seen that the naked body isn't that of Tommo. Hawk's twin has a small but distinctive birthmark on the calf of his left leg and no such mark can now be seen. Hawk bends down to examine the amulet and immediately sees what he is looking for, a small 'M' has been scratched into the surface of the green malachite. 'The Tiki,' he points to the amulet. 'That's his, my brother's.' It was given to his twin by his Maori wife, who died in childbirth, and the 'M' scratched onto the surface is for her name 'Makareta'.

It is a certain sign to Hawk of Tommo's efforts at deception and his determination to make the murder victim seem to be himself. Tommo would have thought long and hard before parting with the Tiki which he greatly cherished as his talisman, the equivalent in his own mind of Mary's Waterloo medal. Then Hawk realises that it is a message to him, Tommo's way of telling him that he is still in the world of the living.

In fact, having received Johnny Terrible's message that Tommo was going after Mr Sparrow, they have each silently concluded the corpse must belong to Ikey Solomon's most accomplished graduate from the Methodist Academy of Light Fingers, the infamous Sparrow Fart, alias F. Artie Sparrow, the odious Mr Sparrow.

Tommo has completed what he had vowed to do and avenged the death of Maggie Pye. The sudden tears Senior Detective O'Reilly now sees streaming unabashedly down the tattooed cheeks of the giant black man are not, as he supposes, for the grotesque corpse on the zinc tray, but for Maggie Pye and the love of his twin. They are also tears of relief that Tommo is still alive.

Using the only currency he knows, this headless corpse lying on a slab of ice is Tommo's payback for all the mongrels who have blighted his life. The ghastly manner of Mr Sparrow's death is paradoxically also Tommo's last gift of love to his brother. Hawk cannot help but think that the pressure on Tommo's brain from the wound to his head has finally driven him insane. For this notion as well, he now weeps.

O'Reilly brings his fist to his lips and clears his throat.

'Hurrmph, er missus, if you'd be so kind as to turn yer back, a matter o' some delicacy,' he says, looking directly at Mary.

Mary turns away from the corpse and the detective lifts the canvas loincloth and nods to Hawk. 'It's another common way o' identification,' he says abruptly, then supposing Mary can't hear him, he whispers *sotto voce* to Hawk, 'Pricks are like faces, every one's different.'

Hawk sees immediately that, unlike Tommo's, the penis is not circumcised.

'Well, what does you think?' O'Reilly asks.

Hawk sniffs and nods his head, but does not reply, not wishing to openly commit perjury. O'Reilly sighs and pulls the small canvas square back into place. 'It's all right to look now, missus,' he says to Mary. As if he is anxious to conclude the identification, he casually produces a gold watch from his pocket. Clicking it open so that the ace of spades on its lid can be clearly seen by both Mary and Hawk, he pretends to consult it.

'Goodness, that's our Tommo's watch,' Mary says quick as a flash, for indeed it *is* Tommo's. Senior Detective O'Reilly grins, the identification of the headless victim is complete, it's been a satisfying afternoon's work all round. He nods. 'Good.' He turns and calls over to the morgue assistant who brings him a clipboard to which is attached a form. The assistant also holds a small glass pen and ink stand. Holding the clipboard in one hand and with the pen poised in the other, O'Reilly asks officially, 'Are you, Hawk Solomon, and you, Mary Abacus, quite certain this is the body of Tommo Solomon?'

'With me hand on me heart,' Mary lies, bringing her hand up to cover her left breast. The question is perfunctory, O'Reilly has witnessed a mother's quick and positive identification and the copious tears of grief still issuing from the giant nigger.

'You'll sign here then,' he says all businesslike, dipping the pen into the open ink bottle and handing it to Hawk. Mary and Hawk sign the paper confirming their identification and the morgue assistant takes the clipboard and departs.

'When can we take possession of the body of our loved one?' Mary asks plaintively, her eyes taking on a suitably sad expression. 'Give it a burial decent folk might attend?'

Hawk is amazed at her assertiveness, her complete presence of mind, she wants the body buried and out of the clutches of the law

12

as soon as possible. 'It ain't in a nice state and we wish to preserve the best of our memories, sir,' she adds, putting the finishing touches to what she hopes O'Reilly will see as a mother's anxiety and grief.

The corners of the detective's mouth twitch slightly and Mary reads this as a sign of his sympathy. 'See what I can do, missus. It's in the hands o' the coroner. He don't like being told his business, though.'

Mary takes a sovereign out of her purse and offers it to him. 'A small contribution to the Orphans Fund,' she says in a half-whisper.

O'Reilly now gives her a genuine smile, knowing himself to be the orphan of particular benefit. 'Might be able to give him a bit of a hurry up, eh?' he says, taking the gold coin Mary holds out to him.

'Most grateful, I'm sure,' Mary says, batting her eyes.

'Mother, that were a bribe,' Hawk says to Mary on their return to the Hero of Waterloo.

'Blimey! And him a detective, fancy that,' Mary laughs.

The coroner, magistrate M. T. Noyes, is happy enough to oblige and he orders the body's release from the authorities and also the immediate return of Tommo's personal effects from the police. Though, unable to resist the temptation to display his infamous wit, and first determining that Mr Cook of the *Sydney Morning Herald* is not present, the magistrate quips, 'In making this decision we have lost our head and must quickly bury the evidence or the case will stink to high heaven!'

By sundown every pub in Sydney will be repeating his *bon mot*. 'Have you heard the latest from his nibs, Empty Noise?' they will say gleefully to every newcomer.

Mary, never one to take chances, orders an expensive black basalt tombstone engraved in gold with the words:

Tommo X Solomon
1840–1861
R.I.P.

In a simple ceremony conducted by the Reverend Hannibal Peegsnit, the eccentric Congregationalist, with only Mary and

13

Hawk in attendance, the remains of Mr Sparrow are duly buried.

Ikey's best pupil, Sparrer Fart, the lightest fingers in London Town, the small boy who never knew his real name, ended the way he'd started his life, unknown, unwanted and unloved, his final epitaph a beak's joke in bad taste. He will lie headless beneath a tombstone, which, when Satan asks him for a reckoning of his life, he won't even be able to call his own.

Hawk wishes Mary 'Long life', which is what Ikey would have done in the same circumstances.

Mary returns to Hobart after the funeral. Hawk gives Maggie's two-room home and all her possessions to Flo, Maggie's little friend, now married to the grocer's son, Tom. He visits Caleb Soul, who accompanied Tommo and himself to the gold diggings at Lambing Flat and has since become one of Hawk's dearest friends, to say his farewell. Then, after telling all at Tucker & Co. that he is going home to Hobart, and attending a gathering in the dock area of the entire company where he receives a handsome crystal goblet in gratitude for his services from Captain Tucker, Hawk sets sail for New Zealand.

On his arrival Hawk makes his way to the stretch of Auckland Harbour where the Maori boats moor and catches a coastal ketch that will take him to the Ngati Haua tribe under Chief Tamihana, in whose household Tommo's daughter, Hinetitama, is being raised.

Hawk discovers that Tommo is dying from the wound to his head and is in constant pain. Often he sinks into a delirium but even when he is conscious, the pressure on his brain renders him incoherent, so that the words in his mouth twist into gibberish. But sometimes he has brief periods in the early mornings when he is quite lucid.

During one such period he asks Hawk to leave his daughter with the Maori until she comes of age and can decide for herself whether she wants the life of a pakeha or wishes to stay with her people.

'The Maori be her family now, even if her name be Solomon. Let her choose later, though Gawd knows why she'd want to be one of us.' In these coherent periods it is the same old sardonic Tommo, ever on the alert for the mongrels.

'I shall see she never lacks for anything,' Hawk promises. 'I will respect your wish, though Mary pleads she would very much like her, as her granddaughter, to be brought up well at home with every privilege and the very best of education.'

'Tell her then to leave something in her will for my daughter, my share,' Tommo replies. 'Although from what I've seen of privilege and education it breeds only greed and superiority.'

Hawk protests and Tommo laughs. 'The Maori have all but lost their land and it has been took from them by educated men, men of the Church, committing a crime in the name of God and the governor himself doing the same in the name of the Queen. These are all educated men, all greedy and superior, all mongrels.'

Hawk, ever the rational one, replies, 'That is an oversimplification, Tommo, goodness is not replaced by greed when a man becomes educated nor is greed absent in the poor. Man is by his very nature rapacious and wealth has forever been the precursor of power, the need to be seen as superior. Hinetitama must have some learning, you would not want your daughter to be shackled by ignorance and superstition.'

Tommo looks wearily up at Hawk. 'You are the only good man I know what's keen on book learnin'. Let my daughter grow up the natural way of her people, she will be taught to read and count and that will be enough.' Tommo grins, it is near to being the old Tommo grin and Hawk's heart is filled with love for his dying twin. 'Unless you can teach her how to handle a pack of cards, eh? You must give her my Tiki.' He touches the Tiki Hawk has returned to him and his expression grows suddenly serious. 'Hawk, there is bad blood in me and it will be in my daughter also. If she stays among the Maori it will not come out so soon. Please tell her to wear it always, that the Tiki will protect her.'

'Your axe? Is this the bad blood you talk of?' Hawk does not wait for Tommo to reply. 'Tommo, there is no bad blood there, what you did was for me and in memory of Maggie Pye. It was justice. You are good, Tommo, as good a man as ever had a conscience.' For the first time the death of Mr Sparrow has been mentioned.

'Conscience?' Tommo smiles ruefully. 'That is the difference between you and me, you would carry the murder on your conscience forever and I have but scarcely thought about it. Mr Sparrow was a mongrel and when I chopped him there was that much less evil in the world.' Tommo looks up at Hawk. 'But it takes bad blood to murder a man, any man, even a mongrel. If they should string me up for it, it would be a fair bargain.'

Hawk sighs and then looks at Tommo somewhat apprehensively. 'Tommo, will you tell about that night?'

It is Tommo's turn to sigh, 'Aye, if you wish, but it weren't a pretty thing to tell of.'

'Tommo, I grieve for Maggie every day, every hour of my life, it would make it more, yer know ah . . . complete . . .' Hawk shrugs, not knowing how to continue.

Tommo sees his confusion and starts right in. 'It takes me five or six minutes to run to Kellet's Wharf from the World Turned Upside Down, the pub where Mr Sparrow stayed. It's fourteen minutes to nine o'clock with the tide turning at some time shortly after nine when the Kanaka ship, *Morning Star*, will sail. I have little time left to swim the two hundred yards out to where she's moored.

'I'm sweating and panting from the run and I remove me clothes and shoes and using me belt I wraps them around the axe holster and returns it to my back. Then I wades in and starts to swim. I'm still breathing 'ard from the run and me 'ead's hurting terrible. It's a calm night and dark with cloud cover, so the moon is lost. The harbour water's cool and welcoming and I strokes me way to the dark shape o' the *Morning Star*, a trading schooner about eighty feet stem to stern. I can see she has her head to the wind, facing the land breeze coming down the harbour and is preparing to sail.

'As I reach the port side I can hear the Kanakas starting to sing as they lean into the capstan bars to take up the slack and begin to raise the anchor. I can hear the click of the pawls and if I'm any judge it's a task that will take anything up to fifteen minutes. It means I can't climb up the anchor rope as I had supposed. But, ah, there is a God in heaven, as me eyes clear I see they've already raised the dinghy but the ship's ladder has not yet been pulled up. Glory be, it's a doddle to climb on board up the rope ladder and soon enough I sticks me 'ead up to take a look over the deck. I'm panting hard but there appears to be no one about. They've already set the mainsail which is luffing in the light breeze and will cover any sound I might make coming aboard. From where I am at the waist of the schooner the Kanaka standing at the ship's wheel and the captain on the quarterdeck can't see me and I can hear the first mate on the quarterdeck urging the men on with the raising of the anchor.

'I look around, there are a dozen or so barrels lashed to the starboard side and the dark shape of the deckhouse with the dinghy atop is to me left. Then I hear a snuffling sound and I go rigid, somebody's coming. But it don't take long to realise, like all Kanaka ships, they've taken pigs on board. Island folk, as you well know, don't like to go to sea without a pig or two. Then I see it, the pig pen, close to the fo'c'sle, Kanakas, the only folk happy to put the pig pen near where they kips down. There's another shape next to it and o' course it's the chicken coop, chickens the second thing them silly buggers like to have on board. All the bleedin' 'ome comforts. The rest o' the deck is the usual mess what come about before sailing. It will be to my advantage, nobody moving quickly, plenty of time to see 'em coming and if I has to, use me axe.'

Hawk looks aghast. 'Tommo, you'd not kill an innocent?'

Tommo grins. 'Nah, just tap him light with the blunt, put him down for a bit. Anyway, it don't happen. It ain't necessary. There's nobody on the main deck and I slips aboard and find good concealment behind the barrels on the starboard side. I'm tucked away so when they tidy the deck there is little chance I'll be discovered.

'I can see the deckhouse leading down to the saloon where I figure I'll find Mr Sparrow. It looks to be a typical trading schooner with the one cabin below decks for a passenger or two and the captain and the first mate in their own quarters aft where it be the most comfortable to sail. From what Johnny Terrible's told me, Mr Sparrow is on his own and does not wish to be recognised, not even by the captain or the crew, let alone a fellow passenger, so it will be him and me alone, if I can get down to him.

'I undoes me swag and removes me axe from the shoulder holster so it's at me side. I'm still bollocky and I starts to shiver again, now me panting's stopped. As best I can, I wring out me wet clobber and get back into it, me clothes clinging to me skin, feeling 'orrible and me feet squelching in soaked boots. Now it's waiting time and me 'ead's hurting real bad.

'The anchor's up at last and the ship turns with the outgoing tide with Sydney now, same as me, on the starboard side. I can see a few lights and I thinks of you and Mama and of Johnny Terrible breaking the news o' Maggie's death to you and giving you the magpie feathers and I silently hopes that me going after the mongrel what done it will some day be of true comfort to you.'

Hawk's eyes fill with sudden tears. 'I thought that I'd lost you too, that of the three people I loved with all my heart, that I had lost two of them on the one night. If it were not for the strength of Mary, our mama, I don't reckon I'd have wanted to go on living another hour.' Hawk grins through his tears. 'She saw how I was and she come right out and says, "Hawk Solomon," like she'd say when we were little 'uns, stern o' face, the scar on her cheek pulled down to the corner of her mouth, "I didn't rescue you from the wild man in the wilderness just so you could snuff it by yer own miserable 'ands! I've lost me beloved Tommo and you, your lovely Maggie, but you ain't gunna do the dirty on me now, so get that inta yer thick nigger 'ead!" She points a crooked finger at me. "Dying is easy, son. It's living what takes the character. Orright? Now, let's get on with it." '

'Yeah, that be our *I shall never surrender*, Mary, that's our mama,' Tommo laughs. 'She's right, yer know, livin's what's the bastard.'

Hawk, hoping to change the sudden feeling of melancholy, changes tack. 'You're on deck, but, with the ship moving down the harbour soon to be out of the Heads, how ever did you think you'd get back to shore?'

Tommo gives a rueful smile. 'Mate, with me 'ead gone an' all, I reckoned there weren't much point to hangin' around any longer. Just so long as I can get a crack at the miserable mongrel. Tell yer the truth, I didn't think much about the next part o' it.'

'Tommo, you were willing to give your life for me and you tell me you've got bad blood. It just isn't true!' Hawk protests fiercely.

'Wait on, it ain't pretty what comes next.'

Hawk can see Tommo is tiring. 'You sure you want to go on?' he asks, concerned.

Tommo nods his head and takes up where he left off. 'It's getting bloody cold with spring not yet come and me sittin' shivering in me wet clobber. A couple of Kanakas pass by and I reckon if I coughs I'm a goner, me teeth are chatterin' that loud I think they must surely hear me loud as a chisel chippin' stone.

'But they goes about their work getting the sails up and trimmed and several others come to join them. We've passed the Sow and Pigs, them cluster o' rocks that stand inside the harbour, and we're just about through the Heads, they've got the flying jib going as well as the topsail with the main and staysail up and under way. I reckon the breeze from the land is now moving us about four or five knots, a perfect night for sail, they'll all be in the fo'c'sle abed not long after we've cleared the Heads. You know how it is, yiz pretty knackered after getting under way.

'Well, it were just like I just said. Bloody ship would sail itself on a night like this. We clears the Heads and turns to port and hugs to the coast to take advantage o' the shore breeze and the crew turn in prompt as I had supposed.

'Now it's only the creaking o' the ship, the bow waves and the sails luffing that breaks the silence. I reckon the only man left on deck is the helmsman and he's got the light from the ship's compass in his eyes, so there's no way he can see the main deck from the quarter. It's dark as hell anyway, best you can see clearly is about ten feet. Besides, the deckhouse is cutting off his line o' sight, so I reckon I am clear to make me move.

'Then I see him, Mr Sparrow, he's coming up from below. I watch as he turns, walking towards me. Gawd in heaven, he's walking straight into a trap I didn't even know I'd set. But o' course he sees the barrels and turns to the right, coming up to the starboard rails not six feet from where I'm hiding. Me heart starts to pump. Jesus H. Christ, I can take him right here and now with the axe, throw it and put the blade into the side o' his skull and he'd be dead 'fore he hit the deck or could even grunt.

'He's wearing a long coat just like the one Ikey used to wear, his 'at is pulled down to his eyes and he's got a woollen scarf wrapped around his phiz so only his eyes are to be seen between his 'at and the scarf. He's looking out to sea and all you can hear is the wash as the bow cuts through the waves. I've got F. Artie Sparrow standing still as a scarecrow, the perfect target, and him no doubt lamenting the good life he's left behind in Sydney and not knowing the next port o' call will be the flames o' hell itself.'

'So that was it then?' Hawk says, sighing, glad the telling is over.

'Nah, too easy, I want the bastard t'know it was me come after him and that he's gunna die. No point him being alive one moment and dead the next without him knowing why. I want to see the fear in his miserable mongrel eyes. I want to see it for Maggie, for you, for meself. It's like he's all the mongrels that ever were and I want to see how their kind take to dying.'

Hawk can scarcely believe Tommo's courage. 'But he could

have shouted and alerted the crew as he saw you coming, anything!'

'Not before I'd a nailed him he couldn't have.' Tommo pauses. 'After that I couldn't give a shit.'

'So, what did you do?'

'I creep up and lift his 'at and give him a light tap on the skull with the blunt and catch him as he sinks to his knees. He's about the same size as me, but I know I'm the younger and stronger, so I slips me axe into the holster across me back and lifts him over me shoulder and crosses to the companionway. It's a bit of a struggle getting him down below and into the saloon. I'm already knackered but I dumps Mr Sparrow on the floor and locks the cabin door and sits down to recover and to await his return to this shitty world. But first I take the precaution of wrapping the woollen scarf tight about his mouth so that he won't wake with a scream and can still breathe through his nostrils.

'Then I takes a look about me. It don't take too long to find his stash what's in a leather saddlebag. There's more in it than even I supposed, gold coin o' course, but mostly it's stuff what's light but can be quickly converted into cash. Diamonds, several gold rings with large ruby and emerald stones and a box o' the finest South Sea pearls you can imagine, maybe two hundred o' the little beauties. There's a stack o' them new five pound banknotes which I can't get both me 'ands around. A fortune carefully put together to be transportable and, I'm telling yer straight, it ain't been gathered in a few days. I am forced to conclude that F. Artie Sparrow has long contemplated there might some day come the need to scarper and was ever ready to escape at a moment's notice. But then I find true paradise, a ball o' opium big as yer fist wrapped in cheesecloth. Mr Sparrow has brought along with him six months supply from Tang Wing Hung.'

Tommo laughs. 'Here I be with a fortune of ill-gained and half a year's supply o' the poppy and I can't do nothing about it. I'm sitting there thinking how bloody typical, Tommo's usual luck, eh? I think I'll find Sparrow's pipe and kill the pain in me 'ead for a while. Then I realise that if he come to while the Angel's Kiss be upon me, I'm history. The craving for opium and the pain in me noggin be so bad I almost think to chop him right there and prepare a pipe and smoke it at me leisure. Then the idea come to me all of a sudden, out o' the blue like. With me craving the poppy

I can't think how there be room for such a plan to come into me terrible aching 'ead, but it comes quite sudden and complete and is worthy o' the cunning o' Ikey Solomon himself.

'I begin to remove Mr Sparrow's clothes, first his Ikey coat, which I can see will fit a treat, then his jacket, weskit and blouse, then the fine leather boots and next his trousers and then his long johns and hose. He's bollocky and there's even less of him than me and I wonder how so much evil can be contained in such a little bag o' skin, bones and misery.

'His clobber fits me like a glove and I'm warm and snug and feeling much better for the change from me own wet garments. Mr Sparrow is beginning to stir and so I pulls him up until he's sitting with his back against the cabin wall and his head lolling, chin on chest.

'His eyes open, bleary at first then with sudden light, he can't talk o' course but the surprise they show is speech enough. He looks down and sees he's naked and jerks backwards against the cabin wall and quickly brings his 'ands to cover his little blue worm.

' "Good evening, Mr Sparrow," I says. I can hear him whimper behind the scarf. So I lifts my axe and puts me finger to me lips so he'll know to stay stum and removes the scarf, though he could have done as well himself his hands not being bound.

' "Tommo!" he says, all surprised. "Where am I?" he asks, still lookin' dazed like.

' "Shush! Where you was before, but now you've got company," says I.

'He looks about the cabin and I can see he's thinking what to say next. Then he turns to me, "How much?"

'I laugh and point to the saddlebag, "Too late for that, mate. I've got the lot and what's stashed in this coat, but you might oblige me by takin' them rings from your fingers."

' "Don't know that they'll come free," he says, still a bit cheeky like. I got to 'and it to him, little bugger's got spunk orright.

'I shrugs and wave the axe. "Easy, always cut 'em loose, makes no bloody difference to me, do it?"

'He gets the rings off without too much trouble and I takes them and drops them in me coat pocket.

' "Righto then, up you gets." I point to me wet clothes, "Put 'em on."

' "But they're wet?" he protests.

' "Never mind, where you're goin' they'll soon enough be dry." I grins, but I don't think he gets the joke. It takes him a while to get the wet clobber on but what fits me fits him fine. I point to a wicker chair what's in the cabin. "Sit."

'He sits in the chair with his hands folded in his lap shiverin' like a captured mouse. I know how he feels in the wet clobber, so I takes a blanket from the bunk and throws it at him and he wraps it around himself, his 'ead an' all. He looks like a scrawny old crone begging for alms.

'I don't reckon he'll make a sudden jump for me, I don't see it in his eyes. I can tell he still thinks he'll use his noggin, talk hisself out of trouble. But he's forgot I were brought up by Ikey Solomon, what could talk hisself out o' the condemned cell with the hangman's noose already 'round his neck. F. Artie Sparrow ain't in the same class o' spruiker. Besides, with the blanket wrapped around him it will be harder if he tries to 'ave a go at me.

' "What you going to do to me, Tommo?" he asks at last.

' "Well now, let's see. I reckon about the same as you done to Miss Maggie Pye. What say you, Mr Sparrow?"

' "She were a whore, Fat Fred fucked her to death, that ain't got nothing ter do with me."

' "Fat Fred couldn't get it up at a whore's Christmas party, yer bastard. What you did was murder Maggie and you thought it were funny, a bit o' fun for the Sydney lads and you, at the same time, gettin' your revenge on me brother Hawk!"

' "No, no," he pleads, "It were no such thing. I swear on me life!"

' "Your life? Right now it ain't worth a pinch o' shit. I've 'ad a chat to Johnny Terrible, he's told me everything, you bastard!"

' "Please," he says, "spare me and you'll not regret it, Tommo!"

' "Spare you? Jesus! Whaffor?"

' "We could go into business, son. I'll cut you in for 'arf o' everything, we'd make a bleedin' fortune you and me." He cocks his 'ead to the side, "You with the flats and me managing the game. There'd be none better in all the colonies." He tries to smile, to crawl right up me arse. "Mr Ace o' Spades, you're the best, the very best there is with the cards, never seen better, a bloody miracle them 'ands. Miracle o' motion and deception. You've got talent nigh to genius, no, correction, you *is* genius."

' "And both of us needin' the poppy regular, eh? A fine threesome, you, me and the opium pipe. Bullshit!" His nose is running and he's commenced to snivellin' and shiverin' and I can see that the courage 'as suddenly leaked out o' him, there's wet tears runnin' down his cheeks.'

' "What say you, then?" he whimpers, his teeth achatter. I don't know whether the shaking is from the cold or his fear, both perhaps. Mr Sparrow spreads his hands and shrugs and appeals to me with the wet eyes, "Please, Tommo, spare me," he cries.

' "Mr Sparrow, I didn't come to bargain, as I see it right now, I ain't got too much time meself. I come to do what I've promised I'd do since I were seven year old and four of you mongrels, you dog fuckers, stretched me over a Huon log in the Wilderness. Pulled down me torn britches and threw me over that fallen log. I remember its lemon-yellow bark were stripped, just like me, me and the pine, both bollock naked, me with me face kissin' the damp forest earth and it fallen to the same by the cruel axes o' the wood fetchers. Then them buggering me, laughing, snotting over me back and me arse bleeding so the blood's running down the inside o' me legs. Them leavin', footsteps crackling through the fern and myrtle bush, laughing, whooping, doin' up their buckles and buttoning their britches. You fuck little boys too, don'tcha, Mr Sparrow?"

' "Tommo, Tommo! I'm like you," Mr Sparrow wails. "They done the same t'me! The very same! Ask Ikey! He took me from Hannah Solomon's brothel where I were a catamite! He said I were too smart to be raped for sixpence by a turd burglar!"

' "Ikey's long dead," I snap. I don't need Sparrow's begging. I don't want him to be like me, even in this.

'He begins to sob again. "It's true, I swear it's true!" For a moment there I'm almost sorry for him, then I remember Maggie and other things I've 'eard about what F. Artie Sparrow's done if a whore angers him, Maggie ain't the first he's done in.

' "So?" I says, "You knew about the mongrels and you grew up and became one o' them, a mongrel yerself and worse than most. Does that make it right, then?"

'He sniffs and gulps back a sob. "I survived, Tommo. I stayed alive."

' "Me too, only just, but I didn't join the bloody mongrels."

'He is silent for a while, sobbing and wiping his snotty nose, pinching at it with his thumb and forefinger. I don't say nothing, letting him think to himself awhile. Then he slowly raises his head and looks at me. "What you gunna do to me?" he asks, his voice real small.

'I don't even really hear meself saying it, it just come out natural, like I've been wanting to say it since I were seven years old and in the Wilderness alone. "I'm gunna kill you, Mr Sparrow, it's what's long overdue for your kind."

'He begins to sob even harder than before, not looking at me, gulping and choking and taking to the hiccups and all the while begging for his life between his blubbing. I've had enough, so I taps him hard on the head with the blunt o' the axe and he slumps out of the chair to the floor. I stretches him out on his back and goes to work.

'Me head's hurting like hell and I know I ain't got much time, the craving for the poppy is buildin' up and I'm beginning to shake for the need o' the blessed pipe. I take the Tiki from my neck and lifts his head and puts it round his neck, then my purse with four pounds and several o' me calling cards in it. I put it in his jacket pocket, then me hunter with the ace of spades on the outside lid and the gold sovereign 'anging on its chain which I fits to his weskit pocket and secures the fob.

'I stands back and looks down at him. Matter 'o fact he don't look that unlike me and with a bit o' splashing around in the sea water and after the fishies 'ave a go at him nobody will be able to tell the difference. Not that I expect he'll be washed ashore before a shark gets to him, though you never know with the ship still hugging the coastline.

'Like I said, in me anger to get to him, to get aboard and kill him, I've not thought too much about escaping after. Now me plan's changed. So I put me axe in the holster to my back and lifts him again and carries him up the hatchway, it's harder even than before. He seems heavier somehow and I'm exhausted as I get up the last o' the steps and dump him on the deck. I'm puffing like a bull mastiff after a pit fight and I'm forced to sit and rest. It's still dark, the moon not broken through yet and I've only a few feet to go to the starboard rail.

'I get up and half drags him and then slumps him over the ship's railing and I'm about to lift him over when I remember something Hammerhead Jack once told me on the *Nankin*

Maiden. How it comes to me at that moment I can't rightly say, it were not thought out, just comes into me 'ead like before.'

Tommo looks up at Hawk. 'Hammerhead Jack once told me if the Maori want to get rid o' someone with no trace they takes him out to sea and chops off his head, so nobody can identify the phiz and the *moko* markings upon it. "The body float but head it sinks like a stone, Tommo, eh. No head, no know him!" He gimme this grin so I don't know if he be serious or what. "No meat on head, on body plenty to eat?"

'I'm only glad Sparrow is out to it. It is sufficient he knew before I tapped him that he was gunna die. He'd shit himself at that, I could smell it as I carried him up the hatchway. Even after what he did to Maggie I can't bring meself to wait 'til he come round to tell him the Hammerhead Jack manner o' his death. So I lops him there and then. Three sharp blows at the back of the neck and the head drops into the waves below like a stone and the blood pours out his neck like a pipe's burst, four feet into the air and arches into the foamy brine below, enough to attract a hundred sharks. I wipes the blade on the back o' his jacket then grabs him by the ankles and tips the rest o' him over the ship's rail. Over he goes, a complete somersault and hits the waves spread-eagled. Good riddance to bad rubbish. With the wash against the bow it don't hardly makes a noise. Then I throw up over the rail.'

Tommo pauses at last and Hawk can see that he's been pretending to be calm, but is terribly upset at the telling, never having brought what happened to the surface before. He puts his arm around Tommo's shoulders and holds him against his chest, his brother is shivering and then begins to sob. 'I got them, I got the mongrels, didn't I, Hawk? Maggie would 'ave been happy knowing what I done for her, hey?'

Hawk is himself crying, holding his brother, sobbing for the agony of Tommo's bitter life. His tiny brother just twenty-one years and some months old, now with his life so nearly over. Hawk can see that Tommo's eyes have lost their focus and his twin is shaking violently. 'Do you need a pipe, Tommo?'

'Aye,' Tommo replies, his voice barely above a whisper.

Hawk has grown accustomed to preparing Tommo's opium pipe. The great ball of opium Tommo carried away from Mr Sparrow is almost used up. It is as though Tommo's life is to be measured by the diminishing size of the sticky black paste.

Hawk finds the oil lamp, its glass like an upside-down bell the shape of a lily and lights it; the flame in the centre of the glass looks like a golden stamen looking down into a lily. Then he takes a small clay bowl and fills it with the black paste which he heats slightly until it reaches the consistency of treacle and with a long steel needle he dips into the bowl and winds a small amount of paste onto its end. This he warms over the flame until the small pearl of opium begins to bubble. He places the smouldering opium into the bowl of Tommo's pipe and watches as his twin pulls the opium smoke into his lungs, his very life seeming to depend on it. Each pearl allows only three or four puffs and Hawk repeats the process until the bowl is empty which takes almost an hour. Afterwards Tommo drifts into a deep contented sleep.

Hawk has long since given up trying to stop Tommo from using the poppy. He knows it is the only way to kill the pain that is slowly bringing his twin's life to an end. Carefully he cleans the pipe and the bowl and blows out the lamp and stores it with the little opium that remains. He has no way of obtaining more unless he should visit Auckland and hope to find it on the waterfront. It is a task he is willing to do if his twin survives beyond the last of Mr Sparrow's supply. Though the idea of leaving Tommo for the three, perhaps four, days it will take to make the journey and return fills him with the utmost concern that Tommo may die while he is away.

Now, as his twin sleeps on his reed bed, Hawk covers him with a blanket. 'I loves you, Tommo,' he says softly, 'sleep now awhile.'

The remainder of Tommo's story comes out over the next week or so. Tommo had the presence of mind to retrieve Mr Sparrow's hat, then wearing the scarf about his face as Mr Sparrow had done, he simply assumed his identity. It seems nobody on board had seen the little villain without his hat pulled down low over his eyes and his scarf wrapped about his face. Mr Sparrow did not even want the captain to know his true appearance when he was smuggled aboard.

Tommo left the ship at Levuka and a few days later caught a ketch going to Auckland and found his way back to Chief Tamihana's village and his baby daughter, Hinetitama.

Over the next three weeks Tommo's lucid periods become less and less frequent, and at night Hawk sleeps on a rush mat on the earthen floor beside Tommo's bed. In the morning he carries him outside to do his business and then prepares his pipe. One morning just after sunrise and three months after Hawk's arrival, Tommo reaches down to touch the slumbering Hawk who thinks he wishes to go outside. Hawk rises and goes to lift him, but his brother shakes his head and now Hawk sees that his eyes, his sad blue eyes, are clear and his mind is lucid.

'What is it, Tommo? Water?' Tommo has neither eaten nor taken anything to drink for two days and Hawk reaches down for a small earthenware dish filled with water and holds it to his twin's lips. Tommo's lips are cracked and they tremble with the effort of swallowing so that most of it runs over his chin and down his neck, brightening the emerald-green surface of the Tiki about his neck.

Hawk places the gourd on the floor beside the bed and takes Tommo's tiny hands in his own. 'Do you want a pipe, mate?' His twin's hands are cold to his touch and Hawk starts to gently massage them, hoping to transfer some of his own warmth into his brother's trembling fingers.

Hawk thinks about the hands he holds, so deceptive, clumsy to look at, ugly even. The palms are criss-crossed with white axe scars, several fingers bent and knobbed from being broken and not set back straight from his twin's time as a captive child in the Southwest Wilderness. Yet Tommo's hands are proved so elegant and mercurial when they hold a pack of cards and so certain and deadly when clasped about the handle of a fighting axe. His brother's hands, always his chief mischief-makers, now look innocent and helpless clasped in his own great paws.

'No pipe, not yet,' Tommo whispers. 'There are two more things I must speak of, Hawk.'

'What is it?'

Tommo tries to rise, his hand trembles as he points to the corner of the hut. 'It's buried in the corner, the satchel, Mr Sparrow's. I don't know how much, but it's a lot.'

'Shall I fetch it?' Hawk says.

Tommo shakes his head, 'Nah, just to know it's there. Jewels, everything, a king's ransom.'

'What is it you want me to do with it?'

'Buy land. For the Maori. Buy it back for them from the pakeha, much as you can.'

'You mean in perpetuity?'

Tommo doesn't know the word and he rests for a moment, panting. 'There is a Maori saying, "Until the sun is dowsed in the sea", buy it for them so it can never be took back, much as you can, spend it all.'

'It won't be easy, I'll have to get a land agent and tell him it's for a big pakeha interest.'

'Aye, you do that. Then give it to the Ngati Haua people forever, tell Tamihana it's Hinetitama's, my daughter's gift to her people.'

'And what of her? Will you not want some of it to go to her, some small portion?'

Tommo's shake of the head is barely perceived. 'Nah, it's tainted.' He brings his hand slowly to his neck and touches the Tiki, 'Give her this, the God Tiki has seen all my wickedness and will protect her from the same.'

'What of your axe, will she have that too?'

'Nah, you keep it, if she should have a son, give it to him.'

Hawk can see that Tommo's strength is fading fast. 'Will you take a pipe now?' he asks. Hawk does not know how to tell Tommo that there remains barely enough of the Angel's Kiss for one more pipe.

To his surprise Tommo shakes his head, refusing the pipe. 'Hawk, I loves you,' his voice has an increasingly hoarse quality and Hawk must strain to hear him. His twin pauses, licking his dry lips, breathing heavily, trying to catch his breath again, 'Hinetitama. Don't let the mongrels get her.'

Hawk, overwhelmed with sadness, places Tommo's hands gently back into his lap, then gathers up his twin in his great arms and begins to rock him. 'Oh, Tommo, oh, sweet Tommo,' he moans. 'Oh, my sweet, sweet brother, I shall guard your little daughter with my very life.' Hawk starts to weep as he feels his twin beginning to slip away from him. 'No, no, stay, Tommo, stay a while,' he chokes. 'Please don't leave me!'

Tommo sighs softly and, safe at last from the mongrels, dies in his brother's strong, loving arms.

Within minutes the first of the death-wailing begins, a great and sudden overflowing of grief, as if by some osmosis the tribe knows Tommo is dead. Those who possess firearms commence to shoot them to announce his passing and show their respect. Chief Tamihana arrives at Tommo's hut minutes later and squats before

28

the grieving Hawk and their noses touch. They hold this nose-rubbing position for nearly ten minutes so that the old chief might show his respect to Hawk and Tommo and their ancestors. Then he announces the *hui* for the *tangihanga*, the wailing for the dead.

Hawk dresses Tommo carefully and his body is carried to the *marae*, the meeting hut, where it will lie in state, for Tamihana has declared that Tommo must have the honours of an important *rangatira* bestowed upon his death rituals.

Tommo is dressed in Mr Sparrow's clothes and boots since they are of a high quality and have scarcely been worn as Tommo reverted to the Maori fashion of dressing. In his long black Ikey Solomon coat and his fine hat he looks more substantial in death than in life.

In less than half an hour the women emerge from the dark line of the forest, carrying armloads of *kawakawa*, the creeper that symbolises death. This they festoon about the meeting house and wave about themselves in the ritual *powhiri* dance.

The old women appear at the *marae* dressed in black and begin the *tangi*, a dance performed together with a high, uncanny wail and much breast beating to express their grief for the recently deceased as well as to summon all the dead to attend the *hui* in the *marae*.

They surround Tommo, moving in a halting fashion about him, wailing, waving the *kawakawa* creeper and singing 'Haere atu, ka tu ka tangi; haere atu, ka tu ka tangi' ('Move, stand and weep; move, stand and weep').

Soon men and women from the surrounding tribes arrive at the outskirts of the village and halt, waiting to be welcomed with true warmth as they have come to pay their respects to the little warrior Tommo Te Mokiri, the leader of the now legendary fifty-five fighting axes, heroes of the Maori wars. Chief Wiremu Kingi of the Ati Awa tribe sends a large delegation of mourners but lies sick abed and cannot come himself, though he sends his chief orator to take part in the *whaikorero*, the oration.

Their women wail, showing their sorrow is of a great and appropriate kind and when it reaches a crescendo, the tribal women dancing the *tangi* return this wailing in a most melodious way, 'Neke neke mui, neke neke mui' ('Draw nearer, draw nearer'). They have been welcomed with the Maori heart.

The women wail while the men weep silently and bow their

heads; all about there is the deep hum-wail of grief as the tribe's tears flow for the dead. Soon the old women, those whose beauty has passed and wisdom has become fixed to their faces, lacerate themselves, cutting the skin of their faces and breasts, arms and legs with a sliver of obsidian until they bleed on all the exposed surfaces of their bodies.

The wailing and weeping for Tommo continues for three days to show the extremity of their grief. Their respect for him is witnessed by the copious amount of tears and nose mucus which is left to drip unchecked so that the song 'Na te hupe me nga roimata, ka ea te mate' ('By tears and nose mucus, death is avenged') may be seen to be true.

There is much oratory performed in this period known as the mihi, where etiquette demands that orators are carefully chosen with the appropriate praises and lamentations given according to their rank. Chief Tamihana has briefed a famous orator, a master of genealogy, ancient chants and local history, who has at his command all the appropriate proverbs.

The orator, who Hawk sees is a consummate actor, creates a great spoken drama on the life of Tommo Te Mokiri. He tells of an ancient time when a great and wise king whose name was Solomon married a black Queen of Sheba, a woman of exquisite beauty, and how forever thereafter each generation produced two sons, one black and the other white, a giant and a small man, so people might know that small men and big, black and white, have an equal part in life. At this remark the mourners look to Hawk who stands at seven feet tall, the magnificent General Hawk, their beloved Black Maori, and then at the diminutive body of Tommo, whereupon a fresh wailing commences which causes the orator to stop until he may be heard again. He describes Tommo's exploits in the great battle of Puke Te Kauere where Tommo got the wound that has brought about his death. He even makes the mourners laugh a moment when he tells of how Tommo was saved in the swamp water by having his head against the great arse of a dead British soldier. He goes on to explain that Tommo's ancestor, Icky Slomon, sits on the Council of the Dead as a Maori ancestor and that his advice is no doubt much respected by the ancestors.

Hawk thinks of poor old Ikey sitting among the Maori chiefs of the past where the luxury of roast pork is the daily fare, 'my dear-ing' them with every sentence and trying to teach them the intricacies of cribbage and the Jewish perspective of seeing every point of view in an argument and so defeating it with commonsense.

There is much wailing and nose mucus as the mourners show their appreciation for the dead Tommo Te Mokiri who has left them his seed in the form of the Princess Hinetitama, an infant to be brought up in the Maori tradition in the household of Chief Tamihana.

While Chief Tamihana and his *tohunga*, the priests, do not allow the supreme honour of a chief, that Tommo's heart be cut out and buried separately in a sacred place, forever *tapu*, so that any person who approaches the place of its burial will meet with certain death, they agree that his body may be placed high up in one of the tallest trees in the forest where it will remain until all the flesh has fallen from him. After the women have cleaned his bones and skull, they will be placed in a cave looking to the east where he can forever greet the morning sun.

Hawk remains a further fortnight during which time he takes a Maori ketch to Auckland and interviews several land agents until he finds an American with the improbable name of Geronimo Septimus Thompson, who he believes he might trust. Using the five pound notes in Mr Sparrow's stash he opens a letter of credit with the Bank of New South Wales in Auckland and, visiting the Government Surveyor's office, he studies the land titles abutting the Ngati Haua tribal lands. He instructs Geronimo Thompson to buy out the small farms surrounding it.

'You will offer two times what the property is worth,' Hawk tells him, 'and allow six months or the next crop to come to the landowner before he must vacate. The name of the buyer must never be known, Mr Thompson, do you understand me?'

'But how much shall I buy?' asks the bemused Thompson. 'Is there a limit? Five thousand acres? More? Farmland only?'

'You must buy everything, valleys, fields, forests, hills, mountains, rivers and streams. If you can find a way to deal with the Almighty I wish you to buy the sky as well,' Hawk instructs him, but then cautions Thompson, 'The parcel must be clean, there can be no farms left unvacated in any part of the land you buy except at its perimeters. I shall return in a year and instruct you further.'

'But, but . . .' Thompson splutters, 'such an undertaking will attract attention, if I have no name for the purchaser, how shall I answer?'

'You will buy the land in the name of the Bank of New South Wales and they will hold the titles.' By doing this Hawk has prevented any possibility of Thompson cheating him.

Hawk returns to the tribe and informs Chief Tamihana that he must return at once to Australia. The old chief commands that a great farewell feast be held on the *marae* in his honour.

During the festivities and much to Hawk's embarrassment, Chief Tamihana invites Hawk's old friend, the one-armed, one-eyed Hammerhead Jack to tell the *rangatira*, the elders of the tribe, and the *tohunga*, and all those gathered at the *hui* about the time Hawk saved his life when the great sperm whale had overturned their whaleboat and his arm had been severed by the harpoon line.

'I am not much Maori, with only one arm and one eye, but my *mana* is in my left eye and it would be my privilege to die for my brother, Ork,' Hammerhead Jack concludes at the end of his talk.

The *rangatira* clap and shout their approval of Hammerhead Jack's sentiments. Chief Tamihana has earlier reminded them of the contribution of General Black Hawk, who with his new guerilla tactics, which the Maori call 'the running away war', made the forces of Wiremu Kingi and General Hapurona achieve victories against the British. They have more to add to the collective memory of the giant black man they think of as one of their own.

It is an altogether grand farewell though Hawk is somewhat bemused at how his reputation as a fighting man and as a general has grown in his absence.

'Chief Tamihana, I am honoured to be counted among you, to be accepted as *rangatira*, but surely you speak of a stranger. I have neither the wisdom nor the bravery you bestow upon me. Of the running away war, it was something I learned in books and I cannot take credit for it.' Hawk walks over and stands beside Hammerhead Jack who is seated among the highest of the *rangatira*. 'We have been brothers in war and I could ask for no braver man at my side. At the battle of Puke Te Kauere it was *this* man who was the true general when we fought outside the *pa*. Without him we could not have succeeded and without him Tommo would have drowned in the swamp. How can I merit praise when it is due so much more to others, to this man, my Maori brother?'

The *rangatira* clap, enjoying Hawk's modesty and his copious praise for one of their own warriors. Hawk promises he will return each year to attend to the needs of Tommo's daughter Hinetitama and to sit with his brothers in the *marae*. He tells them that he knows himself to be a Maori in his heart and is of the Ngati Haua tribe and he wears their *moko* on his face with great pride.

He thanks the *rangatira* and is careful to do the same to the *tohunga*. Priests, Hawk has observed, have long memories for small slights, and finally he thanks Chief Tamihana for the honour they have bestowed on Tommo by giving him the burial rights of a great warrior and for elevating him to the ranks of the *rangatira*.

Hawk will sail in the morning and it is late, with a full moon high in the night sky. Chief Tamihana sees him to the hut they have provided for him in the chief's compound. 'I shall leave you now my friend and we will sail you to Auckland in the morning, I have but one more gift for you which I hope you will enjoy.'

'Gift? I have been honoured beyond any possible merit, Tamihana, I have been given the gift of brotherhood and of your friendship. With Tommo dead there is none I value more than yours and that of Hammerhead Jack.'

Tamihana chuckles softly. 'Ah, Hawk, this is but the gift of one night, an old memory revisited.' With this remark he bids Hawk goodnight and takes his leave.

Hawk is too tired to think what the old chief might mean and gratefully enters his hut. The night carries a cool breeze from the mountains and Hawk wraps a blanket about himself and is preparing to sleep when he becomes conscious of a shadow darkening the door of his hut, blocking out the moonlight.

'Who is it?' he says wearily. He has talked and listened too much for one night and wishes only to be left alone.

'It is me, General Black Hawk, Hinetitama, whose name you have taken for the daughter of Tommo. Do you remember me?'

It is as if time has stood in the same place, for in the moonlight he watches as the woman loosens the neck cord and allows her feather cloak, the sign of a highborn Maori, to fall at her feet.

In the silvered air Hawk can see that she is still as beautiful as when she first came to him. He can remember almost every word Hinetitama said to him that first night so long ago. 'Oh, Black Maori, I have wanted you so very long. I have eaten you with my eyes and I have tasted you in my heart a thousand times. I have moaned for you alone in my blanket and my mouth has cried out to hold your manhood. My breasts have grown hard from longing for you and I have brought pleasure to myself in your name.'

Hawk's throat aches suddenly, for he can think only of Maggie Pye, her sweetness and her brash and unashamed love for him. Maggie so different to this beautiful shadow in the night.

Now the moonlight throws a silver sheen across her skin and he can see the curve of her breasts and stomach. It is as if he is within a dream repeated, each detail the same as before even though so much has changed in him.

Hinetitama crosses the small hut and she lifts his blanket and lies beside him. 'I have never forgotten you, Black Maori,' she whispers into Hawk's ear. She begins to kiss him, as she did before, across his chest and belly, moving lower and lower. Hawk feels himself grow hard. 'Oh, Maggie, forgive me,' he moans silently, for Hinetitama's mouth has reached his trembling hardness and now it engulfs him. Hawk thinks that he will die with the pleasure of her lips and, just when he feels he can bear it no longer, she withdraws and her hand guides him into her so that she now sits astride him. Hawk begins to moan softly.

'Black Hawk, have you learned nothing from your pakeha women?' she laughs. 'You must wait for me, there is a twice greater pleasure when the moment is shared.'

'Aye,' Hawk gasps, and then adds in the Maori tongue, 'But I am only a mortal man.' He can see the flash of her white teeth as she laughs and the fine curve of her neck and the sheen of moonlight as it catches the rounded slant of her shoulder.

'Ah, but did you say this to your Maggie Pye?' She laughs again.

Hawk's eyes open in sudden surprise. 'Maggie! You know of Maggie?' he exclaims.

'See how I have caused you to wait.' Hinetitama laughs again. 'It is not so hard to contain your pleasure when your mind is distracted.'

'Yes, but how? How do you know of Maggie?' Hawk repeats urgently.

'The Maori are everywhere, Black Hawk. Our men are sailors on the whaling ships and those that bring timber to Sydney. Many of our women are widows who have lost their husbands in the wars against the pakeha and so remain barren and unloved for lack of men, some have been taken by the pakeha sailing captains to Sydney.' She laughs. 'As a lover I can't say you have improved, but you have become a great fighter since you left us, a great man who is known by all the Maori in Sydney. You also honoured my tribe when you took Johnny Heki to train you, he is a Maori with my *moko*. Ah, Black Hawk, there is much we know of you, for you are one of us and they are our Gods who protect you now and forever.'

Hawk, taken by surprise at the mention of Maggie's name, has lost much of his tumescence. Hinetitama's voice takes on a mocking quality. 'First you cannot wait for me, now you wait too long,' she teases softly. 'Black Hawk, if you do not make love to me better than this, I shall think your Maggie Pye has taught you nothing.'

With her words and her laughter and her permission to love her free of the constraints of Maggie's memory, she withdraws and lies beside him and Hawk enters her again and now he releases his sadness and his grief for his sweet Maggie and for Tommo's death in Hinetitama's wild and generous loving.

'Ah, Black Hawk, I was wrong,' Hinetitama sighs at last. 'The pakeha woman with the bird in her hair, this Maggie, has taught you well how to please a wahine.' Her lips brush his face lightly and then she rises and picks up her feathered cloak from beside his rush bed and he watches as she moves silently out into the moonlit compound.

'Thank you,' Hawk calls softly after her. 'Thank you, Hinetitama.'

Chapter Two

HINETITAMA

1881–1885

At twenty-one Tommo's half-caste daughter is a great beauty with skin the colour of wild honey and hair dark as a raven's wing. She is small, no more than five feet and one inch, but despite her diminutive frame she has a contralto voice of great power and of a most serene beauty. But from all these gifts from a generous God must be subtracted a spirit headstrong and wilful and a nature as wild as her father Tommo's once was.

Hawk has kept his promise to Tommo that his daughter will be raised to maturity within the household of Chief Tamihana but when she is six years old Hawk's dear friend and Hinetitama's Maori guardian dies and Tommo's daughter is cared for by Chief Mahuta Tawhiao, with the old chief's daughter given responsibility for the young child's daily care.

When Tamihana knew he was coming to the end of his life he wrote to Hawk. The letter is unusual because the old chief, in a missive so serious, appended a note mentioning women's matters, in particular those of a child.

Though Chief Tamihana could well have instructed the letter be sent to Hawk in Tasmania, he wanted his old friend to read it on Maori land while he and his ancestors could look over his shoulder. Hawk was to receive it on his next annual trip to New Zealand to see Hinetitama and to supervise the purchase of more

36

land. The letter, intended for posterity, had been carefully scripted while the note was in the old chief's mission-taught handwriting.

April 1866

My friend Black Hawk,

We shall no longer sit together by the evening fire or eat again from the same pot. I have now seen sixty summers and it is time for me to join my ancestors.

I am writing this letter to you, Black Maori, so that you will hold my life on the page and be its custodian and then, perhaps some day, history will judge me for what I tried to do and failed.

I have had a long life for a Maori man, who does not often see his hair turn white, and who is usually dead while his seed is still strong in his loins. In my time too many of our brave young men have died for some foolish tribal war fought out of false pride or from seeking retribution for some imagined insult.

When I was a boy my father sent me to the missionaries to learn the white man's language and his ways. 'You must see if they have lessons for us,' he instructed.

I studied hard and learned to read and write and spent much time with the pakeha's Bible. I learned that it was a good book from a merciful God and I found it so myself. But I was soon to discover that it was the white man's Sunday book only and all the remaining days of the week the pakeha felt free to disobey the commandments of his own God.

It was then that I first realised that the pakeha's word could not be trusted, not even on Sunday, for it was not founded in his mana.

That his God was good only for births and burials and his word was as worthless as a broken pot.

I knew then that the Treaty of Waitangi was like the white man's word, and that the Maori would never have justice under the pakeha Queen Victoria or the laws she makes.

When I came to my manhood the Maori people had killed more of their own kind than the pakeha. They had taken the white man's gun and turned it on their own. We have killed more than twenty thousand of our people while the pakeha stood by and watched the Maori die, thinking that soon there would be no Maori to come up against them and they could take all our land for their spotted cows.

And so I grew to be a man and I became the peacemaker among the tribes and then the kingmaker, joining all the Maori under King Potatau te Wherowhero so that we could speak with one voice.

Alas, the pakeha did not want us to stop killing our own and they forced us to go to war with them. It was here that you, Black Hawk, became a Maori warrior and gained great distinction, so that you became a rangatira to be forever honoured in the Ngati Haua tribe and among all the Maori people.

Though we fought with honour the pakeha had too many guns and too many soldiers and we forsook the clever ways of our previous guerilla war, the runaway fighting you taught us and we went back to defending the pa and so were beaten, but remained proud in defeat, a worthy opponent.

Now, as I lie dying, I know that the pakeha, in defeating us, has taken everything from us but one last thing. Our warriors still fight in the hills where no pakeha dare go. They have created a redoubt that holds within it the Maori pride. While we have our pride they cannot destroy our race. I pray that it is always there. Ake ake ake. You must speak for us, you must be my elbow and my backbone, General Black Hawk.

I shall die with a curse on my lips for the white man, for what they have done to my people. But there is one exception, Tommo Te Mokiri, who bought back for us, through your hands, the rivers and the streams, the mountains and the hills, the forests and the glades and the good tilling soil all of which once belonged to our people and which the pakeha conspired to take from us. It is for this that I now decree, having talked through the tohunga to the ancestors, that Tommo Te Mokiri's daughter shall be made a true princess of the Maori people.

I go to my ancestors knowing that the Maori mana is the spirit of Aotearoa and that it will prevail. Ake ake ake. In our hearts we cannot be defeated until the earth sinks into the sea.

I go to my ancestors now, where I shall watch over you like a father watches over his beloved son.

Wiremu Tamihana,
Chief of the Ngati Haua Maori.

To this formal letter Tamihana penned his own note.

My friend Black Hawk,

I have kept my promise and now I deliver the Princess Hinetitama to the care of Mahuta Tawhiao, who will care for her as I have done and see that she is instructed in the Maori traditions befitting her high rank.

She is a Maori wahine in all things save one. She is yet a piglet barely weaned from the teats but already she is as stubborn as an old sow. On more than one occasion I have instructed that she be beaten by the old women in my household for disobedience, but she will not bend to their will, no matter how severe her punishment. I think she has this from her father, Tommo Te Mokiri.

When the time comes you must find her a strong warrior who will teach her to be a quiet flowing stream as a woman must be to a man if there is to be peace in his household.

Her singing has brought me great delight and her laughter is always among us. I thank you for the pleasure she has brought me in my old age, she will be a worthy princess of our people.

Your friend,

Wiremu Tamihana.

Hawk has kept his pledge to Tommo and visited Hinetitama every year of her life. Now that she has grown to womanhood he wants her to come home to Hobart, to be with Mary, who wishes above all things to have the company of her granddaughter at her side.

However, to his mortification, Hinetitama will hear of no such thing and asserts her independence, telling him she wishes to go to Auckland to become a nurse.

'But you may do the same training in Hobart, we will find you an excellent opportunity and we will all be together?' Hawk insists.

Hinetitama is silent, her eyes downcast, then she looks up. 'I must stay here, Uncle. I want to go to Auckland to be among the poor.'

'The poor are everywhere, my dear. You will find as many in Hobart as you wish to care for.'

'Maori poor?'

'The poor have no nation, or colour or creed, they are luxuries they cannot afford. Poverty is the one universal brotherhood, my dear.'

'But I am a Maori. I must be with my own people.'

'Only half, the other is pakeha. Grandmother Mary prays that she might have the pleasure of knowing you, of setting eyes upon your sweet face, before she dies.'

Hinetitama gives a soft deprecating laugh. 'I cannot bring pleasure to one rich old woman when so many poor suffer for lack of attention.'

Hawk is shocked at the bluntness of her remark. 'I would not have looked upon it quite like that. Your grandmother has known the worst of poverty and degradation, she will not condemn you for your desire to work among the poor. You must not judge her so harshly, she wishes only to know you as her only grandchild.'

'Uncle, I mean no impertinence, you have always said I must obey my conscience.'

Hawk sighs. 'Hinetitama, it is your duty to also obey me,' he says sternly. 'I wish you to come to Hobart. Your grandmother wishes it, that is all.'

Hawk sees the stubborn set of her jaw as Hinetitama answers. 'Uncle Hawk, when we were young and you would come to New Zealand every year and we would take long walks, you told me about my father, how he wished me to remain among the Maori, among my mother's people, and then when I came of age to make up my own mind.' She looks defiantly at Hawk. 'I have decided to work among my own people. My grandmother does not need me, they do.'

'Your grandmother has promised me she will do as Tommo wished and that you be included in her will. If you obey and honour her wishes you will become a very wealthy lady. You will be able to help a great many more of your people. Be a little patient, my dear,' Hawk pleads. 'A few years to be kind to an old woman and then you may do as you wish, I will not stop you.'

'Ha! You would bribe me, Uncle,' Hinetitama says scornfully. 'I must sit at the feet of an old woman, I must lick her boots so that I may feed the poor. Is that what you are saying?'

'It is not a sin to be rich and then to spend what you have on those less fortunate than you.'

'And it is not a sin to be poor with strong hands and a good heart. The Maori do not need the pakeha money, their handouts, what we need is to regain our pride. I will do more for them working among them in torn clothes than strutting around in new boots and with an open purse.'

Hawk sees in Hinetitama the same idealism he himself felt at her age and he secretly admires her for her determination. God knows the poor and the destitute among the Maori in the city have need enough for someone of their own kind to care about them. Since the Maori wars things have gone from bad to worse for the indigenous people of New Zealand and poverty, sickness, malnutrition and drunkenness promise to do as much to eliminate them.

But Hawk also has Mary with whom to contend. Mary has never accepted that her only grandchild should be raised among the savages and has railed against it for years. Now he must tell her that Hinetitama will not be coming into civilisation. Hawk well knows Mary's hidden agenda, she wants great-grandchildren, heirs to carry on with the business empire she has so brilliantly begun and Hinetitama is her last chance. And so Hawk, putting aside his conscience, tries for several more days to persuade Hinetitama to travel to Tasmania. But Tommo's daughter is resolute in her decision.

Hawk finds himself between the devil and the deep blue sea. In all conscience he can find no reasonable argument with Hinetitama's ambition. After all, she has no aspirations to be a white person, a tribe she is deeply suspicious of. Raised under the influence of Chief Tamihana she is steeped in Maori tradition and in the knowledge that the Maori have been cheated and swindled by the pakeha. She simply cannot see any virtue in learning to be a proper lady or adopting European values and ways.

As the days go by, Hawk finds it increasingly hard to counter her defiance. Several times his anger at her unreasonableness has reduced her to tears, but she weeps from frustration that he cannot see her viewpoint. Hawk notes that after each such occasion she seems strengthened in her resolve.

Finally, having exhausted every argument and plea, he agrees that she can stay. He has been warned of her stubbornness by Chief Tamihana, but he always felt that because of his love for Tommo's daughter over the years and as her guardian, she would obey him without question. It is not the custom for a subservient female member of a family to disobey the wishes of the predominant male in either white or Maori society.

Hinetitama is trained in the Anglican Mission Hospital as a nurse and shortly after she completes her two-year training she leaves the hospital to work among the Auckland poor. She is unusual in this for she is a Maori princess and her bandages and treatments do not come wrapped in a sermon or a plea to repent. Hinetitama brings only her hands and her heart to the slums, together with the songs of her nation, to remind those who have lost their pride, their *mana*, that they belong to a unique people.

Hawk has now taken to visiting her every two years, for despite his letters pleading with her to visit Tasmania, if only for a period brief enough to satisfy her grandmother, she stubbornly refuses, insisting that her work must come first. Mary, for her part, has grown too old to travel to New Zealand.

Hawk grows increasingly frustrated, but realising the futility of punishing Tommo's daughter by withdrawing her small allowance, he deposits a monthly stipend in the bank to see that she has income sufficient to maintain a small clinic. It is obvious to him that she spends little on herself and that she is much loved and respected by the Maori slum dwellers, though whether she is able to do any good among the poor is problematic. It is, he concludes, probably sufficient that she is there among them, a princess of their own, and that the bandages and the salves do less for her patients than her cheerful and compassionate nature and the fact that they see her as one of their own.

Alas, unbeknownst to Hawk and no doubt because of fatigue and the ongoing frustration of dealing with the poor who never seem to improve in their circumstances, Hinetitama has begun to drink herself. At first she is a tippler, an ale or two taken after a long day and for the opportunity to have a bit of a laugh among those for whom she cares, but as time goes on she discovers the false seduction of cheap gin and becomes more and more dependent on grog until she is unable to do without it in her life. She has inherited her father's weakness and his craving.

While Hinetitama continues to work among the disadvantaged, over a period of two years the drink takes possession of her. With her twenty-fifth year approaching, Hawk arrives in New Zealand for his second visit since she came of age only to discover that the clinic has been closed and that Hinetitama has disappeared.

Hawk seeks out the Maori people in her neighbourhood and asks them if they have any news of her. He is a *rangatira* and his *moko* shows him to be of very high rank, so that they must by tradition tell him what they know. But apart from confirming that she is now always drunk and that the clinic has been shut for several months they do not know her whereabouts.

After several days and nights of walking the streets and enquiring in all the harbour-front taverns, he is accosted by a Maori prostitute.

'You want to know about Hinetitama?' she asks him in the Maori language.

'Yes.' Hawk goes to his purse, knowing that information from her kind is seldom given freely.

'No, I don't want your money, Black Hawk.'

'You know me?' Hawk asks in surprise.

'We are from the same tribe,' she answers simply.

'Ah, you know Hinetitama?'

The prostitute nods.

'Do you know her whereabouts?' Hawk now asks.

'She's taken up with the Dutchman, a gamblin' man, them two's gone to Wellington, last thing I heard say,' she replies.

Hawk continues to question her closely but she cannot help him further though she has the name of Hinetitama's paramour. 'It is Slabbert Teekleman.' She giggles and says in English, 'He is known as Slap 'n Tickle, but he ain't like that, you know, nice? He a bad bugger that one.'

Hawk thanks her and tries to press a half-sovereign into her hand for her trouble. 'I have given you sad news, Black Maori, it would be *tapu*. Hinetitama Te Solomon is a princess of the Ngati Haua.' She points to Hawk's face, to his *moko*. 'I cannot take your money. You are *rangatira*.'

Hawk comes away gratified, thinking that Chief Tamihana may have been right after all, and that the Maori, despite their dispossession, have not entirely lost their pride and dignity.

He hasn't lost his touch and he knows that a gambler can always be found if you know where to look. In Wellington he visits the waterside pubs and eventually discovers the Dutchman's whereabouts.

Hawk takes a horse cab into the slums of Thorndon and is finally let down in front of a miserable hovel, made of planking, the single window so crusted with dirt that he is unable to see through it into the interior. He knocks on the door, at first politely and then more loudly until, in the end, he is battering at it with his fist. He is about to smash it in with his shoulder when a bleary-eyed man, with dirty yellow hair and bloodshot eyes of a quite startling blue, opens it, though no more than about twelve inches. Hawk sees that he is clean-shaven and still handsome, though he carries several days of growth upon his chin.

'What you want?' the man asks.

'You Teekleman?' Hawk enquires. It is not the sort of neighbourhood where a man qualifies for any status beyond his surname.

'Ja, maybe?'

'Slabbert Teekleman?'

The man ignores Hawk's question, 'What you want, hey?' It is clear he is losing patience and the door begins to close.

Hawk kicks his foot forward, jamming the door open and starts to push it inwards. 'Hey, nigger, what you doing?' the man shouts in alarm. But Hawk has taken him by surprise and pushes the door, his huge shape filling the doorway. Hawk's free hand shoots out and he slaps the surprised man across the face, sending him reeling backwards so that he loses his balance and falls to the floor.

'Get up, you bastard!' Hawk snarls, moving into the hovel so that daylight now pours inwards through the doorway.

The Dutchman gets to his knees and wipes the blood and mucus from his nose with the back of his hand. 'Please, you don't hit me, please, sir!'

'Where's Hinetitama?' Hawk growls.

'Who?' the man says, though he hesitates a fraction before he speaks and Hawk knows immediately he's covering up.

'Get up, so I can beat the living shit out of you!' Hawk growls again and takes a step towards the Dutchman.

The drunk at his feet pulls back whimpering, scrambling away like a monkey on all fours until he is backed up against the far wall of the tiny room. From the corner of his eye Hawk can see a doorway leading to another room on his left. 'Where's Hinetitama?' he demands again.

The man nods his head to the right and Hawk turns slightly to look at the doorway leading to the next room. 'She dronk.' He gives Hawk a conspiratorial grin. 'Too much the brandy, she Maori, heh?' He shakes his head deprecatingly. 'No goet for grog.'

The doorway has no door and Hawk takes the two or three

steps necessary to get to it. Hinetitama is passed out, sprawled naked on a mattress. She is dirty and unkempt with a mass of black hair spread across the top of the filthy mattress. He is too preoccupied to see that her sweet face is unlined and her small, neat body is still firm and beautiful.

Hawk turns back to the man and takes out his purse and throws two sovereigns to the ground. The Dutchman, still on all fours, scrambles after them grabbing one up, testing it with his teeth and then he finds the second coin and does the same again. It is a gesture Hawk will later recall. Then Teekleman grins. 'I go. I don't make no trouble. You see I go now.' He nods his head in the direction of the bedroom door where Hinetitama lies unconscious. 'She go fock herself.'

Hawk for the first time realises that Teekleman is a big man, six foot at the least and perhaps fifteen years younger than him, a strapping fellow who, if he had the heart, the moxie, might be a bit of a handful in a fight. He takes another step forward so that the Dutchman cowers against the wall. He feigns a punch, pulling back his fist, and Teekleman gasps and brings his hands up to protect his face. Hawk sees the terror of a true coward showing in his eyes.

'G'arn, get yer things and scarper, piss off!'

Hinetitama comes screaming through the door to Hawk's left and jumps onto his back from behind and with her arms clasped about his neck she fastens her teeth into his left ear. Hawk has no trouble breaking her grip and she falls naked to the ground. He brings his hand up to where she has bitten him and it comes away bloodied. Then he sees that his shoulder is already covered with blood which seems to be pouring from his ear. Hinetitama has now got him about the leg and fastened her teeth into his calf, snarling like a wild beast. He leans down and pulls her arms away and jerks her up to her feet, then with the other hand holds her about the neck at arm's length so that she is powerless, though she still tries to kick him, lashing at him, but her legs are not long enough to reach him. She is snuffling like a wild animal, too furious to scream. His powerful hand about her throat could easily close down her windpipe and render her unconscious, but she doesn't seem to care, his niece is a hellcat who knows no fear.

'You bastard! You fucking bastard! Leave him alone!' she screams.

In the meantime the Dutchman has taken up his shirt, boots, his violin case and his jacket and hat and is going out the door, fleeing as fast as he can. 'Piss off, you scum!' Hawk shouts after him. 'If you come back I'll break your fucking neck!'

'I go, I go!' the Dutchman cries fearfully.

Hawk has one hand to his ear and with the other holds Hinetitama at bay about the throat. The ear is bleeding so copiously that the blood runs down the back of his hand and down his wrist and is soaking his shirt cuff and saturating the sleeve of his jacket.

Hawk is suddenly conscious that his niece has gone quiet and sees that her eyes are popping out of her head as she tries to breathe. With the concern for the blood pouring from his ear he has inadvertently tightened his grip about her throat and Hinetitama is choking under his grasp. He lets go of her and she falls at his feet, clutching at her neck and coughing, desperately attempting to regain her breath.

Hawk quickly takes off his jacket, bundles it up and holds it to his ear then drops to his knees beside Hinetitama and touches her on the shoulder with the unbloodied hand. 'Are you all right, my dear?' he asks anxiously. 'I'm truly sorry if I've hurt you.'

Hinetitama lies with her knees up against her breast, still gripping her throat with both hands. She has regained her breath and is panting heavily. Her golden body is wondrously beautiful, caught in the light from the door as she turns her head slightly to look up at him. 'Uncle Hawk,' she croaks in a small, plaintive voice and passes out.

Hawk is suddenly conscious that the light has changed and he turns to see two urchins silhouetted in the doorway. The two boys turn to run but Hawk calls, 'Hey, stop! I need your help!' The urchins turn to face him, legs triggered to the ground, ready to flee like scared rabbits at the slightest suggestion of danger. 'Is there a doctor lives nearby?' Hawk asks. Although his own body shields Hinetitama's nakedness, the two boys can plainly see that there is someone lying on the floor.

'Is she dead, mister?' one of the lads asks.

'No, she's fine.' Hawk removes his bundled coat from his left ear so that they see the blood covering his neck and soaked into his white shirt. 'My ear, it's torn, it needs to be stitched up. Is there a doctor hereabouts?'

'There's Mrs Pike,' the other urchin replies.

'Is she a doctor?'

'Nah, I think she's a sort o' nurse,' the boy says, 'fer 'avin' babies.'

'There's a sixpence in it for both of you, go fetch her, tell her to bring her stitching stuff.'

The boys do not move. 'G'arn, be off with you and hurry.'

'Where's our money, mister?'

Hawk sighs and pulls out his purse, allowing the blood to run from his ear, and takes a sixpence from it. 'One now, one when you return.' He holds the little silver coin up to the urchins.

'Throw it here,' one of them says. Hawk throws the sixpence in his direction and both boys drop to the ground in a scramble, pushing and shoving each other out of the way to reach the small fortune at their feet.

'Damn you, get moving!' Hawk barks. 'And close the door!'

One of the lads has secured the coin and they both run off, to return half an hour later with a stout, big-breasted woman who huffs and puffs as she makes her way through the crowd beginning to gather outside the hovel. She carries a leather doctor's bag and shouts, 'Out of the way! Out of the way!' pushing the crowd aside by banging the bag against them until she reaches the door. The two lads are still with her. 'G'arn, be off with you!' she says, shooing them away.

'It's our sixpence, we's got a sixpence comin' from the nigger man!' one of them protests.

'Honest, missus!' his companion confirms.

Not bothering to knock, Mrs Pike pushes open the door. 'Sixpence! You promise them sixpence?' she shouts into the darkened interior. She turns to the two boys. 'Wait here,' she commands imperiously as she steps into the hovel.

Hawk finds the second sixpence and hands it to the nurse who drops it into the pocket of her nurse's pinny and turns to the two urchins. 'You two stand here at the door, I'll need it open to let in the light, don't let nobody come in, you hear? You'll get yer sixpence later when I'm good an' ready.'

She looks over the heads of the two urchins at the crowd. 'G'arn, piss off the lot'a ya! This ain't none of your business.'

In the time it has taken the two boys to fetch the nurse Hawk has found a threadbare blanket and torn a strip off it and bound his head several times around to contain the bleeding from his ear in order to free both his hands. He finds a bucket half filled with water and a tin mug and splashes as much blood from his hands as is possible. Then he returns with a mug of water to find Hinetitama sitting up with her face in her hands.

'Better get dressed, my dear,' Hawk says to her, handing her the mug.

Hinetitama takes it in both hands and drinks thirstily, downing the entire mug without taking a breath. Then she gets slowly to her feet and, bringing her hands down to cover her pubic region, she goes back into the little bed chamber and begins to get into her filthy gown. She has no hosiery or underwear and finally she pushes her dirty feet into a pair of badly scuffed and worn boots and dumps herself in the middle of the mattress with her legs tucked under her and waits. She has not said a word to Hawk since her recovery.

Mrs Pike, it turns out, is the local midwife, which is a stroke of luck, as she well understands how to insert stitches. She does a neat enough job of Hawk's ear, stemming the bleeding and inserting the stitches which run halfway down the ear by using horsehair and what has the appearance of a small darning needle. It is a rough enough job but soon the bleeding stops. 'It ain't pretty but the parts I 'as to stitch in me midwife's work don't need no fancy darning,' she says gruffly, then adds, 'Better than bleedin' ter death.'

Mrs Pike has become aware of Hinetitama sulking on the mattress within the tiny bed chamber. She nods her head towards the door, 'Bite you, did she?' Hawk doesn't reply and Mrs Pike continues. 'Mouth bite ain't a nice thing, could turn very nasty.'

Hawk rewards her over-generously for her work, handing her a sovereign. 'Ta-muchly, that's very good of you, I must say. Don't see too many o' these around here.' She plunges her hand into the bodice of her dress and moments later withdraws it minus the gold coin.

'You won't forget to give the lads their sixpence?' Hawk says.

'It's too much for the likes of them,' she says sternly, 'I'll give threepence each to their mothers.'

'No! I promised it to them. I'd be obliged, Mrs Pike.' Hawk watches as the midwife reluctantly finds the sixpence and hands it to one of the urchins.

'Thanks, mister!' the boy says with alacrity. Plainly he was expecting a less happy outcome at the hands of the bossy midwife.

'Is there some place near we may stay tonight?' Hawk now asks her.

'There's a wee tavern up the road a bit, the Thornton Arms, you can stay there, they've got a bathhouse out the back.' Then the midwife adds gratuitously, 'They'll take niggers, but I don't know about the likes o' her, she's Maori ain't she? 'Alf-caste I'd say lookin' at her.' She sniffs. 'Brings out the worst of both sides if you want my opinion.'

'I haven't asked you for it, missus,' Hawk says softly. 'We are both Maori, and proud to be so.' He smiles, for he is grateful to the midwife, 'I daresay a coin or two placed in the right pakeha's hands will take care of his sensibilities, Mrs Pike.'

'Oh dear, we are the proper gentleman then, aren't we! No need to be uppity,' the midwife reproves him. Then adds cheerfully, 'Well, must be on me way then, plenty to do, folk breeding like mice, makes a nice change to stitch up a gentleman's ear 'stead of a torn pussy.'

The following morning, leaving Hinetitama locked in her room in the tavern, Hawk bathes and, wearing clean linen, visits a Dr Spencer in a more respectable part of town who examines his ear and pronounces Mrs Pike's work rough but adequate. He is a Scotsman in his fifties with a large belly and a talkative manner to go with it.

He chats as he examines Hawk's ear and then treats his wound with a solution of carbolic acid to stave off infection. 'Stitches, sutures we calls them in the profession, fascinating study, what. Been done since time out o' mind, Ancient Sumerians, Egyptians, Greeks, Romans all did much the same as your Mrs Pike, horsehair! Nothing wrong with that, first-class material.' He pauses as he attempts to wipe away a crusting of dried blood. 'Now if you'd have come to me, m'boy, I'd have used catgut, recommended by the great Doctor Lister himself. Easy to work and doesn't break. If this had been a scalp wound I might have tried something else completely, plaiting.' He looks up at Hawk expectantly, waiting for his reaction.

Hawk, who is only half listening to the good doctor's prattle, feels compelled to say something. 'Plaiting? Like a girl's hair?'

'You heard me right, m'boy. Plaiting. Worked in America once, New York, in the slums of the Bronx where getting your head split open was more frequent than getting a hot breakfast. College chappy, doctor in the Civil War, McGraw, Irishman, nice fellow, apt to drink a bit, hands unsteady, not much chop for stitching, never did it, got his young assistant to plait the hair on either side of the wound together, worked like a charm, union by plaiting, no shaving, stitching, plastering and an excellent result if you ask me, learned it in the American Army, thinks it was probably borrowed from the Red Indians.'

All this is said without a pause and Hawk, feeling he must respond to such verbosity, laughs, puts his hand to his head, fingering his short, negroid, unplaitable hair. 'Not much good if you're a nigger,' he says.

'By George! I never thought of that!' the doctor replies. 'An excellent observation if I may say so, sir.'

Hawk grins, grateful that he has been elevated to 'sir', says quietly, 'From what I've read of the American Civil War it is unlikely they'd have stopped to suture a nigger, Dr Spencer.'

'Quite right, quite right, poor old negro was what the fight was all about though God knows, the niggers don't seem to have gained much benefit from the victory.'

'Doctor, of a more immediate concern, how do I rid a head of hair of lice and nits without shaving it off?'

'Good Lord, m'boy, there's no nits in your hair, I'd have spotted them a mile off if they were there.'

'Not for me,' Hawk replies, growing impatient with the loquacious medical man.

'Oh, in that case you would purchase from any chemist shop a solution of half five per cent oleate of mercury and half ether.' The doctor then proceeds to show Hawk how the delousing might be done.

Leaving the doctor, who has given him a bottle of permanganate of potash to prevent infection to his ear, Hawk takes a pony trap into the centre of town and, with some embarrassment to himself and the young shop assistants concerned, purchases a suitable gown, bonnet, boots, hosiery and underwear for Tommo's daughter at Kirkaldie and Stains emporium. He includes with his purchases a cake of perfumed soap and a towel. As a small apology for his clumsy treatment the previous day, he also buys a bottle of toilet water and a scarf to cover the noticeable bruise on Hinetitama's neck. After these awkward purchases Hawk visits a nearby chemist shop and purchases the delousing solution.

The tavern where they have spent the night has no washing facilities for women so Hawk takes Hinetitama, together with all her packages, to the public bathhouse. He waits outside while she gives herself a good scrubbing down and carefully explains to the female bathhouse attendant how he wishes to delouse her hair.

'Gotta shave it, mister. Ain't no other way. Shave it right orf then wash the 'ead in pariffin,' the woman says.

Hawk produces a florin. 'Do as I say and there's another of these for you, missus.'

The woman sighs, 'It's your money, sir.'

'Oh, and burn her old clothes,' Hawk adds.

'Burn 'em? Seem orright t'me.'

'Just do as I say, please.'

The woman clucks her tongue but protests no further. 'Cost yer sixpence.'

Delousing Hinetitama's hair is a most laborious process involving a towel, the chemist's solution, and a fine-tooth comb, which the woman calls a nit-comb. Tommo's daughter's hair is washed several times but when the process is complete her hair shines long and beautiful.

They sail out of Wellington Harbour on the evening tide, Hawk having purchased the last two available cabins from the Union Steamship Co. The *Wakatipu*, a screw steamer of 1158 tons, will take just five days to reach Sydney.

Hinetitama sulks in her cabin for the first two days. On the third she emerges, having cut and stitched and hemmed the overlarge gown Hawk has purchased for her with needle and thread borrowed from one of the ladies in the next-door cabin through the intermediary services of a young cabin steward smitten by her beauty. It now fits her slender young body and tiny waist almost to perfection. Though by no means mollified, she behaves politely enough towards her uncle while offering no conversation whatsoever to any of the other passengers.

Hawk, for his part, does not expect her to apologise to him or even necessarily forgive him for rescuing her. She has not been asked if she will accompany him to Tasmania and he has, he supposes, effectively kidnapped her.

But as Hinetitama's strong young body recovers, seemingly without any harmful effects from the abuse it has received from bad grog and poor living, her naturally friendly disposition returns and she is soon her cheerful self again, talking to all and sundry and looking a picture.

Hinetitama actually seems hopeful and excited and sings all day, to the enchantment of the Maori crew who soon grow to love her for her informality and friendliness and treat her like the princess they observe she is.

Hawk though finds himself increasingly despondent. First Tommo, a drunkard at fourteen, and now his daughter is well and truly headed up the same path. Finally, after four days at sea and a day's voyage out of Sydney, Hinetitama unexpectedly comes to his cabin and swears she will take the pledge when they arrive in Hobart.

Hawk affects a great delight at this and embraces her warmly, though not without a sense of pessimism. He is experienced enough not to hope for too much and has come to realise that there is a great deal of Tommo in his daughter.

Upon arrival in Sydney Hawk learns that Mary's own trading vessel, the *Waterloo*, a three-masted trading schooner of one hundred feet, is in port and due to return to Hobart in two days. He informs the captain they will take passage on her back to Hobart.

Hawk has some business with Tucker & Co. and also visits his old friend Caleb Soul who has a thriving business as a chemist and manufacturing pharmacist with several of his own successful potions and prescriptions on the market. The elderly Caleb welcomes him warmly and Hawk learns that he has also opened a large retail chemist outlet with the help of his son, Washington Handley, after whom he has named the business. 'Caleb Soul sounds like the combination of a turtle and a fish, not a good name for a business dealing in potions and cures, Washington H. Soul be much the sturdier proposition,' he explains to Hawk.

Hawk also visits Ah Wong, the Chinaman, and his family whom he rescued at Lambing Flat during the riots. Now a prosperous businessman, Ah Wong imports rice and silk from China. He creates a banquet for Hawk and Hinetitama to which he invites Caleb Soul and his son. After the truly splendid repast he brings in his three sons to be introduced to Hawk. He points to his eldest son, 'He born Lambing Flat you lescue him, his name Hawk,' Ah Wong says proudly. Then he points to his second son, 'Number two son yes please, this Tommo.' Hawk laughs, pleased at the compliment to himself and Tommo. 'Number three son,' Ah Wong continues, 'he name Solomon.'

Hawk grins while Caleb and his son Washington clap enthusiastically, 'Three fine sons, eh, Ah Wong, no daughters then?' Hawk says.

Ah Wong claps his hands and says something to a servant who leaves the room and presently returns accompanied by a young girl of about twelve. 'This me daughter, her name, Maggie Pi Wong.'

Hawk is hard put to prevent himself from weeping and as they take their departure from the little Chinaman Hawk embraces his old friend. 'You're a good bloke, Ah Wong, I wish you well.'

Ah Wong looks up at Hawk. 'You want from me, you get anytime for sure, certainly, by Jove!'

The remainder of their time is spent shopping and going to the theatre, both new experiences for Tommo's daughter and each is an occasion in which she plainly takes great delight. In the David Jones Emporium she chooses her shoes and two new gowns with such enormous enthusiasm that the salesgirls, who crowd about her, are as delighted as she is when she discovers something, no matter how small, to her liking. Her taste is plainly for the exotic and she chooses her gowns for their brightness and eschews the dull browns and blacks and deep blues which are the current fashion. The bonnet she buys is simply a riot of artificial blossoms and gaily coloured ribbons and bows.

Hawk cannot help being constantly reminded of Maggie Pye whom he still misses every day of his life and he takes great pleasure in having his beautiful niece on his arm, who, like Maggie herself, barely reaches his waist. Hinetitama's love for Hawk is too old for her to sustain her resentment at her kidnapping and they seem once again the greatest of friends.

The *Waterloo* possesses no spare cabins and the captain is forced to forsake his own for Hinetitama. He and Hawk join the crew in their quarters. The *Waterloo* trades hardwood and hops with the colony of New South Wales and returns with Scotch whisky and good quality brandy as well as an imported English gin. All is purchased from Tucker & Co. in Sydney to be sold in the fifty tied public houses that The Potato Factory Brewery now owns in Hobart, Launceston, Burnie and throughout rural Tasmania.

The mercantile empire built by Mary Abacus and with Hawk's own considerable business acumen embraces timber concessions, a glass bottle factory, several hop and barley farms, fifty taverns and public houses, fifteen business properties in Hobart and Launceston, the majority shareholding in a tin mine at Mount Bischoff and, as the jewel in the crown, The Potato Factory Brewery, the third largest of its kind after the Cascade Brewery in Hobart and Mr James Boag's Launceston brewery.

Mary, once a convict, is now the richest woman in Tasmania and by virtue of her wealth has made it to the top of the business classes, though she is not yet accepted by the true merinos, a rejection which causes her not the slightest anxiety.

As the sole owner of one of its largest private fortunes and one not to be sneezed at on the mainland Mary reckons she has sufficient status and respect for one lifetime. She is a canny and prudent business woman and everything she touches seems to turn to gold.

Mary Abacus has long since discovered that, in this new land, power and influence are not attached to social status but to money. She lacks only one thing to make her life's work complete, she desperately requires grandchildren to continue after Hawk is gone. Hawk, in turn, has steadfastly put off being married and now it is unlikely that he will father children. Hinetitama is her last hope.

'How shall I match the little savage with a good family even if her dowry should be most attractive?' she constantly laments. 'We must have her here to teach her manners and the customs of civilised people.'

Hawk recalls one momentous occasion when Mary's frustration brought matters to a head.

'Tommo were no judge of what was good for his child,' she announced. They were seated on the porch of Mary's mansion set in the foothills of Mount Wellington. Below them all of Hobart stretched out along the shores of the great Derwent River, which in the late afternoon sunshine lay burnished, the colour of sheet metal. 'How can you let her grow up among them savages when she could be brought up proper with no expense spared and married with a dowry to attract the very best of mannered blood? Why may I not have my own lineage?' Mary Abacus asks petulantly and makes a sweeping gesture with a tiny clawlike hand to include all of Hobart below. 'So they may inherit all this and I may pass away knowing I have worked to some avail!'

'Mama, all this as you put it, is precisely why Tommo wished his daughter to be reared by her own Maori tribe. He would see no virtue in his daughter's marriage to a true merino. Tommo saw only mongrels around him, he found greed and avarice everywhere. Then he looked into his own character and pronounced it weak. "Hawk, there is bad blood in my veins, you must protect Hinetitama from it," he said to me. "We must not allow it to come through. She must stay with her tribe until she is of age, you must promise me this."' Hawk shrugs his shoulders. 'Mama, I promised him as he lay dying. I shall keep that promise until his daughter is twenty-one and I am no longer her guardian.' He sighs and spreads his hands wide. 'Then she will make up her own mind.'

'No, she bleedin' won't! She'll come here to become a lady and settle down and have a family.'

'Mama, that's precisely what Tommo feared most.'

'Feared? Why? This talk of mongrels, bad blood? Is that supposed to be me? Is that what I am, greedy, avaricious? Is that what you think of me?' Mary screams. 'Lemme tell you something f'nothing, my boy, everything you see here, everything we've got, come from hard work, from the sweat of me brow. What we have, I've worked for, day and bleedin' night, nobody's done me no favours! And now you're saying I'm a mongrel! You and Tommo, what I brought up from a pair o' brats in a basket over Ikey's arm, is accusing me o' being greedy and avaricious! Ha! That's a bleedin' laugh, that is!'

Hawk is long accustomed to Mary's temper tantrums. She runs an empire and has become used to being obeyed without question, to being indulged and fawned on by sycophants. Mary has grown to accept as her right the dominion she has over most other people and has become corrupted, if not in deed, for she is a hard but fair trader, but in thought, corrupted by the power she commands and the unequivocal respect she demands for her every decision. Only Hawk may disagree with her and hope to get away with it.

'No, Mama, you know I think no such thing. What you have achieved in your life is remarkable, but it has not all come about from the sweat of your brow. Tommo is right, there is a part in all of us that may become greedy and avaricious, in each of us there is a mongrel waiting to emerge if the right circumstances prevail.'

'What do you mean? How dare you say that!' Mary cries. 'I have paid me debts to society, I am an emancipist, an honest woman by the letter o' the law!'

Hawk is hard put to continue and tries to make peace with Mary. 'Mama, please don't take it personally. Tommo only wanted that his daughter should be brought up innocent of the white man's ways. He could not forget what was done to him when he was kidnapped and taken to the Wilderness.'

'Yeah, well, that were different, that was Hannah and David, them two evil bastards, they done that to the two of you.'

'Oh?' Hawk replies, one eyebrow slightly arched. 'There's no proof they kidnapped us, but *if* they did, why do you think they did so?'

'Hatred!' Mary spits. 'Them two hated me and Ikey.'

Hawk sighs. 'Mama, it were hatred, yes. But it came about because of greed and avarice, because of what was in the Whitechapel safe. Not just their greed and avarice, yours too. We stole that money, you and me, we stole it.'

'Half of it were Ikey's,' Mary protests. 'Hannah tried to get it all! Pinch the bleedin' lot!'

'But she didn't, *we* did. It was never *our* money in the first place, not even Ikey's half, he didn't leave it to us in his will, we stole it before he died, remember?'

'He died unexpected like. Before you come back from England. But he gave us his part of the combination, that shows he intended we should have the money. I know that's true!' Mary insists.

'Mama, you know that's *not* true! I worked out Ikey's combination from his riddle and you got Hannah's from the orphan school, from Hannah's daughter, little Ann, who inadvertently spilled the beans. The safe was empty when David arrived, the contents taken by me. We stole it all, but for one ruby ring and Ikey's note which I planted in the safe for David to read.'

'Ikey would have given it to us, shared it if he'd lived,' Mary says petulantly.

'Ikey never shared anything in his life, Mama. Ikey accumulated, he added and subtracted, but he never divided.'

Mary, despite herself, smiles at Hawk's concise summary of Ikey's character.

'Anyhow,' Hawk continues, 'even if he had intended to share with us, only half of it was his to share, the other half belonged to his wife, to Hannah.' He pauses for emphasis, 'And we stole the lot!'

'Yes, well,' Mary now says, patently growing tired of Hawk's persistence. 'Hannah and David kidnapped you and Tommo, they sodding well deserved what they got in return. After what they done to us, to me two precious ones, they ain't entitled to a brass razoo!'

'Mama, we can't prove they did it! That it was them that took Tommo and me from the mountain.'

'And they can't prove we took the money from the safe, can they now?' Mary says triumphantly. She clears her throat. 'Let me tell you something f'nothing, Hawk Solomon, I know in me heart and soul that they did it, took the two of you, my precious mites, my two beautiful boys, and ruined Tommo's life.' She stabs a crooked finger at Hawk's neck, pointing to the band of silvered scar tissue formed from the wild man's rope burns about it. 'And near bleedin' killed you!' Then Mary leans into her chair, arching her back and looking at Hawk with ill-disguised scorn. 'Nothing will convince me otherwise, you hear? Them two bastards are guilty as sin! They done it, I'd stake me life on it!'

'Ah, but Hannah and David also know in *their* hearts and souls that we took their money and nothing will convince them otherwise. I daresay they'd stake their lives on it as well,' Hawk says, then adds, 'And they'd be damned right to.'

Mary says nothing, looking down over Hobart to the Derwent River, the last moments of the sunset now turning it to gold. There is a lovely calm about the little city at this hour when the lights begin to shine from the windows of houses and cottages on the hill behind the waterfront and from the single row of street lamps that trace the line of the harbour. 'That money were wrongly come by in the first place,' she says finally. 'It weren't gained on the straight, them two never did deserve it, it were stolen goods, fenced off the poor for a pittance, or gained elseways in an evil manner in Hannah's vile brothel.'

Hawk remembers how his heart began to beat faster and he suddenly found it necessary to take a deep breath before speaking. He has waited years for this moment and now when it has arrived the roof of his mouth is suddenly dry. 'Mama, we must give it back,' he says at last.

Mary can scarcely believe her ears. 'Give it back? Are you

stark, starin' mad, Hawk Solomon? Give it back! Give what back? Ikey's money? Do me a favour! Over me dead body!'

'Mama, you have used it to make a fortune ten, fifty times as big as the one we stole. Think now, if you don't give it back, then Tommo is right, we must be counted among the mongrels, among the greedy and the avaricious. Mama, don't you see? If we do not make amends we ourselves are sufficient reason why his daughter Hinetitama must stay with her mother's people.'

Mary leans forward and glares shrewdly at Hawk. 'And if I give it back, only Hannah's half, mind, will you bring Tommo's daughter to me now?'

'No, Mama, that I cannot do. I have promised my twin and I must honour my word.'

She pulls back and gives him a short, disparaging laugh. 'Thought so! Yes, well then them two can go to buggery, they're getting sod-all from me!' she shouts, banging her mittened fist against the arm of her chair. 'They get bugger all, you hear me?'

Despite Hawk bringing up the subject of restitution to Hannah and David several times over the years, Mary won't budge an inch and the enmity and the hate between the two families continues to grow.

But now, at last, Hawk is bringing Hinetitama to Hobart to meet the formidable seventy-eight-year-old Mary Abacus, who still runs her brewing and business empire with a grip of steel so that those who work for her dub her Iron Mary.

Mary has had the extreme satisfaction of seeing Hannah Solomon pass away the previous year. She was pleased as punch when David, respecting his mother's dying wishes, buries her in the Hobart cemetery next to Ikey.

Hannah's son, having inherited his business interests from his mother's de facto husband George Madden, has expanded them hugely. David now lives in Melbourne and is a man of considerable wealth. Mary sends an extravagant wreath to the funeral of her mortal enemy with the message attached:

> *Say hello to Ikey from me*
> *when you arrive in hell!*
> *Mary Abacus.*

The day after the funeral Mary purchases the grave lot beside Hannah's. 'So I can keep an eye on the bitch when I'm dead,' she tells Hawk with satisfaction. 'Mark my words, you can't trust them lot, dead or alive!'

Mary, Hawk knows, will be delighted with Hinetitama's unexpected arrival. She will want Hinetitama married as soon as possible and he expects the clash of temperament between the two women in this regard alone to be considerable.

But, in the meantime, he can almost hear Mary saying upon his arrival in Hobart, 'Oh, my precious Hawk, I shall go to my grave a happy woman, I shall have my great-grandchildren to carry on!'

He doesn't quite know how he will tell Mary about her granddaughter's drinking problem. He is doubtful that Hinetitama's taking the pledge will work, she is too high-spirited, too wild to be constrained, and the dullness and pretension of the better folk in Hobart and her stubborn nature do not bode well for the future. Hinetitama, he thinks, will be more than a match for Iron Mary and Hawk does not expect a calm relationship to develop between them.

But he is wrong. From the outset Tommo's daughter and Mary hit it off splendidly. Hinetitama is a Maori in her manners and upbringing where respect for one's elders is a primary consideration. Mary, on her best behaviour for once, seems to like her granddaughter's feisty demeanour. Hinetitama, though always polite, will not be bullied or told what to do and Mary is forced to seek her co-operation in the plans she has for her.

There is, of course, no initial talk of marriage, Mary being much too cunning to shy the filly before the stallion arrives. She merely asks her granddaughter to embrace the conventions of Hobart society. This includes learning how to dress and behave in polite company, the latest dance steps and, of course, the intricacies and mysteries of acceptable table manners. Her rough manner of speaking is put into the hands of Miss Brodie, a teacher of elocution and correct pronunciation favoured by the true merinos. Her pupil's pronunciation is subject to the closest scrutiny, with her vowel sounds given the most attention. Hinetitama takes all this instruction in good humour, she has a marvellous ear and can mimic Miss Brodie perfectly and, if she wishes, she can pronounce her vowel sounds to perfection.

Mary laughs as Hinetitama afterwards takes her through every lesson. Mary has selected one teacher for dress, another for deportment, a third for manners and conversation. These are invariably women with big bosoms and hair drawn back into rigid grey buns, who wear brown or black bombazine gowns and stern bonnets and almost always turn out to be middle-aged spinsters of impeccable character, genteel poverty and in precious possession of an over-pronounced and meticulous English vocabulary.

Hinetitama not only repeats a particular lesson in a voice redolent of her teachers' but she proves to be a clever actress, who takes on their mannerisms as well, often stuffing her own bosom with a small cushion and drawing back her beautiful dark hair into a bun. She will sometimes affect Mary's reading glasses to perfect a likeness.

Her master of dancing is the ancient Monsieur Gilbert, pronounced 'Gill-bear' who dubs himself Professor de Dance and has become a living institution in Hobart. To be tutored by this ageing and doubtfully French dancing master is a prime requisite among the crinolined society and Mary knows she cannot complete her granddaughter's admittedly crammed social education without a knowledge of all the steps in the latest dances practised in the salons of London and Paris.

Although Hinetitama is forbidden to sway her hips in the seductive style of the Maori, she sometimes includes a bit of a swish, a sway and a naughty thrust of the hips into the rigid and pompous dance steps taught to her, rendering them into an altogether different permutation. 'Oh, Grandmother, must I learn this funny pakeha dance,' she laughs. 'It has no joy in it, how can it catch a man or ready him for the joy of a woman?'

Mary delights in these impersonations which usually take place on the balcony of the big house where Mary always waits at sunset to see the parakeets, her talismanic rosellas, fly over on their way to roost in the trees higher up the mountain. Hawk, in all the time he has known her, has never heard her laugh as much. He can see she is greatly enamoured of her beautiful granddaughter and is even beginning to dote on her. Hinetitama, for her part, tries to co-operate with Mary's wish for her education, but she has won the battle of the dress. While she will accept the dictates of fashion, she simply refuses the dark shades and plain bonnets insisted upon by its arbiters in Hobart. She elects to have her gowns and bonnets made in the brightest of silks and satins and even the cotton dresses she wears during the day are of the strongest colours.

This is all observed with a tight-lipped disapproval from her social *milieu*, who regard her as cheap, and her manner of dressing vulgar and ostentatious, although Hinetitama does not seem to notice, or otherwise care for what the young matrons of Hobart may think of her. As for her various tutors, they gossip endlessly among the older society women. While they may privately accuse Hinetitama of constantly drawing attention to herself with her garish finery and her over-bright smile and lack of dignity in front of her tutors, no one is prepared to point this out to Mary for fear of losing their sinecure. They know that the redoubtable Mary Abacus will accept no criticism of her granddaughter beyond the various problems she has given them to correct.

Mary tactfully dismisses Miss Mawson, the spinster in charge of Hinetitama's wardrobe, paying her overgenerously and, without mentioning the matter of fabrics and colour, she compliments the cut and style of the garments the old lady has chosen for her granddaughter. She is secretly pleased that Hinetitama refuses to accept the dull colours of the prevailing fashion. Though Hinetitama is now twenty-five years old she is still a rose in young bud and with her light step, skin colour and raven-dark hair the bright colours suit her very well indeed and Mary thinks will greatly attract the male of the species.

She has also fallen in love with her granddaughter's voice. When her little Maori princess sings to her of a night she often enough causes the tears to run down her grandmother's cheeks for the sheer joy of her song.

Mary gradually begins to introduce males into Hinetitama's life. These are, for the most part, men in their early forties, widowers and bachelors with some breeding or social standing in Tasmanian society. However, Mary has not precluded male members from the more prosperous but coarser business community, who are also invited for sherry and a light supper. With very few exceptions, the men are prematurely bald with stomachs which spill precipitously over their waistlines maintained thus on a bachelor's diet of ale and stodgy food.

Hobart is not a large place and most of the suitors involved share the same clubs or meet at the Wednesday and Saturday races so that the 'Wild Wahine', as one of these hopeful suitors has dubbed Hinetitama, is freely discussed between them. All see her as a filly to be happily mounted and the source of a large and continuing accreditation to their bank accounts. Her dark good looks testify to her tempestuous nature and they roll their eyes in supposed anticipation while speculating on the stamina required to keep up with her primitive savage desires.

But secretly they conclude they are engaged in a simple transaction, no different to a stud bull. In return for their seed well planted, they will have no further obligations and be free to enjoy the fruits of their labour, the abundant dowry that comes with a successful coupling. Hinetitama's half-breed status, they tell themselves, precludes any future considerations or obligations they might be expected to show her as a husband.

Nor is Mary under any illusions. She observes their greedy eyes and reads their sycophantic gestures towards her and the sloppy compliments directed at her granddaughter for what they are and she knows that the only reason the men have accepted her invitation is because of her money.

Despite Mary's extreme wealth her granddaughter is still a half-caste and as Ikey might say, 'Not quite kosher, my dear.' While she hopes for a marriage based on mutual respect she knows this to be highly unlikely. Mary, though anxious that her granddaughter not marry beneath her status, is not looking for perfection. She admits to herself that the potency of the pistol the successful suitor carries between his legs is more important than his looks or even his brains, given her observation that most men seem to be more or less of equal stupidity. She has been told that the Maori blood breeds out and so, if anything, she shows a distinct preference for men of a fair complexion.

But she has not reckoned on Hinetitama's stubbornness. Her granddaughter, while co-operating in most things, refuses to accept any of the suitors Mary introduces. No amount of cajoling or persuasion will convince her and she seems quite impervious to Mary's temper.

'They are all fuddy-duddies and complete ninnies and speak only of commerce, farming, hunting, horses, racing and football. Of commerce I know nothing and of the others I've heard enough after two minutes. They cannot sing or dance and they have no laughter in their bellies like a Maori man. I'd be ashamed to carry their baby in my stomach!'

Mary admits to herself privately that she agrees with her granddaughter, they are a poor lot, men mostly left over in the first place because of their lack of prospects or character. She thinks of taking her granddaughter to the mainland, to Sydney or Melbourne, where the pickings can be expected to be rather better, especially among the burgeoning middle classes. But first Hinetitama must have a veneer of culture applied sufficiently thickly not to arouse the suspicions of a would-be mother-in-law, that is, until it is too late and the nuptials are concluded. Whereupon the family can happily console themselves with the dowry her granddaughter brings to the marriage.

As the battle of wills rages between the two women Hawk's respect grows for his niece, but he knows the fight is one-sided and Mary will not give up under any circumstances. Even though she is plainly enchanted with Hinetitama she will attempt to achieve her ambition for great-grandchildren at any cost.

Hawk realises that Mary is at deadly serious play with Tommo's daughter. She watches her every lesson and makes her practise what she has learned. Although Mary is conscious of her own lack of grammar and syntax, she has always been a great reader and she is quick to correct a grammatical slip or a mispronunciation if Hinetitama should revert for a moment to her accustomed pattern of speech.

'If you know what's correct grammar, Grandmother, then why do you talk differently?' Hinetitama asks her one evening after Mary has corrected her half a dozen times. It is at the time an innocent enough question but is to begin a conversation which will affect Hinetitama's entire life.

'Too old, my dear, can't teach an old dog new tricks. Never had no time for all that malarky, talkin' posh when you ain't. Folks can take me for who I am, common as dirt, or not at all.'

'Why then must I learn all this stuff?' Hinetitama protests, 'I'm common as dirt.'

'Well my dear, no point in beating about the bush. When you're beautiful *and* rich, rising out of a cloud of dust up into the clean air on nob hill ain't too difficult. All it takes is a few manners and customs learned and a voice that don't sound like a cockatoo. But I must be frank my dear, at twenty-five you're well past the marrying age even though you're a beautiful and desirable woman.'

'But a half-caste, eh?' Hinetitama interjects.

'Yes, no point in denying that. So, if we're going to find you an 'usband of the right breedin' stock, with the right pedigree, it's going to take a fair bit of money and manners. I've got the money but you have to learn the manners. Though, Gawd knows, I've searched the length and breadth of this accursed island and what's available and respectable we've already had to tea and you've rejected the bleedin' lot. The whole bunch o' would-bes if they could-bes! Whatever am I to do with you? Maybe the mainland, what say you?'

'But, Grandmother, if you should find me one, what if I don't love him?'

'Love? Tush! T'ain't necessary. Love's for shopgirls,' Mary says dismissively. Then she becomes aware of the distress in Hinetitama's eyes. 'What do you know about love, eh? You ain't gunna miss what you ain't never had, my dear.'

'But I *have*! I have loved,' Hinetitama protests.

Mary sniffs dismissively. 'That's news to me. Hawk didn't say nothin' about you being in love.'

Hinetitama looks defiantly at Mary. 'Hawk don't know *every* thing about me!'

'*Doesn't* know,' Mary corrects. 'Who've you loved then?'

'Never mind, it doesn't matter!' Hinetitama sulks.

'Yes, it bleedin' does! Tell me, my girl.'

'Why? You wouldn't like him?'

'Like him? What's my liking got to do with it?' Mary sighs. 'I'm an old woman wot's filthy rich, Hawk won't marry and you're twenty-five years old and ain't got a man yet, let alone children!'

Hinetitama looks confused and hurt. 'I don't understand?'

Mary shows her impatience and decides in her frustration to come clean. 'Who's it all gunna go to, eh? Who is gunna carry on with it, with everything I've worked for, built? I daresay Hawk can go on another few years, but what then, leave it to the bleedin' Salvation Army? You, my dear, have no idea of business and don't show the *slightest* interest in bookkeeping.' She looks beseechingly at Hinetitama. 'I simply must have great-grandchildren prepared and ready to take over when Hawk dies.'

'But that will be another twenty, maybe thirty years! You'll be long dead, Grandmother?'

'Not too long, I hope,' Mary sniffs, then she lifts her hands towards her granddaughter showing her crooked fingers. 'But what I did with these, with me own hands, won't be dead! The Potato Factory, me beloved brewery, *must* carry on. I don't care much about the other things, they's nice, but the brewery, that's different, that *must* continue!' She takes a deep breath and gives a resigned smile. 'Now tell me, my precious, who is this man you say you love?'

Hinetitama looks shyly up at Mary and says softly, 'He's a Dutchman, from Holland.'

'A Dutchman, eh? Me old man was a Dutchman,' Mary exclaims. 'A tally clerk down at the East India docks.' She thinks of her poor drunken father and how she loved him despite his constant betrayal and state of inebriation.

'He isn't what *you'd* call a true merino, he isn't the right breeding stock and he hasn't got no . . .' Hinetitama corrects herself, '. . . any pedigree. He ain't . . . isn't what you're looking for, Grandmother.'

Mary ignores her protest. 'Tush, go back a generation or two and we're all scum on this island, even the free settlers come from a pretty dodgy lot, scratch one o' them and you'd be surprised what you find underneath. How old is this Dutchman of yours?'

'Thirty.'

'How tall?'

Hinetitama thinks a moment. 'Six feet and a little bit, I think.'

'Healthy? No coughs in his chest?'

'Yes, he's healthy, no coughs.'

'You sure?'

'I'm a nurse, I ought to know.'

'Got all his teeth?'

Hinetitama laughs despite herself. 'Last time I saw him, yes.'

'When was that?'

'When Uncle Hawk found us.'

'He didn't tell me about no Dutchman?'

'That's 'cause he kicked his arse and sent him packin',' Hinetitama says, her grammar reverting to type.

Mary can be seen to think for a moment, then she draws a breath and says, 'Well, never mind, Hawk never were a good judge o' character.' She pauses. 'Do you still love him?'

'Who? Uncle Hawk? Of course!'

'No, not *him*, the Dutchman.'

Hinetitama nods her head and Mary sees a sudden tear run down her cheek.

'Does he love you?'

'I dunno, he never said.'

'Men never do,' Mary sniffs. She looks wan and lowers her eyes as she thinks of Mr Emmett, the man she loved since the first day she set eyes on him when she'd been in the Female Factory. How, after all the years of knowing him, she had been too shy even to attend his funeral. 'You spend your whole life loving them and never know what they thinks of you,' Mary says at last.

Hinetitama looks up surprised. 'You were in love, Grandmother?' She breaks into a smile. 'You *were*! I *knew* it!' she cries, clapping her hands. 'You were, weren't you, c'mon own up, tell the truth?'

Mary pulls her lips into a small grimace as she tries to conceal her smile. 'Never mind that, my girl, what you don't know can't hurt you. Tell me, do you want to have this man's children?'

Hinetitama is momentarily taken aback by the question and she thinks for a moment, then nods her head. 'I suppose? I never thought about it before.'

Mary's manner is suddenly all business. 'Where is he to be found?'

Hinetitama shrugs. 'Wellington, I suppose. Somewhere in New Zealand, who knows. Wellington's where we left hum. What are you going to do, Grandmother?'

'Why find him, of course.'

'Find hum? Go to Wellington?' Hinetitama says incredulously. 'What for?'

'Him, not hum,' Mary now corrects. 'To bring *hum* over. Why else would I bother to find *hum*, my dear?' she teases smilingly.

'Here? To Hobart?' Hinetitama says excitedly and then, as suddenly, looks forlorn, her eyes cast downwards. 'What if he won't come?'

'He'll come,' Mary snorts. 'Don't fret your little heart about that. In my experience there is seldom a man money can't buy, and he don't sound the sort to be too hesitant.'

'But it's been over a year? What if he's forgot me or took up with someone else, he's very handsome?'

'Forgotten me, and taken up,' Mary corrects without thinking. She gives a cynical little snort. 'My dear girl, he'll be suitably reminded then, won't he? In my experience, wallets, in particular, are a splendid way to jog the memory, provided they are allowed to grow a little in size. If he has married someone else then it may be difficult, but if he merely enjoys different company, then a considerable thickening of his wallet will soon cause him a remarkable loss of enthusiasm for the pleasure his new partner brings him.'

'You mean you're going to bribe him, buy him for me? I don't think I'd like that, Grandmother. That's what you've been doing with all the others.'

'Ah, yes, but you didn't love the others, my precious.'

'But what if he truly *doesn't* love me!'

'Don't you bother your little mind about that right now. We'll bring him over and you can decide for yourself. If he doesn't love you there isn't much I can do about it, is there? Besides you're not the sort to be easily forgot, my precious little lark.'

Hinetitama looks doubtfully at her grandmother, she knows enough to suspect Mary's devious mind is at work. 'You promise me you won't bribe him to say he loves me?'

'No, no, of course I promise,' Mary protests, thinking, if she knows anything about men, how unnecessary it is to make such a promise.

Hinetitama remembers the circumstances in which Hawk found the two of them. It is now obvious to her that he hasn't told Mary about their drunken behaviour or the nature of her lover's profession or their predilection for the grog bottle. She is grateful to Hawk for this, but also finds herself deeply concerned. She has managed to stay clean for more than a year and knows that if Slabbert Teekleman returns she will be lost. Hinetitama senses that Mary's efforts to bring her lover back to her are likely to end in disaster for them both.

Hinetitama tells herself she has tried to get over her Dutchman, to forget him, but he has been constantly on her mind. Not a day passes when she doesn't ache to be with him. Just as she knows that even though she hasn't touched a drop of alcohol since she fought Hawk in Wellington, she still craves the gin bottle every day of her life. There is something, some evil devil, deep down in her belly, that needs it. She knows she loves her Dutchman with the same senseless and destructive passion. She admits to herself that he is, by every definition, a scoundrel, a profligate, a drunk and a gambler, but it makes no difference. She loves him, loves the excitement of being with him, and she cannot cast him from her mind. Hinetitama, her heart pounding, gives herself one last chance at her own salvation.

'Uncle Hawk doesn't like hum?' she says to Mary. 'He won't permit it.'

'Didn't expect he would,' Mary barks. 'You leave Hawk to me, an' all.'

But Hawk won't hear of a plan to find the Dutchman and return him to Hinetitama. While he doesn't know the intimate details of their love affair, he has witnessed its consequence.

'Mama, he is a drunk and a gambler just like Tommo, only I daresay not as skilled. I found them in a hovel drunk, with her naked and filthy and him a coward who ran away and left with a curse for her on his lips. I bought him off with two sovereigns. Can't you see what will happen if she returns to this evil man?'

Mary is obdurate. 'Well! If that's all you can say. Why, if she's what you say she is, a drunk like her father, has she not touched a drop of liquor since she arrived? She's a good girl, stubborn as a mule, that I'll admit, but I don't believe she'd do anything silly.'

'Mama, there is a weakness in her. He is a drunk and will take her down with him.'

'Nonsense! Besides, men don't always drink from addiction, often it's from despair at their prospects in life. As Hinetitama's husband he shall enjoy the most excellent prospects. He seems from her description to be a strong enough fellow with good teeth and lungs, tall and fair of complexion. He is a musician also, so he may be a sensitive fellow underneath.'

Hawk cannot believe his ears. Mary, the ever wary, who doesn't suffer fools gladly and can pick a charlatan soon as look at him, is now carrying on with such inane drivel. 'About as sensitive as my black arse,' Hawk says, suddenly angry. 'He is a gambler as well as a drunk, even if he could be made to reform from the grog he will remain the other. She, Hinetitama, has a fixation, that is all.'

'She's in love with him, Hawk, same as you were with Maggie Pye.'

For the first time in his life Hawk turns on Mary. 'How dare you, Mama! This Dutchman isn't worth a pinch of dog shit! He's a useless bastard, and up to no good in every possible way.'

Mary looks at Hawk and says unflinchingly, 'You could have said the same thing about our Tommo, now couldn't you? What about Maggie Pye? She was a whore. I was a whore, reduced to the vilest circumstances. Does that make us bad people? Your Maggie was a fine woman, one of the best I've known, but she was still a whore. We can all reform, Hawk. If we are fortunate enough to get a second chance. Hinetitama loves this Dutchman, why can't we give *him* a second chance, eh?'

Hawk, still angry and unaccustomed to defying Mary or even using coarse language in front of her, wheels around again. 'Mama, I beseech you, listen to me! You don't know what you're talking about. The man's bad, weak, hopeless. He has the look of a gaolbird about him. I simply won't do this to Tommo's memory. Christ Jesus, Tommo asked me to take care of his daughter not to destroy her! I brought her away from New Zealand so she wouldn't ever again have to mix with scum, with rubbish like Teekleman.'

Mary is silent for a moment and then Hawk sees the anger rise up in her. 'Now you listen to me, Hawk Solomon. Tommo's dead, the girl is alive! I can't go thinking about the sensibilities of the dead where the living are concerned. She refuses to marry any of the local prospects and, I must say, I don't blame her, they're a pretty gormless lot. But she *will* marry her Dutchman and time is runnin' out, she's twenty-five years old, not much time left for childbearing and as far as I can see Teekleman has no disadvantages in that particular area.'

Hawk loves Mary with all of his heart but he now believes her power, wealth and arrogance, taken together with her need to create an on-going, living memorial to her life, has totally corrupted her. 'Mama, you mustn't do this, I beg of you. You will destroy your granddaughter, destroy her as surely as you claim Hannah and David destroyed Tommo.' Hawk pauses and takes a deep breath. 'If you persist in this, then I will tell David Solomon that we stole Hannah and Ikey's share of the Whitechapel safe. He will go to the law and I shall testify, admit our guilt and you will be ruined.'

'And you?' Mary sneers. 'It were you who did the stealing, who opened the safe and took what was inside. What will become of you then?'

Hawk shrugs. 'It don't matter. If you let that Dutchman have Hinetitama you will have destroyed me and you have dishonoured my twin!' Hawk sighs. 'What happens next doesn't matter.'

Mary is silent, her hands in her lap, her head bowed. Hawk appeals once more to her. 'Mama, can't you see, what you've done is wonderful, they can't take that away from you, but what happens after you've gone is of no consequence, you can't take it with you, it's all over. Let someone else have the bloody brewery!'

Hawk hears the sharp intake of Mary's breath as she looks up at him. 'Have it? Someone else? A stranger? A man!' she cries. 'Now, you lissen t'me, boy! I built it with me own hands, these stupid, ugly, broken claws!' She throws her hands up in front of her face. 'I've told you how they come to be like this! Men done it, men who wouldn't let a woman have a job as clerk, they done it! Held me down and broke me fingers with their boots, then raped me!' Mary is shaking with anger and tears roll down her cheeks and her nose begins to run. 'The brewery, the Potato Factory, that's me answer to them bastards who done me in at the East India docks! That's me answer to the beak that sent me down. To the vile Potbottom who flogged me on the convict ship and the tyranny of the sanctimonious bible-bashing surgeon Joshua Smiles! Not to mention the utter bastardry o' the male warders at the Female Factory and their soldier friends who lay us on our backs at night and took from us what they wanted! The banks, the fat, pompous bastards in their grey worsted weskits and gold fob chains, in cahoots with the other brewers. "Sorry, Mary, we don't give credit to women," they sneered, then not even bothering to get up and show me to the flamin' door!' Mary takes a breath, sniffs and then continues, 'I'm the first woman in the known world to build me own brewery! To make and name me own beer! You hear that? The first! That's supposed to be men's work ain't it? The male perog-a-tive! Men own breweries, doesn't they? Men with big bellies and bushy curled moustaches!' She sniffs and knuckles the tears from her eyes. 'Well, a woman built this one! Long as it stands with its two chimneys, two fingers o' brick stuck up into the sky for all to see, it says, "Fuck you!" on behalf of every woman what was ever raped and abused and humiliated by a man!'

Mary now points an accusing finger at Hawk, her voice rasps from the anger and disappointment she feels. 'And now *you* want to do the same. The same as them bastards on the London docks. You wish to destroy me.' Her head jerks backwards. 'Why?' she cries, 'Fergawd's sake tell me why? What have I done to you? You who I brought up, loved with every breath in me body. I even *killed* for you.' She suddenly grows very quiet and speaks almost in a whisper, 'My beloved Hawk, I never thought I'd live to see this day!' Mary stops and bows her head and begins to weep softly, 'I am so ashamed.'

'Oh, Mama! Mama!' Hawk cries out in anguish.

Mary looks slowly up at him, her eyes brimming but her voice defiant. 'Well you won't and you can't!' she chokes. 'I'm gunna find that Dutchman and he'll take Hinetitama to his bed and as soon as he's given her a couple of brats it will be your job to see him off this island. What did you say it cost last time? Two sovs, weren't it? Well, I daresay it will take a lot more next time, but I don't care.' She pauses and shouts, 'I WANT MY HEIRS!' Then she brings her hand up and clasps the small gold medal resting, as ever, upon her breast, Ikey's Waterloo medal. 'You know what it says on the back, on this, don'tcha? *I shall never never surrender!* I ain't never and I never shall!' She releases the medal and brings both her hands up to cover her face and weeps and weeps.

Chapter Three

New Life and the Death of Mary Abacus

1886–1892

Slabbert Teekleman simply turns up in Hobart one bright late spring morning in November 1886.

Martha Billings, the kitchen maid in Mary's home, hears the bell on the back door and goes to answer it, thinking it must be the butcher boy. She discovers a small man, who looks to be in his forties and is somewhat red-visaged and battered-looking, as if he's taken a bad licking or two in his time. The hair below his dirty cap sticks out at every angle and is in need of a good wash. At the maid's appearance he removes his cap and clutches it to the region of his crotch. Martha now sees that he has a bald pate smooth as an egg.

'Whatcha want?' Martha asks, summing him up immediately as a nobody.

'I've a note, fer Miss Solomon, miss,' the man replies.

'Give it then,' Martha demands, extending her hand.

The man shakes his head. 'Nah, 'fraid I can't, miss. I got instructions see. I got to hand it to her personal.' He now realises he is talking to his own social level and his confidence is restored. He returns his cap to his head. 'Miss Solomon personal.'

'And what if I said that were me an' all?' Martha says tartly, feet apart, her hands clamped to her waist.

The man smiles. 'Whole town knows who Miss Solomon is, brought back by Mr Hawk over a year now on the *Waterloo*.'

Annoyed, Martha turns and asks the cook what she must do, explaining the man's purpose. 'Well, what are you waiting for, girl? Go and fetch Miss Heenie,' Mrs Briggs instructs, then she pops her head around the door and takes a quick look at the man. 'He don't look like he bites.'

Martha sniffs. 'Wait here,' she orders the messenger.

The man grins slyly, pleased to see the uppity servant girl put in her place by the cook. 'Thankee, missus,' he says, grinning at Mrs Briggs.

'I dunno, young folk don't seem to know their manners no more,' the cook remarks, 'Too much lip that one.' She turns back to the messenger. 'I don't suppose you'd mind a nice mug o' tea and a slice of bread and jam?'

The man smiles, showing several teeth missing with the remainder blackened. 'Thankee, much obliged, missus.'

When Hinetitama arrives he is sitting on the back step with a tin mug of hot sweet tea and a hunk of bread and jam. He jumps up, slopping tea over his hand in his haste.

'Oh dear, you've burned your hand?' Hinetitama cries, concerned.

'Some, not much,' the man replies, plainly embarrassed for creating a fuss.

'Here, let me see your hand?'

'Me 'and's fine, miss. No 'arm done.'

'Cook'll give you another mug of tea.'

'No, miss, it ain't all spilled.' He looks down into the mug. 'Plenty left, thankee.' Then he stoops to rest the mug on the step beside the hunk of bread, wipes his tea-splashed hand on the side of his greasy corduroy trousers, removes his cap and takes a piece of folded paper from its interior. 'Here, miss, I were told to give it to you personal.'

'Thank you, Mr . . . ?'

'Isaac Blundstone, miss, bootmaker by trade.'

Hinetitama smiles. 'Thank you, Mr Blundstone, I'm obliged to you.' She turns to the cook. 'Do we need a bootmaker, Mrs Briggs?'

'Oh, I don't know about that, Miss Heenie. I could ask Mistress Mary, it ain't for me to decide. Food, yes, but not boots, don't know nothing about boots.'

Hinetitama turns back to Isaac Blundstone and looks down at his boots, which are scuffed and in poor repair. 'Bring some of your work, let me see it.'

'Yes, thankee, miss, I do good work.'

Hinetitama smiles knowingly. 'What, down the pub?'

'The pub, miss?' The man looks puzzled.

Hinetitama points to his hands. 'You've got the brandy shakes. You've had a few already, haven't you?'

The man grins slyly, looking down at his scuffed boots and shuffling his feet. 'Hair o' the dog, couple o' heart starters, that's all, miss.'

'Who gave you this?' Hinetitama waves the note. She is excited, for somehow she senses it's from Teekleman, but restrains herself from finding out, fearful of the contents of the note, wanting to know, but not right off, instinctively needing more to add to what might be contained in the note.

'He didn't say, miss. He didn't give no name,' Blundstone lies.

It's been more than a year since Hinetitama's conversation with Mary. While neither she nor Hawk has said a word to her, the servants, the big ears in every establishment, have inevitably gossiped and Hinetitama, who they call Miss Heenie and is a great favourite with them all, has come to know about the terrible row over Teekleman.

'He didn't say, but he shouted you a drink?' She can smell the cheap brandy on his breath. 'What? A nobbler o' brandy, two maybe, where was that?'

'Aye,' Blundstone says, surprised. 'The Hobart Whale Fishery, miss.'

'Card game, was it? You met playing cards?'

Blundstone is clearly impressed with Hinetitama's sleuthing. 'He were, miss. Me? I ain't got that sorta money.'

'Bar fly, eh? Topping up to cadge?' Hinetitama has seen him for what he is, a regular drunk who'll take on the self-appointed task of keeping the drinks coming at a card game and earning his reward in grog both from the publican and an occasionally generous player. It is unlikely, but not inconceivable, that he might not know Teekleman's name.

'He said just to give you the letter, not to say nothing more.'

'Tall, fair hair, blue eyes?'

'Aye, that's him.'

'Foreigner, when he speaks like?' Hinetitama adds, seeking further confirmation.

The man nods again and Hinetitama, satisfied, gives him a

shilling. 'There you go then, that'll buy you the whole dog.' She laughs. 'Or you could use it to sole your boots, Mr Isaac Blundstone, the bootmaker!'

Blundstone grins. 'It's me brother what's the bootmaker, I'm what yiz'd call the prod'gil son.'

The note when Hinetitama finally opens it is written in a competent hand which suggests a fair education.

Dear Hinetitama,

Ja, I have come here to Hobart and also I will much like to see you. It goes well with me. I am staying at the Whale Fishery. You will come I hope so.

Slabbert Teekleman.

Hinetitama goes into a real tizz and spends the remainder of the day alone in her bed chamber arguing with herself, alternately tearful and smiling. When she thinks of going back to Teekleman her heart commences to beat rapidly, though she, on some occasions, thinks this must be a certain sign that she is doing the wrong thing and on others that she loves him. By evening, when a maid is sent up to call her down to dinner, she is emotionally wrung out and exhausted. Claiming she doesn't feel well she tells the maid to ask her grandmother to excuse her.

Mary, upon receiving Hinetitama's message, comes hurrying to her bed chamber, 'What's the matter, precious?'

Hinetitama feigns distress. 'I must have eaten something, I feel unwell, Grandmother.'

'Unwell? Your tummy? I'll call Dr Moses.' She seats herself on the side of the bed and takes her granddaughter's hand.

'No, it's just a small upset,' Hinetitama smiles wanly. 'Best if I don't eat, that's all.'

'You sure then?' Mary asks, looking concerned.

'Grandmother, it's nothing, I'll just rest,' Hinetitama insists.

'You call me if it gets any worse, you promise now?'

'Grandmother, you work so hard, you look tired, it's me should be caring for you!'

'Day weren't no different to any other,' Mary sniffs. 'Can't turn back the clock, I'm gettin' old, that's all, old and cranky,' she adds gratuitously. She bends and kisses Hinetitama on the forehead then rises slowly, though she stands straight as a pencil and, for a woman her age, still has amazing stamina. 'You call me if you feel any worse during the night.'

By morning, with less than a good night's sleep, Hinetitama knows that she must go to Slabbert Teekleman, that she cannot resist the temptation. 'Oh Gawd, help us,' she says to herself as she brushes her hair prior to going down to breakfast with Mary. 'Please let it be all right this time.'

At breakfast, which is served early, just after six o'clock so that Mary and Hawk can be at the Potato Factory by seven when the brewery workers start, she again has no appetite. Fortuitously Hawk is away on a trip to Burnie so that she and Mary are sitting alone at the dining-room table. Hinetitama goes through the motions of dipping her spoon into her porridge bowl, but eats very little.

'Still no good, eh?' Mary enquires, observing her lack of appetite.

'No, Grandmother, it's not that,' Hinetitama says.

'The note?' Mary says suddenly, her own spoon halfway to her mouth. 'Is it something I should know, girl?'

'Mrs Briggs told you?'

'Not much to tell, was there? She said you got a note. Man come to the back door.'

Hinetitama, unable to contain herself any longer, announces, 'Grandmother, it was from the Dutchman!'

Mary remains silent for a while. Finally she returns the spoon, its contents uneaten, to her plate. 'The Dutchman? Slabbert Teekleman?'

Hinetitama nods, amazed that her grandmother has remembered both his names.

'Well?' Mary demands. 'What will you do?'

'Grandmother, I don't know, I'm that scared.'

'Frightened? Lovesick, more like!' Then, realising Hinetitama is asking for her support, her voice takes on a more sympathetic tone. 'Of course you're scared, my precious. After all, it's been almost two years.'

'I'm different now. He may not like me.'

Mary is hard put to conceal her relief, her granddaughter is not rejecting the Dutchman as she's come to think of Teekleman in her mind. 'Course he will, child, don't you worry your little head about that.'

'Whatever shall I do, Grandmother?'

'Do? Why invite him to supper tonight, of course. What does he like to eat? Mrs Briggs will make it for him special.'

'Like? I don't rightly remember. Meat 'n' potatoes, I suppose,' Hinetitama says absently.

Mary laughs. 'Like all men, eh? We'll get cook to do us a nice roast, roast beef and taties.' Mary is suddenly all business. 'We'll send the carriage to fetch him. Where's he staying?'

'The Hobart Whale Fishery.'

'The Whale Fishery? That's a Cascade pub, one of Delgrave's, Ikey used to go there a lot. Do you think he'll agree to move to one of ours?' Mary doesn't wait for an answer. 'Course he will, won't cost him a bean. I'll send him a note, make all the arrangements. Half-six, most men like to eat early, I don't suppose he's any different, eh?'

Hinetitama agrees, thinking that Teekleman is unlikely to be drunk so early in the evening. She has never seen Mary all of a twitter like this before. Her grandmother is seldom her best in the morning and is usually silent, almost morose, her abacus at her side. Every once in a while she grunts and sends the beads rattling along their wires, then writes a number down on a notebook beside her. But this morning she's plainly in excellent humour.

'But what if *he's* changed also?'

'Well, we'll just have to find out, won't we, my girl?'

'What will Uncle Hawk think?'

Mary shrugs, not denying the probability of Hawk's opposition. 'He ain't here, is he now?'

For a moment Hinetitama wonders whether Hawk's absence hasn't been planned by Mary all along, but she is not accustomed to deceit and silently castigates herself for this uncharitable thought.

'Oh, Grandmother, I'm so excited. Whatever shall I wear?'

'It don't really matter, men don't notice anyway.' Mary grins. 'Unless o' course you wear your birthday suit?'

'Grandmother!' Hinetitama has never heard Mary talk like this before. Then she laughs, she's never felt closer to her grandmother and her anxiety is greatly ameliorated by Mary's cheerful assurance. 'Please, God,' she says to herself, 'don't let him be drunk when he comes.' Then she adds another plea to the Almighty, 'And don't let all this be of Grandmother's doing.'

Teekleman arrives promptly in Mary's carriage at half-past six and is greeted at the door by Hinetitama and her grandmother, who has finally persuaded her granddaughter to wear a gown of a modest mousy-brown colour, one of the earlier rejects from old Mrs Mawson's attempts to bring her into line with current Hobart fashion.

'Don't want him to think you're too good for him now, do we? He'll be jittery as a race'orse, no point in shying him right off with silks 'n' satins in the brightest colours now, is there? Modesty, my girl, you need never feel it in front of a man for most have less intelligence than you, but you must appear always to show it,' she declares, then explains further, 'Men believe what they see, women what they hear.' Though she herself has chosen to wear one of her best gowns. When Hinetitama remarks on this the old woman grins. 'Modesty and beauty from you, age and riches from me, mark my words, the combination is irresistible to any man who comes a'courting with a death and an inheritance in mind.'

Slabbert Teekleman is well scrubbed and wears clean though not expensive linen. He is dressed in the manner one might expect from a small businessman of the respectable middle classes and wears a plain woollen weskit without a fob and chain strung across his belly. His boots are freshly dubbined, his hair neatly parted and his beard trimmed. He is a big man, only slightly given to noticeable paunch and is still most handsome in his overall appearance.

Hinetitama watches, smiling, as Mary greets him. 'You are most welcome in our home, Mr Teekleman,' she says, offering him her gloved hand. 'Of course, you already know my granddaughter.'

Teekleman, for his part, seems surprisingly at ease, and Hinetitama observes that he appears to be completely sober. 'Thank you, Madam,' he says formally to Mary. Smiling, he bows and only lightly takes her hand. In doing this he is displaying a social awareness Hinetitama is unaware he possessed. Furthermore, his returning smile reveals he has not lost any of his teeth. Turning to her he offers his hand. 'I am so glad we meet vunce more, Hinetitama, that you and your granmutza invite me here to your nice house.'

Hinetitama smiles broadly, her heart pounding furiously, but she is determined not to show her nervousness and to put the Dutchman at ease. 'I've been that worried all day that you'd change your mind and not come,' she laughs, her words immediately relieving the tension.

'Shall we go in?' Mary invites and turns to lead the way into the mansion. 'Cook has a baron of beef fresh from the roasting oven, I feel sure a big man like you has a healthy appetite.'

A week after the Dutchman's arrival Hawk arrives home shortly after sunset and, stopping only to tell Mrs Briggs he will take a light supper in his study, goes straight to the wing of the house he occupies. He is weary and has a light cold and thinks to take a bath and then read awhile before going to bed. But Mary sends a maid to ask him if he'll have dinner with her, the servant girl adding that Hinetitama is out for the evening.

Hawk thinks the invitation curious. It is the custom for both Mary and himself to dine alone after a journey. Mary is well aware of the rigours of a long coach ride and the accumulated weariness of constant travel over a period of several days. Hawk knows himself to be irritable and not inclined to favour company of any sort. He will catch up with Mary in the morning when she will drill him solidly for an hour, wanting to learn every detail of his business trip.

Hawk finds himself especially tired on this occasion. Normally he would have rested somewhat on the ferry from New Norfolk, but upon his arrival at the little river port he discovered the ferry had struck a docking pylon the previous night and sunk in six feet of river water. The captain, being reputed to have been in an advanced state of inebriation, was blamed for the accident.

Now his back ached from the Cobb and Co. coach ride, where, despite paying for two seats as was his usual custom, he'd been jammed in with too many other passengers, among them two stout ladies who seemed to spend the entire trip complaining about the mishap to the ferry and the added inconvenience of the coach, and on several occasions making pointed remarks that 'someone' among them was taking twice the seating space he was entitled to.

'Tell Miss Mary I am wearied from my journey and wish to bathe and be early to bed and will take supper alone in my study. You will give her my apologies and say that I will see her in the morning,' he tells the maid. Then adds, 'Can you remember all of that?'

The servant girl nods and does a poor imitation of a curtsy before taking her leave. Mary's servants are not expected to be overformal in their behaviour, required only to show respect to their employers. 'Had quite enough o' all that bowing and scraping when I were a maid meself,' Mary would say when she suspected a visitor expected a curtsy or a servant to stand to attention as they passed.

Hawk has removed his boots, socks and cravat and released his starched collar from its gold stud. His braces hang from his waist and his shirt cuffs are unlinked, when there is a sharp knock on the door followed immediately by Mary's voice. 'Hawk, I must talk to you! Will you not take tea with me tonight?'

'Mama, I am greatly wearied from the journey, I beg to be excused.'

'Are you decent?' Mary's voice now asks from behind the door.

Hawk sighs. 'Mama, I have removed my boots and I daresay my feet stink to high heaven,' he says, hoicking up his braces as he speaks.

Without further ado the door to his bed chamber is thrown open. 'Hawk, I simply must talk to you!' Mary repeats.

Hawk groans. 'Mama, can't it wait? I am dog-tired. Can we not talk at breakfast, after I am rested?'

'No, it can't!' Mary snaps. 'I would be most obliged if you'd take tea with me. Mrs Briggs will make you something light to eat, a little cold lamb and mustard pickles perhaps?'

Hawk realises that Mary will not be put off, that if he continues they will inevitably quarrel, an experience for which he has an even greater disinclination than his appearance at supper. 'Mama, allow me to take a bath first,' Hawk sighs wearily.

At the dinner table a thoroughly grumpy Hawk hears of the Dutchman's arrival. Mary tells him that, together with his manservant, Isaac Blundstone, Teekleman has been given quarters at The Ship Inn.

Hawk shows his astonishment. 'You welcomed him and gave him a place to stay?'

'Well, yes, it seemed a proper thing to do, given the circumstances,' Mary says, her lips pursed.

'Proper thing? Proper thing to do! Whatever can you mean?' Hawk cries.

'Well, he's Hinetitama's friend, ain't he?'

Hawk shakes his head, not believing what he's heard. 'Mama, what have you done!'

'It were none of my doing, I swear it! He just come 'ere out of the blue.'

Hawk looks at his mother, holding her eyes. 'Don't you look at me like that, Hawk Solomon,' she shouts. 'It don't have nothing to do with me, ask her, she'll tell yer what happened!'

Mary lowers her eyes, averting his gaze. She is not accustomed to explaining herself or of justifying her actions and he senses she feels vulnerable. 'Mama, are you sure? Are you sure you didn't have a hand in this?'

'Course I am,' Mary snorts indignantly. 'Would I lie to you, me own flesh and blood?'

'Good then, you won't mind if I send him packing? I daresay a little more than two sovs will be needed this time, but I shall regard it as money well spent.'

Mary doesn't react as Hawk expects she will, defending the Dutchman's right to stay as long as her granddaughter wants him to remain, claiming that her love for Teekleman must be allowed to prevail. Instead she shrugs, her expression now completely noncommittal. 'You must do what you think best, my dear, I have only waited until you returned.' Then she adds quietly, 'But if you *must* send him off, then don't tell her, let her think he's left of his own accord. Either way it will break her poor heart, but if she knows it's you done it to her again, this time she will not forgive you.'

Hawk is immediately suspicious. It is an altogether too well-rehearsed reply. He senses Mary is at her most devious. She has the same 'butter won't melt in her mouth' appearance as when she confronted the hapless Senior Detective O'Reilly in the mortuary and claimed Mr Sparrow's headless body to be Tommo's. It is at this precise moment that Hawk knows that Teekleman has been bribed in some manner he cannot hope to match. That money won't buy him off. That, whatever the machinations involved in having the Dutchman return to her granddaughter, Mary has rendered Hawk powerless to prevent Teekleman from staying in Hobart.

She has not forbidden him to send the Dutchman packing, so he cannot chastise or even threaten to undermine her by admitting to David Solomon that they stole Ikey and Hannah's Whitechapel fortune. Unless he should kill him, Teekleman will stay and marry Hinetitama. Mary will have her stallion and Hinetitama will be sacrificed as Mary's willing mare.

Hawk is suddenly very angry. 'Mother, you have done a terrible thing, you will destroy her life. She has Tommo's cravings for the bottle, the Dutchman will bring Hinetitama down to his level.'

Mary has regained her calm and reaching for the tea pot she pours herself a second cup of tea. 'I can't imagine what yer talkin' about. She ain't touched a drop in almost two years and he came to dinner sober as a judge, his linen clean, dressed like Jones the grocer, neat as a new pin, and well spoken and polite throughout.' She places the pot down and adds milk and sugar to her cup and commences to stir it, the teaspoon tinkling softly against the edge of the cup. 'I admit he ain't got the social standing I would have liked for the girl, but who are we to talk? We can't help who we are then, can we? Him a foreigner, her a half-caste, you born black, me a cockney born poor as dirt and not much better than same.'

'Mama, Teekleman is a gambler and a drunk, fer Godsakes!'

'Well, we know all about that then, don't we? Had one of those in the family before, haven't we? Didn't stop us loving him though, did it?'

'Mama, that were Tommo, our own flesh and blood, it's not the same.'

'Oh? Why not? She's in love with him, Hawk. You should see them two together. I've never seen her happier, singing the livelong day, carefree as a lark. She loves him all right, as much as we loved our Tommo.'

Hawk now sees that Mary will not be baited, that she is determined to keep her equilibrium, to stay calm. He tries one more time. 'Mama, I told you how I found them in Wellington, he'll ruin her.'

'People change. He's been here a week and he hasn't touched a drop as far as I know, she's been with him most of the time and except for t'night he's had tea with us every day.' Mary smiles. 'Funny to hear his voice, takes me back, just like me old dad's, all them words pronounced wrong and "ja" this and "ja" that, like turning back the clock, Gawd forbid. I were suddenly a little girl again, tricking pennies from young men stepping out with their sweethearts in the Vauxhall Gardens.'

'Christ Jesus!' Hawk suddenly expostulates, then throwing down his napkin he kicks back his chair and leaves the table.

'Ain't you gunna say goodnight then?' Mary calls after him. Hawk knows that he is finally defeated, that Iron Mary has won the day without shedding a single drop of family blood. He goes to bed furious and humiliated, but nevertheless determined to see Teekleman the next day.

The Dutchman proves to be quite a different proposition to the coward he paid off with two sovs and sent packing in Wellington. He is well dressed, just as Mary has described him, and has a definite air of confidence about him. He is shown into Teekleman's rooms, the two best available at The Ship Inn, by a manservant who, despite a suit of new clothes and boots, has the appearance of a drunkard about him, perhaps an ex-fighter gone to early seed. His rubicund nose looks as though it has been rearranged several times in the past and his ears are tight little knots of flesh. The man is plainly not overacquainted with the duties of a manservant and fails to take Hawk's hat and coat.

Hawk stoops noticeably to enter the room and Teekleman rises from the table he is seated at and where he has been playing a game of solitaire, the cards arranged in sequence on the table in front of him. Hawk's memory goes back to Tommo, to his abiding obsession, how he couldn't for a moment be parted from a deck of DeLarue and at every opportunity would finger them, handle them, splay and spread them as though they were an extension of his own body, which he supposes they eventually became.

'Once a gambler always a gambler, eh, Teekleman?' Hawk says, this opening remark intended to put the Dutchman on the defensive.

But Teekleman is not so easily disconcerted. He smiles and extends his hand. 'Ja, it is goet we meet, Mr Solomon.' He chuckles. 'Last time was maybe not so goet I think.'

Hawk is forced to take his hand and is surprised at the firmness of Teekleman's grip. 'Now look here, Teekleman, I do not intend to beat about the bush. You are not welcome here,' Hawk announces and then feels slightly embarrassed at how the words have come out. They sound overpompous, like a retired colonel from the Indian Army. 'So why don't you piss off!' he adds, attempting to leaven his statement with an addition of the vernacular.

Teekleman does not reply, but appears to look past Hawk, who now turns and sees that Blundstone is still standing at the door. 'Ja sank you, Blundstone, you go now,' the Dutchman says, waving the man out with a flick of his hand. He watches as Blundstone leaves, closing the door behind him. Hawk is fairly certain that one of the little pug's cauliflower ears is well glued to the surface of the door.

'If it's a matter of compensation?' Hawk now says to Teekleman.

'Mr Solomon, I am here because I come myself.' He points to the cards on the table. 'It is just a game, I do not gamble no more, with the flats I am finish. I have goet job and I have now Hinetitama.' He pauses and grins. 'Is goet, ja?'

Hawk wants to smash his fist into the Dutchman's face, he knows the bastard is lying. 'Five hundred pounds and your passage out of here to anywhere you wish to go. Holland, America, you name it. All I require is that you never set foot in Tasmania again.' He knows he is offering Teekleman a fortune, but he is disinclined to bargain and has made him an offer a man in Teekleman's position would find almost impossible to refuse. The overlarge offer is also intended to assess whether, as he suspects, there may be another agenda and Mary has rendered the Dutchman bulletproof.

Teekleman whistles softly and appears to be thinking. 'That is a lot of money, Mr Solomon.' He looks slowly up at Hawk and shakes his head. 'No,' he says smiling, 'I stay. I do not go.'

As with Hinetitama, Hawk's fears seem to have been unfounded. Teekleman has been given a job as a tally clerk in the brewery and, soon thereafter, is promoted by Mary to foreman in charge of transportation, delivering to the pubs Tommo & Hawk ale, the beer most in demand from the Potato Factory. Mary has been careful to put him to work in an area isolated from Hawk's day-to-day influence and it has to be said the Dutchman acquits himself well enough. Furthermore, he drinks only beer, which seems not to affect his sobriety in the least, only manifesting itself by the increasing size of his girth. Hinetitama, for her part, though besotted by the Dutchman, maintains her pledge.

The Hobart society is soon atwitter with the news of the romance, though the gossips are all in agreement that Mary has been forced to compromise and has come down in her expectations for her 'dark little granddaughter', the euphemism they have privately adopted for Hinetitama. They have neatly reversed the fact that Hinetitama has summarily rejected every island suitor, and now gleefully whisper that the island's more mature bachelors and widowers have spurned Mary's fortune and collectively rejected her granddaughter out of hand. This wildly improbable proposition is, of course, happily accepted and confirmed by the motley collection of males who have been sent packing.

Nevertheless, everybody who is anybody in the local society is waiting anxiously to be invited to the wedding. Mary has promised a desperate and frustrated Hawk that she will wait six months before the couple are joined in matrimony, his hope being that Teekleman will inevitably reveal his true colours. When time expires and the Dutchman proves his worth an impatient Mary announces the couple's betrothal. Hawk now begs that the wedding be a modest affair and even suggests that it take place as a civil wedding.

Mary is appalled at this suggestion. 'How can you deny me this?' she castigates him. 'Me, an old woman, what hasn't much longer for this mortal coil! Who never had the pleasure of seeing Tommo joined and denied the same pleasure by yourself! I want this whole bleedin' island to know me granddaughter is gettin' married! I want guests t'come from the mainland and every publican and his wife on the island what sells our beer, all the workers, down to the most 'umble, with their families and the nobs and the snobs and the true merinos, I want the lot, even the flamin' governor!'

'Mama, the workers and the publicans yes, maybe a grand picnic for them. As for the rest they despise us, they'll come to laugh, you'll be giving them more bitch-faced pleasure than they've enjoyed in years. I doubt also that the governor will accept.'

'Yes he will, he knows what side his bread is buttered,' though Mary secretly doubts that Governor Hamilton will accept her invitation. He's a nice enough cove, but his wife, Lady Teresa, is a frightful snob with her nose held high enough to look down upon Mount Wellington, never mind the hoi polloi. Mary takes a final shot at Hawk's objection. 'You've made me wait all this time, she could be nigh six months pregnant by now! I may not live long enough to see me own great-grandchild!'

Hawk gives a bitter little laugh. 'Mama, if you have to cut the umbilical cord with your own teeth, you'll be at the birth!'

'Yes, well, you're not denying me a proper wedding. Next you'll be telling me you'll not give the bride away.'

Hawk feels he cannot protest any longer. 'May as well be hung for a sheep as a goat,' he grins.

'Good, then that's settled,' Mary says, trying hard to conceal the triumph in her voice.

The wedding is truly a grand affair with the governor in attendance at St David's Church, though not at the reception afterwards, which is held at the racecourse, there being no other venue sufficiently large to contain the crowd. Three dozen oxen and at least four times as many lambs are roasted and it seems all of Tasmania is in attendance. Mary has reluctantly made a concession to the local society members by creating a grand banquet for them in the Members' enclosure.

She explains this separation of the classes to Hawk. 'I don't want the nobs and the true merinos walking about among the mob with the ordinary folks chewing a bit of a chop and having a good time feeling obliged to bow and scrape and thinking they's not just as entitled to be there as the nobs.'

In fact, she only visits the Members' enclosure once, to present and to drink a toast to the bride and groom, whereupon the three of them promptly leave the nobs to themselves, joining the picnic on the course. Hawk, meanwhile, remains with the common crowd.

In the months that follow the wedding not much is worthy of mention. Teekleman, having secured the prize, does not go astray and within a few weeks, almost on cue, Hinetitama announces that she is experiencing nausea. 'Morning sickness,' Mary announces gleefully to the cook, 'a little strained broth if you will, Mrs Briggs.'

On time and with surprisingly little fuss, given Hinetitama's size, Ben Solomon-Teekleman is delivered by a midwife, with Dr Moses standing by, enjoying an excellent Portuguese sherry or two in Hawk's study.

The lack of complication in Ben's delivery will characterise him all his life. He is a happy and uncomplaining baby who seldom cries, a child who is good at sports, gathers friends around him easily, is in the middle ranking at school and is seldom less than cheerful. Later, he predictably becomes a young man who takes life in his stride. Neither boastful nor arrogant and oblivious to the wealth at his command, he is much loved by a wide range of mates and accepted as their natural leader. At five feet and ten inches in his stockinged feet he is neither short nor tall but powerfully built, dark-haired and brown of eye with a hint of Maori about his broad brow and strong jawline. A handsome young man by all appearances, he is also an excellent shot and a natural horseman.

His sibling, Victoria, born fifteen months later, has a difficult birth and Dr Moses announces that Hinetitama will endanger herself if she attempts to have more children. She is as fair as her brother is dark, a blonde with almost violet eyes and with a slightly olive skin. While Mary dotes on both children it is to Victoria that she is most naturally attracted. The little girl, much to Hawk's consternation and her great-grandmother's delight, is stubborn as a mule, and, in Mary's last year of life, at three years old already shows an exceptional intelligence. She sits beside the old woman, doing basic sums on the abacus, the bright beads never ceasing to delight her.

'She's the one!' Mary cackles. 'She's the one!' Mary at the age of eighty-five still has all her faculties intact, though she is becoming increasingly hard of hearing. 'Damned good thing too,' she often says. 'I'm tired of hearing all the nonsense people go on about.' She was never one to suffer fools gladly but now she has become a thoroughly cantankerous old woman, the only exceptions being her great-grandchildren, though even they are sent packing when they become too boisterous for her. She no longer goes to the Potato Factory every day but still insists that Hawk talk the day's business over with her as she takes a glass of sherry and watches the sun setting over the Derwent.

At half-past five in the afternoon and half an hour sooner in the winter she is to be found in her accustomed chair on the porch overlooking her magnificent garden. Further off still the city snatches the last of the late afternoon sunlight and finally she looks out upon the river beyond it, that brightest ribbon of water that first brought her as a young convict woman over sixty years ago to the shores of Van Diemen's Land.

Though Mary enjoys the magnificent sunset and the closing down of the day, that is, on those good days when the ever changing Tasmanian weather allows it to occur, this is not the reason she is at her station at precisely the same time every evening. She waits for the green parrots.

'My luck, here comes my great good fortune!' she shouts as the flock approaches, wheeling towards her, seeming to be skidding on the glass-bright air. Her poor broken hand is clasped around the little gold Waterloo medal that hangs from her neck. Then as the birds pass over she releases the medal and clasps her hands to her bosom, cheering them on as their raucous screeching fills the space above her, drowning out her own calls of delight.

It is a ritual which never varies and which is of the utmost importance to her wellbeing. The very site for her magnificent home was selected over several months of observation and only after carefully determining the exact morning and evening flight path of the rosellas.

Apart from Ikey's Waterloo medal, sent to her in Newgate Prison in a moment of aberrant generosity Ikey himself could never satisfactorily explain, the parrots have always signified her new beginning, her second chance and her subsequent great good fortune.

She now recalls how she first witnessed a flock of parrots in flight as the *Destiny II* was leaving the Port of Rio de Janeiro, the convict transport having called in to take on supplies of food and fresh water before proceeding to Van Diemen's Land.

Mary was hidden behind two barrels at the stern of the vessel, having escaped from the ship's hospital where earlier she had lain in wait for the vile Potbottom, to recover her Waterloo medal which he had stolen from her. The departing ship had reached a point between Fort San Juan and Fort Santa Cruz when she witnessed a flock of macaw parrots flying across the headland, their brilliant plumage flashing in the early morning sun.

As the birds rose Mary could see the Sugar Loaf, the majestic peak that towers above the grand sweep of the bay and dominates this most beautiful of all the world's harbours.

With the flock of macaws captured against an impossibly high blue sky Mary felt a surge of exhilaration. It was the first time during the long and dreadful voyage from England that she held the slightest hope that what remained of her life would not continue in abject misery and end in her premature death.

Her kind were usually dead at the age of thirty-four and some a great deal earlier. With seven years of incarceration on the Fatal Shore ahead of her, she had little reason to expect a life free of misery or, for that matter, of her death not arriving at the normally predicted time.

Then, at sunrise many weeks later, as the *Destiny II* lay at anchor in the D'Entrecasteaux Channel prior to catching the early morning tide to take them up river to Hobart Town, a flock of bright green parrots had flown overhead calling a raucous welcome down to her. From that moment, when Mary had seen the parrots enter her life for a second time, she accepted the emerald green rosella as her good luck, her great good fortune. Never a day in her subsequent life passes without her going out to greet them at sunrise and, as she is doing now, to send them on their way at sunset.

The following morning, for the first time in her new life, Mary fails to rise. She is always up before the servants and when she doesn't appear on the balcony, Martha Billings, who usually stands in the garden where she can observe the birds and Mary at her customary place, goes hurrying to the back of the house and into the kitchen to tell Mrs Briggs.

Mrs Briggs, all bustle and fuss, hurries up the stairs and arrives panting at Mary's bed-chamber door. She knocks tentatively. 'You all right, dear?' she calls softly and then, when no sound comes from the room beyond, she knocks more loudly. She hears a faint call to enter and shyly enters Mary's bed chamber.

Nobody within living memory has ever seen Iron Mary in bed and Mrs Briggs is surprised at how small and frail she looks with the blanket drawn up against her chin. 'You must call Hawk,' Mary whispers.

'Oh my Gawd!' Mrs Briggs gasps, immediately bursting into tears.

'Call Hawk, you silly woman,' Mary rasps.

With her hands covering her face Mrs Briggs runs from the bedroom.

Hawk arrives a few minutes later wearing a dressing gown over his nightshirt. He has already shaved but not yet had the time to dress.

'Mama!' he exclaims as he enters. 'You are not well?'

The sight of the frail little woman almost lost in the large brass and enamel bed leaves him with a deep sense of shock. While Mary is an old woman, such is her character that only strangers note her advanced age. Those who have been around her for most, if not all of their lives, see only Mary, or if they are among the unfortunate, Iron Mary, but nevertheless both her friends and her enemies regard her as an indestructible force.

'I shall call Dr Moses,' Hawk says. 'How do you feel, Mama?'

Mary lifts her hand. Even though she is in bed, she still wears mittens to hide the deformity of her hands, they are as indispensable to her as her lace sleeping bonnet. 'No, I don't want him fussing about. Will you call Hinetitama and the children to my bedside but first . . .'

Hawk interjects. 'Mama, you are never taken sick, please let me call Dr Moses.'

Mary doesn't bother to answer. 'Hawk, listen to me,' she says, her voice barely above a whisper. She pats the eiderdown beside her, signalling that he should sit beside her on the bed. As Hawk sits, the weight of his huge body sinks the bedsprings, so that Mary is almost in a seated position. 'Now listen to me carefully,' she repeats. 'In the safe in my office is a brown manilla envelope, it's got a black seal, not red like the usual. Open it, read it carefully.' She pauses to take a breath.

'Then in the drawer of the desk you will find a stick of the same black wax. I want you to reseal it, so it's returned just the way it was.' The effort at talking is taking its toll and Mary rests for a moment, her chest heaving with the effort. 'If the Dutchman behaves well, you will give it to him before you die, or leave it to him in your will.' Mary rests again before continuing. 'If he plays up after I've gorn, tell him *you* now possess the document and send him away. Tell him if he returns you will take the appropriate action.'

'Mama, hush, hush, you're not going to die,' Hawk says, alarmed, putting his huge black hand to her brow. It is cold and clammy and his heart skips a beat.

There is a trace of a smile on Mary's lips. 'Yes I am. If *I* says so, that's it then, ain't it? Do you understand what I'm saying about the Dutchman?'

Hawk nods. 'Yes, Mama.'

'Now call Hinetitama and the children in.'

'Mama, I feel I should call Dr Moses.'

Mary sighs and then remains silent for a few moments as

though she is trying to decide. 'No,' she says finally, 'I've had enough, I heard the birds pass over this mornin' but I weren't there to see them.' It is said as though it is her final word, no different to her dismissal of some proposition put to her in business. 'Go now.'

Hawk taps softly on the door of Hinetitama's bed chamber then opens the door a crack to look in. She is awake but still in bed beside her husband, who is snoring, his fat belly rising and falling well above the level of his head and the bolster it rests against.

In the years they have been together Teekleman has almost doubled in size, his girth well beyond the possibility of joining his fingers about it. Hawk opens the door a little wider so that his niece might see his face. 'You decent?' he whispers.

'What is it?' she asks, climbing out of bed. She is wearing a cotton nightgown to her ankles and her dark hair falls naturally to her shoulders, seeming not disturbed by her sleeping. Hawk thinks how pretty she looks, though a woman now of thirty-two she still appears to be ten years younger. He wonders, as he has so often done, what she sees in the fat Dutchman, for she seems as besotted by him as ever.

Hawk points to Teekleman and brings his finger to his lips. 'Come to Mary's room,' he says softly and then goes to fetch Ben and Victoria from the nursery.

With Teekleman excluded and the remainder of her little family gathered around her, Mary first kisses Ben and sends him off to his breakfast. She holds Victoria a moment longer. 'You shall have my abacus, my precious,' she whispers before releasing her.

'Are you ill, Great-grandmamma?' Victoria asks in the clear tones of a child. 'Are you going to die?'

'Run along now, darlin',' Mary says softly.

'No! I won't and you can't make me,' the child replies, looking defiantly at Mary.

'Go!' Hinetitama admonishes her. 'Do as Great-grandmamma says.'

'No!' Victoria replies, folding her little arms and walking backwards until her bottom brushes against a small chaise longue and she jumps up and wriggles, with her arms still folded, until she is seated defiantly upon it. She hasn't, for one moment, taken her eyes off Mary.

'Stubborn,' Mary whispers, though it seems more a

compliment than an admonishment. Then with a slight gesture of her hand she draws Hinetitama closer so that she is where Hawk previously sat. 'I have made provision in my will for you and the children, my dear. You are to have your own house with servants provided and the income from a trust fund I have set up for the children until Victoria reaches the age of thirty and Ben thirty-two.'

Hinetitama does not appear to grasp what the old woman is saying. 'Grandmother, please don't die,' she cries and bursts into sobs.

Victoria watches Hinetitama crying. 'She can die if she wants to,' she says suddenly to her mother. Then she turns to Mary and announces, 'Great-grandmamma, we don't want you to die, but if you must, then you simply must.'

Mary, increasingly short of breath, still manages a wan smile. She looks up at Hawk. 'She's the one,' she whispers. She lies still for a while then turns to the weeping Hinetitama, 'Now, now, girlie, enough o' that nonsense. Listen to me, I shan't say it again. You shall have the income from the trust fund I have set up for Ben and Victoria, it will take at least until they are thirty years old to learn enough to take over from Hawk. Then they shall each inherit fifty per cent of the trust and you will receive a separate pension.' Mary rests a while, her chest rising and falling in short sharp bursts. 'The principal is *not* your money. *Only* the interest may be used by you and your husband, that is, until they reach the age to inherit,' she repeats. 'Does yer understand?'

Hinetitama, who has her chin on her breast, nods. 'Yes, Grandmother,' she sniffs, though it is unclear whether she does.

'Now I want you to do something for me,' Mary says, reaching for her granddaughter's hand.

'Anything, Grandmother,' Hinetitama sniffs.

'Will you sing me that song?'

'What song?' Hinetitama sobs.

'The Maori one, child, about goin' away.'

Mary nods and Hinetitama suddenly breaks into uncontrollable sobbing. 'Come, come,' Mary whispers. 'None o' that, girl.'

Hinetitama struggles to regain her composure then begins to sing, her voice soft and reedy at first but her lovely contralto gains the ascendancy and a beautiful, haunting melody rises deep and strong.

Hinetitama comes to the end and Mary lifts her arms and hugs her granddaughter perhaps for the second or third time in her life. 'I am most proud of you, Hinetitama, most proud, thank you for my heirs, for Ben and Victoria.' She pauses, then says gently, 'Now you must go, I wish to be alone with Hawk.' Mary turns slowly to Victoria. 'Run along, my precious.'

Victoria jumps from the couch, her small feet landing together with a soft thump on the Persian carpet. She walks the few steps over to Mary's bed and, standing on tiptoe, she kisses her on the forehead, then takes her weeping mother by the hand. 'Come along, Mother,' she commands, leading the sobbing Hinetitama from the room.

Hawk waits until they've left before he resumes his place beside Mary. 'You will keep all the servants,' she instructs, 'they's all of them strays and ain't got no family and nowhere to go, they must have pensions when they are too old to work.' Then she places her hand in Hawk's huge paw. 'I loves you Hawk, I always loved you the most.' Hawk remains quiet, though great tears run down his black cheeks and splash between the cleavage of his dressing gown and onto his dark chest.

After a while Mary asks him to help her up to a sitting position. Hawk does so, plumping and propping the cushions behind her. She leans slightly forward. 'Take it off,' she says slowly. Hawk sees that her Waterloo medal hangs from her neck on its gold chain. 'Keep it for Victoria, give it to her when she comes of age. Tell her how it come about, that it's luck beyond good luck, much, much more, it's her great good fortune.'

Hawk wipes his tears on the sleeve of his dressing gown and reaches over and slips the chain over Mary's head. 'Mama, I will tell her what it meant to you.'

'Tell her about the birds, the rosellas,' Mary says, now almost breathless.

She is silent for almost half an hour and Hawk regains his composure. Every once in a while he can feel pressure from the hand he holds, as though she is about to speak, as though she is gathering her final strength. Then with what must have taken an enormous effort of will, she suddenly sits bolt upright. 'Don't trust the bastard,' she shouts. 'Don't never trust him, yer hear!' Mary, exhausted, collapses back into her pillow.

'Who, Teekleman?' Hawk says scornfully. 'I never did, Mama.'

Mary's eyes open in alarm. 'No! Not him, David, David Solomon!' With this last great effort she closes her eyes and appears to fall asleep.

Around the middle of the afternoon she wakes, though she seems weaker still, barely able to talk. Hawk has sent for Ann Solomon, Ikey's youngest daughter, who at sixteen had left Hannah to be with her father and who has since been cared for by Mary, lacking for nothing and now on a generous pension for the remainder of her life. Ann says her tearful farewells to Mary, of whom she has always been most fond. After her departure Mary calls for Hawk and soon afterwards, with her hand clasped in his, she loses consciousness. Just on sunset, she sighs softly and passes away. Mary has achieved in death what she'd always done in life, gone about things without too much fuss and carry-on.

Hinetitama and the servants will ever afterwards tell how upon the very moment of Mary's death the garden is filled with flocks of emerald rosellas, their terrible screeching rending the air, so that the children and the servants run about with their hands to their ears. The small green parrots land in their many hundreds, some will later say in their tens of thousands, a huge spreading mass of bright emerald and yellow covering the entire surface of the roof and shrouding the surrounding trees and bushes in a whirring of bright feathers. They remain for a full hour, then as suddenly as they've arrived, they depart, leaving the air behind them so still that no one dares be the first to break the silence.

Martha Billings, the kitchen maid, swears on her life that the following morning when she went out into the garden at sunrise, not a single rosella passed overhead. She declares ever after that the little emerald green parakeets changed their path of flight and were never again seen during her time in the big house.

Mary's good luck, her great good fortune, has followed her to the grave, where Hawk later speculates she will lie forever beside Hannah Solomon, quarrelling ceaselessly and giving each other what-for. Though the both of them, he knows, will take time off to lay down the law to a hapless and fervently protesting Ikey. 'Oi vey, I must have a little peace, my dears, a portion of quietitude from your combined vexations, conniptions, quarrelsomeness and cantankery. God forbid I should live through all of eternity in the company of two such raucous and spleenful harridans!'

Chapter Four

HAWK, TEEKLEMAN AND HINETITAMA

Hobart 1892–1893

Mary has left everything to Hawk, that is all but the ten per cent of her fortune bequeathed to Ben and Victoria, the income from it going to Hinetitama until Victoria reaches the age of thirty and Ben thirty-two. Mary failed to explain this disparity between the two ages and no mention is made of it in the document drawing up the trust deed.

Hawk can only assume that Mary believed Victoria was to be favoured. She'd often enough in his presence declared that Victoria was, as she put it, 'the one'.

Iron Mary did not believe in the God-given right of the male gender to take control, leaving the female to fetch, carry, nurture and nourish. She constantly championed a woman's right to look to her own affairs and never relinquished any of her personal power to the opposite gender. She understood the principles of construction as well as any foreman builder and woe betide any carpenter, cooper, brickie, plumber or engineer who tried to pull the wool over her eyes. In matters of accountancy her abacus threatened any tendency to be careless and she knew her beer and its chemistry as well as any brewmaster in the land. While she left the supervision of the company's hops and barley farms to Hawk she nevertheless could gauge the quality and price of the crops as an expert. Iron Mary's querulous eye was everywhere to be found.

It was this fierce sense of independence that led to her constant disparagement and often even to outright hatred. The malevolence felt towards her came not only from the business community in the colony, but also from the chattering females in its society, who saw her as having betrayed her gender. The exceptions were those who worked for Mary, who knew they were better treated and their families more secure than in any other form of employment available on the island. Iron Mary was hard, but she was also fair, there was never any ambivalence about her, you always knew where you stood.

She had even carried the notion of female financial responsibility through to Hinetitama, though she believed her granddaughter practically incapable of counting the change in her purse. Mary made her the trustee for the children's legacy, knowing it was a fairly harmless gesture. Hinetitama could never get her hands on the principal sum while receiving a considerable independent income from it. In her will she had written: *Though you know nothing of bookkeeping, it will be good for you to be charged with this small duty in return for the income it brings you.*

Mary's funeral proved to be one of the biggest yet to be held on the island, though it turned out to be a quite different affair to the one originally intended by Hawk. He decided to give the brewery workers a half-day holiday, informing them they were not duty bound to come to the funeral but that a picnic would be held for their families. However, the workers formed a delegation to ask if they might attend the funeral instead. It was an indication of how they felt about Mary and so Hawk turned what was to be a picnic into a wake. The servants in the big house were invited as well as those publicans and their wives who wished to be present. This was simply a gesture of goodwill, publicans and their wives are seldom included in events of most kinds.

Hawk knew those businesses that depended on the Potato Factory for part of their livelihood would show up at the funeral in their Sunday best. Altogether, he hoped attendance would be kept to a minimum, but now with the workers asking to be at her graveside, it would give things the common touch she would have liked. Mary would have approved of her own people seeing her off without too much of a fuss.

However, Hawk had underestimated the effect her life had had on the people of Hobart and the small towns beyond it. On the day of the funeral the early morning ferries and boats from the outlying districts up and down river were packed and the country roads unusually busy. By noon the common folk had gathered along the route from St David's to the cemetery, removing their caps and bowing their heads as the funeral cortege passed them by. Many wore black armbands or bonnets and it became obvious they had come to say goodbye to Mary Abacus, who, despite her enormous wealth, had retained her common touch and, unlike most of the so-called nobs on the island, never concealed her convict origins. She had given them cottage hospitals, schools and soup kitchens, made work available to the poor and created a widows' pension fund. Wherever a tied pub existed there would be an annual Christmas party for the children of the town or suburb, where no child went without a feed and a gift at Yuletide and, as well, took home a quart bottle of Tommo & Hawk Ale to their parents. She endowed the orphanage and educated and apprenticed its children, finally allowing them jobs in her various enterprises. Half the brewery workers thought of her as the nearest thing they would ever know as a guardian and now they lined the streets. Scarcely a person in the crowd hadn't in some way or another been touched by the little cockney lass who had been transported to the Fatal Shore sixty years before.

The plain folk knew they'd lost someone who could never be replaced in their affections. The *Hobart Mercury* reported:

Hats and caps were removed from the heads of the men and there were copious tears to be witnessed under the bonnets of the women lining the streets to the grave yard. Not an inch of standing space appeared to be available for a hundred yards all about the site of the grave. A great many of the common folk brought informal floral tributes of their own, small bunches and single blooms from their gardens, even wildflowers picked along the lanes. Many brought a single potato as an acknowledgment to her humble beginnings. With due solemnity, they later placed these tributes upon the grave to form a mound of blossom well beyond six feet in height. Mary Abacus never slept under a softer, more perfumed quilt.

There was even talk of the governor coming to the funeral service, but this proved to be a false rumour. Chasms in Tasmanian society were too wide even for Mary to leap, or as Lady Teresa was heard to say at a tea party she attended on the day of the funeral, 'One does not lift one's skirt to step *into* the gutter.'

Hawk, long accustomed to working together with Mary, has none of the usual male reservations about training Victoria to the task of taking over with her brother. Although she is still a small child, Victoria has shown an intelligence above that of Ben, who seems normal enough in all respects, his natural gifts no more than might be expected from a small boy of seven who rides his first pony.

However, Hawk does not see himself as a mere caretaker, preserving Mary's life's work intact for her great-grandchildren to inherit. He has different plans for the Potato Factory which he modestly and correctly believes he has helped to build.

For some time he has realised there is little chance of expanding their interests much further in Tasmania. Scarcely any sizable enterprises are left in which the Potato Factory does not have a finger in the pie. Mary had often talked of opening a brewery in Melbourne, though she knew that Hawk would need to be there to supervise it and she was reluctant to have him away from her. Now he thinks this may well be the way to go in the future.

Hawk, fulfilling Mary's wishes, allows Hinetitama to purchase a home of her own in Sandy Bay and she and Teekleman and the two children move out of the big house, taking four of the female servants and a gardener and stable hand with them.

Thinking he will be moving to Melbourne for several months at a time, Hawk does not wish to buy or build a new home for himself and the big house is much too large for his needs. Retaining Mrs Briggs the cook and Martha Billings as housemaid, he joins Ann Solomon, at her insistence, in Ikey's old home in the centre of town where she has continued to live after her father's death. It is simply a convenience, two people who have always known and enjoyed each other's company in the most platonic way for the best part of their lives, but, of course, it sets the tattletales a-chattering.

Ann's house in Elizabeth Street, though designated a cottage, is large enough for them both, with Hawk taking the upstairs rooms where the ceilings are sufficiently high to prevent him from having to stoop and Ann the ground level where there are rooms as well for Mrs Briggs and Martha. Mary's house is converted into a maternity hospital where company workers' families receive free treatment.

The transfer of power and authority to Hawk is surprisingly smooth. Even the acceptance of him as their new adversary by the other brewers and the business community sees not the slightest reduction in their malevolence. A nigger in charge of the Potato Factory is only fractionally an improvement over an independently minded woman.

Mary, who kept most things close to her chest, has always made Hawk the exception and he knows and runs the business well, seeking among his employees and elsewhere for men, and even women, who can be trained to higher positions. Hawk is an altogether more trustful and benign authority at the helm of the Potato Factory.

However, things do not transpire as well on the family front. Four months after Mary's death Mrs Briggs returns late one afternoon from Sandy Bay where she has spent her Thursday afternoon off visiting her friend, Mabel Hawkins, Ben and Victoria's nanny.

Ann Solomon will be out in the evening to a whist drive, a card game with old friends whom she never fails to join on the same evening every week. Thus, it is agreed that Mrs Briggs is not required to prepare a hot dinner for Hawk and may add a quiet evening to her afternoon off. Hawk is happy to be served a cold collation on a tray in his study upstairs. On this particular Thursday, when Martha is sent upstairs with the tray, she is instructed by Mrs Briggs to ask Hawk if he will see her after he has taken his meal.

'Now this is how you says it,' she carefully instructs Martha. 'Sir, Mrs Briggs has a matter o' concern to your good self, which she 'opes to see you about at your convenience, but hopefully after you've taken your dinner tonight.' The cook looks at Martha doubtfully. 'Shall I say it again, or does you understand it? G'arn, say it just like I said.'

Martha repeats the message without missing a word and Mrs Briggs nods her approval. 'Remember, *a matter o' concern to your good self*, that bit be most important, I don't want Mr Hawk thinking I'm bringing him me own troubles.'

'What's the matter o' concern?' Martha asks fearfully. 'Is it something I've done?'

'I'll thank you to mind your own business, my girl. No it ain't, the world don't revolve around you, you know. Though if you're going to be a stickybeak, we might soon enough find something to your disadvantage, 'aven't I seen you ogling Young Benson?'

'Benson!' Martha exclaims. 'Do us a favour! I'll not have nothing to do with him, he's an orphan an' all.'

'So were you!' Mrs Briggs exclaims, surprised.

'Takes one ter know one, don't it?' Martha sniffs, then lifting the tray she leaves the kitchen with her head held high.

Hawk agrees to see Mrs Briggs immediately after he has eaten and when Martha returns to take his tray he asks her to tell the cook to bring a fresh pot of tea and two cups.

He makes Mrs Briggs sit down and pours the tea himself. Then with milk and sugar offered and accepted, he does the same for himself and leans back in his chair, lifting up the cup and saucer. He brings the cup to his lips and takes a sip. 'Now then, about this matter of concern to myself, Mrs Briggs?' Hawk says, smiling.

'Mr Hawk, I hope I ain't interfering in what's thought to be family and none o' my business, but I've been with you and Mistress Mary nigh thirty years . . .'

'Of course not, Mrs Briggs,' Hawk interrupts, 'you *are* family. What is it you wish to say?'

'Well, sir, it's about Miss Heenie, she's been beaten most severe.'

'Beaten?' Hawk asks, shocked. He leans forward and puts his cup and saucer down on the table beside his chair. 'By whom?'

'Mr Teekleman, sir.'

'The Dutchman? Has Dr Moses been called?'

'No, sir, Miss Heenie will not allow it.'

'Who told you this?'

'Mrs Hawkins.'

'The children's nanny?'

'Aye, she's the only one allowed in Miss Heenie's bed chamber.'

'Does she think the doctor is needed?'

'No, sir, Mrs Hawkins knows something of nursing and says it is a matter o' bruises, nothing broken. Miss Heenie is mending well enough, but waits until the marks are gone.'

Hawk leans back somewhat relieved. 'Now tell me, what precisely happened?'

'Miss Heenie's 'usband come home last Monday dead drunk and she and him had a devil of a row.'

'What time was that?'

'Near on midnight. Mrs Hawkins says they was all asleep like and were wakened because o' the shouting and blasphemy.'

'Did anyone get up and go to her?'

'Aye, Mrs Hawkins, she's ever the brave one. But when she got to her bed-chamber door and asks polite if everything be all right, Miss Heenie, who she can hear crying and sobbing, stops and shouts out she's to go back to bed at once. Mrs Hawkins says there were an empty brandy bottle left outside the bed-chamber door.'

'Thank you, Mrs Briggs. I am most grateful to you. I'd be obliged if you'll not speak of it to anyone.'

'No, no, o' course not, sir. And Miss Heenie's servants, they's all been in the family awhile and knows the same, to keep stum.'

Hawk expects the cook to take her leave, but Mrs Briggs makes no attempt to do so.

'Sir?'

'Yes? Is there more I should know, Mrs Briggs?'

'I can vouch for Mrs Hawkins, I've known her all me life, a sainted woman if ever I saw one, but Young Benson he says Mr Teekleman . . . he's been seen in Wapping.'

'In a public house? But that is his job?' However, Hawk knows it is a foolish thing to do. Wapping is no place to be at night and Teekleman would not be expected to visit a pub in its precinct after sunset. In fact, he is forbidden to do so by the company, one of his predecessors having been robbed and stabbed to death in its dark felonious streets some years back and another, not that long ago, robbed and badly beaten. The public houses in this notorious slum district are territorial, places for gangs and villains to congregate, and are not for outsiders after dark.

'No, sir, it weren't in a public 'ouse,' the cook's eyes grow suddenly large and her voice comes down to almost a whisper. 'It were a *gaming den*!'

'What, playing at cards?'

'I dunno, Mr Hawk, a gaming den, that's all what the lad said.' Hawk can see from Mrs Briggs' wide-eyed explanation that the two words 'gaming den' conjure a depravity in her mind almost beyond anything she can comprehend. A place of dark corners, scurrying rats, toothless old drunkards, filthy, scabrous harlots with their bodices ripped down and murderous villains and cutthroats, the detestable dregs of the seven seas.

James Benson, Mrs Briggs' informer, is one of Mary's numerous rescues from the orphanage. A young bloke, street-wise like all of his kind, he is responsible for stabling and grooming Hawk's thoroughbred and taking care of his sulky, bringing it around to the house each morning. During the day he acts as personal messenger at the brewery and, when he's not busy with Hawk's needs, he is expected to do odd jobs around the house. He has only recently replaced Old McDougall, a long-term family retainer who passed away a fortnight before Mary. Benson is considered by Mrs Briggs to be a bit too cheeky and forward for his own good and has not yet earned her trust, which Hawk knows is likely to take him several more years, if ever. It is because of this that she offers Benson's information to Hawk somewhat tentatively.

'Wapping?' Hawk repeats.

'Aye, that's where 'e said it were, sir.'

If Young Benson's information is true then Slabbert Teekleman has reverted to being his old self. Hawk hopes that it is only an aberration, done on the spur of the moment or as a gesture of bravado when he is drunk and no longer possessed of a natural sense of caution.

While Hawk hasn't yet thought out the consequences of the Dutchman's actions, a husband's right to beat his wife, or even to get totally drunk occasionally, is not a heinous crime in Hobart society. Or in any prevailing society for that matter, provided always such an incident may be brushed under the carpet and doesn't get out into the public domain except as an occasional whisper at a ladies' tea party. The shame of having beaten your wife does not lie in the beating itself, but in the fact that it is something the common people do and is therefore altogether too plebeian. Or as the French might say, it is simply *de trop*, a black mark against one's good standing in the social register.

Hawk well knows that Hinetitama is quite capable of having instigated the fight when her husband proved to be drunk beyond his normal fairly benign state of inebriation and, provided she is not badly hurt, which doesn't seem to be the case, it may be difficult for him to interfere.

The gambling in Wapping concerns him the most. Hawk has a

morbid fear of gambling and its consequences. With the sad life of Tommo always in his mind, he knows that gambling and ardent spirits do not sit well together and the results of combining brandy and cards are almost always disastrous. He can only hope, when he speaks to Teekleman, that it has occurred on this single occasion, the result of a flight of fancy by the Dutchman, and not a deliberate intention, arrived at in a state of sobriety.

Despite Mary's instructions, the ever fair-minded Hawk has not opened the envelope with the black seal left in her office safe. Teekleman has behaved commendably in the past five years and Hinetitama seems happy to remain with him, her wild nature somewhat becalmed by the advent of the children and her temperate surroundings. She has latterly been given the responsibility of overseeing the running of the new maternity hospital, a task Hawk feels sure will utilise her talents as a nurse while keeping her happily occupied.

The Dutchman, for his part, has sired two healthy children and kept his side of whatever bargain he and Mary made. As a result he has sent her contented to her grave, the future of the Potato Factory assured. Whatever it is that Mary held against the Dutchman has either proved to be highly successful in containing his baser instincts, or Teekleman has decided to reform of his own accord. Hawk sees no point in meddling with the past while the present seems nicely intact. Perhaps the only alarming thing about the Dutchman is his stomach, which continues to enlarge to the point where he looks like a perambulating fermentation cask.

Teekleman's rapidly expanding girth seems of no concern to Tommo's daughter. It is, after all, a traditional sign of prosperity among the Maori and an indication that a man is being well cared for by his wife. Hawk tells himself what he doesn't know about the man cannot influence his future judgment, which, as for every other brewery worker, ought to be made on Teekleman's performance and not on his past misdemeanours.

Slabbert Teekleman has risen to be a distribution manager of the brewery. The common name for such a job is a 'cheersman'. A curious job, it entitles him to start at the brewery in the late afternoon where, upon his arrival, he will examine the weekly beer orders made by the various public houses owned by the Potato Factory around Hobart in preparation for his nightly peregrinations.

Over the years, Iron Mary was forced by the rival brewers to build or buy her own public houses as they wouldn't sell her beer in their pubs and successfully bribed or intimidated most of the independents. There was a limit to the number of public houses she could build and, if the company was to prosper, she had to ensure that each of her outlets sold near to its total capacity.

A cheersman therefore has a twofold task, he must be both a bully and a *bon vivant*. It is a task for which the Dutchman is ideally suited, for this ambivalence exists within him. He can be bellicose in the extreme or, if he chooses, he can soon win the approbation of the crowd with the magic of his fiddle playing. As Teekleman increases in size both these negative and positive attributes appear to be enhanced. He is, at once, a bully to be greatly feared and in another guise he seemingly becomes the merriest of company. It is a sweet and sour, hot and cold, merry and monstrous dichotomy seldom found living so conspicuously in one person.

Part of Mary's genius was that she understood this duality in him and cast him in the role of a cheersman. If one of her pubs was not selling the amount of beer expected of it then Teekleman would drop in for a visit. Those publicans unfortunate enough to witness this side of the Dutchman did not easily forget the experience. On the other hand, if a pub succeeded to her expectations, then the publican greatly treasured his visit.

It should be pointed out, in fairness to Iron Mary, that every publican was allowed fifteen per cent of his profits as a means of eventually purchasing forty-nine per cent of his business, a task which should take him about ten years to achieve. Thus it was to his ultimate benefit to increase his sales in what Mary saw as a partnership of mutual profit.

This having been said, she would not tolerate a publican partner who did not give her his very best efforts and a visit by Teekleman in his guise as standover man was the first sign of her displeasure and a warning to the publican to pull up his socks. Eight weeks of poor trading would see him paid out and on the street. The Potato Factory was alone among the breweries in this arrangement, the other brewers using it as yet another example of Iron Mary's stupidity and inability to understand the correct principles of profitable commerce.

Despite the fact that the Wesleyan Women's Temperance

League constantly rails against the company for selling more liquor per Potato Factory outlet than any of the other public houses, Hawk continues the arrangement after her death on the basis that the good it does for a publican and his family far outweighs the bad.

Slabbert Teekleman plays a very fine tune on the fiddle and wherever he goes in his second capacity, a good deal of merriment is sure to follow. He seems to know every jig, shanty and folk song to be sung by the light of the silvery moon and if a new one is presented to him, a few bars sung, even if it should be off-key, he will pick up the tune and present it to the crowd as though it was learned on his grandmother's knee. His fiddle seems to have a magical quality of discovery, constantly surprising with its invention and its ability to make his audience happy. It is as though the bellicose bully is himself, while his fiddle is a happiness of its own, a person quite different in nature to the morose bully who clasps it to the curve of his shoulder.

The Dutchman's entertaining presence in a pub of an evening will guarantee to increase the takings fivefold, while his magic fiddle seems to have the capacity to cause sworn enemies to promise everlasting friendship and send the inebriated patrons home bellowing songs to the moon.

Teekleman the cheersman is always accompanied by Isaac Blundstone, who remains within the crowd buying customers an occasional drink on the house so that a sense of good cheer prevails. He is an expert at picking those among the crowd who might not have the means to hang about, but are potentially among the most roisterous. A drink placed gratuitously in such a person's hands will, he knows, be rewarded by the increased approbation of the crowd and in the greatly improved ambience of the pub.

By closing time, the ex-pug is all sails to the wind and must generally be supported to the coach that comes to pick up Teekleman. It is the last laugh of the night as the Dutchman carries his mate under his arm like a sack of potatoes and unceremoniously dumps him into the coach.

While Blundstone is not in the employ of the Potato Factory, the company willingly accepts the cost of his largesse chalked on the publican's blackboard. The Dutchman himself consumes large volumes of beer as a source of encouragement to others to do the same and, as a further part of the entertainment, he will challenge any man to a chug-a-lug, where, it is claimed, he has never been beaten. The presence of both men can substantially increase the takings for the night and is as happy an arrangement as the two of them can imagine while, at the same time, maintaining goodwill and *bonhomie* with the delighted publican.

Perhaps, after all, Mary was right, some people need only to be offered a second chance to grab the nettle and make good. Hawk hears her voice plainly in his mind, 'We can all reform if we are fortunate enough to get a second chance.' He wishes only that her faith in the capacity of humans to turn over a new leaf might have proved as true for his precious twin, Tommo.

'Have Mrs Hawkins or the other servants noticed any change in Mr Teekleman's habits?' Hawk now asks Mrs Briggs.

'Abits, sir?'

'You know, his routine, his comings and goings from the house?'

'I don't think so, sir. He comes 'ome, takes his dinner with Miss Heenie and then goes out, returning very late, it's what he's always done.'

Hawk, of course, knows this to be true. It is said by some that the Dutchman's work brings him a great deal of pleasure in both its aspects, as enforcer and clown, but with the former giving him the greater satisfaction. Though nobody can deny his almost inhuman capacity for ale, and while he may get merry enough when he has imbibed a skinful sufficient to sink six men in a jabbering heap to their knees, he is never said to be out of control or dispossessed of his wits.

'So what was the difference in his disposition on his return home late on Monday night? I mean, apart from the beating?' Hawk asks the cook.

'Don't know nothing about his dispo . . . dispo . . . whatever, sir. Mrs Hawkins says they was all asleep like and were woke up because o' the shouting and blasphemy and then the screams and sobbing from Miss Heenie.'

'And that was the same night Benson saw him in Wapping?'

'I can't rightly say, sir, he didn't mention what night it were.'

'Thank you, Mrs Briggs, I am truly grateful to you for coming to see me.'

Mrs Briggs rises from the leather armchair. 'Thank you, sir, shall I leave the pot? I'll bring you a fresh cup.'

'No, no, take it,' Hawk says absently, then sees that he has allowed the cup resting on the small table beside his chair to grow cold. The cook is on her way back downstairs when Hawk calls out to her. He hears her ponderous tread as she turns and climbs the three or four steps she has already descended, then her head pops around the door.

'Yes, sir?'

'Tomorrow morning when Young Benson arrives with the sulky, be so kind as to ask him to come up and see me.'

Hawk sits for some time after the cook has left. His first instinct is to take a cab to Sandy Bay and call on Hinetitama. But it is already well after eight o'clock and his commonsense tells him there is little he can do until the morning. He knows sufficient of Tommo's daughter to decide that discretion is the better part of valour, to go around and make a fuss will most probably create an even bigger one. Hawk thinks she is more likely to take her husband's side than his. Despite Tommo's daughter having mellowed somewhat, scratch her skin and underneath is the tiger she ever was. He'll have to approach things somewhat delicately or she'll be likely to send him away with a flea in his ear.

The following morning when Young Benson comes up to his study Hawk questions him closely. 'On how many occasions have you er . . . seen Mr Teekleman in Wapping at night, Benson?'

Benson, cap in one hand, scratches his scalp, thinking a moment. 'Can't rightly say, Mr Hawk, sir.'

'Once . . . twice maybe?'

'Oh no, it be more than that, they's regulars.'

'They? You mean Isaac Blundstone?'

'Aye. But it's late, see, and Blundstone slumps in the corner too pissed to even fart. It's the Dutchman what plays alone.'

'Plays what, Benson?'

'Poker, sir, and euchre.'

'A game between friends maybe, nothing serious, eh?'

Benson grins. 'Not on your bleedin' nelly, sir! It's Benny the Mill what runs it. I wouldn't say it were what you'd call a friendly game.'

'Benny the Mill?'

'Ben Mildrake, sir, a proper villain.'

'Mildrake? But he's in prison, isn't he?'

'Aye, don't make much difference, school's his, he's still the boss cocky on his patch, the dockside half o' Wapping, Andy Handshake runs the top half.'

'Andy Handshake?'

'Another proper villain, sir, Andrew Hindsheek, but they calls him Andy Handshake.'

'Benson, as a matter of interest, how do you come to know all this?' Hawk now asks.

'Cockatoo, sir. Gets me out o' mischief, keeps me out the pub.'

'What, watching out for the law?'

'Nah, law don't come into Wapping at night, sir. Big game, lots of gelt about, there's villains what wouldn't hesitate to 'elp 'emselves given 'arf a chance.'

'Villains watching out for villains, eh?'

Benson shrugs, and then by way of further explanation adds, 'Wapping, sir. It ain't the nicest place.'

'Benson, I want you to stay stum, say nothing, not even to Cook or Martha, but keep your eyes skinned, let me know when Teekleman comes and goes and whether he wins or loses.'

'The first, that's easy, he ain't of a size to be easy missed, but I dunno about the take home. I'm outside on the corner, a cockatoo, I ain't in the room where they plays, nor wants to be. I keeps me nose clean, less you know the better with them lot, know what I mean, sir?'

'Very wise. Well, do your best, there'll be a sov in it for you.'

'Yes, thank you, sir, Mr Hawk, I'll be waiting with the sulky. Will we be going to the brewery, sir?'

Hawk nods and the young man takes his leave. 'He's sharp enough,' Hawk thinks to himself, 'might warrant watching.' He thinks to find out how well the young fellow reads and writes and whether he has some arithmetic.

Hawk calls for Teekleman to be sent to him when he arrives at the brewery in the late afternoon. A few minutes past the four o'clock smoko whistle there is a tap on the open office door and Hawk looks up to see the huge form of Teekleman almost filling the entire door frame. For all his own great size, the Dutchman must outweigh Hawk by a hundred pounds, which would give him a weight of around four hundred pounds in his stockinged feet.

'Come in, Mr Teekleman,' Hawk calls out. Despite the Dutchman being Hinetitama's husband, Hawk has always kept his distance and addressed the cheersman in a formal manner.

'Mr Solomon, you vant to see me, ja?' Teekleman asks.

'Yes, yes, please, come in,' Hawk points to the ottoman, the only seat sufficiently large to accommodate the Dutchman's corpulence. 'Please be seated.'

Slabbert Teekleman first examines the couch suspiciously, trying to decide whether it will bear his weight. Then he gingerly lowers himself into it, first each cheek in a rocking motion, the leather ottoman sighing beneath the weight of his arse. His thighs follow, either hock clasped and lifted into position with both hands to rest in the correct forward direction, though his knees do not touch, his protruding stomach denying them access to each other. His feet are planted like stout stumps, rooted into the Persian carpet, as if they are his anchor points to keep him seated in an upright position. Finally, in what seems his only spontaneous gesture, he slaps a massive paw down onto each knee. It is a process which has taken a conscious effort and some little time to achieve. 'Ja, that is goet,' he says at last and Hawk senses that a part of the elaborate performance is an attempt to conceal the Dutchman's nervousness.

He rises from his desk and comes to join Teekleman, seating himself in a club chair opposite him. The two big men are strangely contrasted. Hawk, though his waistline has thickened somewhat in middle age, does not carry any excess weight and at seven feet remains an awesome sight. His face, now well lined, wears the fearsome *moko* of his Maori initiation and his hair is beginning to turn grey at his temples. It is an altogether imposing look made all the more incongruous beside the fat Dutchman with his straw-coloured hair, blue eyes and florid complexion. While Hawk could well pass for the devil himself in any children's pantomime, Slabbert Teekleman might appear as a grotesque perspiring cherub bursting out of his grey worsted suit. The one man exudes sheer power while the other is a testimony to the extremes of self-indulgence.

'Mr Teekleman, while you and I have kept our distance from each other, you should know that I admire the way you have conducted yourself since you arrived in Hobart.'

Teekleman looks surprised. 'I try alvays my best, Mr Hawk.'

'You have been a good husband to Hinetitama and father to her children and I am grateful to you for this.' While this last is not entirely true, Teekleman sleeps for most of the day and sees little of his children and when he does shows no interest in them beyond a pat on the head, it serves Hawk's purpose to commend him. Hawk is thought by both Victoria and Ben to be the dominant male figure in their lives and he is secretly grateful for Teekleman's neglect as it allows him easy access to Ben and Victoria. For their part, the children seem to like Hawk immensely.

'Ja, Hinetitama, she is goet vummen,' Teekleman mumbles. He senses that Hawk hasn't simply called him to compliment him on his success as a husband and father. 'She look after me well.'

'Wapping, what do you know of it?' Hawk now asks.

'Vapping?' Teekleman repeats. 'We have two pub there.' He squints curiously at Hawk, 'You know already this?'

Hawk nods. 'Do you visit them often?'

'Ja, sometimes, like all za others,' he lies, then shrugs, appearing to be bemused. 'This is my job, I think so, no?'

Hawk nods again. 'And lately, have you visited them at night?'

'Alvays I visit za pub at night.'

'Yes, yes, but the two in Wapping?' Hawk persists. 'Have you visited them recently?'

The Dutchman is suddenly silent, he averts his eyes and fixes them down onto his massive stomach so that his numerous chins concertina inwards. He doesn't know how much Hawk already knows or to what he should admit. Teekleman finally glances up at Hawk. Chancing his arm he says, 'Ja, sometimes I go zere.'

Hawk has earlier in the day sent Young Benson to the two company-owned public houses in Wapping, the Lark & Sparrow and the Emerald Parakeet, Mary having named both public houses, the one after English birds and the other after her new land, for her great good-fortune birds, her beloved rosellas. Benson enquires whether Teekleman has visited either at night in recent weeks. The Dutchman is not stupid and if he has taken the trouble to do so he will have a sufficient alibi to argue his case for being in Wapping. But Teekleman has been too arrogant, or perhaps grown overconfident about his nocturnal perambulations, and hasn't thought to cover his tracks sufficiently well. Young Benson reports that neither publican can recall a visit from him after sunset and that both seem surprised at the question, Wapping is one of the few exceptions where a cheersman never visits at night.

'Mr Teekleman, we value your services very highly. Wapping is a dangerous place after dark and I must from now on expressly forbid you entering it after sunset on behalf of the brewery. I believe there is an existing order to this effect. I know that a man of your standing in the community would not normally enter a place like that at night of his own accord and I thank you most sincerely for doing so in the line of duty.' Hawk pauses and then adds, 'I want you to know it is not required.'

Teekleman is forced throughout to hold Hawk's gaze and now he averts his eyes and appears to be closely examining the fingernails on both his hands which are spread out on the surface of his enormous stomach. 'You do understand my concern, don't you, Mr Teekleman? I feel quite sure Mistress Mary, had she been here now, would feel exactly the same. You are, after all, a part of our family and we would not knowingly place your safety in jeopardy.'

The Dutchman looks at Hawk, his eyes drawn to narrow slits. 'Thank you, Mr Hawk, I am not afraid this Vapping. It is not so bad.' He tries to hide his anger at being told what to do by the nigger and attempts a smile. 'Ja, I have been places much verse den dis.'

Hawk returns his smile. 'Ah, haven't we all, Mr Teekleman, but we are neither of us as young and I trust not as foolish as we were then.'

'I go now, ja?' Slabbert Teekleman suddenly asks, anxious to avoid making a direct promise to Hawk. He is perspiring profusely even though the temperature in Hawk's office is by no means inclement. He begins to move on the couch, his hands firmly gripping the edge of the seat while his huge arse starts to wriggle as if to gain sufficient momentum of its own to attempt the enormous effort required to rise. With a great heave he pulls himself slowly to an erect position, his legs wobble dangerously and for a moment seem unable to carry the burden thrust upon them, then he locks his knees and they steady as the distribution of his weight is adjusted and, panting from the effort, he finally stands upright, his hands clamped to the small of his back.

Hawk rises from his chair and, making a deliberate effort to keep his voice calm, says, 'I hear your wife has had a small domestic accident but is recovering well?'

He waits for Teekleman's response. The Dutchman seems to be thinking then says, 'It is not so bad, a few bruise, I think she vill be soon better.'

'I am most pleased to hear that, Mr Teekleman. Her welfare is of the utmost concern to me. You will be sure to take good care of her, we would not like her to have another such accident.'

Teekleman, who has been feeling increasingly angry, now seems close to apoplexy at Hawk's implied threat. He has the greatest difficulty concealing his fury and his several chins visibly quake and his face turns the colour of new-baked brick as he struggles to restrain his temper. Hawk has no right to threaten him. He has always hated the schwartzer, who humiliated him in Wellington by buying him off and forcing him to run away with his tail between his legs. Now, like the old hag before him, Hawk threatens to possess his whole life, to rekindle the fear he has lived with for five years.

Teekleman believes that while he had an agreement with Mary, it should not carry over to Hawk. The contract with the black seal has become a life sentence he can no longer endure. He has wealth and protection and even a certain standing in society but remains as much a prisoner as if he was incarcerated in a dank prison cell. It is all too much to bear.

Slabbert Teekleman halts at the doorway and turns to face Hawk, who has returned to his desk and is attending to some paperwork. The Dutchman cannot contain himself any longer.

'Mr Hawk, why you do this, eh? What you want?'

Hawk looks up querulously. 'Do what, Mr Teekleman?'

'Threaten me.'

'Threaten you? How have I done that? I am merely concerned for your safety in Wapping.'

'I think this is *not* true!' Teekleman shouts. 'You know something, eh? Mistress Mary, she speaks to you about za contract?' The moment the word escapes his mouth he knows he has made a terrible mistake, that his temper has allowed him to play into Hawk's hands.

'Contract? What contract is this?'

'A paper,' Teekleman replies. 'Your muthza and me.' His voice is somewhat mollified as he tries to play down the importance of the word he has used.

'I have not seen such a contract,' Hawk says truthfully. 'What does it concern?'

The Dutchman cannot explain any further without exposing himself completely. 'It is nothing.' He gives Hawk a feeble grin, then shrugs his shoulders and spreads his hands wide as if to apologise for his outburst. 'Maybe she loses this paper, eh?' he says. 'I go now, please?'

'No, just a moment, Mr Teekleman!' Hawk says, stepping out from behind his desk and coming towards the Dutchman. 'If you wish I shall look through Mistress Mary's papers?' He halts in front of the perspiring Dutchman, a look of concern on his face. 'An agreement you say? We do not break agreements here, nor do we expect them to be broken. Is there something I should know?'

Teekleman is beaten neck and crop and he raises his hand in a feeble protest. 'No, it is nothing,' he repeats, turning back to the door, though Hawk can sense his enormous frustration, his huge body trembling as he waddles through the doorway.

To a man like Slabbert Teekleman Hawk's subtle approach is a form of persecution he is unable to endure. He would rather feel the sharp lash of Hawk's tongue and have him waving the black-sealed agreement under his nose than to suffer the uncertainty of not knowing how much the nigger knows about his past.

He always thought that Mary Abacus would return the document to him when she came to the end of her life, or that she would destroy it, releasing him from its conditions. When nothing was said for several months after her death, and with no evidence to the contrary, he convinced himself that this was what happened. He was free at last to lead his life without constraint. With Mary's death, Teekleman decided that Hawk was not going to take her place and run his life for him. Now he feels deeply betrayed. After all, he has kept his part of the bargain and sired two great-grandchildren for the old bitch. He has served his sentence and it is time for him to be released.

While he would have been afraid to gamble in Wapping while Mary was still alive, his agreement is not with Hawk. He insists to himself, perhaps not unreasonably, that if he can get drunk on behalf of the brewery he has every right to get drunk on his own account. He will gamble wherever and whenever he chooses and, in the process, choose his own companions. Drunk or sober, he will beat his wife if he desires to do so. It is every husband's duty to keep his wife subservient to him and it is common knowledge that a beating will stop a woman from having ideas beyond her station. It is, he tells himself, a matter of respect for his role as head of the household and he cannot be restrained from exercising it.

Hinetitama may be a Solomon, but she is still a half-caste, a reformed drunk and finally only a woman. He, Slabbert Teekleman, is a white man and a Hollander, so he does not have to prove his superiority. In future, nobody, least of all a nigger and a half-caste, will decide how he will lead his life. He has decided that from here on they can both get fucked.

But now Hawk has pulled him up, reminding him that the old shackles persist. It is simply too much to bear and, as he walks away from Hawk's office, he swears he will have his revenge. Halfway down the long corridor, as he passes the stairs leading to the fermenting tower, he suddenly realises how he can destroy the giant black man without placing himself in danger.

It is quite simply done. He knows that Hawk is due to visit Melbourne where he will explore the business opportunities available and is to be gone for four months. Teekleman will wait until Hawk has departed so that he cannot be present to influence Hinetitama, then he'll chuck in his job with the Potato Factory and announce to his wife that henceforth he will make his living as a fiddler working the various taverns at night. With the income from Hinetitama's ten per cent share of the Potato Factory they are wealthy and there is no need for Teekleman to work. He already has a reputation as an entertainer and those taverns and pubs tied to the Cascade and the Jolly Hatter breweries should welcome him with open arms.

'My dear, you are not singing vunce since you granmutza dies, you come with me, we make together beautiful combination, ja.'

With Mary gone Hinetitama has been lonely. Furthermore, her work at the maternity hospital, where she had hoped to practise as a nurse and midwife, has not turned out as she had expected. While the nurses are prepared to have her in the role of owner or even administrator, they will not accept her as an equal who is prepared to work with a birth or a miscarriage in the same capacity as they do. Though they cannot openly object to her presence, they find a thousand small ways to disconcert her and make things difficult.

This proves also to be true with the female patients. Whether or not they have been put up to it by the hospital staff, the workers' wives profess to feel equally uncomfortable knowing that they are being subjected to the ministrations of a member of the late Iron Mary's family. Despite Hinetitama's lack of affectation, they regard her presence almost as though the formidable old lady is herself delivering their children. As one pregnant wife was heard to say, 'Don't want no rich nob poking around in me pussy.' Her words are repeated with hilarity among the staff and finally reach the brewery itself, where the *double entendre* is a cause for much merriment among the men. When Teekleman hears it told he makes a great pretence of laughing and being seen to be a good fellow who can take a joke, but later relays the remark to Hinetitama who finds herself completely mortified and humiliated.

As Hinetitama has no experience in administration and no pretensions or desire or even the ability to be the hospital manager, she has, with Hawk's help, appointed a matron and a manager, and increasingly has withdrawn her presence, remaining only, at his insistence, on the hospital board.

When Teekleman approaches his wife about joining him as an entertainer she is, as the expression goes, 'ripe for the plucking'. Hinetitama is bored and disappointed and while she loves Ben and Victoria dearly, Nanny Hawkins sees to most of their other needs. Hinetitama still sings to them or tells them bedtime stories of the Maori, but otherwise she is given little cause to share in their lives.

She is a woman of thirty-two with her looks, spirit and libido still retained, but the last two have been much dampened by the routine nature of her daily life. Although she has not lost her affection for her husband, Teekleman's increasing size has rendered him impotent and his nightly absences increase her sense of loneliness and isolation. His recent beating has caused her to believe she has lost his love and, as so often happens, she thinks she must be the cause of his anger and somehow given him reason to beat her.

Hinetitama still works among the poor in the slums of Wapping where, during daylight hours, she is a familiar sight. But whereas her work in Auckland involved rolling up her sleeves and nursing the sick and the frail, the poor of Wapping and some of the poorer part of New Town see her in quite a different light. Before, when she worked among her own people, her work involved bandaging the broken heads of women and children invariably caused by the drunken fists of their frustrated, unemployed and usually de facto husbands and temporary fathers. Acting as a midwife to deliver their babies or trying to keep their half-starved children alive through the vicissitudes of measles and mumps, diphtheria, whooping cough and pneumonia, to name but a few of the childhood diseases rampaging through the slums, she felt then that she was one of their own, who offered them from her heart all she had and they responded by loving her and understood when the grog got the better of her as it had to so many of them.

But here in Hobart, the poor want none of her tender ministrations, she is expected merely to give them a handout. As with the hospital, she is regarded as a member of the Solomon family, rich beyond avarice. Her bandaging, nursing and dispensing of cough syrup and ointment, pills, potions and mustard poultices is scorned as mere pretension, a rich woman playing at being Florence Nightingale. They hold out their hands and ask for money, all the while promising to send for the doctor, but, as often as not, a child remains ill or dies and the money gets spent in the Emerald Parakeet or the Lark & Sparrow. The irony of this does not escape Hinetitama, increasing her frustration.

While she has no illusions about the desperate poor, Hinetitama finds herself increasingly disenchanted with this rich woman's life. It is not one she has chosen for herself and her stubbornness precludes her from accepting it as a compromise role. She has begun to despise money and the life it forces her to lead. She is in this frame of mind when, to her surprise, Teekleman comes down to breakfast. She is accustomed to taking breakfast alone while he usually sleeps to well past noon.

'My God, what is this?' she exclaims as he enters the dining room.

'Morning, wife,' Teekleman says, not explaining and walking over to his chair which has been reinforced to take his enormous weight.

Hinetitama rings the bell to bring the maidservant. 'Do you want something to eat?' she asks her husband.

'Coffee only,' then he points a stubby finger to the loaf of bread on the table, 'and brood.'

Hinetitama cuts two thick slices from the loaf of fresh-baked bread and when the maid arrives orders coffee. 'So what wakes you at this hour?' she asks.

'We must talk, ja?'

'Talk? Haven't done much of that for a while.'

Slabbert Teekleman looks up, his belly is so large that he

appears to be seated two feet from the edge of the table but for his stomach, which touches the edge. 'No job no more,' he announces.

'Whatever can you mean?' Hinetitama asks, confused, reverting to the safety of her elocution lessons and the protection of good grammar.

'I give it away, I tell them to stick it up their bums,' Teekleman says, attempting to sound nonchalant.

'What? What did you give away?'

'Me job?'

'What?' Hinetitama shouts, forsaking all pretence at calm.

'Ja, it is so,' Teekleman says more calmly than he feels. He breaks off a small piece of bread and pops it into his mouth.

'At the Potato Factory? You've given in your notice?'

'No notice, I finish, no more work,' her husband announces, chewing on the bread rather more conscientiously than it merits.

'You saw Uncle Hawk before he left for Melbourne?'

'Him? No.'

'Slabbert, what can you be saying?' Hinetitama exclaims, frustrated. It has never occurred to her that her husband isn't well satisfied with his position as a cheersman. After all, it allows him to drink as much as he wishes, and unlike her, he seems able to hold his grog well enough. With Mary's trust fund they are rich and if he spends all his salary on drinks to show what a great bloke he is, what does it matter? She's long since given up thinking of him as her companion and the father of Ben and Victoria. They haven't made love since Victoria was born. 'You didn't tell me you weren't happy. I could always have talked to Uncle Hawk, he'd give you another job if I'd asked him?'

'He found out I were gambling. He don't like that, ja.'

'Gamblin'? That's the one thing!' Hinetitama exclaims.

'Ja, with Miss Mary. It is true. We agree, no gambling. But not Boss Hawk.'

'What does yer mean? 'Course it's the same.'

'Miss Mary sign the agreement, not him. It be her and me, dat agreement. Ja, I have no agreement mit Boss Hawk.'

'What agreement? You had an agreement with Mary?'

Slabbert Teekleman sighs. 'I come here because she bring me, if I don't she tell the police. I go back to Holland, maybe I am hanged.' He shrugs. 'What can I do?'

'What are you talkin' about, Slabbert?' Hinetitama has

reverted to her natural vernacular which she finds puts her husband more at ease.

'I kill a man. In Holland. Long time ago. She, Miss Mary, she find out this.' Slabbert Teekleman shrugs. 'We have contract, agreement, black seal on the paper. I give you baby, I don't gambling, Miss Mary, she stay stom. She don't say nothing the police.' Hinetitama can see he is plainly distraught.

'Why didn't you tell me?' Hinetitama cries.

'Ja, Miss Mary say I don't tell you.' Slabbert Teekleman shrugs and grins. 'She give me goet job, plenty beer, plenty money.' He pauses and looks at his wife. 'When Miss Mary is alive it's goet, ja?'

'You mean you didn't come to Hobart because you loved me? I mean, on your own like? Because you wanted to see me?'

Teekleman looks surprised that she would have such a stupid notion. 'Me, I am Hollander, a white man, I do not marry willing a Maori.'

Hinetitama, who has lost all affection for Teekleman, is less upset by this pronouncement than she is about Mary's duplicity. She shakes her head in denial. 'She bought you as a bloody stud! Jesus!'

Teekleman chuckles. 'I do goet job, ja? Ben, Victoria, my cock it is goet, ja, of course, I am Dutchman!'

Hinetitama conceals her contempt for him. 'So, Hawk found yer gamblin'? What, you and the creature Isaac Blundstone? What did Hawk say?'

'He say, night-time I don't go Vapping, it is *verboten*.'

'And so you chucked it in? Gave up your job for that?'

Teekleman is suddenly annoyed. 'Ja, Miss Mary can say this, not Boss Hawk! When she die I am free man, I go where I like.'

'Did she say you were free when she died?'

'No. But I think so. I always think this, ja.'

'And Uncle Hawk threatened you with the contract?'

Teekleman doesn't answer, instead he counters with, 'Why he tell me I cannot to go to Wapping, huh? Wapping, dat is where I can play cards, poker, euchre. It is not fair, he go to buggery, ja.'

Hinetitama sighs. 'Slabbert, don't be a fool. I'll talk to Uncle Hawk about the contract, I'm sure he'll tear it up.' She smiles. 'You've done your part, you give us Ben and Victoria, he'll understand. He won't tell anyone about,' she pauses, 'you know, what happened in Holland.'

Hinetitama is too accustomed to the Maori way to be concerned about the supposed murder. A fight between two men of neighbouring tribes will often enough result in the death of one of them without recriminations, the fact that Teekleman may have committed a murder when he was young, sometime in the dim past on the other side of the world, means little to her.

'No! It is finished! No more I kiss his black bums!' Slabbert slaps his hand down hard onto the surface of the table. 'Potato Factory, no more!'

The maidservant enters with a pot of coffee and Hinetitama waits until she has left again. She pours coffee for her husband, handing him the cup. 'So what now?'

Slabbert Teekleman smiles. 'We stay here. But like before, in New Zealand, I play fiddle in the pub, you sing, we are happy, ja?'

'You mean you gamble and I get drunk?'

Teekleman doesn't deny this. 'Maybe, a little euchre, sometimes poker, for fun, ja. Drunk? No, no, you sing only, no grog. I tell the publican.'

Hinetitama laughs, shaking her head. 'Slabbert, it's been eight years since I sung in a pub!' But Teekleman can see that as she recovers from her surprise she is beginning to like the idea.

'No matter, your voice it is so beautiful.' He smiles. 'We can practise, soon it will be goet again, first class, okey-dokey ja, you will see,' he jokes.

Hinetitama thinks of the years ahead of her. The children have tutors, already she sees little enough of them, what between Mrs Hawkins and their lessons at sums and reading. She has given up any prospect of being accepted on equal terms at the hospital and the poor of Wapping don't need her love or compassion. She has come to understand that there is a class system no less deeply felt and practised by the poor. What they will accept with open hearts from their own kind, knowing the struggle it takes to give compassion, they will not take from a rich woman with a hot breakfast under her bustle playing at Christian charity for the sake of her soul.

Hawk comes around whenever he can, but he is very busy and when he does he likes to spend time with the children, who quite plainly adore him to the exclusion of their mother.

Though she belongs to one of the richest families in Tasmania, it isn't exactly a family. Teekleman the Dutchman has no status within it whatsoever, Hawk a nigger, respected to his face with much bowing and scraping, is sniggered at and disparaged behind his back, she is a half-breed, a savage with a doubtful past. What passes for the local society, the nice folk, have snubbed her since her arrival and she has returned the sentiment by ignoring them.

It has been a long, long time since she's had any fun. Whatever she has come to think of her husband, which isn't much, though in the Maori tradition she is bound to him, he still plays a wonderful fiddle and she can still sing in tune.

Hawk will be away for three months or more. If she doesn't like working as a singer in a common public house she can creep back into her safe, cosy, boring nest before he returns and resume her role as the good little mother again.

After all, she tells herself, they don't need the money, they will be doing it for the fun, which is different.

'Do you think we can do it, Slabbert?'

'Ja, of course, my dear.'

'We'll have to practise, very hard. I shouldn't like to make a fool of myself.'

The Dutchman brings the coffee cup to his lips and takes a long sip. His revenge has begun, Hinetitama is back in his grasp. 'Ja, that is goet, Hinetitama,' he says quietly. 'Now you are my wife again.'

The first night they perform together is in the Hobart Whale Fishery and Teekleman's fiddle and Hinetitama's beautiful contralto voice, now mature and rich, complement each other perfectly and fill the public house to the rafters.

It is more a concert than simple tavern entertainment, though the voices of the patrons raise the roof when a shanty they know is performed. Late in the evening when mellowness has not yet turned to drunkenness someone shouts, 'Sing the whalemen's song, "John Rackham"!'

It is said to be the song composed for whalemen by Sperm Whale Sally, a dockside whore of the most sweet temperament and voracious appetite for both food and whalemen. As legend has it, an entire whaling ship's crew could be accommodated by this huge and sweet-singing whore, who could consume a leg of mutton, two plump chickens or a goose and a dozen skinned and lard-roasted potatoes while at the same time drink any man who cared to sit beside her under the table.

It is also said that the gargantuan whore, a great friend of Ikey Solomon, was the true mother of Hawk and Tommo Solomon and died giving birth to them. 'John Rackham' is the song which Sperm Whale Sally composed and first sang in the Hobart Whale Fishery, which has ever since flown the Blue Sally flag in her honour.

The Blue Sally is a flag with a blue sperm whale emblazoned against a white background and was presented to any whaling ship in which a member of the crew had successfully eaten more and consumed more grog in the process than the giant whore and then afterwards still possessed sufficient stamina to receive her favours free of charge.

This little piece of blue and white bunting was considered the greatest of talismans for a successful whale hunt a ship could fly from its foremast and it was carried throughout the Pacific islands, Antarctic waters, South America, the Caribbean, West Indian islands, along the coast of Africa and around the Indian Ocean. The song is therefore of great sentiment to the regulars who frequent the Whale Fishery.

Though the sea shanty has been sung on the seven seas for sixty years it is claimed that it has never been matched in the original voice. Now, with the Dutchman's magic fiddle and the Maori Queen of Song, as Hinetitama has been billed, there is an anticipation that Hinetitama might attempt to equal the original, though of course there are few, if any, still alive who heard it performed by Sperm Whale Sally. If there were, they would be too enfeebled to remember, leastways to make a comparison. Nevertheless, the imagination of the patrons at the Whale Fishery is heightened by the prospect and their pulses are quickened with the thought that tonight they may hear more than they have ever bargained for.

The tavern is brought to silence as the giant Teekleman puts up his hand in acknowledgment of the request. In truth, it has been done at the instigation of Isaac Blundstone, who has prompted a patron to call out. Hinetitama has spent two weeks perfecting the song and so is well prepared to render it.

'Ja, this is a goet, I ask her.' He turns to Hinetitama. 'Perhaps, maybe also, you can sing this song, you think you can remember the words?'

'Yes she can! Yes she can!' the mob chorus back. 'Sing us the Sperm Whale Sally song! Sing "John Rackham"!'

Slabbert Teekleman raises his hand for silence. Then when the pub grows quiet again, though this is not achieved without some effort from the more sober among the crowd shushing those who are not far off drunkenness, Teekleman announces, 'Ladies and gentlemen, I give for you, Princess Hinetitama, the Maori Queen of Song!'

There is much applause, whistling and encouragement, for Hinetitama is, in herself, a curiosity, a Solomon by birth and a member of the richest family in Tasmania who is to sing for them in a common public-house entertainment. Many of the patrons have brought their wives and some of their children who crowd against the wall at the back near the doorway.

Hinetitama acknowledges the crowd. 'Thank you, thank you,' she says, 'I shall try to sing this lovely shanty, I don't know that I can do it sufficiently well and I beg you all to help me please.' Hinetitama has become so accustomed to speaking correctly and she knows she must sound quite the toff to the crowd, but she does not revert to her original accent, knowing it will be seen as an affectation.

She is wearing her brightest gown, an off-the-shoulder velvet in cerise, a bright clear red which shows off the light brown skin of her shoulders and arms to perfection. The hairstyle, worn in the modern idiom, is a swept-up look, gathered like a wide garland about the circumference of the head, with the hair smooth and tight pulled from the centre of the scalp, and turned back and tucked under at the peripherals. But she has ignored this flight of fashion and wears her hair in the traditional Maori style, combed smooth, straight and shining to the waist, a raven-dark cascade which shows not the slightest trace of grey. She wears a double tiara of gardenia flowers, and her lips, left in their natural state, are almost the exact match of her gown. She is still an attractive woman and there are many in the crowd, not all of them men, who speculate how ever Fat Slab, the Dutchman, can have captured such a fragile beauty. There are some among them, with several drinks too many below their belts, who crudely speculate that he must surely crush her, if ever he can get it up sufficient to mount her for a smooey. Another remarks that, with his great gut interfering, his plunger could never hope to reach her pouch.

'You must sing the chorus with me,' Hinetitama appeals to the crowd. 'I shall sing it now, so that you may recall it.' She glances at Teekleman, who takes up his fiddle, and to the first strains of the chorus she begins to sing in a fine, clear voice.

So take up your doxy and drink down your ale
And dance a fine jig to a fine fishy tale
We'll fly the Blue Sally wherever we sail
And drink to the health o' the great sperm whale!

Hinetitama repeats the chorus twice so those who do not know it, though there are not too many from the sound of the response, may learn the words. Then to the opening accompaniment of Teekleman's fiddle, which appears to be in most glorious form, she begins to sing 'John Rackham'.

Come gather around me, you jack tars and doxies
I'll sing you the glorious whaleman's tale
Let me tell you the story, of death and the glory
of Rackham . . . who rode on the tail of a Whale

It started at dawn on a bright Sabbath morning
When Lord Nelson's body came 'ome pickled in rum
Every jack tar mourned the great British sailor
And drank to their hero as church bells were rung

I be born to the sound o' the bells of St Paul's
Where they buried the sealord all solemn and proper
That very same day harpooner John Rackham
Rode the tail of a whale around Davey Jones' locker

The watch up the mainmast gave out a great shout,
'A six pod to starboard all swimming in strong!'
So they lowered a whale boat, harpoon gun and line
Three cheers for the crew then the whale hunt was on

John Rackham, he stood to his harpoon and line
'Row the boat close, lads, 'til we see its great chest
Steady she goes now, keep the bow straight
Or this great fearless fish will bring all to their rest!'

The boat's bow, on a crest, held still for a moment
Sufficient for Rackham to make good his aim
Then the harpoon flew screaming to carry the line
And buried its head in a great crimson stain

'Steady now, lads, let the fish make his dive
Then he'll turn for the top and the fight'll begin
Ship your oars, boys, take the ride as he runs
For the Sperm has a courage that comes from within'

Ten fathoms down the fish turned from its dive
As the harpoon worked in, on the way to his heart
Then he spied the boat's belly directly above him
And he knew they'd pay for this terrible dart!

Fifty tons rose as the fish drove like thunder
Like a cork in a whirlpool the boat spun around
The jaws of the whale smashed through its planking
And the sharks made a meal o' the pieces they found!

John Rackham was saved as the fish drove him upwards
He found himself up on the nose of the whale
With a snort he was tossed sky high and then backwards
And landed most neatly on the great creature's tail

'Let me live! Master Whale, I've a child to be born!
Spare my life and I promise to name it for you!'
'That's a fanciful tale,' cried the furious whale
'But how can I know what you say will be true?'

John Rackham he pondered then started to smile
'Not only its name, but its soul to you too!
And we'll make a white flag with your picture upon it
A great sperm whale emblazoned in blue!'

The great fish turned and swam straight to the ship
With a flick of his tail threw him safe in a sail
Then the deadly dart finally pierced his great heart
Now we fly the Blue Sally to honour the whale.

'Everybody now, one last time!' Teekleman shouts. The crowd, flushed by the joy of their own singing, respond even more fulsomely to the final chorus.

So take up your doxy and drink down your ale
And dance a fine jig to a fine fishy tale
We'll fly the Blue Sally wherever we sail
And drink to the health o' the great sperm whale!

There is thunderous applause and much stomping as the final chorus is completed, it has been most beautifully sung and those present cannot imagine how it could be better rendered. Hinetitama is flushed with the excitement and the success of the performance and she is happy beyond words for she has been rescued from a life of tedium and frustration.

Folk crowd around her to offer their congratulations and it is then that Isaac Blundstone, at Teekleman's instigation, places a double of gin in her hands. It is the first drink Hinetitama has had in eight years and as the perfumed liquor slips down her throat her entire body seems to come alive.

Chapter Five

HAWK, DAVID AND ABRAHAM SOLOMON

Melbourne 1893

Hawk arrives in Melbourne on 1 May 1893, the very day of the collapse of several major banks. The banks have long been carrying the euphoric symptoms of gold fever and have finally been struck down by the disease. They have extended credit to too many unlikely projects and explorations devised by dreamers, schemers, believers, confidence men, chancers and those too ignorant to understand what they were doing. The day of reckoning has finally arrived and some of the major banking institutions in the land find themselves victims of their own greed and naiveté. Having over-extended themselves with their incautious lending they are now faced with too many outstanding loans defaulting to have any hope of balancing the books or of continuing to trade. They close their doors to lick their wounds and fail to open them again. Tens of thousands of small depositors lose their shirts and in the process learn that banks are run by men who have no special talent and are as easily infected by opportunity and greed as everyone else. It is a very sobering day for every Australian colony.

Hawk cannot quite believe his luck when he reads in the *Age* that an almost completed brewery project in Ballarat has come to a halt for lack of funds and that it is the collapsed Bank of Victoria which has financed the project. He thinks perhaps that he may be able to bridge the gap and finance the completion and in return be rewarded with a major shareholding in the new brewery.

To his enormous surprise, the company register reveals that the shareholders in the brewery are David and Abraham Solomon. Hawk appoints a firm of accountants to look into the affairs of Solomon & Co. and discovers the Bank of Victoria holds the combined assets of the company against the loan it has given David Solomon to build the brewery. The irony is that among the many harebrained and unlikely schemes the bank has extended credit to, this one has all the hallmarks of a sound investment. It becomes a case of the good collapsing with the bad.

With its line of credit destroyed Solomon & Co. is effectively insolvent and will be forced to declare itself bankrupt as the collapsed bank cannot finance them to completion. They, in turn, now lack sufficient collateral to secure a loan to complete the brewery project from one of the few banks which haven't gone to the wall. David and Abraham Solomon have the makings of a first-rate asset on their hands but for a simple bridging loan and, in the prevailing climate, they have no chance of obtaining one.

The liquidator for the Bank of Victoria will be most anxious to sell the collateral it holds and Hawk finds himself in a position to make them an offer for the Ballarat brewery and also for the entire assets of Solomon & Co. at a fraction of its true value. This will allow the bank with the sale of all the additional collateral it owns from its other loans to eventually pay its own shareholders five shillings in the pound, one of the more creditable performances within the discredited banking community.

Over the years David Solomon has built the grain and timber business Hannah inherited from George Madden into a fair-sized conglomerate that includes wool, coal, timber, mining stock, cattle, barley, wheat and a quite decent portfolio of Tasmanian real estate.

It is an intelligent diversification not entirely dissimilar to the one Hawk and Mary devised over the years. But whereas the Potato Factory has always bought with cash and never taken a loan, David's shrewd business brain has built Solomon & Co. using very little of his own capital. He has financed each new enterprise by borrowing from the banks and using his existing assets as collateral and security against defaulting. In the past he has always retained sufficient assets to recover if a particular project should fail; in effect, never putting all his eggs in one basket.

Though there have been some close calls, the market has always held up sufficiently long enough for him to redeem himself. David seemed fireproof and the bank had come to trust his business judgment and progressively extended his line of credit.

However, this time David has gambled everything to build the most splendid brewery in the colony of Victoria and has been caught well and truly with his trousers down. Hawk, in looking at the prospects for a new brewery in Ballarat, agrees that if it were to be allowed to come on-line, it would have taken Solomon & Co. from a modestly sized conglomerate into the big league. Instead, Solomon & Co. is effectively finished, dead in the water.

Hawk is forced to speculate as to why, as an enormously wealthy and successful man in his seventies, David Solomon would risk everything he has acquired, simply to own a brewery. For a man who has shown such good business judgment it is a surprisingly naive mistake to make.

Then it begins to dawn on him. It is not done out of simple greed as he'd first supposed. The brewery represents something in David's mind of enormous emotional importance. The Ballarat project has the potential to have almost double the bottling capacity of the Potato Factory. The old man simply wished to show Mary Abacus, before she died, that he was superior. That anything the person he hated the most in the world could do, he could do better.

For a businessman as astute as David, this was a childish thing to have attempted. But in some things perhaps we never mature beyond our ability to hate. Hate fostered in the young often brings with it an enormous sense of inferiority, the need to prove oneself in order to overcome the humiliation one has been made to feel as a child. The brewery was not only to be David's ultimate triumph over the adversity of his childhood, but also to serve as a symbol of the fulfilment of his promise to his mother Hannah that he wouldn't rest until he had wreaked her vengeance on Ikey's whore, until he had beaten Mary at her own game.

The day David heard of her passing he flew into a terrible temper, breaking furniture and raging for two days, at one stage invading the kitchen and throwing the pots and pans about, pouring hot soup over the cat and breaking almost all the crockery and glassware while causing the servants to run for their lives. Iron Mary had once again robbed him, cheating him out of his moment of triumph.

With the imminent collapse of Solomon & Co. Hawk instructs his accountants to act as broker and make an offer for all of their assets. While the liquidator may have made more money had he sold each of these ad hoc, the prospect of taking a large debt off his books in one fell swoop is too attractive for him to ignore and he accepts an offer which gives Hawk control of Solomon & Co. at a bargain-basement price. Within three months of arriving in Victoria Hawk has achieved what he'd anticipated might take him three or four years to build or acquire.

On paper it seems to be a brilliant investment. David's assets are soundly based and simply need an injection of working capital to continue to succeed. The ever cautious Mary had accumulated a large number of investments which could quickly be converted into liquid assets. Although Hawk is forced to use a good deal of these to make the acquisitions, he does not stretch his resources beyond anything he cannot cover if things were to suddenly go wrong.

The speculative profit and loss statement shows the new brewery should be in a net profit situation in three years and, had the bank not collapsed when it did, the brilliant David Solomon would almost certainly have pulled off his gamble and paid back his enormous borrowing over a comparatively short period. Ballarat's beer-drinking population is underserviced and, providing the new brewery produces a beer at the right price and suited to the local palate, it is difficult to see how it will not succeed.

In one major move Hawk has established himself as a brewer of some significance in Victoria. The Potato Factory now owns Solomon & Co. lock, stock and barrel and Hawk is in a position to destroy the elderly David Solomon and his son Abraham. For the second time in his life he has David Solomon completely at his mercy.

His intention is to do no such thing. At last Hawk is able to achieve what he urged Mary to do for so long, to make restitution for the money they stole from the Whitechapel safe, with interest added. In fact, the value of the Solomon & Co. assets, if the new Ballarat brewery is included and paid for, is nearly eight times the face value of the original fortune stolen. Hawk calculates that it is at the very least the equivalent of Hannah's fifty per cent entitlement with a decent interest earned on the money over the thirty-eight years since the theft took place. By returning David Solomon's business to him he will have fully satisfied his conscience.

However, the gesture is, to Hawk's mind, too pretentious. There is yet another way which, if taken, will still save the fortunes of David Solomon and his family and serve Hawk's original intention to expand the Potato Factory onto the mainland.

Hawk decides to create a new holding company to be called Solomon & Teekleman under which he will place the Potato Factory and Solomon & Co. as separate identities. The idea is to keep Abraham Solomon as managing director of Solomon & Co. and David as its chairman, while Hawk remains in the same positions with the Potato Factory. At the same time he would hold the chairmanship of Solomon & Teekleman. David and Abraham, Hinetitama and he will own all the shares in Solomon & Teekleman with the combined profits of both companies reporting to it to be divided among the joint shareholders according to their shareholding.

Even in this division of shares, Hawk is scrupulously fair. The Potato Factory is the larger of the two companies though, with the new brewery coming on-line, he estimates by not much more than eight per cent. He calculates the shareholding accordingly. He gives David and Abraham each twenty-three per cent of the shares of the holding company and then converts the ten per cent of the Potato Factory shares owned by Ben and Victoria under the trusteeship of their mother, Hinetitama, into ten per cent of Solomon & Teekleman and the remaining forty-four per cent goes to him.

What this means in effect is that he is the single largest shareholder and his shares combined with those held in trust for the children will always allow his side to control what has now become a giant corporate entity. As the biggest shareholder Hawk appoints himself the chairman of the holding company.

Hawk, going through David's business affairs, sees that father and son are a good combination, with David the developer and Abraham a clear thinker with a cautious mind, his steady right arm.

As David Solomon is already an old man, Abraham, upon his father's death or retirement, will remain as a steady and wise influence in the company, acquiring and building its affairs so the next generation will inherit a conglomerate on a very sound financial footing. Hawk is aware of Joshua, Abraham's six-year-old son, and thinks how well the next generation would be equipped to take over with Ben, Victoria and Joshua sharing the management tasks.

It is all, to Hawk's trusting mind, a nice combination, with David and Abraham running things in Melbourne and himself in Hobart and all of it under his own reasonably benign chairmanship. Ever the peacemaker, he has entirely forgotten the words spoken to him by Mary on her deathbed. 'Never trust that bastard, David Solomon!'

When David learns who owns his company he makes his previous tantrum seem like child's play. 'That nigger bastard! I'll kill him! How dare he! The ignorant black syphilitic bastard! Mary, yes! Mary were a worthy opponent, I hated the bitch, but she was clever! This is the second time that schwartzer has humiliated me! That stupid, dumb whore's son's got the better o' David Solomon!'

Abraham clumsily tries to calm his father. 'But, Father, he's rescued us? Saved us from disaster?'

'Saved us? What you mean saved us?'

'The company, saved from bankruptcy.'

'By a nigger bastard what's going to make us eat shit! You call that saved? You wouldn't know saved if it were jammed up your fat arse!'

Abraham sighs, ignoring his father's insult. 'No, Father, I don't think you're right, he's a good businessman, he sees that it's better to save us than to let us sink. It's commonsense.'

'What do you know, eh? That one's as cunning as the devil, he's stole from us before, now he's done it again, the bastard has humiliated me *again*!' David drops to his knees and starts to sob then as suddenly he stops and throws his head back. 'FUCK HIM! FUCK HIM!!' he screams. 'I SWEAR ON ME GRANDSON'S LIFE I'LL GET HIM! GET EVEN!' Rising, he rushes into the kitchen then outside to the woodpile where he takes up the axe and comes storming back with the heavy axe over his shoulder. 'Out of my way, out my fucking way!' he snarls at Abraham and enters his study, locking the door from the inside.

He remains in his study for three days and with the axe he

progressively wrecks every stick of furniture in it. He accepts only water pushed through a small window and refuses anything to eat. Despite Abraham's constant pleas to come out, it is only after six-year-old Joshua, the apple of David's eye, has cried for several hours outside his study door that David finally emerges.

He is weak from lack of nourishment and the doctor is called and he is given chicken soup and crustless bread and put straight to bed. The doctor recommends that David stay in bed for a week until he regains his strength. But the following morning at half-past six he is up and seated at his usual place at the breakfast table beside his grandson. Since the day he has been able to sit up in a high chair Joshua has taken his breakfast alone with his grandfather.

'Grandpa, are you better now? Why did you break everything? the child asks ingenuously.

'Joshua, my boy, we have lost everything, the schwartzer has taken everything, your grandfather has let you down,' David tells his grandson.

'No, we haven't, Grandpa, I've still got the little wisdoms.' Joshua grins and shrugs. 'So when I grow up I'll be rich, like you said!' The small boy laughs. 'I'll give it all back to you, Grandpa.'

'Rich again? Wisdoms? So much for wisdoms! I am too old and you are too young. That's the only wisdoms we've got!' David brings his hands up to hold his cheeks. 'Oh my God, what shall I do?'

Joshua, seeing his grandfather starting to get upset again, starts to talk. 'Never borrow more than the value of your least important assets,' he declares.

David can't believe his ears. 'And I told you this? I should be ashamed, I don't listen to myself!' he sobs.

Joshua is too young to be aware of the irony of the words he's just recited and begins again. 'When you hire a manager ask him how much he wants, it will always be less than you expect to pay. Then pay him more than he expects in return for owning him body and soul.' Joshua continues, 'Never hire a Jew in case he turns out to be smarter than you or you've married into his family. Roman Catholics have too many children which drives the breadwinner to drink and a drunk can never be trusted to give you a full day's work. Never do business with a handshake, a good contract doesn't have a faulty memory. The eyes in the back of your head must be constantly on the lookout for the knife aimed between your shoulder blades. Hearsay and memory are bad witnesses in a court of law, always write everything down and, if possible, have it signed by the person with whom you are doing business or otherwise a reliable witness.' The small boy stops. 'Shall I go on, Grandpa?'

'Impossible! Impossible! You've learned it all!' David cries, clapping his hands together, real tears now rolling down his cheeks, though he himself doesn't know whether they are from joy at the boy's cupidity or despair at his own impoverished situation.

However, Joshua is enjoying the game and resumes talking. 'If an employee is guilty of doing something wrong in the past, never allow him to forget it in the future. An eye for an eye is what it says in the Bible, but consider a moment, two eyes for an eye, when your enemy is in the dark, he can't hurt you. A bribe only becomes poor business judgment when it doesn't work. On the other hand, a bribe is only a bribe when it's done by somebody else, when you employ it, it is a gratuity in return for something you want. In business a man is always guilty before being proved innocent. Remember, greed is the most important motivation in the human race, forget this and you are out of business quick smart. Revenge is a dish best eaten cold. Never trust anyone except only maybe your mother and even her, think twice and only act the third time, if she is Jewish, the fourth!' David realises that years of breakfast maxims have paid off, the child has learned them as if by rote.

'Enough, enough already,' David cries. 'You are breaking my heart, Joshua!'

Almost from the moment Joshua was born these maxims, and a thousand like them, have filled the intellectual space in the child's mind. David's idea has always been that when his grandson is an adult and forced to make business decisions on his own he will have equipped him with an aphorism for every conceivable situation he might have to face.

Whenever David taught his grandson a new one, he would always end by saying, 'Joshua, my boy, trust nobody except your dog, Spot.' And now, barely stifling his sobs, he repeats the homily and waits for Joshua to complete it.

The child, ever eager to please his grandfather, laughs and claps his hands. 'But always leave a flea under his collar so Spot knows who's the boss!'

It is at this point that Abraham enters the dining room. 'Excuse me, Father, but it is of the utmost importance that I see you immediately.'

David thinks for a moment to send him away, Joshua giving him the first moments of enjoyment since the bank collapsed. Besides it is accepted that his time with his grandchild at breakfast may not be interrupted. But things have changed lately and Abraham's look of concern makes him hold his temper.

'What is it?' David asks, irritated.

'We have a visitor.'

'A visitor? But it is not yet seven o'clock in the morning, tell him to bugger off, come back in two hours.'

'I think you should come, Father, he waits in my study.'

'He, who, why, never mind!' David shouts, slamming his hand down hard onto the surface of the table, but then he rises from his seat and turns to Joshua. 'You're a good boy, Joshua, you've made me proud.

'Who is it?' he now asks Abraham.

Abraham is reluctant to tell his father, afraid that David will not accompany him to his study. 'Father, it is best you see for yourself.'

They reach his study door and David, entering first, very nearly faints at the sight of Hawk seated on the ottoman couch. 'Jesus!' he cries, physically jumping backwards at the sight of the giant black man. 'What the devil!'

Hawk rises, towering over the diminutive David Solomon. 'I hoped we might have a few words, David,' he says, extending his hand, though not expecting it will be taken.

He is not disappointed and his hand is ignored. 'A few words!' David shouts. 'I'll give you two. Fuck off!'

Hawk chuckles. 'No less than I expected, I see you've inherited your mother's charm.'

David ignores Hawk and turns to Abraham. 'What does the nigger want? My blood? Come to gloat, 'as he? Well, you tell the bloody cannibal we'll have no further truck with his sort, we may be poor but we don't 'ave to join him in the gutter!'

'Father, Mr Solomon has a business proposition, one I think may be to our advantage.'

'I'd like to see that when it's got its jodhpurs on!' David sneers. 'What's he want to do, buy the bleedin' 'ouse? He's got everything else!'

135

'I already own your house,' Hawk says quietly.

'Please sit, Father.' Abraham leads David to a chair and then gently pushes down on his shoulders to force him into the leather club chair.

David is fully dressed except that he still wears his bedroom slippers with no hose. He slumps in the deep chair with his chin tucked into his chest, looking directly into his own lap. 'Well, go on, get on with it, nigger!'

'I must remind you, David, that my mother, like yours, was a Jew, that makes me a Jew as well, perhaps a nigger Jew, but still a Jew.'

'And she was also a whore!' David snarls.

'But not a whore mistress, like yours was,' Hawk replies, then smiles. 'I don't expect you to be happy at the thought of meeting me, but I had hoped that, after all these many years, our next meeting might be cordial, albeit not one filled with mutual admiration.' Hawk turns to look at Abraham. 'I'm pleased to say your son is not similarly discourteous. Also, I apologise that I have called on you at such an early hour and without prior notice, but I have business of some urgency to discuss which I believe will turn out to be altogether to your advantage. Perhaps a better outcome than the last time we met.'

David is suddenly transported in his mind to the dark, musty pantry in London where together he and the fifteen-year-old Hawk had opened the safe only to find it was empty but for an envelope addressed to himself. Inside was a gold ring set with a handsome ruby and a note in Ikey's handwriting. *Remember, always leave a little salt on the bread.* The remainder of the fortune had disappeared and, while it has never been traced, David knows with the utmost certainty that somehow Mary Abacus and her nigger boy had contrived to open the safe and steal what he correctly believes belonged to his family.

Now the nigger has beaten him again, humiliated him a second time beyond any possible endurance. Hawk destroyed his prospects as a young man and now he has done so again at the end of his life. He has effectively rendered his entire existence worthless.

'Father, Mr Solomon has a proposition to put to us,' Abraham repeats, 'I think we should hear him out.'

'*See* him out, more like,' David snarls. 'G'arn, fuck off, Hawk Solomon!'

Hawk sighs and removes his half-hunter from his weskit pocket, unclips it from its fob chain and clicks it open. 'You have five minutes to save your company and your arse, David Solomon,' he says quietly. 'If after that you are not willing to hear me out I shall leave you. I had no hand in bringing your destruction about and take no pleasure in it, but I will not again lift a finger to help you.' He removes the watch from its chain and places it on the small table beside the couch. 'Five minutes, gentlemen, and then I'm off to mind my own business.'

A silence follows that must have continued for a good three and a half minutes. Abraham keeps glancing at the fob watch, believing he can hear it ticking away the seconds, though he is too far from it for this to be possible. Another half a minute goes by and unable to contain himself any further he calls, 'Father!'

With less than thirty seconds to go David, restraining his anger, says, 'G'arn then, get on with it, I 'aven't got all bloody day!'

Hawk returns the watch to its chain and restores it into his fob pocket then proceeds to outline the plan he has for the two companies. After he has completed his explanation, he emphasises that David and Abraham would be left to run their own company, provided always it meets with its expected profits and losses and that all major acquisitions are subject to verification from the chairman of the board of the holding company, Solomon & Teekleman.

'That's you! You the board?' David rasps.

'Ah, yes, a board? Yes, well, I daresay we shall have a board, the two of you, my niece Mrs Teekleman and myself, but I shall make the decisions on the simple basis that I control the most shares.' Hawk smiles. 'We shall, of course, discuss whatever is in contention and I shall greatly value your opinions, but the decisions will always be made on the basis of share majorities, whoever might in the future control the majority of the shares will be chairman of the company.' Hawk is thinking that he must keep young Joshua from ever taking over the new holding company.

'Ha, you will be the boss!' David exclaims. 'Just as I thought.'

'Does that surprise you?' Hawk asks him, but David merely grunts, 'And a woman, another damned woman in the picture!'

'You will find this one less trouble than the last,' Hawk says.

'Why, Mr Solomon? Why have you done this absurd and unnecessary act of generosity?' Abraham now asks.

'Ah, it is a long story, Abraham, and I think no longer worth the telling. Let it suffice to say that I do not believe it either absurd or unnecessary. I am most impressed with the manner you and your father have built Solomon & Co. and honestly believe, while you extended your credit with the bank to breaking point, you did not deserve to lose all you have worked so hard to achieve. Quite simply the Potato Factory hopes to expand its interest into the colony of Victoria and eventually throughout Australia, but frankly we lack the top management to do so. I admit I cannot do it by myself. It would seem stupid in the extreme to lose two excellent businessmen who understand the corporation they run simply because of some old enmity between our families. If we cannot be friends then let us be the best of business partners. I assure you, as your chairman, I shall always try to be fair in my decisions and hear you out. But, if you attempt to cheat me, you will find the outcome an unhappy one for yourselves.'

David suddenly looks up and glares at Hawk. 'It's because of the safe, ain't it? The money you and Mary Abacus stole from our family?'

Hawk sighs and for a moment wears an expression of acute exasperation. He knows himself to be as good an actor as David Solomon and so he points to the ruby and gold ring on David's middle finger. 'The only thing I know to come for certain from that safe you are wearing on your finger.' He turns to David's son who has remained standing throughout. 'Well, what say you, Abraham?'

There is a moment's silence when Abraham looks at his father who has always dominated him. He brings his fist up to his mouth and clears his throat. With his heart racing he looks directly at Hawk, 'I accept, sir, your terms are most generous, most equitable indeed.'

'Accept? What? Without me?' David can't believe his ears.

'Yes, Father.'

'Jesus! Me own flesh and blood!'

'Well, that's it then,' Hawk says, nodding towards the seated David. 'I daresay we'll manage quite well without you, David.'

Abraham looks quickly at Hawk. 'No, no, wait a moment, please!' He addresses David, 'Father, be sensible, for God's sake!'

David does not reply, his eyes directed to his kneecaps. Abraham can see that he is near weeping from frustration and anger. While his commonsense has forced him to make a final appeal to his father to accept Hawk's offer, it also gives him a curious satisfaction to see his father with his back so completely against the wall.

David Solomon has always run roughshod over any opposition including Abraham's own cautionary advice, his sheer aggression, bluff and stubbornness often winning the day, when caution would have served him better in the long run. Now this giant black man has him all tied up in knots. For once the bully has met his match and Abraham knows it to be sinful to feel elated at his father's downfall, but he knows that he will always cherish this moment while never again being able to admit it, even to himself.

Abraham Solomon has, of course, heard of the existence of Hawk Solomon, but always as some dark demon, an evil force castigated with the very breath that carries his name. He had no idea that Hawk was Jewish, for David had always portrayed him as the most primitive of savages. Now this huge black man is not only extending an olive branch to his family but also allowing them to recover from disaster, even to prosper again and, what's more, allowing him to personally regain his pride. For the second time in Abraham's life, he has opposed his father.

On the first occasion it concerned Elizabeth, Abraham's sad, disappointed and mostly inebriated wife. When Abraham decided to bring Elizabeth home to meet his sickly mother, half expecting her disapproval, but hoping that by convincing her of his happiness she would understand his desire to marry a gentile, he went to see his father.

Elizabeth came with impeccable credentials except for the most important one of all, she was not Jewish. She was the daughter of the third daughter of an impoverished English lord who had married a wealthy and well-connected Melbourne financier, who boasted of being a 'Fitz', the illegitimate offspring of royalty at some time in aeons past. Her father had subsequently lost all his money speculating in gold shares on the stock market, but because of his wife's lineage and his own pretensions, the family had maintained its social status among Melbourne's better bred while, at the same time, living in relative poverty.

Simply stating that she was a gentile and then presenting Elizabeth's credentials to his father he waited, expecting the worst, but for once in his life he was prepared to stand up to him. To his astonishment, David Solomon had approved of the match after asking a single question, 'Is she a Roman Catholic?'

When told she wasn't, but Church of England he'd seemed unusually enthusiastic. 'Splendid, m'boy, a bit of goy blood can do us no harm whatsoever.' In what was a rare show of affection he'd clapped his son on the back and asked, 'Has she got big tits?'

Not answering, but nevertheless encouraged by his father's approval, the following day Abraham brought his intended home. Leaving Elizabeth to wait in the conservatory he'd entered his mother's bed chamber.

To Abraham's surprise David was seated beside his wife's bed when he entered. This came as somewhat of a shock to him as David's habit was to spend no more than a few moments at her bedside after he'd taken breakfast and when he returned at the end of the day from his office in Bourke Street. Rebecca referred to these visits as 'Papa's passion! A peck in the air, a burp, a fart and always the same greeting, "Ow yer going? Orright? Good! Eat something. Too-ra-loo!"' He would have entered the bed chamber, reached her bed, pecked the air above her head, turned around, spoken, farted, burped and been back out the door before she'd managed a single word in reply.

It was unusual therefore to see David at his wife's bedside in the middle of the afternoon. Abraham had expected to speak to his mother alone and, with the presence of his father, who he assumed must have unexpectedly and untypically come to lend his support, his feelings were mixed. The previous day in David's office he had not talked of loving Elizabeth, nor even of feeling an affection for her, but merely that he had met a girl he liked, a Christian who came from a decent family and he hoped to gain David's blessing to marry her. 'Love' was not a word he knew to use in front of his father, but it was his only hope of success when talking with his mother. Abraham had carefully practised the words he would say to her, but now with his father present, he was afraid they might sound mawkish and pathetic whereupon David wouldn't hesitate to mock him and to make a fool of him in front of his mother. Nevertheless, not one for extemporaneous invention, Abraham decided to plunge ahead with his original plea for her blessing.

'Mama, I have brought someone home to meet you,' he announced shyly, then clearing his throat added, 'Someone I love with all my heart and who it is my dearest wish to marry. Will you give me your blessing, for I cannot do without it, or her in my life?'

Rebecca clapped her hands, delighted at her son's news. 'Oh,

Abie, what wonderful news!' She turned to David. 'To think, all the nice girls I've found for him, the boychick finds one for himself! Her name, if you please?'

'Elizabeth, Mama.'

'Elizabeth?' Rebecca frowned, thinking a moment. 'I don't know an Elizabeth? Not from the reform synagogue, I hope?' She looked immediately suspicious. 'Her surname, if you please?'

Abraham brought his fist to his lips and coughed, 'Fitzsimmons. Mama, she's ah . . . not Jewish.'

Rebecca promptly refused to meet the plain-looking Elizabeth, declaring later that she would rather die than see her only son marry a gentile. She turned and cried loudly to David, 'My son, he wants me to die! I have no time left, but he wants I should die tonight!'

'No, Mama, that is not so,' Abraham cried. 'Give me a chance to introduce her to you, I know you'll change your mind!'

'Not enough boobs to feed a hungry mouse!' Rebecca declared out of the blue, again directing this remark to David. It was true enough, Elizabeth possessed a very small bust, but as his mother was bedridden and had never laid eyes on her, nor David for that matter, Abraham could not imagine how she could have known this.

His mother was a determined woman but she usually submitted to his father's will. He now turned to David for his help. 'Father, I thought . . . ?'

'Stop!' David shouted. 'Not another word! Get rid of the shiksa, you hear! We work with gentiles, we do business with gentiles but we don't marry them! Get rid of the goy!' He looked sternly at his son. 'You hear me, Abraham?' David pointed to the door. 'Out she goes!' Then he added, 'Wait for me in my study after you've sent her home.' Abraham, deeply distressed, hesitated. 'G'arn . . . be off! Oh, and give her a ten pound note for her father, tell him to buy a revolver and use it on himself, he ain't worth a pinch of shit, the stuck up bastard!'

'Thank you, David,' Rebecca cried, taking her husband's hands in both her own and clutching them fondly to her breast. 'I am not long for this world, you must find a nice Jewish girl for Abie before I die, the boy knows from women nothing!'

Abraham, distressed by his mother's stubborn refusal, became even more confused when, upon his return from seeing the tearful Elizabeth to her home, having attempted to comfort her and to assure her that he intended to fight for her, he marched into David's study to have it out with his father once and for all. 'Father, I cannot accept your rejection of Elizabeth,' he cried immediately upon entering.

But before he could continue David held up his hand. 'Sssh! Not so fast, my boy. Not so fast. Close the door. Rejection? What rejection? You have my blessing to marry the girl one hundred per cent.'

Abraham wasn't sure he'd heard his father correctly. 'What? But in Mama's bedroom you . . . ?'

David nodded. 'She's dying, have you no compassion for a dying woman?'

'But why, Father?'

'Your sons will be gentile,' David replied simply. 'It is time we stopped being Jews.'

'Stopped?' Abraham was deeply shocked. 'But we *are* Jews!'

'You are, I am, your mother is, but your children won't be.'

'But Elizabeth could turn, she's agreed to convert. We have already discussed it.'

David looked unblinkingly at Abraham until his son could no longer meet his father's eye. 'She could, but she won't.'

'But Mama? You said yourself, it will break her heart?'

'That's why I wanted to see you, your mother will be dead soon enough.' David shrugged. 'So what's so hard? You'll stay stum until after the funeral.' He gave a philosophical shrug. 'It's not such a long time, just don't shtoop her, you hear? I want your children to be born within wedlock, everything kosher.'

Rebecca died three months later of consumption, much as the family physician had predicted she would. Abraham married Elizabeth and, for the first time in his life, he was truly happy.

When after a year there was no sign of offspring, David started to put on the pressure, demanding that the couple get on with it. When after four years there was still no offspring, David had had enough and he decided Elizabeth was to blame, his son had married a barren woman.

'She must go! Make a settlement, not too much, she has eaten our bread too long for too little!'

But, for the first time in his life, Abraham dug his heels in and stood up to his father and refused. 'Father, Elizabeth is my wife and I love her. If we are not to have children then that's God's will.'

'God's will! God's will! Can't you see the shiksa is too bloody in-bred, she's all dried up inside, look at her tits fer Chrissake!' David, accustomed to having his own way, continued to rant and rave, threatening to throw his son out of the business without a penny if he didn't divorce Elizabeth.

Abraham stayed calm throughout the tirade. 'Father, it's no use, you may do as you wish to me. Elizabeth is my wife and I love her.'

In the end David had no further recourse. There were no substitute heirs in the immediate Solomon family. Ann, his sister, was a spinster and gone over to the other side, Sarah had married and had two children, girls and both quite dotty, not suitable as heirs and unlikely to find husbands, Mark had gone bush on the mainland and was said to have taken an Aboriginal wife.

Abraham remained David's only hope for a grandchild with the unbanished Elizabeth the obstacle.

David, who himself had married late in life, refused to believe that it might be his own son firing blanks. He knew that eventually he would find a way to get rid of Elizabeth. Equally, he was aware that he was already in his sixties and running out of time. His lack of an heir other than Abraham began to preoccupy him to the extent where he grew morbid and introspective.

As often enough happens with men who suddenly become conscious of the fact that their allotted time in this mortal coil is coming to an end, David began to dwell on things spiritual.

In a man as iconoclastic and venal as David Solomon this was a curious notion in itself, but his spirituality took an even more bizarre twist. His son's declaring that their lack of offspring was God's will began to obsess him. Soon he started to believe that maybe it *was* God's will, that he was being punished by a Jewish God for allowing Abraham to marry a gentile.

Though he was wise in the ways of the business world, he was essentially an uneducated and, at heart, superstitious and ignorant man. Reluctantly admitting to himself that his miserable son and his gentile wife had, for the time being, beaten him, David visited Rabbi Dr Abrahams, the rabbi of the Melbourne synagogue.

Since the death of his wife, Rebecca, and the marriage of Abraham to Elizabeth Fitzsimmons, the Melbourne Jewish community had seen very little of the Solomon family, a problem of some significance as it represented a regular source of funds which had now dried up.

And although Abraham's marriage to Elizabeth Fitzsimmons had created a great deal of delicious gossip amongst the synagogue congregation and was seen as a betrayal of the faith, Rabbi Abrahams, essentially a pragmatic man, was sufficiently worldly to know that religion of any kind cannot exist solely on the piety and pennies of the poor and so he welcomed David warmly.

'A great pleasure to see you again, Mr Solomon. Since your beloved wife's tragic demise we have not enjoyed your attendance at synagogue.'

'Too busy,' David replied brusquely, and then lost no time in getting to the purpose of his visit. 'Rabbi, my son Abraham has been married four years and . . .' He paused and shrugged his shoulders, 'Nothing.'

'Nothing? No children, eh?' The rabbi stroked his beard. 'A shame, it is written, every Jew is entitled to a son.'

David nodded. 'Yeah, well we ain't got one!' he'd snapped, then came straight out with it, 'What would it take for my daughter-in-law to become pregnant?'

Rabbi Abrahams looked surprised. Witchcraft and superstition usually belonged to the poorer end of his congregation. He pursed his lips and spread his hands wide. 'As far as I know, the same as always, a boy and a girl and a feather bed, the rest is God's will.'

David was not in a mood to share the rabbi's homely wit. 'Yes, yes,' he said impatiently, 'that's what I mean, God's will. Can you get God to change His mind? Can you pray for a grandson? A pregnancy *and* a grandson?'

The rabbi shrugged. 'The one is impossible without the other.' He thought for a moment. 'You want me to pray? To ask God your daughter-in-law should be pregnant?' He stroked his beard. 'Hmm . . . certainly, it's possible to *ask* Him.' The rabbi could not quite bring himself to believe a man as rich and cynical as David Solomon was so naive in spiritual matters as to expect him to be able to bring his personal influence to bear on the Almighty.

On the other hand, Rabbi Abrahams knew an opportunity when he saw one, though he was not quite sure how far he could go with David Solomon. Certainly the rich old man was a gift from a merciful God, that much he knew for sure. And, furthermore, one which didn't come along every day. And so he decided to hedge a little.

'Mind you in this matter, when the girl party is a gentile, there could be er . . . complications.'

David Solomon was delighted. Complications he knew about, whenever money was about to be discussed the word 'complications' occurred frequently.

'Complications, what complications?'

'You see, it is a matter of ears,' Rabbi Abrahams said, thinking on his feet.

'Ears?'

'Will God listen with His Jewish ear or His gentile ear, that is the question?'

'Both!' David exclaimed. 'How much?'

'Both?' The rabbi looked doubtful. 'I must remind you I am a rabbi, Mr Solomon, a Jew. While I have the utmost respect for the gentile ear of God, I am only familiar with the Jewish.' He shrugged. 'Alas, I am permitted to pray only to one ear.'

'One ear?' David thought for a moment. 'How much for one ear?'

Rabbi Abrahams smiled and spread his hands wide. 'We pray always that God will provide a little Jewish school we hope to attach to the synagogue. A little place of scholarship for our children. Maybe even your grandson?' he suggested slyly.

'Send me the plans, get me a quote.' David jabbed his forefinger at the rabbi. 'Though I warn you, I will obtain another myself, we don't want another incident like your predecessor, that villain,' David paused, 'whatsaname?'

'Rabbi Dattner Jacobson,' Dr Abrahams sighed, referring to the rabbi before him who had been publicly accused of lining his own pockets.

'Yes, that crook, we'll have none of that, there'll be receipts needed and shown, down to the last copper nail.'

The rabbi bowed his head slightly. 'But of course, everything must be kosher.'

'So? What about the other ear?' David now demanded.

'The other ear?'

'Yes, the gentile ear? I *must* have both ears!' David announced. 'I can't take no chances.'

The rabbi rubbed his bearded chin once more. 'For a small commission, say ten per cent, for books you understand, in the school, I could talk to the bishop. We could maybe make a little arrangement?'

Arrangements, like complications, were the things David knew most about. 'The bishop?' David shook his head. 'I'll not do business with the Papists, with them damned Catholics,' David said emphatically.

'Not so fast, not so fast, my friend,' Rabbi Abrahams said soothingly. 'My friend the Anglican Bishop of Melbourne, James Moorhouse, I could have maybe a little talk to him?'

'And he's got the *best* gentile ear? Better than, you know, that other lot?' David asked suspiciously.

The rabbi clasped his hands together and brought them to his chest. 'After the Jews, the best,' Abrahams assured him. 'He is a good God-fearing man who, it so happens, needs a new roof on the baptistery of St Mark's. On the other hand, the Catholics have a brand-new cathedral and God would maybe not be so willing to listen to their needs at the present moment.'

'Fifty per cent now, fifty per cent when the child is born, no commission on the goy roof, but a thousand pounds bonus to you if it is a boy,' David said, extending his hand to the rabbi.

'We will pray for the boy through both ears,' the Chief Rabbi promised, accepting David's outstretched hand. It had been a rewarding day. At the very worst half the cost of the new infant school was paid. Furthermore, with half the price of his new baptistery roof on St Mark's guaranteed and, in the process, a firm relationship established with the powerful bishop, it could do the increasingly prosperous Jewish community in the city no harm. Even if the collective prayers were to fall on deaf ears, the ledger for God's work in the city was suddenly in excellent shape.

Precisely eleven months after David's visit to the rabbi Joshua was born. Rabbi Abrahams, clearly not a man to lose an opportunity to capitalise on this wonderful act of nature, accepted David's cheques together with his bonus.

Carefully folding the two bank drafts into his purse, he addressed his source of pennies from heaven. 'Mr Solomon, God has provided you with a fine, healthy boy, but there has been no bris, he has not been circumcised.' He sighed. 'There is even some talk about, a rumour no doubt, that he is to be raised as a gentile?'

David shrugged. 'It's your law,' he replied with a dismissive shrug. 'His mother Elizabeth is a gentile, my grandson is born a goy.'

Rabbi Abrahams had flinched at the vulgar expression. 'Our law, certainly, Mr Solomon. It is true, your grandson is technically a gentile.' He paused. 'On the other hand, if your son's wife, Elizabeth, is willing to turn, to convert to Judaism,' the Chief Rabbi spread his hands and smiled, 'then it would give me great pleasure to personally instruct her in the Jewish faith. Believe me, it would be a happy occasion for the Jews of Melbourne if I could tell the members of the synagogue that the Lord God has provided Abraham Solomon with a fine *Jewish* son and a grandson to the illustrious Mr David Solomon.'

David was unimpressed with the praise and he thought for a moment then announced, 'No, Rabbi, we will leave things as they are, that is the best thing to do.'

The rabbi was somewhat taken aback, in fact, barely able to conceal his dismay, for he had fully expected David to comply with his request. 'But why, Mr Solomon? Your father Ikey Solomon was a Jew, a member of the first synagogue in Hobart, your mother Hannah was a Jew, also your dear departed wife? You are a Jew, your son Abraham is a Jew? God has answered our prayers, you have a grandson. Why?'

David looked sternly at the rabbi. 'Rabbi Abrahams, I am a plain-speaking man and you have cost me a great deal of money. Not only have the Jews of Melbourne benefited, but I have also allowed you to kiss the arse of a bishop of the Church of England. Mind you, I am not complaining, we made a deal, as you say, I have a grandson and you now have your school and the goy bishop has a new roof over the heads of his Sunday Christians.' He paused for a moment and then said, 'Now, answer me this, please, Mister Rabbi of Melbourne. How do I know it wasn't the gentile ear of God that answered my prayers for a grandson?'

That, with his son, Joshua, the outcome, was the very first time Abraham had gone against his father's wishes. Now, with Hawk waiting for David's answer to his business proposition he has once again defied him. Abraham reasons that if his father, coming to the end of his life, isn't able to accept Hawk's generous rescue plan for Solomon & Co. he, with the remainder of his life ahead of him, has no reason to reject it. On the contrary, he knows himself quite capable of running Solomon & Co. on his own and, without the constant harassment and interference of the old man, he relishes the opportunity.

Abraham can feel his ambivalence growing, but nevertheless

feels duty bound to ask once more for his father's co-operation. 'Father, I have accepted Mr Solomon's offer, I shall not relent. Will you not do the same?' It is the last time he will ask and, for the remainder of his life, he will bitterly resent having done so.

Ignoring Hawk's presence David looks up at his son and bellows, 'Yes! Damn you! Count me in!' The task his mind has set him at this moment is to leap from his chair, cross the room and leave it, slamming the door behind him. But he is an old man and rising from the deep leather chair is an onerous business, though he does so with as much vigour as he can muster and crosses the room to the door, forcing his old legs to hurry. He turns at the door, 'S'truth! A nigger chairman!' then exercising his bad temper he exits, slamming the door behind him as hard as he may.

'I apologise, for my father,' a red-faced Abraham says. 'It has all come as a great shock to him.'

Hawk looks up at David's son. 'I sense you would have preferred him to stay out eh? Well, never mind, it's settled then.' Abraham will later recall how Hawk had clasped his fingers together and brought his chin to rest upon his hands. Then looking down into his lap he had given a deep sigh. 'Thank God, after thirty-eight years,' he'd heard Hawk whisper.

Hawk loses no time drawing up the documents and in a month they are signed by David and Abraham and notarised. He plans to stay another month so that he might learn all he can about the new brewery, though he has learned that Abraham is more than competent to see to its completion and seems anxious to be allowed to do so. Hawk feels they will get on well enough and intends to be home soon with Hinetitama, Ben and Victoria. He does not think of Teekleman as family, but simply as an obese presence to be tolerated. He has since learned that the Dutchman has left his employ, but thinks little of it. Hinetitama is well provided for and her husband does not need to work to keep his household going. Hawk will sort out any other details upon his return.

However, two days after the completion of the contracts Hawk receives a telegram from Hobart.

**TEEKLEMAN DEAD HINETITAMA IN TROUBLE
ANN**

Chapter Six

THE RETURN OF HINETITAMA

Melbourne 1914

September 25th 1914, the day of the big military march past, is typical of that time of the year in Victoria. It commences with a thin pre-dawn drizzle, clears up a little just as the paperboys hurry in the six o'clock dark to their allotted street corners then persists foul all morning, with flurries of rain and sudden gusts of bone-chilling wind that invert umbrellas and send hats skidding along the mirror-wet pavements.

It is miserable weather even for ducks, and the folk making their way from Flinders Street Station to Parliament House lower their heads into the wind and the rain, with one hand placed upon their sodden hats, the other clasping raised coat lapels tightly about their chests, their children, all except the infants, fending for themselves.

If spring is just around the corner as all the newspapers proclaim, then, on a day such as this, it seems in no great hurry to arrive. However, an ever hopeful nature has already set the sap to rising in the plane trees on Bourke Street and, while they still stand naked like up-ended witches' brooms, a more careful examination will show that the ends of the most slender branches are tipped with tender green shoots.

Where other cities might bemoan a rotten rainy day, Melbourne folk take a perverse pride in its weather, fondly imagining they share a climate with England, a place which, in the current nomenclature, they refer to as 'home'.

It is as if in their minds Australia is considered their temporal abode while England remains the destination of the heart and the true home of the spirit.

Because it is claimed Melbourne has four more days of rain a year than does London, its citizens think of themselves as somehow more English than the other cities with Adelaide, home of the free settlers, perhaps the single exception. So ingrained is this premise, that on a February day when the temperature is as likely to soar to over one hundred degrees Fahrenheit, the better folk of Melbourne feign surprise. It is as though they feel it unfair that the weather should turn on them so.

In the middle of a heatwave a stout Melbourne grande dame, taking afternoon tea in the new Myers shop in Bourke Street and dressed up to the nines in a gown she has sent to Paris to obtain and wearing a fur appropriate to a London winter, may bat the air with a cheap Chinese paper fan and exclaim in a superior tone, 'Whatever has become of the weather, it was never this hot when I was a gal?'

But even the rising temperature is accommodated to the myth of an antipodean England. The top people in Melbourne compare the sweltering heat with their notion of an endless English summer, where larks fly in a high blue sky and brass bands play in rotundas on Sunday afternoon in a park redolent with crocuses, bluebells, lilacs and daffodils, an England of quiet country pubs, cricket matches on the village green and small boys fishing for sticklebacks in the local pond.

This sense of Englishness has been carried even further, for unlike the impetuous higgledy-piggledy, stumble and tumble of Sydney, nothing has been left to chance. It is a city meticulously laid out in neat squares, the streets and avenues straight and wide with earnest, clanking trams rattling self-importantly down the centre and generously wide pavements which boast of the city's prosperity and sophisticated demeanour. This is a change brought about by the new wealth from Ballarat and Bendigo gold, which has turned the city John Batman founded into the financial capital of Australia.

However, Melbourne in the old century was not a city to make its better-class citizens proud of their rapidly expanding metropolis, the stench of urine from the back lanes being one of the more ubiquitous characteristics of street life. The Bourke Street East theatre district was used every night by hundreds of theatre-goers and citizens of the night as a common urinal. After sunset the stench and extent of the urine running into it and overflowing its gutters made the footpath almost impassable. The smell of horse dung in every street worthy of a name was omnipresent while the generous dumpings of large herds of cattle and sheep regularly driven through the city added to the ordure.

All said and done, it was a dirty but interesting place, with a street population of German brass bands, Italian organ grinders, French hurdy-gurdy performers and Hungarian musicians, hitching posts and horse troughs and hundreds of street stalls selling every manner of wares. As the sun set there was a migration of coffee stalls into the centre of the city, their owners trundling the strange square boxes with funnels sticking out of the roofs and pitching them in a favourite spot where, with charcoal fires blazing, they appeared transformed into a welcoming and well-lit coffee stall. Hawkers were everywhere, loud and declamatory, selling the latest ballads printed on long narrow pieces of paper clipped to a stick they held above their heads. There were cockatoo hawkers selling caged birds, hawkers selling boiled sheep's trotters, small children selling flowers late into the night and fruit and veggie men and women. Barrowloads of crayfish were sold at sixpence a pound raw weight or for threepence more they came ready to eat.

From December to March, the fish season and the hottest time of the year, when the dusty streets were filled with peel and debris, human urine and horse and cattle shit, the city stench reached a malodorous crescendo with the invasion by fish hawkers. These merchants of the sea used the horse troughs to clean their fish, dumping the fish guts into the gutter and after the plugs were removed from their barrows, oyster shells, fish scales, fish heads and slimy water flowed over footpaths and clogged city gutters in a slushy, effluvium tide that damn near brought its citizens to their knees.

But the Melbourne of 1914 has sobered up and dressed its city fathers in dark broadcloth, top hat and spats and the women from the better classes now dress in unseasonable furs and ill-chosen Parisian finery and, with pinkies pointed outwards, hold bone-china cups of tea and mouth the vowels of England.

Neat cast-iron urinals, exact copies of their Paris counterparts, dot the clean pavements and the city council has erected five underground conveniences with closet accommodation at one penny a time should the requirement be to sit down and an extra penny for a wash and brush. Males in a standing position facing the porcelain are not required to pay.

Perhaps the best example of the now repentant Melbourne is its botanical gardens, designed to be precise and orderly by the German botanist, Baron von Mueller. It adorns the south side of the river and is pruned, mowed and dressed in oak and elm and festooned with the shrubs and blossoms to be found in England and Europe with a token display of the parochial flora.

Only the lazy, mustard-coloured Yarra sidling unpretentiously by is Australian, a laconic country cousin of a river come to visit a rich, patronising and wealthy urban relative.

Despite the cold and the wet, the crowd attending the military parade and now standing three deep in Spring Street remain cheerful. Waving little Union Jacks fixed to lolly sticks, their hearts beat collectively for England and the Empire. Someone with a half-respectable baritone voice and accompanied by a lone mouth organ starts to sing the words to the popular refrain, 'Sons of Australia', and when it comes to the chorus the crowd immediately in the vicinity of Parliament House join in.

> *For Britain! Good old Britain!*
> *Where our fathers first drew breath,*
> *We'll fight like true Australians,*
> *Facing danger, wounds or death.*
> *With Britain's other gallant sons*
> *We're going hand in hand;*
> *Our War-cry 'Good old Britain' boys,*
> *Our own dear motherland.*

They have come to cheer on their troops who are marching off to war to fight in a quarrel Mother England helped to start, but one which their colonial sons neither bother to understand nor stop to think about. 'England calls and we answer' are the proud words on most lips. Young lads, barely out of knee britches, fake their age and grow unconvincing post-pubescent moustaches, hoping to disguise their callow youth and pink unshaven cheeks in their eagerness to join the fray. They carry a collective sense of anxiety that they may miss the so-called 'Grand Picnic in Europe'. The *Age*, the *Truth* and the *Argus* all agree it will be over by Christmas with the German troublemakers taught a damned good lesson by the British Empire.

Not only do the youth answer to the bugle call of the Motherland. Boer War veterans, who should know better, blacken the greying roots of their hair with a diluted solution of boot black. A wag in the letters column of the *Age* notes that never has 'Bluey' been so numerous on Melbourne's streets and in the queues outside the recruitment depots as older men rinse their hair with henna. They all want to join in the mad scramble to fight for a cause more stupid, pointless, morally reprehensible than any in the long quarrelsome history of mankind.

This is a war instigated by pompous German generals with waxed and curled mustachios and their British and French counterparts, who, but for the colour and insignia on their uniforms, can barely be told apart.

Self-important old men, accredited diplomats and posturing politicians, talk of peace and reconciliation while secretly itching to get on with it. In the weeks leading to the assassination in Sarajevo of Franz Ferdinand, the Archduke of Austria, they make and break alliances almost as regularly as the sounds of popping champagne corks are heard in their embassies whenever they celebrate meaningless diplomatic and political initiatives. Some of these barely last longer than the fizz in the champagne they drink in their toasts to peace.

Eventually, with the arcane dialogue exhausted, the pointless assassination of the Archduke gives them all an excuse to declare war. Citing insults more imagined than real as the reasons for taking up arms against each other, these pompous and vainglorious old men have their tailors fit military tunics to accommodate their paunches. If asked, their collective wives, bringing a little commonsense to bear, could have resolved the shambles in a peaceful afternoon around the kitchen table.

The finest, the very best we have to give of our young blood, our tall, strong, colonial sons, will fight for an England they, nor their parents or their grandparents, have ever visited. For some, the last of their forebears to see England had left its shores on a stinking, rat-infested convict ship to arrive in Australia, cowed and beaten.

Now, on this cold and windy September day, to a rousing march played by the bands of the 1st Australian Division together with the 3rd Light Horse Regiment, their fourth-generation descendants wave to their precious sons and brothers who in this passing-out parade each receive the imprimatur of trained fighting man.

David Solomon and his son Sir Abraham sit among the dignitaries on the apron directly above the first set of steps of Parliament House some eight feet above the crowd. David, ninety-four years old, is almost blind and somewhat deaf, a frail old man who must be transported in a wheelchair. Nevertheless, he enjoys the full use of his mental faculties which are mostly employed in voluble cussing and being curmudgeonly. It has been a decade or more since he was last heard to say a good word for anyone with the exception of his grandson Joshua. He turns stiff-necked to his son and declares, 'Is that the band I hear?'

'Yes, Father, won't be long now,' Sir Abraham answers, sensing his growing impatience.

'What's the time?'

Abraham withdraws his half-hunter from his weskit pocket and reads the time out loud. 'Twenty minutes past eleven, give or take thirty seconds of the clock, Father.'

'They're late! Should've passed by at eleven, it's too damned cold to be sitting around.' The old man turns to face in the direction of the Governor-General standing on the pavement below the steps with Major General Bridges and members of the general staff. They wait to take the general salute. 'Sloppy work! By golly, we won't win the war this way!' he shouts down at their backs.

The Governor-General turns towards David. 'Not you, sir! That fat army chappie in the uniform next to you!' He points an accusing finger at Major General Bridges, a man with a high colour and a distinctly bellicose look about him. 'Your troops, aren't they? Should be on time! Not good enough by half.'

The general is clearly taken aback and turns and points at David Solomon. 'Who is this man?' he shouts up at the Governor-General who is also in the front row of the seated dignitaries. Then without waiting for an answer he turns back to David. 'Sir, you insult me!'

Despite the noise from the street below and the rapidly

154

approaching band, the silence on the podium is palpable. Most of those present know David Solomon is notorious for his plain speaking, an old man who doesn't give a fig for the good opinions of others and, with the increasing loss of his sight, most are aware of his irascibility.

'I demand an apology,' Major General Bridges barks, for the band is now less than fifty yards away and the cheering of the crowd has greatly increased.

David, feigning a deafness of convenience, turns to his son and shouts, 'Eh? What he say?'

Abraham leans close to the old man's ear. 'He wants you to apologise, Father. We must!' He is visibly embarrassed and now takes it upon himself to rise and face the officer. Attempting an awkward little bow, he shouts, 'Sir, we apologise most profusely! No insult intended, none at all, I'm sure.' He smiles weakly. 'The cold, General, my father is a very old man and is rheumatic.'

Major General Bridges, only slightly mollified, turns away. The band is almost upon them and he must take the salute with the Governor-General, who has already risen and taken his place on the steps. 'Father, you go too far,' Abraham remonstrates, 'you will need to apologise officially.'

David casts an angry look at his son. 'Apologise? Whaffor?'

Abraham sighs. 'Just don't say anything more, please, Father!'

'It's too bloody cold, I'm freezin' me knackers off, how much longer must we all sit here because of his damned incompetence?' David now says, but the band is upon them and only Abraham hears him. He knows David will continue the altercation with the general just as soon as he can make himself heard again.

'Father, you will do Joshua a disservice,' Abraham shouts into David Solomon's ear. His only hope is to scare the old man into silence with the notion that his precious grandson's carefully planned career in the army might be affected by his rudeness to the general. He knows David will do almost anything to protect Joshua from coming to any harm in the war.

David sniffs and jerks his head backwards as though to refute this notion, but Abraham knows he has won and lets out a sigh of relief. He will send the military man an abject note of apology accompanied by a box of Cuban cigars and once again plead the weather, his father's extreme age and his non-existent rheumatic condition and decrepitude.

Sir Abraham Solomon is a deeply conservative man, deficient in imagination, but meticulous in business procedure and placid enough to have always taken his directions from his mercurial father. Confrontation is not a large part of his character and Abraham, unlike his own son Joshua, both fears and dislikes his father. Often brought to the verge of despair by the old man's unreasonableness, he secretly wishes the miserable old bastard would die, thinking him at least twenty years overdue for the plain pine coffin.

Both he and Joshua have spent their lives attempting to please the old man, but with quite different results. David dotes on his grandson Joshua who can do no wrong in his eyes, while he thinks Abraham, at very best, is an unimaginative plodder with an honest bookkeeper's mind, not at all the sort to advance the Solomon fortunes.

Abraham has spent his life trying to make David proud of him. A naturally shy and retiring man with a passion for racing pigeons, he has, at David's instigation, been Lord Mayor, received a knighthood in 1910, and is now the Grand Master of Melbourne's secret order of Free and Accepted Masons.

These are all positions which David has himself secretly coveted but has made no attempt to achieve. Despite his enormous wealth, David Solomon is aware of his lack of education and the social graces required for public office. His bravado and brusque manner in public are an attempt to conceal a deep-seated insecurity and sense of inferiority he has felt since his early childhood. He is secretive by nature and not at all gregarious, mostly for fear that, despite his wealth, he might be exposed and humiliated as so often happened to him in his childhood.

So Abraham, who has been properly educated in the manners of society, has been forced by the old man to play what is essentially a surrogate role, with his ambitious father calling the shots behind the scenes and taking advantage of the opportunities his son's public persona and position affords Solomon & Teekleman.

As a consequence Abraham has very little sense of his own worth. All his achievements have been reluctant, undertaken only to please the cantankerous old man seated beside him. He is aware that money, placed in the right places and in the right hands, has been the primary reason for his progress in civic affairs. As his father so often says, 'Money will buy you everything, son, except love. The currency of love is soon spent but the money it will cost you never ends.' It is one of David's more benign sayings.

As the mayor of Melbourne, Sir Abraham had the personal satisfaction of having the Solomon family endow the city with a plot of land in St Kilda Road for civic purposes and to finance a new wing for the public library. This sort of largesse could never have emanated from David himself, but Abraham was able to convince his father that the goodwill of Solomon & Teekleman Holdings was at stake. Finally, when it was proposed that the new library wing be named the David Solomon Wing, he agreed even though he had always thought it a crime to educate the masses.

The endowment to the library, in particular, was a quiet source of amusement to Abraham and perhaps the closest he would ever come to avenging himself for the hundreds of humiliations he had suffered at the old man's hands. David Solomon had never read a book in his life, constantly chastising Abraham as a child for doing so. If it had not been for the protection of his mother, Rebecca, his father would have denied him the pleasure of books, believing they softened the mind.

To David, education meant sending his son to the *right* school where he would meet the *right* people and learn the *right* manners so as to be accepted within Melbourne's polite society. It never occurred to him to equate Abraham's education with intellectual progress. Business was all that interested David and he accepted the responsibility of teaching Abraham this himself. In fact, he would later blame his son's conservative business habits and lack of a killer instinct on too much education. 'Too many bloody books when you were a child, that's the problem with you, m'boy!'

Abraham's career as a Freemason was much more to David's taste. While he himself did not join, he liked the idea of a secret society of men who 'scratched each other's backs' and who covertly agreed not to witness against each other in a court of law. He quickly realised how this might be to his advantage, happily accepting that the price of Abraham's elevation was the unspoken promise to employ only Freemasons within the family's vast enterprises. This meant well over two thousand jobs went to the secret brotherhood, which excluded Catholics from its membership. This suited David, too, for he loathed the Irish papists with a fierce and abiding hate. His mother's de facto husband, George Madden, was an Irish

Catholic who had treated David and his three siblings, Ann, Sarah and Mark, with a singular disdain and often enough had beaten them or, as a punishment for some imagined misdemeanour, made them go without food for three days. 'You English made the Irish starve, boy, now you can do the same,' he'd say. David had never forgiven the man, blaming his race and religion for their childhood suffering.

Abraham is aware that his father sees him as a far from adequate replacement at the helm of the giant brewing, timber, pastoral and business empire. He knows that he is, at best, the temporary standard-bearer while Joshua is being groomed for the job of ultimately running Solomon & Teekleman Holdings.

Far from resenting his caretaker role, he looks forward to the time when he can hand over to his son and he can get on with his life free from the restraints of business. The only office he cherishes is that of President of the Pigeon Racing Association of Victoria. Furthermore, he blames his wife Elizabeth's drinking on himself and anticipates a time when he will be able to give her sufficient attention.

With his heart still pounding from witnessing the contretemps between David and the Major General, Abraham folds his arms tightly across his chest in an attempt to crush the anxiety he feels in his gut.

The band is almost upon them with the brass and drums crashing about his ears. Abraham prepares to alert his father that the 4th Australian Light Horse follows. The clopping of 546 horses on the macadam surface of the street and the jangle of their brasses as the mounted troopers move up to take the salute now almost completely drowns out the departing band. Joshua will be the officer riding ahead of the third squadron.

'Is he here yet?' the near blind David cries, grabbing his son's arm. In the din and the cheering of the excited crowd it is impossible to hear him and, besides, Abraham has previously agreed he will tap his father on the shoulder when Joshua's troop appears. David's bony fingers are surprisingly strong as they dig deep into the flesh of his son's upper arm. Abraham sees that the old man's mouth is spit-flecked with anxiety at the thought of not being ready when his grandson passes by.

Joshua's troop rides into sight and Abraham taps David on the shoulder, whereupon the old man brings his hand up to his forehead in a salute intended to be rigid, though his hand trembles so that the tips of his fingers set his ear to vibrating. Abraham sees that the old man is crying and he reaches into his pocket for his handkerchief to hand to him when Joshua's squadron has passed by.

Directly across the street from where the general is taking the salute, black as the devil himself and towering head and shoulders above the crowd, is the magnificent Hawk. He is unseen by David Solomon, but his presence with Victoria is quietly noted by Abraham. During a lifetime of malice and greed, most of it in the name of sound business practice, David has acquired a legion of enemies who would happily slit his throat if they thought they could get away with it. These men, with perhaps one or two exceptions, do not cause David to lose a moment's sleep. On the other hand, David's personal hatred for the giant black man is beyond the sum of all of the others. Abraham decides his father has caused sufficient trouble for one day.

Somewhat stooped, at seventy-three Hawk still stands near seven feet tall with a snow-white crop of woolly hair and the Maori *moko* markings on his proud and handsome face. He provides a natural curiosity for the crowd who try not to stare too blatantly, but occasionally steal furtive glances in his direction. The smaller children have no such reservations and they gawk unashamedly, clutching the hems of their mothers' dresses until they are pulled away and turned about-face to witness the on-going parade.

Standing beside Hawk, her small white hand in his great black fist, is Victoria, Tommo's granddaughter who now lives with him in Melbourne. He brought her over from New Norfolk at the age of eighteen to further her education. She is a handsome young woman of twenty-five who has served her articles and passed the solicitor's examination, but who does not possess, or even wish to embrace, the restrained manners expected of a girl of her social class and wealth. Victoria jumps up and down in excitement, showing her slim ankles and, every once in a while, a daring glimpse of calf as the mounted troopers finally pass and the companies of foot soldiers hove into view, their band playing the popular 'Skipper' Francis anthem, 'Australia Will Be There'. Among them, in the third platoon from the front, is her brother Ben whom she adores with all the considerable love she can pack into a naturally generous heart.

She has observed Joshua riding by, sitting tall in the saddle and ramrod straight and as dashing as can be, with blue eyes and blond hair, the latter inherited from his mother, Elizabeth. Victoria thinks of him as a cousin, though, of course, he is not a relation, and her heart skips a beat at how very handsome he is in his jodhpurs and trim tunic with the polished leather of his Sam Browne belt. She is aware of the enmity between the two Solomon clans, but as Hawk has never dwelt on it, nor fully explained its reasons, it has not assumed any importance in her mind and she feels free to admire the young officer on the big chestnut stallion.

For an instant Victoria regrets that Ben, a magnificent horseman, hasn't joined the Australian Light Horse but has chosen instead to become a foot soldier so that he can be with all his mates. She can see Ben in Joshua's place, every bit as handsome, though darker where his Maori blood comes through, a little shorter and bigger around the shoulders and altogether stronger looking. Whereas Joshua looks like an illustration of a British officer in *Boys' Own Annual*, Ben has a physical hardness about him that comes from working with his hands on the land where he has spent the last eight years of his life, latterly in charge of the company's hop and barley farms and pastoral properties.

Although a uniform sits well enough on his strong frame, it somehow looks temporary. Ben is his own man and no institution is likely to transform him into anonymous cannon fodder. While Joshua will gain his authority from his status as an officer, the twenty-six-year-old Ben needs no rank to make men defer to him. He has been appointed a sergeant not because he marches any better or shoots straighter, or has, for that matter, any more experience at the business of waging war. Ben is their sergeant because they want to go to war with him at their side. Though he has enlisted in Tasmania and will rejoin his regiment before it leaves Australian shores, he has come to Broadmeadows, the Victorian military camp, to attend a special weapons training course and so is today acting as the sergeant of a Victorian infantry platoon. It is a most fortuitous situation as Hawk and Victoria would otherwise have been forced to take the overnight boat to Hobart to farewell him.

The clatter of horses' hooves begins to fade as the Australian Light Horse passes and the infantry brigade are now upon them, the men marching proudly, their chins slightly raised, boots striking the surface of the road setting up a sharp rhythmic cadence, the bayonets fixed to their rifles gleaming against a leaden sky and their heads turned to the eyes-right position to salute the Governor-General.

Hawk is consumed by pride as Ben's platoon approaches them, though, at the same time, silent tears run down his great cheeks. He has no romantic illusions about the war Tommo's grandson is marching off to fight. He has seen men kill men before in the Maori wars and has learned that there is no glory to be found in the slaughter of humans. His heart is filled with trepidation for the lad he thinks of as his own grandson and loves with all his heart.

Victoria also weeps, but rather more from excitement, for she has no sense of Ben's being in danger. Her brother has held her hand since she was a baby and no matter what childish disaster they faced, she always knew he would bring them through it with a self-deprecating grin and a pat on the head. Now, after showing the Germans who is the boss, he'll return to her unscathed and with that same crooked big smile on his silly gob. They'll all be together again, Grandpa Hawk, Ben and herself, all that is left of the disparate little family Mary Abacus gathered around her during her long life.

Hawk hasn't told Victoria that earlier this very morning he has come away from the Sisters of Charity Hospice for Women in St Kilda where for several weeks he has been watching over a dying Hinetitama.

In the inside pocket of his white linen jacket he holds her will, in which she, of sound mind, and in front of a justice of the peace, the Mother Superior, Sister Angelene, and the parish priest, Father Anthony Crosby, has given her proxy to Hawk, making him the trustee for the ten per cent share Ben and Victoria will now own in the giant Solomon & Teekleman Company.

The voting rights on this ten per cent, which have been unavailable to Hawk for the twenty-one years Hinetitama has been away, are the difference between his side controlling a majority shareholding in Solomon & Teekleman or David and his son doing so.

Hawk promised Tommo on his deathbed that he would always care for his daughter but when he took the boat back to Hobart in response to Ann's telegram he arrived to find that Hinetitama had absconded.

In a state of shock he listened while Ann told him the story of how Hinetitama had taken up singing with Teekleman and was nightly to be seen drunk in one or another of the pubs around the waterfront until she was the laughing stock of the town. She told how Teekleman, in the middle of one of his famous 'skols', that is the drinking down of a pint of ale in a bout with another drinker, a competition in which he had never been beaten, suddenly dropped the tankard of ale and clasped his hands to his chest, collapsing to his knees. He was dead from a sudden and massive heart attack before his forehead struck the wooden floor. Without the giant Dutchman to take her home when she looked like making a fool of herself and despite Ann's efforts to dissuade her, Hinetitama had been on a continual binge almost from the moment Teekleman had died. Like all alcoholics, the single glass of gin placed in her hands by the nefarious Isaac Blundstone had been the beginning of her undoing.

Told in a moment of sobriety by Ann that Hawk was returning to Hobart, she'd that very night packed a few things into a canvas bag and disappeared. Hawk arrived in Hobart on the overnight steamer to discover that she was last seen in the drunken company of Captain Ben 'Blackbird' Smithers of the windjammer *The Fair Wind*, one of the sailing ships still plying between the island and the mainland.

Smithers, a former captain of a whaling ship, was notorious as a blackbirder, plundering the islands in the seventies and early eighties, kidnapping Kanakas and bringing them to Queensland to work in the cane fields. He was never apprehended and, like Teekleman, is a drunk and a thorough scoundrel.

From that moment, Hawk searched Australia and New Zealand, even sending detectives to Canada, the new Dominion of South Africa and the United States of America but to no avail. Somehow Hinetitama managed to evade him.

Just before her disappearance Hawk had concluded the deal with David and Abraham Solomon which relied on her shares and proxy in the new conglomerate for him to be chairman. Unable to utilise her ten per cent shareholding he lost his voting majority in Solomon & Teekleman, giving David and Abraham control of the giant enterprise. When David became chairman he immediately removed Hawk from the Potato Factory and Hawk was reduced to being no more than a large shareholder.

Despite his untimely demise, Hawk never sought to find Hinetitama simply to regain her proxy, but because he was guilt-stricken, forced by her absence to break what he considered his sacred word to his twin Tommo. That is, until he received a note from the Mother Superior of the Sisters of Charity Hospice in St Kilda.

The Sisters of Charity Hospice for Women, St Kilda

14th August 1914

Dear Mr Solomon,

Sir, it is with some hesitation that I write to you.

However, after prayer, I am convinced that I have no choice in the matter and so I crave your indulgence.

In recent weeks there has come into our hospice a half-caste woman suffering from delirium tremens, malnutrition and cirrhosis of the liver, in all, an advanced state of alcoholism from which the doctor does not believe she will recover.

She answers to the name of Mary Gibbons, but says that her true identity is Hinetitama Solomon.

I hasten to add that information obtained from alcoholics is usually not to be relied upon. Except, in the case of Mary Gibbons, at such times when her mind is clear, she persists in asking that we contact you as a matter of urgency. It is not usual for someone in her condition to retain such a persistent and consistent obsession and so I am forced to conclude that it may have some validity.

Sir, we do not believe that God will grant Mary much longer on this earth. If this poor demented soul has had any connection with you in the past, then I can only hope and pray that you will see it in your heart to grant her final wish some priority.

I remain yours, in the name of Our Lord Jesus Christ,

Angelene Denmeade,

Mother Superior – Sisters of Charity.

Upon receiving the letter Hawk makes the messenger boy wait and immediately pens a letter to the Mother Superior thanking her for the information and urging her to give her patient all the medical attention she needs without regard to the costs involved. He adds that she is to be given a private room if such exists and asks Sister Angelene to assure Mary Gibbons that he will visit the hospice that very afternoon. With a penny in his pocket for his trouble and the letter placed under his greasy cap for safekeeping, the lad runs off.

Hawk arrives to discover that Mary Gibbons is once again in a state of delirium. He is to wait almost two days before she recovers sufficiently to see him. He takes lodgings at a bug-ridden boarding house across the road, leaving instructions with the sisters at the hospice that he is to be called at any time during the day or night when she comes out of her delirium.

Close to midnight two days later, Hawk is finally summoned to the bedside of Mary Gibbons. A nun carrying a hurricane lantern leads him through the darkened ward to her bedside. She hangs the lamp on a hook suspended from the ceiling and, without a further word, leaves him alone with Tommo's daughter.

The lantern throws a circle of yellow light over the bed and Hawk sees immediately that the emaciated old hag lying in the bed bears no resemblance whatsoever to the beautiful woman who forsook her two children all those years ago.

But he knows almost at once that it is Hinetitama in the bed. On her face she carries the distinctive *moko* markings of her Ngati Haua tribe and attached to a cheap metal chain about her scrawny neck and resting on the coarse material of her cotton nightgown is Tommo's greenstone Tiki.

Hinetitama is by now fifty-four, though she appears to be at least twenty years older. She has always been small, taking her size from

Tommo rather than her Maori ancestors. But now she seems diminutive, a tiny wreck of a woman, her unkempt hair white and her face deeply wrinkled. Her dark eyes are sunk into her skull, though Hawk sees at once that they are clear and follow him closely as he bends over to look into her face. She is toothless and repeatedly smacks her gums together, her once elegant Maori nose and the point of her chin almost touching to give her the appearance of an old crone.

Hinetitama lifts her right hand slightly to acknowledge his approach but it trembles beyond her control and falls back to her side. 'Hello, Uncle Hawk,' she cackles.

'Oh, my dear, what has become of you?' Hawk cries, at once overcome. Tears appear instantly and he reaches for his handkerchief to brush them away. 'Hinetitama, what have I *done* to you!' he cries again in anguish.

'Nuthin', Uncle. I done it all meself. I could never learn t'behave meself. I were always a bad 'un.'

Hawk takes her tiny claw in his hand. Her nails are chipped and broken and while the nuns have scrubbed them clean the brown tobacco stains remain on the first and middle finger of her right hand. 'I searched so hard to find you, how ever did you escape me?'

'Yeah, I know'd that well enough. Always some bugger sniffin' about, askin' questions. Promising rewards.' Her eyes light up and she raises her head from her pillow. Hawk sees there is still a spark of defiance in them. 'But youse didn't get me, did yiz?' She falls back exhausted. 'Nah, it wouldn't'a worked out. It were best I left the young 'uns to you, Uncle. I was never gunna be a good mother t'thum.'

'But, my dear girl, you left everything behind, the most fortunate life. You had so much to live for. Mary's shares made you a wealthy woman. Why did you not come back to claim them?'

Hinetitama sighs. 'Them shares? They's for the brats, had'ta be somethin' good comin' t'them two little 'uns.' She closes her eyes, too exhausted to continue, then in a voice not much above a whisper asks, 'Ow'd they turn out them two?'

Hawk tells her about Ben and Victoria though there is no sign that she is listening or even still conscious. Finally, at the insistence of the nun on night duty, he leaves in the early hours of the morning, with instructions that he is to be called the moment Hinetitama is again lucid.

Over the next week he returns home to dinner each night and leaves soon after, giving Victoria the excuse that he has business which must be conducted at night and continues until too late to return home, which in a sense is the truth. Apart from the occasions when they are allowed to visit Ben, he remains at the boarding house and whenever his niece has an hour or so of clarity he visits her.

Hawk slowly begins to piece together her life, though Hinetitama's mind is too far gone for him to get anything but a sense of her misery and the terribly hard life of a woman who lives rough and cannot get through a day without a black bottle cradled in her arms. To an alcoholic one day is much the same as another, one place as good as another, and the abuse of every kind a poor, drunken woman suffers at the hands of men doesn't alter. She had been abandoned in Cape Town by the nefarious Blackbird Smithers and drifted into a life as a sometime chanteuse, though her drinking made her unreliable as a singer and this soon became a euphemism for practising the oldest profession in the world.

She'd lived in District Six, once the Malay slave quarter, now inhabited by their descendants who had become a mixture of the many races of Africa and were known as Cape Coloureds, a people thought to be neither black nor white and so alienated from either extreme.

District Six is its own private world, in some parts it is still a respectable Muslim community but in others it has become a notorious slum where violence is commonplace and Cape brandy the standard fare for its people. Tucked into a fold on the slopes of Table Mountain, the folk who lived there trusted no authority, kept their own counsel and solved their own problems.

Hinetitama, in the guise of Mary Gibbons, was as safe from discovery and the prying enquiries of any detective under Hawk's instructions as it might be possible had she disappeared into the depths of China. Starting to cough blood and thinking she was dying, she had somehow managed to persuade the captain of a Russian whaling ship bound for Melbourne and thereafter to hunting the whale in the Pacific to give her passage back to Australia.

Gradually Hawk begins to talk to her about her will and makes her see what she must do to ensure her shares in Solomon & Teekleman go to her children. 'It's the one decent thing I done thum,' she says, over and over, 'the one decent thing.'

Hawk tries to persuade her to see Ben and Victoria and tells her that Ben is going off to the war in Europe. But Hinetitama won't be persuaded. 'Nah, they don't want to see me, an old woman what's a derro. I'd be ashamed meself, them two seein' me like this.' Despite Hawk's pleas she is unmoved, the old stubbornness inherited from Tommo still there.

He'd seen the same wilfulness emerge in the next generation, when Victoria, as a child, would stamp her tiny foot and yell at her nanny, 'I won't and you can't make me!' after which no amount of admonishment or punishment would prevail against her. Now as a young woman Tommo's granddaughter is equally certain of what she believes and, while of an altogether sweet nature, she is not easily dissuaded once she determines upon a course of action.

Ben, thankfully, is too easygoing to get into a bind about almost anything. But with Hinetitama's shares and her proxy safely in his pocket, Hawk knows that the cheerful Ben will not lead the family in the next generation, that he has neither the desire nor the kind of intellect to do so. Victoria, as Mary had claimed from the outset, has the brilliance and the willpower and, yes, the sheer stubbornness required to eventually run Solomon & Teekleman.

Hawk reassures himself that Victoria, with her good looks and the wealth she will bring as her dowry, will find herself a good accommodating husband and that this may somewhat soften her nature. Perhaps she will even marry someone capable of sharing in the running of the giant enterprise Solomon & Teekleman. In the meantime he must keep Abraham as chairman, for he has served the company well and Hawk bears him no animosity, knowing that his demise is entirely the work of David. Even though his father has been retired since the advent of Federation, Abraham is still unable to go against the old man's will.

'What you tell them kids about me?' Hinetitama on one occasion asks him.

Hawk smiles. 'I told them how beautiful you were, a Maori princess, with a voice that could charm the birds out of the sky.'

Hinetitama smiles. 'I could sing good, that's the one thing I had goin' for me.' Then she sighs, 'But the grog and tabacca took it away like everything else.'

Hawk continues, recalling the lovely young girl he once knew. 'I told them how, when I visited you each year in New Zealand, we would go for long walks in the forests and, like your mother, you could imitate the birdsong of every species and that you knew all the names of the trees and the plants of the forest and the flowers in the meadows and along the river banks. How, even at the age of ten, you could set an eel trap or weave a flax mat or a fruit basket and cook me a nice fish dinner.' Hawk sighs. 'You were an enchanted child, Hinetitama, always singing and laughing and up to some sort of mischief.'

'What you tell them, the brats, why I left them, hey?' Hinetitama asks suddenly.

'I said that you were a songbird and couldn't stay in one place for long, that you wanted to sing to all the world and that, with some people, it is wrong to try to clip their wings and keep them in a cage.'

Hinetitama squints up at him. 'And they bought that shit!'

Hawk laughs. 'At first, when they were kids. Later they just accepted you were gone from their lives.'

Hawk did not tell her that when Ben and Victoria grew older and asked him about their mother he had been forced to tell them the truth, that she was wild and wilful and drinking heavily and simply couldn't abide the constraints placed upon her in the narrow Hobart society. That Victoria, in particular, is not the sort who can be fobbed off with a fairytale forever. He thinks how sometimes, much to his embarrassment, she says to him, 'Now I want the truth, Grandpa Hawk. Don't tell me any cock-and-bull story!'

Hinetitama smiles wistfully as Hawk talks, then she sighs and says, 'Let it be, Uncle. Let them think of me like what you said. I could sing too,' she repeats. 'It was the one thing I done good.'

She attempts to sit up, struggling to get her head off the pillow, but she lacks the strength and Hawk calls to a nun for help. The nun brings Hinetitama to a seated position in the bed and continues to prop her upright as there are no pillows with which to do so.

'What is it, dearie?' the nun asks.

Hinetitama doesn't reply and Hawk watches as she slowly brings her hand up to her neck, her trembling fingers plucking at the skin, searching for the chain which hangs about it. Finally she locates it and pulls at it to reveal Tommo's little green Tiki from under her nightdress.

'Take it, give it to the boy. Gawd knows it's done me no good, but it's kept me alive, I suppose that's something, eh? Maybe it'll do the same for him. I wore it 'cause me daddy left it to me, but a Tiki is not a thing for a woman to wear.' She touches the little green idol. 'Take it off, Sister,' then looking up at Hawk she repeats, 'Give it to the boy. Tell him it were his grandfather's and now it's his own good luck.'

Now, standing in Spring Street amongst the cheering crowd waiting for Ben's platoon to march past, Hawk decides not to tell Victoria about finding her mother. The gift of the Tiki amulet has taken place two days before the parade by special permission of Ben's company commander Major Sayers. Ben is expecting to return to Tasmania to rejoin his regiment as soon as possible after the passing-out parade and they may not otherwise have been given the opportunity to say their goodbyes to him.

Ben has completed his special weapons training course which involves in the main the Vickers machine gun, but he has, as well, been trained in the machine guns of the Allies, those of the Japanese, the Belgian Browning and the French Hotchkiss. He has acquitted himself well and has also during his time taken control of training a platoon at Broadmeadows and Major Sayers has made it known that he is most reluctant to lose him.

'It was your grandfather's, Ben,' Hawk says hesitantly, not knowing how Ben will take the gift of the Tiki, perhaps thinking it is a piece of jewellery a milksop might wear. 'I want you to wear it and never take it off.' He doesn't explain any further and Ben, somewhat bemused, puts the Tiki about his neck.

'Dunno if they'll allow me to wear it, Grandpa,' he says a little sheepishly.

Victoria laughs at her brother's apparent chagrin. 'Oh, but it's so handsome!' She steps closer to her brother and takes the Tiki in her hand. 'It's a fat little man, such a pretty green colour too.'

'It's the Maori God, Tiki, the creator of life and, as he is said to have created all life, he is opposed to killing. It was given to Tommo by the *tohunga*, the Maori priests, who first asked the permission of the ancestors, it will protect you,' Hawk says.

'I should so like one just like it,' she exclaims. 'If it belonged to our grandfather it's bound to be good luck, you must wear it always, Ben!'

Hawk laughs. 'It is not an amulet to be worn by a woman, Victoria. Tiki is sometimes thought to be the creation of Tane, a female God, who some say was the real creator of life and that Tiki is the male,' he clears his throat, 'er . . . penis.'

Victoria blushes, but then quickly recovers. 'So that's where all the trouble started, is it?'

Now holding Victoria's hand in the crowd, Hawk thinks back on Victoria's innocent remark that the Tiki was bound to bring good luck. Good luck was never a commodity in abundance in Tommo's life, nor in his own, for that matter. With the melancholy he feels at Ben's leaving he begins to reflect on how almost everything he seems to have attempted has, in some way or another, failed or, at the very least, been a source of bitter disappointment to him. He has tried to be a good and honest man, yet those he loved the most he seems to have let down.

He thinks about his beloved twin, Tommo, and of his failure to rescue him when he returned from the Wilderness, tormented, mistrustful and broken in spirit. A fourteen-year-old drunk, mortally afraid of the mongrels, the spectre of whom continued to haunt him all his life, until finally he chopped off their collective heads in one horrific incident when he avenged the death of Maggie Pye.

With Hinetitama's proxy votes now in his possession, this one thing at least Hawk thinks he may be able to rectify. That is, if he should live sufficiently long to train Victoria to take control of Solomon & Teekleman, with Ben there to support her against Joshua, who has always believed that he will inherit the vast conglomerate.

A sense of overwhelming panic suddenly grips him. If Ben does not return what will happen to his beloved granddaughter, Victoria? She has none of the cunning or the guile or even the knowledge to survive against Hannah Solomon's rapacious descendants.

Hawk knows with a deep certainty that David's side, even with the evil old man gone, will somehow contrive to crush Victoria, to steal what Mary Abacus and he have left her. Hawk can barely embrace the thought of this final failure. He suddenly feels older, much older, than the seventy-three years he has lived. His free hand moves to the inside pocket of his linen jacket and his fingers touch Hinetitama's last will and testament. 'Oh God, please let me be doing the right thing this time,' he groans to himself.

Ben's platoon is suddenly upon them and Victoria squeals with delight when Ben, instead of his head and eyes directed to the right in a salute to the general, has turned them towards Victoria and Hawk. And, while his hand has been brought up to slap his rifle stock in the traditional salute, his thumb wiggles in a gesture of recognition and there is a great grin on his gob.

A month after the parade they will go down to Port Melbourne to see him sailing off to King George Sound at Albany, Western Australia, prior to departing overseas in a convoy, but Victoria will ever remember this moment with the band playing 'Sons of Australia' and her brother's thumb saluting them.

Victoria delights in the sight of her brother, the ever cheerful, ever optimistic Ben, marching off to war to put the Germans in their place. She is suddenly aware of being lifted, as Hawk, ignoring propriety, grips her under the arms and raises her high above the crowd so that she might be clearly seen by her darling brother.

After the passing-out parade they are unable to find a hansom cab or, an even rarer commodity, a motor-driven taxi cab, and so return home in the tram where they are packed like sardines in a can with weary folk, their damp clothes steaming in the hot tramcar, carrying sleeping children, returning from the parade. Hawk must bend his head awkwardly to avoid bumping it against the roof and he is grateful when at last they arrive at their stop and are able to walk the short distance to their home.

Victoria, who has hardly spoken a word on the short walk home from the tram stop, pleads a headache from the passing-out parade and goes directly to her room. After the excitement of the parade she is suddenly deeply depressed at the prospect of losing her brother without knowing when or whether she will ever see him again.

A short while later, Hawk, thinking to ask her if she'd care for a cup of tea, pauses at her bedroom door and then turns back at the sound of the broken-hearted sobbing coming from within. Somewhat heavy-hearted himself he retires to his study where shortly afterwards Martha Billings, his housekeeper, comes to inform him that a lad has arrived from the hospice and presents him with the letter the boy has delivered.

'Will there be a reply? Shall I keep the boy waitin', sir?' she asks.

Hawk nods, tearing open the envelope absently. 'Make him a sandwich, Mrs Billings, and give him a cuppa tea. If he's the same lad as before he'll take some filling, he's a lanky lad but thin as a rake.'

'They all looks the same ter me, dirty, smelly and cheeky and always bleedin' 'ungry!' Mrs Billings says. Then ignoring the fact that Hawk is now reading the letter she continues, 'Will you and Miss Victoria be in to tea?' Again she doesn't wait for a reply. 'There's only cold cuts, mind. What with all them going off in the parade, Mr McCarthy's son, Johnny, like our Ben, is also off to fight the Germans. So, without so much as by your leave, he closes the butcher shop and trots off in his Sunday best to see him march in front o' the bloomin' Governor hisself.'

'That's all right, Mrs Billings, cold cuts with a bit of mustard pickle will be just fine.'

'It's not my fault you ain't got a nice roast tonight. Wait 'til I see 'im, I'll give him a piece o' me mind!'

Hawk completes reading the letter and looks up at the old family retainer he inherited from Mary and then from Ann Solomon. Martha Billings is one of the many children Mary rescued from the orphan school and employed. Although young Billings was no different to most of them, hungry with a cough and perpetually running nose, Mary started her in the home and not the brewery. She commenced her employment as a scullery maid and finally, when Mrs Briggs passed on, took over as Hawk's cook. A year later Ann died and Hawk, who could not bear to remain in Hobart with the Potato Factory no longer under his control, brought the plump and perpetually prattling, always complaining Mrs Billings as cook and housekeeper to Melbourne.

As far as Hawk knew Martha Billings had always been a spinster, but Mary, who refused to have a butler, insisted that a cook needed authority over the other servants, and so ought to be a Mrs. She simply expunged Mrs Briggs' spinsterhood. Hawk assumed that Martha Billings had continued this tradition and he never questioned her about her marital status.

Over time Mrs Billings has become so accustomed to this gratuitous addition that whenever she feels sorry for herself, which is frequently, she thinks of herself as a poor widow.

At such times, the man in her imagination is Mortimer, a partner of fanciful character who combines humour, manliness, morals, conscience and kindness with generosity, intelligence and a religious conviction. All of these attributes are of such a high standard that they are well beyond the aspirations of any male who ever lived.

This proves to be a good thing, for Mrs Billings has very little admiration for the living members of the opposite sex who, as far as she is concerned, spill food on the damask table linen and walk into her parlour with mud on their boots. Both crimes are in her mind worthy of the severest whipping if not a lot worse.

Careful not to be seen as potty by her peer group she only talks about her phantasmagorical husband to Sardine, a tabby of no particular breeding, who sleeps eighteen hours a day and will only eat minced lamb and gravy or a nice bit of raw snapper. That is, if she can wheedle a fresh one out of Cox the fishmonger whom she trusts about as far as she can throw one of the sharks, the flesh of which she suspects he substitutes for blue cod.

She has lately taken up seeing a part-time clairvoyant, an Irish woman who calls herself Princess Salome, her alter ego when she's practising her gift of 'the sight', but in the daily domestic answers to the name of Mrs Brigitte Maloney and works as a filleter at the fish markets.

Brigitte Maloney, alias Princess Salome, told Mrs Billings about Cox's shark substitution and so won her trust forever. That, and the fact that Princess Salome demanded the head of John the Baptist on a platter and so obviously shared her deep distrust of men. She could quite clearly imagine John the Baptist coming in from the desert, filthy dirty, his great clodhoppers traipsing dirt around the palace and spilling his food all over King Herod's clean tablecloth. A beheading was a small price to pay in Mrs Billings' estimation.

Mrs Billings is invited by Brigitte Maloney to a free trial seance and when asked about her marital status finds herself forced to admit to being a widow, the alternative untruth being that her husband has abandoned her, an idea which her pride will simply not permit. In no time at all she is in touch with the saintlike Mortimer.

While Mrs Billings greatly enjoys these visitations from the other world her conscience eventually demands that she confess his non-existence to Brigitte Maloney, whereupon the Princess Salome becomes quite angry with her. 'Mrs Billings, can you not see that you were married in another life?' Brigitte Maloney does not wait for an answer from the bemused Mrs Billings. 'So great was your love that no other man, no matter how many lives you may live, can take your dearest Mortimer's place. Perfect love, my dear, is what every woman desires.' She pauses, breathing heavily. 'And perfect love is what you've had!' Now she slaps her hands hard against her cheeks, 'You have had the love of a man who has not been tarnished by life in this mortal world!' The thought is all at once too much for her and she abandons the voice of Princess Salome and begins to talk in her normal voice, 'Oh me Gawd! No comin' 'ome pissed as a newt, no Saterdee night leg over, no chunder on the parlour carpet, no gettin' a backhand when you done nothin' to deserve it, no farting in bed, no gamblin' his wages on John Wren's pony track at Richmond, no bleedin' fist fights!' Then, suddenly remembering her other persona, Princess Salome turns to Mrs Billings. 'You have had a marriage made by God in heaven itself, my dear.'

Hawk has long since ceased to listen to Mrs Billings' prattle. His housekeeper is simply a part of the background noise. Only Victoria can tell her to hush, for it is a toss-up between Sardine the cat and the young mistress as to whom Martha Billings loves the most among the living creatures of this earth.

'It's not that I didn't try, Friday is always a roast,' Mrs Billings persists. 'The tram, by the time it come to our stop, was that full with folks going to the parade it just sailed right past, never mind a poor soul waiting in the cold. I thinks to meself, I might go into town, try that new butcher in Lygon Street, the I-talian. Fat chance! After four trams pass me by without so much as 'ow's yer father, I come 'ome bothered and all f'nothing, me basket empty as a curate's purse. There's no tellin' what's gunna happen next. Mrs Maloney from the fish markets says there's already talk of rationing and doing without!'

Hawk, oblivious to Mrs Billings' prattling, now says, 'Miss Victoria is not to be disturbed. If she's hungry she'll get something for herself later.' He instructs without looking up.

'I'll leave her a nice plate, poor little mite's 'ad a long day of it, all that marching and drums, them horses clopping, boats sailing off.'

The letter Hawk holds is from Sister Angelene to say that Hinetitama is dying and that they don't expect she'll last through the night. It asks if she is a Catholic and whether they should have Father Crosby come around especially to hear her confession.

Hawk, who is dog-tired from the long day, is somewhat confused by this and wonders why Hinetitama, in her lucid moments, hasn't told them herself. He'd left her religious instruction to Chief Wiremu Tamihana, who was educated by the missionaries though never himself became a Christian. Not too impressed with the pakeha God, his old friend probably brought Tommo's daughter up in the Maori way with their pantheon of Gods.

The note concludes by asking him if he wishes to be at Hinetitama's bedside as a comfort to her in her final hours.

Mrs Billings has turned at last and is on her way back to the kitchen when Hawk looks up. 'On second thoughts I won't stop for tea. Will you make me a couple of the same sandwiches you made for the lad?'

Mrs Billings stops and turns, one eyebrow raised in indignant surprise. 'Oh you wouldn't eat what I gives 'im, sir! That's scrag ends o' mutton and yesterday's bread. I'll not be wasting good meat and pickles on the likes o' a poor brat like that!'

'The same for me, if you please, Mrs Billings,' Hawk quietly scolds her, 'I'm sure he's as fond of cold roast beef and mustard pickle as I am.'

'Doubt he's ever 'ad it,' his housekeeper sniffs.

Hawk fans himself absently with the letter he is holding. 'Oh, and tell the lad to wait, he can come with me to St Kilda. There's no need for Brock to bring the motor, we'll take a taxi. Will you please telephone the taxi depot for one and have him waiting.'

Mrs Billings, not at all happy to have been reprimanded, sniffs again. 'Blimey, you'd think it was the boy what's had a bad day.'

In the taxi cab on the way to the hospice Hawk unwraps the sandwiches Mrs Billings has made for him and starts to eat one, expecting the boy to do the same. But the lad continues to hug the parcel of bread and meat he carries to his chest.

'Not hungry then?' Hawk asks.

The lad shakes his head. 'No, mister.'

Hawk smiles. 'You haven't given me your name.' He extends his hand. 'I'm Hawk Solomon.'

'I know,' the urchin says. 'You the biggest nigger in the world!'

Hawk laughs. 'Maybe. In my experience there's always

someone who's bigger, smarter, faster, more cunning or more skilled, son.' He takes a second bite from his sandwich and chews it awhile, thinking as he does so that Mrs Billings makes a nice mustard pickle. 'Well, what's the big secret?' he finally asks. 'You know my name, you keeping yours to yourself then, lad?'

'Billyboysmith, mister.'

'Not mister! We've already been introduced, it's Mr Solomon if you please, Mr Smith,' Hawk laughs.

'Billyboysmith,' the urchin says quickly.

'Yes, that's what you said, Billyboy.'

'No I ain't, I said Billyboysmith, it's all together like.'

'Billyboysmith, all one word? Not two, like Billyboy,' Hawk pauses and then says, 'and Smith?'

'Nuh, me mum says it's Billyboysmith because she says that's the bloke she thinks she 'ad me with if she remembers correk.'

'Well, well, now, I don't suppose I'll forget that in a hurry, Mr Billyboysmith,' Hawk says, amused.

'Yessir,' Billyboysmith says, then quickly adds, 'Mr Solomon.'

Hawk finds himself liking the urchin who has tucked himself into the corner of the taxi cab. He is tall himself, a bag of rag and bones, lanky and awkward, and he knows he doesn't belong and is trying to give the giant Hawk as much space as he can so as not to be a nuisance. Hawk realises that there is nothing about the exchange they've just been through which suggests the boy is a smart alec. He likes the way Billyboysmith has stood up for his correct name.

'Got any brothers and sisters?' Hawk asks between another mouthful.

The boy places his sandwiches on his lap and thinks for a moment, then slowly begins counting on his fingers, his lips moving. Finally he nods, satisfied, and holds up both hands with only the thumb of his left hand concealed.

'Nine! Six girls and three boys.'

'Nine?' Hawk says in surprise.

The boy nods again and grins. 'We got one in the oven, there's gunna be ten of us soon.'

'All hungry I expect. Your father working?'

The boy shakes his head. 'He done a runner. They don't stay long them uncles. They gets me mum with a bun then they piss orf. Me mum does washin' fer the nuns, at the 'ospice.'

'It's not much to keep body and soul together, nine mouths to feed and one on the way.'

'We all does our bit,' Billyboysmith says proudly, then adds gratuitously, 'Every time we gets another one me mum says, "Bugger me dead, where'd that one come from?" and then we all got to remember what "uncle" it were so we can put his name onto the baby's name.'

Hawk throws back his head and laughs. 'You mean all nine have a different father, a different surname?'

Billyboysmith grins. 'One o' me sisters is called Gertiebell, that works good, but another one,' he brings a grubby hand up to his mouth trying to conceal his mirth, 'she's called Nellypoop.' He giggles, 'We calls her Smellypoop!'

'Billyboysmith and Gertiebell and Smelly . . .' Hawk laughs again and waves his hand in a gesture of dismissal. 'Billyboysmith, not *Bully*boysmith I hope?'

'No, sir, Mr Solomon, I ain't no bully.' He pauses. 'But I don't take no shit neither, I can fight if I 'as to.'

'And what is it you want to do when you're older?' Hawk asks.

'Same as everyone, fight the Germans.'

'How old are you, Billyboysmith?'

'Fourteen, sir, Mr Solomon.'

'I daresay it will be all over by the time you're old enough to volunteer, lad.'

'It ain't fair, I'd be good at killing Germans an' all, I ain't frightened of no one.'

'Count yourself fortunate, lad, killing isn't a pleasant business.'

Billyboysmith looks confused. 'I'd be doing it for our King and for England, that's good, ain't it?'

Hawk smiles, not wanting to give Billyboysmith a lecture on the morality of man's propensity to kill one another.

'Some say I look eighteen and could join up. You get five bob a day, they says.'

'Take my advice Billyboysmith and sit this one out,' Hawk says quietly. He still has two of Mrs Billings' sandwiches and almost half of a third. He lifts the open parcel from his lap and offers it to the urchin. 'Here, Billyboysmith, I'm not a bit hungry, tuck in, mate.'

Billyboysmith's eyes grow large and he puts his own packet of sandwiches on his lap and snatches the parcel from Hawk's hands and places it on his lap beside his own. He takes the half-eaten sandwich in both hands and, bringing it up, tears voraciously at it with his teeth. It is as if he hasn't eaten for a couple of days and, in his haste to get the bread and meat down, he barely chews before swallowing. The half-sandwich gone he looks longingly at the two remaining, then sighs and rewraps them carefully and places the parcel on his lap beside the other. Billyboysmith pushes his thin body back into the corner of the cab and, taking up both parcels of meat and bread, he clutches them tightly to his scrawny little chest.

Upon his arrival at the hospice Hawk hands Billyboysmith a sixpence. Billy has to put the two packages down to accept. 'Gee thanks, mister!' he exclaims in wide-eyed surprise, looking at the small silver coin in his hand as though not quite believing his luck.

Hawk sighs in an exaggerated manner. '*Mr Solomon*, if you please, *Mister* Billyboysmith.'

'Ain't I supposed to be "master"? Master Billyboysmith. I ain't grow'd up yet, though I could be eighteen if I wanted.' Billyboysmith pockets the coin and snatching up the two parcels jumps from the cab. 'Cheer'o, sir . . . er, Mr, uh . . . Solomon,' he teases cheekily.

Hawk calls after him. 'What's your mother's name, son?'

Billyboysmith stops and turns to face Hawk, who is having trouble squeezing his huge frame through the door of the cab. 'It's Miss O'Shea.'

'Miss?' Hawk says surprised, then repeats, 'Miss O'Shea, so what's your surname then?'

Billyboysmith nods. 'I'm Billyboysmith O'Shea. She ain't never been married, so she's just Miss Therese O'Shea, sir, Mr Solomon.' He grins. 'It don't make Father Crosby too happy neither. But me mum says she's buggered if she's gunna have a bunch o' bastard kids from only one bastard so's they grows up to be identical drunks the each as stupid as the other, thank you very much, but no thanks!'

'Billyboysmith, you'd better come and see me next week, see if we can find you a job,' Hawk says.

'Yessir! Thank you, sir . . . er, Mr Solomon, sir,' Billyboysmith stammers, this time overcome, and runs off. 'Goodbye, sir,' he shouts from the darkness beyond the street lamp.

Hawk thinks how he has deliberately preoccupied himself with Billyboysmith so that he will not sink into a slough of despondency. But now he prepares himself for the vigil ahead in the little hospice where Tommo's daughter lies dying.

A week earlier he had ordered a lead-lined coffin of a most impressive nature from John Allison, the city's prestigious funeral parlour, and had instructed that it must be properly sealed for travel and its solid silver handles and other 'furnishings' remain intact and were not to be removed. On the lid he had requested a polished silver plaque to be inscribed:

PRINCESS HINETITAMA,
A DAUGHTER OF THE MAORI PEOPLE

He rings the night bell and then enters the vestibule of the hospice, which, much to his surprise, is lit by a lantern hanging from the ceiling. He sees that Hinetitama's coffin stands ready within it, supported by a carpenter's horse at either end. In the dozens of times he has visited the hospice at night he has never seen a light or a coffin in this entrance, yet death, he knows, is a daily occurrence. The Sisters of Charity are simply too poor to afford to maintain a lantern which has no practical use.

Then it suddenly strikes Hawk that the nuns have put the coffin on display to show off its grandness, to give an air of dignity to their hospice. Death is such a poverty-stricken business here that Hinetitama's coffin lends them all prestige, and even, by their terms, grandeur, an object to brighten their selfless lives. A nun arrives carrying a candle and Hawk is ushered into the hospice ward.

The ward is in almost total darkness but for the candle she carries and a hurricane lamp suspended from the ceiling hook above where he knows Hinetitama's bed to be located. The lamp throws a pale yellow circle of light which extends to include a chair the nuns have placed beside the bed for Hawk's vigil. The night sister bids him a whispered goodnight and retires to return to her cubicle, leaving the remainder of the ward in stygian darkness.

It is a darkness filled with the sounds of the dying. Every once in a while there is a scream or howl from some unfortunate caught in the hallucinatory grip of the DT's. The air around the bed smells of Jeye's Fluid, a common disinfectant, though it is mixed with the

179

smoky oleaginous smell of the kerosene lamp. Permeating everything is the insidious, sweet, slightly putrid smell of death.

There are fifteen beds in the ward, some of which Father Crosby has visited before nightfall. These are the Catholics, selected by the nuns earlier in the day for absolution, the dying who are not expected to last through the night.

If these poor souls believe that, with their sins confessed and absolution granted, a merciful God will yet save them from the fires of hell, then the others among the dying must feel that Hawk's huge black presence caught, as it is, in the circle of light, can only be a visitation from the devil himself.

The sense of panic and the sounds of fear palpably increase in the darkness around Hawk as they catch a glimpse of the King of Hades, whose white hair and great dark satanic head almost brush the ceiling as he enters and upon whose terrible face, lit by the light of the nun's candle, can plainly be seen the scratch marks of God's wrath. The Devil has come to take one of their kind, but they know that they too will soon enough follow, to be drawn down to where they will be embraced in a halo of light caused by the eternally roaring flames of hell.

Hawk seats himself in the chair beside the bed and takes Hinetitama's tiny clawlike hand in his own. 'How you going, girlie?' he asks softly.

Hinetitama is too weak to reply but Hawk can feel the slightest pressure of her fingers as she acknowledges him. He knows suddenly that she has waited for him to come, fought to keep death at bay until he arrived. He leans forward and says into her ear, 'I told them you were Maori, girlie. Not Catholic or Protestant, Maori, from a tribe that's proud to claim you as their daughter and a princess in your own right with Gods of your own.'

Hawk pauses, trying to fight back his tears and to keep his voice even. 'Because, you see, girlie, we're taking you back to where you belong. Back to Aotearoa, among the giant kauri trees that sweep the skies and brush the howling wind to a whisper in the forest canopy. Back where your spirit will walk through the flowering meadows and listen to the running of clean water over pebbles kissed smooth by a million years of passing by.'

'My sweet Hinetitama, I'm taking you back to bury you with your own people, near where little Tommo sits sleeping in a cave which faces the sunrise.' Hawk gulps back his tears, his voice choked as he continues, 'You'll sing to him all the songs that only a Maori princess may sing. Your voice will be in the sigh of the wind, contained in the mountain echoes, it will become the soft murmur of the runnels made from the melting snow and be heard in the sudden rushing sound of a late afternoon breeze bending the flax grass. We're taking you back, back to your beloved people, where you belong, my little Maori maiden, my beautiful princess.'

Hawk feels Hinetitama's grip loosen and she gives a soft sigh and the tremors in her hands stop forever. The nightmare is over, Hinetitama has gone to join Tommo in The Land of the Long White Cloud.

Chapter Seven

HAWK AND DAVID – A FIGHT
TO THE DEATH

Melbourne 1914

Hawk leaves the hospice in the early hours of the morning of Hinetitama's death. He has had some weeks to reconcile himself to its inevitability and his tears are now turned inward. Even as a poor wretch, ravaged by years of abuse, Hinetitama remained an innocent, with a heart that never seemed to have hardened to a world of grog and the life of a derro. Hawk tries to console himself with the knowledge that she died aware there was someone who loved and cared about her. After placing his large hand on her brow, Hawk rises wearily from her bedside, his heart heavy, his bones aching. 'Tommo, I let you down, I'm sorry, I'm truly sorry, mate,' he whispers. For the first time in his life he feels old. 'Why,' he thinks to himself, 'must I live to see everyone I love die before me?'

He startles the night sister almost out of her wits by handing her a cheque with the words, 'There is more than sufficient in this to install an electric light system, Sister Brigid.' The Irish nun glances down at the piece of paper in her hands, it is for a larger sum than she's ever seen, larger even than the amounts whispered in the most ardent prayers Mother Superior has urged them to address to the Lord to supply their needs.

'Oh my goodness!' she gasps, holding the cheque to her rapidly palpitating heart. 'Mercy be, to be sure, I shall faint.'

Hawk reaches into his purse and takes out a five pound note. 'I would be most obliged if you would see that my niece is dressed in a new cotton nightgown.' He pauses, then adds a little sheepishly, 'Her hair is still beautiful, will you see that it is washed and brushed? I should like it to hang over her shoulders, over the front, like?'

The nun nods her head, still holding the cheque clasped to her bosom. 'I'm . . . I'm sure that will be a pleasure, s-sir,' she stammers. 'To be sure, I shall see to it meself.'

Hawk places the money on the desk beside the nun. 'Thank you, Sister, I shall make arrangements for the casket.'

Sister Brigid, now somewhat recovered, says, 'You'll be wanting to see Mother Superior before you're to be going now. I shall call her if you'll wait a moment?'

'No, no, Sister, it is just past dawn, you're not to wake her.'

The Irish nun looks surprised. 'Wake her? She'll be up having said her rosary and scrubbed her cell. She'll not be lying abed, you can be sure of that now.'

'No, really, Sister. I crave your indulgence. It's been a long night. I shall visit at another time to pay my respects to Sister Angelene and to Father Crosby. In the meantime would you thank her for the loving care you have shown.' Hawk bows his head slightly. 'I am most grateful to you all.'

The nun, still clutching Hawk's cheque, afraid to place it down, smiles and stoops to look through the slot in her cubicle, which looks into the ward just beginning to be tinged with the light of a new day. 'Electric lights? What a grand thing that will be.'

Hawk decides to walk home to Caulfield, a journey on foot of nearly an hour. He has a great deal to think about and sets off at a brisk pace. The sun rises soon after his departure and he removes his jacket, but it is not long before the sweat runs down his neck and he can feel his starched collar grow damp. It is a small enough risk that anyone who may know him will see him, or even be up and about at such an early hour and so he removes his weskit as well and loosens his tie. Comfortable in his linen shirt and braces, he strides onwards.

In the weeks preceding Hinetitama's death, Hawk has done a great deal of thinking about what he should do about Solomon & Teekleman now that he once again controls a majority of its shares. He has kept the knowledge of Hinetitama's reappearance from both Ben and Victoria at Hinetitama's request, but Victoria will want to know how he managed to regain control of the shares. He decides he must tell her and risk her anger at not being allowed to see Hinetitama before she died. More importantly, he is not sure how he will explain the situation in which they now find themselves.

Victoria has never been told of his aspirations for her to succeed him and, increasingly, she is being drawn to the Labor Party and sees her ultimate career in the law as a means to help the poor and the working classes. Hawk is not convinced that she will happily take to the proposition of one day running a huge organisation dedicated to making money for the already vastly wealthy.

She has, of course, some years previously asked him why her surname is included in the company name. He replied that he thought Solomon & Teekleman was a name which constantly reminded everyone of the enmity between the two families, that one day she and Ben would own a large shareholding in the company and it seemed appropriate that their surname be included in it. Victoria had accepted this explanation at the time but she has on more than one occasion suggested that Hawk, at the annual meeting of shareholders, propose that the name be dropped and they sell their shares to Abraham and Joshua.

'Grandpa, I am ashamed of it! People look at me when I'm introduced and say "*The* Teekleman?", some because they are impressed and others because they despise what the name stands for. Either way I am ashamed to be associated with it, to be a shareholder!'

Hawk has always resisted both requests, putting it down to youthful idealism that will modify as Victoria grows older and becomes involved with the company. But he also knows how stubborn she can be. Now that he is potentially back in control of Solomon & Teekleman he may not be able to effectively manage it. He realises that his eventual ambitions for Victoria may be impossible to accomplish and that he, or rather circumstances, have conspired to leave his run too late.

Sir Abraham Solomon and his stewardship, though not spectacular, have been steady and he has done nothing to harm the profitability of the two giant companies under the Solomon &

Teekleman banner. The times have been prosperous and both have simply continued to grow, finding opportunities to expand without having to seek them out and at very little financial or decision-taking risk.

Hawk is well versed in the affairs of Solomon & Teekleman, but only as a shareholder. He has been absent from the helm for more than two decades and is sufficiently astute to realise that he knows little of the internal workings of the two companies and may no longer be the right man for chairman. Or even if he is, Abraham Solomon would almost certainly retire if he attempted to take over, leaving him alone to organise the affairs of the conglomerate.

Tom Pickles, who is the managing director of the Potato Factory, has requested early retirement. Pickles, a veteran of the Boer War, was wounded at Spion Kop and now has only one lung working effectively, a condition which is exacerbated by the inclement and unpredictable Hobart weather and a childhood spent in an orphanage where, like most of the children, he showed a propensity for bronchial ailments.

Pickles started his working life as one of Mary's orphans and soon proved to be a cut above the usual lad or lass brought into an apprenticeship at the brewery so that Mary picked him early for better things and trained him to accountancy. He had risen to assistant manager of the accounts department when he enlisted for the Boer War, where he was mentioned in dispatches. He returned to the Potato Factory a war hero and resumed his previous job. With Mary dead and Hawk replaced by Abraham, he soon again showed his original promise and was appointed as the manager of the accounts department. When David retired, Abraham elevated Pickles to the position of managing director so that he himself could assume the title of chairman of Solomon & Teekleman.

Pickles has served the company well but, increasingly, is plagued by chronic bronchitis. The doctor has advised him to move to a more equable climate and has suggested Queensland. It is proposed that Wilfred Harrington, the managing director of Solomon & Co., take his place in Hobart and that Joshua, having completed a year of learning the ropes, be given the same position at Solomon & Co. A neat enough arrangement had it not been for the outbreak of war.

Hawk now thinks that it may be possible to broker a

compromise. He will agree to leave Abraham as chairman and, upon his return from the war, allow Joshua to take up his position as M.D. of Solomon & Co., in return for the vacant position of managing director of the Potato Factory and a position for Victoria as a trainee under Hawk's direction.

This is not altogether wishful thinking. Hawk has some reason to believe it might be acceptable. Abraham doesn't share David's pathological hate for Hawk, and has hinted that he would be willing for him to return as the managing director of the Potato Factory under his chairmanship, but only after David has passed on. Hawk has never pursued this idea, thinking it prudent to wait until David is dead.

However, they badly underestimated David's tenacity and physical toughness. He did not retire for lack of strength or the will to continue, but for the singular purpose of training the fifteen-year-old Joshua to take control of Solomon & Teekleman. Obsessed with this mission he has managed to live through his grandson's puberty and into his adulthood. David at ninety-four is still a force to be reckoned with, though recently he has spoken of seeing Joshua take up his rightful role in the company and, then, in his own words, 'Carking it, being rid of you miserable bloody lot once and for all!'

But just when all seemed in place, with Joshua back from Oxford and having almost completed his mandatory year learning the practical aspects of running Solomon & Co., war is declared in Europe.

David is mortified, instantly flying into one of his infamous tantrums. Lacking the strength to break things with an axe, he demands to be wheeled into the kitchen and has the kitchen maid bring him every plate, cup and saucer in the house and stack them beside his wheelchair. Then, hammer in hand, he has Adams, the butler, read the underside of each plate or piece of crockery to determine its origin. Those pieces made in England, France or Germany he smashes. In the first hour after he has been told of the declaration of war David renders a small fortune in Royal Doulton, Wedgwood, Limoges and Rosenthal as well as a dozen manufacturers of lesser fame into a colourful sea of broken crockery that covers the entire surface of the kitchen floor. Exhausted, he is put to bed mumbling obscenities and the doctor is called. The doctor warns him that another such conniption could bring on a heart attack, to which David shouts, 'Piss off, what would you know, you stupid old fart!'

David takes the declaration of war personally. He sees it as a part of the long-standing persecution he has received at the hands of Mother England. Just another part of the personal vendetta she has waged against him all his life. He tells himself that because of his advanced age she is taking this final opportunity to put the boot in. The first time she got her claws into him was when she'd transported his mother and their little family to the utmost ends of the earth. Now she would see him dead and buried before Joshua assumes his rightful inheritance, she would rob him of this one great ambition and see him die without achieving it. David knows from the moment war is declared that not even he will be able to dissuade Joshua from volunteering to fight for the old whore.

While at Oxford Joshua has trained in the OTC, the Oxford University Officer Training Corps, under the direction of the Royal Oxfordshire Regiment. Now he is raring to return to the grand sport offered by a proper war. He has often enough hinted to his grandfather that had he not been trained to commerce he would have liked the life of a professional soldier. It is a prospect totally abhorrent to his grandfather and one of the very few things that has come between the two of them. David's intention in sending Joshua to Oxford was simply so that he might gain all the social contacts and background he would need as the head of an industrial empire. David knew that Joshua was unlikely to do anything of academic note and thought to sneak his grandson in and out of Oxford without Mother England realising he was there, a colonial son making so little impression that the old bitch hardly noticed his presence. But she'd known all along of his whereabouts and promptly set about corrupting his mind with military gung-ho and carry-on.

David has over the years made generous donations to causes serving the interests of both the conservative and the radical sides of local politics and, by sheer attrition and the ultimate size of the accumulated donations, gained a knighthood for Abraham. Like everything else about his son, in his father's mind Abraham's title is intended to bolster Joshua's credentials, the gentile son of a Jew is a difficult concept to grasp but, in David's mind, the son of a knight of the realm, who coincidently happens to be of the Jewish faith, is quite a different perception and will help to bolster his grandson's credentials as a bona fide gentile.

Joshua, ever dutiful, has enhanced this claim to respectability whilst at Oxford by becoming a surrogate Englishman, a complete Anglophile, adopting the mannerisms and attitudes of the English upper class. While at university he has managed to perfect a set of rounded vowels to match his new-found affectations. The ultimate irony is that David's grandson now considers it his patriotic duty to fight for the country for which his grandfather retains only the bitterest memories and feels the greatest antipathy.

Hawk thinks the miserable old bastard will somehow contrive to keep himself alive until Joshua returns from the war and is seen to fulfil his grandfather's ambition. He knows also that Abraham is unlikely to agree to his conditions while David is alive and that it is the ninety-four-year-old whom he must convince, a task which he knows will be formidable.

The certain ascendancy of Joshua to chairman has also been a problem preoccupying Hawk for some years. He has never given up the idea of Victoria usurping him for the same position. Even before Hinetitama reappeared, under the terms of Mary's will Ben and Victoria resume control of their ten per cent of the company shares when Victoria becomes thirty, by which time, unbeknownst to David and Abraham, Hawk's side will again own the majority of shares.

Hawk knows that, with his increasing age, Victoria is his only real hope of getting Solomon & Teekleman back under the control of his side of the family. Ben is essentially an outdoors man and his bum sits more comfortably in the saddle than on an office chair. Although he seems to attract the co-operation of those around him, his is a leadership by example and not out of a sense of being superior.

This lack of ambition in Ben has also been apparent to David and Abraham, both of whom have secretly kept a watchful eye on the young man as he was growing up. They are now certain that Ben will never prove a danger to Joshua and have forgotten about him.

But Victoria is an altogether different proposition. When David first discovered that Hawk's granddaughter, then only fourteen years old, used the abacus with consummate skill, he had her progress monitored and forbade his son to admit her at any stage into any aspect of the company. 'She's another one!' he'd raged. 'Another Mary bloody Abacus! She's not to be employed, not until hell freezes over, you hear me, Abraham?'

'But why, Father, she will one day be a major shareholder, it is as well not to make an enemy of her now. She is still a child but will eventually be a woman, and will marry and have children and assume a woman's place in the home. Surely we have nothing to fear if, when she is eighteen, we bring her into the company where we will be able to keep an eye on her?'

'The abacus!' David shouts. 'Can't you see, it's the bloody abacus!' It is almost as though, in his eyes, the abacus itself is an instrument potent enough to destroy them all. It becomes apparent to Abraham that to the superstitious and ignorant old man, the abacus is a dangerous, almost mystical weapon placed in the hands of a young sorceress who, through some sort of witchcraft engendered by the Chinese counting beads, will triumph over them.

Ignoring the fact that there has only ever been one woman and one abacus, he makes it sound as though there have been a succession of Marys since time out of mind. 'You'll see!' he screams. 'Soon her fingers will grow crooked and her talons grow sharp as a ferret's teeth!'

And so Hawk, unable to place Victoria within the Potato Factory, has her trained in every aspect of bookkeeping and accountancy. After which, she sits for her university entrance examination and wins one of the very rare places for a female student in the law faculty of the University of Melbourne. Hawk, afraid that as the only woman in the faculty she will suffer at the hands of the male students, persuades her instead to gain her articles. By pulling strings, he finds her a position as articled clerk in the office of the prominent city law firm Slade, Slade & Hetherington, in Collins Street.

There are very few women solicitors in Victoria, but Hawk thinks it would be good training for her agile and questioning mind. This proves to be a not altogether ideal arrangement. A female articled clerk is far from welcome in a profession and a clerks' chamber dominated by males. This is even further exacerbated when the other articled clerks in Slade, Slade & Hetherington are confronted by a young woman who is not afraid to express an opinion, doesn't know her rightful place as a female and is a junior. They also discover that she can be inordinately stubborn when she thinks she is right and has the audacity to possess more than a modicum of grey matter and a logical mind to boot. The only other female in the company is the tea lady, Mrs Wilkinson, a timid creature in her late forties in a mob-cap, who addresses the most junior clerk as sir.

Because of all of these things, but mostly because she is female, Tommo's granddaughter is given the work nobody else wants to do. These are inevitably tasks well below her intellectual capacity which she performs generally with her bottom lip tucked under her top teeth, but essentially without complaint.

Her working life filled with tedium, Victoria is hungry for some intellectual stimulus and is astonished when one day Mrs Wilkinson approaches her while she is alone in the firm's library looking up torts for a senior partner and asks her if she would like to attend a meeting of the St Kilda branch of the Labor Party. To her amazement, after a whispered conversation, she discovers the tea lady to be far from the tepid creature she appears to be.

In fact, Mrs Wilkinson proves to be a veritable firebrand who introduces Victoria to the politics of poverty, the rights denied to the underprivileged and the conditions of the working classes. Victoria needs little encouragement to take sides, she has already gained a dim view of lawyers in particular and the business world in general, what Mrs Wilkinson calls 'the lining of fat around the hungry belly of society', meaning by this the world dominated by middle-class males who think themselves superior by dint of money, a privileged upbringing and a stint at Melbourne Grammar.

For the first time in her life, Victoria hears the viewpoint of the other side from men who wear cloth caps and women who cover their heads with cheap scarves and wear knitted jerseys with holes in them, but who nevertheless have fine minds, have read widely and have a mission to fight for the rights of the working classes.

The fact that she is amongst the most privileged of them all in terms of wealth never occurs to Victoria. Hawk has not let her grow up in a wealthy environment nor molly-coddled her in childhood nor ever allowed her to develop a sense of privilege. Brought up on one of Hawk's hop farms near New Norfolk she and Ben have had a natural and easy upbringing, attending the local primary school.

When Ben reached the age of twelve and the limits of the education locally available, Hawk brought in as his tutors Mr and Mrs Wickworth-Spode, recent immigrants to Tasmania. Mr

Wickworth-Spode, a graduate from Cambridge, was the retired headmaster of a boys' school in England and a mathematics and history teacher, while Mrs Wickworth-Spode had been a teacher of English and Latin at Roedean, a famous English public school for girls. Both were fanatical gardeners and with a cottage of their own, all the gardening space they could contend with and a generous salary as well, Hawk was able to attract them to the New Norfolk farm.

It soon became apparent that Ben was an indifferent scholar with his eyes constantly turned to the schoolroom window and the promised freedom of what lay beyond. But the ten-year-old Victoria, who would rush from primary school to sit in on the last hour of Ben's lessons, proved to be a naturally gifted learner, in particular with numbers. She would often confound Mr Wickworth-Spode as her little fingers blurred across the abacus to return an answer to a sum in the time it took a bemused Ben to chew a couple of times at the end of his yellow pencil.

When it was Victoria's turn to come under the total influence of the redoubtable husband-and-wife team, they doted on her and gave their every attention to her education. It was a happy childhood with the rigours of a sound education admirably mixed with the easygoing business of life in the country, and Hawk keeping a sharp eye on their progress when he visited them once a fortnight from Melbourne. Hawk brought Victoria at eighteen to live with him in Melbourne while Ben remained, by choice, in Tasmania learning hop farming, taking over the management and the general supervision of the hop farms when he turned twenty-one. Mr and Mrs Wickworth-Spode retired to the cottage with Mr Wickworth-Spode doing the books for the four estates and Mrs Wickworth-Spode keeping the kitchen supplied with vegetables.

Despite her private tutors and an education which proves to be well in advance of the people she meets of her own age, Victoria doesn't see herself as above her contemporaries. They know her as a young woman with a confident and outgoing personality and friendly disposition.

By contrast, she constantly earns the disapproval of the senior law clerk and even sometimes makes her opinions known in the august presence of one or another of the male partners when she believes an injustice has been perpetrated. She is also prepared to accept their rebukes if she is proved to be wrong, though she seldom lets her emotions override her logic and so she is more often right than wrong, which doesn't endear her to any of the men. If it were not for the importance of Hawk's personal financial dealings with the firm and the fact that her marks in the periodic law examinations are the highest in the State of Victoria, it is doubtful that Slade, Slade & Hetherington would continue to employ her.

Hawk can see that she is unhappy and attempts to mollify her. 'My dear, it is never wise to bite the hand that feeds you, they will not change their ways because you have proved them to be fools. Stay the course, bite your tongue, be patient, your time will come.'

'But, Grandpa, it is not my intention to seem difficult, I wish only that they will be just and fair.'

Hawk laughs. 'Justice requires integrity and there is little enough of that among lawyers. They would sooner get rid of you than have to deal with their own consciences.'

'But it's not fair!' Victoria protests. 'The poor are evicted from their homes so that our clients can build factories on the site rather than find locations where electricity, gas, drainage and roads must first be built. Then they erect sweatshops in which women work for starvation wages!' Victoria has already picked up the vernacular of the Labor Party. 'That is just *one* case I am working on,' she continues. 'What's more they will win. They'll win because there is no one able to oppose them!'

Hawk looks at Victoria shrewdly. 'Have you thought to find out who owned the homes from which the poor were evicted?'

'Of course,' Victoria snorts. 'The rich slum landlords who sell them to the developers at a huge profit but which is still less than what it would cost to develop virgin land with all the utilities to be resourced.'

'Ah, there you have it, the very principle upon which English law is based, the right of property over the rights of the common man. Throughout the history of English law the penalties for damaging property have always been greater than those for harming people. The law has always protected the "haves" and punished those who have nothing. It is very simple, my dear, it is the "haves" who have always made the laws.'

'But, Grandpa, they are hypocrites and the mayor announces to the world at large that they are clearing the crime-infested slums for the benefit of the city when their true motive is to build factories convenient to the city, the railways and the port! The mayor is one of the shareholders in their development syndicate!'

'And what would you have them do? Build homes for the poor with hundred-year mortgages and no interest payments?' Hawk chuckles. 'Ours is a profit-based society with the upper class owning the capital, the middle class utilising it and the working class enduring the consequences. The poor will always be among us and while there is very little profit to a lawyer in defending a poor man's plea for justice, there is a great deal of money to be made out of helping a rich man to exploit him. That, my dear Victoria, is what you are up against and, quite frankly, I don't like your chances.'

'But we are supposed to be an egalitarian society where Jack is as good as his master.'

'In my experience wherever there is a master and a Jack travelling along the same road, it is Jack who carries the master's portmanteau but the master who gets paid for the wares within it. Money, not class, is the equaliser in this country, Victoria, which is perhaps better than class controlling it. No profession understands this better than those who practise at the law.'

Victoria looks up, appealing to Hawk. 'Grandpa Hawk, they are not even clever men, they think to please their clients with sycophantic advice, invitations to the races at Flemington and the cricket at the MCG and suppers of roast beef and claret at the Melbourne Club. They are rapacious, selfish and vainglorious and would step over a beggar rather than throw him a coin. They don't even get their Latin right!' Victoria says in a final expression of her frustration.

'Spoken with all the insight of the very young,' Hawk laughs. 'If brains and Latin were the sole criteria for success in business there'd be a poor living in store for most of us.' Nevertheless, he is delighted with Victoria's strong sense of justice but realises that, while he shares it, his attempts to be just and honest have brought nothing but misery and failure into his own life.

Victoria will often outline a case to him in which she has acted as articled clerk and Hawk learns that she has a capacity to see both sides of a question and draw a quick and accurate conclusion. If ever she should qualify and find herself in charge of handling a case in front of a magistrate, he knows she has a tongue that can cut like a whip and an ability to quickly spot a fool, whether barrister, solicitor, witness, defendant, policeman or magistrate. Victoria may not be a blood relation of Mary Abacus, but she has the same uncanny ability to know what is wheat and what is chaff, what is useful and what is pure hyperbole. Perhaps it is the same instinct Tommo had as a gambler, to know what was real and what was bluff.

At the age of twenty-two Victoria sits for her final law examinations and passes with flying colours. During the course of a celebratory dinner, Hawk, admittedly somewhat reluctantly, points out to her that there may be some future advantage in being counted among the members of Melbourne's society. He adds that while he believes himself not suitable as a black man to make her introductions he can quite easily find the right chaperone to do so.

Victoria is mortified by this suggestion. 'Grandfather, how could you think such a thing? You of all people!' she cries. 'It is everything I am against! They are the people who exploit the workers, who cheat and lie and rob the poor and you want me to join them?' She is barely able to conceal her anger at Hawk's suggestion.

'Not all of them. Not all rich people exploit the poor,' the ever reasonable Hawk protests.

'I can't think of any who don't!' Victoria snaps, letting her indignation override her logic.

Hawk laughs. 'Well, I can.'

'Who? They're all the same. I see them every day.'

'Well, *you*, my dear, soon you'll be richer than most of them. You don't exploit the poor.'

Victoria is scornful in her reply. 'Tush, the money Ben and I get when we're thirty from Great-grandmother's will won't make us rich?'

'Rich enough, but the money you will inherit from me, I daresay, will make you the richest woman in the nation.'

'But that's obscene!' Victoria cries, then quickly adds, 'I shall give it all away!'

Hawk laughs again. 'It won't make a lot of difference if you do. You and Ben will inherit a majority share in Solomon & Teekleman. As fast as you give it away your wealth will be renewed.'

'But, Grandfather Hawk, they are among the worst of the slum landlords and the developers! Did you know that they employ only Freemasons?'

Hawk nods. 'One of David's little innovations.'

'It's not little. Freemasonry, as you no doubt know, requires some expense which, generally speaking, is beyond a poor man's resources. So David made it a condition that anyone who works for the company must be a Freemason and then the company pays for the regalia and, furthermore, as an incentive to join, the company pays their sick and old-age benefits as well.'

'Yes, well, I've always thought it one of the few acts of real generosity emanating from David Solomon.'

'Generosity my foot! You know what that means, don't you? The benefit funds are administered by the Independent Order of Oddfellows, who have strong links with Freemasonry. Grandfather, they are in each other's pockets up to their armpits.'

'I would think that perfectly legitimate. If you're going to pay for the workers' benefits you have every right to choose the friendly society you are going to involve.'

'You still don't get the point!' Victoria exclaims. 'Lots of the company's workers are poor but they are Protestants and now Freemasons. Lots of Catholics are poor but they are forbidden by the Church to be Freemasons. So Solomon & Teekleman deliberately pick their so-called slum areas to buy and then to clear for the building of factories, offices and middle-class homes where the workers' cottages are predominantly Catholic, knowing that their own workers are unlikely to be sympathetic to their plight.'

'My dear, the Freemasons are not villains, in fact integrity, honesty, moral and social virtue are the cornerstones of their beliefs. I feel sure, if they thought Abraham, as Grand Master of the Melbourne Lodge, was forcing his workers to join the brotherhood, they would soon enough do something about it. It is, I believe, one of the strongest tenets of the movement to render practical aid to the less fortunate members of the community. By helping the poorer of his own workers to embrace the brotherhood and by ensuring some sort of sinecure for them in sickness and old age, isn't Abraham doing just that?'

'Yes, but only for his own workers! The unions are powerless to prevent them from going ahead with a particular development by utilising the only weapon they have, to bring the company workers out on strike. As Freemasons, the company employees have elected not to join the various unions. Did you know the company does not employ a single member of a union! Nor can the unions bring the workers from the outside contractors and suppliers out on strike against them, because Solomon & Teekleman are virtually self-sufficient, they largely own all their own equipment and the resources to complete a "slum clearance" as they are so fond of calling it.'

'Just for a moment, let's take the company's point of view. What have they done wrong? You call it exploiting the poor, they call it much-needed slum clearance. They are *not* the government, they are *not* required to make decisions as to what benefits the poor and what doesn't, they are not a social welfare organisation, they are an organisation working within the law to make a profit. Moreover, they can be said to have looked after the welfare of their own employees very well indeed and, furthermore, it is the collective decision of those employees *not* to join a union. I can see that there may be a moral issue here for you and, of course, also for the unions involved, but in the purely practical sense Solomon & Teekleman have done nothing wrong. They are in a commercial sense completely blameless.'

Victoria suddenly stops and brings her fingers to her lips. 'My God, I never thought of it!' She points to Hawk. 'You're one of them, a Freemason, aren't you?' She doesn't wait for Hawk's reply. 'That's why you're defending Solomon & Teekleman, isn't it?'

Hawk laughs. 'Freemasonry is a secret society in that it doesn't disclose its members, but you are quite wrong, Victoria, I am not a Freemason, nor am I defending the company in which both your name and mine appears, but I do try to be a fair-minded and logical human being.'

'But, Grandfather, what I say is true! They have completely manipulated the situation in their favour. John Curtin, the head of the Brunswick branch of the Labor Party to which I belong, says they're virtually bulletproof. Frank Anstey the federal MP says the same. John Curtin says they've got a battery of lawyers ready to defend Sir Abraham's actions every time he passes wind! It's simply iniquitous and this is a company which, in part anyway, you and I own! My name, for God's sake, is Teekleman! How can I hold my head up? How can I live with that?' Victoria cries despairingly.

'Come now, my dear,' Hawk comforts her, handing her his handkerchief, for she has begun to cry. 'It's not as bad as all that, there's still the Potato Factory under Tom Pickles, as decent a man as they come.'

'Tom Pickles! Don't give me Tom Pickles as your example. He is Master of the Grand Lodge of Tasmania!'

'How do you know all this, Victoria?' Hawk asks sternly.

'I heard it at the Labor Party conference last April. From the Tasmanian delegates.'

'Victoria, the Potato Factory has always been a strictly ethical company in its outside dealings, and the workers were always happy. It was your great-grandmother's pride and joy that she neither cheated nor lied in her dealings with others. She would say, "I've done enough o' that in me life and 'ad the same done to me often enough. From now it's all on the square, do unto others what you'd want for yerself."'

Victoria nods. 'According to the Hobart delegate, it's the same there as here, no problems within, with the Freemasonry and health benefits and pension fund thing working, but the company's outside dealings have been described as industrial rape and pillage. All kept very quiet, mind, money and Freemasonry are a powerful combination in Collins Street, but it seems this is equally true of Elizabeth Street, Hobart.'

'Why didn't you tell me how you felt before now?'

Victoria bows her head and is silent awhile, then says softly, 'There was nothing you could do about it.' She looks up at Hawk, her eyes sad. 'I didn't want you to be hurt, Grandfather. You and Mary Abacus built the Potato Factory to be a fair place, a great and good company, you worked so hard to make it the best, now it isn't any more.'

Hawk remembers how, when Victoria was first articled as a law clerk and started to see the lack of corporate morality and greed from the inside and realised she was inadvertently a part of it, he wanted to tell her then that in a few years she and her brother would be the major shareholders again in Solomon & Teekleman, that she would have the power to change things if she eventually became chairman.

But he held his tongue at the time, knowing that it would be eight years before she came of age to exercise her proxy, by which time, with no experience in the company, she would have little chance of competing with Joshua Solomon. He also had to consider that he might well be dead or enfeebled and no matter how brilliant his grand-daughter proved to be, she would have little hope of fighting Abraham and Joshua on her own for control.

Now, with Hinetitama's death and his ability to assume control again and with the declaration of war, everything has changed and the odds have evened up for Victoria. Everything but one thing, Hawk's rapidly advancing age. He is already a septuagenarian and knows he is running out of time. He must move quickly if he is to get Victoria up and running as future competition to Joshua. There is only one way he can do this. He must once again confront David Solomon.

Hawk has no doubt that Victoria will be a match for Joshua Solomon if they compete on equal terms. As two people they are very different. Victoria is brilliant, confident, stubborn with a sharp tongue, perhaps a bit of a bossy boots, but without pretension, loyal and honest and much loved by her friends.

Joshua, on the other hand, seems of an altogether different disposition. On a superficial level he appears somewhat foppish and it would be easy to take him too lightly. But Hawk does not intend to make this mistake, Joshua is David-trained and Solomon-bred and while, on the surface, he may seem the antithesis of his uncouth and irascible grandfather, the old man appears pleased with the job he has done on his grandson and that is warning sufficient for Hawk.

In the year Joshua Solomon has been back from Oxford it is already established among the mothers in Melbourne's social circles that he is the big catch of the season. It seems he has no disadvantages beyond his odious grandfather who, fortuitously, must leave this mortal coil at any time. They titter among themselves and count Joshua's many blessings. He will be rich beyond avarice, is blue-eyed, fair-haired and handsome as can be, he is well mannered and utterly charming, with the affectations and speech of a young English gentleman. To the society matrons with unattached and eligible daughters, Joshua Solomon seems almost too good to be true. To their daughters he is truly to be swooned over. To the patriarchs of Melbourne's business community he represents the new age, the end of the gold-rush mentality with its rough and ready business ways. Joshua is one of the scions who will define business in the new century, just the sort of young business leader to represent the new Melbourne. An Oxford blue in both cricket and rugger where he played in the 1911 Australian rugby tour of England and Wales, starring on the wing in the test against Wales, he now plays cricket for Victoria.

He is urbane, bright, educated and informed. While his Jewish father is sufficient reason for him to be blackballed by the Melbourne Club, he has been accepted with alacrity as a member of the Australia Club. Old codgers in the club, witnessing the young man playing at billiards, turn to each other and remark, 'Splendid young chappie. Wish we had ten more young members made of the same solid metal, eh?'

As Hawk approaches his Caulfield home on the morning of Hinetitama's death he knows that he must somehow force David once again into a corner so that he will be made to capitulate. Hawk knows that Joshua is the key. He must pluck David's teeth first, whereupon he will see Abraham about remaining as chairman. But first he must talk to Victoria and then get some sleep.

In the late afternoon of the day of Hinetitama's death the butler, known simply as Adams, enters the sunlit conservatory of Abraham's Toorak home where David Solomon, wrapped in a light blanket, is dozing in a bathchair. The butler stands beside the old man and announces, 'Mr Hawk Solomon has called and offered his card, he requests that he might be allowed to see you, Mr David.'

'Eh? What did you say? Speak up, man!' David shouts, annoyed at being disturbed.

'Mr Hawk Solomon to see you, sir.' The butler raises one eyebrow slightly, not that David can see this clear sign of his disdain. 'A black man, sir.'

'Hawk Solomon to see me? Tell him to go ter buggery!'

'Sir, he apologises for the lack of an appointment but says it is a matter of some urgency.'

'What, *his* urgency or mine? The only matter of urgency I have is to take a piss. Here, get the bloody chamber-pot.' The old man brings his legs over the edge of the bathchair with some difficulty and places them on the floor. With hands trembling he begins to fumble with his pyjama pants. He can barely see the chamber-pot which Adams now holds at the correct level. 'Tell me when it's pointed in the right direction,' he instructs Adams, 'then close yer eyes!'

'It's about right to proceed now, sir,' the butler says solemnly. He is a big man with a pronounced belly and appears awkward as he bends to hold the chamber-pot at the right height and angle.

After what seems like ages, Adams hears the thin trickle of

urine splashing into the porcelain pot. He keeps his eyes shut until the sound finally ceases and then allows sufficient time for David's trembling fingers to return the fly of his pyjamas to a more decorous arrangement. Placing the chamber-pot down, he lifts David's trembling legs back into the bathchair and tucks the blanket around him. 'Bastard ain't worth the piss in that pot!' David snaps. 'Is that all he said, a matter of urgency? A matter of urgency about what, man!'

'Just a matter of urgency, Mr David.'

'Yes, yes, you said that before!' David says impatiently. David thinks for a moment and then decides that he will take this final opportunity to spit in the face of his last great enemy. 'Tell him he's got ten minutes and damned lucky to get it.'

'Yes, Mr David.' Adams bends slowly and picks up the chamber-pot. 'Ten minutes, it is?'

David appears to be looking about the conservatory until his failing eyesight spies a large wicker chair. 'Take that out, make the nigger boy stand.'

Adams, still holding the chamber-pot, takes the chair from the back and drags it behind him as he leaves the conservatory. 'He's not to be offered any refreshment, yer hear,' David shouts at the departing butler.

Clasping his rheumatic hands so as to appear completely calm and in control, he waits for Hawk to be ushered into his presence.

Hawk's shadowy figure stoops to allow him to enter the doorway into the conservatory. 'Ah, Hawk Solomon, you have dared to call at my house when you know you are not welcome.'

Hawk smiles. 'Would you have met me elsewhere, David?'

'Certainly not.'

'Well then, how else would I be able to say what I have come to say?'

'There is nothing you can say that would interest me, so be out with it and then be gone, I am too old to waste what time I have left in the company of a nigger.'

'Ah, my tidings, whether from a nigger or a white man, will cause you no less consternation, David Solomon,' Hawk replies evenly, not in the least upset by the outburst from the old man. He stands relaxed in front of the bathchair, towering above the supine David, who can see him as a soft image, almost a dark shadow, as if he is looking into a badly smudged mirror.

'There is naught you can do to consternate me now, you have been beaten neck and crop these last twenty years. Yer old and yer useless and yer ready to die!'

Hawk's voice is suddenly sharp. 'I have not come to banter, David Solomon, it is you, Sir Abraham and your grandson who have lost, *we* have regained the voting rights to Tommo's daughter's shares, *we* are again in the majority.'

'We? Who the hell is *we*?' David screams. 'Bah! The boy is not worth a pinch of shit, a bloody hops farmer! And the girlie, the little witch, she is like her mother, nothing but trouble. She and her abacus, opening her big gob and wailing about the conditions of the poor. What does she know about being poor, eh? Tell her to come and see me. I'll tell her about poor! Jesus!' He brings his fist up and wipes his mouth with the back of his hand as though to be rid of a bad taste. 'Now the boy's gone to war, you think she'll take over, do ya? What to do, eh? Count the daily takings with her beads?' He stabs a bony finger in Hawk's direction. 'Now you lissen t' me, yer black bastard, no old nigger and a girlie from the farm who plays with beads is gunna take over Solomon & Teekleman. You've got the proxies, has ya? From that half-caste drunken whore who went walkabout and never come back? You've got her will, has ya? And her proxy? Well, well, ain't that grand.' He pauses again to take breath and spit a gob of phlegm into a spittoon placed beside his chair, then he continues, 'So tell me? How you going to do it? How you going to take over Solomon & Teekleman? You are alone and have no one who knows of the workings of the company! Fer Christsake, you've been out of it twenty years! You'll soon be dead yerself and good riddance to bad rubbish! You think that little snot-nose solicitor girl is going to do it on her abacus . . . alone? Ha! Lemme tell you something for nothing, yer full o' bullshit, Hawk Solomon, and I'll see you in hell first!'

'Ah, but before I do, I shall take over as chairman. It will be tenure long enough to destroy your grandson.' Hawk is surprised how well informed David Solomon is about Victoria. It is, he thinks, a great compliment that they should have watched her so closely. He wonders briefly which of the senior partners at Slade, Slade & Hetherington is in David's pocket.

Nevertheless the old man has instantly put his finger on the problem and, if anything, has managed to gain the initiative.

Hawk is forced to admire him. At ninety-four his mind is still sharp as a tack. The length and content of his tirade alone would have exhausted a man thirty years his junior.

But David has only paused to draw breath. 'You think the government will stand by and let the third-biggest company in Australia with a dozen major war contracts be managed by an old fool? Allow you to put the troops in jeopardy because you want to punish a young man, an officer of the King, who has volunteered to fight for his country? You think they'll stand by and watch my son Abraham be replaced by an old blackfella who 'asn't done a day's work in twenty years? Do me a favour, will ya? Go away! You're fucked, Hawk Solomon!'

Hawk chuckles, hiding his true feelings. It is pointless, he decides, trying to put his original proposal to the old bastard. David Solomon will not compromise, will never capitulate. To get himself and Victoria back into Solomon & Teekleman will be an enormous fight. They could be saddled with years of litigation and interference from a government bureaucracy protecting its military contracts before they eventually win. And, always, there is the sense of time running out for him. Hawk decides that there is little more he can do but try to bluff his way through.

'All that work for nothing, eh, David? All those years teaching your grandson what you know and Joshua will never again have anything to do with Solomon & Teekleman. Such a pity, such a nice lad they tell me.' Hawk pauses. 'Still, you've got plenty of money, I'm sure you can buy the boy a soft job with a large income in a nice gentile firm, a sinecure so that he might remain the darling of the social set.'

But David is not a bit fazed by Hawk's taunting. He presses the electric buzzer at his arm to summon the butler. 'Bah! My lawyers will have your guts for garters! Now you lissen ter me, we'll still be here, still running things, when Joshua returns to take his rightful place. No country-bumpkin, half-arsed female solicitor who uses an abacus to count and calls herself a bloody socialist is going to take his place.' He cackles suddenly, genuinely amused at the thought. 'The nigger and the farm girl are going to run the biggest private company in Australia!' The smile disappears from his face and he sniffs derisively and, with a dismissive flick of his hand towards Hawk, says, 'Be gone with you, you cheeky black bastard!'

Hawk, remaining calm, ignores David's outburst and speaks

slowly, his voice raised so that the old man is certain to hear him. 'I have called an extraordinary general meeting of the directors for tomorrow at 10 a.m. sharp when your son will be asked to relinquish his position as chairman and, of course, I shall see that your grandson, upon his return from the war, finds no position in either company available to him.' Hawk pauses a moment, before adding, 'Victoria Teekleman will replace him and I daresay will eventually become chairman.'

Hawk allows all this to register with the old man and concludes, 'It's our turn now, David, your side is finished. As a director I hope you will be present with your son to witness Victoria Teekleman's acceptance into the company, its latest recruit, the new Mary Abacus. But I don't give a shit whether you attend or not. Tomorrow at ten o'clock sharp I shall accept your son's resignation as chairman.'

The butler comes into the conservatory. 'You wanted something, Mr David?'

'Yes, you will show this impertinent fellow to the door at once, Adams.' David turns to Hawk. 'Be gone with you, Hawk Solomon, I do not wish ever to see you again.'

'Ah, but you will I hope, David. Tomorrow.'

'Be gone! Damn your hide, nigger!' the old man shouts, shaking his fist in Hawk's direction.

Adams steps up to Hawk. 'I'm afraid you must go, my good man. Come along now, we don't want any fuss, do we?' The unfortunate Adams makes the mistake of reaching up to take Hawk's elbow and Hawk, not changing his expression, takes Adams' hand in his own and begins to squeeze so that the butler sinks to his knees, his face turning scarlet and his jowls shaking like a jelly freshly removed from its mould. His expression is a mixture of surprise and agony as his mouth pops open and closed like a goldfish in a bowl as he gasps silently to be released.

'What are you doing!' David demands, not able to clearly see what's going on.

'He's h-hurting me, sir,' Adams says at last.

'Just a bit of good man-ing,' Hawk says softly, and looks down at Adams. 'Come along now, there's a good man, we don't want any fuss, do we?' Still gripping the unfortunate butler's hand in his giant fist, Hawk says to David, 'Tomorrow then. Be good enough to be on time. I shall notify Sir Abraham as well.'

Hawk releases his grip on the poor man gasping at his knees and, bending slightly, takes him by the elbow and helps him to his feet. 'Thank you for seeing me in, Mr Adams. I shall see myself out.'

'We will have the law onto you for this,' David shouts, finally realising what has happened to his butler.

'Oh yes, the law,' Hawk says absently. 'The guts-for-garters men. If you think they will help you, bring all the lawyers in Christendom to the meeting tomorrow. I, for my part, shall bring only one. She should be sufficient to effectively deal with them all, that is, after first adding up their collective fees on her abacus.'

With these final words Hawk turns to depart, leaving the hapless butler to nurse the fingers of his damaged hand by means of squeezing them under his armpit.

'Go to hell, you nigger bastard!' David screams, shaking his fist at the dark shadow he sees as the departing Hawk.

Hawk pauses at the door and turns back to look at the old man and sees that he is weeping, though whether they be tears of temper, frustration or anxiety he can't tell. But with a certainty born out of a lifetime of knowing David Solomon, he knows they are not the tears that flow from remorse. 'Will the wicked old man never die?' he thinks, as he closes the door behind him.

David, in fact, weeps for himself, despite his bravado. He is aware that Hawk is a patient but determined foe and that ultimately his enemy will gain control of Solomon & Teekleman once more. He considers briefly having Hawk murdered, but he is too old and feeble to make the arrangements and Abraham would not countenance any such action. Everything is suddenly falling to bits, first Joshua going off to war and now this.

He has tried so hard to make his grandson everything he himself isn't. Joshua is his alter ego and he is going to die knowing the boy with whom he has worked so diligently and upon whom he has lavished so much affection will come to nothing. David thinks back to the day of Joshua's birth which, in his mind's eye, he sees as clearly as if it were yesterday.

He is standing impatiently outside Elizabeth's bed chamber and when he hears the first mewling cries of the infant he turns the knob on the bedroom door, determined to barge in, but it has been locked from the inside.

'Open this bloody door!' he shouts.

'Sir, I must cut and tie the cord and wash the baby,' the midwife shouts back.

'Bugger that, lemme in!' David throws his shoulder against the door. 'Lemme in, will ya!' he demands again.

But the midwife won't be intimidated. 'You'll stay there until we're ready, sir,' she shouts back.

It is a good fifteen minutes before David hears the click of the key and, without waiting for the door to open fully, he barges into the bedroom, brushing the midwife aside. He doesn't even demand to know the newborn's gender, convinced that whichever one of the ears of God has heard his request, it has also plainly understood that a male child was a mandatory part of it.

David simply walks into the darkened room and makes for the velvet drapes which keep the bed chamber in a semi-darkened state. He rips them open to expose the late morning sunlight.

Elizabeth lies with her infant swaddled and held tightly to her breasts. 'Righto, girlie, let's see him. Hold him up, will ya. Take that bloody blanket off. I want to see the lot of him, all of the little bugger, see he's got everything that should be there and nothing that shouldn't!'

The midwife tries to interfere. 'Sir, she's wearied, the baby is only just born, the mother is weak from the birth.'

'She's always been weak and bloody wearied. Look at her, no bloody tits. How's the boy gunna suckle, eh? Come along, girl, hold him up, let me see the little blighter.'

Elizabeth begins to cry, clutching her infant even more tightly to her chest. 'Father, please go,' she whispers through her tears. 'It's my baby.'

David is genuinely shocked at this idea. 'Your baby? Oh no, you don't! You'll not pull that one on me, girlie.' He points to the swaddled infant. 'That's *my* child. I got him from God and a pretty penny he cost too!' He turns to the midwife. 'You! I'm not finished with you! Hold my boy up, let me see him,' he demands. The midwife, afraid to confront the monstrous man standing in front of her a second time, takes the infant from the weeping Elizabeth and, removing the blanket that covers him, she lies him down on the counterpane, which is folded neatly at the end of the bed. The tiny infant stretches, then balls his fists, screwing up his eyes against the glare which now bathes him in the light, showing the rubbery reddish-brown colour of the healthy newborn.

'See, making fists,' David says gleefully. 'A born fighter already.' He inspects Joshua minutely from head to toe, then, pronouncing himself satisfied with the front, turns to the midwife. 'Turn him over, woman, let's see his tukis.' Finally, having checked Joshua for birthmarks or any other defect, he looks up pleased. 'Good,' he grunts. 'Wrap him up, missus.' Turning to Elizabeth he points to her bosom, 'You'll not feed him with those, girlie. We'll get a wet nurse with big tits. I'll not have him starvin' to death sucking on a couple of bleedin' mosquito bites!'

David leaves just as Abraham arrives, having been summoned from work. Father and son meet at the bed-chamber door. 'It's a boy and he's mine,' David says to his son. Abraham, anxious to be at Elizabeth's side, only hears the words 'It's a boy' as he hastens to be with his distraught wife. This will prove to be one of the few times when the two parents will be alone with their child. David is convinced that the child is his, prayed and paid for, and that Elizabeth is simply the delivery container who, while she is useful, is Joshua's surrogate mother.

At first, Elizabeth objects to David's complete possession of her child but to little avail. David demands that the wet nurse feeds him in his presence so that he is assured the baby receives sufficient milk. He stands beside the nursemaid they have employed to care for the baby while she weighs him every two days, jotting down baby Joshua's weight in a small notebook. As Joshua grows older, David so totally monopolises the child that Joshua's own father seldom gets to play with him. David sees his grandchild as an extension of himself and, from the very first day, he discusses affairs of business with Joshua.

'It's the sounds, see, the sounds of the words. Course he don't understand them, but if they're the sounds he hears about him, he'll get to know them unconscious like, sounds of words like profit, loss, debit, credit, insurance, compound interest, percentage, negotiation, contract. Them's all sounds and words he must later think was born into his head. It don't matter that he don't comprehend yet, it's the sounds, see, like litigation, a lovely sound that, lit-ti-gation.'

'Leave the child alone, Father,' Elizabeth would cry, exasperated at David's almost maniacal preoccupation with her child. 'He's only a baby.'

'Alone? Leave him alone?' David shows his astonishment.

'What do you mean alone!' he yells at her. 'I can't take no chances. It's not my fault there's only *one* of him around.' This last is always said accusingly, guilt is David's speciality and he never hesitates to use it on his daughter-in-law.

Shortly after Joshua's birth, Abraham contracts the mumps which results in him becoming sterile. Despite this explanation for the couple's infertility, David continues to blame Elizabeth at every opportunity for only producing a single male heir.

'You was married four years!' he shouts, holding up four bony fingers in front of Elizabeth's face. 'Four bloody years before Joshua come along, before *I* got him born! Then, only then, Abe got the mumps what made his pistol fire blanks. You and that book-reading bastard who calls himself my son could have made me two more grandsons at least! Instead, you was gallivanting around in the cot using them fancy rubbers!'

'What about you?' Elizabeth objects. 'You had Abraham. That's only *one* child!'

'Rebecca was sick. Sick doesn't count!' David yells back at her. 'Four years you waited. You and him having a good time in the cot, eating me out of house and home, never a sick day between you, and at the expense o' *my* bloody grandchildren!'

On one such occasion, when David's tormenting has driven Elizabeth to distraction, she bends down, thumping her knees with her fists and screams at the old man. 'For God's sake, Father, leave us alone. Don't you realise, your son can't even get it up! He never bloody could hardly!'

'What's that?' David cries. Then, realising what his daughter-in-law has just said, adds, 'That's your bloody fault, girlie! Let me tell you something for nothing. There's bugger-all wrong with my boy a good Jewish girl couldn't fix!'

'Well, then find him one!' Elizabeth howls. 'He's no use to me!'

David stops, not believing his ears. 'You'll not divorce him,' he shouts. 'There'll be no divorce in this house, you hear?' He points an accusing finger at her. 'You leave and I'll cut you off without a penny,' he stammers, barely able to contain his anger. 'You won't even find work in a brothel, girlie! I'll see you in the gutter with the dog shit!' Shaking with rage he grabs her by the arm and pushes her so that she stumbles and falls to the carpet. Standing over her, both his fists clenched, his arms rigid at his side, he screams, 'Joshua has got to have a mother, even if it's only to wipe his arse!' Leaving her on the floor, he walks from the room shaking his head. 'Jesus Christ, I should never have let my son marry out!'

And so, in the age-old manner of men holding women captive, Elizabeth, for lack of independent means, is rendered helpless. Nor can she hope to appeal to her husband to stand up to his father. Furthermore, by keeping Abraham busy and, in Joshua's early years, frequently away on business, David prevents his son from attempting to win the child's affection.

David simply wants Joshua for himself and shortly after Joshua is weaned, his cradle is moved into David's bed chamber with the nurse in an adjoining room and a door between the rooms. The cradle is later followed by a cot and then a cast-iron bed. Most of Joshua's waking childhood is spent within bawling distance of his grandfather and when he reaches puberty and, as David tells himself, needs to pull his pud in private, he moves Joshua into the nanny's old room, so that he still has direct access to his grandson at any time of the day or night.

His tutors, the first employed when Joshua turned seven, are Englishmen, gentlemen fallen on hard times. All are paid well above what their vocations might normally command, as David is aware that they will not long put up with his interference, bullying and bad temper unless the reward for their services is sufficiently high to quell their inevitable disenchantment. Even so, Joshua will have four tutors in all before he is finally trundled off to Oxford.

Joshua's first tutor undergoes a routine which will be common to those who follow him. David interviews him in his opulent office, resplendent in the latest Edwardian style, making him stand like a naughty schoolboy in front of his mahogany desk even though the room is amply supplied with an ottoman couch and four comfortable leather armchairs of similar configuration.

'I am not an easy man to please, Mr Smyth, and in the matter of my grandson you will find me even more particular. Whereas you are a gentleman, you should know right off, I am not. I am a rich Jew and I wish my grandson to be tutored as though he were a gentleman and a gentile, a rich goy. Do you understand me?'

Smyth, who has only recently had his impecunious financial position alleviated by David and all his gambling debts paid, is happy to agree to just about any terms the old man wants to impose. He has been promised superior lodgings and a stipend far beyond the abilities of a second-class degree at Oxford, and he can't quite believe his good fortune.

'I shall do my best, sir,' he assures David.

'No, Mr Smyth, you will do *my* best, which I think you will find a bloody sight better than your best. We will begin with elocution. I desire my grandson to speak like a gentleman.' David deliberately adopts a harsher version of his own accent and lack of grammar. 'If he don't talk proper and drops his h's or his g's like his grandfather, you're in for the 'igh jump.'

'I shall take particular care of his speech,' Smyth promises.

'Yeah, whatever, you look after his speech. I want him posh, not dead common like me.' David looks steadily at Smyth until the other man is forced to drop his gaze. 'What you study at Oxford University then?'

'History, sir.'

'History? What history?'

'British. The history of the British Isles.'

'You mean English?'

'No, sir. That, of course, but Irish and Scottish. The Welsh, as well.'

'Well, you'll teach the boy English history, but no Irish. You understand, no Irish!'

Smyth starts to protest. 'Without a grasp of Irish history it is difficult to get a true perspective on England's –'

'You heard me, Mr Smyth. No bloody Micks! No Irish!'

Smyth looks down at his toes, feeling like the schoolboy David has intended he should. 'Yes, sir.'

'And we'll have arithmetic, addition and subtraction, multiplication and division. Reading and writing, o' course, and Latin.'

Smyth looks up. 'I'm afraid I'm a poor Latin scholar, Mr Solomon, never got much beyond schoolboy Latin. I had just sufficient to scrape into Oxford,' he says, with disarming modesty entirely lost on David.

'Well, my grandson will be a schoolboy one day. That's enough Latin for him. All he needs to know is what it says on coats of arms and the like.'

'In which case I feel sure we will manage splendidly,' the tutor replies.

'Mr Smyth, do you 'ave a coat of arms?' Smyth opens his

mouth to speak and David puts up his hand, 'No, don't answer that, I know you 'ave, that's why you got the job in the first place.' David pushes himself away from the desk. 'That will be all. You may go.'

'Thank you, sir.'

Smyth turns and walks from the study, conscious of David's rudeness, but telling himself he has no choice but to countenance it. David calls after him, 'Oi, boy, you wouldn't know how to use an abacus, would you? A Chinee abacus, yer know, for counting and doing sums?'

Smyth turns to face him. 'No, I'm afraid not, sir.'

'Hmm, be most useful for the boy to learn.' David smiles for the first time. 'Perhaps we can find a Chinaman to teach him, eh? Knew a whore woman once who used the abacus, fast as bleedin' lightnin' she was. Had these broken 'ands, see, all deformed like, but you couldn't hardly see them when she worked them little black and red beads, beat anyone hollow who was usin' a pen and paper to do their sums.'

'Remarkable, sir,' Smyth replies, unable to think what else to say, though he does wonder briefly what a whore would be doing with an abacus.

'Mr Smyth, one more thing.'

'Yessir?'

'You will be polite to the boy's mother, Mrs Solomon, but no more. You'll not speak to her about his progress or, as a matter o' fact, anything else. If I catch you doing so, you will be dismissed immediately. Do you understand me?'

'Perfectly, sir.'

David has so effectively sidelined Elizabeth that she eventually loses heart and spends most of her day in her bed chamber quietly nursing a gin bottle. He puts this down to the inherent weakness in the gentile strain and is grateful that she no longer makes a fuss. He knows that his own mother, Hannah, and even the sickly Rebecca would have fought him to a standstill and most probably would have won. A Jewish mother has resources of resistance and sheer cantankery to a depth impossible to plumb.

Not that Hannah Solomon much cared about how David turned out, other than to instil in him the same hate she had for his father Ikey and his so-called mistress Mary Abacus. Hannah believed that survival in a world where a Jew was considered even lower than the bog-Irish, depended on money and a heart filled with malice. 'Vengeance is a dish best tasted cold,' she'd say to him. 'They's all bastards, David, all greedy. Only thing you gotta learn is how to be a bigger bastard and more greedy. Know what I mean, son?'

David has few illusions about the sort of man he is. Given his parents, he believes he is the logical outcome of Ikey and Hannah Solomon, two of the more rapacious creatures to step ashore from a convict ship. They were formidable in their capacity to create mischief or to make a shilling out of someone else's misery.

Hannah had been the owner of a dockside brothel, the most vile in London. She kept small boys and turned them into catamites. Little girls, orphans from the streets of London, were trained by her for the delectation of paedophiles and the most evil of the great city's perverts and sexual predators. She would, for the right price, obtain dwarfs, nigger women, the deformed and even slobbering idiots from the madhouse, whatever the vile preference or sexual proclivities demanded. That was Hannah Solomon, a business woman who didn't stop to weigh the consequences of any perversion beyond the price it might fetch in the market of the depraved. She believed that if there was a need and if she didn't exploit it, someone else would. And in this regard she was probably right. London, at the time, was the greatest cesspool in the known world, and the exploitation of ragged children abandoned by their mothers to live under the bridges and in the underground sewage system was so common as to be ignored by the law.

However, her four children were well cared for and were too young to be aware of their mother's pernicious occupation. They lived in a pleasant, even by comparison to the houses around it, salubrious, Whitechapel house and were minded by a nursemaid, usually a malnourished Irish biddy, grateful for free board and lodging and a few pennies to spend on gin on Saturdays, the Jewish Sabbath, when Hannah remained at home with her children and the maid was given the day off to get drunk.

This cloistered, albeit lonely life as a child came to an abrupt end when David was eight and Hannah was convicted of the theft of a batch of gentlemen's fob watches and sentenced to be transported with her children to Van Diemen's Land. Though the theft of the watches was no less an act of her own rapacity,

Hannah believed her arrest and subsequent transportation were the result of a clever plan hatched by Ikey so that he and his whore mistress, Mary Abacus, could steal the contents of a large combination safe hidden under the floor of the pantry in the Whitechapel home.

People who hold themselves to be victims seldom bother to examine the evidence leading to the circumstances in which they find themselves and Hannah was no different.

How Ikey might be somehow able to force open the safe from as far away as America, where he'd absconded, Hannah never bothered to explain. Even after Ikey was recaptured and was himself transported to Port Arthur, so that the safe remained unopened in their boarded-up Whitechapel home, she continued to blame them.

Hannah's transportation and the wealth denied her became the basis for her hatred and bitterness and, as both emotions needed to have subjects for vilification, Ikey and Mary Abacus remained the principals accused of her demise.

It was a bitterness and hatred for his father which she nourished in her oldest son during her years as a convict and, later, when, as an emancipist, she took up with George Madden, a successful grain merchant in New Norfolk.

'You must promise me, David,' his mother would say, 'if I should die before that miserable bastard, Ikey Solomon, your father, Gawd 'elp us, or his whore, you will avenge our little family. What we have become is because of them two and they must pay for what they done to us. Listen to Mama, my precious. Every humiliation, every insult, every misery that has befallen you, every moment you've suffered is to be blamed on those two vile creatures who put us here in this Gawd-forsaken place and stole our money. Rich? We was, filthy bleedin' rich, we could've been nabobs, kings and queens. It's them two robbed us, took everything what was rightly ours!'

She would repeat this sentiment every day of the miserable life David endured. Hannah was nothing if not persistent and persuasive and soon David's young mind had become totally corrupted with a hatred for his father and a loathing for Mary Abacus. They were to blame for all his unhappiness, for the beatings he received at the hands of Madden, for every insult and humiliation he suffered working for him.

'Mama, I swear on your grave, they shall pay,' he would tell his mother earnestly.

'Listen to me, David, my boy. You must learn to be a businessman like George, only better. He ain't too well and I don't suppose he'll last much longer.' She smiled and gave him a sly look. 'He coughs somethin' awful at night and sometimes there's blood comes up. I'm happy to say he won't take physic or see the doctor neither. I know he beats you somethin' awful, but we'll get it all when he passes on. Listen to me, poor folk can't take revenge, only rich. That miserable whore Mary Abacus is getting rich with her brewery and what she stole from us, and she'll be respectable soon enough and she'll come after you, you mark me words. What she done to me she'll do again to you and the others.' Tears of mortification would run down Hannah's face. 'We'll be rubbish and she'll be respectable,' she'd wail. 'It's money what earns respect, we must get what's rightly ours and see her in the gutter again!' Hannah would wipe away her tears and beckon to him, 'Come 'ere then, give us a kiss. You're a clever boy, David. I know you won't let your old mama down. Remember, folk don't ask how you got your gelt, long as you've got it. Money ain't got no conscience, nor should you have.'

Soon David equated the only love and affection he ever received with his ability to hate and as he grew to manhood he saw his business success and the subsequent wealth as the means to enable him to become a bully and to use his power to gain revenge for true and imagined hurts and insults. Throughout his long life, Mary Abacus remained the primary protagonist he must defeat. It was a promise to Hannah he was to keep better than she could ever have imagined.

At the age of twenty-eight he'd conspired with Hannah to kidnap Mary's adopted twins, Tommo and Hawk, in an attempt to blackmail Ikey into giving her his numbers to the safe in Whitechapel. The kidnap plan went disastrously wrong but Hannah comforted herself with the knowledge that she'd blighted the lives of both children forever and had somewhat evened her score with Mary Abacus, who loved the boys more than her life. 'It's no more than she deserves,' she'd sneer. 'Them two brats were bastards born of a fat whore, it's all the bitch could love, a whore's sons.' Then she turned to him. 'It's not enough, David. We cannot rest until we have taken everything from them, you hear. *Everything*, we must have it all!'

When Ikey died, leaving his half of the combination to Mary, Hannah, borrowing the passage money from Madden, sent David to England where the fifteen-year-old Hawk was learning how to grow hops in Kent.

It was agreed that the two families would share the safe's contents, dividing it equally, though David and Hannah had already planned for Hawk to be followed and robbed of his share soon after he emerged from the Whitechapel house.

As David lies weeping in the bathchair, he thinks how terribly he was cheated by Hawk when the safe was opened and shown to be empty. How, over the past twenty-one years, in the twilight of his life, he has clawed back his family fortunes and consigned Hawk and his so-called grandchildren, the last vestiges of Mary Abacus, to emotional oblivion by controlling everything the great whore built with her misbegotten gains. Now, he sobs, the nigger is back again, the perfidious bastard has come back to threaten him and his grandson, to destroy his life's work.

David feels a terrible anger rising up in him. It grows more and more intense and he knows he must release it, break something. He finds the spittoon and hurls it to the ground, though it is made of brass and simply clangs and bounces before coming to a halt. He is too weak to get out of the bathchair and the anger grows and envelops him until his entire body shakes uncontrollably and he cannot find the electric buzzer to summon help. His arms, flapping about like a rag doll, are beyond his control. He attempts to shout but his throat is filled with an anger and a panic that leaves him incapable of more than a gurgling sound. His legs are jumping wildly and still the anger grows until it is now beyond containing so that his last conscious thought is that he is about to suffer a heart seizure and suddenly there is only blackness.

Almost an hour later David is discovered lying on the floor of the conservatory by Adams. He appears to have been thrown from the bathchair. His nose has bled profusely from the impact of landing on the tiled floor. The bleeding has now stopped but the front of his pyjama jacket is soaked in blood. His face is fixed in a state of rictus, a grimace not unlike one of his more unusually cantankerous expressions, though it appears to be permanently in place. When the doctor is called to examine the still alive but completely comatose old man, it is discovered that David Solomon has suffered a massive cerebral stroke.

214

Hawk is not to know the news about David until a telephone call from Abraham the following morning asking to postpone the boardroom meeting. Abraham, ever polite, simply explains that the old man has had a stroke and that it would be most convenient if Hawk would be so good as to postpone their meeting for two days.

Hawk offers his sympathy to Abraham, knowing that David's son would be aware that he had visited the old man and that the confrontation may well have been the reason for David's stroke. It is typical of Abraham that he should avoid conjecture and say nothing. 'I may be implicated, Abraham. I went to see your father yesterday morning, it wasn't an altogether harmonious occasion,' Hawk tells him.

There is a moment of silence at the other end of the phone before Abraham replies. 'He was very old. Something like this is to be expected. The doctor says he has no pain.'

'How long will he last?' Hawk asks.

'According to the physician, a week, maybe a little more, who knows?'

'Then we shall postpone the meeting until after the shiva,' Hawk says.

'Thank you, I am most grateful,' Abraham says quietly, placing down the phone.

To everyone's surprise the old man regains consciousness and can even sip a little broth or take a cup of tea, though he is unable to talk and the left side of his body is paralysed. The last known words to cross his lips are a curse for his mortal enemy, the adopted son of Mary Abacus.

David Solomon dies quietly in his sleep three days after Hawk's visit and not even the maid, who habitually brings a cup of tea to his bedroom of a morning, has a tear to shed for the old man.

'Missus, he's dead,' is all she says to Mrs Tompkins, the housekeeper, as she returns the tea to the kitchen.

'Who's dead, girl?' the housekeeper asks.

'Old Mr David.'

'Oh,' says the housekeeper. 'I'd better wake Sir Abraham then.' She points to the discarded cup of tea. 'Is that still hot enough to take in with me?'

'Suppose so,' the maid says, 'but Sir Abraham don't take no sugar.'

Chapter Eight

THE SONS AND DAUGHTERS –
VICTORIA AND JOSHUA

1914

Hawk knows little of women's fashions, but senses that the drama of the occasion may be heightened when they meet Abraham if Victoria appears to be the social equal of the sophisticated, popular and good-looking Joshua Solomon. Therefore he tries to persuade her to dress in the style that might be expected of a young Melbourne socialite whose hair is worn in what is known as the short bob, with curls brushed forward over the forehead. A gown typical of the fashion for the very rich is one such as worn by the pretty Miss Vanda Clarke at an afternoon reception at the Clarke home, Winmarleigh, for the dancer Ivy Schilling, 'the terpsichorean with the most beautiful legs in the world'. Miss Clarke wore a peacock chiffon taffeta gown, with draped bodice and tunic of soft lace and ninon, the bodice finished with a deeper tone of blue.

Hawk, reading the *Age*, has somehow stumbled across the photograph of Miss Clarke and a description of her gown and points it out to Victoria at breakfast. 'Perhaps you could wear something like this?' he says casually. 'You know, done up to the nines.' He chuckles. 'It'll fair sock Abraham and his cohorts in the eye, eh?' He stabs a finger at the paper. 'Miss Clarke seems to be the very height of fashion and you, my dear, are much, much prettier than she is.'

Victoria, who is seldom rude, though often forthright, sends him away with a flea in his ear. In fact, she seems to have tried even harder to appear as plain Jane as possible. Tommo's granddaughter has taken to dressing in a manner you might expect to find on any neatly dressed shopgirl in Myers, wearing a plain black dress, a modest hat and a cheap pair of gloves, except that her face is scrubbed clean, with not the slightest trace of powder, rouge or lip colour.

Despite these extreme efforts to appear to be plain, Victoria has inherited the bone structure of her island ancestors and while she is unlikely to be considered pretty by the fashions of the day she is a handsome young woman with her eyes being quite unusual. They are large and almost violet in colour and have a direct gaze. It is as if they contain an innate intelligence of their own even before she has opened her mouth to speak. They are a weapon of which she is not yet aware. As she grows older and assumes more authority, her eyes will often make people confess the truth before she has demanded or even expected it. Victoria's remarkable eyes will serve her well throughout her life.

Her skin, inherited from her mother, is the lightest olive and flawless, though it is clearly not of the much-admired peaches-and-cream perfection usually accorded the English and to be greatly cherished if it is possessed by a colonial femme. To the astute observer, and there are many such among Melbourne's social elite, Victoria's wheaten hair and violet eyes do not deceive them. Her naturally tanned skin shows that she is a half-breed or, among those prepared to be more charitable, at the very least of Mediterranean extract, a lineage barely considered an improvement on the part-Maori she unashamedly claims to be.

Victoria holds herself erect, even perhaps a little stiff-backed, with her chin at right angles to her neck and even though she is only slightly more than average height, five feet and five inches, she appears to be much taller. While she aspires to the uniform appearance of those women increasingly to be found in the ranks of the Labor Party, her deportment, together with her slightly clipped and correct grammar and rounded vowels, both courtesy of Mr and Mrs Wickworth-Spode, will forever stamp her as being different. In England she would be called a 'bluestocking', here she is simply a misfit, neither Friday fish nor Sunday fowl, a socialist by conviction and an aristocrat by demeanour. To the Labor organisers of the day, in particular those men running the trade unions, she is much too frank, clever and over-qualified to be allowed to play a role beyond that of a general factotum or amanuensis. These two positions are regularly reserved for a female fellow traveller in the so-called egalitarian Australian Labor Party and its corresponding union movement. Only the notorious Muriel Heagney has managed to climb further up the ranks of the unions and it is claimed that the price she has paid to achieve this status is sufficient warning to any other female who feels she might like to attempt to follow in her footsteps.

Victoria Teekleman is cursed with a quality men have never admired in a woman and, like her brother Ben, she is a natural leader. James Scullin, the Labor Prime Minister in the first two years of the Great Depression, was once heard to say of her, 'If Victoria Teekleman had been born a man I have not the slightest doubt that she would one day be running this country. Thank God she is a member of the opposite sex and not a Member of the House.'

Hawk smiles to himself when Victoria emerges from her bedroom, ready to depart with him to the city. He decides that he was quite wrong to try to persuade her to pretension. She is attired in a white cotton blouse with a wide lapel, a knitted cardigan, a sensible grey worsted skirt that shows a defiant glimpse of her ankles, woollen stockings and inexpensive black boots. Her only affectation is a cheap black Chinese silk scarf knotted in the manner of a gentleman's tie but worn loosely with the knot well down below the neckline so that the curve of her neck is clearly visible. Her hair is drawn back severely to a bun at the back of her head. Though neatly arranged, it is not much different to a style any washerwoman might affect and upon her head she wears a broad-brimmed Panama hat with only a simple black band.

However, Victoria still manages to look very attractive. She stands perfectly straight, her chin raised to appear just a fraction defiant. Although in her mid-twenties, she still looks too young to be taken seriously. Hawk suspects men will forever underestimate her, as he himself has in how she should appear at the board meeting. He wonders whether she will ever find a man strong enough to contain her, or will it be Mary Abacus all over again?

In Victoria's own mind, her plain dressing and general demeanour is not an affectation. In the time she has been in

Melbourne she has come to despise the debutantes and, later, the prattling, empty-headed, husband-hunting young women who make up the unmarried social scene. She consciously does not wish to be included among them, even though her name and the wealth that comes with it condemns her to sit at the very top of the social ladder.

It has always astonished her that the middle-class girls with whom she studied accountancy, typing and shorthand look up to these young socialites as if they were on the silver screen and are perpetually gathering scraps of gossip about them as eagerly as a magpie furnishes its nest with brightly coloured bits. It is a curious fact of life that money bestows on a woman an enhanced perception of glamour, whereas a man is accorded the bonus of a superior mind. People mistakenly think that the very rich are somehow more glamorous or intelligent than themselves.

Victoria is conscious of this cultural sycophancy and her manner of dressing is also an effort to be accepted at face value by those who see themselves as having a lower status than herself. She is similarly troubled that women from the so-called middle and lower classes are terribly self-deprecating and believe that they must be less intelligent than men, so that they dare not assume the same responsibilities or expect equal remuneration for their work.

It concerns her deeply that even when women are doing essentially the same work as men, the female equivalent of the job is somehow thought to be second-rate. In the classes she attended in accountancy where the students were a mix of males and females, the women, knowing her name to be Teekleman, seemed disappointed that she didn't live up to their exalted expectations of glamour. They seemed collectively embarrassed that she topped the classes in every subject, almost as though, by beating the males, she was letting down their gender. It was a paradox she would live with all her life as she urged women to slough their sense of inferiority and take the men on at their own game, and to see the male conspiracy for what it was, merely bluff and balderdash.

She would argue with her female classmates, often exampling Addie Keating, the only woman department head at Myers, who ran the toy department, the smallest and most unprofitable area of the store. Miss Keating built it into one of the most profitable within the giant emporium. She was the first woman to travel alone overseas as a buyer, visiting Japan on several occasions and later Europe, where Sidney Myer allowed her an unlimited bank draft to purchase not only children's toys but also any other merchandise. Victoria would point out that Miss Keating came from an Irish family in Bendigo who were down on their luck, and that she'd started as the humblest fourth assistant shopgirl with no influence but a burning desire to succeed. She took on and beat the men at their own game and earned the respect of the great Sidney Myer, who once told his male department heads that Miss Keating was worth two of any of them.

Victoria would become frustrated talking to her female classmates, who pathetically stared back at her blank-eyed. On one occasion, one of them gathered up the courage to say, 'It's all right for you, you're filthy rich! You don't have to work. It doesn't matter if you lose your job!' which brought acquiescent nods from them all.

Hawk also sees why Victoria has dressed in such a severe way for the meeting with Sir Abraham and his legal and accountancy cohorts. She intends to show them that she is of equal intellectual standing and not a dizzy young thing to be treated in the patronising and jocular manner they are accustomed to adopting with the vacuous friends of their own muddle-headed daughters.

Hawk ineluctably concludes that Victoria, despite her efforts, has probably failed in both these attempts as her youth, handsome looks and natural ebullience completely override any conscious effort of plain-mannerliness. She simply isn't common or plain and no uniform she chooses to adopt will make her appear to be so. Nevertheless, in a business world where young women are expected to be seen and not heard and are usually accompanied by a pad and pencil and a competence in Sir Isaac Pitman's shorthand, Hawk silently applauds her determination not to be categorised or taken for granted.

Bringing Victoria to the boardroom of Solomon & Teekleman has not been easy. In fact, the three days it took for David to die and the additional seven for the shiva, the period of mourning whereby the family of the deceased is required to do no work and to remain quietly at home, have been very welcome. Hawk has needed every one of these days to bring Victoria around to his way of thinking.

Abraham has insisted on the strictest orthodox funeral rites for David Solomon. There is no shortage of visitors to his home while the family sit shiva. Even though David Solomon had few friends, probably not even enough for a minyan, the ten males required to say the Kaddish, the traditional prayers for the dead, Melbourne's Jews have all come to witness for themselves that the old bastard is finally dead and buried in his plain pine box.

Hawk himself attends the funeral and stands in line to offer his condolences to Abraham and Elizabeth. Abraham is aware of his presence long before they shake hands and so has time to compose himself.

'I wish you both long life,' Hawk says, offering a frail-looking Elizabeth and then Abraham his hand. He can see that Elizabeth is flushed and, as he draws closer, smells her distinctly peppermint breath. Hawk hopes only that today's bottle of gin is one of celebration rather than of despair.

Abraham, shaking his hand, says, 'I am surprised you came, Hawk Solomon, though pleasantly or otherwise I cannot yet say.'

Hawk looks at him and replies, 'Abraham, the orthodox burial is also a surprise to me, but your father was too big a factor in my life to be ignored in death. To do so would be to convey the impression that our quarrel continues.'

'Oh?' Abraham's head jerks backwards in surprise. He looks thoroughly bemused, not sure quite what Hawk means by this final remark, but certain that his mention of the orthodox ceremony means he understands that the prolonged mourning period gives him valuable time at Hawk's expense.

This is, of course, its principal purpose, though there is another which Abraham will scarcely admit to himself. He knows that David would have resisted with every breath in his body the idea of an orthodox funeral.

'Rubbish! It's all superstitious rubbish!' he'd said often enough in life. 'Waste of time! Put me in a plain box and leave me to the worms! No rabbi, yer hear, and *don't* send a donation! That shlemiel Rabbi Abrahams has already cost me an arm and a leg *and* two ears, he's not going to cash in on my corpse as well!'

Now, by going against his wishes, Abraham is consciously asserting himself, getting rid of the last vestiges of his father's influence. That he needs the time to put his legal representatives and accountants to work to see how they might prevent Hawk from taking over at Solomon & Teekleman allows him to deny this second motive to himself.

When the housekeeper woke him with his usual cup of tea and quietly informed him of the old man's death, Abraham had already decided to give his father an orthodox funeral for these reasons.

Putting on his dressing gown and slippers and without waking Elizabeth, who was sleeping in an adjoining room, he took up his mother's prayer book and put it under his arm. Carrying the cup of tea, he went quietly into David's bed chamber.

After David first had his stroke Abraham had taken the precaution of finding his mother's prayer book. Rebecca, when it came her turn to die, had insisted on an orthodox funeral and, finding herself unable to trust her husband in the matters of her death, had schooled Abraham in the rituals to be observed. Abraham now recalls the long vigil at her bedside where he and Elizabeth had taken turns to sit for three days and nights. How, as dawn approached on the fourth day, he'd read aloud the prayer he'd been required to learn by rote. Even now he can hear his mother whispering the words, repeating them back to him as she lay dying. He also remembers how David, in his red silk dressing gown, sat with his arms crossed, looking up at the ceiling with an expression of resigned exasperation. He had refused to sit with his wife except for the briefest periods and had to be wakened when the time came for Rebecca to say her last farewells. Although it was a long time ago, Abraham now tries to recall the ancient rituals involved in Rebecca's death. He knows he has neglected to perform the first three, the candles, the vigil at David's bedside and the final prayer of confession.

However, he is not unduly concerned, thinking that he can make good with the candles and, when the rabbi arrives, it will be easy enough to be seated beside his father's bed, appearing to have been present throughout the night's vigil. With the prayer book at his side, or perhaps on his lap, the rabbi will assume that Abraham, even though David can't speak, has read the prayer of confession to his father.

Abraham knows how important this last act of contrition is among orthodox Jews, but privately thinks how inappropriate it would have been for David Solomon to show the slightest sign of remorse, even in death. For his father to enjoy the radiance of the Divine Presence after death, as is promised to orthodox Jews, seems somehow to Abraham to be a miscarriage of God's justice. Even though, where a distinct lack of saintliness in life existed, provision has been made for the departed soul to undergo a year of chastisement before entering the Divine Presence, this too seems totally inadequate in David's case. There is a third category, where, according to tradition, only the grotesquely evil qualify for and are subject to eternal damnation. However, Abraham is too honest to place his father in this truly heavyweight division on the scales of wickedness.

Abraham tells himself that his conscience is clear on both counts, the vigil at his father's bedside and the final prayer of contrition. David's stroke has prevented any possibility of a confession and, as for the vigil at his bedside, David was so habitually drugged with an opiate syrup prescribed by the family doctor that he was forced to sleep soundly until well into the morning and it is unlikely that anyone seated at his bedside would even have noticed the moment of his death.

It had been different for his mother. She'd made him rehearse the prayer of confession several times during the week she correctly forecast she would die. 'It is a great mitzvah to be present at the departure of a soul,' Rebecca had told him. 'It will be your duty to request me to confess my sins and I hope to do so with pride.'

She had grown so accustomed to talking about her impending death that the whole family had long since given up protesting. Rebecca tended to get her own way in most things, and it did not surprise them that she would choose the timing of her own death.

'But, Mother, isn't pride a sin?' Abraham remembers teasing her.

'Believe me, in death a little pride does no harm,' she'd said with great authority. 'It's the English Jews got it, not those immigrants from Poland and Russia who do all that lamentation, weeping and gnashing of teeth. That lot, they got no pride!'

'Anyway, what sins could you possibly have to confess?' Abraham recalls humouring her further.

'Sins? Never you mind, my boy! Believe me, I got plenty! You want I should miss you saying the words so I can say them back, my very last words to my only beloved son?' she'd said accusingly.

'Aren't you supposed to say them to God, Mother?'

'Him also,' Rebecca had snapped. Then, finding the confession in her prayer book, she'd marked it with a hairpin. Abraham now sees that the hairpin is still in place after all these years and, not quite knowing why, he opens the book and begins to read aloud the long since forgotten words of the *yezi'at neshamah* in the presence of his dead father. If Rabbi Abrahams asks whether he has performed this particular mitzvah, he won't mention the disparity in time between the death and the reading, explaining only that his father had suffered a stroke and therefore was unable to respond to the words in the ancient ritual of confession.

I acknowledge unto Thee, Oh Lord my God, and the God of my fathers, that both my cure and my death are in Thy hands. May it be Thy will to send me a perfect healing. Yet if my death be fully determined by Thee, I will in love accept it at Thy hand. O may my death be an atonement for all my sins, iniquities and transgressions of which I have been guilty against Thee . . . Hear O Israel: the Lord is our God, the Lord is One.

He completes the prayer and places the prayer book where it can be clearly seen on the bedside table, then he presses the electric buzzer three times to summon the housekeeper.

When Mrs Tompkins arrives, she carries another cup of tea. 'Nice fresh cuppa tea,' she says, putting it down beside Abraham and taking up the old one.

'Thank you, Mrs Tompkins,' Abraham says. 'Now there are several things I want you to do immediately. I want nine candles, well-used ones if you please.'

'Candles, well used? Oh dear?' The housekeeper appears to be thinking. 'I dunno, sir,' she says, 'I shall have to try and scrounge them from the servants' quarters.' She suddenly brightens. 'Plenty o' new ones in the kitchen, mind, kept in case the electric lights should fail.'

'Yes, yes, thank you, I shall require *only* used ones, the more used the better, and don't remove the wax that's melted down the sides. Do please hurry, Mrs Tompkins,' Abraham urges. 'Oh, and while you're at it, see if you can find me a chicken feather, a small one will do.'

'A chicken feather? Don't have chicken on a Thursdee.'

'From a pillow perhaps?'

'That's goose,' Mrs Tompkins says.

'Yes, well, a feather. Find one, please! Oh, and another thing, tell the maid who irons my shirt every morning to make a tear, a big tear where my heart would be, then to bring it to my bed chamber.'

'Tear your shirt?'

'Yes, yes, tear it.'

'You ain't got no old shirts, Sir Abraham.'

Abraham sighs. 'A good one, Mrs Tompkins, a *very* good one!' he says, showing some signs of exasperation.

'Hmmph!' Mrs Tompkins expostulates, clearly showing her disapproval, then she turns towards the door.

'And tell Adams to take the motor car to fetch Rabbi Abrahams, he knows where he lives.'

'Worn-down candles, chicken feathers, torn shirts and Mr Adams to fetch the rabbi, right then,' Mrs Tompkins mutters unhappily as she leaves the room.

With Mrs Tompkins dismissed Abraham walks into the reception room where his mother always kept a silver menorah, the traditional Jewish candelabrum consisting of eight branches. He finds it tucked away in a cupboard and takes it to his father's bed chamber, where he places it on a chest of drawers to the left of the bed.

Then he moves a chair beside the bed and leaves for his own bedroom where, fortunately, the maid has not yet removed yesterday's suit for pressing. Drinking the cup of tea, Abraham waits until the laundry maid brings in the freshly ironed shirt and when she goes to pick up his suit trousers from the carpet where he's thrown them the previous night, he instructs her to leave them. Abraham examines the shirt and discovers that the maid, though it was probably Mrs Tompkins, has made a small, almost tentative cut around the area of the heart with a pair of scissors. Abraham gets into his vest and long johns and, pulling on the shirt, examines the tear in the mirror. Deciding that it does not appear sufficiently contrite, he rips it further to expose a goodly area of his undervest. Abraham is a modern Jew and doesn't habitually wear the tallit, the tassled prayer shawl traditionally worn under the shirt. His mother never threw anything out and he wonders if a little rummaging might produce the one he wore at his bar mitzvah but then decides that Rabbi Abrahams is astute enough to know that, in his case, it would be an affectation or perhaps even be seen as a hypocrisy.

He retrieves his trousers from the bedroom carpet and is pleased to see that they give every appearance of having been much rumpled. Abraham pulls them on and hooks the still attached braces over his shoulders. Leaving the starched collar off the shirt, he cunningly inserts a gold collar stud into its topmost buttonhole to give the appearance of a soiled collar removed. Finally adding his weskit, socks and boots he presents himself once again in front of the mirror. The total effect, taken together with the dark stain of his overnight growth, gives every impression of dishevelment; of clothes and man having endured a long night at the bedside of the dying.

By the time the rabbi arrives the candles of varying sizes that Mrs Tompkins has scavenged from the servants' quarters are well alight and look as if they have worn their way downwards throughout the long night's vigil. Adams steps aside at the door to let Rabbi Abrahams into David's bed chamber. The rabbi observes Sir Abraham sitting slumped in a chair at the bedside with his chin resting on his chest, giving an altogether convincing imitation of someone who hasn't slept a wink all night. Abraham, who is not by nature duplicitous, is relieved when the rabbi nods his approval.

'The vigil of a faithful son, I commend you and I wish you long life, Sir Abraham,' Rabbi Abrahams says as he crosses to where Abraham sits. Abraham rises wearily and they shake hands. 'Ah, he has not been touched,' the rabbi exclaims, seeing David's staring eyes and open jaw.

Abraham points to a saucer on the bedside table on which resides a rather small chicken feather. 'Am I not required to wait for you to say the *Baruch Dayan ha-Emet*?' Abraham asks, hoping he has correctly pronounced the Hebrew words taken from his mother's prayer book.

'Oh, you should have done that yourself, then placed the feather to the lips of the deceased to ensure there is no breath coming afterwards, leaving the body untouched for eight minutes only.'

Rabbi Abrahams points accusingly to where David lies with his toothless mouth gaping, his head sunk deeply into the goose-down pillow. 'It is the task of the eldest son to close the eyes and the mouth,' he says, reproving Abraham. 'Rigor mortis has already set in, now it will not be easy.'

'I'm sorry, Rabbi, as I said, I was under the impression he was not to be touched.'

Rabbi Abrahams shrugs and sighs and points to the candelabrum with the stubs of nine candles still burning. 'And the menorah you don't need. Only one candle to be lit beside the dying, nine is an extravagance, one candle is all that is required to symbolise the flickering of the soul. A Jew's death is a simple affair, a rich man and a poor man are equal in death, so in God's law we keep things simple, affordable, a single candle, a pine coffin, death is no time to show off.'

'I'm sorry, Rabbi, it has been too long since my mother passed away to remember all the details.'

'That is two times you are sorry already. It is unseemly to allow such a distinguished man as your father,' he points to the gaping jaw once again, 'to be like this.'

Abraham looks alarmed. 'What shall I do, Rabbi?'

Rabbi Abrahams shrugs his shoulders. 'It is not for me to say, he will not be seen, it is only a private matter, of respect between you and your father.'

'I thought it important not to touch him. I did not think of rigor mortis.'

'So now he has a big mouth to catch flies?'

'I'm sorry, Rabbi Abrahams.'

'Three times now you are sorry. Perhaps next time the telephone, eh? When you know death knocks at the door you take the telephone and call me and I will tell you what to do?'

Abraham knows Rabbi Abrahams has not been fooled by his bumbling attempt to cover up. The good reb has a reputation for both wisdom and shrewdness and in the work of the Lord is not afraid to use an acerbic tongue when he is confronted by a sacrilegious Jew. Even David had, on more than one occasion, ruefully admitted that Rabbi Abrahams got the better of him, that the rabbi had managed to effortlessly loosen his tightly drawn purse strings when no other man on God's earth could have done so.

Abraham, of course, knows the story of the two ears of God and the resultant birth of Joshua. How the rabbi took a natural and perfectly fair advantage of David's obsessive desire for a grandson. After all, it was one of the few occasions anyone can

remember when David Solomon got his comeuppance and
Melbourne's Jewish community are very fond of relating the story.
Abraham himself derived a fair amount of comfort from the tale,
for it proved that his father was vulnerable and it pleased him to
think that David was made to look foolish for once in his life. But
now he has no desire to undergo the same treatment at the hands
of the famous rabbi.

'What shall I do?' he asks the rabbi again, knowing that if
Rabbi Abrahams decides to advise him, he will by this act alone
have attracted a more than generous donation to the synagogue.

'I can show you, but I cannot help. You understand?'

'Yes, thank you, Rabbi,' Abraham says, greatly relieved.

'You will need a linen table napkin and a woman's stocking
and also somebody else must be here. Mr Adams perhaps? It is not
necessary that this somebody is a Jew.'

'A table napkin and a woman's stocking?'

'For the jaw,' the rabbi explains, 'we must close it, force it into
a closed position, then tie it for a few hours so it won't snap open
again. The napkin is for the eyes,' he adds gratuitously.

Abraham nods. 'Right.' Then he calls Adams, knowing that
the butler will be standing outside the bed-chamber door. The
jowly visage of Adams appears around the lintel, 'You called, sir?'

'Get a stocking from one of the maids and bring a linen towel,'
Abraham instructs the butler.

'A stocking, sir?'

'Yes, yes, man, do hurry, rigor mortis has set in.'

'Hurry, smurry, it won't make no difference, now is already
too late to hurry,' the rabbi looks meaningfully at the hapless
Abraham, 'but not too late for due care.'

Adams returns after a few minutes with both items, and no
doubt there is much speculation and giggling taking place in the
kitchen.

'You must stay to help, Adams,' Abraham commands, glad to
be in a position to assert a little authority of his own. 'And see that
whoever is given the money for a new pair of hose.'

'Certainly, Sir Abraham. May I offer my condolences to
yourself and Lady Elizabeth.'

'Yes, yes, thank you, Adams. Rabbi Abrahams will instruct us
now in what to do.'

'If you please, Sir Abraham, you must place both your hands

on the top of Mr David's head.' The rabbi turns to Adams. 'And you, Mr Adams, will push from the base of the jaw to close it. Then Sir Abraham will tie the stocking about the jaw and pull it tight to the crown of the head where he will tie it like a bandage for a sore tooth. Do you understand?'

'Certainly, sir, I was a stretcher-bearer in the Boer War,' Adams says a trifle smugly.

Abraham is mortified at the prospect of touching the cold, staring, gap-mouthed face of his father who in death wears an expression not unlike the one he customarily assumed when his temper was out of control and he was looking around for something expensive to break. 'Er, I say, can we not have Adams do it with someone else?' Abraham now asks.

Rabbi Abrahams shakes his head and looks scornfully at him. 'It is a task for a loving son, a great privilege and an honour.'

'But you said it was not a religious act?'

'Not religious no, but loving, yes.'

Abraham sighs and closing his eyes places both hands down on the cold skull of his dead father.

'Push now!' the rabbi instructs. 'Push down!' With his eyes still tightly shut Abraham pushes down and he can hear Adams grunting as he forces the jaw to a closed position. 'Now bring the stocking,' Rabbi Abrahams says, 'cup it under the chin and draw it up over both ears and pull tight, then make a knot.'

Abraham opens his eyes and takes up the black woollen stocking in both hands and as Adams removes his hands from David's jaw he quickly loops it under his dead father's chin and draws it upwards, covering his ears.

'Tight! Pull it tight,' the rabbi explains. Abraham pulls hard on both ends of the stocking and finds his hands are now a good eighteen inches above his dead father's head. 'Keep the strain and make a knot. Mr Adams, bring back your hand on the jaw!' Abraham makes a knot and pulls it tight then makes another so that an almost perfect topknot appears at the apex of David's almost bald skull. Abraham notices for the first time that the surface of his father's skull is blotched with large dark age freckles and is, in appearance, not dissimilar to the skin of an overripe banana. He has a sense of having lost his dignity and feels slightly soiled by the waxy, cold feel of the skin. The too close proximity to death is not at all to his liking.

'Now the eyes,' the rabbi says, he looks suspiciously at Abraham. 'You will do the eyes, it is the duty of the eldest son.'

'No, please, no! I do not feel well.'

The rabbi looks at Abraham in surprise and points to the corpse. 'Not so sick as him! Tradition, tradition, it is a great honour, for three thousand years the Jews . . .'

'No! Please?' Abraham interrupts him.

'Tut, tut, it is not difficult, it is very symbolic, you are closing the curtains of life.' The look of scorn appears again as Rabbi Abrahams looks at Abraham. 'It is a great privilege to make this gesture, to bring peace, rest and tranquility to the dead.'

'No, I simply cannot do it! I can't touch him again, not his eyes.' Abraham visibly shudders.

'I shall do it, sir,' Adams says, addressing himself to the rabbi, 'though I must remind you I am not a semite,' he glances quickly at Abraham, 'but Mr David always treated me as his son.'

'Yes, thank you, Adams, I am most grateful,' Abraham says, ignoring the butler's remark. Like himself, Adams took almost nothing but abuse from his father.

Rabbi Abrahams sighs and then shrugs, it is a gesture which makes Abraham immediately decide to double the already generous donation he intends to give in memory of his father. 'As you wish then, Sir Abraham, it is not a religious task.'

Adams stoops over the bestocking'd head of David Solomon and with a minimum of fuss gouges his thumbs deeply into the cold eye sockets and expertly pulls the lids down over the dead man's eyes. Then taking up the table napkin he twirls it into a narrow strip which he uses to bandage the closed eyelids.

Abraham looks down at the now heavily bandaged head of the dead David Solomon. The tightly drawn stocking has pulled his father's jaw so far upwards that his mouth serves as a hinge and the point of the jaw now touches the tip of his nose.

Rabbi Abrahams rises. 'You will, of course, cover all the mirrors in the house.' He looks about him and spies a mug beside the bed. 'And pour the water from all containers near the dead.'

He leans over to pick up the mug. Suddenly his eyes grow wide, 'Oh my goodness!' he exclaims. 'The teeth! We have locked your father's jaw without putting back his teeth!'

Abraham draws back in horror. 'Oh no, you don't! No way! That's it. I've had quite enough!'

'But, Sir Abraham, the jaw will collapse,' the rabbi points to the dead man's face. 'See already it's not so good, it will be most unseemly, Mr David *must* have his teeth, it is a matter of respect for the dead.'

'So, let it collapse, no one will see him!' Abraham shouts in panic, his voice climbing two octaves. 'He's dead, my father's dead, he's not on exhibition! I'm not going through that again!'

The rabbi shrugs. 'That is true but you are the only son, a great privilege!' the rabbi protests.

'No, Rabbi! You've heard me. I'm absolutely not going to do it!'

'It is not such a nice thing you are doing, Abraham Solomon.' The rabbi smiles, 'But on the other hand, I understand.'

'Thank you, Rabbi,' Abraham sighs, greatly relieved. 'I am not sure I feel well, I wonder if I may be excused?'

'Certainly, Sir Abraham, but first I must say the prayers for the dead, it is important that you be present for these.' The rabbi turns to the butler. 'Mr Adams may now leave.'

With the ancient prayer rituals completed, the rabbi quietly instructs Abraham in his further duties. 'You will wrap your beloved father with a sheet and place him on the floor with his feet pointed towards the door and then you will place a single candle at his head. Before Mr Moshe Sapperstein of the Chevra Kadisha arrives my advice to you is to remove the bandages from his head and eyes so your father will look the way a father should when a loving and dutiful son has properly attended to his death.'

'Yes, thank you, Rabbi Abrahams, I am most grateful. I shall make a donation in memory of my father if you will let me know how this might best be done. Some useful project perhaps?'

Rabbi Abrahams bows slightly. 'Now is not the time to talk of such matters, but I am most grateful, Sir Abraham, the Lord's work is never completed. We have a great need to build a new synagogue, thank the Lord our congregation grows. Perhaps I may visit you at some time more convenient to discuss this with you?'

'Certainly, Rabbi. I will look forward to your call. We shall telephone for a taxi to take you home, there is a depot not far away, it will not take long.'

'Thank you, Sir Abraham, I must remind you that the body of your father must not be left alone. You or your wife must not leave him until the Chevra Kadisha comes to fetch him.' Rabbi

Abrahams looks around the room and points to the menorah. 'I think maybe a small miracle, that is the first time I have seen candles that do not all burn down at the same rate.' Then bowing his head slightly before leaving the room, the rabbi says the traditional blessing, 'May the Lord comfort you with all the mourners of Zion and Jerusalem.'

With the rabbi's departure and Elizabeth seated facing the far wall, her back turned on the shrouded body of David on the floor with his feet pointed towards the door and with one of Mrs Tompkins' brand new candles at his head, Abraham is feeling decidedly better. Tradition, tradition, how useful it can be. Expensive, but useful. Abraham decides he will call Hawk immediately and ask for a postponement to prepare for him and his clever little granddaughter. As he commences to wind the handle on the telephone he thinks that David's timely death is the only true example of consideration his father has ever shown him.

Hawk, putting down the telephone from Abraham Solomon, is almost as grateful as Abraham for the extra time David's death allows him. Victoria is proving extremely difficult to convince that she should work with him at the Potato Factory.

'But, Grandfather, you have been retired these twenty-one years, why would you wish to go back?' is the first question she asks after he has approached her with the proposition he has in mind.

'Not retired, my dear, removed, sacked from the chairmanship of Solomon & Teekleman, you well know the circumstances.'

'Well, yes, but does it really matter?' Victoria says, appealing to him. 'We are well rid of the vile company, they exploit the poor at every opportunity.' She shudders suddenly. 'You know how very much I wish my name wasn't a part of it!'

'But you *are* a part of it, Victoria, and will, someday, with Ben, be its biggest shareholder. The three of us already are.'

'It makes me feel dirty, Grandfather. They are singular proof that we must have stronger unions and a government that is prepared to take away much of the power of the large corporations.'

Hawk sighs. 'The working class will certainly benefit by a stronger union movement and you already have a Labor government, but as long as industry can be relied on to pay taxes, even a Labor prime minister will be reluctant to interfere. While I am all for curbing excesses, wherever they may be, it seems to me that the best way to change an organisation is from within.'

'I should much rather work *within* a trade union to make the changes.'

Hawk laughs, applauding Victoria's quick mind. Nonetheless he continues. 'Think of a corporation or company as a human with many of the same characteristics. For instance, Solomon & Teekleman is formed out of two companies, Solomon & Co. founded by David Solomon, and the Potato Factory founded, as you know, by Mary Abacus. The two, when they came together under the same parent company, were diametrically opposed in their philosophies, in other words they had quite different personalities. Like a husband and wife with different cultural backgrounds who are unable to agree on almost anything. Take David Solomon's company, selfish, greedy, unsympathetic, cunning, vengeful and deeply suspicious of those who work for it, these are the characteristics of Solomon & Co. and are a mirror image of the man who founded it.

'On the other hand, Mary's company, in the light of the times, was straight-dealing, open, hard-headed but responsible for the welfare of those who worked for it. Your great-grandmother never forgot her humble beginnings or what it meant to be poor and so she understood the needs of her people.' Hawk pauses and looks at Victoria, 'Do you follow the analogy so far?'

Victoria nods her head, 'Yes but . . .' She knows better than to interrupt, but simply cannot contain herself.

'Yes but what, my dear?' Hawk asks, a trifle irritated at being interrupted when, to his mind, his explanation is progressing along so nicely.

'The bad swallowed the good! Evil triumphed, as it always seems to do in big business! David Solomon won, didn't he!'

Hawk shakes his head. 'I know it looks that way. But David's control came about by a series of unfortunate circumstances which allowed him to take control, rather than what was originally intended, that someone who believed in the Mary Abacus approach should be at the helm.'

'You mean, of course, yourself?'

'Aye. I failed to ensure my control of Solomon & Teekleman.'

'Because our mother left without giving you her proxy? Is that why?'

233

Hawk nods again. 'It wasn't evil triumphing over good, it was my own stupidity. I should have been more sensitive to the emotional needs of your mother. I'm afraid I'm a clumsy, insensitive fool when it comes to that sort of thing. Her restlessness was there for me to see if I'd been looking. David Solomon obtained control by default or, if you like, because of my own lack of foresight, and so he proceeded to create both companies in his own image.'

'Grandfather Hawk!' Victoria protests. 'You are not clumsy and you are the least fool of any man I've ever known, you are the most fair-minded, honest and sensitive person I know!' Victoria pauses then lowers her voice, 'But after all that's said and done, that's my *very* point!'

'What is?' Hawk asks. To his surprise he finds himself slightly on the defensive. 'That you think me weak and David strong?'

Victoria sighs. 'No, "fair-minded, honest and sensitive" doesn't mean weak. But you would be the first to admit that they are characteristics largely missing in big business and deeply scorned by the capitalists. You must see the enemy for what they are! They are not going to change willingly but must be dragged kicking and screaming to the negotiating table.' Victoria takes a breath, 'And if they won't come, they must be punished!'

'Spoken like a true disciple of Labor!' Hawk teases. 'The dialectics are fair enough, though the wording a little too revolutionary for my taste. Capitalism as a system has many advantages but it is essentially based on the very human need that most of us have to want more. Greed being perhaps the most primitive of our many human urges, the capitalist system works very well for those who have the money to exploit it.'

'But greed has no right to exist in a modern society, we are no longer primitive, there is enough for us all, we must learn to share our wealth.'

'Unfortunately, right at this moment the capital on which the system is based is in the hands of those new Australian money aristocrats, the Clarkes, the Armytage family, the Fairbairns, Hentys, Mackinnons, Manifolds and Sargoods to name but a few and, indeed, David Solomon and yourself, my dear. With the exception perhaps of the Clarkes and ourselves, who have been generous in their public donations, they all have every intention of having as much as they can get and sharing as little as they can get away with.'

'But they *must* be made to share!'

'Well, perhaps, but remember they were prepared to take the original risks to acquire it. Taking risks should not go unrewarded or no one would take them. Sidney Myer Baevski was once a hawker, a poor Russian Jew who spoke no English when he arrived, working the small country towns for his living. He endured daily ridicule, young boys would throw rocks at him and shout, "Jewboy, Jewboy, take a piece of pork and put it on your fork!" Three months ago, as all of Melbourne witnessed, he opened his new emporium in Bourke Street, the greatest and grandest shop in Australia and few better in the world. All this in twenty years and achieved by taking countless risks. You could say that he deserves the reward of the risk-taker. Must he also be punished?'

Hawk does not wait for Victoria to reply. 'David Solomon was yet another who started out with virtually nothing. Men such as these, poor boys, Irish, Jews, Protestants, all took risks and some were successful while others failed. It only becomes a problem when the risk-takers are so successful that they control most of the capital, which means they are the only ones who can reasonably capitalise on the essentially risk-free and truly big opportunities that occur in a growing economy such as our new Federation. As capital expands it gains more and more power. Money and power is a heady mixture which very easily leads to corruption.'

'So you agree with me, we need a strong counter-system to control these rich families and consortiums, these money aristocrats?'

'Well, yes and no. Alas, it is my observation that counter-systems, as you call them, tend to acquire the same characteristics and many of the bad habits of the systems they oppose and are therefore often counterproductive. What's more, they are essentially more difficult to remove than big business, because they do not have to survive in a risk-taking world or answer to shareholders.'

'Ha, that may be reasonable speculation, Grandfather. But the unions do have the government of the day to restrain them.'

'Perhaps not as far as you think, let me give you an example, and one I personally experienced. Though I confess it was a little too early for the union movement, it was the start of worker dissent in factories. A Workers' Deputation, as they called themselves at the time, claiming membership of several factories and workshops in the Hobart area, visited Mary Abacus under the leadership of a Scotsman named Hugh Kirk. Kirk was a small-time firebrand and his movement one of many which preceded unionism as we know it today. He had visited Melbourne where he became acquainted with a newly formed group who named themselves the Brewers' Employes' Eight Hours Association and returned home to aim his sights at the Cascade Brewery and ourselves, urging the workers to unite against the bosses and join "the Association". He was a popular speaker among the working classes and had gained some real success in recruiting members as I remember, by calling one- or two-day strikes and frightening some of the smaller workshop owners. But not, it was claimed, without a fair bit of heavy-handed coercion involving several broken heads among those workers reluctant to join. The Potato Factory was his first incursion into the big league and with his new Melbourne association, Kirk demanded that Mary allow his movement to operate within the brewery.

'"Righto," says Mary, "if that's what my people want then they can 'ave it with me blessing."' Victoria laughs despite herself for Hawk brings her great-grandmother alive for her. He continues, 'Mary points her crooked finger at Hugh Kirk, "But first, let's ask 'em straight. You talk to them, tell 'em whatever it is you wish to say, you know, exploitation o' the working classes, snot-nosed kids begging for pennies on street corners, wife dying in childbirth, father of consumption, leaving ten starvin' kids behind, all the stuff what's been goin' on for 'undreds of years and all now blamed on big business. I promise I won't say nothin'. I'll keep me gob shut tight as a possum's bum. Then we'll 'ave the vote, let 'em decide for themselves. Fair enough, Mr Kirk?"

'"Fair enough, missus," Kirk says reluctantly. Well, Mary calls for the works foreman, Ernie Connaghan. "Mr Connaghan," she says, "stop the brewery, close it down the 'ole box and dice, we're 'aving a meeting o' the workers this afternoon."

'Ernie Connaghan looks like he can't believe what Mary's just said, "Can't do that, Miss Mary, we'd 'ave to steam-clean all the pipes, get the yeast vats started from scratch, build up the fermentation vats, take us all night to get under way again, cost a fortune in lost production, what's more, you know it's impossible to close the malt house, barley's piling up as it is with no place to store it."

'"That all right, missus, maltsters don't belong in the Association," says Kirk.

'"You hear that? Cost a fortune, Mr Kirk. My money, not the workers'." She turns to Ernie Connaghan, "No matter, do as I say, Ernie, er Mr Connaghan, Mr Kirk here is from the . . . what did you say you were?"

'"Brewers' Employes' Eight Hours Association," Kirk replies.

'"Yes, well them. He wants to spruik to all the workers, 'cept the maltsters and the clerks in the front office, whom he don't consider the first brewers and the second to be workers, them wearing stiff collars and all." Mary now turns to Kirk, "So what's wrong with the clerks? You got something against clerks, Mr Kirk? I was a clerk once, still am as a matter o' fact, only a bit better paid than most."

'"Clerks can become bosses, missus. Can't trust a clerk."'

Hawk grins at the memory. 'So we close the brewery down except for the malt house and the front office and all the workers assemble in the dray yard to hear Mr Hugh Kirk. And I have to say he does a damn fine job telling the workers how they are exploited by the owners, blah, blah, blah. He's of a fiery Scots temperament and he works up quite a sweat socking it to the bosses, who in this case is Mary and myself, both of us sitting on a dray cart with our arms crossed listening. Then he says, "Righto, we'll take a vote, like the boss said, all who wants to stop the exploitation by the bosses by joining the Association and getting an eight-hour working day raise yer hands."

'"Oi! Just a bleedin' moment!" Mary shouts. "We'll 'ave none of that, Mr Kirk. A vote you shall have, fair and square, but it will be by *secret* ballot, our people will vote with their consciences not with their bleedin' 'ands. Only them and Gawd is gunna know who they are and 'ow they've voted."

'"That's not how it's done, missus," Kirk objects. "We like things to be kept in the open like, democratic, know what I mean?"

'"Democratic me arse!" Mary says. "Sure you want it open so you'll know the names of those who are *for* you and them's what's *against*. All for the future records, eh? Very 'andy, if I may say so meself, being a clerk an' all. Well, I tell you what I'll do, I'll exercise me own perog-a-tive as a boss and put democracy to work. I'll allow a secret ballot to determine whether the people at the Potato Factory want an open vote, a show of 'ands, or want a conscience vote. Now what say you to that, Mr Kirk? Ain't nothing says that's against the rules, is there?"'

Hawk spreads his hands. 'Well, the Potato Factory workers voted in Mary's ballot that they wanted a secret ballot to decide whether to join Kirk's association or remain as they were. Then they used the secret ballot to say they wished to remain as they were.'

'You mean your workers didn't vote for an eight-hour day?' Victoria asks, incredulous.

'Indeed, they did not, but they got it anyway two months later.'

'Well, Mr Kirk's visit did some good then. But, Grandfather, the Potato Factory was an exception, other companies did, and *still* exploit their workers,' Victoria challenges. 'The intimidation from the bosses experienced by the workers during the Shearers' and the Maritime strikes proved once and for all that the capitalists could not be trusted, that a strong labour movement had to be in parliament, that unionism was essential if the workers were ever to be free of what virtually amounted to a system of bondage!'

'Perhaps, but let me make my point. Perhaps as a consequence of this single incident with Mary, for Hugh Kirk was later to become a very big figure in the Tasmanian and Australian union movement, the unions never allowed secret ballots. Today, coercion and standover tactics are more than common in our trade unions. So you see, my dear, power and corruption are not such a long way away in any organisation. We all want control, the bosses have it by owning the means of earning wages and the unions have it by owning the workers. Mark my words, secret ballots are outlawed by the union movement and the next thing they will do is to make joining a union compulsory. In other words, a worker will not be able to find employment without a union card and, as a registered member, they will not be allowed to vote according to conscience for fear of repercussions, not from their industrial bosses, but from their own union bosses. Furthermore, industry will not be allowed to employ non-union labour.'

'But the union officials will be serving in the interest of the workers, gaining advantages and better conditions for them, why would they vote against such laudatory pursuits? Besides, Mr

Curtin says it is a matter of brotherly trust, that a worker must show where he stands at a union meeting, that secret ballots are sneaky and unmanly!'

'Ah, well said, Mr Curtin, how very convenient to the cause.' Hawk gives Victoria a rueful smile. 'But in the end, my dear, it is a matter of freedom of choice. But it is interesting, is it not, that those who have been elected to the House of Representatives achieved this by secret ballot? The so-called common worker must enjoy the right to choose without fear or favour.'

'Oh, I see, the age-old system of divide and conquer. Turn the unions against themselves. Is this then to be the new management weapon?' Victoria snorts.

Hawk looks amused, enjoying both Victoria's lively mind and her strongly held convictions. 'You have the makings of an excellent union leader, my dear.'

Victoria appeals to Hawk. 'But I *am* a member of the Labor Party and I do truly believe they are the solution to the terrible exploitation of the working classes in our country.' Her eyes are sad, as though disappointed that he might not feel the same way. 'Surely you also believe this?'

Hawk smiles. 'Of course. Capital and labour must both be seen to co-exist, to be a viable part of our economy. Both must benefit if we are to prosper as a nation, but there is an ingredient which is essential if each side is to have its rightful share of the good life.'

'And what is that?' Victoria asks.

'Goodwill,' Hawk replies.

Victoria looks genuinely shocked. 'You're not serious? Goodwill? You said yourself, people are greedy and can't be trusted?'

'Well, take Sidney Myer again. He has established a pension fund for his workers, he is a Jew but allows the staff to hold Christian services in the shop at lunch time. He has a choir, a Friday night get-together for his staff, annual picnics and now he has introduced what is called "a spiff", that is, his sales people are paid a penny in the pound commission as an incentive. Is this not the beginnings at least of a caring company?'

Victoria looks appealingly at Hawk. 'You're going to say, when a generous person controls a company and is in a position to make the right decisions, management and trade unions don't necessarily have to be at each other's throats. Is that it, Grandfather?'

'Very good, my dear. If you were to join Solomon & Teekleman and rise to the top it would be a great opportunity to show your character, to show how things might be different.'

'Well, what about Joshua? He has been groomed to run Solomon & Teekleman virtually since birth?'

'We have the majority now, Victoria. We have the say.'

Victoria shakes her head. 'How could you say that! How is that fair? If he were better than me I wouldn't want to be chairman. I would hate that.'

'Better? How can he be? He is the product of his grandfather, he will run the company much as his grandfather did. There is very little of Abraham and a whole lot of David Solomon in that young man, he would be the devil you know and want to be rid of, Victoria.'

'But I would always have to fight him, he'd never give in.'

'Aye, that's true. If you were a union official you'd always have to fight him and he'd never give in. The proposition I hope, with your permission, to put to Abraham is that he remains overall chairman, that I become the chairman and managing director of the Potato Factory and take you with me to train you to eventually run it. Then, upon Joshua's return from the war, he will take over Solomon & Co., whereupon I retire and you replace me as managing director of the Potato Factory.' Hawk shrugs. 'After that it's your personal donnybrook with Joshua.'

'I see, him with one company, me with the other. So that I can learn to practise what I preach, our ideal of a fair-minded company, and Joshua does it his way. The performances of the two companies may then be compared. What if his is better, and greed and bullying proves to be better than sharing the wealth?'

'Well, that's for you to find out, I didn't say it would be easy. If it's a disaster you could always resign and join the trade union movement,' he teases Victoria. 'A little wiser in the ways of the world by then, I daresay.'

'But, Grandfather, you do believe that fairness and honesty will win the day, don't you?'

'I have always tried to be honest and fair in my dealings in life and to be perfectly frank with you my life has been a failure. But that doesn't mean you will fail. The very predicament we find ourselves in at present, with David having snatched control of Solomon & Teekleman, was because I wanted to be fair-minded.'

'You mean you don't think I can do it?' Victoria challenges.

'No, I didn't say that. I said that I had not been successful. But Mary Abacus was, so why not you?' Hawk replies.

'I have never understood why you wanted to join with David and Abraham in the first place, if as you say their way of doing things was so very different to yours? You didn't need to do it, you were already a huge success and, as I understand it, they were in financial trouble. It's never made any sense to me?'

Hawk sighs. 'Because out of something rotten came something good and then out of that something good has come something rotten again and I am stupid enough to believe it might yet come to something good.'

'Whatever can you mean?' Victoria says, puzzled.

'Ah! It's a long story and one I would only wish you to hear if you decide to come into the company so that I might train you. If you don't I will not burden you with it, it is too long and painful and not worth the telling unless it ultimately helps your determination to succeed where I have failed.'

'Grandfather, that is so very unfair!' Victoria protests. 'You want me to make a decision without knowing its entire purpose?'

'Nevertheless, I want you to decide using your own free will. Whatever you decide to do, I shall accept your decision. If I were to tell you my reasons for wanting you to take your rightful place in the company you own, you may well be persuaded by your emotions and not by your own reasoning. I should not want that to happen.'

Victoria spends the next two days alone, taking her meals separately then announces that she wants to talk to Ben who hasn't, as expected, returned to Tasmania. Four days after the passing-out parade he was told to report to Major Sayers, his Victorian company commander.

The major, a scouse, comes straight to the point. 'Look, Sergeant Teekleman, we need you here. I've spoken to your C.O. in Hobart and he's agreed you can stay with us, though in fairness I 'ave to say he put up a fair bit of fuss, no, more than that, he was bloody angry.'

'But why, sir? It was clearly understood that I'd be allowed to return to my own regiment, to my mates?'

The major shrugged, 'Ard luck, lad, we need another instructor on machine guns. Sergeant Freys, the chief instructor, has been diagnosed with cancer, he won't be going overseas with us.'

'But, sir, there are ten other sergeants all of whom did the course with me, all of them Victorians.'

'It's damned 'ard luck. I know. But there are other considerations I am not at liberty to divulge like.' He points to the ceiling. 'Made higher oop.'

Shortly after Ben's instructions that he is to stay with the Victorian regiment it is announced that the troopships which are to take the Victorians and Tasmanians to King George Sound in Albany will be delayed three weeks. There are no official explanations for this, but a major story in the *Age* speculates, as it turns out correctly, that it is because the prime minister and the war cabinet do not want to send the convoy ships to Western Australia without the protection of the battleships HMAS *Sydney* and HMAS *Melbourne* in case the German navy decides to hunt in Australian waters.

Victoria contacts Ben at Broadmeadows and he requests and is granted forty-eight hours' leave. She books two rooms overnight at a small hotel in the Dandenongs so that she might talk undisturbed with him about Hawk's proposition.

Victoria arrives home at ten o'clock in the evening of the second day and goes immediately to Hawk's study to tell him that she accepts the challenge he has given her.

'I am delighted, my dear,' Hawk says, rising and embracing her. 'But now you must tell me why? I cannot believe that my arguments alone have persuaded you.'

'Well no, not entirely, it was Ben.'

'Ben?' Hawk says surprised. 'I didn't think Ben took much interest in business matters?'

'No, he doesn't, but he's got an awful lot of commonsense.' Victoria smiles. '"Sissie," he said after I'd told him how I felt and what you'd said, "the bloody unions are never going to let you rise high enough in their ranks to really change things. Grandfather Hawk is probably right, there are just as many crooks, greedy and corrupt blokes protecting their arses in the unions as there are in big business. The army's the same, full of bullshit artists that don't know their arse from their elbow. What's more, how far do you think you're gunna get as a woman in the Labor Party, eh? You ain't gunna get into parliament, will ya? A woman in parliament, heaven bloody forbid, she might take her knitting into debate! Do a pair of baby booties when the house is in session!"' Victoria is a fair mimic in her own right and she has Ben's soft drawl down pat. '"But, look at it this way, sis, if you join Solomon & Teekleman and you go against Joshua and you beat him, you can do things your way and make a bloody big difference, possibly change the way business is done in Australia. Grandfather Hawk is right about money and power. Mind you, round this bloody place there's no bloody money, it's just power! But it doesn't always have to make you corrupt, does it?"' Victoria concludes. 'Well, that's what he said anyway.'

'He said that?' Hawk exclaims, impressed. 'And that's what made you decide?'

Victoria nods. 'Now, will you tell me all I must know about the past?'

'First you must eat something. Mrs Billings has left a plate in the oven for fear you'd return and starve to death on boarding-house food. Hawk imitates the housekeeper, '"She'd be a shadow, that one, left to her own! Can't even boil an egg, too busy doin' sums on them bloomin' beads! Young girls these days got nothing in their 'eads what's useful. I don't know what the world's coming to, her goin' off and staying in a boardin' 'ouse!"' Hawk then adds in his own voice, 'Better eat something, though, or we'll never hear the end of it.'

'It was a perfectly lovely little hotel and we had a scrumptious lunch before we left, but a little supper would be nice. Will you sit with me, Grandfather? Have a cup of tea?' Victoria smiles. 'I can make a cup of tea.'

It is nearly two before they finally rise from the table and Hawk has told Victoria the whole story of the two families and the bitter conflict which has always existed between them and the reasons for it. He leaves nothing out. Finally he tells her of Teekleman's death and Hinetitama's demise until she returned to die in the St Kilda hospice and that, with her proxy, they once again control Solomon & Teekleman.

When Hawk has completed the story they both remain silent for some time, Victoria weeping softly. 'It is not too late to decide against joining Solomon & Teekleman. I would completely understand if you are reluctant to carry the burden of such a past.

Though Abraham Solomon is a reasonable man, Joshua has been bred to commerce by his grandfather and he may prove equally recalcitrant and unforgiving.'

Victoria looks tearfully up at Hawk and sniffs, 'No, I've made up my mind, I want to be with you.'

'Well then, there is one last task, though more a pleasure than a task.' He rises and goes to his desk and taking a small key from his pocket he opens a drawer and takes out Mary's Waterloo medal attached to a thin gold chain. 'Your great-grandmother asked me on her deathbed to give this to you. It was her talisman, her great good luck. It was only removed from her neck on two occasions, when it was stolen on board the convict ship she came out on by the assistant to the ship's surgeon and when she died. Will you wear it? On the back it says "I shall never surrender", four words which made everything possible for Mary. Will you take it for yourself, the medal and the words?'

Victoria gasps as she is handed the medallion. 'Oh, I know it was wrong, but I was so envious of Ben when he received our grandfather's Tiki. I would so much have liked it for myself.' Victoria, already emotionally exhausted, bursts into tears as Hawk takes the medallion back again and places it about her neck. 'I shall treasure it all the days of my life, Grandfather Hawk. Thank you, thank you,' she says, barely above a whisper. 'I shall wear it with the same pride as did Mary Abacus.'

She goes to bed in the small hours of the morning exhausted but unable to sleep, her pillow wet with tears for the sad past of her family. She sees the dawn light growing through her window and hears the call of the currawongs, always the first of the birds to greet the new day, and then the next thing she knows, Mrs Billings is shaking her. 'It's four o'clock in the afternoon, lovey. Mr Hawk says to bring you a nice cuppa. I've got a nice bit o' fish for your tea and some new taties and them baby beans you likes. I dunno what his nibs thought he was doin' keeping you up so late, you comin' 'ome after a long journey like that. That's men for you, don't think do they, does what they wants, never mind the feelings and welfare o' others, especially us womenfolk!'

Victoria smiles, sipping the tea, her whole life seems to have changed in the last few days but the whingeing rock of Billings can be relied upon to remain ever the same. 'It was my fault, Mrs Billings, he was telling me the story of our family.'

'Hmmph! I could tell you a thing or two meself, but I won't, it's not for me to say, being in service and all.' She points to the Waterloo medal about Victoria's neck. 'Give you that, did he? That were her most precious possession. Never mind the money, it were that she treasured above rubies. Always knew when things were not going good, she'd sit on the porch in her rocking chair 'olding the medal in her broken fist waitin' for them birds.'

'Yes, Grandfather Hawk told me, it was her talisman and her great good luck.'

'Yes, that and them bloomin' parrots. Did he tell you about them green parrots, that were also her great good luck she'd say?'

Victoria shakes her head, trying to recall if Hawk said anything about green parrots. 'No, I don't think so?'

'Well, you saw them yerself, you was three years old.'

'I don't remember. What about the green parrots?'

'Miss Mary, she'd sit on the porch o' the big house in Hobart to watch the parrots come past. They'd fly over the roof going to their roost higher up the mountain. "Here they come, my great good luck," she'd shout for one and all to hear as they passed over.' Mrs Billings warms to the story, happy to be a part of a family legend. 'Your great-grannie, she loved them birds. Well, the day she died, the very minute she went to her peace, the parrots started to come, but they didn't fly over like always, they settled in the garden, on the roof, in the trees, there was more green parrots than there was leaves on the gum trees. Hundreds o' thousands o' them. They made so much racket you couldn't hear nothing, everything was vibrating green. They stayed an hour then they took off, all o' them together. It were like the roaring of the wind, just their wings and the screeching fair blow'd the ears off yer 'ead.

'Well, next mornin' at sunrise I'm in the kitchen garden 'anging out the tea cloths like I always does first thing. I looks up to the porch expecting to see Miss Mary, her in her favourite chair, waiting for the parrots to pass over. But o' course she ain't there this partickler mornin', she's dead, ain't she? But it's time for the parrots to fly over so I waits, remembering the strange thing what 'appened the night before. I waits and waits. You could time them birds on a clock, you could, always ten minutes after sunrise, but they didn't come, didn't fly over. Not that morning, not ever again. The parrots never come back again and if you think I'm lyin' I'll swear it on a stack o' Bibles,' Mrs Billings says. She looks at

Victoria darkly. 'The luck's run out, see. That's what happened to Mr Hawk. There's no more luck, it's all been spent by Miss Mary, used up.'

'Oh, I don't believe you, Mrs Billings, that's just superstitious nonsense,' Victoria cries.

'You mark me words, young lady, the luck's run out with the green parrots.'

Hawk and Victoria arrive at the head office of Solomon & Teekleman on the dot of ten o'clock, having waited in the motor car around the corner for five minutes so that they wouldn't appear over-anxious by arriving early.

They are met at the door by Abraham's secretary, a tall, dour man of whom it is claimed that he has never been seen to smile. There is a greyness as well as a mustiness about him as though he has been locked in a cupboard for several years never seeing the sunlight. 'Sir Abraham is expecting you, sir,' he says to Hawk, while managing to completely ignore the presence of Victoria.

'Good morning, Mr Phillips,' Victoria chirps brightly, but receives no response.

Hawk is impressed, she has done her homework and knows the name of Abraham's private secretary, whom he is certain she cannot have previously met. 'I don't believe you've met my granddaughter, Phillips?' Hawk now says. 'Victoria, this is Mr Phillips, Mr Phillips, this is Victoria,' he says smiling. He can sense that Victoria is more amused than upset by Phillips' original rebuff.

'How do you do?' Victoria smiles, extending her hand.

'How do?' Phillips mutters, averting his eyes and pushing forward a limp hand which scarcely touches the tips of Victoria's gloved fingers before being withdrawn. 'Follow me please, sir.'

Sir Abraham Solomon is seated at the head of the table as Hawk and Victoria enter the boardroom. There are three men around the long mahogany table and another is seated away from the table, in the corner furthermost from the door. They all rise. Abraham in his fifties is a balding, corpulent, clean-shaven man dressed in a well-cut, three-piece, dark-navy woollen suit. He wears a black tie and gold tie-clip, and his starched collar seems to cut somewhat into his jowls. Everything about him, right down to his highly polished black boots, starched shirt cuffs and gold cufflinks, bears the hallmark of those who do business in the big end of town. 'Good morning, Hawk, good morning, Miss Teekleman, may I introduce you to my colleagues?'

Abraham turns towards the three men standing. 'Hawk Solomon you already know, this is his granddaughter Miss Victoria Teekleman.'

'Miss Teekleman, at the far end is Sir Samuel Sopworth, then Mr Bramwell Cumming two chairs up on the right and, next to him, Mr John Miles. Not joining us at the table is Mr Parkin, who will be taking notes as an observer.'

Victoria has heard of two of the men, Samuel Sopworth, who is a famous accountant, and Bramwell Cumming, a notorious barrister known in Labor ranks as the scourge of the union movement. John Miles, whom she hasn't heard of before, has the pinched and fussy look of a successful lawyer, a type with whom she is all too familiar. Parkin is an unprepossessing-looking man in a suit one might expect a clerk to wear, a misfit, and doesn't appear to belong to the same world as the four other men. Though somewhat older, he has a quite startling resemblance to one of the members of her Labor Party chapter, who is a clerk in the railways office in Flinders Street. Then she suddenly remembers that he is also named Parkin, George Parkin, and has on several occasions boasted of his older brother, who he claimed worked in Trade and Customs, and with the previous month's election of the Andrew Fisher Labor government has been made head of department under the Hon. F. G. Tudor, Minister for Trade and Customs.

Hawk has moved to shake each man by the hand, leaning across the table to do so, and when he has completed greeting each of the men around the table, he walks over to Parkin and shakes his hand before returning to Victoria. The men remain standing and Victoria looks at each of them in turn and, smiling, says, 'How do you do, gentlemen, please call me Victoria. It will be easier on us all. Perhaps we can all be seated now, Sir Abraham?'

'Yes, yes, please,' Abraham says anxiously, indicating the two vacant chairs on the side nearest the door. He is a little taken aback by Victoria's unexpected poise. Abraham thinks what an attractive girl she is despite the plainness of her attire and her well-scrubbed complexion. He has grown accustomed to the flighty and fashionable young women Joshua brings home from time to time and thinks to himself that Victoria Teekleman is far more the type of young lady he would prefer to see on his son's arm, unlikely as that is.

The four men resume their seats and Hawk and Victoria take up theirs. On her small notepad she writes *Mr Parkin – Government!* and puts the pad and pencil down in front of Hawk as though she is handing him his notepad. She sees him casually glance down at it.

There is a sudden silence around the table and then Sir Abraham Solomon clears his throat and seems a trifle nervous, glancing first at the two lawyers and then at Sir Samuel, before returning his gaze to Hawk. 'Well, Hawk Solomon, what have you to say for yourself?' Clearly it is an opening line he has practised carefully, though his voice lacks the casual arrogance needed for such a statement. Hawk thinks how much better David Solomon would have used such an opening remark, bringing to it sufficient vitriol to make it hiss like spittle on a hot stove.

Hawk smiles. 'Well, firstly, Sir Abraham, I wish to offer Victoria's and my own condolences on the passing of your father. Although we didn't get on, he was in many ways a remarkable man, we wish you and your family a long life.'

'Thank you, he had a good innings,' Abraham replies and turns and speaks directly to Victoria. 'Thank you, Victoria, I shall pass your kind remarks on to my family.' Victoria looks directly into his eyes and Abraham cannot help but feel that there is something quite different about Hawk's granddaughter, though he is about to find out just how different.

Abraham, of course, has a clear idea of why Hawk has called the meeting. When Hawk called on him to make the original appointment he'd been out of his office and so Hawk had simply conveyed, through the dour Mr Phillips, a request for a board meeting the following morning, preferably at ten, simply stating that it was on a matter of critical importance to the future of the company.

Abraham, on returning to his office, knew at once that something was afoot and made an educated guess as to what it might be. Shortly afterwards he received the urgent call to return home as David had been found unconscious on the conservatory floor. Later he'd questioned Adams at some length about Hawk's meeting with the old man. Adams, sporting a severely swollen hand, proved to have an excellent, if biased, recall of what had transpired, painting Hawk very much as the villain in the proceedings.

David's funeral and the shiva that followed it has given Abraham time to brief John Miles and Bramwell Cumming and to arrange for Sir Samuel Sopworth to be at the board meeting. Not only is Sir Samuel's firm the accountants for Solomon & Teekleman but he, as does Abraham, sits on several government committees and is, in addition, a member of the wartime Board of Industry. Sir Samuel has also arranged for a high government official to sit in on the meeting as an observer, hence the anonymous presence of Parkin from the Ministry of Trade and Customs.

Hawk says, 'I feel sure you will know why we are here, Sir Abraham. As of this moment Victoria Teekleman, her brother Ben and I hold a majority shareholding in our jointly owned company.'

'Ah, so you would like to resume as chairman, is that it?' Abraham interrupts. But before Hawk can reply he continues, 'Well, it may not be quite as easy as you think.' He nods at Bramwell Cumming, the barrister.

'Ah, yes, by no means an open-and-shut matter. In fact, rather more shut than open I'd say!' Cumming glances at John Miles.

'We are at war, the rules change, Mr Solomon, pertinences more powerful than ourselves are brought into play.' He looks to the end of the table at Sir Samuel.

It is apparent to Victoria and to Hawk that the scenario taking place in front of their eyes is well rehearsed, an act, each player knowing precisely his role. She is witnessing the rich and famous scratching each other's backs. Victoria glances at Hawk and she can see his amusement. 'With the greatest respect, Sir Abraham,' she says quickly, 'my grandfather has not completed what he intended to say.'

Sir Samuel Sopworth ignores her interjection, determined to deliver his lines. 'There is a great deal of government money tied up with this company, Mr Solomon. Contracts that are vital to the war effort and which cannot be placed in jeopardy by any sort of interruption, by a . . . er, palace revolution. The Prime Minister, Mr Fisher, and the Minister of Defence, Senator Pearce, have the greatest confidence in Sir Abraham, they have this very week declared Solomon & Teekleman a vital war industry and, I can assure you, they will not take kindly to any changes in management at the very top.'

'They will simply not allow it!' Bramwell Cumming affirms.

'Quite, quite!' John Miles adds. 'Not to be tolerated. War industry. Too important.'

Victoria thinks how Hawk was right about the pragmatism of politics. Andrew Fisher, the recently elected Labor Prime Minister, is already in bed with the capitalists.

Hawk puts up both hands. 'Gentlemen, gentlemen, a moment please, you have not heard us out. In the words of Mark Antony, "I come to bury Caesar, not to praise him." Except in my case there is no duplicity involved, no dastardly plot, no assassination.'

'What do you mean?' Abraham asks surprised. 'It's been all too clear what you intend to do. Good God, man, do you take me for a complete fool? But you won't get away with it, Hawk Solomon, you'll not be chairman just yet,' he repeats.

'Sir Abraham, I don't think any of you are listening to what my grandfather is saying. Perhaps you may allow him to explain our position fully before you all go off half-cocked once again,' Victoria says in a peremptory voice.

There is a stunned silence, the three men on the opposite side of the table as well as Sir Abraham cannot believe what they've just heard from the young woman seated next to the giant black man.

'Half-cocked! Did you say half-cocked?' Bramwell Cumming expostulates. He leans forward and glares at Victoria, intending to intimidate her. He is a large, heavily jowled, bulldoggish sort of a man with a florid whisky complexion, the school bully grown older but not any wiser for the years he's put behind him. 'Damned cheek, who do you think you are, young woman?'

Victoria meets his threatening stare with a calm, clear-eyed gaze. 'Yes, and now you're doing it again, Mr Cumming. It would be so very accommodating if you simply remained quiet for a few minutes while my grandfather completed explaining our position, as the chairman so kindly requested him to do quite some time ago,' she says in Mrs Wickworth-Spode English, whereupon she gives the fiercely glowering barrister a brilliant and disarming smile.

Hawk is filled with admiration for his granddaughter, for it is immediately clear that the opposition's attempts at intimidation have failed and, furthermore, there seems no rebuttal to Victoria's plea to hear him out. To ignore the request and to talk over it for a third time would not only make them look foolish but show the meeting to have been an utter contrivance.

'Would you mind, gentlemen? It won't take long?' Hawk says in a tone of mock humility, then looks at each man around the table as if seeking his permission to continue.

'What is it you have to say then, Hawk?' Abraham finally asks. The tactic they had agreed upon all along was to get Hawk and his granddaughter riled so that they could at once prove his incompetence as a chairman to Parkin. Abraham has forgotten Hawk's ability to stay calm even in David's unsettling presence and so he is reluctantly forced to admit that, as a tactic, it has failed them miserably. In fact, the man from the government observes that Hawk and Victoria remain the most calm of them all.

Hawk scratches the point of his chin and smiles. 'Well, our proposal as the major shareholders is that you remain as chairman, Sir Abraham.'

There is complete silence around the table and all eyes are on Abraham.

'I see, under what condition?' Abraham says at last.

'Well, none really. None anyway which I feel you will object to.'

'That remains to be seen,' Abraham says, clearly trying to recover his composure.

'Well, with your son Joshua away serving his country and Tom Pickles' desire to retire from the Potato Factory, we propose that I take over the Potato Factory. I will take Victoria with me as a trainee and Wilfred Harrington, I suggest, remains here in Melbourne at Solomon & Co. He is also due to retire in three years so that Joshua will return to take his position as was always intended.'

'And your granddaughter? What happens to her?'

'Ah, she takes over from me at the Potato Factory at the same time as Joshua and in the same capacity, as its managing director. The two of them to be the next generation in charge, with you the father figure, guiding them through the narrows, so to speak.'

Abraham immediately sees the sense in the proposal but also the catch. 'Then, when I retire, you, or your grandson and granddaughter, exercise your majority shares and Victoria here becomes chairman, is that it?' Abraham doesn't wait for Hawk to answer him, 'Well, I'm not at all sure that I am willing to agree to such a proposition.'

'Nor should you,' Hawk grins and turns to look at Victoria. 'My granddaughter here informs me she won't agree to it either.' Hawk takes a breath and continues, 'Abraham, my quarrel has never been with you. I have always known you to be a reasonable man and no fool and furthermore, your father has trained Joshua to run Solomon & Teekleman and, I feel sure, trained him well. You will have high expectations of the lad and he must be given every chance to fulfil them. But not without some stiff competition to brace his resolve. Prizes easily won are as easily lost, and I shall probably be dead when all this comes about anyway. We are asking *you* to make the decision when the time comes. You will appoint the new chairman, and you alone will decide between Victoria and Joshua, awarding the prize to the one who has most clearly demonstrated, in your opinion, the ability to lead the company into the future.'

Abraham looks at Hawk aghast. 'You would have me choose between my own son and your granddaughter? After all that has happened between our two families? After all we've done to you, Hawk Solomon?' He looks up to meet Hawk's eye. 'You would trust me to do that?'

'Aye, I must. If I don't, I cannot go to my grave knowing that I didn't do all I could to right the wrongs of the past.' Hawk sighs. 'I have no choice, I *must* trust you, there is no other way to make peace between us. No other way to finally put the past to rest. The rivalry between our two families has gone on for two generations – must we take it into a third?'

'Bravo!' Parkin calls quietly from the corner where he has been sitting.

Abraham leans forward with his elbow resting on the boardroom table and his hand clasped to his brow. 'My God,' he says absently, almost as if he is speaking to himself, 'this places an altogether different complexion on things.'

'No, not different, finally the right complexion,' Hawk whispers.

But Abraham knows that Joshua is not truly his son, emotionally he is David's boy and David Solomon did not bring up his grandson to accept a fair and even contest. He brought him up to be chairman and Abraham knows his son will accept nothing less. He looks up at Hawk and Victoria, 'I will do my best to make the right decision when the time comes.' Then, turning to face the men around the table and nodding to Parkin, he says, 'Thank you, gentlemen, the meeting is adjourned.'

BOOK TWO

Chapter Nine

BEN TEEKLEMAN

'The Click', Broadmeadows 1914

Ben's battalion has three more weeks at the Broadmeadows military camp before departing by ship for Albany, the small whaling town in Western Australia. This is where the convoy of ships destined to take the Australian and New Zealand forces to Egypt will congregate in King George Sound, a narrow isolated passage of water between the mainland and a ridge of island hills that forms a natural barrier of protection for the tranquil stretch of deep water from the rest of the Indian Ocean.

The last two weeks of Ben's stay in the Broadmeadows camp are comparatively easygoing, although the bugle still gets them up at dawn, followed by morning kit and tent inspection, physical jerks, squad and rifle drill, bayonet practice and, if a route march is not scheduled for the day, an afternoon lecture for sergeants on basic hygiene for the troops. In addition, once a week there is musketry practice on the rifle range, an exercise intended to get the platoon accustomed to the Short Magazine Lee-Enfield, known in the military vernacular as the S.M.L.E.

It is a simple daily routine, designed to be busy enough to keep an infantryman's mind on the job and only made difficult by the constant mud. It has been raining for most of September and the men complain that the mud at Broadmeadows makes everything they do seem twice as hard to accomplish, while kit and uniforms are impossible to keep clean. They are not to know that the mud of Ypres, Pozières, the Somme and a dozen other battlefields will one day make Broadmeadows seem like paradise on earth.

Ben has been seconded to the 5th Battalion, 2nd Australian Infantry Brigade and has been given a temporary platoon consisting mostly of city types recruited in Melbourne. Though initially bitterly disappointed that he couldn't return to Tasmania, Ben makes the best of the situation, the consolation being that he will see a little more of Hawk and Victoria before departing overseas. He has a platoon of young blokes who are keen as mustard, but have limited knowledge and, for the most part, no previous experience with a rifle. He has come to realise that all the other standard military procedures can be taught on a parade ground, but learning how to use a rifle is not something a lad from the city can pick up after firing a few rounds at a stationary target on the rifle range.

Ben has never regarded himself as a typical soldier and while he accepts the need for discipline involved in the mindless pursuit of parade-ground drill and obedience without question, he doesn't necessarily believe that it is the best way to stay alive. Taking the initiative and the ability to improvise have always been a part of his character. He also knows he isn't going to change the army mindset and so he concentrates on teaching his platoon useful skills, most of which revolve around three aspects of life in a trench, food, personal hygiene and knowing how to kill, preferably at a reasonably long range with a rifle.

There is nothing much Ben can do about army rations, though he does take several days' worth of standard rations home to Mrs Billings and asks her to experiment with them to see if she can improve the taste.

Martha is, of course, totally scornful of the ingredients she has to work with. She examines the tin of bullybeef, turning it around in her hands. 'Fray Bentos,' she says reading the label, 'sounds foreign to me, foreign muck is it?' Ben shows her how to turn the key to open the can. 'Never seen such an assortment of rubbish in one tin,' she sniffs. 'Wouldn't give it to me cat.' As Sardine, her cat, eats a lot better than any trooper, Ben thinks this is not too much of an indictment. 'Fat and gristle and not much else, if you ask me! Can't do nothing with this,' Martha whinges.

However, she works hard at making culinary improvements

and the results are not too bad, but unfortunately involve several ingredients such as onions, Worcester sauce, tomatoes and a number of other tasty additions that are unlikely to crop up in a front-line trench. But she does create what she refers to as a hurry-curry, which seems halfway practical, as a tin of curry powder is small and long-lasting if used judiciously and not entirely a burden when carried in the infantryman's ninety-pound kit. Furthermore, if a handful of raisins are added to the pot, they plump up a treat and the dish is even further enhanced. Ben purchases two small tins of curry powder for each of the thirty-five men in his platoon. There is a great deal of gratuitous comment about these new field rations and very little of it is complimentary. Curry is a new experience for the city lads and few, if any, of them can cook anything more than the ubiquitous soldier's stew – a rind of bacon boiled in a billy of water. But in the months ahead they will become miserly with the dispersal of their precious tins of curry powder.

However, with the army biscuit and the standard ration of tinned jam Martha Billings creates what will become a culinary triumph in the trenches. To grind down an army biscuit is in itself a major task, because they are so hard. There is a popular myth that, carried in the pocket over the heart, the army biscuit is certain protection against the German Mauser as it is guaranteed to be bulletproof. Most soldiers believe that at the outbreak of war Arnott's, the great Australian biscuit-maker, released a huge warehouse of army biscuits that they'd stored since the end of the Boer War. But the biscuits had grown so hard that they'd defeated even the weevil and couldn't be smashed with the butt end of a Lee-Enfield and so were patently beyond the capacity of the human tooth.

Martha grates the biscuit first then mixes the crumbs with a pinch of salt, a little sugar, baking powder and water until it can be moulded into six small tart-shaped cups. She fills three of these with apricot jam and covers them with the unfilled cups, pressing down gently so that the end result is a flattened disc about an inch high. These are then placed in a billycan with a couple of tablespoons of water in the bottom and the lid pushed firmly in place before being set on the embers of an open fire and baked for twenty minutes.

Victoria pronounces the result inedible but Martha's 'billyjam tarts' eventually become a great favourite in the trenches of Gallipoli and France. They are a major source of comfort to many a young soldier who, standing knee-deep in mud and surrounded by death, with artillery fire whistling overhead, closes his eyes, munches slowly into the hot jam tart, and with a little imagination is transported back to family excursions to the beach and his mum's Sunday baking.

But it is on the rifle, the Short Magazine Lee-Enfield, that Ben now concentrates. By military standards Ben Teekleman is a misfit when it comes to the popular concept of a platoon sergeant. He is relaxed and reassuring, without the need for hyperbole or the traditional overused vernacular of the soldier with three dog's legs on his shirt sleeve. His easy manner makes his men keen to improve under his direction.

At the rifle range while the other sergeants are yelling, threatening, insulting and cussing the greenhorns in their platoons, Ben spends time with each of his men explaining the basics. He watches them carefully as they fire off a round, correcting their action, 'Give the trigger a gentle squeeze, lad, like squeezing a tit, no, no, don't shut your eyes when you fire!' He shows them how to adjust their sights, how to correct an error or bias in the rifle itself, demonstrating the right way to position themselves to maintain firing for long periods without becoming cramped or shooting erratically. Ben strives to give them confidence in themselves, accepting the mistakes they make as beginners and never humiliating them in front of their comrades in arms.

After the second musketry session Ben makes his platoon sit down in a quiet spot under the shade of a large angophora near the firing range and talks with them. 'Nobody gets to be a good shot in a hurry, lads, I ain't yet come across a bloke who was a natural. To use a rifle properly takes patience and some learning,' he grins, 'even a little love and imagination.' He picks up a rifle belonging to one of the infantrymen and almost immediately the Lee-Enfield takes on a different look in his confident hands, it is as if the rifle and the man have a natural affinity with each other.

'Now this thing is a pretty clumsy weapon,' Ben begins, 'it's a rod of steel and a chunk of wood and it ain't friendly neither, it kicks you if you don't hold it tight enough and jams up on you if you don't oil and care for it properly, just like a flamin' sheila.' The platoon laughs and Ben waits until he has its attention again. 'It's heavy and it's a pain in the arse to carry around. Add a bayonet to it and it becomes a top-heavy spear that can't be thrown and isn't that easy to stick into someone's gut.' He brings the rifle to a horizontal position at about waist height, cupping it halfway along the stock with his left hand and working the bolt action smoothly with his right. Although he is left-handed, he works the action with consummate ease. 'But despite all these obvious character deficiencies, you've got to make this clumsy fellow your best friend.' He pauses, then adds, 'And because your rifle is such a cranky sonofabitch, making friends isn't gunna happen overnight. But like all true friendships, with a little practice and a bit of respect, you'll soon enough be the best of mates.' He looks around at the platoon. 'Any questions?'

'Yes, Sergeant!' An infantryman named Cooligan stands up. He is the smallest man in the platoon and at five feet and six inches only just tall enough to make the first intake. He wears a brush of snowy hair above a cheeky face sprinkled with a million freckles and is already known in the platoon as Numbers Cooligan or, simply, Numbers.

'What is it, Private Cooligan?'

'Sergeant, we are to do range practice once a week while we're here, that's six weeks where we fire off two magazines if we're bloody lucky, that's a hundred and twenty rounds.' He clears his throat and looks about him. 'And the best I've done so far is an outer and I think that must have been by mistake, I must a jerked or somethin'. You see, I've never had a rifle in me 'ands before this. 'Cept for Crow and Hornbill, we're all city blokes, so I'll vouch it's the same with most of us.' He turns to the remainder of the platoon. 'What do you reckon, lads?' There is a murmur of acquiescence and several nods of the head from the other young infantrymen.

'Yeah, well it ain't that difficult to tell,' Ben says smiling. 'Can't expect to hit the bullseye right off. One on the outer rim after your second practice on the range, that's not too bad, Private Cooligan. So what's your question?'

'Well, are a hundred and twenty rounds enough practice to kill a German at three 'undred yards?'

'Well, in terms of not firing a shot in anger, that's about all the firing practice you're gunna get. All I can say is I hope it's enough when the Hun aims *his* Mauser at you.'

'Yes, Sergeant, but what if I miss him?'

'Then you better pray he's had no more practice than you, Cooligan.' Ben pauses, thinking. 'While I admit there's nothing quite like using live ammo, firing a rifle isn't the only way to get to know your weapon.' He looks at the faces around him. 'Remember, it's not the bullet that does the killing, it's you. It's you or the Hun and the difference between the two of you is simply practice with a rifle or a bayonet. Practise holding your rifle, practise carrying it, practise firing it with an empty magazine in all sorts of positions, practise squeezing the trigger ten thousand times until you can do it in your sleep. Practise ejecting a spent cartridge, reloading and firing until you can do it in three or four seconds without taking your eye off the enemy position. Practise hitting the enemy in your imagination.' Ben sees the grins on their faces at the idea of this. 'No, really, I mean it, see the Hun in your mind's eye, see the bastard cop your bullet, see him jerk back suddenly, see him clutching at his gut, see him topple, hear him scream out his mama's name as he sinks to his knees and coughs blood. Do it all in your imagination a thousand times. Get so that's what you see without thinking when you fire a shot in anger. Half the skill of firing a rifle effectively is about total confidence in yourself and your rifle. It's about not having to think about what you're doing.' Ben lifts the rifle he's holding up to his chest. 'You can look at this weapon in two ways, as an extension of yourself, a very dangerous twenty-nine inches or so added to the ends of your arms, or you can regard it as something the army gives you to make your life difficult. You can do what you are required to do at rifle drill and no more, or you can work with it after hours, every spare moment you've got.'

'But, Sergeant, I reckon a man would look a proper galah falling about with an empty rifle, going click, click, click, "bang you're dead", when he wasn't doing rifle drill on parade, like when it's not official, know what I mean?' one of the infantrymen volunteers.

'Unloaded rifle, Private Hamill, a jam tin is empty or full, a rifle is loaded or not loaded, or, if you wish, safe,' Ben chides him without raising his voice. 'Sure, it takes a bit of character to play around with an unloaded rifle. I would have thought that keeping yourself alive would be a top priority and that's what this is all about.' He grins. Ben has the kind of easy smile that gives men confidence. At twenty-six he is only about four years older than most of them but they accept his authority as one might an older and more experienced brother. 'There are only two things that can keep you alive in a battle, luck and good practice. I hope you all have a lot of the former, but before I leave you, I'm gunna make damned sure you've had plenty of the second. Then if you haven't the guts to make a bloody fool of yourself in front of your mates, well, I guess I'll be there to bury you as well.'

There is laughter in the platoon and a sense of increasing confidence. Ben hasn't threatened his men with mindless practice and punishment for errors, so that they get to hate their Lee-Enfields, instead he has made them see how necessary the S.M.L.E. is to their survival.

Ben now points to a lanky private who seems to have more bony angles to his body than ought to belong on a normal human being. 'Right, now we all know Private Rigby here is a damned good shot, better than any of you blokes, certainly better than I am.'

The platoon turns to look at Crow Rigby, a country boy from Gippsland who carries the all too familiar badge of recognition of a volunteer from the bush, a permanent squint from staring into the sun. The young private, not yet twenty, blushes furiously and the fresh crop of acne covering his neck and jawline brightens visibly, his elbows rest on his bony knees and he looks down between his legs. It is obvious that he is not accustomed to praise or even to being noticed in a crowd.

'Good on ya, Crow,' someone says.

Crow Rigby has earned his nickname because of an incident on the very first occasion the platoon is taken onto the firing range. All of them are sprawled on their bellies in the standard firing position, legs apart, feeling awkward and anxious, the butt of their Lee-Enfields unfamiliar, tightly tucked into their shoulders to prevent the legendary kick few of them have yet experienced. Each man has his own target which is about to come up in the target butts three hundred yards away. Their instruction is to fire at a rate of fifteen rounds a minute. There is a great deal of nervous anticipation, every man hoping to give a good account of himself while not quite knowing what to expect. Each has his finger lightly on the trigger waiting for the musketry sergeant to give the command to fire. Moments before it comes, a crow cawing and flapping its wings suddenly alights on the top of a flagpole a good twenty yards beyond the end of the firing range. The bird is still wobbling slightly on its new-found perch when a lone rifle shot rings out and the crow explodes in a cloud of black feathers. At three hundred and twenty yards it is a truly exceptional shot.

Placed on a disciplinary charge and marched in front of his company commander, Rigby is asked if he has anything to say in his own defence. 'Er yes, sir, it come on me like automatic, it's the lambing season back 'ome, crows'll peck the eyes out a newborn lamb, can't 'ave one o' them buggers hangin' 'round the paddock, can you, sir?'

Rigby was given only six days' picket duty and then selected to do a special training course as a company sniper. This is his first day back with his platoon.

'Private Rigby, how many times do you think you've fired a rifle, not a S.M.L.E., a rifle of any sort?' Ben asks him.

Rigby is too shy to look up and keeps his eyes on his boots as he thinks, then answers carefully. 'Crikey, Sergeant, I dunno, I been doin' it since I were knee 'igh to a grasshopper.' He squints up at Ben briefly, 'Thousands and thousands o' times, I s'pose, I reckon 'bout six shots a day, though maybe that includes a shotgun, I been doin' it since I were five year old. Awful lot a crows, snakes, and rabbits 'anging about on the selection, Sergeant.'

At the mention of crows the platoon breaks up.

'Thirty-two thousand, eight hundred and fifty times he's fired a rifle against our possible hundred and twenty,' Cooligan shouts out, sending the platoon into fresh gales of laughter.

'Thank you, Private Cooligan, that's very encouraging. Right, now let's be serious for a moment.' Ben, crooking his forefinger, beckons to Cooligan. 'Come here, lad.' The young private gets to his feet from the back and steps between several of the men, zig-zagging his way forward, placing his hand on their shoulders to get to Ben. 'Righto, take your cap off, Private Cooligan.' Numbers Cooligan removes his cap, placing it on the ground. Ben takes a clean handkerchief from his pocket, twirls it into a strip about two inches wide and blindfolds the infantryman.

'Oi, what's 'appening?' Cooligan cries.

'Right, Private Rigby, c'mere!' Ben says not answering.

Crow Rigby unfolds his legs and, rising, walks over to Ben. 'Take Private Cooligan over to the tree, stand his back and head against the trunk.'

'Righto, Sergeant, will I tie his hands?'

There is laughter. 'No, he's going to need them to cover his goolies,' Ben says calmly. 'Now, Cooligan, don't move a muscle, that's an order, ya hear?'

'What you gunna do, Sergeant, shoot me?' Cooligan asks tentatively.

'No, lad, you'll be as safe as if you were in your mother's arms.'

'Do I have to, Sergeant?' the young infantryman pleads, instinctively knowing that somehow his courage is to be tested. 'I promise I'll shut me trap next time!'

The platoon all laughs uproariously. 'Yes, I'm afraid you must, Private Cooligan, it's an order.'

Crow Rigby takes him by the hand and leads him the twenty or so feet to the trunk of the large old gum tree and positions him as Ben has directed.

'Now hold your hands over your privates, lad. Don't want you catching cold, do we?' Ben's voice is perfectly calm. 'Don't move until I tell you. You understand, don't even twitch yer nose?'

'Yes, Sergeant, but I ain't happy, Sergeant.'

'Not supposed to be, you're in the army now.'

Ben stoops over his kitbag as he speaks and from it he removes Tommo's fighting axe. Before anyone can quite realise what's happening, he has straightened up and the axe has left his hand in a whirring blur. It lands with a soft thud, its blade buried in the trunk of the tree no more than half an inch to the side of Cooligan's head and directly above his left ear.

'Shit, what was that!' Cooligan howls as the remainder of the platoon gasps in collective astonishment. To his credit he has not moved.

'Right, Rigby, remove his blindfold,' Ben instructs.

The lanky country lad plucks at the blindfold, his country calm gone, his hands trembling from the shock of what he's just witnessed. Cooligan opens his eyes. The axe handle is sticking out beyond the left side of his nose, but he cannot see the axe clearly as it is so deeply embedded that only the head and a small section of the blade are exposed.

'Jesus!' Cooligan yells. His knees give way under him and he collapses to the ground.

There is complete silence from the rest of the young infantrymen, then someone says softly, 'Jesus and Mary!'

'Right, Cooligan, well done, lad, stand up,' Ben commands.

'Can't, Sergeant,' Cooligan whimpers, the after-shock of the experience bringing him close to tears.

'Come, come, it wasn't that bad, what you can't see can't hurt you, stand up, lad,' Ben says soothingly.

'Sorry, Sergeant, I mayn't, I've pissed me trousers,' Cooligan says in a distressed voice.

Cooligan's confession that he's wet his pants breaks the tension and the platoon roars with laughter, though as much from relief as mirth.

'Shut up! That's enough!' Ben barks suddenly, bringing the platoon to instant silence. Then turning to Cooligan he says, 'Don't blame you, lad, a lot of blokes would have shit themselves.' He rummages around in his kitbag and pulls out a spare pair of khaki trousers. 'Here, take these, lad, get to the latrines, clean up, then back here on the double.' Ben's sharp, emphatic orders help to jerk Cooligan back into action. 'Eyes left, all of you!' He hands Cooligan the spare trousers. 'Up you get, nobody's looking.' Ben turns back to the platoon. 'So what do we do about that, gentlemen? We give our comrade in arms three cheers for being a bloody good sport, eh?'

To the cheers of the platoon the miserable Cooligan, covering the wet patch to his front with the help of Ben's spare trousers, legs it for the latrine block.

'Private Rigby, fetch the axe,' Ben now commands. The country lad retrieves the axe, though not without some difficulty. Ben goes to stand where previously Numbers Cooligan stood blindfolded. 'Righto, Rigby, you've got a good eye, now do the same to me,' Ben says evenly.

Private Rigby hops from one leg to the other, his head buried into his right shoulder and appearing to be all bones and acute angles. 'I can't, Sergeant,' he says at last.

'Why not, lad?'

'I might miss, Sergeant,' he says, grinning.

The platoon, a moment before brought to a nervous silence, now cracks up again.

Ben steps from the tree and, going over to his kit, he removes a small cork dartboard of the type a child might get as an inexpensive extra in a Christmas stocking. It is about half as big again as a human head. He walks back to the tree and fixes the board to the trunk at roughly the same position occupied by Cooligan's head.

'You first, Rigby, and then the rest of you. Take the axe and throw it at the target, see how you go, eh? Ben has now reached the position where he previously stood to throw. 'Imagine it's your only weapon and that there dartboard is an enemy head. Fritz is coming at you in a bayonet charge and he is no more than a few feet away, ten, fifteen feet, you've got maybe two or three seconds. Righto, Rigby, go for your life.'

The young blokes are clearly taken with the game and, with some jostling to get to the front of the queue, quickly form a line behind Crow Rigby, who now takes careful aim, not bothering about the imaginary bayonet-wielding German advancing. Taking a great deal more time than the three-second maximum, he sends the axe flying and they watch it tumble head over handle through the air. To his credit the blade actually fixes into the tree trunk, though almost three feet above the dartboard and somewhat to the side.

'Better hope he was a very fat German sitting on a horse, Private Rigby,' Ben says.

'German general, Sarge, big 'orse, seventeen hands,' Crow Rigby says.

'Well done, anyway. Who's next?'

Rigby and one other young infantryman are the only ones who manage to get the blade of the axe into the tree, while the others either miss the trunk or the head of the axe bounces off the trunk and falls to the ground. They have almost completed the exercise when Cooligan arrives back wearing Ben's trousers. He has rinsed his own under a faucet and now carries them bunched up in his right hand. He sees instantly what's afoot and can't wait for his turn to come. With the rest of the platoon watching, he weights the axe in both hands, then gripping it firmly he takes careful aim, pulls it well back beyond his right shoulder and lets it go with a furious swinging action. Tommo's fighting axe twirls several times in the air and comes to land about twelve feet up at the conjunction of the trunk and the first of its branches, but at least it bites in, the blade sinking solidly into the rough bark. The platoon claps and whistles.

'Real big German on a ladder bird-nestin', Sarge!' Crow Rigby drawls slowly.

Ben thinks what a great temperament young Rigby has for a

sniper. 'Righto, gather around, gentlemen,' he now says and waits until the platoon is once again seated on the grass in front of him. 'Thank you, Mr Cooligan, you're excused tent inspection in the morning and may kip in an extra half hour.'

'Lucky bugger!' several of them shout.

'Thank you, Sergeant, that's thirty minutes, precise, I take it?'

'Aye, thirty-one and you're on a charge. Now, what have we learned from that little exercise?' Ben asks.

'That it's easy to get yerself kill'd with an axe, Sergeant?' calls a private by the name of William Horne, the second of the country lads in the platoon, who is predictably enough known as Hornbill. He is a big, strong lad, six foot two inches with a pair of shoulders that would make him a good ruckman. He is also a reasonable shot, though not anywhere near the class of Crow Rigby. His chief distinction is that, using a pair of pliers and a length of baling wire or a hammer and nails, he is able to fix just about anything that gets broken in a mechanical or carpentry sense.

A small sample of Hornbill's ingenuity occurred when Ben introduced Martha's culinary ideas to his platoon while they were away on a four-day route march. The bullybeef hurry-curry was initially only a limited success as they had not yet been deprived for long enough of the memory of half-decent food to fully appreciate it. But the exception proved to be the billyjam tarts, although they almost came to a premature halt when someone pointed out that they had no way of rendering army biscuits to fine enough crumbs for the required doughlike mixture. That is, until Hornbill was consulted.

'No rucking problem,' he declares and promptly produces a six-inch nail from his kit. 'Always carry one o' these, best bloody tool there is after the one nature give you.' Then, using the steel end of the haft on his bayonet, he hammers an empty jam tin flat. With the six-inch nail he soon pierces the flattened tin with dozens of holes, hammering the nail point through the tin plate and forcing a perfectly burred hole on the opposite side surface which proves to be no different in function to a normal household grater. Hornbill then takes out his wire-cutter which is standard issue and snips a small length of fencing wire from some farmer's paddock and cunningly fashions it into a handle for the grater. 'There you go, good as gold,' he pronounces to one and all.

Private Horne's Gallipoli grater will eventually become a stock item in every trench along the Gallipoli Front, although the Turks, finding them abandoned in deserted trenches, can never quite work out what the hell it is the Diggers needed to grate. They conclude that they can't be bug rakes as the handles are not sufficiently long for them to be back scratchers for the lice they generously share with the enemy.

In civilian life Hornbill is a timber cutter and hails from Coffs Harbour up in northern New South Wales. It seems he was on a visit to Melbourne to help out his uncle when war broke out. His uncle owns a pie cart which he positions nightly outside Flinders Street Station. Or, put into Horne's own slow drawl, 'The old bloke's rheumatiz was worryin' him a treat and me Aunty Mavis took crook so she couldn't push the pie cart from their 'ome in Fitzroy of a night. So I come down to the big smoke ter give 'em a hand 'til she got better again, then the ruckin' war come and I joined up with you miserable lot.'

'Yes, Private Horne, the fighting axe can be a lethal weapon in the right hands,' Ben smiles, 'but I don't suppose there'll be too many of them on either side in this war.'

'Reckon I'd 'ave one o' them 'stead of a bayonet any time,' Horne drawls. 'Not much you can do with a bayonet, it don't even chop timber good.'

Bcn ignores this last remark as it will necessitate a lecture on the uses and abuses of the infantry bayonet. He runs his eyes across the sitting infantrymen. 'Anything else we may have learned?'

'Practice, Sergeant? Everything takes practice.' The answer comes from a serious-looking lad named Spencer, with the stocky build, dark hair and obsidian eyes of his Welsh ancestors. He has a naturally scholarly look about him, enhanced by the fact that he is constantly found wearing a pair of reading spectacles and with his nose in a book. He passed the required army eyesight test simply by memorising the complete eye chart and is known in the platoon as 'Library', as he always seems to know the answer to every question they are collectively asked.

'Right, Private Spencer.' Ben would have preferred someone else to have come back with the answer. He is concerned that rather than think for themselves, too many have come to rely on young Spencer to answer for them. He picks up the axe and absently strokes the slightly curved blade with the ball of his thumb. It is severely blunted from its recent mishandling by the platoon and he thinks how it will take him most of the evening to hone it back to its former razor-sharp cutting edge. 'This is a fighting axe,' Ben pronounces, holding it above his head. 'It was used in the Maori wars around 1860 against the British by my grandfather's platoon, the Tommo Te Mokiri.'

'Your grandfather was a Maori, Sergeant?' Numbers Cooligan exclaims in a surprised voice.

'No, my grandmother was. My grandfather was a first-generation Tasmanian, a timbergetter like Private Horne here, but from the Southwest Wilderness. He perfected the use of the fighting axe for the Maori and made it a very effective weapon.'

'He fought against the British, Sergeant?' Spencer asks quietly.

'Yes, Spencer, the British aren't *always* on the side of God. But that's enough o' that,' Ben says, impatient to continue. 'The point I'm trying to make is that Private Rigby here is a great shot because he's practised most of his life. I guess I can do what I did to Private Cooligan for the same reason. I too have practised throwing a fighting axe for most of my life. Throwing it sixty, perhaps more, times a day since I was seven years old.'

'How old are you, Sergeant?' Cooligan now asks.

'Twenty-six, Cooligan, and prematurely aged by having you in my platoon asking unnecessary questions.'

Cooligan hardly hesitates. 'Sixty times a day, shit that's four hundred and sixteen thousand and one hundred times you've thrown that axe, Sergeant.'

'Thank you, Cooligan, I thought by now you would have learned not to be a smart arse!' Ben pauses and looks about him. 'So that's my point.' He indicates the gum tree with a jerk of his head, 'I apologise for showing off back there, but it's my job to try to keep you alive against the odds. If you can use a rifle better than the enemy it may just one day save your life.' Ben pauses again and spreads his hands. 'So don't despair, you ain't gunna be a marksman right off. Private Rigby here is just as much an amateur with the fighting axe as you are with the Lee-Enfield.' Ben shrugs. 'So there you go, practise, practise, practise. There's few that's born to do anything instinctively except to suck on our mamas' tits.'

This brings a few titters from the seated platoon, but Ben isn't through talking yet. 'Remember, you don't have to be able to hit the badge on a German soldier's cap at a hundred yards to kill him. A metal jacket will make a fair bit of mess wherever you hit him. Remember, you've got a target as big as yourself and the enemy has the same, so always conceal as much of your body as possible. If you've practised holding a rifle, firing it, spending time with your S.M.L.E., then, when you're firing at the enemy, the accuracy will come to you soon enough. Statistics gathered in the Crimean War and again in the Boer War show that only one in one hundred rounds fired will cause any sort of damage, that is, find its mark. You can improve on that statistic. The platoon that uses its concerted and practised firepower effectively and aims accurately is the one most likely to stay alive. The enemy is least likely to directly attack a section of the trenches where the firepower is accurate and sustained. Now, do you understand me, you blokes? Get to know your rifle and you may just come out of this war alive.'

Over the subsequent weeks Ben's platoon is constantly jeered at, the other platoons in the battalion and the company chiacking them mercilessly. They become known as 'Trigger Clickers' because of the manner in which they constantly practise with an unloaded rifle. There is even a chant some wag has dreamed up.

Tiddly-winks young man

Get a woman if you can

If you can't get a woman

Get a Trigger Clickin' man!

However, on the final occasion Ben's platoon appears on the firing range, they achieve the highest aggregate ever scored at Broadmeadows. Moreover, Numbers Cooligan has taken the opportunity to run a book at the camp, betting that the Trigger Clickers, now abbreviated among themselves to 'The Click', who have come to take pride in their nickname, will beat any other platoon in the camp at final range practice. He offers the attractive odds of three to one and he isn't short of punters willing to have a bet as some platoons consist of mainly country lads who know their way around a rifle. After the big win he shares his takings with the others, making every man in the platoon two pounds richer, eight days' pay after deductions.

'So what if you'd lost, Private Cooligan?' Ben enquires while graciously accepting the two pounds Cooligan proffers after the shoot-out.

'No way, Sergeant, I give the scorer at the shooting range two quid to gimme the total score of every platoon in the battalion for all six times we've been to the range. By the time we got to the last practice we was an average of thirty points ahead o' the second best, that's a fair margin to play with.' He pauses and taps one forefinger against the other, explaining, 'Now, with Crow Rigby shooting a possible one hundred or near as dammit every time we go out,' he taps his forefinger a second time, 'and taking into consideration that one or two of us is gunna go off the boil, so deduct say, twenty points, we'd still 'ave won hands down. It's averages, Sergeant, numbers don't lie.' He pauses. 'A champion 'orse don't win every race he runs, but if you know the form of all the 'orses in the race and put him in accordingly, lemme tell ya, he ain't gunna get beat too bloody often.'

'What did you do in civilian life, Cooligan? I seem to recall you were a strapper, that right?'

'Nah, I only said that because I 'oped to get into the Light Horse, Sarge, fancied them emu feathers in me hat.' He continues, 'But they found out soon enough I couldn't ride, never been on an 'orse in me life. Bookmaker's clerk, Sergeant, me uncle's an on-course bookmaker at Flemmo. I pencil for him. Cooligan's the name, numbers is the game!'

Ben waves the two pound notes Numbers Cooligan has given him. 'Well, thanks for including me in, Private Cooligan.'

Cooligan's hair, like all the others', has been cut short back 'n sides but he's managed to persuade the camp barber to keep the front a bit longer so that it looks like he is wearing the hairy part of a snow-white shaving brush above his brow. He constantly smooths it with his palm as he talks, 'Well, matter a fact, Sergeant, The Click was, well we was 'oping, you know, that you could sort a spend it with us? Two quid each in our pocket will go a long way to drown a man's sorrows durin' a night on the town before we embark on the slippery dip. Lads reckon that'd be real good, you know, a final beer or twenty before we all leave 'ome?'

'You're on. Name the time and the place, I'll be there.'

'Hornbill, er . . . Private Horne, says his uncle will lay on the pies at cost price and throw in the sauce bottle, so we thought we'd meet at Young & Jackson's, the pub with the bollocky sheila painting above the bar. Know it, Sergeant?'

'She's called Chloe, yeah, I know it, what time?'

'Tuesday, seven o'clock, er . . . nineteen 'undred hours, Sergeant,' Numbers Cooligan says, clearly chuffed that Ben has accepted their invitation.

It is October 16th, just five days before the battalion will depart on the *Orvieto*, part of the fleet assembled to transport the troops across the Great Australian Bight to Albany and then eventually across the Indian Ocean via the Suez Canal to Britain.

Ben spends as much time as he can with Victoria and Hawk, both of whom are becoming increasingly aware that the war in Europe is not going to be over by Christmas, as all the newspapers confidently predicted when war was declared.

The war of movement had started with the retreat from Mons, where in the first weeks the German successes caused consternation throughout Britain and the Empire. The Germans swept everything before them to come within fifty miles of Paris before they were finally halted by the French and British Expeditionary Forces at the battle of the Marne. But it was achieved at a terrible cost to the Allies, two hundred thousand killed, wounded or missing in September alone, eight thousand dead at the battle of Le Cateau, by no means the biggest battle fought, yet more had died here than Wellington had lost at Waterloo. The battle of Ypres, still going on, promises ten times as many. Slowly it is beginning to sink into the consciousness of thinking Australians that this is no grand excursion in Europe to which the flower of our young blood is being invited but a bloody slaughter such as the world has never witnessed before. They wonder how Britain has managed to involve herself in such an ungodly mess.

With the Turks closing the Dardanelles and thus denying Russia access to the Mediterranean via the Black Sea, it now looks increasingly likely that they will declare themselves on the German side. Most Australians give little thought to what might be. The glory of a young nation proving itself in battle is still the ideal most hold dear to their hearts. As far as the hoi polloi are concerned, all the Allied casualties prove is that we'd better get the 1st Division over there in a hurry so that our lads can have a go and show the Germans what good colonial stock can do in this made-to-order stoush.

The morning of October 21st brings a cloudless dawn which will later be followed by bright sunshine. Victoria rises early and, putting on her dressing gown and slippers, pads through the silent house towards the kitchen to make herself a pot of tea. Passing Hawk's study on the way, she sees his light is still on. She taps on the door which is slightly ajar and pushing it open a little further sees Hawk at his desk writing.

'Grandfather, you're up early?'

'Hmmph, what is the time, my dear?' Hawk asks absently, not looking up or pausing from his writing.

'It is just after five, not yet completely light.' Victoria then realises that the curtains are drawn and Hawk is still dressed as he was the previous evening. She knows her grandfather to be a meticulous man who bathes and changes into a fresh suit and linen every morning. He'd once explained to her that most folk think of black people as being naturally dirty, 'It comes with the chocolate colour, my dear.' From some deep sense of inferiority which he has long since overcome in other things, he has accustomed himself to change his suit and linen every day and, sometimes, if the day has been hot, twice a day. 'You haven't been to bed, have you, Grandfather?' she chides.

'Couldn't sleep,' Hawk says brusquely, putting his pen away and turning stiffly to smile at her, rubbing the back of his neck with a huge hand. She sees his weary face and realises that he is now an old man, it is only his enormous size that still gives him the impression of strength. She has also noticed that the joints of his fingers have become swollen and nobbled with arthritis and that he has taken to holding his pen awkwardly, though, typically, he has not said anything about the pain he must be experiencing.

'Oh, what's going to happen? Will Ben be all right?' she asks in a tremulous voice.

'I hope so, my dear, though it's looking less and less like the grand picnic in Europe the recruitment posters so ardently promised our lads, the great adventure.'

'Grandfather, can't we do what Abraham's done for Joshua Solomon and find a nice safe position for Ben so he doesn't have to fight? Surely you have the influence, if Sir Abraham can, then you can too!' Victoria cries in sudden despair.

Hawk raises his eyebrows in surprise. 'My dear, we don't know for sure that's the case with Joshua, all we know is that he's one of the few selected to go to England for further training, a singular honour I believe.'

'Yes, to be on the staff of one of the fat old generals! What is it? Liaison officer? It's not fair. Why should he get away with it?'

'Well, someone has to do it. Joshua has been to Oxford, he knows the English and their ways extremely well. Why, he's almost become one of them and he's a clever young man to boot. I'd say he was an admirable choice as a liaison officer, wouldn't you?'

'Grandfather, you know what I mean, it was fixed!' Victoria reproaches him. 'It's not like that at all!'

'Well, we can't prove that and nor should we try to. As for Ben, how do you think your brother would feel if we even attempted to remove him from the coming fray?'

Victoria sniffs defensively. 'He needn't know,' she shrugs, tearfully.

'Don't be foolish, Ben would most certainly know. He's not a lad to be easily fooled. Besides, you of all people with your egalitarian Labor views, how could you suggest such a thing? Even if we could, it would be grossly unfair to use our influence in such a manipulative manner.'

Victoria begins to sob. 'I'm sorry! I'm *so* sorry, but I *can't* help it, I don't want Ben to die!' she howls, and rushes towards the seated Hawk, curling up on her grandfather's lap and, like the little girl he used to comfort when she was upset, she weeps against his chest.

'There, there, my dear, we simply have to hope for the best. Ben's a sensible lad and knows how to keep his nose clean. He won't go looking for trouble.'

'Oh, Grandfather Hawk, I have such a terrible feeling,' Victoria sobs. 'Ben never lets anyone do what he can do himself! He'll want to fight the Germans all on his own,' she whimpers.

Letting her weep for a while, Hawk finally reaches into his pocket and hands her his handkerchief. Victoria dries her eyes and then blows her nose. Rising from his lap she stands before him, her eyes red-rimmed and now level with his own. Hawk, with a sense of shock, sees the same sudden blazing defiance in them he has only before seen in Mary Abacus. It is a defiance that brooks no possible compromise.

'Grandfather, so help me God, if Ben dies and Joshua comes home unscathed from some cushy job behind the lines,' Victoria pauses, and in a voice and accent that is more evocative of Mary than her own, declares, 'may Gawd 'elp him!'

Chapter Ten

THE DEPARTURE

Albany, Western Australia 1914

Never before have the Melbourne docks seen a day like October 21st 1914. For the past three days eleven troopships carrying nearly eight thousand men and three thousand horses have departed for Albany, with the Orient liner *Orvieto*, the fastest and the largest ship, departing last. Dock workers are bleary-eyed, having worked double shifts during the several embarkations. Exhausted tugboat captains are hoarse from trying over four days to make some sense of a convoy of ships where each vessel is preoccupied with a hundred tasks at once and seems to have neither the time nor the nous to complete any one of them correctly. It is madness and mayhem and anyone who pretends to know what they are doing is indulging a fevered imagination.

Yet somehow the troops say their last farewells to weeping mothers, sisters and tearful girlfriends. Sons, brothers and sweethearts are embraced one last time and urged to look upon the evening star with the knowledge that their loved one will be on the front porch every night they remain apart, gazing at the same heaven's light and praying for their safe return. Gravel-voiced fathers suck in their stomachs and comport themselves in what they imagine is a military posture, gravely shaking the hands of their sons, exhorting them not to let the family name down. 'Go to it, son, show the Hun what we Aussies are all about, there's a good lad, your mother and me are real proud of you.'

'We've drawn the short straw, lads,' Ben tells his platoon after returning from the sergeants' briefing on the departure. 'We're on the *Orvieto* and so is the top brass, General Bridges and the entire collection of red tabs.' He continues, 'If we should go to the bottom, Australia's part in this war is over. You'll have to watch your dress, mind. It'll be spit and polish all the way and your saluting arm won't get a lot of rest neither.'

'She's an Orient-line ship, Sergeant, there'll be cabins and all, even a ship's library,' Library Spencer pipes up.

'Sure, Private Spencer, though I can't see you loungin' about in a club chair doing a lot of reading, it's steerage for such as you lot, real cosy accommodation. There's two extra bunks built into each cabin and when you're lying down, there won't be enough room between you and the bottom of the next bunk for a highly polished cockroach to squeeze through. One good thing, though, the chow's likely to be a bit better, the high-ups tend to like their tucker, but I daresay the standard will drop a little towards the bottom of the stew pot. I hope you've all brought your curry powder?'

Hawk and Victoria are up early to see Ben off, though they are aware that he will not be permitted to break ranks to meet them. Victoria has obtained a pre-war photograph of the *Orvieto* from somewhere and has marked the exact spot where Ben must stand, roughly midships with the second funnel directly behind him. He is to wave a red silk scarf she has given him, while Hawk, with his head and shoulders well clear of the crowd, will do the same. Hawk and Victoria both count themselves fortunate that the departure has been delayed and over the past three weeks have taken great delight in enjoying more of Ben's company.

Victoria, teasing Hawk, puts the delay down to the generosity of the new Labor Prime Minister, Andrew Fisher. As it will later show she is not that far off the mark. The two German battleships the *Gneisenau* and the *Scharnhorst* visit the capital of Samoa which is only 1,580 miles from Auckland and 2,570 miles from Sydney, and the German light cruiser *Emden*, of the same squadron, is known to be in the Bay of Bengal. Fisher thinks they are much too close to send an unescorted convoy around the coast of Australia. The government of New Zealand shares his opinion and it is decided to send the *Minotaur* and the Japanese light cruiser *Ibuki* to escort the New Zealand troops to Albany. This strategic decision, as well as organising escorts for the Australian contingent from Queensland, New South Wales and Victoria and yet another from Hobart, is the cause of the delay.

Of course, no official explanations for the hold-up are given, as newspapers are forbidden to comment and, as is ever the case in wartime, the wildest rumours spread like a bushfire.

The postponement proved to be a trying time for the men of the A.I.F. They had already said their goodbyes to loved ones and friends and their anticipation was at fever pitch. These were young men trained and ready to go to war, anxious not to miss out on the fray. Now they were thrown back into basic training and the inevitable boredom of repeating the drills and exercises they had long since completed.

In the course of the three-week delay there had been two or three false alarms and any amount of speculation until the troops began to doubt if they would ever get away. A new word for these endless rumours was coined among the Victorian contingent which would go into the Australian language. In the Broadmeadows camp the rear of the sanitary carts that pumped out the latrines carried the name of the manufacturer, Furphy. The rumours became known as 'furphies', in other words a whole load of shit.

The delay also put a heavy strain on discipline. Broadmeadows camp was some ten miles from Melbourne. To an infantryman accustomed to route-marching this distance two or three times a week, carrying a rifle and full kit weighing some ninety pounds, wearing only his uniform and a little change jingling in his pocket, the city was considered a mere stroll down the lane. Army rules required every soldier to be in his blankets by half-past nine but men and officers in their hundreds thronged the streets and eateries of Melbourne until the early hours of the morning during the weeks prior to departure.

Ben, taking the opportunity to visit Hawk and Victoria, was often driven back to Broadmeadows and deposited half a mile or so from the camp at around two. On these occasions Victoria would give her brother a last hug, just in case something happened, or the latest rumour proved to be true and they weren't able to see each other again.

On the morning of Ben's departure, she has accumulated three weeks of tearful farewells and is, herself, somewhat exhausted by the process.

The *Orvieto* is docked at the Port Melbourne Pier, which is just off the main road that fringes the bay, and Hawk and Victoria arrive to find a large crowd already gathered on the road. It is a great disappointment to the crowd that the dockside itself has been placed off limits to civilians. The general grumble is that, in the sea of khaki lining the decks, sons and lovers are too far away to be clearly identified. Nevertheless, there is a great deal of shouting and banter going on, people fashion megaphones from folded newspaper and call out names in the direction of the liner at the top of their voices. 'Good on ya, Billy Thomas!' 'Lucky bugger, Kevin O'Shea!' 'Give me compliments to the King, Danny!' 'Give the Kaiser a kick in the arse from me, lads!' 'Up the mighty Crows!' 'Paris oo la la!' What with the noise of the troops embarking together with the rattle, clank and whine of chains, winches, crane engines and the general mayhem of getting under way, it is unlikely these messages can be heard on board, but they greatly amuse the crowd and do much to quell its disappointment at not getting closer to the liner.

Towards noon the ship's horn gives a baleful blast to warn the dock workers and maritime officials on board to go ashore. Perhaps it is the mournful sound of the ship's horn or the sense of imminent departure, but there is a sudden collective murmur from the crowd which quickly turns to a roar, like a dry river bed suddenly brought into flood. Almost as one the crowd surges forward, the guards stationed on the perimeters of the wharf are brushed aside and helpless to prevent the general stampede onto the wharf.

Hawk and Victoria are carried along with the crowd. To resist would be downright dangerous. So, when the time comes for the tugs to finally pull the giant liner away from its berth, they have a clear view of Ben waving his red scarf more or less from the prearranged position. Hawk waves back with his scarf and it is evident that Ben has seen them, though the noise from the crowd makes it impossible to communicate with him. The liner is pulled away from the dock while a lone tug holds her stern steady and in a surprisingly short time the giant ship is moving to the combined cheering of the huge crowd and the soldiers on board.

Ben is at too great a distance to see that his sister, though waving both arms frantically, is howling her heart out. His last view is of Hawk's snowy hair and the dark dot that represents his face. Hawk is standing head and shoulders above the crowd, still waving the red bandanna. He tries to make out Victoria's white straw hat but she is lost in the sea of bobbing heads and waving hands. Ben, who does not think of himself as either religious or sentimental, whispers quietly to himself, 'I love you both, God bless and keep you safe until I return.'

Ben's prediction is right, his platoon is bunked down in the deepest recesses of steerage with five men in a cabin that would have seemed cramped to three fare-paying passengers. Their kit takes up most of the room and only two of them can occupy the cabin at one time. When it comes to going to bed, three must wait outside in the corridor while two undress and slip into their bunks to allow the next two to do the same. There is no porthole and the ship's laundry is located twenty feet further down from their nearest cabin. They are informed that it will be at work twenty-four hours a day, sending a blast of steamy heat down the corridors every few minutes, so that the sides of the tiny cabins are always damp from the humidity.

Ben quickly realises that the stifling conditions will make rest impossible and loses no time locating a place on deck where his platoon can sleep. He finds an area aft between several large wooden packing cases that is ideal for the purpose as it catches the breeze and will comfortably take twenty-four members of his platoon. Six men will need to remain, one to each cabin to protect their kit, which means every member of the platoon will do cabin duty once every five nights. He sketches out the area and writes down the precise location and pins it on the board in the sergeants' mess, claiming the area at night for No. 2 Platoon, B Company.

Later that afternoon a sergeant named Black Jack Treloar from D Company in the 5th Battalion who is in charge of a platoon of sappers approaches Ben as he is walking down the corridors on D deck. Treloar is a big raw-boned man who affects a dark stubble even when closely shaved. He is known as a bully and has earned his three stripes in the permanent forces where it is said he was once the cruiserweight boxing champion of the Australian army. Drawing up to Ben, he blocks the narrow corridor by leaning against one side and stretching his arm out to bring the flat of his palm against the other. A large semicircle of sweat can be seen under his outstretched arm.

'G'day, Black Jack,' Ben says cordially, 'I hope your blokes scored better cabins than mine, we're in a real shit-hole, hot as blazes, can you believe it, twenty feet from the bloody laundry.'

'Nah, same,' Treloar says, not moving his arm. 'Matter of fact, that's what I want to see you about, Sergeant.'

'What, a sergeants' deputation? Can't see them making any changes, we're foot soldiers, mate, this is the army, besides I'm told the ship's chocka.'

'Yeah, but I hear you've found a nice little space on the deck for your lads to kip down?'

'Yeah, that's right,' Ben jerks his head, indicating the corridor and the cabins behind him. 'Them cabins are not fit for man or beast, put five blokes in 'em and they're jammed closer together than a tin o' sardines.'

'Yeah, right,' Treloar says dismissively. 'Well, I reckon you should share that space on deck, let my platoon in.'

'Love to, Jack, but I can't even fit all my own lads in, six o' them will have to kip down in the cabins, take turns like.'

Black Jack scratches his nose. 'That right, eh?' He looks at Ben. 'That's not good, mate.'

'I daresay there are other places on board, shouldn't be too hard to find a spot.'

'Nah, all took. But I saw your place first, just didn't bother ter make a fancy pitcher and stick it up in the mess, reserve it like?'

'Well, that's tough, Black Jack, but you know the rules, mate. If you got there before me, you should have told us, or posted a confirmation on the sergeants' noticeboard, like I did.'

'You teachin' me to suck eggs or something, Teekleman?' Treloar growls. 'Watch yerself, son, I'm permanent army, not like you lot of toy sergeants from the militia.'

'Sergeant Teekleman or Ben, take your pick, Sergeant Treloar, but not "son" or "Teekleman".'

Treloar chooses to ignore Ben's rebuke. 'You a Tasmanian, ain't yer? Touch o' the tar too, I hear. That's two counts against you in my book, son.'

'I told you, don't call me "son", Black Jack.'

Treloar places his head on the biceps of his outstretched arm and grins dangerously. 'That so? You're asking for it, ain'tcha?'

'Asking for what?'

'A hiding.'

'What? From you!'

'Yeah, none other?'

'What for, Black Jack? The space on deck?'

Black Jack taps Ben's chest with a forefinger then returns his hand to the wall. 'I've 'eard about you bastards. What's it they calls yah? Yeah, that's right, Tiddly-winks young man!' The big sergeant laughs. 'How many pretend Huns have your mob wiped out, or is it killed with an axe? I hear you're pretty 'andy with an axe. You a woodchopper then? Plenty o' them in Tasmania, mostly idjits I hear, droolers.' He smiles unpleasantly. 'If you want my personal opinion your platoon are a bunch o' fuckin' boy scouts.'

'When I want your opinion, Sergeant, I'll pull the chain. Now I'd like to pass if you please?' Several infantrymen have come up the corridor intending to pass and are held up by Black Jack and Ben blocking the way. They hold back, waiting. 'There's men want to pass, Sergeant, we can continue this later in the mess, if you want?'

Black Jack looks up at the half dozen men, but his arm remains firmly jammed across the narrow corridor. 'G'arn, piss off you lot or you're on a charge. G'arn, scarper!'

'Take the port-side stairs, lads,' Ben calls after the retreating soldiers.

'Tell you what, Sergeant Teekleman, I hear there's to be boxing on the foredeck, entertainment for the men. What say I fight you for that deck space, three rounds, winner takes the space. Can't be fairer than that now, can I?'

Ben listens with his eyes fixed on his boots and then looks up slowly, meeting the other sergeant's eyes. Treloar stands about six feet two inches with Ben around five ten but just as broad about the shoulders as the sapper. Treloar has a pronounced beer gut, which gives the impression of his being a lot bigger than Ben. 'Well, I reckon there's nothing to be gained by fighting, Sergeant Treloar, that deck space belongs to my platoon and a stoush isn't going to change that.'

'G'arn, it'd be first fight o' the voyage. A good example set for the men, couple of N.C.O.s having a friendly stoush, boxing gloves an' all, nobody gets too badly hurt, encourage them to do the same, 'stead of pullin' their puds in their bunks at night.' Treloar waits, bringing his head back from resting on his arm. 'Yeah, I thought so, you're a bloody coward, ain't ya?'

'You heard me the first time, Treloar, it's no deal, you're not getting our deck space and two sergeants having a blue is bloody stupid.' Ben's eyes suddenly narrow. 'Now, me being a Tasmanian with a touch of the tar brush, just what did you mean by that?'

Treloar shrugs. 'Ain't too hard to work that out, now is it? Reckon you blokes from the Apple Isle are all cousin fuckers, snot-nosed droolers.' He pauses and nods his head, 'And you, mate, they tell me there's a touch of the Zulu in ya. That right, is it?'

'Zulu?'

'Yeah, nigger, African Abo!'

Somewhat to Treloar's surprise Ben grins and slowly shakes his head. 'You've got a real nasty mouth, Treloar, but you may have half a point there. You see, we Tasmanians go to a fair bit of trouble not to mix our blood with shit from the mainland. As for the other? I'm half-Maori and bloody proud of it, just like I am of being a Tasmanian.'

'I've been to yer little island, son, it's the arsehole o' the known world.'

'Oh yeah? Just passing through, were you?'

There is a sudden burst of laughter from behind Treloar's back. He is unaware that several infantrymen have come up again and are standing behind him waiting to pass. It is obvious most have heard a fair bit of what's been going on. At Ben's put-down of the bully sergeant they prove unable to contain their mirth.

Treloar spins around, furious. 'G'arn, fuck off!' he shouts at the men, but in doing so he is forced to drop his arm so there is space for Ben to pass him.

Ben smiles at Treloar. 'I've got to be off, Sergeant, urgent rifle-clicking practice with my platoon.' Ben stands aside to let the six waiting infantrymen through first. He can feel his shoulder pushing against Treloar's chest and moves backward a little harder than necessary. 'C'mon lads, through you go.' Then he turns around to face the big man once again, 'Been real nice talkin' to you, Sergeant.'

'Yeah, yeah, you'll keep, Teekleman,' Black Jack Treloar growls. 'I'll be lookin' for you, mate.'

Ben has taken three or four steps down the corridor but now stops. 'I'm not hard to find, Sergeant, try leaving a note on the noticeboard in the sergeants' mess.'

The first two days on board are spent settling in, cleaning the Broadmeadows mud from their uniforms and polishing their brass while at the same time, in the ship's parlance, 'getting their sea legs', which proves to be a good thing, for even in the relatively calm seas Numbers Cooligan is sick as a dog while, surprisingly, the remainder of the platoon seems unaffected.

Cabin inspection is followed by physical jerks on the main deck and then breakfast. After which there is rifle drill and musketry practice, though no actual firing takes place. The day then takes on a familiar routine which will continue in much the same way when the convoy sets off overseas. With route marches and many of the other tedious and time-consuming tasks eliminated for want of space the time is taken up with specialist training. Men are selected for all the arcane occupations demanded by a killing machine and are turned into signallers, sappers, machine-gun operators, snipers, clerks, stretcher-bearers and just plain soldiers with a little bit of everything thrown in, though the fundamentals of army discipline are maintained throughout the five-day voyage.

However, talk of the corridor confrontation between Sergeants Ben Teekleman and Black Jack Treloar has spread through the ship. There is a great deal of speculation as to who would get the better of whom in a fight. The fights are on every night in a ring set up on the foredeck and named by the troops 'The Stoush Palace'. It proves to be the most popular entertainment on board and Black Jack Treloar is always there, sometimes acting as a referee and on three occasions even entering the ring himself.

On the first occasion he knocks out his opponent in the opening round and on the next occasion the referee ends the fight in the first minute of the second round, awarding it to Treloar on a t.k.o., the third is another knockout towards the end of the second round. Treloar is a fighter who likes to work the ropes, pushing his opponent into a corner and letting him have it with a barrage from both fists, relying on his strength and aggression to batter through his opponent's defence and put him on the canvas. All three bouts end with a spectacular uppercut and Numbers Cooligan, pronouncing himself an expert, calls Treloar 'a one-punch Johnny'. Treloar's flailing fists invariably force his opponent to his knees while he hangs onto the ropes, whereupon the sapper sergeant takes great delight in delivering the coup de grâce to his undefended chin.

There is something about the way Black Jack fights that makes the audience yearn for an opponent who will take him on. All of the men who climb into the ring with him are game enough but have little previous experience of the sport. They are big blokes, but generally clumsy with their fists and don't know their way around the square canvas. Some may know how to mix it well enough in a pub brawl but getting the hang of the Marquis of Queensberry's rules and a pair of ten-ounce boxing gloves proves quite another matter. It is obvious that Treloar has the advantage of previous experience in the ring as well as being enormously strong in short bursts. He is the undisputed heavyweight champion of the *Orvieto*, though the audience is reluctant to talk him up.

After the confrontation in the corridor, Ben's name is most often cited as the opponent they would like to see, though it is not known whether Ben is a boxer and even if he was he would be a light–heavy, giving Treloar at least a twenty-pound advantage in the ring.

After the way Treloar has disposed of his opponents there are no more contenders for the heavyweight division but there are few outside his own platoon who believe he has earned the title fair dinkum and it is plain he is neither respected nor admired. There is something of the braggart about him, he is rough trade and his platoon of sappers, who are going to war with picks and shovels, is made up of men who have been labourers all their lives and fit much the same description. By way of contrast they take great pride in their fighting sergeant and they begin to taunt Ben's platoon, giving it the sobriquet 'Sergeant Chopper and the Bang Bangs'. Passing a member of Ben's platoon they'll aim an imaginary rifle and say, 'Bang bang you're dead!'

It is childish stuff but nevertheless humiliating and, while none of Ben's platoon will say so, they all secretly wish Ben was as effective with his fists as he is with an axe and that he'd climb into the ring and give Treloar the licking he deserves. They do not have any doubts about their sergeant's courage but would like him to be the instrument of Treloar's demise, bringing the incident in the corridor to its rightful conclusion with the good bloke triumphing over the bully.

Though Ben has won the war of words, the men hunger to see the living shit beaten out of Black Jack Treloar so that there will be no more conjecture. With young warriors the word has never been mightier than the sword. It is not only the incident in the corridor

283

that gives the speculation impetus but also the fact that Ben Teekleman has on a second occasion single-handedly put Treloar's platoon in its place, though unfortunately it does not directly involve Black Jack Treloar.

On the third night out at sea when Ben's platoon is bedded down on deck, six members of Treloar's platoon, no doubt with his tacit approval, decide to teach Ben's platoon a lesson. The story has become somewhat embellished in the retelling, receiving a good start towards mythical status at the hands of Numbers Cooligan, whose accurate accounting is strictly reserved for arithmetical calculations.

However, Library Spencer has written the incident down in the illicit diary the army has forbidden soldiers to keep. His version is without the Cooligan flair but has the virtue of being scrupulously accurate.

They are crossing the Great Australian Bight with the sea uncharacteristically calm and with a full moon in a cloudless sky making the deck seem almost in daylight. Around one in the morning Crow Rigby, who has been placed on guard duty by Ben, sees six men approaching, carrying what can be clearly seen as pick handles. He shakes Ben awake. 'Reckon we've got visitors, Sergeant,' he says quietly.

Ben rises quickly. 'How many?'

'Six, they've got pick handles.'

Ben takes Crow Rigby by the elbow and guides him behind a large packing case lashed to the deck so that they can't be seen by the advancing men. The six would-be attackers move forward in a half-crouch, with one of them four feet or so ahead. He holds his hand up as an indication to advance slowly and quietly. When he is close enough to the first of the sleeping men, Ben leaps from behind the packing cases with an ear-piercing cry and Crow Rigby sees for the first time that he carries his fighting axe. Before the forward man has time to lift his pick handle Ben has jabbed the blunt end of the axe handle hard into the attacker's mouth, taking out several of his front teeth in the process. The soldier gives a startled howl and before he has time to sink to his knees Ben has reached the next man, slapping him on the side of the jaw with the axe head and sending him sprawling to the deck, the pick handle flying from his hands. The third attacker has managed to get the pick handle above his head and as he brings it down Ben parries the blow by holding the fighting axe at each end, then in a lightning-fast gesture he scrapes the axe handle along the pick handle and down onto the hands of the third attacker, breaking his grip and his fingers so that the pick handle clatters to the deck and the man lets out a cry of sudden pain. The axe handle swings up in a curve and smashes into the man's face and there is an audible crack as his nose breaks and he is thrown backwards by the force of the blow to land hard on his arse.

The first two men lie moaning and sobbing sprawled on the deck unable to rise as the third attempts to get to his knees, clutching at his face with one hand while steadying himself with the other. Ben turns to face the next in line but the remaining three attackers turn and flee for their lives.

'Shit!' Crow Rigby says softly, it has all happened in less than fifteen seconds. The rest of the platoon, wakened by Ben's bloodcurdling yell, are barely out of their blankets and on their feet, still somewhat bleary-eyed, when the fight is over. The platoon watches in noisy amazement as the three men on the deck try to get to their feet.

'Quiet, everyone,' Ben commands. 'Help these men to their feet. Private Crow, Private Horne, you too, Private Cooligan.' He is puffing slightly from the sudden rush of adrenaline, but his voice remains calm. The platoon watches in silence as the three privates pull their attackers to their feet and they see for the first time the extent of the damage the axe has done to their collective physiognomies. 'Fuck me dead!' Cooligan says, expressing it adequately for them all.

Ben addresses the three men. 'You all right, lads? Can you walk?' All three nod, the blood from their faces dripping down their chins and onto the deck. 'Righto, no names, no pack drill. Tell the M.O. in the morning that you fell down the stairs or you had a stoush, whatever.' Ben points to the three pick handles lying on the deck. 'Pick those up, lad,' he says to an infantryman named John Parthe who is referred to by the platoon as Muddy. Then turning back to the three wounded sappers he says, 'We'll keep the pick handles, tell your sergeant if he wants to recover them he can post a note on the board in the sergeants' mess. Got that?' The three men nod unhappily, two now have their hands clamped over their mouths, the third over his broken nose. The blood oozing through their fingers can be clearly seen in the moonlight. 'Righto, on your bicycles. As far as No. 2 Platoon, B company, known to one and all as the Clicks, are concerned nothing happened tonight, right? Or would you rather face the C.O. in the morning?'

The three soldiers shake their heads and turn away, stumbling into a half-trot, their hands still clamped to their faces as they make for the hatchway at the far end of the deck. Ben turns to his platoon. 'Let's get some sleep. Well done, Private Rigby, you're off guard duty, get some sleep. Private Spencer, you're on guard.' Ben glances in the direction of the three departing men. 'Stupid bastards didn't even have the sense to wait for a dark night.'

Numbers Cooligan laughs. 'London to a brick them buggers won't be back.' He turns to Ben. 'I has me doubts we can sleep after that, Sergeant.'

'It's an order, Cooligan,' Ben says, stooping to pick up his own blanket.

'Jesus, why don't they issue us with them fightin' axes instead of a stupid bloody bayonet?' Hornbill says ruefully as he wraps his blanket about him. 'Germans would shit 'emselves!'

While Treloar has been strutting his stuff in the boxing ring, he has been careful to avoid Ben. The story of the incident has inevitably reached the other sergeants who approach Ben for confirmation, but all he will say is that there has been a little rough and tumble on deck and that it has been sorted out to everyone's satisfaction.

The three men from Treloar's platoon, reporting to the ship's hospital the following morning, claim to the medical orderly that they had been negotiating the steel steps down a hatchway in the dark when the man at the rear missed his footing and collided with the other two, sending them all crashing below decks. A later inspection would show that two light bulbs were missing over the offending steps, though the ship's doctor, examining them, pronounces himself mystified that no other bruises appear on their bodies. 'You've been fighting, haven't you? What were you using, knuckledusters?' When the men deny this the M.O. shakes his head. 'I'll have to have confirmation from your sergeant, who's your sergeant?'

'Sergeant Treloar, sir,' the sapper with the broken nose and whose name is Brodie replies, being the only one of the three able to speak.

'Treloar, the boxer?'

'Yessir.'

The doctor waves a hand, indicating their faces, 'And you're sure this didn't come about in a fight?'

'No, sir.'

'I'll have to hear that from your sergeant.' The M.O. turns to one of the medics. 'Send a message to Sergeant Treloar to report to me at once.' He looks at Brodie. 'What's your company?'

'D Company, sir, Sappers.' The medic nods and leaves them.

Black Jack Treloar arrives twenty minutes later and confirms that the men are telling the truth and blithely signs the medical report. The M.O. shakes his head, 'I'm not at all sure I shouldn't take this up with your C.O., Sergeant, damned peculiar fall.'

Treloar looks directly at the doctor. 'I agree, sir, and would have thought no different, but it happened on the hatchway stairs aft and I just happened to be close, so I seen it meself. Them bulbs, the lights were missin'.'

'Why weren't the men brought in right away, there's always a doctor on duty?'

Treloar chuckles quietly. 'Well, you know how it is with young lads, sir? They're in the A.I.F. First Division, they didn't wanna be seen as milksops, sir.'

'Sergeant, I've a good mind to put you on report, you have a duty to look after your men, these are not minor injuries!'

'Be obliged if you wouldn't, sir. The lads begged me. They didn't wanna be seen as the laughing stock, there's a lot of pride in the sappers, sir. Fallin' down stairs, it'd be humiliatin', sir.'

'A fair whack of stupidity too, if you ask me!'

'No, sir, with the greatest respect, *pride*, sapper pride, not stupidity, sir.' Treloar would like to put his boot into the M.O.'s groin, silly bastard wouldn't know what side was up. He's only a bloody captain, he thinks, straight off civvy street and now he's playing the fucking warrior doctor.

'Well, I'll overlook it this time, Sergeant Treloar, though it's against my better judgment. Don't let it happen again or I'll see your C.O. is involved.'

Treloar jumps spontaneously to attention and salutes, 'Yessir! Thank you, sir!'

'Dismissed,' the M.O. says in a weary voice.

The three men are placed in the ship's hospital for two days, Brodie to have his nose reset and his hands placed in plaster and the two others, Matthews and Jolly, requiring copious stitches to the lips and mouth and the extraction of several broken teeth, which will be done by the ship's surgeon. There is no dentist on board because in the first A.I.F. intake the standard of recruiting was set so high that a single tooth missing in a recruit's mouth would disqualify him.

Ben, hearing in the sergeants' mess that the three men have been hospitalised, goes to see them late on the afternoon of the day following the incident. On arrival he asks a medic if he can see the three men from D Company.

'You'll have to see Sister Atkins first, Sergeant,' the medic replies.

'How do I do that?'

'Wait here, I'll fetch her.'

Ben is made to wait, standing in the ship's hospital corridor for nearly twenty minutes before he sees Sister Atkins approaching. He has a mind to say something, show her he's a trifle miffed, but a nursing sister, without apparent rank, is given the status of an officer and so he decides to keep his trap shut. Moreover, as she draws closer, she smiles at him and Ben feels his heart skip a beat. A troopship is an unlikely place to fall in love but Ben knows with certainty, even before she has spoken, that he must make every endeavour to develop a closer acquaintance with Sister Atkins. Please, God, don't let her have a sweetheart somewhere, he says to himself, knowing full well that anyone as pretty would not go unattended.

'Yes, Sergeant, I'm told you wish to see the three men who came in this morning?'

'Yes, Sister.'

'Are you their sergeant?' Her voice is light and bright and she smiles again so that the question doesn't appear to be overly officious.

'No, er, they're involved with my platoon, I just want to see if they're all right,' Ben replies a little sheepishly.

'Well, they're not going to die, Sergeant, if that's what you mean? But they've had a nasty fall.' She puts her head to one side as though she is examining him more closely. 'We don't usually allow visitors.'

'I won't take long, Sister.'

Sister Atkins laughs. 'I'll say you won't, five minutes is all you'll get.'

'Thank you, Sister.' He is suddenly desperate to think of

something to say that will impress her but his mind has turned to mashed potatoes.

'Right, follow me, Sergeant er . . . ?'

'Teekleman, Ben Teekleman, Sister.' Then he adds gratuitously, 'From Tasmania.'

'Tasmania? How nice. I have a cousin in Tasmania, though I don't suppose you'd know her, Lucy Atkins?'

Ben is walking beside her and he receives the slightest whiff of lavender water which is enough to send his head spinning. 'Don't suppose I do, but there was a Lucy Atkins in primary school once?'

'Oh, sure, your sister's best friend, was she?'

It is obvious that Sister Atkins has not gone unnoticed on the ship and is up to all the tricks men play with a pretty woman in an attempt to prolong a conversation. 'No really, in New Norfolk, red hair, green eyes, lots of freckles, her mum and dad ran, still do I suppose, the drapery shop.'

Sister Atkins stops, her eyes grown wide. 'My goodness, Sergeant Ben Teekleman, you *do* know my cousin Lucy!'

They have reached the ward door and Sister Atkins enters first and steps ahead, Ben following two or three steps behind her. The ward contains some twenty men. There has been an outbreak of flu on board and there have been several cases of pneumonia as a consequence. Ben silently bemoans the fact that they have effectively come to the end of their conversation.

Sister Atkins stops at the last three beds. 'You've got a visitor,' she says cheerfully. The three sappers sit up in bed and from their expressions it is fairly apparent to the nursing sister that Ben's arrival doesn't exactly thrill them. 'Hmmph, you don't seem too happy about it?' she says, straightening up Brodie's blanket.

'Thank you, Sister,' Brodie says without enthusiasm. The space between his eyes and mouth is swathed in a large bandage, while the damage to the swollen lips of the other two soldiers is uncovered and the ragged criss-cross of stitches can be readily seen.

Sister Atkins turns to Ben, 'Five minutes. Well, I must be off, there's no rest for the wicked.'

Ben is suddenly desperate and he takes his courage in both hands, 'Can I see you, Sister, meet again, talk about Lucy?'

Sister Atkins' pretty lips form a perfect 'O'. 'No, Sergeant, you cannot, you know the rules,' she replies and, turning on a well-polished heel, she exits the ward watched all the way by Ben.

'Bad luck, Sergeant,' Brodie says, happy that Ben has been put in his place. 'Good sort, though, ain't she?'

Ben turns back to the men, remembering suddenly why he's come, 'Oh, g'day, lads.' He glances at the doorway, 'Yes well . . .'

Brodie nods towards the two beds on his left. 'Them other two can't talk, Sergeant, stitches inside their mouth and tongue.'

Ben clears his throat, 'I don't suppose you've ever heard a sergeant apologise, so I won't. But next time you get an order for a night attack at close quarters, point out to your sergeant that it's a full moon, will ya.'

Brodie drops his eyes. 'We was only havin' us a bit of fun, Sergeant.'

'What? With pick handles?'

'Yeah, but we was only gunna hit to the body like, through the blankets, nothing too harmful, plenty o' bruises but nothin' broke. Surprise yiz and get out before youse could do anythin'.'

'That what your sergeant told you, was it?' Brodie doesn't reply and Ben continues, 'In my experience, Private . . . by the way, what's your name?'

'Brodie, Sergeant,' he indicates the two beds to his left with a nod, 'Matthews and Jolly.' The two men nod curtly, unable to speak, though their eyes show them to be less than friendly.

'Yes well, as I was saying, the essence of surprise is concealment, the enemy has twenty-twenty vision the same as you, Private Brodie, you could've read a newspaper on deck last night.'

Brodie glances down at his lap. 'Yes, Sergeant,' he says in a small voice. Then to Ben's surprise he looks up, 'It were wrong, what we done. Your mob didn't do nothin' to us and we didn't find that place to kip down before you done, neither.'

Ben smiles. 'Well, one apology deserves another.' He looks at all three men in turn, 'I'm sorry I hurt you, lads, surprise attacks generally cause an overreaction.'

Brodie looks up at him. 'Not to worry, Sergeant, me nose's been broke twice before by me old man and he didn't never say sorry neither.'

'Yeah, well, what say you, lads? Best to keep our mutual aggression for the Hun.'

'Jesus, Sergeant, when I saw that there axe o' yours, I damn near shit me trousers.' He pulls his hands from under the blankets and Ben sees that they are both in plaster. 'Four broken fingers and me nose ain't too bad, I thought me time was up for bloody certain.'

Ben laughs softly then suddenly grows serious. 'We're all in this war together, lads, if I can help you at any time, I hope you'll come to me.' Conscious that he may have embarrassed Brodie he looks down at the sapper's plaster-of-Paris mittens. 'Don't suppose you'd care to shake hands on that, Private Brodie,' he teases. Ben is suddenly aware of a tug to the back of his tunic and he looks round to see both Matthews and Jolly have their hands extended. 'No hard feelings?' he asks. They both shake their heads and, in turn, clasp his hand in a firm handshake. Then he shakes Brodie's plaster cast ceremoniously, both of them laughing. 'Well, I guess my five minutes is up, lads, better be kicking the dust then, eh? Cheer'o, nice to meet you again under friendlier circumstances.' Ben walks away down the centre aisle of the ward.

'Good luck with the sheila, Sergeant,' Brodie calls after him. 'I reckon you ain't got a snowball's 'ope in hell.'

'You'll keep, Private Brodie,' Ben calls back and there is general laughter in the ward.

The five-day voyage to Albany is without further mishap. In the parlance of the sea, it has been plain sailing. In the way of the army the days become routine, even somewhat boring, so that by the time the ship reaches the tiny whaling port the troops feel as though they've been at sea for several weeks.

What a sight the fleet presents as it lies anchored in the tranquil waters of King George Sound, set against a smudge of distant island hills. Twenty-eight ships carrying twenty thousand young men, Australia's young blood, hand-picked like some exotic fruit to be as perfect as can be, the tallest, straightest, strongest we have to give. They are not to know that they leave as surrogate sons tied to the apron strings of Mother England, but will return as Australians, sons of a nation confident and individual, having completed its final rites of passage.

Chapter Eleven

PEREGRINE ORMINGTON-SMITH

Leaving Home 1914

If Peregrine Ormington-Smith had enlisted as a raw recruit, he would have been culled from the queue outside the recruitment depot. If by some mischance he'd made it inside, he would have stumbled at the very first hurdle, the all-important eye-test. Ormington-Smith wears spectacles, the lenses of which closely resemble the bottom of a ginger-beer bottle.

In military terms Second Lieutenant Ormington-Smith is a dud, plain and simple. Peter Pan would have been a more effective platoon leader. There is simply nothing about him that inspires confidence. He is so hopeless there is a fair bit of speculation that he is the reason Ben's C.O. contrived to keep Ben in the Victorian outfit.

It is difficult to see how Ormington-Smith could possibly have passed muster when the battalion commander was selecting his junior officers, unless nepotism or some other major influence had been brought to bear. Like most sergeants, Ben has grown accustomed to the often mystifying decisions of senior officers, nevertheless he finds it impossible not to believe that any experienced senior officer even wearing a blindfold would instantly conclude that Peregrine Ormington-Smith has a very precarious hold on the practical skills required to navigate his way through life. The battalion commander, Colonel Wanliss, has obviously passed the buck to his C.O. in C Company, Major Sayers, an Englishman from Liverpool, who, in turn, has duck-shuffled it on to his most competent sergeant. Ben Teekleman is to be Ormington-Smith's surrogate nursemaid.

Sayers has on one occasion come close to admitting as much, hinting it was the fault of his battalion commander. 'It's got naught to do with you, Sergeant Teekleman, it's . . . well, it's just the way things sometimes are in the army.'

'With respect, sir, the excuse that there are too many sergeants in the 12th Battalion is bulldust. We have five more platoon sergeants than we need in this battalion.'

'Oh aye,' his C.O. admitted, 'more a question of personnel, officer personnel.' He looked meaningfully at Ben. 'Influence higher up, if you get my drift.' He left it hanging in the air like that, making Ben cope with the hapless junior officer, knowing that the stumble-bum was the reason why he couldn't join his mates in Tasmania.

One of life's paradoxes is that people who are temperamentally ill-suited to a particular vocation actively seek it out. It is as if they want to prove to themselves that they are not who they seem to be. For instance, an irascible and short-tempered person becomes a shop assistant, a tram conductor, a teacher, a football referee or a museum guide and in the process makes a terrible hash of things. Conversely, a timid or congenitally shy person elects to be a policeman, a clergyman, an auctioneer or a choirmaster, with the same disastrous results. These perverse decisions to practise what one is patently ill-suited to preach seems to have no rational explanation and simply emphasises that our perception of ourselves is seldom, if ever, to be trusted.

In an effort to understand where Peregrine Ormington-Smith was coming from, Ben asked Victoria to dig into the second lieutenant's background. She came back with the information that his father had been a colonel on the headquarters staff of General Roberts in the Boer War and was one of the heroes of Mafeking.

The family settled in Australia in 1901 because Peregrine, an only son, suffered from a bronchial complaint and, on the advice of a Harley Street specialist, they moved to a warmer climate. He was just fourteen when they arrived and, shortly afterwards, the colonel purchased a sheep property near Warrnambool in the Western District of Victoria. In Victoria's words the family is 'quite uppity', with Lucinda Ormington-Smith, 'quite a gel', quickly making her mark on the Melbourne Ladies' Benevolent Society and the Red Cross committee.

Young Peregrine somehow stumbled and mumbled his way through Geelong Grammar, where he was the subject of routine persecution because of his impossible Christian and family names, his toffee-nosed English accent and his inability to master even the fundamentals of cricket or football. His chest cleared up and he matriculated, but without distinction. Soon after, much to his father's dismay, he elected to study art at the National Gallery School. After this, little is known of his whereabouts except that he was thought to have become 'some sort of a bohemian'. Quite simply, Peregrine Ormington-Smith began life as a failure and seems to be continuing on in the same vein.

Ben's very first task was to try to persuade his lieutenant to keep in step, for on occasions Ormington-Smith confuses his left with his right. Even when he does march in time, he seems to develop an awkward sort of wobble, his head jerking forward, followed by his shoulders, then his hips and finally his long Ichabod Crane legs. All in all, his body gives the appearance of being jointed in a manner quite different to that of most homo sapiens.

Ormington-Smith stands a reedy six feet and one inch in his stockinged feet but, unlike the angular Crow Rigby who is all horn and hide, he is built on a skeletal frame so rickety in structure and sparse of muscle and meat that a sou'wester blowing with only the slightest malice would knock him on his arse. At the one extremity he has two left feet, both of them size thirteen, while at the other he is almost completely bald. People seeing him in full uniform shake their heads in disbelief and grow fearful for the defence of the country. It is also apparent that the tailor who fashioned his uniform admitted defeat early on in the cutting and stitching process, for his tunic, despite the efforts of his Sam Browne belt to hold it down, hangs from his body like sacking on a scarecrow and his trousers end two inches above the top of his boots.

But it is the lieutenant's voice that marks him for genuine disaster. As high-pitched as a girl's, words issue from his mouth with machine-gun rapidity, so that they bump into each other, some of them breaking in half and joining together as they collide, with the result that Ormington-Smith seems to speak a language which resembles English in tone but makes almost no sense. No doubt this manner of speech has developed as a consequence of the chiacking he received at boarding school for his plummy British accent.

The platoon is forced to master this new language which Library called 'Truncation'. They have learned to respond to sounds rather than meaning. As an example, the word platoon comes out as 'oon', attention as 'shin', eyes right, for some reason, always comes out as 'shite', forward march as 'farsh', and dismissed as 'mist' to name but a few. Library Spencer seems to be the only one in the platoon to understand him without too much difficulty.

'How come you understand him?' Muddy Parthe once asked him.

Library shrugged. 'I don't know, I just can.'

'It's got to do with him reading all them books,' Numbers Cooligan explained. 'Library's that fast when he's readin' that the words come into his mind all blurred, bumping and squashing together, same as the lieutenant speaks.'

Eventually Library Spencer produces a dictionary of the Truncation language which even Ben is forced to swot up.

However, Second Lieutenant Peregrine Ormington-Smith, christened 'Wordsmith' by Library but soon enough adapted to 'Wordy Smith' by the platoon, does not have a malicious bone in his body. And on those not infrequent occasions when the platoon responds incorrectly to one of Wordy Smith's mysterious commands, he doesn't seem to mind too much. At first their apparent ineptitude brought down the wrath of the company sergeant-major and Ben was obliged to cop a fair bit of aggro until the cause of the confusion was corrected by learning Truncation.

Whenever Ben places a member of the platoon on a charge for some army misdemeanour it becomes fairly pointless parading him in front of Wordy Smith for sentence. The lieutenant simply appears anguished and, often biting his nails, he looks appealingly at Ben, sighs and says 'Kitchooty'. This means the offender is to do a day's kitchen duty peeling potatoes or at the handle end of a broom. Kitchooty eventually comes to mean whatever Ben considers to be an appropriate punishment.

The platoon regards Lieutenant Wordy Smith as a kind of invisible presence who depends entirely on Ben to guide their destiny and get them all, including himself, safely through the war. They don't, as might be expected with soldiers who are not much older than schoolboys, take the piss out of him. They accept that they have a sergeant whom they trust and an officer who, while being totally inadequate, doesn't interfere, which makes for a reasonably uncomplicated army life.

In the sergeants' mess Wordy Smith's disinclination to be involved in the daily affairs of the army is considered an ideal situation and Ben is thought to be a lucky bastard. Since the time of the ancient Romans, sergeants have come to the conclusion that the art of war cannot afford the luxury of an officer class and the A.I.F. is no different, regarding the rank of second lieutenant as the lowest possible form of life.

Lieutenant Wordy Smith's reluctance to issue orders and to restrict himself only to those parade-ground commands which are mandatory for a one-pip lieutenant makes running the platoon comparatively easy for his sergeant. As a consequence, Ben must do most of the administration work normally the duty of his platoon commander. Sheer incompetence, and the fact that it is easier to perform around him than to include him, has given Lieutenant Ormington-Smith a soft ride in the army.

All Wordy Smith ever desires is time to write or paint in watercolours. But even in this he is peculiar and contradictory. Without his spectacularly thick spectacles he is certifiably blind, yet his art concentrates exclusively on wildflowers, but only those too small to be noticed in the normal course of observing nature. Using a sable brush which contains only three or four hairs, he will paint no flower in nature that is larger than a tunic button, specialising in those to be found in decreasing sizes down to exquisitely beautiful specimens no bigger than the circumference of a single, minutely small blossom from the pale blue pin-cushion plant. His paintings of tiny green hood, spider and pink cockatoo orchids found on a route-march location show him not only to be a very fine watercolourist but also a very competent botanist. It is as though Lieutenant Wordy Smith is doing some sort of penance for a previous life, one which requires him to find the most difficult way possible to accomplish everything he attempts.

Together with his paintbox and diary, which doubles as his sketchbook, he carries a very large magnifying glass and a small laboratory microscope, the first to locate and the second to unlock the secret details of a myriad of dwarf flora. Wordy Smith paints, identifies, catalogues and writes about floral specimens which one might spend a lifetime crushing underfoot without ever being aware they existed. His field excursions are spent almost entirely on his knees within a radius of ten feet of a plant, crawling through rock and scrub with his nose and magnifying glass inches from the ground and his scrawny bum sticking up in the air. His trousers, despite any amount of washing, always show brown stains at the knees. In an attempt to get him onto the parade ground looking half decent, Ben asked Martha Billings to make him a set of padded leather kneepads to wear on his rambles. When Ben presented these to him, he blushed to a new hue of scarlet, his mouth working to find the words to say thank you, but only managing an assortment of small explosive sounds involving spittle. Finally he gave up and simply reached out and touched Ben's shoulder. He now carries the kneepads in the side pockets of his military tunic, which makes him look as though he is perpetually poised to take off and fly.

The *Orvieto* slipped into its West Australian anchorage on King George Sound late in the morning of the fifth day out from Port Melbourne. There were now twenty thousand men and seven thousand, eight hundred and thirty-four horses on board thirty-six ships, who consider themselves fully equipped, trained and ready to go into action.

However, yet another delay caused them to remain at anchor. A rebellion by conscripted Boer forces in the Cape Colony had raised the possibility of Australians being used for garrison troops in South Africa. It seemed the Afrikaners among the South African recruits, many of them still harbouring bitter memories of their defeat by the British in the Boer War, saw no reason to fight for Mother England. Germany had been one of the very few friendly nations to the Boer Republic during the bitter conflict, supplying them with arms and much-needed medical aid and, if they were going to fight at all, the rebellious men would have preferred to do so for the enemy side.

General Botha, who had himself fought on the Boer side against Britain but now commanded the South African forces, managed to suppress the uprising. The convoy of Australian and New Zealand troops was free at last to sail, bound for the Western

Front to play their part in a war that was going increasingly wrong for Britain and her allies.

The giant convoy leaves on the first of November and this time it is an almost silent departure, with the townsfolk from Albany lined up on a mountain ridge almost too distant to be seen. Once clear of the Sound, the Australian ships travel in three long lines, about a mile apart, with a gap of approximately eight hundred yards between the vessels in each line, while the New Zealand ships follow in a double line observing the same ratios. The convoy is escorted by the three Allied cruisers, HMAS *Melbourne*, HMAS *Sydney*, *Ibuki*, and with a fourth, HMS *Minotaur*, leading the convoy.

The New Zealand troopships had been painted light grey with a small number inside a star at the bow and stern, but the Australians had been less conscientious, leaving their vessels in their original colours, potential sitting ducks in daylight, even obliging the enemy with a large square painted on the bow with which to identify each vessel and supply a perfect target at which to aim. They are almost a week out to sea before someone in the fleet realises that the larger passenger liners and, in particular, the *Orvieto* with the general and staff on board, are conveniently lit up like a Christmas tree for any German cruisers hunting at night. From this point on, the strictest blackout conditions are observed. In an example of Navy overkill which goes from the sublime to the ridiculous, the troops are even forbidden to smoke on deck on the premise that a match struck on a dark night can be observed by a strong pair of field glasses at a distance of four miles.

On November 7th the convoy receives the news that the two German battleships the *Scharnhorst* and the *Gneisenau* have met a British squadron off the South American coast close to Coronel and that the British cruisers *Good Hope* and *Monmouth* have been sunk. There is suddenly a sobering sense of vulnerability among the general staff with the realisation that a single German cruiser, were it to get in among them, could wreak havoc with the three parallel lines of Australian and New Zealand ships. If, for instance, the enemy warship managed to sail into any one of the corridors separating the Allied ships, every ship would instantly become a sitting target for the Germans, while the four Allied cruisers would virtually be unable to fire a clean shot at the enemy for fear of hitting one of their own convoy in the crossfire.

On the night of November 7th, the Cocos Islands thirty-six

hours of sailing away, all lights are extinguished in a practice drill involving the entire convoy and its four supporting cruisers. Sleeping on deck is forbidden, members of the crew pad about the ships in bare feet and complete radio silence is maintained. The Cocos Islands are considered a danger point, since the German battleship *Emden* was last known to be prowling in the vicinity of the Bay of Bengal and is quite capable of reaching the convoy.

To make matters worse, at dawn the following day the *Minotaur* signals to Major-General Bridges on the *Orvieto* that she has been ordered on other service and disappears in the direction of Mauritius. The presumption is, because of the losses of two British cruisers off Coronel, she will be needed to escort a South African convoy from the Cape. The Australian and New Zealand convoy is left with only three cruisers and the *Melbourne* takes the *Minotaur*'s place at its head. They now have a cruiser ahead and one on either beam but nothing to protect them if the *Emden* creeps up at night from the rear and gets in amongst them.

The sun sets gloriously on a smooth sea bringing with it a calm and warm night. They are due to pass fifty miles east of the Cocos Islands in the early hours of the following morning. Ben is unable to sleep in the hot cabin and goes on deck for a spell of cooler air just as the moon rises at eleven-thirty. The sea is smooth as glass and he can see the dark hulls of the convoy, like a great herd of silent and determined behemoths moving on their way. The *Ibuki*'s huge smoke plume is clearly visible in the moonlight. Ben remains on deck for an hour before being discovered by a ship's officer and ordered below. He lies in his bunk thinking of home, of Hawk and Victoria, Hawk growing visibly older, and it occurs to him with a sudden start that Hawk may not be there when he returns home. Depressed, he conjures up in his mind the soft cool dawn of a Tasmanian summer morning and then thinks of the adventure to come. He wonders whether seeing Britain and Europe will change him, though he can't conceive of ever wanting to leave the Tasmanian wilderness with its fast-flowing creeks and the deep-flowing rivers fronted with blue gum and blackbutt that had stood tall and majestic when Abel Tasman the great Dutch navigator passed the island more than two hundred and fifty years before. The trees now tower for almost three hundred feet, brushing the canopy of low cloud that settles above the forest just before it begins to rain. He can't imagine anything comparing with that, no cathedral in Europe could be a grander sight to his eyes. The lights of Paris or London could never compare to a vermilion bushfire raging through the mountains at night. Eventually he falls asleep listening to the throbbing of the ship's engines and the plash-plash of the waves hitting the side of the ship as the convoy moves undisturbed through the warm tropical night.

Summer dawn in the Indian Ocean is as beautiful a display as nature is capable of putting on, with the pink-streaked dawn as sharp as a maharaja's ruby. As the new day breaks, the siren of the *Orvieto* gives a sustained hoot, the convoy is, at that very moment, swinging round the Cocos Islands and the most critical point of the voyage appears to have passed.

At 6.24, the cooks are breaking eggs and beginning to fry the first rashers for breakfast in the galley when the wireless operators of several of the convoy ships and the three escorts receive a short unexpected message. It comes through very loud and clear as if sent at no distance whatsoever and simply reads 'KATIVBATTAV' which makes no sense. Two minutes later the message is repeated. Then the wireless station on the Cocos Islands is heard calling, 'What is that code? What is that code?' No answer follows, but ninety seconds later the same coded call is made, though only once. The next signal to come through is from the Cocos Islands calling the *Minotaur*, which does not reply as she is well out of radio range on her way to Mauritius. The Cocos wireless station tries again and this time adds, 'Strange warship approaching.' The *Minotaur* is, of course, again unable to answer and shortly after the station sends out a general call, 'S.O.S. Strange warship approaching,' and suddenly falls silent.

HMAS *Sydney* is detached from the convoy to hunt for the enemy, leaving the convoy with only the *Melbourne* and the Japanese light cruiser *Ibuki* to protect the convoy. If *Sydney* doesn't find her quarry and the enemy cruiser sneaks up on the convoy, all hell will break loose. With a German warship in the vicinity, discovering the convoy's whereabouts isn't going to be too difficult. The *Ibuki* burns two hundred tons of coal a day and an ever-present pillar of dense black smoke tumbles high into a cloudless sky and is visible forty miles away. A determined enemy warship with a good set of guns and a well-trained crew, if it can get in amongst them, is capable of sinking at least half of the convoy before it is finally dispatched.

The entire convoy witnesses the *Sydney* leaving them and it doesn't take a lot of imagination from the men to know she has gone to meet the enemy. The day is to be treated like any other on board, with physical jerks, inspections, parades and rifle drills as well as the scheduled lectures, but at every opportunity the men's eyes are turned out to sea.

Just after breakfast a message is sent from the *Sydney* to say that she has sighted the enemy ship which is steaming northward and could conceivably cross the convoy's track. The *Ibuki* immediately requests permission from Captain Silver of the *Melbourne* to join the *Sydney* in the impending battle, but this is refused. Both warships now move to a point far out on the port beam to be in the best possible position if the enemy ship approaches, the *Melbourne* slightly ahead of the convoy and the Japanese ship at its centre.

At 10.45 a wireless message is received from the *Sydney*: 'Am briskly engaging the enemy.' Most of the men on board are convinced the enemy must be the dreaded *Emden*, the German cruiser most often mentioned in Australian newspapers as taking a terrible toll on British merchant ships in the Indian Ocean. At 11.10 comes a signal: '*Emden* beached and done for.'

The news, despite the effort of General Bridges to keep it subdued until more is known, spreads like a bushfire through the transports, and there is tremendous pride among the men that an Australian warship has tasted first blood and come out the victor. Whatever activity is taking place on board is thrown into chaos and finally an order from General Bridges gives the troops a half-day holiday.

However, the convoy is not out of danger, the *Königsberg*, the *Emden*'s sister ship, is still thought to be hunting in the Indian Ocean, and that night there is another blackout for the ships. The captains of the transport ships hate the blackouts because they make sailing in a convoy dangerous, with the ever-present risk of one ship ramming another. But the following day news arrives that the *Königsberg* has been definitely sighted off the coast of Africa, at much too great a distance to reach them. From that point on it is plain sailing to Colombo, where they meet up with the *Sydney* again. The prisoners taken from the *Emden* are transported to various troopships, the wounded hospitalised, with the captain of the *Emden* coming on board the *Orvieto* together with several of his officers. The troops are not permitted to go ashore at Colombo and, after coaling and taking on fresh water and supplies, the convoy sails for Aden.

Several days out from Colombo, Lieutenant R. G. Casey, one of the officers in charge of the prisoners, asks Captain von Müller, a tall, thin aristocrat, what he would have done if he had sighted the convoy.

Excessively polite, von Müller replies in an English with very little accent. 'If I had got up to you I should have run alongside her,' he points to the *Ibuki*, 'and fired a torpedo. Then in the confusion I would have got in among the transports. I would have sunk half of them, I think, before your escort came up.' He shrugged. 'I would have been sunk in the end, I expect, I always expected that.'

It is generally agreed that his chances of approaching unobserved on such a bright moonlit night would have been a thousand to one. It is also agreed among the Australian officers who get to know him that he is just the sort to attempt it.

At Aden, while most of the ships are anchored in the harbour, the *Orvieto*, with the Australian High Command on board, docks. Aden proves to be a busy port. Troop transports, either making for India with territorial troops or returning from there with British regulars or native troops, seem to be coming in or out all of the time. On the day the *Orvieto* arrives there are fifty-seven vessels in the harbour and the dusty streets of Aden, set against a backdrop of bare red hills, throng with soldiers.

A small contingent of officers from the *Orvieto* is sent ashore to perform various duties, one of which is to see that the mail from the *Orvieto* is delivered to the Aden Club for posting. Sixteen infantrymen are picked to carry the mail bags to the club where they will be placed under lock and key until they can be put on board a ship returning to Australia. Six of the Click platoon, as they are now known, are among the lucky men selected for the mail patrol. Muddy Parthe, Crow Rigby, Woggy Mustafa, Numbers Cooligan, Hornbill and Library Spencer all draw the lucky short straw, with Wordy Smith as one of the two officers in charge of the ship's mail.

None of the lads has been overseas and, except for Woggy Mustafa, whose father hails originally from Lebanon, they have never seen an Arab and know nothing about the exotic world of the Arabian Nights although, at a pinch, they might admit to having heard of the Pyramids.

Library, of course, knows a fair amount about the Arabs and the British presence in Aden, none of which is considered useful and he proves absolutely hopeless when it comes to the important stuff like brothels, booze, belly dancers and what food is safe to eat, whether the beer is cold and if it gives you gyppo guts.

However, Numbers Cooligan reckons that human nature being what it is, every city has a place where you go to get into trouble and they'd find it soon enough. 'All them what wants to get pissed and plugged, bring your frenchies and follow me,' he declares at the bottom of the gangplank. They are to wait on the wharf for the mail bags and for Wordy Smith to arrive. Ben has given Crow Rigby an exact map to the Aden Club in case Wordy gets them lost.

'Who says we're gunna be allowed any free time?' Hornbill asks.

'Officers have been given the whole day ashore, with my powers o' persuasion, Wordy Smith's not gunna make us return to ship before sundown,' Numbers Cooligan answers confidently.

'Reckon we should do, yer know, a bit o' sight-seeing first,' Crow Rigby says. 'Get to know the lay o' the land, like?'

'Whaffor? We seen it comin' into the harbour, it's a shit-hole.' Cooligan gives a couple of exaggerated sniffs, 'Can't ya smell it?'

'Shit, Cooligan, that comes from that dead dog over there,' Hornbill says, pointing to a dead mongrel lying some fifty feet upwind from them, three crows are already busy pecking at it.

'Fuckin' 'ell, they've even got 'em here!' Crow Rigby exclaims.

'Well, that's yer proof then, ain't it? We 'aven't come fifty feet and we've hit our first dead dog. Plenty more where he come from, mate!' Numbers Cooligan says ominously.

'What do you think, Woggy?' Muddy Parthe asks. 'Yer old man come from 'round these parts, don't he?'

'Lebanon, it ain't like this, we're Christians, mate,' Woggy protests, then adds, 'Me old man says you got to go to the bazaar.'

'Did you hear that, lads? That's a flamin' expert opinion, Woggy's old man says the bazaar. Righto, them what's coming, onward Christian soldiers!'

Lieutenant Ormington-Smith arrives and shortly afterwards the mail bags are lowered by crane. Crow Rigby, on Ben's instructions, takes command and, with each of them carrying a sack of mail, they head for the gate. The provost sergeant at the gate salutes Wordy Smith with the merest touch of his red-banded cap, examines their passes and tells them not to drink the water or any soft drinks and gets the cheerful reply, 'Righto then, Sergeant, if you insist, we'll stick to beer!'

The Arabs waiting hopefully at the gates follow the lads all the way to the Aden Club where Wordy Smith has simply followed Crow Rigby who, in turn, has assiduously consulted Ben's map. Numbers Cooligan, who has been walking alongside Wordy Smith at the rear, gives the thumbs-up sign as they reach the club.

The veranda of the Aden Club, with canvas awning down and electric ceiling fans working overtime though it isn't much past ten o'clock in the morning, is already packed with Australian and British officers off the various ships, the Australians busy getting their laughing gear around a cold and splendidly foaming ale, while the British seem to have a preference for a drink called 'Gin and it'.

The lads from Ben's platoon, trying hard to remember what a truly cold beer tastes like, soon realise they are unlikely to be given the opportunity to find out at the Aden Club, and take the mail bags to the club secretary's office. With Wordy Smith watching, the canvas bags are locked into a back room with no windows which seems to contain several bags of potatoes and onions but little else. The club secretary gives Wordy Smith a receipt, but Crow Rigby politely takes it from him, folds it and places it in the breast pocket of his tunic for safekeeping.

Wordy Smith leaves them at the entrance, having arranged with Crow Rigby to meet them back at the club no later than five o'clock that afternoon.

They all salute him. 'Thank you, sir, have a beer or six for us, won't you, sir,' Numbers Cooligan advises their platoon officer.

Wordy Smith taps the small canvas kitbag he carries, 'No, no, cliffproms splendspes, whato!', which Library translates when they are out of earshot as 'No, no, cliffs promise splendid specimens, what ho!' Library adds, 'He's got all his stuff in his kitbag and he has his kneepads in his tunic. He's taken the day off to paint his flowers.'

'Do you think Ben knows?' Muddy asks.

'Jesus, Muddy!' Numbers protests. 'It don't matter, not for

now anyhow! Let's kick the dust, the bazaar awaits such as us with wonders to behold!'

They walk down the quiet, neatly raked, white-gravel driveway bordered by brilliant red cannas and clipped lawns, shaded by poinciana trees, and out of the gates of the snooty club grounds into the harsh sun and baked earth where Britain's orderly influence ends and Arab chaos begins.

Once through the gates, the lads are immediately engulfed by men in long white robes importuning them, plucking at their tunics and presenting their wares, most of which appear to be of a recreational kind. All of the offers begin with the words 'You want . . .' 'You want jig-jig, soldier?' 'You want my sister? Very clean. You only first time, British guarantee!' 'You want jig-a-jig show, only one dinar, mans and womans, donkey and womans, very nice for you.' 'You want dirty postcard? Only one dinar, six, you pick also.'

'Ere, give us a gander at them postcards,' Hornbill says to an Arab, who has a dozen black and white pornographic postcards which he loops in a two-foot arc from one hand to another. The cards instantly stack into his left hand and he deals the first one to Hornbill as though a croupier in a Biarritz casino.

The card shows a bald bloke with a waxed and curled mustachio, he is barrel-chested with a protruding beer gut and is completely bollocky except for his socks and suspenders. He is chock-a-block up the back of a large female who is on all fours. She is looking directly at the camera, her face devoid of any expression. The centre of her lips is painted into a small bow, which extends above and below the lip line, with the remainder of her mouth visible on either side of the bow. The outlines of her eyes are heavily made up with black kohl and the eyebrows appear to have been shaved or plucked and then painted back in a more intensely arched line with the same substance. Two darkish circles of rouge are apparent on the cheeks of a face powdered a ghostly white. Her hair is swept up in the style of the Victorian era, the whole effect giving her the appearance of a tarted-up possum.

'Shit, it's him again!' Hornbill exclaims as they jostle to have a squiz.

'Him, who?' someone asks.

'Me uncle's got some o' these pitchiz,' Hornbill explains, 'he got 'em from some sailors who were pissed and broke who swapped them for eight pies and a bottle o' sauce.' He stabs a finger at the man in the picture. 'It's the same bloke, me uncle's got twenty o' them postcards, that fat bloke's in all o' them and here he is again!' Hornbill shakes his head. 'No matter what possie he's in, he don't never take off his socks and suspenders.' He turns to the Arab and hands the postcard back. 'Let's see the others, mate? I bet fat Fritz is in 'em all.'

'How do you know he's German?' Numbers Cooligan asks.

'Sailors told me uncle they gets them postcards in Munich, it's the world capital o' dirty pictures and absolute filth.'

'Gee, I'd like to go there,' Cooligan says wistfully.

'Well, you probably can when we've conquered the buggers,' Crow Rigby says.

The Arab hands Hornbill the bunch of postcards and he shuffles through them all, the others jostling and craning their necks to get a clear look. Although the fat female changes from time to time, the bloke with the socks and suspenders is in every one of them. As if to confirm Hornbill's uncle's assertion, one of the poses shows him riding on the back of a buxom Fräulein, who is on all fours. She has whip slashes painted crudely on her enormous bum and he's holding a riding crop aloft and wearing a German officer's spiked helmet and, of course, the ubiquitous socks and suspenders with a set of Spanish spurs fitted to his heels.

'There you go, told ya didn't I, bloody German!' Hornbill says triumphantly.

'Ten dinar,' the Arab says, holding up ten fingers, 'very cheap, special price for you!'

Crow Rigby looks at the Arab and shakes his head sadly. 'Sorry, mate, we'd be happy to buy the lot off yiz if only Fritzy weren't wearing them crook-lookin' socks!'

Hornbill hands the man back his postcards and, laughing, they depart for the bazaar followed by what is obviously, even to the untuned infidel ear, a string of profanities in the Arab lingo.

At the end of a long day of dust and noise, a thousand importunings, strange smells, exotic wares, high-pitched wailing music that seems to drill through the eardrums, too many beers too weak to make them drunk but which sweat back through the pores of their skin within minutes of consumption, it's almost time to get back to the ship.

They've all bought several cheap brass and enamelled trinkets which they fondly think their mums or sisters will find romantic and exotic. They stop for lunch at a cafe in the bazaar and order mutton, potatoes and chickpeas, which Library assures them is ridgy-didge because it all comes out of the same simmering pot and all the germs have been killed. After this Numbers Cooligan tries a small brass cup of Arabic coffee, thick and sweet, which he pronounces to one and all as delicious, but which collides with the warm beer, lamb, potato and chickpeas and persuades the resident contents of his stomach to retrace its steps so that he is violently sick in an alleyway a few minutes later.

They also visit three brothels, the first two have a line of British tommies and Indian troops in turbans a hundred yards long and they decide to try somewhere else. While the queue at the third is shorter, the brothel is in a mean street where they come across another dead dog. Far from the glamorous velvet-draped and silk-cushioned bordello they'd fondly imagined, the brothel turns out to be several small dark rooms, each of which is curtained off into four partitions only just large enough for a man to be placed in a horizontal position on a dirty mattress. Crow Rigby and Hornbill would certainly have had their heels intruding into the next-door partition.

Moreover, the Arab sheilas, except for darker hair and a somewhat duskier skin tone, are dead ringers for the ones on the postcards and even Numbers Cooligan, the only one who hinted of having had previous experience with a woman, decides to give them a big miss. The mandatory lecture Ben has given them about venereal disease suddenly comes into sharp focus. Losing one's virginity is one thing, but being sent back home with a dose of the clap or something even worse is quite another.

Finally, with a little more than an hour to go before they have to retrace their steps to the Aden Club to meet Wordy Smith, they each part with a dinar, a day's pay, to see a live show advertising itself in crude lettering painted onto the surface of a doorway:

Belly dunce Snakes

Plise pulled the bell.

'Whatcha reckon, lads? Must be a classier sort of joint, no wogs trying to get us ter go in,' Cooligan says.

307

'Most likely the opposite, the rock bottom,' Library Spencer suggests. 'Even the Arabs must have some personal standards.'

'I reckon with them whorehouses we've already hit rock bottom, we've got nothing to lose and if Crow or Hornbill gets bit by the snake it'll only make 'em 'omesick! What say we go in, eh?' Cooligan says, obviously feeling better after he'd emptied himself out in the alley.

'Yeah, shit, why not? I'm game if you are,' Muddy says.

'You ring, Hornbill, you're the biggest,' Woggy suggests.

Hornbill steps up to the door and looks for the bell which is nowhere to be seen. 'There's no bloody bell,' he calls out.

A short piece of dirty rope protrudes from a hole in the door directly under the lettering. 'The rope! Pull it!' Library offers.

Hornbill tugs on the rope and, without any apparent sound, the door is flung open by an old man sporting several days of white stubble on his chin, wearing a battered top hat and greasy tailcoat together with pyjama trousers and a pair of embroidered slippers just like the ones Muddy has bought for his mum in the bazaar.

'Ladies and Gentlemans, belly dunce, welcome!' he says, bowing with a flourish. 'One dinar, plise, welcome, welcome!' There must have been a peephole in the door or something, because the old man couldn't possibly have responded so quickly to Hornbill's ring.

'Is that one dinar for the lot, squire?' Numbers Cooligan asks hopefully.

'No, no, naughty man!' the old man says, chuckling and shaking his finger at Numbers' joke. 'Six dinar, you come all, very wonderful belly dunce.'

'What about the snake?' Crow Rigby asks.

'Very, very wonderful snake also!'

They look at each other for affirmation and then Crow nods, 'Yeah, bugger it, let's go.'

The old man stands, blocking their way. 'You pay me now, gentlemans.'

'We pay five dinars for six, fair enough, Abdul?' Cooligan offers.

The old bloke shakes his head. 'Very wonderful belly-dunce snake, six dinars, five dinars belly dunce not take away clothers.'

That settles it, with the promise of a bollocky belly dancer the old man has instantly cancelled Numbers Cooligan's need for a bargain and each of them hands over a dinar, which the old bloke slips into his pocket.

They are led down a dark passageway with half a dozen soot-eyed children with runny noses staring at them silently from passing doorways. Two of the smallest, both boys, wear no clothes and have protruding little stomachs, their tiny brown spigots pointing to their pathetically thin, dirt-encrusted legs.

'Classy joint orright,' Crow Rigby whispers. 'Smell the cat's piss.'

'No cats here, mate, we had 'em for lunch,' Numbers Cooligan replies.

The end of the passageway leads directly to a door which, in another life, was once painted fire-engine red but its brilliance has long since faded to a mostly purplish-brown, the paint peeling in parts to show a dirty white undercoat. The old bloke removes Muddy's mum's slippers and places them at the door. 'Very, very welcome, gentlemans.' He points to Woggy's boots. 'Please to take off the shoeses.'

They look at each other, uncertain. 'If he scarpers with our boots we'll get our pay docked and a month's kitchooty,' Woggy warns.

'Crikey, we've come this far, we might as well have a Captain Cook!' Hornbill protests. 'Besides, even Library could take the old bloke in a blue.'

'We could keep them on our laps,' Library points out, ignoring Hornbill's remark.

They sit down in the passageway and remove their boots and puttees and the old man opens the door using a key tied to the end of his pyjama cord. 'Please to enter, gentlemans.'

'We're not gentlemen, we're Australians,' Crow Rigby drawls, hugging his boots.

They enter a small room roughly the size of your average suburban bedroom. Two hurricane lamps with red-tinted glass, hanging from the ceiling at the far end of the room, cast a pinkish glow over a platform, which is about four feet square and eighteen inches high, and covered with a fitted carpet of Arabic design. The carpet is worn through to the boards at the centre where the belly dancer has obviously performed a thousand exotic gyrations. The platform and the wall directly behind it are vaguely outlined in pink light while the remainder of the room is in almost total darkness and smells of sweat and stale Turkish tobacco.

'Sit, gentlemans, you like coffee? Arab coffee, very, very wonderful, only two shekels!'

They all laugh. 'No thanks, Abdul, Mr Cooligan here may accept your kind offer, but we'll give the wog brew a miss if yer don't mind.'

Their eyes have grown accustomed to the dark and they can now see that the earthen floor is covered with several small overlapping carpets onto which have been thrown eight or nine leather cushions. They all sit down cross-legged facing the stage, preferring to sit directly on the carpet rather than the greasy cushions, their boots resting on their laps.

'On with the show, Abdul, chop, chop!' Numbers Cooligan calls, trying to sound cheerfully confident, though secretly sharing with the others the thought that they've almost certainly blown a day's pay on what, judging from the surroundings, promises to be a real dud bash.

'I fetch-ed belly dunce,' the old man announces and disappears through the door, closing it behind him and, by doing so, further adding to the gloomy atmosphere.

'Shit, what now?' Muddy asks.

'Look, there's ashtrays,' Hornbill announces, reaching out and holding up a large brass bowl he's found on the perimeter of the carpet beside him. 'Anyone got a smoke? I'm out, smoko'll help kill the stink in 'ere.'

Woggy Mustafa fumbles in the top pocket of his tunic and produces a new packet of ten Capstan and foolishly hands it to Hornbill, who removes one and passes the pack around. 'Hey, fair go, fellas! That's me last friggin' pack!' Woggy protests. The packet is returned to him five cigarettes short. 'Jesus! Youse bastards all owe me one, ya hear, the next butt bot's mine?'

'I thought you said your mob were Christian? That's blasphemy, mate,' Numbers Cooligan says, happily lighting up. In the flare of the match he discovers that he too possesses one of the large brass ashtrays.

The door opens and the old man enters, staggering under the weight of a large wooden box with a beaten-brass speaker horn extending from it and reaching into the air well above his top hat. He is followed by a woman clutching to her enormous bosom what appears to be a wicker laundry basket.

'That's for the cobra, I seen it in books!' Muddy says excitedly.

'That's only in India, Muddy,' Library corrects him, 'the fakir uses a flute to entice the cobra out of the basket.'

'Well, the old fucker's maybe gunna do the same here,' Muddy persists.

'Fakir, Muddy, an Indian holy man,' Library laughs.

The woman, undoubtedly and disappointingly the belly dancer, is almost as wide as she is high and wears a red velvet cape which reaches down to her ankles. Even in the dimly lit room it looks much the worse for wear, the hem edged with dirty tassels, several of which are missing, like teeth in a broken comb. The velvet material to which it is sewn is worn down in mangy-looking patches and seems to be attached around her neck by a hook and a curtain ring. It gives every appearance of an old embassy or theatre curtain at the fag end of its life, pensioned off to do the best it can. The fat belly dancer also sports a pair of Muddy's mum's slippers with her big toe protruding through the pointy end of the left slipper.

The old man, wobbling violently at the knees, places the gramophone carefully down to the side of the stage and, staggering back a step or two, is caught in a violent paroxysm of coughing, puffing and wheezing so that he is forced to sit almost doubled up on the edge of the little platform. Finally he seems to recover whereupon he clears his throat and hoicks into a brass spittoon on the floor four feet from him.

'How's yer ashtray goin', Hornbill?' Numbers Cooligan calls as he suddenly realises what the brass bowls placed on the mats are intended for. 'Don't stub yer butts in the bottom of 'em, lads, they may not be empty.'

The old bloke has now recovered sufficiently to wind up the gramophone, then lifting off the lid he sets the turntable going and places the needle arm down onto the thick bakelite record. His hands are shaking like a first-night actor and there is the familiar high-pitched scratching sound as the needle misses its intended groove before gaining traction.

A high-pitched wail, redolent of the music they'd been hearing all day in the bazaar, issues forth, though it seems to be coming from a great distance in fits and starts, as if it has been tortured by being pulled out of the guts of the machine and threaded piecemeal through the enormous brass speaker. The wailing is of such an indeterminate sound as to make it impossible to decide the gender of the singer.

The old man climbs onto the stage and stands beside the woman, who, while being no taller than him, is three times as broad and occupies most of the available space. To maintain his balance, he is forced to rest one leg on top of the basket and his hand on the edge of the gramophone.

The belly dancer hasn't moved since her arrival. She stands with hands clasped in front of her, staring resolutely into the dark. If she can see them she gives no indication. Her face from the eyes down is covered with one of those masks they've seen all day on women in the bazaar.

'Jeez, they all look like nuns planning a hold-up,' Crow Rigby exclaimed on first seeing a group of women in the bazaar. The belly dancer's mask isn't black, though, but is made of a shiny pink material which reminds Hornbill of his mum's knickers.

When they asked Woggy at the bazaar what these masks were called he shrugged. 'It's a face apron,' he claimed, which seemed a fair enough description.

Above the belly dancer's shiny pink face apron appear two hard-as-anthracite eyes buried into kohl smudges, which cover her eyelids and extend into the eye sockets and upwards to end a quarter of an inch below her painted-on eyebrows. She too is a dead ringer for Hornbill's uncle's postcards. Only her jet-black hair is different, either naturally so or deliberately teased. It consists of an enormous frizzy mop which flops in an eight-inch halo about her face and reaches down to touch her shoulders.

'Ladies and Gentlemans, Dames en Heeren, Madame, Monsieurs, Boyses and Girlses, I give you very, very wonderful belly dunce!' the old man announces, as though addressing an audience of several hundred, throwing his head backwards and forwards with the effort, an emphatic spray of spittle exploding into the pink light.

On cue the fat lady comes alive and, with a theatrical flick of the wrist, she unhooks the curtain ring securing the cape and flings it aside in the direction of the old bloke who has stepped from the platform just in time to cop the lot. The heavy cloak hits him on the side of the head and knocks him arse over tit.

This brings a big laugh from the audience but is completely ignored by the belly dancer who is now revealed clothed only in two faded gold tassels which hang from nipple cups glued to her enormous breasts and a pair of Ali Baba pantaloons that balloon to her ankles from her waist. The pantaloons are of the same material as the face apron and Hornbill's ma's bloomers and shimmer in the light.

The belly dancer appears to have a three-tyre thickness of blubber over her stomach and now each of these rotates to the music as she begins to grind her enormous hips. Then, with all her wobbles moving more or less in the same direction, she bends forward slightly and, grabbing her left breast firmly in both hands, gives it a violent twist which sets the tassel rotating. Whereupon she repeats the same exercise with the right tit and now she has everything going, tassels whirring, stomach wobbling and hips grinding as the six lads look on in startled amazement.

It is a bizarre enough sight and they almost feel they've had their money's worth in sheer grotesqueness when the old bloke, having untangled himself from the velvet curtain, lifts the basket lid.

'Bring on the snake! Let's see the snake!' Numbers Cooligan calls out.

'Yeah! The snake! The snake!' the others chorus.

But instead of the snake the old bloke pulls out a bottle about eighteen inches high into which is fitted a long cork. He places the bottle on the stage in front of the gyrating, swirling, tassel-rotating, belly-blubbering, hip-swinging dancer, who miraculously, given her weight, stands on one leg and whips off one side of the pink pantaloons and then the other, not missing a beat.

There is a gasp from the darkness, none of them, except perhaps for Numbers Cooligan, has ever seen 'it'. And, in this case, 'it' is almost a match for her hairdo. 'It' is a thigh beard of monstrous proportions and, like some dark, tangled creeper, it straddles the top of her legs as solid as tree trunks.

Tassels still swinging and everything else going as well, she lowers herself down onto the bottle and using 'it' she neatly extracts the cork from the bottle and with a tremendous flick of her hips the cork flies into the air and is neatly caught in the old bloke's top hat. 'Very, very wonderful belly dunce!' he shouts gleefully.

There is cheering and clapping all around at this amazing display of dexterity and Numbers Cooligan for a start is rapidly becoming convinced they're getting their money's worth and then some. But there is more to come.

'Shit!' Crow Rigby suddenly whispers in a voice loud enough for them all to hear. 'There's a bloody snake in the bottle!'

They all crowd forward to see that the bottle indeed contains a snake curled at the bottom which is now beginning to rise. With everything still moving to the wailing cacophony, which seems a little less scratchy towards the centre of the gramophone record, the belly dancer lowers herself onto the bottle neck and neatly grasps it. She lifts the bottle and arches backwards until she is almost parallel to the surface of the stage. To everyone's horror the snake, about eighteen inches long, moves forward out of the neck of the bottle into the external furry darkness.

'Holy Mary mother of Jesus!' Woggy exclaims, while the others are too gob-smacked to say anything. The dancer, still gyrating and wobbling, though the tassels have now come to a stop, lowers the bottle to the carpet and continues to dance, turning and whirling several times until it seems impossible that her sheer weight and momentum will not throw her from the tiny stage. Then she begins to slow down until she faces them again, her hips undulating slowly, stomach barely wobbling to the music, and opening her mouth she slowly pulls the snake out. In a trice it is wriggling in her hands, its head darting forward, its tongue testing the air, as she holds it triumphantly above her head.

In the weeks to come the eighteen-inch snake will take on python-like proportions and the tit tassels will whirr like Crow's old man's windmill in a stiff breeze. The belly dancer's hips will expand to the size of a buckboard on a sulky and her breasts will become bigger than Easter Show watermelons. They have had their money's worth ten times over. Tired but happy they return to the Aden Club to rendezvous with Wordy Smith.

An hour later they are still waiting for the lieutenant to arrive. Numbers Cooligan finally persuades the reluctant white-uniformed guard in a red fez at the gate to allow him to enter the club to see if the lieutenant isn't waiting for them on the veranda. Most of the Australian officers have already departed for the ship, while those preparing to leave pause only long enough for a final soothing ale. They claim not to have seen the platoon commander all day. At half-past six the lads return to the ship and are put on a charge by the provost sergeant at the gate for staying out beyond the limit on their day passes.

Crow Rigby finds Ben and reports the missing Wordy Smith.

'He may have returned on his own,' Ben says, shaking his head. 'Dozy bugger.'

But Wordy isn't in his cabin or the officers' mess and Ben returns to the lads. 'Did he say anything when you left him?' he asks.

'Yeah, Library translated, he said something about "splendid specimens on the cliff",' Numbers Cooligan says.

Library corrects him. 'No, no, cliffproms splendspes, whato! Cliffs promise splendid specimens, what ho! He had his things with him, in his day kitbag.'

'Any of you men have any experience cliff climbing? Or rock climbing?' Ben asks.

'Yeah, Sergeant,' Hornbill volunteers, 'I come from mountain country, I done a fair bit.'

It is almost seven o'clock before Ben gets permission from his C.O. to leave the ship. They've obtained a length of rope from the chief petty officer, two torches and batteries from the quartermaster and a first-aid kit from the ship's hospital. Sister Atkins, obliging with the latter, seems pleased to see Ben again.

There is only one set of cliffs, to the right of the port as you enter the harbour, though hills stretch further back from them. Ben isn't sure whether he hopes Second Lieutenant Peregrine Ormington-Smith has stuck to the cliffs and probably killed himself or gone into the mountains and become lost. The cliffs seem to be the logical place to start the search, are not too extensive and rise above the sea no more than a couple of hundred feet.

By the time they arrive it's almost dark and Ben sends Hornbill to one end of the top of the cliff face while he takes the other, instructing that they'll meet in the middle, all the while looking downwards and shouting out in the hope of making contact with Ormington-Smith.

Almost ten minutes later Ben hears Hornbill screaming, 'Sergeant, over here!'

When he arrives Hornbill is on his stomach, shining his torch directly downwards. From where he is standing Ben can't see anything and so he joins Hornbill and shines his torch to double the beam. About thirty feet down, Wordy Smith is seen sitting on a ledge looking upwards, squinting into the beam of light. One of his boots and socks has been removed to show a large white foot.

'Doangle!' he shouts at them.

'He's done his ankle,' Ben says quietly. 'Shouldn't be too hard to get him up.'

'Let *me* go, Sergeant?' Hornbill offers.

'Nah, I want the bastard to owe me,' Ben says. 'You reckon you can pull him up if I go down and rope him?'

'Sure, Sergeant, if I can't you can tie him and come back up and we'll sort him out together.'

Ben searches for a while until he finds what seems like the best way down to the ledge. He'll need both hands so he can't take the torch and will have to rely on Hornbill lighting the way for him from the top. It takes him no more than five minutes to reach the lieutenant, whereupon Hornbill lowers the rope and Ben, balanced precariously on the narrow ledge, ropes Second Lieutenant Peregrine Ormington-Smith up and ties his kitbag to the rope as well. The lieutenant seems quite overcome and finds it impossible to get any words past his lips. 'Don't talk, just hang on tight while we get you up,' Ben instructs him.

Making sure Ormington-Smith is secure he calls to Hornbill to have a go at pulling him up. But thirty feet is a fair drop and even though Wordy Smith in appearance seems as light as a bag of chook feathers, without a tree or rock to anchor the rope his weight is too much even for a man as strong as Hornbill to pull up alone.

'Wait on, sir,' Ben instructs and makes his way back up the cliff. It is hard going in the dark and he loses his footing and several times a clatter of small rocks crashes down the cliff face into the sea below. Finally, he crawls back over the lip of the cliff and lies for a moment to recover.

Between them they haul their platoon commander back up and after regaining his breath Ben examines the lieutenant's ankle. It is badly swollen but doesn't appear to be broken, though it is doubtful he will be able to walk. 'We'll manage between us, can you hop on one leg, sir?'

Ormington-Smith nods, it is past eight o'clock and dark, the moon not yet up as they move out with Ormington-Smith between them, his arms clasped about their shoulders and utilising his good foot to hop. They have gone no more than a hundred yards when he suddenly stops, resisting their efforts to move forward.

'What is it, Lieutenant, need a rest?' Ben asks.

'Sketbook!' Wordy Smith says.

'Sketbook? Oh, your sketchbook?'

'Leftit.'

'You what?' Ben can't believe his ears. 'You left your sketchbook? Ferchrissakes, where?'

'Clif-ace.'

'The cliff face, on the ledge?'

Ormington-Smith doesn't reply but gives out a desperate cry, like a child suddenly threatened with a backhander from his father. He removes his arms from their shoulders and, turning, hops back towards the cliff face.

'Bloody hell, we'll get it in the morning!' Ben shouts after him, but Ormington-Smith, as though possessed, keeps hopping frantically towards the cliff face in the dark.

'Shit, he'll kill himself,' Hornbill shouts and together they set off after the lieutenant who has almost disappeared in the dark and is managing a remarkable pace hopping on one leg.

They reach him at last and Ben wrestles him to the ground, but the scrawny subaltern seems possessed and he is hard put to restrain him. Ormington-Smith is whimpering and sniffling like a child as Ben finally subdues him. 'Sketbook!' he howls again.

'Take it easy now, Lieutenant,' Ben says, trying to calm him down, rising and then lifting him to a seated position. He reaches for the first-aid kit slung across his shoulder, takes out a bottle of water and, unscrewing it, hands it to Ormington-Smith. The lieutenant gulps at the bottle greedily, most of its contents spilling down the front of his torn tunic. 'You all right?' Ben now asks as the bottle is handed back to him, he can see that the lieutenant's hand is shaking violently. Ormington-Smith nods and then suddenly begins to weep quietly.

'Oh, shit!' Ben says softly, almost to himself. Then, in a calmer voice, he addresses his platoon commander, 'We're going back, sir, even if I have to carry you over my shoulders. We'll be back for your sketchbook in the morning.' He turns to where he thinks Hornbill is standing. 'Private Horne, help me get the lieutenant to his feet.'

There is no reply.

'Hornbill, you there?' Ben shines the torch and sees that Hornbill isn't where he supposed he was standing. 'Private Horne!' he shouts into the darkness. 'Where the fuck are you!'

'Coming, Sergeant,' Ben hears Hornbill's voice some distance away.

'Get here will'ya, at the double!'

Hornbill comes panting up in the darkness and Ben shines the torch into his face. 'Where've you been?'

Hornbill doesn't reply but hands Wordy Smith's sketchbook to the hapless lieutenant sobbing at Ben's feet. 'There you go, sir, safe and sound, no harm done.'

Ben is almost too angry to speak. 'You could have killed yourself, yer stupid bastard,' he shouts at Hornbill. 'What for? A bloody useless sketchbook, full of pictures of flamin' flowers no one can see!'

'Sorry, Sergeant,' Hornbill says, in a contrite voice, then nodding his head to indicate the lieutenant at Ben's feet, he adds, 'Them flower paintin's, they's everything to him, Sergeant.'

Wordy Smith has managed to get to his feet, hugging the sketchbook and standing on one leg sniffing. Both turn to look at him. 'Thank you, Private Horne, thank you,' he says quietly. 'This sketchbook is more important to me than my life, but not more important to me than *your* life.' It is said in a steady, perfectly modulated voice, not a single word bumping into another or joining together. Peregrine Ormington-Smith will never have a problem with his speech again.

Chapter Twelve

THE CALM BEFORE THE STORM

Egypt 1914–1915

The new and articulate Wordy Smith, while being on crutches for the next ten days, is a changed man. Though it cannot be claimed he has made the transition from hopeless to competent, he has, at least, decided to make up for his previously arcane speech patterns and almost total lack of communication by telling his platoon everything he hears in the officers' mess. Or so he claims.

Ben, who has cause to visit his cabin from time to time, does not let on to the platoon that Peregrine Ormington-Smith shares a cabin with the military liaison officer to the ship's wireless room. Nonetheless, Second Lieutenant Peregrine Ormington-Smith is simply incapable of being deceptive and with a slip of the tongue on one or two occasions his source of information is discovered by the platoon. The wireless subaltern, it seems, has grown so accustomed to Wordy Smith's inability to articulate that he talks quite freely about the messages coming through, airing his opinions on what goes in and out.

Ben realises that his platoon officer, if discovered, will be placed in an extremely awkward position, not quite a court martial as he can hardly be accused of supplying information to the enemy, but he will still be in considerable trouble. He finds himself in a real quandary, as a sergeant he must co-operate with his officer, while at the same time he is responsible for the immediate welfare of his platoon.

Even though the information from 'Wordy's Wireless', as the platoon has dubbed the lieutenant's cabin mate, cannot, in this instance, be said to be critical to their welfare, there is a very sound principle involved which every sergeant in every war ever fought would understand. It is simply that the more hard information you can get from an officer the more likely you are to prevent him from doing something stupid which may get you all killed. After years of saying as little as possible, Ormington-Smith must be actively encouraged and Ben decides to swear the platoon to secrecy.

'No leaks yer hear? We've got this on our own. If it gets out where the lieutenant is getting his information he's up shit creek without a paddle and so is Wordy's Wireless, the ultimate source of our information. We're sitting pretty, lads, so shut yer gobs. That's an order.' Ben looks searchingly into the eyes of every member of the platoon, extracting a silent promise from each of them. 'Righto, Private Cooligan.'

'Yes, Sergeant?'

'You run the two-up school on E deck and you're a bookmaker for the Tuesday-night fights, ain't ya?'

They all laugh and Cooligan colours. 'Me, Sergeant? Never! The army has cured me o' me wicked ways. All I wants is to fight Herman the German.'

'Right, there will be times when the information we get from Wordy's Wireless has to get out to the rest of the ship so, Private Cooligan, you're our official mouth, our Gob Sergeant.'

'What's that mean, Sergeant?'

'When stuff comes from Wordy's Wireless that needs to get to the rest of the ship, you're it. But don't make it look that way, you mix what's real with a fair amount of bullshit, just the way you did a moment ago – you know, but you don't know, you heard, but you're not sure where, something somebody said, putting two and two together, could be wrong but . . . It's a question of mixing the right amount of fact with the correct proportion of crap. Can you do that, Private Cooligan?'

'Can a crow fly?' Crow Rigby quips and they all laugh.

'No, no, I'm serious,' Ben says. 'It takes a fair amount of imagination and at least a pint of Irish blood in yer veins to do it right and Cooligan's got both. What do you reckon, Private?'

Cooligan is flattered. 'I think you just done me a spot-on character reference, Sergeant. Gob Sergeant, eh? Is that a promotion, Sergeant?'

Wordy's Wireless proves to be a real bonus for the Click platoon and adds greatly to their reputation, they now become a valued source of information. Numbers Cooligan performs the role of chief rumour monger with a special brilliance, instinctively understanding the age-old Australian adage that bullshit baffles brains. The information tidbits Ben allows for dissemination spread outwards at an alarming speed and, in a matter of an hour or two, the entire ship knows the latest news. Numbers Cooligan is soon much sought out for information by blokes from the other platoons and, in the nature of these things, anything they know is given to him until there isn't a lot happening on the ship that isn't known to Ben.

However, the very first piece of information Second Lieutenant Peregrine Ormington-Smith brings to the platoon is not from Wordy's Wireless but the officers' mess. Upon hearing it, it is the first time the enlisted men have felt anything but excitement at the prospect of getting stuck into the Hun.

The day after they leave Aden for the Suez Canal and thereafter Britain, Wordy Smith tells them the horrific news brought back by the officers who spent the day at the Aden Club while he went specimen hunting on the cliffs. Several months previously two British battalions of regulars stationed in India, each a thousand men strong, passed through the port on their way to the Western Front. Like those from the *Orvieto* it was an occasion which saw some of their officers visit the club. Now members of the club have received letters from two of the officers who survived to say that one of the battalions has been reduced to three hundred men and the second has been almost completely annihilated.

The news comes as a shock to the thirty thousand Australians and New Zealanders who, from the very beginning, have regarded the war in Europe as a grand opportunity to prove their worth as fighting men while, at the same time, seeing Europe and Britain with their mates. They are suddenly sobered by the thought that they too are destined for the same killing grounds that have butchered both regiments. Herman the German is proving to be less of a pushover than they've been led to believe.

321

If the minimum recruiting age for men had been put at fifty, saving the young men for breeding and for work, the old men on both sides would have soon enough found another way to resolve the conflict. Young men, though, have always possessed a sense of immortality which their elders have exploited since time out of mind. The notion that they are invincible appears to be a part of the young warrior's genetic code. In a peacetime society this is further evidenced by the fact that almost eighty-five per cent of all violent crime is performed by men under the age of twenty-eight. The young male seems to need an outlet for his aggression and, in the process, believes himself to be bulletproof right up to the moment when a high-velocity Mauser bullet churns his innards to mincemeat.

Sobering as the news of the two devastated battalions is, it doesn't seem to greatly affect the desire of the young Australians to fight the Germans but now there is a rumour gaining notoriety on board that the British High Command does not fully trust the Australian irregulars, or believe that men can be trained effectively to fight a war in twelve weeks. This, in their minds, is especially true of the Australians, who, on the last occasion they fought beside British troops, gained a reputation for often ignoring the commands of their senior British officers. In truth, this only occurred in the Boer War on no more than half a dozen occasions when it became apparent to the Australian Mounted Rifles that the British officers, untrained in the guerilla tactics required in South Africa, were attempting to fight a war in the African bush as if they were back in the Crimea.

Britain has always depended on the career soldier who never questions orders. The Australians, faced with similar bush conditions as at home, and living a not dissimilar lifestyle to the Boer enemy, quickly adapted to the hit-and-run commando style of warfare, much of which was conducted in the saddle.

The British regulars took a hiding against the Boer irregulars, whose commandos were made up mostly of simple farmers with virtually no previous military training. But, like many of their Australian counterparts, the Boers rode like the wind and could shoot a man between the eyes at a thousand yards. They could attack a British unit and be twenty miles away before the British had time to pack up and move out in pursuit. In the peculiar African conditions they proved too elusive for the highly trained, rigidly disciplined British regulars, who found it difficult to adapt to this new kind of warfare. Only by sheer force of numbers and the personal understanding and leadership brought to the battlefield by that great general, Lord Roberts, did Britain finally succeed. By the time the war ended in victory for the British forces the Boers had been outnumbered six to one.

The rumour now doing the rounds on board the ships of the convoy is that Britain will use the supposedly under-trained, ill-disciplined and second-rate Australians in India and Egypt as garrison troops. This will relieve the British regulars, at present occupied in this task, to fight in the *real* war on the Western Front. To further substantiate the rumour, news comes through that the Turks have sided with Germany and have declared war on Britain and her allies. The average soldier on board has no trouble making one and one equal two and reaching the conclusion that the Australian troops will be stationed in Egypt.

So when Wordy's Wireless tells them the day after they leave Aden that General Bridges has received instructions by wireless that they are to proceed to Britain, there is a palpable sense of relief. The news spreads as if carried on the stiff nor'easter blowing that morning and by the time the official announcement is made most of the troops on board see it simply as confirmation. Those who first got it from Numbers Cooligan are beginning to show a growing respect for his sources.

However, on a day filled with contradictory news, night brings a further instruction to General Bridges. The *Orvieto* is to sail ahead of the convoy to Port Said. The same message is received by Major-General Sir Alexander Godley, the commander of the New Zealand force headquartered on the *Mauganui*. The two ships are to proceed at their own speed to Egypt.

Wordy's Wireless has suffered a stomach complaint and has been confined to bed for two days when the message comes through so Ben doesn't receive any advance notice from his lieutenant. Therefore it is a tremendous surprise to the troops when the *Orvieto* breaks away from the convoy and sails off on its own. Numbers Cooligan, newly appointed Gob Sergeant, is unable to supply any explanation, which, strangely enough, confirms his status among the troops, as knowing everything seems improbable and is also highly suspicious.

Fortuitously, Wordy's Wireless recovers from his stomach

ailment and is back on deck the following evening, safely ensconced in the wireless room when a late telegram arrives for General Bridges from Sir George Reid, the Australian High Commissioner in London. Wordy Smith reads it to the Clicks at the breakfast parade fully two hours before it is officially announced to the troops on board.

GEN. BRIDGES.
HQs FIRST AUSTRALIAN DIVISION – ORVIETO.
MESSAGE FOLLOWS:
UNFORESEEN CIRCUMSTANCES DECIDE THAT THE FORCE SHALL TRAIN IN EGYPT AND GO TO THE FRONT FROM THERE. THE AUSTRALIANS AND NEW ZEALANDERS ARE TO FORM A CORPS UNDER GENERAL BIRDWOOD. THE LOCALITY OF THE CAMP IS NEAR CAIRO.
GEORGE REID – AUST. HIGH COMMISSIONER. U.K.

The decision is met with utter consternation. When the change in plans is made known to the troops they boo loudly and stamp their boots on the deck to demonstrate their disapproval. To the average soldier the arithmetic is irrefutable, the declaration of war by Turkey and the order to proceed to Port Said can mean only one thing, they are to be used as garrison troops against the Turks.

Ben and his platoon, like every volunteer in the A.I.F. and together with the New Zealanders, have a burning desire to prove their mettle on the Western Front. Nothing short of this is acceptable to them. The soldiers of both antipodean nations take a quiet pride in the fact that they are the finest specimens their people can supply to the war machine, and unspoken, but in their minds, is the notion that they deserve to go against an enemy worthy of their calibre. For them the Turks are simply a bunch of wogs to be kept in line.

General Bridges is forced to issue the exact contents of the telegram together with a personal explanation. He strongly emphasises the particular section of the telegram which stipulates 'AND GO TO THE FRONT FROM THERE'. This somewhat, but not entirely, mollifies the men. There is already a sense of distrust between the private soldier and the officer class which is part of the Australian personality. The convict against the prison warder, the shearer against the squatter, the trade unionist against the capitalist, the people against the politician and, now, inevitably, the foot soldier against those who are placed over him.

The explanation for the diversion, couched in the usual official military language, is essentially correct, but it does nothing to subdue their misgivings. In the eyes of most of the troops it is a heap of bullshit and they suspect the British High Command is going to leave them stranded in Egypt to face the Turks. They are simply told that, due to the early onset of winter in Britain, the site on Salisbury Plain, which is intended for the encampment and further training of Australian and New Zealand troops, has not been adequately prepared.

Three weeks after they arrive in the camp in Cairo a more satisfactory explanation comes out. Wordy Smith once again has come to the rescue. It seems he has an uncle who is a major on the staff of Lord Kitchener, the Minister of State for War. In a letter to his nephew in Mena, the Australian camp just outside Cairo, he gives a much more colourful account of the reasons.

Wordy Smith, perhaps a little naively, simply reads the letter to his platoon.

6th December 1914

Dear Peregrine,

How very disappointed your Aunt Agatha and I are that we shall not be able to give you a warm welcome on your return to England. We remember you as a fine fourteen-year-old lad. Your father assures us your bad chest has completely cleared up in Australia and we greatly looked forward to meeting the strapping young man you've undoubtedly become.

However, we are fast learning that during a period of war the best-laid plans of mice and men are apt to be frustrated. My job is no more important than any other entrusted to the rank of major in the War Office, but it has the singular advantage of bringing me into

*frequent contact with Colonel Chauvel, the Australian representative
with the W.O.*

*And what a splendid chap he is, straight as a die and not in
the least pretentious. It is said he is a disciplinarian and a stickler for
protocol and correct military procedure, though I have not seen this
side of him. He seems happy enough to mix with the lower officer ranks
here at the W.O. and is often to be seen having a beer at the local, where
he is fond of pronouncing the English beer as 'tasting like warm piss'.*

*It was during just such an occasion that he told me in his
own colourful vernacular why the Australian and New Zealand
contingent have been diverted for further training to Egypt.*

*As the official explanation doesn't differ in essence, but
rather in detail, I am confident that Col. Chauvel's version doesn't
transgress the O.S.A. (Official Secrets Act 1912).*

*I shall try to put my amateur theatrical experience to work
to capture the tone and manner of his dialogue, as I feel sure it will
amuse you. I apologise in advance if it doesn't ring quite true to your
acquired Australian ear.*

*The following conversation takes place with yours truly and
the colonel after the third pint of 'luke-warm piss' or, if you like, best
British bitter:*

*'Harry, didn't you mention you had a nephew back home
who enlisted with the A.I.F.?'*

*'Yes, sir, my brother William's son, we were greatly looking
forward to seeing how the lad has turned out, he had a rather nasty
chest problem when he left England.'*

'I shouldn't worry about that, lots of sun and good red

meat, soon fix his chest, pity you won't see him. [Takes a sip of LWP.] Good thing, though, would've been a complete shambles.'

'Oh?' I say, not understanding how meeting you could possibly lead to a shambles.

'The weather, the camp, bloody impossible,' he exclaims.

'You mean on Salisbury Plain, sir?'

'Well, that's just it, isn't it? Bad enough for your own troops and the Canadians, you're accustomed to the mud and the cold, but our blokes are not used to that sort of thing.'

'You mean it doesn't rain in Australia, sir?'

'Well, it doesn't piss down twenty-four hours a day, day in and day out, until you're up to your bollocks in mud!'

'Well, how will they be at the front?' I ask cheekily, 'That's nothing but mud, sir?'

'Hmmph, I daresay they'll do a damn fine job when the time comes, but that's a purely academic observation, the poor buggers would all have been dead from pneumonia long before they ever got to France! Half the Canadians who are encamped on Salisbury Plain are crook, and the others are rioting in the streets of Salisbury!'

'Crook?'

'Yes, down with flu or pneumonia and the other half are close to rebellion. They were promised huts, heated huts for the winter, and they're still in tents, which at night are cold enough to freeze the balls off a brass monkey. What's more, they have no hope of getting better billets until the spring.'

'I'm sorry to hear that, sir. What a good thing the old man changed his mind and sent your lot to Egypt.'

'Had it changed for him, you mean?'

At this last remark I raise my eyebrow somewhat. Chauvel is superior in rank to me and I don't wish to point out that Lord Kitchener is not inclined to listen to the opinions of or be persuaded by a junior officer. 'Well done,' I say, deciding discretion is the better part . . . etc.

'Good God, man, not me! Georgie Reid!' Chauvel exclaims. 'I reported the conditions on Salisbury Plain to him and he telephoned his nibs on the spot for an appointment.'

In case you are not aware, Peregrine, Sir George Reid is your Australian High Commissioner in London, and is well known for his casual disregard for the niceties of diplomacy.

However, being in the W.O., I know that access to the Field Marshal's room by telephone is impossible to obtain. Not even the Prime Minister would think to call him without prior warning and I daresay that pretty well goes for the King as well.

But I wasn't to know that Kitchener makes an exception with Sir George. It seems he enjoys the Australian's disregard for protocol, especially his ability to tell a good after-dinner yarn and generally play the buffoon. (Clever man, what?) Col. Chauvel calls it 'being a larrikin' which is, I believe, a uniquely Australian expression meaning a number of things, both good and bad. It would appear that being a larrikin (good) allows Sir George to get to the great man at any time and to freely discuss subjects which few would dare to broach.

Col. Chauvel then went on to say, 'Georgie saw Kitchener the following morning with my report and told him our convoy would be passing Egypt in a few days. That there was no time to lose, the

Australian troops must be diverted to Egypt at once, and on no account be allowed to come to England where they would only increase the already unmanageable congestion.'

I must say Sir George Reid must be a remarkably persuasive chap, because Kitchener immediately advised the Australian government and the plan was adopted in a matter of hours.

So there you have it, dear fellow, straight from the horse's mouth.

While your aunt and I will be disappointed not to see you, it's been a beastly winter, freezing winds from the north, with January, and possibly snow, yet to come. I don't imagine, with such short notice, that things are all they should be in your Cairo camp – I'm told there's a great shortage of tents – but the prospect of wintering on Salisbury Plain is not one I would wish even on the Hun. You are far better out of it.

The newspapers here have expressed the view that the Australians and New Zealanders are disappointed with the decision not to bring you to England, being of the opinion that the diversion to Egypt means you will not fight on the Western Front.

I am inclined to think this is not correct, as you are much needed in France, where things are not going as well as they might. All things considered, a bit of the Australian 'larrikin' (good and bad) might be a jolly good thing.

The first time I was stuck in a military office job was during the Boer War when I begged for an active-service posting but was refused. Once an office wallah always one, the War Office is unlikely to give me a company command in this one, so it is going to fall upon *your shoulders to follow in your grandfather's (Crimea) and your father's footsteps and to represent the family at the sharp end. I want you to know that your aunt and I are extremely proud of you and we wish you and your platoon the very best of luck.*

That's about all I have to say, old chap. Agatha asks me to send you our Christmas greetings and to tell you to make sure you visit the Pyramids. (Isn't your camp close by?) She also says I must take care to inform you that the damage to the face of the Sphinx was caused when Napoleon's troops used it for cannon practice. She has never been fond of the French – 'Too much side and front but essentially lacking in substance.' She also sends her love and asks you to write a postcard. Though, I daresay, not one showing the Sphinx.

With my very best wishes from your uncle Harry;

Harold Ormington-Smith, Major.

There is some amusement in the platoon at Wordy Smith's Uncle Harry's perception of his nephew, but they feel included and complimented that Wordy would think to read the letter in its entirety to them. Uncle Harry seems like a good sort of bloke despite being an officer and his nephew is so completely inadequate to the task that the Click platoon simply cannot harbour the suspicions they instinctively reserve for the officer class.

None of them can possibly imagine Second Lieutenant Peregrine Ormington-Smith performing as a fighting man, issuing the order to go over the top and, with whistle in his mouth and revolver in hand, leading the charge against the enemy. They look to Ben to lead them with the vague notion that Second Lieutenant Ormington-Smith, with his kneepads firmly secured, his bum in the air and his magnifying glass inches from the ground, will be off somewhere finding his flowers to paint.

'London to a brick, if he's wounded it will be in the arse, a bullet through both cheeks,' Crow Rigby says at tea on the evening they reach the Suez Canal.

'We ought to paint a face on his bum,' Numbers Cooligan ventures. 'For his own protection. Bloody sight better getting a bullet through both them cheeks than the ones higher up.'

They see the Sinai Desert for the first time stretching away to the foot of the Arabian hills, painted pink in the sunset.

'It looks bloody lonely,' Muddy Parthe remarks. 'Yiz wouldn't want to fight in a place like that, would youse?'

The *Orvieto* is put on alert as they approach the ninety-nine-mile canal cut straight as an arrow through the desert and it is thought that they may be fired on by the Bedouins from the east. But instead, in what remains of the daylight, they see the first evidence of the Allies, a tented company who have created a series of small sangars with sandbagged breastworks in a semicircle, the loopholes in the breastwork facing outwards from the canal. Any enemy attempting a surprise attack at night would be met with an outer ring of barbed-wire entanglements. Behind the breastworks, as a fall-back position, are a line of trenches and, behind these, the tents for the men. It is the first sign they've seen of any serious commitment to wage war and there is a great deal of shouting, which brings a number of Indian soldiers out of their tents and up onto the banks of the canal. They are soon followed by two British officers with baggy khaki shorts which fall to well beyond their knees. Shouted greetings are exchanged and they learn from two English officers that they are the Indian Army, the 128th Native Infantry.

'You'll probably join us here soon,' one of the officers shouts.

'Not bloody likely!' a chorus of Australian voices shout back. 'We're off to Britain, mate!'

For the first time the men on board get an actual sense of being involved in something bigger than the A.I.F., a war where others, like themselves, have come from the far ends of the earth to fight with them. It is one thing to be told you are a part of something larger and quite another to experience it.

The *Orvieto*'s original destination of Port Said has now been changed to Alexandria, where they arrive just a few hours ahead of the first ships in the convoy. On the morning of December 3rd, the 3rd and the 5th Battalions entrain from Alexandria for Cairo. They cross the Nile delta with the annual floods rapidly subsiding in the burning sun so that the Nile flats are a brilliant green. People in long white robes are working the fields with wooden ploughs pulled by oxen. A woman walking ahead of a male on a donkey catches their attention.

'Hey, wait a mo! Ain't it supposed to be the other way around?' Crow Rigby says suddenly.

'What yer talking about?' someone asks.

'The bloke on the donkey, ain't the Virgin Mary supposed to be on the donkey?'

'Shit, you're right,' Numbers Cooligan exclaims. 'Look at bloody Joseph, you'd think it was him up the duff, Jesus!'

'It's just like being in Sunday school with all them pictures they show you o' these parts,' Woggy now says.

'You should know,' Cooligan says. 'They're your kin folks, ain't they, Woggy?'

'I told yiz, we're Christians, them lot's Arabs, mate.'

'What say you, Library?' Hornbill asks.

'Well, it's all academic, ain't it? There were no Christians at that time, Woggy's ancestors were either Arab or Jewish.'

'There you go! I told ya, didn't I, Woggy's a bloody Arab, no risk!' Cooligan says triumphantly.

It is nightfall when they finally reach the outskirts of Cairo. Seen from the railway carriages it seems to be a big, untidy-looking city.

Hornbill sticks his nose out of the carriage window and sniffs. 'Smells crook,' he announces. 'Me uncle says every city has a smell, it's mostly from the food.'

'Melbourne don't smell o' meat pies, mate,' Cooligan says.

'Flinders Street Station does, you can smell me uncle's meat pies the moment you get off the train and all the way across Flinders Street.'

'Hornbill's right,' Library says, 'it's the oil they use for cooking mixed with the spices. We smelled it in the bazaar in Aden, though not as bad as this.'

'Wonder if they've got any belly dunces and snakes here,' Crow Rigby says.

The belly dancer and the snake has by this time been told so many times and in increasingly lurid detail that even the six who were present are becoming convinced that the snake was several feet long and the belly dancer's weight around the four hundred pound mark with the three spare tyres around her belly big enough to fit out a Leyland truck.

'There'll be nothing to beat that ever,' Numbers Cooligan says emphatically. 'We'll go to our graves remembering that, lads.'

The train pulls into a railway siding specially built for the Australian troops in the heart of Cairo. The idea is to show the Australian colours by marching both battalions down the broad European streets with the bands playing 'Sons of Australia'.

The buildings on either side of the grand central avenue, some of which must have originally been quite impressive, are now dilapidated, with the stucco damaged, the paint peeling, and the windows dirty. They look as though they've not seen a lick of attention since the day they were built, which is probably true. The whole scene resembles a sort of huge stage set, for the streets have been cleared of traffic and the people, for the most part, have been told to stay indoors. So the hard crunch of boots, the sounds of the bands and the shrill commands against the backdrop of crumbling buildings seem contrived and theatrical.

They pass the Kasr el Nil Barracks where the sound of the bands brings out the Lancashire Territorials of the 42nd Division, who rush across the parade ground to cheer the Australians on.

'Jeez, take a look at 'em, they're all dwarfs,' Hornbill says out of the corner of his mouth. 'I always thought, yer know, the Brits were big blokes.' Indeed the soldiers from the north of England, recruited originally from the coal mines and the cotton mills, are tiny compared to the average Australian and New Zealander, who are astonished to find that they are, for the most part, a head taller than their British counterparts.

'It's meat,' Library Spencer explains. 'Not enough protein in their diet.'

'Meat? Don't they eat meat?' Muddy Parthe asks, astonished.

'Well, not enough, that's why they're so short.'

'Hear that, Numbers, yer mum didn't feed ya enough chops when you were a young 'un. That's why yer such a short arse!' Muddy says gleefully.

Numbers doesn't reply for a moment and then announces, 'Bullshit, I had a chop every mornin' f'breakfast since I was two years old, that's six thousand, five 'undred and seventy chops I've ate, mate!'

'Not enough, mate,' Muddy says, feeling smug.

They pass the barracks and cross several bridges and then march along a long avenue built on a causeway, which starts at Gizeh and runs for five miles all the way to the flooded flats of the Nile. It is almost full moon and towards the end of the avenue when they approach the edge of the desert sand they catch their first sight of the Pyramids etched clear and massive as they rise from the desert. The causeway finally ends and they are marched onto a newly laid road, bathed in the light of a glorious moon, which seems to disappear into the desert.

'Hey, you blokes, lookee there!' Crow suddenly exclaims. 'Flamin' gum trees!'

Indeed they are passing a magnificent group of gum trees standing alone in the desert. A sudden breeze blows up and the sound of the wind high in the trees, like waves crashing on an Australian beach, makes them all suddenly terribly homesick.

'How'd they get here then? Big bastards too, been there a while I can tell ya,' Hornbill, the timber expert, says.

'The eucalypt is the most adaptable tree in the world, it can grow almost anywhere,' Library Spencer calls out. 'They plant it in arid regions to prevent the soil blowing away.'

'Righto, lads, keep the chat down,' Ben calls.

They now see that the avenue of gum trees is planted as a part of the Mena House Hotel, which they soon pass and continue marching onwards until they come to the first valley of the desert and, in doing so, almost bump into the Pyramids standing majestic in the moonlight, taller than any building they've ever seen.

It is here, on a lonely stretch of sand, under a star-sprinkled sky, the great Pyramids casting dark shadows over the pale moonlit desert, that the battalion receives the command to halt.

They are sweating from the exertion of the ten-mile march from the centre of Cairo, so only after a while do they realise the night has grown very cold. They haven't washed or eaten a square meal since they left Alexandria and they're tired and hungry, but mostly tired. Several tins of bullybeef are opened to share around, but most are too exhausted to think of food and roll themselves in their grey army blankets preparing to sleep. Tomorrow they will begin the task of setting up camp in a place where someone has had the good sense to plant Australian gums in the desert.

'Plantin' them gums,' Cooligan says suddenly, 'I reckon it were one o' them prophets they has round 'ere, like in the Bible. He come to them Pyramids to pray like, you know, to one o' them Egyptian Pharaoh Gods and he gets this message back, sorta like a prophecy, the Pharaoh God tells him about us comin' 'ere. So off he goes at the trot and plants them gum trees to mark the occasion.'

'Jesus, Cooligan!' Crow Rigby calls from his blanket.

'Him too! He could've walked right where you're lying, mate, givin' out them loaves and fishes. Bloody old this place, I daresay every bastard in the Bible's been here. Moses . . .'

'So where's this prophet of yours gunna get the gum-tree seeds?' the ever pedantic Library Spencer asks.

'He's a prophet, ain't he? He waves his stick and strikes the ground and says abra-ca-bloody-dabra and, there you go, flamin' gum trees!'

'Ah, shurrup, Numbers! Can't yer see we're all buggered,' Woggy Mustafa calls.

'I thought you said your lot was Christians an' all!' Numbers Cooligan says, wrapping himself in his blanket against the night chill. As always he manages to have the last word.

At the end of twelve days the 1st Australian Division, infantry, artillery, ambulances, transport and the divisional Light Horse occupy the site at Mena which stretches for nearly a mile up the desert valley. The New Zealand infantry brigade and mounted rifles with all their support companies are camped at Zeitoun, on the northern outskirts of Cairo, while Joshua Solomon's regiment forms part of the 1st Light Horse Brigade, together with all its supporting units, at Maadi Camp on the edge of the desert south of Cairo.

At first the Australians discover that only eight and a half thousand tents exist for thirty thousand men. Britain, whose responsibility it is to see that they arrived on time for the A.I.F., has slipped up on the job. In the first few weeks most of the infantrymen are obliged to dig themselves dugouts, which they cover with their waterproof sheets. The officers' messes consist of large, sprawling Arab desert tents contracted from Greek merchants, who seem to be in charge of many of the more prosperous aspects of Business in Cairo.

With the rainy season over, sleeping in the open desert doesn't seem at first to be such a hardship. But there is a downside none of the top brass has foreseen – the desert goes from blazing hot during the day to bitterly cold at night and an unexpectedly high ratio of men are hospitalised with pneumonia until ordnance manages to procure and issue extra blankets to the men.

Over the next few weeks the tents arrive from Britain, pipes are laid to pump water around the camp and the general infrastructure required to create a large working army takes a surprisingly short time to build.

Soon the tents stand in long, straight rows, and to give the men a sense of some permanency in the desert sand and also to prevent it blowing into the tents, the fronts of these are often aproned with whitewashed stones and sown with green oats. 'Desert lawns, mate, so's you won't be 'omesick,' Crow Rigby tells Library Spencer the first time they see one, whereupon they plant their own so that the platoon's tents have a nice neat look.

The roads between the tents are also neatly marked out with whitewashed boulders. Whitewashing stones and roadside boulders becomes the local equivalent of kitchooty. Spacious mess-rooms are erected for the men and the ramshackle grandstand belonging to an abandoned racecourse is turned into the ordnance store. Finally the tramway is extended from the causeway to the edge of the camp.

In no time at all, an Arab shanty town grows up along the perimeters of the valley. And while no houses, brothels or grog shops are allowed, shops of every other description tumble along roads and appear in self-created alleyways. The shops are constructed of bits of tin and box wood, canvas and any material which can be brought to the site and erected in a hurry.

An Arab merchant will arrive in the morning with a donkey cart piled high above his head, and his wife and a helper sitting on the top of the impossibly secured load. By evening, with a bit of hammering, nailing, tying and stretching of canvas and the laying of Turkish carpets, a new shop will appear on the desert sand.

Every imaginable service is suddenly at the disposal of the men, laundering, dyers, tailors who can whip up a brand-new uniform in half a day from army cotton drill mysteriously obtained, news vendors, photographers with painted backdrops of camels set against the Pyramids when the real thing is only a matter of yards away, dubious antique dealers, trinket shops, restaurants with stove pipes jutting out of their canvas and beaten tin roofs with live chickens and ducks out the back, for the slaughter of, bootmakers, carpet sellers, and every few shops there is a tea-room with a crudely painted sign, 'Australians System Afternoon Tea', as opposed, presumably, to 'English System Afternoon Tea'. Miraculously, scones and strawberry jam are available, the former somewhat leaden but the jam surprisingly good, though clotted cream is not on the menu.

Before the winter is over, the little valley that contains the vast tombs of a civilisation more than four thousand years old, and where Numbers Cooligan's biblical prophet first smote the gum trees into existence some fifty or so years ago, has become a dusty, thriving, bustling small city with all the smells and sounds of the Arab bazaar.

Hawkers are everywhere, small boys shouting 'Eggs-a-cook!' 'Oringhes!' 'Boots-i-clean!', selling hard-boiled eggs or oranges and working as boot blacks. Some with dirty postcards call out 'Jig-a-jig-a-look!' The coffee sellers and lime-juice vendors shout their wares and merchants stand outside their shops and beg passers-by not to miss the opportunity of a lifetime and to come inside. On one occasion, when the six 'Aden lads', who are now such firm mates that they seldom go anywhere without each other, are ferreting around the makeshift alleys of the Mena bazaar they are approached by an urchin selling dirty postcards, announcing them as 'Jig-a-jig-a-look!' Hornbill suddenly shouts, 'Betcha a bob Herman the German's in 'em all!'

'You're on,' says Numbers Cooligan as they crowd around the young boy. Sure enough, there he is, the same fat-gutted, curled-moustached kraut, with his balding hair parted down the centre of his skull and brought to two little wings above his eyebrows, bollocky, except for his socks and suspenders and, as usual, chock-a-block up a plump black-eyed woman.

'Told yer, didn't I!' Hornbill says triumphantly, holding his hand out for Cooligan's shilling.

While they are in Egypt, the name Anzac is born out of circumstances less than romantic. General Sir W. R. Birdwood, a British general stationed in India, is appointed by Lord Kitchener to be in overall command of the Australian and New Zealand troops and leaves India immediately to take up his posting. His job is to train the Australians and New Zealanders into a concerted and united fighting division. Before departing he writes to General

Bridges and asks him what he proposes they should call the Australian Division when it is united with the New Zealand Brigade under his overall command.

Bridges proposes 'Australasian Army Corps', but the New Zealanders object to this. To them it smacks too much of Australia and not enough of The Land of the Long White Cloud. They finally settle for the rather clumsy mouthful, 'Australian and New Zealand Army Corps'. Soon afterwards, the clerks in ordnance take to identifying goods received by the initials Anzac, which soon enough becomes the accepted acronym. Thus, in a simple and uncomplicated way, a legend is born.

General Birdwood, as it turns out, is an excellent choice as the commander of the two forces, for he lacks much of the fuss and nonsense and the reliance on due ceremony to which most of the ageing British generals are accustomed and which they demand as their God-given right. His easygoing outlook and genuine regard for the troops under his command will make him popular with the Australians and New Zealanders, who resent the rigid authority the British troops accept without questioning. He seldom if ever judges a man by the shine of his boots or deprecates him for the roughness of his voice or whether he salutes or addresses an officer with the right amount of respect, and actively discourages this form of sententious bullying.

He clearly understands that, in the Australian and New Zealander, he is dealing with a different sort of man. The antipodeans possess a genuine abhorrence of taking pains with their appearance beyond what is tidy and functional.

As General Birdwood once remarked to General Bridges, 'They're tall enough and big enough and, I daresay, more than brave enough, to make splendid guardsmen, but they'd never tolerate the spit and polish!'

To the amazement of their British counterparts, the Australians love fresh air and cold water and, together with their refusal to adopt an obsequious attitude to officers of almost any rank, this distinguishes them from a great many of their counterparts in the various armies collected under the Allied banner.

But it isn't all sweetness and light at Mena camp. Never at heart regular soldiers, Australians off duty consider themselves civilians, full of high spirits and looking to amuse themselves by taking every opportunity to make the most of their time away from home. Like Napoleon's troops and those of earlier British regiments stationed in Egypt, the Australians write their names on the Pyramids. They have money in their pockets and, after two months of being cooped up in transports without being allowed ashore at Colombo or Aden, they have adventure in their hearts. This makes for a highly combustible combination as they invade the bright lights of Cairo and Heliopolis, which proves not to be a city designed for the entertainment of young men and is lamentably lacking in respectable diversions such as sport, theatre or outdoor recreation.

Shepheards and the Continental Hotel, the only two sources of any sort of European culture, are, by tradition, reserved for officers, which leaves only the cafes, the bazaar where some are taught to smoke hashish, and the brothels and sex shows for the men. In the cafes the mostly Greek proprietors serve them poisonous arak and gut-wrenching meals and the brothels, with few exceptions, are diseased and dirty. Fired up with arak and a sense of being out on the town, the young men willingly follow touts to 'exhibitions' of the vilest nature.

The Clicks, led by Numbers Cooligan, set off in search of grand adventure. The tram from the camp is so overloaded with laughing and boisterous men that soldiers are piled onto the roof and bunch out from either of the two entrances, clinging to each other for dear life, all the way to the centre of Cairo.

'If you think Aden was good wait till we get to Cairo,' Numbers Cooligan promises those in the platoon who hadn't been fortunate enough to be present at the now legendary Belly Dunce and Snake performance in Aden.

'How do you know it will be better? I thought you said Belly Dunce and Snake couldn't be bettered?' Library Spencer reminds him.

'Yeah, the best of its kind. But here they're real serious, mate. It stands to reason, don't it, Aden's a pisspot city compared to Cairo. The bigger the pot the more piss it holds, get my drift, gentlemen!' Which is about as close as Cooligan has ever come to a serious aphorism.

Carrying two months' wages in their pockets they show not a scintilla of resistance when an oleaginous tout, with a pencil moustache and dark rings around his eyes deep as a boxer's bruises, persuades them to see a woman copulating with a donkey. On a second occasion, another local low-life leads them to a large room which is more or less in darkness, with a single spotlight positioned over a small stage, under which and, in the presence of several hundred troops, a woman with pantaloons made of a diaphanous net material with the crutch missing, does the splits, picking up shilling coins which the troops throw onto the stage using only her 'it' muscles.

The one curious aspect of this basically boring performance is that she continues picking up a copious number of coins without apparently ever depositing them anywhere. They leave when, to the general hilarity and agonised cries of the performer, some bastard, using a pair of tweezers and a couple of Swan Vesta matches, heats a coin to an almost red-hot condition and throws it onto the stage.

'Shit!' Hornbill says when they're back in the alley. 'That was a shit thing to do, even if she were no lady!'

Numbers Cooligan appears to be thinking, 'If she's done the splits two times a minute, that's every thirty seconds, and what they thrown on the platform was a shilling each time, 'cause she didn't pick up nothing less, then she's making two bob a minute!' He looks at them all. 'Shit, that's six pounds an hour! Jesus, and we felt sorry for her an' all!'

'Yeah, but what I want to know is where all them coins went?' Woggy Mustafa says.

'Where do you expect? In her purse o' course,' Crow Rigby replies.

In the cold light of morning, with their heads pounding something terrible from the previous night's poisonous arak and after a good few of them have freed their stomachs of the atrocious Greek cafe meal taken at some time during their carousal, they collectively decide to give the dirty part of Cairo's night life a big miss.

Belly Dunce and Snake, whether personally witnessed, or given the benefit of Numbers Cooligan's phantasmagorical version, has set the standard by which they now judge these things. Cairo, as far as Ben's platoon is concerned, has been permanently eclipsed by the little pisspot bazaar in Aden.

They also stay away from the brothels, apart from visiting one or two to take a quick squiz at the sheilas, who turn out to be dead ringers for the woman portrayed in various compromising positions connected to the ageing male appendage belonging to the socks-and-gartered form of the ubiquitous Herman the German of

Hornbill's uncle's dirty postcards fame. Thus both the virginity and, with Cooligan, improbably, the exception, the physical health of the thirty members of Ben's platoon remains intact.

Ben, who has attended a sergeants' course on sexual hygiene, hasn't attempted to frighten them, as have so many of the junior officers or sergeants lecturing their respective platoons on venereal disease. He simply says, 'Get a dose and it's a free ticket home, lads. Then they're gunna write to your mum and tell her why you've been sent back. And you, Private Cooligan, could well be the first to go home.'

'Me, Sergeant? Never. Pure as the driven. Left me darlin' at 'ome!'

'Who's that, the cat?' Crow Rigby asks.

The behaviour of Ben's platoon is no more than high spirits. They're all big lads with too much energy, who wouldn't harm a flea unless they found it on their own person.

However, there is a much more serious aspect of behaviour among the Australian contingent – drunkenness, attacks on the local population, desertion, stealing and the wilful destruction of property. There comes a point when the excuse of high spirits among young men bent on having a good time will no longer wash with the senior military and they call for an account.

The supreme commander of the Allied Forces in Egypt, General Maxwell, draws the attention of General Birdwood to the matter and he, in turn, refers it to General Bridges, who writes to the troops appealing to their finer spirit and their country's good name abroad.

What follows is a pronounced improvement, but by early in January some three hundred men of the 1st Division are absent without leave, roaming about Cairo drunk and disorderly, thieving from the local population and defying the local authorities. In the British army this constitutes desertion and they are liable to be imprisoned or even shot, but under Australian law shooting a soldier isn't allowed, nor, for that matter, is it even contemplated and smacks rather too much of the colonial past.

However, General Bridges institutes an investigation and somewhat to his surprise discovers that the trouble comes, to a very large degree, from the older soldiers, mostly veterans from the Boer War or men who have not been born in Australia, though a young Australian-born criminal element is also present.

Bridges, in a covert message to officers of every rank, asks for their suggestions as to what might be done.

Wordy Smith tells Ben. 'You know what I would do, sir,' Ben says at last.

'What?'

'Well, we know it's not lads such as our own who are the villains.'

'That's right, it seems to be the older men, mostly ex-military and, they say, a young criminal element.'

'Yeah well, they're only a tiny fraction of the A.I.F., a pinch of sand in the desert, why don't we just send them back home?'

'What, cashier them?'

'Isn't that only for officers?' Ben asks.

'No, I don't think so, but what you mean is send them home in disgrace?'

'Well, yeah. Most, if not all, of the young lads are here to fight the Hun, they're volunteers and damn proud of having been chosen for the privilege. Let's send the troublemakers home, discharge them from the army altogether, we don't need 'em, all they're doing is giving the rest of us a bad name.'

Second Lieutenant Peregrine Ormington-Smith claps his hands gleefully. 'I say, that's splendid, Sergeant, it's almost bound to work.' He looks at Ben admiringly. 'You know, you really ought to be an officer, Sergeant Teekleman.'

Ben is genuinely appalled. 'Thank you, sir, with the greatest respect, I would consider it a demotion.'

Wordy Smith persists, 'I know you could do my job a lot better than I can, in fact mostly do. More importantly, I most certainly could not do yours. So, in a manner of speaking, I suppose it would be a demotion.' He looks at Ben steadily. 'Sergeant, it's a truly grand solution, but I can't submit it in your name to the C.O.' Ben now sees his platoon officer is visibly blushing. 'He'd . . . well, he'll know I've been talking to . . . er, other ranks, that I've abused an officer confidence, so to speak.'

Ben grins. 'Go for your life, sir. They'll probably think you're crackers.'

Wordy Smith grins back. 'Nothing new in that, Sergeant.'

But it doesn't turn out that way. Major Sayers takes the suggestion to his battalion commander Colonel Wanliss, who moves it further up the ladder to his brigade commander Brigadier

M'Cay, who finally presents it to General Bridges. The three hundred men are sent back to Australia in disgrace, accompanied by a letter to the Australian press from Bridges explaining the reasons why they are returning. Except for the comparatively minor incidents which occur in every army, this very largely settles the issues of hooliganism, criminal drunkenness and violent and inappropriate behaviour by Australian troops in Egypt.

Working on the premise that a young man who is physically exhausted is less inclined to get up to mischief, General Birdwood sets about turning the Australian Division and the New Zealand Brigade into a concerted fighting force. While he stipulates the training required he leaves it entirely up to General Bridges and his Australian and New Zealand officers to undertake. Bridges works his men intensely hard and the training in the desert often goes for twelve or fifteen hours without respite. They march and fight mock battles and do manoeuvres under the glaring desert sun until the shirts cling to their backs. Often they find themselves caught in a dust storm brought on by the howling winds of the *kamsin*. In the first two weeks the average loss of weight over this period is almost eight pounds a man.

Ben is quick to cotton on to the recurrence of a problem which affected his men in their first three weeks in the desert. His platoon, along with their company, will often stop for a rest at sunset, their flanelette vests so wet they can be wrung out by hand. Then, the moment the sun dips behind the highest dunes, an icy breeze will begin to blow. The youngsters, exhausted from eight or ten hours of manoeuvres, think the breeze a blessed relief as it dries the wet vests clinging to their backs. In a matter of days nearly two hundred troops are down with pneumonia and several die. Ben's platoon is bearing up well but Wordy Smith has developed a bad cold and is having trouble keeping up.

Ben visits his C.O. to see if they can be issued with sweaters. Major Sayers sees the sense in this, but upon enquiry discovers that ordnance has no sweaters. The British army, whose responsibility it is to supply the cold-weather uniforms, has, perhaps understandably, not considered that troops training in desert conditions will require warm clothing. It will take several weeks before they can be ordered and transported from Britain and even longer if they are to come from Australia or New Zealand.

Ben calls Numbers Cooligan and Library Spencer to his tent

the following morning. 'Right, you two will go on sick parade tomorrow . . .'

'Whaffor, Sergeant?' Cooligan asks before Ben can complete the sentence.

'Don't jump the gun, Private Cooligan, and I'll explain.'

'Yes, Sergeant, sorry, Sergeant.'

'You'll go on sick parade, I've already spoken to the sergeant on duty and he'll give you a chit, permission to miss tomorrow's manoeuvres, bronchitis. Then I want you to go into Cairo, maybe you could try the Arabs in Mena first, see if you can buy thirty-two pullovers, all of them large.'

'What, jerseys? What colour, Sergeant?' Library asks.

'Not sure we'll be given the luxury of a choice, the essential thing is that they're warm and that they're large. Be too much to expect to find thirty-two large *khaki* sweaters for the use of. Oh, and try not to pay more than ten bob a piece.'

'Yes, Sergeant . . . er . . . and the money?' Numbers Cooligan asks tentatively. 'That's sixteen quid.'

'Isn't that about as much as you've made on that two-up school you run behind the Y.M.C.A. shack of an evening?' Ben asks.

Numbers Cooligan visibly pales. 'Er . . . ah . . . shit . . . ah, what game is that, Sergeant?' Then quickly recovering, says, 'Matter a fact, I'm dead broke, skint.'

Ben hands Library Spencer four oversized white English five pound notes. 'There's plenty enough there to buy 'em and to cover your expenses, don't come back without the goods, lads, *and* I wouldn't mind some change neither.'

The two lads return to their tents. 'Shit, how'd he get twenty quid out the army?' Cooligan asks.

'He probably didn't,' Library replies.

'Whatcha mean? Ya reckon he's payin'? Out his own pocket? Twenty quid? No flamin' way, mate!'

'His name's Teekleman!'

'So?'

Library Spencer sighs. 'You ever drink Tommo & Hawk beer?'

'Sure, it's a good drop. Ballarat.'

'In Victoria it's made by a company called Solomon & Teekleman, they own the brewery in Ballarat among another squillion things.'

'That's him?'

Library nods. 'Not him personally, his family.'

'Shit hey!' Cooligan jerks his head backwards, looking at Library quizzically, 'G'arn, yer bullshittin' me? The beer? That's *him*? Jesus H. Christ!'

Numbers Cooligan and Library Spencer arrive back at Mena camp with an Arab boy who looks to be about twelve years old, leading a donkey carrying a large hessian-wrapped bale half the size of a wool bale on its back. They pull up as the sun is setting over the Great Pyramid and just as the Clicks return, exhausted from an eight-mile march into camp after all-day exercises in the desert. The men drop their kit and rifles and flop down on the sand beside the donkey while Cooligan and Library Spencer help the boy unload the bale.

'How'd yer go, lads?' Ben asks.

'Good. Real good, Sergeant.'

'Righto, let's take a look.'

Cooligan cuts the string tying the bale together and it flops open to reveal a large pile of high-quality khaki pullovers. Library and Numbers Cooligan are both wearing Cheshire cat grins.

'Khaki, Sergeant! Hows about that, eh?' Cooligan says, proud as punch.

'Well done, lads!' Ben exclaims. He is clearly impressed.

'Library 'ere done it, Sergeant,' Numbers Cooligan says in a rare moment of modesty.

'We both did,' Library says, unaccustomed to the praise. 'I did a bit o' thinking and Numbers did the bargaining.'

'Egyptian police, Sergeant. Library thought it out and we went to their headquarters in Cairo, cost a bit but we got the donkey and the boy buckshee.'

Ben is busy counting the pullovers and now looks up, 'There's fifty-two here.'

Numbers Cooligan shakes his head. 'Yeah well, I thought I'd make an investment of me own like, Sergeant.'

'How much did you pay for these?'

'Eight bob each, Sergeant. Cooligan did the bargaining,' Library repeats proudly.

'Yeah, but it become a bit complicated see,' Cooligan says hurriedly. 'Eight bob each, plus the two pound we give the police lieutenant and the quid we give the sergeant in their ordnance, then the ten shillings for the cop at the gate who let us 'ave the kid what's just been nicked fer stealing the donkey, and then just when we's loaded up . . .'

'Hold it, Private Cooligan!' Ben commands. 'Why is it that I somehow know it's all gunna come to exactly twenty quid?'

'Just a mo, Sergeant, or I'll forget where I was . . . oh yes, just as we's about to say "Oo-roo, ta-ta", with the donkey loaded an' all, the lieutenant comes out, the same bloke what's already done us for two quid, and says it's three quid for the police captain or the deal is off!' Cooligan looks at Ben. 'I tried to argue that we done a deal, Sergeant, but he don't want to know. Then I says, "Righto, no deal, gi's back the money!" I'm thinkin' like, yer know, ter bluff him. "No no! No money you get back! Three pound. The captain very hungery!" he says, looking real nasty. They's a bunch o' crooks, that lot, Sergeant, villains to the last man.' Cooligan gives a disdainful sniff and continues, 'Then there's four shillin's for a binder, just lamb and rice at a Greek's, two beers, one and six, a shillin' for the hessian and the string, sixpence for a bunch a carrots for the donkey,' Cooligan smiles benignly, 'and a shillin' to the Arab lad who stole it. And, oh yeah, I nearly forgot, two bob fer me and Library's tram fare to town in the first place.' Cooligan finishes, 'There yer go, Sergeant.'

'And that's precisely twenty pounds,' Ben repeats, a touch sardonic.

'Yeah, that's right, Sergeant?' Numbers says quizzically and looks a trifle hurt at Ben's seemingly critical tone of voice. 'We didn't charge nothin' for walking the ten miles back to Mena with the flamin' donkey!'

'Well done, you two,' Ben says and turns to Numbers Cooligan. 'And your investment? I thought you said you were skint?'

'Yeah well, I come good all of a sudden, like overnight.'

'What, the tooth fairy come?' Crow Rigby asks.

Ben laughs with the others.

'It was me own money, Sergeant!' Cooligan protests fiercely. 'Fair dinkum! I'll swear it on a stack o' Bibles!'

'It's true, Sergeant,' Library Spencer says hastily, nodding his head as further confirmation. 'He had to borrow a quid off me.'

'I wouldn't doubt you both for a moment, lads,' Ben says good-humouredly, then points to the twenty pullovers he's set to

346

one side. 'What do you think you'll get for those on the black market, Private Cooligan?'

'You mean here in the camp, Sergeant?'

Ben nods.

Numbers Cooligan, clearly relieved that he's not in trouble, thinks for a moment, his head to one side, hand stroking his chin. 'I reckon fifteen bob a piece, Sergeant, no sweat.'

'Well that's real bad luck, Private, because I'm buying them from you for eight shillings each. We're changing over to the British system of organising a platoon and a company, there's twenty more lads coming in with us. I owe you eight quid for the remaining twenty pullovers, you'll have it in the morning, Private Cooligan.' He faces the seated platoon. 'Righto, grab a pullover each and make sure you have them in your kit tomorrow. Yeah, I know it's extra weight, but if I find any of you lads without 'em, it's two days kitchooty.'

General Birdwood, on instructions from the War Office, changes the old system of company formation used by the Australians to the one adopted after the Boer War by the British. Whereas there were formerly eight platoons to a company, around two hundred and seventy men with supporting staff, they now organise into four platoons and two hundred and twenty-eight men to a company, the bigger platoons still remaining under a single subaltern.

There is a fair amount of consternation at the news of this reorganisation in the Clicks, who have always seen themselves as somewhat special and have become a very close-knit unit. Furthermore, there are now four extra subalterns in the company, second lieutenants over, and the fear is that Wordy Smith, who is plainly the worst of them all, is going to be taken away from them. While the extra men mean more work for him, Ben doesn't want to lose Peregrine Ormington-Smith. It must be one of the few occasions in military history where the men feel charged with the responsibility for maintaining the poor services of their platoon officer.

Crow Rigby voices their fears to Ben when they are out in the desert the following day. Wordy Smith has sloped off to look under a large overhanging rock some hundred yards away, no doubt seeking out some invisible-to-the-naked-eye desert flora, so the infantryman is free to speak. 'Sergeant, with this reorganisation, does that mean we're gunna lose, you know, Wordy . . . er, Lieutenant Ormington-Smith?'

The others wait anxiously for Ben's reply. 'Can't say, Private Rigby, not much we can do about it anyway.'

'Couldn't we like . . . go to the C.O. and ask him, say we'd like to keep him, Sergeant?' Hornbill asks.

Ben clears his throat, and appears a little embarrassed. 'It's . . . well, it's not the sort of thing a sergeant can do, lads.'

Put this way, they all get the message right off, a sergeant can't be seen kissing the arse of an officer, no matter how he feels about him. That means the men can't do so either.

'There's only one thing the army might take into consideration?'

'What's that, Sergeant?' Muddy Parthe asks.

'Well, with this new formation the platoon becomes the real fighting unit in the army. In the field, once the battle is closed and we're in the thick o' it, the platoon has to be an independent unit. So company commanders and the like get to know which platoons work best for what fighting job. For instance, you lads have been trained with a heavy emphasis on the rifle, I'm trained in the machine gun as well, British Maxim and the French Hotchkiss, so they'll see us as a fighting arm. I think we're potentially a good one, we can already bring more firepower to bear on the enemy than most. But we lack sappers. So, if I'm not mistaken, we'll be given a bunch of lads with shovels to round us out.' He pauses and looks about him, then goes on. 'Now if we can show Major Sayers and Colonel Wanliss and Brigadier M'Cay and some o' the brass looking on when we're on manoeuvres that we're a shit-hot unit, the best there is, well they're not going to change the subaltern, are they now, lads?'

'Jesus, Sergeant, sappers joining us? You mean like them bastards what tried to attack us on board ship?' Muddy Parthe asks.

'Well, yes.'

'More than possible,' Library Spencer says, 'Black Jack Treloar's been sent home.'

'Nothing trivial I hope?' Crow Rigby quips.

'One o' them three hundred disgraced, them what give us a bad name,' Woggy adds a little self-righteously.

'How come I don't know this?' Cooligan laments. 'I'm the Gob Sergeant, I'm supposed ter know everything!'

'No, mate, Library *knows* everything,' Woggy says.

'That's enough, lads, but yes, Sergeant Treloar's platoon is one of those to be broken up and redistributed. I've asked for at least three of them, Brodie, Matthews and Jolly.'

There is a stunned silence.

'But . . . but they were . . . ?'

Ben cuts Muddy Parthe off before he can go any further, 'Yes, the three who went to hospital, they're joining us with some others and I want you to make them welcome. And, by the way, Private Spencer, it's *Sergeant* Black Jack Treloar to such as you.'

'Jesus, now I've flamin' 'eard everything,' Cooligan gasps.

'That's enough, stow yer mess cans, it's time to move out. Private Mustafa, go fetch the lieutenant, make sure he doesn't leave anything behind.'

In the next few weeks the expanded platoon throws itself into training as if it is real war, though this is not uncommon with the 1st Division, all of whom want to make their mark. The young Australians are positively itching to go to war. The new blokes from Black Jack Treloar's platoon work as hard as the rest of them, even harder on occasions. They're naturally fit, accustomed to pick and shovel work, big, strong lads, perhaps a little basic, but tough as teak wood and scared of nothing. Like a journeyman boxer who always finds himself the sparring partner to the champion, they yearn for a chance to shine on their own.

Slogging it out in the desert is bloody hard work and the new members of the platoon give no quarter and ask no favours. Ben though is remorseless, and when the new group gets back to camp or bivouac in the desert at night he has them behind a rifle, sharpening their skills, making them catch up with the Lee-Enfield. They don't complain, which is rare for young soldiers, and from their actions it seems as if they are somewhat ashamed of Black Jack Treloar and want to make up for the bad reputation they've earned. The axe incident on the deck of the *Orvieto* has given them tremendous respect for Ben and, now that they find out he's a good bloke as well, they feel privileged to be in with the Clicks.

Brodie is an instant hit with the members of the old platoon and is immediately christened Brokenose, his hooter now considerably flattened on a face that could never be pretty but which is seldom less than cheerful. He and Library Spencer hit it off together a treat and are soon good mates. This first comes

349

about when Brodie wanders aimlessly into the Y.M.C.A., a ramshackle hut in the camp where the men can write letters home, and observes Library seated at a table writing.

'Whatcha doin' then, Library?' Brodie asks.

Library is too polite to point out that it must be perfectly bloody obvious that he's writing a letter. 'Writing home.'

'Shit hey?' Brokenose Brodie seems genuinely impressed. 'Wish I could do that.'

'Well, what's to stop you? Sit down, there's plenty o' paper, pencils, it's a free world, go for yer life.'

'Nah, can't, me old folks don't read.'

'Well, that doesn't matter, mate, somebody can read it to them, a neighbour?'

'Nah, wouldn't work.'

'Why not?'

'They's ashamed like. Too proud.'

Library looks up at the huge form of Brokenose Brodie. 'You can't write, can you, mate?'

'Course I can!' Brokenose says proudly. 'Me name.' Whereupon he takes up a pencil and on a scrap of paper he laboriously writes *KEVIN BRODIE* in the script of a seven-year-old schoolchild. 'There yer go,' he says, smiling, 'me moniker!'

'That all you can write?' Library enquires softly.

'And me army number!'

Both break up at this and somebody at another table calls, 'Shush!'

'Can't read neither, eh?' Library asks in a half-whisper.

Brokenose Brodie shakes his head.

'Wanna learn?'

'Too old, mate, I ain't got no brains, I'm a fuckin' ditch digger, ain't I?'

'Don't matter, I'll teach ya.'

'Yeah? So I can write 'ome?' Brokenose Brodie says, then he seems to have a momentary doubt. 'Me folk still can't read. Fair dinkum yer reckon yer can do it?'

'Not me, you. *You* can do it, Brokenose.' Library extends his hand which is immediately lost in Brokenose Brodie's huge callused paw.

The training the troops receive at the hands of General Bridges, though vigorous, is simply the traditional British army training from an outdated manual. Little or no advice comes to them from the Western Front, where a new kind of war is raging. The Australian and New Zealand officers must rely almost entirely on drills, tactics and manoeuvres written at another time for war in another place and after this use their own initiative.

The men are also showing that they can think on their feet and make decisions at the N.C.O. and even at the basic infantry level. It is somewhat disconcerting that when, in the mock battles they fight, the officer is killed, the platoon carries on as if nothing untoward has happened. They seem to cope with most situations they are thrown into with an almost cavalier carry-on-sergeant approach.

The troops of the 1st Division have toughened, their bodies almost black from exposure to the Egyptian sun. At the end of January a further ten thousand five hundred new Australian troops and two thousand New Zealanders arrive with Colonel John Monash in charge of the 4th Infantry Brigade. They are fine specimens all but they appear soft compared to the desert-hardened Australians and New Zealanders. Nobody in the War Office seems to have asked themselves whether troops trained to fight in the desert in wide-open spaces under a cloudless sky will be able to adapt to the trenches of Flanders and France. Just how these sons of Australia will react in an actual battle is anyone's guess.

In Europe the men are learning to fight in trenches, often up to their knees in mud on battlefields covered in early morning mist or in a perpetual haze of smoke from heavy artillery shells and mortar attacks. Meanwhile, the Australians and New Zealanders have never seen a bomb or been subject to, or even heard, the roar and thunder of a sustained artillery attack, or the whine of a shell passing overhead, nor, in fact, experienced anything beyond the pop-pop of the 18-pounder field gun a four-man crew can drag into position. Most have never even seen a periscope and few of the thirty thousand men have fired a shot in anger except perhaps at a crow or a dingo. About the only thing they can be said to understand with a thoroughness of purpose is barbed wire and how to crawl through it. Furthermore, most of them can use a Lee-Enfield rifle with some skill and the bayonet attached with a singular and determined efficiency, that is, if you consider an unprotesting bag of sand the equivalent of an enemy.

Nevertheless, the intelligence shown by the men as they work their way on their bellies around a knoll or mount a night attack prompts a senior regular-army English officer, newly arrived to take up a position as adviser on Birdwood's staff, to remark, 'A better division than the 1st Australian together with the New Zealand Brigade has never gone to battle.'

When the platoon and company exercises are completed, Ben's platoon is singled out as one of the three best in the 1st Division. Wordy Smith receives congratulations for their conduct in the field and a personal letter of commendation from General Bridges. In part the letter which Wordy Smith reads to the platoon says:

My only regret is that we did not have an enemy and a battle at hand to test your platoon, for I feel certain you and your men would have come through with flying colours.

That evening after tea the 'belly dunce and snake six', plus Brokenose Brodie, who now makes a regular seventh member of their mob, are seated in the soldiers' mess when Crow Rigby suddenly says, 'Hey, wait a mo, what if, after all our 'ard work keepin' him safe from himself, Wordy Smith gets a promotion?'

'Dead right!' Numbers Cooligan exclaims. 'We wouldn't know how to operate without him! He's like being a champion jockey what's always been given an unfair handicap and is gunna show the bastards he can still win the flamin' race!'

'Nah, it couldn't happen,' Library Spencer says. 'Not even the general is *that* stupid.'

There is a momentary silence whilst they all think about this and then Crow Rigby mutters, 'I dunno, I'm not so sure about that.'

'What?'

'The general.'

Around the middle of March, rumours are coming thick and fast. The British navy, in an effort to aid Russia by creating a supply line through the Bosphorus, fails when her ships are unable to force their way through the straits of the Dardanelles. Like everyone else, Britain has underestimated the Turks and arrogantly assumed the Dardanelles at their narrowest point will be easily breached by her navy and they will sail on to bombard Constantinople and force Turkey out of the war and so, in a military sense, kill two birds with one stone.

The failure of the navy's attempt to force the straits makes a land attack on the peninsula almost inevitable. Though little of this is reported at the troop level, Wordy's Wireless is still working. News is fairly freely discussed in the officers' mess and Wordy Smith briefs Ben daily on what he hears.

The 3rd Brigade has disappeared a month ago and Wordy's Wireless has it that they're in Lemnos practising landing from the sea. Furthermore, Sister Atkins scribbles a note to Ben to inform him that Jolly and Matthews previously from Sergeant Treloar's platoon need to see the army dentist now that their gums have had time to heal properly. In her note she mentions that the nurses have been ordered to get sunhats, which, she says, seems rather curious as they are all working indoors.

Much as Ben tries to see some special message and encouragement in the note which will enable him to make another advance to Sister Atkins, he is forced to concede that hers is simply a duty performed in the interest of the two lads. The sunhat information is couched as though she thinks it is a wonderful example of bumbling army bureaucracy. Ben knows it is strictly forbidden to fraternise with someone of officer rank, but in a moment of lovesickness he seriously contemplates catching pneumonia so that she might be brought to his bedside.

Much of this rumour and speculation about an imminent invasion is given out via Gob Sergeant Cooligan in the hope that it will attract further confirmation from other sources. In the Mena camp Wordy's Wireless has lost none of its potency and has developed into a sort of highly sophisticated rumour cross-reference system. Library Spencer is charged with monitoring what comes back after a soundly based Gob-Sergeant rumour is circulated.

It is surprising how much information can be gathered in tiny scraps from the observations of clerks, the military police, the officers' mess, the soldiers who drive the top brass around, even the barber who cuts the hair of the officers at General Hamilton's headquarters at Shepheards or the corporals and privates who operate the various telephone switchboards. In fact there are a hundred different sources, the note from Sister Atkins being an excellent example of one of them. They learn how, when it is all co-ordinated, it is often possible to get surprisingly close to the truth. The proverbial grapevine has always worked in the army and what Ben is now doing is trying to create a sturdier and stronger vine with further-reaching tentacles.

For want of a better system it works pretty well and they soon develop an instinct for what is true. They firmly believe they're going to fight the Turks somewhere along the coastline of the Dardanelles sometime in early April, though for a while they think the Australians are going to invade Alexandretta and are surprised when this comes to nothing as it qualified on almost all fronts as sound information.

Meanwhile, the Turks have launched a raid on the Suez Canal and although they are repulsed by the British and Indian troops, it becomes apparent from the reports sent in that they are no easy-beats. A new respect is growing for the fighting capacity of the Turkish soldier and they are no longer considered a second-class fighting force unworthy of the Anzacs.

Almost by sheer fluke the training they have undergone in the desert is not entirely redundant, the terrain around the straits is known to be hilly and, though hardly equivalent to the desert, it would appear they will be fighting a war in the open. Besides, they have grown accustomed to climbing steep dunes and rocky ridges and it will be a nice change to have firm ground under their feet as they advance against the enemy. And advance they will. There is not a single man from general to trooper and soldier who doubts for a moment that they will destroy the enemy, even though the Germans are training the Turks.

The first of April is a Thursday, still three days before the leg-weary platoon can expect a day off. Ben comes out of his tent at dawn to another cloudless sky. Though it is still cold, the sun not yet risen, he knows the temperature will climb above a hundred and ten degrees before noon. They are involved in a field day out along the burning dunes which he doesn't much look forward to.

Ben, sick to the back teeth with Egypt, wonders how long it will be before they leave for the Peninsula to fight against the Turks. In the dawn light he takes from the breast pocket of his tunic the letter he has received from Victoria in the previous day's mail. He has already read it half a dozen times but does so again. Rubbing his forefinger and thumb along the edge of the paper he imagines his sister writing it, a cool breeze blowing off the Derwent rustling the curtains as it enters gently through a bright, sunlit window. She will be seated at Mary's old desk, which she tells him Hawk has removed from the Potato Factory and brought to her small study in Ann Solomon's Hobart cottage which she and Hawk now occupy.

Hobart

5th February 1915

My dearest Ben,

You must be thoroughly sick of receiving a letter from me with almost every overseas mail arriving in Egypt, I simply cannot help myself. My mind is so constantly occupied with thoughts of you that my only comfort is to sit down at Mary's old desk and write to you for the sheer relief of getting my thoughts down on paper. I pray each night that you are safe, though God does not seem to be listening, if what's happening at the front is any indication.

Grandfather Hawk says much of what is happening in France is being kept from us. Heaven forbid, what we do hear is horrific enough and, while it may seem unpatriotic, every day you are kept away from the battlefield means another night I can sleep without wondering whether the morning will bring bad news.

I'm sorry to sound so pessimistic and not my usual cheerful self (the newspapers urge us always to sound cheerful when writing to the troops), but Grandfather Hawk brought back the news last night that Joshua, who has already been promoted to captain, has been transferred to be second in command of an ordnance company and is unlikely to see any fighting.

Abraham Solomon, who is visiting us here in Tasmania for a few days, says it is because of his thorough business training, they need men like him because the logistics of war supply require good, sound business principles. In your own words, all I can say is 'Bulldust!' We know perfectly well somebody has pulled strings! And pulled them b . . . . y hard too! It all seems so unfair that he should get a cushy job safe from harm and you will eventually be sent to the front line to fight the Hun.

I can almost see you smiling, I know you wouldn't change places with him for all the tea in China. But please! Please! I beg you to be careful. I simply couldn't bear it if you got wounded, especially knowing you-know-who was safe and sound counting tins of bullybeef.

In a more cheerful vein, I am going up to Launceston next week to see about opening a new warehouse. We are taking a bit of a drubbing from the James Boag Brewery because we sometimes run short of T & H beer in the local market and they, being on the spot, are quick to take advantage. I must say they are keen as mustard and we will have to be on our toes if we are going to keep our share of that market. Grandfather Hawk also wants me to look at a small factory turning out woollen blankets as he thinks he can get a contract from the government for supplies to the troops training here in Tasmania.

He seems a different person now that he is back in control again and looks years younger with a definite spring in his step. I simply don't know where he gets his energy! I am learning a great deal from him, though the thought of taking over if he should pass on is frightening, he is so wise and patient and is completely in control and on top of things. For my part I remain confused and I still have no clear idea of all we own, what's more I am led to believe Tasmania is the smaller part of S & T. We went for a spin in the new Wolseley tourer on Sunday and Grandfather Hawk pointed out a dozen buildings and factory works which he said we owned. It's really quite daunting.

I must end now as this has to catch the mail boat to Melbourne to connect with another travelling via Suez. I have become quite the expert at shipping routes since your departure.

Mrs Billings sends her love, she is knitting you a pair of gloves and seems to be taking ages. Sardine the cat has developed a permanent nose drip and she speaks of little else, being quite sure that 'he is not long for this mortal coil'. She is comforted by the thought that her dear moggy will join her sainted husband, the immortal, though never existing in actual human form, Mortimer Billings. She says to tell you that if you should be cooking rice to add prunes to it as they prevent constipation and give the rice a nice savoury flavour! They should be soaked in water overnight and then the rice cooked in the prune juice together with the prunes. She has never quite gotten over, as she sees it, her appointment as Cook to the Australian Forces Abroad and tells everyone she can earbash for long enough about her billyjam tarts!

Grandfather Hawk says he will write to you at length next week, but to tell you the hops crop is looking splendid this year and everyone on the estate asks for news of you. They all send their love and best wishes, he also sends his love.

Will you get the chance to go to Luxor, I believe it is well worth the visit and, looking at the map, is not far from where you are?

Please try and stay away from the fighting as long as you

are able and give my regards to your platoon, they seem like such nice lads and I am sure are very fond of you. I cannot imagine you being a strict sergeant who they have cause to fear. Taking twenty more young soldiers under your wing must be an added worry though. Grandfather Hawk says sappers can be a rough lot. I hope this is not true in your case? The desert sounds beastly hot, as usual the weather here in Hobart changes five times each day and I despair of ever wearing the right clothes when I go out to work of a morning.

 I miss you terribly!! Write if you can, I constantly long for news of you.

  Your loving sister,
  Victoria.

P.S. Please make sure you always wear your Tiki, I know it's all superstitious nonsense, but our mother said it will keep you safe and she was half-Maori and we are a quarter. I don't know what that's supposed to mean, but just wear it because it's in your blood!

V.

The bugle sounds reveille and Ben goes over to the cook-house to get a mug of hot water in order to shave. Upon his return he sees Brokenose Brodie fully kitted outside his tent, seated on an empty ammunition box with a slate on his lap busy writing. Ben can see by the way he holds himself that the process is one of a most earnest endeavour.

'Mornin', Private Brodie, what are you up to?'

Brokenose looks up. 'Doin' me 'omework, Sergeant. Library's learnin' me to read and write.'

'Good on ya, Private. Soon be writing home to the folks, eh?'

Brokenose Brodie grins but then immediately goes back to work. 'I'm sorry, Sergeant, I can't talk,' he says, his head bowed over his slate. 'I were that tired last night I didn't get me 'omework done and Library's gunna kick me arse from 'ere to Jerusalem!'

The platoon's day is spent out in the desert in a mock battle with the 4th Light Horse Regiment combining with the 1st and 2nd Infantry Brigades to attack one of the high desert ridges. The Light Horse, sent in first to seize the ridge, get there before the enemy, but the 1st Infantry Brigade advancing up the other half of the ridge is held up and the Light Horse are placed in an unsustainable position. If the enemy should reach them before their own infantry they do not have the firepower to hold the position. Ben's battalion with the 2nd Infantry Brigade, who are meant to advance behind the Light Horse, seeing their position is in jeopardy, advances at the double to the top of the ridge faster than seems possible to the two brigadiers, M'Cay and MacLaurin, who are jointly directing the battle. They now see the long line of each company showing dark against the white glare of the sand dunes as they suddenly spring into existence, sweeping, one line after another, across the hillside to take it and bring the fight to an end. A British officer, observing, turns to M'Cay with the comment, 'Could not have been better.' It is apparent to everyone that the Australians are thoroughly trained and ready for the fray.

Late that afternoon when the troops return to camp, instead of being dismissed, they remain on parade and the officers are told that the Australian 1st Division is moving out, and all but the Light Horse and the Mounted Rifles are going to the front. They are to proceed immediately with the evacuation of the Mena camp.

A tremendous cheer goes up as each company is informed. The young infantrymen break rank and are seen clapping each other on the shoulders and backs, sending their slouch hats and caps high into the air. There is no possible way they can be brought to heel. They have waited too long for this moment. This is what they've worked for. At last the time has come for the colonial lads to prove their mettle against a real enemy.

The Anzacs are ready for war.

Chapter Thirteen

THE LANDING

Gallipoli 1915

'Righto, get this into your thick heads,' Ben says. 'We know they'll be waiting for us, it's never easy to invade from the sea, the defender on land always has the advantage and in this case there is every likelihood of high ground involved. That means they'll be looking down on us.'

Ben's platoon is gathered together on a sheltered part of the deck of the *Novian*, one of the transports carrying the Anzacs to Lemnos. They are a day out from Alexandria, hugging the coast of Asia Minor, the weather turning increasingly foul. Ben's platoon is seated under a tarpaulin on the deck where Lieutenant Peregrine Ormington-Smith, together with Ben, is briefing them.

Although they are not supposed to know their destination, there isn't a man in the Australian 1st Division who doesn't have a fair idea of where they're headed after the Greek island of Lemnos. In Library Spencer's words, 'A man would have to be a bit of an idjit not to know that it'll be somewhere along the coastline o' the Dardanelles and that we're gunna get as close to the Narrows as possible.'

'Let me give you an example of what we might expect,' Ben continues. 'We'll probably wait until the moon goes down.'

'Yeah, we've already seen what 'appens when you attack in bright moonlight,' Numbers Cooligan says, obviously referring to the axe incident on the *Orvieto*. Several of the men look at Brokenose Brodie, Matthews and Jolly.

Brokenose brings his big paw up and rubs his flattened nose. 'Yeah, it ain't the best idea,' he says a little ruefully, 'buggers can see yiz.'

Ben ignores the remark, though it gets a laugh. 'The moon should go down around three o'clock, maybe a bit later. That will give us a little more than an hour of darkness to get the men into the boats and start for the shore. The idea will be to land well before sun-up, but with the dawn light to see by. We'll want to be clear of the water and the beach before sun-up so the enemy fire can't pick us off in broad daylight. Hopefully we'll be up and onto the higher ground and engaging the enemy, which will be made a great deal more difficult because the sun will be at their backs and we'll be looking directly into it.' Ben looks at the men about him. 'That's the first wave going in.' He stops, not knowing quite how to tell them. 'But we're not going to be with them, lads, we're going in on the second wave.'

There is a groan from the platoon and it is obvious they are bitterly disappointed, Hornbill and Crow Rigby and several others bury their faces in their hands.

'Ain't that bloody typical, eh?' Numbers Cooligan howls. 'The best there is they leave for seconds.'

When Lieutenant Ormington-Smith told his sergeant of this decision Ben had been forced to conceal his own disappointment. Had he been allowed to rejoin his Tasmanian battalion he would be in the 3rd Brigade and among the first ashore.

'It stands to reason the 3rd Brigade will be the first to land,' he now says. 'They've been at Lemnos a month practising, we're bloody lucky to be in the second wave. So, don't get your knickers in a knot, Private Cooligan. If things go wrong, as they mostly do in battle, going in on the second wave won't be no Sunday school picnic.'

'But, Sergeant, what if them first lot, the 3rd Brigade, do all the fighting and there's none left for us?' Hornbill says and most of the others shake their heads, the possibility too awful to contemplate.

'That won't happen, lads, Johnny Turk is defending his homeland and we're the invaders. What's more, they've got the high ground looking down, they're sitting pretty.' He continues, 'Now, let's get this straight once and for all, the worst thing we can do is underestimate the Turk. In a moment the lieutenant here will tell you a bit about these blokes and it ain't bullshit neither, but let me first give you an example of the logistics involved, paint you a picture of what could happen.'

Ben turns to Crow Rigby. 'Private Rigby, you're an enemy sniper, you're nicely dug in say four hundred feet above the beach and let's say at a distance of three hundred yards. It's broad daylight, seven o'clock and the sun well up, bit of smoke around from the guns but you can see clearly enough. You're watching as our battalion jumps from the boats and starts to wade up to their waists towards the beach, maybe a hundred yards through the shallows. It's gunna take an hour to get all the men onto the beach and into the scrub. Now here's my question. How many men do you reckon, as a lone enemy sniper with telescopic sights, you can take out in a minute?'

Crow Rigby thinks for a moment then squinting up at Ben asks a question himself. 'I've got an offset mounted MKIII Lee-Enfield, right? With an Aldis No. 3 sight on Holland & Holland mounts?' While he has been trained as a sniper, Crow Rigby has elected to stay in the platoon, but his careful question now reflects his meticulous training.

'Well, technically speaking, no, you're the enemy remember, you'll be using a Mauser which is a better marksman's rifle than the S.M.L.E. and the best of your German optics and mountings are as good as, if not better than, any we've ever made.'

Crow Rigby nods. 'Righto, if I had Woggy here to spot for me, I reckon I could get a real good shot off every ten seconds, Sergeant.' He nods again. 'Yeah, that shouldn't be too hard. In theory anyway, it's a big ask in practice.'

'Strewth! Three hundred and sixty dead or wounded in an hour,' Numbers Cooligan shouts. 'That's our whole flamin' company and half another one!'

There is a stunned silence as the men think about what Crow Rigby has just said.

'And that's just the potential of one sniper,' Ben says at last. 'Gawd knows how many they'll have, and, as well, every other Turk not busy fighting off the 3rd Brigade will be emptying his rifle in the direction of the beach, not to mention their gun batteries and their machine guns.'

'Shit, eh?' Brokenose Brodie says. 'And I thought they was just wogs!'

Ben smiles. 'As Private Rigby says, that's in theory, I don't believe any sniper has ever achieved that many kills in one day.'

'Sergeant, the sun, even if it were up an hour or so, would be shining directly into Crow's eyes,' Library Spencer points out rather pedantically. Ben thinks he would probably make a good officer one day.

'Well said, Private Spencer, so let's hope like hell it ain't a cloudy day like today. But that's not the real point, we'll be sitting ducks blind Freddy couldn't miss. All I want you to get into your noggins is that we're fighting a *real* enemy this time and we'll be at a distinct disadvantage. What's more, if you ever get close enough to use your bayonets, it won't be against an unprotesting sandbag.' He looks about him at the men seated on the deck. 'So when we hit the beach don't stand about chewin' the fat, concealment is everything, once up into higher ground we'll probably be digging like wombats, we'll use whatever cover is available and we're not, I repeat, we're not, any of us, gunna try to be heroes! I don't want any of you lads winning a flamin' medal, because it will probably be given to your mum posthumously.' Ben turns to Wordy Smith. 'The lieutenant is now going to give you a bit of a history lesson, it's just as well to know something about the enemy's past form.'

'Yes er well, thank you Sergeant Teekleman, I er . . . yes, ah . . .' Wordy Smith begins, then clears his throat and looks about nervously. Nobody takes any notice, his apparent nervousness stems from the old Wordy Smith who hasn't entirely conquered the mannerisms that went with his previous persona. Among these is the habit of looking at his boots as he talks.

Lieutenant Peregrine Ormington-Smith begins again. 'Yes well, the Turks, better known in history as the Ottomans, created an empire that lasted just six years short of four hundred years. Until just three years ago they still held Greece, Macedonia and Crete. For the greater part of these four hundred years they controlled all of the Middle East from Iraq to Tripoli, they captured Malta, besieged Vienna and controlled all of the Balkans and south-eastern Europe as far as Budapest.' Wordy Smith reels off these names and places quite oblivious to the fact that the platoon, for the most part, probably hasn't heard of many of them. 'Their navy, well actually the Turkish-Egyptian fleet, under Admiral Ibrahim Pasha, terrorised the Mediterranean until it was finally defeated at Navarino by the

French, Russian and English under Vice Admiral Sir Edward Codrington on the twentieth of October 1827. But even after this, none of the great powers were keen to take on such a brave and fanatical enemy on the land.' Wordy Smith clears his throat before continuing. 'For a good deal of this time Russia saw Turkey as her greatest enemy and fought her constantly in an attempt to gain access from the land-locked Black Sea into the Mediterranean. Constantinople guarded the entrance to the Bosphorus and from there into the Sea of Marmara, down the Dardanelles into the Aegean and finally the Mediterranean. Russia never succeeded.'

'Yeah, sir, but all that Otto-Empire, like you says, that was a long time ago, we seen the Muslims in Egypt, they ain't much chop?' Hornbill suggests.

'Wogs in pyjamas,' Numbers Cooligan adds dismissively.

'It's true, the Turks are Muslims, but that's where the comparison ends. They are a fighting nation who goes to battle in the name of Allah. When a Turkish soldier dies in battle he believes he goes directly to Paradise, they are not a people who are afraid to die. Australia has been in existence for one hundred and twenty-seven years, to these people that's the day before yesterday. Believe me, they didn't give up when the Romans invaded, or the Crusaders, the British, the French, the Russians.' Lieutenant Ormington-Smith pauses, perhaps realising that the history lesson is going a bit beyond most of them.

'That's right,' Ben interjects, 'so they ain't gunna be shitting their britches now, they'll be thinking we Australians just hatched from the latest batch of eggs in Farmer Brown's chookyard.'

'I should also remind you,' Wordy Smith continues, 'no more than a few weeks ago in an attempt to force their way up the Dardanelles the combined might of the British and French navies pounded the Turkish forts guarding the Narrows with everything they could throw at them.' Then borrowing his vernacular from Ben the lieutenant concludes, 'And got their arses soundly kicked by the Turks once again.'

There is some laughter at this last remark for it is the first time the platoon has ever heard Wordy Smith express himself in anything but the most correct manner.

'These here Dardanelles where we's goin', Lieutenant,' Muddy Parthe asks, 'is they the same ones Russia tried to get and where the Poms and the Frogs got their arses kicked?'

'Quite right, Private, the Turks have been defending this narrowest part successfully for four hundred years.'

'So that's why we're goin' there, eh? To kick their arses back,' Brokenose Brodie exclaims, pleased with himself for seeing the plot so clearly.

It is probably the first time that the platoon truly knows why they are fighting the Turks and although Sir Ian Hamilton, the supreme commander of the campaign, is better informed than Muddy Parthe, his attitude to the Turkish soldier doesn't appear to be vastly different from that of Hornbill or Numbers Cooligan.

Surgeon-General Birrell has come to him to point out that he hasn't sufficient hospital ships and medical supplies to care for the wounded and has no way to get them off the beaches unless he uses the ships' boats. He is sharply rebuffed by Hamilton who tells him the need to get stores and equipment ashore as quickly as possible takes priority over wounded men.

Hamilton, if he assumes a low casualty rate, has obviously forgotten Europe's long and bloody history against the Turks. As it turns out, very little serious thought seems to have gone into the evacuation of the wounded by the staff officers at his H.Q.

Hamilton's order to the surgeon-general can only be seen in one of two possible ways, either it is a lack of concern for the welfare of the men fighting under his command or he has a low opinion of the fighting capacity of the Sons of Allah.

If the first supposition is correct he is not the only general in this war to have a laissez-faire attitude to the number of men killed and wounded under his command. If the second, which is unlikely, for it is common knowledge among the officers who openly tell their men that casualties could be as high as thirty per cent, then quite simply Hamilton is guilty of gross incompetence. A good commander, given the time, is charged with planning a correct outcome for these components without having to sacrifice one for the other.

On their arrival on the island of Lemnos, just thirty miles from the Dardanelles, the weather hasn't improved. In fact, it is worse, with a strong wind blowing up a rough sea in the large but essentially shallow harbour at Mudros. This, in effect, means a postponement of the April 21st invasion. In the deeper, more treacherous waters of the Dardanelles, there would be no hope of successfully unloading the boats and getting troops ashore under such difficult conditions.

The wind continues for two more days, only moderating somewhat on the evening of the twenty-third. Meanwhile the men are made to practise getting into the small boats from their transports in the choppy conditions of Mudros Harbour. Even in the comparatively shallow water this proves to be a tricky exercise.

Just after noon on the twenty-fourth, the *Novian,* carrying the 5th Battalion together with the Brigade H.Q. and the Indian Army Mule Artillery, sails from Mudros to the Bay of Purnea on the northeast of the island. Although they sail into a stiff breeze all the way, the weather seems to be clearing and by sunset it has practically died down. Squinting into the setting sun, they see five battleships in line astern, slowly heading for the Dardanelles and a place which will eventually become known simply as Gallipoli. On board are the 3rd Brigade who will make the initial assault before the sun rises over Asia Minor.

After the moon sets, Ben's own transport slips its mooring and under a bright moon, sails the thirty miles to the spot on the map where the Anzac landing will take place. They arrive just as the 3rd Brigade is being lowered into boats, each man carrying ninety pounds of kit and equipment on his back. Many of them must climb down the steep sides of the battleships using rope ladders that are swinging wildly from the weight of the frantically clutching soldiers ahead of them, most of whom are fortified with a liberal supply of rum. Even with the practice they've undergone at Lemnos it proves a difficult and trying procedure, as it takes place in the inky darkness and with the added strain of what lies ahead. Fifteen thousand men are going into battle for the first time, in complete silence, jumping into little boats, which, to their great good fortune, are barely bobbing on a glass-calm sea. These are young men from a nation of beer drinkers, their heads a little fuzzy from the unaccustomed rum, each wondering to himself if he'll be good enough, courageous enough and won't let down his mates.

At 3 a.m. the moon sinks beyond the horizon. The cliffs they could clearly see under the moon now disappear in the pre-dawn darkness. The night is so densely dark that you can almost touch it. Only the soft pulse of the battleship's engines sends a slightly hollow sound against the hull to remind you that you are not alone.

It is a curious thing to be alone. You have become accustomed to being identified by your group, your brigade, your company, your platoon, but most of all by your mates. Those blokes you have trained with, who crawled sweating beside you in the sand under the blazing desert sun, to whom you clung, bunched together, on the platform of the tram to Cairo, got drunk on arak in the bazaar, laughed and backslapped, chundered in an alley that smelt of piss and shit while your mate steadied you, jeered, chaffed and constantly mocked each other. You no longer belong to your own silence, this is your true identity now.

Each of you sits silent and remote, realising that the problem is the silence itself. That your mates are mostly known to you by the noises they make, the pitch of their voices, the nature of their wisecracks, their stupidity, shrewdness, shyness, boastfulness, bullshitting, modesty and easygoing comradeship, the expressions they use to announce themselves, their weaknesses and their strengths, never allowing you to see their fear, the fear you now feel yourself and think it must be yours alone.

All these things have been constantly with you for the past few months, they have become as familiar to you as rifle drill so that you can't imagine yourself as a separate part of the whole, or them as no longer a part of your life. And now, when you have to face the moment of truth, they are silent, you are silent, all the touchstones are gone. The familiar voices you have come to rely upon are gagged, the whingers and optimists, the cynics and those who believe with something that shines in their eyes, they're all silent in your rum-heated heart. In the pre-dawn chill there is only the creak of the rowlocks and the slap of a wave against the hull of the wooden lifeboat and the soft pulse of the engines within the dark hull looming up beside your fragile wooden boat.

You are aware for the first time since you stood in the recruitment queue that you are alone, the hard flat wooden seat under your arse turning it numb and the pack on your back the only extension of yourself you are aware of. One towel, one extra vest, socks two pairs, greatcoat, cap, comforter, a change of underclothing (must die with clean underpants, remember throw away the pair you shit yourself in), three empty sandbags rolled up and neatly tied onto your shovel at the back. Three days' rations – two tins of bullybeef, Fray Bentos (doesn't sound Australian), three pounds of hard biscuits (the ones left over at Arnott's from the Boer War). Then the little white bag of iron rations tied around your neck, half an ounce of tea (no fuckin' billy), two ounces of sugar and a jar of extract of beef. Two hundred rounds of ammunition, your rifle and bayonet, the killing load three times as heavy as the food that will hopefully sustain you for the next seventy-two hours, that is if you're not shot right off coming out of the shallows with this heap of shit resting on your shoulders.

In the moonlight you clearly see the cliffs and the land rising steeply from the sea and the fall of land to flatness on the end to the north of a place the Turks called Gaba Tepe on the map, the obvious place to come ashore. But now you only face darkness.

It is a blackness where you know men with cold hands and broken fingernails blow on their clenched fists and wait, their rifles and machine guns oiled, barrels cleaned, spare magazine clips and ammunition belts in reserve, for you to announce your arrival on their land, their beloved country.

They are waiting on the same hills, facing the same coastline where their ancestors fought the Greeks and the Romans, and where they repulsed the Infidel Crusaders carrying their tortured Holy Cross before them into battle, their emaciated bodies and fair peeling skins burnt a crimson colour and their hard, hollow eyes fixed on the cross, prepared to die in the name of the Prophet Christ. Then there were the strutting French and the pompous British, both braided in gold and uniformed in red and blue, both nations vainglorious and arrogant to the point of infinite stupidity. And always, there was the bearded Russian bear trying to shoulder his way through the narrow and jealously guarded sea lanes, never quite learning that he faced a formidable enemy who never failed to singe his fur and send him scurrying back to the safety of the Black Sea.

And now, with spring arrived and the hope of the new wheat already greening the land, the tender shoots broken through the winter-hardened clods and the first of the scarlet poppies in bloom on the thistle and weed-fringed edges of the fields, comes a new tribe of men. Giants with loose shoulders and gangling, easy strides, infidels who have come from somewhere near the bottom of the earth and who are determined to destroy you, murder your innocent children and rape your wives.

And so once again the Turks must defy their entry and, in the name of the Prophet, show them their sharp, snarling teeth and be prepared, as always, to die fearlessly in the name of Allah and so gain a place in Paradise.

The boats are in four long lines, with a little coal-fired pinnace, its stack billowing smoke into the dark night, responsible for towing each line. It is infinitely slow work and, except for the soft throb of the steam engines on the sturdy little boats, one would marvel at the quiet. How can so many young men remain so still when they know that one in three of them may die before the sun sets again?

Suddenly the smokestack of one of the pinnaces sets fire, the leaping flames sending a signal of their arrival for miles, the mirror-calm sea reflecting the orange fire across a wide bay. Shit, if a match struck can be seen at sea for two miles then this inferno must be clearly seen in Constantinople itself. Yet there is no response from the cliffs lining the shore, which, as they draw closer, loom up like dark, unwelcoming shadows. The silence, the fucking silence, remains.

There is a shout, sudden and clear across the water. 'You are going the wrong way, bear over.' But no correction is made and the pinnace ahead maintains the same slow, determined, pulsing course. The voice calls again, 'Bear right, bear to starboard,' but to no avail, there seems to be an inevitability about where you will land, as though the rudder on the pinnace is stuck and it can only move directly ahead. Like all the other men in your boat you wonder what the suddenly shouted instruction must mean. How far are you off course? What will be the consequences? In the dark, how the hell does the voice know, you can't see him, how come he can see you? Why won't the pinnace bear to starboard, to the right, where in the moonlight you supposed the flatter ground to be? Any idjit can steer a flamin' boat in water calm as a mill pond.

And then the pinnace cuts the boats loose and the rowers take over, moving slowly in to the beach, the men behind the oars grunting and sweating in the dawn cold, their oars splashing as the waves created by the prows of the landing boats begin to build up.

The sudden, sharp flash of a searchlight in the distance, then another, both in the direction of Cape Helles, neither reaching you. And at last a half-heard instruction, 'Righto, lads, over the side.' The leap and the obscenely loud splash that follows as you hit the water, the relief as your boots touch the bottom. Tiny waves lap around your waist, your rifle is held above your shoulders as you attempt to wade ashore. Still dark, still safe, though the sky is beginning to lighten, the water cooling, tickling your balls. Then a single shot from the dark cliff ahead, its echo filling the silence so totally that it seems to resonate against the wall of stillness.

And then, in the words of Lance Corporal Mitchell, in the 10th Battalion, 'The key is turned in the lock of the lid of hell.'

Several of the landing boats are scythed by machine-gun fire, killing most of the men on board. Shrapnel pellets rain out of a dark sky, wounding and killing a great many of the men, the young, bright-eyed soldiers of Australia, alive at one moment, preparing to jump, and dead the next. One soldier remains seated as his comrades leap over the side, his sergeant, last but himself to jump, sees what he thinks is panic in his eyes, terror freezing him to the thwart. He reaches out to touch him, their eyes seem to meet for a moment and then the soldier topples forward into the bottom of the boat. He was dead all along, killed without a whimper, the bullet not even disturbing him in his seat. And the bullets and shrapnel pellets fall like summer hail.

The troops thresh through the water, some of them half-panicked but, trying to keep their heads, attempt to fix their bayonets. There isn't any point in firing a shot at the blank, dark wall ahead. Strict orders. 'No rifle fire is to be employed before broad daylight. The bayonet only.' Some stumble against a submerged rock and fall face-first into the surf, the kit on their back slamming them down like a fist to the back of the head, their arms and legs pumping adrenaline to get them up again. Others hit sudden unexpected depths and flailing desperately in the water their packs suck them downwards, mere arms lack the power to pull them back to the surface and they drown wearing full kit in a ring of bubbles. Others drop to their knees in the water with a soft exclamation, a low curse or a surprised bellow as a Mauser bullet smashes into them. They don't see the hole, the size of a baby's tightly clamped fist, or feel the churning together of lung and windpipe and bits of bone as the enemy's bullet enters their chest. The enemy has their range and, even without being able to see clearly, fires into the dark mass of men struggling towards the narrow strip of beach below. Ben is quite wrong, this isn't work for a sniper, this is shooting fish in a barrel. When the dawn finally comes, the surf is seen to wash a frothy deep pink onto the pebbled beach.

The order is for every man to fall in and fix bayonets. It goes further even than this, each man, with his free hand, is to hold onto the sleeve of the man beside him on a beach no more than thirty yards wide. In truth, if anyone had been stupid enough to obey this command it would be the equivalent of being deliberately lined up in front of a firing squad. 'Here you go, Johnny Turk, take your time, aim true, we'll die brave men, steady and stupid to the last.'

Instead, the troops, many of whom toss off their packs as they reach the beach, shouting like demons, rush for the cliffs, men of every company, every battalion hopelessly mixed, sergeants and officers scattered, yelling for their own blokes. Nobody listening. A Turkish battery, concealed in the half-light from the guns of the battleships who commence to pound the cliffs, bursts shrapnel over the landing troops unmercifully. Ears are not tuned to commands, orders have no significance, no meaning, the men no longer know what to do and there is no single command which can possibly make sense. Their briefing has never encompassed or anticipated anything like this. They have landed a mile further north than was intended and, instead of a steady climb, no higher than a good desert dune, they face cliffs and high ground on which no army could or would, in their right mind, contemplate an invasion. In military theory, the Anzacs are defeated before they have fired a single shot in anger.

And so, as the light grows stronger, the Anzacs climb for their lives. The beach behind them is littered with bodies and discarded packs as the men run for cover across the pebbles. Hanging around for orders is certain death, there is no military manual for this, no precedent. And so it becomes a matter of climb or die, clutching onto bush and thorn, root and rock. Boots scuff the hard red soil, sending pebbles and small rocks avalanching onto the beach below. One thought in every soldier's mind is to get off the beach, find cover, move upward, hope you see the bastard before he sees you. Stuff the bayonet, stuff a clip into your rifle. Ram one into the breech and get as far away as possible from a beach which is maybe four hundred yards long but no wider than your mum's backyard and packed with soldiers like newborn chicks in a hatchery.

The immediate slopes ahead of them are very abrupt, rising higher to the north like the walls of some eroding Crusader castle, gaunt canyons are set back slightly further from the beach and appear to be unclimbable. Once up on the slopes it quickly becomes obvious that they are a far more difficult proposition than supposed as they are broken by deep ridges, curving narrow valleys and eroded soil carved into red crumbling gullies twisting in and out of almost inaccessible funnels. Rock outcrops and deep basins, the whole of it, with the exception of the rocky, eroded gullies and cliffs, is covered with dense scrub, much of it vicious thorn. It is a virtual paradise for snipers who, having first had time to study the more likely routes to the top, can position themselves to tremendous advantage. It is not the height of the various ridges that is extraordinary but the steepness and abrupt changes of direction and the general slope which make it almost impossible for advancing infantry and virtually inaccessible for practical or co-ordinated artillery fire.

The entire battle area from extreme north to south is a mile and a half in length and exactly a thousand yards from the beach to the furthest point. In all, it is an area no larger than three-quarters of a square mile. Unbeknownst to many of the urgently climbing troops they often enough rush right past snipers, concealed in the bushes and behind rocks, who take their time to pick their kill.

The sun is well up by seven-thirty when the second wave comes in to run a well-aimed gauntlet of shrapnel, sniper and machine-gun fire. Those on the outer extremity of the beach will lie in the wash and the sun for two days before they are removed. Others, drowned by the weight of their packs, will float to the surface in the next few days. The boats and rafts bringing in supplies will become accustomed to the soft thud of a body as they bump it aside, for if there is no time to attend to the wounded, there is no space left in their minds for the dead.

Ben loses five men from his boat, Matthews and Jolly among them as they sit together one row behind him. Matthews is hit in the throat and, pitching forward, spews blood onto the pack of a soldier named Parker seated on the thwart next to Ben, who grabs him before he pitches against Parker. Warm blood spews over Ben's fist and he sees that the Mauser bullet has torn open Matthews' throat and lodged in his spine. Matthews seems to be looking directly into Ben's face. The soldier's eyes remain bright, alive, for a moment longer, then as suddenly glaze in death. Ben lets him fall forward onto the wooden grating on the bottom of the steel boat, the private's rifle bumping against his arm.

Numbers Cooligan, his eyes wide with terror, grabs Jolly as

he's knocked backwards by the force of a machine-gun bullet, another of which catches one of the navy rowers on the port side. The sailor slumps forward, still clutching his oar until the movement of the boat tears it from his lifeless hands. Both men are killed instantly.

'Oh, Jesus,' Cooligan cries, then begins to sob, his hand holding the dead Jolly as though it is permanently clamped to his collar. The young naval midshipman in charge of their boat signals to Ben that it's time to disembark into the shallow water.

'Righto, lads, into the water, keep your eye out for me as we come ashore!' Ben is surprised at how steady his voice sounds, for he can feel his stomach clutching in fear and Matthews' blood sticky between the fingers of his left hand. 'Cooligan, leave him!' Ben shouts. 'He's dead. Get into the water, will yah!'

Ben makes a quick count as the men leap overboard, he is the last to leave and sees that five of his platoon plus the naval rating are slumped or have fallen. All appear to be dead for none of them moves, and the remaining fifteen of the twenty fighting men in the platoon make it into the water. Twenty yards to his left is another boat drifting helplessly, at least half of its complement dead or dying. Several of the oars are missing though two are stuck in the rowlocks, causing the boat to turn in circles. Ben jumps into the water which comes up to his waist. Shrapnel pellets send puffs of water and spray around him everywhere, the whine of bullets stings the air and the entire stretch of water running up to the beach ahead of him is plopping like sudden rain on a pond. He trails his left hand in the water, trying to wash Matthews' blood from his hand, and is barely aware of the thunder of the guns from the battleship sending salvo after salvo into the heights where it believes the Turkish positions to be. The threshing of the water about his pumping legs is by far the greater sound. Bodies are floating everywhere and he bumps against several. Closer to the beach he hits a pebble bottom, the small round pebbles causing his boots to slip and slide, but he manages to maintain his balance as he reaches the wash.

The beach is littered with early morning corpses lying sprawled as though asleep in the hot sun. Others, only just wounded, are crawling up the beach. Directly ahead of him a soldier lies on his stomach in the wash and Ben sees that a large piece of shrapnel, probably a razor-sharp section of a shell casing, has neatly sliced off his pack without having touched the man, its straps still attached to his shoulders. He has either been knocked unconscious or the shock of the impact has made him think he is dead, but left with his face in the wash he is likely to drown. Ben grabs hold of the webbing attached to the man's shoulders and pulls him up to his knees. There is a sudden gasp and gurgle from the man as he opens his eyes. 'Jaysus, I thought I were in heaven an' all!' he says.

'Keep running, Irish, and you'll live to fight another day!' Ben hauls at the webbing again and the man stands up. 'Git the hell out o' here, lad,' Ben shouts, and pushes him forward across the pebbly beach. Ahead he catches sight of the huge lumbering shape of Brokenose Brodie, his rifle held high above his head as if a signal for others in the platoon. Then he sees Cooligan, Spencer, Rigby and Mustafa all running up to the big man. Horne and Parthe, usually found with the others, are missing from the group. He is not aware that he is shouting, 'Number two platoon, come, come!' though it is quite impossible to be heard above the enemy fire.

This time there is a great deal less confusion on the beach. Several officers doing duty as guides stand calmly some thirty feet from the water's edge and with shrapnel bursting in the air over them they read the shoulder patches of the men as they stumble ashore and immediately direct them by way of hand signals in the general direction of their companies. It is apparent at once to Ben that they have landed too far to the right, too close to the Gaba Tepe end of the cove where the Turkish field guns can more easily reach them. Moreover, the part of the slope they have been briefed to attack is some considerable way to the left of where they now are.

He looks for Peregrine Ormington-Smith, who was in the second of the three boats carrying the platoon. All Ben can see are men milling in confusion, but groups like his own are beginning to bunch and he runs towards the five members of his platoon that Brodie has managed to gather together. On the way an officer sees his shoulder patch. '5th Battalion to my right, Sergeant,' he shouts, pointing. Ben reaches the five men gathered at the top of the beach standing in comparative safety under a slight overhang to the cliff face.

'Righto, lads,' he puffs. 'Packs off for the moment, take a break, the company's down this end,' he says, pointing south to a small fold between the ends of two ridges running parallel down to the cove. 'We'll move out as soon as you've all caught your breath, but scatter wide, nobody within four or five feet of the other, no bunching, you hear? Avoid other groups, a sniper will always go for the biggest target in his sights.' They rest up for five minutes, watching the confusion on the perimeter. There are some troops walking, trying to show they're not afraid or perhaps too dazed and confused to know any better, others have unclipped and discarded their packs and are running down the beach for dear life. Ben looks at the five men. 'We're shitting ourselves, that's an order, when you get back onto the main part of the beach, run like scared rabbits! Packs on, let's be off, lads, full pack, everyone, the only thing we leave behind is our flamin' footprints.'

'And a shit-streak or two,' Crow Rigby quips.

The lads arrive to find Lieutenant Peregrine Ormington-Smith with all twenty members of the platoon in his boat present. Remarkably, his landing boat made it onto the beach without a single casualty. They have taken shelter hard against a clay bank within the slight fold made by the two ridges, which now contains a mass of confused men. Officers are checking shoulder patches and trying frantically to sort them into their correct companies.

Wordy Smith tells Ben that they witnessed the third boat carrying the remaining ten members of their platoon take a direct hit by a large shell. The boat simply disappeared in a huge flash. The only evidence of its existence comes with the afternoon tide when several dozen broken and splintered oars with various landing boat numbers marked on them are washed up onto the shore. They are gathered, with other combustibles, by members of the Engineers Unit stationed at Hell Spit and piled up outside the depot to be used as firewood.

Among these are the oars belonging to the landing boats ferrying B Company of the 7th Battalion. Heading in to the beach on the second landing, four of the boats somehow managed to drift or were mistakenly rowed to the outside perimeter of the cove, coming under the direct fire of four machine guns. All the rowers were almost instantly killed and their oars were smashed or lost overboard. The boats then drifted helplessly, making the troops in them an easy target for the machine guns. The few who managed to abandon ship and get to the shore were cut down. Only two men in the four landing boats survived, crossing the pebbled beach and hiding in the scrub, where they were rescued two days later.

'I cannot tell you how immensely pleased I am to see you, Sergeant, a chap has been terribly concerned,' Wordy Smith says, extending his hand. Ben takes it in his own and the lieutenant shakes it over-vigorously. In his excitement he has unconsciously reverted to the syntax and accent of his English public school.

'Who've we got, sir?' Ben asks, still panting heavily from the sprint. He rapidly counts the men. 'Thirty-four, one missing, five dead in my boat and the ten who took a direct hit in the third, we should have thirty-five.'

To everyone's surprise, Wordy Smith starts to call out the names of every member of the platoon. He knows which ten were in the third boat and abstains from naming them and as he calls the name of each of the four dead in Ben's boat, Ben simply says, 'Didn't make it ashore, sir.' When he's called all the names and each man has answered he pauses and says quietly, 'Private Horne is missing, let's hope he eventually finds us.'

Ben now calls out, 'Privates Flynn, Phillips and Spencer, step up!' Library and the two others move to stand in front of Ben. 'Where are your packs, lads?' Ben asks.

Library elects to speak for them. 'Dropped them, Sergeant.'

'Where?'

'On the beach,' Phillips says while Flynn nods.

'In the water, Sergeant, I . . . I panicked,' Library admits miserably, his head bowed.

'Back onto the beach you three, pick up a discarded pack, a full kit, nothing missing, shovel or pick axe as well. Did you drop yer rifles?'

'No, Sergeant!' the three of them chorus.

'Now bugger off, and get back here at the double . . . and keep yer flamin' heads down!'

The three members of the platoon return humping packs, Library Spencer with a shovel and the other two with picks attached. 'You're on a charge, the three of you,' Ben says. 'We'll sort it out later.'

The situation, by the time the 2nd Brigade arrives in the second wave, is perilous. Earlier, the men of the 3rd Brigade who had survived the landing made no attempt to find their companies, but in the total confusion they set out in isolated groups, 'penny packets', to climb after the unseen enemy. As they attempted to scramble up the rocky cliff face and steep ridges beyond, the Turkish snipers picked them off willy-nilly. Soon enough, some of the most intrepid of these unattached groups reached the first ridge, their shapes silhouetted clearly against the skyline. Those coming behind them, thinking at last they were seeing the enemy, fired at them. Suddenly those keenest and in the most advanced positions found themselves sandwiched between the Turkish snipers still higher up on the second ridge and their own rifle fire coming from below. Many of them perished in the hail of misdirected bullets.

However, instead of waiting for their own troops to catch up with them, they are driven on by the fact that, from time to time, they witness the enemy vanishing into the dark tangle of gullies ahead of them, their shooting dying away, and so they think that victory must be close at hand. They thrust further and further inland, isolating themselves completely. They are encouraged in this perception when some of the Turkish soldiers, seeing the Australians catching up, throw down their arms and surrender. But the attacking soldiers, determined not to be slowed down by taking prisoners, simply shoot them and continue on in pursuit.

The advancing troops are unaware that the Turks, not expecting a landing north of the Gaba Tepe headland, only have a single company guarding the slopes. But not far behind Sari Bair, the very topmost ridge and the most important objective for the Australians, there are several companies of Turkish reinforcements who are no more than half an hour's marching distance away.

Just before five o'clock Turkish shrapnel begins to burst among the troops along the ridges and shortly after nine the enemy reinforcements arrive. The Anzacs near the top of the second ridge see them advancing towards them. The Turkish counterattack moves up the valleys, outflanking the Australian outposts on their left, driving the scattered groups backwards and in the process killing a great many men of the 3rd Brigade.

The Anzacs are not to know that the keenest among them would reach no further than their initial attack in the hours immediately after dawn on the first day until after the surrender of Turkey in 1918. Someone had blundered terribly. Strategically the landing at Gallipoli had failed.

Hamilton, the supreme commander, has vastly underestimated the enemy and, to boot, possesses a sense of geography that is to cost his Australian and New Zealand troops dearly, not to mention the English, Indians and French who also die like flies in what, within the context of the total war in Europe, is considered a relatively minor diversion.

In Australian and New Zealand terms it is a terrible sacrifice. As young growing nations, they can ill afford a vital part of their life seed to be sacrificed in places with names such as Baby 700, Lone Pine Hill, Courtney's Post, Quinn's Post, 400 Plateau, The Nek and what will, in time, become known as Anzac Cove.

But now, with the sun not long up, the Turkish troops have been reinforced and are advancing from the heights above the Australians. The first Australian wave is pushed back predominantly on the left flank where they dig in, hoping to hold the line. The Anzac forces in the centre and the right, or southern, flank are increasingly being sucked into the left flank, thinking to reinforce the line where the fighting appears to be the fiercest. Subsequently, the centre and southern flanks become too thinly manned and are exposed to a Turkish attack, threatening disaster for the whole assault.

It is here, on the southern flank, that the 2nd Brigade coming into the beach in the second wave will be sent. This time, despite the fierce hail of artillery, shrapnel, machine-gun and rifle fire, which is considerably heavier than the reception given the 3rd Brigade in the first wave, the troops are directed to an assembly point, which proves relatively safe from enemy fire.

Here they are organised into their companies or assigned to new platoons if their own has been decimated. The act of reassembling is by no means all calmness and order, instead it is a process of stop–start, with officers screaming commands at confused troops, their own senior officers frequently countermanding their instructions in a similar manner. But somehow the officers and N.C.O.s given the task of organising the troops back into a fighting unit manage to get a sufficiently concerted force together. This allows the brigade commander, Colonel M'Cay, to assemble the means to reinforce the scattered remnants of the 9th Battalion, who are grimly holding their positions on the southern flank against a now increasingly fierce Turkish counterattack.

Shortly after eight o'clock in the morning with the 5th Company in reasonably compact order, Wordy Smith returns from a short briefing. Major Sayers, their company commander, gives the platoon officers their map co-ordinates and tells them they will be advancing up the southern flank known on the military maps as 400 Plateau where they will reinforce the 10th Battalion from the first wave who have been damn near decimated.

'Packs on, bayonets fixed, let's get out of here,' Ben tells his platoon. Whereas the platoon officer would usually give the order to march out, such is the understanding between Peregrine Ormington-Smith and his sergeant that they simply communicate quietly with each other, with Ben, for the most part, instructing the platoon. Anyone looking on from the outside would assume the incompetence in Wordy Smith still exists. However, since leaving Lemnos the platoon commander has shown that he is not beyond the task of leading his troops. He simply understands he has a first-class sergeant who knows the ropes and who will consult him when needed. Peregrine Ormington-Smith is without the slightest pretension and the relationship between the two men is completely free of rivalry.

Moreover, perhaps because of his countless forays into the wild to find the specimens for his flower paintings, Wordy Smith will show that he has a capacity to read the nature of the terrain and that he can anticipate what is to come in the field with uncanny accuracy.

The platoon now begins to climb the steep and arduous slope. With their packs on their backs it is an enormous struggle up the narrow tracks and they find it difficult to keep up with those platoons that have abandoned their packs on the beach and carry nothing but their iron rations about their necks, their rifles with bayonets fixed, and a little spare ammunition.

'S'not bloody fair,' Numbers Cooligan gasps. 'Look at them other bastards, rifle and just their webbing, ammo pouches, water bottle and iron rations, bugger-all else.'

'Ah, stop whingeing, Numbers, it's your fault anyway,' Crow Rigby calls.

'My fault! Shit, why?'

'With a pack on yer back yer can't run away, Ben knows this and so as not to embarrass yer, we've all got to carry 'em.'

'Ah, you're fulla bullshit, Crow. I'll soon enough be watching your skinny arse fleeing back down towards the beach, no risk, mate.'

'No flamin' way, mate, it's much too dangerous down there.'

And so the usual silly young-bloke banter and jocularity goes on among them, to keep their minds from dwelling on the battle to come. On their way up through Shrapnel Valley they pass several hundred dead men and soon realise the danger they face. The stark reality of warfare is beginning to sink in.

The first of the reinforcements under M'Cay, mostly the men without packs on their backs, arrive at the lip of the plateau. His orders are to advance across it so that they can get in with their bayonets among the Turks on the third ridge. With no telephone wires yet laid the brigade commander is unaware that the rest of the line at the centre and the north is pinned down with no hope of advancing and that for him to cross 400 Plateau and, on his own, attack his objective, the third ridge, is pointless. He can't possibly outflank the Turks who are too well dug in on the high ground above the plateau.

The sensible thing to do is to simply dig in and become the southern part of the front line, to stop just before reaching the lip of the plateau and take cover on the reverse slope. M'Cay sees at once that the plateau is covered with the bodies of the 9th Battalion from the first wave. With all their officers dead, the scattered elements remaining have dug in under the lip and are simply trying to survive the Turkish onslaught from the ridge beyond the plateau.

Deciding he has fresh troops and is part of a front line committed to advance across the full front, Colonel M'Cay believes he has no option but to take his men across 400 Plateau and to dig in on the other side if it should become necessary.

This proves to be a suicidal decision as the Turks on the higher slopes are reinforced, far better organised now, and virtually concealed from the Australian forces. The numbers no longer stacked against them, the Turks can stand and fight. What the Australians thought was cowardice in the Wog army was simply tactical prudence, they are in a position to call all the shots and if M'Cay attempts to cross the plateau his men are, almost certainly, dead meat.

Ben arrives with his platoon soon after the first of the 5th Battalion troops are being fed over the rim and told to cross the plateau. Crawling up to the rim, he can immediately see what is taking place. The men attempting to cross are being cut down in waves. Not only are they subject to a hailstorm of Turkish rifle and machine-gun fire, but heavy artillery from behind the third range is raining down on them, cascading scythes of white-hot shrapnel cutting them to pieces.

'We should dig in here under the lip, sir. Then, if we have to, cross the plateau tonight,' he says to Wordy Smith, who has crept up and now lies beside him.

Peregrine Ormington-Smith nods. 'It's not just crossing, Sergeant, unless I'm very much mistaken this plateau dips down into a gully, a basin at its end.' He points to the plateau running away from them. 'This flat ground is like the handle on a spoon. Not only do the Turks have us at their mercy as we cross down the handle but what's left of us will simply be herded like sheep into the spoon. For them it's like looking down into a street jammed shoulder to shoulder with people, every shot they fire will hit someone.' He looks grimly at Ben. 'If we persist in this, the entire battalion is likely to be wiped out, possibly the brigade. I'll see if I can find the C.O., get further instructions, it's sheer madness to continue like this. In the meantime, carry on, Ben . . . oh, er, Sergeant.'

'That's all right, sir, matter of fact, I've been meaning to talk to you about that. It seems to me that while we're fighting, that is in the course of battle, me referring to a soldier as "Private" followed by his name is too wasteful of time, far better to say his surname or even his Christian name and, well, vice versa, they can call me Ben or Sarge. All of this strictly applying only within the platoon, of course?'

Wordy Smith laughs. 'Peregrine, or for that matter Ormington-Smith, is hardly an abbreviation, Ben.'

'Right. In your case, sir, why don't we simply continue with "sir", it's the quickest of the lot.'

The lieutenant nods, not looking up. Ben can see he's thinking, then he faces him. 'I wouldn't . . . er would you mind? I mean, I'd rather prefer to be called Wordy.'

'Seems like a bloody silly conversation to be having with the shit hitting the fan all around us,' Ben says. He slides down the slope, pushing himself backwards on his belly until he is sufficiently far down to stand erect without exposing his head above the rim. 'From now on it's just names among us, no more sergeant or lieutenant or private, just whatever we're called among ourselves.'

'Righto, Ben,' Numbers Cooligan calls quick as a flash.

'You'll keep, Cooligan,' Ben says as a Turkish shell bursts

alarmingly close, sending shrapnel whining over their heads. 'Let's dig in, lads, ain't it grand we brought our picks and shovels.'

'Bastard's right as usual,' Crow Rigby sighs as he unties his shovel from the back of his pack. 'What about them poor bastards who didn't bring nothin', eh Numbers?'

'What gives me the shits is he didn't ask me for *my* permission to call me by me Christian name!' Numbers Cooligan says, conveniently changing the subject.

'Ah, you're fulla shit, Numbers,' Woggy Mustafa says, bringing his pick axe down into the hard earth at his feet.

'Is that a Wog or a Christian opinion coming from you, Mustafa?' Numbers Cooligan asks, picking up his shovel and starting to dig.

'It is a truth that crosses all religious boundaries,' Crow Rigby laughs.

They begin to dig in furiously and, almost as if by telepathy, others on their left and right, those who possess the good fortune to own a pick or shovel, start to do the same.

Brokenose Brodie is wielding his pick with an easy rhythm and Library Spencer beside him is shovelling the clods away as fast as possible as they work in concert, though plainly Library is unable to keep up. He rests for a moment, exhausted, leaning on his shovel. 'I wonder where Hornbill got to?' he says suddenly. The five friends working in the same proximity all stop abruptly, it is as though they have been waiting for someone to bring it up and by voicing their own thoughts Library has somehow admitted the likelihood that their mate is dead, copped one, killed on the beach or in the water.

'Ah, he'll turn up,' Muddy Parthe volunteers at last. 'Look't me, I got lost comin' ashore, separated from youse blokes.'

'Yeah, but in *your* case we was hoping it was permanent, that you'd decided to join another platoon,' Numbers Cooligan remarks.

'Ha bloody ha! If I did, it would be to get away from you, mate.'

Nothing further is said and they return to their digging.

The slaughter taking place on the plateau no more than a few feet above their heads is now apparent to every soldier. The troops are rapidly becoming conscious that going over the lip on 400 Plateau means almost certain death. They all think that if they can wait until nightfall and cross they will be able to get among the Turks with their bayonets.

With their trench no more than eighteen inches dug into the hard red clay, Wordy Smith returns. He is grim-faced as he talks to Ben. 'We're all ordered over the top, Ben. The C.O.'s got his orders. Colonel M'Cay says nobody stays behind and insists on pressing on with the attack, his intention is to take the third ridge before nightfall.' He shrugs. 'It seems we'll be letting down the advance of the centre and the left flanks if we remain here and dig in.'

'The centre and the left flanks are advancing?' Ben asks, sounding doubtful. 'Do we know that for sure? There are no telephone wires up yet, no communication?'

Wordy Smith shrugs helplessly. 'No, it's only assumed.'

'Assumed! Fucking assumed!' Ben cries incredulously. It is the first time anyone has seen him blow his stack and he quickly reins himself in. 'Bloody M'Cay looking for a promotion or something, is he?' he adds bitterly. He turns away from Wordy and looks upwards to the Turkish positions and says quietly to himself, 'As Ikey Solomon would say, "He's fucking meshuggeneh!"'

Platoon officers, brandishing their Webley revolvers above their heads in some macabre form of battlefield tallyho, followed by their men, continue to pour up over the rim, attempting to cross 400 Plateau. By now, less than half an hour after their arrival, the entire area of the plateau is littered with new corpses, a second sacrifice to add to the Turkish killing orgy. Only this time there are vastly more Turks on the slopes above them.

Wounded men, abandoning their rifles, attempt to crawl on their hands and knees back to the safety of their comrades. In the process, they are picked off by the Turkish snipers. Often two or three bullets hit a wounded soldier, his body jerking with each impact, then he lies still, sprawled, spiderlike, with his face against the hard ground, quivering like a rabid dog shot in the street. In a matter of moments his wounds are set upon by a thick swarm of flies. One soldier still crawling back towards the rim has taken a direct hit in the face and the blood pours from his nose, his mouth, even his eyes, though this can scarcely be seen as the flies completely obscure what's left of his features, turning the entire front surface of his smashed and broken head into a blank, black, buzzing horror.

The Indian Mountain guns are firing willy-nilly into the ridge directly above them and are seemingly as effective as a popgun fired at a brick wall, their aim too unco-ordinated to do any real damage to an enemy well dug in and damn near invisible.

It makes absolutely no sense when crossing the plateau to return the rifle fire, it simply delays the run for cover and, besides, there is nothing to aim at. Firing bullets, even machine-gun bullets, into a blank mountainside is a fruitless occupation. The only way they can possibly hope to engage the enemy is by means of a bayonet charge at close quarters. And if Wordy Smith is correct, they won't ever get that far up the slope. In the unlikely event that they make it across the plateau, the handle of the spoon, in any numbers, the spoon is waiting to dish them up piecemeal to the Turks.

'Stow your picks and shovels, get your packs onto your backs, lads,' Ben now orders, then bends down and ties his shovel to the back of his pack and hoists his kit onto his shoulders. Those who watch him are strangely comforted by the sight of the Maori fighting axe in its holster on the side of his pack, a more inappropriate and useless weapon for the circumstances they are about to encounter can scarcely be imagined. But it is their proven talisman and they take heart from it. They also see a red bandanna tied to a buckle on the back of his pack. It is the one given to him by Victoria to wave from the deck of the *Orvieto* when she and Hawk came to farewell him. 'Righto, don't bunch, yer hear?' Ben instructs them. 'Stay well apart, it's no more than a hundred yards across, we can do it in thirty seconds flat, keep low, don't run in a straight line, you all know the drill.'

He turns his back on them and it appears as though he is buckling the chest strap of his pack. None of them see him pull the little green Tiki from beneath his shirt and briefly touch it to his lips. Ben turns and looks at Wordy Smith. The lieutenant nods. Ben turns back to the men. 'Right then, follow me, lads. Keep yer eyes fixed on the red rag at my back, we're going over now, we'll all meet on the other side.'

'Precisely what "other side" is that?' Crow Rigby says softly to himself and watches as Numbers Cooligan makes the sign of the cross.

Chapter Fourteen

BEN AND COMPANY

Shaking Hands with the Shadows

Ben's platoon is positioned on the southern side of 400 Plateau and looking over their shoulder they can see the low black promontory of Gaba Tepe as it intersects the wide arc of Suvla Bay, its Aegean waters sparkling in the bright morning sun. The plateau is covered with low gorse-like scrub, reaching not much above the waist, though it grows in patches with open ground between. It is good cover for a soldier remaining still, but not well suited for forward movement. Directly ahead of him at about four hundred yards is perhaps the narrowest section of the plateau which begins to slope away to an area known as Lonesome Pine, the name of a popular song. This name for the gently sloping hillside came about because among the juniper and scrub stands a single stunted pine tree. Lonesome Pine will soon enough be changed to Lone Pine in the way that Australians have of chopping any extraneous syllable from a word without changing its essential meaning.

Wordy Smith points out to Ben that this southern slope, protected somewhat by the Gaba Tepe headland to the south and positioned at a slightly oblique angle to the sea, doesn't get the full force of the wind. This, in turn, means the juniper and scrub are higher and grow in bigger and denser clumps than on the flatter section of the plateau. He reasons that with the land falling away from the third ridge a man's height is even further reduced, making him a slightly smaller target for the enemy rifle and machine-gun fire. It means they must move in an arc rather than take the shortest route across the plateau.

Ben estimates this will add perhaps another hundred yards to the distance, another four or five minutes of exposure to the hellfire coming from the Turks. But to counterbalance this, Wordy Smith suggests they will avoid falling into the spoon where they can easily be killed, the proposition being that machine-gun and rifle fire is instinctively aimed at the most obvious and nearest target and artillery fire where the greatest force is concentrated.

Ben agrees that the plan is the better of two fairly poor options. He is first over the rim, followed by Wordy Smith and the remainder of the platoon, who are staggered left and right at an interval of approximately four yards between each man. They have practised this drill in the desert where little concealment exists and advancing troops are trained to break into a haphazard formation of single-man targets.

Once on the plateau they can see it is literally covered with the bodies of the dead infantrymen and most of the dead soldiers are already black with flies. Many of them belong to the 3rd Brigade but, after only half an hour of coming over the rim, M'Cay's 2nd Brigade is dying at a much faster rate than during the early morning slaughter. The men trying to cross the plateau form a perfect target for the Turkish artillery, who actually look down at the Australians in a semicircle of heights from Battleship Hill in the north to Gaba Tepe in the south.

If one can imagine an amphitheatre, the plateau becomes its stage and the seats near the top are the enemy artillery positions from which all movement and space on 400 Plateau can be covered. To take the analogy further, the audience in the Greek amphitheatre are the Turks, with rifles and machine guns, and the Australians are the hapless actors.

The Turkish gunfire from the ridge is even more concerted than on the beach. The guns on the plateau have gained a steady rhythm and every thirty seconds a salvo of four shells falls, covering a large part of the plateau as a moving garden spray might water a lawn. Two enemy batteries, one at Chunuk Bair in the north and the other at Scrubby Knoll in the south, are the deadliest. Depending on where the largest concentration of Australians appear on the plateau, these two batteries shorten or lengthen their range like a fire hose playing on flames. The result, no single salvo is missed.

It becomes apparent to M'Cay after the very first troops are sent over the rim that the attempt to get his 2nd Brigade across must fail. A simple estimation of the dead already lying on the plateau after the initial attempt by the 3rd Brigade must tell him that there can be no front line to reinforce. Simple arithmetic indicates there are too many factors against him, the combination of Turkish firepower and the vastly superior and impregnable position they hold on the ridge directly above him means the odds are hopelessly stacked against him. His troops, pouring, as they mostly do, from the handle down into the bowl of the spoon, become, in effect, sitting ducks, unable to do anything more than attempt to conceal themselves from the Turkish guns directly above them. The likelihood of any of them mounting a further attack on the Turkish positions simply does not exist.

Colonel M'Cay is slaughtering his men, thinking only to slavishly obey his misdirected orders without accepting the responsibility to call it off. His men can never reach and effectively reinforce the isolated pockets of the decimated 3rd Brigade who are dug in beyond the plateau and now find themselves pinned down by the Turks. The first rule in the military handbook is that in a rescue operation you do not sacrifice more men than you hope to save.

M'Cay should dig in along a line on the plateau and wait until nightfall for the isolated pockets of the 3rd Brigade to join him in the trenches he has prepared. It is a strategy any junior subaltern could devise and it would save the lives of countless men.

Thus begins a day in which the Turks, far from admiring the courage of the Australians, wonder at the stupidity of the infidels and the commanders directing them. They take great heart from what they witness on 400 Plateau. This is an enemy to be laughed at. Even the humblest Turkish recruit knows that stupidity, even brave stupidity, seldom wins battles.

Stupidity in the time of war is usually put down to a lack of critical information by those responsible for it. It takes a long time for history to point an accusing finger at an errant and inadequate commander, and by then it is usually too late and he is out of the firing line or has been promoted to a higher rank.

Commanders who substitute men for ideas and approach a

battle with complete disregard for saving the lives of the troops under their command almost always turn battles into killing fields without being granted victory as the prize.

On the first day on Gallipoli, from the beach landing in the pearl-grey dawn to the splashed and brilliant sunset over Asia Minor, nearly four thousand men are killed, countless others are wounded. The majority of these deaths occur at two places, on the landing beach and later on 400 Plateau.

Once the foolishness of invading Gallipoli had been decided upon, the attrition rate caused by landing from the sea onto a well-defended shore could scarcely be avoided. It is a price an invading army must expect to pay. But the slaughter at 400 Plateau was not necessary.

However, the manner of fighting the Turk on the Gallipoli Peninsula demonstrated on the first day on 400 Plateau by the brigadiers M'Cay and, to a slightly lesser extent, MacLagan sets the pattern for the Australian commanders on several other occasions.

Gallipoli was always intended to be a diversion, a ploy to make the Turks think that the main attack was to come from the high ground to the north so that they would concentrate their strength and effort on the Australians while the British and French invaded the flat ground south of Gaba Tepe.

In the end, seven months later, two hundred and forty thousand men will have been wounded, over forty thousand killed on the Allied side. The Turks never counted their dead, except in counting them fortunate, for they had been grasped to the bosom of Allah as heroes and consigned to Paradise. But it is estimated that they suffered much the same attrition rate as those who dared to invade their ancient land.

And so more than half a million young warriors were wounded or died in a series of battles and endless skirmishes that never reached further inland than a man could walk at a brisk pace in half an hour from the pebbled beach and which, in the overall scheme of things, didn't amount to a fart in a hurricane.

Ben doesn't rush things, making use of whatever cover is available, effectively using the gorse and scrub or a sudden dip or hollow in the terrain and making a dash across the open ground in between, resting up under the cover after every dash. It is careful progress where time is not the principal ingredient and after a while the platoon grows accustomed to the procedure and uses it skilfully.

However, this method of crossing contrasts strongly with the one adopted by a great many of the men who attempted to make a singular dash for it, running in a more or less straight line directly into the path of the remorseless enemy fire.

It may have been that the men were not properly briefed on the distance they needed to cover to get across the plateau or they lost the leadership of their officers who knew at what pace to take them out. Whatever, in the sudden decision to send them over the rim, a great many soldiers did not appear to have thought out how they might sensibly cover the five or, in some cases, six hundred yards across while carrying a rifle and a ninety-pound pack.

Distance in hilly terrain is easily misjudged anyway and the plateau may have seemed much shorter than it proves to be. Men set off, running for their lives, and soon enough they find themselves brought to an untimely halt, not just by the enemy, but by their own physical exhaustion.

Many bend to grab their knees, gasping for breath unable to move forward. Being stationary or slow-moving targets, they hardly merit the attention of the snipers with their Mausers and telescopic sights, who concentrate mainly on killing the officers. Instead, they become easy targets for the more modest shots among the Turkish infantry and are certain kills for the barking enemy machine guns.

The wounded have to fend for themselves. Officers, those few who haven't been killed or wounded, are forced to press on and not endanger the remainder of their platoons by stopping to check on their wounded men. The wounded beg pathetically for help or plead to be taken back to the line. Others simply cry out for their mothers and some lie down and die, shivering in the blazing sun as the cold hands of death embrace them. They are fraternising with death, shaking hands with the shadows as the Anzac saying goes. While some of the men do stop to help a mate in trouble there is little they can do except attempt to take them back behind the lines and, as often as not, they join the dead or lie wounded beside a comrade.

Ben loses two men in his platoon, both from shrapnel pellets, which even concealment in the scrub cannot prevent. Private Woodridge and Lance Corporal Phillips are killed instantly and

Ben stops to empty their tunic pockets. He's made each man in his platoon write a final letter home and place it together with any other small personal mementoes, such as family photographs, medallions or keepsakes into the left-hand breast pocket of their tunic. Every member of his platoon has been instructed that should a mate be killed beside him, whenever possible he is to remove the contents of his tunic pocket and carry it with him. Under Library Spencer's tuition even Brokenose Brodie has managed a short letter to his parents. He is inordinately proud of this final missive and often reads it to himself or to anyone else prepared to listen. The joke among the platoon is that the letter will be worn out by the time he dies and one of them will have to look up Brokenose's mum and dad to recite to them what it contained.

Dear Mum and Dad,

I am dead when I write this. Our sargent says I must be.

You musint cry, you hear. I am not wirth the tears.

I don't think I will go to heaven. But who no's. The Turk all go there, its called paradice so maybe God will sent me up there to fite them again and get even for gettin meself killt. Dad you is forgived for beltin me a lot.

Your loving son,

Wayne Brokenose Brodie.

P.S. Brokenose is me name here and I can read real good now.

A little further down the slope as they are crossing open ground Hornbill makes a sudden appearance on their left, his legs and arms pumping as he crosses over to them, yelling the while, though his voice is drowned in a sudden burst of shrapnel. He comes to a halt, panting violently just as they reach the cover of the scrub and Ben sees that he is wearing a bandage wrapped about his forehead. 'G'day, Sergeant, 'ullo, sir,' he pants, looking at Ben and Wordy Smith.

'Get yer flamin' head down, Hornbill, and stay ragged!' Ben shouts.

They proceed another hundred yards or so downhill and reach the stunted pine tree where Ben decides to swing to the left into the slight incline on Lone Pine, which leads to the southwestern extremity of the plateau. The juniper and scrub grow thickly here and reach above their heads so that they can walk upright for a good hundred yards or so, carefully making their way through the bush. Perhaps, because of the extra camouflage provided, the enemy firepower is not coming as thick and fast on this perimeter. Ben realises that they appear to be largely alone, and that few Australians have selected this section, thinking it the furthest away from the objective.

Wordy Smith, who has reached the edge of the tall scrub on Ben's right, suddenly calls out, 'Trenches ahead, Ben!'

They hit the ground and wait, expecting at any moment to see all hell break loose from the direction Wordy Smith has indicated. They can now clearly see the mounds of packed red earth some fifty yards ahead and more or less directly in front and above them. The Turkish trench running a good twenty yards or more has been dug into the brow of the hill to cover a wide arch, the centre of which embraces the whole of Lone Pine where they lie, to the right looking down at Pine Ridge and the left over the bottom section of 400 Plateau. The rear of the trench must also look over what became known as Legge Valley to the north and Anderson Knoll to the south. This trench, Ben reasons, must be the most distant point forward from the heights the enemy dominates. In fact, it is one of the very few positions in the Turkish defence that might be vulnerable if attacked with a sufficient force of determined men who can get close enough to use their bayonets. But now, much more importantly, if they are observed and an enemy machine gun guards the entrance to the trench ahead of them, they stand no chance of surviving. Ben has led his men into a trap from which there appears to be no escape. They cannot retreat back up onto the higher ground of the plateau and if they move further south they must cross open ground where they'll be cut to pieces by the Turkish machine guns. If they use their rifles they have no effective target, bullets don't bend into trenches, so their only hope will be to fix bayonets and charge.

Ben calls to Crow Rigby and Woggy Mustafa to crawl forward. 'Woggy, have a look willya, you've got the best eyes in the battalion, see if you can see any movement, any at all. You, Crow, get your telescopic sights onto those trenches, see if you can see anything as well, if you do, don't fire.' He turns to Muddy Parthe, who is nearest to him. 'Pass on, fix bayonets.'

After a minute or so Crow says, 'Can't see nothin', Ben.'

'Three Turkish bodies at two o'clock,' Woggy says, 'legs stickin' out the bush.'

'Sure they're Turks?'

'Yeah, their boots, leggin's, they're not us.'

Crow Rigby swings his sniper's sights to where Woggy has indicated. 'Yeah, he's right, three o' the bastards, flies buzzin' over them, they's dead orright.'

Ben turns to the lieutenant and to his amazement sees that he is clawing at a ground shrub with the tiniest bright pink blossoms. Wordy Smith stuffs the specimen into his tunic pocket and Ben sees that the pocket is filled with floral bits and pieces which his platoon commander has collected on their way across the plateau.

'Wordy, I'm gunna take a squiz, see what's happening.'

'No, Ben.'

Ben looks at Peregrine Ormington-Smith in surprise. 'Uh?'

'I'm going.'

'No, sir, it's best if . . . well, you're the platoon commander, the lads need you to lead.'

'That's a laugh, Ben,' Wordy Smith says.

'Officer should stay with his men, sir,' Ben says, reverting to formality.

'It's an order, Sergeant,' Wordy Smith replies sharply, cutting him short. 'If we get out of this mess it won't be from my leadership and the men know that.' He rises to his knees and removes his pack. Ben sees that his tunic pocket is overflowing with floral specimens and thinks he must be the only officer in the history of warfare who is risking his life with a tunic pocket full of wildflowers. Wordy Smith starts to move forward out of the cover of the juniper and scrub which on this section of Lone Pine appear to have been slashed to not much higher than knee height to increase the line of sight from the trench on the brow of the hill.

Ben grabs Peregrine Ormington-Smith by his Sam Browne belt just as he is about to set off. 'Stay to your left, Wordy, there's more cover, take your time.' He adds, 'We're not going anywhere except straight to hell if that trench is occupied.'

Wordy Smith nods and crawls out of the cover of the tall scrub and juniper into the much lower scrub. His attempt at the leopard crawl on his elbows and knees makes a mockery of the idea that this position presents the most difficult head-on target for an enemy. His long legs push his bum into the air and it now bobs up and down above the juniper and presents a target any sniper could hit without pausing to take aim.

They watch, all eyes glued on Wordy Smith's bobbing bum as he draws closer and closer to the trenches. The scrub has been completely cleared for the final fifty feet up to the trench and the platoon commander must come to a halt before he gets to the edge of the gorse. Hopefully he will be close enough to see if it is occupied, though Ben cannot imagine how, if it is, they haven't spotted Wordy's perambulating movement through the scrub.

'Get ready to charge, lads. Packs off, we'll go to the right, don't bunch, wait for my command.'

They can see that by attacking from the right Ben is trying to maximise every second they have, hoping that by drawing the enemy fire, Wordy Smith will give them time to jump to their feet and get a few yards closer before the Turks in the trench spot them coming. Brokenose Brodie nudges Library Spencer at his side and points silently towards Ben. Library sees that Ben has his Maori fighting axe slung in its holster across his shoulder. 'Them Turks gunna pay dearly,' he whispers.

But Library Spencer knows that Brokenose Brodie's optimism is ill-founded, the chances of thirty-five men taking the trench by charging front-on over fifty yards is pretty bloody slim. If there is a machine gun facing them, then their chances become zero. He can feel the pressure mounting. If Wordy Smith makes it close enough to the trench to listen for sounds of movement and then makes it back unobserved, which, with the bobbing of his bum above the bushes, is highly unlikely, they may need to wait until nightfall before attempting to move out unobserved.

To everyone's astonishment, Peregrine Ormington-Smith suddenly stands up in the scrub some fifty feet from the trenches and, revolver in hand, his long legs taking surprisingly long strides, he proceeds to run up the final steep slope and onto the embankment to the trench, jumping directly into it.

'Holy Mother o' God!' Numbers Cooligan exclaims, as they all rise at Ben's order to charge.

They are in the open running when the lieutenant's head emerges again and, waving his arms, he indicates for them to come forward. 'Halt, lads!' Ben shouts. 'Get back! Fetch yer packs! You, Brokenose, bring the lieutenant's. On the double, we're still exposed! Packs on and run fer'it!'

Three minutes later they are all safely in the trench, for the first time out of the line of fire. They have crossed 400 Plateau and are now on its lower end at the very topmost point on Lone Pine.

The trench is even longer than it seemed and curves around to the south, following the contours of the ridge, and Ben, barely pausing to catch his breath and remove his pack, nods to Hornbill to follow him. 'Bring your rifle,' he says, though he leaves his own and unslings his fighting axe and removes it from its holster.

With Ben leading they turn the corner into the southern section of the trench and immediately come across the body of a Turkish soldier, then several more. Most appear to have been bayoneted, some shot, and soon enough they come across a dead New Zealand soldier and then three more and another eight Turks. The trench is a little deeper at this end and leads into a section with a roof constructed of pine logs. Ben looks into the interior and, although at the extremity it is too dark to see, four or five feet in he makes out the shape of a machine gun stripped down. The moveable parts are laid out on a square of canvas and beside it is a dead Turkish sergeant. The attack on the trench by the 3rd Brigade must have caught the Turks by surprise, and unable to use their stripped-down machine gun.

Hornbill, who has climbed onto the firing platform to look over the southern end of the trench, calls suddenly, 'Come, take a look, Sergeant.' Ben withdraws from the covered section and climbs up beside him. What they see is a dozen or so Turkish soldiers lying dead on the slope and among them three more New Zealanders. Then a little further on they see three more sets of legs protruding from the scrub, they are the three dead Turkish soldiers Woggy has seen previously.

Ben returns to the timbered-over section of the trench, which appears to have been used as some sort of storehouse and is perhaps where an officer slept, the rank-and-file Turkish soldier being thought vastly inferior to his officers. As his eyes become accustomed to the darkness, stacked against the wall he sees a dozen boxes of ammunition and a bag of flour and, more importantly, a barrel of water, a neat pile of firewood and beside it what looks like a tin of kerosene. He moves still further inwards where it is virtually too dark to see without a light and is about to lean his axe against his leg while he finds his matches when suddenly a hand grips his ankle. Ben kicks away violently, jumping back in fright, his heart racing. The back of his head knocks against a hurricane lamp suspended from the ceiling and his arm is instinctively brought up ready to strike downwards with the axe.

'Don't shoot!' a voice cries out of the dark.

'Strewth! You gave me a fright,' Ben calls out. 'Who are you?'

'New Zealand.'

'Shit, you gave me a scare,' Ben says. 'Better come out.'

'Can't, mate,' the voice answers. 'Me leg's broke.'

'Hang on, Kiwi, we'll come and fetch ya, how bad is it?'

'Bullet through me knee.'

'There's a lamp here somewhere, just hit my flamin' head on it, just a sec, I'll light a match.'

Ben strikes a match and locates the hurricane lamp which is still swinging slightly. In the flare he catches sight of the shape of a big bloke seated on the floor, the light from the match briefly shows his blood-soaked trousers and puttees where he's been hit in the area of the left knee.

'Hornbill, get in here,' Ben calls.

'You'll need to find some oil, it went out a while back,' the New Zealander says.

Ben hands the lamp to Hornbill and points in the direction of the small water barrel. 'I think there's a tin of paraffin over there, see if you can get this going.' By now his eyes have adjusted sufficiently to the dark for him to clearly make out the shape of the soldier, though his features are still lost. He moves over and squats on his haunches beside the man, and removing his water bottle he holds it to the soldier's lips. The New Zealander grabs at the bottle and drinks greedily. Ben hopes the water in the barrel he's seen earlier is fresh or he'll be without. He removes the flask from the soldier's lips and takes a small sip before fixing it back to his webbing, though he can feel it is almost empty. 'Owyer goin' then, lad?'

'I could use a smoke, mate.'

Ben calls over to Hornbill, 'You got a tailor-made, Hornbill?'

'Nah, roll me own?'

'Roll one for our Maori friend here, will ya.'

'Hang on, Sergeant, I'll 'ave a light goin' in a sec.'

'How'd you know I's a Maori?' the New Zealander now says.

Ben hears Hornbill strike a match and the room momentarily lights up and he sees a canvas stretcher against the wall. Hornbill trims the wick of the lamp and hangs it back on the wire hook fixed to the log ceiling and the area is filled with a soft light.

'I didn't, mate. I was just bein' a smart arse. Matter o' fact, I'm a quarter Maori myself.'

'Yeah?' the soldier says, then suddenly winces, stifling a groan.

In the lamplight Ben now clearly sees that the wounded soldier sits in the corner, his back against the far wall with both legs straight out. He has torn his trouser leg away to expose the wound and in the blood and gore Ben observes that the kneecap is still intact and that the Maori appears to have been hit below the knee, the bullet smashing through the tibia and the fibula bones. He has done several courses in first aid in the field and thinks the bullet must have missed the posterior tibial artery or the Maori lad would have been long dead from loss of blood.

'It ain't your knee, mate, just below. Lucky that, been the knee, surgeon would've chopped yer leg off.'

'Me granddad didn't have no arm, one eye missing too, maybe it run in the fambly hey,' the big man says, trying to keep calm.

Hornbill bends over both of them tut-tutting about the Maori's wound while he rolls a hand-made, then licks the edge of the cigarette paper and places it in his mouth and lights it. He takes a quick draw on it himself and passes it to the New Zealander. The light from Hornbill's match, brighter and closer than the soft light from the lamp, reveals a broad, heavily tattooed face and Ben is suddenly and painfully reminded of Hawk and home and his beloved sister, Victoria.

'Thanks,' the Maori says. 'Much obliged hey, man.'

'Bring us the lamp, lad,' Ben instructs Hornbill, 'then go tell the others the trench is clear. Tell Wordy Smith to post a sentry, top, centre and down here both sides and to heave the Turks overboard. Leave the four Kiwis, we'll think what to do about them later.' Hornbill brings the hurricane lamp over and places it beside Ben. 'Oh, and leave your first field dressing with me.'

'Jeez, I'm sorry, Sergeant, I'm wearin' it,' Hornbill says sheepishly.

'Oh, yeah, I forgot. What happened?'

'Shrapnel pellet when we was landing, it ain't much more than a graze, but it fair knocked me out, when I come to I couldn't find yiz so they pushed me into a platoon in A Company. Stretcher-bearer bloke done me 'ead.'

'Nice to have you back, Hornbill.'

'Me too, Sergeant. I can tell ya, I were *that* upset losing yiz.'

'Count yerself lucky, lad. We were all shitting ourselves back there, at least you were out of it for a time,' Ben teases.

Ben turns to the big Maori. 'You blokes issued with a first field dressing?'

'A bandage?'

'Yeah.'

'In me pack.' The Maori tries to reach over for his pack and inadvertently moves his leg. 'Oh fuck!' he yells.

'Steady, lad, sit still, we'll get it.' Ben looks at Hornbill who is about to depart and nods towards the New Zealander's pack.

'Sorry, Sergeant, don't mean t'cry out.'

'Not to worry, lad, be my guest, your leg's bust real bad, but it ain't your knee and that's good.' Ben doesn't tell him that the chances of getting him back to the beach are pretty slim, in fact, for all of them. Hornbill hands Ben the bandage from the soldier's pack. 'I'll need two or three more o' these and a couple of pieces of wood for splints, get the field dressings off the four dead Kiwi blokes, get back here as soon as you can.'

'Sergeant, can we get a brew goin', there's water and firewood back there, against the wall?'

'Yeah, sure.' Ben glances at the Maori. 'Like a cuppa?'

The big man nods and tries to smile through the pain. 'Me mum says nice cuppa tea fix most thin's.'

Ben calls out after Hornbill, 'Tell the lads to break out rations, eat something! Oh, and if the dead Turks have water bottles, take them before you toss 'em over the top.'

He turns back to the Maori. 'I'm gunna do the best I can with this, mate, but it won't be much, clean it a bit, bandage it, fix a splint, that's about it for the time being.'

'Thanks, Sergeant.'

'It's Ben. We don't stand on ceremony here. Ben Teekleman.'

'Jack Tau Paranihi,' the Maori says, extending a hand that's almost twice the size of Ben's.

They shake hands. 'Nice t'meetcha.'

'Same,' Jack Tau Paranihi says.

'They issue you with anything to take, Jack?' Ben asks, tearing open the bandage.

'Take?'

'Pain for the use of?'

'Nah.'

'Same as us, eh, not even a flamin' Aspirin.'

Ben uses the gauze pad that comes with the New Zealand bandage to clean out the wound, which has thankfully long since stopped bleeding. He tries to remove the large bone splinters from the wound, which starts up some superficial bleeding again that he staunches. He knows he must be hurting the big soldier, but apart from one or two winces the New Zealander is stoic throughout. 'I'm goin' ta bandage it pretty tight and it's gunna hurt, so hold on, Jack.'

Ben takes out his own field dressing and places the gauze pad from it on the Maori's wound. The Australian field-issue bandage appears to be of a slightly heavier gauze than the New Zealand one so he uses it instead, winding it tightly just below the knee. With the first wrap around Jack Tau Paranihi gives a loud involuntary cry and then grabs hold of his shirt front and stuffs it into his mouth, biting down hard, his eyes tightly closed as he fights back the pain.

'There you go,' Ben says at last. 'At least the bloody flies can't get in. We'll fix a splint for you soon, lad, get you a brew. Have you eaten?'

'On the shup this mornin'.'

'We'll get you something.'

'There's food in me pack hey,' Jack Tau Paranihi says, 'bullybeef.'

Ben shakes his head. 'Only the flags and the badges change, the bloody tucker in every army is the same shit!'

'Sergeant?'

'It's Ben, mate.'

'Ben, where's you get that there axe hey?' Jack doesn't wait for Ben's reply. 'That axe Maori, man, fightin' axe from me own tribe, it's got the markin's.'

'It was my grandfather's, he fought in the Maori wars in 1860.'

'He took it from a dead Maori warrior?'

'No, no, you don't understand, he fought *for* the Maoris.'

'Shit hey? Your granddad, he was a Maori you're a quarter of?'

'No, he was a pakeha, my grandmother was a Maori, her name was Makareta.'

There is a moment's silence and now Jack Tau Paranihi asks, 'Your granddad, he frum Tasmania?'

'Yes, how'd you know that?' Ben asks, surprised.

'Tommo Te Mokiri?'

'Shit, *yes*!'

'His brother, General Black Hawk, and hum, Tommo Te Mokiri, he taught us to use the fightin' axe, they big warriors in my tribe. Not just mine, all the Maori tribes hey.'

Ben points to the tattooing on Jack Tau Paranihi's face. 'Jesus, I thought I recognised the *moko*, it's the same as Hawk's.' Ben thinks back on the stories Hawk has told him. 'Your grandfather, you said he had an arm and an eye missing, did it happen on a whaling ship?'

'Yeah, Black Hawk rescue hum from a whale.'

'His name, was it Hammerhead Jack?'

'That's hum. He give me his name.'

They both shake their heads and laugh, Jack Tau Paranihi for a moment forgetting his pain. 'Jesus, that's weird, here of all places, eh?'

Hornbill returns shortly afterwards with two flat planks taken from one of the ammunition boxes and three more bandages from the dead New Zealanders. Wordy Smith returns with him and Ben introduces him to Jack. Both men then help Ben with the splints so there is no further time to discuss the amazing coincidence.

Ben, with the help of the two others, begins to set the splints. Jack is stoic throughout, biting on the webbing strap of his ammunition pouches, his brow sweating profusely, eyes dilated from the intense pain. 'Steady, lad, steady now,' Ben says as he tries to push back the shattered fibula bone before applying the splint. Blood runs from the corner of the big Maori's mouth as he breaks a tooth biting down on the webbing. It is finally done. 'There yer go,' Ben says, 'sorry, mate.'

Jack Tau Paranihi spits out the tooth and some blood. 'Can't be helped, mate,' he says as Ben gives him his water bottle again and this time the Maori empties it. 'You a good bloke, man, like the ancestor.' Ben is not aware that, by this remark, he means his grandfather Tommo, who is now a Maori ancestor pretty high up in the rankings.

Wordy Smith produces a brown medicine bottle from the canvas haversack across his shoulder. 'Take a sip, Jack, about a tablespoonful.' He uncorks the bottle and hands it to the Maori who does as he's told and hands it back. 'Should help a bit,' Wordy says, returning the cork to the bottle.

'What is it?' Ben asks, pointing to the bottle.

'Tincture of opium,' Wordy replies. 'It helps to have a little botanical knowledge, used to be known as laudanum.'

'Where the hell did you get it?'

'Cairo. I had it mixed, it's almost straight opium, should keep Jack here quiet for a while.'

Ben looks at Peregrine Ormington-Smith quizzically. 'You don't . . . er, you know, take it yourself, do you? I mean, like for normal?'

'Good God, no!' Wordy Smith exclaims. 'I've seen what it can do, some of the chaps in art school got addicted to it, it's rotten stuff, but great as a pain killer. I'm a natural coward, Ben, if I get hit I want to die peacefully.' Ben realises that Wordy's willingness to share the bottle with a strange soldier belies this remark, that Wordy has brought the bottle along for the use of the platoon.

'It works good, man,' Jack Tau Paranihi exclaims. 'Thanks a lot, sir.'

'It's Wordy . . . Wordy Smith, Jack.'

'Mate, we're going to move you onto that stretcher, you'll be better off lying down,' Ben says. 'You all right?'

Jack smiles. 'Don't feel a thung.'

'Good, then we'll do it now.' Ben points to Jack's ammunition pouches and webbing. 'We'll take that off, you'll be better without it.' He nods to Hornbill, who helps the Maori remove his webbing and then moves behind him with his shoulders against the back wall, gripping the big man under the armpits. Ben instructs Wordy Smith to hold the legs together at the ankles and he takes hold of Jack by looping his arms under his bum. 'Righto, one, two, three, *lift!*' The huge man must weigh in the vicinity of two hundred and eighty pounds, maybe more, as they move him the few feet over to the camp stretcher.

'Shit, yer ain't small neither,' Hornbill, a big man himself, says, breathing hard from the effort.

'Lock forward,' Jack Tau Paranihi says.

Hornbill nods. 'Rugby,' he says, explaining to Ben and Wordy Smith.

Later Jack explains how they got to the Turkish trench. It seems the New Zealanders had landed on the beach at roughly the same time as the 2nd Brigade and like them had expected to fight to the north on Baby 700. But his landing boat had become unsecured, breaking away from the steam pinnace towing it, the tow rope possibly severed by a piece of shrapnel. They had been forced to row ashore, landing to the right, the Gaba Tepe side. Half of his boat had been hit by shrapnel pellets and machine-gun fire and those not dead or wounded, sixteen of them, had been bunched together with the Australian 6th Battalion in a company under Captain Hooke. 'Like the pirate in that story,' Jack Tau Paranihi said at the time. They'd crossed over a series of spurs leading down from the southern edge of 400 Plateau, five in all, the last, Pine Ridge, being the tallest. Each of the ridges led into deep gullies and the small New Zealand group, sticking together, somehow became detached from the rest of the company after entering a deep gully between what would later be known as Snipers' Ridge and Weir Ridge. Losing contact they pressed on and eventually found their way alone onto Pine Ridge and decided to go up it. It was the steepest of all the climbs, but fortunately one on which the scrub grew mostly higher than a man's head and so they were able to conceal their approach. They'd surprised a group of about ten Turks near the top who were carrying water and supplies and, as Jack put it, 'got in among them'. The Turks made a run for it and they chased them up the final slope. The guns of the British cruiser *Bacchante*, firing on the battery on Gaba Tepe from the bay, were making such a horrendous racket that the Turks in the trench couldn't possibly have heard them approaching. Foolishly thinking themselves safe, they appear to have posted no sentry on the southern side and the New Zealanders had almost reached the trench before the Turks realised what was happening. Nevertheless, they'd managed to kill four of the bayonet-charging Kiwis at close range.

'But then we was among thum with our bayonets,' Jack Tau Paranihi explains. 'Thum Turks didn't have the stomach for that stuff and they're out the top end o' the trench like jack rabbits and gorn f'their lives down the slope out back! I jump into the trench and see the part what's covered, there's a Turk next to a stripped-down machine gun, but he, or somebody, must'a had a rifle, 'cause as I stuck hum there's an explosion and me leg crumples under me and I don't remember nothink more. When I come to, all me mates'a gorn.'

Ben reasons that the remainder of Jack's New Zealanders, unaware of him lying wounded in the dark recess, had moved on in their attempt to find their company or to follow after the escaping Turks.

Ben and Wordy Smith now talk about their position. To press on over the hill into the valley beyond where the 3rd Battalion lies pinned down will bring them back into the Turkish line of fire. Moreover, not long after they've arrived at the trench the Turkish fire over Lone Pine and further south along Pine Ridge has grown much heavier and artillery and machine-gun fire is whistling over their heads. They are not to know that the Turks have spotted the 12th Battalion pushing towards Pine Ridge and a little later the 6th coming over the southern spurs. This means that Lone Pine is not only receiving aim from the Turks on the Third Ridge but also catching the bullets and shrapnel pellets which miss 400 Plateau. Ben and Wordy Smith were lucky they took their platoon across the plateau when they did. Half an hour later, they would have been in the very centre of a maelstrom of bullets and artillery fire. Leaving the trench now means almost certain death.

Ben calls the platoon together. 'We're staying put, lads, moving on is pointless and suicidal. Our objective was to cross the plateau and try to engage the enemy and we've done the first and we'll attempt to do the second from where we are. There's a good position to mount a machine gun on the northern end of the trench and although it's a fairly narrow trajectory across the valley onto the Third Ridge we can hit the enemy from here a bloody sight better than firing at them pinned down from behind a rock.'

'Machine gun? Where we gunna get one o' those?' Numbers Cooligan asks.

'There's one in the shed back there with the wounded Maori, stripped down, it's a French Hotchkiss, the Turks have got quite a lot of French weaponry.

'Yes, but will we know how to use it, Ben?' Library Spencer asks.

'Yeah, I reckon. I covered all the Allied machine guns when I did a special weaponry course at Broadmeadows, the German ones too.' Ben adds, 'I admit, I've never actually stripped one down, matter of fact this one is the first I've seen in the flesh so to speak, but I remember the system.' He hesitates, 'I think . . . hope.'

'She'll be apples,' Hornbill says. 'I reckon if I can get the blighter assembled we'll know how she works orright.'

Towards noon the machine gun is ready but for a part in the firing mechanism. Hornbill calls Ben, 'Lookee at that, willya. Bastard's perfeck, except for the one small part.'

'What are you trying to say?' Ben asks.

'Well, we're fucked, it's a small high-tensile steel spring behind the trigger, without it we can't fire the bastard.'

'Can't you make one, get it out of a rifle, modify it?'

Hornbill points to a Turkish Mauser and one of the New Zealand rifles, which are Lee-Enfields same as the Australians'. 'I've tried that, no good. The Frogs don't do things like other people.'

Wordy Smith comes over. 'What seems to be the trouble, Ben?'

'Spring in the trigger mechanism's missing, without it the bloody thing won't work.'

Wordy doesn't pursue the usual litany of questions – the have yous or did yous – knowing full well both Ben and Hornbill will have covered all this. He thinks for a moment then looks at Hornbill. 'The sergeant!'

'Huh?'

'The Turkish sergeant Jack here took care of, wasn't he working on the gun?'

'Probably, he was right next to it when I done him in,' Jack calls from his cot. He has had another tablespoon of Wordy's medicine and is reasonably comfortable.

Without so much as a by-your-leave, Hornbill is up the ladder and over the top. They both jump onto the firing platform and peek over the edge. Hornbill has found the dead sergeant where they tossed him overboard. He's rolled down from the top of the trench about ten or fifteen feet and now Hornbill rolls him onto his back and is going through his pockets furiously.

'Nothin',' he says at last, looking up at them.

'Get back up,' Ben says, then, 'Wait on, look at his fist, left fist.'

From where they are they can see the dead Turk's left hand is closed.

Hornbill commences to pry it open. 'Gotcha!' he calls suddenly and turning runs up the red-soil embankment and climbs down the ladder back into the trench. 'Bugger me dead, it were in the bastard's hand all the flamin' time! Imagine that, hey!' He has a huge grin all over his gob as he turns and looks directly at Wordy Smith. 'Blood's worth bottlin', Wordy. How'd yer think o' that an' all?'

'Nine times out of ten it would have been a bloody silly suggestion,' he says modestly.

'Fuckin' genius, mate,' Hornbill says, happily squatting beside the machine gun again.

In another ten minutes, with the rest of the platoon, barring the six sentries, crowding around, Hornbill has the machine gun ready. They've discovered more ammunition stored in boxes in other parts of the trench and they have sufficient to keep pumping away all day if they can get it to work.

Ben slips a strip of cartridges in carefully, trying to remember the steps involved in loading it up, then resting it on the parapet he pulls the trigger and nothing happens. Ben curses and examines the machine gun closely. 'Anyone know what "Firm" means?' he says suddenly. 'Firm with two "e"s?'

'*Fermé*, it means "shut" in French,' Wordy Smith says.

'The safety catch!' several of them call simultaneously. Ben pushes a small lever which doesn't look as though it should be pushed or tampered with and then pulls the trigger. A burst of machine-gun fire fills the air to the cheering of the platoon.

They fill a series of sandbags and place them on the northern end of the trench with the Hotchkiss barrel protruding from it with a sufficient arc to cover the section of the Third Ridge known as Scrubby Knoll within their range, and further south to Anderson Knoll. Standing on the firing platform the machine-gunner can see out quite clearly while still being well protected by the sandbags. To the immediate right Ben constructs another sandbag barricade for Crow Rigby and Woggy Mustafa, which duplicates the area covered by the machine gun.

'They're going to cotton on sooner or later where our machine-gun fire is coming from and they'll put a sniper onto us, try to take him out, Crow. How far do you reckon it is across the valley to the ridge?'

Crow Rigby looks through his telescopic sights, and after a

few moments says, 'About fourteen hundred yards, Ben.' He turns to Woggy, 'What yer reckon?'

'Twelve hundred and fifty the most,' Woggy says. They have learned in the desert that you can bet Woggy Mustafa against a tape measure. He has a wonderful eye, and when he isn't observing for Crow Rigby he takes a turn with the sniper's rifle. Ben has promised him that if they ever take out a Turkish sniper and can retrieve his Mauser, and with Hornbill no doubt able to fix the mount to fit the Lee-Enfield, the German telescopic sight will become his.

The men, having eaten and enjoyed a brew, are now much more optimistic and some of them privately wish they could push on, go after the enemy. They've all been scared crossing the plateau, but the adrenaline rush as they fixed bayonets to charge the trench has made them realise that it is the only occasion they've had to assert themselves. Up to this moment, all they've done is stumble through scrub and climb over rocks under a hail of shrapnel and enemy rifle and machine-gun fire but haven't, as yet, fired a single shot in anger. The Clicks are still virgin soldiers even though seventeen of them are dead with only Hornbill having the distinction of being slightly wounded.

After five hours, around two o'clock in the afternoon, M'Cay is at last beginning to realise that he cannot hope to relieve the decimated 3rd Brigade and establish a new front at the base of the Third Ridge. The 400 Plateau lies thickly spread with bodies and he cannot yet claim a single gain or pretend to have inflicted any real damage on the enemy. The closer he gets to the Third Ridge, driving his troops into Wordy's 'spoon', or as it is now referred to by its military name, The Cup, the easier it becomes for the enemy to slaughter them. The Turkish shrapnel and rifle fire have steadily become more intense as each hour progresses and, with it, the danger of crossing the plateau increases.

In M'Cay's defence it must be said that at no time does he have effective artillery to help him. Churchill's assurance that the British battleship guns standing off the beach would pound the enemy positions remorselessly proves entirely wrong. They are less than useless and, if anything, present a danger to the Australian troops without inflicting the slightest damage on the Turks. They are soon abandoned, used only to fire at Gaba Tepe in the forlorn hope that they might destroy a gun battery thought to be positioned there.

The brigadiers, M'Cay and MacLagan to his north, have only rifles and machine guns firing at an enemy, whose whereabouts he can only hazard a guess at. It is popguns against brick walls all over again. For a short period M'Cay has enjoyed the morale-boosting effect of an Indian unit with four small mountain guns positioned two on either side of White's Gully immediately behind 400 Plateau. The battery is commanded by Captain Kirby and at five minutes to noon it opens fire on the Third Ridge.

Although the sound of their own artillery giving the enemy a little of their own back cheers up the Australians, the Turks, clearly able to see Captain Kirby's battery from the heights of Battleship Hill, simply turn their own artillery onto them and by half-past two the Indian battery is put out of the reckoning. Now the Turks increase the pressure on the plateau, The Cup and, further south, in Legge Valley, on Lone Pine and Pine Ridge. The Australian lambs are being systematically led to the slaughter.

Ben's platoon starts firing the machine gun across Legge Valley shortly before noon. By this time the 6th Battalion, to which Jack Tau Paranihi and his New Zealanders were hastily seconded to reinforce the remnants of the 3rd Brigade, are having a torrid time at Pine Ridge and within Legge Valley. As the afternoon wears on they are driven back and in some parts are surrounded by the Turks coming down from the Third Ridge, who can see an opportunity to move around Pine Ridge and up Lone Pine. If they can do this in any numbers they will surround the Australians fighting on the southern section. Moreover, this will mean that the northern section will be caught in a pincer movement with no hope of escaping. For the Australians and New Zealanders the Gallipoli campaign will effectively be over on the first day.

It soon becomes apparent to Ben that firing at the Third Ridge, while attracting return fire from snipers and creating a contest between Crow Rigby and his team-mate Woggy Mustafa and four Turkish snipers on the Third Ridge, isn't making a great deal of impact. Then he sees the Turkish troops coming into Legge Valley to engage the Pine Ridge front. At last he has a target and the platoon concentrates their fire on the Turks moving in numbers through the scrub. The machine gun works all afternoon to devastating effect, manned by Ben and Hornbill and Brokenose Brodie who has been loading ammunition strips. Hornbill eventually falls from the platform out of sheer exhaustion, and tumbles into the trench fast asleep. Ben too has been forced to sleep.

With Ben working the machine gun, Wordy Smith has taken over command of the rifle fire, manning the side of the trench looking down into the valley with fifteen men while the other fifteen sleep. Three of the men on duty cart ammunition, make tea, prepare rations and fill the machine-gun strips. Even Jack Tau Paranihi is put to work filling machine-gun strips. He has received a spoon of Wordy's medicine every four hours which has managed to relieve much of his pain. By mid-afternoon the trench is working as a highly efficient unit and each of the men has killed or wounded to their certain knowledge a handful of Turks. All the Broadmeadows drill, the ceaseless concentration of handling a rifle, has come to fruition. The Clicks, with fifteen rifles firing at a maximum rate well in advance of perhaps any other platoon on Gallipoli, are almost the equivalent of a second machine gun.

On several occasions the Hotchkiss, together with the concerted fire directed at the same target by Wordy's rifles, forces the Turks to scatter and retreat when they are at the point of reaching the Australian line.

Soon a Turkish gun on the Third Ridge tries to get their range and the ridge just below the trench is pounded all afternoon with shells. Clouds of dust often obscure their line of sight. Rifle shots whistle over their heads and sniper fire constantly hits the sandbags, but miraculously never enters the three narrow slots through which the Hotchkiss and Crow Rigby fire and Woggy Mustafa observes. Crow and Woggy have taken to picking out the Turkish officers, doing to the enemy what their snipers have been doing all day to the Australians on 400 Plateau. They've taken out more than thirty, Woggy's incredible eyes calling the shots and Crow Rigby placing them. Used this way, Woggy's eyes are worth several rifles firing at the enemy.

Ben knows that sooner or later they will either take a direct hit or sufficient shrapnel will explode over the trench and wipe them out. At four o'clock in the afternoon this happens at the southern end of the trench and while most of the shrapnel pellets rain down on the covered section, six of the platoon are killed. Ben orders their bodies to be taken into the shed, as the covered section is now known, so that the trench remains uncluttered. 'We'll grieve them later, lads,' he says, knowing that it is only a matter of time before it happens again and they are all killed. Ben is rapidly coming to the conclusion that there is no escape from Gallipoli other than to be killed or wounded. Victory is simply out of the question. He now has only one objective, to inflict as much damage on the enemy as he is able before he dies. Two more of the platoon are wounded, though not too badly, Library Spencer has a chunk taken out of the fleshy part of his arm and a lad from Geelong, a quiet bloke known to all as 'Moggy' Katz, who played for the Geelong reserves, has lost the tip of his little finger. Wordy Smith proves to be a dab hand with a field dressing and both men continue to man a rifle, with a spoonful of Wordy's medicine to comfort them.

Towards dusk Ben observes that the Australians in the valley below are pulling back and that the Turks are coming after them. In the indifferent light it is becoming more and more difficult to use the machine gun effectively and he is convinced that the Turks will attack them after dark. They have done an enormous amount of damage with the Hotchkiss and any Turkish company commander will want to stop them. Ben is about to pack it in when a Turkish sniper hits the barrel and casing of the Hotchkiss, putting it out of action. Hornbill is called to have a look and shakes his head. 'Barrel's bent, ain't no way.' In the dark and without the machine gun Ben realises they are even more vulnerable to attack.

With the light failing fast, they suddenly observe a soldier coming towards them from higher up on the plateau. The man, running down the slope without a pack, is obviously a messenger. He waves his arms, shouting, 'Fall back, fall back!' With nightfall the Turkish rifle fire seems to have temporarily stopped, only the artillery continues to pound the plateau higher up.

Ben turns to Numbers Cooligan. 'Go get that man, bring him in.'

The soldier, a lance corporal named Penman, explains that the Australians are moving back across 400 Plateau to the original crest and that Sayers, Ben's company commander, has pulled back from a position near the Daisy Patch and reorganised what's left of the 5th Battalion and an assortment of others. Commanding the battalion, he is positioned on the rear slope of White's Valley. 'You're not to try to join him, he wants you to pull back down Pine Ridge where the 6th is pulling back and needs help.'

'How did you know we were here?'

Lance Corporal Penman laughs. 'We seen what you blokes been doing all day to the Turks in the valley. Major Sayers says there's only one platoon in the 1st Division can rapid fire at the rate you can and keep it up all day. He just said, "Tell Lieutenant Ormington-Smith and Sergeant Teekleman well done, we'd love them back with us when he's through rescuing the 6th Battalion."'

'He always did have a black sense of humour,' Wordy Smith says.

'Well, machine gun's buggered, I guess we're no better here than on Pine Ridge, maybe we'll get to look a Turk in the eye before the night is out,' Ben says.

'I'll be coming with you,' Lance Corporal Penman says.

'Good, we lost our "one stripe" earlier, that would be useful, one thing though, we don't stand formal here, what's your name, Lance Corporal?' Ben replies.

'Ben,' the corporal says.

They all laugh. 'Sorry, Corporal, but I'm afraid there's only one Ben in this platoon, we'll have to call you something else.'

'Nibs! Nibs Penman!' Cooligan offers, pleased with himself.

'Nibs then?' Ben asks the corporal.

The corporal shrugs. 'Suits me fine, probably won't be around long enough to hear it much anyhow.'

'Subtle or what!' Crow Rigby cries.

'Aw shuddup, Crow!' Cooligan calls. 'Just 'cause you ain't clever like me!'

'Righto, let's pack up,' Ben calls. 'It's dark enough to get going and the moon won't be up for a while. We're taking Jack with us on the stretcher, I want four men on it. Nobby, Brokenose, Macca, Keith, you blokes first, change every ten minutes with someone else. There's still a little water left in the barrel, fill your water bottles, it could be a long night. Everybody have something to eat now, you've got ten minutes before we pull out. Moon will be up soon, we want to get going.'

The platoon moves out down Lone Pine. The artillery fire has ceased over this part of the battlefield and to the south and while it is a welcome relief it is also a sign of danger to come. The Turks are about to mount an attack on the southern spur. Their plan obviously is to move around Pine Ridge, where the remnants of the 9th Battalion of the 3rd Brigade and the 6th Battalion of the 2nd have been fighting all day and are greatly weakened.

Ben and his platoon make their way down the slope and south to Pine Ridge without any fire directed at them. Perhaps the worst aspect of the trip is the scrub they must move through in the dark. On the southern side of Lone Pine and again on Pine Ridge the gorse is heavily mixed with thorn scrub and their uniforms and puttees are torn to pieces. Jack, lying supine on the stretcher, is, seemingly, one long scratch, the thorns having damn near ripped him apart. By the time the moon is up they have made their way down to the extreme northern end of the spur where it connects with Lone Pine and here they come across a captured Turkish gun-pit linked with a series of trenches which are occupied by Captain Daly of the 8th with a handful of men all exhausted from the day's fighting. They welcome Wordy Smith with open arms.

'Frankly, we're about done in,' Daly tells Wordy. 'We've thirty-five men and half of them wounded. With your mob in reasonable shape we may be able to hold the bastards off, though I think you'll need to break your platoon up. There's a handful of men under Corporal Harrison and Lance Corporal Kenyon in a Turkish trench about a hundred yards to the north, I doubt if they can hold on without help. We've heard down the line of what your lads have done today, I guess we were the beneficiaries down in the valley, twelve men with your firepower could make all the difference.'

Ben asks Wordy Smith to recommend that Crow Rigby be promoted to corporal on the spot. He has lost Mooney, his corporal on the third landing craft that morning and Phillips, his lance corporal, on the plateau, but is reluctant to send Nibs Penman since he doesn't even know the names of the men who would be placed under his charge. Daly, when he is told Crow Rigby is a sniper, immediately agrees to the promotion.

Crow asks Ben if he can take Woggy Mustafa and Numbers Cooligan. Ben agrees and picks the other nine, though none of them seem too happy to be broken up as a unit. 'Give 'em hell, lads, this is your chance to look the Turk in the eye,' Ben says and for a fleeting moment wonders how many of them he will meet again.

Ben can see that Daly, who is wounded, and his lieutenant, an officer named Derham who is actually asleep in the trench at his feet, are exhausted and soon after discovers that both have been wounded. He quickly sets about organising the defence of the gun-pit which is situated in a separate trench behind the front one. It is occupied by a rag-tag of mixed platoons from the 9th, 8th and 6th

410

under Lieutenants Levy and Hooper, both of whom are wounded. Ben breaks up his platoon once again, sending ten of the men to the forward trench and keeping eight in the gun-pit.

Wordy Smith reports to Captain Daly and outlines to him what they've done. 'Sir, there's a lot of Turkish ammunition lying about in crates. I'd like to move it under the section of the trench that's covered?'

Daly agrees. 'Go ahead, Lieutenant, 'fraid we're too bushed to attempt it.'

Wordy Smith sets out to put a detail together to move the crates and returns some few minutes later with two men carrying a Turkish machine gun between them. 'Look what I've found,' he says excitedly to Captain Daly.

Daly sighs. 'We know about it, Lieutenant. Nobody knows how to use the bugger, could've been a godsend.'

'It's a Hotchkiss, sir, Sergeant Teekleman and Private Horne have been manning one like this all day.'

Daly looks amazed. 'Something good had to happen in all this, thank God you came.'

A machine-gun post is hastily constructed out of sandbags near the pit furthest to the south, with Hornbill standing behind Ben to feed in the ammunition strips. Almost on cue the scrub and juniper a hundred or so yards below the gun-pits are set on fire, the Turks hoping the fire will reach the gun-pits and explode the ammunition.

But a God who has been anything but kind to the Australians all day changes the direction of the breeze and the blaze turns back on the Turks, forcing them into the more open ground where they can be clearly seen in the moonlight.

The men in the trenches now realise that they are vastly outnumbered by the enemy who have their bayonets fixed and are charging up the slope towards them. It is one of the few occasions all day when the Australians own the high ground. 'Let them come closer,' Ben yells. 'Don't fire!'

One Turk some ten feet in front of the rest is shouting, 'Allah! Allah!' and is caught mid-word on the third 'Allah' by Crow Rigby, who picks him off from the trench fifty yards from Ben and they all see the man's head explode in a black burst. The remainder of the Turks come charging on, the Prophet's name on their lips, shouting, wildly excited, their bayonets gleaming in the moonlight.

'Don't fire, lads,' Ben shouts again. 'Steady! Steady, lads. Wait until you can see the fucker's eyes.'

At a range of about fifty yards Ben gives the order to fire and opens up with the machine gun. The Turks in the front drop like rocks in a quarry blast and the next line follows and then the next. Seemingly in moments bodies are stumbling and tripping over each other and yet they come, there are no cowards among them. The battle lasts no more than ten minutes, the machine gun and the remorseless rifle fire simply cuts the Turks apart. Finally, with some of the Turks having reached almost to the edge of the gun-pits, they fall back. There are more than two hundred of the enemy lying on the black, smouldering apron left by the fire they'd started earlier. Occasionally a small flame from the spent fire momentarily leaps into life and snatches at the rag of a uniform, sending thin ribbons of white smoke spiralling into the moonlit night.

Captain Daly turns to Wordy Smith, his exhausted face barely capable of creasing into a smile. 'I've never seen rapid fire like that before, your lads certainly know how to handle a rifle.' He turns to Ben. 'Well done, Sergeant, I guess the machine gun was the difference, eh? I doubt we could've held them off otherwise.'

Ben, exhausted himself, grins. 'Bloody good thing the Turks have a habit of leaving them lying around, sir.'

A little later the enemy organises a second attack, but it is no more than a show of defiance. Hornbill, now manning the Hotchkiss, gives them heaps and they soon lose the stomach to try again. What is left of the attacking force withdraws back over the valley to the Third Ridge.

At about 11.30 p.m. Daly receives orders to pull back to the original line at the rear of 400 Plateau. Ben's platoon, though nearly as exhausted as the rest of the men, carries no wounded with the exception of course of Jack Tau Paranihi, Library Spencer and Moggy Katz. They are all badly scratched by thorns and in the days to come almost every soldier who fought across the plateau will suffer from scratches that fester badly. Ben's men are nevertheless in the best shape of any of the men in the gun-pits and so they accept the responsibility for carrying the seriously hurt and wounded men back to the line. Ben, seeing how burdened they are with the wounded, wants to destroy the Turkish machine gun as it will require two men to manhandle it and a third to carry the tripod.

However, Lieutenant Derham and one of his men who is not too seriously hurt elect to take it with them. 'It's saved our lives once and it might do so again, we can manage it, sir,' he says to Captain Daly.

The little party of fighting men under Daly trudge slowly back over Lone Pine. About halfway to the rear they come across a soldier with a broken leg and Derham and his offsider abandon the Hotchkiss, which Hornbill quickly disables, hurling several of its parts into the gorse, and they take the man with them. Light rain begins to fall and the air grows a little cooler. They arrive behind the lines a few minutes before midnight.

So ends the first day of fighting on Gallipoli. They stand exhausted no more than thirty yards from where they'd started digging in behind the rear lip of 400 Plateau shortly before nine that morning. Ben's platoon finds itself with nineteen men dead and three wounded and those still standing barely have the strength to remove their packs. Bruised and cut, their uniforms torn, their faces and arms blackened with cordite and dust, they fall asleep on the damp ground at their feet.

If they can think at all, which is doubtful at this stage, they will be aware that they've killed men they could see, and will never again look at life through the same clear, clean eyes. They have undergone a process of corruption they will be unable to explain and which will cause them to cry out in the small hours of the morning. While some may grow old, where they have been and what they have seen will only ever be acknowledged by a sidelong glance, a knowingness, a look in the eyes of a mate. There are no words for what happens in the organised slaughter of men. It is a thing they've shared, a glory they've felt and a shame they will know all the days of their lives. While they have fought valiantly and with great pride, they have voluntarily lifted the lid to hell and plunged inwards. And, in the process, they have taken a terrible hiding from the proud Turks, whose ancient land they have dared to violate.

GALLIPOLI

Had he never been born he was mine:
Since he was born he never was mine:
Only the dream is our own.

Where the world called him there he went;
When the war called him, there he bent.
Now he is dead.

He was I; bone of my bone,
Flesh of my flesh, in truth;
For his plenty I gave my own,
His drouth was my drouth.

When he laughed I was glad,
In his strength forgot I was weak,
In his joy forgot I was sad
Now there is nothing to ask or to seek;
He is dead.

I am the ball the marksman sent,
Missing the end and falling spent;
I am the arrow, sighted fair
That failed, and finds not anywhere.
He who was I is dead.

– Dame Mary Gilmore

Chapter Fifteen

THE ATTACK ON LONE PINE

Gallipoli and Alexandria 1915–1916

GALLIPOLI
10th December 1915

My dearest Victoria and my esteemed Grandfather Hawk,

This letter is to be shared between you and is, alas, long overdue. I had hoped to get something to you in time for Christmas but several factors intervened of which I will presently write.

I did manage a scrap of paper to Victoria in mid-November wishing you both season's greetings, I hope you received it as there has been no mail from you these three weeks. Something is going on down at the beach and the mail does not appear to be coming in or is not being distributed. The men are ropeable, letters from home and the regular copy of the Bulletin *is what makes life tolerable for us.*

Sitting here in a dugout carved out of the cliff face like a gull on its nest and writing by candlelight has no feel of Christmas whatsoever. I met a cove yesterday who has occasion to visit the ships in the bay below and he told me that the thousands of candles from these little shelters where troops bunk down at night give the impression of Christmas lights. I believe it's also been most inappropriately called 'a fairyland of lights'. Although I can vouch there is very little peace and goodwill to all men to be found on the Gallipoli Peninsula at the moment. There may be a few wicked goblins about but there are certainly no fairies.

To further the idea of Christmas coming, we have had the first snowfall of the year. As there has been no issue of blankets, it is bitterly cold. (Did you buy the blanket factory in Launceston?) Coming after the severe summer heat with very little autumn weather to warn us, the snow, the first most of the lads have ever seen, has been disastrous. We are told nearly eleven thousand troops have been treated with frostbite, bronchial conditions and the like. Several hundred men froze to death on the night of the first fall. Even the snow, it seems, has sided with the Turks. I must end this for the time being as we are to go out on patrol at dawn and I must try to get some sleep. I will take up again tomorrow.

PALACE HOSPITAL

1st January 1916

My dearest Hawk and Victoria,

You will see from the above address that my luck has changed, or has it? I lie on a bed in the sunshine, looking over the coming and going of warships and transports in the harbour below, knowing that I am not, for the present, going anywhere.

Your mail sent to Gallipoli has caught up with me at last and I have a pile of eight letters from you, Victoria, and have taken to rationing myself with one each day. Two also from you, Grandfather Hawk, very precious and much cherished. The constant flow of letters from home has kept me sane and I don't quite know how I would have managed without them. My platoon looked forward to them as much as I did. I was in the habit of reading relevant bits to them and, towards the end, I feel sure they regarded your letters as if they had themselves received them. It is now obvious why they were not received on Gallipoli as they would have arrived over the period we were preparing to evacuate, though, of course, I didn't know this at the time I started this letter.

I have taken a bullet to the stomach which occurred on the last day on the peninsula, in fact only six hours before we pulled out. It is not as bad as it might seem, it was not a direct hit, but a ricochet and has lodged sideways near my spine. The doctors have not operated and there is some talk that I may be sent to England where the facilities for removing it are better. Though I have some pain, it is nothing compared to that suffered by most of the men here and I count myself fortunate. They have shaved my head and I am able to wash my body every day, it is quite the most wonderful experience.

You must both forgive me if I return to the subject of my letter to you from Gallipoli, now three weeks ago. I fear it will be a long one as I have much to get off my chest. You would do well to read it in dribs and drabs to avoid tedium. It is now even more important to me that I write it all down. So, with your permission, I shall finish it, though thankfully in the past tense. This morning, for the first time, I have been

417

able to reflect on being alive and am not yet quite sure how I feel, though I think I am grateful and, perhaps, as the saying goes, time will prove to be the great healer it is supposed to be. And now I shall continue.

What a change has come over us since we first sailed from Egypt keen as mustard to get to the Turk and to show him what it meant to come up against Australians. At the time, I am ashamed to say, we had little opinion of the fighting ability of our foe, thinking him just another kind of gyppo with a broad yellow streak running down the centre of his back. We referred to him, as we did the Egyptians, as 'wogs' and often enough as 'dirty wogs' and yearned to be dispatched to France to fight the German soldier whom we regarded as a white man like us and therefore a worthy foe.

It seems quite astonishing to me that this was only seven months ago and in so short a period I could go from such youthful arrogance to the person I have now become. No matter what you are told at home, the Turk has proved to be a brave soldier who is not afraid to die and loves his motherland as we do ours. He has also given us a thorough trouncing and, although I shall always be proud of the way we fought on Gallipoli Peninsula, the Turk has no less reason to feel proud that he defeated us. You must believe me when I say we were not easy to beat and that we never gave up, not even at the very last disillusioned moment.

2nd January

It seems strange lying here in the winter sunshine without the constant crackle of gunfire or artillery shells bursting over my head. The biggest disruption to the peace and quiet is the occasional mournful sound of a ship's horn in the harbour below or the clatter of the tea trolley down the hospital corridor.

Now that it is all over and I lie once again between clean sheets, I want to put down a few bits 'n' pieces. I do so not because they are important, but because there are ghosts in my life which must be laid to rest. So many of my mates are dead and I must speak for them and the battles they fought in. I feel at last able to write about the previous months. I, who always stared out of the window when old Mrs Wickworth-Spode tried to get me to put my thoughts to paper, now wish to set the record straight as far as I was concerned in the Gallipoli campaign.

Some day, they'll write the history of what happened in the Dardanelles but my mates won't be in it. They will not be included in any report, which will tell instead of plans and attacks and the doings of colonels and generals seeking vindication for actions taken that were foolish and unwarranted and which resulted in thousands of good men dying needlessly.

But Gallipoli was never about charts and logistics or the vainglorious careers of our military leaders. It was about young lads doing the best they could, giving the best they had, showing courage and humour and a love for their mates that was always decent and honest and true. Somebody has to tell of them. I will write about my own men, but you could substitute their names for many others, the young blokes who came to Gallipoli who fought and believed until the last. They were the best we had and I doubt we shall ever fully recover from their loss. Wordy Smith once told me that lads like these, strong and brave, most nearly a foot taller than their English equivalents, are the genetic seed from which a people is made. When you see a thousand young lads strewn across a battlefield, their bodies filled with maggots as they rot in the sun, it is difficult not to feel bitterness and despair at the terrible waste. I am not yet thirty years old though I feel twice this age and when I see an eighteen-year-old lad lying dead or calling out for his mother while he holds his intestines in his cupped hands, I cannot think of any cause that can justify such destruction. I'm afraid the old easygoing Ben has been changed, forever, though I doubt for the better.

And so I am writing down what happened to my mates while it is still fresh in my mind. I will write their proper names at the end of this letter and I want you to find their families and read this letter to them so they know what happened to their sons and can be proud that they raised such men.

But, first, now that it is over in this part of the world, though we still fight the Turk in Egypt, I must tell you of our life on Gallipoli. I have written to you of the landing and the first few days and so I intend to take up from there. Oh, by the way, I was mentioned in dispatches over the incident with the Turkish machine gun late on the first day. I have lost touch with Captain Daly who put me up for it, though I hope they have seen fit to give him the Military Cross as he deserved a medal far more than I deserved the 'mention'. I must say I was a bit embarrassed by it all but the platoon took it in the right spirit and said although there is no ribbon for it, if there was they'd each take turns pinning the ribbon above their tunic pocket. Quite right too, if I got a mention all of us should have.

After the first fierce fighting, when we were eventually driven back and we dug in on a front line that never really changed much for the duration of our stay, things sort of settled down a bit. The fighting went on in pockets, sometimes fierce and sometimes simply an attack on a patrol, or we'd come across a dozen or so Turks up to no good and give them hell. The artillery from both sides (though mostly from the Turk who was better equipped than us in this regard) went on for most of the daylight hours and so did the snipers. On one such day Crow Rigby and a Turkish sniper exchanged shots for four hours until our man seemed to have got the last shot in because we heard no more from the beggar higher up on the ridge. Such contests were common enough and we took a win from one of our own snipers to mean we were superior, like a football match where your side wins against a hated team.

Oh, how we despised their snipers who made walking out in the open in daylight always a dangerous occupation and who forced us to do most of our chores at night when we were exhausted. The biggest danger was going down to the beach to fetch water for the platoon and I lost three men doing this. Ducking or falling to the ground became a habit almost as common as brushing flies from the corners of your eyes. I found myself on one occasion clawing the ground when someone near me snapped a plank of wood free from a bullybeef crate. Without thinking, our ears were tuned unconsciously to the Turkish artillery fire. The snipers' bullets never really stopped and silence was unknown to us, the crackle of rifle fire, the whoosh of a shell passing overhead or the sharp crack, bang and whirr of shrapnel pellets raining down was the only constant.

3rd January

Yet, after the first month, we became so accustomed to these conditions that the men pronounced themselves bored. The only one of us who seemed remarkably adjusted was Peregrine Ormington-Smith who somehow found flowers still growing on ground that was cratered by artillery shells and churned to dust. He would sit quietly in his dugout with some specimen the size of my little fingernail under his microscope and paint it, making copious notes beside it as though this tiny blossom was of the greatest importance to mankind. The man was quite impossible.

The rest of us soon forgot those first few days after the landing when we were too stunned to think and wished only to get off the peninsula and never fire another shot in anger again. In the long period of tedium after the first onrush the thing we hated the most was not being able to see the enemy while they, perched higher up, on the ridge and cliff faces, could look directly down on us. We constantly told ourselves that if only we could fix bayonets and have a go then we'd soon enough have the better of them.

I know you must find this difficult to understand, but day-to-day living conditions were so tedious and difficult that the men thought of fighting, even dying, as a kind of relief from the tension. Most had become quite indifferent to losing their lives. Wordy Smith said it was a type of insanity brought about by battle fatigue and the extreme tension of being shot at all the time without being able to effectively shoot back. He may well have been right. We are different now, none of us the same nice lads who left home ten months ago. Death was such a common occurrence that it seemed almost as normal to us as staying alive. We came to see the business of staying alive not as good management but purely a matter of luck.

But always there was a hunger for victory, to do what you could when you could, so that those who followed you had a better chance. Every day wounded men returned to the trenches, not because *it was critical that they did so, but because they had begged the hospital or first-aid post to be allowed to fight with their mates. They had quite lost the ability to see themselves as individuals, but only as a part of a unit that was not complete without them nor they without it. This changed after Lone Pine, Quinn's Post and the Daisy Patch, where there was so much slaughter and where we lost so many of our mates that those of us who were still alive felt completely isolated and unable to go back to the slaughter. It was as if a part of us had been removed, disabling us as fighting men. I shall tell you later of these three battles which took place in August.*

4th January

Victoria, you must excuse my not pandering to your feminine sensibilities, but I want you and Grandfather Hawk to get a clear picture of how things were here in the summer (June, July, August) and still were right to the end, except that we suffered less from flies and disease in the cooler weather.

I tell you these things not because I want you to take pity on the lads but so that you can understand the life of an ordinary soldier here on Gallipoli. We left Australia not caring what the war was about, it was a chance to fight for King and Country to show what we were made of. Now, with so many dead and so little resolved, I must question why men go to war against each other. If you are to marry and have sons of your own I pray that you will teach them war is a hell to be avoided.

If my life is to be spared there are some things I can never talk about. This is not because I caution myself not to do so, but

423

because men who must kill each other are not given the words for how they feel afterwards.

Not that I regret having come, and if I must die I am prepared to do so, but now I want to know why my country needs to take my life from me, I must know what the higher cause is for which they offer me as the sacrifice. Why all this killing is necessary? On the battlefield, to stay alive was never more than a passing thought, because there was nothing we could do beyond occasional commonsense to increase the probability of survival. We all believe now that it is only a throw of the dice if we come out of this fighting inferno alive or dead. War is a game of chance. A matter of luck.

When a man is shot and killed where you yourself stood moments before, you put it down to luck. God does not get the credit, He loved the man who died as much as you, but it is Lady Luck who is thanked. I confess that each morning as my eyes open to another day it has become my habit to reach for the Tiki about my neck and to hold it to my lips a moment. I do this every bit as earnestly as a Roman Catholic might kiss a crucifix. I do the same before going on patrol or into battle and I do it again last thing at night. Just as our mother said, I have come to believe in it as much as our great-grandmother believed in her Waterloo medal. This little green man that hangs about my neck has become my great good luck and I should be vexed if I lost him.

Let me give you a bizarre example of how our minds were affected in this matter of luck. We all took turns to go down to the bore near the beach for our daily ration of water, that, by the way, was the most precious of substances on the ridge. We were given a third of a gallon each day, which in the heat was only just sufficient to keep us *from dehydrating. I tried to save a mugful for my ablutions etc. With this I had to shave, wash and, if I was careful not to make the water soapy, to get a boil up for half a mug of dirty-water tea. Anyway, I digress. As I was saying, the business of going down to fetch water (each man had to carry four gallons up the ridge on his own) was a slow dangerous journey with a number of rest stops where enemy snipers, ever alert, waited to pick us off. Half a hundred troops died this way every week.*

On the way down from our position to the bore near the beach, along a steep rocky path lay a dead Turkish soldier whom the maggots had cleaned out, and a bit of a bushfire, started by shrapnel, had smoked the carcass to a black, leathery affair of taut skin stretched over bone. He lay right beside the path on his back with one blackened arm and hand straight up in the air as if he was appealing for mercy.

Well, one evening Numbers Cooligan and Woggy Mustafa were sent down on water detail and, passing the dead Turk, Numbers pointed to the blackened carcass and told Woggy that his Irish grandmother had once said that shaking the hand of a dead man brought incredible good luck and the promise of a long life.

'Yeah?' said Woggy. 'God's truth?'

'Would I tell you a lie?' said Cooligan.

'Course you would,' replied Woggy.

'Well, I ain't,' Cooligan said, 'I swear it on me granma's grave.'

Woggy was taken in by the apparent seriousness of the oath and solemnly shook the dead Turk's hand. Of course, when they got back to the line Numbers couldn't tell us quickly enough about Woggy's nocturnal greeting of the dead Turk. It was a big laugh shared all round and Woggy got a hard time from the rest of the lads except Brokenose

Brodie, who asked Cooligan if what his grandmother told him was fair dinkum 'cause he swore it on her grave.

'She ain't dead,' Cooligan said, thinking this hilarious. 'No grave to swear on, mate!'

Well, the next time Woggy was on water detail he went with Andy Anderson, a big lad from St Kilda. Woggy passed the dead Turk and stopped and solemnly shook his hand. On the way back Andy was killed by a sniper. A week later Woggy was on water detail again, this time with Moggy Katz, same thing again, Mustafa shook the dead Turk's hand and a little further down the path Private Katz took a sniper's bullet through the left shoulder. Then another detail on water duty got shot and we had one dead and three wounded in our platoon.

From that time on every member of the platoon going down the path shook the dead Turk's hand. News of the hand soon spread and it wasn't too long before everyone in the company passing by was shaking the hand. Until one day it dropped off, whereupon some wag pushed the hand into the crevice of a rock to the side of the path so that the fingers protruded outwards. To the very day before we fought at Lone Pine in August, every soldier passing by on that particular path touched the blackened fingertips for the luck he thought it would bring him. The black hand, as it became known, assumed a deep significance to those of us on the ridge and I confess to touching it myself.

5th January

Of the many vexations that beset us this past summer the flies were the worst. The greatest relief that came our way was not when the enemy ceased to attack, but when the colder weather killed off the flies.

I first saw the flies on wounded men in April, and thought I had never witnessed such a gross thing, but they were a mere buzzing aggravation compared to what was to come in June, July and into the hot weather of August. We did not always observe the strictest standards of hygiene in the trenches, which fell far short of the standards we were taught before we left. But then it was always supposed there would be water available, whereas we had too little to spare for cleanliness.

The men went for weeks without a wash and the fleas and lice were a constant plague so that every two days we wore our uniforms inside out in the hope that the sun would fry the lice. Every week or so a dozen men from the platoon would go down to the beach where we bathed in the salt water. If you didn't mind a shrapnel pellet plopping beside you every once in a while it was well worth the effort. There were no waves to speak of and it was a bit like bathing in a salty pond, and the cool water of the Aegean after the blazing heat up on the ridges was glorious. We would go in in our uniform and this killed the immediate fleas and the lice, though not the eggs which hatched in the seams and seemed impervious even to being smoked over a fire.

If cleanliness is next to godliness then this was a most unholy place. There was no way we could keep utensils clean other than to lick the surfaces. But always the flies were so thick that to spread a bit of jam on a hard biscuit was to double the weight of the biscuit long before it reached your mouth. You would think there were enough corpses lying around to satisfy them, but still the flies came. We would speak with our hands clamped over our mouths and those who had colds and runny noses soon took the skin from their top lips in the constant attempt to brush away the flies.

I saw one soldier driven to madness in just such a circumstance that he smashed his fist down upon his own nose, breaking it, and the instant flow of blood attracted a swarm of flies so thick that his head could scarcely be seen. I covered him with a bit of a flour bag and he wept uncontrollably for an hour before he could be attended to and we sent him to Lemnos for three days so that he could rest his nerves.

The flies brought sickness which spread throughout the trenches. Our sanitation was not good, as it was never wise to walk to some quiet spot during the day and where there were latrines the queue was an hour long. The men suffered terribly from dysentery and other intestinal ailments and the trenches often went uncleaned with merely a shovelful of soil to cover what a man couldn't help doing when he was down with the squirts.

The rate of sickness, better contained in the cool weather, was far greater than the number of wounded and the men grew weaker each day while the tasks at hand, apart from the fighting, sapped our energy. As well as carrying water up the steep slopes, we made bombs from jam tins, as the bomb factory on the beach could not keep up with the need. We were in constant demand to provide burial parties and no day passed when we weren't called upon to dig further trenches or to help the saps with the tunnelling towards the Turkish lines. We had no relief, no diversions, no back lines, no rest and we existed almost exclusively on iron rations. This frugal diet, intended as an emergency to take into battle, became our daily fare for all the months we were *there, with only an occasional hot meal to break the monotony of hard biscuit, bullybeef, jam and a little tea. Tell Martha the fame of her billyjam tarts has spread far and wide.*

Fleas, lice and flies, dirt and sickness, monotony and always death were our only constants. Death was everywhere. The dead lay under every bush, piled up in rotting heaps, scattered over open ground, and there was a stench beyond any imagining. Turks and Australians rotted equally well under a blazing sun and while the Turks seldom gathered their dead for burial, many of our own could not be reached. They will lie where they have fallen until this terrible time has passed and we can return to bury their bones in quiet graves where the birdsong can be heard once more.

6th January

Yet throughout all this, only a few soldiers surrendered to their afflictions though there were some malingerers and some with self-inflicted wounds, but they were few and far between. Most carried on when they were too weak for any sustained attack. They still thought of victory and wanted to be with their mates. In my platoon not one man dishonoured his nation nor did anything to shame his family name.

I do not say this with false pride, we are well past such shallow and empty sentiment. We were resigned to die and the reason I did not write was simply that I could not imagine what I could say to you. Like all the men who landed here during April I had shaken hands with the shadows and, in my own mind, was already dead. When Moggy Katz was taken off the peninsula with a Mauser bullet through his shoulder he screamed out, not in pain, but in fury that he was leaving and that he had a right to die with his mates. We all knew this feeling.

And now I must tell you of the battles we fought and won and lost and then lost and won and lost again. Late in July we were alerted that we were to make another major assault. Those of us who had been on the peninsula from the beginning accepted the news philosophically. We had long since given up the idea that we could win with one decisive battle. The Turk was too well placed to be dislodged and too numerous to be defeated even if we could kill twice as many as our own dead. Besides, we were ourselves too weakened to sustain an all-out fight to the finish, except to be almost certainly defeated. For us there was only one of two possible endings, we would either be killed or, mercifully, wounded, and our wounds would take us from that dreadful place. Victory was no longer a likelihood in our minds. Yet those who had arrived later looked forward to the coming battle, as we had once done. We had all grown to manhood with tales of glory and honour on the battlefield and this was their turn to prove their courage. They thought us almost certain to win and were most eager for the fray.

We now know that while we thought this a major battle for supremacy of the heights above Anzac Beach, it was only intended as a feint. We were to draw the Turkish reserves from the planned landing at Suvla Bay, the flat ground a mile to the north of our beach, for the twenty-five thousand British New Army troops.

We were to attack the Turks at Lone Pine where they occupied some of the very trenches I had occupied with my platoon on the first day. Now four months later we would try again to take what had been ours within hours of landing. At two-thirty in the afternoon of August 6th we filed into a secret underground trench dug by the sappers for the attack. Three companies, each from a different battalion, formed the front line just sixty yards from the Turkish trenches, though the flat ground between ourselves and the enemy was covered with barbed wire. Another thirty yards in the rear were two companies which would immediately follow us.

Though young men's heads are filled with the derring-do of a bayonet charge, rushing up to an enemy who is dug in and firing from the safety of a parapet at a mass of men who must cover sixty yards before they can become combative is sheer foolishness. I am convinced that my own platoon alone, facing two hundred men rushing at them from this distance, would have eliminated them by means of rifle fire before they ever reached the point of hand-to-hand combat. Add a single machine gun to such a mix and it is lambs to the slaughter.

7th January

At about four o'clock our artillery began to pound their trenches and almost immediately the Turks replied with a bombardment of their own. In the artillery department they always had the better of us and soon shells were raining down, their Howitzers causing great craters in and around us, shrapnel pellets thick in the air so that men waiting to attack and those in the supporting trenches were dropping everywhere. There was nothing quite as frustrating when, with bayonet fixed, you were waiting for the whistle to take you over the top and then were taken out of the play before you could get out of your trench.

My platoon was waiting with me, the miracle was that we still had twenty-six of the original complement with us, these old hands mixed with the new chums to keep them steady, though the new recruits seemed to need no encouragement and were calm enough. In the front, the first over with Wordy Smith and myself were Crow Rigby, Numbers Cooligan, Woggy Mustafa, Library Spencer, Muddy Parthe, Hornbill and Brokenose Brodie, who, by the way, could read at quite a pace and was always to be seen with a tattered copy of the Bulletin in his back trouser pocket. He would pat the magazine at every opportunity to confirm his status as a man of letters.

How these stout fellows had managed to come through everything with hardly a scratch was beyond me, they never ceased to chaff each other and were always first into everything going. Though I was proud of my platoon and especially their ability behind a rifle, these seven had become a fine fighting unit with a reputation for the firepower they could put down together with a Lee-Enfield. All the practice at Broadmeadows and on the Orvieto and subsequently here had paid off handsomely. There had even been some suggestion, Captain Daly and Major Sayers I think the instigators, that if we had come out of this the six lads, with Crow Rigby as their corporal, would have been taken back to Egypt to show the new brigades what it meant to use a Lee-Enfield correctly.

It is best, I've found, not to speculate about these things and to take each day as it comes. Though, I confess, if I had been in charge I would have culled men such as these from the bayonet charges where they could be mowed down from the parapets without firing a single shot. They were too valuable behind a rifle. Though, of course, we are all cattle in this abattoir we called Gallipoli.

We were to go over together when the whistle went at five-

432

thirty. *Waiting was always the worst time, to be sitting ducks while the shrapnel burst overhead, a veritable cloudburst of deadly pellets, and at any moment you imagined that you would take a direct hit. We had stacked our packs behind the lines so that we could run with all our might, water bottle and ammunition pouches and iron rations all that we carried. We expected to fight well into the night and sewed white calico patches to our sleeves and backs so that we could be seen in the dark by our own men. Of course, this proved just as handy to the Turk who could now distinguish us from his own.*

8th January

The whistle went and we were over, it was too late to be afraid now. The new chums were shouting out, 'Here come the Australians!' Some were even singing and all rushed forward as though it was a race at a Sunday school picnic. To use an expression coined here at Gallipoli 'all hell broke loose', it was not yet dark enough to conceal us and a fire started by shrapnel on the Daisy Patch lit us up clearly enough for the waiting Turkish machine guns. Sixty yards at a Sunday school picnic is not much but now it seemed a mile or more. Machine-gun fire, artillery shells, lyddite, hand-thrown bombs and a wall of rifle fire rained down on us. Men fell on either side of us, some sprawled over the barbed wire so that others coming from behind simply used them as mats. I glanced to either side of me and to the back to check my platoon. The ground all the way back from the trenches where we'd started was littered with the bodies of our men, some of whom had taken no more than a single step forward before dying.

We had already decided to go for the trenches we'd

occupied as we knew the layout with the covered section at the southern end. We'd make for this part so that we couldn't be fired directly upon and then we'd come down from the roof of what we'd previously called the shed and jump into the trench. We'd rehearsed this carefully and I'd drawn a map of the dugouts, communication trenches and saps with each man allocated a place to enter and fight. Even the new recruits knew the layout of this particular section and where they should go. Wordy Smith with his long legs was the first over and onto the roof, closely followed by Crow Rigby. The roof was almost safe as the Turks were firing forward and would have had to turn halfway around to fire directly at us. In the confusion they seemed not even to see us about to descend from the roof of the trench down into them. It was exactly how Jack Tau Paranihi had described the way the New Zealanders had taken the trench on the early morning of the day of the landing.

I looked back over the ground we'd just covered to see if there were any stragglers from our platoon, a quick look seemed to indicate that we'd lost a few in the charge and I could only hope that they were wounded and not killed. But what I saw about thirty yards from the trench was Woggy Mustafa trying to come forward, his chest a splash of crimson. He would rise to his feet, take a few steps towards us, then fall and rise again.

Suddenly I heard a cry of anguish from Numbers Cooligan, 'Woggy! The bastards! The f . . . ing bastards!' Whereupon he dropped his rifle on the roof of the Turkish trench and ran straight back into the melee, pushing some of our own troops aside as he ran against the tide of oncoming men and flashing bayonets. He reached Woggy who had risen again and now fell into Cooligan's arms. Cooligan was one of the smallest men in our platoon and Mustafa one of the biggest, but the little man hefted him across his shoulder and, turning, ran towards us. He was no more than five yards away from where we stood when a Turkish machine gun turned on him and cut them both to pieces at the foot of the parapet.

I am not sure what happened next. I know we were down into the trench from the roof. I was not conscious of dropping my rifle nor that I had unslung my fighting axe from the holster at my back. All I can remember was seeing the machine-gunner deliberately turn his gun on little Cooligan and the next thing I knew was that eight Turks lay dead between me and the machine-gunner. And then, apparently he saw me and turned the machine gun into the trench but before he had the barrel around in an arc sufficient to aim at us the axe had left my hand and split his head open, cleaving his skull in half from the brow down to his mouth.

Later Wordy Smith told me that I had pushed them all aside as we'd jumped into the trench and my axe had taken the throats of eight terrified Turks standing between me and the Turk who had killed Numbers Cooligan, my eyes never leaving the machine-gunner. The remaining Turks, about twenty in all, seeing me coming at them with the axe, could quite simply have shot me. Instead they turned and fled for their lives. We'd won our section of the trench and the men moved on to clean up the Turks who'd hidden from the artillery bombardment in several small tunnels, communication trenches, the shed and the saps, killing another seventeen of the enemy.

For my part, I can claim no heroics, I was not conscious of what I was doing, my fury overriding any caution or commonsense.

In truth, I showed poor leadership. I only tell you this so you will know the power of shock and grief and the disregard one has for one's own life in such circumstances.

Numbers Cooligan showed the real courage. By going out to bring his mate back in he had no earthly chance of surviving. Our little Gob Sergeant had thought only to bring Woggy back in, to allow him to die with his mates. We pulled them both back into the trench and cleaned them up the best we could and put them in the shed so when the sun rose in the morning they would be in the shade and hopefully away from the worst of the flies. I will see that they get proper graves. I emptied their pockets so that I could remove the letter they'd been instructed to write home. Woggy had left his envelope open and attached a scrap of paper to it asking for his crucifix to be taken from his neck and included in his letter addressed to his mother. To my surprise Numbers Cooligan's letter was addressed to me. I opened it to find twenty pounds and the following note:

Sergeant Ben Teekleman.

Dear Ben,

I don't have no parents as I was an orphan boy. The bloke at Flemmo racecourse was not my uncle and a real bastard. But I have you and Wordy Smith and seven other brothers now – so will you use this money what's my ill-gotten gains and when it's all over have a beer or ten on me. Tell the lads no bloke ever had a better bunch of brothers and I loves you all. Also, tell Woggy I'm sorry for the hard time I gave him, he is the best Christian I have ever known, bar none, I swear it on my granma's grave (whoever she was!).

It's been a real pleasure, mate.

Wayne Numbers Cooligan

Gob Sergeant, No. 2 Platoon, B Company, 5th Battalion,

1st Division A.I.F. Gallipoli, 1915.

9th January

If we had hoped for a respite after taking the trench we were to be disappointed. We'd clearly driven the enemy from Lone Pine but at a terrible cost, Woggy Mustafa and Numbers Cooligan were but two of thousands who eventually died, a thousand men or more on the first day. The order was to hold on and to expect a counterattack and, indeed, we were not let down in this regard.

They came at us from the start and what followed were three days, wave after wave, of the fiercest possible fighting, a great deal of it at close quarters and with a bayonet, the cruellest of all the weapons and the only one where we touched the man we killed. Often we could feel his hot breath on our faces, and as he died clutching his stomach, the Turkish lad would cry out for his mama, as our own had. I confess with a degree of shame that I found the fighting axe to be a much more efficient weapon than the awkward rifle with its clumsy knife attached to the end of its barrel. Grandfather Tommo's skill with the axe, passed somehow on to me, has, I believe, saved my life on several occasions and, of more importance, has helped to save others. It must have proved a very effective weapon in the Maori wars.

We learned from the enemy the nastiness of hand-thrown

437

bombs. *They have a small bomb about the size and shape of a cricket ball which they throw into our trenches. It has a nasty explosion which can kill but will mostly blow off a foot or blind you. At first we found these very awkward to handle and used to drop a sandbag over them to prevent any damage. But then we discovered that the fuses were fairly long and that we could pick them up and throw them back at the enemy. They soon enough cottoned onto this and made the fuses shorter so that we had to either catch them in mid-air or move very fast to throw them back for they would take anything from one to five seconds to explode. The men became quite expert at it but, alas, losing a hand was a common enough occurrence.*

We have our own version of this little weapon, empty jam tins packed with explosives and any pieces of metal found lying about. These are manufactured at the bomb factory on the beach or by the men in the dugouts and they are just as effective. The men call these bombs 'the hissing death', for the hiss and splutter of the lighted fuse.

For three days and nights we stood face to face hurling these bombs at each other or charging with fixed bayonets. All the while both sides were sending down a veritable hailstorm of rifle and machine-gun fire. Furthermore, when the enemy were not attacking they bombarded us with a constant barrage of artillery shells. There was not even five seconds of continuous silence in the three days of fighting and we were exhausted to the point of collapse, the men taking turns to sleep although the fighting was raging around them.

Even this had its problems, the dead were everywhere, the Turks' and our own. We had no time to remove them from the trenches and no possibility of burying them, they were piled four or five deep in our own trench and even higher in others. Throwing them over the side meant we were unsighted, unable to look over them from the rifle platforms as they piled up in front of the trenches.

If a man, too exhausted to lift his rifle, needed a spell there was little choice but to sit on a dead man. My men slept with the dead as mattresses.

The stench of bodies rotting in the sun was unbearable. We managed to find six gas protectors to help with the smell, and these were shared, an hour at a time, to bring relief from the terrible smell. By the third day of fighting there were more dead than alive and I had lost thirty men in my platoon and every single one of Numbers Cooligan's 'brothers' had joined him in death. As each died beside me I prayed that I would be next. Now I shall have to drink out Private Wayne 'Numbers' Cooligan's twenty quid on my own. I hope to stay drunk for a month if it will help just a little to kill the terrible sadness which consumes me.

Wordy Smith is also dead and I am still too numb to mourn him and them beyond crying in my sleep. I shall try, for the sake of their parents, to tell you how each of them lost his life, though I have not the strength to do so today and will try again tomorrow.

10th January

I shall begin today with the statistics of Lone Pine. On the ninth of August the Turks had had enough. Or perhaps they realised that the main threat to them was the British who had landed at Suvla Bay. We did not know this and fought as if the war must end right where we stood, as if it was our own personal responsibility. We had killed six *thousand of them in the three days of fighting and we had lost two thousand three hundred dead and wounded. Our own dead lay thickly spread on Lone Pine where, when the burial parties came to fetch them, the maggots dropping from their bodies were gathered in bucketfuls.*

Lone Pine was thought to have had the bloodiest hand-to-hand fighting of the war and continued for three days. But on the day following our attack on the Turkish trenches several skirmishes to the north also occurred which, in their own way, were every bit as tragic.

I was not there, of course, still being occupied at Lone Pine, but I have heard about them from some who were, those precious few who lived. I must assure you there is not the slightest exaggeration in any of the details.

The 8th and 10th Light Horse regiments were called upon to take a position known as The Nek, a ridge about fifty yards wide at the Anzac front line and thirty yards or so at the Turkish trenches, so that any bayonet charge from our lines would have the effect of forcing troops into a bottleneck, concentrating their numbers for the Turkish machine guns and rifles. Our trenches and those of the Turks were only twenty yards apart, not much deeper than the average suburban backyard. Five Turkish machine guns covered the ground between them, not to mention the Turks in their own trenches armed with rifles.

The Light Horse were new troops on the peninsula with no old hands among them. This was their first great battle and, like us, they were anxious to make their mark. They told themselves they must prove their mettle and show they could fight as well as their countrymen whom they had watched from the heights to the north as we mounted the attack on Lone Pine the evening before. Bright-eyed and bushy-tailed they stood, four lines of one hundred and fifty men each were to attack at two-minute intervals, their objective the Turkish trenches immediately to their front and the maze of trenches and saps on Baby 700 directly behind the Turkish front line. These trenches to the immediate rear of the Turkish front line were critical to their own attack and were lined with machine guns capable of halting the Australians in their tracks. The idea was for the artillery to pound the Turkish front line and their trenches behind it mercilessly to the very moment of the charge by the Light Horse. In this way the Turks would not be able to get into position before our troops were in among them with their bayonets. Timing was everything, the artillery would halt at four-thirty and at the same moment our men would be over and running.

At 4.23 the artillery stopped, seven minutes short. Three minutes that would cost us countless dead. Seven minutes in which the Turks could get into position, two deep, in their front trenches with their rifles ready, fire a few bursts from their machine guns to clear them and then simply wait for us to come.

Incredibly the Australian officers in command didn't abort the attack. Instead they played by the formula set out and waited the seven minutes. At four-thirty on the dot the whistle went and the 8th Light Horse scrambled from their trenches yelling blue murder. They had barely taken the first step when those soldiers at the front buckled and fell as the machine-gun fire and the Turkish rifles cut them to ribbons. Yet on they went. Twenty yards is not a long way, but they got no further than five yards and not a single man made it to the enemy parapet.

The second line, waiting, saw the fate of their mates but they never flinched and stood the allotted two minutes, many of the dead from the first line lying at their feet where they'd tumbled back into the trench, some clasping at their ankles, begging to be helped. The Turks were jabbering, excited, not quite able to believe the brave stupidity they'd just witnessed. Then the second line went over the top and, like the first, advanced little more than a few paces before they fell in great heaps over the bloodied bodies of their comrades who had died two minutes before them. The wounded tried to move from under the dead bodies, some howling their anguish, others calling for their mothers, but most too stunned to do anything but crawl back. A few made it, most were cut down a second time as they crawled away.

One wonders at such stupidity, but there was so much of it at Gallipoli where men too brave for their own good took orders from officers too stupid to rescind them. Men were fed like fodder into the mouth of hell.

The 10th Light Horse obediently filed into the places of the 8th. By now the men knew they must die, but reckoned still that they must run with all their heart as swiftly as their legs would carry them and so die with honour going forward into the attack. 'I do not want to die running away,' one of the lads was heard to say as he stepped up to wait for the order to go over the top.

'Boys, we have ten minutes to live,' their commanding officer Lieutenant-Colonel Springthorpe told them, 'and I am going to lead you.'

The men shook hands with their mates and when the order came they sprang from the trenches, jumping over dead bodies. Even

442

the Turks could not believe the foolishness as they once again chopped them down to a man. Incredibly, the fourth line followed and they too tumbled into the blood-soaked dust as the attack was finally completed in a terrible defeat. They never stood a chance from the first to the last man dead. Two hundred and forty Light Horsemen lay dead or dying in an area no larger than a tennis court. They lie there still, we left them when we escaped from the peninsula, unable to retrieve them for burial. Of five hundred and fifty men who stood waiting in the trenches for the whistle to blow their lives away, only forty-seven answered to their names at roll call. The battle had lasted less than half an hour.

As the Light Horse lay dying, with the wind howling in the peaks above them, plainly visible from The Nek were the British troops at Suvla Bay making their evening tea. But this is not an indictment of the English who fought valiantly and died in greater numbers even than us, but of their leaders.

When summer comes again the bones of these gallant Light Horsemen will whiten in the sun along with so many others we could not bury with a Christian prayer. No doubt fat officers with bristling moustaches will sip port in clean uniforms at the Shepheards Hotel in Cairo, their chests ablaze with medals and garnished with campaign ribbons while they talk of the glory of this battle, and others like it. These are the names that will tumble carelessly from their lips, Quinn's Post, the Daisy Patch, the New Zealanders at Chunuk Bair. (What splendid fighting men they proved to be.) They will speak with pride that two hundred men attacked the Turks' trenches on Dead Man's Ridge and suffered one hundred and fifty-four casualties, and that fifty-four troopers of the 2nd Light Horse attacked Turkish Quinn's and all but one died. At German Officer's Trench, three hundred of our men went forward with bayonets fixed and one hundred and forty-six lost their lives. These are the only attacks after Lone Pine I heard of at first hand, but dozens of others like them took place and all of them failed. They failed, not because they lacked a full measure of courage, no soldiers ever fought harder or with more determination, but because good fighting men cannot make up for the gross incompetence of those who lead them.

Perhaps I am being unfair for I have become bitter with the months of senseless fighting, but it seems to me that having, in the very first instance, made the wrong decision to attack the Gallipoli Peninsula, those who led us tried to vindicate themselves and enhance their careers by sacrificing the lives of the men under their control. How very much more sensible it would have been if our leaders had let us live to fight a better campaign elsewhere where, in return for courage and determination, there was some small hope of victory.

The Turks, for their part, were simply defending their motherland. How happy they would have been if we'd simply packed up and gone home. When we finally did, they let us go with hardly a shot fired. Make no mistake, we now talk of fooling them, as though our nocturnal escape was somehow a great vanishing trick in a game of blind man's buff. Even some sort of victory. But they knew well enough that we were leaving and were happy to see the last of us. Enough blood had been shed on both sides.

It is claimed their own dead number eighty-nine thousand and ours twenty-nine thousand. One hundred and eighteen thousand men lie dead and no explanation for any of it is sufficiently plausible to convince the mother of a single Australian lad that he died for something of value. We did not die for King and Country or for some great human cause, we died because of the vanity of old men. It should be as plain as the nose on any father's face that his son was murdered. Make no mistake, this was senseless slaughter, men led like cattle to the abattoir, yet we will praise the colonels and the generals and the field marshals and give them more ribbons for their chests.

Speaking of such things, I was visited in hospital yesterday by a major from staff H.Q. who informed me that I am to receive the DCM for the axe incident on Lone Pine. I told him I had no use for it as it cannot bring my mates back to me. He told me not to be so ungrateful and that I was insulting the King.

'Sir, have you led a charge where you lost your entire battalion?' I asked him.

'If I had, Sergeant-Major, I would wear the medal my country gave me with pride.'

'And I, sir, will wear mine with the deepest sorrow.'

'That is enough from you, Sergeant-Major,' he replied. Then, moustache bristli~ ~e turned on his heel and strode from the ward. I have no ~ ~t that the loudest explosion he's heard in this war is the por ~g of a champagne cork.

I neglected to tell you that I have been promoted to sergeant-major.

11th January

I intended to write about the lads and the way they died, but yesterday after the major's visit, I had no stomach for such writing. I do not kno if I can do so today, we will have to see if I have the hand to write it without the shakes.

Wordy Smith

I will begin with Wordy Smith, Lieutenant Peregrine Ormington-Smith, the most unlikely soldier on the Gallipoli Peninsula. I have with me his book of flowers and while the last page is soaked in blood the beautiful little blossoms in the spray he was painting have, with one exception, miraculously escaped the bloodstains. They peep around the patches of brown that often smudge the ink where he has written his notes. Every page is filled with his paintings, right up to this last bloodstained page. Above this half-completed watercolour he has written Ulex europaeus. But it looks to me just like the blossom of the bloody furze bush that has given us such trouble. As you will see, it is plain enough to look at and only Wordy Smith could see virtue enough in it to want to paint it. I am sending his precious book to you, as he told me on two occasions that if he should die I was to have it. It is my most ardent hope that you will find some place of scholarship where it may be placed in perpetuity.

Wordy Smith died as he would have liked, quietly and without any fuss, though he was a hero. His last moments were spent not with a rifle blazing at the enemy but with a paintbrush in his hand. He had taken a much-needed spell from the fighting and had settled with his microscope and box of paints in one of the communication trenches. Earlier in the day I had watched as he saved enough water from his precious daily ration to half fill a small tobacco tin so that he could use his watercolours. When I emptied his tunic pocket it *contained several sprigs and the heads of dead flowers he had somehow gathered, though God knows when he could have done so over the last four days of fighting. He left no letter for me to send on to his parents though. Like Numbers Cooligan, there was a note addressed to me personally.*

Gallipoli 1915

Dear Ben,

You are to keep my sketchbook and if my parents should make a fuss please show them this note. They did not care for the notion that I desired to be an artist and, in their possession, it will only remind them of the son who did not turn out well.

For my part, knowing you and the lads has been the very best period of my life. Now that I am dead I am able to say this, whereas alive you may have thought it sentimental and over-effusive.

And now I require a personal favour. I am the beneficiary of a small bequest left to me by my grandmother in England. I wish you to use it to establish a bursary at my old art school. It is to be called The William Horne Art Scholarship.

By going back to retrieve my sketchbook from the cliff face at Aden, Hornbill changed my life. Perhaps some budding artist in the future may study in a little more comfort because of what Hornbill so generously did for me.

Will you thank the lads for putting up with me, they are

a grand lot and no officer ever was more privileged than I to have them in his platoon?

As for you, Ben, I do not have the words sufficient or laudatory enough to express my love and admiration.

Yours ever,

Peregrine Ormington-Smith,
Botanical Artist.

CROW RIGBY

Crow Rigby once said to me that when he was a kid he was considered the best shot of the young blokes in the district and won the blue ribbon at the local rifle club three years running and had developed a bit of a swollen head. His father heard him brag of it to someone and that night drew him aside after tea. They sat on the veranda for a while looking out over the dry paddock in front of the house, the old bloke sipping at a glass of milk stout. Finally his father looked up at him and said, 'Son, no matter how good you are at something, remember, there is always someone who is better than you.'

Corporal Crow Rigby died after he had been exchanging shots with a Turkish sniper for an hour and the Turk got one through and put a neat hole into the centre of his forehead. Crow would have admired the shot for it was painless, clean and decisive. He'd met his father's 'someone' who was better than him. Like Cooligan, Crow was terribly upset by the death of Woggy Mustafa whom he saw as his eyes. He came to me afterwards and said, 'Ben, I've got a confession to make.'

'I'm not a flamin' priest, mate,' I remember saying. 'What is it?'

'There was this sniper having a go and I got him in my sights, easy shot and I reckon we could have gotten to him after without too much danger.'

'So?'

'I let him go.'

'Why'd you do that?'

'Woggy. He would have got his Mauser telescopic sights.'

'What are you trying to say, Crow? That you didn't want another sniper competing with you? You wanted to keep him as your eyes? What?'

'Nah, he'd 'ave been the best there is, better than me any day of the week, I wouldn't have minded that.'

'Well, what then?'

'It would have been me made him a sniper and I couldn't bear to know that.'

I don't think I understood fully what he meant at the time. Crow Rigby was as fine a man as nature can make with a mercurial riposte that never went without a laugh. If a man may be judged by the laughter he brings into the world then he and Numbers Cooligan must sit equally on the throne of top-notch blokes.

Crow never shirked his duty either and volunteered on more than one occasion when one or another of the men was down with the squirts to do their water duty, often getting back after midnight from the long climb up from the beach. Once when I could see, like all of us, he was dog-tired, I told him I'd send someone who'd just arrived back from Lemnos after scoring three days' leave for a comparatively minor wound. He'd protested, 'Nah, I need to wash.'

'Why ever,' I'd asked, 'you're no dirtier than any of us?'

'Not my body, Ben, my soul. I must go down to the sea to wash my soul.'

'Your soul?' I remember being a trifle embarrassed, it was unlike Crow to talk in this manner and so I remained silent.

Seeing I didn't understand, he kicked one scuffed boot against the other. 'Ben, as a sniper I've killed at least two men every day we've been here. It's not like in a battle or an attack when we're all fighting for our lives, it's seeing some bloke, some poor bastard, it doesn't matter that he's a Turk, who's carrying water to his mates or squatting to do his business behind a bush, seeing him in my sights and thinking I must make a clean shot so he dies well. After a while, mate, well it just sinks in what you're doing, you're murdering men, like they was vermin back on the property. You're not killing in the heat of a stoush, but in cold blood.' He shrugged. 'It's inside you become dirty, Ben, your soul. When I go down that path to the beach to collect water then I'm just like one of the blokes I shoot every day, I'm in a sniper's sights and that helps to wash a little of the dirt off my soul.'

Crow Rigby was a country boy without much education but he was probably the deepest of us all. I shall miss him dearly. I enclose his letter to his parents unopened, though as their sergeant, in the absence of Wordy Smith, I am supposed to read it. There was too much of the private bloke about Crow Rigby to want to know what he said to his parents. Perhaps you, or Grandfather Hawk, will take the motor and deliver it to them and, at the same time, read those parts of this letter you think suitable. Let them know that he was as fine a man as this *country has ever produced and that we buried him facing into the sunrise, so that he would see nothing but the light in his eyes.*

HORNBILL

Hornbill asked me to read his letter after he'd written it, anxious that it be correct. I recall well how he put it at the time.

'I ain't had much education, Ben, I left school when I were nine and me father went timber fetching and took me along when me mum died of the T.B. Timber and fixin' things is all I know and I've not had much occasion to write to nobody before. Me uncle with the pie cart and me Auntie Mavis with the "artyritus" are the only relatives I got and they don't go in much for letter writing. Still an' all, if it's gunna be me only letter, I mean the first and the last one ever they's gunna get from me, I reckon I ought to get the bugger wrote properly, eh, Sergeant?'

Hornbill died manning the Hotchkiss machine gun during a counterattack by the Turks on the evening of the second day on Lone Pine. The enemy made a concerted effort to put our gun out of action, concentrating all their fire on the machine gun. I guess we must have been doing too good a job with the weapon that had killed Numbers Cooligan and Woggy Mustafa. Hornbill swore he'd take out twenty Turks for each of their lives and I feel sure he succeeded. They threw everything at us, firing and coming in with bayonets. We must have killed thirty men, three getting right up to us, one of them close enough to bayonet Hornbill through the chest before we shot them all. Hornbill, gripping the Turk's bayonet in both hands, ripped it out of his chest with a roar, and at the same time fell over the machine gun, using his body to protect it. He must have taken twenty Turkish bullets to his head and chest, though I feel sure he was already dead when this happened. He saved the machine gun and we continued to use it to the very end of the battle.

Hornbill, 'Mr Fixit', never had a bad bone in his body and he died thinking of his mates. I have put in a report in the hope that he will be decorated posthumously for his bravery, though I can almost hear him saying, 'Me uncle would wear the flamin' thing selling pies and tell everyone he won it for puttin' up with me Auntie Mavis and her "artyritus" all them years.'

Dear Uncle Mick and Auntie Mavis,

I am writing this to say goodbye because I am dead. They would have told you by now but I wanted to tell you myself. It was nice knowing you both and I hope you can sell your pies for many years to come and make a quid. I have made some good mates here, blokes I'm gunna miss a lot. We give the Turk heaps, but he give us some back too. It weren't an easy fight.

Try to remember me sometimes.

Your nephew,
Private William Horne, 1st Div. A.I.F. Gallipoli.

Please explain to Hornbill's auntie and uncle that the letter I took from his tunic was torn to shreds and soaked in blood, that is why I have repeated it here.

MUDDY PARTHE

Every platoon has to have a whinger and Muddy Parthe was ours. He could complain better than anybody else about almost anything. Hornbill, listening one morning to Muddy complaining about the sunrise, shook his head, 'He's got real class, lissen to the bugger, just lissen to what he's doing to the bloody sun comin' up.'

Muddy was squinting into the sun. 'Bloody sun, shines on them first, don't it? Warms their 'ands so the bastards can pull the trigger sooner, shines down into our eyes so we can't see 'em. They can see us though, bloody sun's on their side, I'm tellin ya.'

Bullybeef:

'We got to eat this shit and that's why we've got the squirts, bloody stuff rots our guts, don't it? Lookee here what it's called, Fray Bentos, you think that's the name o' the manufacturer, don't yiz. Well, it ain't, see, it's from Argentine where they speak Spanish, don't they?'

'Jesus, Muddy, what you trying to say?'

'Well you take the word "Fray", it's them trying to speak English, they don't know the word "chewed" so they say the bloody meat is "frayed".' He took up a lump of bullybeef and pulled it apart with his fingers, the thin red streaks of meat looking exactly as if they'd been chewed before. 'See, what's that look like, it's been chewed before, ain't it?'

'You're beginning to sound like Cooligan, mate,' Woggy Mustafa says.

'So what about "Bentos"?' Library Spencer asks. 'What's that supposed to mean?'

'Simple, mate, it's them Spanish trying ter speak English again – Bentos, "Bent arse", they didn't know how to say "squat" so they say "bent arse", it's their word for squatting down to 'ave a crap. You've got ter bend your arse to have a crap, don't yer? What they're saying is that what we're eating is "frayed bent arse", chewed shit. And don't you think the army don't know it, we been eating shit ever since we got here.'

'For once you may have a point, mate,' Crow Rigby was heard to remark.

Muddy Parthe died throwing one of their bombs back over the parapet. He'd picked up two Turkish bombs and thrown them back and then one came looping through the air and the fuse must have been cut very short, or a Turk had thrown back a bomb that we'd already thrown back, because as Muddy caught it in mid-air, his hands in front of his face, it exploded. It didn't kill him instantly though. He was blinded and his face was smashed terribly. There was nothing we could do. Wordy Smith poured some of his opium medicine down his throat, where his mouth once was, and he died half an hour later. I can only hope without any pain.

Muddy Parthe was a brave man, he knew that sooner or later a Turkish bomb must get him, that his luck would run out. But it was his job to watch for the bombs and return them to the Turks and it was the one thing he never once complained about. I shall miss his colourful whingeing. When we were going through a hard time, to hear him complain often made us feel a whole heap better. No platoon should be without a Muddy Parthe.

I am enclosing Muddy's letter with this one unopened, though London to a brick he's complaining in it about something.

BROKENOSE BRODIE AND LIBRARY SPENCER

I must write about these two men together for they cannot in my mind be separated. Brokenose loved Library Spencer with all his heart and soul. I mean, of course, in a completely manly way. It is hard for a male to talk about loving another but I cannot avoid the word simply because there is no other appropriate word to take its place. Library made Brokenose Brodie realise that he was more than just a ditch digger, that he was someone who could read and write and hold his own in company. Library told him of people and places and things that would leave him gob-smacked with amazement and the wonder of it all. He discovered that he had a prodigious memory and would take it all in. Brokenose was not stupid, only ignorant, and with Library as his mentor he was like a sponge soaking it all in. He wanted to know everything and as Library Spencer knew everything there were never two mates better suited. Library Spencer, the teacher and reader who loved facts and the truth, and Brokenose Brodie, the pupil who could never get enough of either.

In the tedious hours in the trenches we would often become bored and frustrated, but never those two. They spent hours together with Spencer teaching Brokenose to read and write, Library Spencer using his precious copy of Great Expectations *as the big man's tutor. Library once told me that Charles Dickens was the greatest writer of them all and, if Library said so, who was I to protest that old Wickworth-Spode thought it was Shakespeare. Anyhow, towards the* end Brokenose could read from the great man's book with barely a hesitation.

I suggested on one occasion that he should rewrite his letter home, but he shook his head. 'It was wrote right for them. If I done it better they'd be ashamed they didn't do the right thing by us kids.' Brokenose Brodie, while trying to make up for a life in a dirt-poor family, didn't want to make them feel bad. 'Being poor an' ignorant with too many brats ain't nobody's fault, it just happens to some folks,' he'd once said to me.

Brokenose was the oldest of eight children, who were constantly abused and beaten by a drunken Irish father who worked as a casual labourer at the abattoir. I remember him telling me about his parents. 'Me old man worked maybe three days a week and so we ate mostly quite good, 'cause he'd bring scrag ends and offal 'ome. Saterdee and Sundee, though, we didn't eat nothing we couldn't steal, because me dad and me mum were dead drunk. Me mum couldn't take no more with him and us kids and she'd get stuck in the gin bottle.'

Library was brought up by his mother, a quietly respectable piano teacher who always encouraged him to read and to act like a gentleman. He once told me that he had read every book in the St Kilda library and many of them three or four times over. He never spoke of a father and I can only assume he never had one present in the home. Library was the school swot, the scholarship kid who didn't or couldn't play sport, the brat who knew everything and was bullied because of his brains. Until he joined the army he had never had a friend, had never been admired by someone his own age. He was the loner, the quiet bloke, until Brokenose Brodie, big, clumsy, eager as a puppy and filled *with admiration and love for the man who knew everything, came into his life. There was never a couple more oddly paired or one that worked better in friendship.*

Library Spencer, like Hornbill, died when three Turks managed to get over the parapet into our trench, one of them stabbing him through his back and heart, the bayonet's point coming out of the front of his chest. Brokenose turned around to see if his mate was all right just as it happened. His roar, or perhaps in the confusion and noise I imagined it, seemed to rise above the rifle and machine-gun fire. He dropped his rifle and lunged at the Turk who had his foot planted in the small of Library's back and was trying to pull his bayonet out. The huge man grabbed the hapless Turk by the throat and lifted him clean off the ground, snapping his neck like a chicken. I saw one of the other Turks coming for him and hurled my fighting axe, the blade cleaving the man's skull. Brokenose bent over the fallen Turk and grabbing my axe by the handle he pulled it out of the dead man's head. Screaming, he jumped onto the firing platform and vaulted over the lip of the trench, charging down the embankment straight into the attacking Turks. He killed six of them before they chopped him to pieces with bullets and bayonets.

I don't think Brokenose would have wanted to live without Library Spencer in his life. Both men died having known that they had a pride and a purpose, the one no longer a loner, the other no longer thinking himself useless. The teacher who knew everything and the pupil who wanted to learn everything there was to know together forever. We buried them next to each other, Mr Dickens' book in Library Spencer's hands and Brokenose hugging his slate and stylus. It was a partnership made in heaven where both men are now looking down at me as I write this.

How very much I shall miss them all.

Your loving grandson and brother,
Ben.

P.S. I have written all the names and addresses on a separate page.

B.

R.I.P.

Second Lieutenant Peregrine Ormington-Smith
General William & Mrs Lucinda Ormington-Smith
Holyoak Farm
Warrnambool, Victoria

Private William Thomas Horne
Mr Mick & Mrs Mavis Horne
14 Lambeth Place
St Kilda, Victoria

Private Wayne Cooligan
(Notify only) The Superintendent
Melbourne Orphan Asylum
Dendy Street
Brighton, Victoria

Private Joseph Mustafa
Mr Joe & Mrs Sarah Mustafa
9A Arthur Street
Coburg, Victoria

Private John Heywood Parthe
Mr John & Mrs Shirley Parthe
15 Vere Street
Collingwood, Victoria

Private Colin John Spencer
Mrs Gladys Spencer
51 Alma Road
St Kilda, Victoria

Private Kevin Sean Brodie
Mr Seamus & Mrs Maude Brodie
14A Wight Street
Kensington, Victoria

Corporal Peter John Rigby
Mr Roger & Mrs Sandra Rigby
'Lyndale'
Roadside delivery
Wooragee, N. E. Victoria

Gallipoli

The days will come when men will stand upon the shores,
Of Suvla Bay and Anzac where the fierce sea roars,
Amazed that mortals under such tremendous fire,
Landed at all, and, having landed, could retire.

Men will embark at Anafarta's sandy bay,
Under the peaceful skies of some soft summer day,
And picture to themselves that time, not long ago,
When all the hills were guns, and every rock a foe.

Bits of barbed wire will peep at them from out the grass
And waken up their slumbering memories as they pass,
Old speechless cannon look them in the face,
And ask them are they fit to stand in such a place?

Yes, other men will gaze upon the silent beach,
And thoughts will crowd about the hills too deep for speech;
Sorrow and pride will come and take them by the hand,
To those heroic graves in that forbidding land.

No need for polished marble there, nor sculptor's art,
To tell the world of Australasia's glorious part;
In quiet village church and in cathedral old,
Let the immortal deeds in glass and stone be told.
But at Gallipoli the place will tell the tale,
The yellow sands, the rocks, the beetling cliffs, the gale;
Why carve New Zealand's name on lonely Sari-Bair,
Or tell old frowning Krithia who lie buried there?

Nations may pass away and other nations come,
But time's destructive hand will never mar their tomb;
Those mighty monuments for ever will remain,
The everlasting witness of a deathless fame.

– W. S. Pakenham-Walsh, 1916

Chapter Sixteen

JOSHUA, BEN AND SISTER ATKINS

London and the Western Front 1916–1918

Thus far Major Joshua Solomon has had what every concerned parent would describe as a 'good war' in as much as he has spent it well behind the front line, first in Mena and then in France. Anybody who spends a war ordering boots and bullybeef won't die a violent death, which is a comforting thought to Sir Abraham but one which rankles constantly with his son, the heir to the chairmanship of the giant Solomon & Teekleman conglomerate.

Being the officer commanding an army ordnance company, the chief margarine merchant as the front-line troops call his kind, does not fit in with how Joshua sees himself. From the moment he was plucked unceremoniously out of his Light Horse regiment in Egypt he has done everything he can to be transferred to a fighting battalion.

Joshua is no fool and, while he has been unable to prove that it wasn't sheer bad luck that found him placed in the army ordnance corps, he has a pretty good idea that his grandfather, the deceased David Solomon, may have had something to do with his posting to a safe haven.

His applications to be transferred to a front-line battalion are sent in monthly and are just as routinely refused. In truth, he is damned good at his job and may be said to have contributed significantly to the efficiency of war supplies reaching the front both at Gallipoli and later in France. So much so that he has been promoted to the rank of major, a rare occurrence in an ordnance outfit where promotion is almost unheard of and where officers tend to die in their beds.

Joshua's life in a British ordnance battalion has become as predictable as if he were working eight to five in the city and catching the five-thirty train to Tunbridge Wells each night.

Having bathed and changed into his mess kit, six-thirty every evening finds Joshua in the officers' mess with a gin and tonic in his hand. The pre-dinner small talk among the battalion officers is occasionally interrupted by the crump-crump of distant artillery and at seven o'clock, feeling slightly tipsy but with the sharp edges of the day somewhat smoothed over, Joshua will gulp down the last of four G & T's before going in to dinner.

Dinner, served by a dour, white-coated corporal, a Welshman whose surname, predictably enough, is Thomas, invariably consists of a pot roast rather too well done for Joshua's liking or an occasional leg of pork bartered or purchased from a local farmer. The inevitable mediocrity of the evening meal is somewhat compensated for by an excellent bottle of French red debited to Joshua's mess account. Finally, dessert and coffee are served while the port is passed around. Though there is a war raging just five miles to the north, with the dead too numerous to count, life in the officers' mess of an ordnance battalion in the rear echelon is very little different from the mess routine of peacetime in the barracks at Aldershot.

Colonel 'Tubs' Henderson, Joshua's battalion commander, referred to by his officers as 'the old man', is a regular-army officer and veteran of the previous war who enjoys all the characteristics of a Boer War officer, including a sanguine complexion and enlarged proboscis brought about by his fondness for the bottle. However, he never drinks alone and is fond of saying, 'A chap who drinks alone is a pisspot. Bad habit. Bad habit. Solitary, not up to scratch what?'

No matter how ordinary the food, Colonel Henderson has never been known to complain about it. In fact, he completely ignores Corporal Thomas until after he has served coffee and whatever passes for dessert, always something out of a tin from one of the colonies. Thomas' choice of tinned fruit then prompts the same question from the old man every night. 'The fruit,

Thomas? Which of our allies do we have to thank for this munificence?'

'The Union of South Africa, sir,' Thomas will reply mournfully. 'Will you take tinned cream with your peaches, sir?'

'Jolly good show, yes, yes, just a drop, ha ha, don't want to drown the African sunshine in the fruit, do we?'

Joshua has come to dread those nights when tinned pears are served. These invariably come from Australia and while the colonel's reply to Thomas always remains the same, with the only change being that Australian sunshine replaces the African, it means that Joshua will almost inevitably be selected to remain behind to share the colonel's after-dinner carafe of port.

Corporal Thomas, also regular army, waits until the port is passed around and the toast to the King is pronounced, then he retrieves the carafe (always from the left) and refills it to the brim.

Together with two fresh glasses and a small silver bell he places the newly filled carafe in front of the old man and then, taking one step back from the table so that he stands behind the colonel's right shoulder, he stamps his right boot to rigid attention. 'If that will be all, sah!' he announces at the top of his voice, bringing his hand up in a smart salute.

'Yes, yes, Thomas, don't fuss,' comes the invariable reply. With Thomas departed, Colonel Henderson looks around the table and fixes a bloodshot eye on one of his company commanders. 'Captain Carruthers, a word in your shell-pink,' he'll say, whereupon the remaining officers, barely able to contain their relief, will hastily scrape their chairs backwards and retire from the table, leaving the old man and the hapless officer of his choice to drink out the brimming carafe.

On a bitterly cold night in mid-January 1916 pears are served for dessert and Joshua finds himself selected for the after-dinner port run. He sighs inwardly. No officer has ever escaped before the carafe was empty. If he's lucky it may take an hour, but if the colonel is in a melancholic mood with the conversation punctuated by long silences it could take as long as two. By the time the last glass is swallowed the old man's conversation will have deteriorated to an almost incomprehensible mumble, always involving the Siege of Mafeking, where it seems Henderson was appointed the senior quartermaster.

However, the mention of Mafeking is always the signal that

the evening is coming to an end and the little silver bell may be rung with impunity to summon Gunner Morton, the colonel's batman. Gunner Morton will enter, come to a smart halt, salute and say, 'Permission to transport you to your billet, sah!'

Tubs Henderson, slumped in his chair, will give the soldier a desultory salute and offer the same arm to Gunner Morton to raise him from his chair, whereupon Morton will lead the colonel quietly off to his billet, a cottage on the outskirts of the small French village of Albert, some two hundred yards from the front gates of the ordnance depot. Many a young officer summoned to the port run of an evening, unable to rise after the colonel has made his departure, has been discovered asleep under the mess table by Corporal Thomas the following morning.

With the weather outside bitter, Joshua had hoped to retire to bed early with a book and a bottle of Scotch. He makes a mental note to renew the pound note he'd slipped Corporal Thomas some weeks earlier, together with the suggestion that he go easy on serving Australian pears for dessert. With a second toast to His Majesty and the royal family and an additional one to the speedy defeat of the Hun, he waits, ruby glass in hand, for the colonel to open the after-dinner conversation.

'I say, young Solomon, you're a damned curious case what?' Henderson begins.

'Case? Curious? How, sir?'

'Well, you're a strapping lad, damned fine specimen, all the right qualifications, Oxford, rugby and cricket blue, not at all the type to be found in an ordnance outfit.'

Joshua, realising that, like himself, the old man is a little worse for wear, replies carefully, 'Are you not happy with my work, sir?'

'Good God, lad, not at all! Quite the opposite. Good heavens! You've done a splendid job. Splendid. Promoted to major, almost unheard of what.'

'What is it then, sir?'

'Young, fit officers like you don't usually end up in an ordnance battalion. We're a bunch of old crocks here, jumped-up senior clerks and depot men in uniform.'

Joshua smiles, unable to disagree with this assessment of the officers in the battalion. 'Well, sir, I really can't say. As you know, I've put in for a transfer to a fighting battalion every month I've been here.'

'Quite right too! You deserve your chance to have a shot at the Hun. At your age I'd feel the same way, old boy.' The colonel takes another sip from his port glass and looks up at Joshua. 'I've put through your request for a transfer every time you've made one and, well, it's tantamount to bumping my head against a brick wall. Damned curious what?' He holds up his port glass and sniffs, then squints over its rim at Joshua. 'Tell me, Major Solomon, are you being saved for something?'

'Saved, sir? Whatever can you mean?'

'Politics? Only son? Heir to the throne? That sort of malarky? Never come across anything like it in my life. Not British, you know. Sort of thing they do to a maharaja's son in the Indian army. Not the done thing here.'

'I can't imagine what you mean, sir?' Joshua says again, knowing himself to be tipsy and so trying to keep the annoyance out of his voice.

'Are you quite sure?'

'Of what?' Joshua asks, now consciously restraining his temper.

'Well, I finally grew curious myself. Not usual to have a request refused when it's signed by the battalion commander. Bit of an insult, actually. Slap in the face. Know a chappie in the War Office. We clerks, you know, stick together. Asked him to dig around. Came back to me all hush-hush. You're not to be moved. Stay where you are for the duration. Nothing *I* can do about it, old chap. Orstralian Government. Official request to the W.O.'

This is all the confirmation Joshua needs to act and he immediately writes off to his father. In his letter he threatens Abraham, telling him that if he doesn't have the order rescinded he'll not return to Australia after the war, stating that he'd be ashamed to do so. He points out that his grandfather has left him sufficient funds to live comfortably in England for the remainder of his life, a prospect that would not make him unhappy. In addition he adds:

Father, please understand, this is no idle threat. While I respect you greatly, I deserve the same chance to serve my country as any private soldier and that means carrying a weapon into battle against the enemy.

If you do not see to it that my grandfather's interference is removed I shall write to the Age, *the* Sydney Morning Herald *and the* Bulletin. *If you think you can buy their silence then I will write to the* Truth, *who has long waged war against our family and would relish the opportunity to run a piece as follows.*

I shall tell them that while others lay down their lives for their country the rich and privileged such as me issue bootlaces and count cans of bullybeef in perfect safety five miles behind the front line.

I will not hesitate to add that I have weekend leave to Paris and a private automobile to get me there, where I have occasion to enjoy champagne suppers with beautiful young mademoiselles while my countrymen die in the mud and stench of the trenches.

Furthermore, I shall not be above using the anti-Semitic angle to all of this. 'Rich Melbourne Jew's son . . . etc.' You know how much the Truth *hates Jews and niggers.*

Please, Father, take me seriously in this. I have been trained by my grandfather and I will fight you the way he would have done and you may be sure I shall win.

I wish also to be transferred to the 5th Battalion A.I.F. and not the Light Horse as previously. There are sound reasons for this, the 5th contains the public school company which includes many of my friends.

Although, with the rank of major, I am more likely to command another company in the 5th, it will still be within the same battalion. When, after the war, we all return to Melbourne, it will be most useful for business purposes as all the top families are represented.

Please, I beg you, do not let me down in this endeavour,
Father.

Yours respectfully,
Joshua.

Though mortified by the general tone of Joshua's letter to him, Abraham Solomon takes his son's threat seriously and realises at the same time that Joshua's ruthless attitude towards him will make him an ideal opponent for Victoria when he returns to civilian life. Moreover, his transfer to the 5th Battalion, if it can be arranged, will not be an altogether bad thing. If he should return as the conquering hero with the rank of major, having faced the Boche in the trenches, it will do him not the slightest harm in the Melbourne business community. The newspapers claim that the worst of the fighting is over in France and that things are relatively quiet on the Western Front. Some sort of medal will sit nicely on his son's chest.

Abraham is beginning to realise that Joshua will not have it all his own way when he returns to Australia. Victoria Teekleman is showing a natural aptitude for business. Increasingly she is being allowed by Hawk to do things her way and the results are impressive. The Potato Factory is growing at better than a ten per cent rate per annum so that the Tasmanian-based company will soon be more profitable than its Victorian counterpart under the Solomon & Teekleman banner.

Hawk's granddaughter is proving to be bold but not foolish in her business ventures and Abraham is forced to admire her intelligence and application. Starting with a small woollen mill in Launceston, which Hawk had given her on her own in the first months she'd been placed under his direction, she has, in just under eighteen months, built it to a size where it is now a major supplier of blankets to the Australian army. In addition she has recently lobbied for and submitted, without any help from Hawk or himself, a government tender for the supply of army greatcoats for the troops fighting in France.

John Parkin, the permanent head of the Department of Trade and Customs, who sat in on the conference when Hawk and

Victoria first confronted Abraham with Hinetitama's shares, dropped Abraham a note after the successful contract.

Parliament House

Melbourne

15th January 1916

Dear Sir Abraham,

This morning I was able to write to Miss Teekleman in Hobart to inform her that her tender for the manufacture of greatcoats for our forces abroad has been accepted by my department. While doing so I was reminded of the meeting in your office.

I must say that I was impressed with the way Miss Teekleman conducted herself on that occasion and again during our recent negotiations. She strikes me as an exceptional young woman and well exemplifies the old adage that we should trust our hopes and not our fears.

I trust you are well,

Yours sincerely,

John Parkin

Department of Trade and Customs.

The factory, which has hitherto employed twenty men and seven women, now has two hundred employees, all but sixteen of them female. Using the excuse that the able-bodied men are increasingly away at the war, Victoria has trained young women in the most previously unimagined capacities. She has them working as successful drivers, mechanics and machine operators, occupations traditionally thought only suitable for men. Furthermore, the clerical staff are also all women, with the exception of the chief accountant, who is an old retainer at the factory. Her appointments include a recently retired hospital matron, fearsome by reputation, named Mildred Manning, who has become her general manager.

When Hawk indicated some doubt about the wisdom of this appointment, Victoria responded sharply, 'Grandfather, if Mildred Manning can run a hospital filled with sick people she can run a blanket factory filled with healthy young ones. She's well accustomed to working with nurses and other female staff as well as handling men, who, if you want my opinion, constantly interfere to very little effect on the boards of hospitals anyway.'

The maternity hospital started in Mary Abacus' home for the wives of the employees of the Potato Factory Brewery has, over the ensuing years, become a general hospital. And while it has been taken over by the state, the brewery has an entitlement to a seat on the hospital board. Hawk has given this position to Victoria and she has made it known to him that the old fogies who sit with her on it, all of them men, do nothing but create obstacles.

When the unions complain about the female bias in the blanket factory, Victoria invites the ten most senior union officials involved in the combined trade unions active in Launceston over for afternoon tea. Needless to say they are all men and the affair, which quite incidentally includes tea and cake, features libations of a somewhat stronger and more spirited kind. In addition, there is a case of beer for each of the men to take home afterwards.

After the officials have had a few tipples Victoria points out that she is acting well within the trade-union charter and that factories employed in essential war industries can recruit from anywhere they wish and are not restricted to union labour. She then informs them that every one of her employees carries a fully paid-up union membership card. After she promises to pay the transport and accommodation for three local union officials as delegates to the Trade Union Congress to be held in Melbourne, they leave, assuring her of the utmost co-operation and giving her three resounding hip hip hoorays.

Victoria has also expanded beer production in the Tasmanian brewery and Tommo & Hawk beer has made significant inroads into the South Australian market, taking a ten per cent market share from West End, the well-established Adelaide brewery, which has hitherto successfully fought off all outside competition.

Abraham has been forced to conclude that Joshua will need every resource at his command if he is to succeed his father as chairman of Solomon & Teekleman.

Moreover, Abraham privately thinks the deal David made to keep Joshua away from the fighting was quite wrong and that money and title should not be allowed to buy such privileges. Accordingly, he sets about undoing the elaborate network of safeguards that David, even in his apparent dotage, put together, marvelling in the process at the old man's Machiavellian mind.

Joshua finally receives his transfer to the 5th Battalion in March 1916 and is given command of C Company.

On the 25th of January 1916 Ben Teekleman arrives in England on the hospital ship *Gascon* and is transported from the London docks to the 3rd London General Hospital at Wandsworth where a number of Australian military surgeons and nurses are stationed. Nearly ten thousand Australian wounded have been sent to Britain, and this hospital, and the London War Hospital at Woodcote Park near Epsom Downs where Australian medical staff have also been transferred, are working around the clock with the operating theatres running in shifts, twenty-four hours a day.

It is a week before a surgeon is available to see Ben, and then only because his admission sheet shows that he has been mentioned in dispatches twice and is to be awarded the Military Medal. This is not to say that he has gained preference over cases more urgent than his own, but only over those of equal importance where his credentials as a war hero have shuffled him to the top of the pile.

He is interviewed by a weary-looking doctor with a colonel's insignia on his epaulets, who introduces himself quietly as John Mockeridge. He appears to be in his early fifties and, asking Ben to be seated, apologises unnecessarily for not having had time to shave the two-day growth he scratches absently as he talks.

'You've got quite a record, Sergeant . . . oh, I beg your pardon, Sergeant-Major,' the surgeon corrects. 'I'm . . .' he looks up, 'well . . . impressed.'

'Impressed?' Ben says slowly. 'It's only stuff they give you if you've been stupid enough to stay alive.'

'I'm sorry, Sergeant-Major Teekleman, I had no intention of offending you.'

'No offence taken, Doctor. It's just . . .' Ben doesn't finish the sentence and shrugs instead.

'Well then, let's see what's doing, you'll have to forgive me, I've been operating all night and haven't had the time to read my case notes.' Ben sits silently as Mockeridge reads. Finally he looks up. 'It appears from the X-rays that you have a bullet lodged near your spine, could be tricky, would you mind if I examine you? You'll need to take off your uniform, leave your undershorts on.'

Ben finds himself disarmed by the man's pleasant manner, it is not something he has seen in a military doctor before, or any doctor, for that matter, where arrogance and a disregard for a patient's feelings are the usual distinguishing characteristics.

Ben removes his clothes and the doctor points to his examination table. Making Ben lie on his stomach, he prods gently around the jagged purple scar where the bullet has entered. 'Most fortunate, the object appears to have entered sideways with a loss of momentum. A Mauser bullet coming in clean would most likely have severed your spine and entered your stomach. They're a higher-velocity bullet, slightly bigger calibre and do more damage than a Lee-Enfield.'

Ben is impressed. 'Yeah, it was a ricochet, the bullet came off a rock.'

'Well, there you go,' the doctor says, 'a spot of luck, but we're not out of the woods yet, old son.'

'What do you mean, Doctor?'

'Well, it doesn't feel too bad, but it could have damaged the nerve casing around your spine. Fortunately it has not penetrated through the wall of your stomach. Sometimes taking these blighters out causes more damage than leaving them in. Is it very painful?'

'I wouldn't say it's a lot of fun, Doctor, but I'm learning to sleep on my stomach.' He looks directly at the doctor. 'I'd rather you had a go at taking it out.'

'A lot of pain, eh?'

'I've seen blokes in a lot worse.'

'Well, if I leave it in you'll be sent back home?' Mockeridge offers.

'And if the operation doesn't work I'll be sent back home in a box, is that it, Doctor?'

The surgeon shakes his head. 'No, nothing quite that bad, but you could be a paraplegic, you'd be sent home in a wheelchair.'

'Or it could work?'

Mockeridge nods his head. 'Or, as you say, it could work and you'd soon enough be fit as a fiddle, though I don't suppose you'd be too keen to get back into the thick of things?'

'On the contrary, Doctor, I've seen all my friends die while the Turk quite rightly defended his homeland against us. We were the invaders, the enemy who came to take his home away from him. But in France I'll be fighting *against* the invaders, the Germans. I reckon that's different. I must go back and finish the fight or my mates will have died for no good reason.'

'Hmm, I've never heard it put quite that way,' Doctor Mockeridge says. He pauses and scratches the growth on his chin then brings his hands together, his chin resting on the tips of his fingers. 'As I said, Sergeant-Major Teekleman, it can be a tricky operation, there's a thirty to forty per cent chance it won't turn out well.'

'Those are better odds than I've had in a while,' Ben answers, 'but either save me or kill me, I don't fancy spending the rest of my life as a cripple in a wheelchair. I'd be no use to anyone that way.'

The surgeon looks shocked. 'I can't do that, Sergeant-Major, I can only do the best I can to remove the bullet whatever the consequences. Are we agreed I should try?'

'Agreed. Thank you, Doctor,' Ben says softly. 'Will *you* perform the operation?'

'If you can wait another week, Sergeant-Major Teekleman?'

'Sure.'

Mockeridge writes out a prescription. 'Here, take this to the hospital clinic, it will help with the pain.'

Ben is operated on a week later and wakes up after the effects of the chloroform have worn off to look directly into the hazel eyes of Sister Atkins. 'Good afternoon, Sergeant-Major Teekleman,' she says, looking down at him.

Ben blinks. 'I must have died and gone to heaven,' he mumbles, still not quite in control of his own voice.

'Now, now, enough of that,' Sister Atkins chides, though her eyes are smiling.

'Am I a cripple or what?' Ben asks her.

'Cripple? I should think not. You'll be running around like a puppy in a few days.'

Ben smiles. 'This is a surprise. Last time we met was on the *Orvieto*, do you remember?'

'No, of course not!' she teases him. 'There are so many big, clumsy sergeants pestering me.' She gives Ben a mock sigh, 'How could a girl possibly keep up with all their names?'

'Yeah, thought so,' Ben says. 'Talking about names, may I call you Sarah, Sister? I mean not here, not in the hospital . . . er, other places.'

'Other places? How did you know my name, Ben Teekleman?'

'I had my sister contact your cousin Lucy in Tasmania.'

Sarah Atkins looks surprised. 'Just to find out my Christian name?'

'Well, a bit more, really. I hope you don't think me impertinent?'

Sarah Atkins brings her hands to her hips. 'Now what am I supposed to say to that?' She suddenly parodies her own voice: *'No, Sergeant-Major, I don't think you're impertinent, please go ahead, find out all you can about me, it's quite all right.* Umph! You men are all the same, you think you're God's gift!'

'I've upset you, I'm sorry, I apologise, I had no right,' the words tumble from Ben's mouth.

'No right is quite correct, Sergeant-Major!' Sister Atkins says sternly. 'I must remind you once again that I am a captain and you are a warrant officer, the army forbids any fraternising between us. You know the rules as well as I do.' She pauses and then continues, 'Now you've just been through a nasty op and you really must get some rest. You'll be allowed up in two days and then you'll be in a wheelchair for a few weeks before you're allowed to walk. In a month or so, barring complications, you'll be up and about. In six weeks you'll be allowed to leave the hospital grounds for a few hours, you may even be well enough to go into London. In which case you'll need an escort, someone to be with you in case you have a turn, *and*, if you're a very good boy and promise not to pester the ward sister, then Sarah Atkins, the cousin of Lucy Atkins, the well-known Tasmanian blabbermouth, *may* volunteer for the job. Do I make myself perfectly clear, Sergeant-Major?'

'Yessir!' Ben laughs. He can't quite remember when he has been as happy.

'Now try to sleep, Ben Teekleman,' Sarah says, smoothing his blanket and tucking it in at the side. 'I shall call in to see how you are before I go off duty tonight.' She turns and, in the neat crisp way he'd first seen her walking away from Brokenose Brodie's hospital bed on the *Orvieto*, she walks towards the door.

'Sister! Captain Atkins!' Ben calls out.

Sarah Atkins looks back at him. 'What is it, Sergeant-Major?'

'Thank you. Thank you very much.'

'Will you please rest now or I shall be angry,' she calls, though Ben can see the corners of her mouth twitch as she struggles not to laugh.

A week later with Ben now in a wheelchair there is a ceremony at the hospital which Lord Kitchener himself visits to present to twenty of the Australian convalescents ribbons and medals for valour while serving in Gallipoli.

Kitchener reads a prepared speech, fumbling with his glasses and then equally with the words which are high-flown, pompous and patronising.

Sarah Atkins, watching, sees Ben's head sink lower and lower as he slumps in his wheelchair as if to make himself smaller. Anyone looking at him, though thankfully all eyes are on the great field marshal, will clearly see that he is embarrassed and upset and his face is beginning to colour.

She then looks at the other Australian wounded lined up in the front row in various stages of convalescence, two of them have been carted out onto the lawn still in their beds with a saline drip beside them, and their expressions are no different from Ben's.

Sarah becomes conscious that the turgid speech is filled with sentimental rubbish which might work at a convocation of middle-aged English choirmistresses but which is highly patronising and insulting to the Gallipoli wounded forced to listen to it.

She has nursed these Australians before and was on the hospital ship, the *Gascon*, when the wounded started coming in on the first two days after the landing. Barge after barge filled with wounded men arrived at the ship's side and had to be refused since the medical staff of six doctors, seven nursing sisters and thirty-eight medical orderlies were unable to cope with the influx.

Sarah's mind goes back to the time on the *Gascon*. One barge had waited at the ship's side in the rain for five hours, from six until eleven that night, the men in it having lain on the burning beach a further twelve hours or more, their arms and legs smashed, skulls cracked open, features reduced to a pulpy mess so that nose and mouth are simply bloody holes filled with pink froth and bubbles. Some have gone mad in the sun and now cackle and scream, while others beg to be killed or are silent, staring, completely traumatised. Those who die are pushed down onto the duckboards under which the blood leaking from the wounded sloshes and splashes up through the wooden slats. And still the barges arrive.

One young lad comes on board just as Sarah has completed bandaging the head of a soldier. He seems unharmed, though he has his hand cupped over his left eye. Seeing her, he comes over, stumbling against some of the wounded, apologising. 'Sister, it's me eye!' he cries and removes his cupped hand slowly and Sarah sees that he holds his eye in the palm of his hand, though it's still attached to a membrane that stretches some four inches from where it disappears within the bloody socket. 'Can you save me eye?' the young soldier cries again. 'Please, Sister, can you save it, I'm a sniper and they won't want me now!'

A doctor, one of the six on board, passes at that moment. 'Cut it!' he yells. Sarah looks at him, momentarily stunned. 'With your bloody scissors, woman! Cut the membrane, dammit!'

She takes the scissors from her pocket and snips the membrane so that the lad now holds the eye unattached in his palm. Blood from the empty socket starts to run slowly down his dirt-streaked cheek. 'What do I do with it?' he cries in a panic.

'Here, give it to me,' she says, stretching out her hand. Taking the eye from him she can't think where to put it and so she drops it into the pinny pocket of her uniform. 'Have you still got your field-dressing pack?' she asks and when the young soldier nods she instructs him to take it out and use the swab on his eye. Then, in an impatient voice she will forever afterwards regret, she says, 'I haven't the time to do it myself, there are others worse off, I must go, you'll just have to manage somehow.'

The boy looks down at her, the blood from his eye running into his mouth and over his chin. 'Thank you, Sister, I'm sorry to be a nuisance,' he apologises.

Sarah recalls how she worked all night with the surgeons while the remaining doctors tried to cope with the wounded who didn't require immediate surgery and who could be sutured and bandaged and whose shrapnel pieces could be removed from more superficial wounds. However, the doctors found themselves often enough removing fingers and toes, and on one occasion an ear, on the spot while the soldier's mates held the patient down, with part of his tunic stuffed into his mouth so he could bite on it.

By dawn the pile of arms and legs in the operating theatre was stacked to a height of four feet, leaving just enough space for staff to move around the operating tables. The orderlies were unable to keep up with the removal of severed limbs or find a place to store them. Soon it became apparent that what room there was on board was needed for the living, and the ship's small mortuary was packed with the dead. But the severed arms and legs could not be allowed to decay in the heat, so, together with other bits and pieces, they were thrown, unweighted, overboard. For weeks afterwards they washed up on the beach at Lemnos ten miles away and as far as Alexandria, more than a hundred miles from the beachhead at Gallipoli.

By morning the unventilated ship's hold and the decks carried eight hundred casualties with every nook and cranny packed with wounded men, most of them still unattended to. The rest of the medical staff worked to save the lives of the more critically wounded except for a single orderly who handed out water and cigarettes and occasionally lit a fag or held a tepid mug of water to the lips of a soldier too sick or unable to use his hands.

For the most part, the normal nursing duties were left to those soldiers more lightly wounded who procured the few blankets available, less than fifty, changed dressings, made tea and prepared what food there was for their mates, often going short themselves.

These same men, without complaining, performed a further duty they would never have contemplated in civilian life. The ship's toilets were inadequate and soon clogged hopelessly. With no bedpans available, piles of newspapers were handed out so that the men could defecate on a sheet of newsprint, which was then wrapped into a parcel and thrown overboard. As one wag was heard to remark, 'Most of what's in the newspapers is a load of shit anyway.'

Yet, once on board, those in pain were stoic to the extreme, barely wincing when shrapnel was cut out or lesions stitched. Others waited patiently for surgery, often slipping in and out of consciousness. The ship sailed at morning light, its hold crammed with wounded men, not an inch of deck space available to fit another casualty.

Sarah was transferred to the No. 1 Australian Hospital at Heliopolis where she nursed in a constant state of organised chaos and where the relationships between the Australian soldiers and the nurses more resembled the feelings between brothers and sisters than those of medical staff and patients. In the five months she stayed before being sent to Britain, Sarah lost thirty pounds in weight. She had regained half this amount by the time she met Ben again, yet he thought her nothing but skin and bone and talked constantly of fattening her up.

Now, as she stood listening to the platitudinous nonsense from the old, tired warrior whom all England so loved and worshipped and watched Ben's terrible discomfort, tears began to roll down Sarah's cheeks. She knew it was wrong to love Ben, that he would soon be gone, back to the horrors of France where his chances of returning to her were even slimmer than they'd been at Gallipoli. 'Ben Teekleman, I love you,' she whispered through her tears, 'please don't die.'

When it became Ben's turn to receive his medal she watched as Lord Kitchener bent to pin it to his chest. Then she saw the old man suddenly jerk his head back in surprise and drop the medal into Ben's lap and immediately move on to the next man. She saw that Ben was weeping softly.

Later he told her what had happened. Lord Kitchener, noting Ben's two mentions-in-dispatches and the Military Medal he was about to pin to his chest, remarked, 'Well done, you've had a good war, Sergeant-Major.'

To which Ben replied, 'Your Lordship, there is nothing good about this war, except that good men are dying because of the arrogance and stupidity of the old men who lead them.'

It is to Lord Kitchener's credit that nothing was done about Ben's remark. Those hearing about it from Kitchener's aide-de-camp, who held the medal cushion at the time, simply think it typical of the uncouth Australian soldier who refuses to salute his superiors and deserves the contempt with which the English military regard the rancorously undisciplined antipodeans.

Sarah Atkins, though having to maintain her distance while Ben is in the hospital, spends a few minutes with him each day after she has completed her shift. She will pull a screen around his bed and allow him to kiss her, though only briefly. Soon they both long for the time Ben will be well enough to be allowed an eight-hour leave pass from the hospital so that she can accompany him to London where they will be on their own. But his wound proves stubborn and his recovery is painfully slow.

The day of their first freedom, when it finally arrives in early April, though still cold, is filled with spring sunshine. Sparrows chirp cheekily on the pavement outside the hospital where Ben and Sarah wait for their trolley bus and people smile at them as they pass.

Sarah is dressed in civilian clothes just as if she is a soldier's sweetheart, which indeed she is. She's borrowed a pale blue winter coat from one of the English nurses so that she doesn't have to wear her army coat which will give away her officer's rank. Ben can hardly believe how pretty she looks and when she puts her arm in his he can feel his heart thumping madly.

Sarah has packed a picnic lunch and, after getting off at the Embankment, they walk along the Thames, stopping to admire Big Ben and the Houses of Parliament and visit Westminster Abbey, after which they cross Horse Guards Parade and enter St James's Park. The ground is still too cold to sit on, but Ben removes his army greatcoat, spreading it on the grass and Sarah lays out the lunch. 'It's only hospital sandwiches and a raisin bun,' she apologises, 'but I managed to scrounge an orange and I've brought a thermos of tea.'

'As long as there's no tinned meat?'

Sarah laughs. 'Cheese, lettuce and onions or apricot jam, take your pick, either way you're in trouble?'

'Trouble? Why's that?'

'The apricot jam will make you too sticky to kiss and the onion too smelly,' she teases him.

Ben smiles happily. 'No kiss, no afternoon tea.'

'Afternoon tea? There's only three cups in the thermos.'

'At the Ritz, my dear.'

'Whatever can you mean?'

'Victoria, my sister. It's all arranged. We're to have afternoon tea at the Ritz.'

'Your sister is at the Ritz? The Ritz Hotel? Isn't that very posh?'

'No, she's simply arranged it. Sent them a telegram, I suppose. Victoria can arrange anything, anywhere at the drop of a hat, for all I know she probably did it through the High Commissioner's office who would have sent a flunkey round.'

Instead of looking as pleased as he'd expected, Ben now sees that Sarah has an unmistakeable look of panic on her face. 'But, Ben, places like that are only for the nobs, the very rich. How will we know how to behave? What fork or spoon to use?'

'It's only afternoon tea, Sarah. Sandwiches and cakes, a pot of tea and a glass of champagne. We can pretend to be nobs for an afternoon, can't we?'

'You can't pretend to be a nob. You either are or you're not, the very rich are different, you can always tell, they're not like you and me. The people in those posh hotels can see a couple of country bumpkins coming for miles.'

'Is that so?' Ben laughs. 'Do you know something, Captain Sarah Atkins?'

'No? What?'

'You're a horrid little snob.'

'Me? No I'm not! If you'd ever been in a place like that you'd know what I mean.'

'Oh? Have you?'

'No, of course not. But I've seen them at the pictures. There are at least four different glasses on the table and more knives and forks in one place-setting than we've got in the kitchen drawer at home.'

'Not for afternoon tea, surely? A cup and saucer, a tea pot, a plate for the sandwiches or cake and a glass for the champagne, maybe a cake fork, oh . . . and a teaspoon.'

'A cake fork? There you go. Now there's a fork made especially for cake?'

'Yeah, on one side the tines are joined, to create an edge for cutting through the cake, or a tart or flan.'

'How do you know all this, Ben Teekleman?' Sarah asks suspiciously.

'I saw it in the pictures,' Ben fibs.

'It's not funny, Ben. You're not a woman. You don't feel these things. When you grow up having to make your new dress by unpicking someone else's old one, when you see a pretty pair of shoes in a shop window and know you have to buy the plain pair with the sensible heels that will last you all summer because you can only have one pair, when as a young nurse there are holes in your spencer and your stockings have darns on the darns, you soon learn your place in life and it isn't with the nobs.' She pauses and looks at him with her big hazel eyes. '*And it isn't having tea at the Ritz.* I'm not ashamed of being who I am, I don't want to be anyone or anything else, I'm very happy being me. It's only that I'm sensible enough to know I can't have everything or that having everything is even good for me.'

'You could always marry a rich man, you're way, way pretty enough and quite the nicest person I know?'

'I don't want to marry a rich man, I want to marry a man who loves me and me him. I could've if I'd wanted, there's been two or three officers who have proposed to me, from nice families, quite well-to-do, too.'

Ben shakes his head. 'I wouldn't marry an officer if I were you, my dear. Never know where they've been. In my experience they're a very shallow type of person.'

'What do you mean? *I'm* an officer, Ben Teekleman!'

'Well, nobody's perfect,' Ben answers. 'It's afternoon tea at the Ritz for the likes of us, my girl. Fatten you up. Two country bumpkins from New Norfolk and Toowoomba, to hell with the nobs, what do you say, eh?'

'Are you sure, Ben?' Sarah says, still looking doubtful and suddenly feeling dowdy in her borrowed blue coat, sensible brown lace-up shoes and heavy lisle stockings.

'Come here, Sarah Atkins,' Ben commands and takes her in his arms and kisses her, oblivious of who might be looking. 'I've never been surer of anything, I'm only a sergeant-major, but will you marry me?'

'Oh, Ben. I love you so very much.'

'When? Next week?'

Sarah pulls away from him and is silent for a while, staring at her hands which are folded in her lap. Then she looks up. 'No, Ben, after it's all over. After the war. I'll marry you and have your children and love you forever, but no one has the right to marry while this is going on.'

Ben too is silent, then he takes her by the hands and looks into her eyes. 'Sarah Atkins, will you marry me the day after armistice is declared?'

Sarah smiles. 'On the very hour, Ben Teekleman, while they're still ringing the church bells.'

'We need a glass of champagne to celebrate and I know just where to get one.'

'The Ritz? Are you quite sure, darling?'

'Don't you know sergeants-major are never in any doubt about anything, my dearest?'

Chapter Seventeen

BEN AND JOSHUA 1916

'If any question why we died,
Tell them, because our fathers lied.'
– Rudyard Kipling

In May 1916, after spending a month at the Monte Video Convalescent Camp near Weymouth, Ben is sent back up to London to A.I.F. Headquarters where the medical officers at Horseferry Road pronounce him, though not without a fair amount of persuasion, fit for France. ('Sergeant-Major Teekleman, you've done enough, there's plenty to do here in England to see you out.') He is finally issued with his travel documents and a forty-eight-hour leave pass to commence at five that afternoon. It has only just gone noon which means Ben has five hours to kill and the chief medical officer at the depot kindly signs him out, 'Go on, hop it, lad, enjoy yourself,' thus adding the extra time gratuitously to his leave.

Ben calls the hospital at Wandsworth from a telephone box on Horseferry Road and asks to speak to Sister Atkins, hoping Sarah may be able to spend the extra time away with him. He asks to be put through to surgery and when a man's voice answers, presumably a hospital orderly, he asks again for Sister Atkins. 'She's been called into surgery on an emergency,' the voice says.

'Damn!' Ben exclaims.

'You wouldn't be Sergeant-Major Ben Teekleman by any chance, would you?' the voice on the other end enquires.

'The same,' Ben replies.

'Righto then. She's left a message to say if you've been given your medical clearance for France and have a leave pass she'll meet you at the Eros statue in Piccadilly Circus at four o'clock this afternoon. Don't worry, Sergeant-Major, she's a grand lass even if she is an officer, good luck to you. There'll not be a word spoken about this.'

'Good onya, thanks mate, tell her I'll be there with knobs on,' Ben says this cheerfully so that the voice on the other end won't sense his disappointment. It would have been the icing on the cake to have the extra time to spend with Sarah.

He smiles to himself, remembering how he'd practised the way he would ask her about sharing his forty-eight-hour leave with him. He'd worked up and rejected a hundred different approaches in his head, though shortlisting some of them first and expressing them aloud to himself, trying to imagine what her reaction would be. At the same time, he'd invented cover-up sentences if she refused. One of these emerged as a favourite: 'It was in poor taste, my dearest, I am so very sorry, Sarah,' which seemed to Ben to have a touch of dignity and even sophistication to it and was a damn sight better than simply mumbling, 'Sorry, it's just that I was hoping . . .' which was probably what he'd end up saying because he'd be so nervous and shamefaced he'd forget the rehearsed apology.

When the time came Ben approached the subject carefully. 'Sarah, my dearest, when I go to France I'll have forty-eight hours' leave, do you think you could get the time off?' Then before she could reply he chickened out and quickly added, 'The . . . er, I mean, the daylight hours and some of the evening, you could take a taxi back to the nurses' hostel?'

He was afraid to look at her, afraid of the rejection and of the disappointment he'd see in her eyes. Instead, she took him by both hands so that he was forced to look at her. 'Ben, I'm not a virgin, there was someone when I was sixteen, a boy my parents were keen on, whose father had the general store.' She paused, her lovely eyes fixed on his own. 'Are you very angry?'

'Angry?' he replied. 'No, just very relieved. Seeing we're confessing to each other, nor am I a virgin, though it wasn't the storekeeper's daughter, it was the wife of the farmer next door and I was fifteen at the time.'

'Does that mean it's all right for me to stay the night with you?' she asked a little tremulously.

'Only if you insist,' he laughed, then added, 'I'll try to find the name of a nice hotel.'

Whereupon she opened her handbag, took out a small piece of folded paper and handed it to Ben. 'One of the English sisters at the hospital gave it to me. She says it's nice and clean and not expensive, a boarding house in Paddington. She says the lady who runs it understands about soldiers going to the front and calls it "Doing my little bit for the war effort".'

Ben took the note and wrote to the woman, enclosing a pound note which was the tariff for two nights including a breakfast of soft-boiled eggs, toast and marmalade and a cup of tea.

With four hours to spare Ben has a sudden inspiration, or, rather, he received a letter from Victoria the previous day in which she asked him when he intended getting engaged. His letters over the last two and a half months to her have been filled with Sarah of whom Victoria obviously approves as she demanded to have a snapshot. They'd found a small photographic studio in Penny Lane and he'd sent off a nice photo of them both. In her latest letter she'd written to say how thin he looked and urged him to eat more and then continued: *You both look so happy and your Sarah is quite the prettiest woman, probably much too good for you. My urgent advice is to become betrothed as soon as possible so she can't get away.* Victoria, as usual, had it all planned out.

There's a rather nice shop in Albermarle Street named Garrard's which you may care to visit. They will, I feel sure, have a good assortment of engagement rings. I am enclosing a cheque from Grandfather Hawk on Coutts Bank for one thousand pounds, with it is a letter to the bank authorising you, on proof of your identity, to cash it. You should be able to get a simply splendid diamond ring for about three hundred pounds, three or four carats at the very least, and I urge you to spoil her rotten with the remaining money. Take her shopping to Simpson's or Harrods of Piccadilly in Knightsbridge, a pretty dress, nice shoes, she will choose her own underwear and you won't like the hat she chooses (men never do). Dare I suggest a glamorous nightdress as well? After all, my dearest brother, you are in London and in love and should make the most of it.

Oh dear, I do so worry about you going to France. I know it's not fair to say so, but I cannot help myself, I pray you fail your medical, though just sufficiently to be sent home to fully recover your health or, at the very least, so that you are given a tour of duty away from the front.

News recently to hand from Sir Abraham is that Joshua has been transferred to a fighting unit and is no longer in an ordnance battalion. He didn't say which one, but he seemed pleased. Men are so stupid. Though, on the other hand, you already know how I felt about him escaping the fighting, thinking some special arrangement had been made. I'm glad I was wrong and Joshua goes up considerably in my estimation.

With several hours to spare before he is to meet Sarah, Ben visits Coutts Bank, identifies himself and cashes Hawk's cheque. He immediately opens an account in the name of Sarah Atkins for four hundred pounds and hails a taxi to take him to Albermarle Street where he is deposited at the entrance of Garrard's the jewellers. The top-hatted, brass-buttoned and overcoated doorman looks him over suspiciously as he steps up to the doorway and blocks Ben's path. 'Do you have an appointment, sir?' he asks somewhat imperiously.

'No, do I need one?'

'It is not unusual, sir. Are you quite sure it is Garrard's the jewellers you are looking for?'

'That's two questions in a row and we haven't even been introduced. A bit of a nosy parker, ain't ya?' Ben says, leaning on his Australian drawl. 'What is it? That I'm not an officer?'

'Orstralian are you then, sir?'

'That's right, mate, and bloody proud of it. Are you going to let me in or is this conversation going to go on 'til dinner time?'

'I'm sorry, sir, I only wished to avoid embarrassing you.'

'I'm an Australian, I can't be embarrassed.'

The doorman grins at this and opens the door. 'Beg pardon, sir, I 'ope you find what you're looking for.'

'So do I, mate,' Ben says, entering the shop where he is approached by a stout man who has every appearance of having just stepped out of a very hot bathtub. He is an even-coloured bright pink from his shining pate to his clean-shaven chin and has the palest blue eyes Ben has ever seen. His baldness is fringed on three sides with a neatly clipped curtain of snowy hair. Dressed in striped pants and morning coat, his starched white shirt set off with an electric blue silk cravat, the man appears to be in his mid-fifties or perhaps a little older.

He, too, now approaches Ben with one eyebrow slightly arched and then Ben sees that his eyes go to the colour patch on his shoulder with the bronze 'A' for Anzac and immediately the man's expression changes. 'Good afternoon, sir, may I be of service?' he asks, bringing a pair of folded pink hands up to his chest.

'Thank you, yes, I'd like to see a ring.'

'A ring? And what sort of ring might that be, sir? A signet ring for your good self? A wedding ring, do I hear wedding bells? Or is it, yes, I have an instinct for these things, an engagement ring?'

'Engagement. For my fiancée,' Ben says, then corrects himself, 'to be, that is.'

'Our congratulations, sir. A diamond, is it?'

Ben nods. 'Yes, please, not too big, I don't want to, you know, embarrass her.'

The floor manager, or whoever he is, for he is plainly senior to the other staff who seem to be standing around trying to look busy with only one other person in the shop, smiles despite himself. 'Sir, it is my experience that a young lady is seldom embarrassed by the size of the diamond on her finger.' He seems to hesitate a moment then says in a not unkindly manner, 'I do hope we can accommodate you, sir, but I must tell you that there has been rather a rush on our diamond rings of late and we have no stones left under thirty pounds. Perhaps you could try Hatton Gardens, I am told that there you may obtain what is called a "soldier's stone", a very nice little ring for under five pounds.'

Ben smiles to himself. Unlike the doorman, at least this old bloke is trying to let him down lightly. 'I'd like to see a two or three carat, round brilliant cut, a "D" flawless, forty-six-facet diamond set in twenty-two-carat gold, nothing too fancy, mind. Like I said, I shouldn't want her to think I was trying to show off, but if I cop it in France, my girl will have a bit of a legacy.' All this information comes from Victoria's letter to him and Ben is quietly proud of the authoritative manner in which he delivers her instructions.

The shop assistant, despite an attempt to retain his composure, is obviously taken aback. 'A "D" flawless? Yes, of course. Certainly, sir.' He gives Ben a small bow. 'My name is Johnson, Jack Johnson, I am the manager here at Garrard's.'

'Jack Johnson, same as the heavyweight champ, eh? Nice to meet you, Mr Johnson.' Ben stretches out his hand. 'Ben . . . Ben Teekleman.' Johnson accepts Ben's hand in a surprisingly firm grip.

'Teekleman? Teekleman? Name rings a bell.'

'Oh, yeah,' Ben says doubtfully. 'Not too many of us Teeklemans about.'

'May I suggest a private office, Mr Teekleman? Perhaps a cup of tea, not quite the sherry hour, but perhaps we can send the boy out for a beer?'

'Cuppa tea be nice,' Ben says, suddenly enjoying himself.

He is shown into a small oak-panelled office which is obviously set up for no other purpose than to show important clients the shop's premium merchandise. It has two heavily studded, uncomfortable-looking club chairs upholstered in green Spanish leather with a small display table between them. A second, slightly larger table is placed to the left of his chair and Ben correctly supposes this is for the tea service. There is a picture of the King on the wall as well as the Garrard's *Letters Patent Royal* framed beside it. The carpet is of a slightly lighter shade of green than the chairs.

'Please, do sit down,' Johnson says, indicating one of the leather chairs, then, 'If you'll excuse me just a moment, Mr Teekleman?' Jack Johnson bows slightly again and leaves, to return several minutes later waving a sheet of paper triumphantly. Walking behind him is a pale, sickly-looking, pimply-faced young assistant, also in morning dress, carrying a tray draped in black velvet.

'Ah, here it is, I thought so, I have a letter from Miss Victoria Teekleman of Hobart, Tasmania, received . . . let me see,' Johnson glances down at the letter, 'two weeks ago. In it she suggests we may have the pleasure of a visit from you.' Johnson looks up, plainly pleased with himself. Whatever Victoria has said in the letter has given him all the confirmation he needs to provide Ben with the full Garrard's favoured-client treatment.

The young assistant sets down the tray upon which are placed several tiny envelopes. Jack Johnson, sitting in the remaining chair, opens the tiny flap of one of them and rolls a diamond onto the velvet tray. 'A lovely Kimberley blue–white of two and a half carats, Mr Teekleman.'

'No, no, you misunderstand me, Mr Johnson. I wish to see a ring. You see, I need it this afternoon. I only have forty-eight hours' leave before I go to France.'

'It is most unusual to make up jewellery with a stone of this quality without first ascertaining the customer's exact requirements,' Johnson says a little primly.

'My exact requirements are a ring with a diamond,' Ben points to the beautiful gem sparkling on the velvet cloth, 'bigger than that one and in about an hour.'

Johnson appears to be thinking, then comes to a decision, 'I have an order made up for a client,' he pauses and then, unable to resist the temptation to name-drop, adds, 'well, actually it's the Duchess of . . .' He pauses again. 'Well, never mind, it is not required until late next week when she comes up to stay at Claridges'.' Then he adds gratuitously, 'She has given over her London residence to the military, I believe.' Johnson frowns suddenly. 'Oh dear, a complication occurs to me.' Ben remains silent. 'If I recall correctly, it has two baguette diamonds to the side of the main stone?'

'May I see it, please?' Ben asks.

'Why certainly, sir, though on the hush-hush, we shouldn't like it to get out, I believe it's a surprise for her daughter.'

'Tight as a chook's bum,' Ben says.

'I beg your pardon, what was that, sir?'

'I promise not to mention it to the duchess or her daughter,' Ben grins.

'Well then,' Johnson says, 'if you are prepared to accept this little rearrangement, we can remove the canary diamond at present in it and replace it with the one of your choosing. The transfer will take no more than half an hour, sir.'

'Splendid, Mr Johnson, let me see the ring.'

Johnson presses a small electric bell set into the oak panelling and a few moments later the same pimply-faced lad appears. 'I want you to bring me Number 400 from the safe, and ask Mr James to accompany you.'

The young bloke departs and Ben points to the envelopes on the velvet tray. 'Perhaps you can show me more of these, Mr Johnson.'

Over a cup of tea, which arrives shortly after the departure of the young shop assistant, Ben selects a beautiful three-carat diamond. The lad returns with a small brown envelope and Johnson spills the duchess's ring onto the velvet surface.

Ben picks it up and examines it in a perfunctory manner, it is immediately apparent that it is a beautiful ring. 'Yeah, this will do nicely,' he says, laying the ring back down on the tray.

He waits for the three-carat diamond he has selected to be set into the duchess's ring, whereupon he pays Johnson two hundred and seventy-five pounds in large, white five pound notes and obtains a certificate of authenticity and a receipt from the now entirely obsequious Mr Johnson.

'If it doesn't fit you may bring it in for an adjustment in the morning, Mr Teekleman,' Johnson assures Ben as he walks him to the door. A few paces short he suddenly halts. 'I couldn't help but notice your Anzac "A", sir. My son, Roger, was a corporal in the Royal Engineers and was killed three days after landing at Suvla Bay.'

'I'm sorry to hear that, Mr Johnson, the British lads fought most gallantly, I'm sure your son died bravely,' Ben says, not able to think of anything more comforting to say to the old man.

'It's been a real pleasure serving you, sir,' Johnson says, 'I'd like to think my son had a sergeant-major such as you to lead him into battle.'

'And you, sir,' Ben says genuinely enough, 'a pleasure also. I don't imagine too many N.C.O.s come into your shop. Your doorman ought to leave the judgment of those who do to you.'

Jack Johnson laughs. 'I very nearly got it wrong myself, Mr Teekleman. We have learned to be cautious about judging the Americans but, I regret, we still have a rather patronising attitude towards the colonials. You have taught me much this afternoon.'

Ben shakes his hand. 'No hard feelings. I've got the duchess's ring for a princess, can't do better than that now, can you?'

This time Ben elicits a smart salute from the doorman.

Ben, with the 'almost' duchess's ring safely in his pocket and with Mr Jack Johnson's mention of Claridges', has a sudden idea and hails a taxi cab. 'Claridges', please,' he instructs the driver.

The desk at Claridges' proves more accommodating than his initial reception at Garrard's, though Ben is also somewhat wiser. 'I'd like to book a suite for two nights and will pay for it in advance,' he says to the desk clerk.

'Certainly, sir,' the man says, 'I shall ring for our manager. What name shall I say?'

'Teekleman, and don't tell me my sister has already written to you?'

'I beg your pardon, sir?'

'No, it doesn't matter.'

'Very well, sir, will you require the newspapers in the morning?'

'Only *The Times*,' Ben says grinning. 'Does it carry the football results?'

'Certainly, sir, though I should include the *Telegraph* in that case, it has much the better coverage. When can we expect your party to arrive, sir?'

'About seven o'clock. Skip *The Times*, I'll take the *Telegraph*.'

'Very well, sir, seven o'clock.'

Ben arrives at Piccadilly Circus with half an hour to spare but enjoys watching the people and the large red buses which seem to pass every half-minute or so. There are several dozen soldiers and sailors and a host of civilians all waiting for someone. Somewhere close by a military band plays, though he cannot see it. It is a perfect spring day in May and Ben plans to walk with Sarah to St James's Park and find the tree where they had their first picnic. The precious orange had been carefully peeled by Sarah and shared quarter by quarter between them. Tea at the Ritz afterwards had been a painless experience, with the head waiter being especially attentive. After two glasses of champagne, Sarah, who admitted she had never tasted it before, got the giggles and later, on the bus returning to the hospital, she fell asleep against his shoulder. Ben simply couldn't remember when he'd felt as happy.

Although he's been keeping his eye on the arrival of every red bus Sarah comes up behind him, slips her arm in his and says, 'Hello, soldier, don't I know you from somewhere?'

'Ha, you'll need to do better than that, young lady,' Ben says. 'Will you take afternoon tea or shall we walk?' He kisses her lightly on the forehead and takes her small portmanteau. Waiting to cross the road, he sees that Sarah has borrowed the same blue overcoat as before.

'Let's walk, I've been in a stuffy operating theatre all day and when I opened a window on the bus half the people in it suddenly cleared their throats and rattled their newspapers so fiercely that I hurriedly closed it again. The English can be very intimidating.'

'See that shop over there,' Ben says, pointing at Simpson's. 'We're going to buy you a nice new coat and a dress that hasn't been worn by someone else, the prettiest shoes in the shop and a smart new hat.'

'Oh, Ben, I don't still wear hand-me-downs, that was when I was young and living at home. Now I can afford to make my own, you're not to spend your army pay on me. Besides, do you have any idea what a good winter coat costs these days, it's iniquitous!'

'We'll manage somehow,' Ben says. 'Come along, girl, there's not a lot of time and we have to get to St James's Park as well, the crocuses and daffodils are out and there's a patch of bluebells I want you to see.'

'Oh, I see, been there with someone else, have we?' Sarah teases.

'No, the bobby on the beat while I was waiting for you told me. I asked him the directions to St James's Park and he said, "Ah, the royal park, grand time to go, sir, daffs and crocuses are out and there's bluebells under the elms, with a bit of luck the King's tulips will just be coming out." Ben adds, 'Ah, "the darling buds of May".'

'That's very pretty, Ben,' Sarah exclaims.

'It's Shakespeare, compliments of Mrs Wickworth-Spode, my English teacher. It's about all I remember, that and, "There is a tide in the affairs of men . . . "' Ben doesn't complete the phrase as they've reached the doors of Simpson's.

'Welcome to Simpson's of Piccadilly, madam, sir,' the doorman says, nodding his head and opening one of the several polished brass and glass doors for them to enter.

'All the doormen look like Russian generals,' Sarah says, when they are out of earshot.

'The Brits love a uniform,' Ben says, then takes Sarah by both hands and looks into her eyes. 'Now, there is only one rule you have to promise to observe,' he says sternly.

'What?' Sarah asks, looking suddenly serious.

'You have to pick out exactly what you like without having a sticky at the price tag. And no cheating, you hear?'

'But, darling, what if you're embarrassed?' Sarah looks about. 'It's an awfully posh shop?'

'I've already told one person today that I'm Australian, so I'm incapable of being embarrassed.'

Sarah laughs. 'I'm beginning to think I know very little about you, Ben Teekleman. Perhaps I shall write to my cousin Lucy and ask her to have a bit of a stickybeak. See what she can dig up on the Teeklemans.'

'Well, before she discovers I'm wanted for an armed bank robbery, let's agree to my shopping terms, eh?'

Sarah, somewhat apprehensively, chooses a lovely camel-hair overcoat, the temptation to look at the price tag is almost overwhelming. 'What do you think?' she says, spinning around in it as she pulls the lapels up to her cheeks.

'Terrific,' Ben says, pleased at the happiness on Sarah's face. 'That the one you want?' Sarah smiles and nods and he thinks she looks not a bit like a hardened nursing sister who has seen almost as much death and destruction as he has. 'Righto,' he says to the shop assistant, a pleasant-looking woman in her forties with prematurely grey hair drawn back into a severe bun, 'we'll take the coat.' Ben turns back to Sarah. 'Now choose one for your friend.'

'What, a coat?' Sarah is thunderstruck.

'She's let you use hers every time we've been out,' Ben explains. 'You choose one you think she'll like.'

After purchasing the two coats, two day dresses, a pair of pretty shoes and an evening ensemble with a second pair of grey velvet evening slippers which Sarah describes as 'simply divine', Ben makes her wear the coat out of the shop. As he pays for their purchases he gives the shop assistant his surname and asks her to send all the parcels to Claridges', though he does this while Sarah is busy changing back into her clothes. Then he gives the woman another twenty pounds. 'Ma'am, I wonder if you could, you know, choose a nightdress, silk or something, and some o' that . . . er, French . . .'

'Lingerie?' The woman smiles. 'It will be a pleasure, Mr

Teekleman. But you've given me too much, fifteen pounds will be ample.'

'You've been very kind and helpful, would you buy yourself something nice?'

'Thank you. It's been a pleasure, I hope the two of you are very happy,' the shop assistant says, smiling.

Sarah emerges from the changing booth wearing her new coat which sweeps down to her ankles in the latest fashion. 'How ever are we going to carry everything?' she says.

'It will all be sent to your hotel, madam,' the shop assistant assures her. 'We'll send your suitcase on with it and the gentleman's kitbag.'

'Hotel? It's a . . .'

'Yes, I have given her our address,' Ben says, cutting Sarah short.

Outside again they walk towards Knightsbridge. 'What say tomorrow we do Hyde Park?' Ben says.

'Oh, Ben, that was so kind, buying a second coat for Linda Newings, she'll be thrilled to bits.' She snuggles into him as they walk, her arm clasped about his own. 'I've never owned anything as nice, I do love you so.'

Most of the warmth has gone from the spring afternoon sunshine by the time they get to St James's Park but the light is still good and they stop to admire the policeman's bluebell patch and wonder at the clumps of daffodils and crocuses that simply grow willy-nilly out of the emerald grass. Ben spreads his army coat on almost the same spot they'd sat before, having to move it a couple of feet to avoid a patch of lilac-coloured crocuses.

They settle down on his coat and Ben takes Sarah in his arms and kisses her. 'Oh, my God, I nearly forgot!' he suddenly exclaims, pulling away from her and, on his knees, begins to frantically pat the surface of the greatcoat in a parody of panic. 'Thank goodness!' he sighs, at last stopping, his hand held over a patch of coat.

'What is it, Ben?' Sarah asks, alarmed.

Ben turns, enjoying his tomfoolery. 'Sarah, while I'm down on my knees, will you marry me?'

'I already said I would, whatever's gotten into you, Ben?'

'So we're engaged, it's official, right?'

Sarah frowns. 'Well, yes, I suppose? It's wartime, Ben, I don't want you to make any promises to me you may regret later.'

'But, nevertheless, you agree to be engaged to me?' Ben persists.

'Of course, silly, why do you think we're spending the night together? I'm not a loose woman, some cheap floozy, you know.'

Ben has found the opening to the pocket of his greatcoat and now produces the little black box. 'Sarah Atkins, will you marry me?' he asks, resting on his knees in front of her. He opens the lid of the little box to reveal the diamond ring.

'Shit!' Sarah exclaims involuntarily, jerking her head backwards in surprise. Wide-eyed, she brings her hands up to her mouth, horrified at what she's just said, 'Oo-ahh!'

Ben throws back his head and laughs. 'Is that all you have to say?' He pushes the little box towards her. 'Go on, it's yours.' Sarah takes it tentatively and Ben sees that her hand is trembling violently. Then she suddenly begins to sob, clutching the box to her lap in both hands. She sniffs and brings her right hand up and knuckles the tears from her eyes, sniffs again and then begins to weep, letting the tears run unabashedly down her cheeks and into her lap.

'I'm so sorry,' she says tearfully at last.

'Here,' Ben says, offering her his handkerchief.

Sarah dabs at her eyes then blows her nose, looks down at the ring and starts to cry again, dabbing at her eyes again. 'Oh, Ben, it's the most beautiful thing I've ever seen,' she chokes.

Ben takes the box from her hand and removes the ring. 'Here, let's have your finger,' he commands.

'Which one?' Sarah, still tearful, cries in a sudden panic. 'What hand, I forget?'

'How should I know, every girl is supposed to know that from infancy!' Ben teases. He points to her left hand, 'The one next to your pinkie. That's where they said it goes in the shop.'

Sarah holds her hand out and Ben slips the ring onto her finger, and it is a perfect fit. 'There you go, you're booked for Armistice Day. You have the hands of a duchess, my love,' he says, savouring the private joke. The light is beginning to fade and it has grown quite chilly. 'We need to celebrate,' he decides. 'A glass of champagne is called for immediately.'

'The Ritz? I'm no longer scared of the cake fork.'

'Nah, let's try Claridges'? Victoria says it's a better pub.'

'Does Victoria know everything?'

'Just about,' Ben says.

'Will she like me?'

'It's compulsory.'

'Last time the champagne made me squiffy, it was lovely.'

'C'mon, we'll take a taxi, it's too cold to walk, besides I don't know how to get there from here.'

At Claridges', in the manner of all good hotels, the desk clerk greets him by name. 'Good evening, Mr Teekleman, good evening, madam, I trust you've both had a pleasant day?'

'Yeah, it was lovely, thanks,' Ben replies and wonders momentarily how the clerk knows his name as it isn't the same man he met earlier.

'Your parcels have arrived, sir, and have been sent up, will you be dining in the hotel this evening, sir?'

Ben turns to Sarah, who has a bemused look on her face. 'What do you reckon, Sarah?'

Sarah is too surprised and confused to say anything.

'Tell you what,' Ben says to the desk clerk, 'we'll have it in our suite. In the meantime, will you send up a bottle of good French champagne.'

'Certainly, sir, dinner in your suite, I shall send you up the menu. Do you have a preference in champagne?'

'No, what would you choose?'

'I shall consult the cellarmaster, sir. You may depend on him. Shall I show you to your suite?'

'Thank you.'

They follow the clerk and Sarah nudges Ben. 'What's happening, Ben? Tell me!'

Ben allows the clerk to go further ahead. 'Well, you know how you got a bit squiffy on champagne last time at the Ritz, well, I thought we'd just stay on and get even squiffier. They say if you can get a girl squiffy enough . . . ?'

'Ben Teekleman, how dare you!' Sarah giggles.

Sarah is like a little girl at her first birthday party when they get into their suite where all her shopping has been neatly laid out on the huge bed. Soon the bedroom is in chaos as she once again opens all the boxes. The shop assistant has chosen a beautiful dove-grey silk nightdress with a matching peignoir, and, knowing Sarah's shoe size, she has chosen an elegant pair of slippers with a charming little heel. Sarah blushes violently when she opens the ribboned box of lingerie. 'Ben Teekleman, what have you done! Turn around at once.'

Ben turns his back and Sarah takes each neatly folded item out of the box. 'Darling, they're positively wicked, I can't possibly wear these!'

'Oh well, we'll take them back in the morning then, I'm sure the nice lady who looked after you won't mind, we'll swap them for a dozen each of good sensible spencers and bloomers, shall we?'

'Don't you dare! I've never seen anything as beautiful in my life.'

In the middle of unpacking her shopping a waiter arrives with the champagne in an ice bucket. 'Sir, our cellarmaster, Mr Boddington, hopes that you will accept this with his compliments. It is a 1908 Dom Perignon, a particularly good year and the last bottle he has of that vintage. He lost a son at Gallipoli and this is a small tribute to the Australians.'

'That's very decent of him,' Ben says, slightly taken aback. The English are such a curious mixture of aloofness and warmth, a hot and cold people who constantly surprise.

'May I leave the menu? You may telephone when you are ready for dinner. We ask that you allow half an hour for preparation. Will you choose the wine now so that it may either be chilled or decanted?'

'Would you give Mr Boddington my sincere thanks and please offer him my commiserations, the English lads fought with pride and determination at Gallipoli. I would be happy to have him select a good bottle of red.' He calls to Sarah, 'Red wine all right with you, dear?'

'Lovely!' Sarah calls back, though she cannot remember ever having tasted red wine.

After the waiter departs Ben turns to Sarah. 'That's twice today I've heard of an English lad's death at Gallipoli. We forget that the English lost nearly twice as many men as we did in the Dardanelles campaign.'

Sarah moves over to Ben and puts her hands about his waist, leaning back and looking into his eyes. 'Darling, let's not even think about the war for the next two days. I don't want to go out again, perhaps Hyde Park tomorrow, there are too many people in uniform on the streets, too many reminders of where we've been and where you have to go.' She stands on tiptoe and kisses him lightly on the nose. 'I know this is all make-believe, a fairytale. I can't imagine how you've managed to do it and, what's more, just this once I don't *want* to know. I just want to be with you for the next forty-eight hours.' She smiles. 'And then if they throw us in gaol, I won't mind in the least. I love you, Ben, with all my heart. Right now, at this very moment, I am happier than I've ever been and you haven't even made love to me yet.'

Ben takes her in his arms and kisses her deeply and then draws away, still holding her against him. 'Sarah, I want you so badly and have done so since the moment I saw you on the *Orvieto*. I confess, I have made love to you in my head a hundred times, no, many more times than that.' Ben can scarcely contain himself, his hardness pressing against Sarah's slim body. They kiss for a long moment until Sarah, in turn, gently draws away. Ben can feel his heart pumping, he is nervous, not quite knowing what to do next, waiting for Sarah to encourage him.

'Ben, let me have a bath, darling. Change into my lovely new things. We'll have a glass of champagne when I come out? But I don't want to get too squiffy, I want to love you just the way I am now.' Ben watches as she goes into the bathroom and closes the door behind her.

Suddenly he is depressed. He tells himself he is simply a bit weary. He's been up since dawn and taken the 6.15 train from Weymouth to London and then the underground to Horseferry Road. The waiting around, the anxiety of covering up during his final medical examination, where he knows in his heart of hearts he isn't fully recovered from his wound and the subsequent operation has taken its toll. He tells himself it is mostly the time he's been off his feet. The strength hasn't returned, he simply isn't as fit as he ought to be. His wound still hurts and he wonders if it will always be with him. Then there's been the excitement of the engagement ring and the shopping and the strain and emotion of finding himself alone at last with Sarah. It is as if he has stretched out his arms to take something more than just the war and has had them suddenly filled with something too heavy for him to carry.

He aches to make love to Sarah but at the same time he keeps bumping into the images of the lads in his platoon. Crow Rigby squinting down the telescopic sights of his Lee-Enfield, Brokenose Brodie reading Dickens, his lips moving all the while, brow furrowed in concentration, Wordy Smith painting his delicate tiny blossoms with a brush that appears to contain no more than two hairs. Cooligan, Numbers Cooligan, being argumentative, making a bet, taking one. Woggy Mustafa defiantly Christian, Muddy Parthe working up a good complaint, Library Spencer quietly correcting a fact, Hornbill, smiling, fixing something or other, always tinkering. It is as if the love he feels for them in death keeps intruding into his life, even into his love for Sarah, as if they are somehow participants in the present, perhaps competitors, equally admiring of Sarah, sharing her with him. He wonders if he can love and live without them, whether they have become so much a part of his personality that Sarah will be taking them to bed with her, in some weird ritual in his imagination he doesn't fully understand. They will be her lovers forever while he looks on, Sergeant Ben Teekleman, who managed to kill them all and stay alive himself.

Ben pours himself a glass of champagne, watching the bubbles settle in the glass. Outside his window he can hear the starlings settling in for the night. What a racket they make, an urgency to find a place on a branch or twig, a terrible squabbling in the elm trees, life persisting, tiny wings beating the air with a furious energy, a thousand tiny throats demanding their own brief span, resisting death, fighting it for all their worth.

In those moments of silence on Gallipoli, when both sides had had enough, there had been no birdsong, only the occasional mournful caw of a crow feeding on human carrion. 'Crows. Why is it always the vermin that follow you?' He can hear Crow Rigby saying it. The urgency of starlings had gone out of the air at Lone Pine, The Nek, the Daisy Patch. The charnel fields stank of death, the soil was soaked in it, drowned in a muddiness of young blood. There was so much death about, it became more natural than being alive. Can he now change back again and feel his need for life returning? Can he wipe death from his mind, replace it, even for forty-eight hours, with the life she brings him, the renewal she promises him with her sweet body? Is this woman, any woman, enough? Ben feels corrupted, guilty, ashamed even to admit such a thought, for he knows he loves Sarah more than his own life. Yet the thoughts of death, of decay, of the past, engulf him.

Ben has his back to the bathroom door, facing the window when Sarah calls out to him. He rises. She is dressed in the silk nightdress and peignoir though her feet remain bare, her toes peeping from under the hem of the dove-grey silk. She has brushed her hair and tied it back with a brown ribbon. Her face is scrubbed clean of any make-up. As Ben draws closer he sees the light scattering of freckles across the bridge of her nose and the upper part of her cheeks. Her mouth is slightly open and her hazel eyes are filled with love for him as her arms reach out and she starts to unbutton his tunic. 'Come, darling Ben, come and make love to Sarah.'

Ben entrains at Victoria Station for Dover to catch the troopship to Boulogne and from there to the 1st Division base at Etaples, where he is kitted out with a cold-weather uniform and given, in addition, a tin hat and gasmask.He is also required to undergo a further ten days of training which includes the use of the gasmask and a demonstration and lecture on the effects of phosgene gas.

This is the first of several differences from the conditions Ben had experienced in Gallipoli. For a start, there had been few gasmasks at Gallipoli, and those that could be found were used for only one purpose, to give the troops some relief from the stench of rotting corpses. Any platoon able to obtain a single gasmask to share among them treasured it. If there was one thing every soldier who returned from Gallipoli would remember until the day he died, it would be the stench of the charnel fields where the dead on both sides lay unburied and forsaken.

Ben's headquarters are near the village of Armentières where he is to report to his battalion commander Lieutenant-Colonel Le Maistre who has replaced Colonel Wanliss, who was wounded at Gallipoli. The battalion commander, much to Ben's extreme embarrassment, welcomes him to his dugout some eight hundred yards behind the lines with, 'Well, well, here cometh the axeman!' Ben thinks for a moment that Le Maistre may be chaffing him, but realises almost immediately that the words are spoken in genuine admiration.

Le Maistre points to an ammunition box. 'Sit, please, Sergeant-Major, I've been through your papers and you're just the sort of chap we need. Though, of course, you'll be short of experience in this sort of trench warfare, but then we all are. Different. Quite different to Gallipoli and you'll find it will take quite some getting used to. Thank God, the weather is being kind at the moment. Except for the deeper bomb craters which never seem to entirely dry up, as you can see it is rather dusty. One big shower, though, and we're all back up to our knees in the infernal mud.' He briefly ruffles the papers on the small table at which he is seated. The table and the hard, straight-backed wooden chair with it, appear to have been appropriated from a farmhouse kitchen. Then Le Maistre looks over at Ben. 'Now, much as we'd like to have you here, brigade headquarters thinks differently, that's the problem coming in with a reputation, you can't slip in quietly, as I'm sure you'd rather do, eh?'

'Sir, I am not an experienced sergeant-major, in fact I'm new to the job, I'll be happy to be the dogsbody around the place, earn my crown.'

'No, no, you'll be given your own company just as soon as you return, you're far too experienced a soldier not to be leading men in combat. It's just that brigade headquarters want you to join a special training group, in the 27th Battalion, being conducted by the 7th Brigade. They're a West Australian outfit, damn fine, too. The Joan of Arc Company.'

'Joan of Arc? That's a new one, sir.'

Le Maistre grins. 'I said that deliberately, Sergeant-Major, hoped you might pick up on it. The battalion has, it seems, a great many members of a West Australian family named Leane. They're all enlisted in the same company, so that the C.O., two of the subalterns, several N.C.O.s and God knows how many enlisted men are all Leanes. In other words, the company is,' he pauses and then continues, 'made of all Leanes, Maid of Orleans, hence the Joan of Arc Company.'

'Very clever, sir. Can you tell me what I am to do in the 7th?'

'Yes, you'll be with selected members of the 27th and 28th Battalions to be trained as scouts and as a raiding party. I'm not quite sure what this entails. It seems you are to be instructed in a raiding technique perfected by the Canadians near Messines, last November. Two officers,' Le Maistre glances at his notes, 'yes, here it is, Lieutenants Conners and Kent of the 1st Canadian Division have been seconded to assist as training instructors.' Ben's commanding officer looks up at him. 'I'm sure it will prove to be very useful stuff when you return to us, Sergeant-Major.'

'When will that be?' Ben now asks.

'Haven't the foggiest, old chap. Rather sooner than later I hope, the 5th are in a big offensive planned for some time in July and I want all the experienced men I can find. I have an inexperienced C.O. in D Company, decent sort of chap but he has spent most of his war in ordnance, we're thinking of putting you in with him.' He brings the papers in front of him together. 'Thank you, that will be all, Sergeant-Major Teekleman, report to the Provost Sergeant, who'll give you your clearance and papers for the 27th Battalion part of the 7th Brigade. You're to report to Captain Foss.'

Ben rises and, coming to attention, salutes. Le Maistre grins suddenly and looks up from the table where he is seated. 'Oh, I almost forgot, you're supposed to have volunteered for this assignment, Sergeant-Major, so take extra good care of yourself. Remember, you belong to the 5th Battalion.'

Ben finds himself in a special unit, which simply becomes known as 'the raiding party' and consists of some sixty men and six officers. It is divided into two sections, one responsible for the left half of the attack, the other for the right. As the unit isn't much bigger than a standard platoon, each half is allocated a sergeant, and though Ben is of a higher rank he is asked if he'll act in the lower capacity for one of the teams.

Captain Foss, a big, ebullient man, nearly six foot four inches in height and a good two hundred and eighty pounds in weight, looks and acts naturally as a leader, or, put into the colloquial language of the men under him, 'he doesn't carry on with any bullshit'. He introduces Ben to the West Australian volunteers.

'Righto, this is Sergeant-Major Ben Teekleman, he's a ring-in, a Victorian from the 5th Battalion, 2nd Brigade, but a very welcome one.'

'Tasmanian, sir,' Ben says promptly and the men laugh.

'Tasmanian, eh?' says Foss. 'Well, in that case, if you have any doubts about him you are advised to look at his ribbons, he has earned his crown the hard way but has volunteered to act as the sergeant for our right section. I guess you'll get to know him soon enough, as for me, I'm bloody glad to have him on board.'

Ben, accustomed to big men and himself about average height for the Victorians, finds that he is much shorter than these West Australians. They are magnificent specimens, few of them are under six feet one inch while most are taller. They're hard and well trained and at first he finds the going tough. After almost three months spent on his back, he has lost much of his fitness and the first few days leave him exhausted, so much so that he wonders if he should tell Foss he's not up to scratch.

The whole of the raiding party is withdrawn to a rear area along the railway line between Armentières and Wavrin where they are trained as if they are a football team preparing for a grand final. Each section is subdivided into right and left trench parties, parapet parties, intelligence, linesmen, messengers, telephonists, scouts, stretcher-bearers and covering parties. The Canadians have worked it all out, learning from bitter experience, and they prove to be excellent instructors.

The men's first task is to dig a replica of the German trenches copied carefully from photographs taken by an aeroplane sent over especially for the task. Each night they practise the raid, learning to co-ordinate the various tasks and sections quickly without talk. The Canadians believe that silence, hitherto never attempted, is a critical aspect for the success of the raid. While the practice works well, the aerial photography isn't detailed enough to tell how effectively the trenches are protected, or what state the barbed wire is in or if there are any other obstacles other than craters.

Two nights before the raid Ben is still not satisfied with his fitness. Though considerably hardened by the rigorous work of the past couple of weeks he goes for a run in his full uniform, carrying a wire-cutter and the weapons he will take with him on the night of the raid. He runs along the railway line, passing five or six hundred yards from the German trenches they are to attack. On a sudden impulse he crosses the railway line into no-man's-land and finds himself moving in a circular direction towards the right-hand side of the enemy lines.

At first it is not a conscious decision, he simply wants to feel the nature of the ground they will pass over on the night of the raid. But soon he is taken by the notion of getting as close as he can to the first line of German trenches. Foss, their commander, had some weeks earlier done the same thing, ending up close enough to see that the trenches on his left (the German right) were protected by barbed wire in poor repair and that they were vulnerable to an attack. It is on this premise that the raiding party is being undertaken.

However, it is not known if the right-hand sector is in the same poor condition and this is the area Ben will be moving into with his men. Progressing from one ditch to another, he slowly makes his way to the German lines, eventually coming to the lip of a bomb crater in which there isn't the usual pool of muddy water. He jumps into the crater, a large one that brings him at its extreme end to a point no more than ten yards from the parapet of the enemy trench. He can actually hear someone shouting out a command and a loud '*Jawohl!*', the reply from whomever the direction is intended for. Someone is playing a mouth organ and in the darkness Ben can see a thin curl of wood smoke coming from the trench.

He crawls out of the crater and examines the wire, which is newly constructed, well tied down with stakes hammered into the ground in an ordered pattern and calculated to make it very difficult to penetrate. But further up to his left the newly laid wire suddenly ends and the old wire is partially pulled up in preparation for the laying of a new pattern. However, there appears to be no sign of work taking place or spare bales of wire lying about. The ten-yard gap where the old wire has been ripped up is quite sufficient to put his section through. It seems the Germans have simply run out of wire and are waiting for more to arrive, their ordnance no more efficient than that of their British counterparts.

Ben makes his way back behind the lines and the following morning reports his findings to Captain Foss.

'You're a bloody idiot, Sergeant-Major Teekleman, but thank you.' He thinks for a moment. 'This means Lieutenant Gill can bring four scouts with him to the left-hand sector to cut the wire and guide us through and we'll send only one along with you to your section. Are you quite sure you can find your way through the gap again?'

'It will be around the same time as last night and, if anything, a little lighter, shouldn't be a problem, sir.'

Ben salutes him and turns to depart when Captain Foss calls out, 'Sergeant-Major?'

'Yes, sir?'

'Bloody beauty, mate.'

During the last week in May and the first few days in June the artillery has bombarded the sector to be entered but not so heavily that the Germans will think it a precursor to an attack on their section. The idea is that they should regard the artillery action as routine, their turn to cop a few medium trench mortars. This may well have been the reason why work was stopped on repairing the barbed wire.

503

June the fifth is the night set aside for the attack and the raiding party is given a special set of clothing. They are fitted out with English tunics that contain no badges or identification marks, these being thought to be by far the most common on the battlefield and identical for every English unit. If any of them are killed, the enemy will gain no information from looking at their insignia. Their faces are blackened and their bayonets painted, though the scouts, messengers and carriers, as well as the bombers, will carry revolvers instead of rifles.

They are also issued with a device called a 'knobkerrie', which ordnance will later refer to as a 'life preserver'. This short, stout stick with a knob on the end, in this instance a heavy iron bolt, comes out of the previous century and the Zulu Wars in South Africa. The knobkerrie was used in conjunction with an assegai, a short fighting spear, by the Zulu Impi and used well the knobkerrie is a highly effective weapon at close range. A blow directed to the head will quite easily kill a man. Ben declines one of these, explaining that he would prefer to take his Maori fighting axe and Captain Foss quickly agrees. Ben also shows his section how to use the knobkerrie as a fighting stick in the Maori manner, a skill learned from Hawk as a child. Utilised correctly it can ward off a bayonet attack and, at the same time, kill the attacker.

They are all issued with black plimsolls to quieten their footfalls on the hard ground, though later, with even small falls of rain, these will prove impractical in the muddy ditches and craters of no-man's-land. Finally, an idea from Gallipoli suggested by Ben is adopted and they wear white armbands on either sleeve, covered with similar-sized black ones, which are to be ripped off to reveal the white when they begin the attack.

The two Canadian instructors, both of them extremely popular with the Australians, request permission to come on the raiding party but Foss refuses. 'Jesus, imagine if one, or both, of you blokes got killed because of something stupid my boys did. We'd have a diplomatic incident on our hands the like of which would see me demoted to the rank of corporal, if I was bloody lucky.'

The plan is for Ben and another scout, a lad named Wearne from Donnybrook, a small town southeast of Bunbury, both with wire-cutters, to move up to the gap in the wire and, if it is still there, wait for Gill and his scouts to cut through their section of the wire to the left. If the gap has been repaired, Ben, using his electric torch, is to signal for another wire-cutter to join them. On the command of Captain Foss, who is to move up the centre between them, the attacking units of the two sections, situated in a rifle trench some way back in no-man's-land, are to move up into position. Both sections of the raiding party will then mount the attack, entering the German trenches together.

The concept behind the raid is not to capture the German trenches but simply to surprise and harass them, killing as many of the enemy as possible in the time allotted, and then to withdraw, leaving the Germans feeling vulnerable and demoralised. This will give the Australian infantry, who have not yet experienced a full-scale battle in France or are not familiar with this type of trench warfare, the confidence that the Germans can be intimidated and their trenches entered almost at will. After the fierce and bloody resistance of the Turks at Gallipoli when the Anzacs attempted to raid their trenches, Ben wonders privately how successful this tactic will be. When he questions the ever-ebullient Foss, he is told that the fighting is different here and that a raiding party is not a tactic used in France and will come as 'quite a surprise to the Boche'.

Ben and his scout, Wearne, and Lieutenant Gill and his three scouts leave the rifle trenches just after nine-thirty at the first sign of darkness. At this time of the year the night lasts only until 2.15 so they are aware that the whole operation must be concluded in under four hours. All goes well and Ben and Wearne, following the ditches Ben previously used, reach the gap in the wire without any trouble. At the same time they lay a magnetic wire so that their section of the raiding party can find their way safely home.

Things at first go well in Lieutenant Gill's section. They make comparatively short work of cutting through the dilapidated defences. Gill and a scout named Tozer lie on their backs and cut a front path through the wire, while those behind them expand it. So that the clicking of the wire-cutters can't be heard by an alert sentry, they do not entirely cut through each strand, a skill that comes from much practice. Later the wire can easily be snapped by hand. Gill and Tozer have cleared a passage almost through the German wire when they see that it is destined to come out directly under an enemy listening post. In fact, a man in a spiked helmet now peers over it, apparently looking over their bodies directly below him and into the darkness beyond. Both lie frozen, hardly daring to breathe. The sentry must have been made aware of something because moments later two other heads appear and some discussion takes place. Then, as suddenly, the heads of all three disappear beyond the parapet.

Gill and Tozer, hoping that the other two scouts working further back will have seen the Germans, wait another ten minutes before they begin to withdraw, inching backwards, wriggling their way through the wire, joining those parts further back where they have been forced to cut it. By now it is half-past eleven and Lieutenant Gill, using his electric torch at an angle and in such a manner so that its beam cannot be detected by a German sentry, signals Ben to withdraw.

By the time Ben and Wearne arrive back at the assault group and are, shortly afterwards, joined by Gill, Tozer and the other two scouts, it is nearly midnight, too late to attempt and complete the raid.

The excursion isn't entirely wasted. They have learned a fair bit and at the same time on the following night the raid is repeated. This time, at 11.15, the artillery and medium trench mortars open up and appear to be shelling the German positions considerably to the north and south of the one Captain Foss and his raiders will attack. The raiding party moves into position and with the wires already cut the previous night they are, hopefully, in a much better position to attack. During the day medium trench mortars have played on the area where the wire has been cut to discourage the Germans from looking too closely at it or to repair the section on Ben's side. At 11.25 the guns are switched onto the trenches Foss and his men will attack and they are heavily bombarded for ten minutes. The direct fire into the trenches ceases and a box barrage to either side and the rear is formed around the position to be attacked. This is so that no German reinforcements can be brought up from the rear or the side trenches.

It takes only two minutes for the assault party to reach the German trenches and to leap into them with Captain Foss, revolver in one hand, knobkerrie in the other and a whistle in his mouth, leading the attack. The Germans, thoroughly cowed by the bombardment minutes earlier, are found hiding in dugouts and anywhere else they think themselves to be safe.

A large German sergeant comes out of a dugout brandishing a

bayonet and goes straight for Foss, who has moved to Ben's end of the trench. Foss doesn't see him at first but turns as the German has his hand raised with the bayonet above his head. The raiding-party leader hasn't even had time to bring his revolver around to fire, when the German simply crumples to his knees, the blade of the Maori fighting axe cleaving the back of his skull. He falls, his head actually bumping against the toe of Foss's plimsoll. Foss looks up to see Ben grinning at him ten feet away.

However, most of the Germans are caught completely unawares. The Australians go to work with their bayonets though none of them finds it necessary to use their 'life preservers', their bolted stick, except for one incident when a prisoner attempts to escape and one of the Anzac raiders, his blood up, chases him and brains him with his knobkerrie.

In just under five minutes six Germans are captured and the remainder killed. The raiding party withdraws without a single Australian being killed or injured, though later two of the scouts are killed when an enemy mortar lands among a group retreating back to their own lines.

The Germans grow much more skilled at resisting the raiding parties in the weeks that follow, but the raids are a source of great pride among the Australian infantry. Although the credit for inventing them must be given to the Canadians, the lads nevertheless see their raiding parties as an original contribution to the war in France.

Ben returns to the 5th Battalion where he becomes the sergeant-major of D Company under the command of Major Joshua Solomon and where he will also train several raiding parties.

Foss, when Ben reports to him on the final day before returning to his battalion, shakes his hand. 'I owe you a big one, Ben,' he says simply. 'Thank Christ for the Maori blood in you.'

On the morning of his arrival Ben reports to Joshua in his dugout. Unlike the British, Australian officers share the trench accommodation with their men and Joshua has a small covered section, though open on both sides, to himself.

'Welcome, Sergeant-Major Teekleman, I am as surprised as you may be at this co-incidence.' Then he adds quickly, 'Though not unpleasantly so.'

'Thank you, sir,' Ben says. 'Co-incidence and war seem often enough to be partners.'

'I feel sure we will work well together, perhaps we can set our past aside, what say you?'

'It never bothered me that much, really, sir, I was mostly out of it. In the army you soon enough learn to accept a bloke for what he is.'

'Splendid, then that's settled. I will expect you to be forthright at all times.'

'Thank you, sir, but, with respect, I don't think you mean that.'

Joshua raises one eyebrow slightly. 'Oh, why is that?'

'Sir, our jobs are different, I'll do everything I can to help within that knowledge.'

'I can't imagine what you mean, Sergeant-Major Teekleman? But let's leave it at that.' Ben can see that Joshua is annoyed with him, but is sufficiently restrained not to take it any further.

Ben knows from experience that as the senior N.C.O. in the company he cannot be in Joshua's pocket nor have his company commander too dependent on him. He has learned from bitter experience that his judgment must be his own. He has an unspoken right to re-interpret orders if they are plainly headed in the wrong direction. A sergeant-major is the intelligent go-between, a conduit with a filter at its end and not simply a messenger between the officer and the men. Joshua's inexperience is already showing.

'I want you to create an effective raiding party in the company which I will expect to lead, it ought to be fun,' Joshua now instructs Ben.

'Yes, sir, I shall draw up the requirements right away, you may find yourself rather busy though, it's a big commitment.'

'About time, I wasn't fortunate enough to be at Gallipoli.'

After Ben has been dismissed he ponders the goings-on in Joshua's head. 'Fun' is a strange word to use about a raiding party, designed to kill the enemy at close quarters, whereas the word 'fortunate' is not an expression anyone having been through Gallipoli is ever likely to use. Then he recalls how they all were at the beginning and realises that Joshua's war hasn't yet begun for him. He is as anxious to be blooded in battle as they themselves were. Joshua is a greenhorn and Ben senses that he will have to watch him very, very carefully or his C.O. will soon be dead.

However, Joshua proves to be a quick learner and keen to take over the leadership of a raiding party, even impatient to have them get under way on a real raid. Ben, though, is more cautious. The

Germans are quick learners and they have repaired their wire, laid the odd booby trap and rattles on the wire, mounted extra guards around the clock and, now, as the initial bombardment ends, they rush to stand to order. The chances of catching them off guard are increasingly rare.

Ben suggests to Joshua that he, and not his company commander, should lead the first raid. 'Sir, if you're both an observer and one of the scouts you'll gain a great deal of experience on the job, after which you will be able to take over.'

Ben is aware that he is stepping out of line, but Lieutenant-Colonel Le Maistre has asked him to train a raiding party in each of the companies and he feels responsible. In his mind it is not right to put an officer without combat experience in charge. He has chosen half of his raiding party from men who were at Gallipoli while the other half are new recruits and he feels an obligation to the old-timers and a responsibility for the new. He doesn't want them led by an officer who has never been in a bayonet charge or killed a man in the heat of battle. Joshua can overrule him if he wishes, but Ben hopes he is mature enough not to do so.

Joshua is silent, chewing at the ball of his thumb. Finally he looks up at Ben. 'I know you think I lack the experience to lead men, Sergeant-Major, and you may be right, though how shall I gain it, if not by leading them? I shall lead the raiding party.'

'Very well, sir.'

'Moreover, you will not be on the raid.'

Ben looks at Joshua, astonished. 'I'm not sure I heard you correctly, sir?'

'You will not accompany me on the raid, there is only room for one leader, we have trained two sergeants. That will be all, Sergeant-Major.'

Ben wants to tell him not to be a fool but knows he can't. 'Very well, sir, as you wish.'

'No, Sergeant-Major, there is no equivocation, it is an order.'

The raid takes place two nights later and is a disaster, eleven men are killed and three taken prisoner, with no loss to the Germans, who have seen them coming and led them into a trap. It is Gallipoli all over again. As they rush the parapet the Germans open fire, and if not for a ditch close by, the casualties would have been much worse.

One of the sergeants tells Ben that they were caught in the

open under a German parachute flare not fifty yards from the trench they were meant to attack. Instead of falling to the ground or standing quite still, Joshua ordered them forward. 'Blind Freddy would have seen us coming,' the sergeant told Ben.

A second raid is scheduled four nights later but fails to reach its objective, Joshua pulling them out sixty yards from the German trenches when a German machine gun begins to fire somewhere far to their left.

The next two raids he cancels and then allows Ben to take over when a query arrives from Le Maistre asking why his company has not maintained its quota of raids. Ben takes a raiding party over to a different section of the German line. This part of the line dates from 1914 and a number of solid and large German blockhouses were built. He avoids these as virtually impregnable, designed to resist heavy artillery. Some of them are large enough to accommodate a hundred men. The trench he attacks is approached by using a sap, which he manages to enter by cutting the wire and crossing silently over a covered section of the main trench, entering the saps to the rear where two Germans lie asleep. They die silently, Ben using his fighting axe to cut their throats. Neither would have felt a thing. He signals his men to follow and they come into the main trench from the back and take a dozen Germans completely by surprise, killing them all. It is all over in less than five minutes.

Ben is not to know that *der verrückte Australier mit der Axt*, the mad Australian axe man, will in the ensuing weeks become legendary in the German lines where he is greatly feared. Like the stories among the West Australians, Ben's exploits are hugely exaggerated. In his own right he has inadvertently become a major propaganda item for the Allies. The mad axe man does more to undermine the morale of German trenches and strike fear into every soldier's heart than anything a conventional raiding party can hope to do. Imagination is always more powerful than truth.

The success of the raid only emphasises the way the men are beginning to feel about Joshua, though nobody says anything to Ben or even to their own sergeants. In the way a good N.C.O. knows these things, it is becoming apparent to them that their C.O. hasn't got the stomach for the bayonet and it is now common enough when a raiding party is proposed for the men to bet among themselves that Joshua is going to ring it, another way of indicating a man is a coward without having to come right out and say it.

Joshua has also been drinking steadily, bringing a bottle of Scotch into his dugout with him at night and having very little to do with his subalterns, who, like him, are new to the job and in need of guidance. Increasingly he prefers his own company and while he performs his duties reasonably well, he is often thick-tongued and ill-tempered in the morning and apt to bawl his junior officers out in front of the men. His four subalterns learn to avoid confronting him until noon. Ben more or less takes charge of the company, guiding the platoon commanders quietly, never usurping their authority while keeping an eye on the welfare of the men.

The raiding parties are now almost exclusively under his control and, while he takes care to train each of the subalterns to take command, he is never far from them in a raid, ready to suggest the next move if he thinks they are undecided. The company, despite Joshua, soon earns a reputation for mounting effective raiding parties. In this way the morale of its men remains high and Joshua's lack of leadership is of less concern than it might ordinarily have proved to be.

And then, on July 24th, the Allies mount a major attack at the village of Pozières. For the Australians it is their first taste of trench warfare in France, their blooding against the Germans. The raiding and harassing, or as Le Maistre calls it 'the terrier at the ankles', stage is over, they are going to cross a section of the Hindenburg Line. The Australians are, he assures them, going to do what no Allied army has yet managed to do. To take, cross and hold the German positions on the northern, far side of the village of Pozières and possess their front line.

The Anzacs, having taken the village on July 24th, now extend their attack during the small hours of the morning on the 25th. They do not know that the Germans also have plans to re-take the village fourteen hours after they've lost it. Both sides are planning attacks at the same time.

The Germans have been bombarding the village all day, which is rapidly being reduced to a heap of rubble, but cease at seven on the evening of the 24th.

At eight o'clock the 5th Battalion, led by Lieutenant-Colonel Le Maistre, enters Black Watch Alley, behind the position previously held by that great Scottish Regiment, and prepares to mount the first part of a double attack on the German lines. This is to be a frontal assault to the south of an old Roman road which serves as a reference point for the attack.

Ben and Lieutenant Gray, one of the company platoon commanders who has especially distinguished himself during the raids, creep out after dark carrying tape and pegs and together mark the northern end where the attack is to start. The 7th Battalion, who are to go into the attack with the 5th, are to peg the southern end but, for reasons that never become clear, do not do so and they are consequently not sure where the starting line to commence their attack is intended to be. On the heavily cratered surface of no-man's-land it could be virtually anywhere.

The 5th move out, with Captain Leadbeater in charge of the leading company, and Major Joshua Solomon at the head of D Company beside him. Ben sends the men across the open ground to the starting tape, briefing Joshua just before he takes his company across. Joshua is plainly drunk and Ben quietly instructs one of the platoon sergeants, a Gallipoli veteran, to stay with him. 'Ben, fer'chrissake, mate, I've got a platoon of greenhorns, they're gunna need me to hold their hands.'

'Timbo, you get the C.O. into position or it's your arse, mate. Put the bastard in front and tell him to run.'

At 1.50 a.m. the two companies from the 5th are in place with the two others lined up in the rear. So far the exercise is copybook. The enemy, if they sense there may be someone there at all, simply cover the area with the usual casual rifle and machine-gun fire.

At 1.58 the 1st Australian Division artillery places a heavy curtain of shrapnel on the front trenches of the German lines and the guns of the 34th Division pound the second line of trenches. After only two minutes, thought to be sufficient to send the Germans in the front trenches scurrying for cover, the shrapnel bombardment stops, though the heavy guns firing on the German rear lines continue for another twenty minutes.

Le Maistre gives the signal for the front two companies of the 5th to advance across a front that is heavily pockmarked by shell craters so that it is damn near impossible to keep to a line. Moreover, the Germans, instead of cowering for cover because of the curtain of shrapnel, are waiting for them and their machine guns start to cut the two advancing companies to pieces.

Then, almost immediately, the enemy artillery comes in. The

5th, advancing parallel to the German front line is thrown into wild confusion, breaking into groups who lose the line of attack, some making for the southwest, others for the northwest.

Ben simply stands in one spot, calling his company in and eventually ending up with the greater part of it, though two officers and at least one platoon have become lost. Joshua is nowhere to be seen. Ben has a fair idea where the German trenches are and joins up with Captain Lillie, known as 'the Pink Kid' as he is close to being an albino, who has distinguished himself at Gallipoli. Lillie takes charge and they rush the German position to find that the garrison have fled, leaving only their dead behind.

The instruction is to hold the front line and not to move on to the second and so Lillie gives the order to consolidate and to start to dig in. Despite the chaos, they've achieved their objective and must now wait for the second attack to advance. At 2.25 the barrage on the German second line of defence is lifted and Leadbeater on the left of Ben's company decides against orders to advance.

'Shit, what's he doing?' Lillie cries. 'We're supposed to consolidate.'

'We don't have a choice now, sir, we have to go with him or the Boche will come around him,' Ben says.

Lillie reluctantly gives the order to advance and the whole force sweeps forward towards the German rear lines. To their surprise there is little resistance and where they believe the lines are they see nothing but churned earth and craters. The Allied bombardment has been so heavy that all traces of the German trenches seem to have been wiped out. Eventually, judging by the number of German dead and the equipment lying about, they realise that they have reached the second line and Lillie, reporting the capture, instructs the troops to dig in. They have achieved more than has been asked of them and have done what Le Maistre has demanded. They have taken a section of the Hindenburg Line which has never before been breached. Moreover they've done it without having to look a single German in the eye.

But their victory is shortlived. The Germans now move in. The Welsh Borderers, a British regiment responsible for their extreme right, meets heavy machine-gun fire and is forced back, losing nine of their twelve officers and seventy-four of their men. They are intended to be the support for the Australians on the right. On

Lillie and Leadbeater's left, the 7th Battalion hasn't arrived and only one platoon has made it to the German second line of defence. They join Lillie and the left flank is completely exposed along with the right. Lillie and Leadbeater, the two officers in command of the 5th, are also exposed on either flank with the attacking Germans about to encircle them, coming around on the left and right to once again occupy their own former front line and trap the 5th Battalion behind the German lines.

Ben points this out to Captain Lillie, who, having come this far, is reluctant to turn back. 'Sir, they'll be up our arses like a rat up a drainpipe before we know where we are.'

Just then a message comes through to say that Leadbeater has been killed and his company is in disarray, all its officers having been killed as well.

'We're falling back,' Lillie decides. 'Ben, get the fuck over there and bring them out, we'll pull back to the first German lines and try to hold them there.'

Ben, sensing the direction the Germans might be taking to recapture their own front line, orders Lieutenant Fitzgerald, another one of his raider officers in charge of the 5th Battalion bombers, to move up onto their flank to guard it as he withdraws Leadbeater's company. Fitzgerald, though an officer, accepts the order and doesn't muck about in moving into position on the left flank to protect Ben's withdrawal.

The Germans, using their own bombers, fight to break through Fitzgerald's defence. The Germans have a lighter bomb which can be thrown a further distance than the one possessed by the Anzacs. To make up for this deficiency Fitzgerald and his bombers dash across the open ground so that they can overcome the disadvantage, thus constantly exposing themselves and at the same time drawing nearer to the German bombers.

In the meantime Ben pulls Leadbeater's company back into the German front-line trenches where he joins up with Lillie. Their flank is still vulnerable to the German attack, which is being halted by Fitzgerald's men, though it is only a matter of time before the enemy break through.

'Sir, they'll be breaking through and coming down their own trenches to get us,' he tells Lillie. 'We can't pull back across no-man's-land, they'll cut us off long before we make it. We'll have to stay here and fight it out. We have maybe half an hour if we're lucky to build a barricade to block their advance down the trench from the railway line. We can fight them from behind the barricade with bombs, it's about our only chance.'

Captain Lillie nods. 'Get the men onto it. By the way, Sergeant-Major, what happened to Major Solomon, he's your C.O.? I could use a little help.'

'I've not seen him, sir, must have been caught up in the confusion when the Boche opened up at the start.'

Ben puts the men to work, building a barricade in the trench, using bits of timber and any German equipment they can find lying around. They work feverishly, knowing it is only a matter of time before Fitzgerald's bombers are overrun.

In fact, Lieutenant Fitzgerald, venturing once too often into the open to hurl a bomb, is killed by a machine gun. Shortly after, Gray, who had earlier laid the starting tape with Ben, is also killed as well as two more of the bombers. The barricade, though, is more or less established.

The fight begins.

At the barricade the surviving bombers and those who can crowd in with them throw until they think their arms must surely fall off. The Germans keep coming, hurling their own bombs. Ben positions six snipers who are given the job of shooting the hands off the Germans as they are about to throw bombs over the barricade. They fight for an hour, the Germans only a matter of feet away on the other side of the barricade. The 9th and the 10th Battalions arrive and at last some of the 7th to reinforce the exhausted and wounded men from the 5th.

They manage to mount a Lewis gun for a while, aiming it directly down the trench at the Germans, mowing them down before it is destroyed by a bomb. One of the officers of the 10th moves with another Lewis gun into a cross trench which effectively prevents the enemy from coming over the top of or around the barricade.

On the Australian side the bombers, by now everyone who still has the strength to throw, are standing on the bodies of their mates to get to the Germans on the other side.

At half-past seven, with the men close to collapse, Captain Oates of the 7th arrives with three platoons from his battalion and drives the Germans back almost to the railway. Then a second barrier is built higher up in the German trenches and a T-sap is cut on either side of it to create a broader front and make bombing and rifle fire easier. After two more attacks the Germans withdraw to beyond the railway and the Australians remain in possession of the German front-line trenches almost to the railway line.

It isn't everything Le Maistre has hoped for, but they've achieved more than any other advance on the Germans since the beginning of the war. They've breached the German Line for the first time and now they are holding it.

They have little time to celebrate. The Germans are not going to let the Australians breach their lines. Realising that all their own troops are out of Pozières and can be cleared from the immediate area, they commence to bombard their former front line, making it impossible for those who hold it to retreat.

What follows proves to be the heaviest and most prolonged bombardment of the war. The length of the line the Anzacs hold is just over four hundred yards and contained in it is the whole of the 1st Division, some eight thousand men who cannot advance or retreat and are trapped under the maelstrom of German artillery.

Those who cannot find cover have little hope of surviving. The Germans, who are using their own survey maps of their former trenches, are laying down such accurate fire that whole sections of a trench are often simply wiped out. Men disappear, with arms and legs and heads torn from their bodies. Hundreds, soon thousands, of torsos and limbs and heads are scattered everywhere.

So accurate and intense is the fire that some officers lead their men out of the trenches, preferring to take their chances in the open. Dust rises in clouds that can be seen for miles and the day is turned into dusk.

Oblivious of the bombing, rats now cover no-man's-land in waves, seeking out the corpses, gorging on the flesh of dead men until they simply drag themselves across the ground or lie panting covered in blood and gore.

Ben's section of the trench is hit, killing twenty men who just disappear, and he finds himself cut off from Lillie with just a handful of men a little further down. Some fifty men are now in his section of the front line. Towards the end of the newly exposed section is a blockhouse, not much bigger than a small outhouse but solidly built, probably a place to store ammunition. Dead men lie at its entrance and one wall has been completely covered in someone's blood and brains. Ben moves down to it and pushes open the door. Inside he finds five men, one of them Joshua Solomon, who cowers in the far corner, his knees hugged to his chest. As the daylight floods in he starts to whimper.

'Sir, you had better come out,' Ben calls to him.

Joshua shields his eyes against the light with one hand. 'No way! No way! I'm not going out there,' he cries. 'I don't want to die. Please, I don't want to die, Ben. Save me. Please save me!' He looks about him wildly. 'Sergeant-Major, I order you to save me!'

'C'mon, out you get,' Ben says to the other men, 'how long have you been in here?'

'I dunno,' the soldier replies. 'Since last night I think.'

'Last night? What time last night?'

'When the Germans started to fire on us?'

'What, you mean just after we started forward?'

'Yes, Sergeant-Major, we lost our direction and then we come across this and crawled in.'

'And him?' Ben points to Joshua.

'He come later, Sergeant, about two hours later, he was pissed.'

'Righto, you bastards have done no fucking work, you're gunna have to dig.' He indicates Joshua. 'Leave him there, come on, move your arses!'

The bombardment continues all day and Ben knows that if the shelling continues they will all die, but he sets his men to digging, thinking it better than keeping them idle. 'If we get a direct hit, we're history,' he tells them honestly. 'If we can dig deep enough we may have a chance, dig for your lives.'

As they dig they find the recent dead, mostly limbs and bits and pieces. They throw them over the side, tossing a dead mate's severed head over the parapet like a melon, their hands often wet with blood and gore. And still they dig, their lives depending on it.

Ben prays that they can last until nightfall when he tells himself he's going to have to get them out. At about six o'clock the dust is so heavy that it is prematurely dark. Ben decides he cannot wait. They have had one or two near misses with the trenches on either side of them taking a direct hit, some of the bodies being blown so high into the air that they sail way over their heads. One of Ben's men is killed when a torso lands on his head, snapping his neck. It is only a matter of time before the German artillery find them.

He calls his men together and points to a blockhouse some sixty yards away. It has been reduced to rubble by the bombardment and seems at first sight to be even more vulnerable than the trench in which they are hiding.

'I've been right up to one of those, most have a section underground, we're going to go for it. If I'm wrong we're dead, if I'm right the section underneath may give us a level of protection. I'm giving you a choice, you can stay dug in here and hope for the best, maybe the bombardment will soon be over. Or you can come with me. We'll be fired on trying to make our objective and I can't promise I'm right.' He looks about him. 'If I'm wrong we won't get back, lads. I want you to understand that, there is no return, we won't be able to get back to this trench and we'll all almost certainly die.'

'What if the bombardment stops? We could be safer here than trying to cross over to that blockhouse?' someone asks.

'Quite right, lad, but if I were the Hun and I had us pinned down like this I don't think I'd stop firing until I had so pulverised the position, no further resistance was possible. That's what I'd do. But I'm not the enemy and, frankly, I don't know. I'll give you five minutes to decide. Those who are coming to the right, get your kit together, those staying to the left, my suggestion is to keep digging.'

Ben leaves them to decide and goes to the little blockhouse where he has left Joshua. 'Come on, we're getting out,' he says.

'No, no, I don't want to,' Joshua cries.

'Right, I'm going to count to ten, if you're not out of here by then I'm going to shoot you,' Ben says and commences to count. At the count of five Joshua has crawled out on his hands and knees. Ben jerks him to his feet, but he immediately collapses the moment he is left on his own. Ben reaches down and grabs him under the arms and pulls him back onto his feet. 'You better learn to stand in the next two minutes, we're moving out.' He props Joshua up against the wall of the trench and leaves him.

Nearly two-thirds of the men are standing to the right with their gear. They're a sorry-looking lot, the fight gone out of most of them. 'Come on, sir, we're going,' he calls to Joshua.

Joshua takes a step away from the wall and collapses. Ben turns to two men, veterans he's known from Gallipoli. 'Partridge, Collins, take the C.O. between you.'

Partridge looks at Ben and spits on the ground. 'Fuck him, Ben.'

Ben grabs him by the front of his shirt. 'That's an order, like it or not, he's our fucking C.O., he's coming.'

'He's not worth it,' Collins says, but they both take Joshua and support him.

'Right, we're out of here, it's yonder blockhouse, every man for himself. Go for it, lads!'

There is a mad scramble out of the trenches and Ben waits for Partridge and Collins to manhandle Joshua out. 'What's fucking wrong with him, eh? Bloody legs look all right to me,' Partridge complains again. Whereupon Joshua, seeing himself exposed, jumps to his feet and runs for the blockhouse. 'I should shoot the bastard!' Partridge says.

'Stop whingeing and get going,' Ben orders and sets out at a trot himself. The dust is now so thick that it is akin to fighting through a dust storm and they reach the blockhouse without being fired on. Visibility cannot be more than twenty feet.

Ben is correct, they find a hole in the ground which leads into an underground section of the blockhouse that is untouched by the bombardment. It is sufficiently large to house them comfortably and the men, exhausted and frightened, collapse.

'Righto, break out your rations, see if there's a stove or a fireplace somewhere so we might get a brew up,' Ben instructs one of the corporals, handing him his electric torch.

The man returns in a few minutes, 'Found the cookhouse, a stove, wood and an urn. No water, though, Sergeant-Major.'

Ben doesn't know where he's heard it, but now he says, 'Look under the floor near the stove. Wait on, I'll come with you.' Sure enough, in the centre of the small room used for cooking is a flagstone set in the floor and upon lifting it they see a steel tank of water and a rope with a bucket attached hangs from it. They find six storm lanterns and the interior of the room where the men are gathered is soon lit, dimly but sufficiently for them to see each other and to prepare their field rations. There is a huge sense of relief among the men. The bombardment outside continues and every time a shell falls close the noise within the blockhouse is so intense it hurts their ears.

During a slight lull between salvos Ben calls them to attention. 'Righto, we're not out of this yet.' He indicates the four men he'd found in the blockhouse earlier. 'You four, you'll stand sentry duty for the next four hours. The rest of you eat and get your heads down, have a kip while you may.'

Ben tries to sleep himself but cannot and he takes out a writing pad and pencil and starts to write to Victoria.

My dearest sister Victoria,

I am writing to you from a German blockhouse we have captured near a village called Pozières. You will no doubt read about it in the weeks to come as it is the first major offensive the 1st Division has undertaken in France. The whys and wherefores are not important. What is, is that I feel sure that I won't be coming home to you. That this is the end. The Germans have us pinned down and there is no getting out.

Curiously, it is also the end of a long story because Joshua Solomon is with me, the two of us in the same battle. But, as I write this, he cowers in a corner whimpering to himself. The poor fool cannot, I believe, help himself. What is happening to us all is well beyond cowardice. You do not call a man a coward for being afraid to go over the top when the whistle blows, be he a company commander or a private. He has seen all his mates killed and then all his new pals killed, and, then, because the idea of friendship becomes impossible, mateship now too awful to contemplate, the replacements are received as blank-eyed strangers, who come at night to huddle beside you in the trenches. These are no longer seen as men, only as numbers in a well-thinned roll call after each skirmish into enemy lines. New recruits are no longer seen as whole, but become assorted parts, eyes, skulls, arms, legs, torsos, scraps of unidentified meat. They simply become flesh new-opened, gaping, bloody stumps where once strong arms held their sweethearts close or firm-muscled legs kicked a football and ran shouting urgent instructions across a flat green paddock under a blue sky.

The men who sit huddled in the dust and carnage beside you in the trench become torsos cut off at the waist, like open-mouthed fairground clowns. Heads lolling with fatigue on your shoulder are in your mind already disembodied, tomorrow's 'dirty melons' you are sent out to gather from the mud after each attack. Only the rats are real, they waddle like fat butchers at a meat market and choose the choicest human parts, the intestines, the haggis of hate.

My dearest sister, I do not expect to return from here. The German artillery has us trapped and it has continued now all day and I daresay will do so all night. It is not too hard to understand why our cousin Joshua cowers in a dark corner sucking at an empty bottle of whisky, which he won't relinquish.

It is to drown the noise, the booming, cutting, whining, whooshing, whistling, exploding, blunt and bloody, neverending noise that goes into the senseless slaughter of good and honest men.

And so the male line of our two families will die, here in a charnel field in France. All the hate, all the fierce endeavour, all the malicious greed, come to an end.

Now I want you to do something for me. Kiss Hawk, tell him I love him, and always have. Of all the men I have met in my short life he has always shown me that to be fair and just and honest is the way of a true man. I often think how men fight to put themselves first but he always put himself in the second place. Great-Grandma Mary once told me as a small child how he loved our grandfather Tommo above all sensibility and would have gladly laid down his life for him.

Alas, he has not got the right complexion to blush as you read this to him, but there is no longer need to hide my feelings. You say in your last letter that he grows frail, his huge shoulders stooped, his hands crooked with arthritis, his eyes, his great dark eyes, grown rheumy, but his mind still clear and clean to the intellect. I shall not see him out, I shall not be there to stand by his grave and weep for him. But you will do it for me. Never was there a man I loved as much. Never was there a man who was better at being a member of the human race. In those moments when I have been overcome with despair, and there have been many such as the one I face at this very moment, I ask myself, 'What would Grandfather Hawk do?' and always it becomes clear, he would do the right thing by his mates, by his fellow human beings. I must do the same. My dear Grandfather, if I should die, as I think I shall, I can say only this, you have given me the strength to die with dignity. No better man than you ever lived.

And you, my dearest, I love and cherish you to the last moment of my life. Be brave and good and strong. I thank you and love you with every breath in my body for what you have been to me.

And then there is Sarah, my beloved Sarah. Will you give her half of my inheritance and take care of her when she returns? Treat her as if she was my wife, for I have loved her with my body and my mind is filled with her presence every day. No man could want more than she has given me. Love her, Victoria, as you love me.

And now it is goodbye to the three of you.

I love you all, with all of my heart. Death cannot change that.

Ben.

Ben has barely completed the letter when Partridge comes up to him. 'The C.O.'s gorn walkabout, mate.'

Ben doesn't understand at first. 'What are you talking about?'

'He's ripped off his gear and gorn, tin hat and revolver, screaming like a banshee, told you the bastard wasn't worth bringing.'

'You didn't stop him?' Ben asks.

'Stop him, three of us tried, he's gorn mad, he just knocked us aside, next thing he was out the entrance.'

Folding the letter, Ben finds an envelope and addresses it. He places the letter in the envelope and seals it. Then he puts it in his kit. 'Partridge, you're a useless bastard, but promise me one thing.' Ben points to his kit. 'Inside are two letters, one is addressed to my sister in Tasmania, the other to my fiancée, if you get out of here you see they get them. Tell my sister I said to give you a hundred quid.' Ben grabs up his pad and writes.

Victoria,

Pay this bastard Partridge a hundred pounds when he delivers my letter.

Ben Teekleman.

'There you go.' He hands the note to Partridge.

'Hey, wait a moment, Sergeant-Major, you're not going after him, he's gorn mad, he's a flamin' looney!'

'It's a long story,' Ben says and, taking up his Maori fighting axe, he starts for the entrance. There is a brief lull in the bombardment and he turns to the men. 'There's just a chance the Germans will stop in the early hours of the morning and we'll try to beat a retreat. If it does, get out of here and make for our lines, it's your only hope, lads, take it, don't stay here.'

Ben walks into the open, it is now around ten o'clock at night with the German bombardment lighting up the battlefield in huge flashes as the heavy shells land, sending up towering pillars of dust that catch the light. It is like a scene from hell and he looks to where his trench was before they made it across to the blockhouse. There is nothing to be seen except craters, the lads who stayed are almost certainly dead.

Ben is not concerned about machine guns, there is too much dust. He hopes only to find Joshua cowering somewhere. He doesn't know why he's gone after him, something simply tells him he must. That if he doesn't he will be dishonouring himself, Victoria, Hawk. It doesn't make a lot of sense. But by now nothing does any more. Somehow, something is coming to an end, something dark and ugly and too long in his blood.

A shell explodes about fifty yards ahead of him, lighting up the whole area, cutting through the dust, and then he sees Joshua. He is naked, walking towards the village of Pozières. He has crossed a section of trenches where the German front line stood, now pounded into nothing. Where men a few hours before crouched and hoped, there are only craters and death and the rats scurrying everywhere.

Ben starts to run towards Joshua. Stumbling, he falls and feels his face scrape against the dirt, losing his tin hat. He doesn't try to find it but rises and continues running. Joshua has disappeared into the darkness. But another shell lands and lights him up again. His nude body wearing only the tin hat seems enlarged, bigger than the landscape itself. His nudity is somehow visionlike, as though he is an angel who has come among them, or is man, naked, pleading, asking for the carnage to end, for a new beginning, a new start. Adam looking on the battlefield for Eve.

Ben keeps running, his breath beginning to hurt in his chest. He realises that he is very tired but he moves forward. Another shell bursts and he sees Joshua. This time he is standing in a shell crater and is up to his waist in dirty water. At last Ben comes upon him. Joshua has his revolver and he is firing repeatedly at the body of a dead German strung up on a roll of barbed wire. The German is long dead, his body rotting. An arm falls off and rolls down the side of the crater into the water, and still Joshua fires.

Ben runs into the crater and, taking Joshua's hand, he pulls him out of the hole. Joshua screams as though in pain. On the bank Joshua clutches at his ankle, crying like a small child and Ben, using his torch, sees that his ankle is broken. He lifts him across his shoulder, not quite sure where he finds the strength. Then he begins to carry him across no-man's-land.

Ben carries Joshua for fifty yards and then rests and picks him up again and carries him a little further. Twice a machine gun opens up and he can hear the bullets as they strike the ground near him. Still he continues, resting and carrying. It takes him nearly an hour to cover the six hundred yards. A pistol is fired from the direction of the village, from the Allied lines. He can see men starting to run towards him, his own people. The light seems to hang in the sky forever, bright silver light, sharp, clean, and beautiful. He thinks of Sarah, her body touching his, making love, the soft whimpering sounds she makes and then a sudden lull in the bombardment and into it a single cracking sound, like a twig breaking, as the sniper's bullet hits him. Ben feels himself sinking, melting with the weight of Joshua's body. And he hears Sarah sighing, he is caressing her cheek with the back of his fingers and she looks at him and sighs, 'I love you, Ben, more than my life,' then the darkness comes. Joshua Solomon is mad. Ben Teekleman is dead. The story is ended.

Lest We Forget

A Note on Sources

I and my research team have made extensive use of the wonderful resources of the State Libraries of Victoria and New South Wales and also those of the Australian War Memorial. Numerous texts and reference books have been consulted to confirm dates, names, facts and the overall historical accuracy of *Solomon's Song*. My debt to C. E. W. Bean's *Official History of Australia in the War of 1914–1918* (1921–1942) is obvious. Bean not only edited the twelve volumes of this monumental history but wrote the text of six volumes himself and also produced a most readable one-volume abridgment published in 1946 as *Anzac to Amiens* (Australian War Memorial, Canberra).

Other books used include:

Patsy Adam-Smith, *The Anzacs*, Nelson, West Melbourne, 1978.

—— *Prisoners of War: From Gallipoli to Korea*, Ken Fin Books, Collingwood, 1998.

Australian Dictionary of Biography, 1851–1939, Melbourne University Press, Melbourne, 1966.

The Australian Handbook and Directory for 1874.

A.G. Butler (ed.), *The Official History of the Australian Army Medical Services in the War of 1914–1918*, vol. 1, Gallipoli, Palestine and New Guinea, Australian War Memorial, Melbourne, 1930.

Ruth Campbell, *A History of the Melbourne Law School, 1857–1973*, Faculty of Law, University of Melbourne, Parkville, 1973.

Michael Cannon, *Land Boom and Bust*, Heritage Publications, Melbourne, 1972.

—— *The Long Last Summer: Australia's upper class before the Great War*, Nelson, Melbourne, 1985.

Graeme Davison et al., *The Oxford Companion to Australian History*, Oxford University Press, Melbourne, 1998.

Peter Dennis et al., *The Oxford Companion to Australian Military History*, Oxford University Press, Melbourne, 1995.

Bill Gammage, *The Broken Years: Australian soldiers in the Great War*, Australian National University Press, Canberra, 1974.

Gregory Haines, *The Grains and Threepennorths of Pharmacy: Pharmacy in New South Wales, 1788–1976*, Lowden Publishing, Kilmore, 1976.

R. F. Holder, *Bank of New South Wales: A history, 1817–1970*, in two volumes, Angus and Robertson, Sydney, 1970.

H. Aubrey Husband, *The Student's Handbook of Forensic Medicine and Public Health*, 6th ed., E. & S. Livingstone, Edinburgh, 1895.

John Keegan, *The First World War*, Hutchinson, London, 1998.

Henry Kissinger, *Diplomacy*, Simon & Schuster, New York, 1994.

The Longman Handbook of Modern British History, 1714–1950, Longman, London, 1983.

Philip E. Muskett, *The Illustrated Australian Medical Guide*, in two volumes, William Brooks, Sydney, 1903.

L. M. Newton, *The Story of the Twelfth: A record of the 12th Battalion, A.I.F. during the Great War of 1914–1918*, 12th Battalion Association, Hobart, 1925.

Margaret Orbell, *The Illustrated Encyclopedia of Maori Myth and Legend*, Canterbury University Press, Christchurch, 1995.

Stephen Pope and Elizabeth-Anne Wheal, *The Macmillan Dictionary of the First World War*, Macmillan, London, 1995.

Hilary L. Rubinstein, *The Jews in Australia: A thematic history*, William Heinemann, Port Melbourne, 1991.

Anne Salmond, *Between Worlds: Early exchanges between Maori and Europeans, 1773–1815*, Viking, Auckland, 1997.

Sands & McDougall's Directory of Victoria, Sands & McDougall, Melbourne, 1890–1930.

Elizabeth Scandrett, *Breeches & Bustles: An illustrated history of clothes worn in Australia, 1788–1914*, Pioneer Books, Lilydale, 1978.

G. H. Scholefield, *A Dictionary of New Zealand Biography*, vol. 1, 1769–1869, and vol. 2, 1870–1900, Dept. of Internal Affairs, Wellington, 1940.

Michael Symons, *One Continuous Picnic: A history of eating in Australia*, Duck Press, Adelaide, 1982.

Tasmanian Post Office Directory, 1885–1890.

Fred Waite, *The New Zealanders at Gallipoli*, 2nd ed., Whitcombe and Tombs, Auckland, 1921.

Walch's Tasmanian Almanac for 1885, J. Walch & Sons, Hobart, 1885.